Weep For ISABELLE
a rhapsody in a minor key

By

Mel Month

A historical novel depicting the rise and fall of big physics in the second half of the twentieth century

AvantGarde Press
Stony Brook, New York

This book is a historical novel. The actual lives of well-known people form the basis for the events and situations in the story. For dramatic purposes, several incidents, characters and locales are fictional.

ISBN: 1-4107-3252-5 (e-book)
ISBN: 1-4107-3253-3 (Paperback)

Library of Congress Control Number: 2003091827

This book is printed on acid free paper.

Printed in the United States of America
Bloomington, IN

Published by 1st Books Library
Commissioned by AvantGarde Press

1stBooks - rev. 04/11/03

This Kiss
For My One True Love

Dedication

Dedicated
To the Players
Who gave all they had.
Who could ask for more?

The Players

Maurice Goldhaber	1911
George Kenneth Green	1911-1977
Leland John Haworth	1904-1979
Leon M. Lederman	1922
Isidor Isaac Rabi	1898-1988
Carlo Rubbia	1934
Nicholas P. Samios	1934
George H. Vineyard	1920-1987
Robert Rathbun Wilson	1914-2000
Mickey (Anonymous)	1936

Isidor Isaac Rabi (1962)

Leland John Haworth (1971)

Maurice Goldhaber (1992)

George H. Vineyard (1966)

Nicholas P. Samios (1975)

Leon M. Lederman (1978)

Carlo Rubbia (1983)

George Kenneth Green (1963)

Robert Rathbun Wilson (1978)

Mickey (1977)

The Past:

We do NOT know the past in chronological sequence. It may be convenient to lay it out anesthetized on the table with dates pasted on here and there, but what we know we know by ripples and spirals eddying out from us and from our own time.

Ezra Pound – 1938
Guide to Kulchur (1968)

Now you must wake up.
All dreams must end.
Take off your makeup.
The party's over, it's all over, my friend.

The Party's Over by Betty Comden and Adolph Green
From Bells Are Ringing, copyright *1956*

CONTENTS

Preface

This novel's venue takes you into the world of Science and Technology. With the actual lives of its characters to guide it, the story follows the rise of physics in the latter half of the twentieth century as it is transported by advancing technology and driven by passionate desire into the perilous realm of bigness. The elitist physicists, who hadn't an inkling of the dangerous waters they were entering, demanded more and more particle energy of the accelerator technologists. They did it much in the manner described in Doctor Seuss' Yertle the Turtle and their ultimate end was much the same as poor King Yertle's. It was here in this obstacle-ridden and hazardous territory of big projects that was quite unknown to them, a realm where men tend to lose their bearings and the human drama takes center stage, that these projects simply outgrew the capacity of scientists to handle them. With the ISABELLE project marking the downward turn and the beginning of the end, there followed an explosive decline in the fortunes of Big Science, undone from within by humanity's foibles. Through their antics and games, men, caught in the whirling winds of ambition and vanity, played out the age-old story that inevitably ends up in the vanishing of their dreams. Here on this stage at this time, the sad lady ISABELLE fell victim to man's grasping desire for too much. The gods simply intervened to tell these men that they had gone too far too fast and must stop. Observing the drama, as well as simultaneously being a part of it, my story seeks to record the experiences of this fall from grace. When the struggle between man and his creators had subsided, the end result was simplicity itself: In fighting the will of the gods, there was no man of woman born who could save the dream that was ISABELLE as she fell victim to man's inner need to feed the insatiably hungry beast inside; and in her wake the super lady, known as the Texas Supercollider who sought vainly to replace her, met the same sorry destiny. There is naught we can do but weep for ISABELLE, and to let it be known that all should beware of those awful demons that will only draw the unsuspecting into the quicksand and the same bitter fate. After its meteoric rise in the heady days of the post World War II era, Big Physics was in a shambles by century's end and its promise of glory had turned to dust. Through the medium of the historical novel, I am reporting to you for your entertainment, and recording for those to come, the rise and fall of Big Physics as I saw it and as it happened.

As the sixties were coming to a close, I was knee deep in one of these Big Physics projects. Yet as deeply committed as I was to it, I found myself helpless to interfere in what fate had in store. In spite of all my earnest efforts and an ardent desire to see it through, ISABELLE nonetheless went up in smoke. I looked on in amazement and shock. Only later was I to discover that when adding to the mix a little dab of generalization and a little larger dose of extrapolation, there, staring at me had been a rather remarkable widespread historical phenomenon. Simply said, it is that as research projects grow in size a threshold is reached, which when crossed causes a fast rise in calamities, and that little known to men could arrest the inevitable downward spiral from occurring. Had I known better at the time, I would have understood earlier than I did that there was nothing that an underling like me could do, and most certainly that I could not invoke the spirit of a white knight in shining armor entering to save the day; and so I persisted for many years in that lost cause. Ironically, this ignorance precipitated a lot of good because due to it I came to see and feel and learn about such things. But, as you may have guessed, the subject continued to grow on me because just a little learning is never enough. As my knowledge intensified, my involvement and interest became something of an obsessive need to understand why the fall could not have been averted; and from then on there was no turning back as I was led on a seductive and irresistible journey of discovery of things I had not the least appreciation actually existed. As I moved on in my innocent, eager, and greatly underestimated quest to find the truth, what I found along the way was not an answer, but a seemingly endless series of new and tantalizing and bothersome questions: Why do projects fail when all rationality tells you that they shouldn't? Indeed, with the collaboration of their subordinates, why did the leaders, as smart as they were, not intervene dramatically to save ISABELLE from going down the drain? Why did they stand around and do nothing, refusing to take adequate actions that they knew about full well and that were quite practical? Why did they stick to their rigidly planned course even after all logic demanded a loosening of the reins and the letting in of fresh air? In other words, why didn't they correct their mistakes and move on, which was a perfectly straightforward and reasonable course to set? Why were they so staunchly against accepting help from outsiders even as offers were pouring in? How could it be that they allowed this project to fail so miserably after its wondrous and oh so full-of-hope start? Incredible as it may seem, why did it appear at times that some of them even wished this outcome? Were the mysterious forces underlying irrational motives and behavior at the heart of this gross failure? Is it a reasonable supposition that such irrationality can co-exist in otherwise sane persons? Did they really know that what they were doing was bad? Could they have been so blind about how others privately saw and assessed them? Did they care? Did larger social forces paralyze them, or was it for the most part simply a matter of vanity? Were their claims and assurances of good intentions to be believed unquestioningly, or did they have hidden agendas lying beneath the facade and not easily inferred? And so I went on falling deeper and deeper into the abyss of the human mind and the human heart.

Out of these seemingly endless questions and the resulting clash of ideas within me came the story that you have here. Its central events and the key people populating it are real; and I have been vigilant in ensuring that all the actors in the drama that follows have been given parts identical to those they had in real life. The book follows the lives of ten achievers of high merit, most of whom were great lab Directors, and chronicles their unwitting roles in the decline of projects and laboratories. Somehow there seemed no way to alter the course history had laid out for them as the labs plunged into the depths of social breakdown that ultimately led to the near-demise of today's failing American Big Physics enterprise. As such rise-and-fall cycles go it had a short lifetime, lasting a little more than half a century. Nonetheless, even in its oh too brief productive period on the rise, it yielded knowledge of a high order indeed, telling mankind a large part of the amazing story of the origins of matter and the universe; but the relentless forces of man's darker nature would not and could not be denied. In my detailed account of the main events that took place are found project cancellations, lab reviews held in vain efforts to avert disaster, forced resignations, international meetings to salvage something from the mess, national meetings to attempt to create new beginnings, and other such goings on, all of which are now part of the historical record. On the other hand, when it comes to some of the unrecorded private meetings and discussions that I have chosen to write about, whether they actually took place could not be verified with a high level of confidence. To be sure, however, such get-togethers were allowed in the text only if they fitted well with the natures of the central ten Players, as well as with those of a variety of other peripheral characters who became caught up in the evolving drama. When I first embarked on this writing expedition, I believed that I had already done the two things that had to be done to complete the work. First, I had carefully watched the actors as well as participated with them as we all did our thing, committing a lot of incidents to memory in addition to noting many of them down on paper. Second, I had been diligent in reading and saving newspaper accounts and the like, thereby gaining a deeper appreciation for the public perception of the Big Science enterprise and its exploits. Little did I know then that observation of this sort was just skimming the surface and that if I was going to get anywhere at all, I could not avoid scratching and clawing my way under their skins, as well as rummaging through my own soul. In the end, I was drawn inexorably to the realization that if I was going to find some meaningful answers I would have to go after no less than their minds. But minds are perforce private domains and verboten to outsiders. Nevertheless, disobeying the *stay-out* signs, I did, by hook or by crook, overcome the entrance barriers and managed finally to force my way in.

In this way, although I wasn't looking for quandaries or vexations, I encountered them anyway as I casually and innocently entered that tricky and forbidding realm of intentions where angels should fear to tread. This place, as I soon discovered, is one where all things are hazy, where you can't be sure of anything or anyone, where pitfalls abound and trouble lurks around every corner, and where all things said are intrinsically untrustworthy. Would you trust someone who tells you how pure his intentions are? Would you trust someone to tell you the truth about having impure ones? No, of course you wouldn't because intentions are personal and belong solely to the person having them, and so nothing would prevent him from expressing anything he wants to, whether it be true or false. However, even if he should tell you that he has chosen to share his true feelings with you, keep in mind that by doing so he would be risking the divulging of unflattering and at times even sinister thoughts that are bound now and then to generate negative emotional energy in you. You can almost be sure that this is not at all what he wants to see. It is wise therefore to take such revelations with a grain of salt and not to expect too much truth. It doesn't take a lot of social insight to guess that the outcome of all this is not a pretty picture: by and large, people tend to keep their intimate thoughts private or at least close to the vest, preferring to suppress the possibility of disappointed or even angry reactions directed at them. When people are pressured and under stress, deceit and lying are more than likely to become their standard of behavior; and when they are pushed to their limits, self-deception may creep into their personalities and even end up dominating them. The result of this inevitable social chain is not only to leave a path strewn with pain and loss, but also to make both the people and their intentions very hard to figure out. This is especially the case if you happen to be an outsider, although it must be admitted that even inner circle residents, who have a lot of access, have trouble getting to the bottom of things. You can be certain that it is disillusioning and at times disheartening when you come to realize that intending to find out the secrets of others is one thing, actually doing it is a horse of a different color.

Getting the scoop on what's really going on, by whatever means you can cook up, is a sequence of the most trying, onerous, and sometimes painful chores, but if you want to grasp the true essence of the past, you have no other choice. Society's nature seems to insist that if the past is your aim, then *anything goes* has to be your game. The toughness of breaking through history's well-guarded line of defense smacks you right in the face as soon as you enter the arena, where you are immediately confronted with the big question: how can you get history to open its portals and thereby release the past to you without your shining the light of day on the people involved and what they've done? The simple fact is that you cannot. Opening old wounds and exposing the seedy underbelly is the stuff true history is made of, and therein lies the dilemma of studying this most enticing of disciplines. The job of doing this is filled with unpleasantness, resistance, and retaliation, so enter only at your own risk, and keep in mind that it is not for the faint of heart. In the end, it is no less than a Herculean enterprise, both intellectually and emotionally. This doesn't mean that you should be dissuaded from the effort of illuminating history whenever you can and no matter how hard it might be. I for one am convinced that it is a very good thing to do, believing as I do that there truly exists a pot of gold at the end of the rainbow; but when you take that gut-wrenching slide down its deceptively inviting and safe-appearing arc, you're not very likely to hit the jackpot. Speaking from experience to all of you who develop the inclination to take on the challenge anyway, I feel obliged to make you aware of your low likelihood of striking pay dirt. If however you persist in not heeding this warning of frustration ahead, or of even a total washout, you should always keep in mind that people's lives are meant to be kept from you, so that even if you apply your most earnest and well-meaning efforts, a well-founded and trustworthy history is unlikely to emerge. Those not experienced in such matters might imagine that it can't be all that complicated. To them I can only offer encouragement, but add the admonishment to look before you leap too far, for just below skin depth you'll come to see what you must contend with: minds filled with intermingled intentions, motivations, actions planned, deeds done, and interpretations that are most intricately woven into complex and beautiful but ultimately false tapestries, which are almost impossibly difficult to disentangle and decipher. Distinguishing truth from falsity is indeed a tough business. This being the case, the things you'll have to do to get even a semblance of the truth won't make you a happy camper; and then, when and if you happen to approach close to the promised land, it is most likely that rewards will be few and far between. It is more likely that you'll find under-appreciation and resentment, and if you come too close to the truth, even scorn and ostracism. No, I'm afraid that if you set out to travel this road, the end alone will have to be your sole reward. That's not exactly a powerful incentive to start on such a hard trip, but don't despair, it often turns out that the best comes from unpromising and the least auspicious circumstances. This was perhaps the spirit in which I began my journey. In spite of everything I could see telling me that I shouldn't pursue such a course, I persisted. Having innocently come to the view that I could build a better history of what took place by getting into the minds of the participants, my characteristic optimism persuaded me to walk right into the lion's den and attempt it. I had the audacity to believe that I could not only create a living history but at the same time write an enticing and engaging story. I'm not kidding when I say that I really thought that I could do it, and in quick fashion too, and further that it wouldn't be too hard to accomplish. Wrongheaded as this was, it actually wasn't hard to become convinced of my plan's easiness because the art of combining history and storytelling isn't new, and I was aware of the long and stirring tradition of the historical novel. Why not give it a shot? Others had done it, I thought, so why not me? Although in the beginning some reluctant thoughts entered my consciousness, these ended up being incidental and passing – and ignored. When push came to shove, since I am what I am, I couldn't resist the temptation. Get into their minds, I told myself, you've got what it takes, so just do it.

On the other hand, if you don't have the ambition to be a spinner of yarns, but rather aspire to be a formal historian in the academic tradition, then why do you have to bother with such complicated machinations? In such a frame of mind, you might quite rightly wonder just how important it is to know about intentions and such. If what you're after is plain old-fashioned history, mightn't it be adequate for you to know just the bare facts, which are capable of being made visible and plausible to all? This talk of getting into the soul of others to find the truth could be just a lot of bull, you might think. Furthermore, aside from being a safer and easier way to go, as we all know, agreement concerning facts is a piece of cake compared to agreement about intentions. Wouldn't it therefore be a nice and simple world if we didn't have to bother with intentions at all, but were able to content ourselves with *just the facts, ma'am* as Sergeant Friday of television's Dragnet fame used to say? Yes, there is little doubt that it would be, but unfortunately it would not be the real world, and, for that matter, it would not represent history as well in the truest meaning of that highly misused and underestimated word. At first blush, you may be tempted not to agree with this assessment, but if you'd give it a little thought, I don't doubt that you'd come around. Indeed, sometimes I contemplate such a world, where just the facts are enough to give some sort of decent understanding of it. It would certainly make stories a lot simpler to write, and for that matter life a lot simpler to live. But alas, in our world, facts are not enough because facts alone do not a real life make nor do they a good story make. In the end it is the people and their intentions that really count and they cannot be done without; and so we must steel ourselves and become resigned to having to deal with uncertainty and inference. That is the way it is and that is the way it will always be. However, as strange as it may seem, once having accepted this reality, fortunately for the story-teller or indeed for the true historian as well, it doesn't seem so bad after all because when you come right down to it, wouldn't life be a lackluster subject to write about as well as to read about if the mostly dull observable facts alone were the sum total of the writer's ingredients? This reminds me of high-school kids complaining about their boring history classes being only the memorizing of dates and events. Such is indeed a distressing state of affairs because good history is full of stories replete with gossip and fascinating lives and should be able to snag and engulf anyone who approaches, especially the impressionable young. When filled to the brim with intentions, motivations, and the inner workings of the mind, all stories are intrinsically interesting, and any writer worth his salt has the duty to make them meaningful and readable. Since it should be apparent to all that facts alone are not enough and that intentions matter a whole lot, I have chosen to put a lot of stock in them and have given them big parts to play in my story. The result has been that their inclusion has permitted me to reconstruct the truest picture that I can of the genuine history of the time. Actually it has done more than that, it has ended up giving my novel its very life-blood, and has provided it with the energy to propel the *Players* through to their ultimate and unavoidable destinies. This fork in the road that I have chosen to follow has made all my trials and tribulations worthwhile. Through my struggle to reach into the minds of the actors in the drama, I believe that I have ended up with the truthful history of the times. As for you, it is naturally your call, but in coming to your judgment, I ask you to ponder: is the story I am about to tell you concerning the desires and the self-serving and sometimes sorry deeds of the real people who lived through those times very different from the best-we-can-do history?

By and large, the stories told in this novel deal with the actions, intentions and feelings of its ten protagonists as they lived through the events that are depicted and dissected, sometimes excruciatingly but always necessarily, because of their relevance and importance to our central theme of the rise-and-fall of human dreams and endeavors. At the beginning of the third millennium, some of the major characters are still living and some have since died. In both cases, surely for those dead but in fact even for those living, although I was forced to accept that their intentions and feelings were intrinsically unknowable for certain, I settled on the notion of inferring them in such a way as to be well matched to their known behavior and actions – past, current, and subsequent. This surmising of what was taking place in their minds was further constrained by the actual events that they were involved with in addition to the ensuing events. If my interpretations of their intentions served to strengthen or confirm the uncompromised and untampered with actuality, such interpretations were retained in the story. If they conflicted with the actuality, they were deleted. As for the events themselves, all the major ones and most of the minor ones are real and have become part of the historical record. Although I have already implied as much, I am compelled to emphasize that a few of the minor ones have been inferred by me solely for the purpose of dramatic force and continuity, with their details gathered up and based on hints and comments garnered from discussions and remembrances. Even in these cases, however, something akin to them almost surely took place – although I admit that the few that are actually described in the novel are conjecture and pure imagination on my part.

This method, however, which is not far removed from the common manner of treating man's history, is turned on its head as the novel moves toward its finale. I have here made a supreme effort to overcome the not-to-be-underestimated confusion that comes about when trying to reconcile the historical record with the sometimes widely differing memories of the participating characters. This I have done in a grand flourish by attempting to close the book with a flirtation with fantasy. In one last-ditch desperate effort to get to the bottom of things and find the real truth, the *Players* are invited to a romantic Utopia where all the consequences of divulging that truth are removed. With the apprehension and worry of fall-out no longer a factor, and in particular being unhindered by the threat of social retaliation, they pour their hearts out. Although this excursion is unequivocally fictional, because the thoughts and ideas expressed by the *Players* are fully consistent with reality to the extent that such is known, it rises above the usual fiction and comes about as close to the truth as I could get. It does seem passing strange that fiction should be a valuable and perhaps even a superior way of reconstructing the truth and thereby resurrecting by past – but such is the nature of the irony-filled world we live in. Odd as it may seem to those who have not delved deeply into the mysteries of the past – either the tangible circumstances or the meanderings of the mind – it appears that fact and fiction are not as far apart as many think they are. It is with this as backdrop that I have come to the view that this book can be labeled a work of history, and yet it can also be characterized as a work of fiction. It therefore seems that it is best described as a historical novel.

Finally, since my effort is an exposé of a sort, I realize that it could be quite controversial and will make some people unhappy. This is not surprising, for who would want their innermost secrets revealed? However, at this stage of my life, it is the truth, the whole truth, and nothing but the truth that has become foremost in my thinking, and *calling 'em as I see 'em*, a natural prerequisite, has taken top priority. Nevertheless I want it known up-front that this book has been written with much admiration, gratitude, and affection for the *Players*. They have done the best they could with the cards dealt them and have in the bargain given their lives to the pursuit of knowledge for humanity's betterment. As for me, I have lived through most of the span of time covered by the book and most of the events dealt with; I have taken the trip of a lifetime struggling to find out what really happened; and I have tried my level best to give you the full and unvarnished truth. The result of my strange and exciting journey and adventure into the unknown is the product you have before you, my first novel. I very much hope you will decide to read it. Then you can judge for yourself whether or not my methods, especially the means I've used to infer thoughts and feelings, lead to an interesting story as well as to a true and consistent picture of the history of that turbulent period. So it is solely up to you, the choice is yours; I'm now in your hands.

Mel Month
Stony Brook, NY
January 17, 2003

Acknowledgement

Margaret Dienes is a gem of an editor, a writer's dream come true. What more can I say?

PART I

Point of No Return

Chapters

1. Changing of the Guard

Leland sensed his time was up. You aren't told such things. Rather, they sneak up on you like the darkness does – when you're not looking. Not everyone can accept life's flow with poise and level-headedness; and many don't have the inner strength to face up to it. Some may even lose their capacity to see it. But Leland was not such a type. He consistently looked into himself, and equally sought to know what others were thinking and perhaps conniving. He was forever analyzing. He felt he could look life straight on, unflinchingly; and he had no doubt that he would not be crushed by what he found. The first signs of impending change were vague and uncertain. Nonetheless, he was able to see the handwriting on the wall. Maybe it was because of the way some of his friends as well as his enemies looked at him. Maybe it was because of the way Rabi and some of the other Board members spoke to him – that little wavering inflection in the tone of their voices. It seemed to Leland that they were feeling sorry for him, even bordering on pity. Of course, there was some exaggeration in this observation, but chewing on it over and over again the impression grew in him that the show was over. Still, for a while, he wavered on believing the truth of it. You see, even a man of Leland's strength of character found it hard to take. Then, at some seemingly random moment, the bulb in his head lit up in a glow of comprehension. He remembered well that flash in his brain, that moment of insight. Nobody spelled it out for him, nor had to. He just knew! It was his intuition that was speaking to him. Although a long time in coming, the transition from guessing to knowing had finally taken place. He never doubted that the time would eventually come when the BNL phase of his life would end. He even had anticipated it and verbalized it in his mind. In recollection, he found it amusing that in getting that first glimpse of his fate, although he had been all alone, he did a double take. With no one there to see him, he actually found himself feigning private surprise at his predicament. How funny! Why, he wondered aimlessly, had he found it necessary to indulge in that little fakery of self-surprise? It was so sophomoric. Still, he smiled inwardly at the thought of himself performing that audience-less act.

Once having jogged his memory, he recalled as well the unexpected reaction he had after the realization that his time had come hit home. He wasn't upset, or angry, or scared; rather, he took it all in quite casually. There was no adrenaline surge, no sweat, just a simple and straightforward acceptance of the change and resignation to it. In his earlier imaginings, this was not at all how he had contemplated he would feel. He thought that he would be anxious about such a big change in his life. But he couldn't have been more wrong. For, almost immediately, he found that he actually began to like the idea. Suddenly, in that moment of inspiration when he recognized it had to be and there was no turning back, optimism surfaced and he began to see new opportunities on the horizon. Actually, some opportunities had already been hinted at – he should have known that he would be sought after and courted. In any case, this turned out to be a time when a manner of relief filled his being. It was a moment of happy discovery, a time when hopes began to take hold and he started seriously and optimistically to consider plans for his future. But to take advantage of these anticipated opportunities, he'd have to be careful about how he carried out this transition in his life. Yes, he would see to it that no one, himself included, would upset the apple cart. He vowed then and there that he would control himself during this sensitive period and do nothing to jeopardize the chances bound to soon arise.

As Leland pondered his forthcoming leave-taking as lab Director and the possible new undertakings that awaited him, he thought of times past. Of one thing he was certain: he had no regrets. He had worked hard, perhaps too hard. And he had been oh so lucky. Not every Director can claim a great technological invention on his watch. Still, he had lingering doubts about whether he would be accorded the recognition he deserved. It was perhaps his natural reticence and modesty that held him back from a whole-hearted self-assurance that he would be properly commended for his past achievements. He knew that he had directed and had overseen the beginning of some sort of greatness. But there was something about the place and the community that gave him pause. Maybe it was the people standing ready to take over from him, or maybe it was his loss of trust in the integrity and fairness of the academic experimental types, or maybe it was just his own overly careful nature. But that was all mere speculation and, besides, out of his control. Why belabor it now? Whatever people made of him was their business. He had more pressing matters to consider, particularly his future. Leaving aside any concerns he had about the professional future that awaited him, there was one of a personal nature that he was apprehensive about and caused him some distress – he was worried about his health, and more worried about his wife's. But he knew he had to put such fears out of his mind. After all, there was nothing more he could do than what had already been done and what was continuing to be done. He and his wife were taking good care of themselves and of each other. They were receiving the best medical treatment there was to be had. Yes, he thought, it was indeed a good time to be alive. So sure was he of the great medical progress of the twentieth century that he had boundless confidence in their ability to beat the current attacks on their bodies and so have a lot more years to savor their miraculous tour on planet earth. Thus it was there on that early morning, as he sat quietly in his office, that Leland daydreamed about himself, his past, his legacy, and his future. In a calm and hopeful mood, he imagined himself leaving his directorship as a winner, healthy in body, praised by all for his achievements, and with offers for future positions waiting just around the corner. When it came to the past, he could only keep his fingers crossed. But, with regard to the future, he had friends at the Atomic Energy Commission (AEC), and they had already suggested that he would be a good fit to become the newest Commissioner. Furthermore, the top position was just about to open at the National Science Foundation (NSF), and President Kennedy was looking for scientists who were also good administrators. Just think, Leland anticipated, his face glowing in that pre-dawn hour, in the next year or two maybe he would become the next NSF Director.

Leland had found it hard to sleep the night before. This was atypical for him, and he felt a little tired. But he was determined to fight that feeling. This day was to bring him the first big test of his attitude toward the winds of change engulfing both him and the lab, and he wanted to be up to the challenge. There was still a little time left for him to prepare himself, to wind himself up for the task of meeting with the man he believed would be his successor. He tried his best but as he waited in the early morning hours, before the hustle and bustle of the day's activities got under way, he couldn't prevent his thoughts from wandering into dubiously constructive territory. As important as this meeting was to him, somehow he couldn't focus on it. Actually, what were foremost on his mind were thoughts of the past, a past that just wouldn't allow him the well-earned peace of mind he richly deserved. These thoughts of what had been kept creeping up on him. They were insistent and demanded confrontation. Oddly, this past, apparently gone and unchangeable, still lived within him, as if it were trying to send him some message, perhaps a signal of some kind, to help him cope. Why, he thought, were these remembrances of things past being so persistently activated in him? And why now, when he should be trying to clear his head so that he could be at his best for the demands of the all but certain change looming not too far ahead? Perhaps what kept pushing him back in time were the doubts that kept flashing in his mind, over and over, concerning his ever-increasing misgivings about what the lab would do with its good fortune of the last decade. He was immensely proud of those years. To him the fifties represented the Haworth decade and he hoped beyond hope that it would come to be known as that. But he knew deep down that this was only a wish, perhaps only a reflection of his vanity, because his rational mind knew full well that from here on in it was not to be his affair.

He wondered, in the stillness of the early morning hours, how he would deal with the reality that there was simply nothing he could do about it. It was out of his hands. Others would come to use and possess what he had so painstakingly crafted. They would be the ones henceforth to shape the lab – to govern it, to play with it, to reap the benefits and the goodies, and to suffer the blame and the pain. He would become but a shadow of days gone by. Leland, like all of us as we grow old, would become no more than a relic, eventually a name on a tombstone, to be remembered as it best suits those calling the shots. He, like everyone else, could expect neither to be able to write history before it fully played itself out nor for that matter to set it right from the grave. Like many before him, he had to become resigned to the simple reality that the living cannot write their own history. It wasn't a happy thought, but in the quiet of that early morning, he had raised it to the level of being no worse than bittersweet.

As the dawn of a new day was approaching, he sat in the solitude of his small, neat office in a meditative mood, reflecting on the vicissitudes of his life and the complications it had presented him with. He had always thought of his life as an ordinary one. Nonetheless, given his unaccountably intense urge to examine it, even scrutinize it in excruciating detail, he must have considered it of some special worthiness and significance. During these musings, in order to aid in his self-inquiry, he sought to separate his present from his past so as to get a hold on the past in a detached way. He had put his mark on many things and had a hand in many others. Some ended up being good, some not so good. Were they all willful actions? Did he actively set out and choose to do them? Were they his true intentions? Was he accountable for them and the many things that transpired in their wake as a consequence? Were others responsible? Did he have a right to judge them? Did he have the capacity to judge himself? As these questions hopped and skipped in his mind, he wondered if he really had the capability of viewing his past in a dispassionate manner. If he could, he might be able to see what had truly happened and so discover his involvement and the role he had truly played. But doubts about being able to do this began to predominate. As he pondered the past and its panorama of happenings, as he tried to separate out his relationship to them, he couldn't shake the present from interfering. It wouldn't let go. And, of course, how could it let go? For the past had happened the way it had only so that the present would be what it is. Try as he might, it was a futile endeavor to attempt the disentanglement of past happenings and present surmises. They were inextricably linked, and the present had its say on what the past had been as much as the past had determined what the present was. That's how it was and always will be. The forces and the flow of history demand it. And there is a further demand made by the historical flow, that relating to the future. Just as our past shapes our future, so our imaginings of what is to come cannot but deeply influence our perceptions of what has already taken place. It is all – past, present, and future – a continuum, with the past influencing and merging with the present in much the same manner as the present relates to the future. Time – the medium through which all this takes place – moves on as events follow relentlessly the course fate has set out for them. Yes, it's fate playing its fateful part in the drama that fixes the big picture – life – and determines it all. Thus, Leland not only had his past to confront, made all the more difficult to evaluate and judge by an interfering present, but also had no way to avoid having to deal with what fate had in store for him. In the end, as the doors opened to the sixties, fate spoke and Leland's days at BNL were numbered. But resting was not yet in the cards for him and would simply have to wait. With his age advancing, he was in the process of learning that the only really peaceful sleep is the final one. And, so it was that in 1961 the old guard would have to pass away and, whether willingly or by force, would have to give way to the arrival of the new order.

Was he dreaming? Leland couldn't tell exactly, but there in that dimly lit room he was transported back to the summer of 1947 when he first ventured into the lab that was to be his professional home for the next fourteen years. He found himself in Upton, Long Island, New York, and for the first time saw the terrain from which would rise up the great Brookhaven National Laboratory. What a sorry sight to behold it was – bleak and muddy even on a sunny summer's day. There was nothing visible to the naked eye to commend it. The place did have what would turn out to be a magnificent future lying ahead, but that was still dormant and yet to be even imagined. Leland recalled vividly his sorrowful feelings at this first view. But he loved science so much that even this glimpse of the ugly physical reality at the lab's beginning could not dampen his spirits. He would go with the flow. He would accept it all: being miles from anywhere, the absence of any aesthetic virtues, the dampness, and the dispiriting physical environment. There seemed to be some special strength within him that could dispel all this. So strong was his desire and will to move forward that nothing imaginable could encroach to disrupt his unquenchable thirst for new knowledge and the chance to make it live. With their hearts overflowing with hopes and dreams, the scientists of Leland's day believed fervently that they could understand this crazy world through scientific inquiry. They, including Leland, were so sure that their new method for doing basic research, which came to be called Big Science, would bring forth the secrets of the universe and open the door to eternity. It was in this wildly optimistic frame of mind that Leland came to be a close associate and friend of Philip Morse, BNL's first Director, who had recruited him away from the safety and comfort of the University of Illinois and brought him to this ungodly place. Leland pictured himself in those early days as bright-eyed with a flushed and smiling face. Did this appearance simply indicate the naiveté of an ambitious young man on the make? Did his overpowering ambitions and enthusiasm completely and immediately douse and suppress the desperation that fashioned his very early impressions? Or, was his appearance of optimism really a mask to hide a lingering suspicion that Morse had deceived him? Was it possible that under the surface he still harbored resentment at being gratuitously ripped from a softer academic life for the harder frontier one at BNL? Leland couldn't be sure of any of this, but as he later remembered this time many years before, he would swear that he had very quickly managed to conquer the stranded, out-of-one's-depth feelings of his beginning encounter with the lab, as well as his foggy feelings about Morse's true intentions. In any case, over the years, he certainly beat down any remaining doubts he may have carried. The contentment, exultation, and high spirits that well described him in his BNL days vouched for the fact that he hadn't erred in his choice to come to the East Coast, and also that he was cleansed of any subliminal presumption of Morse's double-dealing. All in all, as time passed during his years at the lab, he was able to piece together and evaluate the chain of circumstances that marked his life there, and he found that any of the early doubts he had were unquestionably and satisfyingly transformed into fulfillment and pride.

Although over all his BNL years Leland couldn't believe it of a man he so admired, Morse indeed had his own private ulterior motives for bringing him in. Leland should have understood, but perhaps he didn't really want to know. Now, however, in the twilight of his BNL years and in the morning silence, he recalled how, in the days just after Leland had arrived, Morse seemed a little distracted, perhaps preoccupied or even a little agitated. It wasn't a big deal, but it was evident enough for Leland to notice and remember. Although Leland didn't pick it up right then, he discovered soon after that what Morse really wanted was out. The implication of this wasn't one to put Leland on cloud nine – for it seems that he was merely the means to that end. But the good Leland simply cast that thought from his consciousness and never came to view it as it really was. As far as Morse was concerned, Leland was sent from heaven, representing Morse's instrument for a graceful exit – and he accomplished his plan flawlessly. In short order, the scheme was carried out. In the fall of 1948, a little more than a year after his arrival at the dingy, barren Upton site, Haworth replaced Morse and became BNL's second Director. Life had again demonstrated – as it does with amazing regularity – its strange ways of bringing one to one's destiny.

Leland didn't see himself in the same league as the great physicists who conceived and made possible the realization of nuclear fission – the same remarkable and vital men who were to go on and inspire the impressive and big accelerator labs that were to spot the nation in the post-war flowering of basic science. What a vision this Los Alamos team had in the early forties! Led by the brilliant and multi-faceted Robert Oppenheimer, they imagined and realized a controlled chain reaction in nuclear matter, liberating a fantastic amount of energy and providing unheard of potential for explosive power. Through the Manhattan Project, one of unprecedented size and organized in an array of secret laboratories spread throughout the entire country, this was to bring into being the atomic bomb, one of mankind's greatest and most dangerous inventions. With it, man would attain the capability of destruction on a scale hitherto unimaginable. Henceforth a single moment of impulsive insanity could result in the destruction of mankind itself. Yes, it was a never-to-be-forgotten and solemn moment in history, one that has since been decisive and of great consequence for the fate of mankind. Of the many people who responded to the nation's call and did the deed, Leland was one. But he never deemed to compare himself to the geniuses that walked the halls of the new Los Alamos lab and made it a captivating and magical place – their greatness flitting about, giving the place an extraordinary and unworldly air. In his eyes as well as in the eyes of others he was of a lesser sort, one whose place in life was to bring to fruition the concepts, the ideas, and the insights of the greats towering above. At the time, issues such as these, dealing with class and stature, were of minor import, and rightfully ignored. Who could be expected even to look at them? During that awesome period, that wondrous time when everyone was blinded by the presence of those flashing, daring masters, that dangerous time when the existence of the free world lay in the balance, what a petty, insignificant, and quibbling matter it was. However, it's not wrong to see retrospectively that there were the greats and the not so greats; and, because their combined presence at that place and at that time had such profound importance to the future of science, it's also not wrong to try to figure out what the consequences of the prevailing class structure might have been. If you were to ask: Was Leland a giant of science? Of course, he wasn't. Compared to people of the likes of Fermi, Bethe, Urey, Rabi, and Oppenheimer, he was undoubtedly a figure of lower stature. But that's simply an irrelevant point. The plain and clear issue, the one that had a deep and palpable impact on the future of basic research, had nothing at all to do with who the people were, but rather was about what they were doing. What the physicists got wrong was the way they came to view the prioritization of the roles science and technology played in basic research. Scientists simply confused who they were with what they did. They presumed and came to believe that what great men did was great for no other reason than that they were the great ones. What they actually did was overlooked and disregarded. So, because that was what the great men did, scientists came to adopt the paradigm that the only science of real weight and worth was of the basic kind. Technology, which was done by a different breed from the great ones, was relegated to a distant second place. As a class, scientists couldn't see that anything else but their beloved "true" science could matter much. Oh yes, getting it done, which demanded imaginative technological insight, had some importance, but it was an importance of a lesser kind. Those who accomplished that part of the basic research enterprise warranted a stature far below that of the great theoreticians and conceptualizers. But in so thinking, the community of scientists was committing a grievous error, and those who followed this line – and most scientists did – had come to an erroneous interpretation of what the Manhattan Project really meant. In a word, they were wrong! By itself, their hard-headedness on this score was neither here nor there, but it led to something that had a more far-reaching consequence. It led to a fallacious extrapolation of how to conduct future scientific research. You see, in the Manhattan Project, the technologies conceived and implemented to build the nuclear bomb were crucial and indispensable to its success. In the end, they may have been more significant than the scientific discovery and understanding of nuclear fission in the laboratory – this despite the fact that conceptualization in basic science is surely great in and of itself. The conclusion is inescapable that in light of the history of the bomb's creation, basic research, or the physics as it's now referred to, turned out to be secondary to man's realization of a new age of technology. So, when a post-war era of basic research was established, why did this truth get reversed with technology taking the back seat? It showed unbelievably poor judgment. Man's monumental act of wartime discovery and creation – some would say folly – lay in the laboratories of Hanford, Los Alamos and Oak Ridge, in the labs at many universities across the country and abroad, and in the multitude of men and women working in tandem in functions as varied as building cities with their complex infrastructures, building massive industrial plants, building and operating sophisticated instruments, handling delicate material, managing delicate human issues, and so on. It clearly was technology that was at center stage, had the requisite priority, and got the job done. Why, in establishing the post-war system of basic research, the scientists, as well as those who blindly followed them and their ideas, missed this striking and transparent truth is truly puzzling and still remains a mystery.

Remnants of this judgment lapse in discerning the right paradigm remain today and have proven to be a significant obstacle to science's advances into the endless frontier, where men are given the chance to unlock the secrets of nature and maybe even touch God himself. But Leland was one scientist who was awake and had his eyes wide open. He didn't miss this point. He saw the correct paradigm. Technology, in its own right, had to be fostered, nurtured, and pushed ever forward; and during his tenure as BNL Director, using his model of how a lab should be run, he saw it flourish and push forward those frontiers of discovery and knowledge. Other labs springing up in that period of enlightenment, using Leland's new model, also flourished. But it didn't last. Sad to say, the power of the old ways was so ingrained in the science community that, when least expected, with success right at hand, it reared its ugly head – and dark days were the consequence. So it was that after Leland BNL entered a barren, paltry period of low scientific productivity that lasted decades. Knowing that, shouldn't one want to scream out in frustration? But emotional outbursts are of no consequence. How could anyone have known back then in the fifties that things would turn out that way? Even if Leland had figured it out, what could he have done differently? Nevertheless, even though he didn't correctly smell out what the future held in store, in his time Leland had great insight into what was best needed then, and he had the instinct of how to proceed that was right on. Although alone in pushing his agenda, he had an uncommon inner strength to stick to his guns. With courage few possess, he was capable of overcoming the precepts of the times and the assumptions of the leaders who preceded him. The capacity to oppose such social forces can come only from exceptional human character, one of boldness and of self-confidence. It can come only from a man with an adventurous spirit. Some would call him dumb for not looking out first for number one, but such selfless behavior represents humanity at its finest. Leland from somewhere deep within himself found a way to stand out in a sea of greatness by fashioning his own special niche, and that helped make him great in his own right. What he saw before anyone else were the true implications of the emerging Big Science – namely that the paradigm of science based on the traditional pattern of original discovery in the ivory tower of a university lab was no longer applicable and that a new paradigm based on the experience gained from the Manhattan Project was needed. Not only did he set BNL on the path to becoming the first lab of the land, but he also single-handedly created a new paradigm for the labs for the age of Big Science. In that, he was a singular man and it's too bad that his insights have not been followed, except in a spotty, inconsistent way. Still, a great deal came from the labs in those wonder-filled few decades. If only that time could have lasted longer!

Leland recalled his first job at the lab. His title was Assistant Director in charge of special projects. Like all bureaucratic titles, on the face of it, it meant nothing. It was what was behind it that really counted. When Leland first heard it, it sounded innocuous enough – not a title to unnerve the innocent and inexperienced Leland. Perhaps his failure to see how hard it would be for him was because he didn't really appreciate how serious Morse was in getting him prepared to take over. Actually, Morse must have had a lot of confidence in Leland's ability to take on the top job of Director because what he gave him was no less than the job of shaping the lab's future for the fifties and beyond. In no time, Leland found himself in the thick of things, both technical and political ones. Before he got the soles of his shoes dirty with mud, he was knee deep in the stuff. He was almost immediately inundated with technical decisions to make; and he had the more difficult job of calming the whiners and complainers, in addition to bringing some sense of perspective to the unreasonably demanding types. He had to temper, console, and direct a bevy of prima donnas. He had to soften the fears of the technical staff. He had to leash the unbridled and clearly unrealistic presumptions of the high mucketymucks. He had almost impossible budget and financial decisions to make in the course of negotiations with the many contracting companies as well as with the Atomic Energy Commission – negotiations of a nature neither he nor anyone else around him knew much about. It was a time of impending chaos. It was a time marked by turmoil, misunderstanding, disagreement, anger, hostility, threats and bullying, and almost universal unhappiness. But such is the wonder and strangeness of the organization's social nature that somehow this tangled and seemingly intractable atmosphere was miraculously transmuted into one of success and pride. Actually, Leland and all the lab's troops experienced large ups and downs – life's wild fluctuations – in living through that restless, feverish, and turbulent time. But when the storms calmed, the players awoke to a dumfounding reality. All through the apparent chaos, small steps were being taken. They were hidden – swamped by the wild ups and downs – but when the rough and tumble settled and quiet allowed an assessment to be made, these minute pushes forward were seen to have added up to something of value. These steps, small as they were, were in fact acting in synchronism, compounding, and finally summing up to a reality so big that it changed the very landscape of BNL and made the lab into a great one. With its new working reactors and accelerators, the tools to do the science of the coming new age, Leland had given BNL an enviable life on the top rung of the ladder. So, although not a genius of science, Leland turned out to be a genius in managing it. He recognized and fought for a principle few appreciated: that it is in the nature of research and development (R & D) and its related projects that when the technologies are right and the projects are right, there's nothing better – not the physics at the end of the line – nothing. When Leland's job was done, BNL was on top of the world. As for Morse, tired and anxious to retreat and escape the trap of directing such an unruly mob of a lab, he had chosen Leland to do it for him. Was this an insightful choice or just dumb luck? Who knows? As it turned out, Leland was just the right man to do the job. And so he did it.

* * * * *

It all happened very fast. In no time, BNL was changed from the morass of Camp Upton to a technological and cultural haven. Directed by the shrewd and incisive hand of the guy in charge, many projects at the lab were kept going all at once. In August

1950, three years after Haworth arrived at the lab, its first reactor for neutron research, the Graphite Research Reactor, was completed by the Ferguson Construction Company. The first BNL research accelerator, the Van de Graaff Electrostatic Accelerator, contracted for by the General Electric Company, started its low-energy nuclear physics program in 1952, and the Cyclotron accelerator for medium-energy nuclear physics research, built by the Collins Radio Company, was finished also in 1952. Some thought it inauspicious that all three projects were plagued with technical and managerial troubles. Although it's not unreasonable to view this as an unfavorable start for the lab, it proved to be an invaluable training ground and actually demonstrated the strength and perseverance of Haworth, his crew, and the lab's top brass in weathering the storms and coming out humming success songs.

At the time, many blamed the adversity, mishaps, and hard days that were experienced on the AEC edict that the lab had to work through private companies. That constraint indeed caused a host of complications, both contractual and institutional in nature, plus some involving interpersonal relations. Since the AEC should have known that using private companies for these R&D projects would make things more difficult, why did they insist on it? Was it because the government believed that as a matter of policy, it should promote technology transfer from the labs to the private sector? Leland wondered about this. He knew the point made sense superficially from the government's perspective, simply because politically the public would easily buy this rather neat and tidy justification for the government to do such work. Yes, on the surface it sounded like an effective and desirable use of taxpayer dollars even though it was far from being anywhere near a generally workable practice that couldn't be easily contested. The truth of the matter is that the use of this approach during the war had strikingly vindicated its validity. The transfer of government-supported technology had worked amazingly well then, attested to by the fact that radar, nuclear energy, and a host of other new-fangled technologies had successfully found their way from government-sponsored conception and development to the industrial and commercial sectors of the country's economy. Thus was carried out and realized an extraordinary accomplishment, proving to be lucrative to the corporate world and productive for the post-war nation. Unfortunately, the government interpreted this success story as a sure-fire proof of the principle, and sought to extrapolate the idea beyond the war years. However, Haworth's years of experience at the lab, where he was responsible for such a wide range of R&D projects, had taught him differently and made him wary of stretching this wartime success story to a peace-time competitive economy. Doing basic research was a far cry from war's call to arms.

Leland brightened as he recalled those days now gone. Formidable obstacles stood in his way at every turn and the effort was trying, tiring, and exasperating – still, he loved every minute of it. A slight smile re-formed at the edge of his lips. They were indeed wondrous years, he thought, when one idea collided and integrated with another, and one project followed another in swift succession. On the heels of the instruments coming on-line came the creations and the discoveries, each more incredible than the one before. But this was a happy moment that couldn't be sustained, as it occurred to him that perhaps it was a unique time and experience, one that was difficult to imagine being repeated at any other time and place. What an immensely distressing thing that would be! His smile having vanished, he sat quietly meditating for a moment, a little anxious about both his future and the lab's. Then, seemingly without reason, his mind, after its emotion-packed meanderings, clicked back to the AEC and its insistence that the lab use private companies to build government projects. Although technology transfer is a worthy and praiseworthy government objective, it is nonetheless wrong to apply the notion to basic research. For R&D and its associated technology development to be effective, you need the capacity to expect and live with missteps and mistakes; the wherewithal to make fast changes of direction; and the ability to absorb unanticipated financial burdens, not as special circumstances but as normal ones. This situation is totally incompatible with making continuous performance gains and short-term profits. Under these conditions and requirements, it's easy to see why private sector companies would have a lot of difficulty with this type of work. They are geared to sustaining short-term profits and gains – for them it's the bottom line that counts. At their cores therefore, labs and companies are opposites, the one stressing the long term, the other the short term. Perhaps the extraordinary emergency and crisis situation of being in a life or death war made this arrangement work before, but in peacetime companies are not generally suited to the management of long-term, high-risk projects. It's a bad match and in the end not workable. But Leland knew that persuading the government of this would unfortunately be an almost impossible task – a bureaucracy set in its ways is as immovable as Mount Everest. But Leland had an even more intractable problem than a government set in its ways: he didn't have a ghost of a chance of persuading his scientist colleagues that there was even an issue here. They were so preoccupied with doing their science – their dear physics – that they could care less about the practical means of getting there. Seemingly controlled by the ivory tower mindset, they seemed to have no clue about how large-scale management worked. It was as if they were telling Leland, "Here's where we want to be and we don't give a damn how you get us there. Just do it, and if the government wants it their way, so be it." Leland was being squeezed between two resolute and inflexible giants, the government and the science community, and got to know first-hand how it felt to be between a rock and a hard place. As he thought about this, that special smile, oft repeated that morning, reappeared. Yes, he did manage the almost impossible task of finding a way to walk that oh so thin line between them. He got the job done and made BNL number one. Knowing all this, one might wonder how anyone could come to view Leland's time on the lab stage as anything short of brilliant. Remembering all this, he felt good inside, really proud of himself. He had an almost uncontrollable urge to beat his chest and cry out, *Hallelujah.* Yet this upbeat mood was coupled with sadness because deep down he knew that the self-centered science community would never give him the credit he deserved. They just didn't get it.

Yes, Leland thought, the late 1940's and early 1950's were great years for the lab and for him, but for the lab those years couldn't hold a candle to what was just around the next bend. The best, by far, was yet to come; and it wasn't just a gift from heaven – like diamonds falling from the sky for anyone to pluck. Although the sixties for BNL were a time of brilliance and success of the highest order, there would have to be difficult struggles and intricate entanglements to overcome to reach that end. Life, Leland discovered, insists that suffering and pain are unavoidable companions of true achievement; and that they have to be borne before the accolades could come pouring in. As it happened, he was the one chosen by fate to bear the brunt of the downside prior to the appearance of the upside. To do what he had to do and what he felt in his bones was right he had first to confront and then oppose the big and the famous. For that, he took the knocks and paid the price; but he also experienced the special thrill that can only come from doing good. As he sat there in the quiet, he couldn't quite picture himself in that role: Was it truly he that bucked the big man? Imagine that, he thought, he had really done it. Although Rabi was not the type to be trifled with, Leland had actually had the gumption to take him on, to win the day, and to live to tell the tale.

Rabi, a man who staunchly believed in an upper class of elite scientists, was, in line with his class, not one to suffer peons. But he was also a practical man, and in order to get along with those who did the work – the peons –he developed a practice of using common street lingo. Many were fooled by this ruse; but it was only a contrivance to mask that inner elitism that was the real Rabi. (Surprisingly, this deeply intelligent smallish big man considered Leland to be a peon, a useful one to be sure, but a peon nonetheless.) Despite subscribing to this un-American doctrine of class, which apparently grew out of his European roots, Rabi was of a separate breed from the ordinary run-of-the-mill snob. He was a true man of action and a man to be reckoned with; and aside from this singular personality blemish of being doctrinaire, for the most part he did have the right approaches and the right ideas. When Rabi said that the university style was the appropriate way for basic science, wasn't he right? When Rabi said that we didn't need large, conservative engineering divisions like the Berkeley Radlab to build machines like battleships to last through the ages, wasn't he right? And when Ernest Lawrence contemptuously proclaimed that the country's East just couldn't do the job, wasn't Rabi great when he looked Ernest straight in the eye and coolly sneered, screw you? Yes, that was Rabi at his finest. With confidence brimming over, for him, anything was possible. So what if Berkeley had a head start, and if Columbia and the other eastern universities had a long way to go to catch up, Rabi knew, from deep within his being, that he was unstoppable. How could he be wrong? He was "the man."

Then, in BNL's high-flying days of the fifties, came the difficult question of what position the lab should take vis-à-vis Berkeley – in particular, who should build the next big accelerator, this time a synchrotron, and what should its characteristics be? Rabi, ever the aggressor, held forth on an energy and size that would be in blatant in-your-face competition with the Berkeley Radlab. He proclaimed that BNL be bold, even be a little wild, and not take the safe and easy path but rather "go for the gold." Would anyone put himself on the line and suggest that Rabi could be wrong? Who would question a man of such eminence, who always seemed to be right? Who would take such a chance with his career, with his future? Rabi was spouting a line that had made him a winner many times; and indeed there was something to be said for his point of view – it made sense and sounded right as well. Nevertheless, in spite of his smartness and worldliness, as events and circumstances were to demonstrate, in this instance, Rabi wasn't right. But who was there to stop him, to tell him that he was wrong? Who was to prevent BNL from taking a step that would jeopardize the grand years that lay just ahead? To take that role, you had to stand up and be counted. As unlikely as it was to find such a type, Leland turned up as the man of the hour. This quiet gentlemanly man showed the steely stuff he was made of and proved up to task. He found the courage within himself to counter the big man. At great risk, he did the required but dangerous balancing act, he walked the tightrope, he swallowed fire, and he lived to tell of it. As these recollections raced through his mind, pride surged within him. It was a memory to treasure. He had done right and he had come out of it whole and with his dignity intact. Not many could claim that.

Still, he wondered now how he would be judged in the future. Although such considerations don't play a role when you're busy with the business of living, Leland had now come to a stage in his life when he found himself thinking of his name, his achievements, and how he would be remembered. But it was far too late to take a hand in shaping any of it. He recalled a saying he'd heard years earlier: "Too soon old and too late smart." How apt it was to what he was going through! It was only now, after he'd already lost control of events and circumstances, and when matters of legacy were in the hands of others only too eager to write their own versions of times past, that how he would be thought of became important to him. So, there he was on that quiet morning, in the twilight of his BNL career, thinking about his life, confused by a mixture of feelings that didn't seem to add up, and filled to the brim with emotion. Nothing seemed to make much sense. Nonetheless, he took great pride in his past judgments and the actions he had taken – it all turned out so well for the lab. However, that didn't assuage the deep concerns and doubts he had about how others would record his role for posterity, and more importantly, about how they would use the work he had done and the monuments and instruments he had left for them.

What had Leland done that was so great? As he mused about his role in BNL's affairs in those eventful early years of his administration, he kept coming back to his standing so steadfastly and daringly in opposition to Rabi. He remembered vividly Rabi's insistent desire – almost a deep-seated psychological need – to go head to head with Berkeley on which lab would be first to go to ten billion electron volts, the highest energy imaginable in the late 1940's. As was his way, Rabi was full of emotion. Be bold, he had always said, and boldness is what he wanted then. He wanted BNL to take on anything that stood in its way from jumping straight to the top. He just had to beat out those snotty westerners. But nobody else wanted a knockdown drag-out fight, with a winner and a loser. No, both the government and the science community leaned strongly toward compromise, with everyone winning. So, Rabi didn't get his way, and when that happened, he seethed. He wasn't the type of man who could forget and go on. He was known to have said, I could have spit blood. That was the way he felt and the way he was to respond. Ruled by his emotions, he was thinking neither rationally nor clearly.

The truth was that Rabi didn't really know what was going on. By not being fully up-to-date on the technology advances being made at the lab, those nitty-gritty details, he wasn't able to see the bigger picture. He wasn't all wrong, but without appreciating the details, how could he be expected to root out and discern the best way to go? He was mesmerized by and too focused on today's battle, while forgetting perhaps the more important need to prepare for tomorrow's. When you're ruled by vanity and not by rationality, you shouldn't be at the helm. Fortunately for the lab, however, Leland was there, as if fate had demanded his presence. It was written that the lab should go right to the top, and destiny had assigned Leland the role of taking it there. It could have been Rabi leading the charge, but "the man" was beginning to exhibit signs of falling from that high horse he had ridden for so long. The toll taken by years of battle was beginning to show. Leland, on the other hand, was different. He was in his prime. He did know what was going on – what the lab needed to do and what its technological capabilities were. He was on top of things. By mustering the strength needed for that critical moment in BNL's history, he became the man of the hour. It was Haworth who could and did bring it all together. He had learned from the master and followed his example and teachings; he also tapped into Rabi's adventurousness. But he went just so far, judiciously stopping before falling off the cliff, as Rabi, at this time of his life, might well have done. Injecting realism into Rabi's vision, he came to terms with the leading lab of the time, as the Berkeley Radlab was reputed to be. In doing that, in spite of Rabi's wishes, he instilled in BNL's scientists, engineers, and the rest of the staff optimism in their future and the will to go on full-steam ahead. Yes, they had become believers. Leland had won them over. Because he didn't push for the moon, they now had full confidence that they could build what Leland wanted them to build. At that time, they would have followed him anywhere.

But Haworth's foresight, his genius, didn't end there. He saw where others didn't. He sensed what could be, where others could only follow their noses or allow themselves to be led unquestioning by the bluster of the Rabi types of this world. How he did this is the essence of the mystery of the mystique of the leader, and will likely remain a mystery till hell freezes over. There is no hyperbole here, for we are asking our leaders literally to foresee things. How can one be expected to sense what might be gained, and then risk sometimes everything on the chance that it will turn out the way it was envisioned or at least be in the ballpark? You'd think that of all the types that might succeed in such a capacity scientists should be perfect for the role. After all, crossing frontiers into the unknown is their raison d'être. But, alas, they are not, and a perfect example of this is when it comes to choosing the right technologies for project building: With the contending possibilities put right in front of them, scientists act as conservatively as the typical administrator, no better and perhaps even a little worse. Maybe this is because they have their eyes so focused on the prize at hand – doing their experiments – they tend to lose sight of the long-term value to both science and society of pushing forward the frontiers of new technology. Leland, however, though a scientist, was of a different sort. This became evident when fate stepped into his life to test his mettle. His inspired sense of when to hold and when to fold proved to be decisive for both the lab and him. At the same time as conservatism caused him to accept a compromise with Berkeley, a defiant spirit and an audacious derring-do drew him to encourage and nurture the fantastic 1952 invention of the alternating gradient (AG) for synchrotrons. Despite the opposition around him, work on this principle, discovered on his watch, was given the go-ahead on his say-so. He said to the three brilliant men who conceived it – Ernest Courant, Hartland Snyder, and Stanley Livingston – *keep going and make it happen.* The science world watched, many skeptically, as Leland transformed, in less than a decade, a gleam in the eye into mortar and steel, and thence into experimentation and the knowledge of the Gods. What a balancing act it was! Borrowing from Peter to pay Paul so as to assure that the Cosmotron would keep churning out data, while the Alternating Gradient Synchrotron (AGS) that would dramatically alter the course of physics was eating funds at an ever-rising clip. But he saw it through and came to taste of the fruit of the victorious. So it was that chance happened to dangle that AGS diamond before him, and although it was hard to see whether it was genuine, fortune was dancing brightly before his eyes as he instinctively lunged for it. Later, as he would look at the sparkling gem he was holding, he knew he had been lucky, very lucky. Of course, the gem would be passed on to others and to future generations, but Leland would always be able to recall that sterling moment when he had held it in the palm of his own hand.

As Leland played out in the video of his mind the details of what had happened, he was once again able to experience the heady moments of 1952. Contrary to what Rabi wanted, Haworth, as the lab leader, had pushed ahead on his two to three billion-volt Cosmotron, while Berkeley was given the higher energy machine of about six billion volts to build. But, as part of the deal, BNL would get their accelerator first, while Berkeley would have to wait for theirs. What an insightful decision that had been. For being first in this instance was to be the key to the lab's rapid rise to stardom, just as being second was to make of Berkeley a falling star that might have shone more brightly but didn't. It's strange how easy it is to pass up the important things in life. Some, including Rabi, thought that getting to the higher energy was the real prize. This may even have been a not unreasonable position to take, but life has a habit of playing tricks on us mere mortals, and those who took that position turned out to be wrong. Different from the others, Leland, taking his turn at rolling the dice, came out a winner: being first was by far the better choice. He could remember as if it were yesterday that day in May 1952 when the machine so casually crossed over the one billion-volt historic milestone, and his heart skipped a beat. "Well, I'll be damned," John Blewett, a young scientist who was to play a significant role as events unfolded, had murmured, as if to himself, but he was actually speaking for everyone watching the event cheerily in the Cosmotron control room that day via the marvel of an electronic oscilloscope. What elation had ensued! But, as happy and simple as the moment appeared to be, it was full of irony. The really important story of 1952 was a different one, hidden beneath the crazily festive hullabaloo of the Cosmotron coming alive. Even as the Cosmotron was being born, although unheard, its death knell was being sounded at exactly the same bittersweet moment. The funeral arrangements and burial would have to wait for some time to come, because for many years the Cosmotron would prove to be a fine scientific instrument. It would realize experiments illuminating the wonderful world of the pi meson, one of the almost unimaginably tiny elementary particles that live for a flash and then disappear forever. Nevertheless, in spite of the good work it was to do, the Cosmotron was doomed in 1952. The reality of modern science is that all technologies must give way when new and better ones come to call, and it was the Cosmotron's fate that its successor technology was being conceived at the very moment of its own realization. The technology of alternating gradients, which opened the door to strong-focusing synchrotrons like the AGS, had such conceptual beauty and practical value that when it worked like a charm as the fifties came to a close, the weak-focusing Cosmotron just didn't have a chance. For Berkeley's Bevatron, that big machine that Rabi had lost out on, fate was even harsher. Being of the same fading technology as the Cosmotron, its demise was foretold many years before its birth in 1956. So it turned out that the fifties did truly end up being the Haworth decade; and all that came to pass in that thrilling and spirit-stirring rise of BNL was mysteriously embodied in the instinctive foresight that was Leland's genius.

Although overshadowed by the glorious coming of the Cosmotron, the real news made in that wonderful summer of 1952 was the birth of an idea for a revolutionary new accelerator technology that was a magnificent example of classic, beautiful science in action. First, a conception was born in the mind's imagination. Then, it flowered into the tapestry of a mathematical kaleidoscope, which when turned and turned led not so many years later, just as the sixties opened, to the emergence of a new type of synchrotron. Strong focusing entered and weak focusing had to give way - one was in, the other out. Such is the miracle of modern science and technology that this new synchrotron, the AGS, had ten times the energy of the Cosmotron, didn't cost much more, and opened wide the doors to a vast unknown. Many of the imaginings and anticipations of science, which were hitherto only men's dreams, would now be open to realization and investigation. When it happened, when the first synchrotrons based on the new alternating gradient technology – the AGS, in addition to the almost identical machine named the Proton Synchrotron (PS) at CERN – burst on the scene and brought science to an altogether new level of potential experimentation, the physics world was replete with happy faces and hopeful hearts. As a memorial to this great discovery, and as a symbol of its immense significance, the moment of its realization coincided, and not just coincidentally, with the moment of the creation of a new branch of physics. The field of high-energy physics, spawned from nuclear physics, was born. Actually, this was only the beginning because following from this imaginative invention advanced research in sciences all over the map would reap the benefits. With the ensuing progress in AG as well as other accelerator technologies, experiments in Chemistry, Biology, Materials, Medicine, and Industry, that couldn't be done before, became feasible. But all this was years away from realization; thus, as he sat in his small, informal office early in 1961, Leland hadn't the least inkling of such possibilities. In fact, the AGS, which generated its first beam about a half-year earlier, would only be formally dedicated in the fall of that year and the great physics experiments were still a year or too off. It's therefore not too surprising that as the sixties got underway no one could predict such a far-reaching outcome. Any foreshadowing of successes Leland may have felt about the future was all whimsical speculation and daydreaming.

Just as Leland couldn't predict the rich and boundless scientific future that would stem from his leadership at BNL in those pregnant days of the fifties, so he also wasn't able to foretell the black days that were to come to the lab less than a decade hence. Nevertheless, he had a sense of foreboding, although he couldn't tell whether it arose because he was being treated so shabbily, so disgracefully, and so unfairly; or whether it was because he was truly picking up cautionary signs and early warnings of what lay on the horizon. In any case, what could he do? He was being cast aside like an old pair of shoes. *C'est la vie*, he rationalized. At that moment, on that cold, sunny morning, with his thoughts roaming freely, he hadn't yet made any irrevocably final decision about leaving the lab. Should he pull the plug and remove any remaining doubts? He felt trapped – caught up in an inner struggle between right and wrong. So mixed-up was he that he didn't even know whether he should be considering himself, the lab, or both. Then there was the Goldhaber question. Even though there was reason enough to believe he would take leave of Upton, and sooner rather than later, it was still only a conjecture that Maurice would be his successor. Would that be a good thing, either for him or for the lab? Would it be bad? Should he stay and fight? Should he simply cut the cord, break the bonds built up over all those years, and let it be? Should he finally pack up and leave the lab to its own fate, sans Haworth? It's hard to know what to do and what's right. Well, he thought, why bother to beat a dead horse? After all, not much, if anything, remained in his hands. To wait and see seemed the sole alternative left to him. Only time would tell. With all this vagueness and lack of clarity about the future, his and the lab's, it wasn't surprising that Leland felt considerable uneasiness about his meeting with Goldhaber not more than an hour away.

Rabi always seemed to be on Leland's mind. He seemed to have his hand in everything. Perhaps of all the reasons Leland could come up with to explain his almost certain decision to leave the lab soon, Rabi was foremost. He tried to piece together the rather strained meeting he had had with Rabi a week earlier. With a picture of Rabi's swaggering entrance in his mind, he recalled what a difficult man he was to follow, his words and movements swerving this way and that and darting about here and there. Even with his short, stubby frame, he was quite a presence. His dress bordered on the formal but it was his face that caught Leland unawares that afternoon and quite unbalanced him. It was bright, red, shining, and had an unmistakably confrontational spirit. The muscles around his cheeks and nose were almost twitching with excitement. His flashing eyes were daggers piercing right through Leland, his lips sneering at him. Towering over Leland from below, he was dominant no matter how you chose to see the scene. Yes, Rabi, "the man," was laughing at him. Finally, he slowed down a bit and sat down opposite Leland, facing him, looking him straight in the eyes.

In an instant, as he stared at Rabi, Leland knew what the bottom line would be. Actually, the dreaded perception had begun to take shape subliminally well before that turning-point moment. Probably it was when he received the telephone call. Would Leland be available to see Mister Importance on his next visit to the lab? How about next Thursday? Would 2:00 PM in Leland's office be okay? Did he have a choice, Leland had thought to himself whimsically? Would anyone dream of refusing? The conversation with Rabi's secretary was quick and business-like, in stark contrast to the human impact that lay behind it. On the spot, it occurred to Leland that 4:00 PM would be better for him. For a second there, he considered making such a suggestion. "Would 4:00 be okay?" he imagined himself saying. But he quickly thought better of it and let it go. You don't play around with City Hall. If Rabi said 2:00, then 2:00 it would have to be. And when the clock struck 2:00 on that winter's day, there he was. The moment of truth for Leland had arrived. There they were face to face, warily eyeing each other. An unpromising and worrisome silence filled the void that lasted only a few seconds, but it seemed like an eternity. Leland was at a loss. Should he act? Should he jump right in? No, he ascertained, it wasn't his show – so he waited. When Rabi was good and ready to lay his cards on the table, the curtain was raised and the performance began. Rabi was an outspoken, direct, and no-holds-barred man. When he spoke, he didn't mince words or beat around the bush. Still, what shot out of his mouth, when it came, took Leland aback. It shook him terribly. He still could feel the adrenaline surge he had. "When do you think would be a good time for you to go?" Rabi bluntly asked. What an opening line that was! Caught off guard, Leland blurted out something embarrassing, something like, "What do you mean?" It was a juvenile reaction, but it did give him a moment to collect himself. Rabi didn't clarify the question, but just smiled enigmatically, correctly presuming that Leland knew exactly what was meant. Leland wondered whether Rabi knew about Ramsey's suggestion that Leland become an AEC Commissioner. The consensus seemed to be that Rabi knew everything, so, why shouldn't he know that? It even crossed Leland's mind that Rabi could have encouraged it, or even instigated it. (Populated by complicated, maneuvering men, what a tangled, unfathomable world this is!) Naturally, such a conjecture would be hard to confirm. One way or the other, would it matter much anyway? What's the difference, he thought? Sure, it could matter at some point, if he had to take into account Ramsey's trustworthiness. But why have negative thoughts about Ramsey, a man who had served Leland's interests well. What did it matter why he did it! Besides, he was a good guy! For that matter, what Rabi was doing was not so bad for Leland either. So, whatever their true intentions might be, Ramsey and Rabi had placed the ball squarely in Leland's court. With a great opportunity at hand, and with only his pride to put a damper in his spirits and hope for things to come, it was solely up to Leland. The next move was his.

Whoever stood pulling the strings the reality was that circumstances were pointing with increasing certainty toward a big change in Leland's life. It would have been unthinkable six months earlier, when the spectacular success of the AGS turn-on took place, that Leland would be leaving the Director's job, let alone leaving the lab. But those six months had been eventful indeed, and what had been unthinkable then had become inevitable now. Although he sensed the winds of change in the air, the substance and manner of Rabi's plain talking shocked and hurt him. The proposal was straightforward and undeniable, more like an order: Go! You've done your job. Now it's time for a change. Those terrible words coming from Rabi's lips were a stunning blow. It was one of those rare times in a man's life when his thought pattern becomes turned on its end. From that moment on, the lab as his life dropped in priority, and Leland began seriously considering and even planning his life-altering move. In that short and meticulously played out twenty-minute discussion, which gave Leland the surrealistic impression of having been rehearsed, Rabi pushed him a lot closer than he ever thought he'd be to taking an action. From that point forward, a new mind-set was created in Leland, and he started to imagine himself in those hoped-for greener pastures of Washington.

Although his meeting with "the man" did seem to be the key to Haworth's change of thinking and ultimate BNL departure, Leland was never entirely persuaded of how important it really was. Was Rabi only a trigger that set off a wish Leland had harbored anyway, or did the puppet-master really fashion the whole show? Despite being circumstantial, there was indeed evidence suggesting that Rabi was decisive. It was actually true that, to save face, he offered up to Rabi at their meeting the little white lie that he was already considering leaving the lab. In addition, he even agreed that April sounded like a good time. He found it hard to imagine himself being so witless and disingenuous, but, yes, he had really said these things. Rabi, the small man with big footsteps, had that effect on people, making them shrink and bend to his will, whether they wanted to or not. Nevertheless, despite what Leland said, he wasn't a hundred percent certain that he would do it. When Rabi left, and he was free of his masterfully coercive and irresistible influence, he remembered thinking that often you say things just because the moment demands it, not because you positively mean them.

Leland had always had his doubts about Rabi. He respected the power Rabi wielded, but he didn't really like him. He certainly had never trusted the man. But when Rabi struck, as many before Leland had experienced, you knew he was a man of substance. Power oozed from his pores as well as from his sharp, incisive tongue. In those years, Rabi ruled like a godfather. For that, he was given the requisite respect and got paid his dues. He certainly had a great impact on Leland's life and career. Although he tried, Leland just couldn't get out of his mind the manner in which the Rabi Meeting swiftly entered its denouement and ended. He recalled still trying to grasp the significance of what was going on when, with unexpected suddenness, the discussion came to an abrupt end. Rabi had finished whatever he was up to, and that meant the meeting was over. Leland felt an overpowering dissatisfaction. The meeting had been so efficient, so quick, and so decisive. He thought afterward that it had been too efficient, that there should have been more consideration given, more give and take. But that's neither here nor there, for when it was over, even though no formal decision was taken, the new course for Leland's life was essentially set. When everything that had to be said was said, Leland felt somewhat unfulfilled. He still wasn't quite ready to call it quits. But Rabi was a no-nonsense type. He believed that he had balanced the ledger with Leland. Nothing more had to be given and nothing more expected. So, when the business at hand was completed, there was no reason to prolong the meeting. No formalities were needed: There was neither a general understanding nor even a handshake. It was a most trying thing for Leland to accept, but when Rabi walked out the door, he knew his time at the lab was past history. And that's the way it was – when the spring of that year came around, he did leave with Washington as his destination. Clearly Rabi had accomplished what he had set out to do – implanting in Leland a new mind-set. Yes, he recalled thinking as Rabi left his office, it might be best for all if he were to go.

Now, as Leland was waiting for Maurice to arrive, he focused his memory on those few minutes he had with the big man. He was pushed to a big decision about his future, but he still couldn't quite figure out why. Whatever the reason, the truth was that he had to have some relief. He needed to get away from it all and especially from all the pressure he was under – with reasons for the stress ranging from professional obstructions to his family's health. Still, he wanted to know why. It puzzled him and even irritated him a bit. He so much wanted answers that made some sense. Perhaps the answer lay in that he wanted a change in his life all along. But, since he lacked the singleness of purpose and the ability to be publicly fully forthright and frank about such personal matters, he couldn't just say it openly and get it over with. No, because of the way he was, someone would have to do it for him. In fact, now that he was giving this possibility some credence, he even recalled doing things that could be interpreted as provocations. Yet there was something missing in that whole line of argument because the actual decision was unquestioningly made by Rabi and implemented through his force of will. That's the way it happened and nothing could change that reality. Even if Rabi was the primary instigator, this dissatisfied him no end and offended him as well. Maybe, all this grasping at straws and overly complicated reasoning was only to hide what really got his goat. Simply put, what Leland wanted to know was why Rabi was so set against him that it pushed him to go to the extreme he had? He had ached over this question time and time again, but nothing seemed to click. It was and remained a puzzlement. Then, as he sat quietly waiting for his apparent successor to arrive, the answer came to him – without announcing itself and without ceremony. Finally, he got it. In that instant of enlightenment, he knew why it was so important to Rabi that Leland should leave the lab. It was so simple that he smiled to himself yet again, and casually, self-satisfyingly, wondered why he hadn't happened upon it earlier and more easily. In fact, he chided himself, why had he not seen it over these many years? He asked himself whether it would have made any difference even if he had figured it out earlier. No, he was convinced that he wouldn't have acted on it anyway, for it would require that he compromise his life's principles, and that he would never do, not for Rabi, not for anyone, not for anything. He was sure of that. Even though it didn't matter much that he now knew, in that moment of discovery, he was very pleased with himself – the puzzle was solved and pride filled his being.

So he sat there smug, imagining Rabi's thoughts and logic, and pretending to read his mind. He was happy in his newfound knowledge and happy in his demonstrated perspicacity. Pondering the clues that had been there all along – but that he had failed to read – Leland could now, finally, piece together the many seemingly unconnected observations and experiences all leading to the decline in the boss-man's use for him. And what was the key to the puzzle that preyed on him – the question of why he was cut loose? It starts with the simple fact that BNL was in a big fix. As the sixties came into being, *doing physics* and *doing technology* were in a bitter fight over a pot of money not growing fast enough. A choice in priorities had to be made, and it's not hard to guess what that was to be. Actually the problem was already in its incipient phase in the fifties, but, at that time, what the AG concept offered for the future was too good to pass up. In that early war over the budget, Leland was exposed and showed his true colors. Rabi knew him well and knew he was of a type that stood on principle and wouldn't budge; he wasn't a man to acquiesce and give in and end up dead in the water. Leland was exceedingly useful then, and worked well with Rabi. But times had changed, and life had passed Leland by. A new day was at hand, and new boys came to rule the roost. As for Rabi, he was getting on and succumbed to the incoming new order. It was now to be: *physics uber alles*! Henceforth, accelerator technology and its experts would have to play second fiddle to the class of experimental scientists and their supporting theorists who were readying themselves to emerge as the power center for Big Science. So it was that Leland came to understand: no, he wouldn't and couldn't go along with that, and so he became dangerous to the new establishment – ergo, he had to be let go.

How many times had Leland heard it emphasized that it was the experiments and their results that were the really important contributors to scientific progress? Naturally, there shouldn't be much disagreement on that point because we all know that it is the results that count the most. On the other hand, Leland countered in his self-argument, were the ends always that much more important than the means? But it wasn't just an emotionless argument in logic that Leland found himself in. There were flesh and blood taking part, men with desires, dreams, and ambitions. They would do anything to have their day and come out winners – even cheat, lie, and betray their unsuspecting friends. As he fought through the intricate issue from its many angles, an understanding was taking shape in Leland's mind: the pooh-bahs were doing no more than judging the relative value of doing their dearly loved experiments with the tedious, unexciting, yet easy-to-handle building of accelerators, concluding that technology was getting far too much attention. That they didn't like at all. They couldn't abide it and would have to make big changes. In the end, it became a classic struggle of man versus man. Some years later, when the dust settled over the field of battle, the experimenters were triumphant: the esteem of accelerator physics and its practitioners was lowered; and the losers' heads were bowed in obeisance to the victors. Leland, then perched atop the NSF, couldn't believe that it had all turned out that way. But the evidence was overwhelming, and couldn't be denied. Still, he kept asking himself why they had to do it. Could they have been afraid that the technologists and the machine builders might get strong enough to take over and lord it over them? Could they have been thinking that society might look on new technology as more valuable and so were compensating – in the psychological sense – for that possibility? Whatever the reasons behind their beliefs and behavior were, the gratuitous downgrading of the accelerator techies became a fact at the labs and had to be lived with.

Leland had actually heard it said that it was the experimental physicists who got the ideas while the accelerator physicists just implemented them. What a put-down! It was such a silly thing to think, and even worse to say. However, it demonstrated that a very important social line had been crossed. A rift had come to pass between two segments of a previously well-oiled social machine – if the parts of the team worked together, they could do wonders; but if they frittered away their energy in opposition, they could destroy each other. He wanted to step in to prevent what he feared could be a long way down for the field he loved. But he knew that was a pipe dream. As he sat quietly on that cold winter's day in 1961, considering the different social classes at the lab and the interrelationships among them, he began to see a historical picture emerging. In the past, one physicist or a very small number working in a compact well-tuned group could both develop the instruments and do the experiments. No distinction was made then between the builder and the experimenter. But today, specialization, coming from the out-of-this-world technological progress made, demanded a division of labor. It demanded that a scientist make an a priori choice of disciplines. You could choose to do experiments or you could choose to design and build accelerators, but for the most part you could not do both. Leland knew that this natural course of specialization would strengthen and intensify over the coming years and that class infighting would follow suit. It didn't have to happen, but unfortunately it appeared to be a phenomenon very hard to avoid; and sure enough that's the way it was. He began to fear for the future of nuclear physics and its spin-off, elementary particle physics, or high-energy physics, as it would come to be called. This strongly exaggerated viewpoint that basic research was the highest of the high – a defensive posture to be sure – had always given him pause. Why were proud and highly successful scientists making such an unwarranted, unnecessary, and ultimately untrue claim? To Leland, research was research; one type wasn't better or worse than another. He had always found it difficult to make the distinctions others made between applied and basic research, as if one were better than another. It seemed to him to be nothing more than empty rhetoric. He knew full well that at the heart of the matter, the difference was artificial – it had more to do with subjective social reality, people's beliefs and prejudices, than with objective physical reality. This became transparent when you looked at particular cases, at least to those who deigned to look. Technologists worked in applied fields like superconductivity, lasers, materials, energy, accelerators, and particle detectors. Did it diminish such research if it was labeled applied rather than basic, or derivative rather than fundamental? Could you even tell the difference? Was work on superconductivity basic or applied? Was laser physics fundamental or derivative physics? Was materials research basic or applied? Was nuclear energy research fundamental or derivative physics? Was the discovery of AG focusing basic or applied research? Was the invention and development of the spark chamber or the bubble chamber or the cloud chamber basic or applied physics? To Leland, being able to pose the question in this way was tantamount to proof – a prima facie case – that scientists who claimed that one branch of physics was more valuable than another based on this distinction, and that one physicist was more important than another because he worked in the right field, were in reality just seeking some sort of higher social status within the academic community. He wasn't happy with this conclusion and he didn't come upon it easily, but his naturally rational way of thinking forced him to it. He couldn't disregard the historical facts and just wish them away. They were there for all to see. He worried about what lay ahead. It seemed that the forces of history were inexorably pushing physics toward some sort of appointment with destiny. And there was nothing, nothing at all, Leland could do about it.

As he became aware of all of this over time, as his understanding broadened, Leland became very troubled. Foremost he was concerned about the future of Big Science, but there was also the question of the personal choice he had made. Not only had he chosen the fork leading to accelerator building, but he had also chosen to focus on the management of the enterprise. Why that role should have ended up being lowest on the totem pole would continue to amaze Leland far into the future. Wasn't the management of science, which had outgrown the capacity of universities to handle it, the reason for the creation of the national labs in the first place? Hadn't science management been the essential ingredient in the successful conclusion of the Manhattan Project? And wasn't that the model for Big Science? Of course it was, so how was one to explain the seeming contradiction? Thinking along these lines, Leland finally began to see the light. He began to understand and to appreciate what Rabi was getting at in their short meeting, which turned out to be quite an education for Leland. He began then to understand the real essence of why there was no alternative but to leave. Rabi had said that Leland had been a great director and had served his purpose at the lab. What Leland now well appreciated was that, although he had been right for his time, what with the AGS about to become a reality, a new type of director might be a better match for the coming winds of change. The new director would emphasize a new era at the lab, one that had three top priorities, experiment, experiment, and experiment. And Leland, filling in the blanks, just wouldn't do for this new type of environment, being, as he was, tied to accelerator building and accelerator physicists. There was his answer, simple, precise, to the point, and devastatingly shocking. Rabi, the crowd in the Physics Department, and the users wanted somebody whose sympathy for experimenters was assured. An appropriate motto for that period could easily have been, users über alles.

Leland should have been able to pick up much earlier the clues signaling the all-importance of the users. Although nobody would come right out and say it to him in plain language, sans the natural tendency to euphemism, there were a variety of hints along the way. He recalled the difficult time he had trying to juggle the effort of doing experiments to the fullest on the declining Cosmotron and of readying the lab for the new era of the AGS. Demands for budget priority and for personnel priority had become the battleground for a developing class war. The demands from influential experimenters for time and priority at the Cosmotron were one important focal point of the struggle, which pulled Leland this way and that, and would have broken the back of one less hardy. Yes, there was great tension at the Cosmotron. The Bevatron had come on at Berkeley with more than twice the energy. The scrimping on upkeep and maintenance and the tendency to shift funds from machine to experiment had led to innumerable Cosmotron faults and shutdowns. The experimenters, under great personal pressure, needed someone to take out their frustrations on and found such a man in the Cosmotron Department head, George Collins. Collins was originally a researcher and, not quite appreciating the demands on him that would come from his management responsibilities, he tried to keep up his work on experiments at the same time. This was a terrible misjudgment on his part as well as on Leland's. For, as a result, George, as the head of the accelerator, became a perfect target for disaffected experimenters. On the one hand, he was looked upon as a turncoat siding with the accelerator sector. On the other hand, trying to do two full-time jobs, running the accelerator and doing an experiment, took everything out of him and made him weak and vulnerable. Thus, Collins had innocently chosen the worst of two worlds. As an accelerator representative, he was on the losing side of the incipient class struggle, while, as an experimenter, he was viewed as a traitor. He was in a sorry plight indeed. What happened next was a painful and insidious letter campaign against Collins that would make a seasoned politician blush. Collins was done for, dead meat, as they say. Still, it was he who had made his bed and, fair or unfair, he would have to lie in it. He would have to suffer the consequences of the choices he had made. Although he was a good friend of Leland's, the pressure on Leland was too great and he had to let Collins take the fall, reluctantly relieving him of his job in early 1960. But this couldn't and didn't solve the real problem, although it didn't have such a bad outcome in the short run, for all that happened was the siphoning of funds from Cosmotron operations into Cosmotron experiments. Although it also made running the machine more trying by substantially increasing the number of faults and shutdowns, the prevailing accelerator-world circumstances assured that the Cosmotron was going downhill anyway. Why not therefore squeeze as much as possible out of the experimental program before it was thrown over and replaced when the higher energy AGS, lying in wait, came on line?

As it turned out, the trouble at the Cosmotron was only a harbinger of the truly bad days to come. Who could have been expected to foresee, without the benefit of hindsight, that its real significance was merely as a training ground? It gave the troops the experience they needed to hone their battle skills and readiness, establish their positions, and prepare themselves mentally, with the appropriately ruthless attitudes, for the bitter, destructive warfare that lay on the threshold of eruption. The hostilities were actually to blast forth a few years later, when the experimenters, while doing their brilliantly conceived and unprecedented experiments at the AGS, would reach their peak strength. With their power towering over the meager strength of the undisciplined, leaderless accelerator class, they were willing and ready to sacrifice BNL's future so that they could eke out what turned out to be a little more advancement for the careers of a few of the elite users. Other than the suffering for so many that came of it, that's all they got. It was a bloody useless war. It was self-annihilating, with no point to it, and certainly no glory waiting at the end. There was only the ruination of a once-great BNL, the lab Rabi and Haworth had together created and set on its dream-like course. But of such consequences, Leland knew nothing. Only the fates had access to the knowledge of what lay before him, and they guarded their secrets with the tenacity of gods. No man of woman born could pry them loose before the time of reckoning came. Leland only knew of the beginning moments of the bad times. He had lived through them and had even been party to them. Even so, he had only a shadowy sense as well as an ill feeling and vague foreboding that no good would come of it. He could see no further than that. Although he had passed through a period when men's wickedness, corruptibility, and sinning nature were beginning to break through their skins, he was blind to its ultimate destructive possibilities – it turned out to be just the tip of the iceberg. The rest – the worst – was yet to come.

Emerging from his sad and full-of-regrets trance, still in the midst of waiting for Maurice to arrive, Leland knew he had finally glimpsed the bigger picture of the emerging class struggle between experimenters and builders. Furthermore, he came to appreciate more the part he played in the developing drama. Yes, now it was as clear as a bell. Tagged as a builder, and with the power at the lab radically shifted toward the side of the experimenters, he simply couldn't continue on as the strong and influential Director he was. He now recognized the somewhat cruel irony that he had played a key part in formalizing, strengthening, and fomenting this class struggle, as well as in his own weakening. True, he had been an unwitting actor, but that wasn't of much comfort. His only consolation was that he could now fit the pieces of the puzzle together. In the wake of the Collins-Cosmotron fiasco, in 1959, Leland had merged BNL's old Cosmotron Division and new AGS Division into a unified Accelerator Department. On the face of it, that sounded good, strengthening the lab's accelerator effort that was so important to its future. But there was another side to the coin. For, at the same time, the Cosmotron and AGS experimenters were being united and melded into a strengthened Physics Department. As it turned out, the experimenters became a strong, coherent force, while the accelerator staff couldn't hack it and, without a power-laden leader unifying them, always seemed to be at each other's throats. They were forever fighting over the crumbs allotted them by the new lab regime, some going to the Cosmotron, some to the AGS, and even fewer being pumped into the development of accelerator technology for the lab's future. Thus, although at the time Leland did not see the full impact and consequences of his seemingly sensible administrative action, it would serve primarily to fan the flames of class warfare and set the stage for future strife. It would soon bring times that would be filled with class jealousy and hostility – between experimenters and builders, between AGS and Cosmotron, and between technology and machine operations – and it would ultimately doom the lab to a life on the edge of failure. But, bringing forth a man's capacity to ignore an impending nightmare, Leland, for the moment, was able to hold any negative thoughts of the future at bay. By pushing such thoughts aside, he could revel in the notion that he had seen through Rabi's scheme of marginalizing accelerator influence by concentration and isolation. How could anyone not be happy with that? Here was a special moment of private satisfaction that he was experiencing. With no one to see it, the muscles of his face almost involuntarily shaped the outward features of an inner smile. He was filled to the brim with vanity. How pleased he was with himself! True, it was too late for him to be able to do anything constructive or useful. He was now almost sure of that. Perhaps that even added to his feeling of placidness and contentment. Knowledge does really make one feel in control, he had thought, even if it is knowledge that one can't figure out how to use. The catbird seat, although one of knowledge and not one of power, is still quite an appetizing place to be. What a perfect moment for Goldhaber to arrive, he thought, as Maurice walked through the open door of his office and closed it behind him.

2. The Greater They Are, the Harder They Fall

Maurice was Rabi's man. He was much like Rabi. Maybe that's why Rabi picked him to be the next BNL Director. They came from the same stock, rose in life the same way, and made the same choices. They had the same spirit and zest for life. They both liked a turn of phrase, a double entendre, repartee, and an off-color reference. Irony was natural to them; it was in their bones. Their philosophical outlooks were hard to tell apart, as were their predispositions towards life's desires. And they both believed in the elite scientist. In this class, their class, were the wisest, the smartest, and the best. They were destined to lead, and even more, they were meant to lead. The only difference between them was that Rabi was the puppet master, while Maurice was the puppet.

As Leland faced Maurice across his desk, both were smiling, wearing their masks of deceit, but Leland's quickly became a memory, as the sudden insight of a Rabi-Goldhaber alliance began to take shape in his mind. He actually became sure of it the moment he saw Goldhaber's face. Perhaps it was the smile, that self-satisfying smile he knew so well, that made it sure. It seemed that the ironic smile Leland had worn only minutes before had been mysteriously transferred to Maurice. Oh, how quickly, without warning, self-assuredness and smugness can turn to tentativeness and self-doubt. Now he finally knew what lay under the surface that the varnished veneer couldn't hide from him anymore. The story, as it turned out, had a more sinister edge than he had thought just moments earlier – it was nothing less than a conspiracy against him. This new revelation caused a shot of adrenaline to pump into his system and made him squirm. The whole business made him sad. But he wouldn't let it get him down – he would push on and see the game through to its destined end. Although Leland had known the gist of it much earlier, having guessed the surface outline of the scheme, he didn't pick up what lay under the façade, the all-important *why* of it. That's what he really wanted to know, and now, he thought, he had a good shot at it.

There were many signals to be recalled from out of the past and analyzed. In a rapid sequence of mental images, he reviewed the situation and wondered how he could have missed it. He brought back how the year before Rabi had supported Leland's notion of making peace by formally partitioning accelerator and nuclear/high energy physics into two equal power centers. As this was uncharacteristic of Rabi, who would always favor the position that true physicists lead and accelerator people follow, Leland now realized that there was even more than the principle of divide and conquer involved. How could he have been so dim-witted and simple-minded? Why hadn't he turned his brain full-tilt on the matter then, when it counted most? Why hadn't he asked himself the reason Rabi would apparently agree to give accelerator physics equal status to what was considered true physics? Although it was self-evident to him that it should be so, he shouldn't have presumed that it was the same for Rabi and his ilk. He had been so slow in grasping the truth. But, as they say, better late than never! Actually, when it happened, it did so with surprising suddenness, just as Maurice wearing his cat-ate-the-mouse grin entered his office and took his place across from him. It was then that the instant of insight arrived – and when it did, the clouds dissipated, the sun shone through, and all became clear. Now he had it, a year late, but he finally understood. It was Leland's neck that Rabi was after.

Although what Rabi really wanted was to divide builders and experimenters so that when the right moment arrived, those pulling the strings, when it suited them best, could let the accelerator-labeled ax fall, the only way to get there was over Leland's dead body. Leland could kick himself for being so dumb. Yet, even when faced with overwhelming facts, he still didn't want to believe that it could be so. How could scientists, of all people, be so two-faced? But, try as he might to self-argue against the point, there was no getting around it – that's the way it was. It was the way destiny had commanded it to be.

Armed with this knowledge, the events of the past years paraded before him, luminous where before they were dark. It wasn't hard for Leland now to see the truth – it virtually smacked him in the face as he gazed at Goldhaber. What a fool he'd been! Rabi had worked it all out, probably well before the AGS, BNL's great new accelerator of the future, became alive in 1960. It was Haworth out and Rabi's pick in, and if the winner had to be Goldhaber, then so be it. Since no one of high scientific stature from outside the lab would take on the job, perhaps sensing an ever so tough road ahead, it was all but certain that Maurice would win and succeed to the Director's chair even while it was warm with Leland's sweat and tears – and Leland had neither the strength nor the allies to alter the course Rabi had set. Evidently, the transition had already begun, and so the discussion with Maurice that Leland had been awaiting since the wee hours ended in substance before it began in practice. Sure they would go through the motions, but the meeting's purpose had been extinguished. No, there was no purpose in it at all because Leland was powerless to intervene to alter fate's no-appeal decision. However, now he understood. He had gone fishing in his memory and had come up with a full catch. It wasn't what he expected to find, not what he wanted to find, but now at last all was known. So, the uneventful meeting took its meaningless course: Platitudes were exchanged. There was a shallow friendliness. They shook hands, and the meeting was over. As for the game, it was a fait accompli, typical for the master manipulator – Rabi had his way and Goldhaber came to take the helm of the BNL ship.

And so it came to pass that Rabi and Haworth were unwitting conspirators in establishing the conditions for class warfare that would rage at the lab through the 1960's and ultimately lead to BNL's hapless fall from the heights. The combatants were ensconced in separate camps, one side in a spanking new Accelerator Department with Ken Green leading and the other side in a strengthened Physics Department that centralized the power of experimenters and users, with George Vineyard as head. But Rabi wasn't of the type that felt obligated to follow the Marquis of Queensbury rules. No, in typical Rabi fashion, he systematically set up the conditions that would assure the outcome he desired. Haworth was dispatched to Washington and Rabi's man was installed as lab Director. As for Rabi himself, he took the role of President of AUI in order to shape and oversee the battles to come. Yes, it was ironic indeed that, just at the moment when BNL was approaching its days of glory, the battle lines for a bitter, destructive class struggle were also being drawn. It was 1960, and with the stage set, the actors in place, and their roles laid out, the camera of history was ready to roll. Rabi, the director, had the boards click for the starting sequence and the action began. But the outcome of the drama was never in doubt. The grand master had seen to that.

One can only wonder at Rabi's ingenuity in the manner in which he set the actors on the stage. The casting was perfect. All Rabi had to do was to set it all in motion, and he did just that. But, although he got what he thought he wanted, the actions, events and consequences that followed were far from what he had in mind. For the class war that resulted was to break the lab apart. Many battles he had planned were won in the early days, but, as the years wore on, the war was lost. Even the best laid plans of mice and men can turn to naught. True, things appeared good for a while, but eventually the hurts he'd inflicted on the way turned around and bit him, and for Rabi the moment of truth came sooner than he had imagined. It seems to be in people's natures that they can't see the errors of their ways in time to change course effectively. In retrospect it appears that success could have been easy: if only this or that had been done, then all would have been righted. Hindsight may be twenty-twenty, but life is unfortunately lived without its benefit. In reality, when people reach a certain age, some younger, some older, they cease to have the capacity to see what's happening around them or to sense what lies ahead. Perhaps it's because of their shrinking horizons, but whatever the reasons, they find themselves unable to look ahead and more and more confined to the limitations of backward vision. And so it was for Rabi that by the early sixties he had already ordered, approved and begun to wear his blinders. With only his memories to guide him, he could do no more than follow his nose. Unfortunately, times had changed; and his past was ill fitted, his nose not primed for the new day. The director would very soon lose control of his actors and his play.

Even as Goldhaber and Haworth were walking through their charade of a meeting, the play, with its accompanying sadness, had already begun; but none of the actors had a clue as to what awaited them. If only they could have seen how it would be! Haworth was neutralized and kicked upstairs, fated to spend his remaining days in Washington, steeped in policy issues, essentially vacuous generalities, divorced from the life and death struggles on the front lines. Although he was tired anyway, what with his own illness and his wife's worse one, he was deeply bothered by what was done to him. What irked him most was how he was summarily booted out, especially since he knew deep down that he was the right man for the Director's job. And then they compounded the error by choosing Maurice, who was certainly not up to the challenges facing the lab, the most notable being whether there was a future for BNL after the AGS and what technologies had to be conceived and developed to make that future come to pass. Although to Leland the right course was as plain as day, it wasn't in the least clear to him that Maurice was aware of any challenges at all that had to be faced. Nonetheless Leland became resigned to his situation and consoled himself that time waits for no one and perhaps in the long run his leaving was for the best. After all, in the game that was in progress, wasn't it quite likely that a man such as he might in fact fan the flames rather than quench the fire? Still, as he watched from the sidelines, the lab went into its relentless slide downhill; and, as it ran its fated course, he couldn't keep a little anger and a little regret from entering his thoughts from time to time. Once, in a moment of sardonic pique, he thought, oh, the hell with it, as ye sow, so shall ye reap.

This fateful decade of the sixties ended up being a turning point in BNL history, when the old were discarded and the new brought in. Who were these new kids on the BNL block? They represented a select group of scientists who were self-assured, fresh, bright, eager and raring to go. They were young at heart if not so young in years, and were ambitious and activist. Like most people given a lot of authority suddenly and unexpectedly, without the benefit of real life experience, they thought they could do more than they actually could. Even Maurice was an activist at this stage in his career, in spite of the image he presented to the world as a sober gentleman. Rationality, or what was represented as such, was the keynote of his modus operandi. Along with Goldhaber in the BNL upper management level for physics and technology were Ken Green and George Vineyard. Ken had that rare combination of dedication to detail and an expansive personality that virtually oozed persuasiveness. He was at once an eager beaver and a wheeler-dealer. He could talk your head off, and, in the end, if it wasn't his argument that got to you, his charming way of holding his lighted cigarette would. Or was it that you'd give in or do anything just to have him shut his mouth? George, on the other hand, wasn't a man of the people, but rather a pretender to the aristocracy, more like Maurice. He had an air of authority and of haughtiness. That didn't much move the down to earth scientist type, but it sure was an asset with the Washington crowd, as he would prove in the seventies when he ascended to the directorship. If not a shaker, a man who could change things, he was definitely a mover, and he represented well his Physics Department constituency. These were the real physicists, as the accelerator lot sometimes sarcastically dubbed them.

When they were catapulted into department chairs, Ken and George found themselves quite unprepared for the power at their fingertips – it was just sitting there, ready for the taking. They came to possess authority previously unavailable to anyone not intimately plugged into the real power, Rabi, pulling the strings from his hidden lair. Meant to be puppets, they actually inherited the real thing. If they had the guts and worked together, the sky was the limit. Alas, that was too much to ask of them. They probably believed their good fortune was well deserved, due to their talent and pretty decent record of scientific and managerial accomplishment; or maybe they thought that Rabi had so much confidence in them that he bestowed those most challenging and demanding jobs on them; but the truth was that their chance had come only because the iron man was melting and fading away. So, even though Rabi didn't at all like what Goldhaber and his team were doing with the influential power base given them, he'd already lost the energy and the will to oppose them. So he simply let it be.

Rabi was the lab's substance and vitality, its life force, and he had been there from the start to guide it as it grew from obstreperous childhood to adulthood. But in life, nothing lasts forever, and Rabi's BNL story eventually began to turn downward. As the lab was growing up, he was superb as the mischievous kid egging it on to greatness, but he would prove not to be able to hack it as BNL took the lead in the community of labs. As the one to beat, BNL was subject to persistent sniping attacks from all sides and this seemed to eat away at Rabi's energy, his drive, and his self-confidence. At the same time, the class conflict heating up at the lab further sapped his diminishing potency. Even his self-esteem, essential for a leader, suffered. As the sixties wore on, he began to wither and withdraw, and with Rabi passing from the picture, a deep power vacuum developed, and those *the man* had placed in power were on their own. Maurice, Ken, George, and a few others, fresh and eager, now had it all. It could have been a time of limitless opportunity for both lab advancement and self-fulfillment. The power-inheritors had a chance to fly, but their wings failed them. Instead, unfortunately for all, the gaping power hole left by Rabi's disappearing act was populated not by bright, optimistic, new leadership, but rather by a self-serving mediocre band of opportunists that took the lab all too close to the edge of doom.

Although it was not easily apparent on surface view, the situation at the lab throughout the sixties and into the seventies was ominous. With Rabi's impact sinking fast and Haworth long gone, there was nothing but inexperience at the helm and destructive conflict rearing its ugly head. This state of affairs should have been enough to awaken the dead, but in the eerie strangeness of the time, not a creature was stirring. Why should anyone rock the boat and introduce risk into their lives? Everywhere you looked, you saw the good life and business as usual. Every now and then, the surface calm would be disturbed by a brave soul who would innocently point to a dark corner where he had inadvertently stepped into some unattended dung. But this type was quickly silenced or taken care of in some harsher way. Who were those sorry doomsayers anyway? Just shut them up. Rabi was okay, it was disingenuously said, so BNL was okay. We're fine as we are. But the critics, who became silenced witnesses, were right. Once the few great experiments at the AGS were done (the AGS provided an experimental vindication of the brilliant Standard Model of the universe with the discoveries of a small violation of a hitherto thought fundamental law of nature by Fitch and Cronin; of a second neutrino by Lederman, Schwartz, and Steinberger; of the nature of the proton's compositeness by Ting; and of a *doubly-strange particle* by Samios), the value and usefulness of the run-of-the-mill ones were rapidly waning. The lab's productive output was precipitously falling. Still, on any ordinary day at the lab you would find a typical rush of people working as if important things were getting done. The truth, however, was quite different. In reality, people were playing at their science as if the world were their oyster, as if the rest of the world would stand still. Under the glossy exterior, there was an eerie silence of thought and deed, perhaps like that of the Hapsburgs in their Austro-Hungarian fortress as the twentieth century was dawning. Just as that sorry bunch had learned many decades earlier, BNL was to learn that time was not on its side. The world was not standing still waiting on the lab's whims, and just as there was nowhere to run for the pitiful few who glimpsed the BNL calamity to come, there would be nowhere for BNL to turn once the point of no return had been reached. That was the legacy that lay ahead. There would be nowhere to turn, nowhere to run and nowhere to hide. There would be no help – only powerlessness, ineptitude, and aloneness inside the lab and silence outside.

By the time the sixties arrived, the post-war science boom was approaching its peak years and excitement was bursting out all over. Sputnik had given basic science a big boost and the outlook for big facilities was big indeed. The only thing science had to fear was fear itself. Kennedy became the new U.S. President early in 1961 and he loved science. As if to signal this, he proclaimed that America would land a man on the moon by the end of the decade. Science was on a high and as Vannevar Bush had predicted – urging in his 1946 report an upsurge in government-supported science – the frontier did appear to be endless. Everyone responded to the tone of the times and was encouraged by the atmosphere of boundless possibilities. The President, in 1963, established a commission headed by Harvard's Norman Ramsey (the Ramsey Panel, as it came to be known) to recommend new challenges and new opportunities for physics, projecting the sense that the sky was the limit. Yes, the era of Big Science was really coming to be.

Filled with top-notch scientists and politically acute types who knew their way around, the Ramsey Panel proposed to the country a round of ambitious projects for the fledgling high-energy physics community that was nothing less than science fiction coming true. It was a gloriously optimistic report for a gloriously optimistic time. Buoyed by the astounding success of the AGS at BNL, and a similar machine called the Proton Synchrotron (PS) at CERN using the same technology envisioned in the insightful *alternating gradient principle*, discovered at BNL in 1952, the Ramsey Panel threw caution to the winds. Its resounding message to the great accelerator builders of the twentieth century, those who had already shone brightly and the younger eager beavers waiting in the wings with great anticipation, was, "We believe in you, you can do it." The wise leaders of an enlightened federal government encouraged them further: "The United States with its youth, its vigor, its know-how, and its might is foursquare behind you. Go ahead and build one of your great tools ten times in strength. And don't stop there. Build one ten times more powerful than that. And what's more, add to the standard type of experiment of smashing a proton beam into a material target fixed at rest, and go for a totally new technology of colliding proton beams, where two counter-rotating beams are smashed headlong into each other, creating collisions with massive energy release." What a call to action that was. What a vote of confidence. And it was unanimous, coming from both the science community and the government. Could any scientist resist such a challenge? Could anyone at all resist?

It was the best of times, ushering in the best the country had. To the fore came the thinkers, the planners and the doers, all ready to work together, all ready to act in unison. In the West, a new lab, the Stanford Linear Accelerator Center (SLAC), was christened at Stanford University. Pief Panofsky, its founding director, saw a niche in the growing competition for particle beams and grabbed it. He conceived a new national lab to be the prime center for beams of electrons and he spearheaded Stanford to that end, leaving the Cambridge Electron Accelerator (CEA) lab at Harvard University and Cornell University's Laboratory for Nuclear Studies in the dust. These were flourishing times but they were also dog-eat-dog times. There were winners, but also losers, for such are the wages of growth. The Stanford initiative was no exception, and it had its negative consequences. In time the CEA lab was disbanded and the Cornell lab was relegated to the second tier.

The competition within the science community was fierce and the consequences of bigness were heavy and bitter; and to add to the human burden, the government connection had its own price to exact. As politicians got a whiff of what was happening, appreciating well the value of scientific research to the country as well as to their constituencies, scientists found that control over their work would have to be shared. The government grabbed its prerogative to exercise its right to choose the geographic distribution of what were, after all, its national labs. Thenceforth, scientists would not simply be able to wheel and deal amongst themselves to make such choices – the politicians who controlled the purse strings were not to be denied. The holders of the real power concluded that the value to any region of the country of a Big Science lab, with its concentration of advanced technology, intellect and practical spin-offs, was too great to leave to the scientists, and that they should be the ones to mete out these plums. According to the new political rules laid down, the East and the West having had their shares, the Midwest would also have to get its due. Thus it was that this new process of choosing a site by national competition with politicians pulling strings behind the scenes had its initiation in 1967 with the selection of Batavia, Illinois, a farming area 30 miles west of Chicago, as the place for the construction of a high-energy national lab. No doubt the unconcealed cozying up of the earthy-voiced immensely influential Republican Senator Everett Dirksen of Illinois and then Democratic President Lyndon Johnson helped pull it off. Clearly a deal had been struck. In fact, it was their combined public announcement that sealed the bargain.

It wasn't an ideal choice for scientists and their families, not one they would have made on their own; but the new process and this choice in particular were good for peacetime science and raised its level of importance to one of national interest. The creation of the new lab, Fermi National Accelerator Laboratory (FNAL or Fermilab), which was to have the newest, biggest proton atom smasher, ten times stronger and bigger than BNL's AGS, was a signal event for Big Physics. Along with all its contributions and continued value to mankind (in medicine, communications, transportation, technology, energy, defense, space, and every other facet of modern life; and add to that a far deeper understanding of the universe than was ever imaginable), science burst on the national scene and was holding its own. In doing so, however, it had found its way to bigness. Ay, there's the rub. Little did these naïve scientists know that this bigness was a very hot item to handle – far too hot for them; and much sooner than anyone could have anticipated it would burn them big-time. The negative consequences were not long in coming and began on the very heels of victory. The most significant and far-reaching of these was the tearing apart of the method of gentlemen's agreements in choosing projects – backroom politics, typical of the collegial style in the world of science and in the university milieu – and the ushering in of a time of free and intense but unfortunately uncontrollably destructive competition among the labs. On the other hand bigness wasn't all bad news, for it also brought with it into the national playing arena Bob Wilson, a scientist of the highest order and accelerator builder supreme. Bob had already demonstrated that special pioneering spirit, building three small electron accelerators at Cornell. But his crowning achievement turned out to be Fermilab. He built it from the bottom up. Bob's artistry shaped the lab's architecture and aesthetics. Eschewing extravagance and luxury while holding fast to a singular scientific-style aesthetic, his management philosophy and approach were lean and mean. He was a master builder. Sad to say, however, the community was not ready for Wilson's vision of science's future and couldn't fathom his depth of understanding of the political world. Without men of Bob's ilk, a couple of decades hence U.S. Big Physics was to fall into big failures. So it happened that Fermilab, Bob's baby, finished in 1972, was to be the last great U.S. accelerator project of the twentieth century.

Any way you look at it, the country did not live up to the hopes and dreams envisioned by the Ramsey Panel. It had told the science community, with the imprimatur of the U.S. President, that the country was ready for three big national accelerator projects, and Fermilab's quick success put it foursquare on a fast track to that end. With only the first and least adventurous having come to pass, the success measure was only one in three. That was not too good, but with a little sophistry you could make that record appear not too bad. You could argue that with the opening of Pandora's technology box, Big Science was here to stay. Whatever the record of successes and failures, in the long run Big Science would prevail and man would eventually reap its rewards both in acquiring deeper knowledge of the workings of nature and in developing and applying practical social benefits hitherto unimaginable. Invoking assurance that there would surely be benefits accruing in the long run certainly softens the appraisal. However, this is much like a check-is-in-the-mail promise and at this point the sophistry breaks down. There is, of course, some truth to this idea of reward in the long run and no one can take Big Science away; it will surely persist, if not sooner, then later. On the other hand, although man must indeed be concerned with the long run, it is the short run that actually governs men's lives. Since for science the long run is measured in centuries or significant fractions thereof, while the short run is measured in decades or less, for us, with limited life spans, what matters is what Big Science can achieve for science and society in the next decade or two. It's the short run that counts. In this sense, the basic science community in the latter half of the twentieth century found that it could not deal well with the onset of bigness. No amount of sophistry, attempting to confuse the long run with the short run, could alter the basic reality that we have not gained anywhere near what we might have from the vast potential of Big Science. The Ramsey Panel presented to the country a bold, imaginative vision that would have impacted and shaped Big Physics well into the twenty-first century. But it wasn't to be. With BNL's flock leading the pack downward, this generation of scientists let it all slip away.

The Ramsey Panel from the beginning sensed the onset of bigness, but they didn't and couldn't have been expected to appreciate the awful events that were to follow down the line in the decades ahead. Even if they had, it's hard to imagine what they could have done to prevent them. In any case, these bad things were the furthest things from their minds as they optimistically issued their report to an eagerly awaiting science community. Getting down to the nitty-gritty details, what did happen between the Ramsey Panel's deliberations in 1963 and the years immediately following the release of their ideas for the future? As it happened, their report was a turning point for science, and in the wake of its hitting the stands, the unforeseen consequences began to materialize. The major ones were the extent of the increased involvement of politics in Big Science – particularly government micromanagement, the rancor and unreasonable demands for priority regarding the balance between experiment and technology development, and the disruptive effect on the science community of the new open and competitive process for determining the geographical distribution of sites. Without the needed foresight, without being able to look ahead and see the pitfalls and dangers lying in wait, the panel simply presumed that BNL would lead the way. And why shouldn't they have? The AGS was a smashing success. By 1961, it had exceeded performance expectations by more than two orders of magnitude; and by the mid-sixties, experiments of momentous impact were on their way. It was a time at the lab such as dreams are made of. It therefore wasn't too surprising that the Ramsey Panel, virtually without consideration, and certainly without realizing the effects it would set into motion, naïvely and blindly subscribed to the gentleman's agreement between Berkeley and BNL that the two labs take turns at building new accelerator facilities. In the panel's defense, they were simply extrapolating from the past. The large cyclotron at Berkeley, the Cosmotron at BNL, the Bevatron at Berkeley, and the AGS at BNL were precedent enough. With simplistic logic, without much long-sightedness, and without inspiration, they saw the next bigger accelerator at Berkeley and the next one after that at BNL. That took care of the first two components of their plan. With them out of the way, there was the third of the panel's recommendation to deal with – a proposal for a new machine that was to incorporate the advanced and as yet untried technology of colliding beams. Again, without any deep thought or prudence, they simply presumed that BNL would be the innovator that would open up this new world, undoubtedly believing that this young, vibrant, and successful lab would be both up to the task and desirous of it. Thus, in the minds of the panel's members, the Berkeley project would provide an interlude on the road to bigness, filling its highly limited site capability in the Berkeley hills to capacity, while BNL would take on the grandeur of accelerator bigness and complexity. It was a rational plan – a good plan. But, with real life playing its little tricks, as it's wont to do, they were wrong on at least three counts. They underestimated the U.S. government's intention of sticking its fingers into the Big Science pie, especially how much it would want to wheel and deal for new big projects as well as to micromanage them by interfering in the littlest of details. They totally missed BNL's inability to deal with the new competitive political environment, and didn't gauge at all well the lab's ability to gear up for a new technology effort. And finally, they failed to sense correctly the strength and resolve of the CERN laboratory across the ocean, with confidence bulging at the seams, itching to get into the fray. CERN, with the adventurous thinker Vicki Weisskopf at its helm as Director-General, was about to embark on a path that would all but knock the U.S. out of the proton game. But that could happen only, and this is not to take anything away from CERN's bold leadership, if the U.S. physics community allowed it to happen. And the physics leaders in the U.S. did just that.

Except at BNL, the sixties were a time when the speed of technological progress for accelerator facilities was breathtaking. Panofsky made SLAC the world leader in electron beam technology. Weisskopf saw a way for CERN to become a contender for world leadership in proton collider technology. And Bob Wilson built Fermilab, which, for a time, was the unchallenged champion of the world. Meanwhile, BNL watched from inside fortress Upton as time passed them by and their edge was being eroded.

Goldhaber assumed the lab directorship in the summer of 1961. He transferred the chairmanship of the Physics Department to George Vineyard, who had been deputy chairman. Just at the moment the AGS was coming alive, the three core leaders at the lab were Maurice, George and Ken Green, chairman of the Accelerator Department. For better or worse, these were the men who had become the ones to take BNL into the new era of accelerator technology. They alone held the key to the lab's future. Haworth had fully broken his ties to the lab. Rabi would still pop up now and then, but he had been sapped dry of any power, and the essence of the greatness he had once had was now gone. How quickly the mighty fall! His well-known and forcefully used rage might be seen now and then, but Rabi was henceforth no more than a shadow of his former self. Ironically, the puppet master's destiny was to become a puppet, a soulless icon to be used as the lab's leadership saw fit. Symbolically, Rabi's role at the dedication of the AGS in September 1961 was simply to introduce Haworth, who returned to the lab for the dedication as an AEC commissioner. Rabi said little of substance whereas Leland spoke of the problem for science that was on everyone's mind – its looming bigness. Although they were words of truth, they could best be characterized as empty, originating as they did from the safe haven of Washington.

A new deal was coming into being, and whether BNL appreciated its importance and consequences still remained to be seen. The role of the newly installed triumvirate running the lab was to deal with science's new bigness, but right from the start the new management team was highly polarized on how best to do that job. Goldhaber and Vineyard stood together at one pole, while Green stood alone at the other. Vineyard, who had worked for Goldhaber as deputy chairman of the Physics Department, tended to defer to his former boss and took a back seat as Goldhaber carried the ball for their side. Goldhaber believed that increased administrative control and more professorial style research in academic physics were the proper Big Science objectives for the lab. That was the way he wanted to prioritize the increased budgets that accompanied and in a sense represented the practical manifestation of the arrival of bigness. Green had a different view of the lab's purpose and where it should be headed. He saw the lab as a factory for advanced technology. He wanted the lab to spend more funds to push forward the technology frontiers to give it the edge on doing the science of the future. For Maurice, with George's support, bigness meant, first, increasing centralized control at the lab by raising the visibility of the top management's leadership authority with a massive enhancement of the lab's bureaucracy, and second, substantially strengthening the Physics Department to do the optimum number and the best experiments with the machines on hand as well as to build a theoretical base for future ideas and experiments. For Ken, it meant greatly pumping up the technical staff, not so much with physicists, but rather with engineers, technicians, machinists and their support staffs. This would give the lab the technological edge it was striving for and the ability for rapid response to new and unanticipated opportunities. It was a classic case of confrontation, with one side wanting an emphasis on the present, the other on the future. Each wanted to spend more, but in different ways, with little overlap and little room for negotiation and compromise. And each side was hard nosed and would stubbornly stick to its points and its guns. This was not a stable situation. It was precarious for both sides and dangerous for the lab. Eventually, one side would have to give ground and back off, and both, together with the lab, would have to live with whatever consequences ensued.

Maurice saw the lab's purpose in the sixties as doing experiments, referred to by many as "doing physics," presumably to give this activity more gravitas. It was strange to hear people talk this way. Is there any doubt that doing experiments is a key element of science? After all, isn't that what Nobel Prizes are given for? Nonetheless, for the newly emerging Big Science, the experiments themselves were just one part – a very important part, but still just one among other important component activities, including technology development and innovation, studying beams and their behavior, engineering, and management. The very difficult but essential job a good lab Director is to keep all these balls in the air at the same time. That would give the lab its best shot at being *the best it can be*. Why didn't Goldhaber do this, and why did he and many others feel that they had to isolate the experiment part of the entire enterprise and give it extra protection? It might have been defensive attitudes and insecure feelings. But perhaps it was no more complicated than that the experimenters, holding all the cards, were ready to cash in and simply wanted higher priority and special treatment – to feast of the resources at hand to their heart's delight. Whatever the true reason, the fear of not getting what they wanted was sufficiently strong that a constituency grew which demanded that technology development at the lab actually be downgraded. That and only that would ensure the experiment component would non-competitively get the priority and support it needed, and that those who held sway at the top believed it ought to have, cost be damned. Maurice was of that ilk, and before he was long in command, he agreed to substantially change the balance of priority, raising the support for experiments while lowering the support for technology. This was a big step and a drastic change from the way Haworth had run things. But that is what Goldhaber did, and there was no one with a strong enough power-base or sufficient guts to stop him or even reason with him. He brought in people with all manner of ideas and encouraged them to compete for experimental slots and for lab support. Then, Maurice set about the task of establishing a management system to see that it all went along according to plan. He expanded the administrative machinery for the experimental program by leaps and bounds. He created a new army of scientist bureaucrats to assess, evaluate and decide on the multitude of proposed experiments, ostensibly because the cumulative time needed far exceeded the limited beam time that was available, but also because it considerably enhanced Goldhaber's control over the process. To further protect the experimental program budget from the demands of accelerator technology, he established a hierarchical structure, including a system of Associate Directors, a council to advise the Director on scientific personnel, and committees for this, that and everything. (This also had the incidental consequence of damping the weak-to-begin-with demands of other scientific activities at the lab.) Thus the means to the desired end was set in place – the rubber-stamping bureaucracy being the means, and the overwhelming of the technology program by the experimental program the end. The one thing left was for the administrators to do the deeds that had to be done.

As the first round of fighting subsided, Goldhaber ended up with a lot more power than he knew what to do with. Taken by surprise, Green felt helpless. He was not at all happy with what he saw but was snowed under by the new power mongers at the lab and became paralyzed. Ken was an idealist and was astonished that the others at the top didn't see things his way. He considered the lab to be the conceiver, builder and keeper of facilities in constant transition. For him the lab's purpose was continuous technological development, upgrades, and new facility creations. Believing that, he felt that money should not be taken from the technology program to feed the experimental program. In that, he and Maurice were at serious odds with each other, and there was little or no common ground between them. There could be no meeting of minds here. Their approaches were built on different philosophies of the laboratory. They were incompatible and the resources to allow both to be simultaneously implemented were not attainable rationally – irrationality, the only remaining alternative, would have to prevail. Thus, Maurice and Ken were on a collision course. There was trouble at the top and in the end only one of them could survive. Their last round was about to begin.

* * * * *

Ken paced back and forth in his big, messy office on the second floor of the accelerator building on the sprawling BNL site. He liked his office, but there was a note of irritation in this thought, for he didn't much like how such an extravagance had come his way. He had inherited it as part of Goldhaber's policy of building and presenting an image of the lab leadership as being authoritative, decisive, forceful, in control of things, serious, and standing far above the run-of-the-mill workers. But what all that fancy language meant was that he believed in leadership by an elite corps and was determined to bring it about – and so he did. In stark contrast, Haworth's regime had been stern and lean, but Maurice couldn't abide that way of doing business. He wanted comfort and an air of extravagance and this was to be the new management style for the lab. Thus Ken became the beneficiary of the director's new policy of largesse for the top people. But it had come at a price and Ken resented that, for he knew that only so many resources were available, and if you spent it here, you wouldn't have it there. He was also well aware that this was a complicated area to delve into – the mystery of budgets – and difficult for anyone to understand. There was already too much talk and fuss about the subject, he thought. Everyone and their uncles had their opinions, none that threw much light, but only added to the growing confusion and rampant misunderstandings. Still, aside from all the babble, this policy had real and practical consequences that caused Ken great concern. Funds for technical support and for R&D, funds essential for the lab to keep up with the new ideas and technologies beginning to take shape, were not forthcoming. Events were taking place and things were changing at an amazing clip, and Ken was troubled that the advances were taking place only outside the lab. Inside the lab Goldhaber insisted that most of the Accelerator Department resources be directed toward experimentation. To Ken, this represented a clear and present danger for the lab. He could already see that in developing new and advanced technologies the lab had begun to lag badly in the previous few years, and on looking forward, he could see no redress in sight. He wondered also about his relationship with Maurice. It could be very important for the lab's future. He had the wrenching thought that it was their philosophical differences, but perhaps it was just their conflict over budget priority, that could explain their sometimes passionate dislike for each other. But it wasn't only their personal relationship that was troubling. That Maurice didn't see that his policy was harming the lab mystified Ken and would continue to do so long after their parting of the ways.

It was a beautiful Saturday afternoon in October of 1969. The grand master Rabi wanted to see Ken. Rabi was coming from the city for an AUI sponsored party that evening and it was proposed that they meet in Ken's office for a chat at about four o'clock. When Rabi's secretary had called on the previous Monday, Ken was taken aback because he had also wanted to see Rabi and was trying to think of a way to make this happen. That Saturday seemed an ideal time and after he had finished the brief formal talk setting up the meeting, Ken was pleased that serendipity had lent a helping hand. What Ken wanted to see Rabi about was to complain about Goldhaber and the potential harm he was doing to the lab. But why did Rabi want to see him? he asked himself. It seemed straightforward enough. It was probably nothing more than that Rabi wanted to see him for the same reason he was eager to see Rabi – the disagreements and conflicts he was having with Goldhaber. As he continued to think more about it, he started to become a little worried. Soon the pleasure turned to apprehension. Then in a moment of insight he felt an ominous letdown as the truth of his situation began to emerge.

Rushing into his mind came that trying and emotion-packed meeting the day before: Ken had been stunned that Goldhaber had come out with what was tantamount to an admission that he was in the process of doing away with him. That shook him and is probably the explanation for his up-to-then inability to see what was staring him in the face. But now, finally, he understood. Adding two and two and reaching the right answer, the whole business began to come together. Maurice must have gotten to Rabi and convinced him that it was the right thing to do to rid the lab of that tiresome Green. It must be a done deal, he thought. Anger tempered with regret began to rise in him as he contemplated that the weasel in the Director's office had reached "the man" first and had done him in. Little did Ken know that the two of them, in some sort of conspiracy, were in it together from the start. But even if he had, it's hard to speculate what he'd have done about it, because Ken was stubborn and not a man to throw in the towel too quickly. No doubt he'd have stayed in there for the duration and given it the old college try anyway. Maybe, he tried to persuade himself, he might even succeed in reversing the Goldhaber strategy, even though the odds were stacked against him. However, no matter how he tried to look at his position, first this way and then that, he arrived at the unique verdict that Rabi was the key. It wouldn't be easy to persuade Rabi to switch sides and back him. It wasn't even clear whether Rabi still had any strength or fight left in him. But Ken was hanging by a thread. What else could he do? It was a long shot, a veritable stab in the dark, but Rabi, trustworthy or not, influential or not, was his only hope. Without Rabi's encouragement and support, Ken had zilch. There was nothing left for him to do but to ask the big power man one last time to reconsider. Unfortunately for Ken, it now seemed that Rabi had already been primed. Worse yet, if Rabi was already in Goldhaber's corner and wouldn't change, Ken would be a cooked goose. His faith and innocence started to crack some as he began to imagine a first-class betrayal in the making. What a fix! Still, impossible as a positive outcome seemed, Ken was the type to persevere and walk the last mile to the bitter end – being behind the eight ball wasn't a position unknown to him. So, forever the cock-eyed optimist, he had to try.

He lit another cigarette, the fourth or fifth of his early afternoon chain. He puffed on it, deeply inhaling, as his face registered for a brief moment a joy that may have come from his innocence and his relative youth, or perhaps from a false sense of immortality. The grimace that followed almost immediately, typical for his smoking sequence, reminded him that he really should cut down, as his wife almost daily exhorted him. Although the addict's joy filled him momentarily, it was the grimace that expressed the true nature of his inner feelings that afternoon. Deep down, he was nervous and anxious about what was to become of him. He was also acutely concerned about all the people who worked with him and who worked for him. He had brought many of them to the lab, persuaded them of the importance and the value of accelerators and technology, and now felt responsible for them in a fatherly sort of way. But most of all, he cared about the lab that he had come to love. Whither it goes, there go I, he had thought. Still, as much as he did double-duty and spared no effort or pain to stem the tide, he felt his hopes ebbing; and so he took another puff and welcomed the tar and nicotine and the accompanying, short-lived satisfaction that allowed him to cast out the truth he couldn't yet face up to.

Ken could almost feel his subconscious hard at work as he tried to draw from it something that would give him a better understanding of what was happening. He took a few steps in his office, which afforded him a little walking room, amused that its grandiosity did after all provide some service. Then he sat close to an ashtray and wondered how it had come to this. When in 1959 Haworth had created a unified

Accelerator Department, he saw it as a great way for the lab to formalize its commitment to the future. As its first chairman, Ken was ambitious and proud to help shape the things to come. But a little over a year later, when Haworth left the lab, Ken began to feel some apprehensions. As he looked about, he found the Accelerator Department was still intact, as strong as ever. But would it remain that way? He was well aware of the also immensely strengthened Physics Department, where groups of experimenters had been given a home with a new, powerful, and unified voice. In itself, that wasn't an issue, but when the amount of resources pouring into these groups caused the amount going into accelerator technology to be drastically cut, this was cause for concern. Ken was deeply worried, but what could he do? The natural thing was to go to the Director and work it out with him – but look at who was in the Director's office! It wasn't Haworth anymore; it was Goldhaber. Could he depend on Goldhaber as he had countless times depended on Haworth? Could Goldhaber be fair to the lab's technology effort when it was pitted against his beloved physics? Not on your life, Ken thought. For a moment he actually believed he might be able to overcome the odds, but that was only vanity. As the reality began to come home to him, it brought on a heavy kind of loneliness. There seemed to be no one connected with the lab that he could turn to. He was isolated and he feared that in time he would come to be abandoned and totally alone. However, the fat lady hadn't yet sung and, slim as the chance was, there was still one avenue left open to him. Rabi was his last hope and he would have to give it a shot. A cold chill went up his spine as that thought passed through his mind.

When the AGS turned on so smoothly, so quickly, and performed so well, the immediate reaction was something akin to shock. As for Ken, he chose to be cavalier about it, calmly and proudly taking in all the plaudits offered as if he had expected that result all along; and there was some, although not much, truth in that response. Having often talked of his superb accelerator group, he had in some weird manner become a believer in his own hype. Still, the extent of the success was indeed stunning, nothing short of miraculous, and, in the quiet of his private thoughts, Ken himself was in awe of the performance of his troops – it was an amazing feat, a tour de force. To give credit where credit was due, Ken's leadership was brilliant. It was an achievement to be deservedly savored. As an R&D project, this was the best of the best. The invention of AG focusing (the idea of placing accelerator magnets in just the right sequence to allow beams of particles to travel in a "circle" tens of miles long, even a hundred, and thus be able to accelerate them to enormous energies) had been all but earthshaking, and its realization had been even more so. Ken's entire accelerator group deserved not only the recognition and tributes from its own time but the earnest thanks of posterity. Ken had thought that the magnificent performance of the AGS project and its subsequent operation not only proved that he had put together an A-class team, but also demonstrated yet again the virtue of pursuing technological advancement as an essential ingredient of scientific progress. However, the honeymoon lasted but a short while. Within the BNL leadership of that time, he was virtually alone in such thoughts, especially the one about a substantially increased technology effort at the lab. Before long, the compliments, the commendations, and the acclaim turned to bland references to the accomplishment as ordinary and not unusual. Ho-hum was not an uncommon attitude. It was a straightforward technical job. It was just standard, everyday engineering. Anyone could have done it. Remember that the same thing was done at

CERN. It was no big deal, the lab was telling him. Now let's get down to the real business we're supposed to be doing. Forget about the machine and together let's focus on the experiments, by far the more interesting and hard part of the AGS complex, continued the guidance, as well as the official counsel, he was getting. Naturally, that's where the resources ought to be concentrated, contended the new leaders of the pack. Ken was astonished at the extent to which he had gotten things so wrong. He had always considered himself a reasonably smart man, but he had missed sensing this changeover altogether. He just hadn't gotten it. And as he sat in his office on that warm October afternoon, he gave himself the luxury of musing on those old times. He wondered if he had ever really perceived things correctly. Had he *ever* gotten it? He went even further and questioned whether he had it even now, at this late date, when the die had long been cast.

In those early days, Ken deeply believed that the lab should take the bull by the horns and get on with it. Events and technology in science were in a high state of flux, and procrastination could truly turn out to be the thief it's cracked up to be. He felt in his gut that it was a time for the lab to throw caution to the wind and follow its star. That is the way of the young at heart, and Ken was that when the lab was adventurous and riding high. True, there was risk involved, but the lab had built a team of the best to be had and everything was on its side. It was number one. For BNL, it was the time of its time, and for Ken it all seemed straightforward. But nothing that involves the feelings and desires of men is simple, and the future, as it unfolded, would tell a story of human conflict, loss and sadness. It could not be avoided, and BNL was condemned to live the oft-told story of the long road down.

The conflict was dark and deep. On one side of the struggle was Ken, who wanted to move on to the next step in accelerator building; but alas, in that he was quite alone. On the other side was the rest of BNL top management, leading an army of followers in opposition. Just about everybody else of importance and influence at the lab had quite a different point of view from Ken's. It was a daunting force for Ken to face by himself. It included, in addition to the lab's top management, the in-house experimental groups, the users, and the many lab scientific advisors from universities and labs all over the country. To stand up to this powerhouse, he had no one except himself and a few silent supporters. He was boxed in, and there was no one on the scene to appeal to. So it was that BNL, which had been the unquestioned leader of the world in accelerator technology in the fifties, came to lose that edge. But, standing on the shoulders of the technology giants of the fifties, the lab became the unmatched leader in experimental high-energy physics in that wonderful decade of the sixties. New names began to come to people's lips. Visions of Nobel prizes danced in their heads. Such was the atmosphere. And many would reach those heights, with their Nobel dreams realized, the likes of Leon Lederman, Mel Schwartz, Jack Steinberger, Val Fitch, Jim Cronin, and Sam Ting, and some would come close, like Nick Samios. Those were glory days at the lab; but unseen by those rushing at headlong speeds, bitter fruit was being planted that would bring painful lessons in the days ahead. A thorough but unpleasant education for the lab was in the making. He who dotes exclusively on his own doings as the world turns will surely forfeit his future. Hubris doth make fools of us all, and so it was that as the lab basked in its own heyday, the world didn't watch and wait, but inexorably passed it by.

In the years following the AGS turn-on, there was excitement in the air. Unfortunately, Ken could not share in it to the extent that he should have been able to. He felt betrayed. He was caught between a rock and a hard place. To his colleagues and the people working for him, he was compelled to present an image of optimism that the lab was indeed readying itself to develop new technology and a new accelerator for future science. He did at times have second thoughts about this kind of little white duplicity, but he couldn't see another way to act. He had always held out some hope and he certainly did not want his team to lose the momentum that had been built up with so much blood, sweat and tears. Still, any confidence he had about his ability to turn things around kept diminishing. In all his dealings with the lab leadership, he was perpetually frustrated, and his self-doubt mounted. They wouldn't listen to reason. Perhaps, he thought, in his pessimistic moments, they had lost the capacity to see and hear, a loss characteristic of a management on the move but set in its ways and too sure of itself. It was a hard time for a man who loved his work and believed in straight talk with straight folks. It was strange for him to have to contain feelings that things might not pan out, while at the same time playing the father figure proud of the ways of his newborn. Then in 1963, when the Ramsey Panel convened, Ken had a momentary sense of being redeemed, even of being vindicated. Others around him who shared his views also took comfort from what later turned out to be an illusion. For a time Ken believed the lab would see the light and begin to move in the right direction. There was still time to set things right. It hadn't yet passed the point of no return. But this was only Ken's hopeful nature at work. Although it was good in many ways to have such a nature, in this instance it just made him easily fooled. He tried to grab onto any little thing that might indicate that a ray of light might be poking through. However, as time moved on, he would have to acknowledge that this was just another of his pipe dreams.

As the Ramsey Panel was doing its work, Ken got strong signals that they were endorsing the Berkeley-BNL informal agreement that Berkeley would build the next big accelerator after the AGS. Then, when their report came out, the recommendation was there in black and white. At first, he saw nothing wrong with it because he thought it meant that BNL would immediately commence doing R&D on the next big machine after that, which was the essence of the original agreement: BNL would give up building early in order to pursue the advanced technology that came with the next step. Working closely and seemingly constructively with Maurice, naïve Ken helped solidify the agreement through discussions at the Berkeley Radlab with its director, Ed McMillan and with Ed Lofgren, who headed the accelerator effort there. As things seemed to be looking up, it was with some chagrin that Ken came to appreciate an important, albeit far-out, implication of the panel's report, one that had entirely escaped him. Goldhaber and his followers and hangers-on did indeed acknowledge that the agreement must and would be honored – so far, so good. But their interpretation of it turned out to be very different from Ken's. What the agreement really meant to them was that they could simply go on with their experiments-first policy, implying that life at the lab could continue without any response at all, for at least a decade or so, to the Ramsey Panel challenge to build bigger and bigger accelerators and ever higher energy particle collisions. To Ken, this was quite unexpected. He thought it had been implicit in the lab's agreement with the Radlab that accelerator R&D for a higher energy machine would be pursued vigorously and immediately by BNL, while Berkeley would build an intermediate energy machine that was compatible with its land limitations. This sounded like an eminently reasonable plan. Unfortunately for Ken and the lab, it wasn't what the upper echelon had in mind. Again, Ken had underestimated the lab's resolve to favor experimentation over technology development, that is, to squeeze what it could out of the present at the expense of the future. With Ken apparently powerless to do anything about what was going on, the lab adopted the attitude of business as usual. Even without significant resistance, the Goldhaber policy was defended forcefully and vigorously. We don't need a new accelerator now, it was said. Let Berkeley have it. Let Berkeley take the risks. We have all we need for now. We have lots of time for the following step in bigness. It sounded a lot like rationalization of a sort, and Ken recalled thinking, "The lady doth protest too much."

As for Ken, not yet ceding the game, he had one final gambit that he thought might make the lab leaders see the error of their ways. What about the new collider technology that the Ramsey panel had talked of? Why not propose strengthening superconductivity research for magnets, he thought? Who could oppose that? Alas, Ken had misdiagnosed once again: the lab response was firm and succinct – no! We won't divert any resources to that. It's not science. It's just science fiction. You can't get enough intensity in each beam to do any realistic work with beams colliding – for practical experiments you need high-density fixed-targets. Colliders are not for us, not now anyway. Ken was jarred by the unreasonableness and finality of the reaction. He was well aware that if you didn't want to do something new and enter the unknown, you could find any number of excuses for inaction. But, even appreciating that fact of human nature, he was caught flat-footed by the strength and resoluteness of the position Goldhaber and the lab took. The best that Ken could salvage, after a lot of wheedling, to the point of begging, was the setting up of a small R&D group to look at superconducting technology for future accelerators. Adding to his humiliation, as if to pay for that puny crumb, he was pressured to take on a task that would significantly strengthen the current lab policy that he abhorred. Backed against the wall and in order to keep his accelerator team going, he agreed to an intensity upgrade of the AGS to enhance the fixed-target experimental program. This Conversion Project would enable the AGS to serve more experiments and give each of them more beam. This was great news for the beam-hungry experimenters, especially the neutrino gang. With big guys like Leon Lederman pushing for the conversion, what could Ken do? So he bit his lips, shut his mouth, and went along. He wasn't proud of himself. He felt like a collaborator in a conspiracy. By going along he found that he lost his honor and integrity, and, in the end, he couldn't even salvage himself. When later he would look back at this period, he was at his wit's end and labored inordinately to come up with reasons for doing what he did. He had to do it, he thought, and the excuses were plentiful: to keep the Accelerator Department together, or to preserve the strength of its staff, or to keep its budget at a workable level. But in his heart of hearts, he knew that what happened was that he lacked the courage to fight the new honchos who had taken charge of the lab. To typify this class of scientist, the CERN builder types had come to call them the physichists – a pejorative name for the user physicists who had taken control – so as to make a clear distinction between them and the poor beaten-down accelerator physicists, who became resigned to their second-class status.

A funny thing happened on its way to the forum, so to say, as the Ramsey Panel report wended its way through the science community. From the moment it was released, unanticipated consequences developed and began to become evident. The first hitch encountered in its implementation was that BNL, with its essentially experiments-only policy, wouldn't strictly adhere to the gentleman's agreement. This seemed innocuous enough. But by not abiding by the spirit of the proposed plan, BNL unwittingly fired the first salvo at it and started the ball rolling against it. The true opponents, the ones who felt disinherited by the BNL-Berkeley establishment's outsiders-keep-out sign, saw their opening and began their attack strategy. These outsiders had their own agenda. It wasn't really that they were against the Ramsey Panel initiative of fast-track accelerator building, but rather they were out to break the BNL-Berkeley hold on new construction. As soon as they were on to the fact that they had something, they gave notice that they wouldn't abide by the gentleman's agreement altogether. Having found a way to stick their foot in the door and perhaps enter the haven of the power-holders, they proved to be a formidable group.

For the most part, what the outsiders knocking at the gate found intolerable and unacceptable was the attempt by the Berkeley-BNL combine to close the door to them simply because they were not in the established sphere of influence. Without free and open access, this system was alternately proclaimed by them to be ill conceived, unfair, or just plain wrong. The fortress mentality of exclusion was not in the American spirit, they concluded. Keeping in mind that this was taking place in the sixties, when freedom and equal opportunity in America were bursting out at the seams, it seems an inconceivable oversight for the Ramsey Panel to have made. What a big blunder it was! They should have known that they couldn't keep burgeoning Big Science contained within the established old boys' club. Although the report didn't spell it out and blatantly insist on the BNL-Berkeley agreement and didn't outrightly preclude others from joining the club, it certainly didn't show the panel's appreciation that for Big Science to maintain its forward momentum, it had to open up. It was one of those instances where a footnote turns out to dominate the message. In this case, the panel became associated with the old, closed way of doing things and its insensitivity to outsiders threatened to blow up the whole report. In the new age of bigness, a free system was essential and everybody had to be given a fair chance to participate. That was the American way and that was the right way.

It wasn't only the scientists who wanted their share of the action. Politicians wanted in as well, particularly congressmen. They all wanted to partake of the benefits – economic, educational, technological, and cultural – that would ensue from the coming of science facilities, universities, advanced technology development, industrial involvement, and the concentration of intellectual manpower. Thus the geographic distribution of labs became a visible issue, and with it the idea of competitive site selection. It was this point that made allies of politicians and scientist-outsiders and was the mechanism through which outsiders could take meaningful concrete action. It came to be the deathblow to the gentleman's agreement and, in principle, to all back-room science deals. Openness was now the byword in the science community. All this should have been recognized and prepared for. Thenceforth, free competition was in. BNL and Berkeley should have seen it, the Ramsey Panel should have seen it, and certainly the science community should have seen it. It still remains a mystery why it was so poorly handled. Yet it was, and the complexities of the process would only intensify. Scientists, politicians – national, state, and local – and others all over the country saw the opportunity to break down the establishment doors and enter the kingdom of science goodies. Big Science is one of those perfect ideas, a combination of everything worthwhile, and as an extra dividend, it not only tastes good but is good for you.

All this ensured that sooner or later the piercing of the BNL fortress was bound to happen. The bubble in which Goldhaber and company were dozing was sure to be pricked, and it was. BNL was eventually driven into the ground by the bulldozers freely roaming the land. As for Ken, he was shown to be right and should have been pleased and praised. But that wasn't at all what followed. Ironically, he again took a pounding to his self-esteem. Nobody at the lab said, good work, you did good, you were right. As other labs zoomed ahead, some of the upper crust accused him of bringing the lab to its knees. This type of talk sometimes caused him to lose his bearings. Was he on the side of right fighting the bad guys in the fortress, hoping and waiting for the cavalry to save the day? Was he treated badly simply because he talked a lot and with too loud a voice? Despite the lack of appreciation he received, was he nevertheless just another inmate of the fortress? In the end, even though he felt the rebel in himself, he had a deep and abiding love for the place he had helped build; and so he had to face the fact that he might just be another reactionary, defending and aiding the established system. If so, what was his alternative, to become a turncoat?

In the meantime, as the struggle for dominance in proton beams heated up all over the country, a man of acute vision on the West Coast was beginning to make his mark. Pief had seen early in the competition the nature and the value of Big Science and instinctively knew the way it would work. He made a critical decision to avoid the big war over protons, and, while everyone else was preoccupied with the struggle over proton supremacy, he quietly won a smaller conflict to create his own electron empire at Stanford. By the time the Ramsey Panel report was done, everybody knew that SLAC was well on its way to becoming one of the great accelerator labs in the U.S., so the idea of new labs in new places already had a precedent. That greatly added to the fact that the competitive atmosphere couldn't simply be ignored. And, in spite of the Ramsey Panel report, it wasn't. The AEC in 1965, just over a year after the report's issuance, asked the National Academy of Sciences to form a site selection committee that would request site proposals from all comers in a process that promised to be open and unbiased. Because Congress would be peering over its shoulders, it would surely have to be. In retrospect, it is remarkable that this simple act of sending a letter from the AEC to the NAS had significance far greater than anyone could have imagined. It let the cat out of the bag. No longer would the establishment be able to call all the shots privately. Smoke-filled backroom decisions were done away with. The wishes of the people would henceforth have to be heard. That little letter was no less than a call to arms. After that, there was no holding back the tides of change, and all hell broke loose as outsiders from all over saw their dawn breaking. What followed wasn't pretty; it was dark and dirty and unsightly, in short, a democratic mess. But the outcome was quite different from the process. There arose a feeling of optimism and a sense of a brighter future, reminiscent of the simile comparing democracy to a sausage: good to the taste when you've got it, but not to be looked at in the making. Suddenly, without warning, a cleansing wind had blown over the landscape and changed it. In the wink of an eye, the BNL-Berkeley establishment stranglehold had been broken. Still, it would take quite some time for the generals of the two old labs and their coterie of followers to see and understand what had happened: that the science they loved, which had grown to an unwieldy and uncontrollable bigness, was about to chew them up and spit them out. Such is the fate of those who won't see what's happening right under their noses, as it was for those unwitting dealmakers, Directors Goldhaber and McMillan, who would thereafter fall by the wayside. This left a gaping power vacuum, and into the breach, with hubris abounding, entered the magnificent Bob Wilson. Leading the attack on the bastion of the status quo, carrying the flag of youth and the future, in strode Bob the colossus. Who could resist him? Who could resist his righteous demand for down with the old and up with the new? He was a charismatic genius with imagination emanating from his very pores, giving hope to the many outsiders who hadn't had it before. A new power and a new leader had emerged, and, as a monument to this revolutionary moment, there arose on the plains of the Midwest a great new national laboratory called Fermilab. It was a sight to behold, represented by its well-known feature, a hi-rise building rising out of the earth like a giant phallus. Bob was ready to take on the world.

Ken awoke from his reverie with a start. Trails of smoke had made their way through his nostrils into his throat and he coughed. He found himself still in a languorous mood. He sat lazily with his chair tilting a little backward, looking at the smoke swirling and curling in all sorts of shapes in the air above him. Through this fog, there appeared a face, and Ken's response, almost involuntary, was a typical Ken Green smile, not a big welcoming one, but rather a subtle one with his facial muscles hardly moving at all and only a little twitch here and there discernible. Actually, it was his eyes that smiled, flashing and darting about; and the smile lingered while his mind had enough time to place a pair of horns atop Bob's head. He laughed silently to himself, exceptionally amused at the thought that in his mind's eye he had created Devil Bob and invited him to call. In this unworldly quiet moment, Ken recalled a dream he had had, in which Bob's head had appeared in precisely the same form. But in the dream, something strange had happened. He remembered it vividly as it recurred in that daydreaming moment: Bob's horned head had bent slightly forward and downward thereby exposing a slow and miraculous sprouting of wings from his shoulders, while at the same time his horns began to lose their shape, then shrank and disappeared altogether. Simultaneously, his fearsome expression had transmuted to a kind of childlike innocence. Here in the privacy of his large office, Ken didn't have to contain the loud and resounding laughter aching to come out. With no one around the building to hear the sounds, he let it out heartily from deep within his belly. His subconscious had expressed well what he dared not utter openly. In his dream, some sort of ironic joke had transformed Devil Bob into Angel Bob. What fun to be alive, he mused, as he realized that in some dark recess of his mind, the answer to a troubling dilemma he had had was there all the time.

Ken's dream seemed to vindicate Bob. Remember that when, in 1967, the BNL-Berkeley gentleman's agreement had been abrogated and Bob's big synchrotron went to the Chicago area rather than to the West or the East, Bob was labeled by BNL, and that included Ken, to be the man responsible for this infamy. But, without it ever having entered his consciousness, Ken had always somehow felt deep down that Bob was not the true villain of the piece. This insight remained hidden from him, repressed in his subconscious. Of course, to label Bob as the master of deceit and the betrayer was very convenient for the entire BNL crowd. In a strange way, Bob had provided them with some measure of guilt relief. Having absorbed all the blame, Bob left them all blameless. But there was a price to pay for this guilt-free trip: they were left with the vituperation and the belligerence that must be borne by the guilty yet blame-free. At BNL in the late sixties, this is exactly what took place, as recrimination and corruption filled the air. It was a bitter and ugly time that came to pass, not unlike a large family in the act of destroying itself.

Because the lab was unable to accept responsibility for its ordeal, a scapegoat mentality arose and grew. People turned on each other as they sought goats to which blame could be assigned. For most of those picked for punishment, the methods used were not very complicated and Ken remembered instances when he had watched the ugly acts perpetrated. A private office would be taken over, a travel request denied, a standard cost-of-living raise withheld, a job opportunity thwarted, and in extreme cases, a private telephone eliminated. There is no end to the ingenuity of functionaries determined to cause pain. Now that it was sure to become Ken's turn to feel the indignities and pain of the poisonous darts he believed were aimed at his vulnerable heart, he questioned why he hadn't interceded on behalf of others when he had the chance. Naturally, there was no answer forthcoming, only another question: why is it that we learn the importance and true essence of things only when it is far too late to do something about them? He could recall his vapid and lame rationalization at those times that this was simply the way people are made and the way things had to be. In Ken's defense, there was indeed a rational basis for such actions. The reason usually expressed to justify this form of harassment was to remove the unproductive; and the lab being a government installation, this was the only way to reach that end. You had to get them to go of their own free will because you couldn't just remove someone without the immense effort of a highly overblown *due process* regimen. In rare instances, it happened that those being pushed out resisted. At such times, moves toward involuntary termination might be initiated. That situation always turned ugly. Fortunately, it didn't happen much, but it was not unheard of. However, most sensed the truth. They knew this was only the beginning, and that rationality would not rule for very long. So it was a hard time for all, with everybody recognizing that things would only get worse.

After Bob won the day and BNL was the big loser, life at the lab worsened considerably, especially for the common worker. Extreme stress entered the picture on a large scale as the lab made its sad journey downward. At this stage on its slide to oblivion irrationality replaced rational decision-making, and not only were the unproductive singled out, but the undesirables and so-called troublemakers also became the targets of scorn. The weak links in the chain and the visible big-talkers came under severe attack, with the most vulnerable and defenseless singled out first. The objective now was to rid the lab of those who couldn't be taught to bend to the wills of the masters in charge. Harassment at the lab became commonplace. The idea was to bring people into line, with punishments meant to provoke ridicule and derision; and for higher-ranking types especially nasty ones were devised, ranging from being ostracized from the lab's social life to being deliberately left out of important meetings vital to their work. A thug mentality began to emerge and quickly spread throughout the institution, with those selected to do the dirty work seeming at times to enjoy their jobs. It was a bad show all around. Since Ken by that time was no longer part of the in-crowd at the lab, and since he had such a big mouth, he found himself to be one of the goats singled out for punishment. He wasn't shocked by this turn of events, and became resigned to the reality that he couldn't dodge the inevitable and would have to suffer. Fortunately for him, at least for the time being, the position he held gave him partial immunity from the usual punishments and indignities inflicted, and shielded him from the full treatment. By virtue of his relatively high place in the hierarchy, he had a substantial degree of protection from any really harsh or iron-handed kinds of administrative disciplinary actions, which for the most part were implemented by lower level apparatchiks. Nevertheless the bigger fish, such as Ken, who had not lived by the rules, by becoming either too independent or too outspoken and defiant, had their own brand of retribution awaiting them; and Ken, who had raised himself up by his bootstraps and risen well above his original expectations, was just about due to experience the fury of an indignant and exasperated man at the top. It was done in such a civilized manner that he was taken quite by surprise. Still, civilized or brutal, he was about to feel the boot of the regime.

Ken had some inkling that the ax would soon fall. Still, when it came, it was unexpected. Ken had gone to see Goldhaber in his spacious office to discuss some seemingly inconsequential personnel matter. Their disagreements on the budget had been a source of trouble between them, but this wasn't supposed to be an issue on that "high noon" October Friday in 1969, so the fact that an important matter was actually on Maurice's agenda caught Ken unawares. As he motioned for Ken to sit, Maurice was just about to end a phone call. As Ken sat on a plush but low chair in front of the Director's ornate desk, he felt uneasy and fidgety. Why had Maurice chosen to make him wait? It seemed to Ken to be a little disrespectful and quite unnecessary. He tried to get hold of himself and not to jump to any conclusions. Perhaps he was just over-reacting to the situation. Nevertheless, Maurice seemed distinctly disinterested, and Ken got the impression that he was acting that way deliberately. He couldn't put his finger on the reason but he had a feeling that a sandbagging was in the works. Could it be that Maurice was putting on an elaborate act as a way to soften Ken for the kill? This thinking added considerably to his discomfort. Even before they started talking, Ken became apprehensive and not just a bit nervous.

When Goldhaber finally put down the receiver, a smile formed on his face – an untrustworthy smile, Ken thought, but he chalked it up to his uneasiness. Why this atypical sense of foreboding came over him he couldn't tell. Perhaps his subconscious had been activated by something in the air. Perhaps all that he had seen happening at the lab in recent years, things that he had suppressed or overlooked in order to maintain his sanity, had been released in an inner emotional torrent. What could Maurice have up his sleeve, Ken wondered, and why hadn't he considered, before he came to the meeting, that he might be blindsided? He had been a trifle overconfident, to put it mildly. Obviously he hadn't properly prepared and now it was too late to do anything about it. In any case, he was about to find out. Maurice's wry smile magnified as he casually observed that Ken's term as Accelerator Department chairman would be up in a few months. A rush of thoughts overloaded Ken's mind's computer and he found himself tongue-tied. Wordless Ken was quite an anomaly and it didn't last long. Within seconds he had composed himself. True, he had been caught off-guard, but he was a man who was good on his feet. Having calmed himself, the old Ken came back to life. He artfully answered that he had considered the pros and cons, and even though his wife had thought he could use a little rest, he felt it his duty to stay a third term to see the Accelerator Department through the difficult times ahead. And so the real discussion began, with Maurice going first. "But Ken, in our last few discussions, you said you were dissatisfied with the Goldhaber administration and wouldn't put up with things the way they were. To me, that meant only one thing." Then, without as much as a how de do, the gloves came off. It was hard to discern what prompted Ken on this path, one from which there was no turning back. Maybe it had been building in him for a long time, and he just couldn't hold back the flood. "Look," he said, "we just don't agree with each other. We don't even like each other. But you and all your lackeys are dead wrong. I'm right. The lab can't go on emasculating and starving the people that made it great. And they're the ones that represent its only hope for the future. I won't let you do it." Maurice was dumbfounded. He couldn't believe anyone would speak to him this way, least of all someone who worked for him. The man who always played the role of the gentleman wasn't prepared for this. Ken had inadvertently found the right button to press that would cause Maurice to lose control. He had a momentary lapse and snapped back at Ken, "It's a done deal, it's been decided." "What do you mean," Ken perked up, "Who decided?" So it was, although it was only for a few seconds, that Maurice had lost that gentlemanly demeanor he so depended upon. He knew almost immediately that he had slipped up. He had allowed himself to be unmasked. Quickly he tried to collect himself and make the best of the tough situation he had gotten himself into. "Relax Ken, I just decided that there should be a change because I thought that's what you wanted. Now, let's calm down. Why don't you think about it for a minute and reconsider. Look, I'm planning to inform the tenured accelerator staff this afternoon that you're planning to step down, and then I'll announce it to the lab on Monday. Why don't you accept this reality and together we can plan a smooth transition. It's really for the best, both for the lab and for you." Ken remembered how at that moment his blood had begun to boil and he had become livid with rage. He jumped out of his chair and blurted out, "Oh, go to blazes." Then he got up and stomped out, angrily making his way down the corridor and out the front door. With a quick pace, he set a beeline toward the accelerator building; and on the way he seemed to find a way to calm himself down. However, he noticed that his body hadn't quite gotten the news, for when he held up his hands, he saw that they were shaking. As he walked briskly along, a strange smile took shape on his face.

There, he thought, it was now over and done with. Strangely he wasn't all that upset. On the contrary, he found that he was quite satisfied with himself. When all is said and done, you can absorb most anything, he thought. You can be scared, awfully scared, but once you face the truth, you find that you can take it. In fact, it wasn't easy for him. It did hurt. But once he coolly thought it over, once the words were articulated in his mind, and once he could lower his emotional level, he found he could live with it. It isn't as bad as all that, he thought. There was even a bit of a silver lining about the whole business – a heavy burden was lifted from his bony shoulders. When it was all over, a warm feeling came over him that day as he recognized something of himself that he hadn't known before – or at least that he couldn't be sure of – that he was a survivor.

By the time he walked up the flight of stairs and reached his office, the whole experience had decayed away in his mind to the point that it appeared as if nothing had happened. It was as if it had all been an illusion. Whatever had transpired between him and Goldhaber and whatever its implications, his understanding of these matters would have to wait. It made sense anyway to let it go for the time being because answers would not come easily and he had a lot of living to do. Although it was undeniable that an uncertain and probably painful period in his life had been set in motion, he knew that the world doesn't stop for you just because you've got something on your mind, no matter how serious you imagine it to be. You've got to grin and bear it and move on. The gory details of daily living demanded attention and there was much to be done. Sure he was hurt, but what did that matter in the larger scheme of things? Life goes on relentlessly, and if you're a man of the likes of Ken, you don't have a choice but to roll with the punches and move on as best you can. If anything, his incentive to achieve had been raised a notch because of what had happened. More than ever, he had to prove he was made of the right stuff, and so he was determined to keep on working until his last dying moment.

On the other hand, he couldn't ignore what had happened, because it impacted more than just himself. As far as it concerned him, there were no more doubts. The game was over and the stadium empty. He was resigned, and in a strange way content with the fact that no one could change the reality that he would have to give up the Department chairmanship. No one could help him and, in truth, he didn't want any help. But he couldn't just walk away from the whole mess. It wasn't only he that was involved. What about the effect on his colleagues? How would they react? Would they accept that it was a done deal or would they rebel against this naked aggression? For Ken knew that it wasn't only him that the physichists, those domineering experimentalist know-it-alls, were after. They were out for accelerator blood anywhere anyone stepped out of line. Some thought obedience to the new regime would save them, but Ken knew differently. Quiet or outspoken, they were all vulnerable. True, aggressiveness was dangerous in the atmosphere that then prevailed, but appeasement wasn't such a wise tactic either. It might work for a while, but eventually you'd have to pay and, in addition, lose your dignity in the bargain. Ken especially worried about John Blewett, a colleague and friend, who worked under him in charge of the development of advanced accelerator technology. What would John do, Ken wondered? Should Ken try to warn him of what probably awaited him? No, he thought, that probably wouldn't help a whit. It was hard to act on the experience of others – you had to feel it for yourself. Ken felt tired and helpless. Was there anything he could be sure of? He snickered to himself cynically as it occurred to him that the only thing he could be sure of was that his time was up. Yes, he thought, this would be a Friday that he would not soon forget. Becoming philosophical, he thought that perhaps all the accelerator folks, including himself, should simply accept things as they were and resign themselves to their fate. Yes, he kept trying to convince himself; perhaps it was for the best. A smile appeared on his face as he remembered Dr. Pangloss' repeated commentary on seeing the many images of the ugliness and pain of the world we live in, "It's all for the best in this best of all possible worlds."

Ken dozed a bit on the bright Saturday afternoon, the day after his fateful confrontation with Goldhaber. He still had a little while to wait before Rabi showed up. He fought the desire to rest a little and tried to imagine what the meeting would be like. But why belabor it, he thought? Once having made the link between what had happened the day before and what "the man" wanted to talk about, there wasn't much doubt. Continuing to feel drowsy, a catnap was far more appealing than speculating about what for the moment seemed obvious. So, he allowed his mind to wander into blank-mode. But after just a few seconds, he awoke with a shudder – his conscious memory wouldn't let him rest. His little gray cells persistently kept on firing. It was no use – peace and quiet would have to wait.

His thoughts meandered about, seeking a place to fix on. So it was that he found himself transported to a time almost a decade earlier, when the new Accelerator Department was in the formative process. With Haworth his boss then, Ken had a lot of say in the workings of the lab. But when the AGS opened the door to bigness, it entered the lab with a vengeance, and with it the inevitable result of big change. He could kick himself for not having given it more thought at the time: for not sorting out what was important and what was not, for not acting with more authority and boldness, for not recognizing deceit when he should have – in short, for not negotiating a better deal for the just-formed vulnerable Accelerator Department. Like all his friends and advisors, he was a know-it-all, and, as all such do, in the end he would suffer for it. Oh yes, he knew what bigness was. He was sure that he knew how to organize and shape a unified Accelerator Department to suit the future. It wasn't hard at all; in fact it was quite straightforward. All you had to do was be rational and logical, and the way to go would fall right in your lap. He remembered pushing the idea that labs didn't just build accelerators as separate entities anymore, but rather they were component parts of complete high-energy facilities. Experimenters and accelerator builders should be unified, he contended. To the simple-minded, non-political Ken, that sounded right, and naturally in an ideal world that would surely be true. In fact, his naïveté went so far as to have him believe that everyone would accept the idea at face value. It was motherhood to its very core – how could anyone object? However, Ken was not in an ideal world, but in the real one. True, the idea of a single accelerator-experiment facility was very impressive and high-sounding. Ken's mistake was that he didn't think it through. If he had, he'd have appreciated that the physichists didn't really want unity, at least not via a unification of equal partners. What they wanted instead is what they actually got: they became the leaders, the accelerator experts the slaves. Poor Ken thought that it would be easy to enter the arena where bigness resides, believing that he could make it a place where rationality ruled. How innocent he was, so confident that by saying the right words he could straightforwardly pull it off and gain his ends. Such beliefs and dreams were rather poignant for a man who had seen as much of how the world turns as he had. However, what blindness to the true reality it really was! He missed the transparent point that political maneuvering followed immutably in the wake of bigness; and in this world of politics, it was dog-eat-dog – it was the jungle where survival of the fittest was the paramount principle, and where the strongest won the day. That was the truth Ken crossed paths with; and it is the bitter truth all must learn, the innocent and cynical alike. To follow the road to a paradise of rational men will lead you only to a world of fools.

It took quite a while for Ken to discover this and finally recognize what a fool he'd been; but before that realization came, he first had to learn life's lessons the hard way, as most of us mortals do. The best that can be said for youthful Ken and the way he acted was that maybe he was just a simple kid thinking he could put something over on the astute but uncaring physichists. He thought, as any rational person would, that if he had all the experimental support people together in the Accelerator Department, he as boss-man could tell them what they could and couldn't do. He could determine what staff was available, where they were needed, and how best to utilize them. He would then choose to place so many physicists here, so many engineers there, and the same for technicians, machinists, and other staff. It was a reasonable idea and a very efficient use of the limited personnel available at the time. It was the coming together of two disparate groups of scientists that he had always wanted and thought any sane person also would want. It was unity, plain and simple, both manifestly and in spirit. Already way ahead of the other labs, it would carry BNL into the latter half of man's century of advanced technology, where glory awaited them.

When Ken offered up this idea to Haworth, Leland said yes and went along. Then, lo and behold, in quick succession, all agreed to it, even the usually argumentative physichists, and so it came to pass. But whatever the reasons, youth or stupidity, Ken and many others would have to suffer the consequences of his innocence – and they were swift in coming and full of pain. The unification of accelerator and experimental facilities, as Ken had dreamed of, never actually happened. In short order, Ken lost control of the experimental arm of the department. It should have occurred to him that such a thing might happen. But he was too lost in his wishes and so couldn't see the transparent reality around him. The experimenters and users in the Physics Department, Ken's nemesis physichists, were very close to the groups comprising the experimental support division of the Accelerator Department; and, with Haworth gone, the Physics Department staff, with Goldhaber and Rabi foursquare behind them, wielded extraordinary influence – they were the real power brokers at the lab. As a result, who would the experimental support teams that were formally under Ken be more likely to respond to when a conflict of authority arose? Would they choose to obey the dictates of Ken, or of their confidants, the physichists? Even though Ken was supposedly their boss, with him having lost any pull he might have had at the lab, their choice was a no-brainer. This point, so obvious in retrospect, was completely missed by Ken and his colleagues and advisors. They were blinded by their sincere wish to do the good things they thought were right for the lab. However, they weren't simpleton goody-goodies. Let's not forget that they were human, and so driven by a quite natural desire to accumulate power. This willingness to use muscle made it a real contest, but Ken and company nonetheless ended up losers. In retrospect, it's clear that Ken wasn't in a healthy situation. The Accelerator Department, soon after it was formed, became divided into isolated camps in opposition to each other: on one side were the accelerator loyalists, pledged to the department chairman; while on the other was the enemy, a sort of fifth column, loyal to the physichists. What a bind Ken was in! "Surrounded by assassins," as dear Jimmy Durante used to say.

Ken did try his level best – you can't take that away from him. At the beginning, when he still had some optimism, he appointed Hildred Blewett, John's wife, as head of the experimental division. That was a reasonable, actually a very good choice. Hildred was effective, fair, and loyal to both the department and the lab. But it wouldn't take long for the physichists to rid themselves of that tiresome woman. It was said at the time that John's failure to support his wife in her trying hour was the straw that broke the camel's back and sent her packing to CERN, eventually ending their marriage. Ken, innocent as he was, was unprepared for such ruthlessness, and he finally succumbed, surrendering unconditionally. The constant bickering between Ken and the Director and between Ken and the physichists had sapped his energy and taken the heart out of his will to win. He couldn't fight the good fight anymore. In time, he was forced to accept the reality that the physichists were to be the true leaders of his experimental facilities division. From then on, he had to live in the essentially untenable state where fully half his staff members didn't recognize his authority. How could he govern under such conditions? Even worse than that, he had to abide the spies living in his midst. It was a sorry plight he had fallen into. He tried to hide his dreadful position, even from himself, but he had become mortally wounded and came to rue the day that he had acted in such haste and with such arrogance in those earlier years with Haworth, when he at least had a chance to do things right.

Ken couldn't get Bob Wilson out of his head, and he began to question his understanding of his own role in the whole affair that blew the community wide apart following the issuance of the Ramsey Panel report. He saw BNL as the good guy, and he defended what he thought to be a legitimate agreement made in good faith between the two great labs, the Berkeley Radlab and BNL, representing the two U.S. coasts. Bob, on the other hand, saw things differently. He said that the country deserved better than the backroom politicking that was then the norm. Ken didn't get it at the time, but life's experiences gave him a tough-to-take education and forced him to abandon many notions about people that he had thought natural and obvious. Having learned the hard way, in life's laboratory, he would thenceforth be far more discerning and astute about what makes people tick and about the behavior of men-in-groups. As he remembered Bob and his words and deeds, Ken began to see Bob's thrust in the larger context of the conflict of the old versus the new, the past versus the future. This was no more and no less than Ken's own struggle at the lab. Without recognizing the true import of the positions he was taking in his fight with the established power structure, he had actually been representing the young and the hopeful knocking at the gate of the old and the entrenched status quo. He had always seen himself as one fighting for new ideas, new technologies, and new projects. He didn't doubt for a moment that just running the same experiments over and over, filling in every blank of what still remained to be measured, was not the only thing a great lab should be doing. A great lab should be looking to the future, pulling the working community along with it into the vast unknown. This was precisely what Bob had been trying to get across and, as it turned out, what Ken would be working toward to his dying day. And so Ken kept returning to Bob and to his dream of Bob sporting the wings of angels. Like Bob, he wanted to try to be of help in the passage from past to future. Unfortunately, just as Bob would have to experience later, he had come up against the immense power and determination of the old, who will fight, by whatever means it takes, to keep for themselves what they believe to be rightfully theirs. Ken and Bob indeed were kindred spirits, soul mates in man's ageless and bloody succession of fathers to sons. It is a harsh and unhappy process that fate has dictated for us, and it is doomed to be repeated till hell freezes over. To ignore this reality is to miss the true essence of living; it would be like having slept all the while during a life that comes but once.

Where was Rabi when BNL was making its fateful decisions of the sixties, and where was his "be bold" exhortation of the fifties? The battleground was full of activity and Rabi certainly should have been there. It was a situation made to order for him. Sadly, he was nowhere to be seen. This powerful voice of the forties and fifties had been dimmed almost to the point of silence. Rabi the powerhouse, Rabi the leader, Rabi "the man" had all but disappeared. What remained was only a shadow. When BNL needed a wise man of strength and stature, Ken tried very hard to understand Rabi's failure to come through; but being comparatively youthful, he could do no better than reach a harsh judgment. Rabi had become merely a figurehead. The little man who was big in heart and spirit had simply become just an ordinary, small man. Sometime, as the sixties wore on, the rapidly aging man, seemingly invulnerable and always on top of things, who knew everyone and could handle anything, began to lose more and more of his battles. His day was done and his night fast approaching.

Ken had always been buffered from Rabi by Haworth's strength. He had never actually felt the wrath of a man noted for outbursts, but, over the years, even without direct contact, Ken sensed Rabi to be untrustworthy, undependable, and certainly not a friend of his. Despite this, he never felt like gloating as he witnessed the fading away of this arrogant man. In fact, he felt quite the opposite. He discovered to his amazement that he actually missed the man. In some perverse sense, he missed his power, his pride, his certainty, and even his arrogance. When Ken had anguished over the incomprehensible stances Goldhaber took on the Berkeley-BNL Ramsey Panel matter, the question of entering the new arena of free competition, and finding the funds for technology to build BNL's future, he would sorely have liked to express his position to a man of Rabi's perceptiveness and high estate. But he didn't see this as a viable option, for, in Ken's mind, the Rabi of old had already passed on. No more would Rabi entrance his willing followers with exhortations like "go for everything" or "anything's possible" or "go for the gold." So Ken, no matter how confident he was that he could lead BNL to ever more glory, had no alternative but to accept that there was no one to appeal to. He felt all alone; and disappointment filled his being. Strangely, his deep emotions of self-loss and lost opportunities spilled over into an overwhelming feeling for a man who, for all he knew, was his enemy. The human drama of a fallen man that had been played out before him filled him with an immense sadness. Although only intermittently, an image kept recurring in his mind for years after was that of a man who had lost his soul, leaving a living shell to remind us all of life's ephemeral nature and inscrutability.

As Ken sat lolling in his reclining chair, waiting for Rabi, all his apprehensions of a strained confrontation, such as the one he had the previous day with Goldhaber, miraculously and mysteriously dissolved. With his emotions brought under control, soothing cool clear rationality spread throughout his body. He knew then that an angry outburst or any unpleasantness just wouldn't happen. How could it? Logic was now his guide, telling him that it would serve no purpose – given where they were in life, such behavior would make absolutely no sense either for him or for Rabi, providing nothing of value to either of them. The change in Ken's attitude, from the right side of his brain to the left, was quick and in his new frame of mind he wondered why he was there waiting at all. Why had he agreed to the meeting in the first place? Why had he wanted it? Rabi wasn't going to do anything for him – he couldn't. Maybe, Ken thought, he was confused and for a moment, when the meeting was being contemplated and arranged, he didn't really believe that the Rabi of old was no more. On the other hand, another explanation might be that he didn't really mean the meeting to be for himself at all, but rather for the others in the Accelerator Department he felt deeply responsible for. Even though the possibility that a positive result could ensue for them was just as slim as it was for him, he had to try to do something. That was Ken – he wasn't the type to just do nothing at all. However, in truth, Ken, without the need to verbalize it, knew the jig was up. The result was a foregone conclusion, and all this excessive pondering and reasoning were mere rationalization. The chances were that he could do nothing, either for himself or for the others. His time of influence was past and he had no choice but to resign himself to his weakness and helplessness. There was simply no way out for him.

After a brief, quiet, and meditative interlude, his thoughts turned to Rabi, marveling at what he had been and saddened by what he had become. Somewhere down the line Rabi had lost his soul and had turned to stone. The great man's heart had been broken, and from then on he didn't appear to care much anymore. Such thoughts made Ken pensive and wistful, and a great sadness overcame him. Sitting quietly, he was suddenly shaken by a spontaneous and intense memory-moment: remembering Rabi and his dying-transition of years earlier. He still couldn't believe that the vigorous bull and his inexhaustible energy had been quelled. In fact, although he seemed to know all along that it had happened – the visible signs were transparent – he never fully accepted the truth of it. As a result, the reality and its consequences, for the most part, lay dormant in some dark recess of his mind. But finally there were just too many open-to-all indications. Also, too many secrets had come to light. Ken could deny it no longer. It was true: Rabi, the thinker, the leader, the man who could move mountains, had died a long time ago. For the first time, having been blind before and unable to fully comprehend till now, Ken became sure of the momentous significance of what had taken place before his very eyes. A man of greatness had passed on. It was the classic and oft told story of irretrievable and unfathomable loss. Although it was not much of a consolation to him, Ken came to realize that no generation was immune to this ageless, sad tale told over and over again and destined to continue to the end of time. He sat still, and in his mind, he paid homage to the man who had been. Then he heard footsteps approaching. He swiveled in his chair and saw the short, stubby, and well-groomed gentleman standing and smiling in the doorway. Yes, Ken thought, he was still "the man" and would always be. He extended his hand, smiled a Ken Green smile, recalled with relish the delectable last drag he had taken, and looked forward to a martini just about an hour away.

PART II

Long Day's Journey Into Night

Chapters

3. Playing with Fire
4. ISABELLE Burned While George Fiddled
5. And the Band Played On
6. It Ended Before It Began

3. Playing with Fire

It was an eerie time at BNL in the late sixties. On the one hand, a sense of anticipation filled the air. The lab, the envy of all, was at its peak of glory, with swaggering Nobels-to-be prancing around its halls. Could greatness be far behind? On the other hand, who, in such an atmosphere swelling with the goodness of being, could have admitted into his consciousness the possibility that a turnaround from this idyllic state was in the making? There were shadowy hints of a downturn appearing in the near horizon; but as the wine flowed freely, as the bounty appeared everlasting, and as the bonds between colleagues and friends seemed true, the place where champions reside appeared to be close at hand. Who among them, reaping such rewards, could have seen a change coming? Then again, if one independent soul had caught a glimpse and seen the light, would he have dared utter a word? Not likely, for those with the courage of gods are rare finds on a planet of mortals. The lab leadership drank heavily of the wine of self-deceit, and strutted about in a manner to reinforce the false image of immortality. The shock of it all was that they were unbelievably unaware of what awaited them. They should have known better. They should have sensed the danger looming. That's what leaders are for. They should have seen the handwriting on the wall and prepared for the coming struggles. But, sadly, they were arrogant and blinded by the dancing dreams before their eyes. And so they saw nothing.

As it is with all human endeavors, there is another side to the visible picture. Superficially the appearance is that of the Garden of Eden as God fashioned it in the beginning. That is what we're meant to see; but under the surface, there is always trouble in paradise. Turn the coin around from the image that is in view – one of self-praise, of self-congratulations, of the smiles of success, and of celebration parties – and there to be found on the dark side is a different picture. But the true essence of human pursuits is not easily revealed, for it is concealed by an intricate mechanism naturally developed for the purpose of preserving what is already possessed and of grabbing even more, despite the cost to others. It operates via parasitic forces that reside within us and gain a foothold because of a powerful human instinct for self-deception, thereby allowing us to deny our unsavory actions and their consequences. These enemies within, not easily discernible and perhaps not even perceived or felt, lie in wait, relentlessly working their way and insidiously eating away at our guts. They can cause us to deceive, to hurt, to abuse, to oppress, to persecute, and to inflict all manner of pain; and ironically, these are all done in the name of the collective good. Ha! Yes, such a thing might exist, but for the most part, it is a fake, a ruse fashioned by the bad to hide the true selfish reasons for the evil deeds they claim they must inflict on others. When the endeavor reaches this stage of its life, it is doomed to failure. For the people involved, there is no hiding from these resident demons that whisper in their ears, *go on.* And don't think for a moment that you or anyone else is immune to them, because, more or less, they take shape and grow in all of us. They are part of our human nature; and when they choose to appear, there is no choice for most except to follow them. To win against such powerful foes is indeed a rare occurrence; and only those few who have sufficient courage and audacity to take the onerous path of confronting them – your own or those of others – have the possibility of beating them. But keep in mind that if you're feeling nervy and daring, and facing up to them is your choice, it were better done sooner than later. Because as time passes and the descent of the collective undertaking doesn't abate, people keep on weakening and losing heart, and, in tandem, the power of these parasites over us continues to grow. This is a lesson universally shared by all who have experienced the awful pain these monsters of the night can inflict. Sadly, however, few are capable of learning this lesson without first experiencing the pain and suffering themselves; and by then it is almost surely too late.

So it was that as the decade of the seventies was fast approaching – hopeful for many – the dark night began to close in on the lab. Its internal strife and squabbling over territory, status, and budget already all but robbed it of any unified purpose. The common mode of conduct was simply each man for himself. The unspoken consensus was to take care of number one. Although the superficial appearance to an outsider may have been one of optimism, under the mask of contentment and satisfaction there lay a mood of despair and hopelessness. This was not only because many couldn't visualize a future for themselves at a lab already in the early stages of stagnation, but also because outside the lab growth had burst forth and there was a rush of enviable activity. For insiders with the guts and the doggedness to look, their poor and inauspicious position was hard to escape. On the other hand, from out looking in, the simple truth was unmistakable that BNL was sinking fast relative to the other labs. The BNL inmates felt stuck in the mud – in a quagmire, unable to move – while others were racing by, flushed and aglow with the beautiful sweat of victorious runners. Needless to say, articulation of the actual prevailing conditions wasn't allowed inside. A fortress mentality had emerged – *if you're not with us, you're against us*. There was an insistent demand, made via peer pressure and threat, that everything outside be looked upon and treated as inimical to the lab's interests. To live under this form of rule and yet maintain a kind of deluded self-pride, most of the garrison's crew immediately complied and became believers, as asked of them; while those who didn't give in right away, if they wanted to survive, eventually found that they would have to bow to the pressure and even to pretend allegiance, if that's what it took. Cave-ins rose daily and would-be heroes seemed to be a dead breed. The secret behind attaining such a base and dastardly state was simple enough. Only visible, resolute, and consistent loyalty was permitted, and there was no slack in this rule. With the use of the usual strong-arm tactics, as well as newly devised ones, there was no tolerance for deviation from the requirement, *love it or leave it*. Any hint that you were not a team player branded you a traitor. It was a type of corruption that would surprise even the cynical and yet it was not something that could not have been foreseen. You might even say that it was not unexpected.

On the whole it was a bad time for those who had to live through it. As the lab moved into the seventies, those deemed to be traitors were systematically eliminated. They were either ostracized by being banished to the lab's Siberia or they had their souls exorcised. Sometimes those who had their fill of the agony and cruelty surrounding them and who simultaneously had the opportunity simply ran away. Still, as time passed, the lab in spite of it all managed to survive, even as the sinister practices continued. Yes, it would survive, but just barely, for, as it turned out, the lab would never again be the vibrant place it had been in its youth. Aging, which is never a happy condition, was to take its requisite toll, sans discount, and leave the lab reeling. Given the prevailing atmosphere and the life-style that had evolved, as one would expect, it was the good guys, those who could find better places, who left, while the weak and the mediocre, those who had nowhere to go, remained to man the bastions of the decaying fortress. These were bad omens for things to come, and there was no escaping the terrible times that lay ahead. The gods had spoken and were preparing their punishment. If one could only have pulled back to take a snapshot with the wide lens of historic insight, one might have seen and understood. Yet, even if that could have been done, would it have helped any? Could it have changed the course of history? Not likely! In any case, at the lab at that time, you couldn't expect such foresight, because that is not the stuff of those who have chosen to bed down with Lucifer.

* * * * *

Mickey, a brash, aggressive man-boy, came on the scene at a time when BNL had lost its way; however, being young, innocent, and blind, naturally this reality passed him by. It was 1966. On the outside, Big Science was on the threshold of the best of times. However, on the inside, it was the onset of the worst. For those whose loyalty, for better or worse, had been fixed by years of commitment, the difference hit them in the face daily. All around them were continual reminders of what had befallen the lab and themselves, thereby reinforcing and strengthening the inner stress and anguish that accompanied the way of life that had quietly crept up on them. Stuck as they were, rationalizing became the way they could get through each day. In the midst of this turmoil of mind and spirit, in walked Mickey, young, hopeful, and above all ambitious. He knew about all the stars, those who had risen to the heights before he had arrived, and those who were making their marks right around him. He wanted to become one of that ilk; he ached to get ahead and to make his presence felt. He was a guy most certainly on the make. To someone with less yearning for action, the lab atmosphere could have been disconcerting, even paralyzing, but it was not so for Mickey. He was the type of person who thought he knew most everything there was to know. However, in reality he had had a most sheltered life with little hard experience to speak of. As a result, he actually knew little of real life.

Mickey had a way of adjusting something seemingly terrible that was happening right in front of him so that after it had passed through his mind's filter, it would come out innocuous and sometimes even hopeful. There were times when he would think to himself that what he was seeing was not really an affront to his sensibility but more like an opportunity to snatch and move a notch up the ladder. It wasn't exactly that he couldn't perceive and appreciate what was taking place; it was more as if he couldn't effectively absorb and realistically assess and process the bad things that came into his view. It was almost as if he didn't want or perhaps was afraid to authenticate their genuineness. Still, every now and then, something would happen that would catch his attention, as if it represented a warning to him. But, with only passing hesitation, he would chalk up the occurrence as just an isolated case. His mind couldn't seem to add up these observations and integrate them into some bigger picture of reality, an inability that is no doubt the lot of the too young and the too hopeful. How mysterious life can be, for actually this weakness of the young could very well be man's one great hope for the future. It is perhaps one of those ironic jokes of the gods that mankind's continued progress stems in large measure from youth's ignorance. Without it, one can only wonder to what depths mankind might otherwise sink.

When Mickey came on the scene, like innocent youth in the throes of making his presence felt, he was saturated with hope. Even though he had come to the lab as it was rapidly waning, this didn't faze him in the least. Somehow, despite the lab's accelerator effort being in trouble, he sustained in himself a fresh sense of something great about those magnificent machines that he had set out to passionately pursue. It didn't occur to him that what he was seeking – becoming part of a grand design – was something of an illusion. Rather, because he so wanted to be part of the thrilling future his mind's eye envisioned, for the time being the fancy was a sufficient replacement for the real thing. Starting out with such artlessness, it isn't difficult to see how he could have so misconstrued the true nature of what was beginning to engulf the lab. As he became acclimated to the place, he began to notice things; but he found that he was capable of convincing himself that what was taking place amounted to no more than common everyday mistakes, easily corrected through straightforward logic via the well-known rational steps of observing, understanding, deciding, and then taking action. So, presuming it to be an easy task, Mickey, as is typical of the young at heart, had the audacious thought that he could be the one to set things right. Hey, no problem, he might easily have thought. All that was needed was a simple application of reasoning and common sense; and he was sure he had lots of those commodities. Thus was born his imagining of how he would reach high places.

For idealists this was an obvious course to take, one that they fervently believed was bound to succeed. And Mickey was most assuredly an idealist. But, as they all are, he too was blind. He couldn't see the more insidious reality lurking underneath that was sure to thwart his tireless rational, though simpleminded, efforts. Nonetheless, he pushed on, worked zealously, and sacrificed much of his time and energy. So deep was his conviction, what with his commonly burning the midnight oil, that his labors might easily have been interpreted as bordering on the altruistic. But, sad for him, the truth was that he hadn't had enough of life's knocks to judge wisely what was really going on all about him. Sheltered, as he had always been, how was he to know that his fellow inmates had built up a lot of baggage in their pasts at the lab, some of which, if it came out, would embarrass and discredit them? How was he to know that these regretted pasts had the danger-ridden potential of getting them demoted or even of destroying their careers, painfully built up over the years with sweat and tears? Mickey, when he arrived at BNL, bright, wide-eyed, and full of aspirations, knew nothing of this. He was but a baby with a lot to learn, and over the coming years, to his distress, learn he would.

Imagine yourself as one of those unfortunate souls who for one reason or another remains at the lab in the face of a looming disaster. To reverse the downward slide, owning up and admitting your share of the guilt is an obligatory prerequisite. But you're stuck with the fact that there's simply no accounting for the nasty and ugly things that went on and that you were part of. You could try to rationalize it all away by convincing yourself that they all took place a long time ago. Then you could continue the old tune: What good would it do to open old wounds? But when you add it all up, that's all bullshit. The truth is that in those days long gone, when the living was easy and when successes could be plucked as if from the air, you didn't give much thought to the other side of the success coin, the dark side – did you? They were days of wine and roses – who could think of much else? Then, when the bad times came, as was inevitable, you found yourself trapped by the unexpected, and in such risk-filled times, who would dare think at all? So, here you are, lips tightly sealed and safe for the time being. Yet, every now and then, a quiet moment would come upon you. Then, in solitude, an unwanted, unasked for reminder of what had actually been done would return to haunt you, and a wasted opportunity now gone forever would enter your mind. Try as you might to avoid such reminiscences, they would come anyway. If only you could erase these thoughts and wash your hands of them. If only you could wipe the slate clean and start fresh. But, sad to say, there's no escaping your past. The burden is yours to bear, and you know it – you know it only too well.

Ironically, what seems to have started the downhill roll was that anyone who was anyone was so happy with the lab. Why shouldn't they have been? Whatever a physicist was doing, whether he was a star or had pretensions to be one, it was the place to be. Sounds good, doesn't it? But not so fast! As it happened, it was the place to be only because there was nowhere else to go. Competition had all but vanished. True, there was the CERN PS facility, but at that time it was miles behind the U.S. in high-energy experimental capability. From this lack of the need to be competitive, a style evolved at BNL, one that led to a state in which the leaders took success for granted, believing they could act solely in their own self-interest, without paying the least attention to the general welfare. The result was a calamity in the making. A dark style developed, where fairness dissipated and eventually more or less disappeared. From there it only got worse. Punishment was meted out when it suited those in the driver's seat, rules were casually overlooked or broken, while blame was heaped on those poor souls with voices that at first wouldn't be listened to and eventually just couldn't be heard anymore. A dangerous combination of fear and deceit took hold. The latter was exposed by the telltale administrative procedures that were established ostensibly to give the workers more of a voice and a say in lab matters: There were committees set up ostensibly to hear people's concerns. There was an onslaught of bureaucratic memos asking for comments on the way things were going. Complaints were incessantly sought out; but what was really meant by this was, *complain at your own risk*. Believe it or not, these techniques were actually used for the purpose of rooting out troublemakers. The truth was that this overdone interest in the views of the workers was in reality a sham, meant not to enlighten management so as to improve conditions, but rather to silence those with the pluck or the inexperience to speak. In fact, the fraudulent trickery worked only too well.

Because the top dogs knew best, who would want to hear what the little guys down on the floor had to say anyway? What a sorry situation! But there was no one in sight who could do anything about it. Any notions that still remained that the lab leadership might wake up and see the light were but foolish hopes. There was only one possible outcome – a steep and swift road down. The trip was a sorrowful sight to behold: due process vanished and with it any semblance of institutional sanity. This bleak state of affairs was the beginning of the end of any possibility for a bright technological future for the lab. Within a few years the lab's great accelerator leaders, Ken Green and John Blewett, were beheaded, cut off in their prime. Both resisted more or less. Nevertheless,

Ken was forced to resign at the end of 1969 as the powerful Accelerator Department Chairman, while, in 1973, John, so angered by his dismissal, had to be virtually thrown out of his office as head of the Advanced Accelerator Design and Development group (AADD), to be replaced by a non-descript functionary, Harold Hahn. These actions, themselves of great consequence, were but the beginning of a reign of terror and a spate of self-destructive behavior that foreshadowed a bitter road ahead.

So it was that Mickey, young and foolish, walked right in where, had they known what awaited them, angels would have feared to tread. When he first set foot onto the Upton site, he was but a babe in arms, quite innocent of the world's cruel ways. He was ready to get on with his new job and his new life. But it soon became apparent that he and the lab were clearly not meant for each other. From the start, there were continual clashes erupting between them. The insoluble mixture of Mickey and the lab was a somewhat strange combination. Despite their being destined to grate on and oppose each other, they had an important similarity in that each had a blind spot: Mickey was oblivious to the dark reality inside the lab, while the lab was oblivious to the meaning of what was happening outside. It was this dual-natured ignorance that was at the core of the friction between them. Because of it, this was no match made in heaven. Yet, in some perverse sense, it was perhaps to Mickey's good fortune that this was how it was. True, he would have to suffer some, but with what strength of character he possessed and with the pluckiness he was able to muster, he found that he had the perseverance and the will to pull through with much of his dignity still intact. In the end he learned from the experience. He would turn out to be a better and a wiser person than the one who had started, even though it was only when it was over that he could appreciate and be grateful for the education he had received. Putting aside the much learning that came to him, both academic and about life, he had a very particular role to play in the ensuing BNL drama. In 1966, as the young and headstrong Mickey blithely strode in, the lab was in the midst of its changeover from rising star to withering vine. Who could blame him for being unaware that what fate had in store for him was to play the unbelieving child yelling that the emperor parading about in his seeming finery was really wearing no clothes at all?

Early in September of 1966, Mickey entered into his new life at the lab and set up shop. As he readied himself for a career of designing and building the great instruments called accelerators, he thought of himself rather grandiosely as part of a breathtaking venture to create those wondrous monuments of Big Science that gave palpable testimony to man's glory in the twentieth century. To such an end, Mickey would be willing to give his all. Whatever awaited him, he sensed deep within himself that it would be worth it. If hard work or sleepless nights or other manner of self-sacrifice were called for, then so be it. In those early days he judged it to be a unique opportunity for him that could not be counted on to come again. He thanked his lucky stars for giving him the chance. So, with an inner urge to boldness and the spirit of adventure in his soul, it was quite natural for Mickey to accept the challenge. And he did, with an overflowing hope in his heart and with all but certain confidence in how he would fare. He studied accelerators in great depth. Convinced of the importance and value of what he was embarking on, he worked long hours and with intense concentration. Loving the university and its ways, he adopted the academic approach of doing scholarly research.

It was a method that had stood the test of time, and he was ever so confident that it would work for him. With the persistence, the determination, and the ability to focus even with distractions all about him, these being his trademark characteristics, he was able to be especially productive, ever writing and succeeding in having published paper after paper – it was an almost non-stop effort. In this way, he was able to learn quickly the material of his new calling.

But even early on he had sensed that something was not quite right in the route he had chosen to learn his new craft. Something was missing, and slowly he came to realize what it was. Mickey had simply presumed that since an accelerator is an instrument of science, it would seem quite reasonable, as with all scientific instruments, to take university methods as the appropriate mode for conceiving it and for giving it life and maturity. But this logic was not quite right; at least the reasoning wasn't complete. It began to dawn on Mickey, as it had occurred to many far wiser people before him, that an accelerator is not just an ordinary instrument of science. It is a really big one, and as such it requires organization and project management, meaning large teams of people, large resource pools, large budgets, and an in-depth appreciation of the applicable implications coming from psychology, sociology, economics and politics. Is the university way of doing things right for this clearly interdisciplinary enterprise? Mickey asked himself. It probably wasn't, he regretfully conceded. Something was wrong with that approach, and he would surely have to do a lot of thinking about it.

This fact of bigness, when given adequate thought, clearly implies that the university alone, as it is constituted, doesn't represent a complete and adequate model for an enterprise like accelerator technology. To make it so, you'd have to fit a square peg into a circular hole. You'd have to change the entire academic infrastructure and that doesn't seem to be too reasonable a thing to try to do. Imagine trying to bring into harmony all those different scientific and social disciplines. No, there has to be a better way to approach the dilemma. Even if you could impose such a change on the university, it would probably be a case where the cure is worse than the disease. Besides, an even bigger hurdle to overcome is that this bigness is not only intellectual bigness but also physical bigness and financial bigness. Trying to shape a discipline out of the addition of all these disparate parts would be only to impose all but insurmountable burdens on the university system. The more deeply Mickey became involved in this issue, the more he came to feel that not only could he not rely on the university model to teach and guide him on the building and financing of this kind of big instrument, but he couldn't even rely on the university, the fountain of intellectuality, to guide him in learning about and understanding the essence and nature of accelerators. Yes, accelerators are science and therefore academic, and when they are sufficiently small, universities can make them, study them, and teach them. Perfect! But the big accelerators aren't at all a good fit to the universities. The resources are simply not there. Duh! Mickey thought, and finally got it. The point was that accelerators would have to be housed in an entirely new type of institution, and of course that's why the national labs, financed and overseen by the government, were fashioned in the first place. Once he gave it due thought, he wondered why he hadn't come to this obvious conclusion earlier. Yes, professors are ideal users of the lab facilities, and universities are useful as management intermediaries between the lab system and the government, but the university itself is simply not a good model to imitate for what the labs are meant to do.

Since Mickey couldn't depend on the university to provide him with a suitable academic package for accelerators, he had a problem. He wanted to learn about the detailed intricate workings of accelerators, so what was he to do? As far as the theory of accelerators was concerned, he would just have to learn the subject by researching it on his own. So far, so good! As for the bigness, after plodding along for a few years, he found the right way for him through a rediscovery of his roots. He was a lover of education and so he did what he had always done when he became aware that facing him was something he knew little or nothing about. Since the nature of organizations fell into that class, he sought an education in this field of study; and in 1971, working at night and weekends, he earned an MBA degree at Hofstra University, about 40 miles west of the lab, about at the limit of his commuting capability. Once he'd accomplished that, armed with degrees in physics and business and with all the research he had done, he was sure he would be able to find a way to unify it all into something coherent that he could use. So in the end he used the universities anyway, despite the fact that they didn't make it easy for him. He did what he had to do – he fashioned his own program.

One might wonder what this enterprising young man gained from all the effort he expended on educating himself in the accelerator business. Clearly, he accumulated a lot of knowledge in a multiple of academic disciplines. Mainly he learned about the secrets of accelerator science and about many of the technologies associated with accelerators. Unfortunately, he found that this type of formal education didn't give him much of an edge at the lab. That's the way it was and still is with the second-class accelerator field. The lab leaders wanted him only to serve their needs, no more, no less. What they didn't want was for him to think things through and come up with new ideas, as professors are supposed to do. That would mean that management decisions would have to be made – more work for them, tough choices to make. Certainly they didn't want that. The upshot was that not only was his status at the lab not improved because of his intense and broad education, it actually hurt him because he came to be considered a troublemaker. "He's always pushing for changes in direction," they would say, "somebody find a way to shut him up and get him off our backs." It's true that when a project is in the middle of construction, proposing that you switch technologies on a dime is not very sensible. However, that's why Mickey studied management. He well knew that in R&D projects, a balance between making changes and moving on is the key to success. You can't just drop what you're doing whenever a new idea pops up. On the other hand, you shouldn't continue on a doomed course just because you've already poured in a lot of resources to get there. He also understood that for a small R&D project, you might totally modify or even abandon it, no matter that you've gone quite far into it, if it's determined that that's the right thing to do. But when an R&D project is big, ah, that's when the balancing act becomes really hard. That's when guts and knowledge are a premium. That's when the presence of management genius may be the only way to get it right. And that's when leadership gets its severest of tests. Sadly, Mickey had come upon a lab in the middle of a big accelerator R&D project, but with a small-minded leadership; and the subsequent conflicts that arose between them thoroughly overshadowed his good intentions, his hard work, the knowledge he'd acquired, and his many scientific contributions. To say the least, for Mickey, this was not at all a good match. So, was his education all for naught? Actually not, for it would prove to be a valuable preparation for him, providing him with the option of running when the lab was rapidly fading. For the present, however, it was of little or no value. Still, even though all the effort and will he'd put into it couldn't stop the merry-go-round from turning, as BNL inexorably proceeded toward its sword-of-Damocles destiny with failure, he didn't let it get him down. Characteristically, he kept marching on, following the drumbeat in his heart in the sureness that he was going somewhere and that he was going to be somebody.

Once the AGS came, BNL was on top of the Big Science world. Come to think of it, it could well be seen as the founding lab of Big Science for basic research. As the lab's foremost leaders, the job of fulfilling its seemingly limitless potential fell to Rabi and Haworth, who together represented the guiding force behind the lab's great leap forward in the fifties. With ingenuity, brilliance and careful attention to a myriad of factors and details, these two remarkable men made the lab the great one, the one to beat. The centerpiece of their achievement, the brilliantly conceived AGS, became the doorway to a hitherto unimagined face of the physical world. With such a wonder of an instrument to lead the way, the lab could now lay claim to those rarest of gems, the stuff that science dreams are made of. All one had to do was to walk right through the door that had been opened wide. Actually, it wasn't quite that easy. The experiments were daunting challenges even to the best of the adventurous searchers. But experimenters like Nobelists Leon Lederman, Mel Schwartz, Jack Steinberger, Val Fitch, Jim Cronin, and Sam Ting as well as almost Nobelists such as Nick Samios would come to the fore to meet the test that life had laid before them. With knowledge, energy, imagination, dedication, and persistence bordering on stubbornness, they proved to be that once-in-a-lifetime aggregation of men on the make, men who could do anything they set their minds to, even unlock the mysteries of our universe. They stepped up to the plate; and one after the other, the home runs kept coming. They looked and felt unstoppable. How young they were, how hopeful, and how bold! But ultimately, sad to say, how dumb they all turned out to be. Yet, how could it have been otherwise? They were after all only human – and it is an unchangeable fact of life that man may reach great heights, but the glow of success and fame is fleeting and must eventually dim. So, in the end, their rationality and brilliance failed them, as, one by one, governed by the untrustworthy emotions of passion and desire, they overreached and took the fall.

As certain as that outcome is, it never ceases to surprise how fast the darkness intrudes on a man's moment in the sun. Some stood tall for a year, some for a decade, some switched directions in a vain attempt to hold on, but when their day of reckoning came, as it must, the sun set for each and all. These bright young pioneers, these explorers of the wilderness could not see the forest as they greedily hacked down the trees around them. In their blustering quest for greatness, they cut their own lifeline to the future. As had many before them, they forgot the past and its lessons. They thought that they needed no one, that they were sufficient unto themselves. First they ousted Haworth. Then, they surely didn't need the abrasive Ken Green or the gentlemanly John Blewett, so they believed. So they rid themselves of these and other tiresome blabbermouths, whose only blunder was to beg them to stretch for where the sun still shone. But they were young and couldn't be expected to know better. How, in the peak of their glory, could they apprehend that sooner or later betrayers, acting in the name of whatever good they imagine, will get their comeuppances? What goes around comes around! As it was, for BNL and its unseeing seekers of fame and laurels, there was nothing and no one to constrain them, and so it was only a matter of a brief time that they had to play their parts in fate's melodrama. Still, despite the fact that some might well have sensed the signals telling them to change their ways, they persisted unaware that the lab's sad destiny lay in wait but a hop, skip and a jump away.

Too busy with their internal squabbles, their discontent, and their mini-wars, all of the lab's staff and users – the management, the technologists, and the experimenters, including the physichists – blinded by triumph and praise, missed what was taking place outside their glory-filled bastion, especially a new generation of science-warriors coming on the scene. Those who were born to oppose the arrogant and aging lab that had had first dibs suddenly sprang up, trained for the fight, and prepared to take on the big BNL bully. They were probably quite astonished at the almost complete absence of will and muscle in their big-talking opponent. Via its self-annihilating tendencies, overconfident cockiness, and years of neglect and error-filled choices, the lab became flabby, overly cautious, and fearful of initiative. Finally destiny did what had been foretold – it stepped in and, speaking loudly and clearly, demanded that BNL be replaced as leader, just as BNL had replaced its predecessor, Berkeley, a decade or so earlier. The succession was sudden, as are all such transitions, and took place in just a few short years. True, BNL tried, in its fashion, to appease the gods by sustaining its gentleman's agreement with Berkeley. This missed the point entirely. What they didn't see or understand were their real enemies. They failed to recognize the barbarians at the gate, the new but ruthless visionaries, come to collect their due of the science bounty. When there are diamonds out there to be had, and while the amazing process of competition remains flourishing, deals such as the BNL-Berkeley one are nothing but distractions and born to be broken. Even in the best of circumstances, they will fall by the wayside under the heavy burdens of their own weight. This is what human experience tells us: words spoken or even signatures on pieces of paper must give way to the far stronger and far superior thrust of historical forces. The puny human will is no match for history's inexorable momentum.

The facts surrounding how badly BNL treated those who wouldn't follow its rules and dictates, when it was swimming in mind-boggling success, kept swirling around and wouldn't give anyone any peace. The issue was discussed interminably. However, it was all moot because following right on the heels of its days of splendor, the lab got its just desserts from a severe and awful onslaught that drove it into the ground. Immediately after the good times rolled by, even while they were still going on, the lab came to sway badly, terribly hurt by inner strife and a series of bold attacks from the outside. Who would stand up and defend the reeling lab in its hour of need? That was the big question of the day, and those who seriously searched for answers found only new puzzles. Where were they all when the heat in the kitchen began rising? Where were those men, both the big and the small, who had gained so much in the lab's days of grandeur? Especially, where were the big winners, the experimental users who became the top influence peddlers? Where was Lederman? Where were Cool and Lindenbaum? Where was Shutt? Where were the young, like Samios and Rau or Sandweiss and Willis? Where was Vineyard? Where were the trustees? Where were all the government reviewers and advisors? Where were all of the lab's friends who benefited so much? Where were the lab's management big guns? And where was Goldhaber, the Director? But most confounding of all, where was the little big man himself, Rabi? Rabi's absence from the fight was most mysterious, a high-octane enigma. If you looked hard enough, as few if any did, you could have seen the possibility. Although, as the fifties came to a close, he had been a man of the highest order and a force rarely come across, soon after, with hardly any signals, his presence seemed to ebb and vanish. So swiftly had the Rabi era come to a close that it left in its wake a power vacuum that in its filling could lead only to pain and hardship; and it was the lab – his lab – that would to be the big loser and that would have to pay the heavy price for his neglect in preparing for such a radical change. His loss left a lonely emptiness at the lab that was particularly hurtful because it was perhaps this man alone who might have been able to save BNL from the ravages of the pummeling and the stabbings that tend to characterize suddenly changing times. In hindsight, it wasn't difficult to see where the lab went wrong. It had depended too long on one man; and, such a strategy being highly unwise, it wasn't too surprising that he wasn't there when he was most needed. The fact is that he simply got too old and frail and had already lost his capability to fight. It creeps up on all of us. When time came for the succession, it was already too late. At least there was one hidden blessing in this sad story, for in all likelihood he wasn't even aware of what was happening to his dear lab. You see, even if he'd understood, he probably couldn't have done anything about it. Still, it was hard not to remember the old Rabi, the one in a million man who could have stood up and confronted the double turbulent instability, the one that was within the lab and the one besieging it from outside. And you just knew that he would have won. Yes, it was hard not to wish for "the man" of old. Unfortunately, his time had long since passed.

As waves of social and political forces swept through the U.S. in the turbulent sixties, society was massively transformed, leaving a greatly altered texture of people's mores, values, and attitudes. It changed their very way of life. At the same time, awe-inspiring and extraordinary changes found their way into the world of physics. So it was that the Big Science invasion began. Similar to what transpired in society as a whole, science experienced a freedom that granted it a loosening of social and political constraints. It was a liberating period, where uptight gave way to anything goes. For science, already well known for its freethinking spirit, this meant an even greater opening of the mind, where anything – to the point of extravagance – seemed possible and everyone wanted in. It was a time to think big, to act big and to achieve big. Although BNL had taken the lead as the decade opened, the changes in the making caught the lab napping. As the action around it began to swell and kept growing, BNL, with its leaders twiddling their thumbs and contemplating their navels, didn't follow suit and began to stagnate. The great lab of the East, in the grips of collective denial, had a hard road ahead of it.

Meanwhile, bigness, sans BNL, was bubbling. First, SLAC, without fanfare, became a Big Science player as the leading proponent and purveyor of electron beams, a niche they quietly and ruthlessly fought for and won. Then the Ramsey Panel saw the vast opportunities that could be had by expanding the realm of proton beams. Surprising to the panel, its report, meant to spur the U.S. to its destiny as number one, instead induced a captivated and persuaded Europe to step in and act first. CERN, which had already matched BNL's AGS with its own version, the PS, quickly jumped into the competitive fray that signaled a new race for science glory. In 1964 Weisskopf, CERN's Director-General, announced that CERN would build the world's first proton collider, ushering in the new technology of colliding proton beams. He further announced that CERN was planning to follow this with the next big step in proton beam energy, a synchrotron almost ten times the size of the AGS. CERN had thrown down the gauntlet. If it could catch the big giant asleep, then proud Europe might once again surpass America, and regain the position it had occupied in the good old days. America, although exceptionally generous to a devastated Europe in the post-war period, still had that competitive desire to win, and, holding the edge then, leapt forward in science, leaving Europe in the dust. Was it conceivable that the great U.S. would buckle under the new European initiative and become a science lightweight again? Bogged down in institutional squabbling and quibbling, it wasn't as impossible as it sounded. Then in 1965, the AEC broke the American bottleneck when they decided not only to build a series of new science facilities but also to institute a system of open bidding for them. Proposals to construct new facilities poured in to the prestigious National Academy of Sciences, which was chosen to run the show and to ensure its fairness. The game started far more quickly than the science community, which had settled into a kind of conservatism, had expected. But politicians don't suffer slowpokes, and it didn't take long, despite foot-dragging and wrangling by the scientists, for a site to be chosen for a big new facility near Chicago. By 1967, the U.S. had acted decisively and had beaten Europe to the punch, at least in the race for higher energy. Proud America was back in the driver's seat.

Meanwhile, back at BNL, because it hadn't won the competition for the site, which would have signaled the opportunity to move forward and reclaim its role as technology leader of the science world, there was consternation and anxiety. Strangely, the worrywarts were predominantly at the working level. The top management and scientific leadership seemed to take it all in stride. In fact, they apparently considered this whole train of events to be of little concern. They had somehow come to the view, erroneous as it turned out, that what was happening around them was nothing more than an extravagant and wasteful diversion. The result was that the Director, by words and action, insisted that BNL would not redirect its attention from what it was already doing. As far as the lab was concerned, only three things were important both to BNL and to high-energy physics, and these were experiments, more experiments, and even more experiments. As for the new technology of colliding beams, because it was uncertain at best, the Director concluded that the lab couldn't afford to be too wasteful on that front. Thus, just as it wouldn't fight for the big synchrotron that would soon rise in the Midwest, the lab decided not to fight for the high-energy collider also proposed by the Ramsey Panel. Instead BNL would stick by its informal agreement with the Berkeley Radlab and, honor being the better part of valor, would honor it. The lab plan was to continue on its path of doing more and more experiments and getting more and more physics data and results. This seemed to the lab's leaders to be the right and reasonable course and it was followed religiously. But that is not the end of the story, not by a long shot, because it was wrong-headed and pitiful decision-making and would have dire consequences for the lab's future. What the lab leaders had ended up doing, obviously not realizing its long-term impact on the lab, was nothing less than to leave the future to others. Casually and without ceremony, they had abandoned the lab's claim to being part of the exciting experiences and the fascinating times that lay ahead. The lab had started it all and assuredly had the right to be a major player in the game; but its current leaders, although they may not have fully appreciated the consequences and implications of what they were doing, chose to cede the whole field to others willing to fight for it. Reduced to its core action, they took a firm stand and risked all on the principle that *experiments now* were of prime importance and were therefore to have unquestioned priority over future technology development that could well be the key to guaranteeing the lab's preeminence in the coming years. How misguided was this course! Clearly, their chosen course violated a cardinal management rule that a proper balance between present and future is of the utmost importance and should take priority over all else – a corollary being that the future should never – that is, never – be sacrificed on the altar of the present.

This philosophy of *grab what you can and let what comes take care of itself* was not at all what BNL's originators had in mind. However, unbeknownst to the lab's incomparable founders and pioneers, Rabi and Haworth, the succession of 1960 was to entirely change the course the lab was meant to take. This they didn't expect; but from then on, the lab would run just as the newly installed men of small minds saw fit. Perhaps the Goldhaber team's priority was to work only with what they inherited simply because they hadn't the capability or the talent for invention. Excuses aside, it must have been a bitter blow for Rabi and Haworth to see their creation in the hands of such meager types. Meanwhile down on the floor, everyone was buzzing with the question, what did all these high-sounding generalities about priorities really mean? The workers there, by way of the real world of hard knocks, soon found out. First on the management agenda was what was to be done with the accelerator resources on hand, that is, the budget and the staff. You don't have to be a rocket scientist to figure that one out. Having overcome the demanding obstacles nature put in their path, the lab's accelerator scientists discovered the secret of reaching seemingly limitless particle energies, and so earned for BNL the reigning place of technological supremacy. Despite this, ignoring the call of the new frontier and the new experimental territory – higher collision energies – to be tapped, the lab came to the mundane decision to raise the intensity of the AGS so as to provide more beam for current-style experiments and to allow more experiments to go on simultaneously. What a letdown! Practically, this meant that more experimenters and more technical people preparing the experiments for the expanding program were needed. Okay, but what about the accelerator experts and machine people? You guessed it: there was less need for them. So they switched their work, left the lab, or simply became dispensable. What a reward for in effect creating the entire basis for the new field of Big Physics! And what did the lab achieve from all of its decision-making apparatus at work? It wasn't something to be proud of, for, as a result, the lab's accelerator experts, especially the high caliber ones, were lost to the more fertile ground sprouting around the country and the world. Although the semi-comatose lab leaders didn't see it, BNL would suffer harshly for this action.

Even if they had come face to face with a better avenue to take, the management wouldn't have been able to recognize it. They were mere amateurs. So they pushed on their perilous path, unaware of what they were doing. In any case, they had the ever-present daily practical matters to contend with. How was the management going to put meat on their skeletal strategy? The immediate and pressing question was how they were to get the higher beam intensity needed to discharge their obligation to the waiting users. Could they really successfully fulfill the bargain with a weakened and demoralized accelerator staff? But the guys who ran the Director's office weren't at all fazed. The top eggheads put their minds to work and devised a plan quite in line with their small intellects. "Why not come up with a new construction project?" came the word from on high. "That would kill two birds with one stone. In addition to providing the increased beam intensity after the project was completed, the idea would allow the lab to maintain for the present the flow of incoming construction funds from the acquiescent and compliant AEC." Furthermore, they believed that, because it was such a straightforward project, even the remaining thinned-out accelerator crew could do it. And so the lab leadership invented, and there came to pass, the so-called Conversion Project. The BNL supporters in the science community and the AEC went along like the sheep they were. But alas, the project was a flop. Technically, it was years before any significant performance increase materialized; and even worse, it was a thoroughly wasted effort because there wasn't much new to be done at the AGS energy, even with the higher intensity. More than fifty million dollars and a few years later, the result was, at best, a mediocre accomplishment. However, it was not only a current bust; the worst was yet to come. Two disastrous consequences stand out. BNL ended up with a greatly weakened accelerator effort, and actually was transformed from technological giant to technological dwarf. But perhaps the biggest joke on the lab was that it ended up with a lower class of experimenter as well, because the stars and would-be stars left for more promising and inspiring higher energy terrain. Life can certainly be cruel!

Yet, that was only the start of the lab's bad times – now those who followed would have to feel, big-time, the mistakes made by their leaders. With the onset of the seventies, everyone in the physics community came to recognize the wrongheaded and self-defeating policies of the BNL administration. Standing out was the harsh judgment made on the inept choice of doing the unproductive and wasteful Conversion Project, a glaring symbol of the leadership's incompetence. Thus, the suffering began. Blame had to be placed and the big question was who would be chosen to feel the brunt of it? It surely wouldn't be the users, who had pushed so eagerly and energetically for the project; nor would it be those community leaders – theorists, physichists, and the like – who chose it for the lab and influenced the AEC to go along; and certainly it wouldn't be the management upper crust that mandated it for the lab's future and carried it to its acrimonious and bitter conclusion. Then, who? Not surprisingly, it was the accelerator experts and especially their leaders who would bear the lion's share of the punishment for the lab's misguided ways. So it was that Ken Green and John Blewett suffered their fates. The whole fiasco had an unreal edge to it, as if the lab were cutting off its head to spite its face. Although the dawning of the seventies was a time of enormous optimism and represented a new age for the field of high-energy physics, for the shrinking BNL enclave the picture was radically different. Being in the throes of internal and external conflict that was harsh and often cruel to the players involved, the lab was in a dark and ugly state. But that wasn't the worst of it – still more remained in store for the cheerless lab. Unknown to the decision-makers at the time, what they were experiencing was but a prelude to a distressing decline that would last for decades. In fact, as the turn of the century would approach, there would still be no recovery in sight. With the passage of time, even the will to play the game and to compete would wither away and die, probably to remain dormant for a long time to come. Whether the disease, if not fatal, can be reversed and whether the lab can be revived and revitalized, only time and another generation can tell. That, without embellishment, is the reality and the pure truth.

It is one of nature's quirks that the mind, the unfathomable mind, the great equivocator, has the disconcerting habit of playing tricks on us. In the memory of many who lived through those trying times, haziness descended over the desperate days as the century wore on and came to a close. Strangely though, they remembered only too well the sixties, a time they retrospectively perceived as one of great success, and of jubilation and dancing. In actuality, it wasn't at all like that: this fabricated and misleading portrayal served to soothe their agonized spirits. Although the outward appearance could have been interpreted that way, under the rosy exterior lay a truth quite different, quite the opposite. For you see, it was then that the roots of the bad times to come were developing and spreading. Sadly, at the time, when things might have been righted, the actors wouldn't or couldn't see the authentic reality. Then, as the lab entered the seventies and moved from there relentlessly to the century's close, the actors, blinded by their past glory and counterfeit dreams, stuck to their parts – and the band played on.

* * * * *

Mickey kept on studying the art and science of accelerators. Day after day, night after night, his learning went on and his knowledge kept growing. Meanwhile the lab leadership was in the dark and struggling to find its way into an uncertain future after the devastating turn of events during the sixties. Mickey, both an idealist and an opportunist – not an unlikely combination – could feel in his guts that this was a perfect time for him. With the lab in such a state, he would help it find its way into the sunlight. There were so many challenging technical and technological issues to be analyzed, so many theoretical calculations to be done, and so many design answers needed yesterday, as some group leaders liked to joke. From Mickey's vantage point, the atmosphere in the Accelerator Department was encouraging. New ideas for lab projects were in great demand and Mickey and his colleagues were only too eager to comply, and kept them coming, one after the other, almost like an idea assembly line. On the other hand, the lab leadership was in a quandary. BNL had lost its edge, while its competitors – Fermilab, CERN, and SLAC – had stolen away with the new-project show. The lab management knew that they had to do something but they didn't know what it should be. Furthermore, since they lacked accelerator know-how, they didn't know exactly what the lab was capable of. That's why they kept changing their demands for new and different designs from the accelerator experts. First they wanted this machine, then another, and this process went on with no light in sight at the end of the tunnel. It must have been tough for the men at the top, because the time was ripe for a new round of accelerator projects. Unfortunately, as the administration and congressional politicos waited eagerly for proposals from the labs, BNL was filled with uncertainty. They were ill prepared for the competitiveness contest at hand. Although it was imperative to put up a good front for the government – projecting confidence and capability – the best the lab could offer up was procrastination and vacillation. It quickly became evident that if

BNL was to get in on the action and be a player, it couldn't be done through technical prowess. The only route that appeared open to them was the political one.

For those leading the accelerator effort at the lab, these were anxious days. They hardly knew what to expect next from top management. They felt like yoyos run by impulsive and erratic children. But for Mickey, it was a good time. He loved the game, and especially its suspense and ambiguity. Some would label that peculiarly odd. But Mickey felt invincible. He believed that the precariousness, the insecurity, and the instability surrounding him could be just what he needed – the opportunity to get ahead. He was so sure that as the others fell by the wayside, he would be one who would be left standing.

It is often said that knowledge is power; and Mickey had accumulated a lot of the former and was getting more every day. He would get a kick out of his dealings with his hierarchical superiors who knew little or nothing about accelerators but still thought they could boss him around. He recalled with a kind of mischievous glee situations where he was asked to pursue a particular design direction dear to one of their hearts. Then, finding that it was a technical blind alley and impractical, he would insist, "No, you can't do that." It was great fun for Mickey to see these ultra-serious know-it-alls squirming. On the other hand, he didn't make many friends that way and it wouldn't be too long before he would have to pay the piper. So, although Mickey got a great kick out of using his knowledge in this unorthodox way, the power he had hoped to acquire with it remained out of reach and inaccessible.

But even at this time, when he was still young, buoyant, free and easy, and full of play, it wasn't all fun and games. It irritated him to be jerked around by the management uppity-ups. They were so unsure of themselves – and with good reason. They didn't know where they were or where they wanted to go – technically as well as politically. So they would shift gears on a dime, and that meant he was pulled off whatever he was in the middle of doing and directed onto something else. The explanations given for such unreasonable actions were that some higher-up or experimental advisor had commented at some exclusive meeting, "No, not this facility, this other one is better," or "This costs too much, try this other approach." For the most part, the options Mickey was presented with either weren't practical, weren't useful, or were even dead wrong. Everything was so tenuous that someone's whim could push Mickey onto an entirely different calculation or analysis. Stressed out as they were, it was hard to blame the top honchos for not knowing which way to turn. Still, sometimes Mickey felt like kicking their butts or hitting them square on their noggins, this especially when they came up with all manner of excuses, some even reasonable, to change previously accepted ideas and designs – and the change orders kept coming, seemingly non-stop. Irritating as it was, Mickey and the other accelerator workhorses had little choice but to comply. They would just grin and bear it and do the job asked of them. Strangely, however, they didn't exactly find these chores disagreeable. The truth was that, even though at times they felt used and often abused, being needed wasn't such a bad position for the accelerator staff to be in, for it did offer them a manner of job security. Although not a word about how they really felt was ever spoken, this fact of life was well understood by all. All, that is, except Mickey! He was a bit different from the rest. For him, it wasn't job permanence that mattered; for him, that was irrelevant. In a strange way, which he was only partly aware of, the way things were going was just the way he wanted them to go. He had another agenda and he actually liked the situation as it was. While the higher-ups were off-stride, he felt that he had the upper hand. The way he looked at it was that he was doing what he wanted to and what he believed was good for him. He was in his element, learning the ins and outs of the accelerator enterprise, and, at the same time, learning the machines from top to bottom and from all sides. As an added dividend, the position he was in also afforded him the amusing and satisfying opportunity of tweaking the authoritarian noses of his pompous bosses. Believe it or not, Mickey was happy to be exactly where he was. At some moments, alone with his thoughts, he would smile to himself as he acknowledged the irony of his situation – having so much fun while around him stress-induced shakiness and fear prevailed.

One day in 1969, Mickey first heard the new idea for a big proton collider at the lab, much like the one CERN was putting into action (the ISR, standing for Intersecting Storage Rings); but BNL's would be much higher in energy. CERN's initiative was the European reaction to the Ramsey Panel recommendations, thus beating the U.S. to the punch. The ISR was fashioned to be a storage ring, operating at a single energy, that of the PS, which would serve as the beam injector. The BNL plan, putting the U.S. back on top if successful, would allow the beam to be accelerated, and so provide beam collisions at many different energies, up from that of the injector AGS to a peak of almost ten times that of the CERN ISR. In addition, the new enterprising American machine would be designed to use superconducting technology, the developing great hope for the future of accelerators and many other instruments of the modern world. He knew immediately that this was what he wanted to spend his time on. Work, Mickey's sine qua non, was the backbone of his way of getting things done, as well as getting ahead, and work he did. First, there was reading to be done and then study, a lot of study. Since Mickey was an impatient and restless sort of person, he began to compute how beams would behave under different designs even before he was truly ready for the beam research he was so anxious to get into. In spite of his rush to get into the real action, he matured quickly. Soon he was writing and publishing papers in academic journals. He found the work stimulating, rewarding, and oh so exciting. He was nothing if not a happy camper.

There was another side to Mickey's chosen profession as a physicist in Big Science. The effort to conceive, design, and build an accelerator was a big one and involved all types of people – scientists, engineers, technicians, administrators, and others – all working closely together. That meant his work included a lot of people interactions. This involved him in seemingly wall-to-wall discussions, and imposed on him the sometimes-exasperating strain that resulted from the collaborations he developed with colleagues, some necessary and some much desired. The endless meetings would tax him the hardest. Although he would always remember this time as exasperating, it was also satisfying, invigorating, and even thrilling – it was one of his life choices that he would never regret. Mickey instinctively came to realize that, besides all the fun he was having, he was living through an experience of far more consequence than the thorny and irksome little business he had to put up with daily with his co-workers: the tussles and the scuffles, the contentions and the conflicts, and the ordinary trials and tribulations that are an intrinsic component of the drama of human contact. How could all that diversionary personal stuff matter much when he was in the middle of the birthing of a team, a family of people working in concert to get somewhere where others hadn't been before? The fact that in the end this team would not succeed did not detract from the know-how, the understanding, and the skills he was gleaning. Mickey was working, experiencing, and learning, and, as time would pass, these days of concerted effort, which would turn into weeks and then into months and years, in some mysterious way would transform him from a boy into a man.

With his will power for work operating at full throttle, Mickey thrived in this atmosphere pregnant with possibility. At times he worried that he was becoming a workaholic and might quickly burn out. But fear was not in his lexicon of rules to live by, and nothing could deter him from his unshakable determination to squeeze from his surroundings all there was to be had, and to make of his life the most he was capable of. He was ravenous to learn and devoured everything in sight as well as all he could dig up. He worked and wrote with anyone who was willing to collaborate with him no matter how much or little effort that individual was willing to contribute. He was ambitious and aggressive, but he also had team spirit and wanted to be part of a whole that was bigger than himself alone. As time passed, ideas flowed from him seemingly without effort, and journal articles quickly followed, and so his paper trail and his knowledge grew. He learned from everything and everyone with the absorption rate of a bright child and so got to know just about all there was to know about designing, building, and operating accelerators. Almost without noticing it, the project he was giving so much of himself to, which came to be called ISABELLE, had become almost an obsession. Perhaps it was because of his passionate desire for her, but this grand dame of modern technology had graciously and perhaps wantonly opened her mysteries to him, and he had come to know her from top to bottom and from stem to stern – every nook and cranny of her being, every curve of her body, and every gorgeous design feature she had to offer. But the lady, like Eve, had been fashioned from Mickey's rib, and so he would come to know more of her than he should have dared seek. From his time with her and his explorations of her, he was led inexorably to her many imperfections. It was dangerous to discover such things; but undaunted, he pushed on and came to know her warts, her blemishes, her faults, and her weaknesses. Having entered the game with an inextinguishable desire to learn the truth and see the light, he had unexpectedly stumbled onto the other side of knowledge gained – the dark side. He could have just closed his eyes to it. He could have just let it go, as most of his BNL colleagues did. But not Mickey! He eagerly gobbled it up with relish and abandon. He had to have it, come what may. So it was that he came to know the truth of ISABELLE. And it was this truth, the one lying hidden in the murky waters, that would prove to be, for better or worse, Mickey's door to the future.

Rena Chasman arrived at BNL a couple of years before Mickey. Contrary to Mickey, who had to go it alone, she had the good fortune to work directly with a couple of the big boys of the accelerator crowd. She came to the lab as Yale professor Bob Gluckstern's protégé; and almost immediately BNL's own John Blewett came to show a special interest in her. Rena had the kind of personality and demeanor that made her easy to feel fatherly toward, and, in addition to Gluckstern and Blewett, many others did.

Perhaps they were attracted to her because of her oh so feminine ways, how she carried herself, how she smiled and spoke and walked; or perhaps it was because of her air of vulnerability. Or, if these reasons don't seem sufficiently satisfying to fully explain the way people felt about and treated her, then perhaps it was just that Rena was a woman and women, rare in the male-dominated world of physics, were not surprisingly given special advantage and privileges. Some feminists might dispute this and say otherwise, but nonetheless, that's the way it was. However, make no mistake about it, she was a fine scientist, quick, smart and accomplished. When a complicated calculation was needed, it can be said without the least hesitation that she could be counted on to get it done right. On the other hand, she wasn't an innovator and, besides, she didn't at all like to rock the boat. There was no drive in her to bring in new ideas, particularly controversial ones, that would cause change – material change or change in the way we see things, these being the ultimate goals of the essential scientist. So, in the science world, where imagination and discovering the unexpected were paramount, she had her limitations.

Nevertheless, Rena learned quickly about the ways of her chosen line of work. As an early feminist, she found a way to combine the new power that the movement gave women with her own natural femininity, and she came to use them together as a means of climbing up the science ladder. She recognized early in her career that her attractiveness to men had given her a special opportunity to advance rapidly. Thus, with determination, energy and a quick and strong mind, she was able to earn tenure at the lab in short order. Mickey, on the other hand, had to wait more than a decade to reach that exalted place that was in universal demand. It was the thing everybody sought, the thing to have, mainly because the group of tenured staff was a club of sorts that gave special professional status to its members and conferred on them the security of their positions that was to all intents and purposes inviolate. Although all the scientists and engineers at the lab wanted it intensely, it was never clear to the innocent and idealistic Mickey whether all this rigmarole really made a difference. But that might have been sheer rationalization, because something deep within him bothered him about the fact that Rena seemed to advance so easily and that he had to fight so ferociously trying to reach the same place. Yes, jealousy could have been a factor but, at the time, being young enough to convince himself – perhaps fool himself – that such things don't matter much, he was able to keep such dark feelings in check and far from his consciousness. Overtly, he chalked it up to the simple reality that she was a woman and he was a man, and that's the way things are in this best of all possible worlds.

Mickey was still in the prime time of his life when he believed that merit would win out in the end. Each of us, his rational mind insisted, presents a distinct and unique image to others, and although first reactions are based on that image, eventually it's what's deeper inside that comes to count. Still, even though Mickey had faith in America's pact with all its citizens that there would be equal opportunity for all, there were times when some cynicism would rear its ugly little head. There was the time in 1971 when he published a paper under his name alone, without informing Rena. He manufactured reasons for having done this in the ingenious way he found for compartmentalizing a problem they were working on together. He persuaded himself that this particular bit was his work alone, and that she wasn't really involved. He had a point, a very small one, that the paper was pure theory, and Rena wasn't really a theory person. Their work together was primarily doing computer calculations and analyzing the results. Mickey chose to view this and theory as distinct, thus giving him the go-ahead sign. Aside from the fact that this point itself is questionable, his reasoning was wrong at its very core because when you're collaborating with someone, everything you publish should be given joint credit. There's no ifs, ands, or buts about it. You see, ideas have a habit of seeping from one person to another even when you're not aware it's happening. So, to imagine that you can draw a clear line separating what's his from what's hers is on the face of it false. Recognizing in the end that words alone can't make right out of wrong, he would always regret what he had done, even though it was an inconsequential peccadillo.

It turned out that as time passed, this issue of *who gets the credit* never amounted to anything because Rena was the type of person to forgive and forget. Thus, their collaboration and rapport survived Mickey's faux pas. Actually, what meant far more to them was that they liked each other and liked working together. These were the key and essential ingredients of their relationship, and gave it its lasting quality. When it came to the incident, from her side, it never hurt their closeness and their caring for each other. Mickey, from his side, taking his cue from her, never let the subject of special advantage become an issue between them. As a result of their cool heads and warm hearts, they sustained their mutually advantageous partnership. Furthermore, with the encouragement of their bosses, particularly John Blewett, their productive association as a team kept growing and getting better. Yet, perhaps what was the most important factor of all was that they were honest to the letter with each other. And so, they worked harmoniously together for many years to come. There was no other way to describe their scientific collaboration than as an ideal one. Not only did they develop a systematic and out-and-out understanding of the physics and technology of the ISABELLE project, but they also helped each other to become better scientists. It was a kind of tribute to friendship and forgiveness as a way of life.

As Rena and Mickey sweated and gave their all to sketch the outline of ISABELLE, BNL's lady of the day and door to the future, the lab was going through hard times. Uncertainty, impending change, serious concerns, and an overall sense of urgency were all around. The lab staff wasn't blind to what was going on. But they weren't privy to the details, and so felt a pressing need to talk of the things they observed and experienced. It was a difficult urge to rein in. To such a degree did it open up people's feelings that they began to obsess with colleagues about their future and particularly what was to become of their professional careers. It got to the point where they found themselves discussing, even with casual acquaintances, private thoughts and matters important to their personal lives. Such is the impact of high anxiety. It was a perplexing time and had many unexpected effects. Many people were brought closer together by the bad things seen occurring around them, and unlikely friendships were fostered. Mickey discovered that, if you carefully sought them out, advantages could be found in this troubled and unhealthy atmosphere. One such person who could be very helpful to him was Rena. What a valuable trump card she could be! Rena had ties to the lab's leadership, and because of Mickey's close friendship with her, as well as her magnanimous openness, he was afforded a rare opportunity for access to people not normally accessible to the hoi polloi. In his defense, he didn't indulge in any pretense and trickery, but rather was prompted by a natural tendency to learn as much as possible before trying to figure out what to do and how to act. Nonetheless, whatever his actual motives were, he came to use people in this way – this being the norm encouraged by the inauspicious and on-your-own atmosphere of the time. This way of life, prompted by the feelings in people living on the edge, became the manner in which most of the staff dealt with the difficult situations they found themselves in. There was much to find out and everyone wanted to know as much as possible. Although lack of trust lay just beneath the surface, openness and apparent frankness was the interacting mode of conduct. The upshot was that there was a lot of talk, both at the top and at the bottom, and there was a lot of news to be had. People-contact dramatically rose. Would you have expected otherwise? When people's confidence in their well-being is shaken or threatened, some lash out, some become paralyzed, and some won't admit what's happening to them. What is common to all of them is their desire to communicate, and so gossip at the lab became rampant. Not unexpectedly, there was a serious downside to this: yes, people saw more of each other, but, unfortunately, two-faced behavior became the governing rule. The big trick, as people came to learn, was distinguishing what was real from what was mere rumor or downright false.

As is well known, talk is cheap and talk there was plenty of. However, when it came to acting, ah, that was a different thing altogether. It's not always easy to know what to do, and this universal verity could be magnified many times over when times are especially tough. At such times, lying in wait just ahead and hidden from view could be a big decision that could easily be harmful to anyone's future. What should any reasonable person do but to try to accumulate as much knowledge as possible in the hope of averting an action against him? It was fortunate for Rena and Mickey that both liked to talk and both had a lot to say. At least this gave each of them a sense that somebody cared. The two, with trust in their hearts, helped each other get through those hard days, with Rena providing a lot of hard information and Mickey contributing advice that Rena much appreciated. Even though they mutually benefited from their working well together and from their warm friendship, because of their relative positions at the lab, there was in those tough times a special advantage for Mickey. Since Rena had tenure and Mickey didn't, Rena became a conduit whereby Mickey came to know things about others that would otherwise be unavailable to him. Concerning the event in 1969 so important to the lab's future, without Rena, Mickey would have had little or no direct knowledge of what actually happened. It was a singular moment of decision for the lab, which Mickey would later come to see as a turning point edging the lab into a downward spiral it could not reverse. In those years ahead, as he slowly came to a greater understanding of this incident, Mickey often thought of Rena and the help she had afforded him in the early stages of his education of how matters of importance were conducted in the Big Science arena. Yes, she had given him a most precious gift. Only with her information and her insights could he have come to appreciate that it was in that period the lab's future course became inevitable, that the die had been cast. Still, even with the help he got, he didn't come upon the right answer easily. Poor dense Mickey found it hard to get it into his thick skull that this moment really represented the critical point for the lab's ultimate decline. It couldn't be, he often thought, because his rational mind told him that the pure will of good people could surely have allowed, in the intervening period, a change in course before the ax fell years later. Nevertheless, the truth was that his logic was not applicable to human affairs, and this indeed was one of those momentous events that mark a point of no return, and it was this event that would resonate in Mickey's mind for years to come, symbolizing BNL's fall from grace.

* * * * *

On a gray, chilly fall Friday in October 1969, Mickey was writing away in his office when Rena entered abruptly, flushed with anger, slamming the door behind her. This was very unlike her. Normally she was reticent and hesitant, even shy, although Mickey thought this was a role that she had learned to play over the years that gave her an edge in her relationships while at the same time suiting her friends and associates. This mode of behavior had come to be part of the Rena persona. But this dark day was different: she was enraged with a passion uncommon to her as she told Mickey the story that had brought her to this state. When she arrived at the lab that morning, a meeting notice in her mailbox informed her that the Accelerator Department tenured staff was to meet with the Director after lunch in his office. She had a queasy feeling that some untoward business might be in the works. Usually the Department Chair would call such a get-together, while in addition the common practice was to supply an agenda listing the issues to be dealt with. However, this case was out of the ordinary: no topic was stated, and it was the Director who had called the meeting, thus bypassing the Chairman. That last point might have clued her in, as she wondered: Is there more here than meets the eye? Rena became increasingly anxious as her thoughts dwelt on that possibility – she couldn't seem to let go of it. Without being able to put her finger exactly on it, she felt there was an unpropitious and ominous tone in the manner the meeting was being organized. However, being cautious by nature, she managed to box up her worries inside herself. She tried to convince herself that there was nothing to be especially concerned about; and she achieved some measure of calmness by the simple act of taking a few deep breaths. Determined not to excite herself unnecessarily, she yielded to the logic of waiting to see what happened. After all, it was only five hours till two o'clock. Then she would have all the answers.

The wait wasn't easy – time has a nasty habit of dilating when one is in a state of intense anticipation. Nevertheless, it does move and when the time eventually arrived she appeared at Goldhaber's office. With about a dozen people seated about, some pleasantries were exchanged; and within a few minutes, it seemed that the action was ready to begin. Maurice's secretary poked her nose in the room, got a nod from the Director, then left and closed the door behind her. At that moment, it hit Rena that Ken was not present, and immediately she felt a surge of adrenalin and a highly disagreeable ache in the pit of her stomach. Quiet overcame the room: Everyone was all ears. In the wink of an eye, Rena's natural smile vanished. Once Goldhaber started talking, it didn't take long for her and the rest of them to realize what it was all about. As was his usual way, Goldhaber was direct, casual, unemotional, and wearing his patented wry smile that Rena was well familiar with. But his words clashed starkly with this affable and business-as-usual deportment. They were sharp and incisive – they were like daggers. He said that Green's term as Department Chairman would be up at year's end and Ken would be stepping down. Continuing, he said he had called the meeting to ensure that the accelerator staff would be the first to know what was happening, especially before the official notice was released to the entire lab on Monday. He paused expectantly, as if he were suddenly unsure of his audience's reaction and of himself. For a brief moment, the silence was deafening – you could hear a pin drop.

Then, without planning or thought, and with a slow but relentless spontaneity, a kind of rebellion erupted. Who would have believed that such coherent action could arise from such a ragtag collection of divided, self-interested, and beaten-down lot? This was totally unexpected and Goldhaber was visibly shaken as the onslaught began. Why was Ken going? He was a great leader. He was the best man by far to take the lab into the future. Was it Ken's choice? The questions and comments came fast and furious. Blewett, red as a beet, blurted out that it was very wrong to do this terrible thing. Even Rena, stammering in her inimitable way, managed to make a remark or two, but they were not memorable lines, more emotion than rational argument. On it went from that fervent pack, filling almost completely the hour's length of the meeting. It was quite a shock to have such aggressiveness, resentment, and unfriendliness aimed at the Director, and quite uncharacteristic coming from a normally compliant set. But as the hostility in the room mounted, Goldhaber, forever the diplomat, seemed to backtrack a little. He was thoroughly surprised at the reaction. He hadn't considered the possibility that the staff's feelings about Green could have been so strong. Astonished at what had occurred, he would have said anything to get out of this bad situation he was in.

Thinking quickly, Goldhaber conceded that he would give some further consideration to the issue. But somebody called what appeared to have been his bluff and asked about the Monday notice. He was caught off-guard at the directness and tartness of the question, and hesitated a bit. Then, with a hardly noticeable quiver in his voice, he promised the staff that nothing would be done against their wishes before further consultation. With the not uncommon falseness and duplicity characterizing the diplomatic way, he had spoken words that in truth meant nothing; in fact, they could have meant the opposite of what they appeared to be promising. However, this was neither the time nor place for argument, and besides, in the heat of the moment, the rhetorical subtlety bypassed everybody. With nothing more to be said, all became quiet. As quickly as it had begun, the rebellion was quelled. Suddenly, the meeting was over, leaving the visitors with a vague feeling of having been cheated. For a moment, this small band of scientists had come together for a cause, but, in the blinking of an eye, it melted before them. The rare opportunity to take a stand, the once-in-a-lifetime chance, was lost. Goldhaber, the tactician, with deceit in his heart, had issued just the right palliative to calm what turned out to be just an unruly mob that didn't have the stomach for a real fight. So, the game was over and the battle decided. Goldhaber sat smugly at his big desk, sporting the self-satisfied smile of the victorious, as he watched the beaten troop get up and steal out into a cold and cloudy late afternoon.

As Rena left the Director's office, she found herself livid with rage. She couldn't get off her chest what had transpired. It was an awful and disgusting thing to do, throwing Ken out that way, she thought – and she had believed Goldhaber to be such a soft-spoken and genteel man. Clearly the incident was an eye-opener and forced her to completely lose trust in that man she had previously thought so highly of. What now? Rena asked herself. She couldn't think of what to do. Instinctively she made a beeline for Mickey's office. Mickey was seated, waiting anxiously to hear what had taken place. He knew about the meeting, and was confident that Rena would tell him the full story and not let him fret about it all weekend. Just then, she burst in and sat opposite him. Tears were beginning to form; yet there was also rage in her eyes. The combination was a stunner for Mickey. A brief moment of silence ensued as they contemplated how to proceed. Then the entire story – every gory detail of it – poured out of her in a torrent. Mickey sat listening raptly as Rena, only slightly stuttering, spoke quickly and movingly, with tears streaming down her vulnerable cheeks. Then, she stopped. There was no more to be said. So, there they were, two friends together, but lost in a world they had yet to learn something about. Mickey realized with a great deal of discomfort that there was nothing he could do to assuage her anxiety, her fears, and her anger. Uncharacteristically, he could think of nothing to say. He was faced with a feeling of helplessness that he would come to know more about as the future unfolded before him. Still, he dug up a few words to console her, saying, perhaps wisely, yet perhaps naïvely, that they would have to wait for the weekend to pass, but that by Monday they would know a lot more. He reminded her that they would be seeing each other early the following week to compare notes on a calculation they were supposed to be working on over the next couple of days. They would have an opportunity then to continue their discussion. Surprised at how smoothly the platitudes were rolling off his lips, he went on. His closing words that day were "Life goes on." Both feeling down and anchorless, they parted to ponder separately this sudden and disconcerting occurrence with its myriad of implications for them and for the lab as well.

* * * * *

There was no magic in solitude. Indeed, what were they to think about, knowing so little of what was really happening? They were new to the hard game of politics, where appearance, innuendo, impressions, and reading between the lines takes the place of rational discourse and straight talk; and where saving face, psychological masks, deception, falsification and lying takes the place of honesty and truth. Furthest from their minds was the reality that to uncover truth you had to find a way to explore the dark recesses of human experience. Although they were on the verge of discovering this on that troubling and doubt-filled weekend, their knowledge and understanding then of the ways of men were still somewhat pathetic. The answers to even the most evident of questions eluded them. Who were the main actors? What were their roles? What was their game and what were they after? What were their intentions and their ambitions? What might they be planning? What were they capable of doing and what was the likelihood of their doing this or that? But what could Rena and Mickey do even if they knew more? They had little or no power or influence to speak of. Perhaps it was better for them to remain unenlightened about the true ways of the world, because a deeper appreciation would only have given their outlook on things a more sinister edge, making life that much more difficult to bear. So, maybe they were lucky in their ignorance. Nevertheless, whatever they were potentially capable of knowing or doing, they were not in the least prepared for the experience that had been thrust upon them. Saying it straight from the shoulder, they weren't in the inner circle, were empty-headed, and couldn't get to first base.

Rena and Mickey had both lived sheltered lives. They simply hadn't the knowledge, the experience, or the capacity to think out a complex human issue with such a multitude of tentacles, which led to so many places, all the way from the clear-cut to the highly unlikely. It is too much to ask that the young and innocent, as they were, could throw any light on such a profound matter, no matter that it wasn't much different from life's not uncommon recurring episodes. Previously unconcerned and untaught about such things, they had no idea of how to influence or control events, even the simple ones. The best they could do was to try to find some appropriate way of responding to their plight. However, what they didn't know was that all their worrying was for naught – the game was already over and the winner determined, with no appeal. Let this be a lesson for all: to be reactive is to be too late. Being proactive is the way – that's the ticket! However, only the older and more experienced among us have enough of an appreciation of politics and real life to be capable of that as well as of taking account of the possible consequences. Isn't it ironic that the young, who most need to prepare for the future, lack the knowledge or the tools to do so, while the old, whose horizons have shrunk and whose need to prepare has dissipated, generally have what is required, but have little or no use for it? A dreamy, credulous idealist might envision the confluence of these circumstances, where the old use their capabilities to help educate and otherwise prepare the young for the future. What a better place the world would be then! Or, what's even more difficult: try to imagine a time and place where the old work ardently, eagerly, and tenaciously to prepare the future for the young. Ah, if only the old could exhibit such selflessness. Alas, doing for others without getting what is deemed to be due compensation, usually amounting to far more than the young can afford, is low on the list of priorities of even the best of the old. Yes, that's the sadness of it all: self-interest is the essential driver of men's behavior for old and young alike, while altruism, being but a distant dream, lags far behind as a human force. There is little or no choice but to accept the reality that the young must wander into the unknown by themselves, without much help from the generation passing on. If anything, the old will fight to their dying breath against passing the torch. So, all alone, the young must get to know and learn to adapt to their own weaknesses; they must find ways to enlist their strengths as well as their deficiencies and mistakes as instruments for their betterment; they must hunt out the faults and flaws of others to use for their own good; they must beware of the chicanery and false teachings of the old; and they must perpetually seek to make opportunities of unlikely situations, finding ways to transform them to their own advantage. What other choice do they have but to search for and discover for themselves the make-up of things, and then to fashion and shape what they've dug up in their best interest? That is the way the social order and men have arranged things – the young must fend for themselves. So it was that the young, inexperienced, and muddle-headed Rena and Mickey struggled through the weekend, racking their brains, trying to understand what had gone on that gray Friday. However, this was nothing but an exercise in wheel spinning futility. In the end, they just waited for Monday to see what awaited them. It seemed to them, as they searched for answers, that they had nowhere to turn to find them, and so they simply came to accept grandma's teaching, *que sera, sera.*

When Mickey arrived on Monday morning, he saw the announcement in his mailbox. He was surprised that it was there that early. Expecting the worst, he anxiously grabbed the harmless looking piece of paper. Even though he saw himself as cynical, worldly, and wise, he was still startled at the words striking out at him like the ratatat from a tommy-gun. When he settled down, he noticed the matter of fact manner of the writing and how innocuous that made the words seem. Yet there was such finality to the message that it made him wince. Then there was the simplicity of it – that's probably what really got to him. Ken Green would be leaving at the end of the year, the note said, and a replacement was being sought. "So that's the way it is," he thought with a sneer and shrugged his shoulders. His face tightened. Anger rose in him, but it wasn't of the pure red-faced kind. It was more of a mixture of hardness and humor that he felt in his heart. Goldhaber, the consummate diplomat, the aristocrat, and the gentleman, had added to his resume the role of betrayer – quite a formidable combination of traits. Was the progression from gentlemanliness to treachery a natural one? Mickey wondered.

The apparent effortlessness and simplicity of Golhaber's accomplishment bothered Mickey. It was so easy: By deliberately lying that a final decision was not yet made, Golhaber calmed the rebels and quelled the laughable revolt. The staff probably didn't believe what was said that ill-fated afternoon, but, resigned to their helplessness, they went along and played the parts their destinies assigned them. In their defense, they might have argued that the result would have been the same regardless of what they did. But for the artfully two-faced Goldhaber, there were no excuses. Without prematurely revealing his hand, he had taken the bull by the horns and acted decisively and ruthlessly. With that, and nothing more, the revolt that might have been quickly became but a memory. There were no records of what took place. For that, you had to depend on those who were there. Mickey was reminded of a humorous line one of his father's friends had repeatedly used when questioning somebody's comment on the past, "Vas you der Charlie?"

Because those who took part in the meeting with Goldhaber would rather not have the event be exposed or even remembered, it sank deep into the recesses of their minds; and from there it was only a short step to oblivion. In years to come, some would have their own private although hazy recollections of what they believed actually happened but, for the most part, forgetting the whole matter was a far more convenient way of dealing with it. Mickey, who hadn't even been a participant, was different. He would continue to wonder how Goldhaber managed to carry out his double-dealing, perfidious deed. Did he act by himself or were others involved? Who might they have been? Undoubtedly he had the experimenters and the users egging him on; and he obviously had quislings from the department's experimental support wing behind him. These supporters were all happy to see Green, the champion of accelerator technology as the top priority of the lab, done for and gone. But for Mickey, even that much wasn't enough. He was convinced there was more to the story than that. He felt it his born-duty to pry into every hole and corner to track down all of those involved, especially those shadowy figures behind the scenes, apparently unsoiled by the sordid affair. In particular, what was Rabi's role and how did the other community leaders fit in, he wanted to know? Mickey would never be able to resolve these questions satisfactorily. In the end, he came to believe that the lab's technological decline during the sixties and its inability to respond to the changing times had crippled the aimless, drifting leadership, and that they were the true culprits. As for Rabi, he turned out to be a victim. The lab's fall from the heights where *the man* had carried it to had beaten down his spirit and made him a cipher.

One point that Mickey kept coming back to, which never ceased to give him a little shiver, was that the quiet, scholarly, and academic Goldhaber really possessed the makings of a decisive and action-oriented leader. Mickey had recurring thoughts that things might have turned out very differently if only Goldhaber also had the vision appropriate to the times and was on the right side. Too bad! But that's all water over the dam, *useless what ifs*. The reality on the battleground was that, with Green departed, the last vestige of hope for a re-invigoration and renewal of the accelerator class at the lab vanished, and the winners, the god-awful, blind physichists, won the day and had their way. It was a pyrrhic victory, however, because without Green's leadership the Accelerator Department was doomed to mediocrity for the rest of the century, and the physichists were to find no comfort in that. Without any effective and strong person to lead them forward into the unknown, the Accelerator Department tenured staff could do no more than put their tails between their legs and run for cover. There were no heroes here, no one who was willing to die for the cause of technology first. Perhaps they thought that by laying down their arms and prostrating themselves before the conquering power they could salvage something and, at least so they rationalized, save themselves for another day. The many who in this way conceded and saved their positions, which predictably became but nominal ones without real meaning or influence, could not, however, redeem their dignity. That was lost to them, never to be regained.

When the Green show was all over, although not easily acknowledging their roles in the dastardly affair, the cringing accelerator dupes realized in their hearts that a profound change had taken place, that their lives had been irretrievably altered, and that things would never again be the same. When the dust settled and as 1969 came to a close, Green was replaced by Fred Mills, and, as the lab entered the decade of the seventies, a mortally weakened Accelerator Department was to be led by a naïve accelerator scientist who, without perspicacity or foresight, could not even see the lab's bleak landscape, much less influence or change it.

Mickey and Rena would never again talk seriously about the 1969 Green incident. It did happen that they would refer to it from time to time while talking about their work and their lives, but any chance that they might explore more than superficially its meaning for them or for the lab was switched off on that emotionally taxing, gloomy Friday in October. But they were survivors, and, typical of the young, they oh so quickly forgot their pain of the late sixties. Ken was out of the picture, and, as the saying goes, *out of sight, out of mind.* Despite his absence and the gaping hole he left in the Accelerator Department leadership, looking to the future, they set about working on the design and analysis of what all the staff hoped was to be the new BNL Collider. The garnering and accumulation of an enormous mass of details for this big and technologically complex machine began as the group of people involved increased – the quantity growing more and more as time passed. Without fanfare, engineers, technicians, and administrators arrived on the scene, bringing realism and some sort of order to the ragtag group. Miniature models and prototype components for purposes of technical testing and cost estimation were made. Blueprints, land maps, and PERT charts to track the eventual construction were already being produced, even though the project was still in the early planning stage. All this essentially paper activity was most welcome for a dispirited accelerator staff. It had the immediate effect of giving them purpose and allowed them to cohere and resurrect, unfortunately only temporarily, a unity and a faith in the future's promise that once had been an intrinsic part of the BNL experience. It appeared for a brief moment in time as if the lab's grand past had returned and a bona fide team was in the making. With the grim dark clouds dissipating and a bit of blue sky beginning to sift through, the void of recent years seemed to be giving way to an aroused hopefulness. So, as the lab moved a few years into the seventies, the new working group, having grown to over fifty people, met at least twice a week en masse. This most satisfying and thankfully gratifying concentration of effort was like manna from heaven. It was a good place to be, and had the welcome advantage of taking everybody's minds off both their past pains and their inner fears for what lay ahead. So, at least on the surface, the survivors had made it through what they believed to be the worst. This unlikely turn of events was well appreciated by Rena and Mickey; and they thrived in the hustle and bustle of the enormous quantity of work thrust upon them. For them also, the spreading attention given to this glorious project-to-be afforded them a large increase in visibility and people contacts, both inside and outside the lab, and bode very well indeed for their futures.

The new leaders, Fred Mills and John Blewett, imagined that this was the dawning of a new era. However, the truth was that this hope of good things to come, manufactured out of thin air, was nothing but an illusion, because such an agonizing past as BNL had experienced cannot be erased with such ease. It could have been that Fred and John knew the score quite well, and they were just projecting optimism to their newly forming team. This gave the team a respite from the nightmare of the past, and allowed them to lose touch with reality for a time, so bringing a bit of brightness into their lives. Whatever was working away in their minds, the new leadership duo succeeded well in injecting some light and hope into their staff. It could be seen on their faces and in the way they had become immersed in their work. There was a togetherness that had been lacking for a long time. No question about it, the rank and file had somehow been fashioned into a team with spirit and productivity – an accomplishment not to be sneezed at. It almost seemed for a time as if the lab could do the impossible and pull itself up by its bootstraps. The effort being expended was intense, and the strategy was working. There was hope, confidence, and expectancy everywhere you turned, even in the air itself, as the picture of a new and fascinating machine began to emerge. So far forward had the project gone that it deserved a special name. John early on had used ISA, the acronym standing for the imposing Intersecting Storage Accelerators, which was an extrapolation from the already running CERN machine, a much lower energy collider called the ISR, which stood for Intersecting Storage Rings. The impressive advancement as compared to the ISR was to be that the ISA would accelerate the beam to an energy more than a factor of 10 higher, in addition to having the capability of beam storage for long periods of time, the ISR's forte. But the ISR had been far less ambitious, and was designed without the capability of changing the beam energy from its injection value of 30 GeV. It also was too early in the technology game to be able to take a chance at the newly emerging superconductivity for accelerators. Yes, the ISA was a truly adventurous dream, worthy of the lab BNL had been. To mark the project's birth, in 1972, Fred Mills, in a flight of poetic fancy, embellished the name ISA with the French word for beautiful, BELLE - and so it came to pass that ISABELLE was christened.

The three years 1969-1972 were good years for Rena and Mickey. They worked hard on the ISABELLE design, made important contributions, wrote numerous papers, and even began to play a substantial role in influencing many of the design choices. With slightly hesitant hopefulness, they ventured to imagine shining prospects on the horizon. The lab had changed and was on its way again, they gullibly thought. Actually, they would have believed most anything, for such is the nature of the young and innocent. Unfortunately, as all must learn, there is no escape from the inevitable. And so it was for Rena and Mickey. Busy with life's daily demands, caught up in the intricate details of ISABELLE's design, they were very slow to sense the presence of looming danger abroad. However, it came to them nonetheless. As 1972 edged toward a close, just as their restoration of faith was at hand, the second shoe fell: their mirage was abruptly dashed as a new wave of trouble at the lab emerged to the surface. The old illness had returned. To the two dreamers, there seemed neither rhyme nor reason to what was taking place. Feeling as if they were giving birth to a new machine, they thought things were coming along as well as could be, just hunky-dory as far as they were concerned. At such an opportune moment for the lab, a repeat of the disruption and crisis of confidence of a few years back was not what anybody reasonable would have ordered up. But, of course, reason had little to do with what was happening. It was men and the power they coveted that lay behind the new madness, reminiscent of the trouble three years earlier. Rena and Mickey could sense the hands of the physichists at work, who, having arduously and painstakingly taken the power from Green in a previous war, weren't about ready to carelessly hand it back to his successors. Lying low and quietly preparing, waiting for the right moment to strike, they were finally ready to show their hands and play another round of dangerous poker. Once the accelerator experts came up with a reasonably good design for ISABELLE, and only then, the time had arrived for the scheming physichists to act. The result was a second stormy flare-up in the Accelerator Department only three years after the devastating first. With the accelerator opposition crumbling at the first sight of combat, as they had before, the physichists again were the hands-down winners. It gained for them exactly what they wanted, every ounce of power to be had, and left the downtrodden accelerator remnants leaderless and without hope. However, in taking it all in their double assault, the physichists all but wiped out any chance for a bright technological future for the once great BNL.

* * * * *

As 1972 began, ISABELLE was going well and the Accelerator Department seemed to have survived the 1969 upheaval. But for the lab, the picture was not so rosy. Goldhaber decided to step down as Director after twelve years of service in order, it was said, to pursue physics research, his first love. His close associate, George Vineyard, who'd become his Deputy Director in 1967, was to replace him at year's end. All this sounded straightforward, but beneath the guise of normalcy it wasn't at all. There was much more behind it than the simple formality of a peaceful succession. During Goldhaber's stewardship, the decline of the lab reached a point where it became evident to all in the community save the die-hard loyalists. This didn't escape the notice of the higher echelon of the science hierarchy, which had to answer to the government for the lab. Undoubtedly they should have acted more quickly, they should have intervened in the lab's hóur of need while there was still time to salvage something, but it's hard to move when you don't know where to go. What was clearly visible was this: Big Science was advancing on a broad front, while BNL was standing still. By 1972 SLAC had its magnificent Linac and had just built an electron-positron collider. Fermilab was completing its high-energy proton accelerator and was readying itself to replace BNL as the number one lab. CERN had begun the hard road to commissioning its ISR proton collider, the first such machine in the world. And, in the midst of this rush for future science glory, where was BNL? This wasn't very difficult to see for anyone with the will to do so: BNL was unmistakably behind the eight ball. Who could miss that? The lab hadn't had the foresight to prepare itself for the coming period, where advanced technology would be the key to moving forward. Yes, BNL's experimental program spoke for itself, but for the future, the lab simply had nothing of interest to show. Because of that deficiency, Big Science politics, a good friend in the fifties, had also turned against BNL and become an enemy. All the slots for the ongoing round of new facilities, all politically determined, were already filled – BNL had simply missed the boat. This represented a clear and present danger to the lab's raison d'être, its very reason to exist.

When things look bleak and you seem to be in disarray and deep trouble, you should always bear in mind that you're still alive. That's the right time to get hold of yourself and begin to think ahead. The future is always in front of you waiting to be taken, but you can't sit around and expect it to come to you. You must reach out for it, you must fight for it, and you must give it your best shot. However, because BNL had been lagging behind for so long, it wasn't in a very good position to act decisively and boldly. Still, where there's life, there's hope: why shouldn't the lab just pick itself up, dust itself off, and start all over again? It's a hard road to hoe, but not an impossible one. Looking at it objectively, its future was in doubt primarily because its present was confused, and, perhaps even more important, the lab had not come to terms with its troubled past. The facts were these: It was a new ball game out there in the Big Science environs. BNL had already been denied the big projects allotted for the early seventies and was not a favorite to catch a prize facility in the next round. In fact, with the other three labs already looking ahead and pushing their technological advantage vigorously and tirelessly, to win a future facility the lab would have to engage in a bitter battle with them. Although the incentive to become a winner again, as the lab had been years before, was indeed great, was there the will to match it?

To survive as a celebrated Big Science lab, BNL desperately needed something technical that was visible and convincing to the community. It had to have some sort of selling point. Even though what you need and what you get only seldom coincide, the lab somehow had to get into the game if it was to survive at all as a high-energy competitor. However, because BNL was weak technologically, the answer it chose to latch onto was to take the political route. But politics is far from a simple game – in addition to hard fighting and the willingness to go for the jugular, it demands flexibility, conciliation, and give and take. Could the lab muster up the courage, the will, and the know-how to do it? Because the lab was far back in the technological race, it made it that much more difficult to make a good case and find an effective political godfather. Meanwhile the other three contenders were heading for the stretch and pulling further ahead. It appeared all but hopeless. But if a direction was to be chosen, despite all the obstacles in its path, the political approach seemed the only avenue open to the lab. When your back is up against the wall, you do whatever you can. If politics had to be the way, then politics it would be. Unexpectedly, adopting this tack, a few years hence there was to be a manner of success, as it indeed would bring to BNL a glimmer of hope and possibility. Yes, an opportunity to rise again would come in the latter part of the decade as a result of this strategy. Then, the big question would be, just as it was currently: could the lab translate an opportunity into a living machine for the science community and for posterity. The only difference was that presently the answer was, *no*; later it would be, *well, possibly yes.*

In 1972, BNL was at its low point and nobody in its leadership knew exactly what to do. The result was that those in charge ignored their real problem of enhancing the lab's accelerator strength and instead entered the blame game. When Goldhaber left the director's office at the end of that year, it was not in triumph and yet not quite in disgrace. There was just a collective but unfocused feeling of defeat and apprehension. With such mindsets, the new leaders had to assign blame, and given the lab's past ways, it wasn't unexpected that they would look in the wrong places to find who would have to take the fall. Vineyard knew he had to do something and, like Goldhaber, he centered his attention for the lab's dissatisfaction and ire on the already weakened Accelerator Department. Fred Mills, battered but stalwartly accepting his fate, was first to go, leaving by year's end. The reason for his early departure was somewhat of a mystery as it was hard to blame him for anything but compliance and dutiful acquiescence to those undependable physichists. You could almost hear the plaintive tone of his defenders as they asked, "What was he to do?" They were right, for the lab had made its bed long before he came. The opportunities that he might have taken advantage of had already been abandoned through neglect or thrown away by the lab's overconfident bosses. Besides, the Accelerator Department Chairman had lost any clout he might have had after the dismissal of Ken Green, who had been the last of the bold pioneers of the lab's wondrous years as number one. Fred, politically naïve and unaware of his vulnerability, was an easy target – in no time he was done for. Once that big decision was taken, the actions followed in quick succession, and the mystery unraveled as the truth of the underlying drama began to emerge.

Fred was replaced at the beginning of 1973 with Ronnie Rau installed as acting chair. Ronnie, a lab Associate Director and a close colleague of Vineyard, was a natural to be given the reins over the unruly bunch of undisciplined accelerator leaders. What was taking place was now evident: the physichists were openly taking over. Henceforth they would make not only the big lab decisions but also the detailed technical and technological choices for future lab accelerators. The accelerator experts were relegated to the position of doing exactly what they were told – no more, no less. What kind of management is this? an unbiased observer might ask. Aren't the experts supposed to play a major decision-making role? For a lab that had a great technological past and could still have a great future, such a direction borders on silliness. It's like cutting off the hand that feeds you. But that's not all. It very soon became clear that the velvet gloves were off and bare-knuckle combat was the order of the day. Soon after Rau took over, an echo of 1969 reverberated through the lab. John Blewett, the last remaining accelerator giant of the lab's glory days, was literally thrown out. An unknown named Harold Hahn replaced him. Harold, who had met Ronnie while they were skiing in Switzerland, had worked in Blewett's superconducting effort at the lab and was considered by John as a trustworthy colleague. But John was a simple man, and even after suffering through this unforgivable summary dismissal, all the way to the end of his days he continued to look with hope toward the future. On the other hand, Hahn was no more than a *yes* man. When John was discarded, he was so dismayed at what he considered a betrayal that, for a long while after, he refused to give up his office. But this impractical response, this childish act of rebellion, was in vain and slowly he became resigned to his fate. After this episode was long over, he would often think about the past, especially the Green episode of 1969. He finally learned, naturally far too late, that surrendering supinely never appeases the power hungry men in charge. At long last he understood that he should have stood up for his friend, not only because he was his friend, which by itself was enough of a reason, but also because Ken was the crème de la crème, both as a technical expert and as a manager. Yes, he should have stood up for Ken because it was best for the lab. John should have fought to the death to keep Ken on board as the irreplaceable leader of the lab's accelerator effort. Sadly, he hadn't, and now it was his turn to feel the pain of loss and disgrace. And so it was that in early 1973, with John's ouster and the Judas Harold installed, divide and conquer had won again; and the sweep of the Accelerator Department was complete. The physichists were categorically in full charge, with no going back. However, there was an ironic catch to it: now, having it all, what were they to do with it? As the old saying goes, be careful what you wish for, because you just might get it.

Meanwhile, almost a thousand miles to the west of BNL, Fermilab's Director was staking his claim to proton supremacy. Bob Wilson was a man of substance who gave much to his country and left a legacy for all. It so happened that he was a builder of particle accelerators for science. Although it is all but impossible to adequately pass judgment on or even articulate well Bob's gifts to mankind, perhaps it can best said of him that he was a master builder of a series of monuments to man's continuing and daring aspirations. Who was this man who did so much and asked for so little in return? Bob was no different from all that are of woman born; yet if you demand that there be something special in the personality of such a high achiever, then it was probably his spirit and his zest for living. He was driven to fight those who would resist the right to discover and learn. He would not abide the uncaring and petty men who would stand in the way of man's quest to fathom the universe and thereby unveil his own soul. He was an American to his bones and believed it his duty to defend the freedom of man to think without constraint. It was in his makeup to appreciate that it is our lot to confront all that would block us from our dreams. A principled man, these were some of his principles and he stuck by them.

Bob's destiny was to fight the good fight to the end and right the world. Such a man was not to be challenged lightly, and it was to the misfortune of any who stood in the way of his search for self-fulfillment. Possessed of a dogged stubbornness, and, being of a fearless breed, nothing could stop him. Only fools would dare try. He made no deals, wouldn't compromise, and had no patience with dabblers and dilly-dalliers. Brimming with the hardiness of a rugged Midwesterner, he was ruthless in his defense of accomplishment and merit. He accepted no excuses. You had to get the job done, and there were no ifs, ands or buts about it. Yet he was also a fair man. He was a man you could depend on, honest, frank, up-front, and ready to give others their due. Patriot that he was, he had a deep and abiding faith in life and liberty and believed passionately in

God and country. An upright man with integrity and forthrightness, his word was his bond and he could always be counted on and trusted. Bob was the quintessential man of honor.

By 1978, Bob's place at center stage was coming to an end. He was to discover, as everyone does, that time takes its toll on us all and makes no exceptions. Thus, even a man with a will of iron and strength of character hard to equal eventually must come to face life's limits. And so Bob, only a man after all, found himself in that ill-fated year at a threatening and precarious crossroad of his life. Although he had always been a risk taker, he feared that this time he might have gone too far. True, he had gone over the safety threshold before, but surviving when you behave that way depends critically on your judgment of whom you're dealing with. In the past, he had always chosen his battles wisely – not a difficult conclusion to arrive at given his record of accomplishments spanning almost four decades. Now, however, he began to doubt himself; and his suspicions mounted that this time he had indeed made a bad mistake by choosing to confront the formidable John Deutsch, DOE's Director of Energy Research. Why hadn't he seen earlier the danger in doing that? he wondered. But that was neither here nor there. The fact was that he had made his move and now it was too late to go back.

John, a professor of Chemistry at MIT, had decided to take some time off from academia to perform government service. He was an astute observer of the ways of the world, and, being acutely ambitious, he wanted to try his hand at the political game. He wasn't the type of man to be trifled with; and Bob worried that John could well interpret the action he took as doing just that. Bob couldn't suppress a persisting dread that maybe this time he actually overstepped the boundary separating wise negotiating from pigheadedness. It occurred to him, with a combination of misgiving and humor, that ten million dollars added to the Fermilab budget that year was not in the least worth putting his job on the line for. What a stupid blunder it was! Sure, in his letter to John, Bob didn't really mean that. There was a lot of history implied between the lines, with the brief note itself being just the tip of the iceberg. Nevertheless, John, a man of enormous pride, may not have been the one to deal with in such a high-handed and cavalier manner. For him, straight talk, man to man, may have been the better way. Maybe Bob's use of innuendo and subtly veiled threats might well make John see red. John, being of an impulsive and pugnacious nature, didn't at all bode well for Bob. No, there just wasn't a way of escaping the fact that the words in the letter, Director to Director, said in effect, after you threw out the formal, legalistic, and too-clever language, "I'll have the money or you can take your job and shove it." There was an even more serious point that came to Bob's mind. John was a newcomer to the Washington game, having recently arrived to work for Secretary of Energy John Schlesinger under President Jimmy Carter. The problem Bob presented him with was peanuts when contrasted with the big issues of the day – maintaining an adequate oil supply and America's increasing need for energy. John might say, "What the hell does this guy want, and who the hell does he think he is?" Putting all these thoughts together, Bob couldn't believe he had done such a dumb thing. Yet he had.

Even though a major component of Deutsch's job as Energy Research Director was to see to the welfare of the national labs, Bob was greatly concerned that John might not care much about the issue that was of prime importance to him: whether or not the distribution of funds to the national labs had been optimally worked out in terms of past performance and future potential. Bob's view was that it was all decided on a political basis – each lab getting whatever their politicos could wheel-and-deal for – and that merit was just a joke. Of course, it didn't matter much what Bob thought, but rather how John felt about it, and whether he would see fit to act to set the situation right. That was the honest-to-goodness reason for the letter: to make John aware and try to get him off his butt. In any case, for Bob, that was the key issue, and certainly not the measly few million dollars for which he had put himself on the line. His qualms and doubts continued to rise. What if John didn't see his all-important question in the same way he did? A distressing and nagging letdown overcame Bob when he realized that John probably wouldn't see it his way, and that in all likelihood John wouldn't give it much thought at all. It was then, in such a frame of mind, that Bob regretted and reproached himself for what he had done. This was a feeling quite new to him. If at that moment he could have, he would surely have pulled the letter back. But that was water under the bridge. He had set the process in motion, and that was that. The truth was that he didn't know what John's reaction would be – all his thinking on it was mere speculation. But whatever it was to be, he knew he would have to live with it.

Bob was filled with anxiety and uneasiness as he asked himself in a self-berating tone why he had gone and done it once again. He wondered self-pityingly whether maybe this would be the last time for him. It grated on him that the delay in getting a response had become just a bit too long for comfort – it was beginning to get to him. The result was an even more severe rise in self-doubt. Perhaps he shouldn't have gone as far as submitting a letter of resignation along with his financial request. Attempting to intimidate Deutsch, as he had done with others in the past, may have been a case of the wrong tactic with the wrong man. In his heart, Bob now knew that he didn't have to take such a burn-your-bridges stand. A do-or-die approach did have its place in the scheme of things, but it began to dawn on him that he chose the wrong time to apply it and so committed a cardinal and perhaps fatal management sin.

Bob found little time for himself in those uncertain years in the mid-to-late-seventies, but that special cool late afternoon in the fall of 1978 was an exception, as he sat in his refurbished farmhouse – the Director's home – on the Fermilab site. As he looked out the window at the setting sun, he wondered at its awesome splendor and at the kaleidoscopic, rich color scheme blazing through the windowpane of his special resting room. That light, in order to enter his life, he thought a physicist's thought, had hurtled through vast and empty space at a miraculous speed, well-known to man, in its immensely long voyage, and then had passed through the multi-layered hazy cover of the atmosphere, so making its colors visible. But soon his thoughts switched to *Planet Earth*. In his mind's eye, he saw the buffalo herd grazing in the pasture he had concocted for them at his environmentally-correct lab, to remind him of the country's early raw western plains and his own beginnings in the harsh, gorgeous mountains of Wyoming. As counterpoint, he could make out the image of the lab high-rise, piercing the sky as if to show man's arrogance toward an awesome, incomprehensible universe. It represented as well a personal gesture of defiance to the compassionless and careless gods, who are blind to our helplessness and deaf to our pleas for guidance. If you looked closely at his face, you could see a few tears glistening. Still, this was one of the rare moments of quiet and meditation he so cherished. As time moved on and the afternoon was closing, his thoughts shifted to his own life and deeds. In a happy-sad frame of mind, he wanted to know how he'd gotten to where he was. Why was he, at this juncture of his life, at such an ill-starred moment under a heavy, dark cloud? How did he get to this point? But these were not questions that could be answered with words, so he became quite still as he closed his eyes and drifted, almost into a dream, as his mind wandered back in time to a not so distant past.

The year was 1965, but it seemed to him as if it were just yesterday. The events that transpired were easy to get at from the formal record, and the tangible results were evident and there for all to witness and touch. However, the feelings – the intentions, the motives, the misjudgments, and the regrets – were different matters altogether. Bob tried his best to snatch those elusive feelings he had had then, but they had largely decayed away. Too bad he hadn't taken more care – a diary perhaps. Alas, he let it slip away. Not in his wildest imaginings did he think that the time would come when he would so much want a reminder of what had been in his soul in those days of action that passed so swiftly by. This aching nostalgia for his inner life of past times filled him with regret, as if he were mourning the loss of something dear to him. However, despite the obstacles he was sure to encounter, he was determined to keep at it and eventually come to learn what he so wanted to know. And, in truth, it wasn't entirely hopeless, for a shadowy remnant had stayed with him. At least it was a starting point, something to work with, something to help him reconstruct his years-past inner mind that seemed so unimportant then but so important now. The difficulty was to separate his true feelings of some past moment from the memory of it at some other past time. Truth and its multiple memories seemed to co-exist all in a mental jumble. They were all simultaneously installed in that mysterious black box – the unconscious sector of his brain – mixed up in some inaccessible soupy concoction. Then, when they exited the box and emerged into his consciousness, they were transmuted into strange conglomerations of superimposed motives and impressions coming from quite different times of his life. That was the best he could elicit from his mind – a neat package with all his feelings merged and wrapped in an inextricable fusion of happy sadness and teary joy. He wanted more, but in life you don't always get what you want; so, for the time being, he settled and rested content with that, hoping that there would come a time when a more complete reconstruction became possible.

In spite of his inability to separate the mixture of images and thoughts buried within him, words to describe what he chose to believe to be his true feelings came pouring into his mind with great clarity and allowed him to recall vividly that exhilarating period in his life. He was able to recapture the combinations of elation and fear, of adventure and foreboding, of confidence and tentativeness, and of triumph and loss. These pairs of contradictory feelings both strengthened and reinforced his belief that perhaps he had truly gotten it right. It might seem to some that such contradictory feelings mixed together might have paralyzed him – like the donkey that saw two piles of oats equidistant from him on opposite sides. But, somehow, maybe because of his decidedly acute penchant for knowing, he was able to handle it, tough as it was. In the process of trying to remember that time thirteen years earlier, Bob came to realize that it may have been the not knowing that gave him the unyielding, indomitable will and the unquenchable desire to stay the course and find the answers. He came to the view that it was exactly these types of ironic and seemingly contra-distinct experiences, part of the complex of experiences that form the human drama, that made his adrenaline flow and spurred him on. Come hell or high water, he would know!

* * * * *

For anyone who knew the younger Bob in 1965, there was no question that he was energized, even to the point of overflowing. In such a state of pent-up readiness, he had a deep-seated need to release this energy through action. In earlier times, he had verged on the recklessness of idealistic youth, but the focus that warranted such latent power eluded him. As a man, Bob had always been in search of a mission. However, the tenacity and resolve he'd acquired, his single-minded persistence, was wasted without a mission to match. Some might consider that seeking to discover the secrets of the universe should have been of sufficient import. Up to a point, of course it was. But many men, some far superior to him at this – man's ultimate and incomparable search for his origin – were playing in that game. Imagine: the scientist and the priest in the same race to discover – what a hoot! So, Bob the realist sought a different play to cast himself in. What he was seeking was another type of big purpose to guide him, one that would be truly unique to him, and one that he had a chance to be tops at. Then he discovered the diamond that, without consciously knowing, he had always been looking for. He found a cause to champion, a cause to make his juices flow. There was a terrible social wrong out there in the world of science, and he knew in his heart that, not only did it have to be righted, but that he was the man to do it. Instinctively he knew what he had to do, without the least doubt that he could see the job through to its successful conclusion. He would, by his sheer will and via his incontestable logic, force the establishment to see the light and mend their ways. With his boundless determination and with the rare combination of conviction and provocativeness, he would push his way into the limelight and lead the leaderless physicists to the Promised Land. As it turned out, he was right on target. The wary, aging science establishment receded without much resistance as Bob the giant came onto the stage. Because Big Science in the United States had become bogged down in the mire of institutional nepotism, as exemplified by the Berkeley-BNL deal to share future facilities, he was just what the doctor ordered. He had seen and understood the danger of rule by fat cats; and he didn't in the least doubt the slow descent to mediocrity that, without intervention, would inevitably follow. He was determined to see that that didn't happen to American physics. A savior had arrived, one who had found a way to inject youth and life into the aging clique of fools running the existing club of elite scientists. The war was on, but it didn't last long. Success followed quickly on the heels of the initiation of Bob's campaign; and he came prepared to celebrate and taste the fruit of a great victory. With all the pomp and trappings of a conquering hero, he saw his triumph become manifest as a great new laboratory sprouting from the intellectually desolate farmlands of the American upper Midwest.

Bob wasn't sure how he had come to be so bold and willing to risk so much. And a good thing it was that he had such derring-do. To take on the passé but stubbornly holding-on establishment required it. But could he do it without help? He wondered whether perhaps he wasn't as alone as he felt. As he tried to imagine who might have the inclination and the moral fiber to side with him, immediately Norman Ramsey came to mind. Recalling many conversations with him on the need for change, Bob felt that he was one man who could be counted on. Norman had become an eminent professor of physics at Harvard University and had also been an important figure in the creation of BNL and AUI back in the late forties. He had a great deal of political experience and savvy and knew the ropes, as well as the rules of the game. He, like Bob, had aspirations for the U.S. to push ahead swiftly with new accelerator technologies, which they both perceived to be pregnant with potential for future basic research. He had been the one who spearheaded the important Ramsey Panel that envisioned and recommended an exciting and challenging U.S. program having new and expanded accelerator facilities at its heart. Going over all this, Bob knew that here was an ideal partner to work with to save physics from the old and tired crowd now running it. They were in full synchronism in sensing the threat to any real progress posed by the current leadership. It had become entrenched and soft. It wanted to move slowly and conservatively to minimize risk, even though by so doing it also minimized the opportunities for scientific breakthroughs. Norman questioned the motives behind this *go-slow and don't-rock-the-boat* approach. Was it no more complicated than that they wanted to keep control by blocking perceived opponents and resisting change of any sort? Yes, it was transparent since, clearly, change and holding on to the reins of power were simply not compatible. Norman knew this was the wrong way for science to go and feared where such a strategy might lead his generation of brilliant and ambitious scientists. When Bob and Norman came to realize they both had almost simultaneously stumbled on this deeper truth about what was going on, they were mentally prepared for concerted action were the opportunity to come up. As it happened, with a new wave of accelerator facilities waiting for the picking just around the next bend, the timing couldn't have been better.

Bob could sense that victory was not far off and just awaited his entrance onto the field of combat. The government and in particular the AEC commissioners were already on board and excited by the prospect of a large-scale development and expansion of their national laboratory system. Big Science, fueled by the wide-eyed expectations arising from the seemingly inexhaustible potential of new and advanced technology, was definitely in. Even Congress began to flex its muscles to get into the act, having come to recognize that science labs were regional plums worth fighting for. When a national lab is built in a congressional district, the local people – the voters – reap very real and concrete benefits and advantages. Education standards rise, the intellectual and cultural atmosphere is enhanced, the area's economic growth soon becomes visible, and investments become increasingly attractive, drawing in new capital. No wonder that members of Congress are ready to wheel and deal for their piece of the pie. As these thoughts rushed about helter-skelter in his mind, Bob tried to focus on what Ramsey's role would be. Because Norman chanced to be a good friend, he and Bob were close and spent a lot of time together. With frank talk, they built a strong bond of mutual trust, and they found a cause they both felt strongly about and were ready to embrace. There was little to counter the proposition both believed in – that to democratize the science establishment was a worthy endeavor. That end appeared to them to be so just and so good that it would even justify an act of conspiracy to achieve. There, he had articulated in his mind what would have previously seemed unthinkable: Yes, they would conspire to pull the rug right out from under the lords in residence by an end run around them. They, Bob and Norman, would together build a new laboratory for the young-at-heart and leave the old fogies behind, squabbling over the old turf. Full of optimism for a bright future, the continuance of their mission was spurred on by the recognition that they were a formidable pair, with substantial technical and political knowledge and acumen. Still, even with all they had going for them, it would be an uphill battle to win this one. They determined their strategy. Having concluded that a bloody fight over the site of the next big accelerator facility was inevitable, they saw their big chance – this was a perfect and practical case to apply their do-good and do-right ambitions. It would be do or die, winner-take-all. Their destiny was set and the action about to begin.

Bob had some concern about the Ramsey Panel presumably having bought into the idea of the Berkeley-BNL deal, which seemed to be in direct contradiction to the direction he and Norman had chosen to follow. Therefore, even though he had not only a warm fondness for Norman but also confidence in his trustworthiness, he forthrightly brought up this question. He was blunt and to the point. Ramsey's prompt answer was equally direct and convincing as well, and Bob did not for an instant doubt its truthfulness: Ramsey had simply changed his mind. Thus, a straight-from-the-shoulder, civilized dialogue settled the issue, and the matter was laid to rest. The last obstacle to their collaborative attack on the establishment was removed. They had no longer to wait, for the time to act was at hand. They were a most impressive team fighting out there on the front lines, with Bob carrying the flag of liberation, leading the siege, and Norman politicking behind the scenes. With Ramsey at his side, Bob finally knew for sure that he was not alone, and together they had raised the curtain on the challenging contest for openness, youth, and equal opportunity. The decisive site battle was launched in 1965 and was all over within a couple of years. A lab in the central plains was established with Bob Wilson as the Director and Norman Ramsey as the President of Universities Research Association (URA), the intermediary management corporation formed to negotiate the contractual arrangements with the U.S. government. Working together, they entered the field with little more than good intentions – no formal army, no munitions or big cannons, just grand ideas and common sense – and yet they won the day. In reality, it was technology and posterity that were the true big winners.

* * * * *

Bob felt a sad smile developing as he sat lazily in the quiet melancholy of a late afternoon in 1978. A lot had happened in the last couple of decades. In 1960, the age of the big strong-focusing accelerators, initiated by the immensely significant discovery of the AG principle in BNL in 1952, started with the thrilling debut of the AGS. Then, in the mid-sixties, came the first round of new accelerator construction of the new era. In 1965, Bob saw his big chance and grabbed it. What a break that was – it made him the uncontested hero of the fledgling Big Physics. But remaining a hero wasn't in the cards for him. No surprise here, for who can stand the glaring lights and mercurial pace of a star for very long, not to mention the incessant attacks on the one to beat? Disheartened and wearying of life in the fast lane, he found himself reminiscing about the past, a little afraid of the unknown that was yet to come. He felt isolated and so alone. His fortune had changed dramatically in the last few years, and he knew things could never be the same again. The possibility of such a turn of events as had taken place never even entered his consciousness. Nonetheless, time and circumstance had played themselves out as they had and the reality of the result was undeniable. As he sat pondering his future, his mind roamed freely as he tried to reconstruct the events leading to his current situation.

He went back to a year that was pivotal for the future of big physics. What occurred then all but ensured that a new round of accelerator facilities was close at hand. In the summer of 1973, a buzz was building that an exciting discovery was imminent. The rumor-mill was in full swing when, in a rare memorable moment of transition, the physics community was rocked. The talk until then had seemed to be nothing but idle chatter, when suddenly it became truth. In November, the results of experiments by Sam Ting at BNL and Burt Richter at SLAC were published in *Physical Review Letters*, with their data demonstrating conclusively the existence of something totally novel and unexpected. This brilliant work done by the two of them in completely different ways – each strongly reinforcing the other – brought out a different and completely original way of perceiving the physical world at its most fundamental level. Later this chain of events would come to be known as the November revolution and irrevocably changed physics and how the universe is understood. In a flash of insight and inventiveness, a new substratum of nature was identified. Instead of the proton and neutron being the most elemental units of nature, it was found that there were three smaller units existing within each of them. Suddenly, with the discovery of these weird and exotic little guys, the true character of all the existing so-called elementary particles became an open book. As might have been anticipated, these proton components aren't really the be-all and end-all of the universe's explanation, but the step taken was so profound as to blow one's mind. Actually, to tell the story properly, a few years earlier, the Nobel Laureate theorist, Murray Gellman, without the benefit of observing their presence, but rather inferring them via an ingenious and wondrous jump of mathematical insight, named these tiniest of elements quarks – referring somewhat whimsically to the line, "Three quarks for Muster Mark," in James Joyce's *Finnegan's Wake*. Thus, the revolution vindicated the quark theory, and a thoroughly original and innovatively modern way of picturing the universe was conceived. For their brilliant work, Richter and Ting were awarded the Nobel Prize only two years later. It would be hard to overestimate the excitement induced by the November revolution. It was an event to trumpet loud and exult in. It was transcendent.

If Bob had had any reasons to hold back from aggressive action before the far-reaching upheaval of 1973, these hesitations were quelled afterward. With doubt for an all-out strike removed, and assured that new accelerators were on the way, Bob pursued his destiny with no holds barred and with all he had to give. He was determined that Fermilab, his lab, would get the next big accelerator facility. After all, he was convinced that Fermilab was tops in performance and stood far and away above the other labs in potential. So, as far as Bob was concerned, his lab had the merit and deserved the reward of building the next big accelerator – this time it was to be a very high-energy collider. To him, the issue, as he had interpreted it in 1965, was simply a question of right versus wrong; and, as he had done before, he would see to it that right would win out again. Ironically, BNL, as it had been in the mid-sixties, was to be his prime competitor. History seemed to be reenacting a drama played out just a few years earlier. But would history repeat itself, as it is sometimes wont to do? It turned out not to be so simple, and Bob was fated to learn that history can teach but is not to be trusted. History always seems to be laughing at all of us mere mortals, and if you look at it dispassionately, you will see that it is the biggest trickster of all.

* * * * *

As the drama of the labs was playing itself out with stories of friendship and betrayal, joy and pain, and success and failure, the government, itself a hotbed of metamorphosis, where sweeping transformations can happen overnight, was equally in the throes of changing times. As the seventies got underway, the AEC had been incorporated into a new, larger administrative structure for energy development, the Energy Research and Development Administration (ERDA). The general idea was to bring atomic energy within a broader authority whose purpose was to handle the country's energy needs in a unified way. This trend continued even further when Jimmy Carter became the U.S. President in 1977. Having an engineering background, it was natural for him to believe strongly in the importance of energy to the country, although it pained to hear him continually say, "nucular" instead of "nuclear." As a major part of his new energy policy, he enlarged ERDA into the Department of Energy (DOE), and brought in the shrewd, far-sighted, and clear-headed John Schlesinger to be the first Secretary of Energy at the Presidential cabinet level. This new powerful governmental unit was created in response to the world oil crisis of the seventies; and the Secretary's authority grew to encompass all manner of energy matters, including national energy policy, energy production, economic implications, and national security considerations. Although ERDA was a step on this road to complete energy centralization, without the oil crisis around when it was formed, it was oriented primarily toward energy research and had the restricted focus of developing better and more efficient ways of producing energy. You see, even before oil became the world's bête noire, the U.S. recognized that energy demand all over the globe was rising rapidly and projected to accelerate over the coming decades. Some innovative ways to generate more power had to be found, and ERDA, bringing widely different possible energy sources together administratively, was deemed to be the answer. At this intermediate stage of the path to full energy research consolidation, atomic energy, or to be more precise, nuclear energy, was to be embedded in the R&D for energy of all sorts, including, solar, wind, electrical, gas, and even fossil fuels.

This notion of bringing energy within the control of a single government jurisdiction, although sound in principle, had what has proven to be the harmful effect of bringing basic R&D, essentially an academic pursuit, into the political arena. The two, scholars and politicos, don't mix very well – one thinks *far ahead* while the other thinks *now*. Nevertheless, in the post World War II period, academia was thrust into a competitive environment for government funding for which it was quite unprepared. When Big Science came into being, academia's basic research quickly became too big for its britches. Even though government funding of basic research has been a phenomenal success and has made science boom, perhaps combining *big* with *little* wasn't too wise. Perhaps it would have been much better to leave Big Science in a small, compact, and more personal unit like the AEC. However, it isn't worth much crying over spilt milk. If you study the evolution of the government's energy organization carefully, then you'll find that each step, one by one, is readily justified. It's just the strange way things are that when you add up all the steps, each seeming to be the correct move, you wind up with an unsatisfactory end.

The impact on Big Physics of the policy of energy centralization was enormous and may very well have been the ultimate source of its stagnation over the next couple of decades. What is known for sure is that in the seventies, with the transition from the well-focused AEC to the broad-based ERDA, basic research in nuclear and particle physics in one fell swoop had its influence greatly diluted and became, rather than the whole ball of wax, a little fish in a big pond. Immediately, politics began dictating a more uniform treatment of the national labs, with merit as an incentive all but thrown out the window. Government administrators and bureaucrats suddenly found themselves with more responsibility, more authority, and, most importantly, more influence. The result, not unexpectedly, was that they formulated new policies, no matter whether these changes were needed or not. Sometimes it so happens that such changes are for the good, but experience demonstrates that that's rare. For the most part, administrative change tends to be misguided and burdensome and at best results in the sustaining of the status quo. More often than not, even though its proponents are only too eager to proclaim that change will lead to reform and renewal, it falls far short of that. In any case, basic research was not immune to the fierce and potent urges of government administrators, as well as those of the labs, to take whatever they could. With new power thrust upon them, they were determined to implement new policies in the attempt – and there seems no other reasonable way to explain it – to put their signature on novel, imaginative work and derive credit and distinction for it. Even though they didn't deserve it, they wanted to be cited along with the true trophy winners anyway. That is the nature of administrative power, and that's the way people who have it tend to behave. Change was their trump card, their modus operandi, although as an end it was secondary for them – authority, control, image, and being the General with all the medals were all that really counted. The upshot was that in the science game, fairness and merit were falling by the wayside, while politics and bureaucracy stood on the threshold of filling the resulting authority void and coming to rule the roost. So it happened that as the infighting in basic research and the Big Science establishment waged on with increasing fierceness, the simple-minded scientists, ignorant of what really was at stake, were losing control of their beloved enterprise. Simultaneously, the cold-hearted and scheming administrators – the barbarians at the gate – were poised ready to take over and well positioned to do so.

* * * * *

Bob should have picked up that this shift from the AEC to ERDA – from contacts of a personal and rational nature with the powers that be to contacts with uncaring, inflexible, and intellectually-challenged paper-pushers lower down on the totem pole – was a signal for him to change with the times. But somehow, even with all his depth of knowledge and wealth of experience, this inference completely by-passed him. To understand this is to explain the inexplicable. Yet it happened. Without reason and logic to guide us, we must bear as best we can the fact that it must have been fate that blinded him. So it was that Bob eventually came to know and appreciate that the circumstances of the seventies were not the same as those of the sixties, and discovered, to his surprise, that what history gave him in the sixties, it was to reclaim in the seventies.

Going back to 1973, a particular policy announcement that year was to have a profound impact on Bob's life. It would also slowly shape the future of the accelerator labs and pave the way for their decline, which began almost immediately, but became fully evident only in the nineties. Nonetheless, although this downhill slide didn't manifest itself for years, still it was there, hiding in the spider's web of history, only awaiting its release. Bob didn't at all like the *new deal* hoisted upon Big Science. Referred to as the "Three-Lab Concept," it was a newly fashioned policy of how to run U.S. high-energy physics. He knew right away that in the long run it boded ill for all the labs. It was a policy in direct contradiction to the philosophy he embraced, and which he thought had been bought by the science community years earlier. Furthermore he didn't miss the obvious consequence that it would immediately harm him and his lab – and in a big way. In fact, that's exactly what happened. Worse, it ended up cutting him off at the knees.

The new policy's reading was innocuous enough. The three big operating accelerator labs, BNL, SLAC, and Fermilab, were to take turns in developing and building new accelerator facilities. But there was danger behind them *thar* simple words. To the administrators empowered to ensure that it was carried out, this plan seemed not only reasonable but ideal: It was such a neat and tidy package promising equal treatment and peace among competitors, a perfect solution for small minds. By digging deeper into its substance, it can't but strike out at you that the idea is quite undemocratic, and further not much more than a prescription for maintaining the status quo. Actually, it was far worse than that. There was a deeply sinister component resting unseen in the new system: Thenceforth, decisions about choices among technical options and about funding were effectively to be made by administrators having little knowledge of what they were making crucial decisions about. The policy wasn't articulated that way. But with the power granted them, the administrators could wield their funding and organizational axes anytime they were so inclined. Who could stop them? There was more to the deceitful genius of the scheme. The plan gave scientists a false sense of continuity, but it ended up encouraging power centers that inevitably became accountable to no one – at least when the administrators weren't looking, were disinterested, or simply wanted it that way. It also took the science per se out of the limelight at the labs and at the same time inserted a system of *rules and regulations* typical of the bureaucratic way. This had the awful impact of discouraging new ideas and novel approaches. It was a prescription for the inclusion of the safe and the old and the exclusion of the risky and the young. What stupidity: the Big Science community had initiated its giveaway of its raison d'être.

When Bob recognized what was happening, he found himself dumbfounded, caught off-guard, and at a total loss as to what to do about it. He had already fought for his way of doing things once before and had deliciously triumphed. He thought the war was over and that the issue of freedom versus control decided. As he recalled those years not too long ago, there was a surge of pride throughout his body. Yes, he had then beaten down the establishment Berkley-BNL combine that threatened the advance of accelerator technology. Standing for freedom and openness, he had come out on top. Nonetheless, here was the old wound returned, come back to haunt him once again. Even though the ensuing period seemed so short, maybe it was just that it was a different decade, a different atmosphere, and a different opposition. Times do change, he consoled himself. Not only was he older, but also he no longer had commissioners Hasimir and Holifield of the little old AEC on his side anymore. However, there was more, a real backbreaker: this time he had to lock swords with official government policy. This was probably the key to his desperate and almost hopeless position. In the earlier battle, the government was persuaded to support him, or at least to give him a fair shot at winning, but this time they literally were in opposition to him. The BNL-Berkeley gentleman's agreement of the late fifties was an informal understanding, accepted by the AEC, but not a policy the AEC had initiated and was firmly committed to. The new situation was different because the three-lab plan had become official ERDA policy. Bob quickly discovered that under his current circumstances, he couldn't, as he had before, just attack his opponent labs separately for their lack of efficiency, their low productivity, and their deficiency in know-how. This time he would also have to confront and challenge the new three-lab-policy itself, at the same time as the government was instituting and enforcing it. What a bind he was in! Could he pass judgment on the government that provided the lifeblood for his lab? Could he criticize the other labs with impunity? Could he contend that his lab was better than the other two and get away with it? Not likely! He faced an awesome strategic and intellectual challenge.

After much consideration and soul-searching, Bob soon found that the only direction available to him was to confront and take on the government itself. But the policy-makers in Washington were no pushovers. Even the articulation of opposition to the three-lab idea was difficult, because the system was created for the express purpose of maintaining stability and of encouraging a future that would ensure steady, controlled advancement. How could he go up against that? It was motherhood! More than that, although the system set up was a phony one, the keepers of it were holding all the cards. As desperate and as remediless as things seemed to be, Bob could only be Bob, and he had little choice but to continue to act in the only manner he knew how – *don't give an inch* was his way, it was in his blood. Then, just as the feud was about to heat up, his opposition delivered against him its pièce de résistance, what to anyone but Bob would have been the coup de grâce. Why hadn't Bob seen it earlier? As smart as he was, he'd been dense on this point. When that big blow struck, he finally did get it. Implicit in the implementation of the three-lab idea was that Fermilab, having just been commissioned, would be taken to have begun the cycle, with SLAC as number two, to be followed by BNL. This would delay any new project for Fermilab for many years. Although it wasn't apparent in the original formulation of the three-lab concept, there indeed had to be a starting point. How could he have missed that killing bomb held in the opposition's arsenal? Although he couldn't have done much about it even if he'd recognized its presence, Bob simply never imagined that the building of Fermilab would be taken retroactively as number one for the upcoming round of accelerator construction. When this became apparent in 1973 and 1974, for a time Bob was crushed. His hopes and dreams of a truly national laboratory, one that would be open and freethinking, one that would have full play to expand on the plains of the great U.S. Midwest, was to be dashed. How could he take that lying down? How could he just resign himself to what he considered to be a disaster for Big Science as well as a slap in his face? He couldn't. His dignity, self-respect, and pride were at stake. He simply had to act. So, as it happened, Bob couldn't and didn't lie down and let it pass. A fight it would have to be, even if it were one to the death. The unhappy result was that for the remainder of the seventies and stretching into the eighties, BNL and Fermilab would remain locked in mortal combat for Big Science supremacy.

Bob didn't know what to do; maybe deep down, without it reaching his consciousness, he wanted out. Overtly, he was caught in a trap, flailing about in a futile effort to unburden and free himself. Release for the time being eluded him, it would have to wait. Although as close to losing as one can get, it wasn't in him to throw in the towel. Conceding was not in his vocabulary. Everything in his upbringing insisted that he not run from his duty to see that right ends up victorious. He concluded that he would keep pushing onward and act as he had in the past, bull-headed as it was. However, this time, in the battle-royal of his life, he certainly had his work cut out for him. Having a tendency toward pragmatism, he recognized instinctively what he had to do to survive and still fight the good fight against the strong establishment that was his opposition – no, his enemy. He would above all maintain his integrity and his dignity. So, even though it was a political, no-holds-barred contest, he chose to be true to himself and go back to his roots of rationality and of up-front, honest argument and persuasion. He chose to work his lab to the bone and devise a next step that would be practical, competitive, and shine above all the other proposals. True to his philosophy, he put forward fresh, streamlined designs that emphasized low cost, novel and a bit risky technology, and high efficiency in component production. It was in diametric opposition to what BNL wanted to do – build a facility that would do most everything and last forever. The two competing lab proposals demonstrated clearly the dramatic contrast between them of how labs should be run. Contrary to the BNL way, Bob's conception was: lean and mean managing, building fast, doing the experiments needed quickly (no straggling here), conceiving and developing the next-step technology, and then getting on with the challenges of forging a brighter future.

Bob wasn't the type to try to cover all his bases before moving forward, but rather it was his way to make a pincer-like thrust to the sea. He wasn't averse to risk: Only by taking chances could his manner of doing things work. Although this was obviously the best, perhaps the only way to do good science, being that science had the intrinsic property of changing at every turn, nonetheless taking the high-risk route had the effect of making a lot of enemies for Bob. Since most people, including unfortunately most practicing scientists, are tuned for stability, the bold and the brave who desire to rush ahead pell-mell, as true scientists should, must themselves bear the risks that that entails, and must ultimately walk alone.

As hard as he sought it out, Bob couldn't find any significant help for his cause. The experimenters, whom he might have expected to be among his strongest allies, turned on him for the mundane reason that the first Fermilab machine built in the late sixties, even though it ultimately became number one, didn't come on line well. He couldn't believe it, so petty was it, yet that was their articulated reason for their unwillingness to go along with him. It annoyed him no end because it was all for their benefit. Somehow they just didn't understand that it was because of his rush to get the machine working for experiments as soon as possible that he had made some mistakes. So what, he thought, that the magnets at the beginning were somewhat unreliable and needed many repairs! Still, they got the opportunity to do their work quicker than anyone could have hoped for. They should have been ecstatic. Bob was thrown for a loop for a while. Then it came to him. Perhaps there was an altogether different reason for their antagonism toward him. It's true that in an effort to save money the conditions in the experimental halls weren't what you'd exactly call plush. Some of the locations were downright unpleasant. Still, he'd got the job done – and fast. Yet Bob wasn't quite satisfied with that explanation. He began to conjecture that maybe it wasn't just that, maybe there was something else. There was the fact that he'd used funds meant for current operations to do R&D for the future – especially on the exciting, but perhaps a little risky, superconducting magnet technology. Yes, he thought in one of those rare moments of insight, gotcha! That must have been what really alienated the experimental community.

Apparently the experimenters were more interested in the present than in the future, a view in direct contradiction to Bob's way of thinking. They presumably believed that the lab funds were primarily meant for their use as they saw fit – for comfortable living and work conditions, and for trying out all the experimental ideas they wanted to, whether good or bad. Their pride demanded it. And damn the new technology Bob wanted to give life to! Bob was torn. He couldn't go completely against the tide. After all, the experimenters were influential, men to contend with. So Bob found himself caught in a budget squeeze. Those who were in the midst of running experiments wanted him to spend more on what they were doing and to forego what the younger set might need in the years ahead. Bob preferred to spend more for the next generation. Unfortunately only so much money was available – the arithmetic was plain and incontrovertible. Where should he turn for a resolution to the impasse? He didn't like the answer, but getting what you want isn't always in the cards.

As the Director of a national lab owned by the government, he had no alternative but to go hat in hand to the Washington trough. That meant he'd have to deal with Bill Wallenmeyer, the Director of ERDA's high-energy physics program. However, Bill, one of the prime formulators of the three-lab policy, didn't want any part of Bob's shenanigans. This was no big surprise. Bill believed in political stability, which to him meant lab stability, which in turn meant equal lab treatment. This was the new policy, his policy, and he would stick by it come hell or high water. Besides, it was only peace he was after, and, as the keeper of it, he would see to it that it was maintained. One thing he certainly didn't want were fights developing among the labs, and it angered him that Bob was just aching to instigate them. Bill was furious with Bob for his contentiousness. So, his response to Bob's request left woefully little to the imagination. Why, Bill questioned, should he allot resources to Fermilab that would encourage Bob in his destabilizing ways? So Bill, equally as stubborn as Bob and possessing the wherewithal to have his way, made clear in no uncertain terms that the policy had been established and that it could not and would not be altered. The three-lab policy he believed in with all the fervency of a father protecting his child would stand. Period – end of story! He was emphatic that there was to be no special treatment for anybody and that was final. Fermilab would simply have to wait its turn. As for Bob, to hell with him!

* * * * *

Bob was in trouble and he knew it. Then, at some moment in the mid-seventies, as if an epiphany had come to him, he settled on what he perceived to be his mission. It would be a do or die effort for the future of Big Physics. He made the choice to risk all that he had accumulated for himself over the years – position, status, and the personal and professional respect of others – rather than, in preparation for his older years, take the safe and secure road of conformity, acquiescence, and compliance. Now, why would he take such a selfless line of conduct? Some would even consider it foolish. But for Bob, the thing most valuable to him was his own self-respect and that's what he prized above all. To earn it, however, he felt it imperative to take a stand for what was right and good. So he consciously chose to walk the narrow line existing between all or nothing, to live at danger's edge with the ever-present chance of being stigmatized as an outcast or falling into the abyss of isolation. He decided to stand tall against those who controlled the money; and if they didn't come through with the cash needed to fulfill his mission, he would scrounge around to get it: he would search out even the most outlandish possible source, take support wherever he could find it, or do whatever it might take. He knew this wouldn't be an easy course because sometimes he would have to do bad things like economizing by sloughing off the weak. But even that wasn't the worst of the trials he would have to go through. Finally, he knew the time would come when he would have to cross swords with the other labs in one on one combat, for all to see, and the only way to win those fights would be to go for the jugular. If it should come to that and if that's what was called for, he was even prepared to go that far.

In the seventies, BNL was the lab that Bob and Fermilab had to counter head-to-head for the next proton facility. As it happened, BNL was the weak link in the chain of U.S. accelerator labs, and was fat and ripe for the taking. At least that's what Bob believed, and all the existing evidence did indeed give credence to that view. It had no technical leadership to speak of, and Bob came to appreciate that, even without any support from the science community or the government, its vulnerability on that score was the only real chance he had left. His trump card was that BNL's vaunted ISABELLE project was bulky and poorly designed, technically inadequate, and far too costly. Perhaps this was its Achilles' heel. In any case, he had to give it a shot – his best shot. Since confrontation and exposure was the tactic he knew best, maybe the only one he knew, he prayed that it be the right one. Thus, convinced that this was his chance, perhaps his last hope, to win the day, even with a creeping skepticism beginning to intrude about his methods and his likelihood of succeeding, he embarked on a campaign to discredit ISABELLE. First, he proposed alternatives that were geared for particular purposes; then he went on an all-out attack on BNL's unreasonable and unnecessary all-purpose machine. How could the science community not side with him? Bob's alternatives would all be far less costly. Any of them would come to life quicker. With Bob's ways and ideas at work and him at the helm, Big Science would move swiftly ahead giving the current generation a sporting gamble at winning big. In comparison, the BNL plan was fiddle-faddle and now-you-see-it-now-you-don't fakery. Its selling point was that it would do anything and was for everybody, not at all like the Fermilab options meant for a select few elite scientists on top of the heap. Was it possible that BNL's unrealistic idea of everything for everybody would win over intelligent and worldly scientists? Bob's counter thrust, in a nutshell, was that he was offering a collider that would efficiently give the Big Physics community and the government what it was paying for, while BNL's device was recklessly extravagant, wasteful, and perhaps most importantly technically challenged. There was a moment while Bob was putting on his show when he became deeply confident that his rational arguments would prevail over BNL's claim that it could do anything it said even without backup, simply because the politicos were on its side and it was its turn. But Bob was wrong.

The big shoot-out between Bob and BNL director George Vineyard came at an ERDA science advisory panel meeting at Woods Hole, Massachusetts, in the summer of 1977. It wasn't really a shoot-out for technical supremacy, as many thought it would be; indeed, it was more like a behind-the-scenes rigged affair – government politics demonstrated once again the meaning of its insinuation into the world of science. Although the physics community believed that its course of action at Woods Hole was to determine what big proton project would be the best next one for Big Science, the meeting was in reality a sham, one that had already been fixed by congressional fiat. What you had here was a bunch of naïve puppets going through their show. The scientists thought that the meeting was meant for negotiation. They thought the idea was to thrash out which technology was better and which lab was better suited to the task. Not at all! You see, the politicians were at work and, unseen as yet, had already made their move. They held the plums and handed them out their way. This was a time for such a plum to be granted. As for the foolish scientists on the receiving end, they would accept with the thought: Hey, great! Why not? Somebody might well have screamed out at them: The losers, you fools, what about the losers? In a heartbeat, without consideration of the consequences of selling their souls, the winners no doubt would silently shape the words, "Damn them!" Although everything was set beforehand and the deal done, no one yet knew that truth. So, the show proceeded on its merry way.

Bob had not foreseen this possibility that it was only a farce being played out. The fact was that he had committed a cardinal political sin by not taking Vineyard seriously. True, looking at his past performance, George was not a very impressive figure. Nonetheless, he turned out to be an able and shrewd politician. In the four years since he took over as Director, he worked Washington masterfully and accumulated substantial political capital, garnering support for the lab from BNL's local congressional delegation as well as from ERDA. So astute and skillful had George become at this role – you could hardly distinguish him from a seasoned politico – that he managed to orchestrate a political act at Woods Hole that completely cowed the gathering of scientific sophisticates.

Consider the scene. In progress were discussions of the minutiae of experimental and theoretical physics as well as of the merits of pursuing a variety of accelerator technologies. The days were filled with endless words and heated debate: What would the self-glorifying physichists discover, as if they had even the slightest inkling? What precise technologies would make the best accelerator, and detector to go with it? How would it be best to coordinate development and construction for the optimum accelerator complex? And so on! However, behind this seeming civility lurked the explosive issue of which one of the two labs, BNL or Fermilab, could better accomplish the ends being sought. Would it be more efficiently and thus faster done here or there? Was one of the labs better prepared? Was one of the labs better – period? When such issues were broached, every now and then, the surface courtesies would be breached, and vitriolic comments would spill out questioning the competence of one or the other. These were tough moments. But fortunately, before the adversaries got too wound up, some statesmanlike scientists would step in to suppress any rancor from getting out of hand. For the most part they succeeded, and so the meeting went breezily along, with the bad blood kept at bay.

Suddenly, without any forewarning to most of the participants, the entire meeting was turned over on its head when more than halfway through something totally unanticipated took place. As the panel's deliberations were uneventfully progressing, with scientists and administrators talking shop in their usual manner and sometimes even trying their inexperienced hands at some horse-trading, heart-stopping news arrived from Washington: Congress had approved five million dollars in initial construction funds for ISABELLE. What a shocker – a bolt out of the blue! Before the panel could make any formal endorsement of what it considered to be the best project to build next, an announcement from the nation's center of power took the decision from right under their noses and made it for them. The impact was an odd mixture of overt reactions and personal feelings. In the announcement's immediate wake, it had an electric effect on the group. Some felt alarm and distress, some excitement and joy, some were in seventh heaven, some were overwhelmed, and some were incensed. The talk, both one-on-one and in groups, was passionate, varying all over the map, from vain and mindless hope to fierce indignation. Then there followed a kind of silence, then a dispiriting resignation, and finally an eerie relief. In such a sequence, the brief emotional interlude burnt itself out, and a semblance of the scientists' rationality and clear thinking returned. Still what was done was done – the action taken was absolutely irreversible.

In retrospect, it was apparent that George had done his job well. Woods Hole would thenceforth represent a historical marker for when the science community was effectively and completely intimidated. With the help and guidance of Washington men far smarter than scientists, George had pulled off a phenomenal political coup. As for the ERDA panel, it capped the congressional dictate by not only endorsing ISABELLE but also topping off the gift with instructions to BNL to double the project's design energy, thus giving it far more value as well as adding more money to BNL's coffers. But, as it is when you do things the Washington way, the deal was not delivered without a heavy price. In this instance, it would be Bob who would have to bear the brunt of the cost of the whole sordid business. Adding to its recommendation that BNL vigorously and immediately pursue the ISABELLE project, the Woods Hole panel, as per Washington's instructions, proposed – perhaps to ensure some manner of peace, or perhaps as some form of revenge for Bob's defiance – that Fermilab cease its pursuit of colliding beams and thenceforth restrict itself to research on a single-ring accelerator strictly for use in high-energy fixed-target experiments. The implication was as clear as a bell: the next accelerator for Fermilab, no more than an upgrade of its current complex, was not to be part of the current cycle of facilities, but of the following one at best. It would be a gross understatement to say that Bob was stunned by what had taken place – by the depth of his defeat. For him, the outcome couldn't have been worse. He was, as they say, up the creek. As seen from the outside, that was the position he was in – bad enough, wouldn't you say? But for Bob the man, the outcome was far worse, the wound far deeper. A little of him died at Woods Hole '77, and he would never again be the same old Bob. As time would pass, as it does for all, he would often wonder at how he could have assessed Vineyard so badly – so underestimated him.

* * * * *

Although Bob was battered, downcast, and almost beaten, he was not the type to go down for the count easily. How could he just abandon his cause that the future be embraced boldly and fearlessly, while he still had an ounce of free American air to breath? No, he would continue to defy the insufferable men who sought to curb him – those wretched bureaucrats and false purveyors of the status quo – until his last gasp of it. Even as he was falling to the earth from the onslaught at his door, he would take a final shot at making his case. So it was decided: he would give one final try at opening the eyes of those who stubbornly refused to see the light. The time he chose for his last stand was in early 1978. With only a miniscule chance of success, Bob chose to march up to the cannon's mouth and fight for scientific freedom yet one more time. He thought he had perceived, or perhaps only sensed, a dim, almost imperceptible light aglow in the blackness at the far end of the long tunnel. It could have been his imagination, but in his current frame of mind he might have grabbed at anything. Sadly, being the man he was, he unrealistically took the mirage to be a figment of hope and he pounced on it. He whipped off a letter to John Deutsch, ERDA's Director of Energy Research. Bob was well aware that by going directly to Deutsch he was going over Bill Wallenmeyer's head, and he knew full well that it was quite a risk he was taking by offending the pride-filled, easily rankled, and score-settling Bill. But, caught between a rock and a hard place, what else could he do? he rationalized. His strategy was simple: he would only ask for a small extra amount for R&D, ten million dollars, so that he could continue the lab's work on future accelerators. It was such a small request, how could John refuse? he thought, conveniently casting from his mind that Bill had already done so. But here was the clinker: to show how important this was to Fermilab and to the future of basic research, he tendered a letter of resignation along with the request. Since it was in his nature to act impulsively, he probably didn't give enough consideration to exactly how aggressive a move that was. In retrospect, he was later to recognize that he had gone too far, but by then it was too late. Somehow, as he was writing that fateful letter, he hoped beyond hope and fooled himself into believing that John Deutsch, whom he persuaded himself was a reasonable man and in the game for the good of science, would take his side and even slap Wallenmeyer's hands in the bargain. But what he had really done was to back this proud, ambitious professor-turned-administrator to the wall, leaving him little breathing space. Bob hadn't thought it out well at all. What he really did was to force Deutsch to choose between Wilson's vision and the consensus arrived at by everybody else. If Deutsch acquiesced, he could, against Wallenmeyer's expressed wishes, simply agree to the small amount of funds asked for. Perhaps that was the heart of Bob's ill-conceived plan: Even if John didn't see things Bob's way, so Bob reasoned, he might still give the money to Fermilab to avoid the extreme act of firing a lab Director. In other words, Bob argued to himself, to forestall a bitter dispute, Deutsch might be willing to agree to his request for such a petty amount of money. That would then give Bob the chance to live and fight another day. Considered in isolation, the strategy didn't seem to be that bad. Nevertheless, it was wrong of Bob to think that John would just cave in like that to what was no more than simple-minded pressure, no matter that it was over a measly pittance. It was naïve of him to imagine that John would casually oppose the physics community to serve the interests of a man who was behaving unpredictably and desperately. Nevertheless, Bob took the plunge and placed his future professional life in the hands of another. Whether he was friend or foe, Bob would discover soon enough.

With his head jerking forward as if a car he was driving had come to a sudden stop, Bob opened his eyes. He felt enlightened, just like when a truth suddenly comes to mind. As he sat in an almost dark room in the Director's renovated farmhouse situated on the Fermilab lab site, he finally saw the light. Not only had he underestimated Vineyard that fateful summer the year before, but he had also underestimated Deutsch and Wallenmeyer. How dumb he had been! Although far past the point of no return, this now became obvious to him. How could such experienced and intelligent men fall for such an indiscreet and prosaic ploy? He could kick himself. He was reminded of the words on a framed sheet of paper that had been hanging on a wall in his long-gone past, "Too soon old, too late smart." Even before the answer from Deutsch would come a few days later, he now knew what it would be. As it hit him, he was surprised at the effect this new insight had on him. It didn't lower his spirits or depress him as he might have expected; rather it seemed to liberate him, as if a heavy weight had been lifted from his shoulders. But that sense of being set free couldn't anchor itself in him, and would soon fly away. As time was to creep by, he would come to rue that decisive action he had taken so rashly. However, for the time being, his predominant feelings were deliverance and relief. The thought flashed through his mind that maybe he had subconsciously yearned for this result all along. Yes, it was his time to leave the stage and, without being aware of it, he'd wanted out – and how better to go than as a blazing martyr to his cause. But that far-out thought passed quickly and fell into a dark recess of his mind never to resurface. He felt so peaceful sitting and gazing out the window at a multicolored glow in the far horizon. It was good – he was alone, quiet, thoughtful, and content. But the moment was short-lived as he was startled out of his reverie by the sounds of his wife Jane coming home. He could hear her steps as she approached. He would have to tell her that his days at Fermilab were numbered and that their lives at his beloved lab were at an end.

4. ISABELLE Burned While George Fiddled

By early 1979, Mickey could not escape the inevitability that BNL would not embrace his design for a leaner, experimentally focused ISABELLE, one that would be better performing, faster to build and accomplished at a greatly lowered cost. He had obviously heard and taken to heart Master Bob's message and come to believe with a passion that it fit the *lady in distress* well. True, Mickey's ISABELLE would not be capable of all the experiments the physichists demanded; however, the significant ones, the ones that might advance the field in major ways and unexpected directions, would work fine. But, all in all, that issue was really a red herring. There was a far more important distinction between the two ISABELLEs, a critical up-or-down one that spelt the difference between success and failure. Through intensive theoretical study and technology analysis, Mickey had demonstrated that, to his professional satisfaction, the current ISABELLE design was fatally flawed. Although privately most other accelerator specialists agreed that he was right in his calculations and scientific interpretations, to Mickey's innocent amazement, almost to a man, none would speak out. Such was the power of a lab Director who wielded a strong political stick and also had a lot of carrots to distribute when it suited his whims. So it was that Mickey learned through bitter experience the ways of men, including the all too human supposedly rational and clear-thinking scientists.

Mickey's firm as a rock confidence was badly shaken. His voice was dimmed and he had no one to turn to. He was all alone. What was he to do? He didn't want to run away, like others who already had or soon would. Yet he couldn't see himself as remaining silent while he was watching and actually helping the lab lurch headlong toward its fearful destiny. Then, in June of that year, even as life was becoming unbearable and there seemed no way out, luck happened by to sing a happy tune for him. It came to him in the form of an idea, a sudden thought that set him on a course that would give him the change of scene he was seeking, yet not make him feel like a frightened jack-rabbit. What he hit upon was that he didn't have to sit on his haunches, waiting on others, reacting to their capricious, quirky, and at times desperate commands. He could be proactive: What about giving another line of work a whirl, he thought? Why not? He might even find a way to do it without running away from what he saw to be his duty to the future of Big Science. And he did discover a scheme to fit his needs. The notion that he came upon was to try to find a place for himself right at the source of Big Science power – Washington. What gall: to think that little Mickey would be welcomed into the city of influence peddling. Nonetheless, it wasn't merely a pipe dream because there was someone there who just might give him that chance and open the door for him. Yet, on the verge of action, just as he was about to take that all-important first step, an alarm sounded in his mind that going in this new direction might mean the end of his days as a practicing scientist. He hesitated for a brief instant, but the alarm was a weak one and was quickly gone, unheeded. Its after-tones would always remain with him, but, except for fleeting interludes of regret, Mickey would never hear them. It was one of those times in a man's life when he takes a big step with little but a passing thought, and without the least appreciation of the consequences. In any case, he couldn't imagine an alternative and so, almost by default, he pressed on. He lifted the receiver, dialed the number, and waited until a chipper voice answered, "High Energy, Doctor Wallenmeyer's office." Mickey asked to speak to Bill and was told that Wallenmeyer was in conference but would return his call as soon as possible. There, the deed was done. Casually, he'd set in motion the wheels that would have a most profound impact on his future life.

* * * * *

Mickey had seen government power in action at Woods Hole in 1977, where he had been an accelerator consultant to the ERDA panel. He had worked tirelessly in preparation for the meeting, writing out all his thoughts and analyses in gory detail, putting in all the care and logic he could bring to bear, and eliminating as much jargon as he could so that all might be able to follow and understand his arguments. He made handouts available and gave talks to the accelerator subgroup, to larger and more general audiences in attendance, and even at informal gatherings among participants who were particularly interested in his ideas. In the end, everyone knew where he was coming from and most knew in their hearts that he was on the right track. But Mickey unfortunately had to learn the hard way that all the preparation, all the work, all the persuading, and even being right would have to recede in the face of a government edict that had the force and majesty of the law. When, seemingly out of the blue, he got wind of the announcement that Congress had approved the ISABELLE project, with five million dollars to start and hundreds of millions more to follow, he did a double take. There was no argument, no discussion, and most importantly no appeal. The decision and announcement were so simple, wrapped as they were in a rosy, optimistic package. Absent the least bit of rationality, the whole affair had an air of unworldliness. Perhaps most difficult for Mickey to swallow was the finality of it all. Period! Game's over!

When he first heard the news, Mickey felt an uncomfortable dyspeptic surge and had to rest a bit to collect himself. How could they do that, he had thought with profound disbelief? ISABELLE simply wouldn't work as designed! Did he do something wrong? No, he tried to reassure himself, he did everything right, everything he could. He wrote his well thought-out thesis in countless memos and papers, spoke of it to everyone within earshot, proclaimed it at lectures and workshops, and screamed it from the rooftops. Nevertheless, not a word of it was taken seriously. Nobody seemed to hear what he was saying or to understand its implications for the future. For quite a while he couldn't come to terms with the reality before his eyes. He couldn't get it through his thick skull that it was a fait accompli. It was over and done with and there was simply nothing he could do about it.

Although it saddened him somewhat, he remembered all the effort he put into trying to understand the ISABELLE design. Burning the midnight oil, he worked out how best to optimize it, poring over the smallest details to make it the best that it could be. For close to a decade he calculated, checked output, wrote papers, made presentations, argued, defended, re-analyzed, and gave his all in the effort to convince the ones who counted, or anyone else for that matter. Alas, it was all for naught. No one was listening. Then, as if he couldn't believe that he had failed to win over the power boys, either inside or outside the lab, he bull-headedly started all over again, repeating the entire process. You see his obstinacy had no bounds. He went on like this, massaging the design again and again, in the vain hope that he could learn to express and convey to them the beauty of his wished-for newborn-to-be. But, in the end, just as you can't change the unchangeable, you can't persuade the won't-be-persuaded.

Mickey had no regrets for having put in all this effort, because the truth was that he loved doing it, even the long hours, the hard work, and the ever-present strain of trying to create something from scratch. Still, he was filled with shock, taken aback because all he had done had not the least impact on those who held the reins of power. Even though most of the technical staff was quietly convinced by Mickey's arguments, those at the top of the BNL heap, with astonishing and disquieting ease, silenced all the potential, but unfortunately all too fearful voices; and, when it was over, they had their way. As it turned out, most, including the accelerator theorists, the designers, and the all-purpose workhorses, followed the lab leadership. They did so regardless of the reality that not far off in the distance they would fall off the edge of the cliff as they marched to the tune of the Pied Piper. In their defense, they probably didn't know what was in store for them, or how soon the ax would fall. On the other hand, they surely must have sensed that things weren't going right. Actually, whether they knew or not mattered little because they were doing the only thing they knew to do. Meanwhile Mickey, powerless, could only look on as the disheartened and pitiful people around him – his colleagues – scrounged around for pittances, willing to do most anything to hold onto the petty privilege of remaining in the nest.

As Mickey watched the sorry spectacle unfold, he vowed that for him it wouldn't come to that. He promised himself that he would never sink so low, especially for such an unworthy bunch of exploiters. Instead, he struggled and searched to discover a way out. Then, without the least appreciation of how it happened, a light bulb went on in his head and the insight was born that maybe there was a freedom train out of his living nightmare. A subtle smile formed on his face as he pondered the humorous irony of an escape by way of going over to accelerator management – Mickey the manager was too funny to contemplate. The inspiration that came to him was simple enough – if you can't beat 'em, join 'em; and the means to get there was even simpler – Bill Wallenmeyer. Yes, by Jove, Bill might be the answer to his prayers and his ticket out of the morass he was stuck in. Yes, but could it possibly work, he asked himself, as he remembered Bill's perhaps saving offer five years earlier?

As he started his attempt at reconstructing the Wallenmeyer episode, an even earlier period, the first part of the seventies, came rushing to his mind. It struck him that, as new as he was then to the accelerator game, he already had an inkling of the influence that could be gained by finding the right place in the realm of management. There was something even more significant to this point than that – something that still holds true. Simply put, if you want to be somebody in accelerator work, only by way of management could you get there. Although he sensed all this, he didn't really know it sufficiently to articulate it; rather it was some sort of subliminal understanding. The truth was that his time for a concrete management role hadn't yet arrived. Still, his subconscious mind seemed to be telling him that a little preparation wouldn't hurt. So in 1970 and 1971, by taking courses at night and on weekends, Mickey earned an MBA at Hofstra University, not far from the lab. Serendipity was speaking during these years as he was preparing for the important moment that was only to come years later in 1979.

However, Mickey realized that his Hofstra experience could be put to good use even before then. That happened in 1974, which was another fortunate step for him, in turn leading to the occurrence five years later that was to save him from a life of stagnation, bitterness, and cynicism at BNL.

With his management credentials in his back pocket, and not having a clue as to what their future significance might be, Mickey met with Wallenmeyer at the 1974 International Conference on High Energy Accelerators in San Francisco. What turned out to be a mutual appraisal was arranged by one of Mickey's colleagues, George Wheeler, an expert in linacs, who came to BNL from Yale and happened to be one of the people who interviewed Mickey for his BNL job in January of 1966 during the New York meeting of the American Physical Society. Wheeler himself spent a couple of years in Washington learning the ins and outs of government, working as a BNL detailee – a detailee being a scientist who spends a couple of years doing government service and then returns to his home institution more experienced and presumably better equipped to help bridge the growing gap between government and academia. It was and still is an effective system, where everyone seems to win. Because he was always a little enamored of management anyway, when Mickey first learned of the scheme from George, he was attracted by it, and said as much. So, since Wheeler had worked with Wallenmeyer and knew him well, it was quite natural for him, during a philosophical conversation with Mickey about the mysteries of management, to suggest that Mickey take a shot at following in his footsteps. Mickey, although not ready just yet, was always open to new ways of thinking, and recognized that there could come a time when this might be the perfect thing for him. Maybe it was a sixth sense or maybe it was just good luck, but Mickey, with the notion of working in management lurking somewhere in his mind, thought that at some future time it might be useful to have such an option. With that in the back of his head, it didn't take him long to decide to explore that avenue, and so he got right down to the practical details of how to accomplish it. As luck would have it, the San Francisco conference was just coming up and Mickey realized that everyone would be there – this was an opportunity he simply couldn't afford to pass up. Without hesitating, he asked George if he could help him to meet Wallenmeyer there. George, being an agreeable guy, assured him that he'd be happy to help, and went on to arrange the meeting that was to be so important to Mickey's future.

Even as time passed and memory faded, Mickey could still remember the dim lecture room after most of the audience had left. He and George waited a while. Then Wallenmeyer, walking forcefully toward them with his big red face bright and smiling, extended his hand, first to George and then to Mickey. Nothing escaped Wallenmeyer's grasp of the moment, least of all the fitting and appropriate protocol called for. He had large hands and a firm, aggressive handshake, which Mickey tried unsuccessfully to match. Besides being a big man, Wallenmeyer had an imposing presence, and Mickey would always carry a picture of Bill seeming to tower over those around him. "I hear you're planning some time with us at headquarters," he blurted out. Mickey was taken by surprise at the forthrightness, the quickness, and the bluntness of the greeting; but finding the strength to keep his wits about him, he replied, "Yes, I was wondering why you never had a theoretical accelerator physicist in your office and I thought you might find one useful." "Okay, just say when," was the retort, and, just like that, their meeting in essence was over. What an impressive character! Mickey thought. The only thing remaining to do was to exchange a few pleasantries, with Mickey hardly knowing what he was saying. Then they parted, just as Wallenmeyer was putting his right arm around the shoulder of a passing friend and moving away laughing, fully involved in his next get-together. Mickey was quite taken by this big, heavy and blunt man with such a seemingly happy demeanor. You see it was only too easy to underestimate Bill, what with his salesman-style smiles and backslapping, but somehow Mickey instinctively sensed that under this mask was the depth and power potential of a man to be reckoned with, and he was quite right. As it turned out, for the next five years, the contact between them was only sporadic, but in 1979 Mickey was ready to take Wallenmeyer up on the invitation he had extended in that dimly lit lecture hall in 1974.

Mickey resigned himself to the reality that a break to pursue a career in management would mean the end of his days in science. Indeed, that's how it was for others who'd been detailed to the Capital before him. Once they had the feel of the big-time, it was hard to take the comedown that accompanied returning – *how can you keep them down on the farm after they've seen Paree*? It was plain to them that management meant power, and who doesn't want that? True, perhaps this isn't the best way to run science. Perhaps management shouldn't be the top rung of the ladder representing authority in Big Science. But the truth is, that's the way it is – you can't go home again and you certainly can't reverse the clock. The creation of the national lab system, the coming of the primacy of government funding, and the influx of politics made the connection between government and lab management so strong that science itself has become secondary. As for accelerator science and technology, it was pushed even further into the background and relegated to a level far down in the order of things. So, if you were in the accelerator field and you wanted to have some influence, management was the only way to go. That meant that if you had a driving ambition such as Mickey had and if you wanted to have any real effect in the affairs of science, then you really had no choice – it was management or bust. Mickey, after a great deal of serious consideration and a lot of wavering, finally bit the bullet and chose the management route. If there was a single reason for doing it, it was probably that he couldn't abide anymore the unending frustration of being a voice in the wilderness. If it wasn't to be through accelerator expertise that he could cause the truth to come out, maybe management could do the trick.

Mickey had mixed feelings about his upcoming adventure, and found the downside ones not easily sloughed off. Yes, there was much excitement in what lay ahead, but he also had misgivings about what would be lost. Science to Mickey had been a labor of love. What a stunning notion is this thing called science. Imagine, man can actually understand the physical world as it really is, in spite of his eyes not having the favor of seeing it – not its smallness, not its bigness, and not its complexities. "There is more to heaven and earth than is dreamt of in your philosophy," said the bard. It almost seems as if the fates set things up in such a way as to keep man in the dark, unable to find out the truth of the physical world around him. But man, through his indomitable spirit, has discovered a way to meet that awesome challenge of the gods via an astonishing combination of rational observation, logic, experimentation, and mathematics. Even though the gods have made the world like an onion with a seemingly endless number of layers, man keeps peeling away and gives every appearance of being on a winning streak. To Mickey that competitive game with the gods is the glory of science. Thus in 1979, as he steeled himself for his Washington move, he felt as if a love he had come to take for granted in his life would have to be sacrificed on the altar of his pragmatic needs.

However, Mickey was not the type to let thoughts of what could have been get him down. Always seeing the positive side of things, looking ahead was more his style. Thus, the picture he formed in his mind emphasized not what he was leaving behind, but rather what lay before him – a new life and a new career in management. It even occurred to him that the loss he would have to bear might not be so bad if his upcoming service were to serve a greater need. If only he could help make accelerators for all manner of sciences, especially high-energy physics, grow to new heights of excellence, wouldn't that be something? And that wasn't a mere fantasy, for, in the transition he had chosen, he would have the thrilling opportunity to make Big Science bigger and better than it had ever been before. Yes, he thought, rationalizing a bit, it is a role devoutly to be wished for.

* * * * *

Waiting for the phone to ring on a beautiful afternoon in the spring of 1979, Mickey couldn't help remembering the past decade and how he came to this fork in the road. He found himself back in 1974 when he first had a flash of light in his mind that said, "Bunch those ISABELLE beams, you fool, bunch them!" When this revelation came, you must understand, the ISABELLE beams were not expected to be bunched, and Mickey was himself part of the trio of beam physicists who were fashioning the design, along with Rena and Ernest Courant – Ernest being a co-inventor of the prized, couldn't-do-without AG principle and a top accelerator scientist at the lab. However, even though Mickey was one of those who devised the currently accepted beam configuration, he didn't find it too hard to do a complete about-face – that's just the kind of guy he was. However, the BNL management and associated physichists weren't so flexible and insisted that the counter-rotating beams of protons remain continuous. Actually, to the play-it-safe BNL management, steadfastness made a lot of sense – after all, that's the way CERN did it and look how successful it was there. Thus, ignorant of accelerator design as they were, the top brass, who wanted it that way and no other, got their hearts' wishes; while at the same time the accelerator experts, compliant as they were, went along and did as they were told.

Being the first to enter the brave new world of proton colliders and fearing the use of yet untried bunches for storage rings, CERN set the precedent, and BNL, having become quite insecure technically, didn't want to stray off the beaten track. Even though storing bunched beams would have made ISABELLE far easier to build, the lab chose to remain within the bounds of established conservatism. What a crock! This wasn't the time to be ultra-cautious, to demand double-sure assurance, to incessantly over-think, to count pennies, and to hold back until it's too late to do it right. No, it was the time to imagine, to put your wits to work, to attempt giant steps, to go for broke, and to fly sans parachute. However, there's no convincing those who won't listen.

At that time in the mid-seventies, Mickey was confounded and not just a little annoyed by the contradictions before him at the lab. BNL had already decided that in order to reach the higher energies needed to enter the new era of colliders, the next machine required the introduction of the new technology of superconducting magnets. Risky as it was, it was absolutely the right way to go, perhaps the only way. And this was the way gullible Mickey thought of BNL – taking the necessary chances to push forward the frontiers of knowledge and technology. But if that's the way the lab was, why then was it so afraid of bunches? In fact, there was an even deeper mystery. Using bunched beams, besides leading to better experimental performance, would considerably lower the risk involved in taking advantage of the up-and-coming superconducting technology. With bunches rotating in the collider, the ISABELLE superconducting magnets would be only half the size. Not only would ISABELLE's magnets be easier to build and almost risk-free, but they would be much lower in cost, and also could be built significantly faster because the smaller and simpler magnets would need only minimal R&D. It seemed like an offer that couldn't be refused.

Nevertheless, as with all bright ideas – and bunched beams was no exception – there was a hitch, a fly in the ointment that couldn't casually be ignored. Some of the smart-asses and spoil-sports in the Director's Office, and surprisingly in the Accelerator Department as well, asserted that bunched beams would not survive the long storage times needed to do the experiments. Mind you, this was only speculation, based on an obscure phenomenon, which, although predicted theoretically, had never actually been observed. But despite the murkiness of the notion, this contention that bunched beams wouldn't work for ISABELLE led to major disagreements and discord among its designers, most of whom were eager to follow the direction of the higher-ups. All of Mickey's work told him that there was nothing of a physical nature that would destabilize bunches in an ISABELLE-type collider, at least nothing that couldn't be handled by established techniques and technology. About that he was adamant. So, as far as Mickey was concerned, there was nothing to worry about. However, for some strange reason, the lab had attached a stigma to the idea of using bunches. This put quite a damper on Mickey's enthusiasm and optimism. What frustration it elicited in him! Why would the lab risk all on magnets so hard to build yet glibly cast aside bunched beams on a far-out conjecture? To say that it was confusing and disconcerting to Mickey would be putting it mildly. What disillusionment it was! It certainly took him down a peg or two.

Having been so sure that he was right and yet having no one willing to listen to him was perhaps not uncommon in the course of life's experience, but it disoriented Mickey and was likely the reason for his flagging spirit. Self-doubt, almost unknown to Mickey, began to creep in. He even saw himself withdrawing a bit from the fray. Then something occurred that abruptly shook him from any incipient self-pity and tore away at the doldrums that were cast on him. At least for the time being, the old Mickey returned for the scrimmage. In 1975, CERN decided to do an experiment at their collider to test how long bunches could survive. Mickey was thrilled. This is what he was waiting for. Either he'd be vindicated or, God forbid, thrown to the lions. The experiment was straightforward enough. One of the beams in the CERN collider would remain in its standard continuous mode, while the one running in the opposite direction would be bunched. It was as if a continuous string would be colliding with a sequence of beads in an X-like configuration. As the experiment proceeded, Mickey's excitement level rose. He was so sure that he was on the threshold of being proved by experiment to be right – something scientists dream about. But, alas, his elation was short-lived, for, lo and behold, the CERN experimenters found that the bunched beam decayed almost immediately while the continuous beam lived on and on. Mickey was aghast at the report from across the Atlantic. He was exasperated and bewildered, and kept repeating to himself, "No, no, no, it can't be so!" This news was so disheartening to poor Mickey that it drove him to a low the depths of which he didn't imagine existed. Could he stand the shame of being so wrong? One thing for sure, his life as a scientist was really being put to the test.

For some, this could have been a mortal blow, but not Mickey. Swaggering Mickey would not be the one to drop the ball. So convinced of his theory and analysis was he that he wouldn't let go. With boundless confidence in himself, he was sure he could find a way to fight back. And, believe it or not, he did find a way. He worked himself to the bone. He re-analyzed, re-calculated, and re-interpreted. In the end, he was able to overcome his inner feeling of shame, to shrug it off, and to argue unemotionally and rationally that he was right. CERN must have erred, he claimed in no uncertain terms. "They're wrong, they made a mistake," he insisted. That is not to say he wasn't disappointed and devastated, but somehow he found the backbone not to back off, not one bit. You see retreat was not in his action lexicon. That was not his way. He was obstinate and stubborn to his very core, and could not be swayed from his resolute and unshakable belief that his calculations were firmly based on well founded, systematic, and theoretically sound principles. It would take more than a quick, makeshift experiment to break his back, and he vowed to stick to his guns.

For reasons Mickey didn't immediately grasp, the BNL management was pleased to hear the CERN results. But after he thought about it more, their reasoning may not have been that complicated. The point was that even though it would have been easier to build Mickey's type of collider, it stuck in their craw to change course, particularly using Mickey's approach; no, they wanted to do it their way. Giving in to that aggressive, troublesome underling wouldn't be easy to take for proud know-it-alls. So, the CERN test ended up relieving them of the embarrassment of having to concede that they were wrong. Furthermore, it made life easier for them; they wouldn't have to explain why they spent a lot of money wastefully, with little or nothing to show for it. As it stood now, all they had to do was let things stay as they were and move along – just business as usual. For them, it was a godsend: The magnets could remain unaltered. Already submitted proposals for particle experiments would not have to be modified. Their desire to appear decisive and certain would be sustained, so that scientists, politicians, and the public could rest assured that the BNL team of experts knew what it was doing and had everything in hand. Thus, that fortuitously ringing CERN bell saved them: saved them technically; saved them administratively; and saved them managerially and politically. What a stroke of good luck had happened by. It was exactly what the lab wanted and the episode was treated as if it were a victory. They were so smug and self-satisfied. They had willed it to be true and it was so. How good it felt to be right! As for Mickey, if they gave him a thought at all, it was that they were amused no end to get this big talker, this bothersome irritant, this pesky gnat out of their hair They were especially cheered to be rid of his incessant whining, and this time for good. They had finally proved beyond a shadow of a doubt that they had it right and Mickey was wrong. Henceforth, therefore, Mickey would have to just do his job, do what he was told, and shut his big mouth.

As it happened, however, it turned out not to be that easy to silence Mickey, for they had underestimated his determination and obduracy. Mickey thought all along that the CERN result was wrong. He was highly confident of his own work and felt that either the experiment had an instrument error, or the data were being misinterpreted, or perhaps the experimental conditions weren't what the experimenters thought they were. Although he couldn't be absolutely certain – indeed it might just have been wishful thinking – he cockily found a way to deny the whole business both to himself and to anybody else. So on his merry way he went, insisting that bunched beams were better on all counts, that they would give better experimental performance, and that they would make the machine less costly and easier to build. Thus, in spite of what appeared to be an end-of-story occurrence, Mickey and the BNL accelerator management remained at cross-purposes. This didn't exactly endear Mickey to the lab bosses; and, given their vindictiveness, bordering on cruelty, he didn't find it an easy time to live through. Treated like an unrealistic daydreamer, he became even further isolated from the mainstream accelerator activity at the lab than he had been before, and learned a little of what it was like to be a pariah. At the same time as all this foolish dog fighting was going on, the unwieldy continuous beam design tended to occupy more and more of the lab's resources and effort. Putting so much into the task of countering Mickey was bad enough, but the lab's failure to pick up the magnet's ultimate impracticality, BNL's Achilles' heel, was tantamount to being unforgivable.

Then two years later, just before the ERDA panel convened in Woods Hole in 1977, a second shocking announcement came out of CERN. It turned out that this seemingly error-free bastion of science in Geneva had flubbed their flaunted bunched-beam experiment. When he got wind that CERN had fully recanted the 1975 experiment showing that bunched beams could not be stored long enough to be of any experimental use, Mickey was flabbergasted. Slowly but surely the admission found its way across the Atlantic that the 1975 results were wrong and the experiment flawed. That such a bunch of top-notch experts in science and technology could have been so careless and negligent was difficult to comprehend. Nevertheless, there you have it. At the root of the problem, it turned out, was electrical noise in the system feeding power to keep the beams bunched. Thus, the bunches were not intrinsically unstable after all. Once the true source of the problem was determined – surprise, surprise! – in no time, the CERN experts found a simple way to eliminate this electrical noise. Then – shazaam! – the bunched beam was as stable as the continuous beam. This put Mickey at a peak in his roller coaster ride, feeling gratified, vindicated, and greatly relieved that his belief and faith in his analyses and calculations had paid off. Later, Mickey would often wonder about the two-year delay in arriving at the correct experimental truth about bunched beams: Could there have been a Machiavellian purpose behind it, more than meets the eye? There could have been some conspiratorial intent to delay the U.S. from moving ahead too quickly. "Nah!" he thought, "CERN was too above-board and wouldn't do anything as underhanded as that.

Mickey was especially elated that the error was unearthed and that the story came out at a highly propitious time for him, right after he had been asked to be an accelerator consultant to the ERDA panel at Woods Hole. Now he wouldn't have to explain why he didn't believe and wouldn't accept the result of the original CERN bunched-beam experiment. It was as if a heavy weight had been lifted from his shoulders. In fact, he almost felt like thumping his chest in triumph. But he restrained himself, although he did go so far as to imagine himself arriving at Woods Hole as man of the hour, entering the arena as some sort of champion and showered with praise. Privately, he couldn't but feel a lot of pride in the work he had done and a shivering thrill that he had been right all along. When all was said and done, BNL and CERN had tried to squelch him, but they turned out to have soft underbellies and it was Mickey who proved to be a giant killer. With that victory under his belt, he could all but see himself walking into the Woods Hole meeting with his head held high. Yes, he could see the glorious picture in his mind's eye. He'd showed them all, and now it was his turn to gloat. However, his reception and his time there turned out not to be like that at all. No, a hero's welcome and the red-carpet treatment was not what awaited him.

Mickey expected to have a great time at Woods Hole, for he had become the undisputed bunched beam man. He had no doubt that he would make himself felt there and that the lab leadership would have to listen to him now that the facts were to be out in the open. As a consultant to the panel, he was assigned to the accelerator subgroup co-headed by Jim Leiss, a top scientist at the National Bureau of Standards, and Boyce McDaniel, Director of Cornell's Laboratory for Nuclear Studies. Mickey respected and admired these accelerator community leaders, both of whom had over the years accumulated a great deal of knowledge about accelerators. When either of them spoke of accelerators, you could count on their being accurate. Perhaps even more important to him was that they were straight-talking men whom he was confident he could trust. As Mickey presented his case for bunches to the subgroup, they listened intently, questioned incisively and at times provocatively, and seemed to understand his every nuance. Mickey had no complaints and was satisfied that he had been given more than a fair shake at giving his side of the story. He wondered, as these preliminaries to the main event were taking place, how things would play out when the word got out to the full panel. He worried a little that some could easily take him to be subversive, an anti-BNL malcontent and spoiler. Although that could very well occur, he found the strength to push aside such negative thoughts. Now was a time for rejoicing. Perhaps he was just daydreaming, but what he really wanted at the meeting was an atmosphere of free and open debate, where impartial and wise judges would decide the winners and the losers. In a fair game of that sort, he felt in his bones that he would come out on top. Unfortunately for him, that's not how it was. As he discovered, that's not the way life works. It's true that he recognized the virtue of using bunches sooner than the rest of the science crowd. Yes, he'd been a little smarter than most, but that minor bit of speedier insight is not what makes a hero. In fact, as the meeting progressed, he came to feel more like the goat in the ensuing drama that unfolded.

Long after the lights had dimmed and the show was over, now and then, that July meeting back in 1977 would come to Mickey's mind. For some reason, he would always seem to focus on a particular moment during an afternoon break. In the broader context of the remarkable things that took place there – front-page stuff of weighty consequence for Big Science – this was such a piddling experience. Yet it stuck with him and alighted into his consciousness via the most innocent-seeming triggers. He would see himself standing with a cool drink having a discussion with Jim Leiss and Mark Barton, who was head of the accelerator effort for the ISABELLE project. Mark, at that time Mickey's boss, made a somewhat snide remark about bunched beams. He was looking straight at Jim and his words were couched in a wry smile; while at the same time, with the hint of a sneer, he extended a condescending nod of his head toward Mickey. Mickey didn't really know what was going on; but luckily, although it wasn't his instinctive bent, he wisely chose to stay out of the give and take between his two higher-ranking colleagues. Silence wasn't his trademark, but in this instance he nonetheless resisted the temptation to intervene. He just stood on the sidelines, looking a bit dumb, with a foolish self-conscious smile on his face. In response to Mark's rather inappropriate comment, even though it was probably just a lame attempt at light humor, Jim, who was naturally dour, looked right back into Mark's face, and with a passing glance to Mickey, said sourly, "He may be right." Mickey recalled thinking, "It's good to be right," privately enjoying Mark getting put down like that, and in addition getting quite a kick out of the special vote of confidence he was getting from Jim. Mickey believed that Jim listened to him and comprehended what was being said during those many group meetings and in their one-on-one discussions. Thus, he concluded that Jim took his views on bunched versus continuous beams seriously. However, although there was some truth to that, Mickey would later come to concede that the incident that kept recurring in his thoughts had little if anything to do with him or with the bunched beam matter. Remember that ISABELLE was spending R&D money, perhaps unnecessarily, at quite a clip, and Jim and DOE didn't like that one bit. Since Mark was the ISABELLE front man, no doubt he and Jim had at least some knockdown drag-out encounters. So once Mickey digested the matter, his verdict was that their head-to-head at Woods Hole was engendered by some disagreement between them about how funds were being spent on the project. Other than that, the only other reason Mickey could conjure up was that they just didn't respect each other that much. However, no matter what the true reason was behind the squabble between Mark and Jim, Mickey was far more intrigued by the question of exactly why this little occurrence had such a deep impact on him and why it stuck in his mind so clearly. That he was never able to figure out to his satisfaction! Maybe, he later would surmise, it wasn't because the incident by itself mattered so much to him, but rather on account of an altogether different reason. Maybe, he thought, it was because this was to be his high point at the meeting, for, as it turned out, from that point on it was downhill all the way.

Poor Mickey, unversed in political maneuvering, seemed to have completely misread the essential reason for having the panel meet in the first place. He thought it was to evaluate whether ISABELLE was technically feasible and whether it was worth doing at all. Anyone with sufficient savvy would have figured out that this was not the case; and eventually Mickey got the painful point. In due course, he came to understand the hard way, by having seen it happen before his very eyes, that ISABELLE was a done deal well before the meeting got underway. The political wheels had been greased, and all the significant actors – with their dialogue fixed – were set and in place. Unbeknownst to Mickey and to most of the others in attendance, the meeting had a larger purpose that was not easily perceived by novices. Speaking bluntly, a ritualistic ceremony was being enacted with the sole intention of announcing that the good, agreeable and peaceful BNL had won the day over the wicked and rebellious Fermilab. The Midwestern lab just wouldn't listen to reason, and thereby became a Washington sacrificial lamb, as well as an example to others who would deign not to toe the line. As for the science community, it was merely a prop put on display to carry the torch and place the crown on the winning lab. It was nothing short of astonishing how well everybody played their parts, especially since most of the scientists present had bit parts and were not made aware of the precise script. What was being witnessed was "Nouvelle Vague" Big Science cinema, and the entire scenario went off without a hitch. If you perceived and looked carefully at some of the hostilities and antagonisms in the arena of action, you would've recognized some jitters reminiscent of an opening night performance, but they were of little or no consequence. When the play reached its denouement, ISABELLE was endorsed and anointed by the science leadership, while, by congressional mandate, the government bureaucrats did their bit by letting everyone in on the already determined level of funding for the coming year. All this was accomplished with no single individual standing out, so that it would be all but impossible to place blame on any specific person's shoulders if things didn't go as planned. There was no particular reason for anything to go awry, but if perchance there was a change of heart, or if a serious slip-up occurred somewhere down the line, it would be no problem for those pulling the strings – the truly responsible, maybe even culpable, parties – to pick out appropriate scapegoats. When it was all done, the ecstatic winners congratulated each other while the down-in-the-dumps losers went off to nurse their wounds. It was quite a sight to see the BNL contingent departing on a high that was loud and raucous, while the Fermilab group almost imperceptibly skulked off subdued and severely rebuked.

Mickey was chagrined as the scene played itself out. He so wanted to understand more of why it had turned out the way it had. As time passed and he became a tad more perspicacious, he arrived at the rather startling conclusion – he was the picture-perfect example of an innocent type growing up – that giving favors and protecting their asses were the prime concerns of the high and mighty. Certainly, as an idealist might have wished it to be, it was not getting a job well done or doing the right thing. It grieved him as he lamented that there were not many men like Bob Wilson around any more. Unfortunately, Mickey was living in a time when the mediocre, scientists and bureaucrats alike, held sway.

In attempting to penetrate the secrets of the system, he uncovered the inescapable truth, obvious in retrospect, that certain people's hides could be saved, using the money-power they possessed, by serving up the dispensable powerless. More generally, having power and control over money being essentially synonymous, those with the most money to distribute bore the least risk. However, on digging a little deeper, Mickey came to appreciate that those who had money-control, although it made scientists bow to their whims, didn't necessarily act in the best interests of science – not by a long shot. And therein lies the real predicament, because that's precisely why mediocrity took over

Big Science in the first place. Having reached this conclusion, you might say, *so what*! But then comes the whopper! As sure as anything, mediocrity does and did inevitably end up in failures, and Big Science was not to be spared as projects began tumbling down. As those who experience it well know, the cost of failure is high; and when failure arrives, it's hard to be rid of it. From then on, it's a whole new ball game; and when Big Science reached that stage in its life-cycle, its life's failure mode you might say, trouble began to hit everyone, the powerful and the powerless alike. That's when the power-holders came to discover that there's no completely risk-free lunch.

No doubt, you shouldn't expect that the average Woods Hole participants could have appreciated all of this, but it is disheartening, actually deplorable, that the smart and the famous among them didn't know better. They should have been able to foresee that the cost of failure would have to be borne by the science community as a whole, and that the future of Big Science itself was being put in jeopardy. What had they done, those convening science gurus blabbing away at Woods Hole? Simply put, they grabbed what they could, these aging sad sacks, and left the next generation, the young, to live with science delayed and science not done. What a pitiful state of affairs – so much risked and so much lost just to cater to the wishes of a few mediocre men!

As for Mickey, by meeting's end, he felt cheated as he sadly had to admit that nobody there cared a whit about whether ISABELLE used bunches or not. He had been no more than a fly on the wall, an observer who watched but hadn't the capability of acting. He saw the tomfoolery and the deceit, but could do nothing about it. So he stood aside and viewed the show, stunned as the true aims of the meeting were accomplished: BNL got even more than what it had sought, the science research budget was set, and Fermilab was put in its place. The underestimated Vineyard certainly knew what he was doing and the Wilsonian opposition was crushed. For those scientists and administrators in attendance who sensed that what had been done was wrong – and indeed a number of such types were present – fear was the predominant characteristic. No one dared contest the outcome, lest it blow up in his face; no one who counted had the courage to speak out; and no one would back up the solitary Mickey, whistling in the wind. Mickey, the dreamer, against all the odds, kept looking for a hero to appear out of the blackness, but alas that was just his naïveté and stupidity at work. For that to have happened he would have had to wait a hell of a long time.

In the two years following the Woods Hole crowning of BNL, Mickey made a last-ditch effort to try to get the lab on the right track. In the immediate Woods Hole aftermath, he even thought there was a chance, as small as it was, that the mood at the lab had dramatically shifted, and that his opponents might have finally seen the light. But his hope turned out to be a false one, and when the air cleared his confidence in a Camelot-like occurrence all but dissipated. A King Arthur there was not to be.

Whatever his own fuzzy and unsettled feelings were, seeing that he and his bunched beam scheme were yet again rejected, he couldn't deny that, along with a kind of post Woods Hole relief at the lab, there was reassurance and expectancy all around. The scientists and the staff were flush with victory and a renewed life. A revived and maybe even revitalized ISABELLE with twice the energy of the old was in the making, and no one could miss the plump budget about to arrive, in keeping with the improved political climate for Big Science. In a dreamlike moment, Mickey imagined that the lab was experiencing the dawning of a new day, but that turned out to be only Baron Munchausen trickery: "No, Virginia, there is really no Santa Claus." It was no more than castles in the air.

Confused by an idealistic, actually desperate, wish that some good could come from it all, a mixed-up Mickey again had to go through the painful process from peak to valley. Although doomed to failure, and he must have subconsciously known that, still he was compelled to go through the motions that one trained in logic and rationality must. He tried to be calm and reasoned, detailing his arguments precisely, carefully, and deliberately. Unfortunately, with no one listening, he was crying in the wilderness. All his words were lost in the clamor of activity and change. Persisting nonetheless, even when the inevitable should have been apparent, he did the best he could: he worked out new designs based on bunched beams; he did cost and schedule analyses; he made comparisons with the current design; and he gave presentations and seminars, including group meetings with endless give-and-take, all in an effort to change things. But it was to no avail. He even tried frantically screaming out that *the emperor had no clothes*, but this just angered everybody around him, even those he incorrectly deemed to be his friends. In the end, his voice lost any resonance it might have had in earlier days; and what was worse, it occurred to him that he had also lost heart. This loss of passion disturbed and distressed him. That, more than anything else, convinced him he needed a change.

At that precise moment the phone rang, and *he was saved by the bell* from his melancholy. He smiled as he heard Bill's voice at the other end. The entire conversation took but a minute or two, and his smile broadened noticeably as he heard Bill's proposition that would give him the change of scene he so needed.

By 1979 ISABELLE had been given a new lease on life. The project was on the go, Washington was foursquare behind it, money was plentiful, and BNL was alive and kicking. After years of a bitter struggle with Wilson, Vineyard had come out on top. Fermilab was squeezed out of the action, and BNL, as it had been in the fifties and sixties, was again to become the undisputed champion of the national accelerator labs. This was all thanks to the new ruling order, which had come a long way since the three-lab concept was proclaimed six years earlier. The system introduced then had withstood the test of time and was now in full swing. It operated in the manner of an oligarchy, where a few strong men in the government and at the labs agreed on a course of action and then dictated to the larger community their choices for the Big Science program. With the autocrats on top controlling the money and the jobs, and having the wherewithal to hand out favors any way they saw fit, the science community leaders were compelled to acquiesce and follow sheep-like on penalty of exclusion from participation in the system's many benefits. Even more was demanded of the working scientists and engineers, the average Joes, who had become putty in the hands of the self-installed power brokers. They would not only have to take what they were given and like it, but would also have to express their satisfaction with the choices by pretending that the decisions were of their own making. How was it accomplished, you ask? It wasn't hard at all. In truth, the process that evolved was rather simple. It went this way: Committees and panels were established as needed, with the membership selected by the ruling elite to suit their ends. These groups issued recommendations as per instructions. Why did they do as they were told – for better or worse? For the obvious reason that the budget, which ended up being the controlling mechanism, was in the hands of the bosses. How could any group dissent when any contrary proposal just wouldn't be funded? It wasn't rational, and besides, deviants who went their own way had hell to pay. The ERDA panel that formulated its plan at Woods Hole in 1977 was a fine representation of the system working letter-perfect. With transparent arrogance and no opportunity for appeal, it gave BNL the thumbs up sign and Fermilab the thumbs down sign, and that was that. What a brilliant piece of forward-looking decision-making that was! There, in that Massachusetts marine paradise, in a groundless, not-to-be-believed perversion of reason, low cost, high productivity, and low risk were penalized – Fermilab's head lopped off – while high cost, low productivity, and high risk were rewarded – BNL's head topped off with a crown.

In practice, most scientists were quite satisfied to live within this system. That's not really very hard to understand, since they derived more than enough benefits from it. Anyway, why rock the boat when it could only end up in pain, even drowning? However, not everyone was scared out of his wits. There were some dissenters, unfortunately very few, who stood fast on principle and asked for some measure of free and open competition. But if someone chose that course to follow, be assured that he had to be very careful if he wanted to end up in one piece. Expressing such opinions was extremely dangerous, since for law and order to prevail, such lone voices in the wind, which might easily spread, couldn't be tolerated, and so were summarily silenced. Ironically, such actions were taken in the name of peace. One man who suffered greatly because of his principled nature was Wilson, who was a staunch believer in freedom and merit. He simply couldn't tolerate the system, couldn't restrain himself, and spoke out thunderously, brazenly repudiating it. To the misfortune of all, as a result of his flagrant words of censure, he was denounced as an extremist. No doubt the system had to respond to such blatant opposition. You see Wilson was an idealist, a veritable extremist, who refused to repent because, in his eyes, he hadn't sinned. And he was right, for it was nothing but the true state of Big Science that he'd pried open for all to see. However, that's exactly what he'd been warned not to do, and so he came to be among the first to feel the full weight of the wrath of the new order, held up as an example to dissuade others from following in his footsteps. He was crushed, no more to be Fermilab's Director; and his lab fell victim along with him. However, little did they all know that the new order had only a short time more to live, that the entire unholy alliance would be toppled over and would come crumbling down in just two short years. Actually, what actually killed it was not Bob, but rather the speed of transitions and upheavals in our modern technological world. This speed is at so high a level that ruling over Big Science was and remains a hard road to hoe. Today's Big Science exists in the midst of very fast-changing technology, and in such a time an oppressively totalitarian-like environment cannot be sustained for long. As demonstrated by the fate of the three-lab system, when the time is not just right, even the best laid schemes o' mice and men are doomed to fail.

Basking in the glow of the Woods Hole verdict, while unwilling to contemplate what might lie ahead, the scene at BNL was one filled with self-congratulation and chest thumping. Confidence was everywhere, even in the air being breathed; and the desire and readiness to whoop it up, get down to business, and take on the Big Science world was infectious. The staff seemed to have uncovered and released an untapped source of energy that had remained hidden for nigh on a decade. So it was that in that pregnant-with-possibility year of 1977, a call to arms was sounded and the lab, with a rediscovered backbone, responded with a collective resoluteness to achieve that had been unseen for many years. BNL seemed determined to get it right and not to foul up such a chance. The halls were filled with hustle and bustle; and the scientists were filled with excitement, prepared for the competition, and ready to move to the front lines.

For a brief moment, a happier past had seemingly come to life. It was good to sense these creative impulses back at work again. And why shouldn't they be buoyant and expectant? Why shouldn't glory be waiting around the next bend? After all, the Woods Hole panel had made its assessment and had wound up with a stunning loud and clear assertion for the entire world to hear: BNL had been deemed to be one hell of a lab, declaring and affirming that BNL was perfectly capable and well placed to build the strongest and best collider in the world. The panel even insisted that ISABELLE should be upgraded to twice its originally designed power, and charged the lab to move vigorously forward, swiftly and without delay. Congress played its part as well: Following its preliminary announcement at Woods Hole, it gave the newly enlarged project its full blessing by formally approving it as a bona fide construction project and agreed to deliver the necessarily enhanced multi-year budget. Once the formal authorizing powers gave their nod of approval, the lab was besieged with all manner of those who wanted in. There were those capable types who wanted sorely to partake of the new action; there were those willing to work at anything asked of them, whether it be technical, administrative, managerial, or even being merely gofers; there were those who, for one reason or another, wanted to be associated with grand undertakings; and then there were those who just wanted to kibitz. The strength of the broad-based support, overwhelming to a lab that such a short time before had been on the brink of falling over a cliff, was astonishing. Anyone who was anyone – and even those who weren't – seemed to rally around the ISABELLE flag. Experimenters, users, and users-to-be – that is, the whole band of physichists – began gearing up and were ready and anxious to get going; and science community leaders fell in lockstep behind the lab.

With all the animated activity surrounding the new champ, most of science's leaders seemed oblivious to the fact that poor Fermilab, which not long before had been the object of their generosity and largesse, was squashed to a pulp. Sad to say, that's the way things are in this best of all possible worlds – up today and down tomorrow. Sure, Fermilab took a ruthless and brutal pummeling and was thoughtlessly and carelessly pushed aside, but there's nothing unusual about that. When you're a loser, what more can you expect? The truth was that Fermilab was just a sideshow to the main event; and no one much cares about what's happening in the wings. Although it was a stark and painful experience for the workers in the Illinois lab, few others even gave it a passing glance. Most were looking elsewhere and putting their money in New York Big Science. For anyone who studies how people tend to behave, this wasn't much of a surprise, seeing that the movers and shakers, the politicians and government officials, and everyone else that counted had all given ISABELLE the go-ahead. So BNL was again at center stage and the place to be. For the lab that had once been great but lost its way, this was another one of those rare moments of triumph to treasure. The world was the lab's oyster, and Vineyard basked in the sunshine of a new day for BNL – his day. It was a far cry from six years earlier, when Vineyard became Director just as the lab was reeling from its long descent from preeminence to mediocrity during the disastrous Goldhaber years. But times were different now. George had entered, a man with the glow of success, and beaming with self-satisfaction and confidence. He was in the clouds, on a high it would be rough to come down from. Unfortunately for him, as he was soon to learn, such a state can't be sustained for too long – not in this world.

When George took command, forward movement was almost immediate and things began to happen and take shape. He seemed to know what to do and perhaps, more importantly, he knew or got to know the right people in the right places. He himself took the role of lab politician, a kind of minister for external affairs. Not long after he took over in 1973, ERDA introduced the three-lab concept. It is hard to imagine a more impressive political victory for the opening shot of an incoming Director. In one fell swoop, BNL gained new life and Fermilab was deader than a doornail as a competitor. Even though Wilson wouldn't accept that assessment right away, he would eventually be forced into concession. But Wilson's unwillingness to admit defeat was of no consequence anyway, and couldn't prevent George's ascendancy to the U.S. proton throne. In any case, whatever Wilson thought or did, there was no question about it: Vineyard was on a roll as political magician. To accentuate that picture of him, in 1977 George reinforced his new persona by putting on a repeat performance when Congress, with unusual suddenness bespeaking some sort of a deal, started construction funding for ISABELLE with a first installment of five million dollars. As if to underline George's newfound political prowess, Congress did so with a dramatic flair that all but floored the Woods Hole gathering and cowed the Big Science community into submission – BNL was to be top dog and that was that. Actually, underneath the polished self-assured manner he learned to exhibit, George was still a scientist and really a novice at the political game. Nonetheless, these forays into politics were the accomplishments of a man of the world, just as if he already had many years of experience behind him. What he had achieved in such a few years was nothing short of a tour-de-force.

George was a man on the make. He quickly learned how to get things done through the age-old but still demanding and thorny method of deal making, where failing was always only a small step away. But to become an adept negotiator, something more was needed, some implacable characteristic, something lethal. He had to cultivate in himself the art of ruthlessness, the capability and the hardness of heart to finish off his opponents. And he did just that – as Wilson would vouch for.

In retrospect, what George gained from the deals he pulled off with ERDA and Congress was undoubtedly a bit more than he could handle, because what he promised meant that BNL would have to change its ways significantly, a task easier said than done. You see the three-lab idea was grounded in the premise that the labs would all be prepared and ready to build the projects they were called upon to do. To accomplish that they would have to be proficient in the appropriate new accelerator technologies called for, as well as primed and geared up to introduce and implement them at short notice. That was the key strategic, can't-do-without point of the Ramsey panel fourteen years earlier in 1963. At that time, refusing to comply, Goldhaber was a holdout; and because of that BNL was destined to fall to the rear of the pack in technological expertise and capability. However, Vineyard, when he came to power, vowed to reverse that policy. He agreed that the lab would henceforth seriously strive toward building the next machine that the government and the community wanted and would perform the necessary R&D to develop the appropriate technology to achieve that end. Whether or not he could come through didn't seem to interest anyone who counted. The essential point was that he promised he would, and ERDA and Congress believed him. Put another way, on a more personal level, he acquiesced to what Wallenmeyer, representing the U.S. government and its policy, interpreted to be the best way for the community to go. Who was there to contradict such power? So, once these two strong men sealed the bargain, although it seems to have been done with no more than a handshake, there was no choice for the weak-kneed scientists but to go along. Thus both Wallenmeyer and Vineyard got what they wanted: Wallenmeyer got his three-lab notion into full swing, which gave him the geographic distribution of accelerator facilities that he believed to be a political prerequisite to getting the optimal congressional support, and Vineyard got BNL a new lease on life at the forefront of science. Peace was restored to Big Science: American scientists ocean-to-ocean were pleased as Punch, except, of course, for Wilson and his dwindling crowd; the community was buoyed up with an eagerness to get going and a child-like anticipation and optimism; and the future for science and technology was pronounced to be secure and full of promise. It was only left for reality to show its face.

To make the deal with Wallenmeyer and company work, George had the onerous job of doing a complete about face on the downward-leading direction the lab unwittingly became committed to during Goldhaber's regime. To get to where he promised he would, George set his sights on fixing the lab's management system, which meant righting the wrongs that had accumulated over the many years of mismanagement, and on bringing order to a staff that had forgotten what it meant to push forward the frontiers of science and technology. The first step was to resurrect a viable and vibrant superconducting magnet technology effort. To do this, he went right to the heart of things and set about the daunting task of unifying the lab's accelerator and physics efforts and of bringing together the accelerator experts and the physichists. With the aplomb of a seasoned veteran organizer, he brought in two lieutenants, Ronnie Rau and Nick Samios. Rau took charge of the Accelerator Department and brought a disgruntled, ragtag outfit to a semblance of order. It wasn't easy and it wasn't without rancor, but he managed to quash the malcontents and incurable complainers and come up with an effective working group for ISABELLE that represented the lab's pathway to the future. When Samios, the second commander in charge, took control of the Physics Department, he found that he had to tame a troop of prima donnas, each going his own way and marching to his own tune, while all of them were forever whining and demanding that their self-interests be satisfied. Somehow he found a way, with a remarkable combination of cajoling and threatening, to transform that unmanageable group into one marked by a rather improbable coherence of purpose and effort. With

Vineyard's imaginative and ruthless methods at the root, in a few short years an enviable leadership team emerged at the lab. It even seemed, for a short period after Woods Hole, that Vineyard, Rau and Samios, the BNL big team, could pull the ISABELLE rabbit out of the hat.

Those who knew the score could only marvel at how far this unlikely trio managed to lead the lab through the dark treacherous landscape of past misdeeds toward the light of laurels and honors. All their instincts and experience told them that it couldn't be done. Only a miracle would suffice – and could scientists really trust in miracles? Yet for a time even these naysayers caught the bug and imagined that possibly George, Ronnie and Nick could actually accomplish the impossible. Unfortunately, their inner mistrust of what they thought they were seeing proved to be a better measure of the truth. Not far beneath the surface, trouble lurked ready to pounce, and this rosy picture of BNL in 1979 was nothing but a sham. Many, perhaps most, were distracted by the rich swirl of colorfully enticing promises and pastel dreams of glories-to-be emanating from the canvas, and they were fooled as well by the self-assured, confident air of the picture's inhabitants and proponents. But, as all would soon come to know, the promises were phony and the dreams were false ones. In time, when the inevitable came and the mask was removed, it would reveal decay beneath, like the dark creature that Oscar Wilde's vision of surface beauty – Dorian Gray – had in reality become. There's a bitter lesson in this story of self-deception and biting off more than you can chew, one that all would do well to learn and heed: beware and be not one of those who race after an easy paradise lest it turn out to be a fool's paradise.

Hints of gathering clouds on the horizon were already discernible as 1979 opened; and as the year progressed, they became looming threats. The sources of these obstacles to BNL playing out the success story of the decade lay both outside and inside the lab: On the outside, CERN was beginning to flex its technical muscles, and a Fermilab rebirth, unimaginable two years earlier, was beginning to take shape. Inside BNL, years of neglect in maintaining forefront accelerator expertise had started to take its toll, as the weakness of its technological core began manifesting itself in technical faltering. Most evident was the lab's inability to decisively resolve issues and difficulties arising in that sphere. Every technical problem became a big deal, with no resolution forthcoming. Yes, the technical staff kept at it, working long hours. But it just went on and on, with nary a reasonable answer in sight. Excuses rather than results became the standard management output and this came to be recognized as their modus operandi.

* * * * *

As the eighties got under way, CERN had already completed its contribution to the accelerator high-energy race, the *modestly* named Super Proton Synchrotron (SPS). Experimental data and interpretations flowed from it and the remarkably built machine became a strong contender for particle energy supremacy. Although the multi-hundred-GeV crown was still precariously held by Fermilab, the fact was that American Big Science management had become hesitant and overly cautious in its decision-making and actions and, by and large, uncertain of where it wanted to go. Thus, despite the advantage of having been far ahead of CERN, the U.S. couldn't find the wherewithal to maintain its lead, and it vanished. So, the challenge from CERN was successful and, make no mistake about it, it wasn't due merely to America's seeming loss of will to excel. Neither was it just a matter of happenstance. Rather it arose mainly as a result of the tenaciously strong-willed management of a proud European lab that was determined to take on and beat the highly touted and thought-to-be invincible United States. The decision to embark on a course of victory or bust – a bold move because it was a long shot at best to imagine ending up the frontrunner – had come more than a decade earlier. CERN's management was aware that to prevail would require a prolonged effort of unremitting industriousness as well as steadfastness and a single-mindedness of purpose possessed by few institutions. You see to CERN this was more than a competition of one lab against another. The men at the helm in Geneva were after something of far deeper consequence: They wanted to demonstrate to the world that the Europeans were well able to handle themselves independently of American largesse, and certainly without the need for American charity. Sure, to some of them it was just a matter of pride, but many others had an enduring and passionate incentive to return to Europe the grandeur of its past – to show that Europe's glory days had not been lost forever when the American juggernaut overran the globe spreading its message that technology and pragmatism would henceforth rule over culture and idealism.

To set the stage for its comeback and perhaps as a test of its own mettle, CERN jumped into the fray early on, back in the mid-sixties, by being the first to take on the daunting challenge of proton collider technology. Success in this venture called for accelerator and technology advances hitherto unavailable and even unimagined. The men of CERN had their work cut out for them. But, as it turned out, luck was walking with them: though they only dreamed that it was possible to beat the odds, they ended up coming out with flying colors. As time would tell, their performance was a technical tour de force, and their triumph was more than anyone could have aspired to. So much new technology did they conceive, develop, and make work, and so much of the lab's staff became technical wizards – the aces of the world's finest accelerator technology specialists – that it made CERN the world's pre-eminent keeper of accelerator knowledge and expertise. This was in stark contrast to the American management of its Big Science technology, where backbiting and technical ineptitude ultimately led to stagnation and second-class status.

The surge of technological and scientific power from the brilliantly piloted, booming, and thriving lab in Geneva was more than a victory of the moment. Not only was it an affirmation that Europe was not less than it had been before, but it set the stage for renowned and top-rank breakthroughs for the entire Big Science world. It came to open wide the doors to a future no one could have either divined or foretold. CERN scientists and engineers had these many years actually been preparing for something, yet knew not at all what it was. What an all-too-human mystery is such a phenomenon! What a perfect example of synchronicity it was as, totally unknown to them, they converged and collided with a completely independent sequence of developments – a sequence that turned out to be just what they needed to be ready and able to embark on a remarkable adventure into a no man's land of accelerators and new science. Scientists, being rational and down-to-earth to the core, might deduce that this was but an example of serendipity – pure chance, a random confluence of uncoordinated events – rather than synchronicity – a still unknown and improbable force of nature, determining certain happenings by a form of collective will. Natural probability and pure luck might indeed be the right answer, but then why did CERN pour so much effort and resources into the enormous undertaking? Could it possibly have been that a mistake or misjudgment was made – one that unexpectedly turned into a gold mine? It happens sometimes!

What started the ball rolling toward yet another nature-revealing secret was a brilliant experimental idea in the ever-boiling mind of a bold and forceful thinker, a pioneer of science, Carlo Rubbia. Rubbia, a reckless and intrepid hulk of a man, who played a big role in the Big Science game, came up with the audacious thought of building a collider where a rotating beam of protons (p) would collide head-on with a counter-rotating beam of antiprotons (pbar) - a veritable p-pbar collider. The beauty of his clever strategy was that, since the two beams are of opposite charge, they could counter-rotate in the same ring of magnets. In a regular proton collider where the two colliding beams have the same charge, two parallel magnet rings would be required. In Rubbia's scheme, the need for two rings, carrying with it a variety of technical complications and substantially higher cost, would therefore be obviated. Another thing: the idea could be implemented readily and without much additional resources in existing high-energy rings either at Fermilab or CERN. If this seems too good to be true, that's right! So what's the catch? The answer is simple: What you gain in possible speed and low cost, you give back in higher risk. Nothing is free, as they say. As might have been anticipated, there is a thorny and troublesome downside to this deceptively simple scheme. Since this world we live in is composed of particles like protons, not antiparticles like antiprotons, sufficiently intense antiproton beams are exceptionally difficult to come by. Antiprotons being incredibly rare, a way to produce, accumulate, and concentrate them had to be invented. Methods for their individual generation had in fact been introduced years earlier, but accumulating and concentrating them remained in the realm of science fiction. A new technology had to be conceived and developed. So you can imagine the enormous amount of resistance to going forward with such a risky endeavor by the stodgy conservative wing of the Big Science community. For Carlo, what this meant was that the road to stardom would be filled with potholes galore.

At this point in the drama, in came CERN's nonpareil team of accelerator experts. With all their hard and dedicated work of the previous two decades under their belts, their know-how was on the verge of bearing fruit. Enter Simon Van der Meer, a calm and thoughtful man, not in the least like the blustery, boisterous Carlo, yet just as daring and insightful. Before Simon arrived, what was missing for the show to go on was a technical genius to make the seemingly impossible happen – to get the sufficiently intense antiproton beams needed to make the Rubbia scenario workable. As luck would have it, Simon was just the man to do it. It was as if he had been preparing and waiting all his life for this moment to arrive. He pulled an idea out of his distant past, which although unrealistic then, given the technological advances of the years since, had in his estimation become doable. It just happened to be a technique he had recently been playing around with, and it occurred to him that it just might work to intensify antiproton beams. If that proved to be true, it would exactly fill the bill for Rubbia's encounter with destiny. So he suggested it, and Carlo bought it. The method, with the imposing name stochastic cooling, was an astonishing concept: millions of particles would be taken and, virtually one by one, brought closer to each other to concentrate them to the level the experiments required. This notion, close to being beyond belief, is what Simon proposed and claimed he could accomplish.

And what Simon said, Simon did! Once the appropriate pbar concentration was in hand, accumulation was straightforward, and voilà, the impossible had become possible. Miraculously, synchronicity dealt CERN a second winning hand, as there in the late seventies and early eighties a marriage made in heaven was consummated. With the CERN Co-Director-General, Leon Van Hove, foursquare behind them, Carlo and Simon raced ahead, and the rest is history. Amazingly, it took less than three years to get the job done. With the technological feat of cooling the antiproton beams accomplished, the collider and its two big complex detectors were built and the hunt was on for the elusive W particle, one of the mediators for directing traffic in the mad, mad, mad, mad subatomic circus. The search, like an archeological dig, required painstaking care, and led to many blind alleys and dead ends along the winding road, but the W was finally found. From its hiding place, lurking in the shadowy sands of the crazy-quilt world of quanta and quarks, it was pried loose for all to see and wonder at. The world of man could offer up to the high priests no more than a Nobel Prize, and, in 1984, Carlo and Simon accepted the accolades courteously and graciously. Still, having approached heaven's gate, even as the lavish ceremony in Stockholm was proceeding, they knew that it couldn't come close to matching the sensation of having come so close to touching the light of the gods.

* * * * *

While Big Physics was bubbling with anticipation, excitement, and glamour as the eighties got started, at BNL the slide downhill rose to such a pace as to make the mind reel. After the all-too-brief high engendered by the Woods Hole accord, reality set in, and in just a few years the science community was gearing up to step in and stop the charade with the simple rationale, "Enough, no more." The straw had broken the camel's back. Central to the lab's predicament was that it just couldn't make a good-enough workable superconducting magnet in a practical way and at a reasonable cost. For years to come, long after the project bit the dust, the question of why this was so would be continually raised. All manner of people, both scientists and non-scientists, were incredulous that some solution to what seemed no more than a rather straightforward technical-management challenge was not found and implemented. The technological issue was not a major one and should have been easily resolved, they thought. And they were right! You see a variety of other labs had managed to do it without any hue and cry. Not that it was an easy job for anyone, but rather what's transparent is that the technology was sufficiently known and available to make manufacturing these types of magnets, perhaps with a little extra effort, unquestionably doable. That's what made it so especially hard to fathom what actually happened: first it was successfully done at Fermilab, then at DESY in Hamburg, then at CERN, and then even at BNL a few years later. Thus, this puzzling question of why BNL so miserably failed ISABELLE on this score has never been satisfactorily answered, and remains mysteriously unresolved. Some say, "Just let it go, it's over and done with. Nothing can be done about it now." But that's so shortsighted, because if it was known why BNL lost its technological competence when it needed it most, perhaps it could help future generations in understanding why so much was sacrificed so needlessly. Perhaps they could learn so as not to suffer the same fate. However, it is quite understandable that people have a lot of other things on their minds, and simply don't have the energy or the will to belabor the whole messy subject. So as time passed, the memory of it dimmed, as all memories do, and the question as far as it could be recalled began to seem unimportant. Still, it is sad to imagine losing such telling details because they did represent the true underlying causes of why ISABELLE fell; why its builders-to-be suffered great loss in pride, status, and prestige; and why the lab was to feel the pangs of having failed for many years to come.

To any passer-by happening on the scene, the lab seemed to be functioning under ideal conditions for running a successful R&D program. Of course these outsiders couldn't distinguish between the lab functioning smoothly and the lab in the throes of hard times. Thus, they came to the view that it had the best possible technical resources to accomplish almost anything reasonable it set its collective mind to. That's what BNL showed the world and that's in fact the way it actually was. As an insider, it was no different: the lab's R&D program had every appearance of being in great shape. Starting in the early sixties, through its own eager initiative and via government mandate, BNL was permitted to take on the challenging and inspiriting problem of finding a way to introduce superconductivity into accelerator magnets in order to realize the capability of building a forefront high-energy collider. What a vote of confidence that was! And what a feeling of self-worth it kindled in the staff! They were so sure they could do it, both the R&D and the construction, and there was ample reason to believe they could. Just think of what BNL had at its disposal, and how it could confront and deal with the responsibility conferred on it: It had top-notch, experienced scientists and engineers; it was accumulating the knowledge and the capability of developing the highest quality superconducting material needed to get the job done; it had claim to the get-up-and-go spirit of American industry, which was ready, willing, and able to be a part of this grand expedition into unknown territory; and it had – as was and still is typical of the openness of academic R&D – easy access to all of the world's accelerator centers and thus to their information and know-how. It was all but unimaginable that anything could go wrong. Yet it did!

R&D funds poured in and an enormous amount of effort was expended. But as the next couple of decades passed, the situation, far from coming to a happy resolution, seemed to go from bad to worse. Nothing would work for the lab, and there was nothing to show for all that was being put into the program. But why, you might well ask? If difficulties were showing up, why didn't the lab seek out answers from outside its borders: from other labs, universities, and any of the places where experts resided? It had access to all of them. So, why, why, why? To put it bluntly, it is hard to grasp and appreciate that BNL could easily have gotten the help it desperately needed from any of these sources, but for some ungodly reason – close to being an urge to self-destruct – was unwilling or perhaps unable to take advantage of this great gift of a free and open climate. The lab actually was given far more than it deserved from its performance: it was provided with all the funds it asked for; and it additionally had the OK and the reassurance from the U.S. government and the science community to do whatever it took to get the job done. What greater encouragement could be asked for? Believe it or not, the lab had what can only be described as carte blanche. But the shock of it all doesn't end there. If you ask how much time the lab was given to complete its mission for science and for the world, you can only conclude that it was given more time than would try the patience of reasonable men. What an awful situation it was, both for the scientists at the lab and for those outside waiting for the successful harvest that couldn't be brought in!

Especially hard to take was the case of the long, extensive, and painful history of the BNL superconducting magnet effort, the centerpiece of the lab's ISABELLE R&D program. The visionary John Blewett started it just as the sixties began. With his foresight, he smartly took *the-early-bird-catches-the-worm* approach, his rationale being to get a running start on working through the rough spots on these tough cookies before others came to realize their potential future value. To justify the superconductivity development program he had in mind to those holding the purse strings, he argued that the magnet staff could use the time effectively by trying first one thing, then another, until they got it right, that is, by doing R&D the way it was meant to be done. Since at the time it didn't seem to be a particularly costly endeavor, and it could very well beat out the opposition should something actually come of using such magnets, then why not? So, management supported the idea, and, for almost two decades, the lab's magnet contingent kept laboring away at it, sweating it out to learn all sides of the art and science of superconducting magnets. Over the years, they developed and accumulated knowledge and experience in a multitude of essential details, figuring out the right mix of titanium and copper for the superconducting coil material, determining the best insulation for the magnet, working out and optimizing the cryogenic system design that would cool the magnets to almost absolute zero, getting a fix on the cool-down method, finding the right vacuum techniques and the type of mechanical stabilization to use, coming up with a quench protection system and a safety network that was at the time without equal. Integrated over time, the effort put into this program was indeed substantial, but it appeared worth it as the lab's understanding and expertise grew by leaps and bounds. When the lab saw what had been accomplished, it took the magnets to its bosom and declared them to be theirs *for better or worse, till death do them part*. Thenceforth, the future of the lab was inextricably linked to how these formidable devices would fare.

BNL declared their magnets to be the ones for the next collider, and the science community acquiesced with nary a peep. That was the way of Big Science – money talks, and money was the big stick carried by the lab to force compliance. As a result of the weak knees, the tentativeness, and the trepidation, complacency ruled the community. It thus came as a scandalous surprise that, after almost two decades of magnet R&D, as the eighties were dawning, the lab was still without a workable magnet. How could such a situation have come about? It isn't a happy little story, but here it is: As enormous as the magnet group's travails were, and as effective as their work seemed to be, it wasn't enough, for the many pieces still all had to be put together into a coherent practical unit that would end up as a working magnet for the experimental purpose desired. And that's where the trouble began. You see having an acceptable magnet meant that the builders and the experimenters had to be in synch on a version that could provide the appropriate beam to the experimenters. Therein lay the problem. The physichists wanted more than the accelerator team could give and wouldn't relent; on the other hand, the magnet types were too proud to admit that they couldn't do what they were being asked to do. This shouldn't have been such a big deal: Why not force the two opponents to closure by some form of compromise? That's the way any reasonable management would act. Unfortunately, because it was putty in the hands of the muscle-bound physichists, the BNL management, even with its money-power, lacked the nerve to do what was right; and so a kind of paralysis set in. The lab came to an impasse, not really cognizant that, without quick corrective action, what it had on its hand was a prescription for failure.

When two needed factions are at odds, isn't this precisely the type of moment where management is supposed to step in? Shouldn't it insist that the two sides get together and come to a successful resolution? Shouldn't the managing troupe ride in cavalry-like to save the day? Isn't that why they're paid the big bucks? Nonetheless, they didn't do anything helpful. Rather they stood on the sidelines, preferring to back the strident and influential physichists, while criticizing the politically weak accelerator leaders, pushing and prodding them to make happen what they couldn't. This was the safe and easy course for the lab's management, and they took it. So, when all is said and done, the question aching to be asked is: How could the lab have done so little with so much? Could it be that poor decisions and bad judgment on the part of the lab's top management were truly the culprits? If not them, then who? There seems no other answer, yet it is hard to accept because the mechanism by which mistakes and bad choices add up to failure continues to elude us. Thus, we are left hanging, without a satisfactory answer. Such is the mystery and galling nature of BNL in the time of ISABELLE. The lab was given everything and clearly possessed all the standard ingredients to succeed. Yet, beyond all reasonable logic, it didn't. Incomprehensibly, the lab's top bananas seemed completely oblivious of what destiny had in store for them. It bowls one over to realize how close the lab was to the edge of failure without recognizing its presence.

Any rational assessment of BNL's magnet program points to the same conclusion: that success should have been had. But that's not the way it was. Even though its beginnings were filled with such hopeful enthusiasm, the program became a dismal sea of troubles and ended in a disastrous crash. Viewed straight on, as it slid in shambles to its inevitable end, it was little better than a band of unhappy people working more against each other than together toward the common purpose they were supposed to be aiming at. Since it seems that further pursuing this line of rational inquiry into the story of the blundered ISABELLE magnet will not bear the fruit of understanding of the project's breakdown, we must pull back and find a different direction to some kind of enlightenment.

Even without poking about in the multitude of poor technical choices made in the magnet program, it's evident that it wasn't the botched magnet that was the sole, or even an important cause of ISABELLE being so ignominiously jettisoned. Think of it: Although a highly dedicated bunch, could those politically simple and innocent magnet-makers have started such a hullabaloo in Big Science? Clearly, they hadn't the capacity or the know-how. No, there is no other recourse but to conclude that the answer to the puzzle, if one can actually be articulated, was not of a purely technical nature. Yet, if not that, then what was it? We can, if we so choose, circle around the lab haystack looking for technical needles, and it might indeed be helpful to do so, but common sense tells us that a better way could well be to probe more deeply into the stack and look elsewhere in the lab's hierarchical structure for some more complete and satisfying explanation. Doing that inexorably drives us to the simply worded but not so simply understood view that the root of the whole miserable mess must lie in that old bugaboo, the management. So, let's look more carefully at how management fits in. That's where all the authority is; thus, at first blush, it seems to be straightforward enough to presume that the cause of the entire affair must be contained somewhere in that bailiwick. Nevertheless, don't be too easily swayed by its seeming obviousness.

The very word, management, connotes rationality of purpose and of method. But that is only a surface view because management is about people, and the presence of people immediately contradicts this assertion. Does anyone really still cling to the notion that people are rational? No, management is far different, far more complex and shadowy, than those in it would lead us to believe. The fact is that management's apparent devotion to logic and sound argument is deceiving; and for those with the courage to dig into its flesh, quite a different picture emerges. So, if you have that urge inside of yourself compelling you to seek out what it's really all about, then dig you must. But beware, for once having begun, you must be prepared to find all manner of behavior – stretching from the all-too-uncommon rational to the deadly irrational kind, with its cheating, lying, deceiving, and betraying. Sad to say, in the matter of ISABELLE, there was precious little of the former and oodles of the latter.

Zooming in on BNL management in the period leading to ISABELLE's demise, we find that it was populated by a thoroughly unreasonable set of people imposing all but impossible demands on those whose job it was to get the work done. This burden was placed on the shoulders not only of those working on the magnets, but also of their counterparts in the many other technical areas comprising the project. Complaints and dissatisfaction were to be found everywhere you turned. Naturally, only an insider could without much difficulty pick such things up. If you were an outsider, you'd have to be pretty sharp and quick on your feet to get the picture. However, without question – either in communication with their managers on the floor, or by applying their leadership training and instincts, or via a modicum of wit – the men in top management couldn't mistake the trouble brewing. Despite their surely knowing what was going on, there were these *see no evil, hear no evil, know no evil* fools in the Director's Office blithely and obstinately insisting to both those committed to and those dependent on the lab's success that all was under control: "Don't worry," they would respond with seeming certainty to the timid questions put to them, "there's nothing to be concerned about, the job will get done as promised." Strangely, those on the floor doing the work, for reasons that seem devoid of common sense, echoed that very reaction, claiming that all was well in hand, that any difficulties that may have been noticed were minor and merely transitory, and that they would be resolved in no time. The staff must have known they were being disingenuous, but they said these things anyway. When you give it a second thought, however, maybe it isn't as complicated as it first appears: maybe they had to go along with the party line if they wanted to continue working at the lab; maybe they were being governed by their instinct for survival; or it may have even been that they were in league with the bigwigs, an unlikely but not impossible scenario. In any case – and this goes for the top and bottom alike – none of the expressed assessments and opinions, which were based on either self-deceptions or downright lies, reflected the way things actually were.

The truth about ISABELLE for all who cared to see was that deadlines passed, money got spent, and still there was not a danged thing to show for it. How could it be anything else but that something in the brains of both the management and technical staffs snapped and they went into a state of psychological denial? At each step, at each failing, they repeated and couldn't let go of their delusion that they could make out the light at the end of the tunnel. So on it went, this incomprehensible process recurring over and over again: another failure, another questioning of it, another excuse, and another promise at rectification that would never come. "No, it wasn't a pattern, it was just an anomalous, singular occurrence, and would not recur," was the contention. Still, that wasn't all there was to it; there was even more to shock one's common sense. If one were to recede from where the action was and observe the scene with a wider lens, one's surprise, bordering on disbelief, would only intensify with the discovery that the lab staff, from top to bottom, was not alone in denying the reality staring right at them. People from all over the world, technical experts, financial experts, and management experts, were trotted in to appraise the situation. What came of this was an endless stream of reviews from every imaginable source: government reviews of all sorts, from those of the DOE to those of Congress; reviews by the National Academy; reviews by independent contractors; and even reviews by his majesty, the lab Director. There was a bitter sort of irony in the Director being in such a situation, acting as if he were an unbiased reviewer seeking the means to solve that lab's problems rather than being the focal point where all the difficulties stemmed from. However, all the reviews were in vain. Collectively, the reviews represented a circular form of action, spinning aimlessly, going nowhere, and accomplishing nothing. Despite the negative evidence all around them, evidence that was even presented openly, the reviewers on the whole backed the lab at every turn. It was all a sorry sight to behold!

Every now and then, a deviation from the sickness of reviewer's blindness took place, and a bit of truth seeped through the thick shield that had been erected to protect the lab as well as the government-community system standing behind it. It was a highly unusual occurrence, but it did crop up. In fact, as ISABELLE approached its appointment with destiny, such happenings tended to increase in frequency, but the rise wasn't really visible until very close to the end. The truth was that the reviews were very important in sustaining the project even while it was rotting at its core, but had little if anything to do with dealing it its deathblow. Well before the fall of ISABELLE, the reviews were distributed something like this: Most were good, reporting that the program would clearly succeed both managerially and technically, and that a little change here, maybe a little there, would do the trick. Bad reviews were rare. On the management side, they ranged from reports that concluded that a wholesale change in the program management was essential to those suggesting that a change in the Director would be the only way out. On the technical side, although highly uncommon even in the class of negative reviews, some of the bad ones even hinted cautiously that the magnet as conceived might not turn out to be satisfactory. So, in this period when ISABELLE was still alive and kicking, the bad reviews were lost in the mass of good ones. It should be said that a free and open system would surely have found even this small number sufficient to be disquieting. Unfortunately the system was what it was, and they were paid no heed. When all was said and done, taking the reviews in toto up to about 1980, the science community and the government didn't find it difficult to accept the good and close their eyes to the bad; and that is what they did, at least for a time. Trying to look at this reviewing process neutrally and dispassionately, the only conclusion that a reasonable person can reach is that it wasn't really serious. As long as the good times rolled, it was for the most part a game of "Hear no evil, see no evil," with a little of "Pass the buck," thrown in; and in this way the charade kept going on while the precious time and opportunity for any corrective actions were going down the drain.

Since ISABELLE was the only game in town – that being the way the three-lab system was set up – more and more people were added to the list of involved and interested parties. This growth made it more and more difficult to contemplate a true overhaul. It was a fat cow that everyone wanted to milk, and nobody wanted to rock the boat and lose out. Furthermore, too many important people had staked their careers on the program as originally conceived, making significant change virtually out of the question. Of those who had invested perhaps too much, the lab Director was the most blatant example. Sadly, as ISABELLE's true insides began to be known and its supporters began to abandon it, Vineyard found that he was unable to bear the shame, and energy-sapped he began to lose control. When the full assault on the poor lady came, George seemed to be only half awake at the ship's helm as he ordered it into the iceberg-infested waters that lay ahead. Because of him, or maybe in spite of him, small technical and management changes were allowed and even encouraged, but they were just cosmetic in a vain attempt to appease the attackers. But it changed nothing in any meaningful way and ISABELLE, with not the slightest switch in direction, maintained its course to oblivion.

Then, without warning, a kind of eerie threshold appeared to be passed. Things had progressed so far downhill that scientists, other experts, and community leaders, both inside and outside the lab, just stopped trying to change things and set them right. The icebergs were looming just ahead, but the lab's staff and others involved too deeply to run away could only catch fleeting glimpses of them in their subconscious minds – invisible by day and only coming through to them as shadows in their nightmares. Without really being aware of what was happening to them, they stopped caring and became reconciled to their fates. What could anyone do anyway? So they busied themselves doing and accomplishing nothing, and, like the rabbit in Alice's wonderland, found a certain type of contentment in that. They acknowledged and even embraced each one step forward, while closing their eyes to the simultaneous two steps back. They squandered resources with abandon and wantonly frittered away their precious time. They began to lose their dignity and their credibility. Without the guts to accept their own accountability in the debacle, they began pointing the finger at others. Reproaches, accusations, and condemnations spread throughout the lab like wildfire; and those too weak to defend themselves had to bear the guilt. The blame game reared its head with a vengeance. The stress level at the lab was pushed higher and higher, and the emotional temperature kept rising. Then a second equally strange threshold was passed, one that made certain that any chance that clear thinking and careful and accurate R&D could prevail was irretrievably lost. It was as if, at that terrible point, the only way to save the lab from itself was to destroy it. A point of no return had been reached and crossed. Now there was no turning back, and a return to reason was no more to be found in the realm of the possible. The lab had gone down as far as it could go, and an explosion became only a matter of time.

Still, there remains a quandary, as we ponder the perplexing enigma of why BNL didn't take action while it still had time. Early on, the problems were strictly of a technical nature and the lab was brimming over with expert scientists and engineers. Why weren't these specialists allowed to correct the design's flaws? Why weren't they permitted to tackle a magnet that could serve the experimenters' needs and at the same time be built expeditiously, and even economically? This was quite possible to do, for the technical and managerial staff were all bright, intelligent, and technically of the highest caliber. Yet, some combination of overconfidence, arrogance, and pride prevented them from facing that the technical options available, the ones that would actually work, implied a more restricted experimental program than the physichists had their minds set on. Perhaps promises were made that the top management felt it couldn't back out of. But then why not just admit that a mistake had been made and a design change would be required? Certainly reasonable people would accept that not everything is possible. However, that was not done. The lab just pushed ahead, blinders intact, refusing to see the threatening reality closing in on it.

Then, as time passed, the true state of affairs at the lab started trickling out, and others began to see what those at the lab couldn't. Advice and criticism from all quarters started to pour in. Unfortunately and sadly, this only made it increasingly more difficult for the lab leaders to act, tied up as they had become in their vanity and self-esteem, as well as in their perceived stature within the community. This was particularly evident in those occupying the Director's Office. Were they thinking of the lab and its future? Were they thinking of themselves and each of his own future? Whatever the reasons for their behavior, they came to what was close to being an incomprehensible conclusion: that clamming up was their best bet. Despite their unresponsiveness, counsel kept coming in, chock-full of recommendations for change and admonitions of danger. Accompanying these communications were attempts at providing guidance and strong expressions of a great many of their willingness to help out in any way they could. Yet, the lab remained adamant and wouldn't budge from its inflexible position to go it alone. Seeing as how the bosses were straining credulity with such an attitude, it isn't unreasonable to wonder why they were so firm, so certain. The input from some of the honest and realistic reviews, as well as from concerned Big Science leaders, spanned such a wide swath of possibilities that the lab certainly could've given a little and picked some of the suggestions to act on. The Director didn't have to be so hardheaded. Yes, it's quite a puzzler.

Some of the more astute critics proposed that changes in the project's scientific goals be made in addition to those in the technical design, having come to recognize that the two were intrinsically and inseparably intertwined. But these suggestions were simply shrugged off. Seeing such unreasonable and unwarranted resistance put up by the lab, and being outsiders not knowing the intricate technical details of the project, their only recourse seemed to be to go for changes in management. Those who took this line ranged from being polite to being demanding. Some attackers went for the jugular, taking on the top management, even the Director, which wasn't such a wise approach if it was serious action they were after. Others with less extreme suggestions limited themselves to asking for newly picked management in the technical areas, particularly in the magnet program. In leaving the top management out of it, this was a little more sensible. Still others recommended the introduction of innovative and modern methods of management. This was a somewhat sly notion, much easier to comply with, since they weren't asking for the top bums to be thrown out. Yet, even here, though done more tactfully, in order for the expertise to be brought in, people addition was called for. Thus, there was no getting around it: the critics, however harsh or mellow their viewpoints, all advised a change in personnel, whether top to bottom or localized, insisting that some people had to go and fresh new faces be brought in. This was unquestionably sound advice, but maybe it struck too close to home by intimating that the lab's top brass weren't up to their jobs. So it wasn't much of a surprise that the lab dismissed all these ideas out of hand. Instead of taking the well-meaning critics seriously and giving them a fair hearing, the BNL management chose to launch a counter-offensive. They insisted that all the critics were on the wrong track by not addressing the central and crucial question of a working magnet and how to get it right. They claimed that there was only one lab problem, the magnets; and introducing all this management nonsense was a red herring raised for nefarious purposes by the lab's enemies. Of course, the critics, being outsiders, couldn't possibly know enough to get into the nitty-gritty of the magnet's guts. Also, the accusation of being an enemy wasn't to be taken lightly. The lab had the clout, and such thinly veiled threats could mean big trouble down the line. So what could they say to all this? They were being told to butt out and they were stumped. More than that, they were defeated.

The only inference that an unbiased and dispassionate observer could have come to is that the top management was being disingenuous. Yes, they did lie, but in a way they were forced to; and they were in the perfect position of authority where no one could call them on it. Although it's easier to see such things after the fact, still the critics should have thought out their strategy more carefully before they acted so incautiously. If they had, then perhaps their attempts at doing good wouldn't have blown up in their faces. They should have been able to figure out that the lab management couldn't abide the criticisms leveled at them simply because they were being singled out as the culpable parties for the lab's weakened technical state. They were being accused of being the ones to blame, and that they couldn't tolerate. Therefore, because they had the influence and the friends, they were able to fend off their accusers and so not have to face the music. As for the critics, they were right, but they had little chance of making stick their interpretation of what was wrong at the lab because the power that mattered was squarely in the hands of the wrongdoers. In fact, because the criticism involved the rather vague concept of management, shrugging it off was quite easy to do for the men supposed to be guiding the lab. They knew that scientists had little or no respect for formal management. In fact, the scientists' collective opinion of it can be encapsulated by the putdown: *when it comes to management, no one knows what he's talking about.* So, when it came to choosing sides, the scientists supported the lab; and so the lab warded off its critics, holding them at bay for the time being, and thereby remained in place at the top.

This leaves us with the persistent question – the one that won't go away: Why couldn't the lab's leaders admit their technical mistakes, both in their own hearts and openly to the waiting Big Science world, and then, released from the heavy burden they carried and with a free conscience, get on with the project? It is here in the exploration of this commonplace situation implied by the question that one can find the essence of what makes management tick and why it's such a multifaceted and knotty business. By connecting rational management with irrational human behavior, it induces us to look more deeply into the human drama, where failure originates. Unfortunately, the stories are full of men who would do most anything, even inflict pain, to hide their guilt. And so it was for the lab's upper crust, as they sank into the morass of self-deception and deceit and crowned it with perverted logic. It's the only way to explain the out-of-touch and aberrant reaction they had to the straightforward choices they had to make. In retrospect, there is little doubt that simple honesty and forthrightness would have been the best policy by far. However, to them, addressing the magnet problem head-on, facing what they had to know were the true facts of the case, and implementing the needed drastic changes would be an admission of guilt, to be followed by condemnation and blame. Of that they were sure; and so, lacking the needed courage to take the heat, they could not take this hard road and opted for the easy one - deny, deny, deny. Without the manliness and the mettle to look into the light of truth, the Director, his lieutenants, and their cohorts planted their heads firmly in the sand.

The management of ISABELLE was poor at best. Although management is more an art than a science – which implies that generalists and those with a common sense approach should make the best managers and often do – there are times and situations when there is no substitute for a manager to have specific first-hand knowledge and experience. This is most certainly the case for R&D projects and so applies almost universally in our brave new world of science and technology. However, one mustn't forget that since management decisions invariably involve a mixture of highly varied and diverse subjects, being an expert in any one is an insufficient prerequisite. That's why finding good managers is so tricky a task. They must be generalists but also experts when the time demands it! Because the expertise needed cannot with any degree of confidence be a priori known, this declaration almost seems to be a contradiction. And it is!

By and large, management is the art of choosing among alternatives with no assurance that other choices might not have been better. If a flashing light were attached to the best alternative then management would be a piece of cake, unworthy of such a grandiose name, and doable by almost anyone. However, life is never that simple and that is why management is not at all a trivial occupation. Usually, there is a great deal of uncertainty about which alternative is best, and in some situations a particular choice made could lead to critical consequences – these are the cases in which managers must earn their keep. It is when stress levels are severe and the stakes are high that the true worth of good management becomes apparent, and this is where the BNL management fell down on the job and demonstrated its low level of competence. The lab's leaders forgot they were in the modern world, where a technical decision is at times the key to whether a project will succeed or fail. By not preparing and being ready for such an eventuality, they carried themselves into the fire and eventually were burned.

At the beginning of the ISABELLE project, the lab chose for it a management framework that left much to be desired. It was an R&D project that the top men had on their hands, and for such a project, the notion that managers need only common sense, intelligence, and an ability to wade through technical jargon isn't appropriate. Here, in unknown technological territory, when a problem appears, the next step must be taken by a special person possessing that special *je ne sais quoi* knowledge that only he has. For R&D, such a narrow dividing line separates success and failure that the wrong move can take you from the high side to the low side with little or no time to think. So, to succeed, thinking and knowing must come before that step is taken, for the most part, well before. It is hard to understand why the lab leaders, scientists who are among the most intelligent and rational of people, didn't realize this, as well as the corollary that there must be room at the top for expert technical knowledge so that it is available when that danger-filled moment arrives. For critical decisions to be made quickly and with the best chance for success, there is no substitute for having the right person on hand to provide the all-important input at the time it's needed.

To see better how BNL came to its low point at the edge of failure, a brief outline of the details of how it arranged to manage ISABELLE might be helpful. Once the project was approved in 1977, the search for a project head led to the appointment of Jim Sanford, who had been at the lab in the sixties as head of the experimental division of the Accelerator Department, at that time under the chairmanship of the accelerator genius, Ken Green. Jim knew next to nothing about accelerators, and wasn't eager or even inclined to learn anything about them. However, in those earlier days, considering that the division of labor was established in the department so as to almost completely separate the accelerator and experimental efforts, that wasn't too surprising. Jim stuck to his job of leading the support team for the high-energy program experiments, while Ken ran the ongoing machine operations and the accelerator technology development for the future. If Jim had any complaints, Goldhaber was there to see to it that he got what he needed. It wasn't the ideal system, what with the awesome power of the Director, but it was workable. However, seeing that ISABELLE was a very complicated and first-of-a-kind accelerator complex – a true R&D project – to appoint Jim as head of it was a stretch to say the least. Jim was a nice enough person and knew a lot about experimental beam lines, but leading an accelerator R&D project was way out of his league. Maybe the men in the lab directorate felt that an experimental type was necessary for the job, a person that they could easily talk to, influence, and order about. However, although they were quite right about Jim being responsive to their whims and malleable, they were wrong about his being able to take on the construction of such a challenging accelerator.

To compensate for this ill-conceived and unsound selection, and probably under pressure from ERDA, the lab established a group made up of the lab's leaders to take responsibility for the project and provide management oversight. Undoubtedly the program managers at ERDA wanted to ensure that high-level people at the lab assumed full accountability for this expensive project, and Jim just wasn't a big enough man. Ostensibly, however, the justification for adopting this form of management by group decision-making was to ensure that the project received top laboratory priority for its needs. This couldn't have been an honest reason because an R&D project generally needs rapid and decisive action, not at all provided by this makeshift system. R&D work is simply not managed that way. The only conclusion that fits the facts is that the reason was phony, cooked up to hide the true, embarrassing one. Actually, the leaders were very foolish to behave so cavalierly: the project did involve a great deal of money and used up a number of valuable lab chips; they would therefore have been far better served had they chosen the optimum and proper head right from the start, when it counted most. Nonetheless, despite the disingenuousness, and even though this management mode was not a very satisfactory one for ISABELLE, sometimes circumstances demand adjustment and compromise. In fact, that's what happened here. Since the project was approved quickly and unexpectedly, and the lab Director was unprepared and off-guard, a quick and not well thought out decision had to be made, and was. Still, if there had been a modicum of flexibility and humility among the oversight group, and if greater weight had been given to the views of accelerator experts, it might have worked. Unfortunately, the scientists forming the management group didn't fill the bill. They were rather a weak bunch that would far too easily cave in when the pressure came and the kitchen got too hot.

The team set up, referred to pejoratively at the lab as the gang of four, was comprised of the lab Director, Vineyard, his two lieutenants, Rau and Samios, and the project leader, Sanford. A key factor to keep in mind is that not one member of this team knew the least bit about the nitty gritty of accelerators. Therefore, when technical troubles surfaced and criticism began to appear, this group was unable to cope. To remedy this deficiency, a Band-aid solution was applied: the foursome was enlarged to include an accelerator expert, and was then called, sarcastically, the gang of five. Mark Barton, then head of the Accelerator Division for the project, was selected as the original fifth member. He apparently didn't fit the role well, probably because he wasn't merely a lackey, and didn't tell the real powers on the team what they wanted to hear, so, not long after being appointed to the gang, he got kicked off; and without much ado, Lyle Smith, a long-time BNL staff member, who had headed the Cosmotron Division of the Accelerator Department in the sixties, replaced him. In retrospect, it seems clear that the gang of four didn't want advice; rather, they wanted someone who would give the appearance of being an accelerator expert, thus appeasing ERDA, but would acquiesce in their wishes and do what he was told. So, even though accelerator problems were increasing in number and import, and they could easily have sought and received advice from on-hand experts, they nonchalantly and carelessly ignored this avenue.

Because the founding gang members knew everything that had to be known, so they thought, the accelerator type on the team was a front man, only for show. If there's any doubt on this point, just look a little closer at the two who were selected: First there was Barton who, although an accelerator scientist knee-deep in ISABELLE, was not a magnet expert, the type of person from whom the gang really needed direct advice. Then there was Smith who was a beam-line man and knew nothing at all about modern accelerators. Not only was he useless for that reason, but he was in fact a ridiculous choice for another reason, one that boggles the mind – he was an unrepentant, well-known anti-ISABELLE activist, and, believe it or not, proud of it. It pains one to imagine such inept decision-making, and for a project so essential to the future of the lab. However there's one thing that you can hang your hat on: these selections strengthen the view that the team didn't really want accelerator advice. Looked at dispassionately and in the light of day, there is not a single plausible argument that this was a management with the desire to resolve technical issues with solid, well-founded, and timely decisions. In hindsight, it is plain to see that no good could have come from this management mode of running the project. A good guess at to what was really behind it was that this patch-work style of management was nothing more than a half-hearted attempt to manage not the project itself but rather the growing chorus of dissatisfaction with the lab coming from both inside and outside. These four arrogant men who were responsible for a great national laboratory thought that they were God's gifts and knew everything. They could deal with the project's technical issues; they could deal with the Big Science community; they could deal with any criticism of the lab; and they could deal with ERDA. And certainly they didn't need any technical help from accelerator experts, who they deemed to be their inferiors – a view validated by the lowly place of accelerator types in the science community's social scheme of things. No matter how you slice it, there was no escaping that the entire management responsibility for ISABELLE rested foursquare on the gang of four. But the gang being an instrument of the Director, it is hard to avoid concluding that the real blame for the inability of the lab to respond to the looming technical failure must lie at the doorstep of Vineyard himself. Ironically, in a way typical of how fate treats the arrogant, what the gang really gave him was the perverse luxury of fiddling while ISABELLE burned till all that was left was its charred remains.

Looking back at ISABELLE, circa 1979, it becomes crystal clear that all but the die-hards believed that only a drastic re-design would suffice for its survival. There was no dearth of suggestions about what technical changes would win the day. They came fast and furious from every imaginable direction, and all who stuck their noses in the affair felt they had seen the light. The very wide range of the advice had the unintended effect of giving the management the perfect excuse for doing nothing. Taking advantage of this luckily picked-up reprieve, the bumbling masterminds running the lab found not happy days but instead only a fool's paradise that wasn't to last very long.

Mickey was the most persistent advocate of change, and he pushed his idea of using bunched beams ad nauseum. From 1974 till his departure for a stint in Washington at the DOE in 1979, he obstinately and unremittingly baited the lab management: He produced a continuous string of provocative papers; presented sarcastic talks making fun of the design and mocking the management; and impulsively sent off a continuous stream of doomsday memos. Such behavior had all the earmarks of one who had a natural affinity for trouble; and this tendency toward troublemaking didn't much endear him to his bosses on high. At the end of Mickey's five defiant, maybe even disobedient, years of championing bunched beams, there must have been a collective sigh of relief at the lab as he exited from their midst. But any satisfaction at his leaving was bound to be short-lived because only the messenger of danger and trials and tribulation to come had departed, while the trouble itself – unseen by most for the time being – remained to haunt the lab and would eventually have to be faced and its consequences dealt with.

After the lab's political war ended in victory – the chief opponents being the redoubtable Wilson and company – and the dust over the battlefield subsided, the lab entered into *put-up-or-shut-up* time. It wasn't long after that, a matter of a year or so, that the lab's IOU's came due, and ISABELLE's hand was called. The attack was on. With all the details drawn into the open, it was plain for everyone to see that Mickey and the other critics of the ISABELLE technical design had been right all along. The proof was in the pudding and the lab's head honchos were caught with their pants down. The blindness of the management at its predicament and the inevitable terrible collapse of the hapless lady still evoke inconsolable disappointment, bitterness, and annoyance at the waste. How sad it is that things couldn't have been different. The lab chose to see only blue skies, and was oblivious to the dark clouds on the horizon. But no one was capable of successfully contradicting that rosy picture. The critics, all saying essentially the same thing, unfortunately lacked the cohesiveness to be an effective and worthy force toward that end. They were a ragtag bunch without the collective will to put themselves on the line and to act decisively and with purpose. Perhaps concerned too much with their own futures, they hadn't the spirit to organize themselves into a unified opposition. They lacked the synchronism without which there can't be a winning campaign of persuasion. True, they warned the lab on an individual basis, but they just hadn't the guts to mount a conspiracy against it. So it was that after the smoke cleared from the opening few assaults, although it was far too late, it became apparent that all the varied suggestions made by the critics were quite right; and even with their widely varied jargon, they all led to one simple end: that the magnet diameter would have to be much smaller, about half the size of the excessively large BNL design. Only then, claimed the critics, would the magnet be doable. And if that were done, so all said, the resulting collider not only would be suitable for most ISABELLE experiments, but also would provide more opportunity for some that the original design couldn't accommodate. What a pity the critics didn't all get together and speak in a coherent and *won't-take-no-for-an-answer* voice!

One can only wonder whether concerted action by the well-meaning critics might have made a difference. It would be consoling to think positive on this point. However, on giving it a second thought, it probably wouldn't have. You see it was the very thing they were asking for – a drastic alteration of the magnets – that engendered such fear in the hearts of the lab management. These leaders, for better or for worse, were wedded to the past, inextricably tied to the magnets fostered and cultivated by them and their predecessors. Sad to say, this marriage to a common legacy came to be their albatross, forcing them ever downward. Yes, this loving attachment, accumulated over so many years, ended up being their Waterloo. It somehow doesn't seem right that being faithful to those who came before you and to your own past could be so wrong. But there you have it – c'est la vie.

As the drama approached its denouement, the commanders of BNL's army couldn't avoid the life or death battle that awaited them, even though they must have sensed that winning it was a long shot. Despite it being the right thing to do, they didn't have the gumption to turn back. They couldn't bear the thought that if they did so, they would have to listen to the growing chorus begging them to alter course or to the one cursing them for their dim-wittedness in not acting sooner. So they just went on, undeterred by the intensifying clamor around them, banking on the lame excuse that it was too late for anything else. Actually, time had passed these BNL men by and they had already turned to ghosts. It's quite true that for them, the chance to pull through with heads high had vanished, leaving them alone with their delusions of what might have been. To the Big Science community looking on, the state of affairs arrived at was plain: too much time had elapsed for the lab's men of leisure to explain away their stubbornly holding on to their much maligned magnets, too much money had been spent, too much of the lab's integrated effort had been expended, and too many unfulfilled promises and assurances had been made to too many important people. The incestuous management style that had evolved at the lab over decades – played like a game of musical chairs, with responsibility and accountability passing from person to person and from generation to generation – wound up forcing everyone to hold on to the common purpose of sticking with the original project design. Insane as this was, the men in charge wouldn't relent, wouldn't give an inch. In the end, they were trapped by their sins. There was no escape, and ISABELLE eventually blew up in calamity; and because for all that time grievous acts were committed, the dues of revenge were high. Thus, as the curtain was about to come down, the hurdle was a great deal too big for average men to overcome and even too much for these brilliant and potentially great men to handle. The hand they were playing was dealt them by the Devil, and while they believed themselves searching for grace, they found only hell.

The eighties brought more bad news for the management of the old, decaying, and tottering lab. The younger Fermilab, after suffering through more than a year of hardship since Wilson's untimely and unnecessary departure, was being revived and reconstituted. It was again poised to enter the two-lab war that Wilson had perspicaciously understood would have to recur. This seemingly eternal conflict between the two laboratories – BNL and Fermilab, father and son – stemmed from their origins and the duplicating work they were created to accomplish. The son was born to do the father's work; but the father, in his struggle with his own mortality, was destined to fight against the succession to his dying breath. No rational resolution could be devised because the problem, which had become like a canker sore, had been implanted from the very beginning and was too deeply rooted to be excised. Since peaceful coexistence had no meaning for either side – except perhaps at some rare moments that merely gave the tired players a temporary respite from combat's agonies – government fiat or persuasion was inadequate to make any peace agreement that could last. A little money here and there did calm the nerves for a while, but appeasement, as always, can only be short-lived. The consequences of original sin could not be denied as once more the troops were marshaled and – with BNL's army ensconced in its fortress at Upton and Fermilab's manning the bastions at Batavia – the continuing bloody saga was set to break wide open again.

The war had been ongoing since Fermilab was brought into being. The new lab was approved for construction in 1967, and right from the beginning its birth was resented and strongly opposed by BNL. Over the years, as Fermilab grew up, there were ups and downs between the opponents, but unfortunately any sought-after stable equilibrium was never found. The period of quiet, meant to follow Woods Hole in 1977 – where Wilson was dealt a deathblow and Fermilab was sidetracked from its quest for dominion of proton facilities in America – lasted only a short time. The deal reached there, rendered by arrogant bureaucrats and foolish scientists, called for Fermilab to rule over synchrotrons and BNL over colliders. The idea was to achieve peace, or at least quiet, by having Fermilab do this and BNL do that. It sounded good in principle, but it didn't hold water because the technology for both types of facilities, synchrotrons and colliders, was the same. More importantly, since colliders had come of age and were the thing to have, the decision was not even-handed and grossly shifted the two-lab competition in BNL's favor. You might say it was nothing if not a slap in Fermilab's face. How could anyone have expected Fermilab to just roll over and concede when it was far better equipped than BNL to take the next step for Big Physics? Anyway, that's what the grand viziers of Woods Hole came up with. However the backlash from this purported wisdom was not at all what was expected and came awfully close to wrecking Big Science. In the immediate aftermath, the effect, whether intended or not, was to push Wilson over the side into the grimy deep waters of oblivion and to send the majestic Wilsonian dream of a truly national lab, Fermilab, reeling. Perhaps reeling doesn't adequately describe the impact, for after Woods Hole, because the days of facilities with accelerators sans colliders were gone, the lab's very future was put in extreme jeopardy. Injudiciously, Fermilab had been left with no apparent viable course. There was no reasonable middle of the road action open to it – it was either fight for its life or die. It wasn't much of a shocker that the choice ended up being the former.

In its search for someone to replace Wilson as Director, it was no surprise that Fermilab had great difficulty in finding suitable candidates. Who would want to have the responsibility for a dying institution that had lost favor with the all-powerful U.S. government? Who would want to step into Wilson's big shoes? With no alternative at hand, the job fell temporarily on the inadequate shoulders of Phil Livdahl, who had been Wilson's deputy for a couple of years. Sad to say, he was a dwarf compared to a giant. Having such a little fish in charge as Acting Director, the lab went into a holding pattern. Leaderless, Fermilab was wasting away; and time, waiting for no one, kept slipping by.

However, there was a fly in the ointment: The men of Woods Hole, stressed out and in a political rush to do as they were told, totally missed the big picture. Filled with self-importance typical of those courted by the high and mighty, they couldn't see the forest for the trees and failed to pick up the threat their actions could mean for their beloved field. You could perhaps argue that their hasty judgment made some political sense. What else could they do under such duress? Nevertheless, they were dead wrong in not contesting the political hacks. They could have mustered the courage to do so, but they didn't. Perhaps they had no cause to fight for. But if that's so, then they were sadly mistaken because they forgot about the key technology issue, presuming that the relative capabilities of the two labs pitted against each other didn't matter much. If one lab could do it, then so could the other one, so they believed. What a bloody stupid assessment that was – close to being unforgivable! You see Wilson had the foresight to prepare Fermilab for what he correctly perceived to be a new technology world for Big Science, while Vineyard and his predecessor, Goldhaber, hadn't done a damn thing in that direction. So it was that Woods Hole gave the wrong lab the go-ahead, and Big Physics in America languished for half a decade.

Eventually the government would tire of BNL's unfulfilled promises and incompetence; and so the tide was bound to shift. It's hard to pinpoint exactly when the attitude changeover at DOE took place, but a good guess would be sometime toward the end of 1978. In conjunction with this, probably because of it, Fermilab simultaneously was given a new lease on life as lady luck glanced at the lab and gave it a knowing grin: for it was then that Leon Lederman, on hearing the whispering of the good lady, saw the light. Leon, one of the early physichists, and ironically BNL's old friend in the sixties, made the choice, perhaps tentatively at first, to give Fermilab a whirl. This was some coup for Fermilab, which had such a short time before been deep in the dumps, and now was to have leading it one of the greats of Big Physics. However, before Leon would fully commit himself, he wanted DOE's assurance that he could act with a measure of freedom to defend Fermilab's interests, and he got all that he needed. Even though the bureaucratic DOE didn't have the capability of doing anything quickly – and it would still be an endless four years before the rug would be pulled out from under BNL – nonetheless, Fermilab, with Leon prepared to take on the reins of command, was given the nod to compete again, this, by the way, being a complete abrogation of the Woods Hole agreement. Thus, having checked all the bases, Leon, finally realizing the true value of accelerator technology, began to take on the persona of the pretender to the Wilsonian throne. He knew both labs inside and out and wisely and correctly concluded that if Big Science in America were to move ahead, Fermilab and not BNL would have to be the one to lead it.

As 1978 entered its second half, Leon was seen at Batavia more and more. Something had transpired, but what it could be was not immediately evident. However, by mid 1979, the fog began to lift when the rumor mill started its buzzing that Leon had all but agreed to become the second Director of the great accelerator lab of the Midwest. Since anyone acquainted with Leon knew he would never accept such a position at a second-class institution slated to fade away, there had to be more to the story. Before long any doubts dissipated and the full picture became plain to see: Leon for quite a time had been spending his time there in order to lead the planning for Fermilab's future, while at the same time negotiating the possibilities with DOE. When all the talk was over, DOE conceded that in the future Fermilab would not be constrained only to the design and development of a very high energy synchrotron, as had been dictated by the Woods Hole panel, but instead would be free to pursue an elaborate sequence of accelerator upgrades, called the Tevatron. It was Wilson who probably conceived this name, but the scheme was all Leon's. The specific agreement arrived at in Leon's discussions with DOE's Deutsch and Wallenmeyer permitted, more accurately instructed, the lab to expand its work on superconducting magnet technology so as to include a collider capability, and in addition to take on a new developmental initiative on beam cooling technology (started by CERN a couple of years earlier) with the aim of building a U.S. p-pbar collider to compete with the anticipated European one. That was some helluva negotiating job! What a way for Fermilab to start its new day and for Leon to start his new life!

Leon, it seems, had found just the right moment to act. After seeing quite enough of BNL's poor performance, the DOE was embarrassed at what ERDA had done at Woods Hole and, with unusual wisdom for a bureaucracy, chose to reverse it. Deutsch and his lieutenants, particularly his deputy Doug Pewitt, wanted to set things right by getting the Director's position filled post-haste and getting Fermilab on its way again. Thus, Leon did well for himself and for Fermilab: in vying for and accepting the position as the lab's Director when the time was ripe, Leon was able to concoct and negotiate a new life for the lab. Incidentally, the arrangement he worked out had the intended effect of making the Woods Hole deal deader than a doornail. So, in just two short years, ERDA's grandiose but, in the end, unrealistic scheme to control a science that was in the throes of an unruly advanced technology, itself in high flux, became merely a historical footnote, an oddity that was to be discarded into that dustbin replete with the missteps of the past. The attempt by rigid and inflexible men to master the flow of modern technology not unexpectedly failed, and the Woods Hole deal was deleted from history's mainstream and soon forgotten.

As the eighties began to unfold, BNL quickly went from being the DOE favorite to being a humiliation for it, and was dropped like a hot potato. From then on the Long Island lab, without special treatment available anymore, would have to fend for itself. Surprised and unprepared, BNL found itself fighting for its very survival as the tides of change shifted to its detriment in the swift way characteristic of the new world of Big Science. The three-lab concept, without much ado, became a distant memory, and the future of all the labs was again up for grabs. What an irony it was that even though Wilson had been forsaken by an unappreciative science and he was gone from power's center stage, his vision of a free and open competitive system nonetheless won the day! In such an setting, left entirely to its own devices, BNL found itself in the soup: Fermilab was on the march, in place to compete with it for a collider; CERN was in the process of building a focused, low-cost collider, and, with its running start, was all but uncatchable in the race for the W; and, as if that weren't enough, BNL's superconducting magnet program was mired in a quicksand that was spreading, threatening to swallow up the entire lab. Even with all these frowns of fortune visited on it, adversity that would make the strongest cringe, BNL had not yet hit rock bottom. Things were about to get even worse as the leadership began breaking apart at the seams. Instead of the men at the top keeping their heads, and coolly and rationally addressing the issues confronting them, they found themselves unable to handle the pressure cooker atmosphere that had materialized around them. With the resulting high stress levels, they began to exhibit paranoid and self-defeating behavior. The gang of four was living in the past; they became paralyzed, losing the ability to take any meaningful action, while George was dazed and without any idea of how to pull the lab out of its free-fall to self-destruction. They could not see the reality and retreated to the never-never land that is the last refuge of the hopeless. They were sure that the bad enemy was somewhere on the outside and not in the lab; and certainly they could not, heaven forbid, see that the true enemy was in themselves. Unable to admit they'd made some bad choices and take what was coming to them, they instead convinced themselves that no options were available other than a fight to the death. And so it was, even as the termites in their minds ate away at the foundation and fabric of the once glorious lab.

* * * * *

In 1981, as Reagan took office, basic science was embedded in President Carter's Department of Energy (DOE), which had jurisdiction over the country's entire energy domain, spanning the wide range from energy generation to energy resource management to energy research to nuclear weaponry to basic science. The trend that culminated in Big Science becoming a little fish in a big pond started with the formation of the DOE in 1977; and the transition was essentially complete by the time Reagan took over in 1981. Although there were good points to it – more money around and more influence if you could figure out how to gain access to them – there were also the bad ones – primarily having to deal with a large, unwieldy, fully bureaucratized system. However, no matter how you sliced it or tried to rationalize it, Big Physics became just small fry in a land of political giants.

This journey of basic research in the high-flux organization of government began with Vannevar Bush's insightful *Endless Frontier* report following World War II. Recognizing the great potential that physics had for the country, and knowing that the only way to do it right and to do it in a big way was to have the government fully behind it, the national labs were established as a government controlled enterprise, and so, what came to be Big Physics was born. To administer the building of accelerators for nuclear research, the labs were naturally made part of the AEC, created in 1946 to consolidate the U.S. Atomic Energy effort. It was a happy union – basic research had a home where it was a dominant force. However, when ERDA was formed in 1974, it swallowed up the AEC, and the labs found their powerful position considerably diluted. Finally, Carter, clearly a lover of bigness, chose to marry Big Physics and Big Government by situating the national lab system, which by then was responsible for basic research in a wide range of sciences, within the greatly enlarged DOE. So, Big Science became merely a fringe element in an overly big and cumbersome structure that was concerned with the much larger issues of ensuring the sufficiency of the country's energy resources and of global security. Still, basic science had a privileged position because it was considered – via congressional legislation – a national trust, with the government the keeper of that trust.

The twentieth century was the century of science and technology (S&T), and to further it in the country's interest the government began a love affair with science in the post-war period that persists to this day. Science needs the government for its funding and the government needs basic research to keep the country at the S&T frontier. It is an ideal marriage. However, as with all marriages, there's more there than meet's the eye. Politicians are attracted to science, not only for the opportunities it affords for technological progress that gives the U.S. an edge in a fast changing world, but also for its importance in educating the young and for raising the cultural value of regions where S&T institutions are situated. No wonder national labs are considered to be political plums! When the astute President Reagan took office, he understood the high value of S&T to the U.S. and was one of its staunchest proponents. He recognized that increased government intervention in the S&T business was something that had to be done. But if he wanted to do it well, it wasn't to be an easy undertaking. Science had demonstrated that it was not the purely rational undertaking it was cracked up to be but, like all human endeavors, was subject to the weakening and self-destructive forces that represent the dark side of human nature. Manifesting this darker realm – particularly demonstrated at Woods Hole in 1977 – science's leaders strongly supported the continuance of deals made long ago and maintained persistently, even to the detriment of progress and even if it meant a threat to U.S. S&T supremacy. This was not acceptable to the Reagan administration, and so Reagan wisely stepped in and ordered S&T commitments to the past null and void and to be for the most part ignored.

Although many of the old-timers holding the power resented this intrusion, it was a hopeful time for the energetic and fresh thinking young people of science, who found relief from an oppressive atmosphere and newfound opportunities to express themselves. The incoming administration in Washington had a special tone of optimism for S&T and a style of advancing swiftly, as if anything in this area were achievable. In spirit, it recalled Kennedy's 1960 insistence and encouragement to land a man on the moon in a decade. If America set its collective mind to achieve something, it couldn't be stopped, he seemed to be saying. Reagan had that kind of faith in man's capability and, like Kennedy, he realized that basic science was an essential ingredient of such an adventure into the unknown. For physics, this meant a demand for pushing advanced technology forward faster than ever and making sure that America would get to the top of world science and remain the best and the first in S&T.

The keynote of this bargain the Reagan team made with science was that science keep moving to bigger and better things. So, for those who were too old or too tired or couldn't keep up the pace, it was tough luck. The resulting environment wasn't suitable for everyone, and the heightened competitive atmosphere put BNL particularly in deep trouble. The lab must have recognized that a tough time lay ahead when the word from DOE headquarters to the accelerator labs was released, instructing them to get on with superconducting magnet technology on the double and launch a strong competition with CERN for the W. Why not? Why should CERN be uncontested and granted free pickings for such a prize? This idea for America to stand up and be counted was already in the wind, but once Reagan took office, it became for real. Unfortunately, BNL – which in reality had the upper hand over CERN because ISABELLE became an approved and fully funded project back in 1977, years before CERN got underway – simply wasn't up to the task. They lagged and lagged, in no great hurry, apparently oblivious to the race that was on hand and to the fact that U.S. pride was at stake. However, nobody seemed to care much until CERN got into high gear. It was then that U.S. concern rose, and questions about BNL's ability to be America's torchbearer surfaced. When finally the demand for results was made, the lab procrastinated and stammered, and when it eventually showed what it had, it didn't make the grade. Having spent two decades coasting on the accomplishments of the fifties, it was unprepared for the sudden onset of a new standard of performance. The policy now was beat CERN or bust, and BNL neither got it nor had it.

On the other hand, through Wilson's prescience and Lederman's inspirational forte, Fermilab was not only ready, it was bursting at the seams to start rolling. Wilson's instinctive foresight had led to an attitude of always thinking of the future, and he hadn't been gone long enough for this way of life at Fermilab to have significantly weakened.

With Fermilab ready to move forward in a determined way and BNL not, a new deal was struck. Leon could not only go ahead with his new lab's superconducting magnets but, lo and behold, could also openly and officially get started on a collider using this new ring. This was truly a Lederman coup, for it meant that Wilson's romantic dream of the Tevatron could now be brought to life. So, the plan Deutsch and Pewitt had devised as Carter was closing out his term was given thumbs up by Reagan and his team, which summarily sent the three-lab concept and the Woods Hole agreement to history's scrap heap.

That all this happened too swiftly was not a convincing defense for the BNL leadership, which had no reasonably valid excuse for not getting in on the action with dispatch. It's too bad that Vineyard and his lieutenants hadn't been able to appreciate sooner the meaning of the noisy, barreling truck coming at them. They were given many opportunities to turn things around at the lab, but they characteristically squandered them all and simply added them to the list of wasted chances. It wasn't that a favorable set of circumstances didn't appear – it did many times. It was just that something inside their souls prevented them from pulling themselves out of the quagmire or even allowing themselves to be pulled out. What perplexing behavior they exhibited! Once bunched beams were demonstrated by CERN to be viable for colliders, it could have been simple for BNL to have incorporated them into ISABELLES's design and use them. At that time, as ISABELLE construction was about to start, BNL was technologically way out in front, and thus, by the oh-so-simple act of switching to bunches, could have easily won the race for the W. Even when Reagan came into office, BNL still had a sporting chance to come out smelling like a rose. At that time, seeing before their very eyes that the colliders both at CERN and at Fermilab were being designed that way, why were the BNL leaders so pig-headed not to have followed suit with a similar type of beam design for ISABELLE? Unfortunately they were in some kind of paranoid shock and all they could think about and see were the shadows of enemies everywhere. There doesn't seem to be a good explanation of what happened, but perhaps, having been propped up for too long by supporting government bureaucrats and by the weak and acquiescent science community, they'd become soft and unfit for competitive combat. They seem to have lost the ability, even the desire, to thrive and survive on their own. Alas, there was no fire left in the BNL belly.

As for Fermilab, henceforth it was the one to carry the American banner for world supremacy in Big Science. But by the time the U.S. opened its eyes to the foundering BNL, CERN could not be overtaken. True, Fermilab did well, but it wasn't good enough. As it turned out, Fermilab was a winner in the advanced technology battle in the physics world by building the first modern high-energy accelerator with superconducting magnets. However, it was too late to bail out the U.S. in the race for the W. CERN, led by the brilliant Carlo and Simon, won that one hands down. BNL, which had every opportunity to be first to develop a superconducting collider, as well as first to spot the W, trashed its own capability and in so doing lost the heart to come through, and these failures became the final nails in ISABELLE's coffin.

* * * * *

There was enough blame to go around for America's rapid descent from being top dog. Certainly the men of the BNL leadership lineage going back to the sixties were the major culprits, but they weren't alone. Wallenmeyer must also bear his considerable share of the responsibility. Consider what occurred around 1977, the period when the judgments at Woods Hole were being made. At roughly the same time, Carlo Rubbia, a Harvard professor in the seventies, wanted in on the leadership of Big Science in America; and he deserved it, being filled chock-full of imaginative and inventive ideas for colliders. Some of them were outrageous and some not even technically feasible; but new ideas, inspired and even risky, were what America should have been looking for, and brushing him off was a terrible mistake, difficult to forgive. In that action-packed, danger-filled, and decisive year, Carlo approached Wilson with his bold and original idea of building a p-pbar collider at Fermilab. It wasn't a formal proposal, more a gut feeling of Carlo's that such a device should and could successfully be made. It became clear in the years that followed that Carlo's instincts were right on target, but in America he was blocked from his mission at every turn. Rubbia and Wilson would have been a formidable duo, but Wilson, by government edict, was forbidden to engage in such a collaboration. Wallenmeyer, the engineer of both the three-lab concept and the Woods Hole accord, and representing the U.S. government, had reserved colliders for BNL. Set on that track, how could he allow ISABELLE, which all thought a safe bet, to be upstaged by a Wilson-Rubbia combine? Besides, he didn't have much faith in the risky Rubbia scheme – so why put good, hard-to-come-by money into it? In response to the rejection, Rubbia – proud, impetuous, and impulsive – flew off to CERN to sell his wares across the ocean to a far more hospitable audience. Not to worry! thought Wallenmeyer and his cohorts. In fact there seemed no one in the U.S. who doubted that BNL would beat CERN in the race for the W, if CERN even dared to enter the competition. You see although CERN had the capability of converting its Super Proton Synchrotron (SPS) into a storage ring, it didn't have a reliable technology for producing antiprotons; whereas the two-ring purely proton ISABELLE, which Woods Hole made a done deal, had no new technology to contend with. Unfortunately, Wallenmeyer had grievously underestimated CERN's desire and initiative. Somehow, unlike him, he wasn't astute enough in this instance to look a step ahead to where he would have seen that his treatment of Wilson and Rubbia could have damaging and insurmountable consequences in the race for the W. Why didn't he think that it just could happen that CERN might be able to transform Rubbia's wild idea into a practical machine? He had a highly straightforward way of precluding that possibility. All he had to do was to encourage Wilson to team up with Rubbia to develop and build a backup to ISABELLE at Fermilab. Why didn't he do that? Didn't he have any inkling that BNL might not be fully dependable? After all, it still hadn't come to a final design and engineering for the magnets. In addition, because CERN was filled with technological ingenuity and capability, why was he so confident that it would not be able to pull a rabbit out of its hat? No, there is no denying that Wallenmeyer, in so wrongly assessing both BNL and CERN, messed up big-time.

Although Wilson had been sorely disappointed, hurt and angry at his powerlessness in the face of the unreasonable Woods Hole dictate that put a collider out of Fermilab's reach, thus making it all but impossible for him to partake of the action being energized in Big Physics around the world, he would have been more than amenable to helping if he had been given half a chance. In fact, in that frame of mind, he might well have been uncharacteristically easy to deal with. But Wallenmeyer was adamant – he wouldn't give up on his three-lab idea, nor would he pull back from the Woods Hole agreement. He could have, but he didn't. Somehow, when it came to these two issues, he couldn't see much beyond his nose. Wilson, another stubborn man, remained defiant to the end; and he would lose not only the war of ideas but his job as well. As for Wallenmeyer, the comeuppance for his arrogance was that his high-energy accelerator bill-of-fare, DOE's flagship basic research program, fell apart. In the wake of his interference with Wilson and his free spirit, BNL fell into stagnation, CERN claimed the W, and America was shoved into the number two spot in Big Science. It may very well be that he lost as much as Wilson did. Maybe it was even more, as his reputation as an enterprising, insightful, and ardent government leader for forefront high-energy physics was irretrievably eclipsed.

To the chagrin of many, Wallenmeyer, through his Machiavellian meddling, had delivered the innovative Rubbia into the arms of a welcoming CERN. The impatient, hot-blooded, and devil-may-care Rubbia, who could not depend on Wilson to provide the means to carry through his bold and arrogant idea, was not to be denied. Without fanfare or fuss, he sought and found a glowing reception at CERN; and within a few years CERN was catapulted to number one as Carlo deposited the W right into its lap. Thus, one of the singular science events of the twentieth century, although upsetting and distressing to Americans, brought joy to Europeans as they watched CERN win an awesome struggle with all the cards initially stacked against it. But win it did, and it deserved all the accolades it received, including a Nobel Prize a couple of years later. As for the blame game in America, lots of mistakes were made and there was no dearth of culpability to distribute, but the two people who stand out as most accountable are Wallenmeyer and Vineyard. Both were in key positions, Bill directing traffic and George at the wheel of the W express. Unfortunately for America's hopes in Big Science, Bill was dozing in the back seat and could recognize neither the value of Rubbia's brilliant fast-in-fast-out scheme nor CERN's capability of pulling it off. Meanwhile George was soundly asleep at the wheel, dreaming of a lab that was more a figment of his imagination than the real thing. Although far too late to redeem himself, Bill was at least sufficiently clear-headed and artful to bail out before the end came. So he left poor George to bear the brunt of the censure and condemnation as George moved relentlessly toward his Waterloo in the summer of 1981.

The final act in the death of ISABELLE was a long and agonizing one for BNL, played out under glaring lights as the physics world watched the entire sad show. Forming the backdrop, CERN and Fermilab, both brandishing the trappings of technological breakthroughs, were fighting it out for big physics stardom. With well-deserved pride, CERN showed off its extraordinary beam cooling accomplishment, and Fermilab made a big deal of its magnets at superconducting temperatures. The two glorious laboratories-cum-warriors, battling it out with their technical muscles flexed, both ready for the good fight, exuded confidence, high spirits, and optimism as they moved closer to the Holy Grail – no less than an understanding of nature's riddle of physical existence. In the meantime, at BNL, the scene was of a far different sort, as defensiveness and despair filled the air. Because of its poor technical performance, and with no potential improvement in sight, it was neither prepared nor permitted to take part in the upcoming competitive search into no-man's land – what BNL had wanted so badly and had come so close to having. Not having qualified, BNL was denied a post at the starting gate. To the lab's leaders and staff, to its scientist supporters, and to its government and community sponsors, this was not a moment to savor. They all knew that it should have been BNL pioneering the march into the unknown territory of the gods. But unfortunately BNL was relegated to the sidelines to look on as others carried out the mission. To keep going under such circumstances, to brave the storm of extreme misfortune, to push ahead when it appears hopeless, to muster that extra drive, to keep the engine humming in case a chance magically appears – to demonstrate such behavioral strength – takes a kind of institutional courage that is rare indeed. Sadly, in the early eighties, BNL could not pass this test. If only the lab had been better led and managed, for in 1981 it still had an itsy-bitsy possibility of being called upon. Instead, a cancer was growing in its midst, which, fed by an elaborate and insidious framework of denial, kept growing and growing and growing.

* * * * *

As 1981 got underway, ISABELLE kept going from bad to worse. Magnets were built and magnets failed. No one could grasp the meaning and potential consequences of what was happening, perhaps because they were too frightening and bleak to contemplate. The result was that to make life bearable, the continual, almost daily disappointments astonishingly came to be taken as the norm. Expectations for success virtually ceased to exist, and a strange kind of casual acceptance of this unwholesome condition descended on the lab and the community.

At the same time, the almost forgotten DOE edict that the labs should encourage the transfer of forefront technology to the private sector was in full force, and this exacerbated the already intolerable BNL situation. To comply, the lab contacted technologically oriented companies with the intention of having them ultimately build most of the few hundred magnets needed to complete the project. This idea, sounding so simple and so right, turned out to be disastrous. The Westinghouse Corporation contracted for half a dozen magnets, with six being built and six failing. A similar contract was worked out with the Grumman Corporation and the outcome was ditto. Because these failures were so all-inclusive, with no extenuating circumstances to hang onto, the lab came to view the matter as a demonstration that outside work was less competent than in-house work at the lab's magnet facility. Ironically, it was somewhat reassuring and even satisfying to the lab that the private sector had failed so miserably. Now it all became clear to them: the lab was fine, it was government interference that was the real problem. Thus, the answer was simple: get the government off its back, let the lab do the magnets itself, and get back to *business as usual*. Undoubtedly, the men in the Director's Office were grasping at straws, but nonetheless that became their position and that's what was proclaimed to be fact. However, indulging themselves with such a patently distorted picture wasn't much help to the lab's magnet predicament. Maybe it made them feel good to have something to point the finger at, but the truth was that the companies were just being used as scapegoats; in fact any inference of company responsibility was both unfair and inaccurate. After all, the companies did only what the lab's specifications asked for. If they were to blame for anything, it was that they didn't do their technical homework well enough to discover what the lab was really asking them to do. No, there's no rational way to come to a verdict other than that it was all the fault of the lab. To put it bluntly, self-deception, data manipulation, and even cheating were most likely the reasons behind the fallaciously promulgated outside-inside discrepancy of performance. Yes, as sure as one can be of anything, the lab was guilty.

Nonetheless, despite the lab's egregious behavior, for a time this story played well inside its walls. It was the government that was responsible; it was the private companies; it was our enemies in the community – it was anybody but us. Because the top management had almost total influence and control over information flow, this misrepresentation that it promulgated had a strangely soothing effect on the lab's workers, management and staff alike. However, on the outside, the impression was quite different, with people being almost certain that the magnet failures, of the ones made inside as well as those made outside, had to have identical origins within the lab management itself. Anxiety within the physics community began to surface and was manifested by advice of all sorts beginning to arrive at the lab from every imaginable source. The variety of suggestions, proposals, and criticisms seemed to be boundless. Some were technical, some political, some friendly and well intentioned, and some belligerent and ill intentioned. But the lab was in denial and not interested in any advice it got. It made no distinctions; all the input the lab got was treated the same way. What does he know? or What can he tell me? were the most favored responses. For reasons still mysterious, defying logical comprehension, the lab rejected out of hand all unsolicited advice. Although not an explanation, it appears that the lab's leaders came to see the lab as their own private territory and as such trespassers were not countenanced.

Instead of heeding the views of those looking in, a most difficult but generally very wise thing to do, the lab began the time-honored process characteristic of all failing institutions, wherein are organized review after review after wishy-washy review. Well-known experts from all over the world were paraded in to assess the project and report their recommendations. So far, well and good, but commonly in such a process, when the results come in, it becomes clear that the review teams for the most part simply conclude whatever the lab wants to hear. You see the true purposes of this mechanism are not discovery and correction, but rather obfuscation and buying time. This is fine if there's time available. But when time is not there and the fuse is short, then it becomes a risky business. Not facing the truth is always fraught with dire possible outcomes. Nevertheless, with the ostensible aim of saving ISABELLE, such a process, ineffective, wasteful, and wrong-headed as it was, was set in motion.

Try to see this mechanism as it actually is! What can be expected of reviewers, mostly technical experts, wise gurus of physics, and mid-level managers, brought in from outside the lab as invited guests? What can be expected of ordinary people who, as guests, are naturally prone to lean toward, sometimes even to promote, the interests of their hosts? What can be expected of people with a tendency to be in awe of top community leaders, and who are particularly deferential to government officials and lab Directors? Isn't it obvious? One thing you can count on: if it's truth you're after, then this is not the way to get it. On one end of the truth-getting scale, the one representing the best that can be hoped for, are reports that are vague and reviews that don't go out of their way to praise the lab. No doubt, reviewers try their best to do the right thing under the circumstances, but still, these types of reports provide the lab with a lot of interpretative latitude, and in the end give it free rein to do what it wants to. On the other end of the scale, the reviewers are weak and grossly intimidated, making their reports, for the most part, downright fiction. So, on the whole, lab or project reviews gotten through this process usually contain gaping loopholes, some big enough to drive a Mack truck through. To be frank about it, it isn't a change-inducing process, but more a leave-well-enough-alone one. In any case, over the years, BNL managers became experts in ferreting out the loopholes in the reviews and ascertaining ways to wriggle through the tough ones as well as to march unencumbered through the easily dealt with ones. As for ISABELLE, the reviews were of the typical variety, more theater than business, thereby keeping it alive despite its faults and deficiencies. Thus, the process worked! With its phony review game operating letter-perfect, it played itself out as envisioned. It must be said, however, that there were a few serious reviews in which practical corrective actions were proposed, but – even if the lab were up to taking the tough steps needed – these were all cases of too-little-too-late, and they couldn't save the project from its fate. Fate is patient, but when your time comes, it acts unexpectedly, decisively, forcefully, and pitilessly.

During the late seventies and early eighties, perhaps because some of the more prominent members of the community's aristocracy thought that the formal review process wasn't hitting the target, the lab was persuaded to commission personal reviews in the hope that these would be more meaningful and fruitful. A few individuals – people who were considered friends, although it's hard to know for sure if people can really be trusted – were asked to spend time at the lab, sometimes a month, sometimes longer, to study the magnet program in depth in order to find out what was wrong and perhaps discover a fix. Within this group, Dave Jackson, a renowned theoretical physicist from Berkeley, among other things known for his capability of converting physical principles and their underlying mathematics into a better understanding of real-world applications, arrived at the lab in 1981. If anyone could get to the heart of the problem, he could. Dave was straight, frank, and true. However, unbeknownst to the lab leaders, he also had a stubborn need to help American science move forward. He had mucho integrity and was strong in character and self-confidence. In fact, if he had something on his mind, it would be all but impossible to shut him up. He was not the type of man to let the lab maintain its status quo if it wasn't deserving of it. If he had to send the lab over, that's exactly what he would do. In hindsight, from the lab leadership point of view, inviting Dave was clearly a big mistake. The last thing the lab's bosses wanted was to make the truth public. But Dave was there in their midst, and what he would say was out of their hands. Not like the run of the mill reviewer, true to character, Dave couldn't be swayed to shave the truth of what he saw; and so he concluded that major changes in magnet design were called for – major meaning starting from scratch or giving it up and taking an entirely different course. And this is what he advised the lab to consider. This was not what the deeply committed lab leaders wanted to hear. Too much water had passed over the dam, too many political chips had been cashed in, and too much money had already been invested in the magnets for them to agree to a wholesale change, thereby admitting they had erred. The lab had gone too far and for its leadership there was no turning back now. So the lab's top guns plowed ahead and, though they were embarrassed by the public disclosure of Dave's conclusions, they had a pow-wow and decided to simply ignore him. The lab had chosen the fork in the road it would take: it would stay the course to the bitter end. It would be do or die while holding on tightly to the design on hand. The dictate from the Director's Office was that there would be no change of direction and that the lab would have to make do – and do well they insisted – with the choices made over these many years. As for Dave, he was a unique man, with the courage to stand up and be counted; but unfortunately he stood alone, and whistling in the wind, he left the lab after a few months a defeated man. You see in 1981 the men at DOE were not ready to listen to the radical thoughts he had, and they didn't.

However, Dave's work and his courageous behavior were not completely in vain. In the coming years, he used the knowledge gained during his BNL stay to help the community finally act decisively and come to terms with ISABELLE's headlong dive. As part of a government panel review of the project in 1983, he advised the DOE that enough was enough. Only at that late date did the DOE came to its senses about BNL being either dishonest or incompetent. But sadly, although Dave would sorely have liked to salvage the project, the DOE's delay had been too long: the ISABELLE cause was a lost one, and it was far too late to keep the project intact.

Another notable person invited to the lab for a long period was Kjell Johnsen, a top accelerator expert, who had led the CERN team in building and operating the first proton collider, the ISR, in the late sixties. Arriving at BNL in 1979, he spent a few years at the lab as a consultant for the ISABELLE project. Some thought this was a serious move by the lab to set itself on the right course, but it was just another maneuver to conceal truths that the lab couldn't bear to reveal – that the ISABELLE magnets as originally conceived were unworkable and that the project was of an age long since past. Under severe pressure Kjell caved in and, good soldier that he was, did what the lab's leaders told him to do, which was to support the magnet program, and otherwise shut up. It's possible that he really believed in the ISABELLE design, and perhaps he even fell for the lab's whole story hook, line, and sinker; but it's far more likely that the fact that his son was working and living in nearby New Jersey had more to do with his behavior. Many couldn't believe that Kjell would let himself be used in this way – to distract outsiders from a truth the lab sought to hide. But he couldn't resist the Devil's temptations. You see labs have great power over the average Joe and, although this is difficult to accept, many people can be bought off rather cheaply. By handing out a little perk here and another there, pretty soon you have a man in your back pocket. And that seems to have been Kjell's sad role to play, caught as he was in Lucifer's net. Anyway, whatever the truth behind Kjell's behavior, the fact is that he stayed and supported the lab's management and ISABELLE all the way until the final curtain descended.

* * * * *

How could the lab have been allowed to keep digging itself deeper and deeper into despair and failure? How could others have stood by and watched ISABELLE being slowly pushed into the dark, moist earth of oblivion? How could they have let the lab's leaders continue on their course of self-destruction? To adequately ponder ISABELLE's sorry fate, we are therefore driven to explore the nature of how the enabler fits into the affair. Some might consider that this is somewhat tangential to the major theme of how and why a potentially great lady came to be destroyed by her creators. Despite there being some sense to this viewpoint, the enablers nonetheless played a role not easily dismissed. Good and balanced judgment dictates that most blame be placed at the doorsteps of the perpetrators who orchestrated and carried through the dark deeds. These are the truly egregious sinners. But the enablers who propped them up, encouraged them, and gave their permission and acquiescence cannot and must not to be let off the hook scot-free. Indeed, how could the doers have behaved as they did without the help and the resources provided them? They simply couldn't, and no amount of rationalization can alter the clear and irrefutable fact that the two, the perpetrators and the enablers, are inextricably linked together. It's as if some sort of conspiracy between them were necessary to make what happened actually take place.

Some of the enablers tried to excuse themselves with the ignorance defense, and others claimed to have been deceived; but these are old, tired, and pitifully lame responses. Putting aside such puny, self-justifying pretexts, there remain the gnawing questions that grate and beg for answers: Where was everybody, all those who, wittingly or unwittingly, became enablers? Where was the lab Director, who had the singular distinction of being both a perpetrator and an enabler? Where was Associated Universities Inc. (AUI), which had the contractual obligation for the lab's work and performance? Where were the AUI trustees, who had the responsibility of assessing, judging, and advising the lab? Where were the government sponsors, including DOE and Congress, who had the task of ensuring the optimal use of the taxpayer's money? Where was the army of reviewers and advisors, friend and foe alike? Where were the technical experts, whose duty it was to frankly and fearlessly express any reservations they had with the design? Where was the prestigious National Academy, the ultimate arbiter of any scientific or technological disagreements? Where were the societies that represented the collective voice of the community? Was there not one brave heart among them all who could cry out that the emperor had no clothes? Alas, there was not a one, and the silence was deafening.

With no determined resistance and with no strong-minded opposition – presumed to mean tacit approval – the lab continued on its merry way, spending freely as the money kept coming in on schedule, with no hitches and no delays. The fact that the expenditure of such a large amount of resources wasn't leading to any tangible output didn't seem of much concern to Vineyard and his crew. They just moved along, acting as if they had it coming to them. As for the enablers, no one said a word to stop the lab from rushing on to catastrophe. The show played on, with money flowing in and money flowing out, and because no substantive accomplishment could be attained, the result was only excuse after excuse, followed by promises that could not be kept. But this couldn't go on forever. Eventually, what goes up must come down. For BNL, laden with do-nothings endlessly feeding themselves and giving nothing in return, the time was short. So, having already gone some distance on the downward side of the up-down cycle, the lab was in for a perilously rocky road, but could do nothing to alter the course it had set for itself.

Then, in 1981, as successes at CERN and Fermilab were coming to fruition and could no longer be denied, the clouds around BNL intensified and darkened. It happened so fast that not only did it surprise Vineyard and his henchmen, but the foolish BNL experimental users as well. Suddenly, a wave of bitterness and hostility against the lab began to take shape. This brought the inevitable consequence of swift government action against it – it was like an elastic band stretched past its limit, which can do nothing but snap. Yet, even at this late stage, the lab was so wrapped up in its own deceit and self-indulgence that it had no idea of the extreme nature of what was in store for it. However, despite the lab leadership being so thickheaded, the bad times were on their way, and the lab was powerless to stop what had become its destiny. So, in the fateful summer of that 1981 turning-point year, the DOE snapped and the full wrath of the U.S. government descended upon BNL, generating shock waves that were felt from coast to coast.

The DOE saw no way out of the BNL problem short of stopping ISABELLE in its tracks. That's the way it is with the government: they'll give you lots of rope to hang yourself, but if you do, better beware, because then, it's "Wham, to the moon!" as Jackie Gleason used to say. For starters, the DOE bit the bullet and launched a full-scale review of the project. The type of review used was one that was all-inclusive, and came to be called a Temple Review. This informal name referred to the review committee's chairman Ed Temple, an official in the DOE's construction division, who fiendishly fashioned exceptionally painful experiences for the labs. When Ed and his review team came to town, all those involved began to quake. He was perfect for the job at hand. Whipping everyone into line with an iron fist, Ed was known to push both his committee and the lab under review to their breaking points; sometimes such a review would last for five days, and forget any free time. It was filled with presentations by the lab's leaders, selected managers, and technical experts; and the sessions sometimes lasted well into the night with incisive and embarrassing questions passing across the table, putting those having to answer on edge and under a lot of stress. Private executive sessions with the lab's top management were scheduled to handle sensitive and political issues. You see Ed used every minute available to him to its utmost, without a moment being wasted. As for the committee's work, it consisted of analyzing the various problems, writing a detailed report, making recommendations to the lab, and most importantly exacting promises for future performance that could then be compared to actual performance during follow-up reviews. This last point was at the core of why Ed was such a success at reviewing a lab: he put it to the test by making it accountable for all its past promises and excuses. Thus, the process, under Ed's persistent, no-nonsense tenaciousness, came to be not a set of independent reviews but a sequence that had a memory; and Ed came to see himself as responsible for assuring that everyone kept the bargains arrived at.

The process was exhausting to all the poor people who found themselves on the hot seat; and it wasn't exactly a piece of cake for those applying the heat. Nothing was too small to take into account. It got to the seemingly ridiculous point where the cost of every nut and bolt to be used in a project had to be identified and justified. Ed's hounds learned the art of sniffing for blood and the lab at their mercy tended to bow to their demands. Yes, a Temple Review was a trying time for all and the experience for the lab was particularly harrowing. The expressed purpose of this exercise in pain was to document the expenditures actually incurred for the project and match them with the earned value so as to ensure that the government was getting what it paid for. Armed with this potent, at times explosive, information, Ed was able to extrapolate it to arrive at an estimate of the project cost and schedule at completion. It may sound straightforward, but to do such a job well requires a man of top-notch technical skill in addition to high-power political know-how. In those days, Ed was such a man. The key questions that he tried to find answers to were: when will the project be done; how much will it cost; will the facility perform according to spec; and, do the data revealed or surreptitiously uncovered compare favorably or unfavorably with past promises made? This was quite a tough assignment for him because in addition to the technical details being sought, delved into, and interpreted, judgments and evaluations had to be made about important and influential people, making it necessary to navigate dangerous political waters.

Ed had brought into being a valuable process, which, when properly carried out, was very difficult and taxing on everyone, but, in the end, was well worth the effort and distress. Since there was considerably wide latitude in interpreting the technical information and the staff evaluations, Ed could use his discretion in giving thumbs-up or thumbs-down to the project he was reviewing. In coming to his decisions, he could apply extenuating circumstances, or he could be driven by ulterior motives, or he could be responding to instructions or orders from above. More often than not, pure politics was the determining factor for the outcome of a review, not a rational evaluation of the project's technical status or its potential value to the science community and the country. Projects could be kept going in spite of poor performance if that's what politicians or other important people wanted. On the other hand, Ed and his team of remorseless tigers could be used as a convenient political way of getting rid of a project that had gone too far astray, and was giving the politicos heartburn.

The case of ISABELLE is a perfect example of this process at work. It was born by political fiat and was to die because it became a political liability. So, Ed was called in to carry out the death sentence. Someone had to do it. Temple went through the motions of the review process he devised, but in the end the politically determined thumbs-down sign was given. But that's the name of the game in politics – when the power-holders want something, they get it. Thus, after a lot of agonizing by the big boys over what to do, they made up their minds, privately resolving during the summer Temple Review of 1981, one filled with acrimony and conduct unbecoming, that ISABELLE was to be put out of the way, to just disappear, leaving as little a trace of its political existence as possible. As a result, BNL found itself in the throes of that vicious Temple Review, the one that would put ISABELLE over the edge. From that point onward, only a miracle could bring it back from the just about dead. All the past promises and excuses made, all the technical mishaps and cheating were brought in to be used to stick the knife in deeper. They could all have been ignored, but they weren't – you see the political battle had been lost. With BNL's political friends looking elsewhere, Temple was loosed to strike the decisive blow. And ISABELLE, on the receiving end, was to be administered a mortal wound.

* * * * *

The 1981 Temple Review of ISABELLE would linger in the memories of many for a long time to come. Full of fury, drama and spectacle, it was a critical turning point for the lab, with grave consequences for its future. BNL got the full Temple treatment, and the men in league with the Director got the worst of it, a lot more than they had imagined possible. It never entered their minds that it would be a full frontal attack and that they would be treated with such insulting disrespect. No punches were pulled here, and the most insolent affronts were saved for the classy and gentlemanly Vineyard. Normally, George had full control of his feelings and emotions, being of a calm and rational disposition, but here, at this time, at one of those moments that change a person's life, he lost his cool and allowed passion to reign. He would later regret it, but that one day during the weeklong review, a force that he was powerless to suppress seized him.

The whole week was full of surprises for the lab, with new ones surfacing each passing day. It soon became apparent that ISABELLE's fate was hanging in the balance. So it didn't bode well that, as the particulars piled up – numbers, questions and answers, commentaries, tone of voice, and back-and-forth interactions – it could be seen that the review was nothing if not a full-fledged trashing of the lab's performance. Ed's team had such contemptuous and even indignant faultfinding with how the magnet program was faring that they kept raising the estimated cost of completing the project. As the days of the review passed, the cost climbed and climbed, and because of that the estimated time to completion, so crucial to the lab's survival as a vital player in the high-energy game, receded further and further into the future. The implication started to become obvious that the ISABELLE experimental program was headed for a huge and perhaps fatal delay. Yes indeed, the lab was headed into very deep and treacherous waters. As the week relentlessly wore on toward its end, the chilling details emerged. The projected cost estimate went clear through the roof, more than doubling, and the time to completion followed suit. It thus became apparent that the review would be not only a slap on the wrist, as most had expected from past experience, but something far worse. It got to the point where an alarming and fateful conclusion was on the verge of being uttered. Adding together the lab's political downturn, its technical ineptness, and the reality of the outside science world passing it by, staring everyone in the face was the ineluctable fact that the project was not worth completing at all.

The possibility that ISABELLE could be finished off rather than finished caused shock and consternation within the Director's Office and the physics community leadership. As the news spread, it elicited a mixture of fear and vulnerability throughout the lab that had not been experienced before. The lab management had expected some criticism, but not the aggressive and venomous hostility they were witnessing. There were anguishing moments all week, but the low point – dramatically speaking, the high point – occurred at the closeout. This part of the review process is meant to be a frank and open exchange between the top management and the reviewers. The closeout's purpose is to go over any shortcomings discerned and then to advise the lab on its best future course. A closeout is usually an affable or semi-friendly get-together. There are perhaps some disagreements as to what exactly a lab should do and how long it should take, with the most sensitive issue almost always being how to arrive at an agreeable procedure for holding the lab accountable for its promises. But for the most part it would end on a positive note, with smiles and handshakes all around. However, this closeout was very different. All the rules of behavior were thrown out the window right from the start as the emotional temperature rose to a hazardous level. Those present saw an open display of the deep mistrust, the antagonism, and the bitter resentment that had built up over years between the lab leadership and the top government officials responsible for basic research. Just the presence of Doug Pewitt, who held the high position of Deputy Director of the Office of Energy Research, should have been a signal that the BNL problem was coming close to being life-threatening.

But no one entering the review show could have guessed just how bad things had gotten. Only after the performance was done were they able to make out how much worse it was than anyone had suspected. Not far into the review, those on the inside track came to have the uncomfortable feeling that this review was not going to be merely a soft rap on the knuckles with business as usual to ensue afterward. They began to sense that behind-the-scene decisions of major import to the lab had already been made. They smelled a rat. But exactly who of the lab's enemies were involved in the conspiracy was not clear at the time; and exactly what lay ahead for the lab still remained a mystery, although it made them cringe to think about it. As for Vineyard, if he hadn't foreseen it before Ed's arrival, he certainly began to understand as the review climaxed that something really big was happening that hot day in June of 1981.

As the closeout played itself out, without knowing the specifics, but feeling deep inside himself that a life or death struggle – more like a free-for-all – was at hand, George simply lost it. It was uncharacteristic of him, yet there he was lashing out at Pewitt with a blistering personal attack. "What do you know of running a lab? You're nothing but a man who couldn't make it! You've got a physics degree, yes, but, when it comes down to the essentials, you're just a lowly bureaucrat." Everyone in the room perked up, and Pewitt, not one to take such reproachful and abusive outbursts sitting down, came back with an equal barrage of his own. "You've got nothing of interest to say, so why don't you sit down and stop wasting everybody's time? If you had done your job as Director right in the first place, I wouldn't be here. Ah, why am I bothering with you? You couldn't run a candy store, never mind a lab!" Technical points and counterpoints were only incidental to the tussling competition. What was especially grave and never to be forgotten was the thorough absence of any trust and civilized discourse. The denunciations and acrimonious invective hurled at each other made the audience shiver with discomfort. Jousting like two angry bulls with a craving to go for the jugular, the whole melodramatic performance continued for what felt like an eternity but actually lasted only about five minutes or so. When it was over, with the combatants weary and tired out, an eerie silence settled in. As everyone in the room pondered what they had just witnessed and meditated for a few moments, they knew in their hearts that ISABELLE had died that day.

* * * * *

When the dust had settled from that shattering review, the changes came fast and furious. The rules governing how the project was to be run were quickly altered. Henceforth, DOE would control all project spending, with a cap of just a few thousand dollars for lab expenditures without DOE approval. This meant that virtually all purchase orders for the project would have to be authorized by the DOE before being placed – reflecting the reality that the project had been put into what was then referred to as a pause state. Although ISABELLE hadn't been canceled outright, it was almost as if the DOE were marking time, waiting for the right moment to let the fatal blade fall. The lesson to be learned was: be wary of playing games with the government and treating the relationship lightly. The government gives the outward appearance of great patience as if it were willing to go along with a lot of misrepresentation and incompetence; but don't be misled by this seeming easygoingness, and most emphatically make no mistake about its power and its willingness to use it when it suits its purposes. When you've got Washington money coming in, it's easy to be led into a false sense of security, feeling as if you've got it coming to you. But remember that the strong fist of the government remains at the ready and when it chooses to act, the results are both firm and final.

Even before the summer extravaganza was played out, seemingly in anticipation of something upsetting about to take place, the lab chose to take some action on its own. It was only nominal, but that's exactly how the top guys evaluated the import of their position – not really that serious, but something worth doing about preemptively. After a little thought, it became apparent that the Director's Office needed some beefing up to fight the soon to arrive Washington formidable entourage. Thus, a position had to be opened up. Ronnie Rau's divisiveness – he'd become too big for his britches – made him a weak link in the chain of command and expendable. So, it wasn't that tough to choose him as the sacrificial scapegoat, in spite of his being a long-time loyal associate of Vineyard. Rau, having the exalted title of a lab Associate Director, was relieved of this post and, thus demoted, began to focus all his efforts on the mundane and ultimately undoable task of cleaning up the mess in the magnet division. In his place as Associate Director a new face appeared in the directorate, Nick Samios. Unfortunately, this was a case of being too little, too late. The lab had sorely misjudged how much it would have to pay for its transgressions, and this minor attempt at preemption and appeasement was ignored by the DOE, so the Temple show was not a whit deflected and went on as scheduled.

After the summer debacle ended, it was a different story. The response then was swift and deep, highlighted by a sweeping management overhaul. The spotlight was on the lab, and act it did. Under the deceptively innocuous banner of reorganization, people's endurance was taxed to the utmost. With the top in total disarray, there were no cool heads to implement the changes that had to be taken methodically, systematically, and meaningfully. At times it seemed that a random uprooting was in progress: some were given new posts; some were left out in the cold to fend for themselves; some were encouraged to disappear; and some were wildly and at times unfairly discredited. Although this was a tough time for everyone concerned, as in all human power struggles, winners and losers were the order of the day, and some big-time.

Vineyard's team, to the extent that it was able to function at all, tried its best to do some good by slowing down the impact on the lower echelon workers connected with the project, particularly those with the magnet program. It did this by downplaying the seriousness of what had happened. This gave many of the ordinary types at the lab the opportunity and the time to decide how to deal with their uncertain futures, which, in extreme instances, turned out to be relocation. It's as if George knew his time was up, and he wanted to leave something beneficial and helpful behind for those who dutifully followed and devotedly trusted him – something decent for them to remember him by.

However, near the top of the management ladder the repercussions came swiftly and decisively. The infighting was fierce, with the mode of behavior represented by stonyhearted ruthlessness, revenge, betrayal, and treachery. In such an atmosphere, where you might not expect a fair distribution of punishment, for the most part it turned out that way – with the most deserving of a harsh fate meeting their comeuppance. This semblance of orderliness was probably due to the rapid succession in the Director's chair, with Vineyard resigning and Nick almost immediately being appointed Acting Director by the AUI Board of Trustees. With Samios the big winner, he was the one thenceforth calling the shots, and the actions came at an amazing clip. The magnet program was given a complete leadership overhaul. Paul Reardon became the lab Associate Director for Projects and, in addition to his role in the Director's Office, was given the job of project head – with Sanford summarily removed – and took over responsibility for the magnet program from Rau. Ralph Shutt, a long-time physicist in the lab's Physics Department and an expert in cryogenics and other technical matters, was called in to give the magnet program a shot in the arm, as was Bob Palmer, an inventive scientist known for attacking technical problems with imagination and ingenuity. Ralph and Bob both had worked with Nick in the bubble chamber program years earlier, and Bob became one of Nick's very close personal friends and confidants. With such strong scientific expertise to call upon, no wonder Nick felt assured that he would soon get to the bottom of the problems of the floundering ISABELLE magnet program. So the old guard had been thrown out and true change was finally had, or so it seemed. You see it's one thing to change people, but quite another to change ways.

The project's top management had indeed been impressively altered. The gang of four was kaput; Rau and Sanford were relegated to stand at the rear and keep their mouths shut; and Vineyard fled the ISABELLE scene, evaporating from management altogether. So, as the post-review period proceeded, with the unlikely becoming the reality, three of the gang of four, Vineyard, Rau, and Sanford, were made to absorb the blame for ISABELLE's pitiful showing. Vineyard and Rau went back to doing physics research, while Sanford, his career shaped to rest on the fence separating management and science, did the best he could in an almost untenable situation and managed to survive in the shadows. Still, they *took the fall* and were made to suffer the shame and disgrace that are the companions of failure. Although perhaps only a rationalization, it may be of some consolation to those who have plunged from the heights that the heavy weight of responsibility that accompanies power over others is lifted from their burdened shoulders. However, when such ill-fated types are taken from the field of play, they leave behind a vacuum that must be filled. In the case of ISABELLE, the power that these three – Vineyard, Rau, and Sanford – had wielded when the gang of four was the force to contend with was sucked up by none other than the fourth member of the gang, Nick, who came out pretty well from the whole sordid affair. In fact, with such a gaping power-hole left to fill, and with no one of consequence at the lab to answer to, Nick became the little dictator he'd always dreamed of being.

Some at the lab would always wonder why Nick alone was saved from the fate of the other three. The Machiavellian types among them said that maybe Nick played ball with the power-mongers of the DOE, that he betrayed his friends and associates as he readied himself to reap the rewards of treachery. Nonetheless, whatever he did to get there, he licked his chops and relished with abandon every ounce of his newfound importance. Nick loved to play with others' lives, and this new role he had so artfully won for himself hit the spot quite nicely. No matter that nasty and obnoxious deals were made, he did attain what he wanted. Nick finally had it all. Well, not quite, because he was appointed only Acting Director. Before he could gain the big one, he would have to butter up the bigwigs, even bowing and scraping, if that's what it took. Although he would eventually win his struggle to get what he had always coveted, he had some hurdles to overcome because he was not the kind of guy that people naturally liked. He had alienated many people by his contentiousness, his loudmouth cursing, and his in-your-face style. So the AUI trustees, whose responsibility it was to determine the next lab Director, looked hard for a new face from outside the lab. A formal search for a new director was called for, and after the candidates were evaluated, one serious candidate stood in Nick's way, Val Fitch of Princeton. An offer was made to him, and he nobly wrestled with it, even going off for a couple of weeks to a retreat in the country's upper west, just east of the Rocky Mountains. This really put Nick through the wringer, and must have rocked his confidence. But he needn't have worried for when Val returned from his soul-searching he declined: Who would be so bold as to walk into such a hornet's nest? Who would risk the ideal life of a professor and researcher for an unappreciated one in management? Who would exchange a success-assured academic career for one destined to end in disappointment, letdown, and, most likely, failure? No, he figured it would be far preferable to have a quieter and healthier life as the university man he'd always been. You see he had reached a time in his life where he lacked the energy, the nerve or the will to tackle the thorny and risky issues roaming around in the lab's spider web of a past. So the prize was left to Nick, given to him by default. When it was offered him, he didn't hesitate – not one to be saddled with Val's compunctions, with his scruples and doubts about what was being asked of him. Brimming with pride and glowing in his appearance, Nick thought of the rewards and paybacks he could now mete out as the crown that he had so single-mindedly sought for so long was finally set on his head.

Nick had put all his ambition and determination – everything he had – into reaching the top. Now that he'd arrived, staying there demanded even more from him. Success depended on his ability to reinvent himself. He needed to make a complete attitude flip-flop and had to do a full turnabout on his conduct and way of thinking: he had to change from a taker and a criticizer to a doer; he had to find a way for the lab to reestablish the old spirit that had been extinguished through the years of poor leadership; and he had to conceive, formulate, and put into action a new direction for the future. In the beginning, as is typical for the honeymoon period of a new Director, he was given carte blanche. "Do whatever is needed to get the lab back on track," came his instructions from all who counted – AUI, the DOE, and the science community leadership. But those nice words, so easily flowing from the lips, belied hidden intricacies and hardships Nick knew little about. For the first time, Nick got front-line experience of what it really meant to be on top with no one to turn to but himself. No more could he show his true characteristics, those of an attack dog growling and biting at his opponents. Now he was the one in the line of fire, unfamiliar territory for Nick. In this new position, he'd have to find a way to acquire proficiency in give-and-take, the humility to compromise, the art of deal-making, and most of all the means to engage in civilized, polite behavior. For Nick as he was then, that's quite a mouthful.

The stress began to mount from the moment he first sat down in that demanding and worry-filled Director's chair. Here, talking the talk was not enough anymore, now he would have to walk the walk, and do it with effectiveness and flare. The times were very tough and danger-filled for the lab. Inside, chaos reigned: ISABELLE was in shambles, especially the leaderless and floundering magnet program. Meanwhile, on the outside, the competitive pressure from CERN and Fermilab was awesome. Sometimes he wondered why he had expended so much of his time and effort just to become a target for others to shoot at. But philosophy was a luxury he couldn't afford, at least not at this time of his life. Besides he was basically a practical man and a man of action. So, despite the overwhelming obstacles before him, he vowed to give it a shot. He hunkered down and he tried, with his newly won power, to do something good, something special that would make him remembered. If the damned community wouldn't give him the honor he rightfully deserved for his discovery of the omega-minus particle, then maybe he could leave a legacy by resurrecting the once great BNL, a feat no one could overlook. Perhaps, he imagined, he could still find a niche in the temple of fame.

Nick strove valiantly to save the ISABELLE project as well as the prestige and illustriousness of the lab he'd come to feel the guardian and defender of. With verve and enthusiasm, he sought to find and implement a solution to the magnet problem. Then, lo and behold, after two anxiety-filled and effort-packed years, Palmer, Shutt and the magnet division proclaimed they'd worked out a solution to a problem that apparently was without one. By changing the constitution of the magnetic material from an innovative but unworkable braid-like structure to an imaginatively used standard known-to-work Rutherford cable, the resulting magnet, they said, was made to order for use in the ISABELLE project, renamed CBA. With such news, Nick, without blinking an eye, broadcasted to the world that his new magnets now had both stability and reliability. Actually, whether that was the case or not for those large and unusual ISABELLE magnets will never be known because only a few of them – big, unwieldy, and costly – were ever built. The real reason so few were made was that during the period the new magnet was being developed times had changed and the needs of the science world had passed the lab by. Machines that could reach very high energy were then the rage, and ISABELLE didn't fit the bill, being bulky and fat, built to provide gobs of data for experiments via high intensity beam collisions but unfortunately without much energy oomph. The trick that fortune played on the lab was that even if a workable magnet had really been achieved, by 1983 nobody would've cared. In the two years since 1981, simply too much happened and the science community, in its wisdom, saw fit to aspire and move on to bigger and better things than ISABELLE. Poor ISABELLE had become an old and tired lady even before she had a chance to reach full womanhood. And poor Nick was stuck with what turned out to be an insurmountable problem: that of having an unfinished project he believed and claimed would work, but one that nobody wanted.

Even the physichists, who counted the most and had been the BNL movers and shakers since the fifties, for the most part, abandoned him. There were still those who gave the impression of caring about the project, but they didn't matter much because they weren't truly sincere. Under their surface concern, what this dwindling number of phony supporters really cared about was not how to get ISABELLE right, or even how to insure the lab's future, but rather how best to extricate themselves from this tiresome, tottering, and passé project. So what do you imagine this two-faced support was for? It's quite simple: to gain their ends there was only one thing they needed, and that was time. And what were their ends, you ask? Those community leaders who had vociferously championed ISABELLE, those who had made commitments to the lab, and those who found themselves saddled with IOU's representing lab promises made – promises that couldn't be kept – needed the valuable time to distance themselves and dissociate themselves from both a tainted project and a tarnished lab. How ironic that Nick's driving though misguided ambition to make his inherited but ultimately unfixable project into a living experimental facility proved useful to these sly, disingenuous people. As for the government officials, whose responsibility it was to oversee the project, to approve the design, and most importantly to approve expenditures, how were they to explain away all that wasted time and effort? How were they to explain the money spent for naught? How were they to get the money still needed to terminate the project and wipe it off the books? And, toughest of all, how were they to find a *creative accounting* gimmick that would erase their guilt in the affair? They didn't doubt for a minute, with all the precedents for doing such things, that it could be done. But it couldn't be done overnight, they too needed time. What a clown of a Director Nick was that he didn't see the pretense, the hypocrisy, and the charlatanism all around him, playing him for a mere Simple Simon. How could he have misunderstood that while he was putting the lab through two years of arduous effort in a futile quest, believing that he was saving the project, the others were busy saving themselves? Smart as he was – this intelligent scientist – Nick just didn't get it.

A few months into 1983, the truth of his gullibility and naïveté finally dawned on Nick – and how painful it was for such a proud man to face up to the way he'd been used. But, even as the hurt intensified within him, his station deprived him of the luxury of lashing out in rage and defiance. Instead, he had to don the civil and well-mannered mask of denial. The position of lab Director for which he'd worked so strenuously – the one for which he'd done such unpleasant things and for which he'd hurt so many people – demanded that he show a stiff upper lip, and he did. But in his guts, he knew the jig was up. Because it was too late, by that time, for him to stop and turn the lab around, he simply had to come to terms with ISABELLE being done for. Nick had certainly given it the old college try, as he vowed to himself that he would. You can't take that away from him. But somewhere along the way, he made a grave and fatal miscalculation. By dedicating so much of the lab's resources toward fixing the project as it originally had been conceived, he allowed the lab to drift for two years, unwittingly placing the lab in more difficult straits than it had been in before he became top dog. Without wanting to, without even being aware of doing it, he had placed BNL in dire jeopardy of becoming a poverty-stricken institution begging for handouts from the government dole – only taking, with nothing to offer in return. However, the *I-didn't-know-what-I-was-doing* excuse doesn't hold water. He was the man wearing the crown – the one all depended on. He should have listened more, should have demonstrated more humility, and thereby should have done better. This persistent need and stubbornness to show that the past he was an integrable part of was justified was perhaps Nick's biggest failure. For reasons hard to grasp, it somehow didn't occur to him that he was letting slide the far more pressing and important problem of preparing the lab for the future and a new beginning. So, while others with more insight, primarily Lederman and Rubbia, were gaining the upper hand on that more urgent score, BNL was wasting its resources and using up its valuable political chips on a lost cause.

All in all, Nick was a loser. Yet, in spite of his weaknesses and deficiencies, he turned out to be the right man to pull the lab through its time of turbulence right after the 1981 paroxysmal earthquake, when people in the lab's camp could easily have lost their bearings. Nick instinctively understood that it was a time to ensure survival, whatever the cost. That was paramount. In fact, it was really the only meaningful option available. By sheer determination and with an unyielding, rock-hard conviction in what he was doing, Nick gave the lab's unhappy lot the will to go on. He shored the lab up and kept it alive and functioning. But the forces outside the lab were just too strong. In that ill-fated and unfortunate two-year period of 1981 to 1983, the science community and the government were working their dirty business. Without any qualms and probably without ample justification, they pulled the rug out from under the lab and cast it adrift. Thus, as 1983 was about to enter its cold winter season on Long Island, in an anti-climax of sorts, the DOE finally canceled ISABELLE and put it out of its misery.

* * * * *

Although Nick pulled the lab together in the aftermath of that killing review of 1981, he didn't have what it takes to lead the lab into a new day. He didn't see that everything was changed from the old days, and that BNL could not be made number one by government and community fiat anymore. Free and open competition was to be the new way, as Wilson had astutely foreseen many years earlier; and henceforth getting to the top would have to be fully earned. The result of this profound change was that for the lab to thrive, even to survive, it had to adapt to the new circumstances – and quickly too – because in 1981, when Nick effectively took over as lab chief, time was not on its side. The only realistic way BNL could recoup and regain what it had lost was to introduce fresh inventive approaches, inspired visions for both science and management, on a grand scale. Unfortunately, this lay well outside Nick's creative imagination field.

As the eighties opened, the lab still had a little time because that happened to be what suited the power brokers. What luck! They didn't want to bust ISABELLE, not just yet, because that would also open up to the public eye their own blameworthiness and guilt in the affair. No, it wasn't for the love of ISABELLE that they held back, rather it was time they were after: time to adjust to their suddenly being placed in jeopardy, time to shred the evidence, you might say. The joke was that in order to save their skins, they had to give ISABELLE and BNL a temporary lease on life. How ironic! Then there were the opportunists who had much to gain from ISABELLE's prolonged agony and sorrow. These ambitious types, lurking in the wings, biding their time, waiting for their chance to strike, finally had it. These cunning foxes were well endowed with the requisite ruthlessness to exploit the chaotic conditions for their own personal advantage and advancement. Nick was such a one.

In the growing darkness of that period, a tiny last opportunity for the lab was to be found peeping through the ominous clouds. It wasn't much, but it was at least a chance. The community and the government together had come to the view that America had to put up or shut up by developing an American option that would be competitive with CERN's new collider initiative. It was almost un-American to just let CERN walk away with the prize unchallenged. Once this notion was out, the burst of nationalism that ensued throughout the country's science landscape convinced the usually internationalist-minded U.S. science leadership that America had to become a contender in the race for the W. So, without anyone anticipating it, and unlikely as it was, it ironically happened that CERN and Rubbia together came to be the means by which BNL was given the chance it needed to stay afloat, and even the chance to make a big splash and a comeback to be remembered. But, as you might have anticipated, there was a catch to making such a chain of events come to pass – the lab had to have the leaders able to heed the call to arms, to bring the troops together, to get them to act coherently, and to move in a direction that would at least give the country a crack at victory over the well-ahead and fast-moving Europeans. Unfortunately, it wasn't in the cards, and America would have to face the fact that ISABELLE was not the answer to CERN's challenge because the BNL leaders simply weren't up to it. Some believed that, although George just kept on fiddling while ISABELLE was burning, Nick might still enter in time to find a way to pull the lab out of its fatal nosedive into that deathly fiery pit. The truth is that he did have a chance, a small window to be sure, but a chance nonetheless. But in the short time left to him, about two years, he would have to mount a bold, aggressive, and Patton-like offensive. Because an action of such daring and brashness tends to leave your flanks and rear exposed and vulnerable, it takes a lot of guts to act like that. Still, when you're going for the gold, only that type of feat will do. You must take your heart in your hands and make a wild thrust for the sea, and so find the victory you haven't the luxury of doubting. "Toujour l'audace," was Napoleon's advice for winning. But Nick, lacking the backbone and the fiber, didn't have the class to pull off the called-for acts of derring-do.

It wasn't that Nick didn't have supporters who wanted to see BNL do the impossible and come through with flying colors. There was no dearth of advice for Mr. Samios. "Make smaller magnets quickly," some said, and "Use Fermilab magnets, they work," advised others. In retrospect, if Nick had had a bit of the humility needed, he might have been able to make a strategy of this type work and come out in front in the big race. But to go that route, Nick would've had to radically redirect the lab and, perhaps more significantly, to change the course he'd already publicly committed himself to. Alas, he lacked the character to follow through on such a plan. He was deaf to these and a variety of other exhortations and pleas because he thought he knew best. He firmly and unalterably believed that what was needed was a holding action. You see for some, following the do-nothing easy road is the only way they know. So, Nick went ahead, and sought and found excuses to justify following this course of inaction. He knew little or nothing of what was really going on, so he did what his past commanded, what was natural for him to do. In the end, a kind of paranoia ruled, where he could only see imaginary enemies knocking at the gate. Thus, he deceived himself about the true state of his lab. "They're just a bunch of jealous bastards, causing all this fucking commotion," he thought at the time. Although it seems so incredible in hindsight, he seemed not to have the least doubt that he could beat off one and all who opposed him. And those he'd pulled around him were no help. They didn't tell him the true situation, perhaps because they also didn't see it or perhaps because they were afraid of the wrath such words would provoke. In any case, they just fed his illusions. "Just these few changes and the magnet will work," Palmer and Shutt, his handpicked experts and presumed saviors, assured him. Wholeheartedly believing in them, Nick was confident that would do the trick and would be enough to make everybody see how right he'd been all along. Heedless of the cries coming from all directions for him to change course, he rushed ahead, doing it his way. That's the way it is with those who come to believe in their own invincibility, and who come to believe that only they know the right path. They forget that we're all only human after all, imperfect beings and in need of all the help we can get. But Nick couldn't see it and, like countless before him, chose the fork in the road that would only lead to hell.

Unhappily for Nick, when the dust settled, he turned out to be wrong about both himself and the direction he'd chosen. He didn't really have within him what he thought he did, and he ended up nowhere near where he wanted to be. In the two years of opportunity he was allotted, he took BNL to the lowest point it had ever been; it had no new project signifying a bright future, and there were no reasonable experiments at the aging AGS that anyone was interested in, save the mediocre hangers-on who had nowhere else to turn. He'd gone about as far down as he could go. Looking back, it's clear that Nick didn't know which side was up, and once he took things into his own hands, it was then – that early – that the mourning season really began. He may not have caused his dream and that of many before him to fall by the wayside, but he was the one to carry her to her grave. Let all who were witness to this fall from grace weep for ISABELLE, in the beginning a princess among projects, but in the end spurned and forsaken by cold-hearted men, and destined never to see the light of day. Now is the time for your tears.

5. And the Band Played On

The decade of the eighties was pivotal for Big Science. It was a time when the remarkable growth in new accelerator facilities in America came to a grinding halt. These national facilities were fashioned to investigate the mysteries of the subatomic world and in their early years were extraordinarily successful. It was a distressing loss for science, for the country, and for mankind not to have the opportunity of extending the experimentation even further into the realm of the unknown by building the imagined and even planned more powerful facilities designed to explore more deeply nature's innermost secrets of physical existence. Too bad! Perhaps it was a signal from the gods who felt that man was approaching too close to their domain and decided that it was far enough. Or maybe it was in man's nature to fear the trip into no-man's land. Whatever the reason, the fate of twentieth century Big Physics was to self-destruct just when it was about to rip open the portals guarding the truth.

When it all started, during the forties in the aftermath of the Second World War, the air was filled with excitement and anticipation. It was a time of daring and action. "Nothing can stop us now," could easily have been the motto of the times, and indeed Big Science had a great run for its money. It was a paradise for winners: physics promised and the government came up with the funds; physics produced and was honored with big prizes; and everybody was happy. In the late forties, the energy of the particles for doing nuclear research was in the millions of electron volts (MeV) and the cost of a facility was about a million dollars ($M). In the fifties, the ante was raised. With fortitude, persistence, and ingenuity, scientists and engineers found ways to reach into the billions of electron volts (GeV, with the G standing for Giga), and the cost was raised to a few million dollars. In the sixties, after the energy door was opened wide by the brilliant invention and implementation of *strong focusing*, up again went the energy, this time to tens of GeV while the cost mounted to tens of millions of dollars. In the seventies, with a growing appetite for higher energy, whetted by knowing that it could be attained, once again the stakes were raised. Despite the miracle of technology substantially lowering the cost per GeV, in order to reach hundreds of GeV, the cost would follow suit and rise into the region of hundreds of millions of dollars. Was there no end to this spending for basic research, as up and up it went? However, contrary to what some nervous Nelly scientists thought, the government didn't flinch, not a bit. The wise government officials knew it was good and said, "Yes, go ahead if you can do it, and don't worry, we'll provide the cash. No problem!"

The boldness of the venture embarked upon was indeed awesome and stirring. The higher the energy region examined, the closer seemed the ultimate truth of the universe. *To stop the search when everything was going so well would be nothing less than a crime!* With that rationale, "Onward and upward in energy," became the clarion call of the titans of physics, whose ambitions were boundless. So, in the eighties, Big Science caught the bug to go even further, and the government, proud of its role in the breath-taking quest, was more than eager to go along. What they all didn't know was that in the attempt of these audacious physicists to take this next giant step for mankind, their reach would finally exceed their grasp. However, at the time, everyone was gripped, not by feelings that perhaps they mightn't make it this time, but only by thoughts of the fame and glory it would bring. You see they all believed that this growth was natural. It was the way things ought to be. This actually wasn't such a hard conclusion to come to, because for decades that's what had been done, and the end was always the same: the sweet smell of success and grand kudos for the men of science – those intrepid pioneers who fearlessly crossed over the frontiers into *terra incognita*. So, why should the eighties be any different? *They shouldn't and they won't,* came the answer, without the least hesitation. *Just give us more energy and the money we need,* said the experimenters, *and we'll take care of building the required bigger facility together with its greater complexity.*

Not everyone was so cavalier. Some even felt a deep-seated hesitancy. But, tight-lipped, they said not a word. How could they speak out? How could they play the hindering spoilsport? Such behavior could be quite hazardous to your health. It is not very wise to get in the way of a high-speed train to stardom. In any case, even if they'd tried, even if they'd been armed with a strong enough reason to slow down the action, there was no way to sidetrack this roaring train – although it must be said that no really good reason to stop it immediately springs to mind. Thus, the physicists, with backing and money galore and the ambitions to match, allowed their minds to roam freely, and so came to imagine and conceive the collider to end all colliders, a fitting tribute to the close out of the twentieth century, when technology came to rule the world. This was to be the big one, the machine of a lifetime, the one that would bring us to the Holy Grail. The particle theorists in their headiness proclaimed that if the energy reached could be in the range of thousands of GeV (TeV, the T standing for Tera, meaning one thousand GeV), a world of fantastical richness would be opened, where the very nature of mass itself would be revealed. They estimated that 20 TeV would be the perfect energy level. Sure, it would be many tens of miles in circumference and cost a few billion dollars, give or take a couple, but wasn't it worth whatever it took for such a glorious objective? These wise men seemed so sure of themselves and so filled with righteousness that everyone bowed in obeisance to the high priests and said, "Yes, you lead and we'll follow."

With the objective settled, the only remaining question was: precisely how much would it cost? Extrapolation from past experience indicated that one to ten billion dollars would be about right. "Great," said all, including the scientists, the community, the government, and just about everybody else involved. So, with lots of hullabaloo and little resistance, the decision was made: "Let's do it." As it was, in the America of the eighties, that amount of money wasn't overly much, being in the same ballpark as the cost a new-fangled airplane, ship, or nuclear submarine. Furthermore, it was a fitting – an almost perfect – way for science and America to end a century marked by technological feats of the highest order. Thus, with the opponents silenced and the proponents – the big boys – gung ho to get moving, the SSC project was initiated. It had everything going for it – the backing of the President and all the important politicians, along with the great scientists of the era; all the money any reasonable group could ask for; all the expertise the project could use; and even the enthusiasm of the average Joe-public, intrigued by the pizzazz and pageantry of the undertaking. Yes, there's no question about it: it should have come to be. Unfortunately, a funny thing happened on the way to the forum: after years of struggle, of toils and trouble – with money, with technical matters, with everyone who wanted to get in on the action, with politicians pulling this way and that, and with a management that was way out of its league – the walls came tumbling down, and the SSC passed into the land of unfulfilled dreams.

* * * * *

Right smack in the middle of the Big Science push further into the high-energy domain, there came ISABELLE, and trouble with ISABELLE meant trouble for American physics. This was bad news for U.S. science. However, because of the messiness and confusion caused by this wretched and luckless project, a sterling opportunity to come out on top came knocking at CERN's door. So, as the eighties opened, popping out like a gift from heaven, here was a chance to beat America in the ongoing particle discovery war. Actually, this wasn't the first such experience for CERN. It already had one when it was the first to build a proton collider, the ISR, in the early seventies, but then, because its experimental capability hadn't yet fully matured, it was not able to cash in on the discovery game. Poor CERN, always the bridesmaid and never the bride! First with the PS in the sixties and then with the ISR in the early seventies, still CERN just couldn't seem to mount any serious European competition for America as the U.S. won the experimental races hands-down. You see coming out fast at the starting gate, when your opponent hasn't had the practice, is a good way to win, a tried and true method. But better be careful to keep cognizant of the plodding turtle at your rear, lest you learn too late, as did the over-confident hare, that to underestimate your fellow-runner is a sure-fire way to end up second. So it was that the soft life – a reflection of the lagging behind of the U.S. in technological innovation and development – was on the verge of exacting its toll, and American supremacy in Big Science, fading fast, was destined not to last much longer.

With ISABELLE floundering in the late seventies, CERN smelled blood. Egged on and led by the formidable Carlo Rubbia, mastermind extraordinaire, it mounted a daring campaign of discovery for the long sought after W particle. Using an inspired and inventive idea that only one of Rubbia's ilk could dream up, CERN was determined not to play second fiddle this time. In management lingo, the plan and course of action Rubbia devised is best described as high risk, high pay-off. This is an approach reserved for those with strong hearts and strong stomachs but it is well known to science; in fact it's science's trademark. Still, at first, CERN hesitated slightly and needed just a little more persuasion to get it into the starting gate. So when Rubbia pointed out the scheme possessed the extra dividend of being relatively low in cost, well how could even the conservative CERN resist? It didn't, and off the *Geneva Express* went on another expedition to overtake the U.S.

The new CERN rapid-action project promised that if the new, clever technology of cooling beams proved successful, the whole shebang – building the new accelerator for beam cooling; building the enormous particle detector to catch the now-you-see-it-now-you-don't W; transforming the existing SPS accelerator into a collider; and finally accumulating and interpreting the experimental data – could all be done in less than three years. The whole idea was incredible, destined to manifest a showpiece of science and technology at its very best. What a man that Carlo was, and how open-minded, in-tune, and activist that guarded, conventional institution of CERN had become! The scheme was indeed ambitious, but, as Carlo convinced the CERN management, if everything worked according to plan, lo and behold, CERN would pull the elusive W particle from right under America's nose. The idea had masterstroke written all over it. Sure, it was risky, but it was also undeniably beautiful. It had the kind of spirit that could easily have borne the stamp, *made in America*. But, in the mid to late seventies, the hapless U.S. was unadventurous, staid and overly cautious, and saw fit to reject the project. So it wasn't to be done in America. Worse than that, the U.S. lost more: it lost the genius Carlo too. Snubbed and rebuffed by the land of the free, Carlo returned to the old country to his European roots. With his plan in hand, he offered the idea to CERN and the rest, as they say, is history. Thus, in 1983, the experiment was completed at CERN and America conceded the race for the W to the new champs. CERN had gambled and won. After two failed attempts, the proud and victorious Europe had taken its great leap forward past America and into the spotlight of honor.

In 1982, it became apparent to the U.S. barons of science, in the government and in the community, that the particle wars had taken a distinctly negative turn. From a war among U.S. laboratories, it had in just a few years been transformed, almost unnoticed, into a U.S.-CERN war. With internecine mini-wars sapping its strength, U.S. capability shrank while CERN's kept expanding. You don't always see your underestimated opponent creeping up on you, but suddenly he's there, and it was your own daydreaming and careless inattentiveness that permitted it to happen. And so it was in the particle science race – negligence and arrogance did the trick. Yes, the U.S. made a number of bad moves to let CERN become a contender for the world's technological throne, like the stultifying and oppressive impact of the three-lab policy, but arguably the crowning one was in 1977. It was then that the Woods Hole ERDA panel chose BNL to build the next U.S. proton collider, ISABELLE, and went on to recommend that Fermilab be prohibited from moving into the collider competition. This was a misguided step for America to take, and turned out to be the critical one that put an end to its first-place standing in Big Science. It compelled its prime lab to wither on the vine while asking its fast waning lab to carry the ball. What goofiness! Probably Carlo was first to sense the winds of change and to realize its international significance. The prescient Rubbia instinctively felt what was in the works. America's muscles were rapidly weakening and he knew it, probably because of his closeness to those making the important administrative decisions, but also because of his rejection from performing his glitzy and alluring act in America. By casually dismissing him, America sent him a message. Of course, it told him that he wasn't wanted, but it also said that this wasn't the place to be – not for a man who has ants in his pants. So, even before the telling story that Woods Hole would formally announce to the science world, Carlo was on his way across the ocean to find his fortune. Ironically, Carlo had reversed the American dream, and if America was going to prevent this from becoming a wave of the future, it had to act, and act fast.

Rubbia began his quest for the W well before the Woods Hole mess-up. Approaching Wilson and giving him first dibs at his idea of a quick way to get there, he found himself bluntly and unceremoniously rebuffed. This wasn't easy to take for a man of Rubbia's theatrical, flaming, and volcanic temperament, yet there's nothing like life's hard knocks to teach one how it really works. But this blow to him was more like a kick in the teeth, because the Tevatron then being planned by Wilson at Fermilab would have been ideal for the job Carlo envisioned. However, BNL and ISABELLE were obstacles in their path, put there by Wallenmeyer in his feeble attempt at totalitarian order in Big Science as dictated by Washington. Wilson might have been tempted to try to pull it off, but his hands were tied by ERDA, which held him back well before the Woods Hole panel made it official. It was BNL's turn and that was that. Rubbia was astonished at the absurdity of the situation U.S. physics had fallen into. Fermilab, its best hope, was being stepped on, and its life was being squashed out of it – and for what? ISABELLE was going nowhere anyway. Rubbia looked at all this in horror. But facts are facts, and he had to face it. He saw the handwriting on the wall, and, once his suspicions were confirmed in the summer of 1977, the truth of America's soft under-belly was revealed and easy for anyone with reasonable eyesight to see. He simply put two and two together, came up with four, and in a flash left for CERN. Leon Van Hove, CERN Co-Director-General in the late seventies, after hearing from Carlo that BNL couldn't find the W soon, and that Fermilab wasn't being allowed to try, heartily welcomed him, along with his fantastic yet brilliant idea. Having Rubbia on hand to spur it on, CERN became unstoppable and was well on its way to particle supremacy and stardom.

When Leon Lederman and Bill Wallenmeyer in the U.S. got a whiff of what was happening on the other side of the pond, they began to get worried. Could the Woods Hole decision have been wrong? Why not? By the fall of 1978, BNL hadn't made a dent in the magnet problem and a behind-the-scenes consensus began growing in the inner circles of power that a change of plan was called for. Leon, as was his way, was hot to trot; and if he could have Fermilab behind him with its constraints removed, he might be ready and willing to take over as head man, eliminating a painful ERDA embarrassment as well. Unfortunately Wallenmeyer wasn't so eager and wouldn't give Leon the thumbs-up sign. Although he knew Leon was on the right track, being a politician through and through, Bill had made many commitments over the years, and those he made to BNL were among his strongest ones, intense and stretching over almost two decades. So he was torn between promises made and doing what was right. This was one time when he found himself caught with his pants down. His many shenanigans finally ended up tying him in knots, and made it all but impossible for him to make the necessary choice of reversing the Woods Hole agreement. Why couldn't he do just that? Because, other than going back on his word – not so tough for a political type – it would also mean abandoning the three-lab policy, the baby he'd made and sold his integrity for. How could he give that up without a fight? So Wallenmeyer was trapped: he couldn't let go of the three-lab idea and he couldn't negate the deals made with politicians and with BNL to keep ISABELLE alive. Even though he knew that it was the right thing to do for the science community and for himself as a man, he couldn't just throw BNL to the lions to fend for itself. So it had come to this: the past was returning to haunt Bill and he couldn't figure out a way to backtrack and leave BNL in the lurch. Similarly, Leon was immovable in his determination to untie Fermilab and set it free to go as far as it could. Thus, with Leon and Bill both being hardened to have their way, the stage was set for a confrontation between them. Even though neither wanted it to be so – they were after all collegial, even personal, friends – events had conspired to make it inevitable. With Bill for the first time in his life tentative and unsure of himself, and Leon full of self-assurance and knowing all the right people, Bill was a goner. How did Leon do it, you ask? It wasn't that difficult: he simply by-passed Bill and went over his head to the higher-ups. Leon, by doing that, not only beat Wallenmeyer over BNL and sent his three-lab policy to the garbage dump, but his action, together with its consequences, also signaled the beginning of the end of Wallenmeyer's reign over Big Science.

Wallenmeyer showed exceedingly poor judgment in having so much faith in BNL that in the end came to be his Achilles' heel. In the past, because he'd had so much success following his instincts, perhaps he just let his guard down. But when you play with fire – and politics is just such a sport – you must always be wary of getting burnt. Bill, for no good reason except perhaps arrogance of a sort, didn't heed the good advice offered by this aphorism. He became careless and made a serious tactical blunder: his support of the East Coast weak sister of the three-lab group, via inaction that he hoped would pass unnoticed, turned out to awaken a sleeping giant, Doug Pewitt. Bill had always underestimated Doug, but he'd grievously erred in doing so. It was a judgment he would have good reason to regret in the years ahead. When Doug, Deputy Director of Energy Research and Bill Wallermeyer's boss, got wind of what was happening, especially Bill's lack of enthusiasm for an immediate response to the collider challenge from CERN, he became red hot under the collar. He winced, and being aware of Bill's untenable position, saw his chance to pounce. Poor Bill didn't know what hit him.

Doug was not only a physicist but a patriot as well. For him, America could not take CERN's challenge lying down. In spite of Wallenmeyer's insistence that the status quo be held to, Pewitt's modus operandi was quick action, and that's what he immediately ordered from his position perched on high. So, confrontation it would have to be. Bill, despite his Machiavellian smarts, failed to notice the influence being amassed by this short, balding, stubby man. Being polite, unassuming, and one to whom a smile came easily, Doug wasn't a hard person to let slip by. But make no mistake about it: under that friendly, comforting, and pacific exterior he possessed the tenaciousness of a wolf on the prowl. Each one of these spirited, aggressive men knew whom he had to beat, and so the contest began to play its course. Towering and intimidating as Wallenmeyer was, it was Pewitt who stepped in brashly with the authority he needed, and with a resolve that wouldn't be denied. It was quite a sight, much like David and Goliath; and just as in the biblical story, in the end, it was the little guy knocking off the giant.

With all Doug's political bases expertly covered, change came fast. Wallenmeyer was pushed aside with an ease that made those who knew him well shudder with disbelief and shock; meanwhile Pewitt intrepidly stepped into Bill's big shoes as his successor over the control of the Big Physics decision-making apparatus. With amazing speed, Doug took things in hand. Yet, though it was Doug's way not look back but to keep looking ahead, there was the Wilson affair that he felt obliged to consider. Although he concluded that firing Wilson had been a big mistake, he deemed that too much had intervened in the meantime to permit any corrective action along these lines. Bob wasn't the man he'd been anyway. His day had passed. His decline – speeded up, maybe even caused by his mistreatment at the hands of ERDA's unwise use of administrative power – was a bad omen for Big Science, but Pewitt, helpless in the face of the daunting CERN-Fermilab-BNL challenge before him, hadn't a chance in hell of reversing it. What did it matter anyway? Righting the world's wrongs was something he vowed to himself long ago that he would leave to others. Doug knew that history is yesterday's news, and he wasn't about to let this unfortunate injustice sidetrack him from and even jeopardize his main objective. In any case, Pewitt wasn't the thin-skinned sentimental type; he was more the pragmatist, and as such, cool as a cucumber, he casually brushed the past aside. Thus, as he set his sights on the future, he gazed at what he'd wrought: Wallenmeyer was off center stage, and Pewitt alone was left with the problem of how to catch Rubbia racing away at breakneck speed.

Pewitt in those days was a thinking man, and certainly no fool. Forever the opportunist, he would've never entered into this joust without an ace up his sleeve. It was so simple and so right, it's still a surprise that the shrewd and astute Wallenmeyer didn't figure out a way of using it himself. If Lederman would take over Fermilab as Director, he would be more than capable of leading the effort for an American collider that could compete with CERN for the W. Pewitt knew he had a worthy brainchild if it could be pulled off; and with him in the driver's seat – presto! – that's exactly what happened. Leon was given the full courtship treatment, and even though he was having some personal problems and hesitated somewhat, within a year he relented. When it was made clear to him that under his directorship Fermilab could move forward on his plan for a Tevatron complex, which would include the new superconducting accelerator already underway and also a proton-antiproton collider heretofore verboten, all his reasons for refusing such an offer vanished. Leon, a brilliant scientist, had always been a master negotiator and so knew a good thing when he saw one. By having it come out this way, he'd made the deal of a lifetime for himself, and also saved Wilson's baby, the great lab of the American Midwest, in the bargain. So, when in mid-1979, Leon became its second Director, Fermilab, as it had been a decade earlier, once again was preparing to become the unchallenged premier U.S. lab.

* * * * *

The impact of giving Fermilab a new lease on life, together with the ensuing consequences, reverberated through the community. First and foremost, there was the prominent reality that a national technology competition had been set in motion: BNL was pursuing a double-ring proton collider with superconducting technology, while Fermilab was planning to use its own distinct brand of superconducting magnets for its projected single-ring proton-antiproton collider. As a competition it was capital, a model that others would do well to emulate: Each rival was driven by a single-minded urge to beat the other to a pulp. But unexpectedly something quite different entered the field of play. Yes, the gamesmen were strongly predisposed to be the first to build a superconducting collider, and in so doing prove to be Big Science's best; but also impelling them forward was a mouth-watering ambition and determination to kick European butt by beating the arrogant Carlo to the W. Perhaps it was fanciful to imagine such an unlikely occurrence, yet for a moment there, pride in the American way came to these internationalist-minded men. Thus, for a couple of years in the early eighties, their self-respect as scientists, Americans, and men spurred them on to fight to overtake the one who'd set his European eyes on being the man-of-the-hour.

As the months passed, it became apparent that the complacent, play-it-safe BNL was falling further and further behind. By mid-1981, a new picture was emerging and Doug Pewitt was there to take a snapshot. Fermilab was moving smartly ahead on its superconducting accelerator, although it hadn't yet seriously started on the collider part of its complex, whereas BNL was stuck in the mud on all fronts. Doug found himself on the horns of a dilemma. Each day, it was becoming more and more clear that BNL was not going to fulfill its mandate from the DOE to timely build the ISABELLE collider, which the science community was depending on. On the other hand, a reactivated and re-energized Fermilab was coming on strong. With this reality staring him in the face, Pewitt's question of which horse to put his money on was a no-brainer. Since Doug was not the type to dawdle over such questions, he quickly made the obvious choice. But then, he was faced with the far more difficult issue of what to do about it. At first, it wasn't clear, as it almost never is. Deciding is one thing, but acting is another. When Doug found himself in situations like this, it was his natural bent to be aggressive and provocative. He would then watch to see what transpires, and only after appraising the situation would he then follow up with his reactions. He would continue in this way until something gave or someone cracked, and more often than not, this method ended up with an answer hitting him smack in the face.

Some might view this type of behavior, and the treatment people get from it, as unwholesome and unnecessarily hurtful. Some might even consider it unacceptable. Granted, a gentler and kindlier approach might sometimes, though rarely, get somewhere; but the plain fact is that if it's the truth you're after, harsh and in-your-face tactics could be the only effective way to get it. To bring out the weak spots hidden under the veneer of excuses, lies, and rosy promises generally requires that they be wrested forcibly. Getting such a job done is not for the tender-foots and weak-kneed, but rather more for the cold-blooded and hard-hearted. If you're easily moved to compassion and tend to fall for the first teardrop, then you're probably not suited for this type of work. You see in life you meet all manner of types, ranging from the unwitting to the fearful to the devious; and you're often confronted with only-friends-allowed stances. So there you are, a manager with a problem: how do you know whom you're dealing with? Don't for a minute expect it to be advertised on their foreheads. So in the end, in judging others, you must trust to your instincts. Or better still, just work on the presumption that everyone has something to hide. Recapping, if you're really in the game to get answers, never underestimate the ingenuity and trickery of those who are bent on concealing their secrets from prying eyes, which includes essentially everybody you're likely to deal with. If you're the type of person who finds such an observation of man's pragmatic ethics to be unappetizing and depressing, the best advice you can get is to just chalk it up to human nature and move on with your life.

Pewitt, crafty and experienced, had the capability, not possessed by many, of pulling off such a strategy of harshness, and in the ISABELLE affair, this was how he dealt with BNL. So it was that in the summer of 1981, the project was mercilessly torn open and peered at through the lens of an all-telling microscope. With Temple's assistance, Pewitt came to see a laboratory suffering from a terminal cancer. ISABELLE had become not a future hope but a deathly sick burden to science and the country. Corrupt practices had spread through the entire project, into its finances, its technical decision-making and implementation, its administration, and its strategic planning. This hopeless mess, with seemingly no way out, confirmed Pewitt's suspicion that BNL was not what it used to be, that its days of glory were gone and days of stagnation and defensiveness had come. As if to mirror this change, Vineyard, a man of high intelligence, who had boundless energy and a deep-seated drive to succeed, became but a shadow of what he'd been and simply couldn't hack it anymore. Doug realized that by pursuing the ISABELLE dream, the DOE was frittering away the future of American science as well as throwing good money after bad. You didn't have to be a rocket scientist to figure out that this was not the way to run a railroad. At the same time, Doug, his mind always whirling with thoughts, knew that when his day of reckoning came, he would be called upon to explain and would be judged on what he did in response to the BNL crisis he'd become inextricably enmeshed in. Thus, from where he stood, after analyzing the case from all sides, his course of action was set. Having recognized that ISABELLE was the problem and not the solution, he knew what he had to do.

Determined to put Big Physics in America back on track on the road to victory over CERN, it was inescapable that he had to give Fermilab free reign. But to make that a reality, his first order of business was to dispose of BNL as a hindrance to the American effort. He set his course on a beeline for the jugular, which meant getting rid of Vineyard. His opportunity came in the form of the ISABELLE project review of 1981, an all-encompassing, top-to-bottom investigation of every wart, mole, and blemish that could be uncovered. As he'd believed would happen, the review exposed Vineyard as nothing more than a Wizard of Oz and BNL as a lab that had known better days a couple of decades in the past but had nothing to offer Big Science in the eighties. With BNL's technical incompetence and embarrassing money shenanigans unearthed and established at the review, Pewitt had the backup he needed to do what had to be done. He forced Vineyard out and he stopped the ISABELLE project dead in its tracks. Although it took a few months for Vineyard to resign and two years for the DOE to cancel the project, the die was cast in that lazy Long Island summer of 1981.

Pewitt, ever audacious, had assumed a role in a drama with profound implications for the future of Big Science. After his presence on stage at the center of power, which lasted but a few years, it would never again be the same. Without being aware of it while it's happening, some people have that kind of important influence on the flow of things. Doug was one such person. By cultivating Leon to lead Fermilab back to number one and by pressuring Vineyard to the breaking point, goading him to let BNL slide across the perilous threshold into self-destruction, he had single-handedly nullified the Wallenmeyer three-lab plan of the mid-seventies. Actually, this was no great loss, for it was neither a very effective nor a realistic plan for Big Science. In fact getting rid of it was a boon, since its removal lifted a burdensome albatross from science's shoulders and freed it to travel to distant shores as it had in the past.

The roots and purpose of the three-lab policy were transparently political; specifically, it was aimed directly at distributing the benefits of frontier science centers to key congressional regions. Give a little to this congressman, a little to another, and pretty soon you'd have a lot of political support. That, at least was the theory behind the idea. But it was a flawed plan from the get-go. Politicians are not simple-mindedly swayed and manipulated. You can't give them, as if out of your largesse, something they already possess. Remember that it is the prerogative of Congress and not of the science community to have the final word as to where a facility will be. That's congressional jurisdiction! It's their perks to give or not, as they would will it. Where do scientists come off thinking that they can horn in? It would've done them far better to be more careful on this score. It's not wise to try to fool father Congress. Simply put, it's their game to play and their territory to rule over, and any congressman worth his salt will not be toyed with.

Congressmen have in their arsenal sophisticated and ruthless ways undreamed of by scientists. Patronage, the punishing removal of someone's job, project initiation, project cancellation, ruining a life, saving a life, and more, all fall within their sphere of capability. You don't mess with that kind of power – not if you savor your skin. Still, some have tried to grab a piece of the action. Even the deep-thinking Wallenmeyer, who should have known better, set out and actually believed he could beat them at their game. What arrogance! How could he have thought that they would allow him to hold sway over their plums to give?

Looking back on it, with the benefit of hindsight, the entire three-lab notion seems rather silly; and we can only wonder at what Wallenmeyer, the consummate Machiavellian, was planning in that devious and devilish mind of his when he first put his scheme into motion. To give him the benefit of the doubt, Bill, really a politically astute man, surely meant the three-lab plan not to manipulate the political virtuosos in Congress, but rather to get his hands on the means of pushing around the more or less politically naive leaders of the science community. He wanted power over Big Science; and he wanted to control a little kingdom of his own; and what better way to get a hold of these things than to intimidate these politically-innocent scientists by convincing them to submit to the idea of a broad geographical distribution of basic research facilities. By pretending to be the middleman between Congress and the science community, he believed he could get them to do most anything. Such was the awe that Congress held for the science community that he had a good thing going for him. It was risky business to play around with such power, but you can't take it away from Wallenmeyer that it did work. This was probably because Congress in any case does try to divide up the federal facility budget pie regionally, and since Wallenmeyer's puny empire was only a blip on the congressional screen, it either wasn't noticed or no one chose to make a fuss about it. Perhaps that's what Bill was depending on all along. On the other hand, scientists as a whole, puffed up with self-importance, fell for Bill's ploy hook, line, and sinker, as he had counted on. Funnily enough, when you give it a second thought, it was quite a cute gimmick that Bill cooked up for himself. Too bad for him that, as a result of his obstinate faith in BNL, it fell apart!

In spite of his conniving gamesmanship and his obvious ulterior motive, Wallenmeyer's three-lab plan had a certain charm for its time in that it kept the peace among a group of highly competitive know-it-alls. But, sadly for Bill, who should have seen it coming but didn't, that time suddenly passed and a new style for a new time found its place on the stage. As the eighties got under way, the talk around the world was of mega-science and international science. Big Science facilities were becoming ever bigger, more complex, and more costly. Thus, the tendency, far from being toward a geographically balanced distribution of forefront centers, was toward a center much like CERN in Western Europe. Simple extrapolation would say that the U.S. was headed toward a single all-encompassing American center. Unfortunately and to its discredit, the U.S. science community has yet to come to terms with this unavoidable and irrevocable trend of the modern world. Worse still, it seems that world science, its system of regional control firmly entrenched, also has not taken the new age of technological centralization to heart.

As 1982 began, most would have welcomed a break from their rising stress levels induced by the destabilizing events and the unsettling realignments of the year just past, but that was not to be. Change, especially the type that attacks the very structural integrity of a social system, only re-energizes more of the same. Without an opportunity to catch your breath, the change continues on in this way, with change begetting change begetting change. There is no respite to be had until the pent-up energy that forced change to start on its relentless course in the first place can find the means to dissipate – can find some relief outlet. Only then can come a cool-down and a time to rebuild. But for Big Physics in 1982, there was no relief in sight. Only more tension, constant anxiety, and lingering, jittery worry were in store. No, as devoutly as it was prayed for, this was not yet to be a year for reconstruction, for the line had not yet been crossed that would permit it. This new year seemed only to promise the same churning change. But wait! Not so fast! There were in fact unforeseen startling developments on the horizon.

* * * * *

In 1982, Fermilab reestablished itself as the American accelerator lab to beat, and hope for BNL as a leader all but vanished. ISABELLE was in shambles. Vineyard was ousted and replaced by Samios; Paul Reardon, an experienced manager but hardly the type to inspire a project rebirth, replaced Jim Sanford, the project head since 1978; and Ronnie Rau, pushed aside earlier, left the field of battle well before the big heat of 1981 arrived. What a top management overhaul that was! It almost seemed as if something good might come of it. The old, tired ISABELLE leadership, the gang of four, was wiped out – and good riddance! In principle, it was a very poor way to run a project anyway, and in practice this was confirmed by the fact that it turned out to be more destructive than constructive. Once out of sight, it was easily forgotten and erased from the history of the times. That's the way it happened, but in thinking about it, perhaps it would've been better to keep the memory alive, not just for historical accuracy, but as a lesson for all of how not to manage a project.

With the gang of four out of the way, in its place, its sole survivor, Samios, emerged from the shadows to take over the reins as a gang of one. This role suited Nick to a tee for he was by nature a one-man show. After years of playing second fiddle, following the orders of others, Nick finally made it to the top of the heap. He was now the lab's commander-in-chief, and he had no one to answer to. It must have been a heady time for him, with all the human resources of the community at his beck and call, and all the money he could effectively use readily available. Looking back, it's a pity he didn't realize early on how easy it would be to waste all of it and more.

At first Nick seemed to be responding to the great challenge he faced. It was now his team running things. So filled was he with confidence and enthusiasm to get going that it didn't even occur to him, in contrast to his predecessors, to doubt that he would get it right. His first order of business was to straighten out the magnet program. Being headstrong and impulsive, he totally trashed its leadership. With Rau, Vineyard's man, shunted to the sidelines Nick brought in his own squad of Bob Palmer and Ralph Shutt, old buddies from the Physics Department. Then, as any new and optimistic Director who thought he was God's gift would do, he unveiled his plan to resurrect ISABELLE. After cutting through its layers of boiler-plate and obfuscation, and plowing through to the core, what remained was this: the ISABELLE name would be changed to Colliding Beam Accelerator (CBA), and the magnet's superconducting coil would henceforth be made using the well-know Rutherford cable devised at the Rutherford lab at Cambridge University in Great Britain. He thus abandoned the BNL trademark braid, which right from the beginning was the key source of ISABELLE's troubles. Getting rid of that braid material was quite a plucky and hard-hitting thing to do, seeing that so many past lab leaders had put so much stock in it, enough to lay themselves on the line. However, mysteriously, Nick's sense of what he had to do just stopped there. As to why it did is anybody's guess. Maybe he really thought that other than that, the project was fine. Maybe he simply lost his nerve. It was such a letdown. For a time, he appeared to be doing well, but then suddenly, as hopefully as his administration began, any sign of progressive leadership at the lab ended and fell with a thud.

As far as Nick's plan went, it was OK. Unfortunately, assessing it fairly and squarely, the verdict is undeniable: it missed the bull's eye by a long shot. Even to BNL's friends and avid supporters, it didn't seem close to responding to the depths of the Big Science community's needs. However, Nick, self-assured, seemed unaware of its glaring inadequacy; and because he was so impetuous and carelessly unpredictable, no one had the guts to tell him the truth. Whether he would've had the ability to listen anyway is questionable, given what's known about his personality. In any case, what happened is that Nick just went ahead doing it his way. Making excellent use of Palmer's ingenuity, Shutt's engineering prowess, and the Magnet Division's quality workmanship, he called for the project's vigorous pursuit of magnet R&D. He demanded a full-scale assault on the problem and wouldn't take less than success. He wasn't disappointed when this first-rate group came through and hit the jackpot. When the test data were finally in, Nick glowed and announced to the world that he had a working magnet, one that would permit the *new* BNL project, the one with the counterfeit and lackluster appellation CBA, to move forward. It was very sad to see Nick addressing an audience that had long since left the theater. You see the day of the big, all-purpose, do-everything-for-every-experimenter collider at low energy had gone. Nick was just too self-involved to notice that the day of high energy at any reasonable cost had come, and the price he'd have to pay for this negligent inattentiveness was high indeed. Magnet or no magnet, there was nobody listening, and Nick was dead in the water. For his lack of vision, his flawed reasoning, and his overflowing self-conceit, he would have to take the fall, dragging ISABELLE, or the CBA if you wish, along with him.

Put in a nutshell, this is what Nick had: the grand opportunity to flower given him when Vineyard fell apart; the seemingly unlimited resources – financial, personnel, and physical plant – put at his disposal; full access to the world's technical expertise; the encouragement and cooperation of the government and the community during his first couple of years when the honeymoon was on; and the power over people that only a lab Director possesses. That's quite a package! With that at our fingertips, how can we speak of him and his leadership during that critical period when he first took office? Starting off on the right foot and doing what's expected of a man just coming into such a top-level position, he made a plan. Although it had a glimmer of sparkle to it and some flashes of technological innovation, it was hardly an inspiration and certainly nothing to write home about. You see his plan really took notice only of the magnet problem. Yet even the magnet wasn't adequately altered to be suitable for a modern machine. Although braid was out and cable in, a very wise and significant change, it still remained the unwieldy, overbearing, and way too costly ISABELLE magnet. Well, that point could be argued ad nauseum, but there was a far more urgent dilemma facing BNL. Even taking the new magnet as a good start, there was more to the ISABELLE crisis than that. What was really the country's objective was to get a working collider, and get it double-quick. Because the magnet was what it was, using it to make a full-fledged collider still had a very long way to go and, as costly as it was, the lab needed a lot more money as well. So, in the end, as a leader, Nick started fast, but ran out of steam equally fast, like a runner who races to the front right out of the starting gate, but by the time he gets to the last turn, finds himself lagging in back of the pack. Thus, when all is said and done, Nick was a man who was given a chance to shine by resolving an incredibly sticky challenge; but he just didn't have it in him, and he fell flat on his face.

In the national context, Nick's plan was a pathetically lame response to what the country's Big Science program needed. It wasn't right for its time nor was it right technically. This was primarily because it failed to address the central issue that the U.S. needed a collider on the double. CERN had thrown down the gauntlet and to sustain the honor and dignity of American physics, it had to be picked up and the challenge accepted. ISABELLE was ill ready to do that job, and so was the CBA. For reasons difficult to fathom, Nick, whose intelligence no one doubted, refused to acknowledge this; he mulishly didn't want to do what had to be done and didn't do it. He went on his way, living in a dream world of his own making. In hindsight, it is easy to argue from what happened that his plan, right from the start, had no chance of gaining community acceptance. Even if the magnet turned out to be feasible, as BNL often trumpeted, CERN still would have almost surely come out on top. Thus the slow-to-get-done and ponderous CBA project, aka ISABELLE, was a non-starter. It had doom written all over it, and for the same reasons that ISABELLE did: its cost was too high, its projected completion date was too far away, and its technical design remained questionable. Nevertheless, Nick chose inflexibly to play the CBA hand to its end. In doing so, there were consequences to be borne, both by him and by the lab he should have led better. They were all destined to experience the stinging and prolonged pain of defeat and loss.

Nick, however, was drunk with power. He could see nothing outside his limited field of vision, fixed by his far too high self-image and kept that way by his bitterness and ill feeling toward Leon and Carlo. These were the exact opposite of the characteristics that make for a top-notch Director. Instead of humility, necessary for foresight and vision, he was full of conceit, bound to blind him to reality; and instead of forgive-and-forget, allowing him to gain a foothold, make friends, and move forward, he had a tendency to paranoia, again reinforcing blindness to the reality before him. So, in truth, he wasn't meant to wear the crown given him. Nevertheless, he had it, and, in fact, there weren't many who even noticed these flaws in him. If you looked around most circles, people all over the U.S. were rooting for him. He was an underdog, and he had quite a bit of charm if you only saw him from afar, and that's precisely the type Americans cheer on. Even years later, some would bemoan the fact that Nick didn't pull the rabbit out of the hat and win the grand prize. Such types went so far as to believe some of the outrageous statements he made, placing the full blame on others – yes, always others, never himself. They would insist that with a little help Nick could have done it. But they were wrong, for his arrogance didn't give him a ghost of a chance of giving CERN a run for its money. Many, thinking him an intelligent, rational man, advised him as to how he might accomplish that end, but he didn't even seem to recognize that a real race was in progress. Was it pigheadedness? Was it stupidity? Was it a form of denial? Whatever it was, he still had a lot of people on his side. Nonetheless, he lost the race anyway and perhaps also his soul.

* * * * *

Though Nick missed the point, Leon was different and did see the big picture. If Nick wanted to play it safe, Leon thought, then so be it. If Nick didn't want to risk losing with the spotlight shining on him and his enemies gawking, then so be it. If Nick couldn't bear the sight of BNL coming out a poor second to CERN, thus exposing his once great lab to the smirks of its opponents, then so be it. If Nick had lost his confidence in his ability to compete in the same ring with the roaring Rubbia, then so be it. If he didn't want to take a good faith shot at reaching the W first by accepting outside help, then so be it. If Nick didn't want to pay the entry fee, demonstrating that there was still the will and some fight left in the old BNL for a place at the starting gate for the next race – this time a really big one – then again so be it. Was Nick just dumb? Leon asked himself. But he rejected that absurd notion and came to believe that the only reasonable explanation was that Nick – yes, it's true, an arrogant bully – was nonetheless a man who lacked the genuine article – real cajones.

Leon, on the other hand, did have the balls, and he wasn't lacking in chutzpah either. He also was an old hand at poker and an even older one at the bluff game. Many colleagues remembered long evenings at his home trying to outguess his every surprising move while the Glenlivet refreshingly flowed. Leon was one who knew which way was up. He had his wits about him and the political savvy to be a big leaguer. He had character, drive, and desire – could anyone ask for a better-suited leader? If anyone was going to take American Big Physics out of its doldrums, he was the man to do it. Unlike Nick, Leon was eager and all hopped-up, full of hope and energy, craving first licks at some new, yet to be conceived accelerator facility, something big and brash enough to shock the world; and he was only too ready to pay the entry fee – scoring big or at least coming off well against the seemingly invincible Rubbia – in order to earn his place at the starting gate.

However, even though BNL was in pretty bad shape, there was still that damnable three-lab restraint standing in his way. Why a deep-thinking man of Wallenmeyer's ilk would stand by a beginning-to-decay BNL for as long as he did still remains locked up in his mind's bag of secrets. As for Leon, he knew Bill well and watched in amazement at the inner struggle Bill was having with his pragmatism versus his conscience. Still, Bill was a man to be reckoned with, and Leon knew it wasn't going to be clear sailing. Doubting that Wallenmeyer's baby could be overthrown quickly, he was actually a bit hesitant at first that Fermilab would be freed to take a shot at Carlo. It all seemed to depend on whether Pewitt had gained sufficient strength to be able to put big Bill on ice. But any doubts or qualms he had on this point vanished when the money to tackle Carlo started rolling in. Doug, a bull of a man residing in that mismatched small frame of his, worked his magic and managed to get Congress to assign two million dollars to Fermilab for fiscal year 1982, beginning in October 1981, to start the construction of their long-sought-after proton-antiproton collider. So, Leon was on his way. But keep in mind that it wasn't just dealing with the Rubbia matter that was driving him. It couldn't be since he knew, although he wouldn't admit it out loud, that he didn't stand much of a chance on that front. No, if truth be told, he had far bigger ideas to wrestle with. Outwardly, he did what had to be done to engage the flaming, blustering Carlo, but in his mind were bubbling fantastical thoughts of things to come in the post-Tevatron era. Most of all, what he really wanted was the go-ahead to conceptualize and design a Big Physics facility archetype – a collider to end all colliders – one that would shock the science world to its very foundations. It was to be in 1982 that his wish came to him.

This congressional ploy to start Leon and Fermilab on their way, engineered by Pewitt in 1981, was curiously and eerily reminiscent of Vineyard's fast footwork in 1977, when ISABELLE was given its first five million dollars of construction money for fiscal year 1978. Vineyard put on quite a show that summer by dramatically orchestrating the gripping announcement that Congress had intervened on BNL's behalf smack in the middle of the Woods Hole 1977 meeting. Just as Wilson and Fermilab had suffered then, so it was for Nick and BNL – first the earthquake of a review in the summer and then this acute aftershock a mere couple of months later. You see when Congress mandated that the Tevatron collider become a real project, it was not only dispiriting for BNL, but it also threatened the very existence of ISABELLE, thus insinuating an alarming precariousness into what BNL's future might be.

There is an element of poetic justice seen clearly when these two occurrences are juxtaposed: just as BNL had done to Fermilab in 1977, so Fermilab did to BNL in 1981. The two events had a striking similarity in their origins in the U.S. Congress, but as history has recorded, there was a major difference in their outcomes. On the one hand, Vineyard promised a collider in 1977, but four years later the collider was on the ropes, close to being knocked out, and two years after that was dead. On the other hand, Leon promised a collider in 1981, one which required two as yet untried advanced technologies, superconducting magnets and the even more intricate and delicate beam cooling, and less than five years later he came through with flying colors. The painful lesson learned by Vineyard was that, if you set out to play with fire without being prepared to handle such a dangerous game, you will likely end up getting burned. He made promises and staked his future on his word, but he had no substance in the lab to back him up – not to mention the enemies in his midst waiting for him to falter. In utter contrast, Leon went to war with his eyes wide open and had complete control of his lab. It's not surprising then that George was a loser, while Leon came out a winner.

As it happened, neither Vineyard nor Leon could accomplish what America really wanted, which was to win the first flashy intercontinental Big Science race. Not unexpectedly, Carlo and his CERN troupe, with strong-willed determination and supreme talent, came out on top on that score. The U.S. just wasn't in the same league and couldn't deny the Europeans their time in the sun. It was their day, and Carlo, Simon, and the rest of them savored it to the fullest: They had the supreme joy of being the first humans ever to sight the awe inspiring jets in their detectors that signaled the discovery of the miraculous W particle. However, the race was not a total loss for Leon, for through his successful – even if late – accomplishments and the way he carried himself, he was able to breathe new life into Fermilab. His feats in Fermilab's interests went even further than that: after the celebrated midwestern lab had suffered through half a decade of being suffocated and humiliated by a vindictive BNL and an intransigent Wallenmeyer, finally Leon brought to it a self-respect and dignity not experienced for years. But actually that's just the beginning of what Leon was able to achieve. With the cunning and artistry of a political veteran, he used his newfound place in the science world to fashion a bold American thrust toward the unknown frontier. His mind kept simmering and he wouldn't let go until a new idea began to take shape. Yes, in addition to the revitalization of Fermilab, he had another red-hot iron in the fire. No doubt, Leon was quite a man! You see it was because of him that the race for the W was not the only earthshaking story for Big Science in 1982, not by a long shot. There was yet a bigger one, of which Leon was the primary architect. Ever the poker shark, he had an ace up his sleeve, and knew the precisely right moment to use it. The fact was that he was after a fish far bigger than the Tevatron. What was that, you ask? With seemingly limitless ambition and imagination, he saw dancing before his eyes out-of-this-world, fabulous visions. Finally, when these dancers in his mind's eye settled down, he could make out what they were telling him, "If you aspire to build, then build nothing less than a mega-science behemoth, a supercollider for America."

* * * * *

The story of the American supercollider starts long before the Snowmass conference of 1982. Its origins could already be detected in the scientists who discovered and developed strong focusing back in the fifties. In the flush of enthusiasm then, they talked of accelerators that could carry particles into the thousands of GeV of energy. They even imagined what was then referred to as a *limitless energy frontier*. This optimism was reflected in the 1964 report of the Ramsey Panel, where it was declared that both very high-energy accelerators and colliders were feasible. This assertion wasn't just idle potboiler. The members of the panel put their names – and important ones they were – on the line by their vigorous and without reservation promotion of the development and construction of these futuristic machines. This encouraged the designers and builders, and hastened the introduction of such fantastical ideas into the world of science; and once the notion of these big instruments for research infected the human spirit of scientists and government officials alike, it was then only a matter of time before attempts would be made at building them. And so it was: as the years passed, palpable machines kept coming – accelerators continued their apparently unstoppable increase in energy; colliders came into being; and the bigness of facilities maintained its relentless course upward. Although designing and planning didn't skip a beat along the way to the ultimate collider, science had to wait until the eighties for a serious try at bringing the big one to life. And the wait wasn't in vain. Thus in 1982 American science – Big Science as it came to be called – spurred on by the prompting of an equally anxious-to-get-going U.S. government, embarked on its journey into the treacherous land of the truly big projects by taking a stab at what came to called the Superconducting Super Collider (SSC).

Before strong focusing, physics experimentation was limited to the energy region of a GeV or so. But once the AG dream materialized, the door to bigness was opened wide. That was fine, even wonderful, but then came the really hard part: scientists and engineers came to see and set their sights on the now visible distant horizon and had to figure out how to beat the odds to get there. First came the BNL AGS and the CERN PS in the sixties. By the seventies, Fermilab and SLAC finished building their base facilities and were running full blast on doing experiments at an intermediate step on the way to the energy frontier boundary, still far off. In those days, BNL wasn't as gung-ho as the other two labs, and it lagged and fell behind on its construction for the future, preferring to keep performing experiments with their 1960 AGS. At this stage of the story, the cost of accelerator facilities was rising at such a pace that the government began showing an increasing interest and involvement: Thus the regional competition for government approval, and naturally to get its money as well, had come into full swing. As the three high-energy labs, BNL, Fermilab, and SLAC, were jockeying for position on the next round of accelerators, each trying the best it could to push the government in its direction, a plan started to take shape. At SLAC, a new electron collider was approved by ERDA on the recommendation of a government panel in 1975; and at the same time Fermilab and BNL continued their jousting for who would be chosen to build the next proton collider. You see BNL, when it saw what was happening, wasn't ready to give Fermilab free reign over the collider field, and, although belatedly, chose to make a fight of it. The beginning of the contest between them was somewhat unusual because it wasn't just a question of who was to get something well conceived. In fact, neither seemed to be quite sure of exactly what it wanted. They both weren't very confident of just how far in energy they were capable of reaching; and to complicate matters they couldn't assess whether they would be permitted to spend the money required to get there. All they could really be certain of was that each didn't want the other to get ahead of it. Thus, a form of destructive combat developed between the two labs and appeared to be the only available option open to them. You see each one felt that to survive it had to have the next project, even though neither really knew what it should be. In fact, there was no consensus in the Big Science community on the right course to take, no vision in the labs as to what to do, and nothing reasonable being proposed to an increasingly ill at ease government quickly losing its trust and conviction in both of the competitors. Thus, irrationality crept deeper than ever into high-energy-physics – and when that happens, it's only a prescription for failure.

Irrationality means people, and the human component of the struggle between the two labs, a soap opera full of melodrama and heartache, was a spectacle to behold. Unfortunately there was no pioneering spirit and the programmatic part of the extravaganza lacked pizzazz. They were fighting over a bundle of cash but offering only pittances and crumbs in return. As the seventies went along and the eighties started, the casualties accumulated. Forced change reached all the way to the lab Directors as first Fermilab's Wilson and then BNL's Vineyard were toppled. With them the many lower echelon men who sided with them felt the hurts inflicted by outrageous fortune. These were bad years all around. The two labs were killing each other and as a consequence Big Physics was falling by the wayside as well. Ideas that would stir men's souls simply weren't there. Something had to be done!

In the midst of this bad business, with American Big Science seemingly locked in a cave of despair, life's randomness was pricked and a sort of synchronicity – perhaps it was just plain good luck – found its way into this lackluster show. For no earthly reason, as the troubling decade of the seventies rolled along, a group of freewheeling, *anything-goes* types, coming from out of nowhere, found each other and began to talk of a new time to come. They were people whose nature it was to remain outside of the mainstream, removed from the sorry agenda being played out – in denial about what was actually taking place before their eyes. Being in such a frame of mind and despite their lowly establishment status, they spoke happily and optimistically of crazy things – wild and impossible things – and they had incredible fun arguing about what these outrageous and unlikely scenarios might look like in some as yet undefined future setting. But this separation of the nerds from the pragmatic was not to last and they began to come together. Slowly, mimicking the merging of two distinct worlds, these two apparently parallel tracks, one inhabited by the outsiders, one by the insiders, came to intersect. Was that another example of synchronicity? However, if you insist on a practical explanation, probably it was because it began to dawn on the down-to-earth opportunists leading the Big Science community that perhaps these playful imaginings might not be all fantasy and that perhaps one of the devil-may-care schemes being thrown out could actually work. Perhaps hidden in that mass of daydreaming, they thought, there could be lying dormant the one realizable dream that would turn flight of fancy into reality.

Sad to say, leaders of the establishment aren't the types that generally possess the capacity to pull themselves, along with the community they serve, out of the quagmire and into the sunlight. Thus, it wasn't too surprising that when push came to shove, when it came to getting something down on paper and announcing it to the real world outside, they got a dose of that destroyer of dreams, the *cold-feet* syndrome. They backed off using that old tried-and-true method of retreating to things that had no realistic chance of coming to pass. They began to talk of a world machine with international collaboration as its centerpiece. They knew deep in their hearts that this was only a pipe dream, but its saving grace was that it let them off the hook from actually having to tackle an accelerator that might be bigger than big, perhaps too hot for them to handle. Whew! They'd found the *do-nothing* answer they really wanted. How relieved they must have been! You see as bad as things were, they were again free to sit back in their easy chairs. So, with no one to tell them otherwise, they simply settled back into business as usual.

Although probably not purposefully manufactured, there was a kind of positive angle to this lull in the action. The truth was that the American Big Physics community really wasn't ready for such a grand technological adventure. It wasn't at all prepared for such an escapade into the unknown, and procrastination gave those with a natural bent to look far ahead the time they needed to work on the multitudinous technical details and to reflect on and mull over the many political and technological unknowns. But, as is well known, *procrastination doesn't give time, it steals it*. That means that each moment of inaction is a moment lost. So, when is the right time to give the go sign? Figuring that out is what true leadership is all about. But there's one thing for sure: Waiting for some sign to tell them when to get off their butts isn't exactly the way bold leaders accomplish their dreams. In fact, the best that can be said in the defense of these so-called leaders is that they believed this blabbering about internationalism might at least be the start of something big. The worst is that they wanted to hold onto their positions and were afraid to leave the comfort of the status quo. So, phony as it was, they all paid homage and lip service to the apple pie and motherhood notion of a world machine.

The truth was that as the seventies ended, national Big Physics wasn't in a position to act decisively – they had a lot lower to descend, a lot more groveling to do before a turnaround was conceivable. Thus, perhaps internationalism could serve an interim purpose. The enthusiasts for a world machine, notably the physichists and the pseudo-builders, opted for talking the talk, as the newly evolving world community sought to make itself heard by developing a forum for discussing and designing a giant accelerator. They found it nice to travel around the world speaking of and imagining a bright future for science and for mankind. Although you can't always get what you want, and you might not actually get to build a world machine, this was a way for the best from all over the world to get together, work together, envision things together, and dream together. Hey, that's not so bad! In fact, once the idea was put into practice, there was something highly advantageous about it not envisioned in its purpose. As it happened, even though the motives for going into this world machine nonsense were more insincere than not because a real machine would almost surely be national, the result of establishing an international body for accelerator technology actually had much to commend it. Though politically it made little sense, technically, by working up ideas and details, even a preliminary design, it could turn out to be a godsend. And that's indeed what happened! In order to fashion a future world machine, the International Committee on Future Accelerators (ICFA) was established in 1976. Any hopes that a palpable world machine would actually get built were all in vain and probably silly. But, by providing national interests with an international consensus on the biggest machine feasible as well as invaluable technical properties, ICFA did serve the world Big Science community well. So it was that during three meetings, in 1976 in New Orleans, in 1978 at CERN, and in 1980 at Fermilab, the idea of a new, bigger than ever, super-duper world collider was conceived and born.

* * * * *

The game of Big Physics pushed particle energies ever higher, allowing man to reach further and further into nature's core. As the decade of the eighties came, CERN and Fermilab were ready again to make their moves across the knowledge frontier, forging new earthly thrusts into never-never land. The prevailing contestants playing in the international arena were America and Western Europe – Fermilab facing off with CERN – and once again a race awaited them just around the next bend. Although early on in the decade the question at hand was about the discovery of the hiding bosons, the intriguing W and Z particles, in a surprisingly short time, even before that contest was over, technological breakthroughs in suprconducting magnets suddenly opened up a new opportunity, one that appeared to permit the building of a high-energy facility previously unthinkable. So the new question on everyone's mind became: Who would be the next world champion, the first to build the accelerator that would tunnel into the deepest reaches of matter to glimpse the power of the unseen universe?

There was that certain feeling of déjà vu about it all. Actually, less than a decade had passed since the previous – pre-W – encounter. At that time, two accelerator builders extraordinaire were vying with each other to test their own mettle as well as that of the two great labs eyeing each other across the waters of the Atlantic. On one side was John Adams at CERN's helm, and on the other, Bob Wilson leading the way at Fermilab. With their then colossal accelerators each measuring over five miles in circumference, these two virtuoso builders came to taste the irresistible elixir that accompanied the march into the dark, foreboding no-man's land, where, with their exquisite machines, they lighted up the night. How fitting it was that these two men of steel, who in the end turned out to be only too human, should be so privileged as to carry the banners of their two continents in pursuit of a tantalizing lure of the gods – knowledge these mysteriously concealed beings held onto so tightly and were so loathe to share with mere mortals.

John, having successfully built CERN's Super Proton Synchrotron (SPS), was subsequently honored by being named, along with nuclear physicist Leon Van Hove, Co-Director-General of the great European lab in Geneva. Meanwhile, in the U.S., Bob had built his Fermilab version at break-neck speed a few years earlier, giving it the strangely understated name, Main Ring (MR), undoubtedly because he wanted to emphasize that, big and important as it was, it was still only the last ring in a chain of accelerators each bumping up the particle beam energy until it reached its peak value. But Bob was a man with a mission, and wouldn't stop there. As soon as he'd completed his lab on the midwestern plains of the U.S., his innate impulse was to go on. With an unquenchable thirst for knowledge and action, and, with nary a pause, he zoomed off into the beckoning new territory of superconducting accelerators. Sadly, both John and Bob would soon depart the scene, bowing to the whimsy of circumstance and human frailty. John's health would cause him to be shunted to the background, leaving the center stage free for that new master particle magician to appear at CERN, none other than Carlo Rubbia, who, just into the eighties, found the key to the W. Bob's case turned out to be radically different from John's. He had the unfortunate habit of confronting strong-willed government officials, but in picking on Deutsch, he found to his dismay that he had acted this way once too often. This time he had gone too far. Not only was he removed as Fermilab Director, but he was also unceremoniously banished to be a bit player and was to be the American star no more. Yet, Bob had a big heart and he continued to fight for life in the big leagues. To a degree, he was successful, and for a few years, although a somewhat unseen presence, he endured as a not insignificant behind-the-scenes idea-man. So it was that, despite their shining years, as all men must buckle and give way to age and circumstance, by 1982 Wilson and Adams had become inconsequential as serious players. However, even as grand old men depart, the young enter the arena to play their parts, and in such a way, life goes on.

The year 1982 was a signal year for Big Physics. It was then that Rubbia announced his victory over Lederman and the U.S. in the race for the W. In truth, it wasn't much of a race seeing as how Leon was held back by a slow-witted DOE and started out far behind. However, there was a lot more to 1982 than even that remarkable occurrence. It was, beyond a shadow of a doubt, a year of years: An unbelievably big American accelerator facility was on the threshold of being launched, and the match for the future international championship of the particle world was about to begin. This was the really big show, the Big Physics extravaganza of the century, the one that was supposed to release the secret of the origin of mass in the universe. In one corner, from Rome, stood Carlo the Great, soon to be crowned the current champion for finding the W and representing that most potent international body of Western Europe, CERN; while in the other corner, standing tall, from New York, pranced Leon the Pretender, representing the mighty United States of America. It was to be the fight of fights, the time for Big Science to shine, and the time when nature would be bared naked for humanity to see all.

* * * * *

That summer meeting of 1982 at Snowmass was one to remember. Inspiring and spellbinding, it carried Big Physics into a realm of bigness that first brought thrills, then bleeding wounds, then crushing loss, and then ruinous prospects and forlorn hope. But the bad part would only come years later. Then, it was a time to treasure and take pleasure in. Participating were hundreds of physicists from around the globe. As well as the business to conduct, they came to feast, to hike, to picnic, to play, to lounge, and to feel the wonderful rays of the warming sun of their Colorado paradise. Here, during this once-in-a-lifetime moment, they spoke in a language few outside their milieu could comprehend. Straining their thoughts, their knowledge, their judgments, and their insights to the limits of their capabilities, their minds and the air around them filled with private mathematical symbols and numbers that danced about as if they were alive – attracting, kissing, repelling, and ever shaping the beauteous orbits that govern the physical world we all live in. How could it be that such purely mental constructs actually embody and imply the tangible and concrete natural world? So mind-boggling is this way of representing reality – you could write it on pieces of paper – that rationality demands that it could only have been fashioned by an Almighty: a being or spirit far superior to the mere mortal men searching for life's meaning. Nonetheless, however the world came to be what it is, it was created constrained to follow these symbolic natural laws. That is some awe-inspiring brain wave! One can only be envious of the very fortunate physicists, because that is the job they get to work on each day – for lying at the heart of physics is to uncover, understand, and develop the capacity to predict the workings of the world via this wondrous, almost unbelievable system of mathematics.

The brilliant men of Snowmass '82 went about as far as they could go. They imagined particles coming to us from dimensions of the universe that we know only through mathematical symbolism. In their mind's eyes they could visualize these visitors flashing their brilliance before us for a split second before returning from whence they came, fleeing back into their vacuum of nothingness – a nothingness that yet is fantastically filled with particles galore, particles of every imaginable and yet-to-be-imagined form. It does sound crazy! Yet, it is a way – perhaps the only way – to explain what is experimentally observed daily at the many high-energy accelerator facilities dotting the world's landscape. So it was that in an atmosphere of fantasy and situated at the borders of reality, the giants of the particle world came to congregate. Yes, they came, they thought, they predicted, they envisioned, and they imagined a glorious future with more and more discoveries reaching down to the minutest essence of what the universe is. They wanted no less than an explanation of everything. No question about it! The Snowmass experience was one worthy of man's special and privileged place on this earth.

However, there was more than pure science that went on at Snowmass. This shouldn't be too much of a surprise because, being ordinary people – in addition to brilliant scientists – these men also brought with them their commonplace humanity. Thus, in their dealings and relations, in their interactions and negotiations, they enacted, as all people do, the ubiquitous soap opera that manifests itself whenever there is human contact. Considering the bad things people do to each other, it would make a casual passerby feel like crying if he weren't already inured to its universality. And make no mistake about it: the high and mighty scientists who came to the meeting of the scientific intelligentsia at Snowmass were no exception. No matter how high the purpose, the behavior always seems to turn out being low – and there was a lot of it at Snowmass. In particular, the big boys – Carlo, Leon, and Nick – were also the starring bad boys. In addition to a variety of underhanded and scheming political aims, they were after self-justification and self-aggrandizement. Carlo came to gloat over his imminent coup d'état in the kingdom of particles and to pronounce his intention that he and CERN would stay on top and would not be dislodged by any of his upstart physicist colleagues. Leon came to show that Fermilab was alive and kicking and was on the verge of re-establishing itself as number one in America and following that the world, although he reluctantly offered comedic deference, as was his way, to the temporary winning streak of the lab across the Atlantic. Then there was Nick, poor Nick, who came to save face. He was the unfortunate falling star as new and far more brilliant ones were springing up about him. While Carlo and Leon came to start the international competition for a world machine – as ICFA had come to imagine such a facility – Nick came to salvage a bit of the leftovers from a generation of accelerators that had bypassed Long Island and left BNL far behind.

Unsettled and confused, Nick entered the Snowmass playing field facing a precarious situation. Floating in a sea of doubt, feelings of anxiety clouded his thinking at precisely the inopportune moment in time when a clear head was called for: He recognized only too well that presenting his case wasn't going to be a mere formality – no, not this time. You see Nick had cashed in one chip too many and was left high and dry on the political front. There were no high-level politicos to pave his road for him. With his high-handed ways, he'd lost these supporters of days past, and had to cope all alone with the uphill struggle that lay before him. Even his well-known fancy footwork wasn't enough to overcome the resistance that awaited him. Only the merit and credibility he'd earned fair and square over the years remained for him to make use of, and he had precious little of both. So there he was with no men of power to appeal to and no past record to point to, alone to withstand the criticism and rebuke of the American Big Science world because he'd squandered the opportunity of a lifetime. He surely deserved what he got as he found himself confronted with the daunting reality that Carlo and CERN had run off with the W prize. Whether he liked it or not, the W was the big item in the ISABELLE energy range - it was no more and no less than what the collider race was all about.

In assessing blame for losing, Nick bore the brunt of it, and rightfully so. The poor choices he'd made and his deficiencies in management talent meant but one thing: defeat for America. Sure, Vineyard should have shared in the reproaches, but by then he'd fled the scene – and to be upbraided, one has to be there to take it. So it was Nick who came to Colorado to face the music. Having fought hard and dirty for the job of boss-man a year earlier, he came to win it, promising to set things right. But he flubbed his chance, broke his word, and got what was coming to him. Thus, when all the arguing and excuses are wiped clean away, what it came down to was that with the W removed as an ISABELLE selling point, the overly heavy, lumbering, and risky project had nothing much to speak of. There in a nutshell was the crux of the matter. Although not voiced openly or too loudly, the big question that lay dormant under the surface, frighteningly ready to spring out, was: Is the project worth going ahead with at all?

As far back as the summer of 1981, Pewitt, with DOE backing, had essentially written BNL off as a loser and had secretly and informally commissioned Leon and Fermilab to replace BNL as the forefront American lab for proton colliders. He had done this for two clear-cut and hard to refute reasons: to save the DOE from BNL's profligacy and to provide competition for CERN's enviable sprint to become leader of the pack. At the time this was taking place, what did Nick do in the face of this looming disaster to American pride and to BNL? Remember, even though Pewitt had self-confidence coming out of his ears, in fact it wasn't a done deal. Nick still had a chance and a little time to swing the field to his side. True, it was only a small chance, but it wasn't zero.

There's no denying that Nick was in a tough spot, and he's certainly bright enough to have recognized it, yet still he acted without seeming to grasp the treacherous significance of what Pewitt had done at the god-awful 1981 summer review. As if in some form of denial, his response was to bring to the table nothing more than business as usual except for the new Palmer magnet and the name change from ISABELLE to CBA. How naïve this once proud and ambitious man had become! Did he think he could fool Congress or anyone else with such a sophomoric stunt? How pitiful this response was to anyone who could see past his nose. On the other hand, in stark contrast to his actions, Nick himself seemed composed and unperturbed, with an air of complacency and self-satisfaction, almost as if he were unaware of the untenable nature of his situation. The *real truth* of whether he was mindful of what was really happening or not is hard to figure out. But certainly he exhibited no evidence that he was awake to the strengthening of the Pewitt-Lederman alliance. In any case, the fact is that he had the strength and the ability to continue playing the game just as if it were his to win or lose.

Nick simply kept on doing things his way. True to form, he took the outward role of Mister Cool on the surface, and it was a performance deserving of applause. One might wonder why he conducted himself as he did. Was there some logic behind it? Actually, there may have been, for he may have believed it would help his own personal career, and it did. He got what he'd always wanted: to be BNL's Director; and remarkably he would remain in that high office for over a decade and a half. Unfortunately, Nick's persistent and mostly uncontrollable masked Mister Hyde, in addition to his antagonism and belligerence toward the establishment, ill-served both BNL and Big Science, and that dark nature of his came to send Big Physics on the first step along the rocky road to collapse and ruin.

Leon meanwhile was a far cry from the doom and gloom that Nick brought to Snowmass. He was the picture of confidence and optimism, striding in as the savior of American science from the BNL menace, and, as an extra dividend, from the CERN challenge as well. Coming with an answer, he as much as said that if they would heed his advice, then even though the W was lost to Europe and BNL was holding it back with its interminable ISABELLE, an American recoup was at hand. By following him and his idea the U.S. would be pulled out of the doldrums it had fallen into, and America would be able to reclaim its rightful status and be back on top where it belonged. Leon, forever the showman, revealed his plan slowly and dramatically, first showing the audience the tip of the iceberg, while holding under the table, hidden from view, the makings of a magnificent undertaking. The Snowmass crowd ate up every word he uttered, in expectation of the revelation they were sure was to come. When finally his plan reached their expectant ears, Leon immediately became the hit of the party. The Europeans smiled outwardly, but inwardly they cringed a mite. On the other hand, the Americans-sans-BNL, who were the majority present, were aglow and all of them hailed the new chief of the champions-to-be. Such was the power of his message that it was destined to shape the futures of almost everyone listening. Entranced by the power of his conception and his inspirational presence, they became hypnotized by what he had brought with him and had so inimitably spoken of. At that historical moment for Big Science, they'd have gone to hell with him if he'd asked them to.

It was a Tuesday evening in July 1982. There was a buzz in the air as everybody – the participants and the multitude of others gathered to hear the word – readied themselves for the big event. It wasn't to disappoint the throng that came to watch; in fact, for the ones lucky enough to attend, it was to turn out to be an experience to savor. Later that evening, there at the theater at one edge of the Snowmass central square, Carlo, Leon and Nick were scheduled to paint their pictures of where Big Science was going. There was high expectation in the air as everyone sensed that it would be a night to remember. To be sure, the performers themselves had done this type of thing many times before and it wouldn't have been surprising if they had felt a bit jaded, even bored by having to go through yet another such occasion. But that night was different. They were flushed with excitement and eager for action, almost like school-kids readying for their proms or preparing for their trips downtown to the main drag. The anticipation was infectious and was to be found everywhere as people milled about waiting for *the happening*. The Snowmass theater-cum-lecture-hall was packed to capacity and the crowd, some standing, was expectant and ready for almost anything – and they got far more than they could have hoped for. The three were well known as formidable speakers, and that night of nights they were in top form. They were brilliant, each one outdoing the others. First one would make a point and emphasize and re-emphasize it; then he would bait the others, push the dagger in a little deeper, and then back off a bit by joking about it. Around they went, each taking his turn, each giving as much as he got, and always they were entertaining. Mini-debates spontaneously erupted, as one of the trio rose from the audience to object, to cajole, and to chide the one at the lectern. The speakers were witty, informative, and exciting; and a lot of fun was had by all as back and forth they went. It was a magnificent show. To have been there was something to cherish forever. It was a moment no one would soon forget.

However, only when one is alone, distant from the glamour and the sparkle of the blinding momentary occasion, can one begin to fathom what really took place. When it occurred, the minds of those there were overwhelmed: by the strutting, the clowning, the ranting, and the vaudevillian gags and jokes of the comedians on stage; by the limelight; by the spectacle; by the dazzling performances; and by the rich colors of a moment of truth. But as time passes, these begin to fade and become dim. Yet there are things that stick in the memory of one who was there, the serious and meaningful things lying behind the masks of revelry, teasing mischievousness, and playfulness. There was Nick with nothing to give but excuses and more promises, living in a time that had long since expired. Then there was Carlo, flaming hot and insightful, but oh so full of self-love, demonstrating and even proving his power and his glory, but leaving one to wonder whether he was speaking to the audience or just to himself. Finally there was Leon, dazzling and inspired, ready to scoop everyone up and take them along for an adventure into the wild. When it was over, there was no denying that it was Leon's night to shine.

* * * * *

Leon came to Snowmass to sell his vision of Big Science in America. Having done his political homework, his voice took on the authoritativeness of a man to contend with – a man on the make. With Pewitt in his corner, the DOE gave him the go-ahead; in addition, both the state of Illinois and its congressional delegation, with whom Leon had a great deal of contact, were eager for Illinois to be in the thick of things. Leon even found his way into the White House and the executive branch of government by way of a spark plug in the Reagan administration, the new presidential science advisor, Jay Keyworth. Jay was a youngish scientist from Los Alamos who came to the capital and caught the spirit of the let's-do-it Reagan team. Excellence in science was his motto and he was raring to go. As it happened, Jay was only Reagan's first gift to science, with a bigger one yet to come.

Keyworth and Lederman hit it off immediately. They spoke the same language and they were both in the right places at the right time for the job they wanted done – to make Big Science really big and more importantly to put America back in first place by giving it the power to excel. Leon and Jay made an awesome couple. Although it took a few years to accomplish, in a nutshell an account of what happened was this: Leon shaped the vision for America to build the biggest collider ever built, and Jay paved the path to the President's ear. Then Reagan, impressed and enamored by the idea of America being first again and of science breaking through the knowledge barrier, worked his magic and – Presto! – Big Science was afforded the chance of a lifetime. How simple it all seems when the facts, alone and bare, are recapitulated! In reality, however, the story of how this very special collider's journey played out is filled with human drama – with desire, passion, and disappointment; and with elation and pain. Some people were overflowing with joy, while others felt the awful pangs of suffering. Some withstood the stress test and survived, others succumbed and fell by the wayside. There were the good and the bad; the compliant and the defiant; the loyal types and the betrayers; the happy and the sad; and the winners and the losers. With the birthing process lasting over a decade, a lot of people were caught in the swirling waters of the whirlpool, and they did what their natures and fates demanded of them. Then, in spite of them, in the end, the gods determined the outcome. Yes, it was a long and hard road that Leon's dream had to travel. But first there had to be a beginning, the initiation rites, and if there was any meaning at all to the Colorado jeu de theater, that was it.

Arriving at Snowmass '82 in droves to see the Big Science supermen do their thing, the crowd came with faith in their future and felt the expectation in the air. Leon started the ball rolling with his proposal for a daring project that he and Bob Wilson called the Desertron. Bob and Leon were close friends, not a typical relationship between a lab's founding Director and his immediate successor. But they were big men with big dreams, and they weren't about to allow the ordinary pettiness, the paltry stuff common to mere mortals to interfere with their grand designs. They were givers of a sort, who sought to spend their time on the stage bringing knowledge and understanding into the lives of others; and they refused to be sidetracked by the trifling and inconsequential squabbles that characterize the dreary lives of most others, those who have little to give but the sweat of their brow. Individually, each strived independently to live his life to the hilt. But when the opportunity came for them to work together at Snowmass, they were an inspiring team. What a dynamic duo Bob and Leon made! They set their automatic pilot on a collider to end all previous colliders, one that would be appropriate to serve as the Big Science capstone to the century that initiated the age of technology. With insight, incisiveness, and effectiveness, Leon worked the politics and Bob worked the accelerator experts. They defined, put together, and worked through the details and choices. They wended their way with dexterity through the myriad twists and turns demanded by the politics and the design. Finally, they ended up with the conceptualization of a great new collider that would dwarf all prior ambitions – just the right one for the right historical moment.

Bob felt young again, yet perhaps with an inkling that this was to be his last hurrah. He could vaguely but unmistakably visualize this to be his final gift to man's glory. It would be a steel and concrete monument, springing up like a fresh wildflower in the great desert of the American southwest. Yes, his exit from life's stage was to be full of sound and fury, signifying what one must go through to make manifest the limitless potential possessed by mankind. You see Bob wasn't of a nature to give in quietly and leave well enough alone. After his rejection a few years earlier, a lesser sort of man would have left well enough alone. But not Bob! He couldn't resign himself to a life with a soft wind and a still night, where he could allow his mind to meander through his memory banks, reminding him of the time he had spent at the center of things. He wanted more than remembrances of things past – perhaps to go out in a blaze of grandeur. So he would make one last defiant gesture to the lords of eternity, and if that meant having to clash with and fight against the weak men who would hold him back from his appointment with destiny, then so be it. He would not go gentle into that good night.

Still, time marches on, and this was to be his parting shot. But Bob being Bob, it turned out to be a humdinger of a shot. He conceived a monster version of his trademarked low-cost lean machine: Get it done quick and dirty; get in and out with no dilly-dallying; and get what you came for and exit fast with the booty. His philosophy for doing science was to merely touch eternity, snatch what can be extracted and quickly retreat to the safe shores of Mother Earth. As for the actual building, he thought it essential not to belabor things, not to be sidetracked, and to stick to the job: Do what was promised; and from all who work alongside you, insist upon their being no excuses, and no *ifs, ands, or buts*. That's the way he'd learned his trade of building the great instruments of science, and that's the way he believed that he, along with mankind, could catch a glimpse of the world of the gods.

Bob was one of that rare breed of men touching all who come into their presence. Persuasion and making things happen were intrinsic to him – he was a man who could talk the talk and also walk the walk. His years of experience and life's hard knocks had taught him well. However, although his methods were the right ones, sadly his time had passed. Age had overtaken him, and, even though the idea of a strictly American super collider to search out the mysteries of the universe originated with him, carrying it through would have to be left to the younger scientists, who would have to try to follow in his footsteps. But, as it happened, there were none with that capability. Thenceforth, men not possessing his genius for enterprising audacity would be taking on the responsibility. Big Science would simply have to do without the likes of Bob. Unfortunately, science would not do as well without him as it had done with him. What misfortune! Now, for all those craving to learn where they come from, sadly they must do without. Bob was gone and hope for this generation to find out about such matters vanished with him. It remains for a future generation to re-discover Bob's ways and re-learn how to brave and conquer the dark waters that hide nature's secrets. Only then can the knowledge engines – accelerators to explore the soul of the universe – be re-started and the light of discovery re-opened.

* * * * *

Given the chance to construct a grand temple of knowledge, the grandest of them all, did the men of science answer the call? Did they heed the advice and the lessons Bob so generously and painstakingly left them? No, they simply didn't have what it takes, and it wasn't for want of desire or for lack of trying. Unfortunately, without the likes of the unique Bob Wilson, they were missing the heart and soul required to pull off the biggest and most demanding undertaking of their lives. Quel dommage! But they'd made their bed, and now they had to lie in it. Years earlier, they'd banished the extraordinary Bob, cast him aside before his time; and when such a thing is done to a man, he ages faster than his nature meant him to. So, when there was a desperate need for him, the *Bob of old* was nowhere to be found. Thus, the arrogant men who'd acted without foresight in letting Bob drift away were left to their own devices. Here lying before them was their possible moment to shine. But they were unprepared – for who could they offer up with the capability of doing the job? No one immediately sprang to mind. So onto the stage came the search process – and resorting to that, when the big test of all you stand for is at hand, is the seal of doom. The truth was that if it were to be done at all, it would have to be done by ordinary men.

Men can only perform within the limits granted them by fickle fate. So, ordinary men do things the only way they know how – the standard way, the traditional way, the conventional way, but most importantly the way with little or no imagination. If Bob had been there, he would have applied his unparalleled patented force of will and made the project a reality come hell or high water. But sad to say – and the Big Science leadership had only itself to blame – no one available could even come close to measuring up to Bob. *Failing* was not a word in his lexicon of possibilities. But for the non-Bobs of this world, that was not the case. Thus, all the effort and resources injected into the collider that was meant to be the granddaddy of them all proved to be insufficient and came to naught.

The difference between Bob's methods and the others' was like that between the rapid-fire, risk-taking, gutsy MO of Patton and the conventional, safe, routine way of Montgomery. In the spirit of Patton, Wilson wanted to engineer a beeline through nature's gate to that land of resplendent illumination of the soul. To accomplish such a feat of daring, he imagined long, very-small-diameter magnets installed in a circular tunnel perhaps a hundred miles in circumference, with the tunnel placed into the ground, segment by segment, near the surface in covered, shallow trenches. It was to be built in a desert-like location far from population centers, at low cost, quickly, and having a design allowing it to perform only at the level needed, no worse and no better. There would be no wasted effort and it would be done in the wink of an eye. As envisioned by Wilson, so swift would the action be that the guards at heaven's gate wouldn't know what hit them. Yes, brilliant Bob had exactly the right idea. What a man! What a thinker! What a genius!

When at Snowmass it began to sink in to the community that Leon and Jay, as if in league with each other, were suggesting that Wilson's massive and grandiose project was really possible both technically and politically, it made many sit up and think. Coming from such highly placed men, it had the air of reality. It just smelled right! Perhaps, many thought, they could get in on the action early in the game. With little formal marketing to speak of, the word got around through lectures and word of mouth, and spread like wildfire. The idea was so alluring that soon it brought a rush of people getting in line to become a part of it. Thus, there in the snow-tipped mountains of Colorado, in the summer of 1982, the Big Science project of the century came into being.

After the glittering pageant at Snowmass, and the Immaculate Conception that transpired there, progress was swift. Everybody in the Big Science community wanted in: the physicists bought into the project then and there; the DOE and the U.S. Congress quickly followed suit; then the industrial community wanted its piece of the pie; and finally came the pièce de résistance when, in early 1987, Reagan decided that the project would rank as a presidential initiative. This meant that money was to be no object – it was Reagan's big and generous gift to Big Science. Taking place a couple of years before the end of his second term, it was a grand gesture by a man of substance, a man who respected physics, believed in the intrinsic value of basic research, and acted forcefully on science's behalf at just the right moment in history.

Once the initiative took place and the money for the enterprise materialized and became available to use, the DOE gave the go-ahead and all the systems' monitors were placed on dead ahead. Big Science had gotten what it so wanted. Then, with the community given the green light, it only remained for the machine to be built and to be made a reality. Although these words fall so easily from the lips, it turned out to be far more difficult than most thought, and became a major test of science's mettle. You see carrying it off, treading into dangerous new territory, was far from a piece of cake. Making a request to do something is one thing, doing it is quite another. Big Physics was to learn from bitter experience the lesson many before it had also come to acquire: Don't wish for something too hard, for you might get it. In hindsight, it is clear that this mighty project, the Superconducting Super Collider (SSC), was a case where the responsibility for it should have instilled more fear in its coterie of leaders than it did. Unfortunately, *fools rush in where angels fear to tread* – and in the Big Physics community, there were more than enough such fools on hand. They imagined that there was more to them than there actually was; they thought that they could do better than they could; and in the end they paid the price that the impudent who have the effrontery to presume infallibility must always pay.

The SSC attracted a multifarious throng, all of them full of excitement, with appetites whetted to cash in on the action. The participation was an amalgam of types from all walks of life. They couldn't get to Texas fast enough. The word was out and the SSC was in. So they came: the scientists, engineers, bureaucrats, industrialists, and a multitude of ordinary folk, all seeking some kind of connection with greatness. When they arrived in the small town of Waxahachie, just south of Dallas, they were brimming with confidence, sure of a bright future ahead of them. They coveted the highest rank they could reach, but accepted whatever they could get. They just wanted to be in on it. Then, with both spirits and optimism in high gear, the project began its forward thrust. It all seemed so right. It was going so well, with everything on track. In no time, the SSC train began to pick up speed and soon, all were convinced, it would be unstoppable. But there was a not easily visible hitch. You see no matter how much momentum the project had it was still vulnerable. It had a product to deliver and a promise to fulfill. If it didn't come through, then kaput it would be. To avoid that, then one thing was absolutely essential – effective leadership. Without it, the project would just weave in and out, back and forth, and get nowhere. So it was a no-brainer that a true leader was simply one thing it couldn't do without. Yet, when the leaders were chosen, not a single *Bob Wilson* was among them. The ones available and the ones selected were weak men, and life in the bigness lane demanded far more than they were able to handle. They found themselves on a train that, once started, kept moving faster and faster, but lacked direction and a coherent station to aim at. The conductor, who was at the wheel at the start, seemed to have mysteriously vanished. Yes, the hapless men of science in Texas were in some kind of frantic, chaotic motion, using up a lot of energy, but getting nowhere. So on it went and, sad to say, the grand design of Big Science began more and more to resemble its predecessor, the project it was meant to replace, the ill-fated ISABELLE.

* * * * *

Nick was not a generous man, Mickey thought one day. Mickey had a habit of going off alone to consider his life at a distance from the glare and the hustle-and-bustle of living it. Being in one of his quiet moods, wondering about the big and famous director-man, Mickey smiled a sardonic smile mixed with a kind of sadness as he recalled how Nick was more the opposite of generous: how he would gloat when others stepped out of line or misspoke; how he would chuckle gleefully when they succumbed to his strong will or severe reproaching, always replete with expletives; and how he would exult when his words openly and loudly beat them to a pulp and they had to scamper to a safe haven out of his reach. Mickey would often ponder over these observations, and then during one of these reminiscing interludes, in a moment of insight, he hit upon the bewildering yet inescapable notion that Nick derived some secret pleasure out of hurting others.

Some refer to such ways of looking at things as *psychobabble*, but Mickey couldn't resist indulging himself. Without such an analysis, he had nothing, while with it his revelation opened the door to a possible explanation of Nick's behavior toward him. Whatever Mickey had done to elicit Nick's disfavor, he could make no sense out of the extent of his persistent attacks and of the venom that oozed from them. Nick would willfully and unremittingly seek Mickey out, seemingly for the sole purpose of inflicting pain. Plainly, there was no denying that the punishment didn't fit the crime – if indeed there was one at all. Why, Mickey questioned in disbelief, would Nick take the time to do this to someone so unsophisticated and naïve; someone so out of his league in the ways of the real world; and someone so much lower on the totem pole? To find an answer – any answer – what else could Mickey do but turn to the area of irrational psychology? Somehow in his perverted way of looking at things, Nick at times was driven to cause others to suffer, acting so in the manner of an obsession. It may seem strange to some, but that's the way life is. There are people who are just made that way.

Some people would just have let it go at that. But Mickey wasn't such a type. He kept digging, searching his mind for clues and a more satisfying solution. Although he may have just been frittering away his time, there turn out to be, as one might have expected, various other levels of understanding to the tales of Nick and Mickey. As it happened, while Mickey trod the many routes he chose to take, he came across one that allowed him to further develop and stretch his view of the matter, one that was grounded in the more putative, less suspicion-inducing cause-effect connection. It wasn't so much that he found this new way of looking at his *Nick problem*, it was more that *it* found *him*. There was this perplexing dilemma that kept gnawing at him and just wouldn't go away: Why was Nick's behavior so personally motivated? Why did Nick choose Mickey in particular to be an object of such hostility and animosity? Finally, why did there seem to be no end to the persecution Mickey had to endure? These questions were always with him, mostly hidden in one or more of his mind's recesses, but every now and then entering his awareness. Then, suddenly, at some seemingly random instant, not during one of his planned meditative periods, an answer leaped into his consciousness: maybe Nick imagined that Mickey had double-crossed him somewhere up the line and became determined to make him pay for it. Yes, Mickey adjudged, as a picture took shape in his mind, Nick must have concocted some scenario with Mickey playing the villain of the piece. Sure, it must be a grudge – a sin of the past. How could this not be the right answer? It had to be. It fit the facts so perfectly.

There was a certain satisfaction in having laid his finger on a possible rational source of Nick's unseemly treatment of him. Simply said, they were acts of vengeance. But knowing that didn't help Mickey much. It didn't tell him what in particular he'd done; and even if he came to figure it out, it wouldn't tell him what he could do about it. Furthermore, it certainly didn't make it easier for him to cope with the memories of those experiences from out of his past, while he was at Nick's tender mercies. He recalled how, when he had to contend with particular penalties meted out to him or with vicious verbal assaults, he became petrified and speechless, completely unable to defend himself. Even while alone with his own thoughts, with no one to gaze at him naked and exposed, still he was filled with embarrassment at the manner in which he'd reacted. Yet, even if he'd had the capacity to de-ice and so unfreeze himself when such undeserved and unfair reprisals took place, what could he have done about such irrational acts of aggression by one no less than his boss? Well, whether or not he would've been prouder had he stood taller against the bully is neither here nor there. What's past is past. At least he'd come to understand a lot more of his dealings with Nick.

Although Mickey had apparently fixed on the outline of what was wrong between him and Nick, his thoughts would continue to linger on this subject that had become so tantalizing to him and so teasing. The truth was that he didn't even know the man. Before Nick began his threatening and nasty acts of retaliation against him, they'd only had a rather small number of face-to-face conversations and these were cordial enough. Other than that, they'd seen each other only formally, at meetings and such. So, despite the fact that the abstract reasoning Mickey stumbled on did provide an explanation for Nick's behavior, nevertheless he didn't have a clue as to the specifics. He certainly hadn't figured out what he'd done to provoke Nick to go to such lengths of vindictiveness. It was a mystery that ate away at him. What could it have been that he did? What could Mickey be missing that could have caused such harsh and continuing conduct from Nick? His behavior was so unnatural that it deserved more palpable causation. But, absent any clear-cut self-interest or other reasonable motivation to make sense of Nick's hostility, Mickey was at a loss.

In time, however, Mickey's tenacious urge to know, his doggedness, and his unwillingness to quit did in the end pay off. Thus, as more and more facts and inferences accumulated, it came to pass that he gained more of a handle on his vexing and discordant relationship with his boss-on-high. With constant pushing and pulling at the problem, taking it apart and putting it back together again, grabbing at it from all sides, and leaving no stone unturned, finally lady luck took him by the hand and showed him the way. An answer he so wanted – one that bore both logic and hard facts – was finally in front of him. Oddly, it had actually been staring him in the face all along. The story he was able to put together was one of men trying their best to do good, but unable to avoid acts of conflict and betrayal; and, as with most such stories, it didn't have a happy ending. Still, Mickey felt good seeing the truth; and as if that weren't enough satisfaction, there was in fact an extra dividend to his stressful mission to understand the nature of a man who so despised him. In his pursuit, he learned much about his nemesis. Yet, despite his newly found appreciation of this inscrutable man, Nick – the ill-natured man, the malicious man, the brilliant man of science, and the family man – always remained a puzzling figure to him.

* * * * *

As a representative of the DOE, where he was serving for a two or three year stint as a detailee from BNL, Mickey came to Snowmass 1982 to examine America's accelerator plans for Big Physics and to evaluate the competition from CERN. Working for Wallenmeyer, head of the Division of High Energy Physics, Mickey was given the particular tasks of assessing any new accelerator proposals that came up, analyzing how they would fit into the DOE's program and budget, and judging how they would stack up in the international arena. That's quite a mouthful for a simple scientist from Long Island; and Mickey was highly satisfied with these plans laid out for him. Actually, he'd been looking forward to his Colorado trip for some time, and he wasn't about to allow any disappointment to creep in. As it turned out, he was to have the time of his life. But things don't always take place exactly the way you expect them to, and for reasons totally unrelated to his assigned duties, this meeting was to be one that would have a profound impact on Mickey's life. It would be an experience that would linger in his memory for a long time to come.

When Mickey chose to spend a few years in Washington, it was mainly because of his intense frustration with BNL's management of the ISABELLE project. Although he was running away from a situation he disliked and couldn't abide rather than reaching for a sought-after desire – not the most auspicious of reasons to act – chance was good to him this time, and he never regretted the move. He got to travel, meet many people, some highly influential, and at times, keeping his ears tuned, he got to know many secrets not meant for dissemination. That's the good side of life in the fast lane. However, political life for the average worker is far from fun and games. On the whole, it's a lot of bureaucratic drudgery; and to top it off, there's the daily intrigue and conflict with the people at your side, who always seem to want to push you to the ground and walk over you. That's presumably how people get ahead in the big town. However, in spite of this unwholesome, down-and-dirty, and potentially harmful side of things, Mickey gained a hell of a lot from the experience. He learned a great deal about the ways of the real world; and having Wallenmeyer to work for was a piece of good fortune almost too good to be true. In fact, interacting with him was a unique education all by itself.

Wallenmeyer was a one-of-a-kind character, combining acute observational skills, extraordinary political acumen, and a gigantic ego. His physical bigness was matched only by his enormous conceit. When important scientific gatherings such as the one at Snowmass were being held, his technique was to send a lot of his people, listen to what they all had to say, read their reports, and then, for the most part, end up doing what he had set out to do in the first place. This wasn't unreasonable, for Bill was way smarter than any of the mostly mediocre people on his staff. Thus, it was no surprise that more often than not Wallenmeyer wouldn't take seriously or use Mickey's recommendations that he had worked on so assiduously and taken so many hours to prepare. For an ambitious and aggressive young man, this was frustrating to the nth degree. After all that he would put into it, and yet constantly seeing his efforts coming to naught, sometimes he would wonder whether he was cut out for such a role. Fortunately, however, these feelings of self-pity and self-doubt would quickly pass as his natural self-confidence re-established control.

When all was said and done, being in the thick of political gamesmanship at this time in the life of Big Science was a really lucky opportunity for Mickey. You see it was just then that physics reached a crucial fork in the road. To be big or not to be, that was the question of the eighties. To be more precise, the question was whether to embark fearlessly on the bigness road where glory lay, even while knowing that it was a road fraught with danger, or to back off to familiar territory and accept the middling, the second-rate, and perhaps the passable status quo. It's better than nothing, you could just hear the weak-kneed scaredy-cats saying. Yes, it's true that all manner of opinion was represented at Snowmass that year, but one thing was sure: everyone knew that much was at stake; perhaps, although no one would dream of uttering it, even the whole ball of wax was at risk. What a favorable break for Mickey to be smack in the middle of things just when this issue of such gravity and importance to science's future was to be settled. So the spinning wheel of fortune apparently stopped precisely where it suited Mickey best: His Washington tour of duty that he'd arranged for himself afforded him the chance to get a grip on the political angle; physics was on the threshold of true bigness; and the result was that politics and physics became more than ever inextricably intertwined. Quel luck! Colliders were a big deal; politics was a big deal; and Mickey was on top of both.

You might think that Mickey's attraction to politics arose out of his disappointments as a scientist. Consider the many rebuffs he received at the hands of the ISABELLE management, who out-rightly refused to heed his advice, and arrogantly never gave his expert opinions fair hearings. Mickey knew he was on the right track, but these know-it-alls wouldn't give him the time of day. With backing from all the *yes-men* they'd accumulated around them, they sloughed Mickey off as if he were a gnat. There was no getting to them. They'd become deaf to reason and soundness. Although Mickey was a truly obstinate fellow, even he had his limits of endurance. So, in the end, he admitted defeat, succumbed to the know-nothings, and left the BNL battleground. For him, retreat seemed the only option open. But, just as he was on the verge of buckling under the iron-fisted and black-booted bad guys, he opportunely remembered the possibility of temporarily working in Washington. Thus, as luck would have it, he had a place to go, a place that represented a chance for a new beginning and a better life. How fortuitous for him was this overlap of present hopelessness and future hope!

If you're looking for a rational reason for Mickey making this change of scene, then taking his background as a starting point, would it be much of a surprise if he wanted to get in on the power game as a means of setting things right at BNL and perhaps settling old scores? For sure, there was that component to the course he decided to follow. However, on the whole, learning about the political perspective wasn't just a means to an end for Mickey. No, it wasn't only as a result of his discontent, and the bitterness he felt over his treatment, or even because of the laudable aim of wanting to help the physics enterprise he so loved. Rather, he was drawn closer to politics and management because he'd developed a voracious appetite to learn more about them. You see he was by nature a knowledge sponge and these areas of study attracted him more and more as his experience with them grew. Actually, it didn't take much IQ to ascertain that these were what were valued most at the labs. Although in private scientists disdained what they considered to be lowbrow functions, outwardly the picture was an entirely different one. Scientists knew who buttered their bread and acted accordingly. They needed the top managers and politicians, sought them out, bowed to their wishes and whims, and, perhaps unwillingly, paid them the necessary respect. Mickey behaved much the same way, but there was an important difference: being an accelerator scientist, Mickey saw Big Science from below, and the respect he paid came to be true. He came to see that it was respect deserved, just as all power deserves respect. Along with this notable shift in attitude, Mickey developed a keen interest in management and politics. So, when he left for the power capital of the world, it wasn't that he was being forced out – as it appeared. The truth was that he really wanted to go.

Although the troubles he was confronted with at the lab undoubtedly triggered his walking out, more likely he took such a drastic and hardnosed step because he developed a sense that this business of management and politics was real hot stuff. He had had his time in the wonderfully mad world of high-energy physics; and now it was time to move on, and what better way than to become involved with this fascinating new line of work. So, management and politics were to find their way into Mickey's life. What a change it was! These branches of learning resided not in the rational, experimentally testable, predictable, law-abiding realm; but rather dealt with people and their behavior, with society and the way it worked, and with the philosophy of living in this ever-surprising, wacky, and irrational world of ours. Dealing with such subject matter, these fields of study had the most interesting character of being open-ended. They weren't at all like science, where the idea is to enclose the system under study (one that is natural, physical, and essentially inanimate) so that you have a chance at fully understanding it, without having unknown factors sneaking in from outside the boundaries to mess up your analysis. On the contrary, in management and politics, you're stuck with those unforeseen bedeviling factors entering the scene from out of nowhere, thus forcing you continually to change your perception if you are to grasp some truth. But this didn't bother Mickey – not a bit. Actually, he perversely loved the fact that, when it came to dealing with people, he could never figure out the whole story, and that there always seemed to be a little more turning up just around the next bend. It was a game to him, and he got a kick out of it. You see at this time of Mickey's life, the notion of uncertainty, of unexpectedness, of guessing which way to turn, of choosing an action, and of seeing how it turned out exerted a strong pull on him. He didn't for a moment doubt that he could play such a sport. In fact, he cavalierly presumed that it was right up his alley. This casual assessment was far from being on target, but he was still on the young side and really didn't think much about the decision he made. He just did it. Thus, full of confidence, he walked right out of a world he knew well and cared a great deal about, and entered a new one he knew precious little of.

Mickey was an eager student. He was a ravenous and insatiable learner, absorbing whatever information he could lay his hands on. Going back to his youth, he developed and always retained the belief that to know was a primal human activity, and his experiences in science strongly vindicated and reinforced that point of view. For him, learning about life in both its physical and metaphysical manifestations was as natural as breathing. But to do so effectively he needed a certain peace of mind, a non-obstructive atmosphere, and most of all the time to think things through. That's the way it was at the university where he'd spent a great many of his formative years. Soon, however, he found that the formal academic-type manner of gathering knowledge he was used to simply wasn't applicable in the real world. Yes, he could read through the political science and management literature – and Mickey didn't scrimp on that score – but before long it became apparent to him that to educate himself in the political sphere, away from the safe harbor of the university, required a lot more than that. In that arena, the right instinctive responses and the quickness of reaction were the keys to making it. However, because these capabilities didn't come naturally to Mickey, it wasn't easy for him to get the point. When he finally did, he knew he had a hard road ahead of him. There are actually many who think that you can't learn these characteristics – you either have it or you don't, they say. But Mickey, always the optimist, wasn't willing to accept such a glib, simplistic, and self-serving aphorism. It's true, he wasn't that good at acting instinctively or swiftly. On the other hand, he was good on his feet – very good at talking the talk; so maybe what he did possess would mitigate the deficiencies he unfortunately had. Thus, with his stubbornness and persistence egging him on, he pushed ahead, determined to make good on the political-management field of combat.

Once he entered the fray, he uncovered a lot of things in himself that could carry him on the road to success. He found things he didn't know were there: he could take risks; he could accept challenges; he could investigate delicate and touchy matters; he could engage in double-talk; he could keep his mouth shut when it was called for; and he could even lie if he had to. Seeing all this, he was able to convince himself that for him to be transformed into a political type not only was possible, but if he persevered, would actually come to be. To reach that end, he concluded, if he really wanted to play the political game, he'd have to develop and cultivate the means to search things out: Don't easily trust what you hear; find things out for yourself and look at them straight on; be bold and tread the treacherous waters where sharks are all about; and, most importantly, always wear a mask, whether it's a true one or not, that has success written all over it. Looked at in this way, the political life doesn't seem at all a savory one. But Mickey was excited by it and enthusiastic about getting right into the thick of things. It was what he wanted, what he sought after, what he was willing to fight for, and in the end he gave it a good try.

Although Mickey had quite a lot of experience with the political playing field before he got to Colorado, Snowmass '82 turned out to be like a minefield filled with deadly traps. There were moments when it came to Mickey's mind that he should perhaps exercise some care. After all, there were a lot of big boys there, men much smarter in the ways of the world than he was. Nevertheless, with abandon and no little arrogance, Mickey was not to be dissuaded from throwing caution to the wind and pushing straight on. And he didn't look back. But like all who are filled with overconfidence, he made a mistake. So assured was he of his ability to ride the political wave that he forgot one of the cardinal rules: Beware of disguised Pandora's boxes, for in the end they will entrap you – so, if you sense one present, stay clear! Unfortunately, Mickey wasn't careful enough at Snowmass, and when one of these boxes appeared before him, he failed to recognize it, and, without thinking, opened it. So, in that full-of-consequence summer in the gorgeous mountains of Colorado, there was no stopping Mickey from biting on some tempting bait, falling into a troublesome trap, and finally having to bear the penalties that risking too much brings with it.

* * * * *

Even with its wild manic-depressive-like swings of ups-and-downs, Mickey loved everything about the Snowmass experience. Topping his list were the endless dialogues: He derived such pleasure in articulating a point, arguing for it, defending it against opposition, and persuading others to buy it. Then there were the special moments when in the midst of dueling, there would come a sudden insight. How thrilling were the acts of expressing it, listening to the responses, and coming up with just the right retorts! Then, when quiet was on the verge of falling on the company, a new issue would spontaneously arise, starting the whole process again. Many people attending found such interplay of language and ideas disorienting and even upsetting. Most of these chose not to participate and ran from the wrangling contest of wits. But not Mickey! He thrived in such action. The more demanding it was, the more he sought it out. He thrived on this most stressful of games and was always exhilarated when engaging in it. Addicted to intellectual battling, he always came back for more. He never failed to get a kick out of the interchanges of words and ideas, and the repartee that would inevitably follow. How appealing all this was to Mickey! How proud it made him to be a scientist!

If truth be told, Mickey didn't come to the mountains of Snowmass only to do his job for Wallenmeyer. You might even say he had an ulterior motive, for under the surface lay a different agenda. Really driving him was the opportunity to take yet another shot at getting the lady ISABELLE to be switched from her present sorry beam configuration to the bunched variety. Buoyed by the failing ISABELLE magnets – feeling all along that the outcome couldn't be otherwise – and by CERN's thrusts forward on the p-pbar collider front, Mickey couldn't resist such a gaping opening. He had to try for perhaps the last time to make the seemingly impossible happen. Having such an important, such a difficult, such an honest, and such an inspiring mission seemed ample justification to take the gloves off. Anything goes! Mickey concluded – including intellectual trickery, ranging from seemingly logical argument to dastardly sophistry, from kindly persuasiveness to insistent browbeating, and from insistent repetition and restatement to the twisting of words and phrases – if that would prove advantageous to his argument. So there was Mickey prepared to open his yap to anyone. But that clearly wasn't enough. What he needed was a forum to compete in and an audience that would take him seriously. Even more, he needed the good fortune to come upon the right person with sufficient power and influence to help him pull off the coup he was hoping for. One thing for sure, he couldn't do it alone. Thus, luck to find a man who could take the required action along with the appropriate persuasiveness on his part represented the dual keys that might do the trick. It was an unlikely scenario, but what else was there to do?

As it turned out, during that stirring and stimulating summer he was surprised and very pleased to find so many of his colleagues willing and even eager to enter the fray and give active and vigorous point-counterpoint combat. Surely among the throng there was that transcendent figure who, if Mickey played his cards right, could give him the improbable victory he so yearned for. Throughout the debates, the bull sessions, and the discourse that ensued there flowed that unique kind of feverish excitement that comes when someone has a definitive, pregnant, and gaining-in-strength cause to sell. Equipped with such a cause sure to pierce even the thick-skinned or the more taciturn among his friends and associates, Mickey got plenty of action. He'd done his homework, was well prepared for action, was in fine form for arguing, and so, on the face of it, was very hard to outdo. Standing by a conviction leading to a desired end that you know is right is indeed a powerful elixir. So Mickey unrealistically thought he'd have a relatively easy time of it. But it didn't quite go that way. He didn't have to look far to find, among the talkative, assertive, and self-assured scientists there, those who, verbal sabers in hand, were only too happy to take up his ISABELLE challenge and give him a run for his money. Thus, when the grand meeting came to a close, Mickey hadn't the least idea of what effect, if any, he'd had.

* * * * *

The sky was cloudless as the hot, glaring sun relentlessly beat down on the central square. It was high noon on a glorious day at Snowmass. The crowds spilled out of the conference center, filling the square with hungry scientists released from the sedentary restraint of listening all morning to what felt like an eternal stream of lectures. Exhausted from the perhaps too intense and over-stimulating wall-to-wall talks, their main concern appeared to be: "What do you feel like for lunch?" The little village was well prepared for this, tempting its guests by surrounding them with a host of beckoning restaurants, where all manner of craving could be readily satisfied. However, although an impressive variety of mouth-watering types of food were easily available, this business of lunch was in fact only a euphemistic way of expressing the unspoken but far more pressing question of whom the attendees would have the chance to sit with.

In addition to knowledge transfer through the presentation of theories, ideas, and experimental results, everyone knows that one of the primary purposes of conferences of all sorts is for meeting people. However, not only does the art of mixing help in building long-term contacts, it also has a highly valuable short-term impact if you develop the knack of congregating with the right sorts. The point is that the people you're seen with plays an important part in shaping your image; and, of course, if you become adept at sitting with one of the stars, you gain an extra dividend in that it does wonders for your self-esteem. There's no getting around the fact that being associated with the authoritativeness of men of influence does rub off on you.

Although there's a lot to be said for image building, lunch in such a resort-like setting provides a multitude of opportunities having a great deal more practical value. It is actually reminiscent of the power lunch, that invaluable mainstay of the corporate world, where you can say a wealth of things you wouldn't dream of saying during business hours. In a relaxed atmosphere, for the most part relieved of any time pressure and with access to anybody that's anybody from around the globe, what's to stop you? So, if you're lucky enough to find yourself alone with a man you're just dying to talk to, then, tête-à-tête, you'll be encouraged, even feel induced to let yourself go and let it all hang out. Don't let such a break pass you by! At such a moment, you're exactly where you want to be. You can talk things out with the aim of setting right a misunderstanding; you can own up and explain a mistake you've made; you can change your mind about a commitment you've made; or you can make a proposition for a new direction to take or for an entirely new enterprise. You can make a deal; you can make an offer to hire someone; you can quit your job; or you can be seeking out a new one. You can pass on your private thoughts and impressions; or you can convey personal information about yourself or others. If you happen to be the ruthless type, you can drop little bombshells – true or untrue – in a manner either subtle or blatant. There's simply no end to the business that can be transacted. Whether you're there to help or to hinder; whether to be honest or to lie; or whether to give someone the right scent so as to put him on target or a false one to push him off course; whichever it is you've come to do, this is the ideal environment to give it a shot. It is a time for wheeling and dealing, a time to clear the air, a time to muddy the waters, a time to make friends, and a time to lose them. But whatever it is you're seeking, remember that such an opportunity as you have on hand – perhaps the chance of a lifetime – may not knock a second time. There may be consequences to endure, even hell to pay, but that's life. Risk is what it's all about. So keep in mind, if you let this one slip through your fingers, you may well come to regret it.

As powerful a means as it is, the lunch game isn't the only way of reaching into the big time. If you already know whom you want to contact; or if you know what information you need; or if you know what you want to transmit, then a lunch really isn't necessary. You could just make contacts privately and independently, one on one, and at any time. Anybody who's important enough to be sought after is surely there; all you have to do is hit upon the means of running into your very own Mister Right. The hitch is that you have to grab his attention, make him care about what you have to say, persuade him that you're worthy of his time and effort, and find a way to finagle your way into his trust. That's no straightforward task! But if you can discover the magic way to get to him, whether it's through your planning or through serendipity smiling on you hardly matters.

There's quite a different route that complete unknowns desperate to rise have to wend their way through. If you're merely a little fellow knocking at heaven's gate, you have to take the indirect approach. This is a tricky business because you have to find a source willing to tell you something valuable and usable; or you have to be lucky enough to find a pigeon that will pass on your message to the appropriate big guy. For this ambitious and aggressive group, the lunch game is delicate, chancy, and full of stress. You have to keep your guard up at all times, and be on your toes should an opportunity unexpectedly turn up. Since you know little to start with, you always face the risk that any information you gain might be misleading or wrong; or that the information you pass on might be misinterpreted, or might get to an unintended ear, where it could be harmful to you. These consequences, important as they are, would best be put out of your mind because over-thinking about them would probably interfere with your scheming. In such a situation, where timing rules the day, as unlikely as it seems, the advice to take to heart is: *buy now, pay later*. You have little or no control over any intermediate steps anyway. So, when all is said and done, seeing that the impact of your actions is bound to occur much later, why worry now? Just take the plunge and keep in mind that sage old maxim, "Everything in its own sweet time."

The biggest practical challenge to a successful lunch break, whether you're a hardy type or an innocent, naïve one, comes right at the beginning when a myriad of people intermingle and flock about. The questions facing you are many: Who's available to join and could prove valuable to you? How long could you afford to wait before making a choice? Would the one chosen be important enough for you to expend all the energy you could muster up? Should you wait a bit longer? If you waited too long, you could end up with the dregs. No doubt, it's tough to come up with the right answers, and then to follow it up with effective, fruit-bearing actions. But once you make the decision to play the game, there's simply no alternative; you have to bear the gut-wrenching burden. If you're not the quick-to-jump, go-for-it-all type of person, you always have the option of taking the safe path by choosing a lunch group before taking your chances on the square, but this tends not to be too productive; more often than not you end up in a group not yearning for the power game – with a bunch of duds, to be blunt about it. So if you want intrigue and excitement and perhaps some juicy bits of information, your best bet is to take your chances alone on the square.

Independent of where you were coming from and what your motives were, the Snowmass Square at noon was the place to be. It was packed with all types. Actually, the majority of the scientific throng that gathered at the lunch break wasn't playing the private information – or misinformation – game in earnest. They were merely going through the motions, spurred on by the gossipy tendency to want to know what's going on and then to pass it on, either as a fun thing or perhaps maliciously. As a general rule, if you want to get something out of lunch, other than food, then best stay as far away from them as possible. On the other hand, although not that many in comparison to the kibitzers, there were politically minded scientific elite as well as true politicos among the mass of people milling about. They were well known, exuded mucho power, and could be diagnosed a mile off. Thus, if you were aspiring to that class and seeking to enter the inner circle and become one of the card-holding members, then these – the players of consequence, the heavyweights – were the ones to be with. Thus, if you happened to be one of the unfulfilled, searching for a way in but not having an inside track to those pulling the strings, then the lunch game was right for you. But there's a catch to the game. Just dreaming about getting to the top is a non-starter. The men holding sway wouldn't waste their time with fools. They wanted something palpable, something that would give them the edge, and something that would give them a winning hand. So, if you had an A1 idea to promote, or if you were in the market to buy or sell something of unmistakably first-rate value, by playing your cards right, you might be able to profit handsomely by clever maneuvering in the lunchtime marketplace. But there's no free lunch. Yes, the jewels are there to be had. But there are always the snakes guarding them that must first be overcome. Therein lies the quandary. The path of opportunity is lined with those who forgot this pitfall. However, Mickey was not to be deterred. Still somewhat young, deadly earnest, and eager to make his mark, he came to Snowmass to seek the jewels and fight the snakes to get them.

* * * * *

At noon on that fateful day, with the fiery sun blazing, Mickey strode into the square. With his back straight, his head held high with chin up, and looking straight ahead, he stepped briskly along, trying to look as if he knew where he was going and exactly who he was looking for. Before long, however, his pace slackened and then slowed to a crawl, as his search for a desirable party was going nowhere. After some aimless wandering for what seemed to be an eternity, the crowd began to dwindle. Soon there were only a few lost souls left in the square without lunch partners. A mild desperation began to set in and he was about to give up and attach himself to one of these. Then, even as his lunch design for that day appeared to be a bust – bingo! – a potential jackpot appeared. Out of the corner of his left eye he glimpsed three colleagues sitting at a table for four in the shade of a large umbrella – highly influential experimentalists who'd do very well as lunch partners. In fact, they were all high on Mickey's scale of men he wanted a crack at. What a pleasure it was going to be to bend their ears, he thought. As luck would have it, there was that inviting and empty fourth chair just begging to be filled. Of course, they could have been waiting for someone, but he dropped this possibility like a hot potato. Any dilly-dallying at such a moment of decision would be a crime! So, without the least hesitation, as if that's where he'd been heading all the time, Mickey, with a wide grin on his face, walked confidently and firmly up to the table and planted himself in the empty seat. Without knowing it – for how could he? – that lunch was to be one he would not soon be able to forget.

Smiles and warm greetings were traded, and Mickey sat at the square table on the side closest to the edge of the terrace where it was perched. Always keeping an eye out for what was going on, he could, with a slight left turn of his face, see the passersby and whom they were with. But at this lunch, he found no need to look at the outside action – no, he had quite enough on his plate right before him. On his right sat Aihud Pevsner, opposite him, Charlie Baltay, and to his left, Won-Yong Lee. Aihud was a professor at Johns Hopkins; Charlie and Won-Yong were from Columbia. The three, both professionally and personally, were closely allied to BNL and its newly installed Director, Nick Samios. As gifted experimenters in the physics of elementary particle collisions for many years and as distinguished members of the group of university users, they'd built strong and lasting relationships with all the important community leaders – and that carried with it a great deal of weight at the lab. Being card-carrying physichists, they knew their way around: they knew everybody worth knowing; they knew how to get what they wanted; and they knew how to get things done. They were comfortable in their highly respected roles, for which they owed much to BNL. As a quid pro quo, they'd seen fit to give unswerving loyalty to the lab.

However, changing times have a habit of changing relationships, both among people and between people and institutions. When the lab was in its prime, the unquestioned loyalty of its experimenters came quite naturally, but when decline and uncertainty entered the picture, due primarily to the tottering ISABELLE, strains began to develop even among the most ardent and valued of the lab's users. Thus, as the eighties commenced, the lab could no longer count on their guaranteed fidelity. But at the time of Snowmass '82, since Mickey hadn't yet resolved his somewhat bull-headedness, such thoughts never entered his mind; and so trying to fashion what he said during lunch on that brilliant day didn't receive even a modicum of consideration. But that was a big mistake. He should have taken a lot more account of the reality of altered circumstances and their consequent shifting attitudes. He should have been far more careful as the most pleasant of lunches got under way.

The lunch was great, with the food being cool and the talk hot. Between bites of juicy fruit and sips of iced tea, the *guerre de mots* went on for close to two hours. First a point was thrown out; then a response quickly prompted a counterpoint, which was then followed by another point; and on it went, back and forth, forth and back. It was a time to savor as intellect and emotion, naturally in opposition to each other, made periodic brief encounters – surprisingly discussion-enhancing – before returning to their respective, separate domains. Mickey was in exceptional form as he slowly and deliberately shaped his arguments. At the heart of the discussion – the luncheon question de jour – was the question on everyone's mind that year: "Can ISABELLE be saved?" Since the four of them were scientists to their very cores, they were more tuned to the unwavering logic of the physical world than to the unruliness and unpredictability of the realm of socio-political man. Thus, they interpreted the question as one dealing with engineering and physics. With that presumption, the answer was as simple as the question. The result was that, in their political naïveté, they far too easily agreed that of course ISABELLE could be saved. Such was their ivory-tower existence that none of them could imagine that real life might have very different plans for the sad lady of Long Island.

And why should they have had any dark thoughts? In 1982, ISABELLE was still alive, and where there's life, there's hope. On top of that rational and quite correct statement of fact, here were four scientists on a three-week sojourn to paradise, four optimistic men enjoying the warm sun, the good food, the safe atmosphere, and the luxury of only having to talk the talk. Life was good to them and they couldn't imagine it otherwise. Logic would argue that the conversation about ISABELLE should have ended on that positive note of confidence that the project would indeed succeed. But something odd happened on that beautiful summer day. They gave up the small talk, and chose instead to explore the intricate and tricky details of the ISABELLE dilemma. Why? You might wonder. Actually it's hard to say. Perhaps it was simply because they were in a devil-may-care mood where anything goes. More likely, however, it was because one or another of them felt subconsciously that they were being a tad overconfident. But whatever the true reason, the fact of the matter is that the discussion turned to a much more interesting and serious question, and a far more difficult one to boot. The shift happened when Mickey, chomping on a large piece of pineapple, without thinking and with a dumb-looking smile on his face, interjected: "Yes it could be saved, but how?"

This was Mickey's baby, the other three felt, as they sat back oozing with self-satisfaction. They believed that Mickey had really posed a non-question – it being their presumption that *Nick's on top of things, he'll take care of it.* So Mickey, who'd brought up the issue in the first place, had to convince the others that a problem was there at all before getting to the delicate and sensitive political question of how to solve it. Since the two issues were inextricably intertwined, Mickey craftily sidestepped the first one and went directly to the *how* question. "Have patience," he told his audience of three, "I'm sure you'll see the problem after you've listened to my proposed solutions." Mickey started out by laying the groundwork for his case. He set down the two conditions that had to be adhered to in any solution. It felt good taking the lead in opposition to these three cocksure – more like gullible – academics waiting on his every word. He was also in great spirits and took special pleasure in showing off the political knowledge he'd picked up in his three years in Washington's DOE office. First, he pointed out, the project had to be completed quickly, probably in record time, and in any case much less than two years. Since CERN had not yet announced any firm evidence that the W had been found, BNL, representing America, was still a possible competitor to be the first to see that elusive particle. Second, any plan had to be low in cost so as to allow the project to be completed with the construction funds already set aside by the DOE. This would avoid the risky step of having to go back to Congress for approval of the significant cost overrun that was projected at the infamous Temple Review a year earlier. So far, it sounded to all of them simple and straightforward enough, nothing to argue about yet. Thus, with only minimal fuss, the table quickly and unanimously bought into these conditions. Mickey paused and looked around. Yes – he could see it in their faces – he'd gotten by the first hurdle without their even suspecting it. They didn't quite get it yet, but in fact they'd accepted the fact that there truly was a problem.

Mickey, being a scientist, trusted the premise that once the conditions for a solution were clear and distinct, the solution itself couldn't be far behind. He counted on the fact that the others felt the same way, and he was quite right on that score. When it came to BNL's collider problem, this rule turned out to apply perfectly. Thus, the communication fog at the table lifted and Mickey now had both the go-ahead and the means to express how BNL might be able to save ISABELLE by taking the path leading to his favored solution, probably the only realistic and practical one. But first he thought it necessary to prepare the other three for a bit of a shock. So he chose to show them the light indirectly in two steps - first he would sketch his general point that the magnets as currently planned didn't satisfy the agreed-upon conditions, and only then would he deal with the more troublesome and perhaps difficult-to-take specific solution he was thinking of. Here's the way Mickey argued his case: The incontrovertible need was for low-cost magnets built and installed within two years. Herein lay a dilemma for the lab because the Palmer magnets that Nick was proposing for the renewed ISABELLE could not possibly satisfy the conditions that the lunch foursome had agreed upon. They had much too high a price tag and producing them didn't have a chance in hell of being done in time. Thus, the cat was out of the bag. Mickey had asserted that BNL was on the wrong track, that Nick's judgment was flawed. It was then that a gnawing suspicion began to take shape in the minds of the happy-go-lucky *lunchers* that with the two conditions lumped together – short time and low cost – a probably insurmountable obstacle was bumped into. It did seem inconceivable that Nick could have missed this rather obvious point; however, the logic leading to that conclusion was incontestable. The group appeared stumped. What now? They must have thought. But, being sensible people, they easily found the right thing to do. They wisely chose to drop the issue temporarily, giving the newly introduced critique now facing them a chance to sink in and their minds the opportunity to roll it over and get used to it. An agreeable silence fell upon them, and the four of them sat for a minute or so enjoying the warmth of the noonday sun. During that respite, they pondered a bit the complex issue they had entered into and wondered if and how they should continue exchanging their diametrically opposed views.

However, Mickey wasn't the type to just let things go. He'd already made some sort of a mark on the others, but still he ached for a lot more satisfaction. There was unfinished business to attend to, and he wanted to finish it. He believed that if he set his mind to it he could keep the little game that was underway going. That wasn't exactly obvious because there certainly was something to be said for not getting too serious in that breathtaking atmosphere of their mountain retreat. On the other hand, scientists aren't made that way. For them, a problem and a solution went together much like a horse and carriage used to. It would be hard to persuade any of the foursome that there wasn't a rational way out of the hole BNL seemed to be trapped in. This being the case, their response was a foregone conclusion, and Mickey knew exactly what to expect. At the very least, the talkers sitting in the sun would try to come up with a reasonable and workable way for BNL to go. So, without any words to the effect being spoken, the game was put back on course. Mickey, never doubting that the game would be allowed to continue, didn't cease in his preparations and, when the time came, was chomping at the bit, on the verge of making himself felt again. Since Mickey was sure that he'd sufficiently discredited the *leave it to Nick* approach, he believed he could just ignore it. That left only one alternative remaining, and Mickey was now ready to articulate it. Lo and behold, like a magician, he made that practical solution appear. He almost couldn't contain himself as, with an immodest amount of self-congratulation in his tone and without the least bit of doubt, he posed the rhetorical question, "Why not use the magnets already designed at Fermilab?" Mickey paused for a moment. Had he spoken the unspeakable? Was he getting into excessively treacherous waters? Could the pride of BNL's leaders permit them to buy into any idea of a bailout? Worse, could they bear the shame they would almost surely experience if they had to take help from their archenemies? Finally, could Mickey's somewhat rattled colleagues, being so closely attached to Nick and BNL, give his views and assessments a fair shake? No doubt about it, Mickey had put himself in a very tough spot indeed. Despite all the levelheaded, prudent, and in-his-personal-interest reasons for Mickey to pull back, he was simply not to be deterred. He pursued this *combined-lab* line of argument by pointing to the production line already set up at Fermilab for the magnets being used in the new Tevatron ring. By continuing to produce them at the then current rate of ten to twenty per week, the line could supply the couple of hundred needed for the two ISABELLE rings in a few months, six months tops. The table was stunned by this arithmetic and there was a brief period of numbness as everyone tried to absorb its meaning and the surprise of its apparent simplicity.

A shaky quiet filled the air around the table. The three Doubting Thomas types, Charlie, Aihud and Won-Yong, seemed a bit undone by Mickey's disclosure, and became fidgety. They stared at Mickey in disbelief and there unmistakably was mistrust in their eyes. There simply had to be a catch somewhere! There had to be something wrong with Mickey's cunning little stratagem! Mickey looked back at each of the other three in turn as their minds whizzed about at full tilt. He thought a little about them. But when he got to Won-Yong, he couldn't avoid the conclusion that there was something wrong with his reaction. Although Won-Yong appeared to be just as taken aback as the others at the direction the discussion took, there was no earthly reason why he didn't immediately recognize the solution Mickey put on the table. It was an enigma that he didn't forthrightly acknowledge it. You see he and Bob Wilson, who had taken up a professorship at Columbia about a year or so after leaving Fermilab, collaborated on a proposal for an electron-proton (e-p) collider to replace the ailing ISABELLE project. In their proposal, which was distributed to a few people for appraisal more than a year prior to Snowmass, they suggested using the Fermilab magnets for the required proton ring. Mickey, the DOE monitor and advisor for the grant that Columbia had received for this work, simply latched onto Wilson's clever scheme of using Fermilab magnets to build the e-p facility quickly, and shrewdly applied the notion to the two proton rings of the ISABELLE collider. It was as simple as that: without the least trouble, out popped the numbers for the cost and time to complete. They were so low that it caused one's head to whirl and made one want to jump for joy. With every imaginable detail falling perfectly into place, it was almost too easy. Yes, it certainly was a great idea, one that could, almost risk-free, pull BNL out of the mud and into the light. It was a clear-cut way for the lab to place itself squarely back into the mainstream competition for physics laurels and fame. Hoping to find some sign of concurrence, perhaps even a little appreciation from the rest of his tablemates, for devising what could be a viable plan for saving ISABELLE, he was disillusioned to find that he was barking up the wrong tree. No, there wasn't a nod of approval, there wasn't a commendation, and there wasn't even an encouraging word that said, *good work for all you've done.*

Mickey was particularly disappointed with Won-Yong, who should have known better and should've been more honest and forthright. Strangely though, he too seemed reluctant to give any visible support to Mickey's two-lab ploy. Siding with the other two, he acted dumb, as if the scheme was as much a surprise to him as it was to the others. The three of them tried one way after another to pour cold water on what Mickey thought was an inspired design. Instead of rationally discussing it, they put the onus on him to explain his brainchild and to prove its validity and its worth. Thus, the pressure fell more and more on Mickey as the conversation took a turn from being rational to being personal. It's too simple, they insisted. This was followed by rapid-fire questions that came upon Mickey from all angles. The probing was relentless and moved at a fast and furious pace, leaving Mickey with little chance to get a word in edgewise, never mind mounting a defense. On and on went their questions and their almost accusing commentary: With all those accelerator experts staffing the ISABELLE project, why hadn't one of them come forward with this? Why hadn't Palmer come up with it? Why hadn't Nick seen it? It seemed to them improbable that everyone at the lab had missed it. Clearly they were mulling over the whole business. They questioned Mickey's credibility, implying that there was only a low likelihood that he was the only one to see something that on the face of it was so transparent. How could they accept such an absurdity as that? "Mickey, how come you're so smart?" they only half jokingly asked. Mickey got the distinct impression that the three were almost angry with him.

However, mixed with all these doubts, Mickey somehow got the feeling that they wanted him to go on. True, they had a deep-seated aversion to hearing what he was telling them. Thus, they were disinclined to listen to him any further; nonetheless, oddly enough neither did they want him to stop. Something intuitive seemed to tell them that Mickey had more to divulge, things it would do them well to be acquainted with. So, because they wanted to know more and because he'd been the one to whet their appetites, Mickey felt obliged to take on the thorny matters that were implied by the assertions he'd made. The *Can ISABELLE be saved* and the *how* questions having been dealt with, there only remained the issue of *why*. This third and last issue comprised a group of questions that was the most complex of the three. It asked: Why was BNL so intransigent? Why was it willing to risk the life of such a grand dream? Why wouldn't it listen to the advice of so many men of unquestioned wisdom? Why wouldn't it entertain any thought of compromise? Finally, why would it rather let ISABELLE wither away than deal with Fermilab? This was a formidable task Mickey had taken on. The truth was that he was beginning to experience the onset of a tinge of cold feet. He'd have preferred to call it a day rather than tackle the gory details. He wasn't as confident as he had been when he began his *sermon* that he could handle such a tangled and convoluted set of issues demanded by the group of *why* questions. So there in a rare panic-stricken moment, he missed any potential simplicity, but could only visualize a knotty and even intractable confused jumble that lay before him – the twists and turns, the labyrinths he could well find himself trapped in, and the tortuous paths he'd have to maneuver his way through. How could he unravel such a perplexing set of questions he now had to face? However, he'd already committed himself, and there was no turning back. Thus, because he sensed from his three colleagues an earnest and true wish for him to continue and because it wasn't in his nature to give in easily, he felt encouraged to try and so proceeded to deliver an indictment of BNL and its management.

Once Mickey became resigned to the tough task at hand, his mood was swiftly transformed. He took it as a challenge and found picking up the gauntlet irresistible. So his mind began to work double-time. How could he manipulate such a complicated mess, involving inferences, judgments, and betrayals, so as to simplify it into a statement that could be delivered in a few minutes, make sense, and actually throw light on why the BNL brass were behaving as they were? At first it seemed impossible. But before his company of listeners could pick up any hint that he was in hot water, he hit upon a way that he thought just might work: Why not focus on the irrational refusal by two BNL Directors to jump at the chance of getting Fermilab's magnets to complete ISABELLE one-two-three? Yes, that's the ticket! He could manage that and get it done in short order. Of course, with so little time available, most of the psychosocial stuff would have to be omitted, although, Mickey being Mickey, some would surely creep in through innuendo. So he had it, and immediately began to feel better. His self-confidence returned, and he started to prepare himself for the denouement of his get-BNL hour.

Mickey smiled, trying to give the impression that he knew exactly where he was going, while all the while he was just hoping that the little gathering would become a little receptive to his point of view. He commenced with the provocative remark, "It's worse than anything you might imagine." That seemed to catch everybody's attention; and they listened intently as Mickey proceeded. The story Mickey told was about an incident that occurred in 1981, less than a year before Snowmass. Leon had chosen his good friend, Bob Wilson, to be his emissary on a mission to try to lend a helping hand to BNL and thereby to the wobbly American Big Physics enterprise as well. Bob visited Vineyard at BNL and proposed to him the very same idea that the lunch foursome were just discussing, to wit that it would be both suitable and wise to use Fermilab's Tevatron magnets for the ISABELLE collider. Leon had already cleared his side of the road, should Vineyard acquiesce to such a saving-the-day arrangement. He cleared the way with the government crowd, working the halls from Wallenmeyer on up, and ending up with the A-OK sign; and together with his staff waded through the logistical and financial preliminaries for Fermilab to do the job should it be called for. But his efforts were in vain. It's true that Leon's heart wasn't a hundred percent behind this scheme. What Leon and Bob really wanted was an American plan whereby BNL would build an e-p collider using Fermilab magnets and Fermilab would build a p-pbar collider to compete head-on with CERN. However, there seemed little chance of Vineyard and Wallenmeyer going along with this because it would openly put Fermilab back as the number one U.S. proton lab. So Leon gave up on that, and instead he sensibly chose to compromise, leaving BNL on top, with a little help from its midwestern friend. Still, despite Leon's good will, and even though the whole deal was almost entirely for the benefit of BNL and the country – only peripherally for Fermilab – Vineyard saw fit to give Wilson the cold shoulder. It's really hard to imagine these two gentlemen, George and Bob, clawing at each other like two alley cats. Yet it happened. However the outcome left them in radically different shape. Vineyard walked away from the duel with his arrogant head held high, and moved on to his day-to-day functions; on the other hand, poor Bob was left to lick his wounds and had to skulk away from BNL a beaten man.

Outwardly Mickey told the story matter-of-factly and without passion, but inwardly he remembered his disbelief and low feelings when he first heard of the episode. It was in late 1981 at a DOE review dinner at Fermilab at which he and Bob's wife Jane happened to be sitting beside each other. Jane was an up-front, straight-from-the-shoulder person. However, for a brief moment during their conversing, she looked into the distance and with tears in her eyes, emotionally recounted Bob's recent experience at BNL, detailing emphatically the snubbing he'd received at Vineyard's hands. How Bob was hurt by it all! Mickey would never forget the look of profound regret that appeared on Jane's face. It was almost as if, through her, Mickey was able to peer into Bob's most inner feelings. Yes, Mickey felt very privileged and honored indeed to be so trusted with such private thoughts from a lady of Jane's insightfulness and moral character.

It's quite true that, being only a DOE monitor and advisor for the Wilson-Won-Yong research grant, Mickey was but a bystander watching the show. Nonetheless, this galling and deplorable affair caused him more than a little distress and melancholy. How could such a giant among men as Bob be treated so badly, not only once, but twice, first by Deutsch in 1978 and again by Vineyard in 1981? Mickey was at a loss as to what to make of it. Perhaps Vineyard could be forgiven for such deficient and unseemly behavior, taking into consideration that he'd just gone through that esteem-ripping summer confrontation with Pewitt in addition to the fact that he was on the threshold of resignation and disgrace. However, it was hard to forgive the other ISABELLE-BNL leaders, particularly Samios, who was one tiny step away from the Director's chair. There isn't the least doubt that he could easily have stepped in to bestow the proper civility and respect befitting the extraordinary and unique Mister Wilson. Too bad Nick wasn't more of a man! Suddenly, Mickey realized that he'd already been thinking about this more than he should have. So, he brushed aside any downbeat thoughts of the past and got back down to business.

Lifting his head and facing the others, who were expectantly waiting for him to say something, Mickey exclaimed with some pride, as if proclaiming himself the winner of the lunch debate, "So, what do you think of them apples?" The reaction to Mickey's discourse was puzzling, to say the least. For two of them, Won-Yong and Aihud, it was more like a non-reaction. Won-Yong said nothing at all. He simply smiled inscrutably, as if he knew more than he wished to say. Perhaps he was caught between a rock and a hard place. Being closely allied to both BNL and Bob, it's clear that he didn't want to bad-mouth either, and certainly wouldn't want such a thing to get out. Aihud also smiled, in his case, with a kind of phony wisdom. It wasn't that he said anything that was inaccurate, but in truth he was being two-faced. Acting the wise man, he gave the younger Mickey a fatherly pat, saying: "Yes, yes, I understand your strong desire for action and justice. But have a little patience and soon you'll learn how life really works. Just give it a little more time." Perhaps, being a member of BNL's Board of Trustees, he also could have known a lot more than he was letting out. You see Aihud, a university experimentalist, had, over the years, come to depend on the labs, and no doubt came to believe that to stay in their good graces, he'd do well to keep his mouth shut. Finally there was Baltay. His reaction was one hell of a surprise to Mickey. Aihud and Won-Yong, in the spirit of the lunch, appeared amused at the whole episode. However, with their patronizing attitudes, their taking all that was said so lightly, and their lack of seriousness, they ended up frustrating Mickey more than anything else. Charlie, on the other hand, was an entirely different matter. He seemed genuinely distraught, almost as if Mickey had wounded him. Mickey was caught off-balance as Charlie kept hammering away at him and just wouldn't let up. He strenuously persisted in his defense of the BNL way, and was either unwilling or unable to let the moment pass. Aihud and Won-Yong were ready to let Mickey walk away with his self-proclaimed victory – of course taking everything he said with a grain of salt. As for Charlie, however, what to the others was lunchtime banter, to him was dead serious. To the question, *why wouldn't Nick go for Leon's magnets*? Charlie, obviously annoyed, countered in a somewhat angry tone of voice: *he must have had a reason*. Even though he didn't provide any, he unthinkingly demanded that Mickey take it for granted that there were some and respond to them. Mickey, perplexed at this change of mood and at Charlie's irrationality, took the comment as a kind of question and pondered the issues involved. The other two, taken by surprise at what was happening and not knowing what to do, quietly looked on. It was hard for Mickey to put himself in Nick's shoes, but that's how he tried to respond to Charlie's pique and apparent loss of self-control. Still, he wondered why Charlie wasn't providing a proper defense of Nick's position by giving specifics himself. Why did he expect Mickey to speak in opposition to himself? Nevertheless, he felt that Charlie needed a little coddling and decided to take on the challenge. "Perhaps Nick didn't believe the Fermilab magnets could do the job," Mickey stammered. After a pause, he continued, "After all, the smaller magnets require that the beam be bunched, and maybe Nick still believes bunches won't work." But everyone there knew that experiments had been done at CERN expressly to test bunches, and they had been shown to work fine.

Furthermore, the two new colliders being built at CERN and Fermilab both used bunched beams. Charlie appeared flustered but said nothing. Mickey continued, "Maybe George and Nick simply didn't trust Leon." With that statement, the atmosphere at the table went through a complete turnaround. For no apparent reason, Baltay – his face having been flushed with anger just a few moments earlier – altered his demeanor drastically: He just sat there, silent and glum, as the other three followed his lead. Charlie's tirade thus ended, and with it so did the lunch.

The four scientists sat for a short while, wordless and completely drained of energy. Then, suddenly, Aihud rose with a start, peering at his wristwatch, "Hey, the lecture's beginning." With that, the other three stood up. They all smiled knowingly at each other as they noticed that the restaurant had already completely cleared. Quickly they prepared for the short walk back to the conference hall. Although the transition back to the lecture theater took but a few moments, once again there was a dramatic change in atmosphere. The melancholy mood disappeared in a flash, replaced by the usual banter of such a group, including jokes, word play, references to physics, and repartee. As they strolled through the square, all was lightness and fun, and who was to say that there was more to it than that? Mickey and Charlie, however, were to discover that substantial consequences from this lunch in the mountains of Colorado were still to come. As it happened, both would have good cause to remember that sunny afternoon for a long time afterward.

* * * * *

The next day, before dinner, Mickey felt the first stinging impact of that consequential lunch. It was damp outside and he stepped briskly into the apartment lobby, where he was to meet a friend and colleague he and his wife were accompanying to dinner. He was looking forward to the evening and was deep in thought, oblivious of the other ten or so people moving about. Suddenly he heard himself being addressed by a voice he well knew, "I was just thinking of you, and I *wanna* talk to you, buddy." Startled, Mickey, in acknowledgement, murmured something under his breath as he looked up into the face of none other than Nick, who appeared grim and threatening as he motioned to Mickey to follow him to an out-of-the-way spot under a nearby spiral staircase. The two men stared at each other. Mickey had an astonished and questioning expression on his face, while Nick was glaring with an unremitting and bitter hatred in his eyes. Mickey, caught totally off-guard, couldn't grasp how he might have precipitated such a belligerent and offensive attitude. However, before he could catch his breath, Nick blurted out, "You've got a fucking big mouth." Mickey, jolted by the dirty tongue of his boss, the Director, was dumbfounded and literally speechless. Overtaken by surprise and feeling uncharacteristically timid and nervous, Mickey experienced an overwhelming urge to apologize. But why should he do that? What had he done to deserve such outrage and fury? Then, with nary a tick of the clock, it hit him that something must have happened at the lunch the previous day. But how should he respond when he didn't know what was on Nick's mind – what crime he'd presumably committed?

Mickey had to think fast. In the few instants he had available, he desperately tried to reconstruct the lunchtime exchanges. There had to be some kind of an explanation contained in the dialogues that took place. As the memory of the frank and unreserved ISABELLE chitchat returned to him, he was sure he'd hit upon the answer. *Someone must have spilled the beans*, he thought. Of all the four of them, he'd been the most plainspoken and unfortunately the most artless. He knew full well there were risks involved in being so blunt and in not mincing words. However, only now did he come to appreciate how dumb he'd been. He really believed that his three companions would be more discreet. But he obviously was mistaken, because at least one of them immediately went off and blabbed his mouth off. What a trusting jackass Mickey had been! Now the price would have to be paid, and this was just the beginning. There he was, caught red-handed and standing red-faced in front of the prosecutorial Nick who had *j'accuse* written all over him. There was little doubt remaining that this was the right analysis. What other causal connection could there be?

What could Mickey have been thinking when he let loose that barrage of insults – and to Nick's friends, no less? He was well aware that Nick was strong-willed, proud, ruthless, and relentlessly vengeful. For Mickey to have done what he did was akin to inviting Nick's wrath to be visited upon him. Yet, even though he'd seen this facet of Nick's character in action before, and despite his being answerable to Nick in the BNL hierarchy, still, he'd ploughed on anyway. How stupid of him to speak of BNL and Nick in a manner so disrespectful, so disparaging, so scornful, and so contemptuous! Aside from his damning and blasting remarks, Mickey recalled some of his more rational technical comments: how he had voiced strong doubts about Nick's magnets and supported, with equal vigor, the idea of using Fermilab's magnets. Had he been too bold in entering the political sphere, an area verboten by Nick without his explicit permission? Had he gone too far?

Mickey later regretted that when confronted by Nick he'd not said: "But, Nick, you know I'm a fan of bunched beams and smaller magnets. I've been saying that for years." However, there was nary a peep from him by way of defense or counterattack. Uncharacteristically bewildered and tongue-tied, he simply bowed to Nick's aggressiveness. The little he did say appeared to be false, as if he had something to hide; and in truth he did. Yes, he feigned ignorance and gave the very best performance he could to appear naïve and guiltless, or at least *guilty with explanation*. However, even though Mickey was indeed guilty as charged, surely Nick was over-reacting because, no matter how you sliced it, *the punishment simply didn't fit the crime*. Thus Mickey could come to no other conclusion than that his mere words of the previous day could not be the full explanation of Nick's vehemence and raging tantrum. Despite the apparent rightness of the explanation he conjured up for the taxing one-sided confrontation between the two of them – one a big man of high station and full of official authority, and the other a little pipsqueak – Mickey felt in his bones that something was missing, that he didn't have the complete picture. He wondered: Was there more here than meets the eye?

As the true story seeped out to Mickey a bit at a time, his instincts proved to be right. His original conjecture, that Nick's angry outburst was triggered by Mickey's bad-mouthing of the ISABELLE management, turned out to be only a side issue to the real show. The actual cause was hidden in the shadows of private human transactions difficult to get at. It was something that lay on an entirely different track, something that Mickey could never have guessed, not in a million years. It was well outside his field of vision, not something he would normally come across in his everyday dealings. You see it wasn't the sort of knowledge that could be gained from systematic reasoning alone, but rather the kind that's picked up by being at the right place at the right time, by having a keen ear for seemingly irrelevant details, and by being, at heart, a veritable gossip. Someone who wasn't of Mickey's ilk might easily have taken the puzzle to be complete by accepting the original premise. But not Mickey! He had a gut feeling that an important piece of the puzzle was still missing, and it wouldn't give him any peace of mind until he found it. So, he persevered and it paid off, as in the end the missing link was unearthed. With fate playing a helping hand, with a lot of accidental good-fortune, with a strong determination to find out the truth, with the stubbornness of an elephant not to forget, and with the willingness to work assiduously to put together seemingly unrelated facts, over the span of the next few months, he was able to glean the clues and solve the mystery. When it finally came to him, everything fell perfectly into place. He had it and there wasn't the least doubt about it. So, when all was said and done, it wasn't logic and rationality that did the trick, but rather some *words-can't-describe* feeling inside of him that kept egging him on and that kept him going. Yes, it was instinct mixed with a good-sized portion of good old-fashioned luck that finally gave him the satisfaction of glimpsing the truth.

So it was that the Snowmass lunch followed by the grim and harrowing Nick-Mickey confrontation it caused together turned out to be for Mickey a noteworthy learning experience. Although the Snowmass meeting still had almost two weeks more to go, this collision with Nick under the spiral staircase turned out to be Mickey's high point – although his low point would probably be a far better description. It was both odd and astonishing how an encounter of such consequence took place at such breathtaking speed. Before he knew it, the one-sided lashing by Nick was all over. There was no chance to reflect on it, no chance to explain or defend himself, no chance to go over it with Nick step-by-step, and no chance to see if some sort of amicable resolution was possible. In the blink of an eye, Nick, annoyed and appearing weary, left with the acrimonious parting words, "You're a bloody fuck-faced nuisance." A stunned Mickey remained under the staircase for a moment, settling himself, trying to calm himself before his damnable dyspepsia set in. But, even with his sensitive stomach, Mickey had a knack for surviving tough spots. He wasn't one to let even such a numbing attack get to him. Fortunately for him, that was one of his strengths and he knew it. Many years before he'd vowed always to live by the rule "*pick yourself up, dust yourself off, and start all over again,*" and – knock-wood – for the most part, it worked for him. So he breathed deeply and counted to ten. Then, lo and behold, magically, he recovered his self-control. Not a trace of his tumultuous experience was visible. The old talkative, amiable, take-things-as-they-are Mickey was back. Improbable as it was, a mood transition from a doubt-ridden, apprehensive, and anxious state into a more congenial one had occurred in an instant. With his self-assurance and his confidence in the future returned, he felt good being back in the driver's seat. Just at that moment, he caught sight of a friendly face a few yards away. No, Mickey would simply not allow his upcoming evening to be lost to the antics of one such as Nick, whoever he was, Director or not. "Anything wrong?" came the voice of his colleague who was peering at him from just outside the nook under the staircase. "Hi! No, there's no problem, none at all. I've just been waiting a few minutes, relaxing and thinking about life and such." Mickey's face lit up as he fashioned a healthy smile from ear to ear. "What's your pleasure for dinner?"

* * * * *

With the passing of the summer of 1982, fall began its changeover from green to gold and red; and there was a taste of the approaching cold, bare emptiness of winter in the air. Mickey, beginning his third and last year at the DOE Germantown office, situated a little north of Washington, was 150% engrossed in his work. Other than the politics, which he'd become more and more attracted to, his days were filled with performance reviews, financial and technical analyses and assessments, countless reports to write and submit, and planning bull-sessions lasting for hours on end. Although this was all-consuming work, it was also quite a lot of fun. Yet, even with the glut of assignments on his plate, he managed to find the time to meditate on his Snowmass experience. He reflected on what had actually happened at his memorable lunch, on his stinging encounter with Nick, and on the presumed consequences that he was sure were in store for him. Although he tried to deny it, supported by the fact that no further incident had taken place since the Nick flare-up in July, he knew in his bones that the Nick affair was not over. He constantly speculated about how it would play out; and the more he thought about it, the more anxious he became. Then in early October, he got an answer of sorts, and he didn't like it one bit. That retaliation could be engineered so quickly, so blatantly, and with such finality shook him to his very core. When it came right down to it, what happened wasn't as bad as all that. After all, he wasn't hurt bodily; his job wasn't taken from him; and he wasn't blackballed in any way. However, by withholding money from Mickey, Nick did find a way to cause him and his family a taste of some pain and suffering. But, as you no doubt anticipated, there was far more to it than that. By the action Nick took, Mickey was given stark notice that if he didn't toe the line, there could be hell to pay. Transgression against the big boss wouldn't be tolerated or ignored. If Mickey didn't shape up and become one of the good boys, Nick would have his satisfaction. The upshot was that Mickey was force-fed an unhappily learned lesson: He wasn't as free as he thought he was. He was made to understand that he couldn't just spout off at the mouth in the manner that was promised by the principle of academic freedom, at least not unless he was willing to pay the going price.

Mickey had been awarded tenure five years earlier; and, always the optimist, he firmly believed in what it represented: academic freedom, the truth, and all that jazz. Actually, he was still a believer, and thus his immediate reaction to what was done to him by Nick and the lab was one of indignation and resentment. *Something was terribly rotten in the state of Denmark*! It could've been that the impact he felt was exaggerated by its unexpectedness. As it happened, the jolting discipline leveled against him took place on an ordinary day. Picking up his mail on the way to his office, as he usually did, he opened an envelope, which was innocuous looking enough, except for that telltale "private" stamped on it. It was his salary notice for fiscal year 1983 (fiscal years for the U.S. government start in October). He read and reread it, staring at it unbelievingly. The lab had assigned him a zero raise! There was no accompanying explanatory note; and no reasons for the action were specified. There was just the bare, stark fact of it. Somehow

– notwithstanding that he was actually working at the DOE for Wallenmeyer, who had more than once voiced his approval of Mickey's performance – it had been decided by the lab that Mickey's progress for the year was worth zip – nothing. What a shock – to have to pay such an out-of-line and undeserved penalty at a time when the country was just coming off a period of double-digit inflation. This menacing and nasty deed had all the earmarks of Nick's handiwork. Yet, even though Nick was known for his vindictiveness and quick-tempered impulses, Mickey never believed he'd go this far. Nonetheless, it was indeed Nick's intention to give Mickey a punch in the belly he wouldn't easily forget. *You don't fool around with boss Nick with impunity*!

When Mickey cooled off, he tried to come up with some sort of rational understanding of Nick's behavior. Maybe Nick felt that his reputation was impugned by Mickey talking to his close friends in the way Mickey did. Then again, maybe he judged that Mickey overstepped the line where big talk went from good-natured fun to anti-establishment treachery. But Mickey simply brushed off these interpretations as being so far out as to strain credulity. In fact, if past experience was any guide, Mickey never imagined that he could actually have much influence on things. How could Mickey, the guy with the bit part in the drama, possess the wherewithal to harm or offend Nick? He wasn't even a player in Nick's high-class league. No, Mickey concluded, this whole line of reasoning was ridiculous.

In any case, Mickey couldn't escape the reality that he was a big talker and a loudmouth. On the other hand, it's also true that BNL played no small role in making him that way. *Just do the calculations you're told to do, and otherwise keep your yap shut*, they as much as said to him. So, treated like a comparative nobody in the lab's power hierarchy, Mickey felt free from the responsibility of having to watch very carefully every utterance he made. Since he already had a well-developed tendency to say what was on his mind and let it all hang out, the tactics of BNL's management, far from pulling him into line, actually resulted in an intensification of this characteristic. So he became a freewheeling and cavalier type, saying anything that came into his head, the unvarnished truth included. He called it as he saw it! He told it like it is! Others might be more inclined to say that he came to have an even bigger mouth. But no matter how you refer to what Mickey became, it's not at all what the lab's brass had in mind. Instead of a do-as-you're-told assembly-line-like accelerator scientist, they'd helped create what they came to see as their Frankenstein's monster.

Although Mickey felt quite sure that Nick was behind his salary chastisement, the full BNL management went along. What could they all have thought he'd done to deserve such an extreme reprimand? Perhaps they questioned his trustworthiness and his loyalty to the lab. It's quite true that for years Mickey tried to persuade the lab to redirect its ISABELLE course and design the machine properly: in particular, to use bunches and make smaller and cheaper magnets. Because the lab was dead-set against going that route, could the management possibly have deemed this to demonstrate an anti-BNL attitude? But the fact is that his campaign failed – it was all to no avail. Although his voice screamed loudly and forcefully for change – some claimed he would settle for no less than revolution – alas no one was listening. The status quo held fast, and *business as usual* remained the lab's motto. So, in the end, when Mickey conceded the fight in 1979 and left for Washington as a BNL detailee, the lab's management was the winner. It was Mickey, running off with his tail between his legs, who was the loser. Yet, throughout all his trials and tribulations, including the Nick episode at Snowmass, Mickey stuck it out at the lab – until 1999 when he retired – and never once gave going elsewhere the slightest consideration. If there was even an ounce of disloyalty in his blood, then he certainly would have abandoned the lab for greener pastures. But he didn't. No, the truth was that Mickey never had the least intention of causing BNL any hurt. On the contrary, he'd always been meticulously loyal and true to its best interests. If anything, he had become emotionally attached to the lab and its future, come hell or high water. Far from being disloyal, he was loyalty personified.

Mickey just couldn't let the Snowmass matter and its aftermath rest. But, even working painstakingly through the details of his past, he wasn't able to find the *gotcha* clue - the one that would satisfy him. Something was missing and it wasn't in his nature to let it pass. No, he would push on until a persuasive conclusion was reached. He would persist in his attempts to uncover some semblance of truth. Hot and bothered by what was being inflicted upon him, he broodingly grappled with the particular question of what the lab and its management leaders were saying by this latest spiteful and malicious action against him. Were they expecting loyalty to Nick personally, no matter what Mister Samios' decisions might be? Why so? Take the ISABELLE case. Wasn't it possible that the so-called loyal staff was wrong about it? Wasn't it possible that the physichists and the lab's top management were intimidating them? Wasn't it possible then that Mickey was right and Nick wrong? Did that never cross anybody's mind? Mickey became profoundly disturbed by where his thinking was leading him. Did they simply want unquestioning obeisance? If so, then how would a freethinking tenured scientist fit in? What happened to the university-like academic freedom that BNL was so proud of in its early days? Was it possible that the lab was not the place he thought it was – that it was no longer what it was fashioned to be when it was brought into existence thirty-five years before? It pained him as he came to recognize – leaving aside his own victimization, which was no more than a slap in the face, undoubtedly suffered by many others before him – that the lab had descended to the level of BNL first, truth a distant second. Was that what Big Science had wrought? Was that what all of science had to look forward to – institutional loyalty *uber alles*?

Mickey's shock at being forced to conclude that BNL was dumping academic freedom was a complex of feelings: It began with simple dismay and was followed by distress, which turned to exasperation, then to resentment, and finally to rage. Was Rabi's inspired creation of 1947, built in the image envisioned by the ingenious and forward-looking Vannevar Bush, to be destroyed by a bunch of barbaric charlatans? No, of course not! He couldn't just take it lying down. You see Mickey, with a kind of child-like innocence, believed he'd stumbled on an issue of right versus wrong. You can't simply let a thing like that go, you've got to do something about it. To become convinced that he should indeed act, he asked himself: "If not you, then who; if not now, then when?" From then on, for Mickey, it became a matter of principle. That wasn't to be taken lightly. It was well worth going to bat for, even giving one's all for. At stake here was not only his silly little salary dispute but also the duty of all scientists to speak out for what they found to be right and true.

Mickey was thinking big thoughts. Unfortunately, he was on the threshold of learning that it's one thing to uncover injustice, but quite another to do something about it. But he was still relatively young, and if the young are to learn anything at all, it's bound to be the hard way. So he made the free choice to take up the sword of justice and fight for right. Since you can't win the big war without first winning the little battles, he decided to take a stand on the issue of BNL's attempt to squelch his voice by punishing him financially. That's where he would draw the line in the sand. The Don Quixote in him had been awakened and he took on the challenge in his usual systematic way, seeking out everybody he could think of. He explained it all to them – everything – leaving out nothing. He cajoled. He pleaded. He begged. He was ready to prostrate himself if only they would ally themselves with him. He called on Larry Leipuner, chairman of the BNL Council that represented the tenured staff in laboratory policy formulation; then Bill Wallenmeyer, his boss as a detailee in Washington; then Jerry Hudis, the lab's legal counsel; and then Bob Hughes, the President of Associated Universities (AUI). It didn't stop there: he went lower in the hierarchical chains of command – associates, assistants, chairmen, run-of-the-mill scientists and engineers, and veritably anyone who would lend him an ear. So on it went, this doomed struggle for justice and for scientific freedom of speech. Sadly, but inevitably, Mickey was stopped cold at every turn. Then, when the dust settled, he was a beaten man, feeling all but dead on the ground. Everybody that he complained to and pleaded with – people from the lab, from the government, from AUI, and from the science community – without exception advised him to accept it and stay quiet. "Don't rock the boat," was the gist of the response in a nutshell. Leipuner – then Chairman of the Brookhaven Council, where complaints by the tenured staff are supposed to go – even told him that a few years back he'd been treated in the exact same way. He too had tried to fight, but finally had to concede and resign himself to his fate. The solution for him was to simply become one of them; and his advice to Mickey was that there was no other recourse for him than to do the same. Poor Mickey, who yearned to fight the good fight for right, found himself flat on his back on the mat, where most idealists tend to end up. The view from that position is a stunner. All he could do was groan as the establishment crowd screamed for more blood.

The frustration and disillusionment Mickey felt was disheartening, as if his spirit had been wrenched from him. However in spite of being down-in-the-dumps, he unwittingly provided himself with some comic relief, which proved to be just what the doctor ordered to purge him of his disconsolation and clear his mind. When he first came to understand that he was totally powerless, and he could think of nothing left to do, he actually imagined becoming a whistle blower. Why not, he thought? Others had gone to the media – why shouldn't he? But fortunately it wasn't an idea he acted on hastily. To his credit, Mickey realized before it was too late how absurd and ridiculous the whole notion was, and wisely dropped it.

When it was all added up, was all this thinking wasted and in vain? Actually not! For, as Mickey came to appreciate how uninterested the media would be in his petty affairs, the truth of his situation hit him like a bolt from the blue. Who, he asked himself, gives a damn anyway? Who cares about his salary or his puny thoughts about academic freedom? Through bitter experience, he'd come to know that no one really cares, at least not enough to risk his neck or his comfortable life. More than that, he came to realize that he was not the first but that many before him had waged this battle, and, except for a very few bright and shining historical figures, came up with the short end of the stick. No, from where he stood, it was a lost cause, because no one that really mattered cared a whit. So, when all the talk, along with the high sounding principles, was set aside, Nick, the embodiment of il Duce's spirit, could do whatever he wanted to. That was the way the system was devised, and the way all the leaders wanted it to be. What a pity it had to be that way, Mickey thought. Still, when everything seemed so bleak, his sense of humor came to the rescue and he smiled to himself. You see there's a catch in the system. Even Nick had his limits; he was constrained not to touch the tenure system because, as long as the system remained firmly anchored, he and the other top guys were secure in their positions. And who knows what would happen to them if *tenure* was eliminated? Thus, it was absolutely forbidden to meddle with it. It was sacrosanct! So in the end the joke was on Nick. Wasn't it ironic that since the lab had granted Mickey tenure in 1978, he was a beneficiary of the very system that he'd always ranted against, the system that put Nick and his ilk where they were and kept them there?

Mickey felt a certain sense of victory that at least his job was safe and that Nick couldn't touch it. Sad to say, his private smile was short-lived as it entered his thick skull that, aside from firing him, the Director could do almost whatever he wanted to make his life miserable. So far, Mickey was hurt only in his pocketbook, but he feared that this was not the end of it. Shaken, and with the fight drained out of him, he backed off; and, as many had done before him, he put his little tail between his legs and ran, like all the other sheep-like creatures around. He thought briefly of confronting Nick, but to what end? Nick knew what he was doing and so did everyone else. Yes, it was Nick who'd ordered Mickey's zero raise. There wasn't the least doubt about it. In Mickey's exploration of the whole salary affair, through his badgering and provocative questioning, more than one person, a couple very high in the chain of command, had verified that fact. The truth is, Nick had the power to do it and that was that – so much for academic freedom and so much for a free and open science environment. Nick was the boss and he ran the show his way. Still, Mickey, the cock-eyed optimist, believed fervently that, in all he'd done, he'd done right; and deep down he felt certain that someday he would be vindicated.

The story of Mickey's hard-luck Snowmass luncheon, where he awakened Nick's wrath and unwittingly directed it onto himself, didn't end there. There remained one loose end that Mickey still hadn't been able to figure out and tie in. So far, he'd connected the verbal lashing by Nick under the spiral staircase and his zero raise to his eager-beaver lunch-tongue. This, he was thoroughly convinced, had to be the source of Nick's infuriation with him. But even though that was perfectly true, Mickey still found it difficult to believe that that was all there was to it, that there wasn't something else that, when sighted, would flash the "Gadzooks, I've got it" sign. He kept hammering away at himself about what that missing link could be. To trigger such severe and brazen responses from Nick, there simply had to be a cause that was more important to Nick and more palpable than the nebulous and fuzzy reason of Mickey's talking too much at Snowmass. He kept chewing on it, endlessly speculating on what it could have been.

Undoubtedly it wasn't very satisfying, knocking his head against the wall like that. But what else was he to do?

Perhaps, Mickey thought one day, it dealt not with him alone, but had something to do with the relationship of Nick with his friends. Yes, maybe he'd inadvertently stumbled into a delicate situation that prior to the lunch he wasn't involved in at all. That conjecture actually seemed quite plausible to Mickey, so he began to pursue that line of inquiry. Where could he start? One thing was certain: that at least one of the three spoke to Nick after the lunch. If he could figure out who, then at least that would be a beginning. But, which one? Or maybe there was more than one of them in on it. As for Won-Yong and Charlie, they were from Columbia, Nick's old stomping ground; and the three of them were thick as thieves. Aihud's ties to BNL were deep and long-standing; and he too was a close friend of Nick's. In fact, all four were members of that elite club of physichists who always stuck together. Wasn't it likely that at least one of them hit a homerun with Mickey being the ball? Mickey dissected every exchange he could recall from the lunch, but it was all old hat. What he was trying to do was blindly wade through the fog of verbiage and discover the path that could lead him into the sunlight. But, nothing he remembered saying was new or had sufficient force to flash a "eureka light" in his head. Over and over again, he stubbornly reviewed the details, refusing to give up, but this was a hard road and he could plainly see that he hadn't yet ferreted out and unraveled the elusive secret.

Mickey began to think that maybe he was barking up the wrong tree again. But he wasn't one to easily throw in the towel. So he continued for days on end, whenever he could find a moment to spare, analyzing each word, each communication, and each reaction in the minutest detail, but without finding the key. Then suddenly it came to him – the break he'd been hoping for. It was an insight that seemed to come from nowhere. It just spontaneously popped up in his head: It wasn't his big mouth at all! He knew at that precise moment that the answer lay not in what he'd said but rather in some effect that'd come from it. Of course, that's the answer! Mickey gleamed and could hardly contain himself. Nick must have reacted to that effect, whatever it was, and not directly to any opinions Mickey had expressed. Mickey felt the thrill that could only come from making a breakthrough. However, that it had to have been a big deal for Nick to be able to generate such fanatical antagonism and fury gave him a slight reason for pause. "Why wasn't it then obvious?" he asked himself. Nevertheless, despite this little bout of misgiving, which passed quickly, he knew he was on the right track. He'd done no less than break through the truth-clouding fog that'd kept him from knowing and understanding and stepped into the daylight. Thus, having passed through the portal of truth, it wasn't long before he was able to fit most of the pieces of the puzzle into their proper place.

As Mickey continued connecting the puzzle's component parts, the picture was just about taking shape. Yet there was still that damnable missing piece! But there was hope because, being situated in Washington, the gossip capital of the world, he was in the optimum position to come across such things. Here in the city of politics Mickey was privy to information he might not have otherwise picked up, unless he happened to notice such stuff while looking through a science magazine or the science section of a newspaper, or unless by chance he found himself in the circuit of the relevant grapevine. He was particularly lucky because he was working for Wallenmeyer, and nothing that happened in high-energy physics slipped by Wallenmeyer; in fact little could be done without his OK. Mickey came to appreciate this reality early in his sojourn in the capital, and always kept his ears tuned when he was around the big guy, listening to his every word, going over them with a fine-toothed comb, and forever attempting to decipher every nuance of the one and only Machiavellian Bill. In this way, Mickey came to know things well before they were open to public knowledge. Thus, the missing link in his Snowmass lunch-initiated experience appeared before him. Unfortunately, it got lost in the mass of detail that was at times overwhelming, and the connection eluded him. As it happened, at one of the periodic staff meetings at DOE's Germantown office, a discussion took place about the planned big SLAC Linear Collider Detector (SLD), and big Bill mentioned that SLAC Director Pief Panofsky was looking for a top-notch physicist to lead that effort. This occurred during the summer of 1982, and there it was staring him in the face – the missing link was none other than Pief. But how was Mickey to know then? How could he have guessed that Pief was even involved at all? After all, it was only talk, a dime-a-dozen piece of gossip.

Even as Mickey was heading for his lunchtime destiny at Snowmass, unbeknownst to him, Charlie Baltay was nearing a major fork in his career. He was in the throes of making a choice that would deeply impact and entirely change his future. Two extremely attractive job offers had been tendered him, both giving him the opportunity to reach the land of Big Science stardom. What a luxury it was, yet what a dilemma as well. Panofsky, in the midst of building a new form of electron collider, the SLC, had approached Charlie and asked him to consider coming to Stanford from Columbia to lead the effort for the challenging new detector, the SLD, one that would be able to take advantage of the SLC project's full capability. This was a dazzling alternative to staying put on the East Coast. Nick, not to be outdone, and perhaps even as a response to Pief's offer, had come up with the idea that Charlie remain at Columbia and take on the leadership role for one of the major detectors for the ISABELLE-CBA project. For Nick, serendipity was calling! Charlie was a godsend. You see Bill Willis, who had that role, had been spending more and more time at CERN and, for reasons both professional and personal, told Nick that he wanted a change of scene. This put Nick in a tough spot, doubly so because, not only was he going to lose Bill, but it was also at a precarious time for ISABELLE and for BNL. The move and the timing that Willis chose could be seen in only one way, as a slap in Nick's face. Why else would Bill be making such a seemingly selfish move at such a critical juncture for the lab after all that BNL had done for him and his career? Willis, a long-time experimental stalwart, was big-time stuff and his relocation was an embarrassing loss. But, as if a gift from on high, Nick was presented with Charlie, a real up and comer, who not only could soften the loss of Willis but also might erase entirely his untimely defection. This boded well for Nick because, if he could persuade Charlie to remain at Columbia and help lead ISABELLE and BNL back from the brink, it could save both his hide and his pride. But, although Nick had come to expect, as a matter of course, that life would be kind to him, this time, with Pief as his opponent, it was far from a sure thing. According to Pief's plan, Charlie would move west for a bright new future at Stanford and become an integral part of SLAC's pragmatic and uniquely devised push into Big Science country. It was a difficult call for

Charlie – Nick or Pief, Pief or Nick, which one would it be? With two such auspicious offers in hand, it was his career choice of a lifetime, and at this sensitive moment of decision, in walked the innocent, simple-minded, and talkative Mickey with his two cents worth.

As the summer of '82 took its course, these details of Charlie's inner struggle slowly seeped into Mickey's mind. Still for him to make it all fit, to place the missing link into the chain, he had to work on it, and for that some sort of trigger was required. That, it turned out, came in the form of Nick's harsh judgment on Mickey's 1983 fiscal year salary. Once that happened, Mickey's mind began to work double-time. It was then that the particulars of the Nick-Pief-Charlie negotiations began to cohere in his thoughts, and he began to appreciate what his words at the Snowmass lunch might have meant to Charlie. Mickey had as much as said that ISABELLE wouldn't fly because it was way too costly; that even if completed it wouldn't perform well; that the DOE was not inclined to support it because it had no chance of being a meaningful CERN competitor; and, as if that weren't enough, he implied that when it came to accelerators Nick and the lab leadership didn't have a clue about what they were doing. These words he had spoken echoed in his mind, and Mickey knew the puzzle was solved. How straightforward and simple it was once the missing link was properly inserted. Seeing for the first time all the clues assembled together, he found it obvious why Nick had reacted so angrily and hatefully to him. Even though Mickey hadn't had the least idea that he was meddling in such a delicate matter, he'd been doing just that; and opening his yap as he did may have been the straw that broke the camel's back, tilting Charlie just enough to push him over the line and send him packing to the West Coast.

Once this chain of circumstances was established, Mickey's eagerness to know it all was finally satisfied. Because he'd discovered what really followed his Snowmass lunch-talk and so came to understand why he had to suffer the painful consequences, he felt he had the right to say, "Gotcha." Still, Mickey was not entirely through with this episode in his life. There remained the open issues of what Charlie and Nick really knew and exactly why they acted as they did. So, Mickey – not the type to leave well enough alone and wanting to close the book on the whole messy business once and for all – was prompted to question the motives involved in the story. Was it possible that Charlie was unaware of the actual state of affairs at BNL? Asked another way: Was the picture Mickey painted truly an awakening for Charlie, and did he leave BNL for the West because of it? Or, perhaps it wasn't that straightforward: Did Charlie, well knowing which way up was, simply use the words spoken at that fateful lunch as a pretext, making it easier for him to break the news to Nick that he had chosen SLD over ISABELLE, Pief over him? Mickey naïvely wondered if people could be so callous about others' careers merely to cover their own sensitive asses. In his innocence, he couldn't believe it. On the other hand, life was cruel at times and people did do bad things. Still, could it really have been that Mickey was used by Charlie just to let Nick down more easily and by Nick as a convenient scapegoat to appease his own inadequacies?

Once Mickey phrased the questions, he knew that it wouldn't be easy to come by satisfying answers using the direct route. How absurd to even contemplate that Nick might open his inner self to Mickey! So, without giving it a second thought, Mickey discarded that notion. On the other hand, Charlie was an entirely different matter. He had done Mickey harm – a severe injustice. He was beholden to Mickey, at least enough to divulge the truth. More than that, Charlie was somewhat of a good fellow at heart. Maybe he would own up and tell Mickey what lay in the shadows of his mind. It wasn't very likely that Charlie would give him the unqualified and unequivocal truth. After all, did he really know the truth, considering all the rationalizing that was surely going on in his brain? Nevertheless, it was worth a try. What did Mickey have to lose? So Mickey, anal retentive by nature, couldn't resist the temptation to telephone Charlie in a last-ditch attempt to put the finishing touch to the affair. He did so in mid-October 1983. Always pushing the envelope and always looking toward the blunt approach, he wanted to know what Charlie had told Nick, especially how he had characterized Mickey; he must have said something god-awful to unleash in Nick such vituperation and such unbridled venom. Mickey shuddered as he recalled that terrible one-sided Donnybrook that took place only hours after the so-magnified-by-its-consequences lunch. But rehashing that was for another time, perhaps when he actually got in touch with Charlie. Thus, continuing with the problem at hand, Mickey tried to work out how he should handle himself when he spoke to Charlie. Should he be matter-of-fact and ask his questions plainly? Or, as he was tending to lean, should he confront Charlie and ask him why, knowing what kind of a person Nick was, he had to open his big mouth? Did he really have sufficient cause to tattle to Nick? "Look at what he did to me," Mickey thought he might say. So, leaving his preparation at that, he dialed Charlie's exchange with an avid determination to squeeze the truth out of him. But as the phone rang – first one ring, then two, then three, and then four – he managed to get hold of himself and, without rhyme or reason, became calm. However, after all that pre-telephoning analysis, with his self-control returned and intact, Mickey was thwarted and didn't get a chance to speak to Charlie. After the fifth ring, the voice of a young lady informed him that Charlie was on travel, and that he would be returning the following week. Mickey told her, "No, no message, I'll try again another day."

When Mickey and Charlie did finally connect, Mickey, in a tone as tranquil and sober as he could muster, related to Charlie what had happened between him and Nick, including both their confrontation at Snowmass under the spiral staircase and Nick's subsequent action on Mickey's salary. Actually he wasn't gentle-as-a-lamb as he was hoping to be. Somehow his underlying resentment and ill-tempered feeling couldn't be fully suppressed. However, it turned out that how Mickey conducted himself didn't much matter. You see Charlie wasn't even aware that Nick had done these things to Mickey; and once he was told, Charlie immediately recognized that he was the one who almost surely had precipitated them. His reaction was disarming to Mickey. Charlie freely admitted that he probably was the one who incited Nick's unseemly behavior, but that it was done unwittingly. Then he caught himself, as if realizing that what he was saying gave him the appearance of being pretty dumb. Although everything he'd said up to that point was quite true, he knew then that he'd have to open up and be more forthright, converting half-truths to more or less the real thing. Charlie paused for a slight moment, and then continued. He said that even though he knew Nick's temper was hot and that Nick was willing and able to lash out, he had to do what he had to do. He had neither the justification nor the luxury of taking the journalist's stance of not revealing sources. Thus, he was forced, by both his past friendship with Nick and his probable future need for him, to name names, and so Mickey became involved. He simply had no other alternative. In other words, Mickey deduced, Charlie was pleading guilty with an explanation, the explanation being that he was under great pressure and therefore not thinking clearly enough about the possible impact on Mickey. "What could I have done?" He asked Mickey. Mickey was stuck. He couldn't tell Charlie that he should have lied – and lied to a man that was his friend. So Mickey had no answer, and, tongue-tied, said nothing. Thus, in the end, Charlie's apologetic words and manner softened Mickey, who seemed, anyway, to have lost his will to hit back. Charlie closed his successful defense by insisting that he was sorry for his role in the matter and for any hurt Mickey had suffered. That was it! The telephone call was effectively over, as they concluded it in the standard civilized way with a little light patter. Charlie's contrition had done the trick and appeased Mickey, even though he knew that Charlie's apology was just one of the little white lies we all live with daily. So, although not a hundred percent satisfactory, as far as Mickey was concerned, the loop was complete and the case was closed. What was done was done, and thus this chapter in Mickey's life ended. For him, the future still lay ahead and there was no use crying over spilt milk. When it was all done with, and Mickey was alone with his thoughts, he did the feel-good thing by rationalizing that all of us have to live with and ultimately come to terms with the inevitable consequences that life brings with it – whether these consequences come from our own actions or from those of others, and whether we're aware of them or not.

6. It Ended Before It Began

As the curtain fell on Snowmass 1982, a new world order laid its claim to accelerator-based Big Science. It recalled a time decades earlier, when, in the wake of the creation of the atomic bomb, Big Science was fathered in the United States. Thus, America became the original superpower in basic physics. On the other side of the Atlantic, competition was generated in Western Europe by CERN, which was created in 1952 to jump-start science in a Europe devastated by World War II. This Geneva-situated basic science laboratory became the base for European accelerator power and a contending counter-force to American hegemony. Once Europe got going, a Big Science structure emerged with two giant superpowers vying for world supremacy. Although American science was the undisputed leader in the early days, CERN, playing catch-up, worked its way up until it broke through to the top by the early eighties. The United States, not the type of country to accept such a take-over lying down, took the big step in Snowmass 1982 to pick up the gauntlet and take the CERN challenge. The basic science game of the century had begun.

Generally, organizational strength is secured when there is a central authority that can act swiftly and decisively, whereas weakness results from divided power's tendency toward internal dissension and its consequent slowness to take action. This is just a rule of thumb because centralization of power can become a corrupt dictatorship and distributed power can generate a productive consensus or gainful and breakthrough competitiveness. So in the end there is no escaping a complex system of checks and balances, and the good judgment of the people involved. In the particular case of basic science, the keynote is rapid change. It is a field whose raison d'être is discovery, and the faster the better. This implies that it is best to have centralized power and unified action. Rapid flux goes well with a single commander in charge. It's most emphatically not good if you have to wait for a bunch of representatives to figure out what's best for each one's home unit before doing something. By then the world will have passed you by. Your opportunity for discovery and glory will have vanished. Thus, basic science needs great leaders, each with his own empire to rule over and the wherewithal to build the instruments – monuments to mankind – capable of detecting and mining nature's well-guarded secrets.

From a closer look at the nature of the two science giants, it soon becomes apparent that the two superpower units exercise their hierarchical authority very differently, each having its strengths and each its weaknesses. A major strength of the European model is that its functioning power is localized in a single laboratory, CERN. However, CERN's political governance, controlled through a conglomerate formed from the countries of Western Europe, is divided at the top. This Council is the lab's ruling body, meaning that CERN's high-level decision-making authority is distributed among its member states. In America, the situation is reversed. American Big Science rests in the hands of a single controlling political unit, the U.S. government. The authority over basic science is vested in a single agency in the executive branch, currently the cabinet-level DOE. That is its strength. However, the American system also embodies a major weakness: political reality, enforced by the U.S. Congress, demands that the Big Science establishment not be localized in a fixed, single geographic unit, but instead be dispersed as a set of independent national laboratories. Politicians must satisfy their constituents, and this results in the scattering of U.S. science centers along with its consequent competitive tendencies; and, although this could be a good thing, it can also lead to non-synchronous behavior, and worse, disruptive monopolistic practices, even to the point of labs acting destructively against each other.

With the ability to cohere their divided units being the essential ingredient for being quick, decisive, and successful, the contest between America and Europe therefore comes down to which one can be first to become unified in forging forward-thrusting rapid-fire action. The CERN member states must be able to act together as if they were one, contrary to their natural tendencies compelling each country to protect and defend its own turf. The difficulty in forging unified action in the American system lies one level down, where resources from the central government are distributed to separate and independently operating fiefdoms. With each competing for its piece of the central pie, it is difficult to expect them to put the nation first, themselves second. So you see that in both models, concerted action is limited by the inertia and the resistance inherent in any system requiring agreement among constituent parts whose interests are generally not in accord and sometimes not even compatible. The components are certainly not designed to be like that, but, even if they aren't that way to begin with, the natural forces of survival and self-glorification in time make them that way.

By the early eighties, Big Science, using these systems of doing business, was a well-managed enterprise, thriving on both sides of the ocean. For more than three decades one success followed another; and the factor most responsible, most credit-bearing for this, was the motivating influence of physics research – that bold and defiant search into the basis and meaning of the world we all live in. But there's a fly in the ointment, and even that most powerful of reasons has its limitation. The forward thrust of the endless frontier was on the threshold of coming to a screeching halt.

To infer that this is the case for Europe as well as America, despite their governing systems being so very different, look at what was happening in that decisive, turning-point decade of the eighties. CERN was sustaining its determined movement upward: LEP was well on its way, the p-pbar collider was on the verge of coming to life, and Rubbia was beginning to imagine a really big collider. America, on the other hand, had seemingly already reached its peak in the seventies with Wilson's wunderkind in the farmland of the Midwest. It was still very much in the game, but the signs indicating what was in store for America were indeed ominous. There was ISABELLE dragging the U.S. into high-energy physics oblivion. There was SLAC, limited by space and earthquake-infested California, having nowhere to go. Although Richter had high hopes of developing a linear collider with a challenging, inventive, and all-new technology, it was to end up being a false dream. And then there was Fermilab, Wilson-less and facing a dull, do-nothing future. This picture made things appear very optimistic for Europe and very bleak for America, and that, in fact, was the gods-honest truth. At the time, Europe unwisely inferred from this merely temporary state of affairs that it was intrinsically better than the U.S. Why not? It had been so far behind, and managed to find a way to leapfrog into the lead. However, appearances can be deceiving. You see Europe and America aren't really very different at all. It's just that in Big Physics,

Europe has always lagged a little behind the U.S.; and unless it is to act in a superhuman way, *whither goest the U.S., so goes Europe, just a little later*. In the end, *bigness*, ever so enticing, will have its way and overpower Europe in the same way as it was to trounce the American giant a mere decade hence.

What goes up must come down! *Ay, there's the rub*! And in Big Science, the culprit causing the downturn is bigness. You see as physics becomes bigger and as technology becomes more intricate and sophisticated, more and more strains among the system's multiple parts can be expected to appear. As the stresses, induced by the diverging interests of the separate components – the CERN member states in Europe and the national labs in the U.S. – become manifest, what choices do each of the units have? When push comes to shove, is there an alternative to looking out for number one? Ideally, the needed course of action to stop or prevent this outcome is plain: each superpower has to look into its various units and get them in line with top management policy. To accomplish that, there are only two choices: devise policies that satisfy them all, or make the units satisfy policies designed for winning via cold, hard, favoritism-eschewing logic. Trying to make every element happy means pouring in sometimes excessive resources to correct persistent mistakes and mismanagement, while making everyone toe the line requires weeding out the weak links and letting survival of the fittest reign. Either coddle them or insist on them shaping up or shipping out. Throw money in or throw the dead weight out? That is the question. Looked at in this way, it becomes clear that if you want to get things done and if you want to come out on top, there really is no alternative to eliminating the non-achievers. They're wasteful and their wastefulness is infectious and contagious. So, even if in the unlikely circumstance that there's money to burn, in the long run, it's best not to burn it. Unfortunately, most organizations cannot hold back from spending if money is made available. There seems to be an inescapable tendency to take the easy way out. If the funding agency doesn't demand that there be a correlation between money allotted and useful output, between funding and performance, then why should they? It is simply a matter of human nature; and to put off the gratification, the sense of being important, and the feeling – although a false one – of having accomplished something requires men with hearts of stone and minds of gold.

In Europe, if the existing system is going to allow more and more coups, continued ascendancy, and maintaining the golden times in full swing, it eventually must face up to the reality that it has no choice but to change its mode of governance. If Europe is to stay in front of the U.S. in the long run, then its system must be made to converge toward the ideal of a single authorizing and controlling unit governing a unified operating system. Wow! That's a lot to ask. Yes, it's not very likely to happen, but it isn't impossible. In fact, high-level people in Europe are talking about a way of functioning, which, if applied to CERN, might work. Wouldn't it be something if CERN governance would come from a single science body representing a unified Europe? Actually, this is not as ridiculous as it sounds in light of the current idea of forging the disparate European states into a European Union. Still, that is a mighty big leap – don't hold your breath waiting for it – for, as history teaches, creating a truly international body won't be as easy as formulating one on a piece of paper. Eventually CERN will have to confront the tough choices managements everywhere have to deal with: Will

Peter give more to save Paul when trouble comes, and will Paul return the favor when needed? Will the countries fight against each other with self-interest ruling, or will they collectively and sympathetically appreciate the vagaries of life and come through when called on to sacrifice? Will they actually be able to *do the right thing*? Probably not! It flies in the face of all that past experiences teaches. However, maybe Europe can pull off this unification thing and, because it's almost a violation of human nature, do what's close to impossible. History has witnessed such things before, although only rarely. Still, you never know!

Then there's American Big Science. Here, the basic problem is to get the small number of fiefdoms to work in concert toward a unified objective. Although not impossible, it takes more than a bureaucratic body like the DOE to do it. Such a U.S. government agency is beholden to Congress and furthermore becomes committed to – you might even say allied with – the labs it's supposed to be monitoring for fitness. Far from being independent and hardnosed about performance, it comes to act more like a congressional clearing house and a lab lackey. What is needed is a governing entity that does more than unquestioningly accept the fancy administrative jargon from the labs. These are for the most part excuses meant to deceive the powers-that-be that meaningful, authentic, and clear-cut action is just around the corner, or that corrective action for some detected problem is in the works when it isn't. To overcome this dark side of self-interest working to conceal the truth, a way must be found to look honestly and dispassionately at the performance and productivity of each lab. Only by digging through the contrived protective image can falseness be revealed and the labs genuinely judged. But who can be entrusted to act in such an independent and honest way? There is little doubt that the prime prerequisite is some single enforcing corporate body that most assuredly doesn't have the close ties to the labs its meant to assess and rank, and one with the power to re-allocate resources after passing judgment. In other words, the DOE must assign to others power it now holds. Of course the Congress could order such a course by law if it had the will to do so. Ha! That'll be the day! The truth is that it's an enormously touchy thing to do. You see the government doesn't give power away; the government amasses it. There's even a more sensitive issue: For such a body as envisioned to really have teeth, it must be given the authority to go as far as to focus resources into a single big lab similar to CERN, if that is what is deemed optimal and necessary. That's asking a lot, probably too much. Even though this power center undoubtedly wouldn't want to or have to go to such an extreme, at the minimum it has to have the threat of being able to do so in order for its suggestions, orders, or dictates to have any weight at all. However – not to worry – the U.S. is nowhere near such a venturesome paradigm.

There was very little likelihood of such ideal administrative structures being set in place in either America or Europe. But the world doesn't seem to care much about these piddling matters of little men. It just keeps chugging along. Tuning in as the seventies were coming to a close, Europe hadn't yet experienced the full impact of the de-unifying forces, bound eventually to make themselves evident, and was moving smartly along, especially in the new-tech arena. (Still, and make no mistake about it, unless something was to be done to prevent it, dissension among CERN's member states most certainly would in time begin to rear its ugly head.) Meanwhile, on the American science scene, the leadership still hadn't come to terms with the shortcomings of the national laboratory setup: a scheme for true unification still remained in the realm of fantasy. Under the American system that had been in force for many years, the actions that were needed to keep bigness from causing physics to fall flat on its face weren't taken: There were no rewards given for good performance – on the contrary, Fermilab was punished for it; good money followed bad, pouring into the failing ISABELLE project; and there was no attempt to focus resources so as to foster the bigness that was lying ahead. The reality in the U.S. national lab system was a far cry from what was needed to keep up with CERN's thrust forward in accelerator technology. Unfortunately, with DOE's manner of distributing its high-energy budget, the best that the U.S. could expect in the short term was a state of modest decline or zero growth in operations for existing experiments. So, as the eighties made its appearance, it was a sad time for the plodding, unwieldy American giant. But what a thrilling period it was for Europe, flexing its technological muscles and spreading its wings.

In the meantime, on the field of play, where experimental operations were old hat and new-technology projects were the name of the game, its policies and its technical failings put America into a tailspin, while Europe remained on the rise. So, as the eighties got underway, the CERN model seemed to be the superior one, and Europe began pulling further ahead of America in Big Science. With no end of that trend in sight, America, with its potentially awesome change-inducing power, had to do something about it. Then, just when everything was so bleak, and everyone so down in the dumps, a turnaround was on the verge of taking place. There, from out of nowhere, came that full-of-promise, inspiriting Snowmass summer of 1982.

* * * * *

Having beaten the U.S. in the race for the W, CERN was riding high in 1982. But the competition for who was best had gone much further than that. There seemed to be no end to CERN's strength; and the Geneva powerhouse was advancing quickly along a broad technology front. American Big Science, on the other hand, was falling apart at the seams from within and couldn't seem to come anywhere close to mounting an effective counter-offensive. BNL and Fermilab conceded the battle over proton colliders to CERN, while CERN continued expanding its accelerator capability by also entering the arena of electron colliders. Its new Large Electron Positron collider (LEP) was parading out with a flourish of European trumpets as the U.S. was squashed deeper into the mud. SLAC, which was supposed to be carrying the electron banner for America, hadn't the resources, the money or the land, to launch a similarly large project. However, despite the looming dark clouds, SLAC did in fact represent a glimmer of hope for America on the electron front. Looking further ahead to the next generation of electron colliders, Richter introduced a chancy, high-risk competitor to LEP, a collider built with an imaginative and exciting new linear accelerator technology. But it was a real long shot and, in truth, CERN had little to fear from this SLAC initiative, which was more a plucky, highflying coup de theâtre and not nearly enough to displace CERN as top dog. In the proton arena, America was pitifully exposed and things looked very bleak indeed. By giving up on BNL entirely, and instructing Fermilab to focus its efforts solely on its new superconducting magnet technology for the Tevatron, America sacrificed its small chance to win the W prize. With the U.S. resigning and leaving the field, CERN claimed victory and the big battle of the early eighties was over. America, rather than remaining on an obviously losing track, chose instead to regroup and look ahead. Following the wisdom of the old lyric, "*Pick yourself up, dust yourself off, and start all over again,*" it set its sights on a comeback in a future war, one that was closer than anyone could have imagined.

In hindsight, it is apparent that CERN had leapt in front by building an unparalleled expertise in accelerator technology in the sixties and seventies. As for the U.S., losing the W was hard to take, but nevertheless it was good medicine. As America entered the eighties, it finally saw the light, and began preparing its campaign for the next round of competition. Why, during the previous couple of decades, it had come to lose faith that big-time technology investment was the right road to hoe is one of those mysteries hard to fathom. After all, with the completion of the phenomenal Manhattan Project, technology investment might quite properly be referred to as a particularly American way. In any case, the U.S. regained its footing, and by the time of the 1982 Snowmass conference, it was rarin' to go. This was to be the first step on the road to the U.S. becoming number one again. Going into that once-in-a-lifetime meeting, there was a lot of apprehension about what lay ahead for high-energy physics in the country, although for the few with that distinctively American "We can do it" attitude, there burned a slight flicker of hope. But coming out of Snowmass was an altogether other matter. Everything seemed to fall into place. Somehow, during the course of that stunning extravaganza that changed the science world, the American get-up-and-go spirit was revived. The U.S. Big Science enterprise put on a really good show, but in truth that's a gross understatement of what went on during that dazzling summer in the mountains of Colorado. Indeed, it was much more than that: as it happened – for those fortunate enough to have been there – it was a life-changing and never-to-be-forgotten experience. No one was the same after that. In a brief three-week span, the U.S. completely altered its course, changed its image, and breathed new life into the dying spirit of Big Physics in America.

What the U.S. did at Snowmass '82 was no less than set the stage for the development of what was to be the first project in a new era of mega-science. Furthermore, it put into motion a new bout of competition for which superpower would become the new mega-accelerator champion of the world. America and Europe were at it again! With rare brilliance, those remarkable individuals who had the Snowmass vision launched a new shining star into the kingdom of the labs. It was one that was meant to lead America and the world into the era of mega-labs, thus enabling man to go where no man has gone before and to shine the light of day on the breathtaking and mysterious secrets nature was hiding deep within its fearful restricted zone. CERN, caught off-guard by the quick-to-awaken America and the boldness of its move, had no immediate reply prepared. However, the towering strength of Geneva could not be outdone for long, at least not while there was still time to get in the game. With Carlo to spur it on, CERN would soon respond with its own candidate allowing it to participate in the brave new world of mega-science. And so the entrants took their places at the starting gate of the exciting race for who would be the first to expose and liberate those as yet unseen and even less understood tiny and fleeting particles nature has so tantalizingly packed into her Sphinx-like master-control box of riddles and miracles.

* * * * *

The post-Snowmass air was flush with excitement and exhilaration, and yet people felt some queasiness in the gut, as if they sensed some ominous consequences. Once the word of what took place was out, it became clear that there would be winners – but naturally there would also be losers. The price would have to be paid, and keep in mind that progress doesn't come cheap. The first on the list of losers was already selected. So, even as the BNL contingent packed to leave Snowmass, it was painfully clear to them that the jig was up. They should have sensed the beginning of the end a year earlier, at the acrimonious, unnerving, and deplorable Temple Review, where Vineyard met his Waterloo. They should have worked their butts off to avert what was to happen in its aftermath. Unfortunately, the truth of the lab's position in the world of Big Science still hadn't yet fully sunk in. However, after the Snowmass meeting passed into history, even though the final curtain hadn't yet descended, only the diehards could have failed to see the impending doom staring at them.

Those at BNL's seat of power not unexpectedly couldn't face the truth of their past doings. They couldn't bear the thought that the lion's share of responsibility rested with them – that the choices they'd made over the years had finally brought the lab to this. Among the most prominent of the guilty parties was Nick. As the lab's man-in-charge, he tried in desperation to keep hope alive by persisting for another year in the fiction that he could save the cursed project. But ISABELLE's days were numbered. The time of the lady he helped shape years earlier had since passed. Nick should've appreciated this. He should've been more insightful and more flexible. He had all the technical expertise anybody could ask for at his beck and call, and could have set a course to redesign the project to suit the time that was. As the number one man at the lab, foresight and the courage to act on it should've been part of his makeup. That was his job and that was why he was put there. Otherwise, why have a Director at all?

If not his sole role, the Director's cardinal and indispensable one is to make the tough choices that match the lab's output and investments to the needs of its stakeholders. For them – the science community, the government, and industry – ISABELLE had to be shaped to beat out CERN in the stretch, even as Rubbia raced toward the temptress W just about coming into view. It certainly wasn't meant that the project should simply be made into a slightly recast ISABELLE-of-old, thereby placing the desired-by-all W into Carlo's eager hands with nary a fight. However, Nick couldn't or wouldn't acknowledge this reality. Logic and down-to-earth reasoning were well outside his field of vision. There were actually far different things on his mind. Poor Nick was in fact in the throes of an age-old conflict, the war within himself. What he was actually being driven by were the pangs of an old nemesis, an uncontrollable hubris that blinded him to his past and impelled him to throw good sense to the wind. Trapped by his past actions and associations, Nick could not escape from a burning desire to have been right. So, leaving rationality in the dust, he did little more than rename ISABELLE, and proceeded to spend those two critical years from 1981 to 1983 rallying the old-guard troops to march to the drums of his too-little-too-late CBA.

Unfortunately, the effort Nick and his staff expended was just a waste of time. It fooled no one except himself and his inner circle. You see the CBA was just the old lady herself with a new name. Nick's plan, after Pewitt's 1981 onslaught, which, ironically, had given him the throne, was to get the magnets to work with the minimum of possible change and then foist them on the funding agency and the community. The concoction he dreamed up contained the almost unbelievable presumption that all of them were asleep and wouldn't notice that it made no response to the vital issue of big Carlo running unopposed toward the grand prize. Nonetheless, misguided as he was, what Nick managed to do was not a trivial matter to pull off. His scheme required the major and conspicuous concession that the braided superconductor, the key ISABELLE innovation, held on to for almost twenty years, had to go. Imagine the uproar when all those – and there were many – who had staked their careers on the braided magnet heard the news! Yet, despite this formidable opposition, Nick wended his way through the resulting minefield and, with Palmer and Shutt behind him, identified the braid as the culprit, and discarded it as being impractical for an accelerator magnet. With that obstacle out of the way, Palmer, Shutt, and the other magnet brains soon managed to find a way to introduce the standard and universally used Rutherford cable. Thus, Nick wasn't anywhere near being a management wimp and could act decisively if he was moved to do so. Then why, it might be asked, did he stop there? You see, although he solved the superconducting material problem, he didn't at all alleviate the more serious and pressing issue of the magnets' size, which remained way too large for their cost-effective use in the miles of tunnel needed for the ISABELLE rings. In the end, Nick bought this cute idea of replacing the braid with cable. But it was no more than that – a cute idea. Yes, it was a technical success, but ultimately an unimportant one. Actually, it turned out to be the basis for the propagation of a fatal misjudgment: It allowed BNL to maintain its delusion that it could use very large diameter magnets. If only Nick could have seen that it was this design feature that was the project's Achilles heel, things might have ended up differently. Unfortunately, he couldn't see it.

Believe it or not, that switching of the magnet material was the whole of Nick's solution. Then, once having himself accepted it, amazingly, he was persuasive enough to convince the lab and its followers that his way would suffice to save ISABELLE, and that the lab need go no further. What a selling job it must have been! He was telling them all to ignore the enormous cost-to-complete; to ignore the highly uncertain time-to-complete; to ignore the sapping of the resources from a physics community wanting to get on to a bright new day; to ignore the fact that CERN would surely find the W soon, essentially eliminating the physics case for ISABELLE-CBA; and, to top it off, to ignore the reality that Fermilab, already In 1981, had been given the mandate to explore the ISABELLE performance range with a collision energy coverage more than twice that of ISABELLE. Yes, Nick persuaded his followers and supporters to back him, probably either because they were committed to BNL in order to further their careers, or because they felt it was the only right and proper thing to do as a quid pro quo for past favors. How demeaning it must have been for them when they were asked by their colleagues to articulate their reasons for giving BNL and CBA the thumbs-up sign. However, despite the weakness of Nick's case, he felt invincible and saw no reason to change in any extreme way. In fact, Nick wasn't far from wrong. Before the 1981 Temple Review, indeed there was no coordinated opposition strong enough to effectively counter ISABELLE. Thus, it could very well have been that Nick and the lab might have gone on muddling through and come out unscathed. It's incredible but true that this state of affairs could have kept going on, with U.S. high-energy physics being dragged down further and further. Too bad Nick wasn't able to recognize that the Temple gang had changed everything.

As it happened, in spite of Nick's intransigence, big change did actually happen – because in walked a man named Pewitt. Nick failed to see the determination and the power in Pewitt's eyes. So, he persisted in what seemed to be the only way for BNL, the only way he knew. Probably the crown he'd gained in 1981, going to his head, blinded him. Nevertheless, Pewitt accomplished what a lesser man couldn't have. In that memorable slashing review, he almost single-handedly changed the course of Big Physics history: He stopped BNL dead in its tracks, removed Vineyard from office, and set the stage for an American revival and comeback. Being brash and abrasive, Pewitt wasn't a well-liked person. But he was an astute and perceptive man, and had his ears finely tuned to the political goings on of the time. Even more, he had *being right* on his side. So it wasn't very surprising that a year later the insightful, decisive men of Snowmass wisely discerned the BNL delusion and, in their struggle and resolve to manufacture a visionary plan for the future, took the crucial first step that would wind up ridding the physics community of that tiresome project. These brilliant and courageous men knew what they had to do and did it: that for the sake of the science community's future and even for the sake of BNL itself, ISABELLE, by that or any other name, had to take the fall. Although it would take yet another year for the deed to be done, so it was to be.

* * * * *

The signs of danger loomed ominously around BNL. No one knew exactly how things would play out, but the facts were plainly there for all to see: including the fortress mentality at Camp Upton, the appearance of cracks in the walls, and the unwillingness of the lab to admit how near disaster lay. What a trying time it was, and to think that it was just an accident of history that put Nick in the driver's seat to rule over BNL as ISABELLE fought for her life! In any case, being where he sat, it was all up to him. Although the falling of the government ax was more imminent than anyone thought, Nick refused to budge, not an inch. He was a bull-headed man and would push on to the bitter end – doing it his way – while warding off all those who might imagine they could oppose him with the threatening reminder he'd once expressed at an unguarded moment, "Après moi, le déluge." Such was Nick's arrogance that it never occurred to him that the world of Big Science could – or might even want to – get along without him. So on he went. With his wrong-headed scheme to pull BNL out of its nosedive under his arm, he proceeded onward toward the cliff's edge, the Pied Piper playing his merry tune, leading his followers to their inevitable sorry fate.

The truth is that, as 1983 began, Nick wasn't done for – not just yet. While he was pursuing his destructive course, an opportunity for redemption unexpectedly appeared. Not many are given such last-minute reprieves, but fortune happened to choose Nick to be one of the rare recipients. All he had to do was pick up this lucky break and run with it. The fact is that a decision was made in the halls of power that ISABELLE-CBA was to be given one last chance: a HEPAP (High Energy Physics Advisory Panel) sub-panel was to be formed that would revisit the project and make recommendations to DOE that coming summer. By itself, this wasn't really unusual because those who stride through those halls generally shun the responsibility of themselves taking any bad-guy actions or ones that might be construed that way. Instead, when a change is desired or deemed necessary, *why do it yourself when you can get a committee of experts to do it for you?* That's the democratic way, isn't it? In the particular case of ISABELLE, it was probably quite wise of the moneymen to let the scientists do the dirty work for them. Scientists after all are easy pickings – *a little carrot here, a little stick there, and pretty soon they'll be eating out of your hands*! You see the idea for the 1983 sub-panel almost surely originated with those who wanted to rid themselves of that irritating and threatening Long Island project.

However, it must be remembered that there's a catch to this way of doing things. When a bunch of independent types from the academic sector are brought together as a committee to make a decision, anything can happen. Keep in mind that BNL still had a number of supporters: government officials and scientists, particularly the lab's many experimental users. So, although Nick didn't deserve it and his chances were slight at best, because of the government's aversion to appear to be directly attacking an institution it had created, he had some cause for hope that ISABELLE could be rescued from the jaws of the hungry tiger.

However, to the misfortune of both BNL and the science community, Nick was not the man for this moment and was not up to the task. That's undoubtedly why, after two years with Nick steering, the lab found itself in this god-awful situation. You see to make something positive out of this last-ditch hope required that he change his ways. Unfortunately, he still clung to the notion that it was his opponents who had the changing to do. Thus, sad to say, he didn't have it in him to respond successfully to the challenge before him. A man like Nick simply can't admit the error of his ways because all his instincts and his nature drive him precisely in the opposite direction. He interpreted the opportunity handed to him on a silver platter to mean that finally he was to get his long-sought forum to persuade the community and the DOE that he was right, and that he'd been right all along. He'd even go further, claiming and believing that it was the others – all those bastards, especially Leon, Pewitt, Keyworth – who were in the wrong. *To hell with them all, they were only out to get him anyway!* So he persuaded himself that this was to be his time. Now he'd show them all the kind of man he was, the man who would make his CBA work and would beat the technological pants off all those who had the insolence to doubt his capacity to end up on top. Sure, he knew there'd be many enemies on the HEPAP sub-panel, but there'd also be friends, enough, he thought, to carry him through to win the day. So he got on the phone, marshaled his allies, and began his campaign of persuasion, all the while unrealistically convinced of his ultimate victory.

The half-year leading to his fateful hour in the summer of 1983 passed quickly for Nick. He loved a good fight, especially the joy of vanquishing an enemy; and, anticipating the sweet taste of victory, he found the action during that period to be exhilarating and life-giving. Being a very stubborn man and filled to the brim with false self-confidence, he wasn't much fazed by almost anything, not even when the stunning announcement came from CERN early that year that Rubbia had discovered the W and Z particles. If Nick had had an ounce of humility, he might have hesitated. He might have stopped to consider how it affected BNL and the country; and how the lab might conduct itself in light of this new state of affairs. But not Nick! Whatever fleeting thoughts he may have had about a different line of attack, he'd gone too far and taken too many with him to turn back now. So he moved forward on his unalterable course. It's truly mind-boggling that a man with such a high IQ could have treated Carlo's coup, such an important event, so casually. Yet he did. Perhaps the stress of the previous few years simply got to him. In any case, he deceived himself with the thought that it didn't matter much – *who cares about that anyway*?

Ignoring what was happening across the Atlantic, Nick worked hard in preparation for his big Washington moment. He was overbearing in his tracking of the progress of the magnet effort, bugging the daylights out of Palmer, Reardon, Johnsen, and the rest of the staff, insisting on knowing every little technical detail. He was tireless and had energy to burn. His attitude and comportment were infectious, as everybody – working themselves to the bone – tried to imitate him. Strangely, it was a good time for Nick. But the end of it came quickly. In the twinkling of an eye, the HEPAP sub-panel meeting was upon him. So he and his entourage packed off to Washington to talk of the CBA and present his case. Nick's moment of truth had arrived.

What a letdown the BNL show was! One by one the lab's contingent went on stage to perform. They spoke with conviction and showed their slides and overhead projector sheets with the assurance of winners. But in the end it was the same old claptrap. There was nothing new, just the usual stuff heard many times over in the past; but to them, their line represented the new-wave BNL and was the lead-in to their pièce de résistance: the revelation that the lab had successfully built some short versions of the new Palmer-style magnets as well as completing a couple of full-size ones. Some of the speakers, particularly Nick, couldn't resist the temptation to cap off their talks by proudly emphasizing that all their magnets actually worked. Hello! Why shouldn't they have worked? With self-deception written all over the claim, Nick was clearly oblivious of the obvious. He truly appeared to believe, with little reason, that such a limp series of achievements would be enough to assuage all the hurts inflicted on the American science community by the ISABELLE fiasco. No, the lab's presentation wasn't an inspiring one at all, and, when it was all over, it lacked the panache to turn the tide. However, despite this lackluster performance, Nick did have a short-lived success that demonstrated his considerable talent for building support for the lab. You see, when the sub-panel vote was tallied, the result was a tie. What a shock! Nick was shocked because his political head-count was off the mark. The group of conspirators aiming for *American Excellence* was equally shocked, and for the very same reason. To top it off, the average politically innocent scientist was also shocked, but for him it was because the vote violated all logic and reason.

The panel was in a quandary. There were many hours of ensuing discussion on the floor, in addition to a great deal of arm-twisting and all manner of persuasion in the corridors. But it was to no avail. Each member had his mind made up and stuck to his guns, or perhaps simply had to honor the commitment he'd made. Thus the panel, unable to come to a clear-cut verdict, deemed it necessary to give the members a chance to think it over and search their consciences. The chairman therefore declared the vote to be an interim one, setting the stage for a follow-up meeting where a definitive verdict could be reached. Although alternatives were considered, for such an important judgment – to continue the big BNL project or to kill it – the panel conceded that a re-vote was the only way. Presumably, the consensus was that someone would change his mind, or perhaps be convinced or intimidated to do so.

Thus the time came for politics to enter the dispute at full volume. In fact, the surprising finding rendered by the equally divided panel set in motion a swell of anti-ISABELLE political wrangling. The idealistic rebels, who had engineered the panel's assemblage in the first place, believing without the least doubt that the result would be a pro-forma "*no,*" were not about to let their Snowmass trade-off, already in the works, be derailed by a sorry bunch of professors. They were determined that those politically naïve members of the panel would not be allowed to put a wrench in the spinning wheel of progress and block the road to American excellence in science. Meanwhile, Nick, on the sidelines watching the action, began to feel the shaky ground under him begin to shift, and his bit of remaining hope became mixed with a growing and aching anxiety. The truth is that he was no match for the political bigwigs who had set their sights on something far surpassing the little daydreams of Nick the bully.

There still remained the details to work out of how to proceed. The HEPAP sub-panel members were exhausted by the struggle just endured and didn't really have a handle on how to resolve their impasse. So they chose to take a reasonably long break of a few weeks, hoping that in the interim an answer would materialize before them, either magically fair or politically realistic, or maybe, miraculously, the two combined. They planned to meet around the July Fourth weekend for a few days for a final showdown. So as to be far from the political pressures of Washington, as if it were really possible to escape the long arm of political power, they chose the out-of-the-way Nevis Laboratory, ironically a part of Nick's alma mater, Columbia University, located just north of New York City. As the members gathered, there was anxiety and high anticipation in the Big Science community. To relieve the tension, everyone wanted an answer ASAP. But, as it happened, one was not quickly forthcoming. The first day passed, then the second, but not a word came out of the Nevis silence-vowed stronghold. The politicos on hand and the science power-holders were taking their own sweet time to make sure that there would be no mistake. This time the outcome would be what it was supposed to be. This boded ill for BNL and its assailed lady in distress; and one could imagine the stress induced in the poor scientists as the steam of political reality descended on them. Meanwhile on the outside there was quiet, and all people could do was wait. The holiday passed and still there was nothing but silence out of Nevis. More time passed and at BNL hope diminished as uncertainty and fear mounted with each hour that went by. People could think of nothing else: "Any word?" they would ask. "Not yet" or "I haven't heard a thing" were common responses. Anguish grew at BNL. Nick's hopes and confidence, along with those of the lab's staff and followers, were clearly flagging. Nick sensed that he had lost control of things and began to fear the worst. Then the sub-panel disbanded, but what was agreed to was hidden behind an iron curtain of silence. The members had committed themselves to a vow of non-disclosure. "The results of our deliberations will come directly out of Washington at the discretion of the DOE," was the best anyone could get from the members. So the silence persisted and more days went by. Suddenly, after a quiet July weekend, the political blackout was lifted, and the HEPAP sub-panel's decision was announced, hitting Long Island like a bomb.

On Monday, July 11, 1983, the headline in the morning edition of *Newsday*, Long Island's major newspaper, carried home the dreaded death notice, "LI Atom Smasher Doomed by Panel." It continued by identifying the underlying deal that had been cooked up, "U.S. Unit to Urge Substitute Project." The cat was now out of the bag, where all, including the public, could see it. In the *New York Times*, on July 14, James Barron wrote, "Builders of Atom Smasher on L.I. Keep Death Watch Over a Dream," and a day later, William Broad said, bluntly, "Big Accelerator on Long Island Gets a *No Vote*," as well as "Panel Favors Scrapping of Brookhaven Project." Earl Lane, a *Newsday* science journalist, wrote of "The *Rise and Fall* of an Atom Smasher," and said, "Brookhaven Atom Unit Voted Out." The reporting went on in this vein for more than a week as more details became public. In one *Newsday* article, Earl Lane wrote: "A national advisory panel of physicists yesterday dealt a death blow to the partially completed atom smasher at Brookhaven National Laboratory when it accepted a bold plan to build a super atom smasher far surpassing the power of any existing machine." Finally, in a *New York Times* piece a few days after the original announcement, William Broad named one of the key men behind the Snowmass political deal that was supposed to save American Big Science by bringing *excellence* to it and by giving it sufficient strength to fight Carlo and the CERN colossus: "The President's science advisor, Dr. George A. Keyworth, has publicly called for a stop to the project, and the Department of Energy is expected to concur." And, of course, the DOE did.

* * * * *

The end was a long time in coming, but when the final blow was dealt, it was all over in a flash. ISABELLE, the lady who embodied so much hope in a lab filled with dreams, was done for. What remained for future generations were only those agonizing words of dying and death plastered in everlasting black and white all over the newspapers. No, there was no reversing those terrible words now! At the lab, it was a time for grieving, for sadness and reflection over lost dreams. However, that's not at all the way it was. After the mortal stroke – the *coup de grace* – was delivered, the reaction instead was one of outrage. There was hostility, anger, and aggression everywhere, as havoc and mayhem reigned. No one knew what to do and what it all would mean. All the buzz was second-guessing, sour grapes, and Monday morning quarterbacking. The reactions were not generous to the physics establishment, which was cursed for having sold the lab down the river. Although the lab's response couldn't retrieve the past, it is not uncommon for people to react this way to the experience of crushing and ruinous loss. What alternatives were there? No doubt, underneath these masks of resentment, indignation, and wrath, there were depressed spirits, heavy hearts, and unremitting demoralization. Yes, unseen at the surface, but deep inside, there was melancholy and profound regret that the deed had actually occurred. But that's the way things are. There's no going back in the game of life.

Actually, the end shouldn't have been the shock it was. You see dissatisfaction with the lab and its project had been building for a long time; and the signs were transparent, open for everyone to see. The government simply lost confidence in BNL and saw no way of avoiding the elimination of the project. At the same time, throughout the community, scientists feared financial reprisals and resource burdens if ISABELLE were to limp along eating up funds. Where would the money come from? So, with no good end in sight, both the government and the science community saw no alternative but to give in and acquiesce to the inevitable. It was all so rational, so right. But the lab wasn't governed by reason. No, it was irrationality that ruled there.

It's not difficult to see why an average BNL staff member should be ruled by passion and emotion. But more should be expected of a leader. Alas, Nick hadn't the needed qualities. If anything, he fomented these irrational feelings in the others around him. The truth is that Nick just wasn't a man of substance and foresight. He didn't have the ability to think things through, to understand, and then to accept what can't be changed. What happened was over. Now he and his followers had to live with it and get on with their lives. Unfortunately, that wasn't Nick. No, he was incredibly agitated, fit to be tied, and, to the lab's detriment, it was his revenge-seeking heart that controlled him. He felt no less than betrayed. Being livid with anger, he chose to see others as responsible for the predicament he was in. As for himself, he felt entirely blame-free. Guilt, he was absolutely sure, rested elsewhere. This way of looking at the mess around him, the view according to Saint Nick, was expressed in the prevalent language of that awful time after the death blow was dealt: "Damn those bastards. We did what they asked for. First, they wanted a machine that could do all sorts of experiments. Then they changed their minds. Then, when we found all the problems and solved them, they pulled out. They kicked us in the teeth. Damn them all. Why couldn't they have let us finish? We were so close, why couldn't they have waited just a little longer before pulling the rug out from under us? It was that traitor, Leon, damn him. We knew we couldn't trust that Judas, selling us out for a few pieces of silver. Let him rot in hell". This sort of talk naturally didn't do much good for the lab. But it did serve to salve Nick's aching heart. By getting it all off his chest, it somehow relieved him. He wasn't the bad-guy of the piece. Not at all! He was the victim!

These feelings and attitudes, particularly the one of being done in, would linger for a long time in the BNL milieu. However, Nick found somewhere inside himself the strength to overcome his base instincts to bash the bastards that did this to him. Soon after ISABELLE fell, uncharacteristically, he picked himself up and chose to take a more common sense and conciliatory line. He told the HEPAP sub-panel in a formal communication and at the same time wrote to the lab's more than 3000 workers, "We are deeply disappointed with this recommendation, which was made in spite of highly favorable reviews of the project." Although in the previous couple of years, there really weren't any favorable reviews of the project, there were some technical teams made up of scientists and engineers brought to BNL under various auspices, groups answering to organizations of the science community or of the government or even answering to Nick himself, that attested to America's need for the ISABELLE facility and to the fact that the new magnet design had a good chance to be practical. It wasn't anything to write home about, but it did offer Nick the opportunity to save face after the fact, and he grabbed it. Was this a new and improved Nick? Unfortunately not! Nick, the statesman and the diplomat, the true leader in times of institutional rebuilding, didn't last very long. It was an unexpectedly hopeful sign; and for a short while, even the skeptics came to believe, against their better judgment, that maybe people can sometimes change for the good. In any case, his short-lived guise of the good guy wasn't really him. Eventually the true person under the mask made his way out. Thus, after a short respite, just long enough to get the burial done, Nick was back to his old ways and his old tricks. *You can't keep a bad man down*, to vary the old cliché. So, before long, with his real persona intact, the real Nick was back in full swing.

Nick instilled his preferred stance in his committed supporters all around the lab. He thrust upon them – those truly loyal to him and those bound to him, forced to feign loyalty – his own sentiments and demanded that they follow his lead. Eventually they all came, sheep-like, to see his views as their own. Thus, the old Nick was back again, the ruthless Nick, the take-it-and-like-it Nick, the be-absolutely-loyal-or-else Nick, the never-does-any-wrong Nick, the if-you-don't-like-it-get-out Nick, the always-right Nick, and the blameless Nick. Yes, the true Nick returned. As for who was really to blame for what happened, the names of the guilty parties, the wrongdoers, flew vituperatively from his mouth in every direction: this one didn't do enough; that one went too far; this one was a damned traitor; that one couldn't stand up when it counted; this one succumbed to the pressure; that one was a sniveling weakling; this one didn't know his ass from his elbow; and that one knew even less. But, as if induced to do so from deep within his soul, he always returned to Leon, the Devil incarnate, the man of evil, upon whom he heaped the worst that his gutter-mouth could conjure up. Using a tongue dipped in poisonous venom, he persisted in blaming that damnable Lederman, his erstwhile colleague from the Columbia club, whom he fingered with an unnatural conviction and who thereby became the lab's symbol for all its troubles. It was a stretch, to be sure. One might well wonder whether there was much truth to Nick's claims about Leon, or even whether Nick wholeheartedly believed it all. The portrait Nick painted of Leon – that of a man in the image of Dorian Gray, pure on the outside, fiendish on the inside – was patently false. Still, there could have been some rationality and method in Nick's foul play: the position he took vis-à-vis Leon had the distinct advantage of deflecting attention away from himself as villain of the piece.

Thus, Father Time passed over Nick, and, smiling his mocking, duplicitous smile, gave Nick his most earnest desire, the BNL crown. Poor Nick! Yes, he got what he wanted, but it came to him only to have its wondrous and illustrious jewel unkindly ripped from it. That's a reminder to everybody of the sage dictum, advice it would do well to heed: "*Be careful of wishing too hard for something, for you just might get it*!" Such is the manner in which the gods play with us mortals and make fools of us all. Yet, for what it was worth, ambitious Nick did in fact manage to capture the BNL throne; and the fact is that he turned out to be a man with extraordinary staying power, a ruthless man, very hard to dislodge. Nick was indeed a man to be reckoned with. He had that rare ability to see bright glimmerings in a sea of dark forebodings. Some might think that to be so is just a form of self-deception, but there's a lot to be said for keeping your head and moving forward despite all the odds stacked against you. And that's the way Nick was; that's the way he planned things out; that's the way he worked things out; that's the way he played out his role; and that's the way he led the lab. With tenacity and fervor, even as the threatening clouds were gathering ominously overhead, Nick, year upon year, sustained life in the old place, kept the staff going, and kept the faith. True, BNL would never become what it once was, but instead had to rest content with mediocrity. Nevertheless, despite the necessity of drinking undeservedly, but still rather plentifully, from the far-too-generous government's overflowing trough, under Nick's guidance the lab survived.

Actually, for Nick personally, even as the lab was reeling from its painful loss of ISABELLE, or CBA, as Nick liked to call it, things were not as bad as all that. After all, undoubtedly it was because BNL was then in its worst hour that he had risen to become the lab Director. You see the times were such that most of those eligible for this high position were scurrying about like scared rabbits trying to find a hole to hide in. But not Nick! This was his big chance, and nothing could keep him from the opportunity to play his role on center stage. When you think of it, finding the right man for the job gave AUI quite a difficult time. Where can one find a heroic figure to step into perilous quicksand to lead a battered pack of losers? How can one decide a priori how any man will fare in such unprotected, inauspicious, and treacherous circumstances? Nonetheless, with Vineyard thrown out in disgrace, AUI had to find someone to replace him. They tried as best they could. They looked here, there and everywhere. But there were only softhearted men around – no one with the fighting spirit to try the seemingly impossible, no one with the guts to walk right up to the cannon's mouth. So, in the end, AUI turned to Nick. He wanted it; he sought it out; he worked hard for it; and finally he got it – he became king of the hill.

Sure, Nick wasn't the knight in shining armor come to save the damsel ISABELLE in distress. But still he became king, and it was the misfortune of ISABELLE that paved the road that took him there. So how could he let her cancellation get him down when the perception – nay, the inevitability – of that happening was probably the underlying reason for his fulfillment of a long-time dream to reach the top? Mind you, it would be quite a stretch of the imagination to think that all this was part of a master plan on Nick's part. It almost surely wasn't. But in life, sometimes circumstances, bad as they are for others, play into your hands and serve your own needs and ends. Looked at in this way, things were pretty good for Nick. In a sense, it was a promising time for him: He was the Director of BNL; the lab was still there doing business; it still had a budget that wasn't to be sneezed at; it still had thousands of employees needing to be led; it still had its full complement of local political, academic and business support; and it still had a future that could have interesting possibilities. The conditions were perfect for Nick: he had inexhaustible energy and perhaps the capability to bring BNL back to life – to take it from the ignominious depths it had fallen into, back to the heights of greatness where it once had been. It could have been his time for fame. If only he could've braved the flames and pulled BNL out of the fire, he could've been somebody.

But there was this black spot in the rosy picture, an imperfection that would leave that depiction ever in the realm of potentiality, never to be realized. You see Nick simply didn't have the heart and mind to be a leader in the trying times he found himself in. How so, you ask? It was simply because he wasn't the master of his fate. Inside his very being there lay that personality defect that he just couldn't control: He couldn't forget the past. He couldn't forgive any hurts done him, real or imagined. He couldn't just take things as they were and move on. To his misfortune, he couldn't escape those deep and dark cravings that came from the innermost regions of his soul. What dominated him was a desire for vindication and revenge. His vision was that in the end all those who had betrayed him would pay dearly for their transgressions. From his position on high, he was able to and indeed would target his attacks on these enemies, especially the sorely hated Leon. He would see to it that they would all suffer the bitter experiences and humiliations that he had gone through; that they would also come to feel the painful flames of betrayal; and, foremost in his twisted mind, that they would come to know and appreciate the strength of the man they were dealing with and to feel the full force of his wrath. Through his iron fist, they would soon come to learn the error of their ways and come to regret what they had done to him and to his lab. Such was Nick's frame of mind as he planned for the lab's future. As for his own future, he'd come to see that as indistinguishable from BNL's. Together, he and BNL would march ahead and lay waste all their enemies of yore and all that stood in their path to glory. So it was that in the end, ironically, ISABELLE came to be Nick's obsession. Such is the playfulness of the gods that they lure the ambitious with false promises of brilliant stardom. Nick, a greedy weakling in the grip of a delusion, envisioned in his mind's eye how from the ashes of ISABELLE would arise a Phoenix, a new power-packed BNL purely of his creation.

* * * * *

As the shock of 1983 faded and, along with the cold winter wind, reality set in, anxiety began to surface. Fueled by worries of what was to become of them all, this uneasiness and restlessness manifested itself in all the wide variety of types involved – the scientists, the engineers, the technicians, the administrators, and the many others working in the Big Science arena. Naturally, this attitude of worry was to be found in those who were confounded and distressed by the events that had unfolded that year; but oddly it also found its way into those who were euphoric that honesty and rightness had finally triumphed. Yes, all of them started to feel vulnerable as their thoughts became filled with uncertainties about what the impact might be on their own lives. Rapid change always seems to instill in people doubts about their futures, and the swiftness of the harsh and ruthless blows dealt to BNL was ample enough cause for concern. Not unexpectedly, people asked the clear-cut, self-evident questions, the straightforward and self-serving ones: When will this new supercollider come to pass? Will I be given the opportunity to be a part of it? Will I fit in? Will the work be fulfilling? What do I do till it happens? On the other hand, over and above the day-to-day effects the big change in the making would have, there was a more complex source for people's doubts and lack of trust in their futures. Considering that they seemed to have lost their bearings as well as any control they may have had over their surroundings, they searched for a more concrete, a more palpable reason for their feelings. It really wasn't that hard to find the logical and undoubtedly correct explanation for their misgivings. It lay quite openly in the widely felt mistrust of their leaders that was growing in the community. Troubled by not being able to guess what was yet to come, they felt a disquieting pall of foreboding. Both as individuals and collectively as members of participating groups, they felt a growing apprehension about whether or not they counted for anything. Some were just plain discouraged; some became alarmed; some became filled with consternation; some were frightened out of their wits; and some even panicked. Were their interests being looked after, they asked? To that there was no disagreement. The universal answer was, "No!"

There was a common remembrance of that transforming summer of 1982, that summer of sweeping and organic change, that things-will-never-be-the-same summer, that summer when Big Physics leaped across the frontier into daredevil *bigness* from where there was no return. It was then that the physics establishment, the labs, the universities, and the government agencies, made the choice to sacrifice ISABELLE in order to gain the supercollider – to choose one at the expense of the other, to give up the lesser in order to gain the greater, to sell their souls for what they believed to be the betterment of mankind. Thinking about it in light of the killing of ISABELLE, the many community members not fully committed to the ambitious plan started to appreciate that a trade in human cargo had taken place that summer. Now, suddenly, its deeper meaning sprang out at them: When would it be their turn? When would they be sold down the river for a few pieces of silver? When would they go the way poor ISABELLE did? As a result of such cynical thoughts, their feelings of control over their environment and their futures began ebbing. It even got to the point where job security, that untouchable academic entitlement, which they had come to so depend on, was beginning to course downward and was on the threshold of a rapid decline. They began to ask the unthinkable: Could the worst happen? Could they find themselves out of a job? Adding fuel to the fires of speculation, secrecy was rampant. Thus, those who weren't part of the inner power circle – and few were – found themselves in the dark. Plans that would hurt them might very well be in the works, but they wouldn't know about them. Someone around them, their boss, their supervisor, or perhaps some competitive colleague, could be out for their hides, but they wouldn't know either who or why. Yes, it was hard going for the average Big Science Joe. Yet, what could they do? They had no voice and no one to speak for them. It was take it or leave it time! But where could they go? Would it be any better elsewhere? In any case, were they really sure about all this?

Basing such inferences and feelings that the bottom was falling out solely on the trade-off made at Snowmass wasn't about to earn anybody high marks on the logic-based common-sense test. The fact was that there were sound, logical reasons for the choices made there. BNL messed up big-time technically, thereby delaying the project to the point where it became obsolete. Furthermore, the lab failed to deliver on its promises so often that, with its credibility lost, it passed the point of being in the least trustworthy. However, there was far more to what was happening than purely rational analysis can explain. Indeed, there was an intense emotional component to the consequences of the Snowmass decision. Just think of it! The community had taken this giant step into uncharted territory, setting a very scary precedent in issuing up a sacrificial lamb. Perhaps people didn't respond full-scale immediately, but a year later, when HEPAP did its thing, consummating the execution of ISABELLE, it sent a shock wave through the Big Science community, and even pushed some over the edge. With that as backdrop, wasn't it natural to ask who would be next? The reasoning behind the action taken by HEPAP was, *we had to do it*, with the emphasis on *had*, but was that very far from *we wanted to do it* or *we did it to get even*? Anyway, when ISABELLE was done in, the shit hit the fan. Skepticism went on a rapid ascent. That actually made good sense because at some point a sell-out is a sell-out, no matter how you slice it. Thus, it would seem quite reasonable for an individual to ask, "When will it be my turn to get shafted?" However, this is really a rhetorical question, because more often than not, when an answer is found, it's already too late to do anything about it. As such, it isn't difficult to figure out that just the asking of it, whether overtly or only in the mind, represented a paradigm shift in people's outlook and behavior: Rationality was thrown out the window and the result was that trust in the community's leadership started to descend. Once this trust got low enough, reaching a certain threshold, irrationality began to rule and objective evidence and truth, such as it was, became secondary to the inner life. For a person in such a state, the mind's image of things begins to transcend and therefore overrule what the eye sees and what the ear hears. Then what the mind imagines becomes the crucial factor in how life is perceived, how motives are fixed, and how deeds and exploits are determined and played out. Unfortunately, this is the nature of the environment the Big Science community found itself in as it was on the threshold of its biggest project of the twentieth century. To win this one for basic physics research would be its biggest challenge since its great victories of decades earlier, and time would tell that it was perhaps a step too big to have risked so much for.

The line between an act of considered judgment and one of betrayal is often a fuzzy one. But once the deed is done, does it really matter which interpretation is the better one? Some poor guy got the shaft. Now, It's merely the past tense. It's over and done with. Why bother over something that can't be changed anyway? Yet, is it wise to jump so quickly to this conclusion? Even if you're not the one being *sent over* this time, you could well be next in line. Then it would do you well to pay heed to how others around you are faring, and why they were treated the way they were.

Let's slow down here and take things another time from the start. One thing is certain: Any interest you might have in asking questions and searching for answers surely depends on where in the scheme of things you're sitting. If you happen to be one of the group making the calls and pulling the switch, then that's one thing. In that case, you probably know full well what's going on. But if you're in the class of the vulnerable ones, if you could soon be on the receiving end, if you could be close to feeling the pain and the shame of the black boot, then the chances are you're in the dark. If that's where you're positioned, then *search and discovery* would seem to be your best bet. Think for a second: Since knowledge is power, why hesitate? Don't! Seek it out! And don't let up on questioning your every move! Which side is this one or that one on? Can you trust him? Should you play the fool? Should you play up to him? Should you tell him all you know, or just a part of it? Should you give him small talk and no more? Can you open up fully to him? Is he part of a secret power cluster meting out the verdicts? Is it all being done through backroom politics in smoke-filled rooms? In an atmosphere where consensus-building is absent; where openness is dead; and where whispering, suppressing truth, concealed decision-making, and underhanded dealing represent the standard mode of conduct – in such an atmosphere, can anyone count on due process being followed?

In the ISABELLE case, the big question was who and what was behind the sell-out of BNL. Did the community decide openly, taking all interests into consideration fairly; or did a few power-laden individuals who had it in for the lab finally have their day and cash in? To a disinterested person this would appear to be an open and shut case. Certainly the process had a high degree of openness: it included many DOE reviews; the momentous 1982 Snowmass conference; town meetings with community participation galore; HEPAP meetings; and a HEPAP sub-panel formed specifically to look into the issue, with active representation from all sides. Would anyone question that the community went out of its way to bend over backward in order to ensure a balanced process that gave BNL chance after chance after chance to explain, to correct, to change its management and its ways of doing business, and to do what it promised it would do? Some argued that BNL was given too much slack. They claimed that more discipline would've been better and would've had the added advantage of setting the right example for the future. All in all then, with this history, how could any reasonable person escape the conclusion that BNL was given due process and then some? No, there is not the least doubt that the ISABELLE cancellation was via community consensus, if that expression is to mean anything at all. Yet, despite this reality, even after the multitude of opportunities given to BNL to mend its ways and start anew, many, especially BNL's followers and friends, refused to accept the honesty of the process and the fairness of the result. To them it was a Judas kiss. To them, mendacity, hypocrisy, and knavery lay behind the act, and the word betrayal seemed to flow easily and naturally from their lips.

However, in the supercollider's heyday of the mid-eighties, those in the catbird seat, feeling invincible and indestructible, didn't take much notice of the BNL sore losers initiating and propagating these notions of perfidy and treachery. The new priests considered such types to be heretics and gave them little or no consideration. They were blind to the suffering of those who had lost. Looking back, this may not have been the wisest of courses for the leaders of the new project to follow. To ignore people who later may be important and even essential supporters isn't the mark of a high-class strategist. But the winners were basking in their time of holding the reins and leading the pack. As for the losers, let them fend for themselves. To hell with them! They should've joined the winning team when they had the chance. "*They still could*," came the word from above. All they had to do was to bow down to the new kings-of-the-hill. These high-flyers were cavalier, believed themselves to be infallible and invulnerable, and didn't give a hoot about what anyone else thought. Gone and forgotten were the questionable things they did to get where they were. But be that as it may, it still seems worth asking, *was it sensible to forget*? Was what they did in the first place right? Is there any justification for a killing or, if you insist, a sacrifice? Is there any defense that can be made at all? Can any reasoning make right out of wrong? It may very well be that there are no words that can suffice, because it seems that a nagging doubt will always remain about whether trading one life for another, whatever the excuse, won't somewhere down the line turn on those who practise such a risky business.

In spite of the dangers inherent in sacrificing one for another, the Big Science community couldn't resist the temptation to do just that. The fabulous scientific fortune promised by Reagan and his philosophy of excellence was too much of an opportunity to pass up, and if a sacrifice had to be submitted as the price exacted, then it would be paid. BNL, as it happened, was both a stumbling block and an unprotected sheep ripe for the offering. It was an irresistible combination. So a phony war was arranged for the world science community and the public-at-large. But the outcome was a foregone conclusion: a piece of BNL's flesh, ISABELLE, was given to appease the demands of the Washington gods. Unfortunately, there was no contingency plan to aid BNL in its hour of need. As the shaky and hurt lab sought to find a path to recovery from its painful and protracted ISABELLE experience, the rest of the community couldn't have cared less. The fact is that BNL took the best shot it knew how, but still came out second-best, and found itself down at the bottom of the barrel. It was now left to churn out experimental data of little consequence with grandfather AGS. The truth was that BNL could do little more than contemplate its navel, as the champs were looking ahead to brighter, challenging days, luxuriating in the splendor they imagined lay ahead of them.

With Reagan's check delivered as promised, the victors stretched for the shining star beckoning in the distance. Those leading the parade were sure they could reach the object of their desire. However, the new and exciting supercollider was as yet merely a figment in the minds of dreamers. Still, they felt as if it were already a real and tangible thing, almost palpable to the touch. But could they actually pull off the basic science coup of the twentieth century? Were they built of strong-enough fiber? They had done similar types of projects before, although those were but faint shadows of the plans now on the table. Nonetheless, as complex, as daring, and as close to being impossible as the task was, there were moments when it was hard not to believe that these men, so buoyant, so full of self-assurance and know-how, could reach the pot of gold. Drawing on their sterling performance of past days, these men partaking of this adventure-filled feast had permeating their bodies and souls that special mixture of hope and anxiety, of recklessness and caution, and of desire and fear, that – when found in the right proportions – impels men to strive to achieve beyond their means. But did they possess these characteristics in the proper proportions? Were they the right men for this challenge of a lifetime? Ah, these were questions that only time could fashion answers to! So it was that Big Physics – or, perhaps more accurately very, very, very Big Physics – arrived in America.

The original idea for a super-duper multi-TeV energy collider arose during the ICFA workshops of the late seventies. (The energy unit TeV stands for one thousand billion electron volts of energy.) To pierce nature's armor protecting its hidden knowledge, they needed a machine many times more powerful than the existing Tevatron at Fermilab, with its particle energy of about one TeV. After a lot of rumination, a consensus among the influential theorists was reached and led to the madcap desire of upping the ante to more than twenty times that. With the confidence of thrill-seeking youth and the choice of that energy range, Big Physics set the size scale for the collider of the century. The AGS of 1960 at BNL operated at an energy of 0.03-TeV, with the ring carrying the rotating beam of protons being one half mile in circumference; the Fermilab tunnel of 1970, with 0.8-TeV protons racing through it, was a little over three miles around; and the new collider with particles envisioned in the multi-TeV energy range would have to be a pseudo-circle more than 50 miles in length. Wow! What a jump! The planners needed brazen ambition and a rich taste for risky business to embark on such a challenge. But starting is one thing, pulling it off quite another. Once having set out on the journey, could they really bring home the bacon? However, for men with such voracious and lusty appetites for fame, and with such wild fancies, the consummation seemed no more than a formality. Worrying about whether or not it could actually be done was a waste of their emotional energy and their valuable time. Just give them the dough and wind them up, then in a flash a magic carpet would carry them off to the land of their dreams. For their part, all that was needed was to put their shoulders to the wheel and get down to the nitty-gritty of doing what has to be done. No problem!

Once the seeds were planted in these spirited men in search of their dreams, the work to build concrete reality out of imaginings began in earnest with an impressive flurry of activity. In the wake of Snowmass 1982, where the Desertron was conceived and discussed, and following the HEPAP recommendation of 1983 for a multi-TeV collider, a series of informal, almost ad hoc, workshops was quickly organized at a variety of locations around the U.S. After a little consideration, the notion of a low-cost, promptly made machine near the surface somewhere in the desert southwest, the brainchild of Bob Wilson, was deemed brash and plainly impractical. It was regarded as elitist as well because, by keeping experimentation to the minimum required to get what was wanted, it wouldn't involve widespread segments of the community of physichists. Who but Bob could have pulled out of his magician's hat such a problematic, such a tricky, and such a precarious machine? For anyone available to tackle it, it was simply out of his depth. So, not unexpectedly, the community turned in another direction. However, Bob's daring and full-of-flare stratagem managed to insinuate into the minds of scientists the feeling that it truly might be possible to search for and find the Holy Grail. Although his plan might not be right for a modern, up-scale machine, they surmised, to build a supercollider some other way, maybe bulkier and more costly than Bob would have liked, began to make sense to them. There was of course the added money needed to undertake the construction of a more conservative collider. Then there was also the enhanced *bigness*. That latter point no one even thought worthy of any serious consideration. But as far as the money was concerned, there seemed to be no issue here. The universal assumption was that the government would cough it up. Yes, there wasn't the least doubt that the money would be had. The people involved actually thought very little of these matters of money and *bigness*. What really pumped them up and what really gave great appeal to this idea of a machine-for-all was that it would garner more support from the all-important *physichists*.

As it turned out, Bob was not to be in the thick of things as, being a builder, he most dearly would have loved to be. However, his role, as the supercollider story unfolded, couldn't have been done without. He pushed the community forward, using his stature, his persistence and any other quality he could dig up. He pressed on, against the odds, when others not of his ilk would surely have folded. He whispered ideas. He turned men's thinking in ways they couldn't have done on their own. He talked of fantastical discoveries and of greatness-to-be. He was an inspirer of men. He imbued in scientists what had been his youthful trademark, the belief that what seems to be impossible is not always so. It can be done, he insisted. It will be done!

The buzz about the new machine that would change high-energy physics consumed the community, and all manner of ideas – about whether to do it, when to do it, and how to do it – roamed the land. In this way, the stage for the supercollider was set. It only remained for the community leaders and the government bosses to give their OK. With ordinary folk, the hoi polloi of science, putting on a show of record-breaking initiative, the higher-ups found themselves under a great deal of pressure to do something about it. How else were they to react? The little guys had already set the example. As a result, the big shots felt the need to measure up and not just take the usual slow-as-a-mule establishment road. So, in quick order, they got their act together pronto and their voice was heard. The anxiously waiting scientists were well prepared for the *yes* that came, and when it did, it acted like *the bang* of a race-starting gun. CERN was stunned that America could move so fast and so decisively. And the U.S. didn't waver in its resolve. In a heartbeat, the contenders, with CERN lagging well in the rear, left the starting gate. Whether CERN was prepared or not, the race was on.

In America, with the green light flashing, action on the supercollider came at a breathtaking pace. Formal workshops were already being planned; but now that they were sanctioned, they followed swiftly. The accelerator scientists worked day and night putting together a preliminary design of the collider. Meanwhile the physichists weren't sitting around twiddling their thumbs. On the contrary, they matched the accelerator types, developing ideas for the massive and complex detectors that would be needed for the envisioned experiments. As time passed, from labs all over the country came reams of paper containing an immense amount of intricately technical information. Not to be outdone, the administrators and technical managers called in were no slouches either. From them flowed memos galore that glued the pieces of the project together, while in addition there appeared an endless number of reports overwhelmingly detailing exactly how the project would be made to come to pass. There were the financial and personnel requirements; the physical plant requirements and layouts; the scheduling and budget plans; the checks and balances that would be associated with the project's progress; and the project justification, including what it would accomplish. What an exciting time! It was like the energy release coming from the letting go of an elastic band stretched to its limit. Suddenly, after a long wait and an inordinate amount of stress, there it was. Once set in motion, the work energy seemed boundless, and along with that the work ethic flourished. It all happened so very fast, not much more than half a year, give or take a couple of months. Looking back, it all seems so simple: first, the knockout blow was dealt to ISABELLE when the DOE formally cancelled it in October of 1983; then came the thumbs up sign, turning on the supercollider's lamp of life, where before there was only underground activity; and finally the project was given the official imprimatur: The Superconducting Super Collider (SSC) was on! With such an unimaginative designating title, it's a wonder the whole enterprise survived its birth. However, nothing could derail it, and nothing could detract from the grandeur of this spellbinding endeavor.

The naming of the supercollider, like a baptism, endowed it with identity; and once this official recognition was granted, the DOE made a pot of money available for R&D. When that big step was taken, all the pieces needed to impel the new project forward began falling into place. It was real, people thought, and they all wanted in. Accelerator builders saw their chance to get in the ground floor; physichists were ripe to claim first dibs in the supposed mind-blowing experiments-to-be; and particle theorists, the high priests of physics, visualized their names in lights as being first to predict what would be discovered. With verve, energy, and hope in their hearts, they all, young and old alike, flocked to the new center of the Big Physics universe.

The interest and involvement of high-level officials, from the government, from industry, and from lab directorates all across the country, also jumped by leaps and bounds. *Money talks*, as the saying goes. Thus, they took charge of the distribution of the R&D funds; and, doing so, these leaders of the Big Science establishment took over ownership of the project. They proclaimed its urgent importance for the future of U.S. science, and firmly established it as the highest priority item in the high-energy physics budget. So it was that the supercollider took flight and began to fly faster and faster. In the summer of 1984, a Central Design Group (CDG) was formed, based at Lawrence Berkeley Laboratory (LBL). It was managed by Universities Research Association (URA), which also happened to be the prime contractor for Fermilab. But URA had a unique quality not possessed by any other lab-managing organization: it was veritably national in character. You see it was governed by a consortium of almost all the research universities in the U.S., a total of about 80. Thus, in a single imaginative step, the marriage of the SSC to academia was accomplished and everything seemed to be coming up roses. Soon 150 accelerator physicists and engineers were hard at work on a preliminary design for the imposing, endlessly talked about project-cum-monster. But it didn't stop there. Not skipping a beat, it kept growing at lightning speed. In the short span of two years, the CDG, having grown to a staff of 250 scientists and engineers under the leadership of Maury Tigner, a Cornell scientist, came out with its Conceptual Design Report (CDR). Here the community was provided with its first glimpse of the full-fledged SSC.

The Berkeley group had a variety of prototype superconducting magnets built at labs around the country, and in 1985 it chose a high-field magnet using the well-known, established technology launched at Rutherford and Fermilab. The SSC magnet design also made use of the further improved magnet technology developed at DESY in Hamburg. The DESY magnets were built for their proton ring as part of their electron-proton collider, a new type of collider in the modest Tevatron energy range. However, the CDG didn't just sit on its haunches and use what was already available on the shelf. No, it made its own advancements in magnet technology as well. Most particularly, it came up with a significant increase in the current-carrying capability of the magnet's superconducting material. But the CDG work on the crucial choice of a magnet wasn't its only preoccupation. The accelerator scientists and engineers working there were truly a bunch of eager beavers. They set their fertile minds on many issues that might prove to be future stumbling blocks to the SSC's smooth, unhindered construction. They studied a multitude of potential problems, ranging from beam stability and beam loss to particle radiation effects to a variety of crucial engineering issues, including those related to vacuum and thermal properties. Yes, these were serious men, hard-working men, clever and even brilliant men; and they vowed that no stone that could lead to trouble would be left unturned.

This 1986 CDR was profuse with technical details. When taken all together, it became the base design for the SSC, the rose of the accelerator world. In addition, the report contained the all-important estimated cost and schedule. That was what all the big boys were interested in. So as not to give them heartburn and, perhaps of even more significance, so as not to inflame regional conflict, the cost estimate made was site-independent. This strategy wisely left open the delicate and possibly explosive question of where the SSC would be situated. Getting down to the number everybody was aching to know, the preliminary cost estimate for the SSC presented to the DOE was a little over three billion dollars. This was substantially more than Bob Wilson had in mind for his Desertron. But, to the astonishment of most, this flagrantly extravagant, even outrageous, cost didn't seem to upset the government bureaucracy; actually it hardly raised an eyebrow. On the contrary, they seemed to have expected it, and may secretly even have liked the fact that it was so high. You see the government's job is to spend money, not to save it. Although one may find it strange when first confronted with this reality, the truth is that spending more raises a bureaucrat's stature, while saving only lowers it. In any case, whether it is valid or not, or whether it's made honestly or not, the argument is that the more the government spends, the better it is for the economy. Naturally, the expenditures should be done for productive ends; but in the instance of a Big Science project, that goes without saying. It therefore appears that the designers at LBL did their part well – they had a high price tag and didn't name a site. Thus, in 1986, the proposal was submitted to the DOE and scientists near and far took a collective deep breath. Although they felt exceptionally pleased with themselves and quite confident of the outcome, they were mighty anxious as they awaited the government's answer. You see before the champagne starts flowing, it's always best to see the pledged commitment, the contract, in writing.

* * * * *

The making of the SSC was a big step for American basic research. Fermilab, some fifteen years earlier, had cost one quarter billion dollars to build. When this number is compared to the annual high-energy physics budget, including both operations and construction, in the early to mid-eighties, which was around one half billion dollars, then clearly the SSC ushered in a whole new ball game. With the amounts being bandied about for the SSC, no doubt the high-energy bureaucrats would have sorely loved to push ahead. On the other hand, their Washington competitors had other ideas. They weren't about to let the SSC suck them dry. You see everyone has a use for money. That's why the status quo is such a tough nut to crack. So, if it's a big change in the budget you're after – any government budget, for that matter – then good luck! Nonetheless, here was the worthy SSC asking for quite a pretty penny. If you were a government man, how would you like them apples? On the face of it, that's not so hard to answer. The tendency would be for the government to stand still, either drag its feet or out-rightly say *no*. But the SSC was a very special case. It was in the midst of a love affair with Reagan and his science lieutenant. Still, going ahead with the project meant that there would have to be a substantial increase in the basic research money supply and that implied a very hard sell – to Congress, to the Office of Management and Budget, to the bureaucrats who feared the worst for their areas, to the gurus of the science enterprise at-large, and to the many jealous doomsday preachers. But, as it happened, fortune was smiling on the knowledge-seekers, and there turned out to be enough smooth-talking Big Physics salesmen to garner the loot and get the project aimed at deciphering the code of the universe off the ground.

However, there's a great deal more to the big money regime than merely a lot more cash. It's not that handling money isn't tough enough by itself. It is: What exactly do you spend it on? How much can you afford? Can you put it off? Is it absolutely necessary now? Are you overspending? Should you continue negotiating? Should you hold off a bit? Is there a good deal to be had waiting just around the corner? These are questions common to all uses of project money. But at a certain level, a qualitative change arises as the system passes over into the state of *bigness*. With a sufficiently large number of people, each looking for his piece of the pie, the typical management ceases to be viable. It just doesn't work anymore. It requires a special kind of team to manage the onslaught of people problems that stem from the state of *bigness*. When that state comes to pass, with big money there for the picking, it is a time when people lose their grip on themselves. Only number one counts; each Doctor Jekyll becomes his alter ego Mister Hyde; and irrationality becomes the ruling mode of conduct. Yes, *bigness* fosters badness! The scientists who came to run the big new supercollider were totally unprepared for the ensuing level of bad behavior: coming from the squabbling for position; from the disputes and the wrangling over sweet deals and honey-dipped contracts; from the misrepresentations of human worth and product value; and from just plain greed. It's not that these human failings don't take place in any organizational framework. Of course they do. But when you enter into the state of *bigness*, try to imagine the number of them and the rapidity with which they pile up one on top of the other. It is then, when the sheer numbers begin to overwhelm the management, that, for that particular management, *big-bad-bigness* has intruded its way in. In the case of the management of basic research, the top was and is comprised primarily of scientists. That's the way it was designed. Unfortunately, that's not a very auspicious entry into *bigness*. You see the management of Big Physics was borderline workable before the SSC arrived on the scene. Then, when the giant project came, although the science leadership couldn't fathom it, Big Physics found itself on the edge of a precipice, ready to fall headlong into the black pit of failure.

Here's how the state of bigness works. Big money is like honey, sweet and desirable. Take honey. It's just there in the tree out in the open, begging to be had. It's so inviting, so tempting. Why not reach out and grab a handful? You can almost taste it! However, hopefully before it's not too late, you notice those bees hovering about. Remember, bees can and do bite. So you'd best beware of easy pickings, lest you end up getting hurt, or worse still, destroying what you've so wanted. Like honey, money is seductive and irresistible; and it also has its hoarder-bees and self-styled protectors; and the bigger the bucks, the more attractive it is and the fiercer the competition. All the while, standing on the sidelines, are jealous outsiders aching to get in and get their crack at it. They can be kept out for a time, but it gets harder and harder to do as they become more determined and their numbers grow. The more money involved, the more intruders there are, the faster they gather and swell, and the more vicious they tend to be. Occasionally dangerous bears penetrate the barrier and channel their way onto the premises. The management bees must always be on the lookout for such types. Alas, they must also be strong enough to counter the interlopers. These uninvited guests aren't stakeholders in the venture, but they have the itch for action and booty, and, more often than not, the power to back them up. So, what are the poor guards at the gate to do but let these trespassers have their way? When the new arrivals become aware of the size of the take, when they see what the sweet plump beehive has to offer, their fascination intensifies. Then, once they catch the craving bug, once they take a sample-taste of the loot, it's indeed difficult to keep them from what they've come to perceive as their share of the entitlement. In this way, on goes the process, spreading relentlessly and insidiously. The more money there is, the more claimants there are, leading inevitably to the result that more resources become necessary to manage them. Thus, even more money has to be found. And then comes the clinker! Is any of this added financial burden being put to productive ends? *The answer my friend is blowin' in the wind, the answer is blowin' in the wind.*

Thus, *bigness* is a money attractor. So, if the project is to keep going, more and more money has to be brought in. With all this money floating about, someone has to keep track of it, if for no other reason than that the government requires it. Yes – you guessed it – a bureaucracy, the smaller the better, is called for. Its job is to control, distribute, and police the flow of the ever-increasing money being moved around. However, at some point, the bureaucrats just won't be adequate, they won't be sufficiently perceptive or agile enough to deal with the onrush of tricky-Dicks skimming off the top. So, finally, those who still want to salvage something of the project must concede and allow a full-blown administrative hierarchy to come into being. Scientists as a rule don't want such a beast. They prefer a more collegial style of management, where informality and trust are the defining characteristics – idealized, to be sure. That gives them the higher productivity they want. You see they just want to do science, and not be bothered with hierarchies, chains of command, formal procedures, rigid communications networks, and other stuff like that. Unfortunately for them and for Big Science, *bigness* demands a big administration, and *bigness* will have what it wants or else chaos will reign. So, take your choice: Is it to be the big SSC or a big bust?

Thus the big project is swallowed up by a big administration. This administration develops and evolves, along with its natural tendency to accumulate power, to grow uncontrollably, and to become an end unto itself. Thereby even more money is eaten up. Once started, the process of administrative growth accompanying *bigness* is next to impossible to curtail. The organizational distance from the money input to its productive use gets longer and longer. Controlling fund-flow gets harder and harder, until at some level it becomes an accounting nightmare. No matter how hard an honest man might try to inhibit it, this insertion of administrative measures for the purpose of prevention unavoidably and inevitably leads to money slipping through the cracks. How ironic! The intended solution by way of a watchdog administrative system ends up being a major source of the problem. And on the vicious circle goes! Losing money implies the necessity for more money; then, of course, there is a need for more control, more management, more bureaucracy, and thus even more money. Where will it all end, you ask? The fact is that nothing can be done about it. It is just the way things are! The tides generated by *bigness* are too powerful and must run their course to the shore. Thus, if you must be big, you have to pay the cost it entails. In other words, you have to pay for having money. The meaning of this is clear: to maintain your *bigness* and keep the wheels of the enterprise churning away, you have to get the cash to support the big project's voracious and unquenchable appetite. Keep in mind that you're not actually doing more, perhaps you're even doing less, but it simply costs more to just get the chance to do what you want done.

As if all this weren't enough, there's yet another factor to take account of, one that even surpasses in importance the loss of the productive use of funds. And what might that be? The answer is the risk factor. Now you might be a little skeptical of that. You might even become flippant and whimsical. Isn't every endeavor risky, you might ask?

Isn't stepping off the curb risky? Isn't merely living risky? Of course, all that is quite right. But here we're talking about *bigness*, and *bigness* has its own special brand of risk. Of and by itself, *bigness* actually increases the risk of failing to successfully complete your project. The way it works is that a big project naturally induces big stress in all who even come close to it. Then, from that big stress, there follow more and bigger mistakes. There's the rub: mistakes can be killers if they're not properly looked after. If they're neglected, they'll just pile up and eventually overcome you. Your project will then be kaput, and maybe you along with it. However, even if you handle them right, still their very presence leads to higher risk, then to higher stress, and then inevitably to more mistakes. You might find that you can't keep up with the mistakes. There's just no time. Correct one and look up to find another or two or three or more in its place. But if you don't correct the mistakes or somehow take care of them, you're a cooked goose. Yet, that's the nature of *bigness*. When you first choose to enter its arena, you'd do well to check whether you've got the stomach for it. If the project were small, where mistakes aren't so costly and stressful, perhaps you could catch them in time and save the day. There'll just be some delay in completion and some additional cost. But the project will be there. You might even be commended on being so resourceful in overcoming the obstacles and crossing the finishing line. However, in the state where *bigness* prevails, you mightn't be able to stop the merry-go-round as it inexorably leads you nowhere except to the darkness of oblivion.

If you're still not convinced that getting into the *bigness* game is like going to stand on a volcano ready to blow, then there's even more. Consider this. Suppose you're a man of unparalleled persuasiveness. Suppose you're able to keep the money flowing even as you incessantly keep increasing the cost-estimate, keep delaying the project completion, keep changing the technical design, and keep making promises you only fail to come through on. That's quite a mouthful! But that's not all. Suppose the government, in spite of all this, continues to remain supportive and helps the project management raise the cash that becomes essential to have. Actually, it's tough for it to back out being that it played such an instrumental role in starting the mammoth project in the first place. Thus, even though the project appears to be falling apart, the feeding of it shows no signs of abating and it goes on. With that as backdrop, the big questions are: Where is the project going and where is the money going? It turns out that there is a most insidious impact of the *bigness* phenomenon that cannot be resolved merely with more money. You see in order for the project to ever be completed, the incoming money, at least enough of it, has to be made to go into it and to be used for it. However, in the *bigness* state, slowly but surely, the management tends to shift its interest from doing science to raising and handling funds. Thus, because it is the management's interests that determine its priorities, and it is its priorities that determine where the money goes, then more and more money will, as sure as anything, end up in financial administration. So, as the failing project enters into its later stages of *bigness*, finance becomes the predominant and driving concern of the enterprise. From the top management well into the organization's structure there develops an all-engrossing preoccupation with money. Then, the apparently sole questions that prey on the minds of the now all-important moneybag men are: How much is coming in and how much is going out? Unavoidably there is a lessening of attention paid to the enterprise's true science and technology raison d'être. At that juncture, the project doesn't seem to have a ghost of a chance of coming through. From then on, it is a slippery slope, and the downhill slide is on. As its course downward gains momentum, the chance of stopping it diminishes and the end approaches a certainty. The decision process for the wide range of project organization matters, technical, production, marketing, and even financial, first begins to develop cracks; then it experiences the formation of lesions; and ultimately, without potently forcible, even Herculean, intervention, it breaks down completely. As this happens, starting from the top and moving down the management ladder, mistakes, accidents, and failings in all areas, administrative as well as technical, begin to increase, and nothing that is humanly possible – barring the unlikely massive overhaul of the project management itself – is capable of bucking the trend. At this point, the *bigness* effect has come into full bloom and the influx of more money, so acutely yearned for at first, is futile, and becomes nothing more than money flushed down the toilet. Finally the truth is apparent: money has been transformed into the kiss of death. If there were a moral to this critique of an all too common occurrence, it is simply that it's a mark of wisdom to hesitate before taking the last step and crossing the line into the realm of *bigness*.

* * * * *

What came to be the SSC was first proposed at Snowmass as a big project, but not that big. That's where Wilson put forth his less than one billion-dollar daringly imaginative Desertron. A short time later, Leon came down a little closer to earth with his claim that he could use anti-protons; and so, by having to build only one ring, he could keep the cost down to one billion. Thus, the first-blush ideas were for a quick-and-dirty, low-cost machine! No luxury! No gold plating! Just the old-fashioned way of doing science with Band-Aids! You do what you have to do to get the job done! But as the community of high-energy physicists got into the spirit of such a striking and enviable endeavor, slowly but surely they edged toward the more formal and the bigger. The original concept became transformed into an honest-to-goodness super collider, one that would provide more energy; would be built deep underground in a standard tunnel with the usual cross-section; would develop and use far more advanced and complex magnets; and naturally would cost a lot more money. "Hey," they seemed to say, "We can do it! Just give us the cash and we'll give you the best that money can buy!"

Maybe that was the right way to go. Maybe it was the only way to discover the true secret of the universe's mass. In any case, as the proposal wended its way from the science community to the DOE, it became, with its price tag of over three billion dollars, what can only be termed a really big project. That wasn't really much of a surprise seeing that the whole evolution of the idea of a U.S. supercollider was done with government complicity and consent. That's what the government men wanted and that's what they got. Nonetheless, when it came to putting signatures down on paper, the government officials were a tad nervous and tentative, not as sure as they were when it was only talk. After all, their first-hand experience with defense projects had already given them a taste of *bigness*, and it wasn't anything to write home about. There was no escaping the stark and off-putting institutional memory of the mistakes, the missteps, the promises not kept, the unconscionable overspending, the charlatanism, the chicanery, the book-cooking, and even the downright face-to-face lies. Did they really want a repeat performance of that in basic research? With all that knowledge of how defense fared under their belts, they well knew the risks in saying *yes*, and so took their own sweet time about doing so.

But, even though there were many obstacles, from the government as well as from the science community, standing in the supercollider's path and delaying the verdict, the big step was finally taken. To make the SSC a real project, the *go – no-go* question actually had to be taken all the way up to the hallowed office of the President. That's where it would be determined if basic research would be permitted to cross over the line into *bigness*. There was much drama in this moment of decision. Try to picture the scene with President Reagan, seated in his luxuriously leathered tall-backed chair, listening intently, while his science advisor, Jay Keyworth, made the case for Big Physics and the SSC. Jay had done his homework assiduously and was well prepared. As a prelude to his arguments, he informed the President that he had the firm backing of a large number of important political, government, industrial and scientific leaders. Then he briefly summarized the major points that he felt would interest his boss: what the project would accomplish; how much effort it would require; and what resources would be needed. Then he capped his presentation with his personal view that the plan could be made to work, and ended up with the all-important bottom line. There was a short pause. Reagan thought about it, but just a bit. You see it wasn't his way to belabor decision-making. Then, without further ado, he came to the judgment that the SSC was worthy of endorsement. Smiling at the younger man sitting opposite him, he said, "Throw deep," echoing the sentiment of that great Oakland quarterback, Kenny Stabler.

The President, in giving Big Science the green light, impressively demonstrated his out-and-out trust that the scientists, who said they could do it, would carry through on their promises made. The formal process was quite straightforward: The DOE recommended "*go*" and the President, always looking hopefully to the future and with a strong faith in science and technology, didn't have a problem going along with that judgment. It's not that he was an easy mark. On the contrary, he was actually a very tough cookie. But how much time can a man sitting in the Oval Office give to any matter that, after all, amounts to but a mere blip in the great big U.S. budget? For the most part, letting his instincts carry the ball for him, he'd no doubt given it just the right amount of thought it merited. Yet, in that oh-so-brief "OK" moment, he'd paused ever so slightly, questioning whether the science community really appreciated what it was getting itself into. However, his hesitation was short-lived as his attraction to modernity quickly overcame any passing doubts that American science was up to the task. Thus, the men of Big Science passed the point of no return, and the last chance to reconsider the course they'd chosen – strewn with the bodies of other men who'd tried before them – was gone. But whether or not they really had the opportunity to hold back didn't matter much anyway. You see the *physichists*, the ones who really counted, were so bloody cock-sure of themselves that virtually none of them had a slightest tilt in that direction. So, from that moment on, there was no stopping science from entering into the waiting – the awesome and humbling – jaws of *bigness*.

Once Reagan nodded his assent, the show was on although the formal decision to proceed with the SSC project was made a little later in January of 1987. Make no bones about it – this was a fateful decision in the life of American Big Science and was, one way or another, to change it for keeps. Just think! If the men of science were up to the job, what happy days lay ahead! On the other hand, if they couldn't measure up to the task, what heartache was in store for them! However, when it all began, who among them could have accurately guessed the actual outcome? This was a new and untried experience for science. It was an enterprise of such high risk that, in hindsight, it would've been much better if things had been done differently. Surely, some cool heads – some more cautious and questioning types with a more temperate outlook – should've been included in the project's leadership to remind the far too self-assured *physichists* that this was not going to be a piece of cake. On the other hand, when you're entering into entirely new territory, winning can never be a sure thing. So who knows? Perhaps it was a time to throw caution to the wind. Yes, naturally there was lots of risk in going ahead, but remember that if the project could be brought off, there would've been a very high pay-off for science, for the country, and for all mankind.

For its part, the government came through with flying colors. The project, bigger by a long shot than anything basic science had ever done before, had to be pushed through the halls of power against a lot of resistance: There were congressmen who, as a matter of principle, wanted to keep government small and the budget down; there were those who represented jealous scientists, constituents in their districts; and there were those who believed that Big Science of the basic variety was either a luxury that the country couldn't afford or an item very low down on the scale of priorities. But the smart eggheads running the show, both government officials who'd come from academia and highbrow scientists, figured out a way to do it and made it happen by doing an end-run around the opposition. They made a beeline right for the President, and he came through. The man in the White House didn't really need much persuading, and, without much fuss, he made the SSC a *presidential initiative*.

The expression "*presidential initiative*" wasn't empty bureaucratic jargon but was an awe-provoking process. Almost immediately, this special status conferred on the project brought with it the palpable, envy-of-all benefit of so-called new money, miraculously springing up from that most complex of mechanisms, the U.S. budget. The principle behind this new money – similar to congressional earmarked funds – is that it mysteriously materializes and is tacked on to the existing annual budget of the area in receipt of the largesse, in this case high-energy physics. Wow! But where, you ask, does the money come from? If you're of a cynical bent, you'll insist that it's being taken from somebody else's pot. If that were to be so, then, wherever in the budget you happen to be placed, especially if in a scientific discipline, you might have a legitimate cause for concern. But this way of thinking totally misconstrues the whole remarkable process. Strangely, the U.S. budget is not a zero sum game, not at all like a family budget with its fixed amount in – fixed amount out mechanism. No, somehow the U.S. budget has what is referred to in economics as a high elasticity. The upshot of this is that although many areas given government money suffer every year, rest assured that it's not strictly speaking due to any presidential initiative. One thing appears certain: the SSC didn't cut into the budget of any other science. In fact, the funds for the singled-out SSC project were not taken, even in part, from the existing DOE component of the budget. Even more, going down another budget level, the funds for basic research in physics as well as other scientific areas, that is, the amount already allotted to the Office of Energy Research (ER) of the DOE, was – believe it or not – untouched. Thus the government demonstrated, in as dramatic and concrete a way as it's possible to do, its astonishingly no-strings-attached support for basic research. What power the government has! What extraordinary power lies in the presidency! As if to validate these truths, in no time flat, the high-energy physics annual budget shot up to well over a billion dollars. One can only marvel at such inestimable power that can double the budget for a field almost overnight with the stroke of a pen. Yes, it's quite a thing to have the President on your side.

What a magnificent gesture of respect for basic science the whole business was, so much so that you'd have expected every scientist – the ones directly involved, the ones on the periphery, and even the ones just watching from the sidelines – to be proud, honored, and pleased as Punch. But life is not that simple. In fact, the reaction wasn't at all what you'd think. In sciences other than high-energy physics, there was more resentment than anything else. Now, how do you explain that? Perhaps it was no more than the "*Why not me*" syndrome showing its ugly face. So it was that jealousy could be seen everywhere! Odder still, in time, even the receivers of such beneficence became unappreciative of the government's generosity. What a shocker that was! They should have said, *thanks, thanks, and thanks again*. They should have undertaken, with as much determination as they could muster, to fulfill the promises they'd made. They should have sworn to each other and to themselves to give their all to come through, no matter the sacrifices to be made. But they didn't. It was almost as if they felt they had it coming to them. How maddening! What arrogance!

* * * * *

After the initial exhilaration and self-congratulatory rejoicing, the act of starting off on that risky and rocky road to *bigness* began. But right from the beginning, both inside and outside the mini-community of the beneficiaries, it instilled in many a measure of trepidation and apprehension; and some became more than a tad nervous. As the stress mounted, the cynics among the non-SSC scientists saw their chance to go on the offensive: "Creative accounting, as good as it sounds, doesn't always end up the way it's supposed to," they argued. Continuing, they asked, "The money has to come from somewhere, so why shouldn't the SSC-lovers ante up and pay the tab?" Of course, that was the whole point of going the *presidential initiative* route. But the anti-SSC scientists weren't thinking too clearly. With only weak and stressed-out men acting in the project's defense, there was a tendency to believe the troublemakers. By following these naysayers, establishment scientists came to believe themselves unburdened of any responsibility if things were to go wrong, thus relieving somewhat their anxiety and tension. Actually, the carping wasn't all just running off at the mouth. In life, anything can happen. Circumstances can change, and what's valid today may become invalid tomorrow. Thus, the words of the cynics began to have an impact. Second thoughts began to creep into the thoughts of the men of science. It began to dawn on workers in non-SSC high-energy physics, in other branches of physics, and in other scientific disciplines that whatever the future held for the supercollider could have a substantial impact on their own fields of research. Bluntly said, suppose this high-profile project had to have additional money, either because of underestimation at the proposal stage or because of mistakes and delays that ensued later; and further, suppose the funds needed were not accounted for in the original SSC budget contingency fund as authorized at the presidential level. What then? Mightn't they quite rightly presume that if it came down to a priority contest, the SSC would win out? Didn't they have reasonable cause to be concerned that money would indeed come to be taken out of their hides?

So it was that the troubling and tormenting worry began its relentless spreading and intensification throughout the science community. First there appeared a kind of unfocused and restless disquiet that soon became transmuted into a nervous agitation. Then came the stage of anxious foreboding and dread. Finally, the lives of the scientists came to be haunted by good-old-fashioned fear of what was to befall them. Such feelings of vulnerability and insecurity could not long be ignored; and many came to believe that they couldn't just sit back and watch, but that they had to figure out some kind of pre-emptive course to take. However, no matter how dissatisfied and querulous they were, with the choices already made by the *Big-Science* big wheels, what could *Little-Science* little guys do? Confronted with the reality that what the bosses had done, as well as what more they could still do, could very well hurt them, they were at a loss. Here they were sitting on tenterhooks, wondering how they would fare in the times ahead, which to them was serious business, yet they came to be branded as mere worrywarts. No, they didn't at all like their position, and they also didn't like what was taking place around them. Were they being forced into acts of conspiracy? Was rebellion their only alternative?

Even though the apprehensive non-SSC types knew full well it was right for scientists to stick together, even though they wanted to support their brothers and be good soldiers, they nonetheless felt the stronger urge to look after number one first. It became clear that to keep themselves solvent and to keep their own little empires thriving they had no choice but to mount a campaign against the SSC. Unsure and tentative at the beginning, they found somewhere in themselves the means to overcome their instincts to be good and began to walk the dark and dirty road of betrayal. To start, they built a case that the project's *bigness* was beyond the capability of the scientists entrusted with it, and screamed their breakthrough finding from the rooftops. They particularly hit hard at the incompetence of the SSC's leaders to do as they claimed they would. But the SSC proponents weren't about to take these loose accusations lying down, so it didn't take long for them to fight back. They responded with every reason and excuse in the book – and then some – to vindicate themselves and contradict the verbal assaults leveled at them. Rather than be defensive and answer the charges made against them, they chose the offensive route and launched a blistering counter-attack. Although lots of harsh language was used, the gist of it was that their opponents were interested solely in themselves and not in their country; and further that they were nothing more than jealous of the SSC's grand mission and its overwhelming government support. Yes, it was said, they were alienated and disenchanted losers who were non-competitive and so resorted to the low blows that had their origins in sour grapes. However, in spite of their appearance of being mean-spirited and a bunch of whiners, the SSC's envious rivals for money and fame – the *bad guys* in this internecine strife – did have a genuinely valid viewpoint. Their logic was irrefutable, to wit that if the SSC proved to be harder to complete than first presumed and promised, it would end up being hard and dark days for both Little Science and Big Science, as well as all the science in-between. You see this humungous hungry hulk of a project – this brother rat – might just swallow up all of its siblings and set back science for years to come.

Despite the SSC's efforts to stifle and quash the rising tide against it, the nasty tempers, the troublemaking hostility, and the righteous indignation within the science community only grew. Inevitably, it followed that an informal coalition spontaneously sprang up that brought together in common cause a wide range of people almost spanning the complete gamut of the sciences. They were all in the same boat, they resented and hated the SSC. What strange bedfellows find each other in times of discontent! In truth, they thought primarily of their self-interest, their own wants and needs, yet they insisted in high-sounding but hollow-ringing words that it was all for the community good. But it mattered not a whit what words they spoke because the end they had in mind couldn't be hidden either by obfuscation and deception, or by the obviously transparent use of euphemistic language. No, even though there wasn't universal agreement among the amateur conspirators, what was behind it all, what the end was that they really sought was crystal-clear: that the SSC should vanish from the face of the earth – just go away. Some wanted to fully de-fang this threatening danger-filled menace by transferring a substantial part of its power to none other than themselves. Failing that, some wanted to simply take the project down from its high horse a notch or two, that is, make it smaller and more amenable to control, or delay it until new technology would do that job for them. Then there were those who wanted blood, and would settle for nothing less than altogether getting rid of this powder keg waiting to explode, this jeopardizing-to-all supercollider.

Even without any centralized planning, the conniving plotters settled on an approach they could all go along with. What a beauty this line of attack was! The strategy that ensued came to be expressed, in short, as a plea that the project be put on hold so that R&D could be done on new and more sophisticated technology. The claim was that, in this way, the size and cost could be greatly lessened, thereby bringing down the risk for all to a more manageable level. Was this really well thought out and sincerely rendered advice? Was it just the schemers wanting to return back to their pre-SSC safe and easy life where money arrived yearly like clockwork? Or, was it a ploy to block the SSC from moving on its fast, albeit risky, track? What do you think?

Undoubtedly, this particular argument came about as a result of the serendipitous discovery at just this time in the eighties of the new so-called high-temperature (HT) superconductors. How lucky they were! How else could such a ragtag group of intriguers have come to closure? Still, you've got to give them credit – they picked up the idea and ran with it. In any case, whatever it was that made them do it, the project's antagonists rallying around these new HT materials portended hard times for the SSC. *Wait a while*, the SSC adversaries unfairly and underhandedly proposed, *and when these new materials become usable, the SSC will be much better: more reliable, less costly, and more straightforward to manage*. Although all this would have been quite correct if their premise had been right, the fact was that the use of HT technology in the SSC didn't make much sense technically. Superconducting wire and cable simply couldn't be manufactured from this new stuff. You might have to wait generations for some reasonable chance to actually make magnets with it. Even worse, it might be that accelerator magnets are fundamentally an unsound and illusory application for HT superconducting material. Nevertheless, as wrong-headed as the idea was, in the game of money and politics, who could judge which of the scientists were right and which were wrong? The project's leaders were thus put on the defensive. With their backs against the wall, they were forced into the contention, which was hard to articulate and back up, that, even if these new types of materials became fully understood and practical to use, they still wouldn't be suitable for accelerator magnets in the foreseeable future. Cunningly, they'd been shoved into the position of having to argue a case that was right on target but was understood and believable only to those steeped in superconductivity R&D. So suppose you were one of the guys holding the purse strings and the political power to say *yes* or *no*. There you were listening to the pro-SSC and the anti-SSC scientific experts, all carrying impressive academic credentials. Those in the black hats said that waiting a bit would make the project small and manageable, and would also be the saving grace for all of science; while those in the white hats said that the suggested delay would unnecessarily set back Big Science for decades to come. Which side would you believe, and what would you do?

* * * * *

The deep gulf separating the pro and con factions on the question of how the SSC might fare led to interminable squabbling. With the true bone of contention hidden from view – the motivating sore point actually arising out of the mean-spirited envy and covetous greed of the anti-SSC group – the snarling dispute had little if any meaning to those not in the inner circle. So, as the politicians and the public watched in dismay the out-in-the-open knock-down-and-drag-out quarrel, they were at a total loss as to what to make of it. For the schemers, this was far better than they'd anticipated: The less truth there was out there, the better it was for them. Now there isn't any doubt that the naysayers didn't plan it exactly the way it turned out, but luck was with them and they actually got what they wanted: First the opportunistic sharks who wanted the SSC out of the way planted the seeds of the idea that the project leadership was both impatient and wasteful. Then they broke the vicious story wide open with a donnybrook of flying words. The media rumormongers and gossipers could hardly contain themselves. Oh, how they loved the contentiousness and the bickering discord coming from the reputedly sober, rational minded, and logically thinking professor types. How could they resist such a juicy item? This was right up media-alley! Thus, the SSC, along with all of its trappings, was brought under the bright and unfriendly light of public scrutiny; and once started on its do-good path, the media, right or wrong, is unstoppable. No, there was no escape for the SSC from the newsmongers' noses for scandal-real and scandal-made-up. Even though the newspapermen and the rapid-fire TV reporters knew little of the technical issues at hand and even less of what was really going on, they latched onto the story and pressed on, squeezing every last drop of hearsay and proprietary information they could out of it. Exaggeration and misinformation filled the printed pages and the airwaves. *Impatient* was transformed into *rushing recklessly ahead without thought*, and *wasteful* became *squandering spendthrifts throwing money down the drain*. Yes indeed, shooting for the big-time is not for the squeamish and the faint-hearted. The SSC had made its bed, now it had to lie in it.

Whether the con view was correct isn't the point, for undoubtedly it wasn't. As tough a project as the SSC was, its mission to explore the essence of the universe was well worth the risk and the cost it was asking the country to bear. Nonetheless, the opposition to the project, only months after its formal initiation by the President, was remarkably effective in its political action. As sure as anything can be, there's simply no denying that its dirty business was done with exceptional aplomb. Somehow those who sought an end to the SSC managed to shape and exploit an authoritative and persuasive argument against the project, one that could be understood as well as articulated and repeated by non-technical strategists and politicos as well as scientists and engineers. The major two points were that the SSC wasn't really ready to go forward, and that the management wasn't sufficiently competent to get the job done. The language was plain spoken, sans jargon, and could easily be taken up and used by any of the project's enemies whenever it suited them to do so. Thus, it became a thorn in the SSC's side, and would remain so even after the current onslaught was neutralized. However, as it turned out, the rescue wouldn't come from either the SSC's management or from its supporters. The best they could muster was the most pathetic of responses. "It's only negative spin, with no real substance," cried out the pro-SSC innocents. But no one heard. Unfortunately for the project and the country, most were listening to the anti-SSC forces. *Ain't that politics for you*? Just go which way the wind happens to be blowing! Still, as unlikely as it seemed at the time, the SSC would be saved from this assault. But before that was to happen, it first had to suffer awhile and be taught a painful lesson in politics.

Once the anti-SSC bandwagon got itself together, people of all sorts began popping out of the woodwork to put in their two cents worth. The attacks became stronger, more strident, and harder to contend with. There were many types that joined the chorus of naysayers: those who had legitimate grievances with the SSC; those who were habitual complainers; those who had pet peeves and other axes to grind; those who stood to gain from the SSC's demise (and these included the *physichists* performing old-hat particle physics experiments, thus making the high-energy physics family a house divided); and those who had some inner need to express an opinion about things whether or not they knew anything about them. But they all ended up in the same camp with the same question: they began to wonder whether such an imposing and uncertain endeavor was necessary. This way of thinking inexorably drew people to express doubts and misgivings about the value of Big Science itself. "Why," they asked, "does it have to be big. Hasn't *Little Science* served well enough?" Why indeed! Sure, if *bigness* can be done without, why not? It's costly. It's risky. It goes without saying that *bigness* should only be resorted to if it offers something of signal and unique import. So, there appears to be something missing from the whole row about *bigness*. Why argue about the obvious? Well, it doesn't take much of an intellect to figure out the answer to that one. The truth was that most who were clamoring that science, as a whole, should be protected from that risky, unnecessary *bigness* were among the large number of scientists who were dependent for their research on *Little-Science* government grants. Granted, there might well have been some principled men among them. However, it wouldn't be such a leap of faith to buy the inference that these were in fact very few. But if you swallow that, then the conclusion is forced on you that it was no more and no less than self-interest that was driving these claiming-to-be pure idealists out to save science. How sad that it's come to this – that deceit and falseness should in the end prevail!

It was strange to hear *Little Science* being trumpeted as the wave of the future, while the big variety was said to be passé. How ridiculous can you get! Nonetheless, Big Science was portrayed as a dinosaur soon to be extinct, determined to drag the little guys down with it. There was this stark image of Big Science as the dragon wreaking havoc with its last breaths of fire and *Little Science* – it has such a nice ring to it – entering to save the day. Can you believe it? Yet, it's the plainspoken, I-kid-you-not truth that many scientists and government men actually fell for this claptrap. The self-deception (or, is it possible that false-hearted men were playing out an act of cunning duplicity?) ran so deep that some people even said that little was as good as big, even better. Whatever was inside men's souls driving them, all this talk was a lot of hooey because there isn't a doubt in the world that to move ahead physics has to get big, and what's more, even bigger. You see, it's big instruments working in tandem with higher energy particle beams, or with more highly concentrated beams, that allow scientists to peer into the secret depths of nature. The bigger the better! That's just the way it is. However, this self-serving ploy that *Little Science* was a genuine alternative generated the illusion that *bigness* – Big Science – was wasteful. Well, perhaps *big* isn't as efficient as *little*. But wasteful? No, it wasn't true then and is in reality just a lot of nonsense. Nevertheless, despite the truth, a political point was scored for *little* and against *big*. Yes, the SSC was indeed vulnerable, and with this added checkmark against it, another point was chalked up on the nay side of the ledger.

Because the SSC was elitist in nature, involving very few of the country's scientists, while at the same time being a cash-eating machine, it was forced into a defensive posture. Perceiving this vulnerability, the men of *Little Science* saw their chance and went on the offensive. As the *big-little* war went on its merry way, there just didn't seem to be a happy middle ground where the two could peacefully co-exist. The *Little-Science* men felt threatened and wanted Big Science at best removed, but at least substantially downsized, castrated you might say. They were hellishly effective in the pithiness of their pointed remarks and questions: "What we do is just as good as what your monstrosity will! Who cares about the obscure stuff you're doing? Who does it help anyway? What we're doing is important today! Besides, in time, we'll get the answers that you're looking for our way, and at a much lower cost!" Somehow the *little scientists* couldn't see much past there noses. They appeared unable to recognize that the polarization of science into *big* and *little* that they were causing could only hurt scientists everywhere because the one clear sure-fire result of it was that scientific progress would be slowed down.

There is a certain subtlety in the issue of the impact of slowing down basic science. The consequences to the nation and the world could indeed be profound. History is replete with cases where being first in making a fundamental discovery was crucial to a country's future – for its quality of life enhancement, for its survival, or for its military conquests. It was science, in the term's broad sense, that led to: weaponry over the centuries for purposes of both defense and offense; pioneering travel across the face of the globe that saw man's awe-inspiring taming of the earth; the breathtaking development of industry and technology over the past few centuries; the spectacular formation and distribution of power for the masses across the country and across many other parts of the world; the explosion of man's commerce and mobility; the incredible increase in man's life expectancy; and the bringing forth of the fantastic and precarious nuclear and space ages. But, impressive as it is, that's the past. In making the case for doing future basic science, it's a whole new ball game. It was a hard sell in days gone by, and the same is true today. You see, the practical gain from basic science are highly speculative and cannot be pinpointed with precision because they depend on things not yet done or not even imagined. That scientists of the past, even under these challenging and exacting circumstances, found ways to amass the resources to support their work just adds to their fame and glory. However, that they brought home the bacon throughout history doesn't alter one iota the reality that they still must fight for support today. Thus, there's no getting around it that the *big-little* fight over the SSC was a losing situation for everyone. As for the bureaucrats holding the moneybags, they were in somewhat of a pickle. They knew little or nothing about basic science, yet they had the job of determining the winners and the losers. What should they have done? What side should they have chosen, Little Science or Big Science? How should they have distributed the funding between them? No doubt, it was a dilemma.

If the SSC and Big Science were to be waylaid, it's probable that future generations would sooner or later reap their unknown benefits anyway. So, would it be that bad? Perhaps not, but there would be a price to pay! You see, without *bigness* now, the current generation of scientists would unfortunately remain ignorant of the full potential that these explorers of the unknown had right at their fingertips. They'd be the real losers. How sad it would be for them to have to leave the earth without knowing the outcome of their dreams! Why, you want to scream out, why might such an awful thing happen? Mundane as it may seem, it could well come to pass because those jealous, carping, and big-mouth *little scientists* weren't able to learn the simple rule of behavior that lets freedom ring: live and let live. Without this, how could science be expected to flourish, or even survive? How could it prosper while scientists persist in weakening their colleagues, undermining them, trying to shoot them down, and dragging them through the mud? Doubtless, with this kind of stuff going on, science is in a lot of trouble, and the most vulnerable Big Science is in real hot, nay boiling, water.

The war that started over the SSC clearly demonstrated the inability of scientists to appreciate the importance of making peace with their colleagues. They should have known what all scientists should know: that they should even go a lot further than merely abiding the presence of their brothers. They should help each other in any way they know how: to correct a colleague's mistake; to improve his status and position; to aid him in recuperating from a downturn; and to mature, ripen, and advance his work. This mode of conduct is well worth following, not only for the class of scientists, but for any family or group where people doing all sorts of things are operating in close contact. Like many other human endeavors, science is carried out by an amalgam of individuals who have a common purpose and methodology: Their educations and backgrounds for the most part coincide; they tend to converge toward the same way of thinking; and they inevitably end up having similar ways of doing things. But, digging deeper into scientists' lives, you find that specialization has considerably altered the detailed day-to-day work they do. Sometimes scientists belonging to the same societies and associations and working in the same universities or other institutions become so attached to their own disciplines that they haven't a clue about what the others are really up to. Yes, it just may be that as time goes on, the differences between scientists are more and more outweighing their commonality. Perhaps, the notion of unity in science may be becoming a thing of the past. But that doesn't mean that there shouldn't be unity among scientists. It doesn't mean that one scientist is more important than another. After all, they're still part of the same family. They're still professionals with the common objective of understanding nature. They're still members of a group that, even as it stands on the verge of breaking apart, nevertheless is begging to have its coherence sustained.

Even though the men of science are bound by science's credo to criticize their colleagues when the evidence warrants it, and always to be as self-critical as is humanly possible, they still have to find a way to live and work together in harmony and fellowship. If they don't, they risk being overwhelmed and degraded by grasping outsiders. To remain intact and prevail over those with envy and spite in their hearts, scientists surely should accentuate their commonality, embodied in their belief that the world is rational and amenable to observation and logical analysis. Well, if you buy that apparent axiom, then all well and good. It's certainly a sufficient reason for scientists to stick together. In any case, if they don't close ranks, they'd best beware, because jealousy is all around them, from those who covet the fame and money in the Big Science arena to those who crave for themselves the attention given the field to the miracle-believers, as well as the *deconstructionists*, who don't accept science's central premise as axiomatic. In the end, there's simply no alternative. Scientists must protect themselves as a group. At the very least, they must stop their interminable internal squabbles. If not, it'll only make it that much easier for these *barbarians at the gate* to attack and crush Big Science. And wither goes Big Science, so goes science. Make no mistake about it: science's enemies stand ready to knock it off its ascendant position and are quite willing to make their move to do it.

Despite the irrationality of the anti-SSC faction and the attacks on the project growing daily, the men of the SSC, besieged as they were, with their backs against the wall, were not bowed by the scorn heaped on them. Although the siege was hard to overcome, it strengthened their resolve and spurred them on to come out fighting. However, the determined men of *Little Science* were sly devils. They'd somehow managed to establish a consensus that the project's *bigness* was a threat to the very integrity of all of science. Unfortunately, the SSC scientists mistakenly treated the assault of the *little men* as you would a fly on your arm that, to be rid of, simply had to be brushed off. But they were wrong. The reality was that the anti-SSC numbers kept going up until finally they reached a level where they could no longer be ignored. False as their viewpoint was, the anti-big self-appointed protectors and guardians of science found a way to express themselves. They sparked and generated a cause around which their troops could rally and build up strength. Then, with their power concentrated, they could mount hard-hitting campaigns. However, all this belligerence was of little consequence. You see, the SSC was hardly a threat to the men of *Little Science*, or indeed to anyone for that matter. Its *bigness* was indeed jeopardizing and hazardous, and, should it explode, its falling debris could indeed rain on those close by. But in that case the appropriate reaction of those who feared such an eventuality should be to just stay clear or, better still, to aid their brothers in distress. Why then did they insist on trying to derail it and work so hard to that end?

Perhaps the motives of the naysayers were not as pure as loudly proclaimed in their rhetoric. Was it actually a case of *the lady doth protest too much*? They said that what they were doing was for the good of science everywhere, and for all scientists. Yet, it's hard to escape the compelling impression that their thoughts were primarily of themselves and of their own kind. No, it's not very wise to believe those who insist that they're being altruistic and doing something just for you. It's best to be wary of such types. It's best not to pay attention to them if all they have is words without palpable backup. No, there's no question about it: As a general rule, it does make good sense to always beware of those with high-sounding phrases. On the other hand, *always* may be too strong a term. For, every now and then in the course of history there do appear naysayers in a class of men who stand bigger than life itself. There are glorious and saintly individuals such as a Christ, or a Gandhi, or a King, as well as inglorious and evil ones like a Genghis Kahn, or a Hitler, or a Pol Pot. But it's way out of line to claim the righteous men as examples to justify pre-emptive acts of betrayal against your brothers. Making such an argument is pure sophistry. You see these were historical giants. The people railing against the SSC were no match for such saints and devils. They were just puny self-interested midgets, and, no matter what they said, their cause was of no significant import to humanity's future. They were negativists. They were obstructionists. They would try to bring down anyone who tried to stand tall above the run-of-the-mill. They were the defenders of the status quo. They were only little people playing minor political games. They were ignorant and uncaring, unaware of the self-defeating and painful-to-the-rest-of-their-family long-term consequences of such games. Their language may have been big talk but their meaning was small potatoes.

In looking back at the whole *big-little* affair, the struggle that erupted turned out to be instigated by a bunch of charlatans who trumpeted their call to arms. As for those who followed that call, how were they to know that the appeals to help save science from the *big bad* SSC were merely words and ideas full of sound and fury, but signifying nothing? Can they be blamed for their misjudgment? Probably not, because with the measly information available it's never easy for people to know the right thing to do. In the end, however, in the case of the SSC – life forever being full of ironies – it turned out that the critics, these little men of *Little Science*, were not as important a factor as they would have liked to be. The truth is that if the SSC had to die on the vine, it wouldn't be because of those blustering *little scientists* on the warpath, but rather solely of its own doing. T'would be its own unmanageable *bigness* that would kill this glorious beast.

* * * * *

"With the SSC funded by new money through the use of the powerful presidential initiative funding mode, not a stitch will be taken out of your hide," the government contended, "you have absolutely nothing to fear." In this way, the government attempted to allay the concerns of *Little-Science* folk and Big-Science giants alike. "This method is a budgetary safety net," the government continued, "that's the point to it." But none of the numerous members of the opposition believed a word of this. They had a sense of foreboding that sooner or later some future SSC resource needs would confiscate money they believed was due them. So what were they to do? They had so many questions, and there were so few answers. What if the SSC budgeters misestimated? What if they inadvertently left one or more items out? What if they slyly did so deliberately to low-ball the estimate for political ends? "That project is so big," they pointed out, "giving a little more to them could eat us up alive." Then there was the reality staring at them that all they had was the pledge of government bureaucrats. With nothing tangible, nothing concrete to back up their promise, could they be trusted to honor their word? "OK," they argued, "you're still giving us most of what we had in the past. But how can we be sure of its continuance into the future? With all the construction money required for the SSC by presidential fiat, can we really expect you not to cheat a little here and there if you found it to your advantage?" They were quite right to be so pointed. The government gave the *Little-Science* men only their reassurance. They got nothing more from the bureaucrats than a handshake. But was that enough? Probably not! To be satisfactory, the government men had to demonstrate in a far more palpable manner that they truly meant business. But how could they do this? How could the government certify its sincerity and veracity and give evidence of its credibility? So, the men of *Little Science* were caught between a rock and a hard place. With the SSC wrapped in the protective custody of the U.S. government, what next?

Thus, as the government, which wanted to travel the road of excellence with the SSC, tried to find a way to break the impasse, the army of do-gooders formed to defend the integrity of science as a whole came out in full force. They would speak out against the big project at every opportunity. They diligently sought out each and every forum that would allow them to present their case, and there they would spout all the self-righteous indignation of fanatics who believed fervently in their cause. They would give testimony at congressional hearings; they would get in touch with all levels of government officials, including their own districts' congresspersons; they would write letters to the many science magazines; they would include their ideas on *bigness* in lectures given at universities, at labs and at meetings of science societies and associations; they would travel the tricky-to-maneuver, precarious media route, a tough road to hoe because journalists and the like are at their core unpredictable, having a strong tendency toward gossip-mindedness yet technically being almost totally unversed; and they would try to influence personally whomever they could, including colleagues and associates, magazine editors, and anyone else they could pull within hearing distance. They came to see themselves as guardian angels and vowed to be heard regardless of the consequences and whatever the cost might be. Nothing could appease them save the blood of their foe.

In their fight for fairness, the SSC antagonists were up against not only the project, full of politically green scientists like themselves, but also the mighty and potent force of the U.S. government. Too bad for them! As long as Uncle Sam stood in their way, the grinding road leading toward their ultimate desire of pushing the SSC into the grimy deep was indeed a hard one to travel. But that's life! America and the SSC were *in like Flynn*! You see that big, fantastic, and breathtaking project was something the U.S. government had come to want badly. What good fortune the SSC had! Having such a formidable powerhouse on its side was much like being born under a lucky star. Why was the U.S. so enamored of the project, you might ask? No difficulty here! It was simply because the SSC represented all that America and Reagan wanted to stand for:

the pursuit of excellence; Big Science; the challenge of the frontier; modern technology; breaking new ground; and forging a bright future for the country's young. It would encourage and allow America to go where no one had gone before; it was the new wave of the twenty-first century; it would trigger a continental competition with a strong and worthy opponent in Western Europe, a contest America was just itching to engage in; all-in-all it was the mark of being number one. What chance did the *Little-Science* SSC opposition have against the awesome strength of the American presidency? Certainly the U.S. government didn't have to appease the naysayers, those faint-of-heart, weak-kneed university professors, those without the spirit to give of themselves what it takes to reach the unknown, and those who haven't the stomach to search out glory and seek the path to their destiny for greatness. The fact is that America has no need to pay off anyone, and emphatically not the bumptious and loud-mouthed, but in the end spunkless and easily cowed SSC scientist-foes. Nevertheless, even with its power to intimidate by force, and even though it didn't have to give the SSC adversaries a damn thing, still the U.S. government found an inventive strategy to make everybody happy. That's America for you! It didn't have to do *good*, but it did anyway.

When the U.S. government wants to resolve an issue – with emphasis on the word, *wants* – you can bet your bottom dollar that, if it's a question of money, it's tantamount to a sure thing. The SSC – non-SSC funding dispute was just such a problem. How could the government effectively demonstrate its good faith to the men of *Little Science*? To the U.S. this wasn't much of a big deal. All that was needed was a good idea, and in no time flat a sharp and clever Reagan official got it. To prove beyond a reasonable doubt to the suspicious, mistrusting skeptics that, as promised, the SSC would not, over time, come to eat up the existing structure and institutions, a series of parallel investments for the non-SSC labs was proposed. Grants would be made throughout the country for new projects in order to strengthen the infrastructure of the national lab system, and thereby ensure all the labs a meaningful, forefront future life. Do you see how the effective use of a little money can go a long way? The remarkable and humbling U.S. government, in one swooping administrative gesture, neutralized the complaints of the entrenched scientific establishment. The overanxious, nail-biting worriers had said, "Yes, it's new money from the restricted and privileged presidential fund now, but eventually the big, the giant SSC will need more and take away first our people, then our work, and then our budget. So, in time, we will diminish and die." But the masterfully diplomatic and boundlessly resourceful U.S. government, with a strong mind to have both the SSC and the complete science establishment satisfied as well as working at full tilt, came up with just the right riposte. By beefing up the labs' infrastructures, not only did it give them new future worth, but it also represented a conspicuous, palpable commitment to all of science's future. That straightforward and hard not to appreciate government act rendered the arguments of the opposition moot and devoid of any impact. The insurrection was thus crushed.

Did the U.S. really love science this much? In Reagan's time, when excellence was the byword, apparently it did, and the President's men did their level best to match reality to his vision. In the case of the dispute between the SSC and smaller science, the man who inspiringly shaped the perfect solution was Alvin Trivelpiece. During Reagan's second term, he was appointed Director of DOE's Office of Energy Research (ER), which had oversight responsibility for the system of national laboratories dotting the country's landscape. Trivelpiece was a theorist in plasma physics before coming to the DOE and, after he left the government as part of the natural revolving door effect, he went on to become the Director of Oak Ridge National laboratory (ORNL). Could it be that seeking such an outcome played a part in his dedication to his job? Could that have influenced his favoring the labs, including the one he would come to lead? Of course, anything is possible! But if you weigh all the factors together, especially the man's character and his past actions, in all likelihood you'd conclude that he did what he did because he felt it to be a national obligation to sustain the strength and vitality of the national laboratory system's infrastructure. Being a man with an earnest desire to serve science and to serve his country, why wouldn't it be quite natural for him to seek to find ways for the DOE to invest in the future of its banner laboratories? That he did, and he did so with decided brilliance. How, you ask? He devised the plan, which came to be called the *Trivelpiece Initiative*, that accomplished the dual objectives of planting the seeds for the future of the national lab system and of alleviating the establishment's anxiety and fears over the SSC. Not only that, but he actually made it happen. Here was a man who was given an almost impossible problem, who came up with an exceptional idea of how to manage it, and who saw his solution come to pass. No doubt, that was indeed a virtuoso performance. Yes, Reagan sought men who would help carry the country on the road to excellence, and he certainly found one in Alvin Trivelpiece.

The Trivelpiece idea was that, while the SSC was being built, commissioned, and operated, the ER budget would allow for new projects to be constructed in the DOE lab system, with the aim of advancing non-SSC basic science on a broad front. This served to ensure that *Little Science*, though overshadowed by the big colliders and accelerators, would keep moving forward and prosper in the emerging era of *bigness*. The plan also had the added attraction of being a safety valve, just in case the SSC didn't pan out, and caved in under the crushing weight of its bigness. Although, in the late eighties, this seemed to be a very unlikely occurrence, *better safe than sorry*, as the saying goes. Thus, by placing the *Trivelpiece Initiative* on the front burner and in a fast-action mode, the government proved that it considered science and technology (S&T), both little and big, to be hot stuff with high priority. What a reasonable outlook the U.S. had! What foresight! What high-class fairness! How excellent for the country! Furthermore, by example, the government taught scientists a couple of lessons they would do well to follow: that it's wrong to tear at each other's reputations, and to rip their brothers off by snatching their funds; and that, with a little compromising give and take, they could live side by side in harmony. In a single action, the Trivelpiece agenda combined the largesse of promoting American S&T with the pragmatism of hedging its bets on the SSC. It certainly made a lot of sense: Why burn your bridges before assuring yourself that *bigness* could work in basic research? Thus, with the guidance of this forward-looking policy that was devised, the U.S. set aside the money to keep the entire national lab system going full bore while the SSC experiment in *bigness* took its course. If it turned out that a retreat became necessary, the Trivelpiece scheme was optimal for American S&T because a viable alternative would be maximally ready to proceed. As time passed and events unfolded, it became abundantly clear that this strategy was both very wise and one quite practical to implement. Yes, Trivelpiece came through in princely fashion.

* * * * *

The new projects envisioned in this unique program of deals were aimed at being modest, about a half billion dollars each. In the first phase, special attention was paid and consideration given to the flagship high-energy particle physics laboratories, SLAC and Fermilab. This was a well-reasoned way to start the ball rolling because it was these two labs that had the most to be alarmed about with the SSC behemoth getting ready to emerge from its cocoon. After all, once *big-boy* got running, *anything they could do, it could do better*. So, in a keen and insightful manner, the *Trivelpiece Initiative* got underway.

In 1988, SLAC's Linear Collider prototype and Fermilab's superconducting Tevatron, both built in the early eighties, were already operating in fine fashion. But to ensure the viability and productivity of these labs into the future, the newly configured budget would allow for their facility growth well into the nineties. For SLAC, this meant the construction of its B-factory and a substantial upgrade of its Positron Electron Project (PEP). (The "B" stands for a short-lived elementary particle, which, when produced and studied in large enough quantities, would throw light on the tiny violation of one of nature's conservation principles – that violation, by the way, leading to the beyond-belief fact that our world is made up of stable matter and doesn't simply explode into pure energy as anti-particles floating about annihilate the matter.) At the same time as SLAC's strengthening was in progress, Fermilab was given the go-ahead to build its proposed Main Injector project and to upgrade its p-pbar collider. This strategy made good sense for high-energy physics as it approached the era of the SSC. SLAC was given the chance to show its stuff in the competitive world of particle research with electron beams, while the Tevatron at Fermilab was to remain the highest performing proton collider. Then a few years later, when the SSC would come on line with its more than fifty miles of tunnel burrowing through the kingdom of the worms, particle physics research would reach its zenith of hitherto unimaginable performance heights.

Having quickly taken care of SLAC and Fermilab, the emphasis of the *Trivelpiece Initiative* turned to the scrutiny of areas outside high-energy physics (HEP). In this second phase, the government's intention was to finance new major facilities at non-HEP labs to enhance frontier research in biology, chemistry, medicine, materials, and other fields of physics. On the face of it, these investments were designed to help calm the nerves of people who were truly sweating bullets over the SSC as it plowed relentlessly ahead. If that objective alone did well, then the outcome of the initiative could be stamped, *mission accomplished*. But even if some of the loudly expressed distress, misgivings, and antsyness over the onrushing SSC were feigned just to squeeze more money out of the DOE, that was OK too. You see, the Reagan government was an enlightened one and knew well that basic science is good in and of itself. Thus, first and foremost, it wanted the research done for the good of mankind – naturally, so much the better if done in America. So it treated all that rigmarole of psycho-mumbo-jumbo as a sideshow meriting not the least bit of concern. It treated these peripheral motivational issues as niceties to which it paid little heed. Although there might well have been some truth in them, nonetheless they were but petty matters and immaterial in the larger scheme of things. All in all, Reagan and his men considered that why scientists did what they did was of secondary interest; and the chickenshit and *Mickey Mouse* games they played were of virtually no importance to them – *just a tempest in a teapot.* When taken down to the essentials, basic science of all types had such a low cost-benefit ratio that it would be foolish not to take everything possible out of it, to squeeze it dry. Thus, the U.S. government, with so much to gain and so little to lose, flexed its muscles and demonstrated its power and resolve to preserve science as a whole even as Big Science stood perched to wedge a path into its midst.

Once the objective was established, the management of the initiative began; and Trivelpiece proved to be just the man for the delicate, knotty, and multi-faceted negotiations required. With Buddha-like composure, nerves of steel, and the poise of a seasoned veteran, he was unflinching in his resolve; and ultimately he got what he wanted. Without a hitch, the initiative was cleared with the President's science advisor, with the Secretary of Energy, with key congressional leaders, and with the Office of Management and Budget (OMB). Showing his prowess and creativity as a man of administrative meticulousness as well as one of high political capability, Trivelpiece wisely dug deeper into the hierarchies and made sure to clear it with the appropriate staff members. They were the ones that made things really happen; and he didn't want them to feel passed over and ignored, and then end up dragging their feet. With the thoroughness of a man in masterful command, he next turned to the labs from which he needed categorical acceptance and flat-out, unconditional agreement on the specifics of the agreement. Again, this time bargaining and haggling it out with the lab Directors around the country, he came through with flying colors. Thus he traveled the tough negotiating route, wending his way through the intricate maze into the open sunlit field where everyone was ready to give his plan the A-OK. Finally, sometime in or about 1988, the job was done and a deal was struck.

High-energy physics, with the substantial enhancement of SLAC and Fermilab, was to get what it had already been promised. Next in line, nuclear physics would get a flashy new collider called the Relativistic Heavy Ion Collider (RHIC) to be located at BNL. As the counter-rotating bunches of heavy ions would explosively crash into each other, scientists would be simulating in breathlessly tiny miniature the initial moments of the creation of the universe, thereby catching the first glimpses of that momentous event for all of humanity. BNL was perfect for the job. It was well prepared for this project because RHIC was nothing more than a sensibly corrected version of that ill-starred, hapless lady, ISABELLE. Designed for bunched beams, with reasonably sized magnets similar to those already in use at Fermilab and DESY, and to be contained in the tunnel built for ISABELLE, it was about as straightforward a collider to build as any could be. Of this RHIC project for nuclear physics, one might say that, after a pause of a few years, it served as a continuation of ISABELLE and an ironic tribute to her sad memory.

Moving on with his plan, Trivelpiece next opportunistically seized the moment to make magnanimous and generous offerings to other sciences. He saw to it that the worlds of biology, condensed matter, medicine, chemistry, and low-energy nuclear physics also got their chances to advance toward the technological frontier. The practitioners of these fields were thrilled by such bountiful manna from heaven. In these areas, with scientists studying the intricate nuclear, atomic, and molecular structure of the materials of their trade, it happens that neutron and light beams are the favored probes. From the government's viewpoint, all it had to do was to give its national labs the resources and the opportunity to design and build, first the accelerators that would spew out such beams, and second the associated experimental facilities that would make use of them. Yes, it was really going to happen. How bizarre that the SSC, long before the bulldozers started doing their thing in Texas, should bring about and unwittingly sponsor this superb, first-rate growth in such a wide variety of sciences! What a fertile mind Trivelpiece had to perceive that this was exactly the right moment to translate a fanciful notion into a practical reality! And he did it! Trivelpiece's vision was a trio of new machines: the Advanced Light Source (ALS) alighting onto the Berkeley hill at the Lawrence Berkeley National Lab (LBNL), situated not far from the San Francisco shoreline of the central California coast; the Advanced Photon Source (APS) rising from the plains of the great American Midwest at Argonne National laboratory (ANL), just south of Chicago; and finally the Advanced Neutron Source (ANS) revitalizing basic science at the old and tired Oak Ridge National Lab (ORNL) in central Tennessee. What a beauty of a plan it was, well thought out and reasonable, one that would be good for science, good for the country, and in truth good for everybody! The imaginative Trivelpiece, finding himself at the right place at the right time, seized the opportunity given him to fashion one of those rare win-win situations where there are no losers.

The Trivelpiece saga didn't end there. Not being a perfect concoction, it wasn't as seamless as it might have been. Yes, it might have worked smoothly, but, unfortunately, hidden in its interior specifics, there was a time bomb ready to go off. And it did! The hitch was that the source of neutrons for the ANS project was to be a nuclear reactor. Alas, poor project! The word *reactor* had become anathema to the hoi polloi as well as to the Congress that represented them in the nation's capitol. How irrational people can be? *Ain't that the truth*! You see this wasn't planned to be a power-generating reactor, where there is a tiny risk of some serious event. It was merely to be a an exceedingly low-power research reactor, with every safety precaution to be taken double-fold; so that even in the worst case scenario there would be no impact on the public welfare. Thus, although it was the right thing to do and the proper way for America to go both scientifically and technologically, the attempt to do it was like waving a red flag in front of a foaming, raging bull. There was simply no clearheaded thinking going on. Rationality was nowhere to be found. The top men who chose to go ahead with this approach were reacting solely from the gut. So why did Trivelpiece, a thoughtful man, proceed with the idea and propose a reactor anyway? It wasn't that the decision-making upper crust was so naïve that they didn't see the danger ahead. They did, but somehow ORNL convinced the government that together they could push it past a not-too-vigilant public. Both the government and the lab were wrong, and when what they were doing became known, political mayhem erupted.

The project in fact was conceived and designed to be especially safe, far safer than common sense and scientific reason would dictate. Furthermore, it would be especially good for the country to gain expertise and experience in the tools necessary for the production of the nuclear power necessary for its long-term future. Nevertheless, in spite of these oh so rational reasons, Trivelpiece's suggestion of it as part of his initiative was quite a blunder. It is a fact of life that mistakes in political judgment are not unusual, but this one was a doozy. With the choice of being technically correct or politically correct before him, he no doubt should have stuck with the latter. Of course, that's just the 20-20 vision that hindsight provides.

Probably he did what he did because the ORNL scientists and engineers hadn't the will or perhaps even the capacity to leave reactors behind. He could have insisted that an accelerator-based project producing neutrons was a far better alternative from the political standpoint. But he didn't. Being a consensus type of person, he went along with what ORNL wanted. The lab's staff had been working on reactors for many years, knew them well, and didn't want to change their ways. In addition, they didn't know much about accelerators and didn't want to go through the hard game of learning anew. This was natural for an aging staff in a lab that had grown rapidly decades earlier, and by the late eighties was saddled with old men who couldn't imagine giving up their privileged positions to the more energetic and more flexible young. Trivelpiece listened intently and seriously to all of them, but then, taking a course that in retrospect is difficult to fathom, he bewilderingly began to believe that he just might be able to sneak the idea through the public opposition to nuclear energy. How could he even have contemplated going in such an unlikely-to-succeed direction? Since the Three Mile Island incident, the bad-tempered distaste for nuclear power in both congressmen and the people they represent, without rhyme or reason, has reached irrational proportions. Thus, in our open and freewheeling circus of a society, Trivelpiece and ORNL were engaging in wishful thinking in the extreme. At the very least, Trivelpiece should have remembered the doomed Clinch River Breeder Reactor project from the seventies, also proposed for the state of Tennessee, that suffered a knockout blow at the hands of an angry Congress, driven by an even angrier anti-nuclear public. Being a man of broad experience and political acumen, the mystery of why he was blind to the reality of the position he was taking must remain without a satisfactory answer. Maybe it really was because he was thinking of his own future and wanted his plan to be advantageous to ORNL. That was the politic and self-interested thing to do. However, that's neither here nor there. Suffice it to say that he should have known better but unfortunately didn't.

Despite Trivelpiece's setback, this little story about a man and his mission, no more than a blip in the flow of history, has a nice-and-tidy happy ending. What more can you ask? For, as the *bard of Stratford-on-Avon* has writ, *all's well that ends well.* But it wasn't merely a simple change of plan. It wasn't just, *OK, let's do it this way and not that.* After a bitter inner-lab struggle, and under mounting political pressure to modify the project by expunging the reactor from it, ORNL finally succumbed to the public will. As the eighties passed into history and the nineties came, the lab transmuted its project from being reactor-based to being accelerator-based. In this manner – replacing the ANS in the Trivelpiece agenda – was born the Spallation Neutron Source (SNS), *spallation* being a method of producing very intense neutron beams in an accelerator-based reactor-less system. However, because ORNL was woefully lacking in accelerator expertise, ahead of it lay a hard road to hoe.

Strangely, DOE, being ultimately responsible for seeing to it that the project was done properly and expeditiously, wasn't much perturbed by this turn of events. Finding a silver lining in an otherwise very tough situation, they even came to like what happened. You see, when *bigness* in basic research entered the government bailiwick, the DOE recognized that some sort of consolidation in the national lab system had to be undertaken. After all, how many big projects can be afforded? So, should the number of labs be reduced? That didn't appear to be a politically viable thing to do. Then what could be done? Nobody wanted labs just sitting around doing nothing, least of all the labs themselves. Then, as luck would have it, some smarty-pants administrator came up with the bright idea that perhaps the labs could work together in designing and building big projects. Each lab would simply do what it does best. Thus, get a little done here, a little done there, put it all together and *eureka*, the object of desire emerges. Unfortunately, it isn't that simple. The truth is that it's a mighty tall order, mainly because it removes the high motivating factor that comes from a lab identifying itself with a particular project. Nevertheless, DOE was chomping at the bit to try out the concept, and here was ORNL giving it the perfect opportunity. Who was to stop it? Thus, the SNS project became a test-bed for an ambitious new management undertaking, with five labs, ORNL, ANL, LANL, BNL and LBNL, working in concert as a kind of consortium to get the job done.

So it was that DOE's long-term strategists welcomed the chance to try out this rather iffy approach to managing the national lab system. They well knew that in the coming era of *bigness*, the decline in frequency and number of new projects was inevitable. Therefore if the one-to-one lab-project correlation were to be maintained, the clear implication was that not all the labs could share equally in the available annual funding process. The Congress wouldn't like that one bit. Besides, it would be a highly inefficient way of using government money and people. You can just imagine the scene: Some people, at labs with projects, would be working their tails off, while others, at labs without, would be busying themselves doing nothing. On the other hand, working together in an all-for-one fashion might be a great equalizing mechanism and possibly even the wave of the future. Furthermore, another plus for this way to go was that it provided a way to attack the problem that the national labs were aging and the system, as it was currently constituted, didn't permit a straightforward way of rejuvenating itself. Just think: With the status quo intact, the government would eventually be forced to willy-nilly fire the old and hire the young. Not only would this be ethically wrong, but it would also suffer from the deficiency of not dealing effectively with the continuity-of-knowledge question. However, this new idea of pooling the expertise and resources of the labs might be a way to bridge the gap as the succession of generations, from old to young, proceeds. *Yes*, the administration said in unison, *this type of lab cooperation could well be the answer to our prayers*.

Thus, the ORNL problem of aging reactor personnel, who would become guinea pigs of a sort, became a possible administrative solution to the pressing dilemma of project *bigness*. The five chosen labs could set a precedent by working together toward a facility to be located at a site other than their own, ORNL in this case. It could even be a springboard for a whole new way for the national lab system to operate. Thus, the stage was set for the DOE lab management trial balloon to be launched, and the five labs were asked to join forces to build a billion-dollar-plus accelerator facility to produce neutron beams to serve the many sciences and scientists yearning for them. So, because of his imagination and his quick response to the challenge generated by the public's unreasonable fear of nuclear energy, Trivelpiece found the means to recover from what could have been a disastrous reversal of fortune for him; and, in the bargain, gave the country a possible way out of an even more significant – almost intractable – problem than the one he'd originally set out to resolve. He was quite a man, this Trivelpiece! First came his brilliant initiative. Then he was thrown off balance by the ORNL nuclear reactor fiasco. But when a way out chanced by, he grabbed it and did what had to be done. He got right up off the mat and saved the day. In the end, the *Trivelpiece Initiative* came to fruition. It will always be remembered as his scintillating life-giving contribution to the U.S. national lab system. Yes, his positive, upbeat legacy will go on in spite of the great difficulties the SNS was to encounter, as well as what was to happen to the SSC.

* * * * *

Immediately after the announcement that the SSC would be a presidential initiative, the word was "*go,*" and the politically sensitive site selection process got underway. You'd better believe that there were lots of states vying for the right to host this scientific plum. The DOE received 35 proposals that met the criteria set forth in the guidelines established for the open competition. What a tribute this was both to the American way and to Bob Wilson's winning clash with the entrenched and shortsighted scientific establishment of the sixties! In quick order, a site selection committee was formed, under the auspices of the National Academy of Sciences. This gave to the process the requisite weight and credibility as well as the all-important appearance of being unbiased and honest. For the most part, the National Academy was true to science's creed of calling a spade a spade. The task was actually made easy for the Academy because the DOE kept the final choice, which after all was a political one, to itself. Thus, the committee did its job examining and assessing the proposals, and whittling the number down to seven. Its work thereby being done, it passed this short list on to the DOE for its review and final selection, the stage of the process where the heavy-duty, dog-eat-dog political wrangling would play out its course. As for the scientists, they could only stand on the sidelines in suspense, kept on *shpilkes* as they awaited the verdict from on high that would shape their lives for years to come.

In November 1988, with the presidential election just a hair's breadth away, the DOE announced the winner to be Ellis County, Texas. Reagan wanted this giant step in science to be unequivocally recognized as his initiative, and also had a penchant for Texas to be the place the new laboratory should be located. And he got what he wanted on both counts! Yet, even for a president, it wasn't as easy as *one-two-three*. The competition became sorely rancorous toward the end, when a fierce struggle erupted between Texas and Illinois. The contest was so close that up to the very day of the public heralding of the verdict, the governors of these two powerful states made pronouncements to their constituents and to the country to the effect that their states should and would win out. The Governor of Illinois pulled out all the stops with his conviction-packed pleas that the rational choice was Illinois because the existing high-energy lab, Fermilab, would be an ideal home base for the project and would give it a head start over all the other proposed sites. To him it was a no-brainer since the lab already had substantial accelerator technology strength, a highly effective lab infrastructure, and its Tevatron primed to serve as the injector for the new complex. He went further and implied that choosing Illinois would give the project a faster completion date and be a hell of a lot lower in cost than if it were located elsewhere. But all that bluster was to no avail. Despite the irrefutable logic of the Governor's message, it would not be common sense or rationality that decided this contest of powerful states. There could be only one winner, and because the project had been magnified by its *bigness* and its correctly presumed social value, there could be only one way to get to the end of the line – politics, plain and simple. Of course, it was quite natural for the Illinois Governor to know all this. It's just that he had sweet reason and a sound pragmatic case in his back pocket. So, why shouldn't he play these cards to the hilt? Still, he knew deep down that, even though Fermilab might make the SSC come to pass a little sooner and at a little lower cost, it would be *Mother Politics* that would ultimately fix the outcome. How could it have been otherwise?

For a representative government like that of the United States, that's the way it should be, for the Congress is an assembly of elected officials each of whom has the duty, naturally, to serve his country – but also to bring home the bacon to his state. Why should they not have the privilege of influencing the distribution of federal facilities, including those of science? If not they, who should have the power to divide up the pie and hand out such favors? Should scientists or their like do it? Is it enough of a pretext that the choice can best be made by informed critical reasoning at which scientists fancy themselves tops? No, it can't be so! For, logical argument and rational dialectic cannot be the proper means to answer the question as to which state be given the authority and the federal funds to build and operate a major laboratory like the SSC. What manner of logic can ascertain the preferability of New York over California or of Colorado over New Mexico or, indeed, of Illinois over Texas? Yes, it's quite right that choosing the state offering the minimum cost or the one claiming the earliest completion date could fill the bill. But, even when cases are made in such a vein, they inevitably end up being full of factual flaws and holes of uncertainty. Taking away the chaff and looking at the core, you see that the states can offer no more than promises. Well, that's neither here nor there, because they can all do that. So you're still stuck with how to choose. The truth is that what one state can do, so can another. So, what alternative is there to making it a purely political decision – one where men fight it out with no holds barred?

This state versus state issue recalls Illinois Senator Charles Percy's public anger when he heard that a scientific committee had been given, or simply took upon itself, the right to voice such a siting decision. The committee had been created by the DOE to review proposals from states competing for the right to build a new type of electron re-circulating accelerator facility. The two leading proposals were from Illinois and Virginia. The question to the committee came down to which design was the better one. It wasn't actually asked where the facility should be situated. However, having concluded that the Virginia design was technically superior, it took its mandate a step further and recommended that the Virginia site was therefore the more appropriate one. Percy found this a very bitter pill to swallow. As a senator, he was chagrined at being by-passed, not even consulted. Furthermore, representing Illinois, he was offended and not a little embarrassed that a bunch of scientists ignored his state so cavalierly. He had to respond to such a put-down and to such arrogance. So, once the DOE made the announcement, he made his own. With marked annoyance in his voice and red as a beet, he declared publicly that Illinois was quite able to build and operate the design worked out by a group of scientists and engineers in Virginia. The committee, he went on, although representing the best of the country's technical expertise had gone too far.

Choosing the site was none of its damn business. Doing science and making technical evaluations was for scientists. But federal facility distribution – site selection – was fully the responsibility of politicians. Thus, in a succinct and direct manner, plainly articulated, he reprimanded the scientific community for overstepping its bounds and realm of authority. However, despite his fuming oratory – his outward indignation and inner humiliation – the Continuous Electron Beam Accelerator Facility (CEBAF) for nuclear physics research was actually built in Newport News, Virginia, as the eighties came to a close and the nineties opened. Although by the time he made his presence felt, it was a lost cause, perhaps to salvage a little face, he saw fit to speak out against the state of Virginia for taking part in such a rotten affair. In retrospect, Percy may have just been grandstanding, for things weren't at all what they seemed to be. Actually, the innocent scientists involved were merely pawns in a game being played by the two states. Yes, it was really a political contest all along, and when the dust settled, Virginia won and Illinois lost.

All in all, although Percy got the short end of the stick in this case, he made a compelling case for the political process having the last word in choosing the sites for technological or scientific facilities. Because, in fact, for the most part this is actually the way the U.S. arranges for the distribution of all its facilities, what Percy's persistence and articulation really relayed to his political colleagues was, *keep your guard up at all times, lest you lose power that's rightfully yours.* Still it's not just a game of power, for who is to say the political way is not really the best way to make such difficult choices? Keeping in mind that real people make decisions and that each comes with a healthy share of bias baggage, can anyone suggest a better one? Yes, Percy demonstrated a lot of perceptiveness in the positions and actions he took. Perhaps he was emulating the great Illinois Senator Everett Dirksen, who showed a great deal of political foresight in recognizing the economic, educational and cultural value of scientific facilities for his state well before *bigness* thrust it into the minds of most politicians. Remember, it was the Republican Dirksen who worked out an arrangement with Democratic President Lyndon Johnson in 1968 to locate what came to be Fermilab at the farmland site in Batavia, Illinois.

* * * * *

By the time the SSC came along, the great value of having a scientific facility in your backyard had become clear to everyone. That's why so many states vied for this really big one. As it turned out, Texas was simply too strong politically for the others to have any real chance at this prize scientific laboratory, although Illinois did give it a good run for its money. In the end, Texas won because it had enormous political strength and its politicians chose to exercise it. Besides Reagan having a soft spot in his heart for Texas, there were Vice-President George Bush, Senator and Vice-Presidential candidate Lloyd Bentsen, House Speaker Jim Wright, and a host of other supporters in high places. With such men willing to put themselves on the line, where else could the SSC wind up? Thus, the SSC came to be centered in the heart of the wealthy land of cattle and oil, just south of Dallas. The politicians having played their part, it wasn't long before a procession of scientists, engineers, managers, hangers-on, and a myriad of other types descended on the small town of Waxahachie and set up shop for their believed-to-be thrill-packed venture into science history.

Only two months after the site selection announcement, in January 1989, Universities Research Association (URA) became the prime contractor to manage DOE's new SSC laboratory. In quick succession, URA established a Board of Trustees, named SLAC Director Pief Panofsky as its chairman, and designated Roy Schwitters to be the project's first Director. Roy, a Harvard physics professor, was an experimentalist in particle physics with wide experience in the conceptualization, design and management of large detectors. With extensive work at SLAC and Fermilab under his belt, he knew first-hand the ins and outs of the national labs: He knew the top people and how to work with them; he knew what labs wanted and needed; he knew their ways of doing things; and he knew how to get things done. How much more perfect for the job can you get?

Roy had youth, ambition, and know-how; and he gave every indication of being an up-and-coming star. But there was even more than that. His past placed him very close to the one who was undoubtedly the SSC kingmaker. Yes, history had seen to it: Roy was Panofsky's man. A little over 15 years earlier, with Pief's encouragement and under his tutelage, he'd been the key scientist for SLAC's big detector for the 1973 experiment in the SPEAR Electron-Positron collider, the experiment that inspired and galvanized the so-called November revolution in particle physics and garnered the Nobel Prize for Burt Richter. That Nobel Prize ended up being a critical turning point in Roy's life. Young and impatient, it was hard for him to see it slip through his fingers. He felt he'd done the central and vital work, and, being overlooked that way, he always harbored a deep resentment for not sharing in this honor. Poor Roy, so badly treated! However, unbeknownst to him at the time, Pief also believed that life hadn't played fair and square with Roy in this affair. Thus, although Roy was indeed a deserving candidate in his own right, Pief saw to it that he was given this greatly sought after SSC position, perhaps as some kind of guilt-induced payoff for the previous negligent oversight. So it happened that Roy's capabilities and achievements were finally recognized.

The case of Roy and the SSC directorship was a classic example of the ironic twists of fate that make bad things happening to you often turn out to your good fortune. Out of bad may well come good! So, although Roy could only bemoan his lost Nobel dream, that occurrence was actually a door opener of equally grand proportions – or even more. But fate works in strange ways, and here's part of the story. Before he was finally noticed and given his due in 1989, his unhappiness back in the seventies at not being rewarded the way he thought he deserved led him to look elsewhere in the particle physics landscape. He left off working with electrons at SLAC and switched to experiments with protons. This greatly broadened his technical experience and placed him smack in the middle of the growing proton collider labs. He did a lot of work at the forefront Fermilab and even toyed with the idea of leading one of the teams for the planned ISABELLE detectors. Thus, even without the big Nobel prize, and perhaps even as a result of not having it, he gained enormous knowledge and experience as well as visibility. He became very well known around the world, and seemed almost to be preparing himself for the opportunity of a lifetime with the coming collider to end all colliders. The fact was that with all the scientific and technological knowledge he'd gained over the years, all the managerial know-how he'd picked up, and with the many contacts and associations he'd made, from lab directors down to technicians, he gave every appearance of being the ideal choice. That's exactly what Pief saw. As a result, Roy was given his big chance, handed to him on a silver platter by *Godfather Pief.* All he had to do was pick up the raw jewel from the platter and cut it just right.

As it turned out, however, life, with its bag full of ironies, wouldn't comply. Roy was not the master gem-maker he was first thought to be. There were crucial missing links in his resumé that weren't apparent to his choosers. In retrospect, you might be tempted to condemn them for their oversights, perhaps even for their incompetence at selecting the right person for this position that meant so much to the future of high-energy physics. However, you should be cautioned not to judge them too severely or fault them too harshly. You see, management at the heights is not an easy place to be. The things you must do are demanding, complex, and problematic; they're full of troubles, stress, and pain; and never are they appreciated. So, there they were, Panofsky and the URA chiefs, with the DOE breathing down their necks. They simply had to come up with a leader for the SSC on the double. The DOE had the go-ahead, had the cash, and had to have someone to assign it to. A Director just had to be set in place. But who? What sort would be needed? It isn't that tough to come up with a list of characteristics. It would be: someone who was technically adept; someone who could handle personnel; someone whom the DOE would approve of and the science community would accept; someone who could negotiate with all manner of people – scientists, government administrators, and hard-nosed industrial types; someone who could fit in with the Texas upper-crust – politicos, financial wizards, and party-goers; someone who could walk through the corridors of Congress and relate to the men in residence there; and someone who could deal with the executive branch, from the various science offices to the Office of Management and Budget, to the President himself. Whew, that's a tall order! So, should Pief and the others be hauled over the coals because they fell short of their assigned mission? Surely, that's going a little too far. They undoubtedly tried their best. Besides, there probably was nobody at the time who would have been right in the part being auditioned for. Who could have known when the selection was being made that what Roy lacked would mean the difference between success and failure? The truth was that on paper he looked to be about as close to an on target match as was possible. However, it was the intangible qualities, the ones hard to diagnose and those that in the end make the real difference, which he was missing. He lacked that certain sense of humor that would allow him to live in the midst of contradiction, deceit, and betrayal; he lacked that savoir faire about the job, that certainty of who he was and where he was going, that would allow him to push on when things seem totally out of hand; he lacked the ability to expect the unexpected and to be flexible under extreme stress; and he lacked the inner resources to keep his head and find that ray of hope when all about him are those who see no hope to hang onto. So it was that being young, smart, knowledgeable, ambitious, logical, persuasive, and, especially, charming were not enough for what was needed – or perhaps just not relevant.

As time would tell, he didn't have the sixth sense that drives men to invade unknown and uncharted territory successfully. Roy, unaware of the treacherous nature of his SSC journey, naïvely walked right into one such territory, that of *bigness*. There, instead of finding the key to the universe as he'd set out to do, instead of reaping the fame and glory that accompany profound scientific discovery – rewards he believed were already rightfully his from days gone by – he was to become lost in a no-man's land and ultimately abandoned in a desert where it appeared nothing could bloom. Was Roy the cause of all that befell him and the SSC? If only he'd been a mite better, could things have turned out differently for basic Big Science? It's hard to say and leaves us with persistent and gnawing doubts about what could have been. One thing seems sure, that he can't be relieved of all accountability. As pilot of the caravan traveling across the frontier of *bigness*, it seems self-evident that Roy certainly must share some of the blame for the SSC's sorry fate. On the other hand, placing the entire burden of responsibility on Roy's faint-hearted and ignorant shoulders hardly seems to be fair or accurate. You see, Roy was just an ordinary man. How then could he have brought about such a disproportionately extraordinary event? No matter how you slice it, he couldn't. If you believe the fiction that he could have done it, then you're only experiencing an illusion, a trick that the mind plays to help all of us indubitably *better men* move forward into the vast and unknowable future. However, if not because of Roy, then how and why did the SSC suffer such a sad fate? Was the cause of it bigger than the man himself? Was it bigger than any man who happened to be in Roy's shoes? Was the outcome inevitable right from the start? Is it really possible that Big Science was just moving forward too fast, and was therefore guillotined by jealous gods guarding nature's secrets? Yes, it has a nice ring to it, but in the end divine intervention is also not a very satisfactory explanation of the SSC story.

All the bidding states offered a dowry for the privilege of marriage with the SSC, but Texas outbid the others by a long shot, as only Texas can. This vast state, blessed with whopping wide-open spaces and money to burn, promised more than ample land for the project and a pile of special financial grants to universities. Ostensibly the SSC was a national objective going to further the cause of Big Science in the U.S. However, the technology, the knowledge, and the culture that the SSC would bring to the state that won it surely aroused the enthusiasm of the Texans and spurred them on. No doubt that spiced up with a healthy dose of self-interest, an act of altruism for the common good is made far more palatable!

By tradition and history, Texas was an action-oriented, pistol-packing state; and so, almost immediately after the Texas site was chosen, it went on the move. The state empowered the Texas National Research Laboratory Commission (TNRLC) by filling its coffers with hard cash. Formed two years earlier in 1987 to oversee the Texas interests in the grandiose and high-flying project, the commission ensured that scientists and politicians, as well as government, university and industry officials from all over the country appreciated just how serious Texas was and how generous it was willing to be. It obviously did that part of its job very well indeed. As part of its current purpose, the TNRLC set up a peer-reviewed program to administer and distribute 100 million dollars of Texas taxpayer money over a ten-year period to energize and cultivate SSC-related R&D. Despite the natural tendency of any state to foster and support its own research universities and academic infrastructure, Texas, in the spirit of the American science tradition of open and fair competition for federal funds, opened the competition for Texas money to universities throughout the United States. Since the federal government intended – more accurately insisted – that the SSC laboratory be truly national in character, it put the state under a great deal of political pressure to go this route. Still, although political force was unremittingly applied, nevertheless, this commendable plan for the countrywide distribution of Texas money for SSC R&D and its implementation was a purely Texas initiative. It showed beyond a reasonable doubt the acute sensitivity and the political wisdom of this aspiring, always-looking-to-the-future state. Not only did this action demonstrate the willingness of Texas to accede to and comply with federal policy, but it was also an example of Texas stretching out its hands in its ongoing efforts to become part of the American cultural mainstream. Any way you look at it, it was a wise and gallant gesture.

Meanwhile, back at the Waxahachie ranch, Schwitters grabbed the reins of his newly found power base, and with gusto rounded up his team and began to set the SSC wheels into motion. With everybody behind him, it seemed easy at the start. Temporary makeshift offices were completed and local workers were hired as administrative assistants, secretaries, technicians, and the like. The eagerness with which people approached their jobs was infectious, and the top dog became puffed up with pride and confidence. On the technical side, by July 1990 there was a lot of promise on all fronts. One of the many significant accomplishments was that the scientists and engineers under his close leadership completed the site-specific conceptual design of the facility with remarkable dispatch. As for the Collider itself, although still just a figment in the ambitious minds of those who came to Texas, it was beginning to take on the character of being Schwitter's machine. As time passed, his imprints were to be more and more seen throughout the design. How full of self-importance he must have been! There he was on top of the basic physics project that was to rock the twentieth century. Who could resist the pride that came from having the country's – even the world's – scientists waiting on your every word and ready to jump to your commands? How could he help but feel the honor of it all? However, slowly a subtle change began to take its inexorable course, with hubris being the causal culprit. Roy began to think of himself as infallible and swaggered about like a man with the world in his palms and not a care or worry in sight. He was so sure of himself. He knew exactly where he was going and how to get there. And he had good reason to think as much! With all the obstructions from the community, especially those who feared the project or were jealous of it, cleared away, and with Congress in his back pocket, in quick succession he got the *go* signs from the myriad places that had to be dealt with: The tough negotiations with DOE's Office of Environment, Safety and Health (ES&H) represented a big hurdle, but ES&H finally agreed that the project complied with all its required rules and regulations and signed on; the budget was reviewed and approved by all, including the executive branch's independent tight-fisted Office of Management and Budget (OMB); and the science office of the President together with the DOE, which was already primed and in the *go* state, jumped on the bandwagon. The SSC wunderkind gave every sign of being fully on top of things, touching base with all the important characters who were needed for the project's formal approval as well as those who were a must for consultation. Everywhere he went and whomever he saw, he walked away with the thumbs-up sign. Thus, with all the necessary "*OKs*" in his grasp, Roy was in seventh heaven and ready to roll.

The year 1990 was a big one for the SSC. The action was fast and furious. As soon as the site footprint was completed and in hand, the state of Texas began land acquisition. Later in the year, the dreaded Environmental Impact Statement (EIS) was not only completed but, with the wheels having been shrewdly and discreetly well greased, was accepted without the least fuss by the federal government, the government of Texas, and the local community. So, with the worrisome and delicate issues of land for the SSC and the project's environmental impact firmly settled with trouble-free agreements, there was no stopping *big-boy* now. The merry-go-round was on and the off-button nowhere to be found. Not even the Director could have blocked it's forward thrust or even altered the project in any significant way, for although it wasn't yet transparent, the SSC had by then taken on a life all its own and Roy's influence was fast diminishing. But what could all this negative thinking matter in the least bit to him at this stage? After all, he had the ball in his hands and he was running headlong toward the goal line. What he hadn't an inkling of was that strong defensive back bearing down, ready to blindside him. So, on went oblivious Roy. With no idea of what lay before him, and in truth no desire to know, he ordered the SSC train to keep moving *full-speed-ahead*. In the meantime, at the Waxahachie site, far from the shenanigans in Washington and Austin, the SSC stage was set and the actors were in place. All that was needed to start the ground quaking and shaking was little more than a faint signal from the Director. Once that nod came, the first major construction at the SSC site began in earnest in 1991.

The SSC was off to the races and all seemed to be going right. But that was deceiving, for there was a hidden darkness and a foreboding not readily open to view. It's not that the truth couldn't have been uncovered. But most of the people involved weren't tuned in or weren't susceptible to perceiving that type of unpleasantness, or at least they weren't ready for it then in 1991. Either they were innocents, as so many scientists are; or they wouldn't apply the time and effort needed to dig out the dirt; or perhaps they didn't want to know, preferring to be happy while ignorant rather than unhappy knowing what lay beneath. Overspreading Waxahachie was an outward tone and atmosphere permeated with hopeful prospects, buoyant enthusiasm, and defiant optimism. But it was only a fool's paradise, for the air reeked thick with false promise. Yet, the fictitious and counterfeit nature of what was apparent couldn't be diagnosed. Being so deeply engrossed in their work and embedded in their dreams, the scientists and the rest of the SSC troupe simply couldn't see the forest for the trees.

There was, however, one sour note that surfaced right near the start, back in 1989. But it passed so quickly that most didn't pick up the uncomfortable signal that all was not as rosy as it appeared. It had to do with the official name for the new laboratory. Filtering the notion along the grapevine, through the halls and back alleys of the government, the powers that be let it be known that they might look kindly on the enterprise if the name of the new laboratory were to include the name of Ronald Reagan. It so happened that the President was very proud of his backing of science and technology, and was particularly taken by the great new American collider designed to push into the unknown lying beyond our ken. It was even leaked that the name, the *Ronald Reagan Laboratory for Particle Physics*, would be looked upon in a favorable light, especially since Reagan had personally applauded the project and put himself on the line with his presidential initiative money. Alas, the people with influence at the SSC and in the science community didn't want any part of it. What incomprehensible folly, what sheer stupidity – to slap your benefactor across the face! Yet it happened, and it still remains a mystery today as to why they behaved that way.

At the time, two reasons were put forth that at least had a modicum of plausibility. The trouble with them was that they both were based on philosophical differences and grudges of a sort. They lacked any pragmatic quality normally attributed to scientists. But why expect *the scientists* to shine through? Those running the SSC were after all only men. So, why, just as with all ordinary men, shouldn't the irrational sides of their natures hold sway? First there was the fact that the men of the SSC had strong differences in political ideology with the President. You see, scientists have a strong tendency to be Democrats, and, as such, how could they be expected to tolerate the idea of associating their laboratory with the name of Mister Republican himself? As a logical explanation of what was done, it leaves a lot to be desired. But then, men will be men – or sometimes children? Moving on the second reason, maybe the guys running the SSC had, as a matter of principle, a deep-seated opposition to Reagan's policies. Since the basic scientists of the *post-Manhattan-Project* generation, following Oppenheimer's example, leaned in the pacifist direction, far from the militaristic, perhaps more worldly and realistic Reagan. Thus, it shouldn't be much of a surprise that, for the most part, they felt and expressed an intense emotional aversion to the technologically ambitious Strategic Defense Initiative (SDI), commonly known as Star Wars. It's quite true that its proposed technologies didn't hold together well and were on the risky side. But, on the other hand, of all people, scientists should be supportive of bold and adventurous forays of the high-risk, high-payoff variety. These are their stock in trade, the reason they give for government funding of basic research. If it's good for the goose, as it's said, then why shouldn't it be equally good for the gander? If *science* can indulge in basic research, then why not *defense*? So, here again, if policy conflict were to be the reason for the conduct of the SSC's top tier, then scientists were behaving more like petulant brats than wise men. The result could've been foreseen. Acting like little people, spitefully and peevishly for personal satisfaction, and not at all for the common good of Big Science, they would have to be brought down a notch or two. And they were! How could the smart, reasonable men of science have been so dense? Despite the politically wise move it would've been and the honor it would've brought to the SSC, it seems that in a fit of collective pique, the SSC crowd denied the President his wish to be a visible part of this great scientific adventure. What asinine outrageousness! What a colossal blunder! What arrogant elitism! What addle-headed, myopic mindlessness! It's hard to believe, but in all likelihood, they probably didn't give it much thought, but what a whopper of a mistake they made, one that turned out to be something like shooting yourself in the foot, or even worse.

When looked at dispassionately and thoughtfully, it's quite understandable that some of the top-echelon scientists would've wanted the name of a distinguished and famous scientist to represent the grand lab they envisioned. That in fact was the basis for the names given to the Lawrence Berkeley lab and Fermilab. However, this manner of determining the names of labs is more the exception than the rule. You can easily see why. It takes quite a bit of courage to choose one over the many others proffered because what's one man's favorite may not be another's. To get a consensus is bound to be a rare occurrence. So, what's generally found are bland names that are chosen by searching for the least offensive ones, a particular popular method being to choose a name that identifies the lab's geographical location. However, when it came to that unique lab that was to house the SSC, there's a compelling sense that somehow it should've had a special name to match its majestic stateliness. Yes, a great scientist would've fit the bill quite well. Although this was undoubtedly tried, it seems evident that there was a lot of trouble in getting agreement on which the right one would be. However, picking a great scientist is not the only method. Scientists are not the only people who made the SSC come to be. Politicians also played an important part. So, why not choose one of them? Once you reach this point, it's quite obvious that one person in this class stands out above all the others. Not only was Reagan the key individual that carried the SSC from fantasy to reality, but he also gave all of science a great deal to be thankful for. Yes, he undeniably was a man of vision who saw the virtue and immense value in Big Science. More than that, he was willing to vouch for it and send science into the really big-time. Although the impetus Reagan gave science was immeasurably significant, the know-it-all scientists at the top high-handedly brushed off the President's contribution. Insolently, they rejected his claim to have been a player; and, as it turned out, in so doing, they irretrievably threw away their generation's chance of a lifetime to view the deep-lying innards of an uneasily yielding nature.

The men in the Big Science game shouldn't have forgotten one of the prime lessons of the *bigness* experience: the SSC was a political animal, born in political wars and the product of political maneuvering and action. Naturally, scientists were a big part of the show. But they just did the begging and then stood aside waiting for the benefits. They did as they were told and only entered the political combat zone when they were called for. Is there anyone among us who doubts for a moment that it was the big men of politics who fueled the Texas juggernaut that did the trick for the SSC? What an impressive list of *big-boys* it was: George Bush was Reagan's Vice President and Republican candidate for the 1988 presidential election; Jim Wright was the perennial Speaker of the House of Representatives; and Lloyd Bentsen was a leading U.S. senator and the 1988 democratic vice-presidential candidate. In addition to their national prominence, all of them were Texas strongmen as well as figures of enormous personal stature and importance. Just think of it. These men and their multitude of followers stood ready to back the SSC and to place it in their beloved state of Texas. It was one of those offers that couldn't be refused. And after a little soul-searching and inner squabbling, Big Science didn't. Although it's quite true that these Texans won the SSC prize for Texas, it's also true and even more important that they, along with the President, won it for science and posterity. These were men of foresight and vision, who saw science as the wave of the future. They were irresistible and commendable men. They were great men. And above them all stood the man with the baton, President Reagan himself. No, there's just no escaping it: Big Science should have acknowledged its obligation to the President, for he was the political glue that pulled it all together and made it work. Naming the lab after him was a once-in-a-lifetime political smile from Lady Luck. It should have been lunged at, seized, and embraced as the honor that it was. Instead, what the unwise and thoughtless men in charge of the SSC did was to gratuitously and ignominiously rebuff the President's outstretched hand and slam the door in his face. What addlebrained numbskulls they were! What political nitwits! What shortsighted fools! Then, having done such an imprudent and dim-witted thing, what were they left with? The science community was left with nothing but a lame, politically neutral, unimaginative and unmemorable name, *The Superconducting Super Collider Laboratory.*

It would have been well for those scientists involved if they'd remembered the biblically originating aphorism, "As you sow, ye are like to reap." But this invaluable bit of advice was not heeded in the *Reagan snubbing affair*, and the ungenerous political action they took represented a point of no return for the SSC. From that point on, only a short time after the project began to plant its Texas roots, the life of the SSC started to turn sour; and then, going from bad to worse, the slide couldn't seem to be stopped. It's true that the connection between the contemptible spurning of Reagan on the name issue and the SSC's sharp downturn of fortune could well have been purely coincidental. An alternative political explanation could equally have been that at roughly the same time the political might of Texas peaked and its political fortunes were on the threshold of plummeting to the earth – kerplunk. Just prior to the presidential election of 1988, when the SSC was given its Texas home, there seemed no end to Texas political power and no visible reason not to think that it would go on forever. However, just after the SSC became a Texas reality, the Texans in high places began to drop like flies. Bentsen lost his vice-presidential election bid; Wright was ousted from the House because of a petty book scandal; and Reagan himself was gone from the presidency after serving two terms, and thereafter ceased to be of any political consequence. Only Bush remained, but he too was to be lost to the SSC four years later when Bill Clinton beat him out and took over the Washington *White House*. In hindsight, it seems pretty clear that having Ronald Reagan in the SSC laboratory name could have provided a great deal of protection for the tottering SSC. It could even have saved it. Would Congress really have wanted to be on record as having eliminated a beloved-by-all *Ronald Reagan anything*? Too bad the high-energy science community wasn't smarter! Unfortunately, that opportunity to be clever, to show foresight, and to do the right thing was lost back in 1988 when the men of the SSC acted so self-servingly, so unintelligently, so unthinkingly, and so disgracefully. In the end, when all is said and done, it's hard to figure out exactly why the SSC went the way it did. However, one thing seems sure: the SSC leadership's lack of political acumen played an important part in its decline; and dating back to the Reagan snubbing, the fortunes of the new lab moved steadily on a downward course till it reached its last stop – right in the jaws of oblivion.

* * * * *

There was a mixture of intense feelings intermingled with a flurry of purposeful and resolute activity that gripped Waxahachie in 1991 as the big project began to move toward its appointment with destiny. The SSC had signed in and was ready to make its mark. Large construction equipment started to reshape the Texas landscape. Trucks and bulldozers rumbled in. Tunneling devices began to carve their way through the resisting earth and rock. The ground, undisturbed for so long, was no match for the modern crushing machines. Eventually, it gave way, and soon a gaping hole became visible. So was initiated far beneath the surface a more than 50-mile circular-in-cross-section excavation worming its almost circular path through the Texas plains. At ground level, there was action all around the site. People bustled about with that happy sense of being part of a worthwhile and glamorous adventure. Temporary structures to house the burgeoning administrative offices sprang up out of the dry earth. Key technical components of the project began to materialize: Superconducting magnets were contracted to be manufactured by the corporate sector, in particular General Dynamics, Westinghouse, and the SSC industrial partner, Babcock and Wilcox. Concurrently, a magnet factory in expectation of the multitude of magnets to be tested, modified, and inventoried was promptly and hastily erected. The initial stages of the injector complex started the transformation from design drawings to the real stuff. The ion source, which would ultimately spew out those precious proton beams, and the 250-meter linear accelerator, the first links in a long accelerating chain, were both readied for testing and placement in their fast-being-completed structures positioned securely in the earth to ensure perfect safety. Simultaneously, work on the other four links of the chain was begun: The Low Energy Booster, the Medium Energy Booster, and the High Energy Booster were on track and preparing to be ensconced in their separate compartments; and the capstone of the SSC, the magnificent collider ring itself, began to show signs of palpable coming-to-life. Just imagine the moment when the king of rings would be all done: thousands of sparkling magnets having the force of angels would be set in place in an almost circular concrete tunnel winding though 54 miles of hard-yielding terrain, deep beneath the surface; and finally, when the last magnet would be put in position, there it would find and kiss the first. The stage would then be set for man's rendezvous with the gods. Yes, the fire of life would be lit in the desert plains of Texas. With the Big Physics frontier but a hair's breadth away, you could almost taste the imminent presence of the fruits of heretofore forbidden knowledge.

By the fall of 1993, 15 miles of the collider ring was already dug. Then, suddenly, without so much as a how-de-do, it all stopped. The planning, the effort, the imagination, the production, and the construction, all the stuff of the modern organization, just ceased. Scientists all over the world went into shock; and silence reigned in Waxahachie. The unexpectedness of it took your breath away. Not moments before, the SSC was humming along seemingly seamlessly with the speed of a healthy enterprise certain of its longevity. The lab staff grew swiftly and assuredly, and in short order reached 2000, including 250 foreign scientists from 38 countries. In fact, it was actually much bigger, filled to the brim with many scientific personnel from research universities and other institutions around the country and from all over the globe. All of them were robust men committed to doing science, R&D, and whatever else they could to help the project reach its grand design. Poor souls! Those sad dreamers believed that, out of the sweat of their brows, an intellectual and scientific oasis was really about to spring up in that dry desert-like zone south of Dallas. In truth, they were on the right track. It was so close to becoming a reality. But, alas, it turned out to be only a mirage. Their awakening to the real world was quick, rude, and rough. *Bing, bang, boom*, and it was all over! The place they mistook for a waterhole was nothing but a place for tears. Like the Lady ISABELLE a decade earlier, this dressed-to-kill damsel turned out to be only a flash in the pan, superficially enshrined in multi-colored brilliance but without the promised substance underneath. As the fates would have it, the project ended before it began.

The puzzle as to why the SSC had to end, and why it had to end so brusquely and unceremoniously is indeed a tantalizing one. Baffling as it was, it elicited no dearth of answers from the many people involved. Everybody and his uncle were sure they had the right ones and were not bashful about making them known to all within earshot. Opinions abounded and flew about right and left. One person said this, another that, and it didn't take long to realize that the only outcome of a search for a straightforward reason for the downfall would assuredly be unvarnished disappointment. You might listen to someone give a reasoned viewpoint or some carefully thought-out analysis and think, "Yes, that's it!" However, not long afterward, you'd hear another person present an entirely different case in total opposition to the first, and – will wonders never cease – you'd find yourself reacting the same way. Actually such complicated situations, apparently with no unequivocal answers, are not that uncommon. Such cases have a familiar ring to them. In fact, if you've tangled with them before, you'd surely know either that no truly unique answer has really been grasped or that no easy to articulate, standard answer can be found. But surely no suggestion is being made that if you persist and struggle hard enough you absolutely won't or can't come up with something satisfactory. Perish the thought! That a rational solution actually exists to the puzzle of why the project failed goes without saying. For, as we all know, our world is of an undeniably law-abiding objective nature. Isn't it?

OK, let's presume that somewhere there's undeniably a true and clear answer that explains the SSC's downfall. But how does one get to it, and how does one recognize it for what it is? Well that's the problem! You see any answer worth the effort of searching for has to lie in the minds of the people who were at the center of the whole affair. But if you listen to what they have to say, which is usually more than you want to hear, you're more than likely to get a whole lot of self-serving mumbo-jumbo. If you accept this argument – actually quite a reasonable thing to do – then it follows that you'd do well to beware of the sophistry all around you. The technique that people use to confuse you and derail you from the right track, whether knowingly or not, is simple enough. In most instances, an unwitting conspiracy is established. Immediately a straightforward answer to an intricately complex set of human actions – the SSC fiasco being a case in point – is presented. Whether it's true or not is immaterial. Any reasonably relevant and cogent declaration or contention will do just fine. Then, it's repeated over and over again, and voilà it's picked up by others as well as the media, and embraced and swallowed as if it were the truth, the whole truth, etcetera, etcetera. But don't fall for it. It's too good to be true and should be recognized as such. So, your rule should be to maintain your skepticism of such apparent ease of discovery. Thus, just in case you haven't inferred it by now, here, in recap form, is the essential block to finding the real down-to-earth story of what happened to the SSC. You see, for the most part, the answers voiced are merely opinions, and although they may reflect a small part of any objective truth, they mostly echo the minds conceiving them – dominated by self-interest. To get at the real truth and not just the truth according to so-and-so, is a ball game of a vastly different kind.

Complex as the origins of the SSC's downfall are and difficult as it might be to disentangle the many intertwined reasons, still, it could be some fun sport to give it a stab. Who knows? It might even be a blast, and there could be something to learn from it as well. If more motivation were needed to pursue this arduous task than the sheer pleasure of a challenging intellectual pursuit, then let's say it's for the purpose of remembering and paying tribute to the pain and suffering the demise engendered in so many. However, if you're the practical sort, then stay the course because passing on that knowledge might help others in situations of a similar nature. If even that is not persuasive enough, then let it be said that our common humanity demands that we not ignore the SSC's rise and fall, but delve into the project's depths to search for reasons and causes. You see, all the people involved in the SSC, and there were many who suffered, deserved more of an answer than they got. They had a right to as scrupulously clear an explanation as could be uncovered. They had a just claim to a fit and proper eulogy. But what they were given fell far short of that. To be blunt, it was just a lot of pap! In the end, there was no one to speak for the little people. That being the case, it behooves us to explore the bloody mess and to uncover the dirt. Don't shirk the duty to do so. Dig on.

The project's leaders gave their own self-serving and unsatisfying version of the events. What the guilty parties seemed to care about most was justifying their own roles in the play and shifting the blame to others. Would that these so-called leaders were the only ones deserving of our disdain and contempt. No, there were others who could have eased the grief at the sorrowful loss. Unfortunately, these too were remiss in their duty. The many double-dealing, here-today-gone-tomorrow types from the government and the community, who joined the parade when the SSC band in shining uniforms with trumpets blaring victory tunes marched by, also had the responsibility to own up and express their mea culpas. They too could have given the event some meaning to those who were hurt and, along with the project, died a little too. There must have been some of all these men who could have stood up to console those who lost dearly. Actually, not much was being asked of them, just a few kind and honest words to help, even a little, soften the burden that befell them all, the little and the big alike. But where were such wise and heroic figures to be found? Even one! The truth was that such a one was not to be found. Of all the gung-ho types who led the march to fame and fortune, there were none of the likes of Bob Wilson. Who, among those at hand, could tell the people who put so much of their lives into it why it had to end? Who could step up to the podium and tell them why it had to be? Who could tell the folks of Waxahachie? Who could tell the people of Texas? Who could tell all the politicians, the government officials, and the scientists who worked so diligently and tirelessly to make the SSC dream come true? No, there was no one. Except for the phony platitudes and downright lies, there was only silence. There wasn't a man who could say it from the heart, and tell it like it was. No one could do it. Did any of them really know or could they see the truth if it were staring them in the face? Everyone seemed to feel more comfortable hiding from any answer of substance, as if they feared finding it. Thus, for the most part, they stopped looking; or perhaps they never even started probing; or, what's even worse, perhaps they felt more comfortable merely expressing the opinions de jour. As a matter of fact, they simply turned their backs on the whole stinking mess they'd created and slinked away.

The strange thing about the whole affair is that what seems to be the truth was actually staring right at them. It was deceptively simple. All the time, it was just lying there in the nature of man himself waiting to be found, open to view to anyone with the guts to lift the veil and look. To be sure, it was the dark side of man's nature that was the true cause. That being the case, could it really be expected that the men of the SSC, puny and shaking as their numbers were called, had the capability and the courage to stand up and be counted? Surely not! And there you have it! That weakness of spirit, that lack of depth and daring-do undoubtedly explains their reticence and reluctance to go headlong into the problem; they surely didn't have the strength of character or the nerve to search their own souls. They just weren't man enough! However, on second thought, one shouldn't be too hard on them seeing as it's hard for anyone to set about exploring this most forbidding of places. Still, if it's answers you want, then there's no alternative but to reach into yourself and face the music. It's not happy music, actually more like a dirge. You see, the set of circumstances such as the one the SSC losers had to face originates in the inexplicability of man's folly, his need at times to destroy his own dreams and, unnaturally, to inflict pain on himself. Surely, it's asking too much of them to have had the fortitude to go there. But now, almost a decade after the SSC had its encounter with death, there aren't many, if any, excuses for not seeking out the dark needs that lurked in the hearts of the SSC men, as well as the dark deeds that followed. However, from this vantage point of a later time, even though on the normally accepted historical scale it is really not much later than when the SSC's fate was sealed, looking in a detached manner at past events doesn't seem so uncomfortable. And if the players won't do it, then the duty rests with us. Thus, we must forego caution, and rush in where angels should fear to tread.

* * * * *

As with all complex human situations, the best that can be done is to develop a catalogue of the many potential circumstances and answers, and the many possible states. When organized according to some well-chosen classes, there's a chance – a slim one, but you can always hope – that some pattern will emerge that leads from the confusing hotchpotch of unreliable testimony into the bright light of understanding. Once you choose to alight on this particular cataloguing route, you shouldn't lose sight of the fact that you've set your sights both lower and higher: lower because you've given up on a single, straightforward result – doubtless the right thing to do; and higher because it demands extraordinary willpower and hard work to sift through the myriad entries in the catalogue. Just imagine what you've gotten yourself into! Think of all those painstaking, laborious hours you'll have to go through in the probably vain effort to reach a satisfactory resolution. Think of the small chance at being successful in the endeavor. Think of yourself gazing at all the possibilities, each one imploring you to accept that it's the right one. How can you do otherwise than make the big push and examine each and every one of the multitude of reasons, from serious to whimsical, that have been thrown into the pot? No, there's no short cut! Then, from examination, you move on to judging them in gory detail: Which ones are pertinent? Which ones have been shaded or simply invented by deceivers to throw you off the track? Which ones should be discarded as not being germane, not material, out-of-tune, non-contributory, or just plain false? Which ones should be retained as treasures and jewels? Which ones can be held up to the light as the crème de la crème? Which ones should be taken up and used to the utmost to discover clues about that elusive pattern that leads to understanding and truth? After you've done all that and more, then comes the hardest part of all. Presuming you've come to the point where you're able to conjecture a pattern, it's still not enough. You now have to take the components of the pattern and test them for consistency by trying them out. For that you must rummage through the psychosocial nature of the men involved, indeed you must do no less than poke around and grope your way in the dark through their minds. There's a lot of vagueness and ambiguity in all this. So, unless you're tenacious, persistent, strong-stomached, and persevering, and unless you've got the heart to shrug off the bumps and take it, come what may, this is not a job for you.

For gossipy types, this scouring through other people's minds could make for quite a bit of fun. But bear in your own mind that the aim of this exercise is serious, to wit to illuminate the links clarifying the underlying reasons and hidden intentions behind the behavior and actions of those responsible for bringing down the SSC. Through this process the idea is to bring into focus a unified picture and the enlightenment that comes with it. To reach this goal, you should recognize before you start that there is no avoiding naming names. You must unerringly shine the light of truth on the ones who did the deeds and to root out why they behaved as they did, leaving no stone unturned. Only then can all the loose ends be tied together and the truth emerge.

Getting to the heart of the matter is surely a worthy campaign. You're to be enthusiastically applauded if you choose to take it on. Bravo! But be advised not to jump into the breach too hastily. This heart-and-soul and often wearisome exercise, you see, is a thankless task. The search for truth is a dangerous sport and the faint of heart should not undertake it lightly. If you embark on this journey up-river into the swamps, be wily, be astute, and always be wary of where you might be led. However, it wouldn't do you well to be put off and so deterred by these perhaps too stern words of caution. Better to unbind yourself from the shackles of conventionality and move forward to that strange place that's both murky and filled with enlightenment at the same time. It's a mean assignment, this stirring up a hornet's nest, but you'll be the better for it.

As you pass through the door through which there's no returning, the questions will pour out at you: Do you share in the responsibility? Do your friends? Do your enemies? Do those whom you have venerated? Do those whom you have trusted? Who can bear the light of truth when the spotlight is thrown upon them? Can you? Can you battle against the vindictiveness and wrath of those exposed – those who have little reason to self-limit their natural or built-in urge for revenge? Can you absorb and tolerate the physical and mental torture that could well be inflicted on you? Can you handle the false disrepute and dishonor thrown in your face? Can you live with the shame of ostracism? Alas, whether or not you had the least intension of doing the *exposé bit* before, surely after hearing of what awaits you, there is cause to fear that you've been disabused of such apparent folly. If that's so, too bad!

An old story warns of the menacing power and resolve of a wounded animal, and advises that it is better to kill it than to wound it. For, if you don't take its life, then it will return to strike at you once again. Add to this the case where the animal has friends, associates, or self-seeking allies willing to wreak revenge on its behalf and you will be close to a description of a pretty commonly occurring human situation. With the risk-filled plight of having revenge lying in wait, the act of pointing the finger and placing blame is a forlorn and sorry road to take. No, the life of a *truth-teller* is not a happy one. So you can be sure that finding such a one isn't going to be an everyday occurrence. But surely that isn't too surprising. Do you truly expect to see figures hanging about ready to thrust themselves voluntarily into the mouths of hungry tigers? Probably not! Yet, without them, is there any hope that the guys in the black hats can be thrown in the hoosegow and those in the white hats can ride into the sunset?

Frankly, there is such hope. It isn't very satisfying, but can beggars be choosy? If a man won't step forward, then life's experiences tell us that fate indeed enters to balance the scales and set things right. True, fate does a good job. Unfortunately, it waits its own sweet time, as if it's seeking man's help, or willing to give men a chance at redemption. So it remains for us to ask if we should help fate via our intervention. Doubtlessly by now you've concluded that it's wiser to stay on the sidelines and leave well enough alone. That's what most would do and what we've come to expect from humankind. However, fate is begging for a hand. Can we just sit back and do nothing as it pleads for our becoming engaged? So, why not give it a shot. After all, as we're told, you only live once. Yes, that's the ticket! Let's ignore the sound advice of leaving it all to fate. Undaunted by the potential danger involved, let's walk right into the tiger's lair and push on toward the bitter truth, letting it bring what it may.

Enough of this wavering, philosophical gibberish! Having been wrapped up in more than sufficient whetting-the-appetite chatter, let's get on with plain speaking and the what-we're-here-for question at hand: why did the SSC end up going south? There's just one last little point to clear up before getting down to the nitty-gritty. Here we have before us an issue that has irrationality written all over it. To deal with it, however, we're bound by the constraints of conscious thought, a product of the rationality of our minds. There is simply no alternative open to us but logical reasoning and argumentation. You might be wondering whether rational means of comprehending can actually throw light on irrational behavior. Although not absolutely certain, it's probably not something to lose sleep over. Besides, it's all we've got. *There just ain't no more*! So, working within that limitation, let's take the plunge and enter the learning zone.

Here's the plan of attack: Having accepted the fact that a single all-encompassing, all-explaining answer is not going to just jump out in the "Eureka, I've got it" manner, then we must bite the bullet and go swimming in the amorphous, clear-as-mud waters of complexity in search of that pattern that carries us home to the real McCoy, the genuine article, the naked truth. As prescribed, first we formulate our catalogue of potential reasons by methodically dividing the countless opinions and perspectives that have found community currency into a small number of classes. With such classes, we develop prospective patterns. Then, devising consistency tests, ones that look for contradictions, ambiguities, accord, and agreements, we analyze them in the hope that among them we can pin down that pattern that screams out at us, "*I'm the one*!" Yeah, right! Anyway, let's plow ahead. There are many reasons out there just waiting to be picked up. In an attempt to put some order into them, let's consider the community to be made up of groups that have glommed onto one or another class of such reasons: One group's constituents concur that some particular class hits the bull's eye; in another they've reached a consensus that a different class is behind it all; and in still others there's common consent revolving around various other classes. After modifying, shaping, and honing the classes, finally, we've arrived at the moment of truth. It's time to pose the big questions: How many classes are there and what distinguishes them? *And the envelope please*! Opening that precious piece of stationery, we find that there are six classes. Some may indeed find another number and slightly different classifications, but be assured that they won't deviate in any substantive way from these: political reasons,

reasons linked to money, social reasons, reasons stemming from international affairs, reasons of competence, and last but not least, the ever-popular class of miscellaneous reasons. In short, we can refer to the classes with the simple titles: politics, money, sociology, internationalism, incompetence, and all-of-the-above. Maybe a little time and a little thought for each of the six will bear fruit, and an answer will come falling out like manna from heaven. It's not very likely that we'll be so lucky. But rest easy; far chancier things have come to pass. Whatever, it's worth a try. So here goes!

* * * * *

Politics

Perhaps the answer to the puzzle of the SSC's undoing lies in the class of political causes. What a trendy notion that was in the science community at the time the SSC took the full count. Unfortunately, getting to the root of things is not a popularity contest. However, you can see why scientists were attracted to this source, even though seizing upon it and proclaiming it as truth were just picked out of a hat and not at all in the usual manner of the scientific hunt. Plainly said, it took the onus off them. That was it – no more, no less. And besides, after the fact, government bureaucrats, arch targets for blame, are always easy to bash and trash. Actually, seeming strange at first blush, political officials didn't really seem to mind being considered in this light. They even got some sort of positive boost out of these slings and arrows being hurled at them. How ironic! Complaining about them, sneering at them, and reproaching them all seemed to attribute to them a special brand of importance – they were men to be feared, men it would be folly to cross, and men to be listened to. The psychology behind it was really quite simple. How powerful they must have been to deserve such bad-mouthing, such degrading assessments, and such contempt, yet still survive to fight on. The truth is that, unfair as it may appear, this type of scenario could and sometimes did lead to substantial future increases in influence. On the other hand, for the most part, what they acquired in this fashion wasn't the real thing, but rather only a sort of faux-power that didn't last very long. Nevertheless, it was more an asset than a liability in the Washington scene. You see, in this setting, it's the image the men in political residence projected and people's opinions of them that were what really counted. Thus, in this strange world of politics, it suited the SSC losers to denounce the politicians and the bureaucrats, just as it suited the politicos to be on the receiving end. It was all a sham, but that's the way it was.

However, Washington did play a key consequential part in the ravaging of the SSC, and cannot be nonchalantly dismissed. Since most if not all Big Science enterprises are controlled and funded by the government, this causal source is actually a not unreasonable first guess. Here's the picture: Congress appropriated money for the SSC and the Executive disbursed and controlled it. Together, these two government branches, being responsible for the wise and proper use of the taxpayers' money, had the job and duty to ensure the public that this Big Science project, or any project, was using it properly and legitimately; some would even insist on it being used optimally. With power over the money flow, the responsible government careerists and administrators, both elected and appointed, wielded the ax that could mean life or death to the SSC and the scientists' dreams. Since the government men were running the show, straightforward logic would dictate that they had to be the predominant bad guys. Who else should be sought to paste on that label but those who held the reins of power? Although it's the case that scientists are politically naïve, they're certainly not begging for logic; so they conveniently chose to see it this way. Because no one stood up to object to this deduction, it wasn't hard for the public and the media to buy the package as well, thereby further reinforcing the scientists' conviction that they were right. Of course, they could've easily been on the right track, but just because it was plastered over the newspapers and even reported on television is by no stretch of the imagination good enough to bet your life on.

Many at the SSC claimed out-rightly that Congress did it in. They reasoned from the chain of circumstances that led to the 1993 end game that the ones behind the dastardly deed represented a cabal of young and newly installed congressmen, headed by Sherwood Boehlert, Republican of New York, and Jim Slattery, Democrat of Kansas. Taking advantage of the anti-spending mood in the government, which reared its ugly head because of the large annual federal deficits and the accumulated debt from the previous dozen or so years, and the whopping, king-size loss of Texas political influence, they found the perfect moment to strike. They were ambitious men, as most politicos are, and, with the SSC at a low point and highly vulnerable, it was payback time. Politics is a tough game to play in; and politicians are vengeful types with long memories. But scientists-cum-professors, living in their ivory towers, were innocent of this, or ignored it to their risk and detriment. Meddling in the political sphere is a dangerous business. Still, many scientists who'd staked their careers on the SSC continued to do so. But when they played an influential part, in league with DOE bureaucrats, in the decision to dismiss out of hand Boehlert's upstate New York district as a possible SSC site, they'd gone too far. Sherwood's revenge must have been sweet indeed.

These political men, looking for blood, had a mixture of double-speak and common sense in their minds, and malicious spite in their hearts. But it was the time of their time, and they were the center of attention. As it happened, this was an especially auspicious moment in history for them to take action against the big, poorly managed SSC. Government bigness was being raked over the coals, given the full Washington treatment. All they had to do was to lump the SSC into this all-encompassing menace of bigness, rail against the real thing, and the SSC would be caught in the whirlwind. There was even more favoring the aims of the riled-up duo. Their anti-SSC show coincided with hard times for the old Texas machine that had wielded power unscrupulously when it was holding all the cards. The fact is that you make a lot of enemies when you're sitting in the driver's seat, and the Texas team was no exception. Now that it was falling fast, it was ripe for the taking. Boehlert and Slattery, who were heretofore pipsqueaks in the congressional scene, weren't about to let their big chance slip through their fingers. So they stepped right up and acted decisively. They grabbed the reins and took their fifteen minutes on center stage.

Too bad the SSC and Big Science were sitting ducks ready to have their throats slit. Almost in shock and without much fighting back, they came to suffer the fate of lambs going silently to the slaughter. So, the deed was done, and it was Congress that proved to be the killing instrument. Although the hidden-from-view contest that was actually taking place was a classic young against old struggle, this internecine congressional opposition expressed itself as *big-versus-small* government. Therein lay the opening for the fatal strike at the SSC.

For years – too many, to be sure – the old guard politicians wielded excessive, out-of-all-proportion sway; and, propped up by the orderly but ultimately detrimental seniority system, the old-timers had accumulated inordinate power, especially in the Senate. The newcomers, desperately yearning for a way to move in and enter the club, found the cause that would get the succession going. As it happened, the SSC got caught in the crossfire and suffered the fate of such as are so unfortunate. The rallying cry of the young bucks in Congress for less government spending and for just plain less government rang true to the ears of the new guard that had begun to flex its muscles in the House. Rebelling against the bigness of government, they were driven to extol the questionable virtue that small government is better government, and, by logical extension, that small science is better science. Can it be so? Surely not! Small Science is clearly not better than Big Science. On the contrary, Big Science is the only means available to push science into the twenty-first century. As for government as a whole, small government is transparently not better for the poor, the old, the infirm, and the helpless. Despite this clear-cut case, the simplistic argument of the virtues of smallness in government caught fire. This was no doubt a result of the increase in strength of the country's rich and powerful, in alliance with the growing number of conservative *interest-groups*, all of which wanted lower taxes and especially tax preferences. For this group, the aim was simply less interference, and particularly less regulation – in a nutshell, less government. More and more this informal coalition enhanced their ability to elect congressmen who proclaimed the virtues of smallness, and this did not bode well for Big Science, saddled with a weakened and highly vulnerable SSC.

As the war waged on in Congress, you've got to give these two small-time congressmen from New York and Kansas mucho credit for seeing the linkage between big government and Big Science. With that as their focus, they certainly made themselves part of a force to contend with in Congress. Sadly, they also made themselves felt by scientists all over the world, but nowhere more painfully than in Waxahachie. Using the *big-versus-small* attack mode against the Texas collider, they won the day, and the SSC, cast aside, lost its bid to live on.

This politics-centered chain of events and circumstances leading to the SSC finale is about as true as anything else perceived and written about the event. However, if you take this sequence as the full and authentic picture of what happened, you are buying into a purely political cause for the SSC's woes. Doing this, by implication, you're accepting the preposterous scenario that the SSC leaders were innocent bystanders who happened to bumble their way into the killing meat grinder of an internal political war. That could not have been and was not so. Nonetheless, there is a measure of truth to the politically oriented version of the SSC story. The facts were plain for all to see: science was getting bigger and bigger just as smallness was being praised as apple-pie-and-motherhood in Congress. Furthermore, Texas political strength had indeed withered and lost its massive clout, what with the sorry Jim Wright "book deal" episode, the election-loss departure of Lloyd Bentsen from the political scene, and the George Bush 1992 election loss. Still, it is a stretch to take politics as the central thesis for the SSC's collapse and disgrace. Just think of it. Suppose politics was the true culprit. Then, if it weren't for Slattery and Boehlert, the SSC might well have pulled through its dark hours of the early nineties. Can you really believe that these two little congressmen were akin to the burping Mac bringing down the superconducting Yertle? Give us a break! How naïve can one be? Is it conceivable that the all-the-rage Reagan credos of excellence and American leadership could so easily be pushed aside – and by nobodies to boot?

No, the story behind the SSC's fall has far more to it than the shenanigans in the halls of Congress. Boehlert and Slattery were just silly geese who believed themselves to be more than they were. As they basked in the glory of their moment to shine, fools that they were, they were merely a drop in the flood that brought the SSC to its knees. There were clearly other reasons and others who bore a lot more accountability and blame. Still, there were many who were deceived by the bogus outward signs that the SSC fell to the whims of Congress. There was a kind of cleanness to this point of view. So, many fell for it. It also helped ease the grief. Poor science! Poor Big Science! Poor SSC! Just pin the label "*vanquishers extraordinaire*" on politicians, and then the loser-scientists could turn their backs on the entire affair and wash it from their troubled minds.

As it happened, many sought this pin-the-blame-on-politics road to consolation. There were those who chose to put the blame on the little power-and-fame-hungry guys from New York and Kansas; there were those who chose to put the blame on the ill-starred weakening of the Texas political contingent; there were those who chose to put the blame on a fiendish lawyer-legislator who, by cashing chips due him from some congressional colleagues, dreamed up some machinating amendment to a congressional bill that would bring the earmarked SSC money to one of his own pet projects; and there were those who chose to put the blame on a few congressmen do-gooders imagining they could redirect the money marked for the SSC to some worthwhile cause such as improving the quality of life in the decaying inner cities. Then there were the SSC staff and the physichists, who, by self-servingly putting the onus on congressmen and perhaps even believing it, sought to escape any blame themselves for losing the SSC. So there you have it. The majority of scientists simply took it as self-evident that profound political involvement, particularly that of the Congress, was the cause of it all. In a way, there was some truth to the claim, but only to a degree, and a minor one at that. When the whole picture is lying before us, there'll be little or no doubt that they were all barking up the wrong tree.

* * * * *

Money

Perhaps that old favorite money was at the core of whatever killed what was to be one of the modern wonders of the twentieth-century technological world. On its face, money was the explicit instrument for the action that untimely halted the SSC in its tracks. Wouldn't you say that for a government project, that's axiomatic? Well, cutting to the quick, withholding the cash, as expected, did indeed spell the final curtain. In the fall of 1993, Congress simply stipulated in a bill that all funds to be used in furtherance of the project were to cease at once and any to be thenceforth expended or appropriated must be only for its orderly shutdown. Wow! What a kick in the teeth! Looking more carefully at what was done, you can see that Congress, although it halted the project dead in its tracks, didn't just suddenly stop the money flow. So, for at least another year, even though the SSC was doomed to oblivion, the cash kept rolling in. That demonstrates with crystal clarity that money, important as it was, wasn't correlated one-to-one with the project's performance, but rather seemed to have little to do with whether it was progressing or not. Thus, it certainly had no causal relationship to the SSC's failure.

You might wonder why Congress didn't just say: *The project's done for – finis – so don't expect any more cash! This far and no further*! To better appreciate this, note the legal meaning of the qualifying word *orderly* in its SSC-ending legislation. This signaled the government's intention of satisfying all contractual and civil obligations that had been entered into in its name, such as the issuance of reasonable severance pay for employees, the reimbursement of the State of Texas and private contractors for federally allowable expenses they had incurred, and generally giving all organizations with rightful claims what was due them under federal law. And the government stuck by its implied promise.

Come to think of it, it was perhaps because of all this fuss and focus on money that some designated it as the crucial factor. But their deduction wasn't quite right. Although, beyond the shadow of a doubt, the role of money was big-time stuff, exactly how it played its part didn't just step right out at you and announce itself, "*I'm here*!" However, since important it was, it behooves us to delve more deeply into the details of how money wended its way into the SSC affair.

To explore the money angle further, let's start by examining its well-known use in the expression, "*Money is the root of all evil.*" True, everyone knows, or thinks he knows, what it really means. However, it's actually shorthand and isn't that obvious. More precisely, the more accurate statement of the idea is to say, "*The love of money is the root of all evil.*" Ah! Now you might be able to sense where we're headed. The distinction between the two ways of saying the same thing is at the heart of the matter. What it demonstrates is that money, in and of itself, being both neutral and fungible is not the essential point of the saying. Even though money is the visible medium, the expression in actuality explores the relationship between love and evil, with love ironically the force that leads to evil. So it was with the SSC and its extinction. You can use the shortened version, "*Money was the root of the SSC's demise.*" But what this really means is that human behavior and emotions laid the foundations for and brought about the SSC's death, with money being the means by which it was implemented. This is not to imply that money is not a key component of the plot. Not at all, money is the transaction medium and is the means of transforming ideas and feelings into actions – of converting the dark motives to get rid of the project into its murder. You could say that the full-length version of the expression might well be, "*The malicious intent energizing and propelling the money was the root of the SSC's demise.*"

Thus, it seems that we've done away with money as the "*Eureka, I've got it*" solution to what put the SSC six feet under. What a pity! First out went politics, now it's money being tossed out the window. But what else is there to do? They simply don't work. Putting the weight of the killing deed on either Congress or the money belt just doesn't fit the facts of the case. Yes, money was the mechanism for inducing the SSC's final sad and people-devastating moments; and Congress was the agent for guiding the flow of money that put an *orderly* end to its life. But as sole determinants and prime movers, money and politics don't cut the mustard.

Even together, they don't quite hack it. Sure, Congress and money have a very intimate connection. In fact, Congress is none other than the government's *Mister Moneybags*. So you might think that by combining money with politics, the mind's light bulb would flash and enlightenment reign. No dice! Even though Congress and its money were vital to the SSC right from the beginning and all the way through the rocky road of its life, when it came to the project's demise, the legislation Congress adopted was, to politically sophisticated Washington, a no-brainer. There really was no free choice to be had. As it happened, Congress spent a great deal of time and thought debating precisely how to close out both the project and the financial books. To be sure, there were lots of hand-wringing emotional speeches, on the one hand, decrying why the project had to go, and, on the other hand, devoted to why it should be brought back from the almost-dead. But it was all a lot of grandstanding because the result was inevitable. Thus, finally, when the verdict was announced, Congress bowed to the will of fate. The men of Congress voted and the outcome was what had to be – that the money intended for SSC building funds was transmuted into burial costs.

Thus, we can't but conclude that money and politics, alone or together, aren't able to account for the project's staying down for the count. There's simply no recourse but to look for and find some other factor at play – at least one – which accounts for the SSC's too few years of life, begun with such hopes and dreams, as well as for its heart-rending closing chapter. But to uncover another source, you have to dig more deeply into the facts of the case. Only then will it strike out at you that it wasn't money as used by the Congress that was the key, but rather the coveting of it by the SSC's power-bosses that forced the SSC to be silenced. Pushing along these lines, you'll be led inexorably to the human side of the story, the insatiable grasping for more power and its accompanying money-grubbing greed. If you don't stop there but go on even further, you'll eventually come to the appalling conclusion that the SSC fell into a self-destruct mode and sent itself into its grave. What a shocking and perverse scenario that is! However, we're getting a little ahead of ourselves. The point here is that you can't go very far toward understanding what happened to the SSC with money alone, or even with politics added to the pot. No matter how you try to isolate money or politics or both as the sole cause, people and the psychological baggage they carry with them penetrate your oh-so-simple picture and demand attention and consideration. So, even though the two popular causes do play central roles in the story, the upshot is that you can't point the finger at them for the whole bloody endgame. For any valid and compelling explanation, you simply have no alternative but to include people in the mix. To coin a phrase, "*Money doesn't kill projects, people kill projects*!" Although without much doubt that's true, still you can't just willy-nilly completely remove money from the equation. You see, money, like people, is intrinsic to the project and can't be easily dismissed. So, when it comes right down to it, there are at least three items to take into account: money, politics, and people. Yes, that's easy to say, and no doubt you can add more to the list. But, more important, what's the linkage among them? How do they combine to crack the code to the puzzle of the fall of the SSC? Try this on for size: Money went along with the SSC people who used it badly; the SSC itself was a political creation instigated by dreamy-eyed scientists, but was far beyond their capacity to build successfully; and the project's death was a testament to men's rapacious appetite for glory, and their loss of faith and that dauntless spirit of resolution needed to go the distance. How does that grab you? If you find this a little too wordy and complicated, and if you'd prefer a nice, clean, simple shorthand way of saying it, take this: *money was the means to the SSC's end, but it was people that did the ugly killing deeds.*

But let's get back to money. There's not the least doubt that it was important. However, if it wasn't in the domain of causation, then how did it make itself felt? Actually, there was a lot of variety in its impact: There was the way people used it; there was the way people responded to acquiring it; there was the way people behaved once they possessed it; and then money was also a way to gauge people's performance and to appraise to what extent they lived up to their promises. So, let's switch from money as a causal factor to money as an instrument for influence or accomplishment. Looked at from this vantage point, there are two overall groupings: How did money affect people when they had it and when they didn't get it? And how did assessors check up on how money was being used or abused?

Perhaps getting the funds for the project was too easy for the young and inexperienced SSC scientific leadership. By not knowing so many things about money – how to care for it, how to control it, how to spend it wisely, how to spend it efficiently, how to save some for a rainy day, and how to make it available only to honest and deserving enterprises and supplicants – the men in charge regrettably let it slip right through their innocent little fingers. But how can you explain how such intelligent and knowledgeable people could be so imprudent, so injudicious, so dim-witted, and then have to suffer such harsh consequences? Would you say they were wasteful? Were they spendthrifts? Was the unseemly amount of money thrown at them simply beyond their ken, not consciously thought about? Could it be that it was actually the money-greenhorns themselves who unwittingly led to the ensuing drastic and irreversible consequences? Even as the money kept pouring in, there was never enough. There was a seemingly never-ending return to the government trough for more. The project came to be like a "black hole" with money vanishing as quickly as it came, never to be seen again. It needed more, and then some more, and pretty soon still more. It ate money like an addict out of control, gobbling whatever it could. Still, there was never enough.

In 1988, the project's first formal cost was estimated at about 3 billion dollars; then, in short order, it was raised to 4 billion, and with nary moments of pausing thoughts, it went relentlessly upward, till, in 1993, it reached over 8 billion. Each request was accompanied by promises that this would be the last one – *yes, absolutely, for sure*. But, without fail, not long afterward, the project's leaders were again on the doorstep begging for yet another refill of their coffers. *We forgot this, or we forgot that*, they explained. At times they were more specific: *we didn't know we were supposed to include the detectors in the cost estimate*; or, *sorry, we didn't realize the full extent of the complexity of the injector*; or, *we didn't get adequate contingency funds for such a big and complicated project*. Then, towards the end, came the straw that broke the camel's back.

By then the SSC's big shots had learned more of the ways that Washington worked, and they'd become more sophisticated in their demands for more. They believed and acted as though they had everything in hand and had everyone under their thumbs. To their misfortune, in truth, they'd only become too big for their britches. Here's what happened: Once again, they were in the capital with hands outstretched and palms faced upward. This time, irrationally confident that *the force* was still with them, they firmly contended that for the project to perform as advertised, they would have to increase the magnet dimensions a little, actually by about 25%, and for that about another billion was needed. How easily rolled the word *billion* from their tongues! In addition: *It was you*, they accused the all-powerful government, *that really caused a delay in the construction by not providing enough money per year. This resulted in higher inflationary costs and substantial increases in the salary sector. So, better make it 2 billion more*! *We're sure*, they went on, *that you can well appreciate that all this escalation and delay wasn't at all our fault. But, don't worry about it*, they continued, *now that we have all our bases covered, just rest assured and sign the check*. It was a time like all the other times, they thought, and the game was to be played as it had always been. As for the project, as before, it was not much closer to getting done and there still seemed no end in sight. But the leaders, perpetuating their chronic self-deception, as they had during all those other visits to the capital, cried out, *yes, we see a light at the end of the tunnel*. Doubtless there was a tunnel that had to be passed through in order to reach the land of dreams-fulfilled, but in reality there was no light. As dismayed but powerless onlookers, those who could look at the project dispassionately, could plainly see, this was a mirage, coming from greed's blinding glare.

Stubbornly, recklessly, and oblivious to the dangers ever so close by, the project's leaders moved forward along their chosen path. It's hard to comprehend, but even as the clock ticked toward the eleventh hour, they remained unaware of the harm they were about to inflict on others and on themselves. Perhaps they lost any chance they might've had to change their course because they actually found a way of life for themselves that was strangely rewarding. Because they kept getting what they asked for from those money-fat Washington bureaucrats, who had themselves become implicated in the big lie, they concluded that what they were doing had to be right. So why stop? Everything was the way it ought to be and all was right with the world. Money kept rolling in; money was casually spent without a care; and their importance was apparently rising in direct correlation to their spending growth. True, the project was going nowhere, but that didn't seem to bother anyone, so why give it a second thought. Project or no project, it was a good life, a fine life. They felt on top of the world, squarely seated in the *Catbird Seat*, and that it would last forever. What fools!

Meanwhile, outside the inner circle, people began to catch a glimpse of the truth. What with the project performance nil and the cost going through the roof, the wonder of it all is that it took so long. But as time went on, the cost-estimate numbers grew and grew to such an extent that it finally became clear to the big cheeses in the capital and even to a few of the open-minded scientific elite that something just had to be done. But who could actually take action that had a chance at being effective? Scientists were utterly powerless to go up against their muscle-bound SSC cousins. Over a barrel, if they opened their yaps, it was tantamount to career suicide. The executive branch of government, the DOE, the Office of Science and even the White House, made some attempts through reviews and backroom politicking, but it was half-hearted because they weren't united and were unable to alter that circumstance. Fragmented into splinter groups, some favoring the SSC and some agin it, they could find no way to pull together, and the result was paralysis. Thus, it fell to those on the Hill to take action. There, via the legislative process – the wheeling-and-dealing and chip cashing for votes – there was a way to reach a collective bargain and get something done, even make a radical move.

Not only did the Congress have the mechanism for taking a far-reaching step, but it also had a built-in institutional memory, thereby affording it the vast experience of the past to tap into. This was invaluable in the case of the SSC because in fact Congress had seen it all before. Overrunning costs for big defense projects had provided it with quite an education in cost estimation. Although the men of the SSC didn't know it, this was bad news for them. You see, once the defense-SSC linkage through their bigness was made, it would be hard to stem the certain-to-ensue anti-SSC tide. Starting with small numbers of congressmen, the demand for SSC accountability began its upward spiral. Independent cost-estimates were ordered from both the project itself and from the DOE administering it. The emphasis here is on the word *independent*. The old friendly, incestuous-like reviews just wouldn't do anymore. In short order, the poor SSC was inundated with cost-estimators and project assessors from every which way. Then, as if to top it off and provide verification of the other reviews, the congressional Government Accounting Office (GAO), created for just such a situation, was brought in to report on the state of the SSC directly to Congress. Thus, the project was placed under a cruel and all-telling microscope. The truth could not be withheld any longer. Discomfort in Waxahachie mounted as an army of scientists, engineers, bureaucrats, accountants, and a conglomeration of other professionals and onlookers descended on the town with blackness in their hearts.

When the teams of evaluators and appraisers issued their reports, they were replete with dire warnings of what the SSC had in store for it. The project was chastised for continuing to tolerate every management failing in the book. The reviewers singled out the cost estimate for censure and emphatically charged that it wasn't near being adequate. *Just look at what has already been spent and compare that with the earned value* (what the project has acquired and what has become a concrete part of it), the members of the official accounting teams, particularly the GAO, sneered. Thus, barring any visible action, unlikely at best, any cost estimate the project made or could come up with was dead on arrival. They were treated like the hot air they were. Now the sky became the limit as the independent cost-estimators began to run wild. *If you want to hear what the real cost will end up being, then listen closely*, they said: *At best it will be 10 billion, but probably closer to 12 billion*, or, claimed the pessimists among them, *it could even reach 20 billion*. Once the reports hit the street and were open to public scrutiny, the SSC's fate became a foregone conclusion. The end was closing in fast, as the project's promises began to sound hollow indeed. The pleas that had worked wonders in the past now rang false. Wither goest the SSC from this place, you ask? Is there any doubt? Yet, despite the signals flashing in bleak, dark shades and blaring in deafeningly painful tones, still, the outcome came as a shock to most. Suddenly, the *go – no-go* threshold was crossed and the Congress, in a kind of collective pique, blurted out, "*No more*!" And that was that. It was all over but the formalities. Then, when the congressional legislation doing away with the SSC was signed by President Clinton, leaving no one to appeal to, the dream so tightly held by so many scientists for so long simply passed on. Poor SSC! Poor dumb project! Poor science! Poor generation of twentieth century scientists! But, you know, life is like that: When it hits home, it always seems to hit unexpectedly, and always like a ton of bricks.

Was it really money that was responsible for all of this? Not by a long shot. Just as those who proclaimed a purely political basis for the SSC's end were off-target, so were those who subscribed to a purely money basis. To be sure, the purely-money proponents, just as the purely-politics proponents, also had a lot of good points on their side. But when all the claims and arguments for money as the sole cause were added up, the sum missed the mark and the backers of money alone didn't hit the bull's-eye either. In the end, the backers of both groups didn't see the forest for the trees. As it happens, politics and money, in this context, are merely trees. Then what, pray you, is the forest – the pattern – you ask? Ah, that is the question!

* * * * *

Sociology
I
Science Comes Face-to-Face With Progress

If not politics or money, then perhaps the root of the SSC's failure lies in the realm of sociology, that old standby used to explain a wide-ranging set of human phenomena. In fact, all human undertakings and affairs of collections of individuals fall under its purview, including intra-group identification and inter-group rivalry. Just look around you and you'll see the powerful social forces that are at work in virtually all walks of life.

The social factor is of such weighty significance because by nature people tend to partition themselves into competitive groups. By appearance, by interests, by capability, by profession, by gender, by religion, by wealth, by birthright, and by any number of other ways that man can devise, people have a deep-seated urge to set themselves apart from others. Historically, as well as anthropologically, the driving spirit behind this segregation lies in the reality that there is power in numbers. If you act in concert with others *of your own kind* you are more likely to prevail. This is true whether your aim is defensive or warlike, to consolidate or to appropriate, to favor or to injure, to profit or to share, to surpass or to suppress, to achieve or to plagiarize, to praise or to denounce, to build or to destroy, to upgrade or to downgrade, and a multitude of other motivations.

As you can see, the self-interest of the individual has crept its way into our discussion. Being intrinsic to any analysis of group dynamics, in one way or another, it had to happen. The fact is that as exclusive social groupings are shaped, since people together with their own personal desires and dreams are implicated, it inevitably transpires that psychological forces must and do enter the picture. As it happens, since we are interested in downfall and death, it is the dark ones, cousins of jealousy and fear, that grab and engage our attention. Although these detrimental and poisonous human sentiments and emotions are common within groups, they are fiercest between groups. You see, isolation breeds and reinforces such feelings. How ironic that group formation and development – meant for unifying people to fulfill their human identity or to determinedly carry out and consummate some prescribed mission – should also abet and perpetuate the mean forces of mistrust, exploitation, despoilment, thievery, and hate!

In the modern world, with technology, particularly communication, running wild, groups have become far more dynamic than they've ever been before. It's gotten to the point where they shift ineluctably with the changing wind. In America, it sometimes appears that group distinction has entirely disappeared, that unification of human identity has stretched its glorious wingspan to encompass all, and that the reality of the *melting pot* has come to pass. Actually, for groups in the U.S., as well as in many countries of the "*first world,*" it's true that the earlier unbridled and savage inter-group and class rivalries have moderated and become more restrained and civilized. At times, it even appears that the moves toward diminishing, subduing, and pacifying have been so effective that extreme hostility and harsh aggression have gone away. But don't be fooled by this false impression: The dark forces in man have only assumed more subtle guises, and universal unity still remains but a dream. For a while science seemed immune to the de-unifying disease, but in time dissension came and grew, and ultimately science too succumbed.

* * *

Sociology
II
Unity Versus Specialization

As communities go, the science community has in the past been a rather well-knit group. The main impetus for scientists to unify, and to shape strong personal bonds, is a direct result of their common purpose and way of life. They do the same things; they want the same things; and they experience the same things. Scientists have similar beliefs and philosophies about the natural world as well as similar methods governing their day-to-day activities, ranging from observation and experimentation to rational thought, discourse, and argumentation. Taken together, these creeds and methods are meant to lead scientists to their ultimate identical objectives of testable knowledge and understanding about our world. Thus, scientists have much reason to identify with each other; and it would therefore seem to be quite natural for them to seek togetherness and to cultivate each other's interests.

The primary means used by scientists to achieve and sustain closeness is the standard one of creating and fostering societies, associations, institutes, and other such organizations. This gives them the means to make presentations, to argue their cases, to meet together, to stimulate each other, to learn from each other, to work together in close contact, to collaborate on experiments and ideas, and to foster new thinking. Up to now this has been good for science and has worked smoothly and effortlessly. However, in the last few decades, science has seen a rich and ever-expanding specialization phenomenon entering the mix. This means that business as usual for these organizations can't work as it has. They simply must adapt to the changing circumstances where one scientist may not have the time or the will to get involved with what another is doing.

In spite of specialization pushing science in the direction of de-unification, many scientists believe that the spirit of science unity continues to hold on, though ever so tenuously. Through their common ethic and similar methods, the argument goes, scientists have been able to withstand the breakup impulses in their midst. The hope is that their commonality of interest has allowed them to survive the incursion of specialization, at least for the moment. But it is simply not so. The incentives and temptations to split apart have grown and spread. In ever-increasing numbers, organizations designed to represent the interests of one or another particular scientific area have sprung up. In this way, modernity has finally caught up with science's vaunted unity, which has held its own for so long. What we are witnessing is doubtlessly its closing chapter. Specialized groups have formed and continue to do so in increasing numbers. Group isolation has spread. Scientists now know less about each other than ever, and have come to care less and less for each other. In many circumstances, they have come to attack each other. They have also become jealous of any favors given to colleagues whom they have begun to view as their opponents, even enemies, fearing them and imagining infringements of their fame and funding. Under such conditions, how can unity come out unscathed and intact? In truth, it is already dead, only scientists just haven't yet recognized that reality.

Today, as the twenty-first century begins to unfold, science unity is going down the drain before our very eyes. All the indicators point to it. Science, instead of building more and more sophisticated instruments for the betterment of all, is muddling along, continuing to segregate itself into small exclusive groups, each tending to its own needs and particular interests. Aside from their own specialty, scientists have acquired the inclination to see the endeavors of their fellow practitioners as foreign and subordinate. Professional groups are fostering this trend by encouraging the formation of both separate bodies and ad-hoc entities or sub-units within societies, each representing particular sciences, groups of sciences, or sub-sciences. In addition, totally separate professional entities representing particular groups are being established. Worrisome as it is, there seems no stopping this trend toward segregation. Although it can only lead to hard times, the splintering due to the continuation of inevitable specialization seems to be here to stay. The strange thing about this whole business is that specialization is quite natural if any field is to advance and prosper. It is both necessary and desirable. Progress demands it! What a bummer – to have something so good and so bad at the same time! But what's to be done about it? What can anyone do? Actually, not much! You see, the truth is that life is full of such contradictions. So, when all is said and done, there's clearly no alternative but to grin and bear it and to roll with the punches.

Where, you might ask, has all this rapid change come from? Surely, there's no difficulty in answering that one: it's from the impressive rise in science sophistication over the last half century. Yet it is more than that. You see, a marriage of science and technology has in fact taken place. Even more than that: both have been advancing forward at breakneck speed, and are making dramatic strides that show no signs of abating. Actually, science and technology have always been strongly interdependent. Progress in one leads to progress in the other. In such a manner turn the wheels driven by the engines of human enterprise. However, in today's world, the two have become so enmeshed in each other that quietly, without fanfare, the two have to all intents and purposes become one. They have merged so intimately that we now refer unabashedly to a field of Science and Technology (S&T). But the world is moving forward at such a fast pace that even before getting used to its new name, S&T finds itself in the throes of a wholesale state of restructuring. New and unexpected S&T groups are stepping up and making themselves felt everywhere you look: some represent completely new technological areas through new inventions; some represent combinations of traditional sciences transformed into new interdisciplinary branches; and some represent sub-elements of old sciences that stretch the boundaries of the ones they've sprung from. Thus, who would deny that Pandora's science box has been opened, and S&T can never be the same again? As for S&T unity, it has fallen off its perch on the wall, and nobody can put Humpty-Dumpty back together again.

The story, here given in a nutshell, tells it all. Once upon a time, science was a small, unified group. But then, being good, useful, and in demand, it expanded and began to fly. It became rich and varied. More and more people were attracted to it and newly formed scientists flocked to its call. So it grew even more, and became bigger and bigger. Its renown and importance mushroomed. There was so much in it and so much for scientists to mine that they became more focused. Specialists, experts in particular parts of the grand whole, emerged and flourished. All was good. Specialization and unity lived together in peace and prosperity. Then, as time passed, it became very big indeed – too big. One scientist thought he was better than another and worth more. He wanted more recognition and more accolades. What he was doing was more important, more urgent. As it happened, this manner of thinking and the demands that followed from it sprouted up like burgeoning weeds, infectious ones that spread across the heretofore-peaceful land. Thus, the skies over science began to darken. Time moved on its inexorable course forward, and the clouds became ominous. What could the aging scientists do? They'd tried everything to stop the deadly sickness in its tracks. What more was there? So they withdrew from the field of combat and began to reminisce about the good old days, when the sun shone brightly. But that era, along with their memories of happier lives, was gone. They remembered how close they were *way back when*. Unfortunately, that togetherness had all but dissipated and melted away. Ah, if only those days could return again! Sadly, however, their dream-like remembrances were only of things long past. Still, what a time it was, that time of unity! But, as is the way of life, all things pass. And so it is that today specialization reigns and unity has become nothing more than the daydreaming of the old-timers.

* * *

Sociology III The Establishment Under Siege

In the orb of institutions representing physics, we are still apt to find a group like the American Physical Society (APS), clinging to the past by a fine thread and continuing to maintain its claim to speak and act for a unified field. Striving tirelessly and sparing no effort to stem the rising tide of emerging competitive sub-groups residing inside the society, many of them dominated by technology, might well be a worthy ambition. But it is a futile course to take. It's like trying to plug up a collapsing dam with your fingers, even as cracks persist in forming all over the map. In truth, institutions like the APS are caught between a rock and a hard place. Philosophically, they're for unity; but in order for them to serve their members in the free and open manner the members have come to expect, the emerging sub-groups must be afforded the voice and forums they insist upon and deserve. After all, the members pay their way. Their will can't just be ignored. So the science institutions are in a quandary. What are they to do? In the end, they may be forced to choose between the two non-overlapping alternatives, unity and specialization. And if that's the way things go, is there anyone who doubts that their philosophy of unity would be abandoned in favor of the pragmatic solution that entails presiding over a kingdom of faction-ridden, cutthroat competitors, fighting like the dickens for recognition and the best soapbox in the house?

The fresh and original types of groups bursting forth upon the scene range from brand new branches of physics evolving from their father building-blocks, to fields that inventively combine physics and technology, to sub-groups formed by dividing units into sub-components designed especially for experimentalists, or theorists, or engineers. What we are witnessing is a conglomeration of smaller highly competitive representative bodies replacing the small number of larger essentially non-competitive ones. But surely that isn't bad! No, not at all! After all, it is progress, and quite in the spirit of the democratic way. What a truly juicy innovative mess of separate and diverging interests that is! On the other hand, what difficulties this poses for the establishment institutions that govern and represent science!

Yes, the trend toward splitting and splintering is undeniable. This spells tough times for all of science's component parts: for the societies, for the science community itself, and for the funding agencies. Where do the newly fashioned groups belong in the science community – in the universities, in the national labs, or perhaps in the industrial labs of the nation? Which ones are the different societies to represent and how is the division to be figured out? How are the funding agencies to establish their areas of responsibility, and how should they divvy up their pot of cash? With great difficulty, it might be said! You see, all these institutions stress and focus on stability; and are characterized by an inflexible, unyielding, and enduring inertia. They were built that way and designed exactly for that way of operating for very good reasons – to give scientists a sense of confidence about tomorrow, to ensure that their soap-box will still be there and their next meal will be awaiting them, thus calming their nerves and optimizing their productive work. But, what with the massive S&T changes in the works, these reasons ring hollow today. Times have changed! So, what's to be done and how? How do you wake up the Establishment? How do you reform the institutions? How do you reshape them? How do you transform them? How do you fit static-oriented institutions into a dynamic reality? Said another way, how do you fit a square peg into a circular template? However you look at it, the threshold for the realignment of science, more precisely of S&T, is upon us, and all scientists best beware of what lies on the other side of the line that there is no choice but to cross.

Dispassionate logic tells you that universal fragmentation in science (yes, in physics, but also in biology, medicine, chemistry, geology, and the many others), being but another face of the phenomenon of specialization, is no more than a natural outgrowth of the remarkable expansion of this century's S&T. This being the case, just an ounce of common sense demands resignation to the unstoppable genesis and course of modernization, demands submitting to what can't be controlled by man, and demands learning to live with what fate has prepared for us. It is surely best to take up and embrace what the gods have chosen for us with grace and equanimity. But, man being man – self-centered, self-indulgent, stubborn, contrary, and tough to tame – such is not the case. When it comes to the Establishment, relishing and thriving in the status quo, change is never easy to submit to. You might think that, even for those who must sacrifice some of their long-possessed positions of high esteem, prestige, and power, a composed and tranquil acceptance of the inevitable is both practical and desirable. However, such a rational reaction to life's shifting sands is not a realistic expectation.

* * *

Sociology
IV
The Young Demand Their Piece of the Pie

Yet, is it so difficult to understand why those holding the scepters find them so hard to surrender? Consider the plight of the scientists and societies of long standing, the VIPs of the in-groups. There they are, safely and securely ensconced on top of the world. Then, one day, the carpet is yanked from under them. Their balance is shaken as they begin to feel the loss and pain that the progress they initiated and cultivated has brought with it. No, they are not at all happy about what they have wrought. How foolish they were to have believed that they could indefinitely remain unaffected by the winds of change! How foolish they were to have believed that the young would not take full advantage of the destabilizing specialization in progress by standing up and fighting to the death for their time in the limelight – their birthright! How foolish they were to have believed that they could beat off and prevail over the iron wills and youthful muscular frames of the boys-turned-men, keeping them from what they were certain was rightfully theirs! It is sad to watch the scientists who have aged, and as the old are wont to do, look back to the good old days, when life in science was unified and simple. When you think about it, in actuality, the past probably wasn't at all the way they recall it, but nostalgia makes things that are gone and irretrievable appear far better than what is staring them in the face. Yes, it is very sad to see them resist to the point of madness what is in the end irresistible. Whatever was true long ago, the fact is that time passes; things change; and the flow of history cannot be undone.

Thus, the old have a lot more to deal with than a radically changing social structure in the world of science. At the same time, it is also their sacred duty to pass the torch to a new generation. But the old don't easily make way for the young. They desperately try to hang on. Of course, as their minds and bodies begin to fail them, it fast becomes a losing battle. Nonetheless, they seem to be possessed of an uncontrollable inner urge to keep pushing till they drop. And don't underestimate the ingenuity of the old in putting off the succession that they subconsciously fear so much. Of course, as nature demands, there's no doubt that they'll eventually have to give in; and the young, standing ready to enter the arena, will end up running the show, as the young must.

But, in the meantime, before reality is forced upon the old, self-deception rules their lives. One method of keeping their hopes alive is to build alliances with the governing classes of other scientific disciplines. In this way, they've come to fashion new combinations of sciences, referred to as interdisciplinary ones, in which they're still capable of making contributions. What they're attempting to do is to strengthen and forge new interdisciplinary bonds as if to demonstrate that a commonality of interest and purpose still persists across the boundaries of the different science disciplines. But these bonds are only skin-deep; and the work is not substantial science, but rather on the superficial side. The truth is that the whole idea of interdisciplinary work is much in the nature of a scam, designed to confuse and obfuscate. For a new area really to be meaningful and lasting, you need dedicated people who become thoroughly committed to the subject, and are willing to submerge and engross themselves in it. No, interdisciplinary science is not an alternative to specialization. Frankly speaking, its true underlying purpose is no more and no less than to propagate the myth of unity in science.

On the unity versus specialization front, here's the situation in science today: The days of unity are fast ebbing. The similar methodology that scientists enjoyed and still possess, which worked so well to keep them together in the past, just doesn't do the trick anymore. Specialization, together with the massive penetration of technology into science, has come upon the scene with a vengeance. Because the forces of specialization and those of unification are in direct opposition to each other, it is inevitable that a competition for supremacy must surely be the result. And such a contest does indeed exist. But the science warriors going at each other are playing, in parallel, another major game – one that, in significance, surpasses by far the abstract and ideological specialization-unity issue. You see, specialization is for the young, while unity keeps the old propped up. Thus, intertwined with the philosophical contest and inextricably tied to it is the age-old struggle of young versus old, a rivalry that can end but one way. Sadly, as that end is approached, contentiousness and antagonism prevail. However, if this inimical bad blood is not successfully dealt with, because it's probably the root cause for failure of one kind or another, dire days for science, particularly Big Science, most certainly lie ahead.

* * *

Sociology
V
The SSC Confronts the Bureaucrats and the Old-Guard Scientists

In principle, the SSC was just another one of those specialized claimants to America's allotment of fame and fortune set aside for science. But the case of this big project was very different. You see, specialization, being fragmentation of a sort, implies that the parts arising from the *mother whole* are smaller. Take a piece of anything, break it up, and surely the parts are smaller! But that's not the way specialization works. Yes, it's quite true that when new areas are created, they do indeed start small. But they don't necessarily stay that way for long. Some of them begin to grow; and sometimes they grow far faster than they would have if the unwieldy and ponderous unified science had remained as their landlord. That's in fact one of the prime movers for specialization – the breaking of the shackles that hold fledgling areas back and prevent them from marching to their own drummers. This freedom to stretch to the limit, to flare out, to shoot for the sky is a state devoutly to be wished. And that's exactly the way it was for science in the past. Out of the newfound freedom emerging from the ashes of World War II came specialization: and with it came high-energy physics, and with that came Big Science, and with that, after less than four decades, came one of the biggest imaginable projects, certainly the biggest accelerator project that could be conceived. Yes, the SSC had arrived, and from then on science would be governed by new rules, the rules that bigness dictates.

So it was that into the midst of the feuding one-upmanship that had insinuated itself into the once unified science, swaggeringly strutted the SSC. Full of confidence and conceit, and proud of their impressive product-for-a-fantastic-future, the men of the SSC offhandedly and recklessly walked into what turned out to be a maelstrom. They certainly had their work cut out for them. Their first order of business was to take care of that ever-present matter of garnering enough political and financial support to make the seemingly impossible come to life. Since the SSC was really big as science projects go and demanded a great deal of money, the way to do it just didn't pop out of the air.

How could the funding agency, the DOE, be persuaded to take it upon itself to dole out the enormous amount of funds needed? It most assuredly wouldn't be easy because the money-meisters of the DOE were already committed to many other undertakings. These projects and programs were on the books and their claimants, hardened veteran men of research who wouldn't just nonchalantly take *no* for an answer, were on the DOE doorstep calling for their piece of the promised cake. Furthermore, since it's a zero-sum game, if the SSC got into the act, from whom would the bureaucrats take the money to satisfy the *big one*? Do you really expect ordinary run-of-the-mill bureaucrats to be able to make the tough choosing-one-over-another decisions that spell life or death to science researchers? After all, for the most part, they're just bean counters. They're the ones who went to Washington because they couldn't hack it in the science game.

Lacking in judiciousness and knowledge, who above them would be so ill advised, so brainless, as to give them such authority? Frankly, it's a very good thing that they don't possess such god-like power over the basic research enterprise.

In any case, the funds the SSC asked for just weren't available in the DOE budget. So, when confronted with this monster project, the Washington crowd hesitated first and then, as you might well have anticipated, they did nothing – not uncommon for weak-kneed administrators. This actually is the course that the DOE bureaucrats chose to take. This is the way they responded to the challenge posed by the SSC idea placed in front of them. They knew that by simply floating along with the tide, they were holding back progress and increasing the dissension between the young, who wanted to fly, and the old, who wanted to remain planted firmly and safely on terra firma. Nevertheless, without the budgetary insights needed or the guts to buck the tried-and-true do-nothing approach, that's what they did. So, between 1982, when the idea for a big American collider first surfaced at Snowmass, to 1987, when Reagan himself got into the act, the SSC lingered in limbo.

Within the science establishment, there were a few who, once they grasped what the SSC could mean for physics and for mankind, were ready and eager to go for broke. Unfortunately, without the consent or encouragement of either the higher-ups or the DOE, they were stuck in a rut. What a bind they found themselves in! Should they aggressively move forward alone in support of this grand venture into the unknown? It was a risky road to ride. It was unknown territory and they'd be laying their futures or their reputations or both on the line. Then there was the perennial question of money. There was just too little of it. Certainly that fatal stumbling block would have to be removed before the project could push off from the starting gate. So they held back and thought it over. Perhaps they should just stay put and leave the glory to future generations. Actually, that wouldn't be so bad. Like their craven and spineless colleagues, they could continue to stuff their eager little mouths with the honey all around them, like *Pooh Bear*. No, it wasn't at all easy for ambitious yet also pragmatic men to choose which fork to take: Should they throw caution to the wind and shout out in favor of the SSC, even take the plunge with it, or should they let the opportunity for an acclaimed and ennobling legacy pass them and their generation by? Should they give up the soft life to help science march into the wilderness or stay put? For the SSC to move ahead, the need was for selfless men, heroes. But, sad to say, such were in short supply.

* * *

Sociology
VI
Which Side Are You On Boys?

When the SSC was first envisioned back in 1982, it was conceived as a major step in advancing the science frontier. But was science satisfied? *No*! Was physics satisfied? *No*! Was particle physics satisfied? Well, *yes and no*! The "*No*" people were all confused at the beginning and had many questions to contend with: Should they go against their instincts and support this unasked-for giant? Should they stand unified as scientists as a show of solidarity? Where did their loyalties really belong, to science as a whole or to their own particular specialties? Would it hurt them in the end to go along with the SSC? Should they risk their own well being for something so distant from their ken? What if they were for it and then it didn't fly, would they be left holding the bag? Most scientists found themselves in a real fix. They didn't really know enough about the SSC to make an informed judgment. Actually, very few could appreciate either its vital scientific significance or its technological value and intricacies. In any case, rational discourse and clear-headed thinking weren't at all the key to the view they came to.

So, what did determine the position they finally settled on? The truth is that they were afraid of the project's bigness, afraid that it would swallow them up, and jealous of the fame it could bring – none of it to them. Thus it was the classic human dilemma pitting the self against the community. As such it was no contest. Altruism being but a figment of the idealist's imagination, inevitably self-interest must win out. This is one of the primary dictates of human nature. As it happened, although the collective conclusion came fast, it wasn't immediate. First, scientists argued a lot, both openly and privately; and presumably they also experienced slews of conscience-wringing bouts. But when the show was done, a consensus arose. It was that, except for an elite few particle physicists, the interests of scientists as a whole lay in opposing the big new project. Once that occurred, the word went out across the land, and the floodgates were opened. Anti-SSC sentiment spread like wildfire; and it became open season to pounce upon, assault, and condemn this wondrous and majestic but unwanted colossus that sought only to enlighten mankind.

Make no mistake about it, single-minded, committed, uncompromising, and relentless men will find the means to express their opposition; and when it came to the SSC, they were determined to make an end of it. The dirty talk, the tale telling, the news mongering, and the name-calling, occurred behind the scenes in private meetings behind closed doors; it occurred in the open with all to see and hear; and it occurred at high-level government reviews, lab reviews, funding agency reviews, and congressional hearings. The words were flying and they were everywhere. They were strident, they were spiteful, and they were vicious. But why, you might wonder, was there such a passionate reaction to the appearance of the SSC? It's true that in this modern era of rapid change in S&T, it's not unexpected that the clashing of interests would shoot up in frequency and heat up in steamy intensity. It's not even so surprising that the building up of specialized groups with separate and diverging concerns has led to just the things that people were trying to avoid: polarity, discord, hostility, loss of unity, and a bad taste in the mouth. Sure, it wasn't intended to be that way; but it nevertheless was. Still, the steely and unyielding will to send the SSC into the cold darkness of oblivion leaves one dazed, flustered, and shaken.

However, if you give it a little extra thought, it isn't that hard to figure out what there was about the SSC that made people fear it so much. When the SSC came on the scene, science specialization was already proliferating here, there, and everywhere. OK, so the SSC played its part in specialization overspreading all of science! But that certainly isn't the whole picture. What about the red-hot, kill-crazy, and ferocious hatred of it? Yes, what about it? Certainly, it had to be because of the SSC's unprecedented bigness. You see, following along with specialization was the ever-widening and oh-so-intense competitive pressure for financial and political advantage that represents the other face of the specialization coin. Now it begins to become clear. Seeing that Goliath about to enter into their midst must have scared the living daylights out of most every scientist. It was their careers and their beloved research that were at stake. No, there's no doubt about it! It was the deadly combination of extreme specialization and bigness that stimulated the formation of circumstances ripe for the passion-filled frenzy and the stormy shenanigans that erupted in science's center stage.

Once the condemnations by those who were embittered and felt cheated got under way, they just couldn't be stopped, and a lot of people were hurt. Whether you were a good guy, a bad guy, one committed to the SSC, one heatedly and irately against it, or simply a bystander watching the goings-on, you were vulnerable to the pummellings that were flying about. Finally, when the bloodlust was satiated and the acrimony subsided, the result was that most of the science community was torn asunder. So it was that the SSC made clear to all that science unity, much vaunted and cherished by the old guard, was irretrievably lost. Kaput! Finis!

* * *

Sociology VII Bigness Kills

When the SSC began its bumpy ride with destiny, it had already been conceived as something really big. Indeed, it was touted as the first project of an emerging era of Big Science for basic research, and that it was. But a project that has crossed the threshold into bigness has a habit of developing a life unto itself; and, that done, the project then has a tendency to run away from the people who thought they had it in hand. Its creators may be the ones to start the ball rolling, but the umbilical cord soon breaks and the project can't be held back. It flies freely, unencumbered by its origins, and can't even be prevented from jumping off a cliff to its doom if fate so demands.

It just might be that ordinary people, those good people who conceive, build, and manage man's glorious monuments to the gods, aren't given the capacity to envelop and control the process of creating big accelerators once they grow past some size. It appears that men are made a certain way and can't, except in rare instances, handle projects in the realm of bigness: There are too many people involved; there are too many interests; there are too many technical details; there is too much sophistication; there are too many areas impinging; there are too many interfaces and interactions; and there are too many factors strongly coupled to each other. People just can't fathom it; it's beyond their ken. Furthermore, the methods and theory of organization, meant for dealing rationally with bigness, have severe limitations, some often fatal. Frankly, it's not surprising that these methods don't work well because they're merely straightforward extrapolations from small projects to big ones. However, that's the wrong thing to do. You see, projects that are big are qualitatively different from those that are small. In the realm of bigness, it is irrationality that rules. And how can rational means be used to govern irrational processes?

Those fearless leaders of science should have figured out that they were in for trouble, because it had all happened before. Why didn't they seek advice from the leaders of the earlier big defense projects, who had to face the identical daunting reality? They might have learned from those who already had gone through the experience. They might have made good use of finding out about the *hows* and *whys* of their predecessor's singular successes and, more importantly, of the many failures endured. They might have learned that success in bigness can take place only under very special and unusual circumstances – to wit, when the country or the world is at stake, or when a time of high national urgency is at hand. Just imagine what you'll have to deal with when you set out on a bigness expedition: You'll have to be prepared for setbacks. You'll have to be prepared to turn a new leaf many times over, and then do it again. You'll have to be prepared to start all over again from scratch, and leave everything you did in the past behind – forgotten. You'll have to be prepared to tolerate mistake after mistake after mistake, and then search for yet another way. You'll have to be able to depend on the funding agency to be patient and understanding, or at least compliant with your wishes. You'll have to be allowed the luxury of inefficiency; and, if that's not already asking for too much, you'll have to granted the right to be wasteful. Now, just consider this for a moment! How can such circumstances be permitted unless you're in the midst of a life-and-death situation? No, a big project can't be taken as an ordinary occurrence brought about by ordinary people. Bigness can't be taken for granted, and those who take the plunge must expect hard times and countless failures before that once-in-a-lifetime bright light might shine on them. Unfortunately, the SSC men just didn't get it; and because of their ignorance of the true nature of bigness, they tasted of the same bitter fruit as those before them who didn't call on history to teach them and so weren't able to follow up and heed its lessons.

Bigness thus eventually became a killer of the mortal men of the SSC. How, you ask? It's just this: There appears to be some level of size at which a project becomes self-powering, growing solely on its own accord. From then on, it cannot be fenced in, but simply becomes bigger and bigger. However, it's not only size, for, in crossing that line into bigness, it has entered a region where jeopardy and treachery lie in wait. A project in the throes of bigness acts much like a cancer. It threatens all that is around it, and is quite prepared, and even, strangely, looking forward to self-destruct in the cause of the Devil's work. All those doomed men who are part of such a project tend to enter a twilight zone and cease to listen to or even hear the pleas from every direction that they change their ways. You see, they can't hear, for the project takes over. A role reversal takes place: the men of the management are transformed into automatons – zombies – who have no choice but to follow the dictates of the reigning project; and rationality is no more the guiding principle, but rather the project comes to be run by Lucifer's rules. Then, as the end nears, the project turns on its makers and on itself. So it was with the SSC, and in such a way did it meet its fate.

* * *

Sociology
VIII
The SSC – Waylaid and Murdered

Meanwhile, the men of the science community who had no influence or direct involvement in the project stood on the sidelines outside it and watched in dismay. Some were continually frustrated in their attempts to intervene or help in any way. Some hated the project from the *get-go*. But before long, for all of them, the reality of their own personal situations began to sink in. They started to wonder whether or how long they could remain immune to the looming messy debacle. Unremittingly, the state of affairs in Waxahachie went from bad to worse, with the SSC swelling ominously, threatening to burst, and menacing all in its path. Seeing this, and without a chance in the world of doing anything about it, their hopes for an SSC turnaround came to nothing. Discouragement overcame them, soon metamorphosing into concern for themselves, then into fear, then into resentment, and finally leading to an unwanted but last-resort lashing out in a gnashing-of-the-teeth opposition to the project. In this way, the science community, with no clear-cut alternative, broke ranks; and, even with Reagan's 1987 money and assurance firmly in place, its support for the project flew the coop.

Once the true nature of the positions of the non-SSC scientists took shape in their minds, there was no assuaging these men, who'd fretted endless hours and came to feel an utter helplessness, reaching the point of being unbearable. Who could help them? How could they be given respite from their down-in-the-dumps, gloomy outlook? How could they be encouraged to recover their optimism? How could they be made to breathe easy again? Well, as it happened, when Reagan opened the starting gate and let the SSC loose, the government tried its damnedest to turn the anxiety-ridden community around and set things right. In fact, in its wish to see the SSC come to fruition, if anything, it went overboard in its make-everybody-happy approach. It's true that a happy scientist is a productive one, so the idea had much to commend it. But appeasement doesn't work very often. Nevertheless, it was the government men's call, and that's the way they chose to go.

First, there were the sound, cool-headed, cheerfully upbeat, and aiming-to-please words – coming from government and science leaders at the highest level – that in the unlikely event of SSC problems, even big ones, the rest of the community would absolutely be free of any consequences. But, to the cynical lot in the science community, that was not enough. Even the calm, reassuring, we-have-everything-under-control tone didn't resonate with them, and wasn't enough to give them a restful night's sleep. Then came the presidential initiative funding mechanism that they were assured would, without a shadow of a doubt, protect them from any financial mishap at the SSC. But that also was not enough. Finally, in an all-out effort to relieve the stampeding panic that had overspread the community, the government, determined to demonstrate to everyone its capability of taking care of all the sciences and their futures, set out on an unprecedented course. So came into being the *Trivelpiece Initiative*, whereby substantial government investments were made. In particular, there were new projects approved at six of the national laboratories around the country. What awesome power! What confidence the government showed in Big Science and in the whole idea of scientific basic research! Surely that would carry the science community through its qualm-filled, jumpy, and nerve-wracking days!

In fact, giving the science community everything but the kitchen sink did work for a while, at least long enough for the project to get underway, but alas, in the end, that approach proved not to be enough. It appears that trust had totally vanished, so that promises and even demonstrations simply didn't suffice. The collective community mind had become so convinced of the mischief, the loss, and the harm the SSC would bring to science that, come hell or high water, it had to go. Thus it was that the SSC-instigated transition from consternation, to alarm, to rancor, to rage, and to warlike hostility took its fateful and unpreventable course.

The anti-SSC forces steeled themselves to the task at hand. American science was at stake, and it had fallen on them to save it. There was no choice, it was their duty, and it soon became their mission. There was no quarter to be given as the righteous came out swinging in damnation of the sinners. This was no job for the meek and the timid of heart. They had to be rock-hard, and they were. Yes, they kept their most abusive faultfinding and reproaches to privately persuade the men-on-high in Congress, those who held the purse strings and the power of life-and-death over the SSC, to come over to their side. But they knew that in addition they had to go public, and they did so with pretty harsh accusations and denunciations of the big, lumbering giant. Wither goes the community, so go the *big boys*! Now, how did they know this, these innocent scientists? Somehow, they did, and in this particular game, where their futures were held in the balance, they acted like political pros.

Sneeringly, they queried the community, "Why do we need the SSC, anyway?" It's just a big white elephant. Its time is over, and it'll surely fall and break of its own cumbersome weight. Do you want to go down with it? It's obscure science, merely an ivory tower game for the elite; and it's being done only to satisfy the greed and the drive-for-fame of a few. And think of this: it will never be useful to society! That's just not right, and we shouldn't allow it. Then again, don't you think that science should be more socially aware? Don't you think that we need more practical uses of science, and more applications for society's needs? No, there's no value in this project now, either for science or society. Thus, don't you think we should wait a while till perhaps technology finds a better way, rather than putting everything in one basket that's sure to sink? Wow! How convincing were their arguments! How persuasive they were! So it happened that scientists from all over the country responded in unison, "Down with the SSC!" Thus, in the end, ruthlessness, remorselessness, and mercilessness won out. Nothing less would do than to bring the project down, and if that meant that with it would also go high-energy physics, then so be it. At this point, the community had gone too far to turn back, even if it wanted to. No, nothing could be done to stop the anti-SSC express from rolling through the land of science. The deed was done, and history, as it always does, would have the last say.

* * *

Sociology
IX
The Social Solution Strikes Out

How do you like that? Here's another compelling case to account for the SSC's downfall. On its face, sociology gives every appearance of being right on track, apparently incorporating the full range of potential reasons from the de-unification of the science community resulting from specialization to the close-to-the-edge disintegration of science togetherness triggered by the giant SSC ready to eat everything in sight. Even why Reagan's brilliant maneuver to assuage the community didn't work is explained. You see, on that score, it wasn't the lack of money that bought out the worst in the anti-SSC scientists. They recognized in their hearts that the SSC was just too big to be handled by men of their own ilk, research oriented men; and they didn't at all trust the government to honor its commitment to them in the event that the SSC went down the tubes. So the establishment scientists reacted the only way they could, with harsh vocal and public hostility.

OK, so the anti-SSC scientists were loud-mouthed and made terrible nuisances of themselves. But was that really enough to send the Texas laboratory to oblivion? You have to wonder: Did they truly have the know-how and the power to prevent and knock off a feat of excellence the country would've been only too proud to show off to the rest of the world? Look, the Presidency had started it off, the Congress was originally foursquare behind it, the project's political backing was breathtaking, and the DOE was bound to it, lock, stock, and barrel. Could politically innocent scientists have changed all that? Could they have managed all by themselves the elaborate undertaking of political treachery that was required? Surely not!

Actually, on second thought, they did have words working for them, and it's true that words can sometimes do what first appears impossible. Could this have been a situation where that applied? Not likely, because their words were attached to phony ideas. The scientists said there wasn't enough money to feed the SSC. But to the U.S. government, the SSC's cost was a pittance. The scientists said that the SSC men couldn't handle such a big project. But the government had been through it all before and pulled it off. Why not again? Furthermore, to be effective, the scientists' words had to get through to congressmen and influence enough of them to change course and put their shoulders to the killing cause. Ha! The scientists didn't have the leverage. Their words didn't have much substance, and surely didn't have any teeth backing them up. There's simply no reason in the world why Congress would heed mouthing-off scientists, doubtlessly only envious men seeking their piece of the country's science pie, afraid that the SSC would whisk it away and run off with it. Congressmen are far too sophisticated to fall for such a cheap shot. Besides, this was something the government was showcasing, and was S&T at its finest. No, there's not a chance in the world the scientists could've pulled it off alone.

The upshot is that we're back where we were when we thought that money or politics alone could do the trick for us. Yes, it's quite right that, just as with them, a strong prima facie case can be made for a social solution. However, as before, although social factors were undoubtedly intimately connected with the guillotining of the big project and may even have played an important part in it, by themselves they leave gaping holes and just don't cut it. In the end, compelling as the argument is, the social solution is not the winning wild card. But don't be discouraged because we've yet to find the pot of gold. There's still more to explore. Maybe as we travel along the road to finding the truth about the SSC, that surmised *pattern* will spring out at us and make our day. So, let's not give up prematurely. Let's just try harder. As the *Fat Man*, in search of the diamond-encrusted *Black Bird*, urged his cohorts, "*On to Istanbul!*" In like manner do we urge you, "*On with the quest!*"

*****

Internationalism
I
No Help From Abroad

In the years just after the SSC went down for the count, one of the more prevalent excuses was the inability of the project to realize a true internationalism. On its face, this doesn't appear to be a very promising direction to take. However, although a long shot, it is nevertheless a possibility. So there really is no choice. Sitting there, waiting to be looked into, it simply must be given its due consideration. Besides, being such a weighty concept, and such a big word as well, it just wouldn't do to simply ignore it.

It's quite true that internationalism is a powerhouse of an idea, one that we would do well to respect. History is full of countries cooperating in war and trade. But don't let its seeming all-pervasiveness fool you. If you happen to be someone who's dreaming the dream of internationalism, bear in mind that it's something to challenge the spunkiest and most resolute among us. To be sure, trying to convert an apparently natural nationalism, which induces potent and often destructive competitions, into an everyone-wins internationalism is a hard road to hoe; and more often than not, it falls flat on its face. You see, the truth is that countries tend to think of number one first. Yet, when internationalism works, it shows men at their very best. Understand that as it is with countries, so it is with projects. Thus, let's turn to the case of the SSC.

What a grand idea the SSC was when it first saw the light of day back a couple of decades ago. It was entrancing and stirred men's souls. However, right from the start, the project rejected internationalism and instead was purposefully and openly – even *in your face* proudly – fashioned on nationalism. Thus, it took a lot of chutzpah for the SSC to go in search of international cooperation when it fell on hard times. Remember that the SSC was born in 1982 as a purely American project. Its purpose was to foster American basic science, make American S&T the hallmark of excellence, and get America to be first again in Big Physics. But things don't necessarily turn out the way people want them to. For the SSC, slowly, as it wore on and began to falter, with no light at the end of the tunnel in sight, internationalism was resurrected. It wasn't brought in because of principle or for the good of world science, but rather for a purely pragmatic reason: If it worked, it could well end up calming a beginning-to-waver U.S. government. Of course, there was the added dividend that it would also pull in a little extra cash. Who wouldn't want that?

Those pointing the finger at international snubbing as the straw that broke the SSC's back picked out and underscored the fact that, when asked, foreign governments made the choice that their own scientific enterprises should not become SSC partners. "*The bastards just wouldn't come through for us*," was the commonly heard American refrain at the time. However, the SSC didn't have much purity and honor in its heart either. Keep in mind that in shooting for international collaboration, the SSC's top echelon staff hoped only that by persuading CERN, plus Germany, Japan and other countries to share in both the benefits and the cost, they could make the U.S. government see the importance of not leaving the SSC in the lurch. The idealism associated with international cooperation was the least thing on their minds. All they wanted was something of an insurance policy against any rash action by the U.S. to give the project the heave-ho. But the cute trick didn't work. Foreign interest was zilch, and the scheme flopped.

When the project found itself in desperate straits, the "*we're-in-it-together*" argument was trotted out and brought to the fore. *Science is intrinsically international*, the Americans argued. *It is for everybody. You must help us*, they persisted, *just as we would come through if you were in need.* Nobody admitted it openly, but the SSC had desperation written all over it. Toward the end, enticements of unprecedented user privileges – among other come-ons, such as particular management rights – were offered, and there was a lot of begging going on. But it was too late! Still, the answer was "*No*!" There was to be no new partnership with the courted foreigners, and no financial help for the SSC would be forthcoming from abroad. The answers were brusque and final. That was that! It appears that no one was in the least fooled by the SSC's ruse. At the end of the day, the only thing that could be said about this gambit was that it was a dud and didn't pan out. These countries oceans away were deaf to the pleas of the American scientists; and they stayed out of what they rightly perceived as an internecine American dispute, and a breach of trust internal to the U.S. between the science community and the government. It certainly had nothing to do with them. Thus, when all was said and done, no international savior stood prepared to enter and try to pull the SSC out of the threatening inferno it was engulfed in. The SSC therefore had to meet its fate without such aid.

In spite of the package of glaring evidence that spoke against it, there were still some earnest and thoughtful people who suggested that it was this inability of the SSC to muster and build up any significant international involvement that caused it to tumble with a thud. They were good people, even if a little naïve, and they really believed the song they were singing. But they didn't really know what was going on, and in their heart of hearts they didn't want to know. So they did the next best thing: they hid their heads in the sand.

Looking back, this explanation of an international cause for the SSC's sad outcome is quite a stretch. How lame it is! How ignorant its proponents were of the reality of the time! Would the great and powerful government of the United States permit such piddling nit picking to prevent it from a deep exploration into the atomic nature of our world? Would it allow the inability to pry a little loose change from abroad to block it from the incredible challenge of making what was little more than a gleam in scientists' eyes into a palpable, practical, integrated facility complex for a precedent-shattering, adventurous scientific investigation? Nevertheless, unlikely as it might seem, in the air was this notion that international chicanery – other countries' lack of loyalty, lack of reliability, lack of trustworthiness, and fickleness – was the thing that did the SSC in. So widespread was it that you have to wonder what it was that gave it such credence. It cries out for an answer: Why did so many put such stock in it and attach such weight to it?

* * *

Internationalism II Big Science Bought and Sold in the International Marketplace?

Internationalism in and for science is long-standing and has an enviable tradition. What an irresistibly attractive ring to it that word *internationalism* has! Originally the strong linkage of science to internationalism comes from the characterization of science as intrinsically having no borders. To the extent that science is knowledge and rests in the minds of men, and since there is no natural impediment to men communicating with each other from anywhere to anywhere, this is true. But it is a somewhat trivial point, applying to all sorts of knowledge. If men wish to communicate, then of course they can. Thus, the notion that science is something special in having no borders and being inherently international is really nothing but a crock, because so is any other kind of information or knowledge that can be communicated by word.

However, the sheer national value of S&T demands that governments enter the picture and speak their piece. If there were reason to prevent the dispersing of certain information or knowledge, then undoubtedly borders of an incorporeal nature could be concocted and raised; and it is the governments' responsibility to see that it gets done. This info blocking by intangible means – classification, intelligence networks, and other onerous methods – is an old story in a world of countries continually at odds with each other. Countries, for reasons of national security, when the knowledge is deemed important enough, have always expended no end of effort to achieve confidentiality and concealment. Much has been learned from this widespread and concerted drive to keep the veil of secrecy non-porous and intact, one being that to establish effective control over information and knowledge is not at all straightforward and very pricey. Whisperers, deceivers, and both innocent and not-so-innocent informers are everywhere. At the same time, opponents are always seeking information or knowledge that you possess. It's a perfect match! Whether the opponents are seeking particular info, or whether they are simply going fishing, if the informers are not weeded out, the info will inevitably wend its way through the well-known and well-trodden channels of intrigue. The upshot is that if you want to stop it, you have to pay through the nose – and still it's an iffy business.

As it happens, basic science has a high communicability component. When combined with the technology it fosters and uses, it has always been a pivotal factor when war is at hand. But it also plays a big role in countries' peacetime defense efforts. In both circumstances, countries would certainly be profoundly distressed were the knowledge that they've created and nurtured within their physical borders to be either carelessly or traitorously disseminated to outsiders for who knows what ends. Heads could roll for such acts of folly or betrayal. However, pure scientists generally consider themselves to be immune from this secrecy constraint, arguing unreasonably, perhaps because of their ivory-tower innocence of the ways of the world or their unrealistic idealism in man's oneness, that their work is not usable anymore for the waging of war. Actually, it may well have been so in the good old days some decades ago. But it *ain't so* today. Nuclear energy for war and peace and space exploration, as well as a number of other areas contingent on basic science that have serious national security implications, patently contradict this presumption of being exempt. In addition, there's the ever-deepening connection of basic science to technological development. It would surely give government officials a good deal of heartburn to see some of that material flowing freely around the globe. Thus, as more and more basic science becomes valuable enough for a country to consider it proprietary or classified information, requiring unswerving and determined protection from eavesdroppers and unfriendly ears, the whole idea of science-without-borders has become an outdated notion and is but an empty reminder of foolhardy days gone by. It then behooves countries and their science institutions to figure out ways to contain the knowledge of the basic science that has become designated as privileged material, and to prevent it from leaking across borders via the mind-to-mind conduit. Of course, it's not likely that zero-info-outflow can truly be achieved. But there's always the fallback position of instead aiming for a leakage slowdown, so that at least some advantage gained from either the discovery process or through spying can be kept. If not the ideal aspiration, it's certainly the pragmatic way to go; and surely it's the next best thing to an unrealistic leak-proof perfection.

Reality tells us that the whole issue of national security in today's basic science endeavor is something of a red herring. For the most part, the free passage of basic science results is not inimical to the well-being or safety of countries around the world. That's not entirely true because some of the technology used to build and operate the facilities could very well bear on national security and be of value to enemies or potential enemies. But, by and large, this specific information is a rather smallish component of the overall basic science enterprise, and can be dealt with separately. Thus, a good case, based on both cost and content, can be made for making basic science exempt from the rigorous rules – very costly to implement – devised to keep classified material away from prying eyes. That being the case, you'd expect that scientists would be pushing hard for a free-flowing, open system for basic science. That would maximize science progress and on the whole optimize scientists' ability *to be the best that they can be*. Sad to say, this ideal situation has yet to be realized and isn't likely to be, at least not for this generation of scientists.

As it happened, modernity combined with the darker side of human nature and arm-in-arm walked right in. Along with that entrance there was built a *wall* that clamped down on free access. Strangely, it wasn't the various governments that did this. For their part, they essentially gave basic science its sought-after exemption from national security controls. These governments rightly deduced that protectionism in the area of basic science was uncalled for; and although logic is not generally a government's best suit, rationality won the day this time. But, knowing this, can anyone make heads or tails out of what subsequently evolved? Since the governments can't be faulted for making the *wall* go up, then who erected it? That's right! It was the scientists themselves who wanted it and, in the end, got it. This is really funny – a case where government officials were filled with logic, and scientists found wanting in it.

What is this *wall for science* and what is it for anyway, you ask? Well, the *wall* itself is nothing more than a representation of the authority and the muscle to parcel out to outsiders access to the country's Big Science facilities; and its goal is to give the country that chooses to activate it in its interest an edge in doing the experiments. For that nation's scientists, that edge gives them the best shot at being first, and in their way of seeing the world, that's what really counts.

So it was that the government, recognizing that national security wasn't an issue to be concerned about, gave full responsibility for it's country's basic science facilities to the scientists themselves. Thus, by government consent, the scientists thereby became the effective owners; and, as such, they were the controllers of the experimental information garnered and the knowledge to be derived from it. Whether they chose to share access or chose to lock up the facilities for their own private use, the call was theirs alone to make. In a nutshell, then, here's the principle by which science, specifically Big Science, has decided to play the game: *When countries come to own advanced and unique facilities with the capability of developing and using forefront technology to acquire knowledge and its products, the knowledge comes to resemble a commodity, and can be treated as such. In particular, as any commodity, it can be traded in the international marketplace.* No doubt, scientists don't much appreciate this cold statement of reality. Was this truly their vaunted, pure-as-the-driven-snow science that was being referred to? The statement was distasteful to them, and to many it was downright offensive. It made them seem callous and inflexible. But there it is! That's what they'd done; and, once the cat's out of the bag, in matters such as these, only a miracle-man can put it back again. So, from then on, science, like many other forms of intellectual property, could and would be bought and sold on the bartering market. In Big Science, the implementing mechanism is access to *unique facilities for a price*. At the same time, irretrievably lost was that special character that set science apart from the money-grubbing real world. What a far cry this was from the time, not so long ago, when science stood, with squeaky-clean hands and with nobility, high above the fray!

* * *

Internationalism
III
Internationalism Suffers a Knockout Blow

It's apparently an inherent part of men's social nature to want to be first in achievement. Winning the game is an age-old human wish. Contrast that with altruism, back a distant second, and relegated to an obscure notion deliberated, debated, and endlessly hashed over by idealistic, unworldly philosophers. Well, it's no contest. Being first, yes, that's the ticket! Has anyone not experienced that accompanying surge of adrenaline? What a high it is! As an individual, a man yearns for it, resolutely seeks it out, and grasps for it when the opportunity is there. But man doesn't live and act alone. He's part of a nation; and it's more often than not that his nation gives him the advantage he needs to reach his heart's desire. So it is that men and their nation join together, and nationalism, the force that drives a group of men to get to the top in front of others of other nations, comes into being. If America can help a scientist win the game against nationals of other countries, then why shouldn't the American grab at the chance? In like manner, why shouldn't a European, or an Asian, or anyone from any other country of the world do the same? Thus, it is a fact of life that, even when confronted with compelling pressure from the world science community to conform with the ideal of science internationalism, the deeply ingrained, irresistible compulsion to be first just can't be denied.

Once upon a time, scientists who were into basic research stood tall and were able to withstand and refuse to give in to the strong pull of nationalism. In fact, they were a kind of nation unto themselves, divorced from the standard ones. In those old days, when basic science was small and politically invisible, the question of gaining an advantage by virtue of their particular nationhood didn't much occur to most scientists. Then it was easy for Americans, Europeans, and others to relate to each other as equals. They collaborated; they shared; and the give-and-take was free and admirable. In those times, they were innocent of the dark forces of nationalism and its uses to enhance self-interest. There was considered to be no difference between them, whatever their country of origin. International science was on a high. "*Liberty, equality, and fraternity*" was the prevailing motto for science. Open and free competition was the predominant spirit of the times. Perhaps it was naïveté that held sway and made it all possible. In any case, it was a good time.

In those days, the facilities were small and the technology straightforwardly transferred or imitated. Thus, science seemed to be blessed with the ideal conditions for universality to work. It was to any scientist's advantage to cultivate his counterparts in other countries. Experimental ways and problems could be exchanged. He could cross one of the big ponds to participate with his scientist friends there. He saw no difference between himself and his colleagues from other nations. This was the picture of internationalism as scientists saw it; and it was good to be a part of it. It was a win-win situation, with everyone gaining. No one even gave a second thought to politics intervening in the dream world they were living in. There simply was no reason for anyone or anything to intrude. They were so sure that this was an everlasting gift bestowed on them by the gods. It was the natural way for science and they had a right to it. It would surely last forever.

However, nothing in this world goes on indefinitely. Everything changes. For science, it was bigness that entered upon the scene and obliterated its fantasy way of life. As things stand, to keep basic science free-flowing across national borders in today's world of growing bigness requires that scientists, even as they wheel-and-deal and negotiate with each other, also be able to rely on, to bank on, to be confident of, to be sure about each other, and then to show some generosity toward each other. But isn't that too much to ask? Consider the situation where a big facility in one world region is not available in another. The scientist that doesn't have it in his own region naturally seeks access to it in the other. Sure, there's an implied promise that in time the favor will be returned. But, who really knows what will happen when the time for potential reciprocation is indefinite, maybe a decade, maybe more? That's how long it takes for a high technology, costly facility to come into being. Surely it's asking too much of ambitious men, looking to make names for themselves and advancing their careers, to be so trusting and bighearted. Under such conditions, a fully free competitive system is undeniably not a viable option.

When you think about it a little, this conclusion that the scientists' view of internationalism just can't work becomes quite clear. The fact is that if it's to work, human nature – that urge to be first – would have to be violated. To appreciate this, consider that scientific knowledge is built on a foundation of experimentation that in the age of bigness requires an elaborate infrastructure of facilities and technology. The chances are, therefore, that some region will have a particular facility to the exclusion of the other regions. In fact, with so few facilities being simultaneously built because of their bigness and the time it takes to get them operational, you can see what this implies: Those who have ownership of the facilities also have first crack at the acquisition of the knowledge that derives from them. That being the case, why should an American want to give first dibs to a European or other foreigner if he doesn't have to? And, naturally, vice versa!

Here's what actually happened, and it shouldn't really shock anyone: As particle physics facilities grew in size and complexity, over time, the rules of the game changed. Because only a few countries or regions held the capacity to pull off the experiments, scientific national elitism began its upward surge. The entire new state of affairs that evolved seemed to sneak up on the world science community. Although signals were there to see, nobody noticed them, and most scientists did in fact come away with the impression that a new way of life had made a sudden, irrevocable appearance. In any case, there it was: Scientific knowledge coming from small, easily duplicated equipment – once you knew how to build it – wasn't the key any more. Now, to be competitive, you needed elaborate physical facilities created with forefront building, manufacturing, and technical capability. You see these were instruments – uniquely possessed – that only a very small number of nations had the capability of generating. Both scientists and politicians quickly saw the significance of this. Only those countries with the technological and industrial capacity to build such complex measuring tools could do the science unless, out of sheer goodness, they allowed others in. Thus, the handwriting was on the wall. It was only a matter of time before the illusion of science internationalism was exposed.

Pulling back to get a wide-angle view, we can get a glimpse of what took place as bigness came on the scene: It was no less than a revolution, dragging basic science kicking and screaming into the twenty-first century and beyond. Such was how Big Science made its grand entrance. Thenceforth, owning the infrastructure that only a modern first-world state could have came to mean, as it so often did in man's history, that the possessors had the power to offer it up or to withhold it as befitted their interests, or indeed to do anything with it that it suited the owners to do. To be sure, technological know-how has been used in this way since time immemorial; and you better believe that there is no impediment to basic science know-how being used the same way.

Let's get down to brass tacks, and ask the two questions of real substance: Who were the power-holders, the owners of the instruments, and were they ready to share the wealth – the knowledge to be gained from the experimental output, which only they possessed the capability of acquiring? To the first one, why, it's the scientists in league with their governments! Who else? To the second, you'd think that idealistic scientists would instinctively answer, "*Of course, let's level the playing field. What's ours is theirs. We're all equals in this grand international scientific enterprise.*" But if you expected that, it's to be hoped that you didn't hold your breath in the waiting for it to alight. You see, at stake were the bread-and-butter issues of scientists' careers: Who gets there first? Who gets the fancy-titled job? Who gets their country's acclaim and tribute? Who gets their colleagues' recognition and commendation? Who becomes *number one*? And finally the pièce de résistance: who wins the big one, the Nobel Prize? Surely you're not too surprised that scientists, being just ordinary people after all, succumbed to nature's call for self-aggrandizement and self-glorification. Like others before them, and no doubt many others to follow, they played the innocents, but furtively palmed the money placed before them. So it was that Big Science stole idealism from the scientists and brought in the hour of nationalism in basic science.

* * *

Internationalism
IV
The SSC Stands Alone

Let's go back to the time when *little science* prevailed, and when the facilities that were needed for it were correspondingly small. No elaborate technological and industrial backup infrastructure was required back then. So, in quick order, such facilities could straightforwardly be cloned by anyone determined to do so. Trying to contain the knowledge of how to do the experiments, keeping it hoarded all to yourself, was both wasteful and useless. *The info will out*! You see, people will talk and the know-how will find its way out whatever you do. Thus, surely it's far better to take the easy path that also happens to be the right way: be true blue internationals, share facilities, work together, and remain friends with your colleagues across the oceans. And that's the way it was. As the old-timers remember it, "*Ah, that was a good time.*" Basic science had no borders of any kind; good old-fashioned fair, see-who-comes-first races were the order of the day; and the picture then was that of the scientist in open and free international competition.

Then Big Science entered the story. When that happened, everything changed, and with it went the good life. You see, when facilities reached a certain bigness, they couldn't be imitated or duplicated unless the industrial infrastructure was there, and unless there was a willingness to make huge investments in money, people, technology, and time. Under such conditions, owning these facilities provided a ready-made advantage and a means of getting the jump on your competitors from abroad. All that needed doing was to prevent physical access. But, because basic science thrives in an atmosphere of openness, why go to such an extreme? If the facilities couldn't easily be replicated, why bother with such a nasty and hostile approach? There was after all another way – a civilized way of accomplishing the objective of doing good science, and with a fair crack at being first in the bargain.

Rather than knocking each other off, wouldn't a far better way be to sit down together and talk, to somehow come up with a deal on either a quid pro quo to everyone's liking or on a satisfactory access charge? How simple it would be: Set up an impartial and evenhanded negotiating system; set up a system, fair to all, to manage international cooperation in the building and usage of the needed large projects; set up an access system limited to those who've joined the network; set up a system to ensure the equalization of long-term resource usage; and you're on your way. Once it's going, here's how the overall system might work in practice: if you're American, you can go here and do this experiment; if you're European, you can go there and do that one; if you're Japanese, you can go to an agreed-upon location and do another one; and with appropriate charges or trades, you can easily find the means to mix and match fairly, that is, according to the resources invested in the system.

It's a pretty good arrangement, and equitable too, don't you think? And it's perfect for Big Science! Because large facilities, advanced technology, and an extensive industrial and managerial infrastructure are necessary for its effective operation, this form of international trading is about the only thing rational people can do. Actually, a little thought would tell you that such a system is inevitable anyway, and in time will surely come into use. In one fell swoop, this type of solution throws the claimed necessity for internationalism à la times-gone-by on its red face. The old-style altruistic internationalism wouldn't work anyway in the age of Big Science. It goes against both man's intrinsic competitive nature and his desire and need to be nationalistic. After all, man is what he is! So, when all is said and done, in the era of bigness, it's negotiation and cooperation that will eventually hold sway. That's the civilized way. That's the right way.

However, that's not the end of it. Even after discarding altruism as an impractical approach in modern times, there's a crucial matter that still remains. It is a question that's likely to decide the future of Big Science for a generation or even more. Indeed it is the heart of the matter: Will the men of science behave rationally and negotiate in good faith, or will they be irrational and withhold their facilities from foreigners for a short-term advantage, but to the detriment of all in the long run? It's only common sense that screams out for the road of discussion and cooperation to be taken. But, men being men, they could well reject this *reasonable nationalism* for a form of pain inflicting and self-destructive behavior – not uncommon in man's history – that originated from Lucifer's implantations in the dark recesses of men's minds so long ago.

In theory, seeing that facility duplication is cost-prohibitive and really not too smart, a rational international framework for Big Science indeed sounds good. In practice, however, it's tough going – that is, if it's possible at all. In the case of the SSC, American scientists saw no international competition that could match them. Seeing nothing much to gain from being international goodie-goodies, why should the Americans just out-and-out give the Europeans the chance to beat them? Actually, the situation wasn't quite that straightforward. CERN might've been able to get in the game, but as bad luck would have it, the big Geneva lab was bogged down in financial troubles, and seemed to be foursquare behind the eight ball. Since there was no one else that was competitive, the SSC had clear sailing, and chose to give CERN the finger. Perhaps you could call that a reasoned, albeit dastardly, way for the SSC to go. But that wasn't all there was to it. The U.S. insensitivity to CERN's plight had another reason behind it. Americans were still stinging from the loss of the W race. Not only that! There was also Rubbia's arrogantly rubbing it in. Putting it all together, if truth be told, what the American scientists really wanted to do was to stick it both to CERN and to the *big clown* himself.

As history tells the story, in 1982 the SSC came into being as Americans beamed with nationalistic pride. That's the way it was! The SSC was born as a national facility, with the U.S. seemingly unnecessarily thumbing its nose, not only at CERN and Carlo, but also at the many earnest, although misguided, men who, at the time, were pushing for a world machine. Believe it or not, the manner in which the project was established was no less than an act of anti-internationalism. Well, that's neither here nor there. In any case, it didn't turn out to be one of America's finest hours. At the beginning, Americans thought they were on top of things because only they could muster the technology and the resources to build such a gigantic instrument. That was indeed true, but, as time would tell, it was far from enough. Not aware of what awaited them, they were sure they had it made. If Carlo and CERN could risk the store and win, so could America. However, the comparison was only skin-deep. Yes, like Carlo, the Americans were arrogant. On the other hand, unlike Carlo, they weren't able to transcend their self-defeating impulses and get the job done. Thus, although fate smiled on Carlo in the early eighties, the SSC wasn't so fortunate in the early nineties.

Toward the end of the SSC's short life, the American scientists came down a mite from their high horses. They believed money was their problem and pathetically, with desperation and anguish in their hearts, pleaded with the international science community to help out. What they were selling was the chance to participate in the experiments once the SSC got going. For that privilege, an up-front entry fee was being asked. A few miniscule contributions were in fact made, one noticeably from India; but these were all chicken feed, nothing but a pittance for the greedy monster being shaped.

However, the CERN leaders held back. They vacillated, as if to punish the Americans for the transgressions inflicted on them. You see, it was nothing but a show they were putting on. They were just leading the Americans on by the nose. They had no intention whatsoever of coming in to save the big American project. On the contrary, they far preferred that the project just cease to be.

As it was in the early nineties, CERN might have stepped in and kept the SSC alive by providing the asked for entry fee. But why, in God's name, would CERN donate a half to a billion dollars to aid a foe when this would work against its own self-interest? Why not just let it blow in the wind and eventually bite the dust of its own accord? That would serve them right, those cocky Yanks. The fact was that if it should really happen that the SSC were to go belly-up, it would also give Europe an open field to reach for the high-energy gold. You see CERN, in spite of its financial woes, was in the midst of trying to develop and fund its own big machine, its vaunted LHC. In fact, the more the SSC wallowed in difficulties and faltered, the greater the chance that the LHC would be given the *go-ahead* sign by the CERN member states. Sure, the LHC was smaller than the SSC, but it was still a collider to be reckoned with.

However, CERN, beset with thorny and challenging cash deficiencies, also wanted and needed new money from outside its own boundaries – from outside the European community. Thus, like the SSC, it was trying as well to extract all it could get in entry fees. However, it wasn't going to be easy going, for as the money situation stood at that time, around 1990, the competition between the U.S. and CERN for foreign funds was stalemated. Since the U.S. set the tone of combat by imperiously going off on its own when it was riding high, CERN, when its chance came, responded in kind. So, because both were immovable and inflexible as could be, they were determined to fight it out until only one was standing. It turned out to be a dog-eat-dog, knock-down-drag-out escapade, and the earth upon which Big Science rested shook and quaked as the battle to the death went its course.

Since CERN wasn't going to help the SSC, the Japanese were the last hope for America to make an international sale of consequence. Although having S&T ambitions of their own, the rich Japanese, anxious for Big Science, were aching to get in on one of the big projects. Without the technological infrastructure to do it by themselves, for them, the question was simple: would it be the SSC or the LHC? Japan had strong bonds with the U.S., dating back to the late forties, and surely had a tendency to apply its support in that direction. All else remaining equal, the Japanese would probably have chosen to join the SSC; but undoubtedly more important to them was being on the winning side, a not unreasonable strategy. However, once the bitter dispute between CERN and the U.S. got underway, they procrastinated and waited for the dust to settle before committing themselves. Thus, the Japanese held off on making their pick. Then, suddenly, in the fall of 1993, the SSC's end came; and when the SSC fell, the Japanese knew where their precious and constructive money would go.

But there was more than meets the eye to the Japanese holding off on taking action. The fact is that they also had another reason for their less than friendly behavior towards the SSC. They remembered the image and the reality of the "*ugly American*" in the wake of World War II a half-century before, and began to glimpse it in the current actions of

American scientists and leaders. Not having been consulted before the full SSC management was set up or before the technical design was completed, the Japanese felt that they were being treated as merely a checkbook, and they didn't much like that. So, as it turned out, the special Japanese-American relationship was lost to the SSC, and the Japanese waited to see which side would come out on top in the Big Science cross-Atlantic battle.

As the SSC's final chapter began, it found itself abandoned by both Japan and Western Europe. There was no help to be had on the international front. Thus, the big floundering project had no recourse but to go it alone.

* * *

Internationalism
V
Why the SSC Fell Remains Elusive

True, having pitiful international backing might have been the straw that broke the camel's back. True, politicians might have used this fact to build up a negative slant on where the SSC stood and where it could be expected to go. True, seeing the project falter in its attempts to get foreign support might well have pushed the Congress over the edge. Yes, it could've happened that way. But it surely didn't. Actually, the SSC's destiny was determined long before this eleventh hour. If internationalism had anything at all to do with the project's ride down the dark road from which there is no return, it no doubt played but a peripheral role. Yes, in the drama's denouement, there was a lot of talk by the anti-SSC contingent about how foreigners didn't consider the project reliable enough to invest in. However, don't confuse the SSC's inglorious folding up, during which the international community made itself felt, and did its unseemly and unworthy deeds, with its long journey downhill. No, the failure to attract international partnerships was hardly responsible for its sad fate.

As to why so many still insist on claiming that it was the absence of international money that pushed the SSC into an early grave, a compelling answer doesn't immediately spring to mind. All the evidence, solid and circumstantial, when looked at with a critical eye, points to other causes: politics, money, and sociology, to name just three. Certainly, if you had to select just one reason, international disloyalty and falseness would be low on the list, in all likelihood at the bottom. But then we're back to the puzzling question of why so many still persist in the opinion that internationalism was at the root of the SSC's trip to the vast void of nothingness.

It's quite a brainteaser! However, taking a wild guess, perhaps it stems from a form of self-delusion that allowed people to relieve themselves of their own responsibility in the entire sordid SSC affair. Why not? Holding up the *internationalism solution* as the right-on rationale for what took the doomed project away to its final resting place did indeed shift the culpability away from blameworthy individuals for actions they may have devised or for things they might've done. By believing it themselves, even if wrongly, first they muddied their thoughts and then conveniently fully banished those troublesome and distressing memories from their suffering minds. Actually, it's not uncommon for people to go to great psychological lengths and logical convolutions in order that they might see themselves in a better light. In fact, facing reality as it is only rarely makes an appearance in the soul of an everyman; rather, it is the mark of the little seen heroic figure.

Thus, the full and true story of the SSC was lost in a blur through a combination of intentional and unintentional self-serving but false interpretations of events. It certainly can't be too surprising that people subconsciously, or sometimes purposefully, used the prevailing confusion to alleviate their guilt and gain relief. Under the topsy-turvy circumstances of the time, people were able to get away with saying just about anything. In such an environment, human nature alone suggests that they would resort to the mental contrivance that minimizes their pain. Yes, maybe it's this victory of imaginings over actuality, fiction over fact, that provides the answer we're seeking. Maybe that's exactly the reason why many people were so quick to offer up the *internationalism solution*. Oh, by the way, it might also be of some interest to you to ponder the possibility that the distortions of truth implicit in this little investigative account could be an explanation, to a degree anyway, of why historical truth is so hard to come by.

* * * * *

Incompetence

The fifth and final high-circulation cause for the end of the SSC was that it fell apart from within because of incompetence of one kind or another. Confronted with the considerable political and technical challenges of bigness, a state in which you always seem to be on slippery ground, the SSC's laboratory management might just have been too weak and too inexperienced to take on such a daunting charge. The Director and his troupe might've been able to deal with something smaller, but, as the argument goes, this was far over their heads, and way too hot for them to handle.

Clearly there's much to be said for this view. How easy it was for the top cookies of the SSC to underestimate the formidable job given them! How easy it was for them to miss the signs that said, "Beware, danger ahead!" How easy it was for them not to foresee the life-and-death struggle that lay ahead! How easy it was for them to fall into the trap that *hubris* sets for blind men! How easy it was for them not to see that they were presiding over an enterprise whose card to be played was the *Queen of Spades*! How easy it was for them to be not in the least aware of the onrushing failure train they were riding! So it was that, with arrogance filling his cup, the SSC's high priest surrounded himself with naïve incompetence. These men, meant to manage the SSC, were well out of their depths in the league they'd come to play in. You could argue that their end was foretold in the stars and was meant to be – that they were meant to fail, that it was the will of the gods, that it was their destiny. Maybe so! Yet still, there is the nagging doubt that makes you wonder whether greater men could've withstood the gathering storm forming just ahead of them that was to be the SSC's fate.

Failure is something you can't quite put your finger on. It starts out slowly. Little things happen. Mistakes ensue in response. Then the mistake rate speeds up and they accumulate, until, before you know it, you're face to face with the big monster that failure really is. It lures you into its lair, and then it traps you in its net by making you believe that each little step is nothing much, nothing to be concerned about in the least. Then, one fine day you find that you've gone too far to turn around and make your way home again.

Think back about the failure that befell the SSC. How might it have occurred? It could have started innocently enough, perhaps with a perfunctory or careless mistake. "*It's no big deal, we can take care of it later*," the managers might've ascertained. But left unheeded, such mistakes have a habit of becoming compounded. Yet, seemingly oblivious of that possibility, the managers blindly and thoughtlessly moved on. In their cockiness, they smugly and complacently hid the smoking guns, under the misguided certainty that these telltale clues wouldn't be discovered. How dumb! And yet, how human! What they'd gone and done is to superimpose their own misjudgment on top of the mistakes already made – and that, be assured, is a volatile mix, very likely to be on the verge of exploding.

This chronicle of man's pathetic conduct is an all too common one, as many have learned the hard way, and it very likely happened that way in the case of the SSC. The process of mistake and misjudgment repeating over and over, piling up one on top of the other, became overwhelming to the fault-ridden SSC brass. This situation they found themselves in, that they'd permitted to come about, caught them completely off-guard, vexing them and worrying them sick. In their minds, a kind of disorder took shape. They became unsettled, befuddled, and flustered. As a consequence, the chain of events that had placed them in such straits changed the way they perceived things to such an extent that soon they could no longer tell what was true and what was false, what was real and what was imagined. The big shots of the SSC had entered a state of psychological overload. They became unable to face their new circumstances. They even reached the point of becoming conspiratorial. They trusted no one except their fellow travelers, holding everyone else at bay. In this way, they isolated themselves from the real world. Promises were made but not kept as they tried anxiously to keep up the charade. Persisting in their tendency to over-reach, they allowed the messes to expand to such a degree that they got to the point of being unmanageable. Then, what could they do but leave them behind to fester? So the process churned along. On and on the failings went, large and small, in a seemingly never-ending sequence. To anyone with eyes to see, the SSC tower, resting on a rotting foundation, couldn't do other than to topple. But the men in their fancy offices hid themselves from real-life matters in a make-believe world. The truth was that in order to survive they refused to see – or perhaps they just couldn't anymore.

With no visible demands on them for discipline or accountability, the project's headmen, their staff, and the dwindling band of faithful physichists went along their merry way. Even with the mounting threat at their doorstep, they still didn't get it. Being unable to deal with what they'd wrought, they simply ignored it; and being unwilling to fess up to the roles they'd played in the oh-so-sad display of ineptitude, they ignored that too. Thus, their very presence became an almost insurmountable barrier to any viable solution as well as an embarrassment. However, since anyone who was anyone was also part of the whole ruinous and tangled muddle, who was there to step in to clean it up? With each review, the cost estimate climbed and the time-to-completion was further delayed. And what was the SSC laboratory's response? The tired excuses, incessantly used and overused, were taken out of their mothballs and brought forth. Yes, they were placed in shiny new boxes, but inside they were nothing but the same old ones. Then, not unexpectedly, there were oodles of promises made, some new, but for the most part, the same old stuff. It didn't much matter anyway, because the promises, old or new, were for the umpteenth time not lived up to. The truth about the project was that, although a lot of work was actually being done, it wasn't moving any closer to its aimed-for target with any dispatch. It just kept going on incoherently, in a meandering waltz of undirected, unguided, and purposeless random motion. However, as the SSC danced the *dance of death*, it slowly retrogressed in a downward drift that was relentless, and simply couldn't be stopped until the bottom was reached. At that low point, a pall set in, and all the good men of the SSC could do was to talk the talk. The chance and the ability to walk the walk had passed it by. Only blue-sky thoughts now remained as their hopes of last resort.

Since neither the scientists reviewing the project nor the government officials responsible for overseeing it believed what the SSC's management was saying, after each review episode the DOE heaped more controls, more constraints, more inspections, and more safeguards on it. You'd think that should've put the fear of God in the bunch at the Waxahachie ranch. But a funny thing happened on the way to the forum. As the cost of the project went ever upward and the project itself moved ever backward, a new twist entered the strange tale of the SSC. The SSC's upper crust, contrary to the way reasonable men might be expected to construe such a predicament, came to fancy themselves to be less vulnerable and more favorably situated. Had they taken leave of their senses? Had they been pushed over the edge and gone bonkers? Maybe, but still there they were in their *Alice-in-Wonderland* way of life, acting as if the world were their oyster. Rather than running for the nearest hole to hide in, they seemed to be swelling with an ever-increasing dosage of swaggering cocksureness. Was this a tactic to agitate and unnerve their opponents? Was it a way of shoring up their friends? Did they really have a rational basis for their behavior that outsiders couldn't imagine? Was there someone or something behind the scenes that made them truly invincible? Or maybe they were just bluffing, and merely represented a collective *Wizard of Oz*. In any case, they acted as if they were as enduring as the Rock of Gibraltar; and the pooh-bahs of the SSC took easily to this state of affairs. As the political power brokers, the Texas bigwigs, and the prestigious and well-connected scientists scrambled down to Waxahachie to catch the flavor of the world-wonder-to-be, the SSC Director and his beaming men, with chests thumped up, greeted them all with friendly welcomes and embraced them with open arms. Smiles and handshakes abounded and a perverse kind of happiness filled the Texas air. Industrial concerns and big consulting companies also were Texas-bound to join the party, coming to partake of the action, perhaps sensing a fat cow to be milked. To top off this curiously outlandish, absurd, and even preposterous picture, without hesitation, the government kept the SSC in the money.

It often happens that our thoughts are governed by our desires and by what we think should be, and not by what is. So it was that, with their backs to the wall and being of weak character, the crowd at the SSC ranch in Waxahachie chose to believe the happy-days portrait before their eyes as painted by their partners in self-deception. It was a false image, as could quite clearly be seen by glimpsing underneath the glossy exterior, where calamity lay waiting to be loosed. But, sadly, these were fainthearted and unheroic men, men who were timid and running scared. What can be expected of such types? Thus, not being able to face the true nature of the reality of their lives, they came to feel that things weren't all that bad at the ranch.

However, despite their willful misconceptions, their wishful thinking, and their delusions of grandeur, the show kept driving inexorably toward its final scene where reality would make its grand entrance. If only these men could have sensed the fool's paradise they were living in. But, alas, they were fools; and where else should fools reside. So they accepted as true the contradictions and lies that hopped and skipped around them. They became believers. After all, if things were not what they appeared to be, then why was so much being given them? And they were quite right! The cash kept flowing in even though only promises had to be given in return. No productive output was demanded of them; *make-work* was more than sufficient. No end of distinguished national figures came to pay their respects, unobtrusively taking their cut of the action. Yes, everything was hunky-dory; everything was just as it should be. So it was that these conditions became a way of life: The high muckety-mucks of the SSC, courted by the big-money Dallas elite, were filled to the brim with a dream-like optimism. Ah, it was a time to remember! Who had the energy to think much in those days? There were parties galore and the world-class opera in Fort Worth to go to. What with the gala affairs, the honoring banquets, the cocktail parties, the hoedowns, and all the other hoopla, it was indeed a high time in the old Dallas town! But the glamour was but a will-o'-the-wisp; and the lights were just about ready to dim before the curtain descended.

Maybe unseen, and certainly unheeded, were two little-known congressmen, each seeking to make his mark. These little Macs of Washington did indeed burp in 1993, and Yertle – King Roy – came tumbling down, falling from his perch on high onto the dirty ground where mere mortals walk. Without the least doubt, if there were any single cause for the demise of the SSC, management incompetence – and you can throw in a little technical incompetence for good measure – would be a prime candidate. However, you can't just ignore the other classes of reasons – politics, money, sociology, and internationalism. You see, if these are not also taken into account, you might, without too much difficulty, contrive ways that the SSC could well have squeaked through. To be sure, it would've been shakily and at high cost; nevertheless, there are means by which management malfeasance could be scotched and checkmated, thereby allowing the SSC story to have a happy ending.

Try this scenario on for size: Imagine that near the end, as a last-ditch attempt, you could put the SSC back on track simply by dealing with Schwitters and his immediate underlings. Why not? Take all the stops out! Be brash! Show them your contempt! Walk the tightrope! Be ruthless! Just throw the bums out! Thus, with one quick thrust to the heart, you would be ridding the project of the parasitic leeches sucking the life out of it.

No matter how well connected they are, incompetent people can be replaced, you know, presuming, of course, that the will and the determination to really set things right as well as the guts to brave the storm are there. After all, no one is indispensable. The project would do just fine *sans* Roy. Maybe, by now, you're beginning to feel a little queasy. *Would it be possible to be a little less extreme*, you ask? The answer is emphatically, *no*. You see, by the early nineties, the SSC had sunk to such degrading depths that going for anything less than the top of the heap would be nothing more than a slap on the wrist. No, doing the job right means shooting for the jugular and expunging the king himself. Sure, it's a tall order to knock off someone that so many are committed to. To get to such heights in the first place, you must have collected lots of chips on the way up. Despite that excuse for backing off – and there are any number of them if you're resolve is fading – still, it's what has to be done when an enterprise is so far in the dumps. Now don't be discouraged. It's not impossible. However, there's just one hitch. There has to be someone made of the right stuff, someone with the know-how to pull together an influential and effective band of conspirators, and someone with the spirit to brave it out to the bitter end. It seems like a tough haul, doesn't it? But the beauty is that it really can be done. Just find the man, find the will, and, lo and behold, the way will materialize. However, needless to say, there wasn't such a heroic man about, and a regicide there was not to be.

So there it is. Indeed, the management, along with its incompetence, might well have been done away with. Yet, it didn't happen, and truly for the simplest of reasons – that it wouldn't have reprieved the SSC from its death sentence anyway. For who was better than Roy that could've replaced him? Sure, there would've been a new name sitting in the top man's chair. But would he have been made of different fiber? Would he have been able to instill life into a dead project? Not a chance! Thus, it's hard to escape the conclusion that, by itself, incompetence cannot account for the doleful end suffered by the SSC. Like the others, therefore, the *incompetence* class must also be shelved as a solitary cause.

* * * * *

All of the above

You might well be convinced by now that looking for a *magic bullet* is just an exercise in futility. Yet, perhaps the way we've chosen to look at why the SSC had to die while still in the womb is a bit askew. Perhaps our mind-set is off the mark. Perhaps we've been following the wrong scent. Perhaps we've been fool enough to be shadowing decoys all along. With just a little tilt of the kaleidoscope, perhaps that elusive *pattern* would suddenly appear in rich, blazing colors on its inner screen. That would be a moment to remember, the glorious instant when the curtain parts and the light of truth is seen for the very first time!

But how do we unearth such a thing – something that hasn't been thought of and that hasn't been understood before? We've presumably covered all the bases: We've scrutinized in gory detail all the commonly asserted reasons; we've plumbed their depths; and we've taken them apart, reconfigured them, and scrupulously studied them in their new guises. We've gone about as far as we can go; but still, finding the real thing has eluded us. It's so frustrating. This *standard model* that supposedly provides us with the set of all possible causes for the big project biting the dust just doesn't seem to work. So, what do we do? How do we proceed from there? Of course, it's obvious! Let's pin the blame on something altogether different! Ha! Easily said, but *where's the beef*?

After meticulously and painstakingly categorizing them, after analyzing them past all endurance, when people still can't figure out which one of a complex set of reasons fits the facts, many are ready to just give in and let it pass. To set themselves down easy, they latch upon that favored compound reason known as "*all of the above*." If you're such a one, then don't try to wriggle out of what you're really doing! Face it! It's no less than an admission that you've failed as a detective in finding the true culprit. *But sometimes what else is there to do*, you say? Don't be silly! Don't give up the ghost so easily! You can't just stop there! Don't you feel that there must be a better way because, for such a severe, untimely, and hapless occurrence, as was the case of the SSC, this vague *non-answer* is painfully unsatisfying?

On rethinking, maybe simply dismissing "*all of the above*" out of hand as a cop-out isn't the right thing to do either. Since it is so popular with so many, perhaps it should be treated with more respect. In fact, it behooves you to give it a shot and at least attempt to put together a plausible reason from elements of the five classes that have been introduced. These classes surely cover all the tracks. So, by piecing well-chosen elements together, you might be able to plumb the depths, to unravel the puzzle, to disentangle the whole messy SSC affair, to decode the clues, and thus to finally crack the case. Yes, it's certainly worth a try! By taking a little from this class and a little from that one, a satisfactory answer might indeed materialize, thereby giving you a tale worth telling.

True, if all the pieces don't fall into place like those of an intricate jigsaw puzzle, then you're out of luck. You'll be left with nothing except the loss of all that wasted time and effort you invested in the undertaking. Of course, you could always just settle for that over-rated and over-used notion that the cause was pure chance, the roll of life's dice, or merely bad luck. Why not? Just take *chance and luck* as the answer, and let it go at that. It doesn't sound all that bad. To be sure, if it were so, or at least if it were believed to be so, there's something to be said for it. It would certainly help perk up the unfortunate losers at the SSC project, who could then retain some of their pride. By taking it as true, they might even be able to relate to their grandchildren, with a degree of honesty, how they missed the SSC boat by just a hair. Hey, wait just a minute here! *Bad luck*? *Pure chance*? That's just plain silly! It doesn't cut the mustard – no, not one bloody bit! It would be equally valid to claim that it was those damnable red ants that pervade the dry plains of Texas and made everybody oh so miserable when they came to Waxahachie to call. Stooping to such a level makes the entire exercise of extracting the truth and learning some lessons from the SSC's sad story pointless and ridiculous. Now, that's not where you want to go, do you? There was so much pain, so much suffering, and so many damaged dreams that it is something of a sacred duty to see to it that some sense is made of the whole sordid business. No, *chance and luck* just won't do! It's absurd to imagine that they were behind what took the SSC out. So, let's just stop this nonsense. It's simply not worth belaboring the point more than we already have.

Without giving it a second thought then, let's simply discard them. Let's move on and continue with our search for more promising ground – for the one causal factor that works, the one that's compatible with all the evidence. Let's cut the bull and get serious, dead serious!

One sure thing that we've discovered is that the standard classes of possible causes give an abundance of clues but, in the strange case of the SSC, not one of them provides a single definitive explanation. So which way should we turn? With no clear-cut way to go, we find ourselves stuck in a rut. Of course, we could accept defeat. We could throw in the towel. But giving up when we've already come so far toward an answer goes strongly against the grain and is surely not the right thing to do. Furthermore, rationality, being all we have to help us in our truth-hunt, unequivocally tells us that there has to be a better way of seeing through to the essence of such a big event. So, believing that there is an answer to be found, and also believing, as science-minded men do, that we will somehow fix upon it, on we go with our quest all the way to the bitter end! Thinking about some kind of reasonable answer to our baffling and vexing question, remember the advice that Mick Jagger gave us many years ago, "*You can't always get what you want, but if you try hard, sometimes, you get what you need.*" Mick was right: we may very well not get the simple answer to our knotty brainteaser that we so want, but, by trying hard enough, we may end up with the true one. OK, it will almost surely be a complex solution, involving all the five standard classes of reasons we've been exploring. But, so what if it's difficult and complicated! So what if it's not a breeze to describe! If it's the best we can get, then the truth of the matter is that it could indeed be all that we need. Actually, if we really come by that kind of answer and get it in hand, who could ask for anything more?

To state it simply, the big task before us is to extract from each standard category the relevant material, and then join and fuse them all together into the integrated and unified explanation we're seeking. But, to get ourselves going, we must first hypothesize the *pattern* that we're looking for. After all, it would be pretty dim-witted and foolish to start knitting an Afghan blanket without first devising a blueprint to show us the way. Similarly, we need the *pattern* spelled out for us so that we might weave the elements of the classes into the reality lying in evidence before us. And what, no doubt you're wondering, is that *pattern* we should be aiming to fabricate? Why, it was staring us in the face all along. True, we didn't recognize it for what it was. But that was because our classification wasn't done astutely enough. Nonetheless, it was there.

All the while we weren't able to sense its presence, *bigness* was lurking in the dark, doing its dirty work. Yes, it was *bigness* that brought *money, politics, sociology, internationalism,* and *incompetence* all together into a deadly stew that poisoned the SSC and eventually did it in.

Take *money*: It was big money that first gave the giant project its chance. But it also brought with it big trouble. Everyone wanted a piece of the big chunk of Texas bucks, and they came in droves to have their chance at it. So they came and they fought over it without respite. Everything was oversized: there was the big moneybag state of Texas; there was the big Washington money arriving right on schedule; and there were the many power-packed, cutthroat competitors fighting to get their grubby hands on the loot.

Some who came, mainly subcontractors and companies with products and R&D to sell, just wanted their share of the cash; and, with so much of it around, they weren't skittish about grabbing all they could get. Then there were the SSC insiders and supplicants, most of whom wanted the influence and the power that came with money. So they too wanted to feed at the SSC trough. The result of so many wanting their piece of the action was that there was a lot of mean, ornery infighting and ill-natured, ferocious disputes going on. Could the SSC survive such threatening goings-on within its body? No, *bigness* was preparing to take its toll.

Then there was *politics*: The SSC was born in political maneuvering; it thrived in it; and it died in it. Big men were called for and big men were there. The Texas politicos gave birth to the SSC; the Reagan team instilled life and reality into it; and the withering away of Texas political strength, combined with Reagan's departure and the ambitions of a few conniving members of a Congress with rapidly changing faces, finally gave it the legislative kiss of death. You see, *bigness* means big political power, but it also means big political vulnerability!

And what about *sociology*? Naturally, it played a very crucial part in the tearing asunder of the SSC. The U.S. science community was torn apart by the big monster thrust upon it. Divisiveness, intolerance, selfishness, betrayal, and treachery showed their ugly faces, and pushed the doomed project into an untenable defensive posture it was never able to shake off. Attacked from within by the project's own self-serving and ambitious family, eating away while the big structure decayed; and from the outside by its jealous and fearful science compatriots-gone-sour, terrified of being eaten alive by the giant come among them; the SSC had no one on the scene man enough to save it from its sad fate.

As for *internationalism*, it was a latecomer to the death scene, and entered the playing field only to help thrust in the final stabs. True, U.S. nationalism was very strong at the start, and certainly infuriated the other Big Science countries. Still, when the SSC was on its last legs, and the international community had a chance to demonstrate its all-for-one – one-for-all qualities, the idea of internationalism was a big flop and fell flat on its face. This showed, once and for all, that in the nationalism versus internationalism war of philosophies, the self-interest intrinsic to nationalism always wins out. So it was that when the SSC was in need, in answer, the true colors of internationalism – a cowardly blend of yellows – were hoisted up to blow in the wind, and the poor project was left to fend for itself.

Finally, there was *incompetence*: The *bigness* of the project asked for much from the men running it; but the SSC management couldn't come through and was ripped apart by it. The management succumbed in the face of the myriad demands of *bigness*, and became weak and indecisive. It couldn't handle its own technical staff, which kept dropping the ball. With mistake after mistake after mistake piling up, unheeded, the SSC's management was ever in need of more money and forever in a begging mode. It couldn't handle the companies that came to Waxahachie to claim their share of the loot. With no teeth or smarts, Schwitters and his henchmen just gave them everything they asked for. Then, the pièce de résistance, the project's management couldn't handle the all-important politicos. The SSC top guns – really duds – were either scientists or recycled bureaucrats, and neither of these types had the capacity to weather the changing winds and swirling storms of the political world. When strength of character and the courage to stand tall were so needed, these men simply withered, wilted, and wasted away. So the SSC, abandoned by all, approached its bitter end alone.

So there you have it. Maybe one class was more important than the others at one time or another, but their order of importance changed continually as the long death march went its route. In the end, all the standard classes played their essential parts in the unfolding drama. So it was that, ironically, "*All of the above*" was the right answer after all. And what about *bigness*? In truth, *Bigness* is the glue that makes it possible to tie together the proper choice of the elements of each class that jointly caused the SSC's head to be unseemly and unkindly cut off. It made all the SSC's deficiencies bigger. It exaggerated them; it worsened them; it activated more of them simultaneously; and it made them uncontrollable. Ultimately *bigness* was the project's death knell. Yes, just like ISABELLE a decade earlier, it was *bigness* that killed the SSC.

* * * * *

Six Feet Under

No matter what the underlying causes, the facts of life and death are exquisitely singular and immutable. They are firm and unyielding, and lie well outside the pale of human understanding. From them, there is no appeal. And such is the fate of all earthly things. So it was that by an act of the Congress of the United States of America to mark the event, the SSC passed away in October 1993. The formal announcements were definitive, unconditional, and final. On October 26, URA's Bulletin reported coldly but with somber undertones, "This afternoon, the House passed the revised Energy and Water Conference Report by a vote of 332-81. It now proceeds to the Senate, where quick passage is possible before going to the President for signature and enactment." That was it: *death by decree*. The New York *Times* actually foresaw and predicted the end a week earlier, when on October 22, Michael Wines screamed on page 11, "Conferees, After Final Wrangle, Officially Kill the Supercollider." His text started, "A congressional panel officially killed the $11 billion Superconducting Super Collider today, but not before a final bitter wrangle between the members of the House and Senate conference committee over how lavish to make the burial." It went on, "The House members prevailed, just as they had Tuesday, when the House voted for the third time in 16 months to delete the supercollider's budget from an annual water-projects bill." Wines also brought out the political side of the congressional struggle with his comment, "The clear loser was Senator J. Bennett Johnston, a Louisiana Democrat, who had led the Senate's charge to save the project but who conceded defeat after Tuesday's vote in the House." It was a long and politically packed fistfight lasting for two years. But in that short time the extraordinary Texas strength, which over many years had systematically been built up in Congress, dissipated, leaving only a shadow of what it had previously been. It was a textbook demonstration – as if any convincing at all were needed – of how swiftly things in this world can change. Bennett Johnston, an old powerhouse and still a man to contend with, was, in the SSC's hour of need, acting alone on behalf of the creaky project. However, without the vigorous help of a strong

Texas contingent, he couldn't by himself hold back the budget cutting zeal of the rapidly changing House, where Newt Gingrich and his cohorts in conspiracy had begun to show their political muscle, the result of which was that, within a few years, they opened wide the floodgates to an onrush of congressional conservatism. It was the time for the new kids on the block to strut their stuff; and those little guys in the House, Boehlert of New York and Slattery of Kansas, won the day for the lofty sounding conception of fiscal integrity that was really no more than highly overrated flimflam. Anyway, that's the way it was done; that's the way the SSC was doomed.

Although in just such a manner was death's seal planted on the SSC's burial casket, the forces actually governing and directing the action originated in an unearthly realm. Yes, the fate of Big Physics rested in hands far beyond the ken of mortal men. To their misfortune, the men of science, filled with conceit and audacity, and far too brash and arrogant, attempted to approach too close to the business of the heavens. In hindsight, they should have recognized that there are limits to knowledge aspired to and should have settled for less. You don't fool with the gods! Thus, because foolish men tempted the fates once too often, in a fit of ill temper these fickle ministers took the grandest of all dreams from humanity and dimmed the lights in Texas. Using *bigness* as their destructive instrument, determined to preserve their privacy, the gods made themselves felt and made it clear to mankind that their domain was off-limits to living men. For science's gross effrontery, the harsh punishment meted out was that the waiting-to-be-born star conceived by men with hopes for glory, that temple for man's enlightenment meant to honor the gods, was ripped away and not to be. So it was that the SSC passed into oblivion, into the *obscure darkness* that's forever.

* * * * *

The Professor and his Student
A Parable of a sort
I
The Old Man's Story of Big Physics Begins

Once upon a time, there was an old professor and his young student. They studied particle physics together and became close – friends, you might say. The old man, his active work-filled days far behind, had learned well the ways of the world. He knew much, but time had taken its toll; and, for him, *doing* was a thing of the past. On the other hand, the youngster, his future still before him, was ambitious and anxious to get moving. He knew little of what life held in store for him, but his youth gave him the self-assuredness that whatever it was, he would be able to conquer it. One day the bright-eyed inquisitive young man asked of his mentor, "Why were we stopped from doing the great experiments? We're scientists. That's what we do. It would've been so cool, such a thrill, to uncover nature's knowledge storehouse. So why weren't the facilities completed? Why was the opportunity of a lifetime so callously taken from us?" His mentor smiled knowingly, with a wisdom that can come only with age. He thought a bit before answering, and then said, "That's the way the world is. There are ups and there are downs. Fortune chose us to be at a place and time when we are on a down side.

But I can see in your face that maybe I'm being a little too glib for you. I guess I should try to clarify what I want to say. Let me see: How about this? Perhaps it was because we'd gone too far, too fast; and so the gods insisted that we had to be stopped. We're only human after all and can handle only so much of the glaring light of truth."

Seeing that his student wasn't in tune with these remarks, the professor shifted gears: "I've no doubt that these words seem woefully inadequate to you. However, I can tell you that I've been through such disappointing experiences myself, and, although for me it's all over, I can frankly tell you that I feel your pain in not being able to push forward with all your heart. God knows your generation deserves the right to probe into the unknown just as mine had." The old man stopped for a moment to rest. A bit winded from the emotion he was feeling, he took a deep breath, shook his head, and went on: "Before going on any further, I must get it off my chest and admit to you my generation's culpability in putting you in the spot you're in. For sure, we of the older generation didn't do right by you. However, although you should know that it was more innocence than greediness, more misjudgment than mendacity, that brought us to this state, there are no excuses for the mistakes we made, and I won't attempt to offer any. Because the lamentable loss you've suffered is final and irreversible, I can only tell you how much regret I feel in my heart for what happened. I can well understand that the price you've had to pay for our mischief is not easily forgiven. But I sincerely and profoundly hope that you can see it in your heart nonetheless to do so."

The professor stared expectantly at his student. But all he could detect was a kind of glumness. The silence that ensued caused him some discomfort, so he continued talking: "A thought just occurred to me. Perhaps it's worth briefly stepping back and going over it all for you. I'm not doing this in the spirit of *mea culpa*; nor am I trying to justify either my generation or myself. In fact, I can promise to tell you all that I know, and to give it to you straight from the shoulder. There'll be no watering down in what I have to say. Maybe it will be of some help to you or maybe it won't, but it's the best I can do." He turned, averting his eyes from those of his younger colleague, as if he were ashamed of his role in the affairs he was on the verge of talking about. Then, turning back to face the youngster and seeing no objection, he went on. "If you don't heed history's failures, you are bound to repeat them," the old man told the young one in a tone of voice that mocked the old cliché. Somehow, triggered by that thought as well as the manner in which it came to him, a strange mixture of defiance, amusement, and remorse overcame him. It was in such a state of mind that he continued: "I couldn't resist saying that. It is so *à propos*. Just look at what happened: First there was that distressed damsel, ISABELLE, dead in 1983! Then, following so soon in her fateful footsteps, there was the SSC, dead in 1993, only a decade later! Wouldn't you agree that our failure to learn the lesson of that dictum's stark and unyielding truth of man's life on earth played perhaps the key role in the predicament you find yourself in today?"

He paused for a short spell, wistfully reminiscing about those Pollyanna days long gone, days when anything was possible, and when golden dreams and rosy expectancy filled the air. *Too bad that such opportunities were lost*, spoke the voice of his conscience. *You shouldn't have let it all slip away from you. You should have been better than that.* Holding back the tears that were just beginning to well in his eyes, he collected himself and carried on in his renowned *Herr Professor* style: "I'm going to tell you an abbreviated version of the story of Big Physics. Although considerably shortened, it's still quite long, so I hope you're ready to spare the time to listen. It's a story of great deeds and great men. But it's also a story of old age, a time when men must leave the stage. In this story, telling of my experiences and that of my colleagues, the men of physics refused to accept the absolute dictate about learning from the past that history demands of us. Alas, when finally we became painfully aware of the consequences of not abiding by this hard and fast rule, it was by then far too late. To be sure, however, our lives were not in vain. We did give birth to Big Physics; and we did dream intoxicating and magical dreams, many of which came to spectacular fruition. However, I'm loath to acknowledge that we came to like the seat of power way too much. No, we didn't graciously and timely tender it to our worthy younger successors, but instead we had to be thrown out in shame and disgrace, as the enterprise we'd built began to tumble down around us. Still, in the end, our legacy remains – both the knowledge of the gods we'd wheedled out of them and the inspired monuments we'd constructed. And that, my friend, now belongs to you.

"Yes, when it was our time to show our stuff, we really did do great things. As a result of our promoting, advancing, and nurturing the growth and development of world accelerator facilities in the last half of the twentieth century, we opened a secret entrance that allowed basic science to play with nature's many mysteries. What a knockout the new physics turned out to be! It reached heights it never had before, and gave us a hitherto unimaginable understanding of the universe we live in. So it came to pass that Big Physics entered the arena of the knowledge circus, and in quick order was the favorite of *the center ring*. It flourished famously everywhere; it went great guns; and it shook the world."

* * *

The Professor and his Student
II
America Nurtures its Would-be Competitors

"America's political agenda and implementing policies were shaped by the prevailing circumstances in the wake of World War II: The policies were governed principally by the perceived need to preserve the West's freedom from being destroyed by the aggressive and imperialistic Soviet Union; they were highlighted by the determination to help reconstruct a devastated Europe by means of the ingeniously devised Marshall Plan; and they were envisioned and formulated to prevent via the brilliantly executed Berlin Airlift of 1948 a forceful military takeover by the Russians. The thinking that lay behind the policy was that rebuilding Western Europe would be developing an ally with which to foster and cultivate a free and prosperous world.

"Seeing as how Science and Technology had been so vital in America's victory over the Nazi menace, and was the bulwark of its defense against communist incursions, the U.S. embarked on a course to sponsor and encourage the intensification and expansion of new S&T. Since basic science was seen to be the father of all S&T, it became the beneficiary of this new U.S. worldview. Thus, Big Physics was generated and on its way.

"In tune with what the U.S. was doing in Western Europe, America became entranced by the intriguing notion that free and open competition among countries on a world-wide scale was a prime road to progress; and that helping a competitor nation get on its feet would, in the long run, be better for both – and for all. Internationalism was thereby on the move and, although it was not new to the current breed of idealists, America had brought a form of heretofore-unseen realism to the idea. Sure, helping another potential power implies that, when it becomes strong enough, it will turn around and take you on. But that's the point of the policy! So it shouldn't be too surprising when it happens. If anything, it's just that sort of competition that should be desired and anticipated. We should be looking for it to come, and pleased when we see it. After all, that's what true internationalism is.

"As it happened, in a spirit of unprecedented optimism after the war, the U.S. virtually gave Western Europe its capability to do basic high-energy physics. Both politically and financially, the U.S. was a prime mover in the establishment of the CERN Laboratory in Geneva. Perhaps more importantly, it's hard to see how CERN could've become a thriving research laboratory without free access to American accelerator and experimental know-how, not to mention American dollars. So it was that America did exactly what it set out to do: it helped create its very own equally strong science competitor.

"It was in this way that the *America-versus-Europe* race for supremacy in basic physics research started. How right the American idea of international rivalry as a generator of ingenuity and productivity proved to be! In an amazingly short time, scientific instruments of unheard of dimensions were imagined, conceived, and ready to be built: the age of the giant accelerators was upon us. As early as the fifties, CERN had already become a booming lab, bustling with talent. It had truly become a contender. So, as wanted, anticipated, and planned for, a passionate U.S.-CERN competition in building accelerator facilities and doing Big Physics experiments got underway. The U.S. quickly leaped ahead with the invention of strong focusing at BNL in 1952, a monumental step that opened the door to almost limitless bigness in facilities for basic science. But CERN, not to be outdone, quickly picked up the idea, and, without skipping a beat, was back in the race. It was a breathtaking time, and a hard-fought game. And, in leapfrogging fashion, the contest was to continue without abatement into the twenty-first century."

* * *

The Professor and his Student
III
Europe Flies Ahead

"Because of the soldiers returning after World War II, and in preparation for the onrush of the baby-boomer generation, the fifties and sixties were a time when

American universities experienced a breathtaking expansion of whopping proportions. As the soldiers came home from their gloriously winning fight for freedom overseas, the U.S. government, with astute shrewdness and judiciously applied foresight, gave them their due – the opportunity to prosper and start fresh lives, to own their own little bungalows, to raise families, and to learn to their fullest potential by being afforded entrée to the university campuses across the country. To become major beneficiaries of the nation's insightful largesse, American universities were required to make discrimination of all sorts a thing of the past. They came through with flying colors. The universities opened their doors to all, and underwent a level of growth unmatched in the annals of university history.

"Flush from its dynamite performance in the noble U.S. victory to keep the world free from tyranny, and being a field of special importance in America's determination to push the frontiers of technology ever outward, university physics reaped its hard-earned and rightful rewards, surging ahead by leaps and bounds. What an inspired time it was! Research abounded. Advanced technology and basic physics became in-things to do; and young men flocked to the campuses to partake of the knowledge feast. They came to learn physics and technology; they came to learn to teach them; and they came to become researchers. To complement and enhance this swell of university physics, and to a somewhat lesser extent to egg on and further the causes of many of the other sciences, the government established a system of national laboratories, poured more than ample funds into them, exuberantly championed them, and encouraged them to function to the utmost of their capability. It was a science Camelot in the making. For scientists, it was a dream come true. Progressive and highly advanced work in experimental physics rushed forward at an unprecedented pace. Accelerator technology bloomed, and struck it rich. The fertile panoply of technologies materializing at the labs was transmuted into a wide array of particle accelerators that came to dot the nation. These brilliant contraptions were sprouting up everywhere you turned; they kept proliferating with abandon; they were upgraded when they had the inherent capacity to generate higher energy particle beams; they were superceded by newer facilities when the particle energy they could produce reached its limit; and, all the while, these magnificent machines kept getting bigger and better. Paralleling the accelerator building, original and inspired methods of doing experiments with particle beams were being dreamed up, fashioned, and put into action. In this way, the U.S. experimental program in high-energy physics, without looking back, sped swiftly and confidently toward its destiny.

"As was the American way, scientists from Europe were welcomed into American accelerator-based facilities. Meanwhile, although at first propped up by American know-how, Europe, by the sixties, was beginning to flex its accelerator muscles. With competitive facilities springing up across the Atlantic, American scientists began to venture to Europe at an ever-increasing rate. A most productive international collaboration ensued. Physicists were so enamored of it that they began to think of it as just the highly anticipated appearance of their imagined *international science*, as if it were a phenomenon natural to science sure to just go on and on. But, as it happened, it was only unrealistic idealism at work, and the idyllic picture lasted for but a brief historical moment. Yes, the illusion was fleeting and, within a few decades, would pass away like an evanescent dream. In retrospect, from no more than an elementary application of human behavior, it's obvious that it couldn't last. It was like giving a child the tools and the opportunity to take up life's challenges; but forgetting that when the child and his buddies grow up and become equals, the urge they'll have to beat the other guy and become winners will take over. Oh yes, the games people play to stay ahead of the pack, extending even to hitting a guy when he's down, will begin to intrude and eventually become the predominant mode of conduct. The ugly face of competitiveness, in the end, always wins out over the friendly, but unfortunately deceptively false and misleading, face of altruism.

"By the seventies, CERN caught up with the U.S., becoming comparable in experimental methods and technology and even a little ahead in accelerator technology. This was a stinging and hard-to-take shock to many of the men in charge of American science, who, given their past experience, perhaps thought of themselves in some super-human guise. But it really shouldn't have startled and jarred them so. Just think of it a little: It is certainly the case that, at the time, heritage-proud Western Europe had a far greater incentive to excel than America, and so was bound to mature sufficiently to pass the U.S. at some point. So why shouldn't it be then? To be sure, because the U.S. was just rambling along at a casual clip-clop, blind to Europe's spirited, enterprising attitude, driving gusto, and galloping opportunism, there was simply no avoiding the U.S. loss of its early lead. As it happened, this wide edge in ambitious aspirations and resolute purpose, apparently not evident to the looking-the-other-way Americans, ended up by propelling CERN into the position of accelerator-facilities top dog by a long shot at century's end. It was something like the plodding turtle with one thing on its mind – to win – overtaking the over-confident, arrogant, bumbling, and cock-sure hare. Too bad the U.S. science leadership was unable, or perhaps unwilling, to see this eventuality. There's little doubt that things would've turned out a lot differently if it had."

* * *

The Professor and his Student
IV
Halcyon Days Remembered

"Looking back over the last half of the twentieth century, we see three distinct stages to the international practice of high-energy physics. These three phases can be characterized by the relative number of scientists from either side of the Atlantic Ocean doing experiments on the other side. In the first phase many more European scientists came to America than the reverse. In the second phase the number of scientists traveling in either direction was about equal. In the third phase American scientists were ready and anxious to work at European facilities in ever increasing numbers, while the opposite was the case for European scientists, who'd become well satisfied where they were, thank you. The trend is unmistakable: from clear and unchallenged U.S. leadership in the fifties, to roughly equal status in the seventies, to a growing CERN advantage in accelerator and experimental development during the eighties and nineties.

"It seems straightforward enough. What's up today comes down tomorrow, as on goes the inexorable cyclic nature of things. However, life is only that simple if you pull back and look at it from afar. On the other hand, if you want to know reality as it is, with all its warts and blemishes, you've got to approach closer. But, in doing that, you almost surely won't be too happy or comfortable with what you find. Yet that's the price you have to pay for a God's-honest view of the truth zone. Nonetheless, bravely taking the plunge and delving in greater detail into the three periods, as anticipated, we come face to face with a worrisome and troubling picture: an eye-opening observation about the behavior manifested on the two sides of the Atlantic. Of course, scientists would like to believe that they're of the same character everywhere. After all, aren't they internationalist in nature? But the facts don't back this up. Their actions speak a whole different story. From the picture before us, the only conclusion we can reach is that there's a big difference between the scientists on the two sides of the ocean.

"OK, let's get to the crux of the matter: The first period was one of U.S. paternalism, where the U.S. extended a helping hand to Europe. That was the American way and hearkened back to the way the U.S. had treated a devastated Europe, even its archenemy Germany, just a decade earlier. Then came the second phase when a reversal took place. During this period, the crossover point was reached, when Europe became the technology-equal of the U.S. and began to pull ahead. For a brief moment there, it was an ideal time, when there was a quid-pro-quo, and it almost seemed as if true internationalism could actually work. Alas, it was only so during that particular interval when roughly as many Europeans were traveling west as Americans east; and this much-to-be-desired time quickly passed into history. Then the third phase arrived. As it started, an unexpected and unforeseen phenomenon came to the fore. When the European science leaders took over as number one in accelerator technology, they might've been expected to behave the way the Americans did in the fifties and sixties. If they'd actually taken on the American way, then all the high-energy physicists would've continued to be competitive, continued to be maximally productive, and continued to be level-playing-field participants in their claims to fame. In such a perfect framework, world physics – unattached to anything, with nothing to push-off on – would rise all by itself, like a person pulling himself up by his bootstraps. Yes, it would've been a time of equal opportunity for everyone, a time when all men could take their best shot for glory, a time of true internationalism, and a time when science and humanity would be the biggest winners of all. Unfortunately, real life and the true nature of mankind entered the picture, and that's not at all what happened."

The old man took a deep breath and appeared tired, but he was determined to finish his tale: "In the beginning, and at least until the crossover point in phase two, scientists on both sides of the big pond stuck firmly to the idea of free and open access to national facilities. This gracious and civilized manner of handling experiment access was made possible because of a combination of American generosity and the fact that it served the self-interests of all concerned. Everybody gained from the high-minded idealism that pervaded the atmosphere of world science. Physicists contributed what their means allowed them to, and they were permitted to be equal participants in the experimental scene and *be the best that they could be*. Whether the experimenters were from Europe, America, or anywhere else on the globe, they all became beneficiaries of the giving spirit of the times. However, although it wasn't fully evident, this pretty picture chock-full of goodness and nobility was nothing but a screen covering a build-up of nationalistic fervor threatening to blow the counterfeit façade sky high.

"As the seventies progressed, the real game being played, the one that was to be deadly to the future of Big Physics, was between the U.S. and CERN; and it was a doozy of a contest. You could feel it in the air – there was big change in the wind. With equalization being close to a reality, American magnanimousness was needed less and less, and naturally diminished. So far, so good! In parallel with the waning of overpowering American influence, competitiveness was climbing, on the way to becoming the dominant force in high-energy physics research. Hold on! I ask you, wasn't this exactly the way it was supposed to be? Of course it was. Everything was A-OK and right on target. All was exactly as it should be. Here's what was expected to follow: Competitiveness would be raised a notch; then there would be gestures of noble European bigheartedness; this would in turn lead to another step-up; and on would go the good and productive times. This was *true internationalism*, and it was good. However, there was a fly in the ointment. You see, unless bridled and shaped to do so, competitiveness doesn't naturally work in that way, as we'd all presumed. Unfortunately, there were no such controls turned on, and the dark side of competitiveness was just about ready to show its nasty, menacing face.

"Yet I still experience the joy of being a physicist in those days of the sixties and seventies. High-energy physics was young and vibrant, and was advancing at an unprecedented clip. There was so much to be done, so much to discover, and so many opportunities available. As a proton man, you could go to BNL, or to Fermilab, or to CERN to do your experiments. There was no discernible difference. All doors were wide open to you. You could get on a plane and go to Europe if that's where you decided to put your experimental gear, or you could stay in America to do your experiment. It was your choice to make. Yes, it was so easy to believe then that science had no borders. It was a time when the spirit of internationalism seemed genuinely to be on the up and up. Who would be so bold as to suggest that getting and keeping it wasn't just a piece of cake?

"Let me shift gears a little and tell you the way experiments actually worked in those halcyon days. It might well give you a feeling for why the scientists then were prone to confuse easy-to-understand international collaboration with the subtle most-difficult-to-attain *true internationalism*. Here's the picture: The available high-energy accelerator facilities were much the same on both sides of the Atlantic. Thus, it really didn't much matter where you did your experiment. You went there, got your data, and went home. Remember this was before the era of the proton colliders really got going. So, for the most part, the experimental method was via the fixed-target mode. Beams of particles were extracted from the accelerator, split up, and sent along the many beam lines. These lines were aimed at targets made of dense materials placed at the ends of the beam lines at a variety of locations around the accelerator. When the beams collided with the target material, the particles emerging were again split up and the various secondary beams were transported to the experimental setups to be examined in detector equipment situated at the ends of the secondary experimental lines. As you can see, with so many locations to choose from, there were many opportunities for the well-traveled experimenters."

The professor hesitated for a moment. His head turned a bit upward and away from his student, who was waiting for him to continue. You could almost notice a tear beginning to form, as he appeared to be overtaken by a nostalgic memory. But his silence didn't last very long. Slowly, his head lowered, and he faced his student with teary eyes. Then, with a shaky voice, he started to speak: "Yes, our generation was young then, and rarin' to go. We came from everywhere imaginable, from universities and institutions all over the world to do our thing – to do what we loved most, to do physics. We worked day shifts, night shifts, and who knows how many hours in the day! If beams were sent to us down those secondary lines, we were there to use them. We were there despite the sometimes-terrible conditions. Nothing could keep us away: not the damp environment, not the ramshackle experimental buildings out in no-man's land, and not the fussy equipment that so often refused to submit to our wishes. It didn't really faze us much. We simply braved it all, and, in the end, came through just fine. The truth is that through it all, we were happy to be there, happy to be high-energy physicists, and happy to be alive. It was our time, and we grabbed it with both hands and with gusto."

At that moment, the student, although loath to do so, interrupted the teacher from his reverie and asked him if he could possibly go over again how the experiments were done in those days gone by, when the student was but a toddler. The professor, made aware of how far he'd strayed from his intended course, pulled himself together. Naturally, he was only too willing to comply with the request; he was even a little flattered that his student was paying attention and seemed genuinely interested. Seeming to have gotten a second wind, he began: "This was the fixed-target era, before colliders came into their own. Experiments, except in rare cases, were done outside the accelerator proper, therefore permitting experimenters to move in and out without unduly involving or upsetting the facility. When a group of experimenters completed their data taking, they would just move out, taking their equipment with them, and another group would move in. Because the experiments were very small compared to today's collider standards and furthermore were localized to regions outside the accelerator proper, sometimes quite far away, it was feasible to do many experiments simultaneously. Space was ample and was no issue; and so the only limitations were how many lines were built at the facility and how intense the beams flowing through the lines were designed to be. However, compared to the freedom to do what you wanted to, these were nothing but minor nuisances.

"*But how did the universities fit into all of this*, I sense you thinking? Am I right?" The student smiled nervously and nodded in assent. "Well, at that time," the professor went on, "the universities played a major role in the experimental enterprise. They had the responsibility of conceiving, designing, and building a substantial fraction of the experimental devices. In many instances, the entire detector was built at one or a few collaborating universities, and brought to the area at the accelerator site in toto and ready to go. Actually, universities still have a role to play in today's experiments; but it's much less. What with the monster detectors used in colliders requiring big money, up-to-date technology, and great complexity, centralization is the only way, and that means the labs run the show. Thus, the universities really have little to do except provide the physicists – the users."

Then, without warning, an all-absorbing melancholy overcame the professor. There was a hint of a smile on his face that started from the edge of his lips and moved up his cheeks. He became dreamy-eyed, as if transported to a distant place, appearing self-amused and beguiled by his thoughts. He remained in that pose for almost a minute. Then, perhaps sensing the stillness, he squirmed just a little in his chair. He lifted his head and looked straight at his student. It was almost as if he were asking for permission to go on. But his student refused any eye contact. The old man appeared to be a bit befuddled. With his head bowed, his strange smile returned; and slowly, with a quivering tone of voice, he began a brief reminiscence: "How I remember that word *users*! It was such a strange way for people to describe themselves. When you think about it: who would want to be called a *user*? It has such a negative connotation. As if thinking of ourselves that way weren't enough, others thought even worse of us. The accelerator folk used to refer to us pejoratively as physichists. Well, why shouldn't they have resented and disliked us? We treated them like underlings. It must have been hard on them. They were, after all, physicists, no different from us. I wonder why we behaved so insensitively and so unfeelingly toward them, so haughtily superior. Sometimes I think of it, and it really bothers me that I could've been part of it. And it wasn't only how we treated them. There was also the problem of the distribution of funds. They fought us like hell over money; but we invariably won, always ending up with the lion's share. We had all the influence and position, you see, and took full of advantage of our superior place in the order of things, sometimes quite unfairly, I might add. Well, there's no use crying over all that now." For a moment, the professor became derailed from his train of thought, as he wondered out loud, "Could it possibly be that this quarreling and infighting might have played some part in the calamity that was to befall us all?"

Catching himself from going any further off course, he looked up, wiped his forehead, smiled, and continued, "But all that's for another lecture. Let me get on with this one. Recall that in the fixed-target way of doing things, the users would build their equipment at their home base, send it to an accelerator facility, get their results, and then return home to analyze their data. Although their experimental detectors weren't just little things you could carry around, these scientists were still in the small-science regime; and the principle of freedom of access was straightforward to apply and easy to embrace. Not only did this way of doing things provide for effective and motivating competition, but it also allowed for a quid-pro-quo check. How many experiments were done here? How many there? How much money was CERN spending to support Americans? How much was America spending on Europeans? How many scientists were traveling in one direction? How many in the other? And so on. So it was quite easy to tell if things were skewed one way or the other. The main point was that as long as the accelerator facilities on either side of the ocean were similar and being used equally, it was natural and easy to accept the ideas of internationalism and science-without-borders. But, sad to say, things changed *on the way to the forum*. Rapidly advancing accelerator technology made colliders feasible to build and operate. Because the precious and highly valued collision interaction energy was much higher in colliders, the fixed-target mode of experimentation soon became obsolete.

"In colliders, however, the experiments had to be done within the accelerator itself, using enormous detectors surrounding the circulating beam. So big were the detectors that the users themselves found that, along with those running the big collider-accelerators, they too had entered the age of bigness. As I've already indicated, the immediate consequence of this was that detectors, because they were so big, tended to become the province of the labs. From then on, the universities had less and less of a say in the matters of high-energy physics. Yes, they could remain cheerleaders, but that was about it. It was the labs that came to rule the roost. Thus, in parallel with the fixed-target mode of experimentation giving way to the collider mode, university influence of any substance and import was transferred to the labs.

"As for the university experimenters, they were caught between a rock and a hard place. The universities kept pressuring them to stay home and take care of the students, while the labs insisted that they take care of their long-time experiments on the lab site. Since they cherished their professorships at the universities, they were firm in their determination to hold on to them; however, to do the physics they were intent on doing, they had to play ball with the labs. It was a quandary for them, and, by the way, still is. They were stuck with two masters and dual loyalty, a circumstance very difficult to maneuver in. It's not a very healthy situation for high-energy physics, but nonetheless, there it is. When you come to think of it, it just could be that this corrosive and precarious state of affairs was one of the ripples that combined with others to build up into a tidal wave that sent American high-energy physics into its all-too-stormy and rough-and-tumble downward slide as the twentieth century took its leave of us."

* * *

The Professor and his Student
V
Big Physics Brings World Physics Down to Earth

The professor and his student took a short break to relieve their over-filled bladders. But so intrigued was the student, that he was chomping at the bit, anxious to quickly return to get on with the rest of the story. He did just that, and soon after, the professor followed. Buoyed by the youth's enthusiasm, the man that teaching meant so much to didn't waste a moment, immediately moving into the next episode in his sad tale: "We left off at the point in our story where Big Physics was born, with all its myriad consequences for scientists and science alike, including the psychosocial, the economic, the political, as well as the day-to-day practical ones. As the particle energy in the new collider designs went up and up, the required facilities, for both accelerators and detectors, became bigger and bigger, and fewer and fewer. I should call your attention to that little phrase I used, *fewer and fewer*. It appears, at first glance, to be innocuous, but in fact its consequence for high-energy physics was indeed profound. The fact of really big collider facilities portended a future when high-energy facilities would become less and less practical to duplicate. Yet any experimenter worth his salt would surely want to be at one of the very small number of available facilities. So, if this condition of *few facilities – little choice* were really to come to pass, we would have a case of too many mouths to feed with too little food on hand to feed them. Nevertheless, it did indeed happen that facilities started to become limited to a single lab in each world-region and unique to that particular region.

"OK, so you have the general sense of what transpired. Now let me tell you about some of the historical details of the experimental transition that took place. Then you can judge for yourself whether things could have been different or not. The technology that permitted the accumulation of protons and anti-protons to a level sufficient to make collider experiments at very high energy worth doing was developed over the decades of the sixties and seventies. Colliders, with their much higher experimental capability compared to the old-fashioned fixed-target mode, were without a shadow of a doubt the way to go. Thus, once it became clear that it was practical to build them and that they could be made to work, a new mind-set took over the high-energy community, and a new way of doing experiments was in the making.

"With the technology to do them available, the age of colliders arrived with a bang: *Fixed targets* were out and *colliders* were in! Here's what then took place: By the eighties, the size, cost, and complexity of the facilities became so high that it could only mean, as I've already mentioned, that they'd have to be few in number. No one really wanted to think about what that implied, but the truth was that, if the trend continued, at some point growing facility bigness would inevitably reach the point where, for a given facility type, that number would become one. For a time, experimenters, trying to keep their universities interested and involved and to sustain a semblance of independence from the labs, still provided large pieces of equipment from home. But before long this practice began to decline and for the most part came to an end. It was that old illusion people have that the past can be kept alive in an ever-changing world. How innocent we were in those days! Anyway, thenceforth, despite the efforts to forestall or even avoid it, the facilities for high-energy collider experiments became the comprehensive, A to Z responsibility of the labs that housed them.

"Thus, these facilities – the whole kit and caboodle – were now under the out-and-out, unqualified control of government laboratories in particular world regions. The result was national centralization; and that presaged the urge and determination for each of the world's regions to accumulate Big-Physics power; and out of that arose the too-hard-to-resist temptation to use that power; and that, my friend, meant big trouble for internationalism. The upshot was that the international community's adherence to free and open access for all came to be on the verge of being severely tested by the reality of the market place as well as by the deep-seated and potent driving force of collective national pride. Until bigness, in the form of colliders, arrived, world physics, and national physics as well, flourished. The physicists seemed to have it all: Ideas came from out of the blue; experiments quickly followed suit; success was around every corner; and knowledge of our universe and of advanced technology flowed freely and abundantly from all of this. Seeing all of this happen before their very eyes, how could the physicists think other than that they were the best and that the way they did things was the best? It's quite true that most other groups weren't able to establish and work harmoniously in a system characterized by freedom of access and open competition; but scientists were different. Yes, they naïvely believed that it was natural to their class to be able to do so. They further believed that they could continue on in this way indefinitely, unstifled and unimpeded by irrational passions, by greedy self-seekers, and by the pernicious face of nationalism.

"Actually, there were a variety of circumstances from the past – interpreted by the scientists as evidence – to back up their assessment. To be sure, the examples were nothing to sneeze at, for they managed to combine hardy competitiveness and friendly across-the-ocean collaboration into a blooming and vigorously thriving internationalism. It was a dream of an idealist come true. There was the BNL-CERN competition of the late fifties and early sixties; the Fermilab-CERN competition of the seventies and eighties; and a SLAC-CERN competition in the eighties in the area of electron colliders. Besides CERN, the U.S. was also in direct competition with other basic science centers around the world: SLAC versus DESY (Hamburg, Germany) in the seventies and SLAC versus KEK (Tsukuba, Japan) in the eighties. Even if I haven't covered all the bases, I'm sure that you can see by now what an out-of-sight, *très bon* thing high-energy physics had going for it. It almost appeared for a while as if the world science community had worked out a scheme within which free and friendly competition and crowning achievement could walk along happily together, hand in hand. But soon, unforeshadowed and unanticipated by anyone, this inimitable and as-good-as-they-make-'em system – in which the facilities were national but the science done in them was international – came face to face with its muscle-bound and invincible nemesis: yes, it was bigness – stemming from the so-desired highest-that-can-be-gotten energy of the upcoming colliders – that came upon the stage and promptly put an end to this wayward fiction."

* * *

The Professor and his Student
VI
The Sad Legacy of Men Who Overreached

"With bigness came political visibility. As facilities grew in cost, the politicians wanted to know what they were getting out of it; and it didn't take them long to figure it out. For a man with a district or country to represent, having a national lab in his backyard was quite a plum. What he saw wasn't just the basic science that, on the face of it, the facility was built for. That was the least of it. There was so much more. There was the enhancement of business, technology, and education that came along with it. There was the influx of first-rate, high-class workers, particularly scientists and engineers. Furthermore, it was an attractor for high-tech enterprises, academic institutions, and even industrial concerns. All in all, it raised cultural standards and played a part in the modernization of the community. So, contrary to what scientists had presumed to be the case, basic science took a back seat to the forefront technologies that the national labs generated. That's what the countries truly valued as national treasures. In fact that's the way it had always been, but *smallness* kept it well hidden in the background. When facilities were *small*, they simply weren't worth enough to create political tensions over. Why should a politician cash in some of his hard-won chips unless it was for something substantial? However, when bigness came on the scene, the political floodgates opened wide. Once this happened, it was a completely new ballgame. The science community, with its deeply held belief that it could determine alone and without interference how science was conducted, found that others, stronger than it was, also wanted to run the show. With the advent of bigness, technology and money became the issues of critical value and central concern. Everyone wanted in on the action. Governments wanted to control both the technology and the cost, and business wanted to get its share of the pie. In the face of such power, the science community was helpless.

"As it is, scientists are members of a collegial community. Yes, a few daring and fearless men did crop up in the sixties and seventies, and did have the force of will and the management know-how to build some relatively large facilities. But when bigness – the true kind – showed up as the face of the future, the community put its tail between its legs and ran scared. Where were the leaders then, those who were empowered with sufficient ruthlessness to carry off such endeavors of bigness – the building of truly big accelerator labs? Unfortunately, there was no one with spirit and heart big enough to step up, grab the ball, and run with it. There was simply no one willing to take on such a venture, so risky to his career and to his self-esteem; or perhaps no one really knew how to get the job done; or perhaps the community just didn't get it, didn't really understand what was going on in its midst. So what did the physicists do? To be blunt, they hid their heads in the sand. Just give a moment of thought to the scheme scientists worldwide actually devised. What foolishness and naïveté they showed when the best they could come up with was to present to their governments, via the International Committee on Future Accelerators (ICFA), the idea of a world machine. They innocently thought they could apply the CERN model of internationalism to the national technological giants of a competitive world prospering beyond reason. In reality, the conditions in which CERN was created, the coming together of the devastated countries of Europe in the forties, were a far cry from the modern geopolitical state of affairs. In a nutshell, the idea of a world machine was silly. Everyone in the know recognized immediately how out of touch it was with human nature and world affairs; so, as it happened, the influential politicians simply ignored it. The truth is that it was nothing but a diversion. You see, the men of Big Physics were at a loss as to what to do, and needed a little breathing space. This gave it to them. But there was a price to pay for this little excursion into idealism: It was to cause Big Physics to languish. And, frankly, it will remain so until scientists come to see the light and do what has to be done: embrace the inevitable nationalism, make it work, and devise a system to make World Big Physics be *the best that it can be*."

Talking about making the choice between internationalism and nationalism brought the teacher back to the emotion-packed feelings he had had when he was in the middle of the disputatious debate. He had believed so deeply in the grand notion of internationalism in science, and found it disheartening to have to adopt the *America first* mode of conduct. He wondered whether he could explain or at least describe this forced conversion, but deep down sensed that it wasn't even worth the effort. Why did it matter anyway? It certainly wasn't relevant to what he was talking about. Besides, his student surely didn't care about it, at least not at this time. In any case, he realized that his time for deliberation was done. He just had to get on with it and finish up.

Just as he was about to start talking, it occurred to him that, when all was said and done, his student and friend didn't really want to hear any excuses for what happened to American Big Physics in its twilight season. OK, no excuses! On the other hand, the young man did deserve, at the very least, to know some of the facts and the reasons behind them. So he steeled himself for the task, and sprang into it: "Not long after the world machine idea surfaced in the mid to late seventies, the notion crumbled at the Snowmass 1982 conference, where the idea of an American supercollider was born. Yes, it's true, America chose to go it alone; and as a result that was the end of internationalism for basic science. With the American big one off and running, it could've been a big boost for American science. But what could've been is surely not what interests you. The question you'd like answered is certainly, what actually took place? Well, I'll take a shot at that one, and do the best I can in the short time we have left.

"Soon after the 1982 meeting, in the wake of winning the race for the W, CERN, with its new star, Carlo Rubbia, took up the gauntlet and prepared for the emerging new game against America. This time the U.S.-CERN contest that erupted within the staid and conservative world science community would be between two labs, CERN and the SSC, both of which had pretensions to become giants. CERN, run by a conglomerate of countries from Western Europe, seemed no match for the great superpower of the western world. But this didn't in the least put off Carlo the giant killer. He'd been through the mill before, and had a good feeling for what to expect. He knew in his heart that he would emerge on top, the world's champ, just where he'd been when the W found its way into his waiting hands. Who could beat out Carlo the king anyway?

"As it happened, the U.S. had not fully appreciated the weakness generated in its own Big Physics enterprise through years of hostility, backstabbing, spiteful enmity, and bad blood within its national lab system. The consequence was a distressing and pitiful lack of inspired, gutsy, and iron-willed men of science who could do the seemingly impossible. Furthermore, America hadn't counted on the opposition being led by a fierce and passionate visionary like Carlo Rubbia. Here was a big bruiser who played hardball for keeps and was not one to mess with. Carlo was a man of many faces and very difficult to fathom. He could be a charmer and a cajoler. But beware of that beguiling mask he wore, because he could be easily transformed into a master manipulator and deceiver. Even after the U.S. decided to go forward with the SSC project, Carlo fought back with an almost fanatical will and burning desire to win. Underestimating the formidable and irrepressible Carlo was undoubtedly one of the American science community's biggest mistakes.

"The intercontinental engagement was being played out during phase three of the U.S.-CERN war, when more Americans wanted to work in Europe than the reverse. You see, in the eighties, the SSC was still far off, and CERN was way ahead in high-energy experimental facilities. Using this advantage, Carlo, in an attempt to cow U.S. scientists, began to touch on the subject of an international entry fee for doing experiments. At the same time, he went even further along the intimidation route by emphasizing at every opportunity how much better of the two Europe was. Although it wasn't true, at least not yet, his approach seems to have worked, for he scared the living daylights out of the

Americans. With America already injured by catty and venomous infighting, Carlo saw his chance to pour salt over the open wounds. Yes, he was certainly ruthless, and took from the American physicists what they needed most, their self-confidence. Even as he was dealing with the American opposition, Carlo found the energy to turn inward toward his home base and formulated an ambitious plan for the Large Hadron Collider (LHC) project. He instilled in the CERN top echelon the incentive and the desire to compete with the great superpower across the Atlantic. This, in itself, was no mean task. But he went further and convinced them that they had the capability of doing so, even in the era of bigness. With Rubbia as the project's leading proponent and CERN's world ambassador, they even began to believe that CERN could actually come out on top. In truth it was unlikely, but not impossible! As it turned out, Rubbia was right on. What happened was more than he could ever have imagined possible.

"In 1993, as Congress dictated, the SSC threw in the towel. Its sudden and irretrievable demise exceeded even the hopes and dreams of Mister Pollyanna himself. Within a few years, as the twenty-first century was dawning, the American competition lay dead in the water, and CERN was alone as the world leader in Big Physics. With the SSC out of the way and CERN still holding the ongoing experimental edge, Carlo was the hands-down winner. With Carlo egging on the CERN management, they really stuck it to the arrogant Americans by negotiating a highly inflated LHC entry fee of about half a billion dollars. Frankly speaking, don't be surprised if it actually turns out to be even more than that. Anyway, there you have it. That's the story: Big Science internationalism came to its resting place six feet under; the notion of an entry fee was in; and a United States, mortally weakened in Big Physics, bowed its head and paid up for a place at one of the big detectors for the LHC, scheduled to be ready sometime between 2005 and 2010. The LHC is still not a sure thing; but American Big Physics, at least for this generation, is indeed at its journey's end. In a word, it's kaput."

As the professor expected, the student wasn't convinced. The impression emanating from the youngster was that of blaming the old man for his predicament. The boy was obviously confused, and sat for a moment in the silence that engulfed the room. Then he defiantly sat up in his chair. His face scrunched up in exasperation and resentment. His eyes widened and his mouth and nostrils flared. Passion oozed from his every pore. He looked like a bull ready to attack. Although he appeared to have something to say, he was tongue-tied. However, after a moment or two, the redness in his face faded. Becoming somewhat calmer, he found himself able to speak. Quite unsure of himself, in a tremulous voice, he broke the silence, and poured his heart out: "I still don't get it. I just don't understand why you and the rest of your professor friends did what you did, and especially why you couldn't do any better. You're so smart. Was that really the best you could do? Others were able to make big facilities before you, men like Ken Green, Pief Panofsky, and Bob Wilson. Even if the SSC was bigger, so what! All you had to do was imitate what the successful builders of the past did, only do more of the same. It can't be that different, that much tougher. Ah, what's the use? I guess your generation was just self-destructive. Something inside of you forced you to fight each other, and eventually kill each other off. And with the dead bodies went the SSC and my future too! You simply couldn't get your egos in check. But, why? It's so self-defeating, so stupid. Why did you have to play those mind games? Why was it so important to you to beat the other guy? Why was it so important to show the others how much better you were? Why was it so important to you to show them who was boss? Why couldn't you just go out there, take yourselves as you were, be men, and get the job done? I can only tell you that from where I stand, it sucks! There's just nothing for us young guys. You simply left us no alternative but to fend for ourselves. I guess I'll just have to go out and be a banker or some such thing. Or, perhaps being a waiter or a taxi driver is all I'm suited for." The student, brusquely shaking his head, abruptly stopped speaking. He appeared to be totally discouraged and worn out. While wondering if he'd gone too far, he looked at the gray, downcast, and wrinkling face of his teacher who felt a great heaviness in his heart. Time had indeed taken its toll of the old man. The professor was despondent, and dismayed at the student's outburst. He hadn't at all anticipated the turn things had taken. But words had run out. There was simply no more to be said. He appeared terribly old as he turned and silently shuffled out the door, leaving the student alone to ponder his future.

PART III

Emberglow

Chapters

7. A Tale of Two Labs

With all the yarns spun, the tale is done. The actors have left the stage. It is now left to you to try to understand these men and their plights as they passed through history's grinding machine. Then, if it so moves you, you are free to cast your judgment upon them.

In the beginning of their journey, they were all filled with boyish hopes. As the landscape appeared before them, with the awesome mountains they had to conquer in full view in the distance, they welcomed the challenge with open arms; and they praised the Lord for the opportunity to take it on. Dreams of inspired feats spurred them ever forward; and they were further emboldened by their spirited and boundless confidence that in the end they would come to touch the stars. It's not as if they really had a choice, for the desire and the need to excel was in their bones; it was instilled in them throughout their upbringings and from their past experiences; and perhaps it was even deeply embedded in their genes. Being young, they blindly plowed ahead, oblivious to the reality that lay in front of them, never even giving it a second thought. They hadn't yet guessed that on the other side of the hill would be still another challenging height to scale, and that eventually they would come upon one that would beat them and throw them down on the mat for the count. Thus, ignorant of the ways of the world, they went on. That's how it is with the young and foolish – thank heaven for that. When all is said and done, don't we just love them for such brashness in the face of awesome nature? Don't we just love them for their brazen audacity, the hallmark of the pioneer? Without such nerve and such impudence, how could these men of fortune exist? Yes, frontiersmen they were – all our actors – and as such, they glimpsed the forest with stars in their eyes, even as they failed to assess the deceptive trees that would turn out to halt their trek into the unknown land. Still their journey was to the good fortune of all, a guidepost to mankind and its destiny. For, although they weren't able to cross the great divide themselves into the land where lay the ultimate truth, they left maps for future generations. They threw out lines of breadcrumbs to follow for those who would stoop to pick them up; and it very well might be that one of these lines could actually lead to the place where shines the radiant light from which all in our universe originates.

All these men, who were determined to push Big Physics to its limits, innocently stretched beyond their reaches and in the end grasped the bitter fruit of defeat. In looking back and studying their stories, it has become clear that they were up against a foe that they really had no chance to overcome. It was the most formidable opponent of all, and only too late for them did it come into focus, when they finally were able to make out that it was none other than they themselves.

* * * * *

By now, all the events have gone by. They are forgotten by most, either because they meant little to them, or more likely because they meant too much. Yet, for some, the memories linger on. One of the major threads of our story dealt with two great laboratories: one – BNL – erected in a godforsaken, desolate former army camp on Long Island, sixty miles east of New York City, the other – Fermilab – rising up out of the sprawling farmland on the Midwest plains, thirty miles west of Chicago. The first-born sprang from the flatlands near the town of Upton in 1946, and the younger lab was born twenty-one years later on the fallow earth of Batavia, under the dark cloud of being passionately resented by its older sibling in the East. Over the decades following the coming of the second-born, there was an unending series of divisive disputes, hostile skirmishes, and inimically-minded, at-each-other's-throat sniping, all characterized by that special ferocity and bad blood of brothers at war. Big Physics in America was a house divided against itself.

With each lab grabbing what it could, there never seemed to be enough to share. Just the other's presence in the competitive bidding for new projects, facility upgrades, enhanced operations, and such was like having a red flag waved in front of an enraged, foaming-at-the-mouth bull. Each wanted more money, more people, and more work, even if it couldn't handle any more and would only become overloaded. So long as it would ensure that the other wouldn't be able to get at the government booty, such conduct simply couldn't be resisted, couldn't be overcome. As it happened, time was not healing; and, as the hands on the clock kept turning, there was no alleviation of the smoldering enmities and jealousies. On the contrary, things just got worse. Panicky apprehensiveness, spiteful grudge-bearing, and contemptuous loathing were pervasive, and any idea of fair play, of giving the other an even break, or of an *entente cordiale* were about as far from view as it is possible to imagine. The animosity, the resentment, and the acrimony were all but irreversible and there seemed no alternative but a continuing battle to the death.

Following none of man's rational rules, as often happens in life, the *adversary named change* was not where it was expected to be. Here's what happened: The two American labs were going eyeball to eyeball, with venom in their hearts, under the mistaken notion that a winner would emerge that way. What a surprise they were in for! They had an obsessive fixation for gnawing away at each other, eating at each other's guts, and remorselessly undermining and crippling each other. But that turned out to be not at all a contest to determine which one would come out on top, but rather to be a process that sapped the energy from them and served only to gravely weaken both. Thus, there they were: out of gas, damaged, de-fanged, and ripe for the taking. That was a state of affairs that no one – not the muckety-mucks of the science community, the government, or the labs themselves – foresaw coming. Now isn't that a crock of bullshit? How could they have missed it? The two labs were hacking away at each other and emasculating each other. *But the labs insisted that they had things under control*, you could've heard the clowns-in-command sheepishly bleat. Such fools were these men given the responsibility for keeping America *number one* in Big Physics that they actually believed this garbage. Of course, we now know with the benefit of hindsight that to find the real competition they should've been looking across the Atlantic. Frankly speaking, well before the two labs began their warring ways, they really should've been doing just that. After all, looking ahead was their job. Why else were they put on top to lead the flock? In any case, if they'd taken the trouble to look – little as it was – that would've sobered them up some, and certainly would've caused them to change their ways at home. While the two lumbering labs were slugging it out in America, and flushing their superpower advantage down the toilet, Western Europe's CERN lab –

coming of age, ripening, shooting up like a streak of blue lightening, and exhibiting scintillating performance – erupted on the scene and made its move to become the world leader in Big Physics.

Although a little late on the uptake, when the United States finally noticed that a foreign player had entered the fray to vie for the top spot in basic science, it clearly had to pick up the challenge. Being the great superpower of the western world, it was not of a nature to suffer such an upstart lightly. However, with their blue-ribbon labs, BNL and Fermilab, completely unprepared to carry the country's torch, the government, with a wealth of resources at its disposal, found a different way to face the European threat to American high-energy physics supremacy. Choosing to ignore its two labs that squandered money, lost their imagination, and blew their lead, America began readying itself to build a giant accelerator – a super giant – such as the world hadn't yet seen. Launching such a thing into the Big Science wars would then be America's fitting response to the European try at overtaking it. In such a way did the U.S. plan to return to its proper place *sitting on top of the world* as befits such a mighty power. Via its apparent capacity for prevailing at the bigness game – meaning that it had big money, unlimited ingenuity, and the spirit of *toujours l'audace* – it set its sights on recapturing what it had temporarily lost because of the internecine bloodletting in its national lab system. Thus, America, let down by its own prodigal labs that frittered away their chance to beat CERN to the long-sought W particle, altered its course. Overtly, America continued scrambling to bring the W prize home, although it was clearly a lost cause. However, behind the scenes, some of the deep-thinking, free-wheeling American minds were turning their attention to the really big one that they were oh so sure would be the basic-science capstone of the twentieth century.

In the meantime, BNL and Fermilab, the two siblings locked in mortal combat in a dance of death, were reduced to being but pawns in a bigger game that America was conjuring up. Adding insult to injury, blown into their faces was the dust whipped up into the air by the European feet racing swiftly by en route to the W. By then, the two U.S. labs just couldn't have missed the reality that had come about. Doubtlessly, they must have begun to realize the shocking truth that their unseemly, self-defeating behavior toward each other had forfeited either of their claims to stardom. How distressing it was! Still, that wasn't all! There was even more bad news coming to knock them for another loop. Hitting them head-on was the awful truth that there was no turning back. Their course in life had been fixed, and there was no one to blame for it but themselves.

As for the labs' scientists, unappetizing as it was for them, there was no recourse but to continue on with the life they'd arranged and settled into. They'd put themselves in a box with no way out. What an intellectually impoverished way of life it meant, but that's what they were stuck with. Just imagine what it was like! There were no incentives to motivate them: There was nothing worth fighting for, nothing to shoot for, and nothing to put their hearts and minds into. No, there was no *gold* on the horizon to spur them onward. What a measly existence they'd come to! They had to go to their labs each morning to put in their *nine-to-five* hours, go through the motions of doing useful work, and then leave at the end of the day with nothing of worth accomplished. It was not a condition to be wished on any man, even your worst enemy. Nonetheless, that's the way it was. These once vital men of two once-great labs could only watch as spectators as others took the reins of power and, with prestige, honor, and stature dancing in their desirous gazes, pressed on to secure their places in history. As for the losers, they were left holding the bag filled with rotted fruit.

No matter how much thought and muscle they were willing to put into it, the two labs simply didn't have the ability to change what they'd wrought. There was nothing left for them but to go on smacking away at each other. You see, that's all they knew how to do. Only now they were fighting, not for the whole pot, but rather for the scraps thrown to them by the newly arrived cake-eating SSC elite. What a heartrending lesson was learned! Back in the days when the two truculent, trigger-happy labs were in the midst of their pre-SSC cutthroat rivalry, what they thought were diamonds worth fighting for, and even dying for, were only ordinary pebbles in the grand scheme of things. They were off on wild goose chases, letting the golden goose slip from their grasps, while CERN and *Master Carlo* were on the track of the real thing. So it was that the two brother-labs sold their souls to Lucifer, and now it was too late to be released from the pact they'd made with him. You don't fool with Mister D! So, in the end, they'd left themselves naked, with no open options available. They could only persevere and hope for the best, while lying in vermin-infested beds of their own making.

* * * * *

With life's ironies seeming to show no bounds, as time passed, the two American labs – notwithstanding their continuing onerous ill-will for each other, and their still being at cross-purposes with the Establishment for bringing in the SSC in the first place – actually came to see a measure of their heart's covert desires realized. It was such an unexpected gift from heaven; yet, there it was, as clear as day, before their very eyes. The American super giant began collapsing under its own overbearing weight, and soon fell to earth with a thud. To top it off, the only other big collider in the works, the LHC pseudo-giant across the Atlantic, began to experience severe growing pains and to exhibit the classic symptoms of over-reaching – conspicuous anxiety, money deficits, and incessant delays. Being at the bottom of the barrel for more than a decade, each of them, BNL and Fermilab, almost forgot what it was like to be top-drawer and to wear the crown. But it was now again within eyeshot. Although it wasn't apropos to openly party and display their jubilation, this sweet bounty made for much private rejoicing. One might well question whether the suffering or the death of others should be joyously celebrated at any time, publicly or privately. Certainly it wasn't apt to beat the drum or sound a fanfare for either the sorry fate of the big U.S. collider or the good possibility of the same happening at CERN; and whether it was cricket to take some inner satisfaction or keen pleasure from these occurrences was dubious at best. Nonetheless, they did feel some perverse sense of vindication in the fall of the SSC behemoth as well as in the hoped-for and expected descent of CERN's mini version.

Well, all that is neither here nor there. Despite the seeming unfairness, the reality is inescapable: It was a clear-cut and unambiguous victory for the two self-seeking-above-all-else labs. However, there was a second side to the victory coin. On the darker side, you could see that the victory was in fact a Pyrrhic one, because what they cherished so deeply, basic science, was to be the ultimate loser in the whole messy big-collider business. Still, on the brighter side of the coin, the two mischievous siblings came out of it all still alive and kicking; and, strangely, they were valued and appreciated more than they had been before the days of the SSC. Thus, as unexpected as it had seemed just a short time before, with the twenty-first century fast approaching, the two combative labs that had behaved so greedily, so recklessly, and so imprudently were nevertheless given another chance.

The egregious, unmitigated failure of the supercollider had the unanticipated effect of making life easier for the two American bad-boy labs – and, as the saying goes, *don't look a gift horse in the mouth.* The new rules were not half bad for them: go with the flow; give as little as needed, for not much is expected; don't reach too far or extend yourself too much; live the good life; and, above all, don't worry and be happy. What a difference from such a short time before! Then, so much had been demanded of the physicists, and so much had been willingly and wholeheartedly given. That was a time when magic filled the air. However, the SSC changed everything. First it came, and then after its potential existence was untimely ripped, a strange result ensued. You'd think hard times would follow. But no! Life in the two brother-labs became like one of those lazy, hazy days of the summers of our youth. All was tranquil; tension was unknown; there was nothing much to do; there was no one to look over your shoulder; there was no one to judge you; and there was no prize to win or greatness to attain. You only had to sit quietly on the veranda, in a slowly rocking hammock, with a warm breeze clearing the sweat from your brow. Of course, the summer must end; but that didn't get anybody down, for tomorrow, when winter comes, was time enough to think about that.

For the community as a whole the story was very different. The profound loss of its quintessential, once-in-a-lifetime world-beater turned Big Physics upside down. Just as the SSC died that fall day in 1993, so also did the dreams of the men who dared to imagine extracting nature's tightly kept secrets. And with their dreams gone, they lost heart; so, slinking away, they passed the torch to those unseasoned younger men who coveted it. It really wasn't much of a torch, what with Big Physics being but an emasculated version of what it had been before. But, fittingly, it was far weaker men vying for it. So it was that the life of Big Physics passed from one generation to the next just as the curtain was about to fall on the twentieth century.

Ending its half-century run on the big center stage, the Big Physics play was replaced by a different one. The new show, compared to the one just completed, was one of a lesser kind performed by new actors of a lesser breed. The old actors were gone; and with them went the driving ambitions, the ingenious inspirations, the passionate zeal, the spirited desires, the lusting after the impossible, and, sad to say, any hope for scientific and technological glory.

Time marches on and a new era came upon Big Physics. It was a hard blow to take for those who'd seen how it was in the days of yore. They simply couldn't take it. So, soon they faded into the background, retreating into a nostalgia-filled memory bank. There was an all-around new play on the stage; and in contrast to the one preceding it, it was puny. However, for the physicists, it was the only game in town. Yet, if truth be told, that's all the new guys knew how to do anyway!

So, even without the SSC, the show went on. There were new plans, new physicists, new programs, and there was new building going on. Fermilab completed its Tevatron upgrade construction, and expanded its experimental program with their *highest-in-the-world* energy of 1 TeV. How meager that sounds when compared to what the supercollider would have generated had it lived! BNL, on the other hand, built what the lab said was a new collider named RHIC, albeit four-times-lower-in-energy than the Tevatron. In reality, however, it was nothing more than *sad Lady ISABELLE II*, seeing as how it was erected from the remnants of her decaying carcass. This machine was limited to a few hundred GeV in energy; and only experiments with beams of heavy ions or polarized protons had a chance of turning out anything original. So you can see that it wasn't much to write home about.

That's what took place at BNL and Fermilab. In the larger context, American Big Physics, acting far too rashly in search of a way to remain big, hastily depleted its budget by more than half a billion bucks betting on CERN's LHC collider. Only desperation could account for such an action because this European mini-version of the SSC was already on shaky ground, with its completion date being pushed almost ten years into the twenty-first century. Anyway, that's it, folks! There ain't no more! The fact is that this new incarnation of the Big Physics enterprise couldn't hold a candle to the thrilling genuine article that existed before the twentieth century took its leave; and the conceptions envisaged were but a mere shadow of the collider aspirations of the American men who'd fought and lost their bid for science's jewel in the crown.

But such is life, with its up-down cyclic ways. Too bad the current lot were not the eager beavers and spitfire go-getters who preceded them. Still, those now-gone men of action and their deeds of the past are not forgotten. Their spirits live on in the many achievements they realized, and in the frequent visitations of these ethereal wisps to the minds of those who seek to advance by standing on their shoulders. Their memories linger in the ideas they gave to those who followed them, and in the concrete they poured, out of which came their grand and still highly valued accelerators and colliders – monuments of twentieth century Big Physics for all humanity.

In a way, these men, who played the game of life to the hilt, and gave their all for mankind, still live. Naturally, they live in what they left behind. But there's more than that. Their souls as well remain in the air that physicists breathe. Thus, they endure; and if you seek them long and hard enough, you could well catch a glimpse of them. Just hold on for a moment! There they are! Don't miss the chance! Look with all your might! *It's those grand old players, the actors from a dream-filled past. It's them all right, still strutting their stuff, but now on the street where sorrows lie hidden beneath laughing faces. Yes, they're on the avenue where shattered schemes are on the tips of the tongues of all its strollers – on the Boulevard of Broken Dreams.*

8. On the Boulevard of Broken Dreams

So many questions remained unanswered. Perhaps, Mickey thought, there were no clear, unambiguous answers to the puzzles he'd stumbled across. However, he wasn't about to concede defeat that easily – no, not Mickey. So he set out to try to discover what actually took place. In his naïveté he believed that the historical facts would suffice. But after compiling the innumerable details of what had transpired, he found that he'd ended up with nothing but the obvious remains left for all to read about, to see, and to touch. There simply was no critical discernment and no penetrating insight that sprung from them. Yet he persisted in searching through them and analyzing them as fully as he could, trying, as it were, to extract blood from a stone. As you can well imagine, soon he had to face the truth, which was that alone they told very little about what he wanted to know. The facts themselves, as he found them, were straightforward enough. Here's a brief outline: ISABELLE's life was snuffed out first; then, the SSC was given birth to keep U.S. science in the number one spot; and finally the super-duper Texas collider also fell from grace and was axed. So it was that American Big Physics crumbled under the heavy burden of these big projects that, if realized, could've made posterity sing its praises to science and to America. OK, that's what happened. But it's a superficial picture; it's highly unsatisfying; and it gives an understanding of no depth at all. Thus, driven to know more, Mickey vowed to go further and explore the *how* and *why* of it all.

Impelled onward by the many gaping holes in the story, Mickey knew what he had to do. It was evident to him that ISABELLE was at the core of what had transpired because it was from that experience that the Big Physics ball started its relentless downward roll. If he could only get to the heart of the ISABELLE matter, then, he felt confident, the story would open up to him like a blooming flower, and all would become clear. Thus he came to accept that he would have to face the question of the hour – why did the ISABELLE project fail?

With any reservations about how to proceed out of the way, and the judgment to tackle the ISABELLE *why* question made, then the fun began. This was because to find answers to that one, he had to know who did what and when; and to learn the honest-to-goodness truth about these things, he had to dig through the memories of all who knew anything about the gory details. But how does one do that? The only thing he could think of doing, in addition to seeking and researching the written record and other tangible evidence, was to go the standard route of the historian or journalist: interviewing and asking for answers from the ones involved, at least those who were alive and willing to talk to him. There were so many things he wanted to know: Who made the decision to do this or that? Were reasons given? Did anyone resist? Was the first choice made stuck to? Did change ensue? Were the losers treated with respect? Were they smashed to a pulp? When things began to go awry, were there those who demanded changes in direction or leadership? Who were they? Did they get their way? Did they come out bloodied? Were there forced removals? Who led the attacks? Who did the deeds? And on and on the questions piled one on the other in his mind. He wondered about how he would pose these questions, and about how he would act when there was a real person opposite him. He knew that when in the thick of things he'd have to think fast on his feet. He also knew that he wouldn't have the luxury of shirking confrontation; yet he'd surely have to be judicious at the same time. Difficult as it all sounded, the more he thought about it, the more he became persuaded that it was the right way to go, and the more he was determined to do it.

So it happened that Mickey bit the bullet, sought out the ones involved, and gave them the third degree – of course with the greatest of care, with kid gloves, and with the utmost diplomacy. Yes, he did it all with the fervor and aggressiveness that was characteristic of him. To be frank, he had the will, but the whole business was essentially *all Greek to him*. Still, even though he didn't know a hell of a lot about the process, he assiduously went through all the motions expected of someone seeking out a true picture of days gone by. It was a hard game to play. Nonetheless, would it were only as easy as a game of questions and answers; and, in the end, it all turned out to be nothing but wheel spinning. You see, when it comes down to snatching truth from a stingy reality, the rules of the discussion game are dramatically altered from being rational to being irrational.

Naturally, if you speak to someone, he'll give you answers – at least a lot of words. However, the result of all the time and effort expended, as Mickey found out, was only that more questions were raised: Was what Mickey told correct? Did the interviewee really know anything? Was he talking through his hat? Was he guessing? Did he want to throw Mickey off the scent? Was he frank and candid? Was the truth frightening to him? Was he telling Mickey about true reality or some dreamed-up version? Was he telling Mickey what he thought Mickey wanted to hear? Was he being deceitful? Was he betraying anyone? Was he being false? Was he trying to be honest and to tell all? Was he credible? Mickey was shaken by the magnitude of the problem he'd latched onto. As the questions roamed through his mind, caroming off each other, he was thoroughly taken aback by the onerous task he'd embarked upon. What was he getting himself into, he thought?

Doubts about what he was doing began to creep into Mickey's mind. Even belief in himself was slipping as he questioned and wondered whether he was getting anywhere. Did the type of inquiry he'd opted for really prove to reveal anything of value? Did he deal adequately with the transparent stonewalling? To what extent was there deception and even lying? How much of what he was being told could he believe? Was it *the truth, the whole truth, and nothing but the truth, so help you God*? With so much uncertainty still swirling around the affair – the many doubts and ambiguities about what he was hearing, and his feelings of insecurity about whether he had the ability to sort things out – how could he put much credence in his interpretations or confidently buy into the saga he was piecing together and giving words to? Actually, it's quite possible and even likely that the renditions of what took place that he picked up were nothing but speculations or even fabrications, all related to him as sure-fire recollections. Nonetheless, Mickey stubbornly pursued this line of attack. Always the optimist, he pushed the approach as far as it would go, and then some. But not even the ever-persevering Mickey could sidestep the inescapable limitations of people's memories or the deliberate attempts to mislead him and steer him off-course. So, inevitably he became stuck in the mud; and there he was, flailing about, yet stubbornly seeking the magic portal that would lead him out of the morass into the light.

Still, as off-putting and disheartening as it was for him up to that point, it was only the beginning. His upcoming quandaries would be even worse. No, there's no avoiding that once you've walked through the door armed with that all-too-simple question of *who* did *what*, and once you've posed it, you'll find, as Mickey discovered, that this seemingly innocuous question forces you across a threshold where an entirely new vista unfolds before you: That oh so innocent-sounding question takes you into a hugely expanded and totally different topology with strands sprouting in a chaotic spider's web of offspring.

Mickey mused on the strands he would now have to deal with. What a mess, he thought! So many people! So many unanswered, perhaps unanswerable, questions! What caused each person involved to act as he did? Was he filled with selfishness or selflessness? Was he motivated by a rational incentive? Did his behavior have any altruistic component? Did he act out of sheer nastiness? Did he mean for things to happen the way they did? Did he have something else in mind when the project started? Could he originally have had good intentions that later got out of hand? What were the consequences to him and to others? Did he have an accomplice or maybe more than one? If so, who were these men in the shadows and what were their interests? What principles did he embrace when he acted, or were principles a consideration at all? Was he the leader of a cabal? Was he a follower and an idealist or was he a mere bystander, one who got sucked in simply because he was close to the action? Could he at first actually have been against the project's success, but for one reason or another changed his ways and maybe even his views when the outcome became undeniable? Could he have become frightened of being seen as a fifth columnist? So the questions in the story continued to wind their relentless course toward a Byzantine labyrinth of evermore entanglement. Still, always at the end, there remained that tantalizing *why* – the quintessential question wherein lies the heart of the matter.

Mickey was in one hell of a pickle. It wasn't his first sticky situation by a long shot, but this one was a real toughie. There'd be hell to pay if he didn't get things right-on, if he stepped on the toes of the big shots, if he didn't give fair treatment to all, or if he cast blame incorrectly. Yet, he was in the dark. How was he to figure out, with virtually no help, why ISABELLE lived and died as it did? He just didn't have a handle on it, and there was simply no one to turn to. Still, he was determined to find a way out of the dilemma, and not to let this once-in-his-lifetime chance to pursue the truth just slip away. It was an irresistible quest; and if there were no alternative but to push ever deeper into the exploration of the past and the men who were part of it, even though it gave him some measure of trepidation and pause, that's what he would do. Whatever it took, he was up for it. If he couldn't get the info out of people by cajoling, by persuading, and with plain man-to-man talk, he would simply change course and generate the truth otherwise: he would acquire it from direct observations and his memories of formal events; from his re-interpretations and search for consistency of the comments and tales garnered from others both publicly and privately; from existing chronicles made currently and in days gone by; and, last but not least, from some manner of resurrection of the past in his own brain, a method that he'd yet to craft. It was a tall order indeed; but that's what he wanted, and nothing would get in his way. Thus, Mickey, forced by society's immutable character to seek for answers from within himself, was drawn into the complexities, the hazards, and the chancy haziness of the mind – both his own and the oh so guarded ones of others.

So it was that Mickey's adventure and inquiry continued to shift inexorably into a world of intent, intrigue, and conspiracy. In following that road, he had to be prepared to bear the intense unpleasantness – the nasty goings-on and the spitefulness of many – that you can be sure lies en route. That's what hunting down the truth about others is all about. It's intrinsic to the process. Who's going to be happy having someone snooping around in his affairs? Yet, even after braving it out and hanging in, as far as reaping a rich harvest is concerned, the best Mickey could think of doing was to look to heaven in prayer and rely on fate to smile on him by permitting the past to yield up its secrets.

Yes, it's a hard game to play, this getting at the truth. So what else is new? Isn't that why historians are paid the big bucks? Mickey smiled to himself impishly. He knew very well that serious-minded historians were always taking on *missions impossible*. But, in the same breath, he also knew that adopting the historian approach wasn't his way. For him, there had to be a better way, and certainly a quicker way. In truth, he'd always known that in stretching to comprehend the rationally incomprehensible, he would reach a point where he'd have to make a leap in his thinking over a natural divide, and, by so doing, move from an objective approach to one mixed with imagination and filled with fantasies. But it was hidden inside some gray cells deep within an inaccessible region of his brain. Then, suddenly, in a single moment of insight, perhaps because he yearned so much for a way out of his predicament, that very thought reached his conscious mind. What an ironic discovery he'd come upon – *that only through fantasy is one able find the truth.* OK, but even if that's the case, what next? In which direction should he go? Which forks in the road should he take along the way? How might he get to that desirable end where the *why* would give an inch or two or even more? How could Mickey find the means to cross that great divide where fantasy and truth come together, then kiss and make up? What methods could he use to get from here to there? Ah, those were questions worthy enough of giving your all to.

What with the questions laid out for him, now it was time for Mickey to find the combination code to unlock the answers. He pondered his impasse. Certainly he was in a cul-de-sac if there ever was one. How could he get people to open up and tell him all? Of course, behind that, there was always the follow-up, vexing question of whether they still knew the truth anymore. In fact, was there really any truth to find out, or only interpretations, subject to the vagaries and self-serving modes of the human mind? *Blast it all*, he thought! He knew very well that this philosophizing wasn't going to get him anywhere. He'd been through it countless times before, and what came of it? Zilch! There had to be another way. OK, so take it for granted that people wouldn't pour out their souls to him. That being the case, then perhaps he might find a key that would reverse the process. Perhaps somehow he could find a way to get into their minds. What a thought! On the face of it, the notion sounded just plain silly. Anyway, no precedent came to mind. Yet, where there's life, there's always a chance. Mickey actually believed that cliché, and lived his life that way. He wouldn't walk away just because it seemed impossible to break the case wide open. So he persevered, and stayed on it. Maybe, just maybe, he'd get lucky and discover that fabled pot at the end of the rainbow.

Mickey's mind wandered and his eyes glazed over as he tried to envision a place where people, in particular *the players* he'd assembled in his head, would be released from life's social shackles, from promises given, and from the intertwined commitments entered into. If only he could find such a place: a place where people would be free to speak their minds without hindrance, without intimidation, and without fear of any consequences; a place where all could tread safely through the minefields of their memories without shame and without fear of indictments, vilification, and retaliation from those around ready and sometimes eager to pounce on them. Yes, he thought, it would be something else again if there were such a place and if he could get to it with his full entourage. What a show of shows it would be! Wouldn't it be a glorious occasion, one that could be treasured for a lifetime? And he wouldn't be greedy. He would ask for just one day to meet the men who'd come into his life's field of experience, those who'd helped shape his past and make him what he'd become, especially those giants who came before him and created the world of science and technology he reveled in. He tingled and shivered at the thought of seeing them face to face: those who taught him; those who wished him well; those who meant him ill; those who knew him well and those who wouldn't even grant him a passing glance; those who admired, appreciated, and encouraged him; those who disliked and obstructed him; and those who sought to hurt and harm him. It was not for him to pass judgment, and so he would take them all to his heart. He would cherish the memory of such a time, and enshrine the moments he'd be privileged to have with them. What wouldn't he give if such a thing could be made to happen? Why not, he thought? Life is full of mysteries. Stranger things have actually taken place. After all, *there's more to heaven and earth than is dreamt of in your philosophies*, he thought with a smile both mischievous and full of eager anticipation. So, earnestly and passionately, he wished with all his heart for such an experience to come to pass.

* * * * *

One early morning, as Mickey sat wearing his thinking cap, putting his brain to work on the problem he'd set himself of how to fathom the minds of *the players*, it spontaneously flashed in his own mind that, in actuality, he'd already had the good fortune to visit that special land where honesty, forthrightness, and truth prevailed. Not only that, he'd been there with these men who stood like giants above others. He'd been given the extraordinary opportunity to have discussions with them, to socialize with them, to question them, and to parry words with them. Was his mind playing tricks on him? No, at that moment when this remembrance alighted into his consciousness, he was convinced that it wasn't just his imagination, and that there really had been that one magical day, believe it or not, when such a thing did come to pass.

The image that came into his memory was that of an ordinary day. But, of course, it wasn't. It was a different and special one, one that apparently defied natural law. He recalled seeing in his mind's eye an object resembling Aladdin's lamp. In the flash of an instant he believed with all his might that he could reach out and rub it, and so release the genie that could grant him that one wish he sought so much to have fulfilled. Stretching beyond his true capability, he managed to reach the lamp, and out popped the genie. With his mind in a whirl, he couldn't think too clearly, and he blurted out not the fabled three wishes, but just one – to go to that place he so yearned for. Then, to his amazement, it happened. How? God only knows! But, with an intervening phase where there was only darkness, the duration of which he couldn't discern, he found himself transported to the fable-like land of his dreams.

* * * * *

As he sat in an armchair, with his memory running at full speed, Mickey was unable to bring the complete experience back. His mind just wouldn't click it into the *on* state. It was oh so close, but still it evaded him. If only he could catch the thought-experience of that charmed and transcendent happening that took place sometime earlier – but he knew not when – then maybe he could even figure out how the transitions were made. Unfortunately, it just wouldn't come back to him.

Then, without rhyme or reason, out of the blue, it came into his mind that he'd actually had access before to this apparently regulated and restricted, at times forbidden, part of his brain. Yes, he knew that this wasn't the first time he'd remembered the circumstances, the ambience, and the feel of that mystical trip. In fact, he realized at that moment, that the memory had returned many times. Generally, it would come, stay awhile as bits and pieces of that wondrous day, and then go back into its hiding place, vanishing from his consciousness until the next time. But, at some rare moments, quite unpredictably, he would remember the occurrence in excruciatingly fine detail. Perhaps, he thought, with unflagging optimism and a boyish appetite, that this was such a time. So he sat in the cool darkness of a soon-to-come daybreak with eager anticipation.

Still, memory is not the same as the real thing. Oh, how he keenly ached to go back again! But, as much as he wanted it, the bona fide miracle seemed to have been a once-in-a-lifetime wish come true, one that just wouldn't return. On the other hand, he was afforded those terrific memory moments, and he gave great thanks for that. When one came in full bloom, it was an exhilarating mind-expanding experience, when every detail of his get-togethers in that magical place was spontaneously brought to the fore with great clarity. However, even in that case, there was one minor complaint. He wasn't really a grumbler at heart, but it did irk Mickey somewhat that when it came to the transitions, notably the back-and-forth journeys themselves, he couldn't latch onto the full story. With their mysterious changes of venue, try as he might, he always came up empty-handed. He chuckled as he thought that empty-headed would be a more appropriate description.

Mickey's inflexible will, stiff-necked pride, and obstinacy compelled him to want to know it all. So, when opportunity chanced to knock and he would again get to experience one of these interludes of remembrance, he vowed to be as vigilant, alert, and attentive as he knew how. Yes, he would do his utmost to discover the true nature of his curious voyage. But, sad to say, that was a commitment he wouldn't be able to keep. You see, those sly spirits that permitted these thought-excursions were always way ahead of him. By using inter-experience forgetting, and by making the mind-trips, as with the original, highly controlled, ultra-active, and rushed, there simply wasn't the time for the needed concentration to put the pieces of the puzzle together. Thus, Mickey was able to glean only what they wanted him to know.

Watching the dawn approach from his bedroom window, Mickey's consciousness of his mystifying and enigmatic travel began to expand. Appreciating that this was a signal of things to come, he gasped at the thrilling prospect that he might well be on the verge of a thought-memory. He started to fill with anxiety, and hoped beyond hope that it would be one of the biggies. Maybe this time he would even be able to snatch the essence of the transitions, the back-and-forth transfers from his dreamland, with their mysterious and baffling changes of venue. Yes, he would keep his eyes wide open, and his ears well tuned. Oh, to be able to better understand that momentous, breathtaking, and unique – actually quite bizarre – passage to *the other side*, to grasp its full meaning, and to discover its true nature! What a coup it would be! Wouldn't it be something if he could actually learn to be able to get there at will? Wait a minute, he thought! Better not to be too greedy! It would be too bad indeed if he actually were asking for too much. Perhaps it was more than the powers that made him a chosen one – those powers beyond our ken – wanted him to have. He certainly didn't want to antagonize or infuriate them. It's not too smart to annoy or anger gods. So, Mickey, with second thoughts, concluded that it would be best to take only what they offered him and let it go at that.

As he waited for the special moment to arrive, with the sun just about ready to show its fiery face on the eastern horizon, he became somewhat concerned. Time was passing, and still there was no sign of his enthusiastically but impatiently expected time-travel. Maybe they were upset with him. Maybe something he did made them mad at him. Yes, he thought pessimistically, spirits are known to be impulsive and vindictive. Clearly, he was overreacting, but that's the way it is when you're hooked, and no doubt he was addicted. He just had to see that damnably desirable place again. So, he caved in. Trying to set things right, he promised himself, in ritual appeasement of the gods, not to delve too deeply into the transitions if only he could get another fix. As he was in the midst of this humble, obedient, and pleading mood, suddenly, without warning, the thought-experience arrived. His entire body was quivering with pleasure, as his mind erupted in a kaleidoscope of images that could mean only one thing: Yes, it was one of those bewitching and magnificently mesmerizing memory moments that'd come upon him. As a trigger, no elixir or lamp was within arm's reach, nor any Open Sesame or Abracadabra within earshot. Mickey, seeing no rational alternative, imagined that maybe the moment of truth arrived precisely with the juxtaposition of the disappearance of the full moon – resulting from the onset of the brightening glare of the morn-to-be – and the sun's appearance in the eastern sky. Or, more likely, maybe it was because he'd shown the requisite respect and honor for the superior force that had afforded him the fabulous opportunity for *tripping the light fantastic*. But whatever made it happen, the time was ripe for remembrance.

All at once, the many facets and features about the true excursion began pouring into the conscious sector of his mind, and, strange as it may seem, except for how it started and ended, he could remember the rest of his visitation in astonishingly meticulous and minute detail, just as if it were happening again right then and there. He found that he was able to see the whole fabulously enchanted experience in his mind and describe it, each scintilla of it, without a shadow of a doubt creeping in.

As the thoughts, the images, and the impressions piled up, he was overcome by a spirited yet lighthearted feeling – a feeling that he could do anything, and that anything was possible. In conjunction with this, he felt the return of his characteristic self-confidence, accompanied sometimes by an intemperate bigheadedness and sometimes by a condescending over-assurance. In that frame of mind, Mickey quite forgot his compact with those supernatural denizens of the air. He simply blew them off, as he pledged to himself that this time he would not be negligent. This time, before all the facts and implications of the current thought-expedition could escape his mind, he was determined not to err as he had before but to record them as his legacy for the many generations of young scientists to follow.

The experience itself wasn't too different from earlier occasions. After that first instant of flashing rich-colored brilliance, he fell into a sort of semi-consciousness. Everything became pitch black, and he could feel a kind of soothing bumpiness, as if he were driving in a car along a road with slow, relaxing ups and downs. Awakening with a start, he felt an intense anxiety when he realized that the hour was fast approaching, and that this was his last chance to go over the questions for the discussions he was to have on his day of days. Peering out the partially tinted windows, he could make out that the car was speeding along a divided highway, lined by a sequence of weeping willows and with a lush green well-tended landscape on either side. He noticed that not a house or living thing was in sight. Then he could see, as if it were in front of him, the entrance to a tunnel being approached. But somehow he just couldn't resist being lulled off into a semi-sleeplike condition, the kind that comes with a mild sedative.

Le Petit Village

After the mind-hazy ride through paradise-like terrain and then through a long dark tunnel, followed by an interval of deep, dream-free sleep, Mickey found himself standing at the edge of an out-of-the-way little hamlet, a place seemingly made especially for a charmed circle. Behind him were mountains rising quickly, with small rolling hills along the way up, until they reached a summit – a crown – that seemed to be watching over the earthly matters below. A beautiful day greeted Mickey with the sun shining brilliantly in the cloudless sky above. But his eyes were fastened on the dazzling image of the café-lined street that lay before him. Shrubbery and colorful flowers and plants were set exquisitely along the multiple paths paved with multi-pasteled stone. In some areas Mickey counted four parallel paths. It was a place clearly designed for walking, with not one motorized vehicle as far as the eye could see. There seemed to be a bicycle path, but there was nary a bicycle to be seen on the pathway or anywhere else. In fact, there wasn't a sign at all of any means of transportation. The people simply moved along on their own steam.

It occurred to Mickey that this was almost identical to the picture he had of Shangri-La. In this version, a mass of men and women were casually strolling about on a lazy summer afternoon, surrounded by the Café des Artistes, the Luxembourg, the Pam-Pam, the Moulin Rouge, the Rosemary and a number of other cafés lining the paths along their entire length. Wow, Mickey thought, what a place! The promenade's walkers appeared so unhurried and relaxed that he imagined them to be residents of this tiny village situated in some valley in the middle of nowhere. As he looked around and became more accustomed to the atmosphere, he saw that walking about was only one of the many activities that could be indulged in. Some of the people there had chosen to while away the hours on one of the street-side patios, reading a book or newspaper or magazine and sipping one of the aromatic coffees of distant lands. Some would amuse themselves by watching the passersby. Some would group themselves at tables in heated debate. Yes, Mickey was quite taken by this Utopian and picturesque vision.

Yet, absorbed as he was, he couldn't help comparing it to a hazy image that spontaneously came to him from out of his past. At first he couldn't quite zero in on it and put it into focus, but slowly the smokiness dissipated. Then he saw in his mind's eye what his fanciful thought was, magnified and jazzed up by the melodic strains of the *Boulevard of Broken Dreams*. Brought back to him was the great Tony Bennett's rendering of this song many years before, when it had quite an impact on an impressionable, susceptible youth. How could he ever forget it – that picture Tony painted of smiling, happy faces covering lost souls inside? Such a close facsimile was it to the scene he'd come upon that he felt as if he were in that make-believe land. Boy, was he thrilled to be afforded the singular opportunity of being able to see it all now in close-up: the diligent, earnest readers; the single strollers with their confident strides and proud demeanors; the lovers holding hands; the coffee-drinkers relishing the taste to the very last drop; and the expressive animated discussions all about. Although the people appeared to be happy, that was only a first impression. As Mickey continued to watch the unfolding show, he detected something quite different as he began to notice their intense gazes, their passionate eyes, and their fast-passing frowns that vanished almost before they formed. Guided by the insight in Tony's lyrics, Mickey came to sense that underneath the gleaming surface veneer lay a far more involved and tangled interior wherein were stored the experiences of a lifetime. It was no surprise to Mickey that, accumulated from life's unavoidable dead ends, missteps, missed opportunities, misdeeds, and frustrated, thwarted schemes, there built up in people's souls the disappointments, the sorrows, and the regrets that are the lot of us all. What a sight to behold! There was both happiness and sadness in the same people at the same time. Mickey smiled at the irony inherent in that – oddly humored by it, and yet baffled at the disparity between what could be seen and the unseen truth. Yes, the song had given an extra dimension to his current experience. Lucky for Mickey that whenever Tony's voice and that haunting tune came to his mind, the paradoxical, maybe even self-contradictory meaning of those entrancing and spellbinding lyrics always helped give him a better understanding and a keener sense of the mystery of the human condition.

* * * * *

As Mickey walked along one of the pathways, gazing on either side to orient himself to the unfamiliar surroundings, he stopped in his tracks when he looked ahead and saw up close the imposing structure at the center of the square that marked the end of the line. His head snapped back and his neck tightened. Confronting him was this tall edifice stretching upward at least a couple of dozen stories. He was jarred by its distinctively modern architecture. How anomalous it looked when compared with the other buildings in the enclave, mainly Bohemian-style, renovated and strengthened old wooden frames. But Mickey's eyes were glued to the space-age avant-garde structural marvel. Its four sides were made of smooth flat jet-black reflecting-square segments connected at various angles. Going up, the angles of the shiny flat segments got smaller and smaller until each side of the building became a vertical plane at right angles to the adjoining side. From the sky, the four black sides formed a square. As the building was followed upward, along with the angles of the connecting segments straightening out, its floor area shrank by about three-quarters. Finally, topping off the rising pyramid-like tower was a spire containing electronic gear, which Mickey guessed was an antenna. He stared at the cold angular geometry and pondered its incongruity and its awe-inspiring eeriness in the midst of an otherwise quaint-looking town. At the front entrance, there was a sign at the center of a circular grassy area, surrounded by pieces of variegated and pale multi-colored marble, which read *Visitor's Bureau and Administration* in dark blue lettering on a speckled white background. Above the words was a blood-red insignia that had a circular area about ten inches in diameter and contained gold-colored lines of varying lengths emanating from an explosive-appearing center. Except for its coloring, the sign's logo reminded Mickey of spark chamber pictures of the aftereffects of particle collisions when beams hit head-on in colliders. He stared at the sign, still a little shaken by the whole experience. But then, hearing a tick-tock in his head, he was wrested away from his overly engrossing ruminations, and he began to move forward.

Mickey walked through the grassy area along a flagstone pathway, crossed a narrow semi-circular roadway, and ascended the ten steps to a high translucent door that opened automatically as he approached. He entered a large lobby. To his right was a reception area with only one piece of furniture: a big, ostentatiously ornamented, and expensive-looking desk made of dark brown shiny oak. In the high-ceilinged chamber there were marble statues, some of Greek and Roman origin and others dating back to even older civilizations. The long opulent staircase facing the entrance led to a level far enough away that he could make out none of its details. It was quite an intimidating welcome, if there ever was one. The bareness and lifelessness of the hall caught Mickey unaware and disrupted his natural inquisitiveness and desire to explore. He just stood there, momentarily transfixed and disoriented. This state couldn't have lasted more than a few seconds, and then the spell was broken when he looked up and noticed an attractive woman who, just then, appeared at the bottom of the stairway. Without in the least acknowledging Mickey's presence, she moved briskly toward the desk. She was tall and wore medium-height black pumps, a gray suit, and a pale green blouse. She also had on elegant, stylish, and tasteful jewelry: an emerald broach on her lapel above her perfectly-proportioned breasts, a cameo around her long narrow white neck, a silver-plated digital watch on her rather small left wrist, and chic emerald earrings, but no rings on her long-fingered beautifully shaped hands. Her dark glistening hair was tied in a broad bun at the back, her large dark eyes sparkled, and the full lips of her wide, sensitive, and sensuous mouth were painted in a pale sandalwood tint. She had all the earmarks of a raving beauty – a sexy movie star, the likes of a young Joan Crawford or Kim Novak. Yet, despite her stunning appearance, she conducted herself in the manner of a stern, let's-get-on-with-it businesswoman. All in all, she was some classy lady. However, before he could dwell on this, the woman was standing at the desk officiously summoning him to approach. On each of the desk's four sides was a high-backed, heavily leathered chair. The woman sat behind the desk with her back to a large stained-glass window and motioned to Mickey to sit on the side opposite her. As he sat, he noticed her nameplate, Ms. Virginia Holt.

Without any informal chitchat, she opened a folder already on the desk. Examining it briefly, she looked up unsmiling and stiffly informed him that two appointments had been made for him. Mickey, who'd said nothing up to that point, interjected somewhat timidly that he had hoped to see each person separately because one-on-one contacts would make for more profitable and productive get-togethers. For the first and last time during their first brief meeting, a slight smile crossed Ms. Holt's face as she said: "Yes, we know. This point was considered, but there simply is not enough time. You must understand that we get many such requests and naturally we try to satisfy them all. We're sorry we couldn't give you all that you expected, but we did the best we could." She waited to see if Mickey had anything to add. When he didn't react, she continued, "So, getting to your day, we have scheduled your first appointment at the Luxembourg, with Mr. Goldhaber, Mr. Haworth, Mr. Samios, and Mr. Vineyard. That will be at three o'clock, precisely 23 minutes from now. Your second appointment will be at the Moulin Rouge, with Mr. Green, Mr. Lederman, Mr. Rubbia, and Mr. Wilson, at half past five. Unfortunately, two and a half hours is the maximum time available for each meeting since your departure must be promptly at eight. Walking along any of the pathways leading from our central building, you will have no trouble finding the locations for your meetings." Mickey was uneasy and a tad nervous at the formality of it all, but he managed to calm himself down sufficiently to be able to squeeze out his second comment, tentative as it was. He reminded Ms. Holt that he had also asked to have the honor of seeing Isidor Rabi. "Oh, yes," she reacted, in a manner suggesting to Mickey that her failure to mention this part of his request was just an oversight, "we tried to arrange for you to have some time with Mr. Rabi but unfortunately during your stay here he will be visiting the New York city area." She paused for a moment, perused a few sheets in her folder – probably some sort of schedules, he thought – and then lit up when she seemed to figure out a possible solution: "We could arrange for Mr. Rabi to have dinner with you if you can be available this coming Thursday evening." "Yes, of c-course," Mickey stammered, "that would be perfect." "Fine," she said with self-satisfaction; and making the decision on her own, she went on, "you will have from eight to eleven next Thursday evening; a car will come to get you punctually at a quarter past six." Mickey started to give her the address where he could be picked up, but Ms. Holt brushed it aside with a wave of her hand and closed the conversation: "Yes, it's all in your file. Don't worry about it. But time is pressing, and since your time here is very short, you had better be off. It has been a pleasure meeting you and we hope that your discussions here at our little village are apropos and satisfactorily meet your requirements and expectations." With that, she rose from her chair, stepped briskly toward the staircase, and began her ascent.

Mickey followed her movements till she disappeared from view. For a while he sat motionless, ruffled and quite off-balance. Bewildered by the turn things had taken, he felt he should take the time to settle down and compose himself. Everything that had happened so far was curiously oddball. He had anticipated none of it, and that made him feel that he was out of his league. Yet that is not to say it was unwelcome. In fact, the more he thought about it, the more he liked the way things were going. Everything appeared to be coming up roses. So, why not go with the flow? Mickey then remembered Ms. Holt's reference to *23 minutes*. Quite some time had elapsed since then; so he realized that he better get cracking. After all he'd already been through in getting there, it would verge on the ridiculous for him to be late.

Since no one was there to tell him what he should do next, Mickey presumed that he was meant to leave on his own. So, without thinking much about it, he simply got up and left the building. As he walked back along the flagstone pathway he saw that the hi-rise he'd just left was set off from the low structures of the street he was then facing by about fifty yards. As he walked toward the action, he surveyed the cafés he could see. Although each one was independent of the others, they almost touched on either side. They seemed to be designed to fit into a limited space, like the downtown area of a big city.

Mickey, with his scientific brain working overtime, had a yen to figure out the size of this well hidden site he'd somehow lighted upon. Clearly located in a valley, he thought, probably there wasn't more to it than what he'd seen. What you see is what you get! Continuing along, stepping up his pace a bit, he couldn't resist trying to accumulate as many facts as he could. To get some sense of the real size of the place, he tried to focus on the distant location where the roadway terminated. He was confident that the far-off mountain range began its upward climb from the spot where the street ended or not far from it, but whether that point was half a mile away, a mile, or even more, he couldn't ascertain with any assurance.

But Mickey couldn't escape the fact that time was rapidly slipping by. He turned and looked back, observing that, driven by the setting sun, the shadow of the towering, imposing mass of steel and stone had begun its creep along the street. That meant that the west was behind him and what he could see in the distance up ahead were eastern mountains. More than that, it meant that the day was passing, and everything he'd been waiting for and building up to was imminent, approaching at breakneck speed.

Mickey rushed along, and it was obvious from his flushed and exultant face that he was really getting a charge out of the whole experience. Yes, he got a kick out of tackling these natural-to-him self-challenges. But, oh, how his spirits skyrocketed when the dynamite hard-to-outdo things to come entered his mind. Then, was he on cloud nine! Why not? There was so much he still had to look forward to. Sure, he should've been thinking about and making preparations for his meeting just moments away. But at that instant, he was just a playful little boy moving about in a land of his dreams. Lightheaded and without a care in the world, he felt as if he were floating on a cloud filled with goodies he was destined to partake of. How inspiring and exhilarating it was to be where he was! How stimulated and energized he was! How stirring and exciting was this time in his life! How glorious was this day of days!

No, there wasn't a moment to lose. The hands on the clock were relentlessly turning, and he had appointments to keep. He was feeling the pressure and hurried along the almost mystical street of sorrows and broken dreams, close to jogging now and jostling a little with the mingling mass on the crowded pathways. Suddenly a curious thing occurred. The experience of being on Tony's *Boulevard* was so thrilling, so uncanny, and so mesmerizing that for a brief moment he needed no more than that. Stopping in his tracks, he'd forgotten why he was there in the first place. But fortunately that was only a short-lived memory lapse. He glanced at his wristwatch, and realizing that it was five minutes to three quickly snapped him out of his reverie. Recalling Ms. Holt's encouraging comment that he would easily be able to get around her little village, he scurried off to find the Luxembourg.

At the Luxembourg

Mickey saw the Luxembourg a little way down the street to his right, about a quarter of a mile from the hi-rise. As he approached the café, he had to wend his way through a good-sized, concentrated group of people milling around in front and then past a number of loungers sitting at closely spaced outside patio tables, each fitted with an oversized red and white umbrella. Above the door was a sign identifying the café in red neon lights over a dark gray background. He pushed open the heavy wooden door and found himself in a bustling environment with people squashed together all the way from the doorway to the highly active bar about twenty feet away and slightly to his left. To his right, smart looking, energetic, and nimble waiters, carrying coffee, sandwiches, cakes and other goodies, were serving the small, closely packed tables. Everybody seemed lively and carefree, the conversation was spirited and earnest, and the mood was animated and cheery. Appropriately from the jukebox came the happy strains of Louis Prima singing his fifties' hit, "*Enjoy yourself, it's later than you think*," and all seemed to be following the advice to a tee.

In less than a minute from when he first entered, and just as he noticed that further to the right, past the tables, the room drifted toward a dark interior, he was whisked away by a tall business-like man in black formal attire. After pushing through the tiny spaces between tables, with not a word spoken, Mickey followed the man toward the rear. The sounds of the crowd began to diminish as the two men passed through a dim and shadowy vacated space, separated off from the rollicking exuberance of the front section. As Mickey's eyes became accustomed to the very low-powered lighting, which gave this back part of the room somber and eerie overtones, he saw that they were approaching what he sensed to be an exclusive curtained-off area of the restaurant. As they got closer, he saw that it was really a series of private rooms, each opening through a separate richly and deeply – almost gaudily – colored curtain, embellished with unreal, enigmatic figures bordering on the grotesque. The tuxedo-suited humorless man pressed a button and the left-most heavy and almost soundproof curtain parted and Mickey passed through the short, narrow archway leading into a smallish room.

This was the moment he'd been waiting for. As he moved toward the circular table at the room's center, the first words he heard were, "Well, look who's here." Nick had taken the initiative and continued his warm, yet mocking greeting by grabbing Mickey's left arm and accompanying him to the empty chair at the far side of the windowless room. Nick then reclaimed his seat opposite Mickey and established a light friendly tone by kicking off the introductions in his inimitable style. He started by addressing Mickey first, "You know George and Maurice, of course." The two were seated on either side of Nick, Maurice to his right and George to his left. Next to Maurice came Leland and then Mickey. Nick went on, "Leland, I don't think you know this gentleman; well, meet Mickey, my alter ego." This produced chuckles and guffaws all around, as Mickey and Leland turned to each other, smiled, and politely shook hands. There they all were, at a cozy table for five; and Mickey, with his big chance finally having arrived, felt that he should take control and start the ball rolling. Although he was the one who had asked for this gathering, and had this golden opportunity handed to him on a silver platter, he was finding it difficult to begin. All the thought and preparation that he'd put into it, and all the scenarios he'd gone over time after time, simply weren't enough and hadn't readied him for this moment now confronting him. Still, he had to act, for it was put-up or shut-up time.

Mickey always thought of himself as a plain talker. He saw himself as the quintessential rational and up-front modern man. At heart an egalitarian, positions and titles meant nothing to him. You see, he firmly believed that people were all equal, just humans – some better, some worse, but all entitled to the credit and respect they earned. He was a scientist to his very core and unquestioningly believed that logic was the essence of human communication and contact; and in this interaction mode he was convinced that he was top-drawer. With such a personal resumé, you'd think that he'd be in full emotional control and carry the ball in a no-nonsense business-like manner. That's exactly the way he'd imagined it would be. However, contrary to his expectations, it wasn't like that at all. As it happened, he was full of misgivings and forebodings. He was uneasy, agitated, and all tensed up. He almost found it hard to speak. Why was it so? Why was he in such a state? Why was his throat dry? Why could he not find the words? Why was he nervous? He felt his right hand trembling a bit and quickly pulled it off the table, out of sight of the others. Mickey's head was bowed, but he caught a glimpse of the four former BNL Directors around the table, all of them looking at him. The silence, short-lived as it was, was surely somewhat off-putting. Add to this that they were still wondering what Mickey really wanted and why they were there, in spite of the forewarning they'd received, including an informal agenda with some sample questions. This incipient concern about what was going on was especially true for Nick, the worldly cynic, who was peering at him quizzically. Mickey knew he was on the spot and had to overcome this bout of anxiety and apprehension he was experiencing. Then, like a true trouper who in spite of stage fright manages to perform, he came to his senses and miraculously found a way to go on – just in the nick of time. Thus, before his hesitancy produced any meaningful and recognizable uneasiness and embarrassment, he somehow found the means to pull himself together. Strangely, this mild discomfort at the table generated the positive effect of enhancing the level of anticipation. If planned, it would've been pure genius. But it wasn't. It was serendipity playing its tune and doing its part on Mickey's behalf.

Mickey started by thanking the four for taking the time to help him in his quest for a better understanding of BNL's eventful history over the past half-century. There were assenting nods, and Maurice interjected that he too would be interested to learn more about how and why things happened the way they did. Mickey continued: "Because I prepared for one-on-one interviews, I hope you won't mind if I address particular questions to each of you. But let me assure you that there is no formality here. If anyone wants to say anything at any time, please feel free to do so." As he uttered these words, he realized that he'd become far too serious-sounding and should've bitten his tongue before saying what he just did. Wishing he could retract those remarks and feeling a little foolish, he attempted to rebound by adding with a snicker, "Surely that's redundant – even a bit silly – for who could stop any of you from butting in and getting in your two-cents' worth anyway, and who would want to?" This seemed to do the trick. Any discomfort or second-thoughts in the modest gathering that Mickey had brought about – by his being over-anxious and white-knuckled when he first sat down at the table and by unnecessarily being so stilted and de rigueur a few moments before – were now quelled. Some smiles appeared; and the relaxed atmosphere that Nick had brought on at the start returned to the little group of five. What a perfect way to begin! Who could ask for anything more? It's just what Mickey wanted. So he took a deep breath, and the game he'd come for started.

* * * * *

Leland

"Leland, I hope you don't mind me calling you by your first name." "Of course not," he brushed off Mickey's gratuitous comment, "just go right ahead with your questions." Mickey was not only embarrassed by this exchange, but felt somewhat stung by having committed yet another faux pas. However, put in his place, he took his medicine and got on with it: "I've always presumed the importance of your leaving the lab in 1961 to be that it signaled a change in policy, whereby greater stress would be placed on the experimental program and less on accelerator development. When it got down to the practicalities of daily life at the lab, this policy shift came to mean that resources, manpower, and money were transferred out of accelerator technology into experimental support. To make clearer what really was happening at the lab at that time and to test whether my assumptions have any validity, my three questions to you are these: Was this change of policy contrary to your position? Was this why you left the lab? And, who was behind your being pushed out, if indeed that's what happened?"

When it came to serious matters, and he did take Mickey's questions seriously, Leland was generally pensive, reflective, and sober. His natural tendency would have been to let sufficient time pass before answering. However, this situation called for an on-the-spot response. There was simply no time to mull it over. So Leland absorbed it all in double-quick time and, after only a brief period of deep thought, he was ready. "You know," he said, "the late fifties was not an auspicious or a happy time for me. My wife became seriously ill; and that, you can well imagine, was very stressful and took a lot out of me. At the same time, the Cosmotron was experiencing the pains of having to carry on and learn to live with the bigger and better AGS facility just about ready to move in. Everybody saw the handwriting on the wall. They became ruffled and very nervous about the imminent change. What's worse, a users' rebellion was brewing that found its focus in George Collins, who was then heading the Cosmotron program.

"In the eyes of the users, George came to represent the bad guy who always took the side of accelerator development over the experimental program. They were right, except that it wasn't George's doing, it was the lab's policy and mine. I've no doubt that George believed in the course we'd set, but he wasn't the one calling the shots. What could've exacerbated his predicament was that he was actually part of the user pack, and so was probably seen as a betrayer of the first order. He was expected to be on their side, come hell or high water. It was awfully unfortunate for him to have been obliged to move against his own kind. The truth was that George was a good person in the role of leading the Cosmotron effort; unfortunately he was too thin-skinned to be able to handle all that faultfinding and carping and nitpicking; and mostly he wasn't able to wise up and pick up the knack of tolerating the personal attacks being leveled at him. With his highly charged emotional responses to them and with his lack of self-control, he came to look guilty in the view of the insurgents. So George proved to be the perfect scapegoat.

"To smother the whole mess, I decided after a great deal of soul-searching that I had to relieve Collins of his job, and that's what I did. I replaced him with Lyle Smith, whom the users found more to their taste. This whole business was bitter medicine for a lot of us, and it was especially taxing for me because rightly or wrongly I felt that I'd double-crossed George and committed an act of treachery.

"Then on top of all that gut-wrenching stuff, there remained the onerous and thorny matter of money. How could we make our budget fit the changing times? Remember there were burgeoning demands for more and more, and then some, resulting from the increasing number of accelerator and experimental opportunities that arose swiftly during that awesome and inspiring period of technological enlightenment. But the money to make everybody happy simply wasn't there. Unfortunately, each of the two sides, experimentalists and accelerator technologists, thought it was far more important then the other. With both competing for the same funds, what could you expect? If one group got the nod, then the other one screamed blue murder. Those of the losing faction were ready to tear apart anyone in sight they believed was responsible. If the situation were reversed, then naturally, it would be vice versa. And we, mainly George and I, were the lucky men to have to pick and choose. Believe you me, it's not much fun when the money doesn't keep up with the growth potential, and two forceful and self-righteous gangs are gunning for the same pot. As it happened, we chose to favor the accelerator mob, the weaker of the two sides, making it much harder on us. As the leader at the front line, George felt the brunt of the rage and fury. But make no mistake about it, I got my share of the dirty doings.

"With all this closing in on me – my wife's sickness, the Collins affair, and the budget gap – it just seemed too much to bear. I woke up one morning and there I was, smack on the verge of throwing in the towel. Giving up is bad for anyone's self-confidence, you know; and, not only for you, it's especially bad for the morale of the troops. Where would I go anyway? What would I do? So I didn't take an action of such finality lightly. I hesitated; and it was a good thing for me that I did. As luck would have it, something came to me from out of the blue that pulled me clear out of the rut that I'd dug myself into. You might say that, stuck in a corner being battered to hell, I was *saved by the bell.* Yes, fate stepped in, in the guise of Norman Ramsey, who offered me the chance to be named a commissioner for the Atomic Energy Commission (AEC). Wow! What an opportunity! It was a way out of the whole stinking business. I could just pick up and walk away from it all. Could anyone resist such a temptation?

"As you can well imagine, Norman didn't have to do much arm-twisting. Nonetheless, he put some highly appreciated icing on the cake anyway. He informed me that should I choose to go, I'd have a good shot at becoming the National Science Foundation (NSF) Director in a few years. This was music to my ears. Thank heaven for Norman! It was without a shadow of a doubt the right thing for me to do. What good fortune! This bountiful gift of freedom, together with the sweet bonus, arrived at just the right moment, when I needed it most.

"I must say, though, that I felt a smidgeon of guilt having to leave things at the lab as unsettled as they were. However, I didn't find it too tough to rationalize away the abandonment argument by convincing myself that this new way of serving the science community and the country would be a remarkably worthwhile endeavor; and, in any case, it would be far better than for me to continue beating my head against the wall at BNL. Still, at the end of the day, it turned out not really to be a question of choice, of rational decision-making. When I added it all together, I recognized that all of us grow old and tired and must make room for the young and eager; and I didn't doubt for a minute that it was time for me to go and leave the big problem of future accelerator development at the lab for others to grapple with."

For an instant, everyone was caught up in Leland's emotional remembrances. Empathy filled the room and freely flowed to him. The air was charged with feeling. Mickey instinctively sensed in his gut that the meeting could easily get away from him. There was just too much heart, and not enough brain. Having his target in full view, in addition to knowing full well that a lot of business still remained to be done in the short time available, Mickey chose to try to get things back down to earth. He did it by acting as if he were unaffected by Leland's powerful, yet sensitive, account. He nonchalantly came back with the unruffled, matter-of-fact, and perhaps a little provocative rejoinder: "Just for clarification, and please excuse my bluntness, but does all that mean that you were pushed out to make room for someone who had more sympathy for experimenters than for accelerator types?" Leland thought a bit and then spoke: "I wouldn't put so much emphasis on whether or not I was pushed out. Certainly there was never any talk of that sort. It seemed to me at the time that the prevailing circumstances were the real factors that favored such a move, and I chose not to fight against the tide. On the other hand, it turned out that resources were indeed shifted in the way your comments implied; so looking at the situation in retrospect, what you were driving at may actually not have been too far from the truth. In fact, on rethinking, it is possible, although far from certain, that I was indeed encouraged to leave because the users didn't agree with my policy. Continuing along in that vein: if it really happened that way, then as far as naming names is concerned, I can only say that Rabi was not in my corner." There was a lull of a few seconds as Mickey savored what he interpreted as a very solid beginning.

* * * * *

Maurice

Quite taken by Leland's forthrightness and candor, Mickey was exceedingly pleased with this first step down the road of *whys and wherefores*. Enthusiastically believing that in this way he'd be led to the nexus of cause and effect, and thence to the gospel truth, he breathed deeply and turned to Maurice. But Maurice, after thinking a little about Leland's remarks, wasn't quite satisfied with them, and felt compelled to react. So, before Mickey could begin phrasing his next line of questioning, Maurice began to give his take on what had transpired in those early days around 1960: "While Leland was speaking, as a sort of comparison, I was trying to bring to mind my understanding of what took place in that period over forty years ago. As I recall it, the transition of Directors was very simple. Leland had already served more than two terms; and the Trustees felt that, by itself, independent of personalities, that was a sufficient term of office. Thus, in order to set the right precedent, a change was demanded. And a change there was. After the search committee could find no suitable candidate from outside the lab, I was asked by the AUI Board to be the lab's next Director. What could I say but *yes*? But I want you to know that I accepted the assignment only because I thought I could be of service at a time when we had a good chance to reap many scientific gains from our unique new AGS machine. I strongly believed that I was well suited to that assignment. I absolutely had no other motives. That was my sole agenda – period! As for Leland leaving the lab, he alone made the choice that was best for him. I'm sure that it wasn't easy for him to make that tough life-changing decision, but after taking into account both his professional and his personal circumstances at the time, there didn't seem to be much doubt about what he had to do, at least as I saw it. It is important for me to state emphatically here and now that I played no active role either in the succession or in his departure from the lab. Personally, I'd always believed that Leland was a very effective Director when technology development was the lab's main concern. Unfortunately, when experiments and users came to the forefront of the lab's primary mission, I came to see that he wasn't the man for the job. So it seemed to me to be only logical that his time had expired. But that was my opinion – nothing else – and everyone certainly has a right to that. Because I had that viewpoint, I did in fact agree with the Board's verdict. But as for any direct involvement in the changeover, I played no part in the whole business, except of course to accept the offer that was given me. From my vantage point, c'est tout!"

Vineyard, having been close to Maurice at the time, concurred with this assessment, and he nodded to him with an encouraging gesture. Leland, on the other hand, had no intention of saying anything or of reacting in any way at all. He just remained quiet and sat staring at his hands on his lap. As for Mickey, he conspicuously ignored Maurice's tart remarks, which he took to be an inappropriate and unnecessary defense of both the lab's and his own actions. Looking at his watch, and seeing no useful purpose in prolonging the discussion of the Haworth-Goldhaber difference of opinion, he quickly changed course and went on with his truth tracking.

"Maurice," Mickey began, "my questions for you relate to the time a few years preceding the end of your tenure as Director in January 1973. It was almost at the end of the sixties, and you were about midstream in your second five-year term. What I would very much like is to try to better understand the circumstances that led to Ken Green's resignation as Chairman of the Accelerator Department (AD). Remember that Ken had become Chairman of the newly expanded Accelerator Department in 1960, about two years before you became Director; so, it wasn't entirely unreasonable that he should decide to leave that post in December 1969 after having served two terms. That does indeed seem roughly to be the typical time-of-service for a high-level position, much like that for the lab directorship or the U.S. presidency.

"However, my personal recollections as well as those of some of my colleagues indicate that the idea that Ken would give up the Chairmanship of his own volition doesn't hold water. We saw it in Ken's demeanor, in his conduct, and in his comments at the time. There just appeared to be no other interpretation than that he was very unhappy about having to leave a post he was so smitten by, so attached to, and one that he ministered to so well. In fact, everything seems to point to his stepping down not being voluntary at all.

"All of us who had the good fortune to know Ken perceived him as a most determined and go-getting man who was extremely excited about superconducting magnet development and the new BNL-destined collider on the horizon. If you listed the few men who might've been indispensable to BNL, he'd most certainly be at or near the top. And he deserved to be there! He was one man who'd have walked that extra mile for the lab, so dedicated was he to its future. In fact, if you allowed him to get started on the topic of superconducting accelerators, he'd talk your head off and simply couldn't be stopped – and I can vouch for that from my own firsthand experience. I recall, ironically with a good deal of fondness, how irritating it was to have to sit there and listen to him go on and on about those magnets that would revolutionize high-energy physics and make possible unheard of machines and experiments. Yes, he was a big talker, but one, I might add, who had something worth saying. How knowledgeable he was! How persuasive he was! It was as if he wanted to transfer whatever it was he had directly to you, enthusiasm and all; and, if you resisted, he was just about ready to shove it down your throat. However, despite these practices that just overwhelmed the listener, he was a man designed to inspire young physicists and engineers to work themselves sick. That, I must point out, was good for them, good for him, good for the lab, and good for science.

"All in all, most of the working accelerator professionals of the sixties had exceptional regard for him. He led them and they willingly followed. Anyone knowing him had to be infected by his boyish eagerness and passionate zeal. Who would want to see him go? Anyway, getting back to the point, when you look at his exemplary qualities of curiosity and inquisitiveness, and his attraction and devotion to the biggest technological challenge of the day, it would appear to be highly unlikely that he would've abandoned the enterprise, and deserted all those who believed in him, by freely electing to resign. He just wasn't the type to quit of his own accord."

Mickey paused to catch his breath. Just then, something clicked in his mind, telling him that his *Ken Green excursion* had perhaps carried him a little too far afield. If he had any lingering doubts about it, he was quickly set straight as he caught a glimpse of Maurice's icy stare directed right at him. Mickey's immediately instinctive reaction was to apologize and plead for patience. But fortunately he was precluded from doing that by the calming voice of reason in his head that said, *it'd only make things worse, forget it, just let it pass and move on.* It seemed like really sound advice, so he chose to heed it. Maurice, on the other hand, didn't at all like the way things were going. He took umbrage at what he saw as Mickey's insensitivity, even insulting attitude, toward him. Yet Maurice somehow found the strength to have common sense overrule his passions and prevail. So he backed off from voicing his resentment and waited for Mickey to pick up where he left off. Mickey, looking squarely into Maurice's defiant eyes, was set to go. He presumed that Maurice – not with words but rather with the bitterness in his face and eyes that couldn't be camouflaged – was trying to intimidate him. However, Mickey was stubborn, and was determined to remain steadfast in his tough, no-quarter-given questioning.

So, with Mickey and Maurice both prepared to tangle, the show resumed with Mickey speaking: "I'm almost ready to pose my questions to you, but there's one final crucial point I must bring in. An incident took place on a Friday afternoon in October 1969 that I would like to explore with you. You called a meeting in your office with the AD tenured staff to inform them beforehand that you would be making an announcement to the entire laboratory on the following Monday. Aside from boilerplate, the memorandum would tell the lab that Ken was resigning and that a search committee was being established to determine a successor. According to some of those present, under pressure from Ken's staunchest supporters at the meeting, who were in the majority, you agreed to put off the announcement. But something happened over the weekend that gave you sufficient confidence to go ahead and make the announcement anyway, despite your promise not to. Shortly thereafter, Ken made it known publicly that he'd accepted what had befallen him and indeed planned to step down at year's end. The combination of his formal resignation, his clear-to-everyone resignation to his fate, and his private instructions to his friends that any trouble would be counter-productive took the sails out of any incipient rebellion. However, although you won that personal campaign against Ken, it further widened the rift in the lab between the accelerator technologists and the experimentalists – a schism whose adverse and potentially ruinous effects continue to plague the lab to this very day.

"Keeping in mind all this as background, finally here are my questions to you: Was Ken truly forced to resign? From your perspective, what really happened at that October 1969 meeting in your office? Did you thoughtlessly and tactlessly choose to ignore the resistance of the staff to what you were planning to do? Did you actually renege on your promise to them, as some of them claim? What happened that weekend that gave you the confidence to go ahead with the announcement despite the raucous meeting the previous Friday? Related to that, but in a more speculative vein, since it is known that Rabi was at the lab that Saturday for an AUI Board meeting, was he involved? Might he have been the missing link that could explain your apparent lack of candor? Lastly I would like to ask you if you resigned as Director two years later of your own accord and, if it was not fully voluntary, did the Green episode play a part in it?"

The room was silent for a short time while Maurice was pondering the questions, but to Mickey it seemed forever. They all sat waiting in that bare, square room some twenty feet on each side, with nine strong lights, uniformly distributed in threes and in depressions in the high whitish ceiling. For the first time Mickey noticed the erotic nature of the wallpaper. The images, in light green on a beige background, evoked the dark and deep mysteries of the Asian subcontinent, and reminded Mickey of a scene in David Lean's movie of the E.M. Forster novel, *A Passage to India*: *He could see in his mind the ruins of that palace in a deserted location where weeds ruled the land. There were shrubbery, wild vines, and masses of heavy foliage protruding through the spaces between the granite remains of striking images of acts of untold pleasure and gratification. The people, now long defunct, had been replaced by free and yelping monkeys passionately guarding their possession with threatening motions and gestures. They lived the good life, imitating the sights shaped for eternity in stone by those who wanted posterity to tell the story of their presence on earth and their lust for life.* As he pondered this, in an interlude lasting but a minute or less, Mickey thought he heard some whispering around the table. His head jerked up, and he felt somewhat embarrassed for being remiss in neglecting his guests. Even if it was for only a very short period, he still felt as if he ought to say something by way of an explanation. Alas, he had none. So, he was relieved that just then Maurice began to speak.

"I'm not sure I know how to respond to these questions you've given me. They are highly provocative and have an accusatory tone that I find quite annoying and troublesome. Since I can't bear to leave such allegations and insinuations left hanging in the air as if they were true, you can well appreciate that I would very much like to take you on and rebut them. The concern I have is that I can't seem to recollect much of it, in particular the fine-tuning and the motives that seem to be what you are predominantly preoccupied with. Remember you're referring to things that happened some thirty years ago, a very long time indeed. However, in spite of my lack of readiness, I think it's important that I try to present my side of the story. It shouldn't surprise anyone that it's quite different from yours – probably best described as being a hundred and eighty degrees out of phase. Well, enough of these preliminaries! No more à priori excuses! Just permit me to say that, with the opportunity you've given me – and I very much thank you for that – I intend to give it my best shot.

"It's true that Ken wanted to remain as Chairman of his department and strongly resisted my initially friendly broaching of the subject of his stepping down. Frankly, this surprised me no end. How could he not have appreciated that his time was up and that he wasn't wanted anymore? The truth was that it wasn't I alone who thought this way. Rather the majority of the lab directorate as well as the AUI Board also felt that the laboratory needed new blood in the accelerator leadership. As far as we were concerned, because of his abominable managing of that double fiasco – the AGS Conversion Project's abysmal performance and our loss of the 200-GeV Synchrotron to Wilson and Fermilab – Ken ought to go. We agreed – all of us, to a man – that his staying on would be only a hindrance to the lab's revitalization and restoration we all wanted. A new era was dawning, and the laboratory needed to attract the right people to decide how best to do world-class A-1 physics and at the same time build the new machines that were a match for the full-of-promise, possibly epoch-making, future that we all believed in and that lay before us for the taking. Although he might have been well suited to do the construction, he just didn't have the capability of doing the rest of what the job demanded. Ken simply wasn't the right man. He was too stubborn to seek the middle ground; he wasn't a team player; and he was a bulldog lacking the requisite finesse. The lab needed the right balance of experiments and accelerator development and, because it was universally agreed to at the top that he wasn't fit for that delicate job – requiring both good judgment and a cool, rational outlook – we decided to look outside for someone up to the task. Thus, since it's bluntness you want, my straight answer to one of your knife-edged questions is, yes, in a way Ken was forced out.

"Getting to the meeting in October 1969, I do have some memories of it, hazy as they are. The first point I want to make is that my motive for calling it in the first place and for acting as I did was out of deference to the tenured staff and regard for their feelings. I must admit to being quite naïve about the whole business. I felt that, before they saw it in a cold memo issued by me to the whole lab, I should inform them that Ken was resigning. I didn't have to do that, but I chose to anyway. I wanted to show them the respect that I believed was due them. Although it should have dawned on me that Ken might put up vigorous resistance to the decision, it somehow didn't occur to me. I still find it hard to understand how I could've missed it. Worse yet, I failed completely to anticipate that some of the accelerator staff would become so uncontrollably incensed. So, on the day of the meeting, there I was, uncharacteristically unprepared for such a strong emotional outpouring. The aggression and antagonism leveled at me were about as intense as can be; and the conduct of these otherwise sane men was totally out of line. Certainly I didn't deserve such treatment. Under the circumstances, I did the best I could. After they worked themselves into a dither, what could I do but try to calm everyone down? I assure you that the things I said and did were for that purpose, and that purpose alone. That was it. There was no more to it than that.

"As for that so-called commitment I'm supposed to have made and that accursed finger-pointing at me for reneging on a promise, that's all no more than a lot of poppycock. I would never do such a thing, and I didn't. The simple fact is that it is not in my nature to behave that way. Besides, I simply didn't have the authority to be able to follow through. All high-level personnel matters are integrated decisions made by the top lab management in full consultation with the AUI Board. Tacit agreement from all of them as well as formal AUI approval is required for all such actions. That means that the Director can't make them unilaterally. There are no ifs, ands, or buts about it. The rule is firm and unqualified. There are no exceptions, no mitigating circumstances. How could you think that I would flout such a deep-seated imperative and tradition? How it really happened was that in discussions lasting over a period of weeks, perhaps even a month or more, the deal was crafted and the entire matter settled. Yes, it was all irrevocably decided long before the October meeting in my office. By the time that was called, there wasn't a chance in hell of turning back, regardless of the passionate feelings of the AD tenured staff. Even if I'd wanted to, I was powerless to pull it off. However, because of the extreme character of the feelings that were exhibited at that messy Friday affair, I did inform the Board and the top lab management that weekend. I told them everything that had transpired, but, as I'd expected, it changed nothing. Too many had put themselves on the line for it. Any possibility of reversal was a lost cause.

"Then there was Rabi. You particularly implicated him in your picture of some sort of conspiracy. If you're an outsider trying to get a slant on what's going on in the inner circle, why shouldn't you grasp at that straw? After all he was a man who carried with him the aura of power. He was perfect playing the role of the man behind the scenes, directing the course of events. And it's true: he had his hands in everything. You couldn't do much at the lab without his concurrence. Why shouldn't you believe that he was the one pulling the strings? Well, I'm not going to argue with you about that. The fact is: how could he not be involved? Of course he was. But, for a man who wanted to know everything and for the most part got what he wanted, that wasn't unusual. However, if you ask whether he masterminded the whole thing, not a chance! It was a consensus decision, pure and simple.

"And that, Mister Mickey, is *the Ken Green story of 1969* to the best of my recollection. I hope it helps you and sets your mind to rest. But, given your attitude and your mind-set, perhaps that's asking for too much. Anyway, to cap the story, I should review the historical details. They're part of the public record and are rather straightforward: When the informational meeting was held on that Friday afternoon, the resignation announcement had already been prepared; then it was copied over the weekend and sent out on Monday as scheduled. No fuss! No bother! No second thoughts! No last-minute reprieves! Take it or leave it, what I have told you is the unadorned truth – the whole megillah. There is no more to tell.

"Finally, you asked about the circumstances of my leaving the Director's office in 1973, after a little more than two terms. Here there's no mystery. I resigned when my second term ended because, after putting in more than my share of administrative service, I'd fulfilled my obligation to the lab and the science community. It was time for me to get back to what I really love and that is doing physics research. I'd certainly earned that privilege. I deserved no less. And that's exactly what I did.

"Well, there you have it, the Goldhaber point of view of history in a nutshell. I'm not sure it gives you exactly what you wanted to hear, but let me assure you that it's as close to the real truth of what took place as you're likely to get. Having seen and experienced much in my lifetime, I'm well aware of the difficulty of recreating the past. So I've come to the viewpoint that such a difficult endeavor as that ought best to be left to the full-of-energy younger generation. I guess that means you." Maurice formed a mischievous smile, and while nodding to Mickey, extended his arm as if he were saying, *it's your show*.

Mickey had a hunch that Maurice had pulled off a coup using the old selective memory game. No, he wouldn't do that, not right in front of his Director-peers, and not here smack in the middle of getting-it-off-your-chest territory! Indeed, everything pointed toward Maurice having told the truth as best he knew. How could Mickey do other than give him the benefit of the doubt? On the other hand, Mickey continued to reflect, whether planned or unplanned, don't we all shave the truth a little? As time goes by, doesn't the truth as anyone sees it go through a process of filtering and become shaded or even modified by the conveniences and demands of the moment of each recollection? That awful lesson hit him, as it always did, like a ton of bricks. Although it had that effect on him, it shouldn't have, seeing as how he'd learned and accepted long ago that memories are relative, depending on when and why the remembering takes place and of course on who is doing the remembering. That's just the way the mind works. It helps you make your arguments, justify your conduct and behavior, get through the day, and survive the pains of ill fortune. So it is that once an experience – an action, an event, or any happening – gets into the mind, it is no longer subject to the rules of rationality and reasoned judgment, but rather comes under the sway and jurisdiction of the iron grip of Darwinian logic. Damn it, Mickey brooded! Wasn't that exactly the reason he came to this place of truth – to get away from all this vagueness and ambiguity of the human mind? Had he bit off more than he could chew with this endeavor he'd undertaken? Was he capable of finding that needle in the haystack – that funny thing called truth? Was it even there at all? Wait a minute! Mickey collected himself. Why was he thinking in such a juvenile manner? Why was he going on so half-cocked and like a chicken without a head? Was it merely because Maurice had put up a brilliant defense, contrary to Mickey's expectations? Was that what sent Mickey into this muddleheaded fluster, this scatterbrained frenzy? Well, if that's what the reason was, Mickey was simply going to have nothing of it. Who knows? Maurice could well have been right on the money.

Thus his misgivings and reservations about his mission and his self-doubt were just part of a passing thought flashing through his mind. You see, Mickey the pessimist was a contradiction in terms – an oxymoron. It wasn't more than that his momentary insecurity arose because he'd half-wanted Maurice to be more shaken. He certainly hadn't expected this offering up of such a cogent description of Maurice's version of things. Perhaps he didn't want to, but Mickey really had no choice but to be impressed by Maurice's adeptness and skill in telling the story. And even if Maurice was a bit disingenuous and told it solely as he wanted it seen, still that was no reason for Mickey to give up the ghost and quit the field.

Mickey knew that he couldn't dwell on such philosophical issues for long. He would have more than enough time for that later. Catching himself from wandering off course any more than he already had, and without a moment to lose, he got back to the business at hand. He complimented Maurice on the responsiveness and directness of his answers to the pointed and maybe even overly aggressive questions put to him. Boy, was he happy with himself for making that concession when he so much didn't want to! It made him feel on top of things. Yes, he was in control again. Just then, Mickey glanced at his watch and noting that it was closing in on four, with a smile and a shrug, he commented that time was fleeting, and turned to Vineyard.

* * * * *

George

Before Mickey could return to the questioning, George interjected that he didn't know how everybody else felt, but he needed a break. *A great suggestion* was the consensus, and without hesitation the five of them trooped through the curtain opened by Mickey, who, thinking ahead, had discovered the location of the Open Sesame button. Heading for the men's room, they meandered around the empty tables in the adjacent darkened chamber and then marched down the narrow dimly lit hallway situated immediately to the right of the bar. About ten minutes later when they'd all returned, they found a light snack awaiting them: pitchers of lemonade and iced tea, and a plate of chocolate chip and raisin oatmeal cookies. Each one filled a glass and took his seat. Drinking and munching, they were in a jovial mood. Mickey had mixed feelings about this, knowing he would be the one to have to transform the lightness back to the seriousness befitting the subject they were there to talk about. Still, the atmosphere was upbeat and full of promise; and Mickey reveled in it. Except for him, the other four were talking up a storm. Obviously, whether they'd been friends or enemies in the past, they had much to say to each other. But to Mickey, the words melded together into a din without meaning. He was deep in thought about how he would handle his questions for George. Then, he was suddenly snapped out of his solitude when Nick, as unpredictable as ever, quipped, "Where's the gin?" Mickey wondered whether this was Nick's typical sort of backhanded criticism aimed at him; or, on the other hand, maybe it was just Nick's way of helping to keep things on the light side. Choosing to presume the latter, Mickey in the same vein piped up, "If there's anyone who doesn't need liquor to loosen him up and cut to the quick of things, it's you, Nick." In the meantime, the other three seemed to be having a heck of a time, and getting a kick out of the whole affair. In particular, Maurice was exceptionally perky. He was clearly caught up in the spirit of one of those as-good-as-they-come leisurely interludes, where time appears suspended. Happy as a clam, he cried out, as if to himself, "Ah, just what we all needed."

Mickey couldn't help but feel good about the zestful, free-and-easy, happy-sounding chatter around him. But for him, this break was an opportunity to clarify in his mind and to develop the right and proper, suitably politic wording for the Vineyard questions; and he took as much time as he could. Then, feeling a pinch of nervousness about the clock moving relentlessly on, he took a last throat-moistening sip of lemonade, and, even before all of them finished their munching and gabbing, he jumped in and began to speak: "Before I get to your specific questions, George, I think that to refresh all our memories it might be useful for me to briefly review some of the relevant history dating back to the early sixties. So carry yourselves back to that time when BNL was on top of the world. The AGS had come on line beautifully and was a smashing hit. Yet, as outstanding a feat as that machine was, somehow the lab was unable to grasp the true extent of its significance for the future. A new era for physics was emerging, but the lab's management – with a head start over any would-be competitors – just couldn't sense the true nature of what lay ahead, and so couldn't take advantage of its position. Even as the lab's leaders wallowed in the praise, the tributes, and the flattery for what they'd achieved, others, quicker on the uptake, were readying themselves to take the new road and steamroll right over them.

"Perhaps it was living in a dream-world fantasy of the past, but BNL was steadfastly and stubbornly prepared to stick by and implement the by then infamous Berkeley-BNL gentleman's agreement, giving Berkeley the right to build the next big accelerator project. It should have surprised no one then that in the emerging sky's-the-limit physics era the laughable coast-to-coast agreement went up in smoke. Any reasonable man couldn't have missed the many signals floating about: the Ramsey Panel report, the unimaginable beam energies envisioned to be right around the corner, and the talk of fabulous colliders. Nonetheless, BNL and Berkeley were stuck in their long-outdated world of make-believe. They saw themselves as thriving and on top of things, when in reality they were already in the process of decay. This was especially true of BNL, seemingly oblivious of the reality that this was the time for building giant machines and doing bigger and better things, not just redoing old-hat experiments. However, the BNL top men were slow-thinking men, and even after Fermilab was chosen to be the site for the new-day big-as-could-then-be-built accelerator, they still couldn't admit their shortsighted policy and persisted in their illusion of perpetual grandeur instilled in them in the lab's heyday.

"In January 1973, when you became the lab Director, BNL had already passed its prime and was on its way downhill. That was also the year of the electrifying *November revolution*, when the quark was finally lured from its hiding place and forced to reveal itself. Suddenly, excitement filled the air. What more was there lurking in the shadows? But to explore those *little fellows*, new big heretofore unheard of machines were demanded. Now was time for labs to demonstrate what they were made of. Unfortunately, by then, the AGS, once the crown jewel of high-energy physics, had become but a mediocrity. The name of the game was now high energy, as high as could be gotten, and the AGS just didn't have it anymore. Meanwhile, outside of BNL, *the high-energy game was busting out all over*. The electron machines all around the globe were busy as bees, and were moving smartly and expeditiously forward; while Fermilab and CERN were hard at work on the great push for ever higher proton energies. These two labs had their eyes set on the collider to end all colliders, or at least a step toward it. Not only were they vying for physics supremacy, but also they had that special urge of the scientific mind to stretch the bounds of man's understanding of the universe. And for that, the quark was the little beast you had to follow. Thus, as it became clear that, with the right machines, new physics – for a red-blooded physicist, the chance of a lifetime – was on the threshold of being discovered, the words capturing the imagination of the world of physics were *colliders* and *quarks*.

"With good reason therefore, as the seventies progressed, a furious and frenzied competition for accelerator facilities ensued. The prizes, knowledge and Nobels, were worth a lot to scientists; and the men racing were ready to put in all the effort they could muster to get their hands on them. This was a new apply-everything-you've-got breed. These men were hard and mean, and determined to be first. They were the perfect matches for the new order of free competition. But *free competition* more often than not means that you're in an unpredictable and chaotic mess of a fight, one that's career making but can just as easily be career breaking. Yes, it was a new day, with incredibly desirable prizes, and a new way of contending for them. But before you were able to get started on the quest, first you needed the machine; and this time, the right collider, the means to a winning end, was up for grabs. The day of gentlemen's agreements was over; and BNL, with no pre-arranged understanding to bank on anymore, would have to fight it out like all the others. Unprepared for such mud-slinging, gladiatorial jousting, the lab seemed doomed to a humble-pie dessert.

"Political know-how is central and imperative to how labs fare in the American national lab system. Unfortunately, although in the years following the lab's formation in the forties and the fifties, its political performance was the envy of the science community, by the early seventies, BNL seemed to be dying, and there was no one to halt the progression of its apparently terminal sickness. In only two decades, the lab had fallen from its political penthouse on Fifth Avenue to a dump in lower Brooklyn.

"How could it have come to that? When the lab began, the men who ran the place had an outstanding collective acumen about the way the world worked, manifesting itself in BNL's rapid rise to the top. But somehow this political acuity, insightfulness, and perspicacity got lost along the way. The management became but a shadow of what it previously was. By the mid-sixties, when BNL should've been preparing to keep up with the fast-changing times, particularly the raw combative conflict of free competition, it simply wasn't on the ball. The Director and his troupe of partygoers were too busy redecorating their offices, basking in the glory of past deeds. They simply didn't have the clarity of mind or the time to pay heed to what others were doing and what actually was happening outside their self-made fortress. So, while the BNL sun was setting on the East Coast, the sun with a new shining light was rising in the Midwest.

"Perhaps it happened that way because BNL's great leader of the early days, Rabi, who'd been the guiding force behind BNL's express thrust into the limelight, wasn't what he used to be. By the sixties he'd become weary, old, and tired. Unfortunately for the lab, Rabi forgot to pay sufficient attention to the all-important succession. After the fact, you could see the quandary he was in. Who was there that could fill his big shoes? Who could equal the matchless Rabi when he was young and in his prime? There was no one who could take the political reins he had handled so well for so many years. He was irreplaceable, so what else could he do but just forget the will, wander away, and leave it to others to take care of the after-Rabi era?

"Thus the lab seemed destined to continue its slide downward. Then, out of the blue, *there was you*! How could anyone have guessed that hope would pop out of nowhere in the guise of someone like you? On the face of it, what did you have to offer? First you were a university professor, then you came to BNL as a theoretical physicist, then you became Chairman of its Physics Department when Goldhaber succeeded Haworth, and then you were chosen to be the lab's Deputy Director in Goldhaber's second term. What kind of political credentials are those? To be frank, they're squat! Nonetheless, wonder of wonders, you ended up having what it takes.

"So it was that fortune smiled on BNL. True, you got the job because no one of high stature from the outside would take it on. But what luck that turned out to be. When you came on board in 1973, you gave the lab its big break when it needed it most. You gave the unbelievers – all reasonable men – the surprise of their lives. You seemed to take naturally to the political component of your new job, learning the ropes with astonishing ease and speed. Then came your big test. In the summer of 1977, with dexterity no one thought you had, you executed a once-in-a-lifetime political coup that transformed you into one hell of a big winner. You orchestrated quite a show. Remember the drama that filled the air with electricity when Congress approved ISABELLE smack in the middle of the Wood's Hole meeting of DOE's HEPAP sub-panel. It was a time to treasure, a time when everything seemed to be coming up roses. ISABELLE was alive!

"Meanwhile at home the lab focused its resources on the new dream project, applying thought and effort at a level unseen there since the fifties. High hopes swelled in everyone. Everywhere were scientists and engineers, with dedication and passion, putting the finishing touches on the design, working through the engineering details for the multitude of components, debating the anticipated physics, and bringing to life the detectors that would be the project's capstones. Then, to top off the lab's new style, the one that you brought with you, massive R&D was appropriately being concentrated on the especially intricate magnet that ISABELLE still had to see realized. The people doing all this felt pride in what they were doing and worked themselves to the bone both for science and to bolster the project that would make the lab great again. They actually believed that they could do it – pull the lab from the quagmire and up by its bootstraps.

"But it was only an illusion, a trick of the mind. In spite of all the work and resources that were poured into the project, ISABELLE never amounted to anything. In fact, it was only a short four years later when DOE made the decision to toss in the towel and dump it. So, from the champ of 1977, you became the chump of 1981.

"I've often wondered what happened in that brief four-year span to have caused such a turnaround. Actually, it isn't difficult to comprehend. As I see it, DOE's Doug Pewitt visited CERN in early 1981, saw what was going on vis-à-vis its new collider, and decided on the spot, perhaps with a little prodding from Leon back home, that the U.S. had no choice but to launch a competitor to Rubbia's antiproton project to find the elusive W particle. It's quite likely that his first reaction was that ISABELLE ought to be the one to carry the ball for America. However, Pewitt was of a type to let free competition reign. He was a straight-from-the-shoulders, no-nonsense man. To him, playing favorites was a no-no. Being a pragmatist, and being well aware of ISABELLE's less than stellar technical record, he resolved that if BNL was unwilling or unable to do the job, then he would support Fermilab's collider proposal. This strategy of giving BNL first dibs made sense because ISABELLE seemed well on its way to becoming a real machine, while Fermilab's product was still in the conceptualization stage. So it would seem that, by giving the lab a fair shot at being first, Pewitt was not the devil incarnate as he's often portrayed at BNL.

"It was primarily patriotism that drove Pewitt. He wanted America to be first, and would do whatever was necessary to that end. Doug was a man of action and, although reasonable to a degree, he wouldn't suffer naysayers and had no patience for dilly-dallying. You were either with him or against him. After Doug saw all he had to see at CERN, he returned home with his game plan set. However, for some reason that has always eluded my understanding, you wouldn't go along with his idea of shaping ISABELLE into a CERN competitor. That was a really bad mistake on your part. Pewitt was the wrong man to say *no* to. Knowing the two of you, it wasn't any great shakes to predict that you and Doug would fall into a bitter feud. And you did. This dispute erupted with explosive force during the chaotic Temple Review at BNL in the summer of 1981, which culminated in an embarrassingly quarrelsome public display of emotion, a shouting match with the angry words of men who felt betrayed. The upshot is that you managed to outrage and infuriate Pewitt to such a degree that within the next few months, you ended up resigning and ISABELLE construction was placed under DOE's direct control; and then two years later the already comatose project was formally canceled. This was quite a comedown from the hope generated by your striking political success of 1977. Would that it had ended differently! But when two foaming bulls engage each other, head to head, horns interlocking, it's hard to see an outcome without one flat on his back. Too bad you were the one to fall.

"Well, that's my Reader's-Digest-like condensed version of ISABELLE's sad fate. However, there's just one loose end that I'd like to explore with you. In late 1980 or early 1981, when BNL was still not able to build a practicable ISABELLE magnet, Wilson came to BNL as an emissary from Fermilab to persuade you to accept Leon's offer to provide Fermilab magnets, which had been proved workable, to fill the bill. This idea made considerable sense to DOE: It would satisfy Pewitt's desire to mount an

American competitor to CERN. It would get Wallenmeyer off the hook for having too long endorsed the fast-failing ISABELLE. It would satisfy Leon because it would give him the appearance of a hero saving the day for America. And finally, logic demands that it should have satisfied you. But mysteriously, it didn't; and therein, in your seemingly inexplicable reaction, is a most puzzling dilemma, one that strains credulity and belies the mind's supposed rationality. Consider the likely outcome if you'd gone the other way: It would've given you a way of privately washing the lab's dirty laundry; it would've suppressed the project's technical and financial problems that came as a result of the lab's persistent and obstinate attempt to cling to an unsatisfactory and possibly unbuildable magnet; and it would've presented you with the most desirable image of being a political mastermind. Yet, as good as all this sounds, unfortunately you blocked it from being done. Now George, why in heaven's name did you give *thumbs-down* to such an eminently reasonable proposal? And more, why did you treat Wilson so badly in the bargain? Did he really deserve to be rebuffed and so humiliated? Poor man! He had to leave the lab, not only having failed in his mission, but also having been demeaned in the process. It's hard to understand why you couldn't have been more gracious.

"Whew! Finally, I'm done. Now it's time for my explicit questions. One way or another, they're all connected to that most extraordinary chain of events leading to ISABELLE's free-fall, from its high point to the shadow of death. As succinctly as I can, here goes: Why did you reject the Fermilab-DOE offer? Why didn't the lab give Wilson the welcome a man of his station deserved? What were the reasons behind the angry and contentious public exchange between you and Pewitt at that hostile Temple Review? And to close, were you compelled to resign, and if so who was involved and how were they able to exert such influence over you?"

When Mickey stopped talking, he looked straight at George to see if he could discern the nature of his response. But he couldn't penetrate George's inscrutable mask. So he sat quietly for a moment, somewhat numb. He became sapped of energy, and he felt spent. He tried to rest and calm himself. Then suddenly a change occurred in him, all of itself. Self-doubt began to fill his brain, as his mind raced along on its own steam. There was no stopping it. He found himself quite unable to shake the spell of a turn of second guessing himself: Had he been too blunt or too harsh? Had he been sufficiently fair and even-handed? Had he tried too hard thereby making his account and portrayal of the events overdone and unnatural? Had he put too much preparation into it, giving it too much rigidity and causing it to be of low believability? Having waited so many years to ask George these things face to face, he hoped he hadn't screwed things up. Apart from his self-absorption, he also wondered about George: Might he be embarrassed and angry at being so put on the spot? Might he just be unresponsive and distant? However, Mickey had little to worry about on both these scores because George was a worldly person. He'd anticipated frankness on Mickey's part and, like Mickey, he was prepared to be up-front, blunt, and unguarded. There was to be no mincing of words from him either. He was determined to speak straight from the shoulder. Yes, he'd come to this party ready to give as good as he got. Mickey, still unsure of himself and uncertain of George, continued to look anxiously at the man on the hot seat, who was deep in thought. Although he guessed that was a good sign, he remained in suspense and keyed up, full of tension. He waited with bated breath. Then George slowly and deliberately lifted his head and smiled, not a wide and happy smile, but a subtle and ironic one. He was on the verge of speaking, but hesitated theatrically, drawing the attention of the others at the table. Mickey realized at that moment that any fears he might've had were needless: George was in complete control of himself as well as of the situation. Mickey's itchiness and thirst to know what would come next heightened as he gazed at the man preparing to answer him and maybe even uncharacteristically bare his soul. But George was now in command of the performance, and he took his own sweet time in starting the show. So, as eager as Mickey was for responses to the difficult queries he'd posed, he had to wait until George was good and ready.

"Look," George began, "your story is not all wrong, but to get it closer to being right, you have to go further into the real but hidden intentions of the men involved. Bob and Leon did agree to provide the Fermilab magnets for ISABELLE, that's true enough. But I never believed for a minute that they really wanted to help us. I talked with Bob when he came to the lab and I also discussed the matter with Wallenmeyer and with Pewitt. There wasn't the least doubt in my mind that these were not people the Director of BNL should put any trust or faith in. I didn't come to this judgment lightly. In as much detail as was humanly possible, I scrutinized their proposition to me, and the counsel they were offering as well. I went over their ideas and advice with a fine-toothed comb. I set up a critical evaluation with my staff, examining and re-examining every word said and written. I probed and searched. The study was exhaustive. I analyzed every possible consequence. I inferred every implication that there could possibly have been. I theorized all manner of things. I conjured up trial balloons. I played devil's advocate. Believe it or not, I looked hard for any good points there might have been. I explored as far as I dared go. I plumbed the depths of their overture. I poured over what they said they were giving the lab till I was blue in the face. Then I looked at the nuances. I read between the lines. I tried to insert what was left unsaid. And, after all this effort, after all this painstaking diligence, after all this critical thoroughness, after all this meticulous attention, and after all this vigilant wariness, what do you think I ended up with? You might criticize it as a foregone conclusion. You might say that given the history of the two labs, BNL and Fermilab, my reaction was predictable. Nevertheless, the truth is that I perceived there was more to their apparent gift than meets the eye. For me, their credibility was in dire short supply; and I came to see in their proposal the telltale signs of treachery. I simply couldn't avoid what was plain as day. So it was that I came to appreciate that their true intent and real purpose was not to help us but rather to delay us.

"The stench of an anti-BNL vendetta seeped at me from all sides. Such were the times that even the extreme interpretation of these *honorable* men being in a conspiracy against the lab seemed quite probable. To this day, I still believe that there actually was one. So, you can see why I felt that I – and I alone – had to be in the driver's seat, that I had to be the one calling the shots. I just couldn't play the featherweight with all those heavies out for my hide. Thus, surrounded by would-be assassins, what was I to do about their *offer*? I figured that once I gave Fermilab control for manufacturing the project's magnets – its key component – BNL would become totally vulnerable and at the mercy of its enemies. I believed that, once the lab was beholden to them, more than likely, Fermilab would drag its feet and keep BNL's needs as a low priority while pretending and contending that it wasn't so. Remember that by then Leon had already started work on his own collider, which quickly became an American competitor to ISABELLE. How could any reasonable man expect that, once in the game, the Fermilab management would voluntarily and purposefully give BNL an edge? Not on your life! So I came to believe that what Leon and his associates-in-crime really wanted was for me to admit that ISABELLE was in trouble and couldn't be completed without assistance from the outside. However, doing so would give Fermilab free reign to take the initiative and do what it wanted to in order to pull ahead. Then would come their scheme's true raison d'être: it would make BNL weak and easy pickings to knock off. That's the way I saw it: Could anyone disagree that they were trying to trick me into agreeing to take a back seat to Fermilab as far as the next American collider was concerned? Could anyone disagree that the real meaning of that is that ISABELLE would be a dead duck? Could anyone disagree that, to top off the blackguards' stratagem, Fermilab would be put in the catbird seat where it always wanted to be? How could these men – men of science, after all – ask such a self-defeating thing of me? Did they think that the great lab I was directing and I were simply playthings to push around at their whim? How did they have the gall to ask me to put my bare, unguarded neck into Leon's eager claws? Never! I couldn't and wouldn't go for that.

"What I've given you so far is my analysis of what was going on at BNL vis-à-vis ISABELLE in the first half of 1981. I think it's about as true an account as you're likely to get. However, regardless of whether or not I'm right, I hope it gives you a sense of why I acted as I did. OK, let's get on with it. Taking this picture I've painted as background, let me now turn to your particular questions. To your first and perhaps most important one, I've already given you my answer: Briefly restating it, I rejected Leon's offer to use Fermilab's magnets in ISABELLE because I was convinced that it wasn't made in good faith. Although there was some rational reasoning behind my arriving at that viewpoint, it wasn't pure logic that pushed me to see it that way. It was more that gnawing feeling in the gut that just wouldn't let go of me.

"Turning next to your accusation – actually more like a denunciation – that I mistreated Bob during his BNL visit, I must be frank and tell you that I don't think I did. On the other hand, since, at that moment in time, I was agitated and alarmed at being ganged up on, and ready to explode emotionally at the slightest provocation, perhaps I wasn't as gracious as I might've been. For that I can only plead *mea culpa.* Come to think of it, I probably should've been a bigger man than I was: I should've been able to overcome my self-indulgent feelings that both I and the lab were being victimized; and I should've been chivalrous enough to behave more generously towards Bob. The truth is that whatever I felt about him as a competitor and as a man, he did do a lot of good for our country's science program as well as for the glory of physics. Yes, I should've been more respectful of that. Still, I think you do me a grave injustice by claiming that I acted in some kind of insulting or contemptuous manner toward him, although I must admit to my mind being just a bit hazy about what actually took place. In any case, if I in fact did humiliate or degrade him in any way, I'm truly sorry about that. I certainly wasn't cognizant of doing it. Although nothing can be done to alter what happened, if I did him wrong, I hope Bob, wherever he is, can find it in his heart to forgive me.

"Before I tackle the question relating to Mister Pewitt, I must say something about how Wallenmeyer fitted into the picture. My impression of him was that he was on the fence, but that should be no surprise to anyone who knew him because that's where he inevitably turned up. Whenever there was an issue of two sides or more, you can be sure it would be most difficult to tell where he stood. That was his way of leaving his options open to choose whichever proved to be the most favorable side to come down on. I wouldn't want to pass judgment on him, but that's just the way he was. In the past, he'd always been a strong and visible supporter of the lab. Then he began to change. When the lab needed moral support, he wasn't to be found. When the lab needed someone to speak up for it to Wallenmeyer's superiors in the DOE and to the big wheels in the halls of Congress, he wasn't there. When the lab needed unforeseen financial assistance, he didn't put his heart into getting it as in the past. More often than not, the money didn't come, and the lab management was left to its own devices. Moving funds around to correct a problem, when there isn't enough of it to go around, is like putting your finger in the dyke, and every time you do, a new hole opens up somewhere else. Eventually, the whole thing will collapse and you'll find yourself inundated with the unwelcome flood – not of money, alas, but of censure and condemnation. Nevertheless, despite being left in the lurch, the lab was managing to squeeze through.

"Perhaps Wallenmeyer's wavering should have sent me a signal that I would've done well to heed. However, in spite of his fading support for the lab, I continued to believe in and depend on him. In hindsight, I now know that by the early eighties he couldn't be taken seriously anymore and I should've been looking elsewhere. The truth about Wallenmeyer was that by then he'd ceased to be a central player in the high-energy physics political game. Over the years, all his shenanigans just caught up with him; and his influence and power dwindled to almost nothing. At one point John Deutsch almost fired him because John came to find Bill's finagling with the budget and with people too much to take. No doubt I should've seen the circumstances changing before my very eyes. I can only attribute my unfortunate attitude and outlook to mistaking illusion for reality, false for true, and desire for evidence. I simply turned a blind eye to what was really happening. You see, insight just picked up and fled from me. Thus, being about as wrong as I could be, I chose to keep my stock in Bill. I believed to the end that he would come down on our side, and that this would give us an eleventh hour win. But that turned out to be a big mistake: Not only was I thick-headed about Wallenmeyer's decline, but I didn't at all count on the empowerment and the rapidly growing clout, potency, and sphere of influence of that insidious Mister Pewitt.

"Doug Pewitt wasn't a subtle man. Sarcasm flowed effortlessly from his lips; and his ruthlessness and cruelty knew no bounds. All in all, he was an openly nasty and extremely unlikable man. I had no doubt that his intentions were anything but honorable. He had blood on his mind, and BNL and I were his targets. What ate at me most was the way he publicly raked ISABELLE and the lab over the coals; the way he berated and impugned us; and, in the end, the way he damned and doomed us. If there was any single person responsible for wiping out ISABELLE, it was this odious and menacing little man.

"As disagreeable as it is for me to do, I guess I must now address that terrible Temple Review that changed my life. It was there – in front of my friends, my university colleagues, and my lab associates and staff – that he excoriated me, chastised me, indicted me, condemned me, and applied the coup de grâce that ended my days at BNL. Yes, it was there that I was driven to plunge over the edge and explode. In hindsight life always seems simpler than it was in the living of it, and this case was no exception. I can easily and clearly see now that I should've controlled myself. After all, I was the lab Director and my top priority had to be the lab. Emotional venting in public may be the privilege of some, but for those in executive positions, where diplomacy and statesmanship are paramount, it is *verboten*. It is not easy for me to admit, but the fact is that I became so enraged at the treatment the lab and I were accorded that I lost it. I simply broke down. I guess all of us have our breaking points, and Pewitt, with Temple as his helper in goading, found mine. The result was my public outburst: What a temper I was in! So provoked, so exasperated, so seething with acrimony and resentment was I that I flew off the handle and allowed my passions to reign. I stewed. I smoldered. I fumed. I stormed. I raised hell. I was fit to be tied. I vented my spleen. I bristled. I saw red. Then, as quickly as it started, with my tantrum drained away and my body exhausted beyond imagining, I quit and became quiet. But in that moment of pique, in that fit of mad anger, down went my career.

"When that awful summer finally ended, a pall fell over the lab, even though superficially the business of daily living went on as if nothing had happened. However, for me, as you can well appreciate, things could never be the same. Although nobody told me to resign, I knew there was no way for me to come back and deal with the Washington men I found to be so dishonest and utterly distasteful. I felt that my authority as a lab Director and as a man could never be resurrected. So, for the good of the lab and its future, after much soul searching, I came to the decision, entirely on my own and with no pressure at all from the Trustees, to leave the post I'd worked so hard at over the years. The official act of resignation was arrived at that fall during a regularly scheduled meeting of the Board. It was all very proper and polite – civilized, you might say – but the handwriting was on the wall. Although they affirmed their prior support for any decision I made, I knew they wanted me to go almost as much as I understood that I had to leave. In the end, we agreed amicably, respectfully, and courteously, as gentlemen should, that it would be best if I stepped down, and that's what I did."

You could have heard a pin drop. The room was silent. Not a peep! No one stirred. George became a little flushed, filled with some manner of inner excitation. Then suddenly a change occurred. A kind of relaxed serenity overcame him, and he sat, tranquil and composed, yet wide-awake, with just a hint of a self-satisfied smile on his long bony face. He seemed at peace with himself and with the world. As for Mickey, he was exceptionally taken by George's forthrightness and candor. He was also relieved and very pleased that this delicate exchange of versions of ISABELLE's descent had gone as smoothly as it had. There'd been absolutely no rancor or personal animosity in George that he could detect. However, there was more to George's performance than an unimpeachable exhibition of laying-it-on-the-line straight talk. Upon reflection, Mickey came to realize that he'd been witness to an astonishing private from-the-heart statement. He had a decided urge to express admiration for how George so vividly and expressively portrayed that time when grim, distressing, and forbidding circumstances and events weighed heavily on him and cut right to his heart. However, given the situation Mickey found himself in, that was easier said than done.

In what manner could someone of Mickey's common-man station presume to address this aristocratic man of such stature and achievement? Could he casually remark to this gentleman, *well done, George, you did a great job*? Such comments coming from Mickey were surely inappropriate and out-of-line. George was the big man of the two, while Mickey was just the little guy. If Mickey said anything, it would have to be humble; and although he felt humble at that moment, it wasn't in his make-up to show himself in that way. Not only was it unnatural for him to conduct himself so, but also he couldn't abide the phoniness of trying to be someone he wasn't. Thus, with apparently no way out, he was locked into inaction. He looked around the table as if appealing for help, but the others sat with heads bowed in silence, trying to absorb and digest the combination of melancholy and esteem they all felt for George. A short time passed and no one spoke. What could Mickey do? The show being his, there was simply nothing left for him but to bite the bullet and say something; and whatever it was to be, it would best come quickly. He began to feel an increasing pressure to act. Yet there was precious little time to think. It soon became clear that his only alternative was to trust his instincts, cross his fingers, and pray. So, that's what he did, and without knowing what would come out, he cleared his throat, stared at George for perhaps a little longer than necessary, then carefully enunciated, almost in a whisper, "George, I think I can speak for all of us and thank you for presenting us with a very special experience. You gave us a rare glimpse into your inner feelings. It was a wonderfully generous thing for you to do." As commonplace and innocuous as this commentary was, there was wholehearted agreement, and gestures of approval sprung simultaneously from all the men sitting around the table. After such an unimaginative response, it was quaint and not a little ludicrous to see Mickey fill with pride and self-satisfaction that verged on smugness. However, this swellheaded self-conceit, this vain and pompous appearance he had, wasn't to last too long.

He looked up and his muscles tightened as he found himself face to face with Nick, who was staring at him from across the table. This brought him back to reality. Self-congratulation was clearly premature seeing as how he was on the threshold of the biggest and most difficult test of his trip to wonderland. It was after half past four, and that gave him less than an hour to engage Nick, his erstwhile nemesis. He knew that action was demanded on his part. However, despite the immediate need he felt to move on and begin the Nick part of the show, he nonetheless couldn't let go of George, at least not just yet. You see, at that very instant, there came to him an evanescent moment, one with time standing still. It was an involuntary psychic event. His thoughts whirled about as he converged on the matter of what had happened to the tall patrician gentleman after the turmoil of 1981 when he had his date with destiny.

Like many in similar circumstances who had preceded him, George, after being the top dog for so long, found the road back rocky and tough to navigate. After he was cut loose from the power game he'd played in the Director's office, he took the standard steps to return to the *status quo ante*. He tried to reactivate his full-time research in solid-state physics, where he'd spent his early career. However, going back to science after spending years in administration isn't a piece of cake. Yes, all his old buddies were behind him. Yes, he worked as hard as he was able to. Yes, he gave it his best shot. Still, there was that well-known barrier experienced by many returning scientists who were tempted by the political call or who were persuaded to serve. Nevertheless, with optimism in his heart, George thought he might just beat the odds. But, like many gamblers who strive for that illusion, he couldn't get the better of the laws of chance. He was bound to fail, and he did. You see, nothing from the past would suffice anymore. An irrevocable change in science's character took place while he was away, and there was simply no way to turn back the clock. It was sad to see him try to reestablish himself. He put everything he had into it. But, nothing seemed to be sufficient; and, even though everyone was rooting for him, ready and willing to help, it just wasn't to be.

What in particular happened, you ask? The university community stood foursquare behind him. Many academic positions were offered. The most prestigious institutions of higher learning in the country opened their doors to him. They were all prepared to honor him and to give him his due, his reward for the service he had performed. He did make a stab at it. He spent 1982 and 1983 first at Harvard University and then at the Institute for Theoretical Physics in Santa Barbara. Unfortunately, with the young having stepped in and moved steadily ahead during the years of his absence, he felt inadequate and out of place. No doubt about it, he was ill equipped for an academic comeback. Outmatched and out of his depth, his scientific performance was simply not up to snuff.

However, being the man that he was, George didn't give up easily and looked for an alternative way to make himself still count. He sought a productive future by grasping at the oft-taken road of committees and boards, and became an advisor and consultant to labs and government agencies. Although this seemed to work for a time, fortune wasn't riding along with him: He could never find the right fit that would again give him a sense that he still had value and merit, that he still was a man of consequence, and that there was still something left in him that was of worth and usefulness to science. As the months passed, he would've settled for some moments of solitude and contentment, but even that eluded him. In time, he became a man without a purpose, without the ability to serve his community or his country. After his fall in 1981, it seemed that any path to vindication was unattainable. Then, in 1986, when all seemed lost, a ray of light shone on him as he was elected to be President of the American Physical Society. His schedule of service was to act as Vice-President in his first year, as President Elect in his second year, and finally as President in his third year, 1988. As it happened, he completed the first year, and began to serve the second as President Elect. But lady luck didn't remain with him long enough, and in February 1987, before he had the opportunity to serve his year as President, he died. This short, woeful resumé flashed through Mickey's mind as he peered at the stately man. He wondered why fate had been so unkind to George as this unblessed man neared the end of his life.

Suddenly Mickey's mind clicked back to what he was there for that magical afternoon. With the all but instantaneous interlude of remembrance over, even though it was dominated by melancholy thoughts of lost opportunity, he strangely was invigorated. Now he felt prepared to deal with big bad Nick. Meanwhile, unaware of what was going through Mickey's mind, Nick was looking impatiently at him, puzzled by the long pause and wondering what was coming next.

* * * * *

Nick

Of all these brief contacts that Mickey sought so diligently, so unflaggingly, and with such tenacity, he felt most skittish about the one fast approaching. He could sense the stress building up in him along with the fast-forming burning heartburn in his gut. It was a sensation that he'd come to know only too well. Much like the pain of an old war injury that comes back to a soldier when something dreaded is about to take place, this stress symptom, originating deep within his subconscious mind, unfailingly returned to Mickey with the appearance of such pressure moments. No, there was no way he could fool his all-too sensitive gut. Mickey smiled ironically to himself as the thought occurred to him that his gut had the capability of foreshadowing what his conscious mind could not. However, this time, just as his gut was, he too was aware of the confrontation that was just moments away when he and Nick would come face to face, eye to eye. As he considered what it would be like, Mickey became shaky, apprehensive, and even a bit fearful about what he imagined would be a kind of showdown. Oddly, however, despite his feelings of being vulnerable, insecure, and wholly alone, he was actually looking forward to it. Imagine that these two contradictory reactions could coexist in his mind! Yes, far from wanting to distance himself from this upcoming war-of-words, to keep it at arm's length, he craved it, and couldn't wait for the opening round.

Over the years, Nick and Mickey hadn't gotten along. That's probably putting it far too mildly. The truth is that a lot of bitterness and hostility formed between them. But, with Nick being miles above Mickey in the hierarchy, Mickey couldn't figure out how to fight back, and so resorted to make-believe, a sort of imitation of *Walter Mitty's* secret life. What else could he do? He saw himself as some kind of white-pure David pitted against the malevolent and iniquitous Goliath. He romanticized the two of them as archenemies, dueling, as in days of yore, over some valuable treasure. Or he imagined himself the White Knight charging in to rescue the damsel in distress from the blackguard Nick. Too bad none of this romantic fantasy could come to real life! Just try to envisage Mickey rushing in to save the abused and suffering Dame ISABELLE from the tyrants in control! What a sight! More than that, if Mickey had actually won the day, what a change that would've made in BNL's history! Sad to say, such flights of fancy are but the stuff of dime novels and B-movies, which Mickey, by the way, had a heavy dose of when he was in his pre-teen years. But if you're waiting for such things to happen – for the good guys to wipe out the bad and rule the day – you'd be well advised not to hold your breath. The fact of real life was that Mickey had nowhere near Nick's muscle-power and sway; and he suffered over and over again from Nick's inner need to lord it over others. That was just the type of man Nick was. To Mickey's misfortune, his inflexible and willful resistance to the sort of restraint on his freedom that Nick demanded, coupled with his determination to go his own way, had the unsurprising effect of intensifying Nick's resolve to rein him in, tame him, and force his will on him. But Mickey was strong-headed and just wouldn't yield. There was simply nothing, not even Nick's shamefully vile and chilling methods, that could push him to succumb and concede. No, Mickey would live his life his way no matter what the consequences.

Although the memories of those old times lingered on, Mickey knew that there was nothing to be done about them. All that was over and done with long ago. He could imagine no alternative but to just let them rest in peace. Time heals, they say. So why not pour some soothing balm over these perhaps unsavory remembrances? That ought to do the trick. Actually, he didn't in the least need any artificial aid in the forgive-and-forget department. You see, the funny thing was that there was no more animosity toward Nick left in Mickey. It simply fled the coop. There wasn't even a trace of a desire for revenge. All the resentment and anger he once felt had vaporized and was gone. In fact, he felt some hard-to-explain sympathy for this aging, little man staring at him from across the table. Somehow, in time, a transition in his emotional temperament toward Nick had taken place, and, for reasons not apparent to him, Mickey had simply lost any lust for retribution.

But all this was beside the point. Here was Mickey's chance of a lifetime, and he wasn't about to let thoughts of past offenses against him and hurts inflicted interfere with his unquenchable thirst to know and understand the history Nick had stored in his brain. Thus, for the sake of discovery and with his newly found attitude toward Nick, Mickey was prepared – no, determined – to let bygones be bygones.

However, a coin has two sides. It takes two to tango, you know. A change in Mickey just wasn't sufficient. Nick would have to comply as well. Would he? Mickey wondered. As he remembered the kind of person Nick was in the old days, it just didn't jibe with the fact that Nick actually agreed to speak with him. Why, he thought, why did Nick make this trip to the land of truth? The optimist in Mickey said that miracles can happen and maybe time applied its healing ways, chastened Nick, and made him see the error of his ways. But, on the other hand, the pessimist in him insisted that people don't spontaneously change, and Nick certainly wasn't the type to bury the hatchet and make a fresh start. Then there was a further, perhaps more troublesome concern. Nick wouldn't be pleased with Mickey's version of things, not at all; and Mickey worried about how this volatile personality facing him might react to being point-blankly opposed, impugned, and even accused. But Mickey had gone over all this ground before; and, when all was said and done, now simply wasn't the time to hesitate or get cold feet. So he cast out from his mind any remnants of nervousness and anxiety. He threw caution to the wind and went ahead in the firm belief that Nick, by virtue of his being there, would go through with the game Mickey devised and answer the questions put to him. So, reassured that Nick needn't be a cause for alarm or apprehension, Mickey was ready to go. Yes, all would be smooth sailing.

"Nick," Mickey began, "before getting down to business, I want to mention and commend you on your impressive resumé that abounds in successes and honors. You were top-notch both as a scientist and as a lab and community leader. Anyone would be proud to have been what you were and achieved what you have. In your time, you were a man to reckon with. You weren't satisfied with just a share of the pie. No, you wanted it all. So, moving at full-throttle, with spirit and tenacious resolve, you aimed to get it. You played life at full-tilt, all the way to its limits. You were a man with a surfeit of energy, bursting at the seams for more and more action, always hustling, always looking for an edge. You were a man of the street. With you, there were no holds barred; and the word *no* was simply not in your vocabulary. Some fuddy-duddies might have questioned your tactics, but in this hard world, new ground is broken only by the fearless, who cross into unknown territory with abandon. If you had worried over every little detail, over the necessary *collateral damage*, you'd have done better just to stay home, sticking to the staid rules, and getting nowhere. That way, only few get hurt, but nothing of real worth gets done. Yes, you were indeed quite a man. One thing that surely can be said for you is that you gave it your all. You were the best that you could be. But, like the heroes of Greek tragedy, you had a flaw. It was the hubris in you that sapped you dry and drove you to the brink of disaster. However, all that is recorded in official and personal documents and in the memories of those who lived along with you in those highly charged times, jam-packed with glory and heartbreak. It is all past history. So let me not belabor the obvious. Still, there are some loose ends. Actually, that's why we're here. Its my big chance to ask you about these irksome issues that only you can throw light on. Now, seeing as time is marching on, let me move on to my background statement and my questions for you. I assure you that I will not mince words. I'll give it to you straight-out, free-tongued and blunt, just as I expect you would and in fact undoubtedly will.

"With your permission, I plan to explore two periods in your career. These two chapters in your colorful and eventful professional life that I want to bring up concern, first, the circumstances surrounding the DOE's cancellation of ISABELLE in 1983, about a year and a half after you became lab Director in 1982; and, second, the bizarre end of your tenure as Director fifteen years later, after three terms. Before posing my particular questions, let me give you all a brief review of the pertinent history spanning the almost two decades from about 1980 to 1997. So if we're all in accord on this, here goes!"

Some Background
The ISABELLE Affair

"With Pewitt on the warpath and carrying the DOE banner, ISABELLE was put on hold in 1981. Vineyard was desolated and literally wiped out by this action. By the end of the year, he was out of office, and you were in as Acting Director. You took to it like a fish to water. It was as if your new job and the challenge it entailed were made to order for you; and you jumped in with both feet. You stepped into the raging ISABELLE battle confidently, intrepidly, and skillfully, bringing with you the impressive duo of Bob Palmer and Ralph Shutt along with the formidable and potent resources of BNL's Physics Department. To put the project back on track required nerve and brains. But even armed with those, it would still be a tough and demanding road to hoe. Nevertheless, with faith and optimism, you scooped up the challenge and impetuously flew into the hornet's nest. Making the wise choice of going headlong into the technical accelerator shortcomings double-quick, you got off to a good start. The main glitch in the project lay in the design of its magnet and the implementation of the few hundred needed. To be sure, it was the lack of a workable superconducting magnet that was the central obstacle to the project's being wrapped up, sealed, and delivered. If not dealt with and overcome with dispatch, it was destined to become ISABELLE's Achilles' heel. Looking back, I've gotta hand it to you, Nick. With Palmer and Shutt showing their stuff by getting the bugs out of the old magnet, you managed to emerge parading out a shiny new one, the winner you believed everyone was waiting for. You really thought success was in your grasp, didn't you? But was it?

"Not quite! As jeopardizing as the magnet was to the project's coming to fruition, there was still something even more critical that had to be faced, and here is where you faltered badly. Just at the time when you were giving your all to fixing the ISABELLE magnet, other labs around the world were beginning to stake their claims on the *new physics* ripe for the taking. The collider race was in full swing, and the competition for new discovery was fierce. BNL was neck and neck with CERN in the push for the W, the first of the precious particle plums. But Fermilab was on the verge of waking up; and even the electron labs were beginning to show signs of life in reaching for the high-energy frontier. Being at the front line must have been daunting for you. Still, wasn't it clear to you that your job, pure and simple, was to make BNL *number one*? I'm sure that deep down that's the position you wanted the lab to be in. But for some reason you didn't pull out all the stops; for some reason you held back. Why Nick? Naturally, I can't be sure. But I put it to you that there was a catch, and that something embedded in your psyche prevented you from taking the right and proper course. You see, to be on top, you had to squeeze in ISABELLE PDQ. And for that, those big unwieldy magnets had to go. But you just couldn't do that, could you? You couldn't take that gallant, daring step. Why? Because it might embarrass those who had stuck with the magnets far too long? Because it might embarrass you? What piddling, measly reasons! Nick, didn't you see that expeditious construction was a must, else the project would end up being nothing but a waste of time, money, and effort, more like a fossil, an old-world thing of the past? It would've been so easy for you. Just rid yourself of those awful, tiresome magnets! You just had to be yourself. No discussion! No excuses! Just get it done! And more, didn't you relish the idea of taking on Carlo, of whipping him, of tearing him to shreds? Nick, why didn't you do it?

"To remind you of a few of the specifics, Nick, let me ask you to take yourself back to about 1980 when CERN was just beginning its quest for the W. ISABELLE, then an all-purpose experimental facility, was way ahead of the incipient CERN project, whose sole purpose was to force the W to show its face. ISABELLE had the lead because, designed with two proton rings, it didn't need to develop the new technology to make beam cooling a reality. On the other hand, CERN, with only a single ring available to compete with BNL, required beam cooling to make the necessary rare antiprotons. But BNL's advantage, as real as it was at the beginning, was short-lived. Those fat, good-for-nothing magnets were dragging both the lab and you down. Always those damnable magnets! Soon CERN was breathing down your neck, Nick, and then pulling ahead as Carlo's daring cooling strategy remarkably ended up working. You must admit that given these facts it is puzzling that you and BNL didn't adopt the obvious objective of going like blazes, hell-bent for the W. All you needed were small, quick-to-build, streamlined, practical magnets to fill the already done tunnel. Surely you and your boss, Vineyard, could have accomplished that – of course, presuming the will was there. As a matter of fact, more than one way of getting an appropriate type of magnet were unveiled and proposed. Unfortunately, they were all ignored or discarded for one phony reason or another. But the one opportunity you missed that strains credulity and greatly compounds the mystery is your out-and-out refusal of the offer by Fermilab to use its magnets. Why, in God's name, didn't you grab them? Well, it's pointless going over that again. Nonetheless, it's as plain as day that a well-trimmed, sleek, W-directed, speedily-built, Johnny-on-the-spot ISABELLE, completed in the early eighties, would've given BNL and the U.S. more than a fighting chance to beat CERN to the W.

"Even today, it boggles the mind to recall that you didn't jump at the chance to use the Fermilab magnets and go for broke for the W. Everything seemed right for such a policy to work: the DOE was eager for it, especially Pewitt; and Fermilab, perhaps under pressure from the community and the DOE, signed on to the idea. Sure, changing in midstream – from an all-purpose facility for the physicist masses to an elite one for a single class of experiments – would've been a nervy and somewhat precarious move; still, despite that, all the signs pointed to its being the right thing to do. OK, Vineyard didn't go for it. But you – young, bold, ambitious, and ready to take on the world – were surely the right man for that tough job.

"When you look at the big picture, latching onto the W wasn't the only big-time advantage to be gained by taking the small-magnet plunge. Actually, the benefit to be had from going that route went a lot further. It would've also given BNL a leg up on all its competitors in the future push for higher energy colliders. In fact, pursuing this line of attack could've changed the entire mood and direction of Snowmass '82 and shaped a different future for Big Physics as well as for BNL. But why bother belaboring this? You've heard it all before. Anyway, it's water under the bridge. But there's one thing I feel compelled to express to you: those fateful decisions made by George and you in the early eighties were the immediate and direct causes of ISABELLE's harrowing and crushing culmination and BNL's emasculated and aimless future. How could you have let it happen? Right there in black-and-white written in the historical record are the distressing, hard-to-take outcome and consequences for BNL: ISABELLE floundered; Snowmass '82 gave the Big Science community a new supercollider lab to take to its bosom; CERN in early 1983 announced the discovery of the W; and BNL was abandoned by the high-energy community. You were the loser, Nick, and Carlo won the whole shebang handily, without a serious and determined fight from either BNL or America. In the fall of 1983, the shocked, humiliated, and out-for-blood DOE cancelled ISABELLE; and with the lab devastated and in disarray, morale plummeted. No imagining could've played itself out more catastrophically for BNL. There just couldn't have been a worse finale."

Some Background
ISABELLE's Aftermath

"Fortunately for BNL, however, you were there to pull it out of its doldrums. Manifesting a high degree of leadership and an uncommon insight on the human condition, you managed to do what was seemingly impossible by setting the lab on a course to revitalization and renewal. You gave the staff the sense that, once again, there was a captain at the helm making sure that the ship was being steered on a worthy course, one that they could take pride in. Specifically, you bet the lab's future on a new collider for nuclear physics. The early eighties turned out to be a time when nuclear physics was being reshaped to study nuclei using the quark picture. For that, the plan was to use collisions of nuclei at relativistic energies. Brilliantly, you proposed to transform the ISABELLE carcass into a new machine that would serve that end. You just loved to coin new names, and you called this new facility the Relativistic Heavy Ion Collider (RHIC). Then, after a few years of stimulating effective and dedicated work at the lab, and by virtue of your inimitable persuasiveness, lo and behold, you did it, and BNL was resuscitated with its new RHIC project; and along with it came a welcome transfusion of new blood. There may be disagreement among scientists on whether ISABELLE-cum-RHIC, that you brought into being, had any worthwhile physics to offer. However, one thing is undeniable: it saved the lab from oblivion and gave the staff new life and the will to go on. Just think of what you did: In agitated and topsy-turvy times, you brought the lab back from the brink of a meltdown, and gave it the chance to live again and look toward a brighter future. These are awesome accomplishments and make you special in anybody's book.

"Time passed quickly after the 1983 ISABELLE collapse. BNL was close to *crossing the bar*, and hopelessness filled the air. But you were a man with a mission to accomplish. What a tough assignment! Instilling life into a near-corpse requires a tough and durable spirit, a heart of steel, an ingenious brain, and a superhuman will. How were you able to withstand the treatment you got? Being raked over the coals; being endlessly berated; being held in contempt; being condemned for any scourges or calamities plaguing high-energy physics; being blamed for any periods of tight money or other forms of hard times befalling it; and sometimes even being blackballed. But somehow you were able to summon up the courage and the guts to get through it. You let all this abuse roll off you, and then emerged from the black, sunless tunnel still alive and kicking.

"But survival was merely the beginning. The lab was on doom's edge. So you did anything that had to be done to keep it from tottering and crashing to the ground. Sure there were some untoward things among the actions you took. But you didn't shirk your duty. You simply laid your conscience to the side. You simply shunted these actions from your consciousness and moved forward. After working tirelessly in those tumultuous eighties and nineties to make something of the lab, you looked around at what you had done, and you saw that it was good. No, the lab wasn't what it had been back in its glory days, but there's no denying that it was strong and healthy. It was building facilities, doing research, and an overall credit to science and the nation."

Some Background
The Tritium Affair

"Your years as Director were eventful years, full of change. You radically altered the landscape, and made the lab whole again. Could anyone proclaim other than that you were a ringing success? But before you knew it, you'd finished your first five-year term as Director, then your second, and were nearing the end of your third. Then, without your least anticipating it, your past came back to haunt you. One of those damnable, hard-to-purge skeletons popped out of the closet to hex and vex you. Unfortunately, you didn't recognize the signs flashing around you for what they were. You didn't recognize that the jig was up. You were overflowing with pride, and frankly, too cocksure of yourself. So, with no one stationed on the watchtower, you were unprepared for the gathering clouds appearing over the lab. You simply didn't see that bird of ill omen descending on it. How suddenly it all happened! In 1997, in the immediate wake of your choice to stay on for an unprecedented fourth term, without warning and with astounding suddenness, the roof caved in on you.

"To understand it all, however, you have to go back about a dozen years earlier. That's when your trouble really began. You didn't know it at the time, but nonetheless, it did. While you were intensely pre-occupied with the matter of straightening out the lab, from out of nowhere, what seemed to be but an awkward little insignificant matter was brought to your attention. You thought it innocuous enough. No problem! Your staff would readily deal with it. It was hardly worth the consideration of such a high-level wheel as you deemed yourself to be. True, you were preoccupied with the bigger matter of the lab's survival. But this was a nuclear issue. You knew what happened at Shoreham, Clinch River, Three-Mile Island, and Chernobyl. This was big-league stuff. You should have seen to it. Anyway, as it happened, back in the mid eighties, during periodic lab-safety testing, very small amounts of tritium were found to be contaminating some local drinking water-wells. You and your safety experts cavalierly chalked it up to a common phenomenon, related to the piping, and occurring in all manner of systems of waterworks; and it was left at that. However, unfortunately for you, as the years went by, the tritium contamination got worse and expanded in the groundwater. This was atypical if it were merely a piping problem. Worse for you, as the nineties progressed, for a variety of unrelated reasons, government safety inspections at the labs were mounting at an inordinate rate. Then, one fine day as 1997 was approaching, as was bound to happen sooner or later, some Washington bureaucrat rummaging through old safety records, accidentally discovered this history of years earlier. When this was made public, all hell broke loose and the now infamous Tritium Affair began.

"It must have been a nightmare for you: People living near the lab became scared as hell. People from all over the island began fuming, consumed by irrational worries about their drinking water. The so-called concerned citizenry was awakened into a fury. The media were on top of this *delicious* story like a shot, and took up positions to point their fingers of blame and condemnation at anyone and anything at the lab that moved. The lab came to be held accountable for all manner of sickness and imaginary cancer rate increases. Anti-nuke and anti-lab groups sprouted up like wildfire. Local activists saw their chance to stir up the waters, and quickly got into the act with their two-cents' worth of know-nothing bluster. Even national activists couldn't resist the call, and came to partake of the frenzied feast. The Southampton celebrity crowd, with supermodel Christie Brinkley and actor Alec Baldwin at the head of the charge, led a political campaign capped by visits to the Secretary of Energy and President Clinton himself. The media got a real charge out of that. Politicians, not to be outdone, entered the fray with a vengeance. They saw their chance to get attention and free publicity. Doubtless such visibility would be quite a boon in name recognition and votes at the next election.

Representative Mike Forbes, the lab lying in his congressional district, became the powerful voice of the people living in the neighborhood; and Senator Al D'Amato, who used to be your friend, Nick, became an incensed and savage adversary of the lab and came also to assail you personally. Finally, as if all that weren't enough, the Suffolk County Health Commissioner, Mary Hibberd, became so exasperated and infuriated at the lab's negligence that she wrote you a damning letter insisting that you stand up and publicly explain your actions. So, with 1996 closing and 1997 beginning to show its face, it was a pretty bleak time for the lab. Things weren't looking good at all, not one bit!

"However, if you thought that this represented the peak of the nightmare, and that things couldn't get any worse, you were sadly out-of-tune, quite mistaken. In the wake of this onslaught by the lab's neighbors, augmented and strongly fortified by outlanders, intruders, and gatecrashers, what quickly ensued were trials and tribulations of Job-like proportions for both you and BNL. The lab became inundated with DOE officials of all sorts who, programmed for aggression and molestation, were void of any understanding, empathy, or fairness. The truth was that it wasn't a mission to uncover and ascertain the truth of what transpired. Rather, it was a plot to incriminate the lab, its Director, and AUI for negligently endangering the public safety. They were looking for the worst, and nothing could prevent them from finding it. They pried into every nook and cranny. All the lab's documentation was gone through with a fine-toothed comb. When they caught the scent of the minutest of details that would help to more deeply implicate their helpless prey, they would follow it like hound-dogs readying themselves to pounce. So it was that the lab's past, with all its fuzziness, its vagueness, and perhaps even its indeterminateness, was opened to the light of day. It's not too healthy to have your paper-trail history revealed and paraded out in raw form. Under the circumstances, and taking account of the type of people involved, you can well imagine what was highlighted. Right! It was the deliberate misinterpretations of events concocted by BNL's enemies to make the lab appear culpable. This was the view of things adopted by the lab's reviewers, the media, the activist groups, and the hoi polloi. How could you fight that? Then, when the official government reports arrived on the scene, as expected, they were hypercritical, pointing the finger of damnation at – surprise, surprise – the lab contractor, AUI, and the Director. So, all three – the lab, AUI, and the Director – were stuck in a head vise, and were being squeezed. They were castigated, scathingly slashed at, relentlessly railed at, and, all in all, skinned alive. They were reproached, rebuked, and reprimanded. What a hell of a mess it was! There were exaggerated claims and denunciations against the lab; there were livid people out for blood; and there were limp and vain attempts by the lab at some sort of defense, naturally falling on deaf ears. The lab was accused, condemned, and judged guilty as charged. Its fate was sealed.

"But the game wasn't over and done, not just yet, and the show continued to go on for a little while longer. The enrapt onlookers, the audience as it were, were glued to their seats waiting for the final scene to be played out. Eventually it approached as things began to spiral out of control. Under such extreme pressure, even a seasoned veteran and a hardened street fighter like you, Nick, one who doesn't give up easily, wilted in the blistering, consuming heat. So, on March 7, 1997, a week before your 65th birthday, you changed your mind about remaining on as a four-term Director and announced your resignation effective April 30. It was almost 15 years to the day that you were formally appointed to your first term after serving months *on pins and needles* in an *acting* capacity. However, that wasn't the end of it. There was even more bad news coming. Soon after that initial thunderbolt of your resignation, an ominous and destabilizing aftershock arrived when Secretary of Energy Peña fired AUI as lab contractor. Both the spectacle and the speed with which these almost unprecedented actions took place were breathtaking. Before our very eyes, in the flash of an instant, an era passed."

Some Background
The AGS, an Alternative Neutron Source?

"In the mid to late eighties, you'd already been the lab Director for a few years. By then, you were deep into your efforts to make something of a lab that had come unimaginably close to losing its bearings. As it happened, Lady luck was playing her part. The Trivelpiece initiative to appease the labs so fearful of the SSC was in its formative stage, and a real life for RHIC suddenly became a rather good possibility. In addition, you'd submitted a proposal to DOE to upgrade the old High Flux Beam Reactor (HFBR). What happy days would ensue if both these projects were to be approved! Actually, although not a likely prospect, it was possible that things would turn out exactly that way. Wouldn't that have been a high point for you! Wouldn't it have made all you'd been through in putting the lab together again worthwhile! The nuclear physics community would be thrilled with RHIC; the neutron physics community would be overjoyed with their reconditioned new and improved HFBR; and naturally you and the lab would be full of pride and very, very gratified, nay exultant, to again be able to serve the science community as BNL had in the past. You'd all be ready to break out in song, *Happy days are here again.*

"Although it looked as if things were going great guns, and the bells of optimism were loudly ringing, there was in fact lurking in the shadows a highly unwelcome *guest.* In 1985 and 1986, routine tests showed incontrovertibly that tritium contamination was present in some wells on the lab site. Although the amounts were very small, the fact that they represented significant increases over the previous few years was an ill-boding tip-off that trouble lay ahead. This observation alone was reason enough to pursue the investigation further. Oddly, however, the lab reaction to it was almost 180 degrees out of phase. Instead of enhanced examination and inquiry, deeper probing, and complete open-mindedness, there was a spooky and thoroughly unjustifiable silence on the entire matter, except for murky pronouncements from the management that the situation was nothing out of the ordinary and was well in hand. No public out-of-lab reports were issued. The outside was, to all intents and purposes, kept in the dark. What a risk to take! Weren't you concerned about the dire consequences not only to you but to the lab as well should the secret come out? Tell me, Nick, was it guts and daring, going for the whole ball of wax; was it a well thought-out plan of attack; or was it plain old-fashioned shortsightedness?

"As it turned out, this strategy pulled you through the eighties and early nineties. Still, it was an injudicious course to take, particularly so because there was no significant – if any – health hazard to either lab personnel or the surrounding population. However, as ill conceived as being silent was, there was an even worse judgment made. No carefully detailed, documented follow-up studies were done to find the actual source of the tritium. For a scientific lab, that's akin to being a criminal act. Both you and your staff did no less than violate the time-honored principles you were educated with as scientists. Just look at what you did: in 1986, by shutting down one of the experimental wells that might well have thrown light on the whole matter, you actually adopted the *head-in-the-sand* management approach to running the lab. I know it sounds harebrained, but that's what happened. You fixed on the speculative culprit, *leaky sewer pipes,* and simply took the pipes to be the guilty agents. That was it. You left it at that. It's quite true that it was politically convenient to explain this ticklish situation in such a manner, but it wasn't at all worthy of the high priests and arch-stewards of an exalted national laboratory.

"Nick, I put it to you that you knew only too well what the source of that leaking tritium was. Even if you didn't know it right away, immediately after the discovery, you almost certainly did when you sent DOE the proposal for the HFBR upgrade. In fact, weren't you privately informed that the spent-fuel tank of the old HFBR was leaking and had been for a few years, at least dating back to the early eighties? Yes, you were indeed privy to what was surely the true source of the tritium that was radioactively polluting the drinking water. Come on admit it! You knew it was the aging HFBR, didn't you? Truly, I can well imagine how you must have felt. What a bummer! This wouldn't have been good news at any time, but at that particular juncture in the mid eighties, it had all the earmarks of a calamity in the making. Just as you were beginning to see some light at the end of the tunnel, this sour-tasting and touchy breakdown of the HFBR's reactor safety system showed its ugly face. This truly was a very precarious situation for you.

"Seeing as how the lab was in the midst of delicate negotiations with the DOE, if such information were to see the light of day, who could predict what the outcome would be? It wasn't unlikely that people would come to question whether BNL could be trusted to handle radioactive material. They might even begin to doubt whether the lab could be trusted at all. At the very least, it would jeopardize BNL's chances of landing the new RHIC and HFBR construction projects. Thus, the ball was in your court, Nick. What were you going to do? What was the right thing to do? No doubt you were in quite a bind. Your options seemed highly constrained. In fact, did you have any at all? I can imagine you thinking: If only the safety question brought up by the tritium leak could be ignored for the time being or maybe even suppressed. There, the words were released and became free-floating in your mind. For someone with your brainpower, it wasn't long before an idea of what had to be done clicked into place. The *Eureka-bulb* flashed in your head: If the research reactor upgrade were funded, then the issue would be resolved because the upgrade included replacement of the spent-fuel tank. A clobbering would be turned into a feather in the lab's cap! A defeat into a victory! A shellacking into a romp! A chump into a champ! Yes, all would then be well again in this best of all possible worlds. All you had to do was be patient and keep mum. It just seemed so right. How could something so reasonable end up being reprehensible? How could it be the wrong way to go? With such thoughts, you became convinced; and so you started down the road of dishonesty, hypocrisy, duplicity, and deception.

"Going that route naturally entailed a great deal of risk and raised gnawing ethical questions. But, in the frame of mind you were in, these were alien concerns. You were so sure that the fates were playing on your team. Foremost in your thinking was to keep the lab strong and competitive; and the way to do that was all too straightforward: get the HFBR upgrade and, as part of it, the tritium leak would be automatically eliminated. It was so logical. It was so inviting. It was so seductive. Being able to toss out the window the entire safety matter with all its menacing tentacles must've seemed like the perfect way out of the dilemma. So don't overanalyze, just do it, you must have thought. Just put off the tritium headache from getting to the outside by delaying an in-depth analysis. Then, once the Upgrade Project approval arrived, poof, like magic, your potential plight would simply evaporate. It would be as if it never existed. No annoying predicament! No vexed quandary! No dilemma! Just peace and a bright future! Could you ask for anything more?

"As a matter of fact, Nick, you did have an alternative. You could always have refitted the old BNL workhorse accelerator, the AGS, to be a source of neutrons. Of course, the neutron beam community preferred reactors because they felt comfortable with them. It had been their experimental source of neutrons for years. What did they know about accelerators? To be blunt, literally nothing! So what could you expect of them? On the other hand, they could have adjusted. They could have adapted to the reality of the times. They could have been persuaded to do so. They could have been made an offer they couldn't refuse. Certainly if there was no other alternative, they would've seen the light. After all, we all have to compromise. We all have to sometimes accept less than our ideal.

"In truth, the AGS-solution wasn't quite as straightforward as I'm painting it. But it was a viable way to go. It was a way out of your dilemma. Furthermore, if you went that route, you would've ended up being *Mister Honesty* himself. Who knows? Maybe the DOE would have been taken by your frank sincerity and high-minded uprightness. So impressed might the DOE managers have been that maybe they would've listened to the full story and chosen to go with the HFBR upgrade, leaving the AGS option for when it might be an absolute necessity. Stranger things have happened; although I must say that it wasn't too likely seeing that at the same time Oak Ridge National Laboratory (ORNL) was asking for its research reactor, similar to BNL's, upgraded. What with Trivelpiece closely allied to ORNL, perhaps that was insurmountable competition. Frankly, the more you think about it, the more the AGS-solution appears to be the best option you had.

"From the BNL perspective during the mid to late eighties, there was considerable merit in building up the AGS capability as a neutron source to serve the reactor community. First, it would give the lab another upgrade project; second, it would enhance the lab as a forefront developer of new technologies for experimental facilities; and third, it would help to sustain the AGS as a forefront, actively functioning user facility in the post-fixed-target era. But most important of all, it would be a very politically attractive alternative because of the growing public antipathy toward reactors - irrational, pig-headed, and self-defeating as that attitude is. You might actually have ended up being a hero to the neutron physics community, providing them with a source that the public embraced. No more would they have to do their research surreptitiously, always looking over their shoulders, wondering if the ax would soon fall. Of course, it may well be that this all seems so transparent and straightforward to me because I'm saying it with the benefit of hindsight. But that doesn't alter the fact that your unwillingness to seriously entertain a full-fledged AGS-based neutron facility as your option of choice is a perplexing puzzle – a mystery that you hopefully will throw some light on.

"Well, I'm just about done. All in all, Nick, this picture I've painted doesn't make you or the lab's staff look too good. Well, frankly, how could it be otherwise? How can those who've taken part in a cover-up appear any way other than dishonorable and shameful? After all, such are stories not of heroes, but of cowards. Still, as harsh as my indictment is, given the evidence, my scenario is not at all strained, but flows effortlessly and naturally. I believe you'd be hard-pressed to come up with an equally forceful and convincing one. However, even if it happened exactly the way I've portrayed it, who am I to presume to condemn your choices, to reproach and to reprove you, and to pronounce you guilty? In the end, whether or not you were justified in acting as you did I can only leave to your own conscience and to history's judgment. I wonder, however, if perhaps you should've taken Ibsen's, *An Enemy of the People* more to heart."

Mickey's Questions to Nick

"I have finally reached the point where I can pose my Nick-questions. I can only commend all of you, especially you, Nick, for your reasonable forbearance and your patient condoning of my long-windedness. Anyway, Nick, I have three questions for you: First, since you're a most formidable person, there seems little doubt that you could've negotiated a good deal with DOE to use Fermilab magnets. That would've given BNL a leg up on racing CERN for the W. So, why didn't you take Fermilab up on its magnet offer? And, if you were dead set against dealing with Leon, why didn't you at least try to fashion a streamlined BNL-style magnet that would allow you to engage CERN in the competition? Second, in the mid to late eighties, why did you jeopardize your career and put the future of the lab at such risk by choosing to ignore the tritium contamination problem? And why did you hold back on proposing the AGS as an alternative neutron source? Lastly, with hints of looming accusations of lab safety violations in the air as 1997 approached, why did you take such a big chance of losing it all by seeking an unprecedented fourth term when it would have been wise and quite natural to voluntarily leave the battlefield before the Tritium Affair erupted?"

Nick's Response

Mickey looked at Nick and wondered about the ponytail he'd come to sport, guessing that it was like a teenager's seeking to find an identity of his own by exhibiting his wish to be different from the class of his origin. Although uncommon in a man of Nick's age, thumbing your nose at your own kind isn't unusual in people who've experienced shock or the stinging pain of being cast aside. Putting it in Nick's type of dialect, this new image was saying, "*Fuck you, world.*" There was defiance written all over him. Yet Mickey also noticed a kind of melancholy sadness in Nick's face, and he felt sorry for this man who'd gone so fast from so high to so low. Such a waste! So much so pointlessly, so futilely lost!

After his fall from grace, Nick still had a job with a good salary because of BNL's formidably potent tenure system. But he experienced a loss that was not measurable in money by being deprived of any chance for an honorable and acclaimed legacy that he could be proud of and cherish into his old age. Instead, he was left with a dark cloud over his head – with an impression-at-large, rightly or wrongly, that he used his high office not to benefit science but to further his own personal interests of career, fame, and power over others. It's hard for common folk to fathom what Nick sacrificed to the god of vanity. The best this poor soul could hope for following his diving crash was that people would forget his past deeds and even forget him in toto. It must be hard for a man of such pride and promise to have to live with such an outcome to a life that began with so many hopes, ambitions, and dreams.

Even as these thoughts were speeding through Mickey's mind, he knew they were mere speculation. The truth was that he actually hadn't a clue as to what made this remarkable and imposing man tick. Perhaps Mickey was reading too much into what might be nothing but a passing frown or an involuntary muscular spasm. How could he presume to discover from an exterior view – carefully developed, embellished, and nurtured over many years – what any person really believed or felt inside? No, he knew he couldn't uncover the real man behind the mask merely by observing him. For the true Nick to be found, the man would have to let it all hang out, and more, he'd have to spill his guts. Yet, even then, Mickey would still have to interpret, to search between the lines, to extrapolate, to mix in deeds and occurrences not even hinted at, and ultimately to resort to intuition. No doubt it was a very tall order. However, Mickey, ever the optimist, believed he would hit upon the means to catch a glimpse of the real Nick in the response the pony-tailed man was readying to make.

Mickey lifted his head and looked around the table. How pleased he felt at that instant! There they all were, and everything was clicking for him: the time was right; the stage was set; and the actors were in place in this remote truth-telling village off the beaten track. All that was needed was the director's go-ahead. So, taking a surreptitious peek at his watch, Mickey, breaking in on a couple of hot tête-à-têtes, cut in, "OK, Nick, you have a little over half an hour before we have to part company and go our separate ways; till then the floor is yours."

Nick pushed his chair back and stood up. With his head lowered, deep in thought, he paced about the small bare room, slowly circling the table. When he returned to his starting point, in turn, he stared intently into the eyes of the four others seated, shrugged apologetically with a tone that seemed to say, *c'est la vie*, and fashioned a wide grin. With a surprising swiftness, his face lit up, and the glum, out-of-sorts moroseness, undoubtedly elicited by Mickey's assault, was transformed. From deep within himself, he somehow found a way to retrieve his well-known but now long-gone attack mode. Mickey and the others knew immediately that the old Nick, the one with fire in his belly, insolence in his eyes, and fury in his heart, was reappearing for this special engagement. Strangely, this combative, militant personality, perked up and ready to speak, produced a reassuring and upbeat effect at the table. An air of expectancy arose at the prospect of hearing this embattled veteran of many such word-wars defend himself. Nick stood behind his chair, slightly bent over, with his hands on the chair back. All eyes were trained on him. He hesitated theatrically until the other four were on the edge of their seats, burning to get on with the anticipated bravura exhibition. Then it came.

"What the hell," Nick started, "what's done is done, and what's gone is gone. But, I can still sing, and sing I intend to do." With a challenging gaze, he looked at all of those seated. They stared back at him in awe, transfixed by this still-proud, fallen man. It was a moment to remember. It seemed as if a man, presumed dead, suddenly was resurrected. Nick lifted his hands from his chair, waved them with a flourish, stood erect and tall, and continued with a mixture of dignity and bravado, "I've had a good run for my money. Sure they got me with the glaring sun blinding me, but I'm not ashamed. I gave them a good fight to the bitter end. My life had its ups and downs, and I had good times and bad. Sometimes you have to be ruthless and I did what had to be done. They were all close calls that I had to make, and *I called 'em the way I saw 'em*. Unfortunately for me, those with the ultimate power saw what I did differently and determined that I would have to take the fall. Look, if you want to play the game of hardball politics, you've gotta be willing to suffer the consequences. I didn't expect to be the one to get the short end of the stick. But I was ready for it; and, when it came, I picked myself up and found a new life. I played with everything I had. It was my way, and it was the best I knew how. I played to win and I've had my share of the sweet fruits of winning. But you have to be prepared for the bitter kind as well, and I tasted of those too. I have no use for those who whine and look for excuses, and I won't go there. There won't be any complaining from me. I tried to climb the steep hill, got oh so close to the top, but couldn't quite make it. Sure, I was beaten back. Sure, I was bloodied. Sure, I was knocked about and tossed off like a wet towel. Sure, I was cast off into oblivion, or so it was thought. But, look at me. I'm still here, bowed a little, but not out of the game. There's still a lot of living to do in these old bones. Nobody's gonna get rid of me that easy. And don't make the mistake of thinking I was all wrong! The fact is that if you consider slowly and carefully what the outcome actually was, you'll make out a picture that you perhaps wouldn't have expected to see. Remember it's what happens in the final round that really counts. As a sport's philosopher once quipped: *The opera ain't over till the fat lady sings*."

Nick was proud of the words he'd opened with, and appeared invigorated and energized by them. Now, he knew, was just the right time to get to the beef: "Let's review the facts as they are today: RHIC is for real. It wasn't but a short time ago that we had lift-off, and soon afterwards we achieved honest to goodness heavy ion collisions. I remember the talk that was going around in the eighties. Most believed we were losers and said as much. Naturally, it was all behind our backs. Who had the guts to say it right to our faces? They thought we couldn't do it. But we ignored them all, with their mischievous chatter, and stuck to our guns. And, by heavens, we came through. By any measure of performance, we did real good. Remember how BNL was dying from the Machiavellian machinations of Pewitt and company and the dirty double-dealing Snowmass crowd! Well, we showed 'em that they couldn't just casually brush us aside. Yes, we were down for a while. Nonetheless, we still had some fight and spirit left in our creaking bones. We found the stamina deep in our souls and the means to work our way out of the fire they threw us in. And, just as I said it would, RHIC turned out to be like a Phoenix rising from the ashes of ISABELLE. What an eye-popping stunning miraculous phenomenon that was! You've got to admit that it was something worth setting our sights on, something worth putting the sweat of our brows into, something to hang our hats on, and something we could relish in and be uplifted and fulfilled by.

"Compare all that we were able to do with what happened to those dirty no-good sons of Benedict Arnold, particularly those betraying shit-heads, Burt and Leon. They wanted to roll over me, but look at them now, eating crow as we go on our merry way, and having to eat dirt with their labs having nowhere to go. Anyway, they got exactly what they deserved, what with their trying to finish me off. They're just a couple of phonies. Then there's the SSC's Mister Schwitters, a Judas if there ever was one. He too got his comeuppance, and boy was it big time. Today, as we at BNL do top-rung mainline physics, the big SSC-that-was-to-have-been is nothing but a piece of junk, and Mister Bigmouth himself is right there on top of the heap. So, from where we now sit, with a full perspective, we came out OK, didn't we?

"I can see Mickey getting a little antsy about the time. But hold on a bit, relax, I'm not forgetting your questions. You asked why we couldn't beat out CERN for the W, and here is my take on that. Over quite a long period of time, we ran into magnet trouble and, with everyone bearing down on us with hellfire and brimstone, we had to scramble mightily to find our way back from what at times seemed to be like the fires of hell. But Leon, Pewitt, and the rest of those bastards wanted to take advantage of our setback and tried to finish us off. But in the end they all turned out to be paper tigers. I shouldn't forget to include in that bunch Mister Wallenmeyer. On the other hand, maybe he isn't even worth mentioning because by that time he'd already become a flunky and a softy. After Mister Deutsch almost fired him, he probably got the scare of his life and didn't have any more fight left in him. So, abandoned by both the DOE and the science community, there we were all alone. We knew we had to dig in for a long campaign. We had to be continuously on the alert for snipers shooting for our budget and headhunters aiming for our staff. Surrounded by enemies, there was simply no one in those so-called halls of power who'd take the risk of trying to push through to us and extend a helping hand. As for anybody pulling any strings for us, not a chance! So, if anyone thought we had it in us to win a race with CERN for the W, he was on another planet. We were so far down in the dumps that we couldn't even get our juices flowing to approach the starting gate. A race? Forget it! If you want to know what was on our minds at that time, it was keeping alive. Where was our next meal coming from? We couldn't stop for a moment. There were no breaks for us. No rest! Just keep going! It was our life on the line. Coming first in a race? Ha! Survival, that's what we had our sights set on.

"Yet, in spite of it all, despite being left entirely to our own devices, and with not a bloody soul ready to lift a finger for us, we still managed to push on. Alone and forgotten by most everybody, with no one to turn to, we stuck it out. Then in time we were able to break out of our isolation and ostracism. We did the almost impossible and found a way to pick ourselves up by our bootstraps. Yes, we ended up coming through it all in one piece. Slowly and deliberately we worked our way out of the mud, through the fog, and into the sunlight; and when we emerged some years later, lo and behold, we were on top again. OK, we didn't get to win the race for the W particle. But we won something we needed that was far more urgent for our future. Through hard work and consistently high-class performance over many tough years, we returned from the almost dead and once more earned the trust of our country. What a show we put on! Would anyone deny that?"

Nick paced about for a brief period, oblivious of his attentive audience waiting eagerly for him to resume. Then he lifted his head, and wearing a self-satisfied smile, went on: "In the nineties, after the SSC was done away with, good fortune smiled on us and we found ourselves on easy street. So, you see, when you're down on your luck and your situation is grim, and the best you can come up with is that you can just about glimpse the light at the end of the tunnel, I can vouch for the reality of that light. Counting on it was really the only chance for us when we entered that long, dark tunnel, where we were badly sandbagged, where we were shamefacedly defeated, and where we were made to say *uncle*. But in the end we forced all our adversaries and foes to feel our presence. We took the wind out of their sails when we did finally come out the other end into the sun with our heads held high. That was a time made in heaven.

"Winning is such a great feeling; and, yes, we did it. We came out first, ahead of the whole pack. We prevailed while the others faltered. We were sitting pretty in that grand place on top of the world. What a high it was! It was sheer euphoria. Unfortunately, being in such a state blinded us. We compromised ourselves by putting our guard down just a little too prematurely. Negligently, to be sure, we left the gates unattended. There wasn't a lookout perched to warn us. Well, why should we have had guards? Everything seemed so rosy. But, as it happened, it was a most regrettable and deplorable miscalculation, because just then – when all the visible signs were favorable, when life seemed all-promising, and danger was farther away than the eye could see – that tritium shit hit the fan. It's hard for me to explain why, but the truth is that I didn't see it coming. Actually, we were all fools, and none of us foresaw it. It just snuck up on us. Then, before we knew it, we were blindsided. Too bad! It was so good for a while. But, *c'est la vie*. I guess that's just the way things are: You've gotta take the bad with the good.

"I'm sure I'll get no disagreement from any of you when I say that this whole radioactivity business at BNL was nothing but pure nonsense. There wasn't the least justification, there wasn't the an ounce of rational foundation for the harassment inflicted on us, for the condemnation heaped on us, and for the vicious attacks made on us. Nonetheless, even though it was all a lot of baloney, they swooped down on us in a panic, some to the point of hysteria. The little shits at the DOE were the worst. To legitimize what they were doing, and to keep their skins from being singed, they wrapped themselves in the mantle of the safety mantra. Then there were the others: There were the bloody do-gooders trying to make names for themselves on our backs by carrying signs, blocking the lab's entrance, intimidating our personnel, and making all-around nuisances of themselves. There were the lawyers lured by the greenbacks they saw as easy pickings that could be wrested from the government by bullying and coercing those scared-shitless bureaucrats. There were the mediocre so-called technical experts, some of whom had gripes and bones to pick with the lab and others who simply had nothing better to do. And finally there were the people who lived contiguous to the lab. I don't cast any blame on them. In fact, they were the real victims, not because of the radioactivity, but rather because of the activists and lawyers who saw a fat cow to milk and went whole-hog for it! These poor folk were mercilessly riled up and preyed upon by those ready to take advantage of their irrational fears and technical naïveté. Sad to say, these neighbors, once accepting, even proud of the lab, were transformed into bitter opponents.

"That's quite an assault-group that we had to contend with. You can well imagine the confusion, the turmoil, the chaos, and the alarm at the lab. Being right in our face, the activists were undoubtedly the toughest to take. I guess they were out of either gainful or voluntary work after they got rid of the proposed nuclear plant at Shoreham, and so needed something new to keep them going. And there we were, playing right into their grubby little hands, ready to be hit. Bluntly speaking, and you wouldn't expect less from me, they were all know-nothings who didn't care to know anything, thank you. The gang that really got my goat was that rat pack from Southampton with those high-falutin resident actors to lead and goad them on. Outwardly they were out to keep *the Island*, even the world, safe from the menace of radioactivity. What a lot of hooey! In truth, they were really nothing but safety-mongers, who didn't give a damn about honest-to-goodness safety. They had neither the knowledge nor the interest for that. Actually, what they really wanted was some free publicity, and also to keep the southeastern shore of Long Island as their private playground, with no room for anybody else. *The Hamptons are for us, all others stay out, and nobodies especially unwanted* would be just the right motto for what they were up to."

For a short spell, Nick became pensive, "You know, in quiet moments of solitude, I sometimes entertain thoughts about all those men who carry weight in high places, the likes of the ever-present politicians and the rest of the Washington crowd. They're supposed to stick by you, aren't they? Yet things don't always turn out the way you think they should. I worked so hard trying to cooperate with them, to be as helpful as I could, and to assuage any concerns they might've had about budget, performance, and such. I even took the extra step of trying as best as I knew how to befriend them. But then, when it really counted, when it was my ass on the line, when I needed them most, they let me down. They were nowhere to be found. They simply disappeared. Vanished into thin air! Actually, they were nothing but scum. They just up and fled, leaving me all alone to hold the bag." Nick paused, preoccupied, swept away by his inner contemplations. A bit downcast, he wondered about how much of what happened he brought on himself.

Then, in an abrupt about-face, the old combative Nick returned: "They just wanna make me puke. Look at them now, they're just a bunch of nothings. The truth is they just had no character, no sense of loyalty. They deserve all they got. From one who's been there, let me say straight out that you just can't depend on politicos, not any of them. I played their game. I trusted them. But when the going got a little rough they ran like scared bunny rabbits. Yeah, all in all, it was a magic show gone awry, with me the one left in the meat-grinder. And let me tell you, that's no fun, no fun at all."

Nick stopped and walked around for a bit, his mind working full-tilt. Then he started the engine again: "I have to admit that I was overwhelmed by the whole damn tritium mess. If you want to know what it was like, just imagine yourself being overpowered by an angry mob with everybody trying to grab a piece out of your hide. Frankly, you, Mickey, reminded me of one of those grasping warlocks when you were spouting all of that planned deviousness and conspiratorial crap about the period back in the eighties. For the record, I did not – and I stress, *not* – contrive or plot with anyone to keep any information on any safety matter from the lab staff or the public-at-large. That's *no* – *N, O*! Period! I reiterate emphatically that it's nothing but make-believe. Be assured of that! And I simply consider it self-denigrating to go into it any further, and unworthy of you to expect me to."

Nick bowed his head a bit and just stood still for a time, trying to recall how his end came. Then he looked up, and, not quite so defiant, continued: "It became clear to me in 1997 that the party was over when those government dupes were sent into the lab to wipe out the administration, meaning me and AUI. They stayed for months searching for damning evidence to lynch us with. Yes, that's what they came for – to squeeze us out and to extract the life-blood out of the lab. That was their assignment, and that's what they set out to do. You know, when everyone is afraid of their own shadows and all the documentation, including private memos, is opened to prying eyes, it isn't difficult to find skeletons in the closet. They're always there. To be sure, they're in the shadows, trying to stay out of open view. But once you decide that you want some found, once the determination is there, then it's merely a question of choosing the right door. So these executioners came, went through the motions, and nailed us to the cross. Whether there was any truth to the stories they contrived and whether they were hurting anyone didn't matter a whit. I always found that dame who led the DOE contingent an interesting though unlikable character. I forgot her name, but I do remember her well. She certainly was a tough cookie. But even she went down the drain a little later when she didn't seem to know her place in the Washington scheme of things. Perhaps, in her pushy way, she aimed too high, and stepped on some toes she would've been better advised to avoid."

Nick suddenly looked a bit tired and seemed ready to wrap up. But there was still more to be said. So, maintaining his typical macho bravado, he plugged along: "In the end I did get through it all in one piece; and with my hide still intact, here I am rarin' to go again. Don't get me wrong now: I well know that my time on the big stage is passed – over and done. But don't worry about me. You see, I'm ready to take life with whatever it has to offer. I've always been that way and I certainly don't intend to change at this late stage. Looking ahead is the way to spend our time on this earth, at least that's what I believe, and as long as I have an engine and some gas left to fill it up, I'm gonna keep going with as much get-up-and-go and verve as I can muster.

"Yet, as much as I want to keep focused on the future, the past keeps coming back to me. I guess you can't escape what you've been and what you've been through. But I've nothing to be ashamed of. Actually, it's quite the opposite. The truth is that I'm proud as hell of myself for all the good I've done for BNL. OK, maybe I'm a little conceited, but just think, it was I, and I alone, who found the means to raise the lab up again from the lowly depths to which it had sunk. This I did in spite of the fact that all around us were our enemies, sniping at us, hitting at us, and trying to ruin us. In the end, however, we managed to beat and outlive them all. And let me tell you outrightly and unabashedly that it was I who did it, who guided the lab through its most difficult hour, and now stand tall for having done so.

"Now, about my resignation: Of course I was pushed out. Consider my predicament in 1997 after the roof fell in: I'd lost the support of big Senator Al. Obviously I pissed him off somewhere along the way. Maybe I didn't give him the real lowdown about the tritium business, or maybe I didn't give him the info early enough. That bit of disinclination or shilly-shallying on my part could've made him imagine that I wasn't being fully up-front with him, that I wasn't being as forthright as he expected me to be, and, frankly speaking, as I should've been. Anyway, I couldn't depend on him anymore. Then there was Bob Hughes and his successor at AUI. I certainly couldn't count on them. They were just pussycats, and didn't know their political asses from their elbows. They couldn't find the right corridor to go down in the Rayburn building if the lab's life was at stake. What could I expect from them? Finally, there was the just installed Energy Secretary, Peña. Right from the start, we didn't hit it off. Perhaps my reputation of being blunt and of going my own way got to him, and he preferred a more agreeable and compliant type. Anyway, the upshot was that there was no love lost between us. As for any trust, there wasn't a speck. In any case, he was the new big DOE chief-man on the scene and was out to make a name for himself by knocking people off. As it happened, I turned out to be one of the poor dispensable guys in his path to the Washington heights. So, you see, there was simply no one of any consequence for me to turn to. I was merely one of the men lost in the mayhem. The only way I could be of service to anyone was as a scapegoat, and that's exactly what I became. My only choice was to write the big R-letter or get fired. It's true that I liked a good fight, but I wasn't completely nutty. So I gave up and quit the field of battle.

"Oddly enough, for some strange reason, as 1997 got underway, even though all concrete indications were to the contrary, I still thought I could pull success out of the bag. I really believed that I could finish out three full terms, and then either leave with my pride intact, or even go on to a fourth term. However, on that score, fate and I didn't see eye-to-eye. Not unexpectedly, fate got the best of me, and things didn't work out the way I wanted them to. Yet, in spite of the rough treatment given me, the bad press I got, and the terrible accusations that were leveled at me, coming from every which direction, I was saved by that godsend, the lab's tenure system. Thus, in the end, I came out A-OK. Yes, as unlikely as it was, even as I was staring into the face of that deluge of overwhelming criticism, not only did I finish three full terms, but I also left the Director's office with the assurance and the full confidence that I could do then what I always wanted and planned to get back to – doing physics research.

"Sure, I could've left in January of that year before the whole tritium fiasco exploded; and because – believe it or not – I actually thought of doing it, I could kick myself for not. Mister Blume, who was actually more involved in the tritium affair than I was, did do it. He flew the coop well before everything came apart at the seams. The lucky shit! That left me holding the bag *all by my lonesome*. It hurts even more that I didn't go that way because my leaving early had some logic behind it: Remember that back in early 1982, I was actually serving in the capacity of Acting Director for a few months. So, in principle, I could have counted those months as part of my first term, thereby ending my third term around January, just before that infernal period of torment hit the lab. If only I'd taken advantage of that luck-fashioned technicality, I would've averted being the butt of the entire safety onslaught. Although a satisfactory explanation of my decision still eludes me today, the truth is that at the time I simply couldn't let go of the directorship on my own. Maybe deep down, as Mister Freud might've diagnosed, I wanted to go out in a ball of fire. On the other hand, it could simply have been that, overconfident as I was, I wanted to squeeze more out of my position than there was to be had. The truth is: I liked being the big man. I liked directing the traffic at the lab. I liked ruling the castle. I liked being catered to. I liked the idea of being there to protect my legacy. Unfortunately, although I didn't get it, I'd already been defrocked, and these rights and benefits of office weren't mine to have any more. So, in the end, I bit off more than I could chew. I was just far too greedy. In any case, my hesitation about voluntarily relinquishing the throne and simply walking peacefully away – that terrible error in judgment – cost me a lot. However, on the whole, you must admit, although it wasn't fashioned on glory, I did indeed go out in a blaze."

* * * * *

Closeout at the Luxembourg

As Nick finished, he looked cool and composed, at ease with himself. He was also grateful, and especially appreciative of this opportunity afforded him to vent and give his side of the story. As he sat down, you could see developing on his face this wide, uncharacteristically guileless, *je-vous-remercie-beaucoup* smile. He was clearly pleased with the performance he'd given. Mickey gazed at Nick carefully, and for an instant seemed to discern a cat-that-ate-the-canary look. But the thought passed as quickly as it came. It was simply not the time to grope for such half-baked, impugning notions. No, it was surely the time *to praise Caesar, not to bury him*. The reality was that in some mysterious manner Nick managed to generate an air around the table that was thick with good feelings. Now certainly if you knew Nick and his past, you wouldn't have guessed that such an occurrence could ever come about – no, not in a million years. Nonetheless, it did indeed happen. No more than a few minutes into his shared reflections of things past, all the guests – yes, all – were heartily rooting for him to come through. They were actually eating right out of his hands, rapt in his every word. Somehow, Nick, by speaking so earnestly, so passionately, and so much from the heart, by leaving himself exposed and vulnerable, and by being unguarded and believable, simply won them over, hook, line, and sinker. And when he was done and after the decompression of tension set in, a kind of quiet empathy, mixed with a *douceur-de-vivre* sensation, filled them all.

Later Mickey would interpret this strange and unexpected mood this way: All of Nick's audience didn't want the discomfort of having him fall apart in front of them; and since he came through for them and didn't, everyone's relief spilled out as good will. Well that's one way of looking at it, although it's far more likely that the collective feeling of understanding and compassion experienced that afternoon was much deeper than that. In any case, whatever the reasons behind Nick's triumphant afternoon celebration, all implicitly concurred that he was due the rave reviews given him by his peers. Under a great deal of stress, he did a lot more than make the best out of the hard undertaking of explaining a difficult set of past circumstances: He kept his head and systematically described his innermost feelings during such arduous times as most don't and shouldn't have to live through. That, one can hardly deny, is no mean task! Yes, Mickey had to admit that Nick deserved the admiration and esteem he received, and the warmth and friendliness that were tacked on.

On the other hand, Mickey was keenly aware of the fact that not all his questions were satisfactorily answered. Some of the rather important details were lacking in Nick's seemingly off the cuff, impromptu performance – like why he refused to bring in an amended ISABELLE-CBA magnet design, or why he didn't just drop the too-hot-to-handle HFBR and go for the AGS as an alternative neutron source. But Mickey knew that, at that take-your-breath-away Nick-moment at the Luxembourg, expecting every detail to be addressed would be mere quibbling. The man was really good, and put on a sterling act. There was simply no two ways about it. In fact, such was the satisfaction of those at the table that they were almost ready to break out in applause. But, curbing their instincts and holding back from such sophomoric ostentatiousness, they maintained an appropriate decorum and kept their reactions in the form of silent plaudits.

As the five of them sat contentedly in the waning minutes of the emotionally charged afternoon, the seconds ticked by. All eyes were glued on the man of the hour. But the moment was fast passing and would soon be relegated to the realm of soft, bittersweet memories. There was a little chatter at the table, with everyone wearing happy smiles. Then, all too soon, it was fade-out time. Yet even as this altogether unique afternoon was nearing its end, Mickey couldn't get Nick out of his mind. Passing through his thoughts was the picture of Nick in days gone by, especially those demeaning and confidence-bruising bouts just before the curtain on his directorship descended. Yet despite all that Nick had gone through and endured, his show that afternoon demonstrated beyond a doubt that he still remained quite a fighter.

As everybody rose from the table and stretched, the atmosphere was chatty and genial, abounding in *gemutlichkeit*. Mickey was beaming and thanked them all for giving of themselves and providing him with an exciting and informative afternoon. There were warm and amiable handshakes all around. In the midst of such good will and friendly spirits, how could Mickey, the little guy surrounded by big-wheels-that-were, feel anything but a strong bond of kinship with the four Directors? Although he started out critical of these men, full of faultfinding, and having considerable bones to pick with them, he ended up with genuine respect for their impressive levels of accomplishment and for the indomitable spirit they exhibited in the face of highly formidable adversity. He so wanted to linger and extend the afternoon's experience, whose significance he would never fully be able to grasp. But time waits for no one and nothing, and it was time to go.

Hesitatingly, he began his psychological transition to the next beckoning and full-of-promise appointment he was preparing to embark upon. Moving toward the exit, he noted that the curtain was already parted. As he passed through the open doorway, he couldn't help turning back for an instant. That's when he glimpsed the four of them freely and harmoniously conversing, laughing politely, showing a large measure of simpatico, buddy-buddy with each other, and without the least trace of discord or friction. The sight, brief as it was, gave him a rush of adrenaline, followed by a warm feeling of satisfaction and fulfillment. But time marches on. Quickening his pace through the shadowy room and past the bar, he left the Luxembourg, thinking, with a smile on his face: What a fabulous afternoon! Outside, he turned right and walked along the rightmost pathway. He noticed that although it was still light, the sun had dipped well behind the high-rise to his rear, leaving the street mostly in shade. Daylight was on its way out and dusk was not far behind. Lights were beginning to appear in the cafés lining the street. Mickey's day was ebbing. But there was still a fair way to go. Moving swiftly and breathing heavily, he crossed over the walkways to the leftmost one as he saw to his left the red and blue neon sign for the Moulin Rouge Café.

As Mickey's upcoming thrill-instilling rendezvous came closer, the one just past was still on his mind. He kept returning to Nick. Particularly, he thought of a story that Nick told at one of the frequent project review dinners Mickey was at. It's true that these dinners are usually unexceptional. To be honest, they're almost always *boresville*. But this one – ah, this one – was different. Not long before it took place, Nick had been unrelentingly hammered at Snowmass '82, so it's not hard to see that this was one after-dinner talk no one wanted to miss. A combination of the lab's taking it on the chin and Nick's immense talent and reputation as a speaker generated an atmosphere of high expectancy among the throng gathered. They weren't disappointed. Nick was in great form. For the occasion, he chose to relate Aesop's fable about the Frog and the Scorpion. *The Scorpion wanted to cross the river and asked the Frog to help. The Frog feared the Scorpion's intentions, but he feared the Scorpion's wrath even more, should he refuse, so he agreed. The Scorpion proposed to rest on the Frog's back while the Frog swam across the river. The Frog retorted, "If I let you ride on my back, I'll be vulnerable, and you'll be free to bite me." The Scorpion replied, "I won't bite you, because if I do, I'll drown too." The Frog was appeased by the Scorpion's logic and went along with the deal. Despite the irrationality of doing it, in midstream, the Scorpion bent over and stung the Frog on the neck. As both were sinking, the Frog, shocked at the Scorpion's suicidal act, shouted out, "You've killed us both – why did you do it?" As the Scorpion went under, he cried out, "I just couldn't help it – you see, it's in my nature."*

What an intriguing and mysterious story for Nick to tell after what happened at Snowmass! Although he felt betrayed there, did he really want to be seen as the naïve simpleton-like Frog? On the other hand, was he painting a picture of himself as the menacing hard-to-fathom Scorpion? The most evident interpretation is that Leon, the betrayer, was the Scorpion and Nick, the betrayed, was the Frog. But that simply doesn't jibe with Nick's character. In his eyes, he's the macho man with the big cajones. Nick, playing the weakling? Never! There's no way he'd exhibit himself as the poor dumb Frog. Still, how could you see it any other way? Well, as it happens, there is a way to see it differently. Remember Nick's flagrant threat to the community at around the same time. *Après moi, le déluge*, he said, meaning, *if I go, you go with me*. Looking at the fable with that in mind, and interpreting the statement as the threat that it was, would make Nick the Scorpion and *the community* the Frog. So take your pick: Was Nick the Frog or the Scorpion? Wasn't it exactly what you'd expect from Nick to leave us with such a puzzle? Just then Mickey saw the entrance to the Moulin Rouge, and he reached out and opened the gate.

At the Moulin Rouge

As Mickey shut the wrought iron gate behind him an attractive young woman greeted him. Her light colored outfit matched her sparkling wavy blonde hair; and she had a warm and loving face designed to melt the hardest of men. She smiled flirtatiously as she brazenly stepped up to Mickey; then she whirled around with a flourish, like a dancer, as her skirt twirled and raised, showing off her exquisitely shapely and ever so appealing legs. Her sleeve grazed his left cheek and her sweet and fragrant aroma enveloped and enchanted him. She led him arm in arm down a winding stone pathway situated to the right of the main entrance; and they moved at a moderate pace toward the back of a garden patio. They passed several tables, each occupied by cheery, buoyantly spirited, and carefree patrons, engrossed in a world of their own. Mickey found the atmosphere enviably convivial and festive. In those flitting few seconds as he was walking down the path, he felt an aching urge to be part of it; yet, at the same time, there was a hint of it all being less than genuine. The scene intrigued him, but unfortunately everything was happening so fast, he didn't have a chance to think through that peculiar mixture of impressions. Hustling along, they reached the back and turned left toward the café. Adroitly skipping ahead and holding the door open for him, the woman motioned for Mickey to enter the annex at the back of the restaurant and to go straight ahead, then veer a little to the right, toward an alcove jutting out near the far side of the room.

The recessed area was bright, with a large circular table separated far enough from the others to allow a good measure of privacy. The table, set comfortably for five, was in a right angle formed by two large picture windows. So engrossed in the details of the physical layout was Mickey that the men already seated totally escaped his attention. Glancing outside through the window in front of him, he noticed for the first time the grandeur of the multi-peaked nature-made mountains behind the village's man-made jet-black central structure. The mountains were not far away, and the white on the snowy tips contrasted sharply with the building in front. As he turned back toward where he'd entered the room, he was sad to see that the woman was gone. It occurred to him that not a word had been spoken between them. Strangely, although their contact lasted but a minute or two, her unexpected precipitate disappearance somehow made him feel as if he'd lost something. But this was no time for reflection: There was simply too much remaining to be done, and too little time in which to do it. Suddenly, while he was absent-mindedly musing, he got a wake-up call, abruptly tearing him away from his self-absorbing contemplation.

"Friends, the man of the hour has finally arrived," a voice well known to Mickey proclaimed. His head pivoted downward and he saw Leon's grinning face. "Welcome to the land of wizards and kings, and the land of happy faces," Leon went on. "Will you deign to join us?" Mickey, taken by surprise, answered self-consciously, "Wow, what a welcoming committee!" He felt his face warming and couldn't believe that he was actually blushing. However, there was no way Mickey was going to allow that involuntary reaction to take him over. So, resolute in his will not to be intimidated and without flinching, he was determined to get down to the business at hand.

Looking around the table, he saw his second foursome of the day: To his left was seated Ken with a cigarette dangling from the left side of his mouth. To Ken's left was Carlo who, Mickey was startled to see, was also smoking. However, unlike Ken, he didn't appear to be too comfortable with the cigarette. The way he put it to his mouth seemed to Mickey to be – although barely noticeably – an effeminate gesture; or, was that just the way romantic Europeans did it? Next to Carlo was Leon, holding court and setting the party-like mood for the occasion. Finally, Bob sat next to Leon with his head bowed a bit. He seemed to remain separate, a bit aloof from the rest. That didn't surprise Mickey much because to him, Bob was always a man of mystery, standing apart from most. Although he could only see Bob's profile, he could make out a faint, enigmatic smile on the tanned, wrinkled face of this man who'd lived life to the fullest. Mickey had always thought the world of Bob, who, with his unique blend of the outdoors and the intellect, was an honest-and-true American. He was a man who towered above other men, yet one who entered the fray with all he had to give. Just then, Mickey noticed the empty chair right before him, between Bob and Ken. It was the choicest seat, with a view of the glorious western mountain range. It was just like Leon to be so gracious as to leave to Mickey this panoramic vision-to-die-for of the awesome place they'd all come to visit. As Mickey sat down, he heard softly in the background the dreamy low sounds of Edith Piaf singing *La Vie en Rose*. It was a moment of fantasy one could only wish for, and Mickey had the fabulous good-fortune to be living it. His mind was in a dither. What luck! How amazing for him to be here with these four giants of science, men of a rare breed, builders of the big accelerators and creators of Big Science! It was the stuff dreams are made of.

Mickey was taken by the fun-and-games atmosphere. He marveled at how well these four brilliant men fitted together, especially considering that their personalities were poles apart, that their careers spanned a variety of differing time periods, and that some of them had, in times past, fought each other with passionate zeal, vigor, and unyielding determination. After each of them had accomplished so much against such great odds in such a harsh world, a little jeu d'esprit and joking around certainly wasn't too lavish a reward to ask for. That they had actually come to be in this amazing locale, *Le Petit Village*, where they could together indulge in monkeyshines and saucy humor was indeed miraculous. It was, all in all, a well-deserved celebration of their historical feats.

The truth of the matter was that Mickey wondered whether it was his place to be there at all. After all, he wasn't in the same class as these high-powered men who'd wowed the science world and won their wings by shooting the moon and hitting sockeroo homers. It briefly crossed his mind that he might ignore the implied protocol and simply join in the high jinks and hoopla. But Mickey knew the apparent invitation to him was only semi-serious, and that they were playfully pulling his leg a bit. The reality was as plain as day: he no way fit the bill. No matter, each of us has his place in the scheme of things, and Mickey's was just not on the same level as these men who had aspired to fashion a new world. Nonetheless, he did have a perfectly valid reason to be there with these great men in this logic-defying blessed stead. To be sure, it was one with a not-to-be-easily-cast-aside consequence and weight. And what was Mickey's reason for being there, you ask? It was no less than to uncover the truth about what really happened to Big Science in the latter half of the twentieth century. That was no mean task. Does anyone doubt that his purpose merited him being there?

As the thought of why he was there broke into his consciousness, Mickey snapped back to reality. He had a job to do, and it had to be now or never. So, after taking a deep breath, he began to speak: "Although you all seem so chipper – and don't get me wrong, it's wonderful to see your spirits so high – what concerns me is, will you still feel the same way at eight, after our tête à têtes?" But it wouldn't be as easy as a meager attempt at lightheartedness to break into that tightly knit group, appease the rowdy gang, and grab their attention. "Don't you worry about that; I think I can speak for all of us on our side of the table in declaring that nothing you can disclose or express can in the least dampen our spirits or ruin our fun and gaiety – our *allégresse*," quipped Carlo. "Go right ahead and say whatever you want," interjected Leon. As if on cue, all four, banging the table with their fists, chorused, "Here, here." "Let's have some order here," railed Bob, with a mocking, jesting frown. All went quiet, and after a slight pause, Bob went on, "Let the gentleman speak, or he'll never get his work done." "Work?" asked Ken incredulously, "I didn't sign up for any work." Carlo stood up and, with flashing eyes and flushed face, posed a question filling Mickey with alarm, "Why don't we get some of Leon's special Scotch whiskey and forget about all this question and answer nonsense? What can it possibly teach us anyway?" "That's a brilliant suggestion, Maestro," the chorus chimed in. Not knowing what to do, Mickey found himself smiling nervously and self-consciously. It appeared that the only thing open to him was to sit back and wait, keep his fingers crossed, and hope that serendipity would come to help him out. What he was trapped in was a veritable circus; and the devil-may-care, make-fun-of-Mickey mood of joviality persisted for a time that seemed to Mickey much longer than it actually was. You see, he'd totally lost control of the meeting and was powerless to do anything about it. So he sat still and prayed.

Then, out of the blue came the blonde, smoothly and quickly gliding toward the table. Yes, it was the *Le Petit Village* beauty, come to be his savior. Holding a tray with five glasses and a bottle of Leon's favorite, Glenlivet Scotch, she immediately drew everyone's attention. Carlo, having had his fill of prancing about, sat down, readying himself to partake of this treat. As the woman poured, she seemed to dissipate the spell that had befallen the group, and the unruliness subsided. Ken then lifted his glass, and with his bony face breaking out in a huge smile, he echoed Leon with the toast, "To happy faces." As the blonde left, Mickey, pleased at the quick turn things had taken, thought, "Thank you, God."

As they all savored the smooth whiskey, the lull in the action continued and seemed to have taken hold. *Fantastic*! Mickey thought. This was just what the doctor ordered. Yes, the *Glenlivet* served Mickey only too well. Not about to let the unexpected opportunity pass, he glommed onto it, hoping it wouldn't just slip from his grasp and fly away. Stepping up to the pitching mound, ready to throw, he began by laying on the table a sequence for the interviews. He pointed out that it might be best to have them in chronological order so that they would roughly relate to separate decades proceeding from the sixties to the nineties. He conveyed his preference that Ken's questions pertain primarily to the sixties, Bob's to the seventies, and both Leon's and Carlo's to the eighties, stretching into the nineties. That appeared to everyone to be a reasonable starting point, and, almost in unison, they all nodded acquiescence. Mickey could've been knocked over by a feather at the utter about-face that had taken place. Where he failed, the blonde, with such charming ease and poise, found precisely the right moment to enter and, poof, just like that, she quelled the group's obstreperous attitude and behavior. What a gift, given purposefully, from her to him! Mickey imagined.

So, the show would go on. And it did. With the agenda set, Leon, as if to put the finishing touch to the group's rowdiness, interjected, "Here's to good questions and even better answers." "Here, here," piped up the harmonious chorus, and with that the glasses were emptied. You can well imagine the relief Mickey felt that finally things seemed to be going his way. But his sense of being on top of things didn't last long. Almost immediately, a twinge of panic took shape in him as he realized that it was already after six. There wasn't a minute to lose. *Get started*, he urged himself. Now, what was it that he planned to say? Unfortunately, his mind was blank. What lousy luck! Just at the moment of truth, how to get the ball rolling escaped him. Nonetheless, he was in the spotlight, and perform he would. *It'll come back to me*, he reassured himself. As he got set to allow his first words out, he could make out in the background Piaf's "*Je ne regrette rien.*"

* * * * *

Ken

Mickey, in a lame attempt to sustain the lighthearted atmosphere began: "I hope you'll excuse me for being so slow in getting underway, but being in the presence of the best of the best leaves me somewhat tongue-tied. Since you all know me, you might find that hard to swallow, but there it is, there's no end to the wonder of things." This brought a few laughs and smirks, but they were half-hearted. "Enough of this drivel," Carlo interrupted somewhat jokingly, his big round face flushed from the three glasses of the Lederman potion he'd imbibed. Leon was not so generous and followed impatiently and more soberly with, "OK, let's get on with it." "I think you'd better start," opined Ken in a chummy, well-meaning, and fatherly manner. Meanwhile the clock in Mickey's head kept ticking away, as he apprehensively and nervously tried to begin again. But this time, he vowed, he'd be more disciplined and focus himself on what had to be done. Forget the small talk! No more of that! Just at that instant, Mickey felt the butterflies in his gut begin to depart. His confidence was quickly returning, and all the ideas he'd formed in preparation for this singularly unique occasion came rushing back into his consciousness. Yes, now he was ready to take them on – to take on the world, if need be. He felt as if he'd been transformed into a new man in the blink of an eye. His brain was churning at a high clip: *Bring on the big guns. Here I am. OK, let's get to work*, he thought. In this frame of mind, he turned towards Ken and his words started to flow.

"Ken, the projects you've led you've executed with precision, seasoned wisdom, and virtuosity: The brilliantly designed, perfect-for-its-time Cosmotron was completed expeditiously in the early fifties, despite the difficulties encountered with government-ordered industrial sub-contracting. The masterfully conceived and ingeniously developed AGS was on its mark, ready, and set to become a going concern as the fifties ended. It was on its way to growing into the BNL shining star throughout the lab's glory-packed sixties. And then, in your final years on earth in the seventies, you gave BNL a parting gift of what later became the judiciously conceived, farsighted National Synchrotron Light Source (NSLS), the lab's trend-setting foray into light-producing electron facilities – one, as it turned out, that was in high demand by university and lab science departments and industrial R&D labs for many years, and, in fact, still is. That's quite a record. But my questions to you are not directly related to your insights and your sweeping and consummate track record, which speak for themselves. Frankly, what interests me here is not what is historically documented, but rather the people that made it all happen and particularly what was going on in your mind. What ambitions stirred you? What lit your fire and turned you on? What aroused and motivated you? What piqued you? What raised your gander? What finally got your goat and pushed you over the edge? Stuff like that! Specifically, I'd like to go through with you what drove you to do certain of the things you did?

"Your resumé is chock-full of high-class science. However, you also had a deep appreciation and immense talent for engineering. It was, in fact, that combination, the hallmark of the accelerator facility builder, that allowed you to play in the machine-game, where you did your most important work. For almost two decades, during the fifties and sixties, you positioned yourself as a top-notch builder and manager of science facilities at BNL. The truth is that, along with Haworth and Rabi, you were one of the prime movers in the creation of the first Big Science lab. It's this aspect of your life that I'd like to explore.

"In the late fifties, Haworth merged the Cosmotron and AGS Departments into the Accelerator Department (AD) and made you its first Chairman. This ostensibly wise marriage of departments concentrated the lab's accelerator strength and put the lab in a strong position to become a leader in the emerging era of big accelerators. However, in working out this arrangement, he was compelled to accept compromises that would end up haunting and hurting the lab well into the future. As long as Haworth was in command, and with you as his lieutenant, these worrisome and menacing implications of the power redistribution he'd agreed to were held in check. But when Goldhaber took over from Haworth, the door was opened for these suppressed demons to spring out and do their dirty work.

"As it happened, without Haworth backing you up, you just didn't have the oomph to stop the worst from coming to pass. The source of the danger to the lab, which was not fully appreciated by Haworth when the negotiations took place, was that the reorganization also unified the lab's experimental work into an expanded and strengthened Physics Department (PD). On its face, this power concentration, just as in the accelerator case, seemed to represent the wave of the future, good for the lab, and good for its staff. But, unfortunately, these two newly constituted and highly reinforced and fortified departments had very different ideas as to where the lab should be heading. This polarizing of the lab's muscle and potency turned out to be laying the groundwork for a ruinous confrontation. How cruel and unkind fortune can be! To cause an ambitious administrative action that appears a priori to be exactly the right thing to do to end up being so adverse and detrimental to the institution's future!

"The ultimate aims of the two new packed-with-punch departments, different as they were, left no room for rapprochement. There was no way they could fight it out, then smoke the peace pipe and iron things out. Kissing and making up were not in the cards. Their distinct targets were simply irreconcilable. The AD's end goals were to build new accelerator facilities – a much higher energy synchrotron and a new collider, as recommended by the Ramsey Panel – and to develop and enhance future technologies designed to push facility capability past the current boundaries limiting the research frontier. However, the PD, rather than pouring resources into what some believed to be a pie-in-the-sky future, sought to prime the AGS pump and exploit its experimental offerings to the fullest. Its motto was: more data as fast as fast can be. Therein lay the impasse: the AD with its orientation toward building accelerators and future technology, and the PD shooting to squeeze all that was humanly possible out of the extraordinary instrument they had in hand. It was a classic contest of the present versus the future. As a consequence of their irreconcilable differences, the campaign for which of the two departments would rule the roost was on.

"In truth, the struggle between the two strengthened departments was no contest, none at all. In the sixties, the experimental types, later pejoratively referred to as *physichists*, were the big cannons of science, the men with the names on the tips of everybody's tongues, the men with the all-important university credentials, the men who were Nobel-destined, and the men who made the lab Director quake. The accelerator types, on the other hand, were just little pistols. Yes, they were the builders of the machines that made the entire high-energy enterprise work; but they acted behind the scenes. Compared to the experimenters, they were nobodies, forced to merely remain shadows lurking in the background. In reality, they were the earth-shakers of Big Science, but no one knew exactly who they were. So it was that in possession of overwhelmingly more firepower, the victorious department in the hostilities between the two armed camps was a foregone conclusion. Does anyone doubt which side took home the booty? Yes, you got it right: The PD clobbered its opponent AD, and the winners and champions of the lab's facilities were the *physichists*!

"Thus, BNL, egged on by the highly influential and persuasive experimenters, chose the route of increasing the AGS intensity so that more and more experiments could be done. It was one of those offers the lab couldn't refuse! You see this was the will and desire of the triumphant side, the PD and the *physichist-users*. And its wish was the lab's command! But the price paid by the lab for taking that fork in the road – ignoring the one whose sign read *World Big Science Ahead* – was high, far higher than even the pessimists imagined.

"As time passed, BNL technological know-how and overall expertise in accelerators flagged; and the lab that was the leader of the pack became the laggard. On the threshold of the seventies, BNL was falling fast and was soon to be well behind Fermilab and CERN. These two labs, fast becoming the crème de la crème, were on the verge of making their big push forward, moving at a pace that made everyone's head spin. When the extent and meaning of this metamorphosis from BNL as top dog to BNL as a joke was finally becoming recognized, your place at the helm of accelerator work at BNL was in its twilight. Because, during the sixties, the lab had lost much of its accelerator capability, you became branded and stigmatized as being the man who caused the lab's fall from the heights. That's right! You became the scapegoat for the entire mess.

"What a miscarriage of justice that was! Yet it happened; and once the powers that be tagged you with the blame-label, your end came quickly. You were blamed for the fiasco of the AGS conversion upgrade. Who else? Certainly not the conquering *physichists* who'd demanded it against your better judgment! Then came the attack that really must've hurt. You were deemed responsible for the subsequent state of discontent, disarray, and squabbling in the AD. Who else should take the fall for that but the AD Chairman who'd been emasculated by the Director in league with the *physichists*! So the die was cast. Everything was in place for your being kicked out. And that's indeed what happened.

"In January 1970, you were summarily forced out and replaced by Fred Mills. Fred was a good and simple man. He was hard working, and an able and smart physicist. But a leader? Heavens no! There's simply no getting away from it. He could never fill your shoes. But who could? Anyway, there was Fred, the newly installed AD Chairman, with the job of pulling BNL out of the quicksand it was immersed in. As you no doubt expected, he could do nothing to help matters. There simply was no one as far as the eye could see that could. Actually, when you were in command, there was still a smidgeon of a chance for the lab to pull out of its slide. But with you gone the situation became hopeless.

"As time pushed its way into the seventies, you were entering into your closing chapter, and any possibility for a quick BNL renewal went with you. Thus, the cards portended dark and distressing days ahead for the lab. Quel misfortune! Poor BNL! There was this star that passed so closely by. Just a slightly extended lunge by the lab would've done the trick and brought the gleaming brightness to its bosom. But it wasn't to be. The lab was destined to miss its chance to catch that beckoning star. There's no doubt that fate did indeed offer the lab the opportunity to be a winner; but BNL couldn't see it for what it was. Too bad! Yet that's the way it was, and who can argue with history?

"Cutting to the chase, here are my questions for you: First, let me explore the 1964 period, when the Ramsey Panel recommended that the U.S. pursue both a very high-energy synchrotron and a collider. Remember there was no burning atmosphere of competition and there was no Fermilab at that time. So why didn't BNL pipe up right away and make a grab for at least one of them? In the wake of the phenomenal success of the AGS, the lab was on a high; why didn't it take advantage of this celebrated and illustrious achievement? It's almost unimaginable that the AEC wouldn't have gone along with such a plan. As history would confirm, this was a critical moment for the lab. Non-action was close to being suicidal and a clear-cut case of reprehensible management. So, Ken, what was your specific role in this whole business? Outwardly, it appears that you went along voluntarily with the lab's mainstream. Is that true? Being the accelerator boss-man and czar, why didn't you push for a fully new higher energy accelerator facility in that early period? Didn't you see its importance for BNL's future? As my analysis leads me to conclude, were the *physichists* the ones who blocked what was surely the right way to go? Did they simply overpower you and mow you down? OK, let me now move ahead to a few years later, to 1969. That was the year you were thrown out as leader of the AD. Why do you think the lab acted in such a self-defeating manner, by ridding itself of its best hope – you? Was it because the AD was really responsible for making the poor, futureless management choice of choosing to upgrade the AGS for higher intensity and more beams? Or perhaps it was because you screwed up the project? My impression is that the choice was really made by the lab's top management as part of the Goldhaber strategy. Is that right? Do you believe that the true and sole purpose of the AGS Conversion Project was merely to suit the whims of the *physichists*? Could it have been that they were the ones who wanted you out because you were pointing the finger at them? Finally, going back to the beginning of the sixties, do you think that Haworth's departure as Director in 1961 was a contributing if not the essential long-term factor in causing the events of the sixties that eventually brought BNL to its knees?" At this point, Mickey quit. He was struck by the sudden quiet at the table. He looked up at Ken who seemed deep in thought. Then, as the ticks on the clock kept passing, he became somewhat fretful and restless, as he anxiously awaited Ken's reply, which was quite a while in coming.

Ken lit up and held his cigarette close to the ashtray. He turned his chair toward Mickey and stared not quite at him but past his head into the dark room behind, as the cigarette burned *unpuffed.* For the moment, Ken's mind was far away from the business in front of him. Meanwhile Mickey waited impatiently. But he needn't have worried, for soon the bony-faced man returned. Ken then took a slow drag and looked into Mickey's eyes. "I'm inclined to say that on the whole you've got the picture right," he said in a slow, thoughtful way, "but I can't. That's mainly because I really don't think I was as insightful as you paint me. As I recall the merger of the two departments and my elevation to Chairman, I didn't have a good hold on what the Haworth-Goldhaber deal meant. What I'm getting at is that I actually thought it was the best thing in the world that could've happened. I wasn't in the least conscious of any darker significance. The truth is that I didn't think much about it. I took it at face value, liked it, and left it at that. Foremost in my mind at the time wasn't at all the political angle. Rather it was that I just loved to build these damn machines. They nourished me. They inspired me. They set me on fire. Bringing them to life intoxicated me. You may not know the feeling, but it is some truly mysteriously magical moment when your creation comes alive. It's like you've performed an act of God. I'm sure Bob knows what I'm talking about. It's spiritual. It's transcendent. Anyway, I guess I was good at that kind of stuff. Since that's what I loved doing and that's what needed doing, that's what I determined to do. My mind was set. And nothing – no, nothing – was going to stand in my way.

"On the other hand, when it came to planning for the future, I'm not sure that I stacked up. For better or worse, I didn't push hard for something new for BNL in the mid-sixties. Later in my life, I was always to regret that. You see, so much did I love to build that it was both in my heart and in my guts to press for BNL to go on the move again. So it's hard for me to explain my behavior. Maybe it was because I had a soft spot for Berkeley that I simply couldn't overcome. Since some of my formative years were spent at the Radlab, my subconscious mind might have compelled me not to oppose my fond old friends there. I hope you'll forgive the little sidetrack self-indulgence in that psychological mumbo-jumbo crap. I just couldn't resist saying it. In any case, the gist of what I'm trying to express is that, whatever the reason, I was in favor of keeping our agreement with Berkeley, and there seems little doubt now that BNL's hesitation – and that includes mine – delayed the lab and put all of us behind the eight ball.

"Then the decision came down from no less than the duo of Senator Dirksen and President Johnson that the new synchrotron would be built near Chicago and neither at Berkeley nor BNL. How frustrated and disillusioned I was! If not Berkeley, why did I split my effort? Why didn't I let the Radlab fight for itself, and go whole hog for BNL to get what at the time was *the big one*? The whole thing was quite a blow to me. Bob would get to build it now, not me! I was crestfallen. Drained from me was the will to put my heart and soul into anything. I would wake up sometimes and think, *no, it didn't happen*. But it did. I just couldn't believe it. Finally, I had to face reality. I simply wasn't able to see the stinging setback coming and, in that failing, I let down not only myself but also the two labs I cherished most.

"Still, even after all the pain it caused me, even after the ensuing self-doubt and self-pity that engulfed me, a slight spark remained in me that could be built upon. In time the healing process set in and the hurt of losing the synchrotron to Chicago started to fade. I found myself pushing harder than ever for BNL to go for the collider. The fact is that we were already working on superconducting magnets for that purpose, and had been since the early sixties. You see I wasn't completely blind. I did have the foresight to urge the lab to be in the vanguard of superconductivity for accelerators. The way I see it is that after my recovery from the lab's defeat in the synchrotron competition, with renewed spirit and vigor, I wanted to go much faster and make up for lost time. However, to my misfortune, by then 1969 was upon us and it was too late for me.

"My impression of what lay behind the events of my ill-fated year is that the lab simply lost confidence in my ability to lead. Goldhaber and his band came out in full force and tore me to shreds. The accusations were devastating and ruinous. You can well appreciate that the whole mess with the Conversion Project didn't make *my case for the defense* any easier. Looking back, I guess they felt they had to get rid of me, at least in my role as the top accelerator man. Let me tell you that it was hard for me to just walk away, for I did so want to get into the new superconducting collider business and lead a proud department at the lab. But unfortunately life isn't always kind to you, and I obviously wasn't meant to get my heart's desire. Was the Director right in acting as he did? Probably yes, but I don't really know. I may just not be the right person to address that question."

Ken paused. He was breathing heavily, and needed time to calm down. No one spoke, but all four waited for him to compose himself, as they knew he would. Then Ken's face brightened and with no noticeable aftereffect of his minor *panic attack*, he continued: "I hope you're satisfied with what I've told you about myself, specifically how I felt and the role I played in the lab's fall from grace. Now let me try to say something about Haworth and Goldhaber. Leland was a man I came to have a great fondness for. He was made to order for managing people, and, as my boss, I took to him like a little duckling to water. By the end of the fifties, it wouldn't be an exaggeration to say that we were a spirited team in the service of science and our lab. We saw eye to eye. We made things move and got a lot done. I believe I can venture to say that together we did much to make BNL the world-class place it became. As for Goldhaber, I better leave it at the fact that there was no love lost between us. Despite my divergent feelings about these two men, I must say that both gave much of themselves and tried their damndest to make the lab the great lab that for a time it was. I worked for about a decade with each of them, and so I could go on and on about each one. But I guess you wouldn't want me to do that, now would you? No, no, don't worry yourself to a frazzle about it! I haven't the least intention of taking over. It's the furthest thing from my mind. After all, it's your show, isn't it? Anyway, let me get to a few details about them on the particular matters you've broached upon. Even though I'm talking about men of real substance, of whom much can be said, I'll attempt to give you the *big-picture* version, and so be brief and to the point.

"I think I'll start with Goldhaber, the one who's so tough for me to talk about dispassionately. I'll try my best to be straight and unemotional, but I can't really promise I can stick to such a resolution. To be frank with you, as far as he's concerned, I'm not really on firm footing. So perhaps the less said the better. In retrospect, sure Goldhaber should have worked harder for new facilities and not put as much resources into the AGS experiments. In the long run, that surely would've been much better for the lab. But, as I said before, I didn't help as much as I might've either. So, if you're gonna assess blame for the lab's accelerator enterprise falling apart in the early to mid seventies, some of it surely has to fall on me. I must say though that in 1969, Goldhaber didn't treat me right. If he'd been more astute, and if he hadn't listened to those blasted, selfish experimenters all the time, maybe together we could've salvaged something from the growing disorder, maybe even prevented the whole damned mess lying in wait. But that's all water under the bridge. No use belaboring it now! It's just the way things are. He was the Director. He was the boss. And it was his prerogative to do what he deemed best. He wanted me out. So that's the way it was.

"Now on to Leland and his leaving the lab in 1961. Although this period in his life wasn't a good time for him for a variety of reasons, I believe he would've stayed if the atmosphere had been better. He wanted so much to set the lab in the right direction for bigger and better things in the future. But, unfortunately for him and for all of us, Rabi and Goldhaber insisted on putting greater stress on experiments. This flew smack in the face of Leland's view of things, and he fought them tooth and nail. But in the end he came out with the short straw. I always had the feeling that Rabi wanted to make some sort of deal. I guess Leland simply couldn't accept the accelerator share he was offered. I guess he couldn't abide working to implement a policy he didn't believe in.

"One thing is sure: they couldn't come to an understanding. But that's not much of a surprise. Rabi just wasn't a compromising kind of man. There was only one way he knew, his way. You know it's always hard to do business with a one-tracked mastermind, and that's exactly what Rabi was. So Leland, quick-witted and smart as a whip, saw the handwriting on the wall. He was backed into a corner, with not a bit of slack to move in. So he did the only thing he could. He kept a stiff upper lip, swallowed his pride, and gave up the lab he'd come to feel one with. In my humble opinion, if you're interested in it, he acted accordingly and properly. Yes, Leland was a stand-tall man up to the very last instant.

"By way of contrast, at the very same time, I didn't understand a whit about what was going on. Maybe it was because I was younger than Leland, and had much less experience of life in the real world. Maybe it just wasn't in me. How naïve I was! Actually, as I recall, I couldn't believe that the lab management and the whole BNL community didn't see the importance of accelerator technology the way I did. What a fool I was in those days! So you see, when it comes right down to it, Leland was a wise man and I wasn't. It's as simple as that. Well, for what it's worth, Mickey and friends, that's my take on the way it was."

Mickey watched Ken savoring the smoke as it billowed around his head. Quiet filled the air. So moved was Mickey by Ken's opening up so on that fabulous early evening in *Le Petit Village* that he shivered a bit. Ken's words meandered through Mickey's mind like the cigarette smoke above him. He kept returning to and finally fastened on Ken's self-effacing remark about not being so good at being able to see ahead. Somehow that notion evoked the memory of Ken in the seventies, before his passing away from all earthly obligations. What an exceptional and exemplary man he was then, having the pluck and spirit to come back as he did after the deplorably shabby and reprehensible treatment he'd received! The ideas he fashioned during that decade for a BNL light source certainly belied his lacking any foresight. However, he had far more to offer than that. Not only was he way ahead of everyone else in anticipating the tremendous research value of a user facility for experiments in all manner of sciences, but he also had the persuasiveness as well as the fortitude and skill to see that it got off the ground. And to do this after all he'd been through! It was nothing if not amazing. Even in his waning years, his love for the building of new devices came through loud and clear. Against all odds, he was able to bring forth from deep within himself the remarkable and rare managerial knack of making a shaky lab get off its ass. As unlikely as it was, he got BNL to move in a new and untried direction, to fight the daunting Washington inertia, and finally to win a brand new light source project. That was Ken's doing. He conceived the whole thing. He designed the facility. And he gave the lab the zip to pull it off. Yes, Mickey concluded, he was more of a man than his modesty would suggest. Too bad Ken didn't get the chance to build the light source himself, he thought, with a wistful melancholy.

You could have heard a pin drop. The table stood in an eerie stillness. Then – perhaps it was the silence, or perhaps some sort of sixth sense in his mind – something broke Mickey's trance. Actually, the whole episode had lasted no more than a minute. But, once Mickey awakened, his time for reverie was over. With a jerky motion of his head, he peered at the man who'd occupied his momentary nostalgic reminiscence. "Ken," he began, "I cherish those all-too-brief periods I had the good fortune to spend with you. How I thank that lucky star looking over me for the day it caused us to first cross paths! You see it was you who inspired me to enter and rove about in that breathtaking world of fantastic machines. How I thought the world of you when you were my boss in the late sixties! How I admired you no end in the seventies, when you taught me so much about what it meant to be a scientist! How I stood in awe of your inventiveness and tenacity in the face of so unfair and uncalled for adversity! You showed them how a real man should conduct and acquit himself by steadfastly and unflinchingly withstanding those vicious assaults on you and living on. Do you remember that during the seventies for more than five years we occupied adjacent offices in the AGS building? Well, you may not be aware of it, but during that time I developed a deep fondness for you; and those warm feelings are still with me, and always will be." Ken smiled knowingly as he turned his head to the far-off mountaintops. As he took a deep puff, holding the smoke far down in his lungs, a mixture of contentment and longing appeared on his face. Mickey felt a tear starting to form, and he began to lose control of his cheek muscles. But, catching himself, he shook his head and, with tearless eyes, looked toward Bob, another of his idols.

* * * * *

Bob

Bob was calm and pensive, with a wistful air about him, as he gazed out at the western mountains. For the moment, all was quiet at the table, and Mickey took the opportunity to remember old times. He recalled those early mornings in 1976 at one of Bob's Aspen summer workshops on new accelerator facilities. Mickey was an early bird in those days, and by seven in the morning he would be earnestly working in one of the offices set aside for scientists to talk about their dreams and to begin planning to bring them to life. Lucky for him, Bob was of the same early-to-rise ilk and would often turn up at that cock-a-doodle-doo hour as well. Mickey wondered whether Bob was being opportunistic and did that on purpose, with the true aim of talking to Mickey about the nature and limitations of the big colliders just around the bend, or about other designs being cooked up by the workshop's accelerator teams. No doubt that was merely Mickey's wishful thinking. The truth was that Mickey didn't really consider himself in Bob's league. So the thought took a hop, skip, and a jump, and quickly fled his mind. In the end, Mickey chalked up the fortuitous get-togethers to good luck; and indeed it was. What a thrill it was for him. There they were, just the two of them, with no one else around, talking shop about designing big machines, about creating new technologies, and about ensuring the stability of beams. Yes, Mickey thought, what good times they were!

Treasuring these moments, Mickey tucked them away in his mind to be brought out when he felt the need to convince himself that at least some of the big boys were capable of friendliness toward the hard-working aspiring young, or that some men of consequence actually wanted the expert opinions and advice of the dutiful plugging-away nobodies. Mickey, in the prime of his professional career, imaginative, creative, and youthfully ambitious, found the entire experience in Aspen to be something worth writing home about. But nothing could compare with those stolen morning-moments with Bob. They were by far the high points of his three-week stint. To Mickey, they were singular occasions that over the years became magnified in his mind to mythic proportions. They became indelible and precious memories that he would harbor close to his heart for the rest of his days. Oh how he loved being with a man so high up on the totem pole, talking of big-time stuff, like science's future and the technological frontiers. It made him feel as though he were a part of that elite, stationed high above the clouds with the gods-on-high. He was young then, when he was innocent enough to indulge himself in such illusions.

However, now, in the realm where truth was the prime rule, there was no place for such pleasures and fantasies as diversions and flings with gods. Dreaming and fancies were out, and pragmatism and realism were in. Mickey had a down-to-earth job to do; and to do it right he had to get the rational part of his mind in high gear. For this tough task, he needed clarity of expression, well controlled pacing, unquestioned believability, and beyond-a-shadow-of-a-doubt trustworthiness. And what was this challenging and tricky mission? It was no less than to elicit from Bob the truth that only Bob would know. To wit, Mickey had to dig out of him how he felt about the things that happened to him in his most eventful life, and about the men who played central parts in his ups-and-downs, principally those men responsible for doing him wrong. But to do all that, Mickey had to drop the little-guy mask he was wearing, get a grip on himself, and face Bob as an equal. That was a lot to ask of anybody. How was Mickey to visualize himself as even-steven with this giant of a man? How was he to talk with this peerless, quintessential king of men, a man who was so aloof from the world of ordinary men, so above it? How was he to assure Bob that he was worthy of such confidences? Of course, he should have been able to see ahead and prepare for the moment when he would come face-to-face with Bob, but things happened so fast that the very notion of choosing the appropriate image – of finding just the right mask and wearing it convincingly – completely eluded him. Actually, there was really no need to chide himself, for it wasn't something he could learn anyway. No amount of thought or practice would've done the trick. The fact was that there was no choice open to him other than to depend on his own natural instincts and on the devices for persuasion he'd built up over the years. So there he was, again on the threshold of put-up-or-shut-up time. Ready or not, this was the take-it-or-leave-it moment. Having waited so long for the opportunity, Mickey, not surprisingly, chose to take it. So, head first, he plunged right in.

"Bob, even though I'm well aware of your reputation of not taking too kindly to being praised to beat the band, forgive me for perhaps embarrassing you a bit by speaking from the heart," he opened. "My only excuse for doing it, despite your disinclination for it, is that I'm under the spell of a compulsion. Difficult as it is for me not to respect and comply with your implicit wishes, I must tell you that you are a great man and, compared to your deeds, words are but puny shadows. It may not be my place to say this, ordinary guy that I am. But being here with you, having this once-in-a-lifetime chance, how could I resist? Without overstating the case, I can say without the least hesitation or ambiguity that, having given mankind the monuments you so selflessly erected during your far too few years on the stage, all men are the better for your having been there. These fruits of your genius represent you and will do so until only the ravages of time send your concrete godly instruments to their final resting-places. Your conceptions, your noble and far-famed creations, are your legacy. Explanations or justifications for them are certainly superfluous because they speak for themselves. Although I am one of your ardent fans and appreciate all you've done, the young – the new generation and future ones to come – may not. What a loss it would be should men of the future not be afforded the chance to fathom the phenomenal impact you've had on science! No, it simply can't be allowed to happen. And it won't, for the evidence is palpable and will persist. In fact, I have no doubt that your name and your gifts to humanity will live on in the annals of science achievement as long as men have the will to record and maintain greatness.

"As with all men of substance, you too have risen to the heights only to have to endure the inevitable fall. Not surprisingly, your decline of fortune leaves many unexplained holes, which you, and only you, can help me explore. Thus, my investigative inquiry into the long journey down of high-energy physics in the last quarter of a century brings me to you and the part you played in it. It turns out there are certain nebulous matters that baffle me; and only you can throw light on them. Try as I might, I just haven't been able to penetrate to their core truths. You see there's simply no alternative but to come to you. So I hope you'll see fit to respond to my queries and help fill those bothersome gaps in the story. The questions I have for you deal with some of the men of Big Science and the way they navigated the stormy sea of their fiercely lived human drama. What I'd really like to know and better understand are things like: What was behind a particular occurrence? Did it really happen the way it's usually portrayed? Did so-and-so really do what was ascribed to him? What were your motives? Are the inferences many people make about your involvement and the feelings you had right or wrong? What's your take on the others implicated? What is your opinion of their intentions? And so on! My quest is to find the reasons behind the actions and events that transpired in your lifetime, and why the actors did what they did.

"Let me start after you finished building Fermilab in the early seventies. Oh, how the lab was riding high then! More precisely, the good times began rolling once you'd resolved that annoying magnet blunder and physics results started pouring in. Having been so economical in your building of the Fermilab facility, to the point of your stingily parceling out every penny, many doubted that you'd be able to bring it off and get the facility to be so productive. Do you recall the insufficient magnet insulation you chose? That was some predicament you got yourself into! It caused the magnets to fail far too frequently, thereby interrupting data collection. That must've taught you the lesson not to step on the toes of the *physichists*, who'll have their way no matter what the cost to the careers and morale of their supposed colleagues! The result was no end of frustration, manifested by a hell of a lot of whining and then mean-spiritedness. It was blood the experimenters came to want – your blood. However, throughout this period of facility unreliability you remained upright and steady. And in the end you stemmed the angry tide aimed directly at you. Keeping your head and holding on, you worked out all the wrinkles and righted the wrongs. Eventually, the results began streaming out in droves, and Fermilab was on its way to the top of the physics world.

"Along the way, like all great men, you were necessarily ruthless at times. You made enemies, and some, particularly the vindictive or jealous ones, didn't want you to succeed. They did all they could to throw obstacles in your path and tarnish your reputation. Nevertheless your vision of how Big Science should be conducted – *get in quick, take what's there, and get out quick* – proved right, and all those naysayers and nonbelievers had to eat crow. There was no better example of this than your competition with the father of the Big Science labs, BNL. While you were pulling swiftly ahead, BNL was stuck in quicksand and couldn't find any forward thrust. By pursuing the outdated *go-slow, watch-your-step, don't-be-rash, wait-your-turn* philosophy for facility building, the old lab kept sinking and falling further behind. While BNL was paralyzed, refusing to look ahead, the circumstances were perfect for Fermilab to make a bold move for the future. And you were there, ready with ingenious ideas for making superconductivity work for the next step in the rolling thunder of twentieth century Big Physics.

"But the vagaries of life, the ironies we all live with, unobserved and unforeseen, entered the picture. Unfortunately for you, and, as it turned out, for Big Science as well, as the decade of the seventies passed its mid-point, the political tides shifted. That's politics for you! In just a few short years, an entirely new world can crop up. As it happened, the change that took place boded ill for you. When President Carter took office, he chose to kill off the AEC and to embed it in ERDA. To most, this action meant little, but to you it meant a great deal. How is it that you didn't see that with the demise of the AEC would go your political clout? But even that wasn't the worst of it. At the same time, while Illinois seemed to be taking a nap, New York took the initiative and gained the political upper hand in Big Physics. This confluence of events wasn't at all what you expected, and for some strange reason, you didn't appreciate its significance. Methinks you misread the tealeaves.

"In spite of the signs telling you to change your ways, to cut down on your aggressive tactics, and to hold back and wait for your day to return, you kept pushing as you'd done so many times before. But this time, in 1977, you pushed too hard; and, as it turned out, it was once too often. All the signals and advice you were receiving, from friend and foe alike, were to keep cool and be patient until the environment for a political comeback became feasible. If that weren't enough to dissuade you from impetuously, recklessly, and foolhardily placing your head in the noose, then certainly the fact that John Deutsch was simply not a guy to tinker with should have been. But there was no stopping you, and your arrogance and insolence won out. With little thought and a hot head, you pounded out an ill-conceived offer to resign and sent it off.

"Actually, this was but one in a series of such letters that you meant as threats in order to win more favor and funds for your beloved lab. *It's more money or I go*, you were saying. And in previous instances the ploy worked! Washington caved in and the little extra funds for Fermilab were conceded. However, this time it was different, and the letter you unthinkingly wrote turned out to be the last in the succession of them. Was it that you were getting on and perhaps weren't as indispensable as you thought? Was Fermilab just not worth it anymore? Was Deutsch simply a man who would not be intimidated? Was it perhaps all of these reasons? Who knows! But the fact is that this letter of resignation was accepted, and you were out the door. You didn't intend for it to come out that way, but when one rolls the dice, snake eyes do turn up sometimes. Still, that you should suffer such a loss – the job you so treasured, your base of influence and operation, and your chance to lead Big Physics to undreamed of places – for only ten million dollars or so makes no sense at all. You see, this contest was nothing but petty gamesmanship and one-upmanship, and there were no winners. Only second thoughts, regrets, disappointments, and blighted hopes followed in its wake. But boy, you certainly miscalculated! How could you have missed the warning signs? How could you not have sensed the danger lurking in Deutsch's heart: his pride, his determination, his obstinacy, and his inner need to make himself felt? Well, that's all past and part of history's vast vista of missteps and misjudgments. Although it's probably not much of a consolation, it wasn't only you who misread the true state of affairs. Deutsch erred too; and his may have been the worse of the two blundering gaffes. He failed to see that without you he would be stuck with a dispirited, weak, bloated, and ineffective BNL. What a pretty mess the result was! In fact, by pulling back and viewing the big picture, it is evident that, in the end, although you lost much, the biggest loser of all was American Big Physics. Indeed, it was this choice of Deutsch to favor BNL and precipitously drop Fermilab that led step-by-step to CERN and Carlo traveling freely and unopposed to the pot of gold – the W and the Nobel.

"After what you went through, most men would've folded and joined the never-to-be-heard-from-again choir of overthrown and beaten, ruined and forlorn castaways. But not you, Bob! No, as taxing and grim as things were in those dark and tortured days, there was still life left in you. Although you were untimely ripped from the scene, you weren't yet ready to go down for the count. In your never-give-up fashion, you found the means to pick yourself up and re-enter the ring. So it was that you returned a few years later to fight yet again. Just as some doubting Thomases were ready to give up on you, you bounced back by showing up at Snowmass '82 armed with a daring new concept you fashioned, giving it the colorful name, the Desertron. It was an ingenious idea put forward at the perfect spot and at the perfect moment for Big Science. What a prize package you delivered! What a gift you bestowed upon that undeserving lot who'd treated you so carelessly, so callously, and so hurtfully! What a vision you set forth for the future of American Big Physics! With that virtuoso inspiration you single-handedly transformed Snowmass '82 from a doomed-to-dullsville conference into an extravaganza. Just the recollection of it raises my spirits. How exciting it was! How pride-filled for you! How thrilling for me! How electrifying for everybody lucky enough to have been there!

"Oh yes, Snowmass '82 was indeed a glorious occasion. But understand that such a unique event didn't simply spring up spontaneously. Indeed, how does an ordinary, run-of-the-mill conference reach such heights? In fact, it took hard times to bring the Rocky-Mountains affair to fruition and to life. It took the gathering of dark clouds and the visitation of ill winds. American Big Physics was in deep trouble and had to find its way back to the sunny skies and peaceful breezes where inventiveness and success thrive. It was that trip, from despair to dreams to hope that made Snowmass '82 what it was. However, to go from the dark to the light, the evil BNL star had to be exorcised. That was the unspoken reason that impelled the physics community to congregate in Colorado. That's what sowed the seeds of the heaven-sent brilliance that was ushered in and that flowered at Snowmass. So it was that as the new splendid and scintillating star shone in the Rocky Mountains, BNL – as if by some conservation law or as if a kind of duality were at work – came to suffer the consequences of its misguided and heavy-handed ways, and of its corrupt and injurious deeds. Often it happens in life that out of a bad circumstance there arises a good outcome; and such was the case at Snowmass '82.

"Perhaps it shouldn't be too surprising that it was out of the winter of your discontent that emerged in you the masterly stroke of genius for a giant collider, which ended up being the centerpiece of the Snowmass show. It was as if the fates demanded that you suffer first as prior payment for permitting you to deliver the restoring transfusion to a wasting away and about-to-totter high-energy physics. And the bed of thorns you were made to endure was indeed bitter and dignity crushing. When Washington snatched from you and deprived you of your pride and joy, that was a maliciously outrageous and gratuitous act of vindictive retaliation. But even that wasn't enough for the greedy spirits that play with men and their frailties. Another dagger was at the ready to prick your woe-filled heart. Compounding the appalling injustice already done you, you were about to feel pangs of pain inflicted by the menacing old BNL, flailing at any outsider nervy and brash enough to enter its Upton fortress. When you did just that, you, BNL's archenemy, were ideal as fodder to appease the inhabitants' insatiable desire to hurt. So it was that you came to Long Island, innocent and eager to help. How is it that a man of your depth and experience of life wasn't able to anticipate what awaited him there? Nonetheless, without the least armor for protection, you walked naïvely into the jaws of the hungry tiger.

"Here's what happened to you at BNL prior to the big event of 1982, and after your lamentable, leading-to-no-good episode with Deutsch in early 1978. About a year before Snowmass, as the autumn of 1981 approached, ISABELLE was floundering, and you visited BNL to propose that it use Fermilab superconducting magnets to solve its magnet problem. You told Vineyard that in this way ISABELLE could be finished quickly and perhaps, even at that late date, beat out Carlo for the W. With Leon's approval and Wallenmeyer's encouragement, you set a price for both magnets and aid that anyone would have jumped at. However, the outcome of that trip must have surprised even one as worldly as you, because, not only did Vineyard decline the offer, but he also snubbed you to boot. You must have been wounded to the core and sorely humiliated by the scathing treatment you received – ignored for needlessly long periods, contemptuously scorned at times, and then sent away with nothing but a foul and rank taste in your mouth. But even more important than you being insulted and demeaned, as you were, the BNL response meant that the proposed scheme that would have saved ISABELLE was scotched.

"Ironically, this harrowing, galling, and deplorable treatment at the hands of Deutsch and Vineyard was the very thing that gave you the impetus and the drive propelling you to Snowmass '82. It was up there in nature's breathtaking and inspiring mountains where Big Physics history was made, where you sold your alluring and glitzy American dream to a keyed-up and oh-so-receptive audience, all agog, intoxicated by your boldly venturesome spirit. You aroused these men of science who came to find their way to the Promised Land. You stirred their blood. You lit their fire. And you awakened in them the belief they'd almost forgotten that in the Big Science realm, anything was possible.

"Behind this chain of circumstances that led you to that final brief high point in your illustrious life, there must be fascinating and intriguing tales to tell. That we could hear of them from your lips would truly be a dream come true. But, as we've all no doubt come to appreciate: *You can't always get what you want!* So I will settle for far less and limit my questions to the two particular issues I've been highlighting: First, what was the real story surrounding your resignation, not the hand-me-down versions full of guesses and inferences? Also, focusing on Deutsch, what do you believe was the part he played? Was he being fed information? Did he act alone? Did anyone have influence over him? If so, who? Second, what exactly happened during your 1981 visit to BNL? Did you have any prior inkling of what was to transpire? Did Vineyard really treat you as badly as the grapevine reported? Did you go with only goodness and purity in your heart? Did you perhaps have a hidden intention? If so, what was it? There, that's it! I've finished!" Mickey paused for a slight instant; then, looking toward Bob, but not able to make eye-contact, he resumed: "You know, it never ceases to amaze me how simple the questions sound when taken down to their bare essentials. The answers, naturally, are something else again."

Bob sat still, head bowed, engrossed in his own inner world. It wasn't a long time, maybe a minute, but to Mickey it felt more like an hour. Mickey searched his mind for something to say, something that might alleviate the fidgeting, the jittery nerves, and the tension in the air. But not a word was spoken. They all waited for Bob to stir. They waited in silence, with respect and heartfelt esteem for the man whose magic lit the byways that showed them and their ilk the way to fame and glory. Then, the moment of stillness passed. As Bob lifted his head, he was suddenly transformed from being seemingly downcast to an uplifting vivacity. His face was red with passion and his flashing eyes darted to and fro. Belying this spirited image, he spoke in a calm, deliberate manner: "I am a simple man. As time flew by, as my experiences amassed, and as my life slipped away before my eyes, I never forgot the plains and mountains of my youth. I can still visualize in my mind's eye the plains where buffalo once roamed in droves and the mountains from where hordes of horses streamed down. How they gleamed in the sun and sparked my youthful invincibility! I had dreams in those days: dreams of palaces and kings, of frontiers to conquer, and of mysteries to unveil. In the memories of those times, I have been allowed a measure of comfort and tranquility. Actually, they've always been a solace to me when life became disheartening and almost unbearable, when distress seemed on the verge of overwhelming me. Nonetheless, although adverse and ill-fated things did happen to me, as they do to all of us, on the whole life was kind to me. Whatever came my way I simply took to be part of life's fickle chanciness! Appreciating that I was what I was – no more, no less – I was determined to live and work as best as I knew how. My way of life, instilled in me as a youth, was always trying to discover what was good and true, and to expose what was bad and false. And that became my guidepost and my MO!

"It seemed only right that having been given the gift of life and society's faith and investment in me that I should give something back to the community of man, something that would advance it and that it would value. As it happened, science was in my bones and so gave me the means to fulfill that bargain. I had a knack for probing into the mysteries of nature; and so, for better or worse, I chose that to be my life's work. I vowed early on to dedicate myself to this end, honestly, plainly, simply, and with the cards that the heavens dealt me. This I promised to do, and to stick with it, even if there were self-sacrifices to be made along the way. If I'm to be judged by my peers and by those who follow me, let these qualities and my ambitions be taken as the measures of me as a man.

"Looking back on my life and what came of it, I cannot but conclude that luck smiled on me and made me a favorite of the gods. How blessed I was that my stars permitted me to taste of my dreams! Could anyone ask for anything more? As it was, I was a builder, driven to build temples and monuments to search for and discover life's fountainhead and genesis. To let me strive for my heart's desires, destiny placed a silver spoon in my mouth. What a break it was for me to have been born in the land of the free, where a simple man might think big thoughts and build big things! With such grace bestowed upon me, I attempted to erect cathedrals that would be pathways to the world's soul. It was an impossible dream right from the start, a youthful ambition that I had no chance of ever wholly realizing. Nonetheless, it was my destiny. It was all I could do. It was all I could give to mankind. Though bound to stumble and founder in my unattainable mission, there would be no rest for me until the *Graveyard Express* made its last stop. What more could be expected of me?

"I struggled with every ounce of strength within me to reach the unreachable, but, in the end, inevitably I lost what couldn't be won. Still, it cannot be said that it was all in vain. No, not at all! In our youth, we take a stab at the impossible; and, in old age, ideally, we pass on that ambition to the young at heart. So it is that the cycle continues, and, at each peak in the cycle, more of the truth of the world is recorded and pocketed by mankind. As a man who's become older and wiser, I'm well aware that we humans may never comprehend the full panorama of our wondrous heaven-built world. But who can say that it isn't worth a shot to try to find out what it's all about? Certainly we should give thanks that, generation after generation, youth is ignorant enough to try for the golden scepter that will explain all. It would be a sad day indeed if the young were to know what the old do, and too soon become old fools fearing to press on.

"In my youth, as I strode and tramped the many highways and byways, pulling out all the stops and going all-out to discover the hidden meanings of our physical world, I found to my dismay that, in addition to the gods, human nature itself blocked my path to heaven's gate. Too bad for those of us who aspire to know all! In doing so, we become intertwined with other men, and unfortunately our natures prevent us from working together for too long as a coherent team. Eventually the destructive face of competitiveness begins to show itself. We start to disagree, to have falling-outs, to misunderstand one another, to clash with each other, to cross swords, and finally to grasp at each other's throats. Thus, as the gods have willed it, we are drawn to plant the seeds of our own ends. That is what has been ingrained in us, and it is unalterable. Upon entering the arena to play the game, what we find is inevitably more than we bargained for. Yes, when it comes right down to it, it is not the gods that stop us. It is ourselves alone! No, there are no special beings to do the things humankind has achieved on earth. Great thinkers there are. Great doers there are. Great builders there are. Great scientists there are. But there is no ideal human being among us. There are only plain men. Still, look at what they've done and what they've come to know!"

Bob stood up and paced about for a moment or two, then sat down and continued: "In hot pursuit of how the world works, science was my game. The contest whetted my appetite and electrified every fiber of my being. It animated and exhilarated me; and it galvanized me into action. This way and that I went, down this lane, up that blind alley, into a murky dead-end or a no-man's land, and then back out only to enter the maze once more to try again. For a time lady luck shone a special light on me: ideas just popped into my head, and discoveries alighted with almost every throw of the dice I made. Then I came upon the elusive quarks and embarked on their hunt. With zeal, eagerness, and hope in my heart, I jumped right in, holding the firm belief that the good times would simply continue on and on. But all good things must come to an end. Although I didn't fully realize it then, in the seventies the uncovering of treasures and the lucky strikes were over for me. As it turned out, I'd already had my last hurrah. Before I could set out and really get anywhere on the great quark adventure, alas, my time had passed. By then the last glory-bound grain had already sifted through my life's sieve.

"So, as it turned out, the *quarks* got me. No, of course, it wasn't the inanimate, conceptual *quarks*; but rather it was men who did me in. While you were talking, Mickey, my mind wandered back in time, and I began to recall those grim and trying periods in the latter half of the seventies and early eighties. Oh yes, it was those men, Deutsch and Vineyard, who struck those cruel and callous blows that shook me to my very core. They humiliated and embarrassed me. They engraved on me the stigma of the victim, making me feel ashamed and disgraced. They caused me to begin to doubt myself, to doubt my philosophy of living and my capability. They stole from me my balance and equilibrium that gave me the wherewithal to sail fearlessly into uncharted waters, and acquit myself like a man. They darkened my life, made me sullen and lonely, and triggered the return of my black moods. They made me bristle with hatred in my heart, made my angry passions rise, and made my blood boil. They caused me to lose my temper frequently, to become enraged in fits of indignation, and to snap at my friends, taking things out on those I should've been embracing. They made me lash out at the gods for having forsaken me. Yet, in spite of what they inflicted on me, in a strange way, I don't visualize these wayward men as devils. After all, they were merely men, doing the best they could, imagining that what they were doing would be good for them and for the world of science over which they were presiding. In the end, they were much like all our lot. So how can I do other than forgive them their trespasses and the sorry consequences that followed, both to me and to our dear high-energy physics?

"The truth of the matter is that I have no choice but to forgive them, for, you see, I was not entirely blameless in the affairs. I was a free man in a free nation. I could've behaved better too. I didn't have to push them to their limits of endurance. I didn't have to prod and goad them past the line where reasonable men are transformed into irrational beasts. You understand that there's more here than meets the eye. The deeper I go into my exploration of this part of my life, the brighter becomes the moving light of truth out in the distance as it edges closer and closer. As I begin to see it more clearly, I recognize what it's telling me. Perhaps it wasn't the *quarks* that got me. Perhaps it wasn't even the men. Furthermore, perhaps it wasn't the gods either. Then who shoulders the responsibility, you ask? The shining beacon of truth spells it out clearly and unequivocally: It is I myself who must bear that burden.

"I suppose this is as good a time as any to tackle some of the particular points you raised. About your overall interpretations of my run-ins with Deutsch and Vineyard, I really haven't much to add. Yes, I believe that Deutsch was a man whose pride was overwhelming and got the better of him, and that Vineyard was a man who lost his way in the ISABELLE storm that swept over him. On your specific queries: It's likely that Deutsch was influenced by the committed-to-BNL Wallenmeyer; and I can tell you that, knowing myself, the intentions I had for my 1981 visit to BNL were strictly honorable. However, that said, how can I deny the inescapable truths that Deutsch and I were at odds with each other from the moment he appeared on the political scene, and that my BNL trip had to be colored by my deep devotion to the lab I gave birth to? Now please don't take what I'm saying as being evasive. I can comfortably guarantee you that I'm not. It's just that such points are intrinsically hard to pin down. The best we seem capable of is to attach to them a kind of maximum likelihood. And that's what I've given you. Anyway, other than these few details, I'm in full accord with the way you've pieced together what happened to me. Thus, all in all, your versions of the John Deutsch and George Vineyard episodes, implications included, couldn't be closer to my memories of them.

"Please forgive my rambling, but being here on this incomparable of days, gazing at the setting sun and at the mountains not far from the ones that I grew up with and that lit up my youthful eyes, I can't but reflect on my past, and try to pin some sort of label on what life on this earth of ours made of me. But how does one pull it all together and sum up the experiences of a lifetime? The thing that keeps coming to me and sticks in my mind is that despite all the bleak, despairing times, when all seemed hollow, futile, and empty, stale and flat, I never – not once – lost my faith in life and the freedom of man. That's quite a mouthful. Perhaps that's the reason I've always taken for granted that I had a good life and was a happy man. Yes, through thick and thin, all the way to the end, that's the way it was. There seemed to be a source within me that determined that it should be so. No matter what befell me, this *happy* source radiated and wiped the *bad* clean out of my thoughts. How simple it was. I just had to follow my bliss and being happy fell right onto my lap.

"On the other hand, maybe it was too pat, just a bit too easy. On second thought, that picture of my life and the way I saw it might well be a gross oversimplification. How could I then and how can I now ignore that along the way there were many an instance of unhappy moments, of melancholy times, and of deep regrets? Doubtless you can all well understand that. These experiences are universal. Who among us doesn't have them? Yet, in spite of them, most abide and many flourish. Now I ask you, this power we have over adversity and its consequent despair and feeling of aloneness, where does it come from? At first I thought it was given as a gift. But what about its apparent universality? Does that mean that it's a gift to all? Not likely! Then there's the simple fact that to live with some measure of optimism each and every one of us must learn to build in ourselves the capacity to endure the hardships and the downers, to brave the turbulent and tempestuous waters, and to bring to bear life's most demanding need to hang tough? Yes, we must acquire it for ourselves with our own efforts. So I ask again, where does that power come from? Methinks it is not at the stars in the heavens, but at the stars in ourselves where we must look to find the answer.

"As I bring to mind some of the more fierce and malicious acts done against me and the hopelessness that permeated through me in the aftermath, difficult as it is, I find myself able to reconstruct in some detail just how I was affected. I remember the sensation that filled me when I successfully pulled through a particularly rough one of these bouts. Oh, how good it felt! I had the impression of possessing an abundance of strength to have overcome an extreme case of life's seemingly endless string of obstacles. I somehow found the means to convince myself that even though I'd lost that particular vicious confrontation, I could come back to fight another day. So, why feel downhearted and beaten? Then lo, something within me clicked, and my spirits would rise. I'd overcome, and could go on with life's next round. At such times, I believed that nothing anybody did could phase or perturb me. It was as if I were invincible and, being all-powerful, could I be anything other than a happy man? Can you imagine Superman unhappy? Aha! So that's how, even as we must deal with cruel and venomous men, and with the most demanding and morale-busting of circumstances, we can still walk on to the next encounter, smiling all the way.

"However, as the experiences of living piled up and old age crept upon me, I came to appreciate that this sense of invincibility is but an imaginary figment, one of life's most powerful illusions. It is formed in us in our youth, and serves as a fantasy impelling young men, or whoever is under its spell, to enter arenas where the survival instinct should give them serious pause. It's as if Darwinian survival is temporarily suspended. But, as you can easily appreciate, this illusory process eventually has to start showing cracks. The false feeling of invincibility can't and doesn't last forever; and, being but a man after all, it came to ebb in me. It's strange that I didn't see before that once I'd lost the illusion of invincibility, the associated sense of being a happy man also became untenable. The connection is as plain as day. Feeling invincible and feeling happy are just two sides of the same coin. But somehow I simply missed that plain and simple truth. I believed I could hold onto the *happy-man* bit, even as my wrinkles proliferated and *invincibility* slipped away from me. How foolish I was back then! Still, I thank heaven for it being so.

"As time passed following the Deutsch incident and as I began to age noticeably, I came to miss being the Director. Over the years after it was taken from me – after I in effect threw it away – slowly but surely these moments of melancholy and moroseness, even despondency, intensified and were not so easily shaken as they'd been in my more youthful pre-Deutsch days. Is it really possible that not being the Director anymore might've brought on these pangs of depression? No, it couldn't have been that alone. But if not that, then what? Is there anything else that could be the cause behind it? Unfortunately, even after thinking long and hard about what it could be, I must admit that I haven't found a fully satisfactory answer, that is, except for the obvious fact of getting older. As you no doubt gather, that explanation has never been a favorite of mine. So let me put it to you, all of you: Is it simply getting older and trying to come to terms with your mortality that generates these moods of gloominess, hopelessness, and utter dejection? To be frank, I must tell you that as an alternative answer, I once thought that maybe it was because I so terribly missed that sleek black Director's limousine that used to pick me up and drop me off."

* * * * *

Interlude

No one at the table was ready for that kind of moving confession. They'd just witnessed the crying heart of a once-great man. When it was over, all were spent and everyone needed a pause. Mickey was especially touched by Bob's candidness about his inner feelings. He felt a little shivery and knew he had to compose himself. He took the opportunity of the momentary silence to do so. However, although he was quiet on the outside, the truth was that nothing could stop his thoughts from zipping right along. Images of Bob in times past played out in his mind: Bob deep in thought, Bob morose and distant, Bob smiling an inward smile, Bob grinning, Bob laughing heartily, Bob speaking purposefully and convincingly, and Bob joking around and having a ball. Bob was a man of many moods and many faces, and seeing them slide-projected in his mind that way somehow made Mickey feel blue. Oh, how he missed that man! But this mood of pining for a long-gone past, this nostalgic wistfulness passed quickly. Mickey surreptitiously looked about and saw that a little more time was still necessary to bring the table back to equilibrium. Quietly, he lowered his head and let his mind wander where it might. He was reminded of something he planned to say before Bob started speaking. It was right there on the tip of his tongue, ready to spill out. But, although anyone knowing Mickey would find it hard to explain, it remained unsaid. What he wanted to say was that *he came to praise Caesar, not to bury him*. What a gaffe that would've been! You see, the encounter with Bob was as pure as the driven snow. Thus, even though the quotation was reversed, the implied accusation of falseness and betrayal that underlies Marc Antony's ironical expression was entirely inappropriate. If anything, the inversion would've made the remark worse in that respect, and a jarring addition to the proceedings. How fortunate that Mickey resisted his inclination to say such a stagy and needling thing. Since it was in his makeup to play the game of quips and repartees, it was indeed a lucky break that this time somehow he passed up the chance. It made him feel good that his on-the-spot instinct to desist served him well on this special occasion.

As Mickey sat quietly, it struck him that Bob's impassioned words of wisdom caused the interviewer to lose sight of whether or not his questions were actually answered. Thinking it over a bit, he guessed that Bob was indeed responsive, but to uncover specific replies required a lot of digging. Bob gave every indication that he agreed with Mickey's suppositions that Deutsch fired him through pique, and that Vineyard did in fact degrade, dishonor, and humiliate him during his BNL visit. He also appeared to acquiesce in Mickey's guesses that Deutsch had been in league with BNL and that Bob himself had somewhat less than one hundred per cent goodness in his heart when he arrived on Long Island with the plan to save ISABELLE and Vineyard. In dealing with these two issues, Bob chose to be cagey and not absolutely forthright as he was with everything else he uttered. So, when it came right down to it, to come to the assessment that Bob was truly affirming Mickey's conjectures required that Mickey read quite a chunk into what was actually said. These points being important to his inquiry, Mickey did have a quick-passing urge to pursue them further, but he just couldn't find the nerve to press Bob for clarification. Bob, the giant killer and the lost soul, was let off the hook. Maybe it was because Mickey lacked the cold, calculating opportunism to attempt to take advantage of a man he so respected; maybe it was simply out of courtesy for this straight-shooting gentleman who befriended lowly Mickey from the Director's perch on high; or maybe it was because Mickey couldn't take the chance of offending someone who so freely and generously agreed to be on hand for Mickey's show in truth-country. Actually, it's hard to figure out why Mickey held back. Each one of these many reasons sounds perfectly plausible. Yet, there's still one more; and, if none of the others is appealing, perhaps it was that Mickey was in awe of this commanding man, this *Master Builder*, and simply became tongue-tied. Anyway, since Mickey, in all probability, had the answers he was seeking from Bob, why he didn't continue to pursue it more does seem moot. In any case, that damnable passing of time was beginning to intrude. So Mickey knew that thinking-time was over, and that he had to move on.

Mickey sensed the need for a breathing spell, a respite from the all-consuming, mental-straining Bob-experience of the past half-hour. So, even though there was less than an hour and a half to go before *closing time*, Mickey asked the silent lot, "How about a break?" With a collective sigh of relief, "Good idea," chimed the chorus. In nothing flat, as if they were on their marks at the starting gate, all of them paraded around a corner about twenty yards into the room and towards a door with a get-the-job-done, but tacky blue colored picture of a bathroom sink pasted on it. When they returned to the table, having been gone only a few minutes, they found clean ashtrays and refreshments awaiting them. There were cold drinks and two temptation-filled plates of sweets, heaped full of chocolate chip and oatmeal-raisin cookies, praline and cherry-filled liqueur chocolates, vanilla halvah, and white chocolate with nuts. As their eyes scanned the appetizing table, their faces lit up, and they breathed oohs and ahs, much like children. Then they caught sight of a fresh bottle of Glenlivet with schnapps glasses just aching to be filled beside it. Immediately, Leon made a beeline for the whiskey and, as he'd done countless times before, filled the five glasses to the brim. As each man lifted a glass, Leon entertained the toast, "To Mickey, for inviting us to this hallowed place where we can all be redeemed and purified, and so reborn." Mickey didn't quite pick up Leon's slight tone of sarcasm and became flushed with pride. Although he was beginning to feel a little woozy and faint, he could just about make out the echo of the chorus, "To Mickey." For an instant, as they all stood there, glasses raised, time stood still. Then, in a flash, with the momentary spell broken, they all drank heartily of the spirits to the very last drop.

Ah, just what we needed, Mickey rationalized, some of the best fast-energizing food there is. With that, he reached across the table, over the veritable caloric sweet-fest, and picked up a praline from one of the platters. He'd gained a few pounds over the past couple of months, and so he knew he shouldn't be indulging in such stuff. Nevertheless, he went for the chocolate anyway. As the chatter heightened towards a high-level din, Mickey stood up and paced about the room for a minute to slow down his heart rate, which had unexpectedly begun to rise. Then he resumed his seat and cleared his throat, making a lot of noise so as to catch the attention of the other four. He thought he could break up the antics of this high-flying gang just like that. What a fool! Meanwhile, the other four were having a ball: eating, laughing and talking up a storm. If they noticed Mickey at all, they certainly didn't show it. In any case, they weren't about to stop their carousing merely on his say-so. So, when it came right down to it, Mickey had no clout and carried no weight in this circle. There was simply no recourse at all available to him. You see, only when those who really controlled the show willed it to be so could Mickey get on with it.

The wisecracking, joking, and overall good cheer bewildered Mickey. What a turnabout from the heavy-hearted mood that had hovered over them just a short while before! He did try for a brief period to get into the prevailing spirit, to participate in the merriment and the freewheeling conversation, but he wasn't able to. Even though he could hear the laughter and savor the feel of it all, his heart just wasn't in it. The truth was that he was at a loss. So preoccupied was he with how to rein in this unruly bunch and get to work that he couldn't even decipher what precisely was being said. What a bind Mickey was in! He was powerless to intervene. He could only watch as the relentless clock ticked away. What was he to do? Being realistic, he chose to let them have their fun. What else was he to do anyway? Fortunately, there was also a practical side to his nature, so he took the opportunity to decide on how he should proceed and to pull together his thoughts.

It thus came to Mickey that he could just sit back, let matters run their course, and use these few moments he had in a profitable way. Leon, next on the agenda and sure to be a tough nut to crack, certainly deserved some prior attention and thought. Yes, what questions should he ask him? There were so many holes to fill about this man whose impact spread far and wide, through every corner of the high-energy enterprise over the full half century of its existence. His long arm seemed to reach into every nook and cranny. There were all manner of high-energy undertakings that Mickey approached; and in each one, Leon's name was bound to come up in one context or another. If it was a mind-expanding experiment, Leon was somehow involved. If it was a decision to build a new accelerator or collider, Leon was part of it. If there was a policy choice to be made, you guessed it: Leon was not far from the action. And if there was a conspiracy in the making – to do good, bad, or both – wasn't it just like the ubiquitous Leon to be right in the thick of things?

But it was quite ridiculous to imagine such a broad exploration in the limited time available. Mickey simply had to resign himself to the fact that he couldn't do it all. So the key question was, what priorities should he set? Yet, difficult to deal with as that question was, it was merely the beginning. What tone should he use? Should he be heavy or light-handed? How could he get Leon to be more disciplined and less full of fun? Should he be mortician-serious or play the tongue-in-cheek game? Did Mickey have to give it to Leon straight from the shoulder, or was it possible to cut the truth loose by cajolery? But why was he bothering with these issues? *How* to approach Leon wasn't really at the core of his dilemma. The real question was *what* to engage Leon in. Blast it, Mickey thought, it's hopeless; the problem is simply solution-less. How could he manage to get to even a small fraction of Leon's multifarious involvements? The more time he had to consider the whole problem, the more anxious he became. How impractical his objective seemed! Impossible would be more like it. Yet, in spite of the daunting challenge before him, Mickey knew that he was going to put everything he had into it and give it his best. That was Mickey. That's the way he was. There wasn't a doubt in the world of what was in his mind on that score. He would do whatever he had to do to get the job done.

"OK," Mickey spoke up, almost shouting, "let's get the ball rolling." The moment he said it, he knew he'd made that same serious blunder he'd made before. You don't tell these guys what to do. Not this crowd! But it was too late to take back. You don't get second chances. So Mickey was in for it. He had to face the music. And it came almost instantaneously. Immediately after his dim-witted, clumsy attempt at taking over, he got his answer. There was a sudden lull, a silence that lasted no more than a second or two. The four of them looked up at each other in surprise, as if to say, *what luck*! There were gleams in their eyes, hints of smiles on their faces, and mischief in their hearts. Oh no, Mickey wasn't about to dodge this bullet.

It was Ken who began Mickey's well-deserved lesson in behavior, "Order please! Let's have some order here so we can get started." "The man wants order," Carlo added mockingly, "well, we shouldn't delay. Let's give the man, this so important man, exactly what he wants." Leon, not to be outdone, put in his two bits in much the same vein, using a taunting, mimicking tone: "I wholeheartedly concur. If he wants order, who are we to keep it from him? Look, he invited us here. Shouldn't the man running things get what he asks for?" "Yes," they all shouted in unison. Then, spontaneously, they all started to bang the table with their fists; and, in singsong mode, the chorus began chanting, "OR-DER, OR-DER, OR-DER, ... Mickey was beside himself as the unrestrained banter just wouldn't let up. Chaos had taken over and Mickey was helpless to change it. So he just sat there, his face in his hands, bemoaning his rotten luck. *Why did he start off in such a dumb way*, he thought? *Why couldn't he foresee what the result would be*?

However, the situation wasn't really as bleak as Mickey imagined it was. All was not lost. Once the group's tension-energy was released, after these prank-filled, clownish men of science had their fill of sport and play at Mickey's expense – a few minutes at most – then, just as suddenly as the disorder had arisen, it ended. Leon, clearly the ringleader, was the one who came to Mickey's rescue. With his two arms in front of him waving up and down, he gestured for the table to calm down. While performing this ritual, he asked the group, "What do you think, shall we give him some order?" This proved to be sufficient for the exuberant, joke-loving pack. They recognized this as a signal for a change in course, and, in the manner of a well-oiled team, followed suit. Perhaps they closed the curtain on their little show because the fun's object was subdued and there was simply nothing to be gained by going on. The group's purpose was served. Why pursue it any further? They put Mickey in his place, and showed him who was boss and who wasn't. Thus, since that was accomplished, once given the cue, they all simultaneously came down from their high. The four talked quietly amongst each other for a short while. Then, as the din subsided, Mickey sensed he'd been given his chance to step in. So he did.

* * * * *

Leon

"Leon, during the couple of decades closing out the twentieth century, a chain of events unfolded that sent Big Physics reeling and into a downward slide, leading to its current depressed state. This is especially true in America where high-energy experimentation has sunk to an ill-boding low ebb. For many of the drama-like links in the chain of stories that brought about this state of affairs, it turns out that you were a major actor. This shouldn't surprise anyone. After all, you're *Mister High-Energy Physics* himself. Although you made your merit-packed mark in the extraordinary days of Big Physics majesty and splendor, it is well to emphasize and keep in mind that you were also a player of some weight in the dark threatening days that have come to plague the field.

"With Big Physics in a veritable fight for its life, the least we can do is try to better understand its plight. And that, Leon, is precisely our goal. That's why we're here. So how do I approach this dialogue with you? To cover as much as we can of this ominous *decline phase*, what I would propose to do is bring back some critical occurrences that transpired, review them, and give you some impressions I have of them. Then, after I pose my questions, the idea is for you to respond with your observations, interpretations and explanations about the links, particularly the missing ones and those that are shadowy and uncertain. Of course, if you would favor us with the intentions and motivations you had along the way, and in addition clear the air about any misunderstandings and misinterpretations that were flying about – and perhaps still are – that would be a delicious icing on the dessert cake. So, if it's OK with you, I'll get cracking." Without blinking an eye, Leon stared right into Mickey's face and, with a flourishing wave of his arms, proclaimed, "Onward, my good man. Give me your worst."

Mickey's Portrayal of Big Physics
The Seventies

"In the beginning, in America during the post World War II period, Big Science came into being as a result of the vision of a few great men, men of the ilk of Lawrence and Rabi. Of course, it was Vannevar Bush who made the dream manifest with his breathtaking insight to develop a system of national laboratories for basic physics research. At the center of this grand enterprise were the big accelerators. Proudly showcasing its AGS brainchild, BNL led the way in the fifties and sixties. This inspired machine opened the door that paved the way for labs all over the world – those in America and Europe and subsequently in Japan and other countries in possession of the necessary technological infrastructure – to partake of the feast of the mysterious particles making up our universe. Once the AGS, based on the ingenious AG principle, came to be, accelerator facilities flourished around the globe. However, sustaining the advancing knowledge frontier required that the energy of accelerators keep going up and up, with the size of the facilities getting bigger and bigger all the while. And for a time, the getting-bigger route worked like a charm. Everything was coming up roses. But, alas, the glory days couldn't last. You see, there was a fatal flaw growing like a cancer in the Big Physics body, which eventually would block the extraordinary burgeoning expansion of the house of accelerators, and bring the entire enterprise to a crashing halt.

"The fact of life that stole the accelerator show from science was human nature itself. Although the bright and fruitful face of competition allowed the field to blossom for a time, its dark face was bound sooner or later to come to the fore and bring to an end those all-too-brief glory days. Yes, it was jealousy, greed, and a kind of inner pernicious urge to wreck and devour what man creates that eventually came to rule and dominate the conduct of high-energy physicists. And when this ugly side of humanity erupted, there was no stopping it from its destructive course. What a disintegrative and ruinous process came to infect and permeate the accelerator facilities in the seventies! Having free play within the high-energy institutions, it percolated in them with a vengeance, particularly among the three top proton-using labs: BNL, Fermilab, and CERN.

"Here's a short and *sweet* outline of the BNL-Fermilab feud: BNL was the early leader in the sixties, with CERN closing in fast as the seventies approached. The newly built Fermilab entered the fray in the early seventies, and, with its substantially higher particle power, quickly became a contender to be reckoned with. The combination of the science being basic and the labs being big demanded that the government run the American show. And for the sake of peace and quiet among the competitors, the straightforward easy road was taken, with the U.S. having an informal understanding – actually a dictum from the federal funding agency – that BNL and Fermilab take turns in any new facility developments or major upgrades. That's all well and good in the abstract. However, when put into practice, well, that's a different matter altogether. Since Fermilab was brought to life with a major high-energy synchrotron, the powers that be presumed that BNL would take the next step in leapfrog fashion. However, a funny thing happened on the way to fulfilling this plan. With BNL weakened by internal stresses in the sixties and early seventies, Wilson, in command of Fermilab and making all the calls, seeing the Upton breach, didn't waste a minute and strode right into it. So there you have it. Here were all the ingredients for generating hard times.

"The cutthroat rivalry that had emerged in high-energy circles was bad business all around. On one side was an impatient, incomparably full-of-fight, hard-hitting and uncompromising Wilson as Fermilab's el supremo. On another was a government with a penchant for order, tidy stability, and harmony, insisting that things be done its way. Then there was BNL, expecting what it deemed its due, the next big proton facility, to be handed it by the government. The ensuing result of this about-as-far-as-you-can-get-from-ideal mix was a confrontation that admitted not a chance in hell of coming to an understanding and striking a deal. So a harsh, no-holds-barred competition erupted – something not unlike a to-the-death war. With bad blood driving all sides, unseemly and vengeful acts were the order of the day. None of that free-market-type competitiveness that's paid so much lip service in America would determine the winner. No, the outcome was a foregone conclusion because it was politics, pure and simple, that dictated the lab that would be number one. Nobody seemed to give a damn about what was happening to basic physics and what was the right way for things to get done. Nobody seemed to care about what was the productive way to go and what was the common-sense thing to do.

The politicos simply declared by fiat that BNL was to be the champ of American labs. That's right! Fermilab was summarily quashed and shoved to the sidelines, while BNL was lifted up and proclaimed the centerpiece of America's winning strategy. Ha! To imagine that you could come out on top without having talent and experts at the ready, without planning and preparing for the fight! To think that you could achieve the winning margin so arbitrarily, just like that! How utterly stupid! And how unfair! Still, that's the way it was. That's how politics works its mysterious and at times ungainly and inept ways.

"However, despite its enormous strength and resources, the U.S. government doesn't always get what it wants. You see, sometimes what politics decides, reality negates. And that's exactly what happened in the Vineyard-Wallenmeyer-Wilson affair. This is the way it went: ISABELLE, the vaunted BNL collider project, began falling apart because of the lab's inability to support the project's excessive weight. At the same time, by government edict, Fermilab was unfortunately prohibited from advancing its more reasonable proposed projects. How ridiculous it all seems in retrospect! With so much potential, America was about to be left behind the eight ball – with zilch. The truth of the matter, hard to take, was that because of the government's counter-productive and un-American suppression of free competition, and because there was absolutely no flexibility in the hardened bureaucratic system, the U.S. – believe it or not – just went and put American basic physics in a car going downhill with no brakes. Meanwhile, across the Atlantic, the European CERN lab had no such political constraints. Unfettered by fracture-forming infighting and political friction, it plowed into the lead, as the U.S. sat twiddling its thumbs, seemingly waiting for a *je ne sais quoi* that wasn't coming.

"Time passed and the U.S. labs weakened even more. Finally, the U.S. Johnny-come-lately politicos, the rulers of Big Science, came to understand and to appreciate the implications of what they'd done. When they finally got it, they acted in the manner natural to politics. They adjusted quickly and harshly: BNL was thrown to the wolves and Fermilab was given the OK to make its move. Wow! A complete hundred and eighty degree reversal – just like that! Isn't the rapidity and extremeness of political change mind-blowing?"

Mickey's Portrayal of Big Physics The Eighties

"But political change doesn't happen automatically. People do it; and for good change, you need good people. In America, the beginning of the eighties represented the onset of the Reagan era. In those years, the U.S. wasn't the type of country to cave in just because the going got rough. How fortunate that was for High-energy Science and Technology (HST), which found itself in a really bad way when Reagan and his troupe came on the scene. If anyone was going to free it from its *sticky wicket*, it was *President Ronnie*.

"The fact is that during the late seventies and early eighties, the U.S. HST position was dramatically altered from a decade or so earlier. No indeed, it wasn't at all rosy:

BNL was in a shambles, in total disarray; Fermilab faced CERN alone after years of government neglect; and CERN, already way out in front of the U.S., was continuing to move smartly ahead at a fast clip. Then, Reagan arrived, and a glimmer of hope appeared. Still, having fallen far behind, and watching CERN recede in the distance ahead as it continued to pull away, what was the great American giant to do? Although the solution wasn't a piece of cake, Reagan well understood the mighty U.S. He knew that if he found the right course to take, by flexing the power-packed American technology muscle, the U.S. could face up to the challenging European HST opposition and end up coming out on top. So it was that the Reagan years were a time of hope for American Big Physics.

"The idea that emerged of how to reassert American supremacy in high-energy basic research in the eighties was to combine the adventurous spirit of American science with Reagan's passion for excellence throughout U.S. society. It was a simple and elegant plan. Just push the S&T frontier to the limit of American know-how, and so much the better if the facility that rises to the surface is so expensive that no other political power on earth could compete. It was in such a climate of far-sighted astuteness and clever nationalistic thinking that the SSC was born.

"Along with Reagan came a whole new set of political rules for Big Science. The old-guard ways were discarded: deals in smoke-filled rooms were done for and individual freedom prevailed. Cutting to the chase, that meant that *anything goes*; and that's the way it was when Snowmass '82 sallied forth into the spotlight. So there the physicists were, in the mountains of Colorado, worried sick about the state of their revered physics and aching to be led out of the darkness and into the land where dreams come true. Then, at the perfect moment, the sly purveyors of wild *castles in the sky* dangled before the eyes of the panting, trusting born-again souls in their Disneyland paradise an offer they couldn't refuse: *Here folks, here's an American super-duper dream! With it, you can make your mark on the world! And it's almost free! All that's required is that you rid yourself of the piece of junk that's holding you down! Don't resist! Be daring! Be tough! Be smart! Just do it!* So it was that over the next year, following that fateful time at Snowmass, a trade was made by the scientists of the high-energy community to appease the political appetite and save Big Physics: an American supercollider, the SSC, was to be exchanged for ending the life of ISABELLE, the sacrificial lamb, which would be sent to the scrap heap. Presuming that this marvel could actually be built, it was a very fine idea. And why couldn't it be made? After all, scientists were full of knowledge, inventive, and ingenious; and they were certainly capable of building big things, as they'd amply proved by deed. Even to the tough-minded realists, this sounded like a pip of a prize, full of treasures to be mined, and well worth pursuing. Yes, with a little luck, it could work; and both the government and the U.S. science community bought into it. Thus, with the answer they'd been waiting for handed to them fully free of further charge, scientists became believers. *Only good days lie ahead*, they imagined.

"I've thought a lot about where this scheme came from. It didn't just materialize out of thin air. Some person or persons hatched it. But who? Who were the masterminds behind it? I put it to you, Leon, that you and Keyworth were the architects of this plan. Actually, when you think about it, when you look at it dispassionately, doesn't the plan make a lot of sense? The SSC would, when completed, stand in magnificent grandeur and be the defining achievement of Big Science. It would be the epitome of science excellence. It would bring new life into American basic research. It would pull the community out of its doldrums and cynicism. It would perform the onerous job of cleaning house. Yes, it was indeed a solution to the high-energy dilemma that just a short while before seemed to have none. So, all in all, if you did conceive this little gem of ingenuity, then I, for one, think you should be proud of it.

"However, even the best thought-out and shaped plans often turn on you. To be sure, a plan is just a plan. In the doing of it, things are rarely the same as in the thinking of it. Somehow, that's something you hadn't anticipated, something you missed. Thus, when you and your plotting cohorts tried to translate your strategy into reality, politics entered the picture again. Did that surprise you? It shouldn't have. You should've guessed that the politicos would invariably insist on their pay-off. As it happened, what they demanded and what they got for the SSC was an open competition, where politicians and not scientists determined the site of this prized national facility. This was not at all what you had in mind. Although you didn't admit it in so many words, you wanted Fermilab – a greatly expanded Fermilab – to host this new super machine. But the new political rules-de-jour played against you, and Illinois would have to fight for it in open political combat. There would be no special advantages given for technical or scientific reasons. Did you really think that these hardened veterans of political warfare would let scientists have the last word about such a juicy plum? If so, you were pretty naïve. These are the guys that have all the power. They hold the purse strings. They know money like the palm of their hands. You couldn't stand up to them. You were just putty in their hands. No, it wouldn't be as you imagined and wanted. It would be politics, politics, and more politics.

"As it happened, a stronger state also had its eye on one of the high-tech prizes of the century. Texas, with massive political strength in the eighties, chose to compete. Surprisingly, you thought up to the very end that your logic and having Fermilab behind you would win the day. But, as events demonstrated, you were dead wrong. With politics ruling, in 1987 Texas won hands down. Because you put all your chips on Illinois coming out on top, and Illinois lost, you too became a loser."

Mickey's Portrayal of Big Physics
The Nineties

"Being a prime loser must have been very distressing for you. Still, the story had an even gloomier epilogue for U.S. Big Science. Six years later, in 1993, the SSC, bloated and bleeding from internal and political stresses, sank of its own weight, much as ISABELLE had a decade earlier. However, in and of itself, that awful punishment was not sufficient to appease the gods. For America's reckless profligacy and decadent squandering, the ministers roaming the unseen dimensions had a little more mean and pitiless cruelty to inflict. By throwing a healthy dose of salt on the deep and still open losing-the-SSC wound, they demonstrated only too well their displeasure with the way American science manhandled Big Physics. The second administering of comeuppance to the already tottering American high-energy enterprise came from the other side of the Atlantic. In the wake of the sunken SSC, CERN took full advantage of America's bumbling blunders to open its throttle and zoom forward, now unchallenged by the discouraged American juggernaut. The LHC, given a tremendous boost by the SSC's appalling and shocking fate, was vigorously set moving full speed ahead. CERN was now the big daddy with all the candy. Thenceforth, that's where America would have to go, crawling on bended knee, to beg for its chance at a Big Physics crumb. Sad as this story is for American science, that's the way it was."

Mickey's Questions

Mickey looked at Leon, wondering about the provocative presumptions he'd made. Did he go too far in questioning the integrity of this man he so admired and respected? But Leon, head bowed in thought, showed not the least sign of exasperation, resentment, or pique. So Mickey breathed an inaudible sigh of relief. His interpretation of Leon's calm, undisturbed, and tranquil demeanor was that it was a go-ahead sign. Thus, he felt quite safe in going forward with his questions. What luck, he thought! Then he began to speak: "With that background, voilà, I'm ready to probe your role in this ISABELLE-SSC affair and put my suspicions, inferences, and judgments to the test. First, what role did you play in the two-project trade of the early eighties? In particular, were you Keyworth's connection to Big Science and he yours to President Reagan? Asked more bluntly, were you two the primary conspirators concocting the trade?

"My second question is a little about how the SSC project was established and shaped; and more specifically about how you let it slip through your fingers. However, before I actually state the question, please bear with me while I review a few points. I really don't want to take up any more of our valuable time than is absolutely necessary, but I fear that without taking this little sidetrack, the question would make little sense to anyone. As Snowmass '82 approached, you worked together with Bob on the groundbreaking notion of an American supercollider. What a momentous gift to United States Big Science it would be! Then when you stood at the podium on that memorable Tuesday evening in that Colorado paradise and presented it, you were nothing short of dynamite. Oh, how you stunned the throng with your unique blend of colloquial lightness, joking around, depth, and brilliance! Your words and ideas still ring in my ears. I'll not forget them till my dying day. How charismatic you were! How magical you made it all sound! So moving and persuasive were you that I imagine you could've sold the rapt audience the *Brooklyn Bridge* if that was your wish. With the picture you painted, using swashbuckling strokes, you not only made the eyes of the young gleam with excitement and hope, but you also did the seemingly impossible by stirring and whetting the appetite of the fast-getting-staid American science establishment. In its original form, the supercollider concept was of a large Wilson-style machine, which you and Bob referred to as the Desertron. The idea was to build *el cheapo* in the desert Southwest where land was both flat and plentiful. But nothing like that actually happened. As it turned out, the project started to get bigger and bigger; and once its underlying capability *to answer the unanswerable* became known, once big money got into the act, and once politics entered to run the extravaganza, you simply couldn't hold onto this major scientific undertaking anymore as if it were your own. It didn't belong to you. It belonged to Big Physics and to the country. Yes, as hard as it is to believe, the project had become bigger than you and Bob combined. It had outgrown the two of you.

"So it was that the Desertron was transformed into the SSC. What a big beauty it was to be! What an American beauty! Boy, did you want it bad, maybe even more than when it was *small* and desert-bound! Well, that's not so hard to understand. After all, it was your baby, and you believed it to be your property. It was only right that you should be the one to carry it to world glory. At least that's what you imagined. That was your dream. But somewhere along the way, you made the blunder of your life. Instead of thinking *SSC, SSC, and only SSC*, you unbelievably and implausibly chose to tie the big project to the future of Fermilab. What could you possibly have been thinking when you made that almost politically-infantile move? You see, that put you in an exceedingly weak position to become its leader. You forgot the cardinal rule that the political will always comes before personal wishes. The politicos may well have wanted you, but they sure as hell didn't want Fermilab attached. Since it was decreed that the enviable chap to head the colossus-to-be had to be chosen before a site was selected, it followed ipso-facto that by refusing to give up your Director's chair at Fermilab, both politics and fair play demanded that you be disqualified for SSC leadership. You were out in the cold, and it was you alone who put yourself there. It was a classic problem of dual loyalty. By openly exclaiming your support for Fermilab as the SSC site, your credibility as being site-neutral was reduced to zero. Smart, worldly, and aware as you are, you must have been cognizant of these implications. So finally I've arrived at my second question for you: By identifying yourself so closely with Fermilab, didn't you deliberately, or perhaps subconsciously, take yourself out of the running to be SSC Director? I recognize that this question may be somewhat speculative, but how can I overlook the plain and simple logic that forces me to it. However, if you believe my thinking to be faulty, then try this question: Why didn't you go all-out for the SSC by giving up Fermilab? You must've known that there's just no way on God's earth that you could've gotten both!

"Now, getting to my third and last question, why do you think that, as this new technological century opens, the world's sole superpower is ready to take a backseat by deferring to CERN as today's Big Science giant? And, as a follow-up, why do you think the U.S. is willing to humble – even humiliate – itself by paying an exorbitant entrance fee for a few American scientists to work at CERN's watered-down version of a supercollider-to-be? OK, Leon, I've finished. That's it for me. Now it's your turn. The ball's in your court."

Leon Reassures Mickey

"I think you're asking for a lot," Leon petulantly blurted out. "When I agreed to do this gig, I hadn't the least inkling that you were going to tread in such personal waters. I didn't think for a minute that what you had in mind was to put us through this torture of self-examination. If I'd known, maybe I would've thought twice about it. What I imagined was that you were interested in the historical details, and certainly not what was in my heart and soul. Well, that's over and done. Maybe I should've probed you a little deeper. Knowing you, I should've figured that you probably had something up your tricky little sleeve.

"Come to think of it, and to be perfectly honest, what intrigued me most was your uncannily impressive guest list. It was so strikingly remarkable, so extraordinary, that I didn't think you had a chance in hell of succeeding. I remember smiling, treating the whole thing as if it were some sort of joke. I guess I was fascinated to see if you could really pull it off. However, I can't say that I wasn't attracted by your inspiration and outrageous initiative. Thus, on the off chance that you could make a reality of it, I found it hard to resist the delight that would come from the opportunity to rediscover and reach out to old friends and old enemies alike. And then, almost as if you really knew what makes me tick, you poured it on with the seducing skill of a temptation-wizard. I was still hesitating, you understand, but at just the right instant, you introduced the pièce de résistance. You pointed to and emphasized the one thing that could push me over the edge. And it did! How could I refuse that very special enticement you placed before my eyes? How could I not say *yes*? What a cunningly crafty one you turned out to be! How psychologically shrewd! How clever! How insightfully diplomatic! Giving me that once in a lifetime break to meet my most admirable and steadfast colleague, my most intimate and trusted ally, my tried and true companion, my old confidante, and my sorely missed Bob. What a treat that would be! One final fling! How could I pass up such a chance? The truth is, Mickey, far from being displeased with what you've done here, I give you my most heartfelt thanks. These brief moments I've had with Bob more than compensate for the stress you've inflicted on me. Actually, what you've accomplished is beyond thanks. But, what more can I say? It's the best I can do."

Leon stopped dead and stared out the window at the mountains and the shadows forming along their slopes. Mickey was becoming uneasy. It was an awkward moment for him. What was Leon driving at anyway? Did he really get what he came for? Was he perhaps gonna crap out? Noticing Mickey's discomfort and apprehension, Leon, in a moment of generosity, added with a roguish smile, "I'm just joshing you with this quibbling. So let me set your mind at rest. You know me. It's not my natural inclination to balk when up against the wall. I've been in far more problematic and demanding situations than this, and never once have I reneged. So relax! I have no intention of going against my nature at this point in my life. I said I would go through with your interrogation, and I will.

"Frankly speaking, Mickey, since truth-telling is the keynote here, I should confess to you that I would've come anyway, even if I'd known your true intentions and the type of questions you were going to spring on us. Naturally, I might well have objected. But, in the end, I would've agreed to your proposition. You simply made the party too tempting to miss." As Leon made this last remark, he was looking straight at Mickey, with his bright eyes opened wide and with a hint of a smile on his rosy, wrinkled cheeks. With his arms up and in front, and with his palms facing upward and tilted at an angle, Leon appeared to be paying a small tribute to Mickey and his one-for-the-book smash hit. Not being the type that got many compliments, Mickey was surprised at the gesture. The best he could manage in return was a self-conscious nod, and a sequence of motions that simulated the doffing of his cap at Leon. Meanwhile the other three at the table looked on and smiled approvingly. The scene was frozen for a couple of seconds, allowing Mickey to savor the vote of confidence and the flattering commendation from these elite barons of Big Science. Then the moment ended abruptly as Leon resumed on a note of acceptance: "Being of a compliant nature, here I am ready to participate. However, I have to admit that I've been caught a little off-guard. Since I'm sure you'll all want me to be at my best, please permit me to presume a guest's prerogative and take a couple of minutes to collect my thoughts. So, why don't I just take a little stroll around the room and see what I come up with in the way of answering Mickey's queries? Therefore, if you'll all excuse me, I'll be right back." As he rose and walked thoughtfully toward the dark side of the large room, Leon's face had that rare combination of being glowing with spirit, yet at the same time being meditatively somber.

A Mickey Interlude

After Leon left the table, the ensuing break in the action released any pent-up emotional energy in the remainder of the group. Taking full advantage of the relaxed atmosphere, the others became engulfed in a gabfest. Seeing the three old but still full-of-verve men having such a good time brought out in Mickey a warmhearted, compassionate feeling for them. It occurred to him that there being such serious and potentially explosive matters under discussion, it might be unseemly to be feeling so good. Nevertheless, that's exactly how he felt. The entire get-together he had contrived was in fact going so well, how could he not be on cloud nine? How could he not be bursting with pride? How could he not be luxuriating in his delivery of this enchanting occurrence? The truth was that the self-satisfaction he was experiencing was bubbling inside him, and seemed to know no bounds. Was it really he who did it all, Mickey asked himself, a bit of self-doubt entering his mind? You see Mickey couldn't recall much of how the whole thing got off the ground. In fact, if truth be told, he could remember none of it. Could it be that he wasn't acting alone? Yes, Mickey thought, maybe it was the gods-on-high who, while somehow ensuring that Mickey got the credit, actually willed it and brought the grand event in the valley of truth to life? In any case, what did it matter how the party was arranged? Who could recognize the difference anyway? He smiled privately as the thought don't look a gift horse in the mouth spontaneously popped up in his head.

While pouring himself a little lemonade, Mickey happened to glance out of the window in front of him, noticing that dusk had arrived right on schedule. That meant time was quickly running out on his day-to-end-all-days. It would soon be but a memory. However, *nothing*, he reflected, *no, nothing is going to spoil that warm glow in my soul*. Partaking of the tart liquid in his glass, he thought: *Ah, just what I needed. That really hit the spot.*

With a moment to himself, Mickey's mind veered toward times past, and he thought about that amazing man who was then on the questioning block – that man of profound achievement, of sparkling wit, of daring bravado, and of prodigious ingenuity. What a lucky day it was for Mickey, that day when he first crossed paths with Leon. You see Leon did a lot for him, important things that had a deep enough impact on his life to even alter its course. Mickey tried to get his mind to focus. But it wandered about for a while. He could visualize so many incidents – Leon here, Leon there, Leon everywhere. Then finally his mental kaleidoscope settled. There was this one particular situation that Mickey often thought about; and, sitting quietly in that dimly lit room, with the din of agreeable, idle chatter around him, it came to him again.

In the early eighties when Mickey's troubles with Nick started, Leon was the only one with the guts to come to his rescue. Mickey was always puzzled as to why Leon would go up against Nick, thereby risking the wrath and well-known temper of that little guy with the big fists, always itching for a scrap. Many possible reasons did occur to him, mostly relating to Leon's famous naughty streak. Sure, Leon could've simply wanted to stick it to that bigmouth upstart from Columbia whose high opinion of himself wasn't in the least matched by his scientific merit. But, because Mickey was not inclined to think of Leon as being gratuitously mean and spiteful, he stuck that explanation at the bottom of the pile. To Mickey, Leon was a big man, a man of stature, and so not prone to pettiness. Actually, the view that Mickey favored most was that Leon wanted to do the right thing and what was best for science. Mickey believed that at the core of that impish elf was the heart of a tough and practical man, a get-it-done-and-no-excuses man, and a man who could be ruthless when it was called for. Mickey believed that despite the reputation Leon had of being frivolous and somewhat of a clown, he was a man of derring-do who dreamed of stepping across the line into the forbidden zone and returning with the *God Particle* in hand. In the end, he believed Leon to be a noble and majestic knight inspiring all the world with the glories of science. In Mickey's mind, there wasn't a shadow of a doubt that Leon was one of the foremost role models for Big Science of the twentieth century. Yes, Mickey indeed had a soft spot for Leon, and there was good reason for it.

So vivid was Mickey's memory of what took place in the fall of 1983 that the picture show of the time played out in his mind as if it were happening then and there. How could he ever forget that telephone call to Leon? In just a few minutes, it transformed Mickey back from an embittered, resentful, and desperate bit player into the bright-with-anticipation, upward-looking, and irrepressible dreamer he was. Yes, Leon was Mickey's harbinger of good times ahead.

In 1980, just three years earlier, Mickey pulled out of his hat the idea of educating would-be accelerator builders. Universities couldn't do it. No one else was taking a shot at it. So Mickey set his mind to the task. From scratch, he created the U.S. Particle Accelerator School. Even today, more than twenty years later, it remains a going concern, with thousands of students and teachers having passed through its rigorous regime of formal courses and study. It has become an ingrained part of the accelerator community; and, being a *good friend* to the young and ambitious, it is amiably referred to by them as USPAS, pronounced, "*ooss-pass.*" But before USPAS got to the state of being so widely and so firmly accepted as a part of the high-energy enterprise, it had to pass through the fire by overcoming the obstacles laid before it by Nick. Now Nick may not have had anything against USPAS as such, but he certainly had it in for Mickey. So, as it happened, the birth and growth of USPAS was indeed a rocky one, and it was up to Mickey to see it through those initial hard times.

That day when Mickey made his case to Leon on the telephone, USPAS was at a critical juncture in its formative and still vulnerable stage. The School was in urgent need of a savior, and judicious and astute Leon turned out to be the man to fill the bill. By that time, three summer programs, one each at Fermilab, SLAC and BNL, had been completed. Determined not to slacken off after the initial three went off so well, Mickey immediately started preparations for the fourth to be held at Fermilab in the summer of 1984. But, unfortunately for USPAS, Nick inserted himself directly in Mickey's path, thus preventing him from going ahead with his plan. Why, you ask? It was the Baltay incident at Snowmass '82 that got Nick's goat and triggered his enmity. Too bad that Nick was such a vengeful man with such a long memory. There was absolutely nothing that could make him forget what Mickey did. After the Snowmass flare-up – the presumed act of disloyalty and treachery, the nasty and obnoxious confrontations, and the ill feelings engendered there – Nick always thought of Mickey as a traitor. No matter what Mickey did to try to assuage and pacify Nick so as to turn him around – explaining, giving excuses, apologizing, and pleading – the man was adamant and just couldn't be shaken from his deeply held view that Mickey deserted BNL and sold out to ISABELLE's enemies. For a betrayal of such proportions, Nick resolved that Mickey would pay dearly and keep on paying until all hell freezes over. Actually, this shouldn't be much of a surprise to anyone. You see, forgiveness was not in Nick's repertoire. Over the years, his mind was shaped in such a way that he could think only in terms of inflicting punishment. That was his way, and that's what he'd come to like doing.

The truth about the Baltay affair at Snowmass '82 is that Mickey inadvertently stepped into the middle of sensitive negotiations that were in progress between Nick and Baltay. Unknowingly, Mickey may have actually pushed Baltay over the edge. Whether it was true or not didn't much matter as Mickey came to be seen by Nick as being the bad guy, the cause of Baltay's choosing SLAC over BNL. As for Mickey, far from being a scheming Machiavelli, his role was simplicity itself. Talkative Mickey just talked too much. It was all truth that Mickey was blurting out, but Nick wasn't the kind of boss to tolerate that kind of interference by any of his underlings. Furthermore, Nick didn't go for that *innocent by ignorance* argument. So Mickey would have to pay the price and absorb Nick's penalty. He would have to suffer the stinging lashes from Nick's store of whips. From Nick's point of view, he had to do it. There was simply no alternative. He had to set an example for others. Transgressors had to be given what they deserved. The men on his staff couldn't be allowed to go shooting off their mouths whenever they felt like it. No, nobody on Nick's watch would step over the line without bearing Nick's harsh consequences. He would see to that.

Because Nick was constrained in how far he could go by government policy and academic tradition, he couldn't just out-and-out fire Mickey. But make no mistake about it, Nick could cause him a lot of pain and hardship, and he wasn't in the least averse to doing just that. Holding down a dissident's salary was a common tactic used by harsh bosses; and this is exactly what happened to Mickey. It may not sound so terrible, but anybody with the least acquaintance with compound interest can easily appreciate that this action taken against Mickey hurt him a lot. Losing over a quarter of a million dollars over the years is not peanuts. Nonetheless, through it all, stubborn Mickey absorbed all the blows, both to his pocketbook and to his morale, and just kept going. There just seemed no way to dampen his spirits or quash his optimism. Both were irrepressible, indestructible and through it all remained intact. As for Nick, having Mickey under his very eyes, conspicuously unbeaten, unbowed, and even making a little niche for himself in the science-education community, made him see red. He wanted to see Mickey's knees buckle. He wanted to see Mickey stumble and fall, and beg for help. So clearly he needed another line of attack. If money wouldn't do the trick, maybe something else might. Since Nick was so adept and ingenious at figuring out how to make people feel his wrath, if anyone could find a way to make Mickey crawl, it was he. So it was that Nick set his mind to work on it, and, in due course, Mickey was blindsided. He didn't see it coming at all. You see he didn't count on Nick attacking USPAS.

In October 1983, Mickey arrived at his BNL office one fine morning and found in his mail an ominously threatening memo from Derek Lowenstein, the Chairman of the AGS Department. On its face, it was business-like, written in that straightforward, no-nonsense, passion-free bureaucratic style. But, looking under the surface, it was charged with icy hostility, belligerent antagonism, and venomous ill will, all directed at Mickey. It informed Mickey that henceforth he would not be funded for any official travel except with direct instructions from and specific approval of the Chairman. Taken literally, what that part of the letter expressed was that BNL would allow Mickey to travel only if Lowenstein signed his trip authorizations and vouchers. However, since Lowenstein wouldn't sign for USPAS travel, the impact was the prevention of Mickey from traveling on USPAS business. And here comes the twisted-thinking bottom line! Because without Mickey's leadership there would be no USPAS, the memo's deeper intent was to bury USPAS in the cold, dark ground. That's the real point. For all intents and purposes, the memo declared USPAS kaput. Mickey knew that Lowenstein, although a cunning and devious man, was ultimately but a mere bureaucrat, a surrogate who did what he was told. Thus, there's no way on earth that he would dare take such an extreme action on his own. It doesn't take much IQ to figure out who was really behind it. As sure as anything, it was Nick. Not only did it have his MO written all over it, but all logic and rational thinking supported that conclusion. If money wasn't enough to make Mickey *say uncle*, then Nick would get him to throw in the towel and beg for quarter another way. Yes, for Nick, it was payback time again, and this time it was in spades. In hindsight, from Nick's perspective, it made good sense. He would get to Mickey by killing off what Mickey loved most dearly.

Once Mickey ascertained what was really going on, he was at a loss. What was he to do? Did Nick successfully knock him out? Was USPAS really to be taken from him and eliminated? Now it's true that Mickey wasn't the type to shrivel up and not put up some sort of a fight. But Nick was a tough-to-surpass champ when it came to this sort of game, and Mickey found himself with very few options. He couldn't just grin and bear it, the way he did when it was only money. This time, the life of USPAS was at stake. To get the better of Nick this time, he had to go out and get someone to help him. There was simply no alternative, he'd have to give up his independence. How tough it was for him to do this! Yet, that's exactly what was called for. He had to search out and find someone brave enough to counter Nick, and he had to find a way to persuade that man to pull him out of the quicksand in which he was sinking. Was it possible that Mickey could actually manage to come through the fire with USPAS still alive? Did such a man as he was seeking exist?

No doubt, Mickey had his work cut out for him. What was to be his game plan? How could he get from here to there? How should he proceed? Well, what he did was run the gamut of possibilities, taking the game one step at a time. The first thing that came to his mind seemed to him to be the natural one. Yes, why not go to Nick? Perhaps the little man with the hard heart could be influenced. Perhaps he would listen to reason. In retrospect, it does sound a little foolish, but nonetheless, that's what Mickey did. He was actually able to contact Nick and speak to him. But, alas, with a flick of the wrist, as if Mickey were nothing but a gnat, Nick brushed him off. He said that he had many more urgent matters to contend with and couldn't be bothered with Mickey's petty little problems. Mickey could still hear Nick's words over the telephone, "I'm the Director here and I can't concern myself with every individual's foul-up." That was that. Mickey recalled thinking at the time: *What a dumb thing to say! Isn't that one of the more important jobs of a lab Director?* Anyway, Mickey found out the hard way that Nick wasn't about to back off merely because Mickey asked him to, and promised to be good in the bargain. What a stressful time it was for poor Mickey! Stunned and powerless, it seemed to him that he would have to watch helplessly as USPAS – the School he brought into being and was in the process of expanding – was casually bumped off. Was that really to be Mickey's fate? If he didn't know already that Nick was a master in the art of hurting others, it became evident to him with this distressing situation he found himself in. However, even with the deck stacked against him, Mickey was determined not to prostrate himself at the feet of this self-serving bad egg. After all, this was America, the land of the free, the place where anything was possible. There simply had to be a way for Mickey to extricate himself from the mess he was in.

When all was said and done, Nick and Mickey were two hellishly proud and stubborn men. Neither would give an inch. So an all-out duel there would have to be, an *affaire d'honneur*. But it was hardly what you'd call a fair fight. On one side there was Nick the heavyweight, with authority, prestige, and the potent striking force of a great lab behind him. On the other was Mickey the featherweight, a man of little account, a babe in the woods, with no one and nothing to back him up. Well, perhaps he had his handy-dandy slingshot tucked away up his sleeve. Still, despite the odds against him, Mickey chose to stand up to the brute force of the man in command.

What did he do then, you ask? Since Mickey still had his telephone (for some hard-to-explain reason, probably just an oversight, Nick didn't have that taken from him) he called everybody he could think of, bombarding them with his complaints and pleas. There were so many of them: Wallenmeyer at DOE; Hughes at AUI; Reardon, BNL's Associate Director for Accelerator Projects; Sanford, Head of the just slain ISABELLE project; Palmer, Adair, and other physicists, Nick's close buddies whom Mickey knew well; and a host of scientists and administrators from all over whom Mickey considered personal friends as well as friends of USPAS. He put on all the charm he could muster, he cajoled, and he used every power of persuasion he possessed. He argued till he was blue in the face about the value and necessity of accelerator technology education. But it was all to no avail. Sad to say, the reactions he got were damnably disheartening. What a bunch of chicken-hearted, lily-livered milquetoasts! What he got from all of them would make you wanna puke! *Sorry, I'd love to help, but I just can't. Why don't you try so and so, he might be able to help you? Why don't you try such and such tactic – that might work?* And on it went in that vein! Yes, it *is* hard to believe. But that's the way it was. That's the gist of what Mickey got in answer to his ardent, desperate peas for help. No, there wasn't one bloody bulldog among them. Not one man with balls! Slithery spineless eels are what they were. Sure, many offered words of support and encouragement, but nary a one would intervene. Not one would lift a finger. There was simply no one who would come to his aid, to help him keep this unique educational endeavor – USPAS – alive. Notwithstanding it being a dire emergency, a matter of life and death, still, all of them refused any involvement at all, offering only excuses in its stead. When push came to shove, they were just a bunch of sniveling, cringing, wimpy, gutless cowards, slinking to their safe havens, away from Nick's wrath, with their tails between their legs.

The disillusioned Mickey indulged himself in a lot of soul searching. Most assuredly, he had good reason to feel sorry for himself. His position seemed hopeless. Certainly, in his place, most would've knuckled under, ceded the field to Nick, and groveled in obeisance. But not Mickey! There wasn't even the whisper of a thought in his mind to yield. You see Mickey was an action-oriented guy. Nothing could change that! He was a go-getter from the get-go, and he would remain that way till the day he died. Thus, although he didn't have a clue as to what to do, he resolved to plow ahead anyway. His natural optimism told him that something would come up. So, discouraging and unpromising as it seemed, for Mickey it was, *on with the show*!

When Mickey was subjected to the injustice of Nick's attack on him, his instinct was to be quick on the draw. He acted impulsively and immediately. He was somewhat nervous as he began making contacts, but he believed that others would side with him because they surely knew the difference between right and wrong, and Mickey was doubtless in the right. But, Mickey unfortunately greatly overestimated the important men of Big Science. His rash, reckless, and overzealous response to Nick's action only made matters worse. Although there wasn't much Nick could add to his harassing and taunting of Mickey, what Mickey did turned out only to enrage, energize, and encourage Nick more than ever. So Mickey had to learn the hard way, again, that sometimes it's better to think first before you shoot your mouth off. And Mickey did learn, at least for a while, for thinking is exactly what he did.

After a week or so of reviewing and assessing his situation, he came to realize that he needed no more than a little travel money. It seemed so obvious once he saw it. After all, that's all that was taken from him. So why raise the ante and make a big deal of it? All Mickey had to do was find someone who'd provide him with the cash. That's all that was necessary. That's all he needed for his ticket home. *It can't be that hard to achieve*, he thought. He need do no more than find a man who was willing to tweak and prick Nick's smug vanity and overweening self-importance, a man who controlled a goodly amount of money, and a man who was willing to apply an itsy bitsy amount of it to Mickey's good cause. Of course, it would have to be a man who would also be able and willing to brave the storm sure to come from Nick's resentment and displeasure. Mickey wondered whether there really was such a man who could fill that bill of fare. Over the next day or so, he thought long and hard about it. Then, in a lightening-swift instant of insight, the obvious smacked him in the face. An electric brainstorm flashed through his head, and it hit him: *What about Leon*?

Wow! That's gotta be the answer to my prayers, Mickey thought. Suddenly, everything began to fall into place. Mickey had the good fortune to have worked closely with Leon as DOE's Fermilab Project Officer during Mickey's three and a half year Washington stint in the early eighties. In addition, while organizing the first USPAS program in 1981, which was held at Fermilab, Mickey had need for a lot of contact with the lab Director on matters pertaining to organization, personnel, and finance. With these connections to the man, it's safe to say that Mickey knew Leon well. So it's something of a surprise that Mickey didn't come upon Leon as the right person to approach sooner. Well, OK, Mickey was a little slow on the uptake in this case. However, he did get there. He finally saw the light. How obvious it was! Leon fit the profile to a tee. Furthermore, there was simply no reason – not a one – that spoke against him being just the man Mickey was seeking. Leon was, in a word, perfect. It gets even better. Leon also was precisely the type of man to accept the challenge Mickey was ready to spring on him. Could Mickey ask for anything more?

Mickey was filled with excitement. He knew he had the solution he was searching for. But, before contacting Leon, with his heart beating fast, he waited for a few minutes to calm down. This gave him the opportunity to think a bit more rationally about it before going off half-cocked. Actually, thinking more about it wasn't about to change Mickey's mind. The truth is that nothing could stop him from trying the *Leon solution*. Thus, firmly believing that getting Leon to help had a good chance of working, a belief tempered by the reality that this was probably his only chance to counter Nick's venom, he laid his hand on the telephone.

Yes, Leon is in and would be happy to speak with you, came the pleasant voice from the other end of the line. *Just wait one minute, please*. Then, praise the Lord, Mickey had his prayer answered: He got to talk to the Director who he was sure would get him out of the jam he was in. Being on a high, as well as a bit on the nervous side, his words came out in a ratatat manner. He told Leon the whole story, every gory detail. Leon listened intently, without interruption. The whole conversation took less than fifteen minutes. But that brief call changed everything for Mickey. As it turned out, it was an unqualified success. Leon, Director extraordinaire and Nobel laureate-to-be, was persuaded that it would be good for everybody if USPAS continued to live. Not only was he pleased with the program at Fermilab in 1981, but he was also convinced that USPAS had long-term viability. There was a slight pause. Mickey was on pins and needles as he waited breathlessly. Then it came, the exact words that Mickey wanted to hear. Leon thought it a good idea to have a second program there in 1984. He therefore agreed without the least hesitation to put up the needed travel funds for Mickey to organize it. Mickey was beside himself. He never imagined it would come out so well. It was a dream come true.

But that wasn't the end of the call. Leon had even more to offer Mickey. As if giving him the 1984 program weren't enough, Leon in fact did much more than simply agree to extend the life of USPAS by a single year. He also assured Mickey of all the necessary help in establishing a central office for USPAS at Fermilab, funded through DOE. That would give Mickey both the cash and the wherewithal to run the USPAS programs for years to come, without any need at all for either BNL or Nick. And that's what happened! It was even better than if Nick hadn't stuck his big nose into the whole USPAS business at all. Yes, ironically, it turned out that Leon, with a little help from an unaware-of-what-he-was-doing Nick, made USPAS far bigger than Mickey had any right to expect. What a turn of events! Nick had actually provoked the outcome, vis-à-vis USPAS, where Mickey became free of him. Godfather Leon had seen to that.

It never ceased to amaze Mickey how much happened during a telephone call that lasted less than fifteen minutes. On the surface, the details and implications of what Leon agreed to appeared straightforward enough: how to set up budget accounts, how to move money, how personnel for USPAS would be hired and paid for, and so on. However, underneath the business-like exterior, lay something of a human drama. Leon, by interfering in the affairs of another lab, committed a grievous violation of club rules. What an audaciously valiant and bold-spirited thing for him to do! How daring it was! Yes, Leon was quite the man. And it wasn't the money. After all, only a measly amount of less than ten thousand dollars was involved. No, it was that the gallant Leon, counter-punching Nick on Mickey's behalf, saved USPAS as it struggled through its infancy, thus giving it the opportunity to live to a ripe old age. As it happened, over the years, Leon continued to prop USPAS up and so allow it to grow and thrive. Today, thanks to him, it's still going strong.

In Mickey's eyes, Leon was much more than the chivalrous knight come to rescue those in distress. To him, Leon was the consummate new-age scientist. Not only was he a forward-looking visionary, but he was also a down-to-earth practical doer of big things. He wanted to take science into no-man's land with instruments that could only come by pushing forward the frontiers of high technology. And he was a man of the world, skilled in the black art of politics. He knew what was important, and he knew how to get it done. He was also willing to take the necessary risks that went along with making things happen. Mickey remembered fondly the time that he'd spent with this man of many faces and talents. What good fortune that the fates allowed him to come to know such a one as he! He marveled at the myriad of incidents and chance steps taken that ultimately ended up in their meeting. *Ah, how strange life is, how good*! Mickey mused.

All was still. All was well with the world. Mickey sat motionless. His mind was bathed in a restful, untroubled, serene dimness, inhabited by dream-born faces, wavy, flitting figures, and harmonious, friendly shadows. Suddenly, Mickey's head snapped upward with a jolt. Oddly, having fallen into a doze, dreaming of Leon and times past, he was jarred awake by the complete silence that had come over the table. As his eyes opened, there was a burst of friendly laughter. Leon was already seated in his chair. Looking at Mickey questioningly, he chided him in a fatherly, albeit light and pleasing manner: "Well, can we get started?" "Of course, of course," said an embarrassed Mickey, "forward ho! The show must go on."

Leon's Angle Conspiracy

Leon hunched over and hesitated, waiting for the right dramatic moment to enter. When everyone's attention was fixed on him, and they were almost to the point of impatience, he leaned back, smiled sportively – sprinkling the look with a little dash of mischievousness – and took the stage: "I hate to disillusion you, but I'm not exactly the jolly, amiable do-gooder, the silver-tongued jokester, that I'm cracked up to be. Nonetheless, that's the role I chose to take on many years ago and, because I am what I am, I always played it to the hilt, and still do. It's the mask I use to make me distinct and noticeable. Because of it, I'm remembered; I'm able to influence; I'm sought out; I'm afforded the chance to put on my little performances, and voice my viewpoints and ideas; and I'm given entry to the community's shindigs. It's all part of the show the elite put on for the crowd of onlookers. It whets the appetites of those outside the inner circle, and allows them to relieve their tensions and anxieties by exercising their wagging tongues. Sometimes I wonder whether there's any point to the whole business, other than it being a lot of fun. Who knows? Maybe I'm just rationalizing, but it might well serve to catch the attention of and attract science-minded people. Perhaps it makes them think: *Hey, I could do that, I could be a physicist*; or, *I could be a better physicist.* Others it could make conclude: *Yeah, it's probably something worth supporting*. So, when all is said and done, it could end up spurring people to do more work for Big Physics, and perhaps encouraging the government to invest more in it. Actually, to be candid about it, I can't really say our acts do these things; but, you gotta admit, it is a possibility.

"I can see you getting a little fidgety, Mickey. I know what you're thinking – that you didn't get that rascal Leon to come here to spout his spiel, to strut his stuff. Well, don't you go getting yourself all worked up about it. I'm the type that guarantees satisfaction. So not to worry, not in the least! You can rest assured that I came here in total good faith. The fact is that my intention here is to take off the garb of the fun-maker that has been my trademark all these many years. What I have to say you'll be getting straight from the shoulders, with no holds barred. I'm going to tell it like it is – the truth, the whole truth, and nothing but the truth. That's what I believe your assignment was. That's what you meant for us to do, and that's exactly what you're going to get. In a nutshell, we're supposed to be honest, right?" Leon, ever the showman, paused and looked at Mickey mockingly, with that question mark plastered over his face. But Mickey was on the lookout for something unexpected from the master stunts-man, and answered unhesitatingly, "I couldn't have said it better myself. Yes, that's what we're here for – you're precisely on target." It was in this relaxed, amusing, and lighthearted manner that Leon's opening up of himself began. Although it was to be a selective revealing of his soul, as are all confessions, Mickey still was elated to the nth degree. Never in his wildest dreams did he imagine he would get to hear Leon speak explicitly and unabashedly about what he did and what made him do it.

"You've opened two big bad events in my sweet life," started Leon in his typically blunt yet tongue-in-cheek style. "In the case of the overthrow of ISABELLE, yes, it was a tough time for Big Physics. But when it happened, I believed that it wasn't all that bad. In fact, there was a silver lining attached to it. We, the purveyors of the grand venture of high-energy exploration, did it for the greater good. We were looking forward to a new world that would close out the wonder-filled, now-legendary twentieth century, and lead us on to the next one on the highest imaginable note. On the other hand, the lynching of the SSC was an altogether different matter. Oh, that terrible occurrence of 1993 was indeed a very sad day for physics. Its repercussions are still being felt today and will undoubtedly continue for a long time to come. When it happened, we were stopped cold, and found ourselves hurled into a sticky mud, where we were inextricably stuck. We'd put all our money on that SSC horse to win, but it turned out to be scratched before the race got underway. The politicos were deaf to our pleas. Those whom we thought of as our friends abandoned us without a second thought, acting as if they were pleased to see us out of their hair. Our colleagues from the other sciences wouldn't even give us the time of day. Even before the body was cold, to them, we were past history. We'd certainly mishandled the golden egg we had right there in the palms of our hands. It happened so fast: One day, poof, it was gone – lost, perhaps until a new and better generation comes to rediscover the dream we had. But, as for us, the aging generation of Big Physics, there would be no further chance at the grand prize. We were alone, penniless, with no one to turn to, and nowhere to go.

"Now, keep in mind that I'm not implying there was any unanimity as to why and how such a dark event came about. The disagreements at the time were indeed profound. To give you a feeling of the wide range of prevalent views, get this: Some thought of the downfall of the SSC as a treacherous betrayal by false friends; some thought of it as an attack from the small-minded political enemies of science; and some even thought of it as being a form of suicide, where the men of the SSC so feared failing the awesome task they were trusted with that they encouraged and were party to its demise. Did I hear you ask, *which one is right*? Well, frankly, I really think it was a modified form of the third view. The argument goes like this: Those guys who were invested with the responsibility of guiding the SSC and seeing it through began to feel it slipping through their fingers. That's when their subconscious minds got to work. How could they take the blame for its burial in the deep dark earth? How could they bear the shame? What would happen to them and their careers? So they opted to let it go down – even give it a little shove – rather than admit their incapacity to go on, their cowardice, their infirmity of will, and their feet of clay. However, who cares about my opinion anyway? I'm afraid it'll have to be left to historians to pin that question down."

Leon stopped speaking for a moment, reflecting on man's limitations in fathoming the past. Then his face reddened noticeably. He sat quietly, as everybody waited, all ears. Suddenly, his outlook seemed to brighten, and he lit up, all aglow: "Damn it! I shouldn't be wasting all of your time beating around the bush with a lot of philosophical balderdash. Anyway, if I remember correctly, you didn't ask it explicitly, but I've chosen to presume that you'd like me to address my part in this double whammy of big project cancellations. So let me get on with it. To start, I'll address your two major concerns about ISABELLE and me: Did I really try to help BNL in its hour of need, and did I conspire in a negotiation to trade ISABELLE for the SSC?

"First, I'll tackle the easier one for me, about my proposal to give BNL assistance. Even though I know this may not satisfy the many who are predisposed to view me as something between an artful bamboozler and a steely, cold-blooded charlatan, I must tell you that I really did want to help BNL with ISABELLE. Everything I did backs that up.

I simply did my utmost to make the deal work. Not only did I make the offer in the strictest confidence, but also I did so only after coming to a firm understanding with Wallenmeyer that Washington would back it up. Besides, I deeply wanted both high-energy physics to flourish and American Big Physics to be on top again; and around 1980 BNL was the key. So Mickey, with all this to support my claim of high-minded purity in the help-BNL matter, can it really be rationally construed that I acted the way I did if I wasn't being honest and honorable? I think not.

"Because I was well aware that BNL considered me a turncoat for trying to breathe life into its hated competitor, Fermilab, I removed myself from having any direct involvement in the negotiations. To get the job done, the transaction that I hoped would successfully take place was conducted via an emissary. Although Bob was kind enough to do this most difficult of dealings, I take this opportunity to declare unequivocally that I was behind the scheme full-bore, and his visit and proposal to Vineyard were with my absolute and unqualified blessing. I assure you that that there were no strings attached and no fine print at the bottom. Everything was totally above-board and in full view. Sure, I well appreciate that it's no easy matter to convince those prone to suspiciousness – especially the ones who, with meager if any cause, mistrust me – but, take it or leave it, the way you're hearing it now is the way it was. It's just too bad that Vineyard's BNL inner circle didn't trust me and so vetoed the deal." Leon looked very pleased with himself for getting these things said, things he had wanted to get off his chest for a long time. The truth is that it was quite easy for him to do. You see, here he was occupying high moral ground, and surely that tends to make your spirits rise, as well as loosening your tongue. However, what was coming up next was going to be a lot different. Thus, before continuing, he took a brief time-out. He was quiet except for some wriggling and squirming in his chair. His eyes were a little sad as he pensively looked outside at the darkening sky. Then he perked up, and took a swig from his glass of Glenlivet as he prepared himself for the more difficult ISABELLE question connected with the SSC.

"As for the tradeoff that sold ISABELLE down the river, what can I say but mea culpa? Yes, it's true, I was a member of that cabal that laid the groundwork and paved the way for ISABELLE to meet its dismal and miserable fate. But what else was there to do? Reason simply couldn't make Vineyard, Samios and the rest of the BNL first-stringers see the light. Ironically, it was as if, in their unconscious minds, they were driven collectively to make a sacrifice of ISABELLE. So determined were they that nothing could make them change their ways. Thus, in the end, it was called-for – nay, demanded of us – that our little clique act to lay the terminally ailing project to rest. So it was for the good of the high-energy enterprise and for the future of Big Physics that we complied and did what had to be done. However, I particularly want it known that I didn't play my part in the wretched affair because I was vengeful, or spiteful, or even because I bore any ill will toward BNL. But the old lab just didn't give us any options. It was on the skids and was creating a master-dilemma for U.S. Big Science. You couldn't just look the other way. Something simply had to be done about it. ISABELLE was hurtling downhill at an accelerating pace, unable to stop, and threatening to take the whole of high-energy physics down with it. Thus, my cohorts-in-intrigue and I became convinced that BNL had to be abandoned. So, when all is said and done, I must plead guilty to the charge set down at my doorstep. Indeed, I did my share in the conspiracy that led to the execution of ISABELLE.

"So, you see, even before the idea surfaced of getting something in return for sending ISABELLE over, the fact that it had to go was already fixed in the minds of a select few of the top men of the high-energy physics game. But there was something of a problem in getting such a notion off the ground. You can be sure that just eliminating ISABELLE without some quid pro quo wouldn't sit well with the community. Frankly, it wouldn't sell at all. Then, serendipity smiled on us, and we were miraculously favored with the missing link we were seeking, the grounds to get the action going.

"What luck! During the years, one on either side of Snowmass '82, a confluence of things transpired that added both the rationale and the wherewithal to the assurance we already felt in our guts of the absolute necessity to commit the extreme act of ridding the community of that tiresome project eating away at the innards of American Big Physics. The thing that made it all possible – the missing link – was that Bob came up with the Desertron. It was the skeleton of a project we immediately recognized to be the one that just might allow us to carry out the previously unthinkable act and save the day for high-energy physics. From the moment Bob's insight became known, we three conspirators, Pewitt, Keyworth, and I, knew we had our reason for an ISABELLE sellout.

"Each of the three of us had a vital role to play, crucial to the success of the venture. Remember, we weren't coordinating each other's efforts. We were purely independent agents, except for unplanned conversations and the spontaneous passing on of ad hoc information. We didn't work it all out in some smoke-filled room. Still together, we were quite a team. Unbeatable, as it turned out! Pewitt was sure Vineyard would be the death of all of us if he wasn't stopped in his tracks, and as 1981 was closing he ruthlessly did away with the ruinous tall gentleman. Keyworth, Reagan's eager and ambitious science advisor, fervently believed in and promoted his ideas on excellence in Big Science and found a way to get the President behind the high-flying, flamboyant Snowmass pitch. Finally, I was convinced that the high-energy particles that would be generated by the Desertron would make it the quintessential collider project, the accelerator flower of the twentieth century, and, during the year leading to the summer-of-1983 HEPAP meeting that rang ISABELLE's death knell, I discovered the means to persuade and bring the Big Physics community along with us. Frankly, it was through one of those offers that couldn't be refused. The resulting circumstances surpassed being favorable and auspicious – they were perfect. Thus, the three of us, only too eager to lead the growing bandwagon, climbed aboard the first coach of the Reagan Excellence Express and raced on into the land of the SSC.

"But what did we three and the others who climbed aboard the glory train know of the deceptiveness of politics? How were we to know that ISABELLE was only the first installment to be exacted? How were we to know that our dignity and self-respect – not just ISABELLE – were part of the bargain? How were we to know that in this instance politics was just the Devil in disguise? Yes, indeed, how were we to know these things? To be honest and candid, we didn't know – not any of it. We were young in the ways of the world. Actually, we were in the formative stage, just beginning to get our hands dirty. We simply didn't have a clue about what any of the hidden political implications were. All that seemed to matter to us were our unquenchable and uncontrollable ambitions.

"What fools we were to believe and trust Lucifer's lying eyes that cast a spell over us and sucked us in with dreams of fathoming the heavens! Sure, we should've been more watchful. We should've been more insightful. We should've read between the lines. But, believe me, so enticing was this SSC that we didn't stand a chance in hell of not giving in to it. What a catch this would be for a scientist! What a mouth-watering temptation it was! Imagine: coming face to face with the universe's deepest secret, *mass* itself! Who could resist an opportunity to take that challenge on? But, when we chose to follow the call of the *pied piper*, we found that things weren't at all the way they seemed. Yet, how were we to know that we were only being lured by a false beguiler? You see, the fact was that the SSC and ISABELLE weren't at all the true currency in the transaction; rather it was our very souls. But, being innocents, how could we be expected to discern the difference? So, thinking we were God's gifts, thinking that we knew everything there was to know, we followed the beckoning charmer. Captivated by the promise of stardom and ennoblement, we were ensnared by the come-on. It's true that we had a vague inkling that great, perhaps even life-threatening risk lay in our path, but the light that seemed to be assuring us acclaim and exaltation blinded us. So we chose to gamble and hazard the trip anyway.

"For our initiation, treachery was demanded of us, and we complied by betraying BNL. Then, when the sacrifice was carried out, we looked the other way as ISABELLE's blood flowed. But somehow, with visions of glory dancing in our heads, the reality of that awful occurrence totally escaped us. In any case, we had our places booked and our tickets in hand for the Waxahachie-bound express. So, leaving the nightmare of agony behind us, and panting with excitement at what lay ahead, we boarded the train that was to take us to our dream. However, when the train reached its destination, we found that the roads weren't filled with gold nuggets just for the picking; it wasn't the land of milk and honey we imagined it would be. Actually it was a place where only the hard of heart and the politically inured might have a crack at survival. Since very few had the stomach to slog through the dog-eat-dog world at the end of the line, most who came on the *Dream Express* rued the day they chose to do so.

"As it happened, our Texas supercollider experience lasted for a little more than five years. But soon the political windstorms rose with an awesome ferocity. We became tempest-tossed as the Washington-induced blizzard erupted. Only novices after all, we just didn't have what it takes to stay the course, and we were overwhelmed. After the calm returned, not only was ISABELLE gone and forgotten, but the Devil called politics had also snatched the SSC from us. So it was that the curtain descended on the dream whispered to us by deceiving gods, the dream that fanned and inflamed our desire to savor the knowledge of the farthest reaches of nature's origins, and the dream that ultimately drove us to treachery. Well, it's over now. Although we eventually learned that the dream wasn't real, only wishful thinking and wistful daydreaming, by then, with the SSC disbanded and junked, it was far too late. The truth of the matter is that we were younger then; and, typical of the young, we lunged for a brilliantly shining star far off in the distant sky. Alas, it was only a mirage. It was an illusion put there by mischievous gods only to tease us for their sport. Too bad! What a fantastic breaker we could've ridden, what a high we could've had, if only the story of the SSC, so full of mankind's hopes and dreams, would've managed to have a *happy ending*."

Leon's Angle
It Had To Be Done

Leon meditated a bit. His mouth felt dry. He stretched over for the lemonade, but then noticed the Glenlivet bottle. It was irresistible. He filled his schnapps glass and swigged it in one gulp. Boy, it felt good. It warmed the cockles of his heart. He sat still for a moment, wondering if he should just stop there. Of course not! How could he? How could he finish his side of the story of the decline of high-energy physics without mentioning Fermilab or CERN at all? No way, he thought! He certainly would've liked to take a break just then, to think it over a little. But he knew there wasn't time for that. So he jumped right in. "Up to this point," Leon began, "I've ignored the roles played by Fermilab and CERN in the harrowing, stab-in-the-heart failures of ISABELLE and the SSC. This was a great oversimplification – too great, I trust. So let me rectify that right now, while I still have a little energy left in me.

"Back in the latter half of the seventies, Bob had already been pushing for a Fermilab collider for many years; and when I became the Director, my inclination was to proceed in the same direction. After a lot of study about what would be best for Fermilab and for America, we came to the view that the right way to go was to develop an antiproton source that would provide beams for a single-ring proton-antiproton collider at Fermilab. We firmly believed that such a facility would be particularly low in cost; would permit the highest energy beam collisions than could be had anywhere in America or the world for years to come; would be the simplest and most readily operable instrument then available; and would be the quickest facility to get running and generating experimental data. We were well aware that our scheme would put us on a direct course to cross swords with BNL, which was by then in the process of building its already Washington-approved two-ring ISABELLE project. But, in the spirit of the free and open competition that America stood for, we were ready and willing to answer the bugle call, and fight the good fight with everything we had.

"But things didn't work out the way we intended them to. Divisiveness ruled Big Physics in America: Disparaging, damaging quarrels, and irate, fuming words of discontent and outrage were the order of the day. As it turned out, while all this bickering and backbiting between Fermilab and BNL took place, the clock did its thing, relentlessly ticking away. In this way, time became our enemy and passed us by. Carlo, ever the opportunist, recognized his chance to leave the U.S. in the dust, and seized it. He flew off to CERN, and persuaded the top men there that they could beat the pants off the U.S., which was frittering away its long-time advantage in internal strife. They agreed with him that the U.S. was in disarray, and gave him carte blanche to go ahead with the utmost dispatch. And that's exactly what he did: He built a CERN proton-antiproton collider and beat us to the punch. By the time we in the U.S. woke up to our plight, it was too late and Carlo was too far ahead to catch.

"What about me, you ask? Let me take you back to 1981. I'd brought Fermilab back from the brink after Washington pounded it to a pulp because in the mid seventies Bob, against Washington's will, chose to take on BNL in an American collider race. You see Bob didn't have the least faith in BNL's ability to be America's prime competitor to Europe's CERN lab; and he was inflexible and wouldn't yield. So, in 1978, Deutsch callously threw him into the dumpster. What a bonehead goof that was! Think of it: Throwing out the one man who might be able to keep the U.S. on top! Anyway, there I was in 1981 trying to fill Bob's big shoes. Actually, by then Washington had become quite concerned about BNL, and had already given me the green light to move on the idea of a single-ring collider at Fermilab. But playing the game of catch-up with Carlo way in the lead was nothing but a fool's errand. I tried, but deep down I knew it was a lost cause. The truth is, early in 1981, I still thought BNL had a chance to win the race with CERN. You see, in their collider design, they didn't need antiprotons, which made the single-ring scheme so damned hard; so, even as late as it was, I believed they might just be able to pull it off. Add to that the fact of Washington's insistent prodding, and you'll appreciate that I couldn't very well refuse to put Fermilab's resources behind BNL. Thus, convinced that Fermilab couldn't win the race for the W, I resigned myself to the *East Coast solution.* Since our low-cost superconducting magnets were already being produced in assembly-line fashion, it was perfect for BNL and would give it at least a little chance to overtake Carlo. So, against all my better judgment, I stood ready to support ISABELLE, and did in fact give it my best shot.

"Why they didn't accept my good-faith offer will always remain a mystery to me. The only reason that comes to mind, although I wasn't completely cognizant of it, is that by then the BNL management had already become completely paranoid. Help from any outsider was anathema to them. This was especially the case for help from Bob or me. We were the epitome of what they saw as evil. Under such circumstances, how could I help them? No, on that score, I was fully impotent. Understand that there was no rationality behind their behavior. For reasons I've never been able to fathom, I became cast as the worst in their eyes, no less than the devil incarnate. I guess that sometimes you have no choice but to accept things as they are. That's what they believed, and nothing on God's earth was going to change them. I resisted accepting the truth of this state of affairs for about as long as I could, probably too long. But finally it got through my thick head. And when I at last came to understand the situation I was in, it became clear that I had but two choices: Either I grabbed a seat on the train to conspiracy alley, or it was a rest-home for me. Anyway, when the dust settled, Carlo became king of the eighties, and I became a co-conspirator in the killing of ISABELLE in exchange for the Washington promise of an American Big Science dream."

Leon's Angle
Which one will it be?

Leon felt tired. Still, he was determined to go the distance. He wasn't the type of guy to just walk away. Besides, here was the chance to explain himself! He certainly wasn't about to let that pass. So he took three or four deep breaths and carried on like the true trouper he was. "OK, I feel myself beginning to wind down. So, before I fade away from the spotlight, let me take a stab at the issue Mickey calls my dual loyalty dilemma, referring to the fact that my heart was divided between the SSC and Fermilab. Of course the predicament was of my own making, originating with my proposal at Snowmass in 1982. After that, things began to happen very fast. Once ISABELLE was dispatched in 1983 and the SSC came into the picture with the political speed of light, the problem hit me like a ton of bricks. I was flabbergasted. The swiftness took me utterly by surprise and I found myself totally unprepared to come up with a rational answer to my quandary: Should I do the honorable and principled thing and stay on as Fermilab Director, or should I do the pragmatically sensible thing and give it up in order to make a realistic, credible fight to become the leader of the SSC? My choice was between right-and-proper idealism and down-to-earth realism. Which one was it to be?

"I must say that, looked at in this way, my plight was indeed dramatic. It's the stuff theater is made of. However, although I know, Mickey, that you won't like it, I'm afraid I'm going to have to disappoint you. The truth is that I didn't have to make the choice at all. You see, those men making the decision as to who would be the SSC Director wanted someone who'd carry with him a broad coalition of support. What that really means is that these guys, particularly Pewitt at DOE and Panofsky representing the American physics community, wanted someone whom everyone felt comfortable with and liked. Well, who could fit into that slot? Presuming that they intended to choose an eminent scientist, I guess it would have to be one who was also sociable and friendly, one who had a lot of experience with labs and projects, and, here's the clincher, one who'd made next to no enemies. Sure, I passed the *eminent scientist* criterion, and I was certainly sociable and friendly, as well as being very familiar with labs and projects. But when it came to the question of enemies, I've not the least doubt that the physics community is packed full of those who dislike me for one reason or another. Not only that, there are many who positively despise me. Some would even like to have my head on a platter. So, in the end, given the *broad support* condition, who would even look in my direction? No, for someone as controversial as I, there was about as much hope as finding Hitler in heaven. I was simply out in the cold.

"I sometimes wonder about that *no-enemies* constraint. Think about it: If you're looking for someone who's made no enemies, you're probably looking for some bland soul who hasn't lived very much in the real world. And if you find such a one, he'd surely be unfit for the ruthlessness that big money, beyond a doubt, brings with it. What could those guys have been thinking when they inserted such a condition? It's almost as if they got it ass-backwards. They should've been looking for someone who'd made a lot of enemies and came out in one piece, for someone who'd passed through the fire and came out ready to play some more. Yes, such a person might well have been able to survive in the dog-eat-dog atmosphere that the SSC was sure to engender. Such a person, hardened to life's realities, might well have brought the SSC through its dark winter days and into the light of spring. It just seems very strange that the decision-makers, all smart men, could've been so wrong. Yet, when you look at what actually happened to the SSC, wouldn't you have to agree that my assessment wasn't far off the mark?

"Actually, in my case, the conclusion that I was persona non grata is supported by more than theoretical inference. As it happened, by direct personal contact, it was made plain to me that they didn't want me. When I spoke to Pewitt and Panofsky about it, although I didn't ask them point-blank if I was in the running, they made it perfectly clear to me that the Director's job was earmarked elsewhere. Looking into their eyes, I came to understand not only that the answer was *no* but furthermore that there would be no appealing the verdict. It couldn't have been made plainer to me. I simply had no realistic chance of winning the SSC Director's chair.

"So Mickey, put yourself in the position I was in. What would you have done? This is the way I saw it then: Why should I give up Fermilab? From that position, at least I could fight for my lab to be the SSC site. Since the SSC Director was to be chosen before the site selection, as Fermilab Director, I could never be made the SSC's top man. However, if I could get the SSC to be built at Fermilab, I could at least have some influence: I could try to ensure that no big political or technical gaffes were made, that mangement decision-making was as good as it could be, and that political support stayed at peak levels. The more I thought about it, the more I liked being in such a position. Frankly, it would've been perfect for me. Think about it a little: Weren't these exactly the things I'd be best suited for anyway? After all, I was getting on in years, and being an experienced and wise advisor, helping the young through their trying initiation into the real world, is certainly the best an old man could aspire too. So why not? Why shouldn't I shoot for that? It would be far better than fighting those picayune skirmishes, both inside and outside the lab, that are a Director's bane to bear. Yes, better to be involved in issues connected with the big picture, from a place where the clashes and conflicts tend to be on the philosophical level. No doubt about it, that's far better for a man coming upon his golden years. Thus, driven by a confluence of reasoning and instinct, that's what I went for.

"Getting back to the question of why I wasn't looked upon favorably to become the SSC Director, I'm not sure I can provide any further enlightenment. However, I should perhaps point out that, at the time, there was a lot of negative prattling chatter about me making the gossipmonger rounds: *No, not Lederman, he'll just stick up for Fermilab*! Or, *no, not Lederman, he's just a clown; nobody will listen to him, so he'll never be able to get the job done*! Or, *no not Lederman he's too old*! So you see, if getting a consensus on your side was the key to becoming the SSC Director, it sure as hell wasn't gonna be me. Nonetheless, after a lot of soul-searching and trying to work it all out as dispassionately as I could, I've become persuaded that the real reason they didn't opt for me wasn't my cozy ties to Fermilab – that is Mickey's dual loyalty – nor was it that I'd made too many enemies to be effective, nor was it my advancing age. If you're interested in speculation, mine is that the choice was really made by none other than *Mister Serendipity*.

"As a matter of fact, if people friendly to me had been in command of the selection process, does anyone doubt that I probably would've been the one to come out on top? As it was, the ones with the votes that counted were men who gave me the *thumbs down* sign: They were men who grossly mistrusted me; they were men who feared the power I would inevitably accumulate; they were men who were vindictive and were seeking revenge for past deeds of mine; they were men who would damn me, see me rot in hell first, even if I was the right person for the job; and they were men who were pushing somebody else, with Pief, the Chairman of the SSC Board of Trustees and smack in the middle of the anti-Lederman camp, staunchly behind his protégé Schwitters. Of course, there were some who sincerely but wrong-headedly believed that I wasn't up to it, and there even were a few who were behind me. Anyway, as it turned out, at the end of the day, when the votes were in, there were just too many against me. Of course the crowd that did it all, the faction that came up with Mister Schwitters as the winning name, was stacked against me from the get-go. Men in high places, like Pief, saw to that. But, speaking with the utmost candor, I can tell you outrightly that I have no regrets. True, if I'd been more judicious, more sensitive, more astute in the way I handled people during my lifetime, then maybe I'd have been the one picked. But that's water over the dam. Besides, if I were that sort of person, does anyone here believe that I'd have been well enough equipped to see the SSC through as it meandered along the hazardous road it had to take? I think not. In any case, I wasn't the chosen one; and that's the be all and end all of it. So you see, Fermilab was all I had, and I was determined to give my all to it."

Leon's Angle
Sign-off

"Well, Mickey, that's my story. That's my take on ISABELLE, the SSC, and the people behind those awful disasters. Be assured that it's the best I can do for you. Still, they're only my views – mine alone. They're the way I saw things. If it's absolute truth you're looking for, methinks you're barking up the wrong tree. I don't imagine you'll get it from these lips. Even if such a thing were to exist, I'm not at all confident that we humans have the wherewithal to find it anyway. And even if we did find it, do you think we'd recognize it? Do you think it would give us a better understanding of life, and help us to be better people? I wonder!" Leon stood up, reached for the bottle of Glenlivet, and filled the five glasses. He lifted his. Then, as the other four did likewise, he smiled broadly and said, "A toast to Mickey! May he discover the truth he's so zealously and passionately searching for!"

Leon sat down and heaved an audible sigh of relief. *Whew, it's over*, he thought. But, alas, his wrap-up, his closeout, and even his toast turned out to be premature. Just as he was beginning to unwind, just as he was beginning to feel an unburdening – the experience of an expanding circle of lightness overspreading his body – it suddenly struck him. There was a third question that he'd overlooked. *Oh, drat it! Maybe I could just let it go and call it a day*, he thought, wondering if he could. But he knew he couldn't. It simply wasn't in him. He was one of those types who like to dot their I's and cross their T's. If he says he'll do something, then, by god, he'll do it. So, even as a relaxed chitchat overtook the room, he interjected: "Oh, sorry about that faux-ending. I know it isn't good form to leave the stage with a flourish only to have to return. Unfortunately, that's what I have to do. What a bummer for me! What a letdown for you! But if you'll all bear with me, it'll take only a minute or two."

Leon turned to face his interrogator: "Mickey, you appeared keenly interested in the post-SSC period, and especially curious about the quandary America found itself in. In particular – and I hope you'll permit me a little leeway in my paraphrasing – you asked me: First, why did the U.S. lose its spirit? And second, why did it not only leave the field wide open for CERN, but, in addition, actually go on to help CERN complete the coup de grâce by paying through the nose to buy some of the LHC leftovers? I presume you'll allow me to give my imagination free reign on these issues. After all, I can't really speak for the U.S. high-energy community but only for myself. The best I can do is tell you, as a man with considerable access to the science power centers around the world, what I honestly felt and what others told me. I'll also favor you with my inferences gleaned from our deeds and the manner in which we American high-energy types conducted ourselves.

"Gathering all the pieces, then adding them up, my surmise is that the U.S. acted as it did because, having ignominiously lost their supercollider dream, their very future, the country's physicists became tired and scared, and old before their time. They also didn't have the energy to fight anymore. So where was the spirit to come from? I guess what happened is that we all lost our will and succumbed. We simply gave in to the stress and strain of not knowing what to do. Then, in a weakened state of mind, we took the easy way out by laying on the table the cash demanded of us for any pittances CERN might be willing to dole out when the LHC came to life. You see, we didn't only lose our spirit to fight, we also lost our pride.

"Well, my dear friends, that's the sad ending we have to live with. *That* is *that*! Now, you all know that it's not my trademark to end up on such a disagreeable note. But what could I do? Mickey wants the unadulterated truth. He wants us to tell it like it is. So this is what we're stuck with. OK, I think I've talked myself out. It's sign-off time and time for me to quit. And I guarantee it, this time it's for real!" Leon jokingly mimicked his earlier sigh of relief. When he looked up at the others, all of them were staring at their laps, deep in thought. Seeing that no one was reacting to his good-humored gesture, at least not fast enough to suit him, Leon was incredulous and, feigning displeasure, threw up his arms in disbelief. "That's it folks," he gesticulated, "it's all over. The show's done and there just ain't no more to tell." Clearly, Leon was donning his acting attire, for he knew full well that the silence was one of approval and not dissatisfaction. However, he found it hard to abide that everyone was so glum. What he really wanted was for them to perk up, not to take things so seriously, and above all to smile at the passing parade. Or perhaps it was just that, when all was said and done, Leon was a comedian at heart, and couldn't tear himself away until he got his closing laugh. And it actually worked, at least partially. As Leon finished, you could see the heads lifting and the smiles beginning to appear.

Mickey couldn't seem to find the words to express his delight with Leon: both because of the opportunity he gave them all to have a glimpse into the inner workings of his *little gray cells*, and because of the frank opinions he expressed about others. Mickey's inability to find the words – when this moment following Leon's stagy finishing touch was screaming out for them – may have been due to exhaustion from such a long and emotionally taxing day. But, at the last instant, good old Mickey somehow found the means to pull himself together. He knew he had to say something, and he managed to come through with an old favorite of his: "Leon, you did the impossible: You brought tears to our eyes and put smiles on us all, and both at the very same time. That is a feat only a rare few are capable of. I can only say that you were too much and left me, for one, without words that could possibly match such eloquence as you've expressed here this evening." At this point, everybody seemed to loosen up: they began to shift about and started to converse with each other; and, as the chatting went on, hearty laughter began to materialize. Whew, Mickey thought, the men-of-old that he was coming to know so well had returned. Somehow, Mickey had wrested the table from its doldrums; and – get this – he'd also given Leon his craved-for laughs to boot.

* * * * *

Carlo

Mickey was thoroughly spent, actually not very far from just crashing. However, the day wasn't quite over yet. There was still one more matter to deal with. And for this one, he certainly had to have all his wits about him. It's strange how sometimes something comes from out of nowhere to help you when you need it most. And this is what happened to Mickey in this instance. Somehow, delving into that just about depleted energy fountain deep inside him, he found the strength to go on. He turned toward Carlo and, though tinged with sarcasm that Mickey simply couldn't resist, gave the big, hulking man-of-the-hour the admiring tribute he rightly deserved, "King Carlo, the undisputed champion of the energy game, are you ready?"

Carlo smiled a wide-eyed, cheeks-ablaze, winning smile, which was ever so friendly and inviting. But the more you looked at it, the more you recognized a touch of the devil in it that, for some strange reason, made Carlo even more appealing. There was such a boyish appeal in his big, red, glowing face. But this image didn't just come about all by itself in the natural course of his life's experiences. Not at all! He worked hard for it. Then, gradually, over the years, he'd evolved and polished this façade that had the effect of making him most difficult to resist, even for the hardest of hearts. It fitted oh so well with the fact that he was such a sweet charmer when it suited him. It was quite obvious that he was out to unbalance Mickey, and this mask he'd donned was the first step to that end.

As Carlo wriggled about in his chair, a hush came over the room. He knew well how to respond to a compliment when it contained a slight tongue-in-cheek edge: He spoke around it. Effectively, he ignored it. Hesitating just a bit more than might be appropriate, his voice finally emerged: "Before we start, Mickey, I want to tell you right up-front that I have absolutely no wish or intention to make things rough on you. Now, I can understand that you don't believe this. True, I'm not a mind reader, but I can easily imagine what you're thinking: *He's going to be a tough nut to crack.* Come on," Carlo cajoled! "Admit it! That's what's running through that mistrustful little brain of yours. Isn't it? But it's simply not the way it is. It's not the way I am, regardless of the reputation I've been grievously and unfairly saddled with. So don't you give it another thought! The truth is I'm going to be easy pickings for you, putty in your hands. In case you haven't noticed, I'm the nice guy of the bunch! So go ahead and give me all you've got. I can take it. Ask away to your heart's delight. I'm a pushover, easy game for a man of your worldliness."

Mickey stared at Carlo, trying to find the key that would crack the code of this man of mystery. How was he to approach such an enigmatic personage? Here was this thundering and swaggering colossus of a man, who, at the same time, was a cocky, saucy, and impudent little boy. Yes, Mickey knew he had his work cut out for him. Carlo was a bag of contradictions to all who knew him, and Mickey found to his dismay that he could make neither hide nor hair of this man who'd managed to reach the pinnacle of Big Science. *Just how should I deal with this heavy mass of a man when there's simply nothing to latch onto, nothing but undependable, continually changing versions of him? How indeed does one deal with a dashing chameleon?* Mickey pondered the issue before him, quite unsettled and flustered by the task.

Who was this debonair mastermind anyway? And what was he really made of? In the few seconds available to him, Mickey allowed his mind to wander as he thought about it. Carlo was an ambitious man, a tough man who had fought his way to the top of a dog-eat-dog competitive racket. Robust and tall, with a potbelly on him that was not unattractive, he was a man of great vitality; a man who loved good food and drink; and a man who took great pleasure in the art of playing, laughing, flirting, and romancing. Yes, he was a man of the world, one who cherished living to the utmost of his being. But most of all, he loved his work: When the idea for an experiment came to his fertile mind, he would do anything to see it through to its end. He would get to that goal line no matter what it meant, no matter whom he had to walk over, no matter how nasty and ruthless he had to be. Wherever it took him, that's where he wanted to go. Whatever he would find there, whether it be bitter or sweet, he was determined to squeeze out the truth from its hiding place, and hold it up as a trophy: *Here world, here's the how and why of our existence, here's what made it all come to pass. And don't you forget that I'm the one who's giving you the key to the universe.*

Unfortunately, all this drifting and roaming about, trying aimlessly to get to the bottom of Carlo, wasn't getting Mickey anywhere. He began to think that maybe his inability to find a good way to react to Carlo had little to do with Carlo himself. Maybe it was more that he was simply overtired. The more he thought about it, the more it seemed to be right. But if it was so and if he was going to be able to proceed in the optimal way he wanted to, Mickey simply had to beat that fatigue and drowsiness that'd overcome him. But, how was he to do it?

Then as if in answer to his prayer, Mickey got a second wind. He felt it happen deep within him. The old Mickey just up and spontaneously came back: In a fast-as-fast-can-be transformation, he found himself aroused, burning with the fiery glow of excitement, uplifted by what he imagined lay ahead, and rarin' to go. Now Mickey was ready. His exultation at this rare opportunity to lock swords with the big man showed plainly on his face as he looked at Carlo admiringly. Then, slowly and deliberately, he began to speak.

Magnetic Carlo According to Mickey
A European Science Magnate

"Carlo, you are a true hero. In your wild and vivid imagination, you believed, against all conventional wisdom, that a most exquisite and tricky idea you dreamed up could unravel the mystery of the W. *Poof, it'll happen just like that*, you said. Most others, lacking your brash and nervy bravado, would've taken one look at what had to be done, determined it to be unfeasible, hopeless to pursue, and stopped right there, dead in their tracks. But not you! Undeterred by its ball-busting formidability, you unflinchingly went on, embarking on the next step, and then the next. You kept knocking down obstacle after obstacle, until, in the end, you transformed what was an improbable idea into a tell-all science machine. Then came the pièce de résistance: You made the machine sing! And what a song it was! What a humming-irresistible song! What a memorable song! It was no less than a song that opened wider the door to the universe. Can't you hear its strains now, this *chanson d'amour* sung for all of mankind?

"You pulled the whole thing off so sure-footedly and so quickly that it still shakes me when I think of it. Imagine: You went off to CERN just as the decade of the seventies was coming to a close, and by 1983, history was made. Dragging the ghostly W kicking and screaming out of its obscure corner was one hell of a feat and a dazzling sensation both for science and for you. It was a job well done, and no manmade commendation could do you justice. Anyway, with that triumph under your belt, there you were, on top of the world. Having reached a peak of immaculate fulfillment few others would even dare try for, you could've blissfully and deservedly rested on the kudos, the tributes, and the laurels that followed. But, no, not you! Your vaulting ambitions and eager aspirations weren't about to stop there. Perish the thought! Carlo, being a perpetual motion machine, kept his motor churning with not the least sign of slowing down. Quickening your pace, you set your sights even higher. You switched your attention to Europe's next head-to-head fight against the American superpower across the ocean and the gigantic colossus it was preparing to unveil.

"It must've been quite a thrill for you to return home to Europe, to your roots, and then quickly become a savior of its honor. It was good to be a big hero, and it didn't take you long to become acclimated to the respect and position afforded you in the old world. Oh yes, you felt right at home there, and immediately you looked to the long haul. Taking your cue from the U.S., you adopted the spirit of nationalism, and immediately took up the cudgel for European Big Science in its rivalry with America. After the brilliance you exhibited in uncovering the secret hiding place of the W, you were catapulted into the role of CERN's ringmaster, with the exhilarating, challenging mission of taking the Geneva lab as far as it could go.

"Unquestionably, you were the right choice for the job. With no hesitation at all, as if you'd already conceived and digested it all, you fashioned a way to defiantly respond to the new American threat to Europe's single-minded will to hold onto its newly won position as front-runner. Seeing the SSC already on the move, still you had the audacity to intrepidly plan a counter-offensive. No, you weren't a lily-livered wimp, ready to back down at the first sign of a high-powered, major-league impediment. In spite of the many confounding political and administrative roadblocks you had to contend with, in spite of the limited managerial options available to you – breathing room that you could hardly maneuver in – you were still able to give CERN a new raison d'être, a new hope for the future, and a renewed sense of itself as a winner. Allowing your fertile mind to roam freely, it didn't take you long to imagine your next step. You came up with just the right European reply to the American Supercollider; and you called your dream the Large Hadron Collider (LHC).

"Thus, as the eighties passed the mid-way mark, the trans-Atlantic race for particle supremacy was on again. Each side got cracking, and pulled out all the stops to demonstrate its superiority, braving the drudgery and the grind of the work needed to do it. So enticing was the dream, and so compelling was the prospect of winning that both the U.S. and CERN spared no effort, taxing themselves to the breaking point to maximize their chances of reaching the finishing line first. With all the means they could muster, they stretched to their utmost in the attempt to reach and surpass the frontiers of technology, seeking there to ascertain the precise engineering solution that would transform a state-of-the-art concept and design into a practicable, working experimental instrument.

"For CERN, being up against the power-packed U.S., it was a confrontation sure to dishearten the timid of heart and weak of spirit. But you were not the type to fold under pressure. Your destiny was to go on to the bitter end. You really had no choice. It was embedded in your nature. You would fight on all the way until it led to a knockout – one way or the other – and the referee pronounced an end of it. So you worked yourself to the bone; you traveled incessantly around the world seeking allies; and you put your mind on double duty. Now, why did you do all this? That's simple! What you were looking for was no less than the key to the kingdom of victory; and, being up against the world's sole technological superpower, you weren't going to get it just like that. Yet you kept moving on, putting everything you had into the effort. This you did even during times of waning hope, as it was during the late eighties and into the nineties, when your situation was dolefully bleak. Nevertheless, you somehow kept CERN plodding along, even as the U.S., with its massive economic and technological might, pulled further ahead. With the LHC as CERN's strategic underpinning, and acting in the capacity of Director General (DG) of CERN from 1989 to 1993, you managed to find a way to breathe life into that ponderously bureaucratic, discouraged, jumpy, and full-of-qualms old Swiss lab. And it was a good thing for the CERN fuddy-duddies that you did in fact keep the lab's wheels turning.

"As it happened, during your last year as DG, *Lady luck* once again was walking with Master Rubbia. For the second time in a decade, with CERN languishing well behind the U.S., American Big Physics once more dealt itself a deathblow. Just as ISABELLE self-destructed in 1983, so the SSC did the same in 1993. So it was that history put on its repeating act and yet another time pulled American Big Physics out of the game. So there was CERN, once again left alone to make an unchallenged run for physics immortality. But this time things were not at all the same. In the earlier eighties' episode, using antiprotons in the CERN SPS, you plucked out the W and made your way to Nobel stardom. In the later case, just at the moment the free ride to glory jumped into CERN's lap, fate stepped in and called for your exit from the field of play. Now, without you, it's a whole new ball game. Whether those carrying the LHC forward towards its destiny can follow in your footsteps, only the wily and slippery fates can say."

Magnetic Carlo According to Mickey
Can the LHC make it without the King?

"The death of the SSC along with the no-competition open road for the LHC was all well and good for CERN. But for you, the story of 1993 was quite a different one. Your first term as DG expired that year, and the many enemies you'd accumulated along the way finally caught up with you. You were not renewed! That second term you were just dying for wasn't to be. You'd think those high-level reps of the CERN member states would've known better than to dislodge you. How unappreciative of them not to recognize you for what you'd accomplished! How unthinking of them not to damn well know that they couldn't replace the genius they had on hand with just anybody who had the appropriate accent! Nevertheless, that's what happened. Well, *c'est la vie*! Anyway a new leadership arrived on the scene, and CERN, sans Carlo, went along its merry way with its mini-supercollider.

"OK, so the LHC supercollider, as conceived, isn't anywhere near the equal of the never-born Texas pipe dream; but at least it has a chance of being the real thing. In fact today, the big European project is moving ahead. Actually, I shouldn't just let those words flow from my lips so casually. Yes, to be sure, the LHC is pushing forward, but you certainly wouldn't say that it's breaking any records for speedy construction. The truth is, speaking bluntly, it's on a rather slow and tentative course. The management seems unsure of itself, while the project is lagging badly. Is there any doubt that the LHC is exhibiting many of the characteristics signifying impending failure that were observed in the SSC? There are the ever-recurring magnet mistakes and mishaps; there's the hazard-packed staff demoralization; there's the mounting number of excuses for the things that simply don't get done or get done wrong; and then, to top it all off, there are the periodic cost-estimates that keep going up and up. No, it doesn't look very hopeful, not at all!

"Although the new CERN top management undoubtedly wouldn't admit it, I, for one, would be utterly surprised if these Johnny-come-latelies didn't miss you something awful. What wouldn't they give if only they could have around them your capacity to get people to put their shoulders to the wheel and their minds to work at double speed; your way of explaining away delays and persuading the higher-ups to have patience and cough up the cash; your magical accounting schemes; your indomitable drive and imagination; and your ability, against all odds, to get things done? Too bad they don't have you to get them out of the mess they're in. They're simply going to have to depend on their own devices, which – and this is strictly entre nous – have very little oomph indeed.

"As for you, there's no surprise here: *You picked yourself up, dusted yourself off, and started all over again.* Left by CERN to fend for yourself as a free agent, without skipping a beat you sallied forth on a new adventure, searching for ways to solve the world's on-the-way energy shortage. As I understand your position, you perceive it as a crisis bound to happen, and sooner rather than later. Although many question that assessment, I say you're probably right. I must tell you, I most fervently hope you're not, but I fear you are. Frankly, imagining the potential consequences of the western world without enough energy gives me the shivers. However, difficult as preventing this unthinkable scenario might be, I dearly hope that you'll continue the good fight. Certainly I haven't the slightest doubt that if anyone can get that *impossible* job done, it's you. And, in truth, I think few would argue with that."

Carlo, acting a trifle impatient, but secretly pleased with the praise being heaped on him, saw the right moment to jump in: "OK Mickey, let's cut the bull; get down to brass tacks and skip to the nub of what you're after." Carlo sensed that he was going to be asked questions he might not find easy to answer, and was becoming a little antsy at how slow Mickey was in getting there. But if this was some kind of intimidating tactic on Carlo's part, Mickey wasn't going to fall for it. Nothing, positively nothing, was going to deter Mickey from his original line of attack. He took a passing glance at the tough and vigorous Carlo, and thought: *This man is about as sturdy, resilient, and self-assured as they come; he can take anything I'm capable of dishing out.* No, there wasn't the least reason to alter his plans. Mickey knew he couldn't back down now anyway, not even a little. He would just go ahead as scheduled and give Carlo the worst he was capable of. However, before going on to the questioning of Mister Big, Mickey had a couple of things still to deal with, matters that he just couldn't let pass. Since a little nervousness caused his throat to be filled with some phlegm, he first had to clear it. It took a bit more effort than he'd have liked. It made him feel self-conscious. But then, when it was finally done, he started in speaking.

"Let me make it clear, Carlo, that everything I've said about you is deeply felt and comes from the heart. It's not at all bullshit! But, as time is passing, I'll heed your advice and move on with a mite more dispatch. Although I too would like to get right down to my questions for you, they'll certainly make a lot more sense if I finish up these preliminary remarks. So, if you give me a break and let me go on, I do promise to try to be more concise. But I have to tell you that, as of now, *I'm dancing as fast as I can.*" Mickey looked at Carlo, and then at the others. Seeing no objections, he took it to mean he had *thumbs up* to go on. And so he did.

Magnetic Carlo According to Mickey An Inscrutable Man

"Allow me to travel back in time with you so that I might remind you of something that took place in 1983," a re-invigorated and animated Mickey started up. "In the early spring, a few months before ISABELLE was cancelled, and about the time you announced your discovery of the W, you visited Bill Wallenmeyer and company. I was stationed at the DOE in Germantown when you arrived there. If you recall, you had quite a private session with Bill. The whole staff was aware that the subject had to be the W, ISABELLE, or perhaps even both. We all had our guesses, but, in reality, we knew squat. All of us were consumed with curiosity, just itching to find out what you two guys really talked about. Eventually, I did find out. How simple it was! Yet, how unsatisfying! In fact, it was quite a surprise.

"According to Bill, you were a most avid supporter of ISABELLE, and tried your damnedest to persuade him to do whatever was necessary to save it. When I heard this, I was floored. Now Carlo, listen here, you knew accelerators like the back of your hand. Why would you help to prop up a project that was so poorly designed technically? The magnets were horribly over-designed, being far too big, far too risky to make assembly-line style, and far too costly; the direct current beam was better suited for the accelerator Stone Age than for a modern state-of-the-art collider; and the combined injection/beam accumulation system was a joke and sure to bring big trouble, that is, if it worked at all. I could sympathize if you were lending a hand to a real-life dying lady seeking your help. But help ISABELLE? What *a puzzlement*!

"Then again, if it wasn't for that sorry damsel in distress, could it possibly have been for Nick and his BNL cohorts that you demeaned yourself? Really? For that arrogant bunch! You must surely have known they were all out of control and on the verge of big trouble. You must have known they were up to no good. So why, Carlo, why would you foster the perpetuation of the two-faced, unsavory, and irresponsible behavior of such men, behavior about as close to being unscrupulous and illicit as one can imagine of scientists?"

Mickey stopped for a moment after that onrush of provocation. He could feel droplets of sweat forming on his brow and sliding down his cheeks. Using his forearm, he could absorb some of them. But they kept coming. He could hear himself breathing heavily. What was he to do? There was no one to turn to for advice. There was nowhere to run. The best thing he could do was just to sweat it out. So he took a momentary pause to help settle him down. As he felt his heartbeat slowing, he looked up at Carlo, who didn't appear fazed in the least. He, along with the others, were just sitting there placidly, awaiting Mickey's return.

Magnetic Carlo According to Mickey

The Last Days of Big Physics Internationalism

Having found a way to contain his severe, but thankfully short-lived, emotional reaction, a sufficiently recovered Mickey went on: "Let me now move ahead a few years into the early nineties. You were serving as the CERN DG during those critical years when the SSC was in uncontrollable chaos and moving irrevocably toward its doomsday assignation. After studying the SSC's demise in as much detail as is humanly possible, I have firmly concluded that you – and that includes CERN and the LHC – were not, and I repeat emphatically, *not*, a material causal factor. Of course you were there, right in the thick of things, if not in body then most certainly in spirit. The slyly ambitious types, aspiring to move up the ladder, used you as a phony threat to the SSC; and everybody, absolutely everybody, talked about you incessantly. However, in reality, you were entirely peripheral to the main event. As far as being a vital factor, as far as playing one of the starring roles, forget it! If anything, all three – you, CERN, and the LHC – had minor, bit parts in the heavy drama that culminated in the death of a dream. So rest easy, it wasn't your doing. The truth is that you beat the pants off the U.S. because American Big Physics, hoisted by its own petard, blew up wholly of its own doing, with not the least help needed from you. So there it is: you got exactly what you wanted without having to lift a finger. However, like it or not, as for any responsibility for the SSC's decline and fall, other than two-bit stuff like public and private gratuitous tongue-wagging, you get a sparklingly spotless bill of health.

"Whoa! Hold on to your horses! Don't go running off half-cocked thinking you're such a lily-white pure model citizen of the world. On the contrary, in the matter of European-American Big Science international relations, you weren't exactly *Mister Clean*, not by any stretch of the imagination. *What did I do*? I hear you ask, in the manner of a boy caught with his hand in the cookie jar. Well, here's the answer, straight and undiluted. Typical of your modus operandi, you found a way to insinuate an annoying and ultimately injurious cog into the already precariously churning wheels of the U.S. high-energy physics program. Wasn't it in the mid to late eighties that you began your campaign against trans-Atlantic internationalism – actually American Big Physics – by saying, *put up or shut up? Pay to do experiments at CERN or stay out*!

"OK, I guess it's true that after the way American physicists treated you in the mid to late seventies, why should anyone have expected you to go out of your way to help the U.S.? And you didn't! But you went much further. Blind to the pain of your American colleagues, acting hardheartedly and callously, you gave them what you deemed their just desserts. *Mister Eagle Eyes* that you were, you set your revenge-filled sights on that particularly weak link in the American high-energy program: its disgraceful deficiency of experimental capacity, resulting from its condemnably negligent lack of Big Physics facility development and construction in the seventies and eighties. You saw the chink in the American science armor, its Achilles' heel, and you attacked in your inimitable pit-bull manner. As U.S. experimental Big Physics was helplessly floundering, instead of extending a helping hand, you chose to give it the big boot in the ass. Now that wasn't a very nice thing to do. That wasn't very high-minded, or noble, or knightly. Well, why should anyone be surprised at that? Frankly, you'd have to look far and wide to find someone who'd have believed that victory-or-bust Carlo would actually play by the Marquis of Queensbury rules."

Mickey sighed. The muscles of his face tightened, as if he were berating himself. *It's only the truth according to Mickey*, he thought, somewhat regretfully. Then, as the others at the table stared at him somewhat incredulously, Mickey knew he had to go on: "But, when you take all the known facts and the inferred intentions all together and add them up, who's to say what's right? When you kept battering the fast-sinking American's, who's to say it couldn't have prodded them to get their act together? Who's to say it might not have actually goaded the U.S. into taking their high-energy physics program to heights it hadn't seen for a long time? Imagine if the SSC had actually come to pass! Of course, as we all know, it didn't. I'm sure that didn't cause you any sleepless nights; but too bad for American Big Science."

Mickey paused, trying to find just the right words that might get him out of the holier-than-thou passer-of-judgments hole he'd dug for himself. *Ah, what the hell*, Mickey thought, as the words began to pour out again. "Carlo, I imagine that my thinly veiled impugning of your motives and what you did screams out for elaboration. So, by way of explanation, here are some of the details: After the humiliating and debasing ISABELLE ordeal of fire, U.S. Big Physics was right on the edge of collapsing from the sheer weight of the disgrace and wasting of its resources. Having staked everything on the *belle-dame*, the men who ran U.S. science, via a series of shabby and fourth-rate decisions, left high-energy physics in a state of crippled, corrupt, and scandalous impotence. Any available experimental facilities were low-grade, lackluster, and mediocre. And, believe it or not, nary a forefront collider was to be found in the country; nor were any future ones that had any chance of bearing frontier-fruit on the horizon. To all intents and purposes, American high-energy physics lay prostrate and paralyzed, unwittingly knocked out from within the Establishment by a bunch of figurehead ciphers, men of straw.

"Meanwhile, across the Atlantic, CERN, with no management snafus to speak of, and coming off its inspired, dazzling, and overcoming-all-the-odds-against-it victory in the race for the W, was in tip-top shape. Because its experimental facilities were up to snuff, it was no surprise that many more American experimenters were clamoring to go to CERN than those seeking to go the other way. Yes, it was a good time for CERN. It was riding high, all teed up, prepared for anything, and ready for action. Surely it was the master of its fate. It coaxed and enticed all comers, and feared nothing at all that the world could offer up.

"In the past, the situation had been the reverse. Remember the fifties and sixties when experimental physics at CERN, in its infancy, was struggling to come into its own. Then, the U.S. facilities were in their prime, and in great demand by Europeans and Americans alike. I remind you that at that time America acted with high-minded and noble generosity of spirit by opening its doors and its resources to Europeans. But change is the keystone of history; and although man continues to make the mistake that it is otherwise, the truth is that nothing remains the same. So it was with the European high-energy facilities vis-à-vis those of America. Throughout the seventies, change was in the wind, as CERN moved to catch up to the highly over-confident U.S. It was unwanted and unacknowledged by America. But it nonetheless happened anyway. In the mid-eighties the crossover came: Now scientists wanting to do experiments in Europe outnumbered those wanting to go the other way. What a striking and dramatic difference from a scant two decades earlier! As the eighties came to a close and the nineties began, this tendency only intensified, as the gap continued to widen. This was a situation real-life dramas are made of. What was CERN going to do? Would it exhibit the magnanimity of the Americans some decades earlier? Or, perhaps it would travel a more ominous and ill-omened route.

"Now, Carlo, consider the situation: Using your achievements, your wits, your brains, and your charm, you made it all the way to the office of CERN DG in 1989. In parallel, by the early nineties, the SSC was on the ropes, and feeling foul pangs, the pricks and stabs of its accursed fate. But you were blind to its anguish and misery. Even as the bedeviled project was approaching the agony of its final days, you stepped into the picture with vengeance in your heart. As the wretched pack, trapped in woeful Waxahachie, was bearing the aches of a dream-not-to-be, they pleaded with you to intercede on their behalf. But did you even entertain the thought of doing so? I put it to you that you didn't. On the contrary, your tendency was to move in the opposite direction. *Internationalism be damned,* you said with your actions and deeds! *Collegiality be damned! Memories of the good old days be damned! Old friends be damned! I'll have my way, and you'll get what's coming to you!* That was your lame and ungenerous answer. Sure, on the face of it, these men deserved neither your pity nor your assistance. When they had the chance, when they stood on top of the world with the SSC in their hands, they were hostile rather than friendly, unsavory rather than inviting, nasty rather than kind, and selfish rather than munificent. But, Carlo, they really needed you, and were begging. For old times' sake, why didn't you let bygones be bygones and come through for them? Why didn't you demonstrate the right and good way a man should act? Well, needless to say, you didn't. I guess you found it to your liking to imitate them rather than set an example for a different and better way to go.

"Anyway, there the Americans were, a sorry sight indeed, reduced to supplicants, beseeching you to come up with some cash to help them through their hard times. But you were hard as stone. To be blunt, you said: *No, I've got my LHC to think about. For you, nothing!* And you didn't stop there. You went even further. You took the hard stance that the SSC-versus-LHC state of affairs should be exploited by charging the U.S. for the privilege of using CERN's current experimental facilities. It appears that you were prepared to hit the Americans with the second half of a double whammy. Not only were they to pay dearly for a falling-apart SSC, but, in addition, you were going to see to it that they would also have to pay through the nose so that a not insignificant number of U.S. high-energy physicists could keep plying their trade. Those poor American high-energy types! Didn't your heart bleed for them? Even a little?

"Oh, how you wanted that *entrance fee* policy! You hammered away at it unrelentingly. So persistent and persuasive were you that, in the end, you pushed through just such a policy on Americans experimenting at CERN. It wasn't an easy course shift to carry off. Tradition stood smack-dab in your way; and many on both sides of the Atlantic were dead set against it. But, when push came to shove, no one had the muscle or the balls to stand up to you.

"Actually it was the circumstances prevailing in 1993 that really allowed it all to come to pass. With the SSC canned, the U.S. high-energy physicists were left with precious little in hand, and nothing – zilch – to look forward to. What luck for you! You were precisely where you wanted to be, firmly ensconced in the *catbird seat*. And what did you do from this position of dominance and sway that was thrust upon you? Why, you made the bitter pill given the U.S. physicists even more difficult to swallow. *You cough up the money*, you said, *and I'll open up the CERN facilities for you to use. I'll do even more than that. If you pay enough, I'll let you take part in some LHC experimentation when it's up and running*. Wow! Can you think of hitting anyone worse than that? OK, you can argue that, as DG, you were supposed to be looking out first and foremost for CERN. So who's to say you shouldn't have taken that pragmatic route, going all the way by squeezing everything possible out of the situation? I'll grant you that. But, I ask you, Carlo, isn't there place for even an itsy-bitsy dose of idealism in this tough, dog-eat-dog world of ours?

"Now, don't get all worked up! I'm almost there. I'd like to comment on just one more thing before getting to my specific questions for you. So bear with me. To make as clear as I can this matter of internationalism in American-European high-energy experimentation, let me go over it briefly. And I do mean brief! Just a couple of minutes, no more than that! Scout's honor! The focus of what I want to talk about is the *entrance fee* for doing experiments. When it first hit you that you might implement its imposition, because of the particular circumstances in the eighties, it may have made a lot of sense. In the first place, the notion wasn't entirely yours. DESY had already used it for its HERA electron-proton collider a few years back. However, when you look at the amount of money involved in that instance, it was chicken feed. Now let's get into the CERN case. Once you got into the act, it was an altogether different story from the DESY one. When you do something, it's bound to be big. Well, what do you expect from big Carlo? So it was that you brought the *entrance fee* into the big-time.

"At the time when you started your drive for the fee, on the political front the SSC was going great guns while the LHC was struggling to stay afloat. Given that condition, it was quite natural for you to be searching for a way to gain some sort of an edge. One thing to do was to propose a scheme that would be of mutual benefit to both projects. It was straightforward and reasonable enough: CERN would make resources available to the SSC, and the U.S. would return the favor with funds for the LHC. Characterized by a quid-pro-quo, it had all the earmarks of a good deal all around. Furthermore, internationalism would flourish, and everyone would be a winner. Could anyone imagine a more perfect scheme?

"But the U.S. procrastinated. You knew, of course, it was all a sham. America wasn't really planning to go along. I can well imagine how you were boiling on the inside. Then, suddenly, a drastic alteration in the political status of the SSC took place. It was a total reversal of fortune. The SSC had come on hard times. Only then did the U.S. adopt the position of buying into the on-the-table internationalism idea. However, at the same time, your anticipated collider found its niche, came into its own, and was smoothly humming along. Try to envisage yourself then: on the European side of the Atlantic, everything was hunky-dory; but there were grim and dire signs coming from the other side. The SSC was in deep trouble. *Three cheers! Bravo!* I can imagine you thinking. But, in the midst of your weasel's glee, it struck you that there was this loose end to deal with: What about your idealistic plan of money passing in both directions across the ocean? Of course, how could you do other than withdraw it? Since the U.S. hadn't accepted it when it had the chance, why should you stick to it with the SSC in the dumps? You therefore had the justification. Just jump the gun and toss the whole plan out the window! And you did. Thus, you returned to the vindictive CERN experimentation policy you really wanted before all this goody-goody internationalism crap raised its head: You demanded that America pay an *entrance fee* for using CERN's experimental facilities.

"Things were beginning to look real good for you, Carlo. With the SSC going down fast, and the LHC shooting ahead at an enviable clip, a state of euphoria came to grip CERN. Having provided your lab with a kind of heaven-on-earth, who would have the audacity to object to anything you did? So your newly introduced international policy on CERN experiments, uncontested, just kept rolling along. Perhaps for the sake of world science you should've reconsidered that policy. But you didn't. Today the impact of your decision is that the SSC-less and substantially weakened U.S. Big Science community is contributing funds for the construction of the LHC facility as payment for no more than the promise of having the privilege of sending American scientists to participate in future experiments there when it comes online. Why did you have to rub salt in the wound? Whatever your reasoning was, there is now an accepted and probably entrenched *entrance fee* for doing experiments in high-energy physics across national borders. I ask you again to recall that the U.S. did not pull the same stunt in the early days when it was way ahead; on the contrary, it stuck by the accepted principle of free access for science that you have now trashed. The claim of scientists worldwide that science is international has become but an empty hope and a long past dream. Free access is no more, and who knows where this trend will lead world science as the days go by.

"Now don't go getting the idea that I'm judging you or taking any particular stand on this issue. In truth, I never believed either that there was a practical possibility for a true form of internationalism to work or that it represented some sort of absolute good. Actually, assessing things rationally, how can you conclude other than that it's nationalism that truly rules over our real world? Just look around you! *What about globalism*, I hear? Don't be silly! That's just an imaginary figment, manufactured by the large worldwide corporate marketers. However, in spite of how clear the opposite is, still, science is dominated by men spouting the internationalism line. So you see, Carlo, you're stuck. You simply can't escape it: you'll always be remembered as the man who burst the high-minded bubble of the internationalists. As for the internationalism-that-could've-been, the fact is that it's become a lost cause. Big Physics will just have to do without it, as, yet again, pragmatism has triumphed over idealism, and this time you were the instrument of its doing."

Mickey got off his chest some troubling things about Carlo that he'd wanted to for years. But it wasn't at all as satisfying as he thought it would be. Actually, it was quite the opposite. He felt ill at ease, to say the least. In fact, the mood of the entire group became highly uncomfortable. An oppressive pall fell over the table. Everyone felt awkward. It was a very unnerving situation. Anxiety ruled as they all tried to anticipate the next step in the action. Carlo was deep in thought, waiting for Mickey to get to those bottom-line questions he kept continually promising to give. As for Mickey, his breathing became irregular, and he had a little difficulty catching his breath at times. He fidgeted about in his chair, and was as nervous as hell. But he had to do something. He couldn't just let the solid effort of the whole day blow up in his face, especially as he was so close to the finishing line. So he began to think of words and phrases – frankly, any kind of nonsense that might free him from the tightness he felt in his chest and abdomen. Then, lo and behold, after only a moment or two, his self-composure returned. From *down* to *up*, just like that! He wasn't sure how the others felt. But he hoped they would take their cues from him.

Although it felt as if it were much longer, the entire dispiriting episode of self-doubt lasted but a minute. Yet, following that bleak and inauspicious minute, he was miraculously transformed into a high-spirited state, eager and bursting to tackle anything that anyone might hurl at him. Now he was gung ho to move on. He felt invincible. Thus, with his spine straight as a board, he defiantly looked Carlo in the eyes, and started in on the questions he'd developed for the *big man* facing him: "First, why did you support ISABELLE so zealously, particularly near its end, when you knew full well that it could only be a threatening drain on American Big Science? And second, why did you knowingly attack and eventually wipe out the vaunted, even though quite unrealistic, principle of free international access for science?" As soon as the two questions fell from his lips, Mickey realized he'd forgotten an important-to-him third issue that he meant to address and that simply couldn't be ignored. He just had to get it in.

Instinctively, before the fast-on-his-feet Carlo could get a word in, and talking with a swiftness he didn't think he had in him, in a manner suggesting he was afraid *the hook* was about to remove him from the stage, Mickey exclaimed: "Hold on, I have a couple of extra-credit questions for you. Even though the answer to the first of them seems to be common knowledge, I thought, *why depend on gossip when I could hear it straight from the horse's mouth.* So here's number one: Was your leaving the DG's office in 1993 forced on you or was it purely voluntary? For number two, I want to ask you something related to the all-absorbing and worthy interest you developed toward the end of your tenure in the matter of how to provide the world with safe and affordable nuclear energy. As an aside, let me say that this subject, of such profound significance to the future of mankind, is certainly deserving of the attention of a man like you. Anyway, my question on this topic is: Was your departure as DG in any way connected with your wish to have CERN be a prime participant in this wild new adventure of yours?"

Mickey paused for a second or two, and breathed an obvious-to-all sigh of relief: "Well, I'm sure you'll all be very happy to hear that I've finished. But, Carlo, before you answer, I want you to know something of my opinion of you. In the matter of the races, one for the W and the other for the building of a supercollider, in my humble view, you won them both fair and square. For the dedication, the spontaneous creativity, the managerial imagination, and the technical inspiration you exhibited in attaining these triumphant ends, you are to be commended, admired, and envied. If there's any meaning at all to the word *genius*, it applies perfectly to you. I salute you for what you've accomplished. I only hope that future generations will remember your selfless sacrifices and your immense contributions." *Here, here*! The chorus chanted. "Carlo," Mickey concluded, "in awaiting your turn to speak, you have shown a great deal of patience, not a quality you're well-known for, I might add. But now, finally, the floor is yours."

Carlo's Case
To Spill the Beans or Not To – That is the Question

"You didn't leave me much time to speak," Carlo began in a teasing manner. Then, addressing Mickey head-on, he continued, "I can see in your face that you're worried. But you know me. You don't have the least reason for concern. So why don't you just sit back and relax! There's lots of time. Besides, everybody knows I'm a fast talker." Mickey took the ragging in stride, but he was starting to feel the heat from the hot seat because Carlo was right-on about the time getting short.

How well the day was going, Mickey thought. What a shame it would be to lose the momentum built up just as it was about to end! Unfortunately, Carlo was just sitting there quietly in solitary contemplation. Why wasn't he opening up? As Mickey anxiously waited for Carlo to get his engine running, his apprehension mounted and intensified. What an opportunity would be wasted if Carlo were to pull out and jump ship! How awful to be left hanging like that! Perish the thought! Well aware that a chance like this would almost certainly not recur, Mickey knew that this was the moment. It was now or never.

No, he vainly tried to reassure himself, the worst simply can't and won't happen. Carlo would surely come through, just as all the others did. There isn't a valid reason in the world to believe otherwise. Still, he couldn't escape a growing uneasiness. He knew it wasn't a rational reaction. Still, there it was. Perhaps his edginess stemmed from his desire to see the day pass without a hitch. On the other hand, maybe it was because he didn't want it to end at all. Well, all that's neither here nor there. But, one thing was sure: Mickey wanted some straight answers from this great hulk of a man. Yes, Carlo had done a lot for Big Science. You might even say he was one of its crown princes. But there was more to his brilliance and to his achievements than meets the eye. There was another side to his story. And that's what Mickey really wanted to uncover. He wanted some light shed on Carlo's dark side. But therein were things that only Carlo could know and talk about. Yes, that was the whole point. It was these hidden secrets – that most enticing part of the unfolding human drama – that Mickey was seeking to draw out of him. However, there was nothing he could do except sit tight and hope, for Carlo held all the cards and it was up to him to play them. Mickey found himself sitting on pins and needles. He wanted to say something that would prod Carlo to get on with it. But he remained silent. He felt in his bones that, in the end, it would be worth waiting for. As for now, he decided it was best to do nothing.

Then, just as if Mickey's wish for Carlo to break out of his funk were granted, Carlo's mood changed. Brightening up and grinning broadly, he conceded, "OK, I give in." Even though Carlo spoke with that inimitable gruff tone of his, to Mickey it sounded light and airy. To him, it was very reassuring. The important thing was that Carlo appeared to be friendly; and Mickey interpreted that to mean he would be forthcoming and responsive. In that same manner, Carlo continued: "I guess it's your lucky day, Mickey. In thinking about my situation, I swayed this way and that. Should I defend myself? Should I answer some of those vile insults you leveled at me? Should I lower myself and respond to some of that crap you were spouting? Or maybe I should say to you, *drop dead, I'm outta here*! After all, what's done is done. Why dig up old wounds? I know the others have done it. But I'm a free agent. I can think for myself. I can be different if I so choose. The point is that it was up to me to decide. So, back and forth I went. This way and that! First yes, then no, and so on! But then, suddenly, something crept into my consciousness that flashed the verdict in my mind. You see, while you were asking your questions you appeared to be so serious. I know it sounds strange, but as I gazed at you, in spite of some of those ugly thoughts that were coming out of your mouth, I sort of liked you. In a way, although I can't explain it, I felt sorry for you. I never expected you to be the way you were, and I certainly never expected that reaction from me. Nevertheless, that's exactly what happened. Anyway, as you were speaking, at one moment I simply wasn't hearing what was being said, and I vowed: *Carlo, be restrained and give him what he wants*. Now, I want you to know that, contrary to the gossip about me, I do sometimes keep my promises. At least I keep the ones I make to myself. Well, I do sometimes. In any case, you'll be happy to hear that I intend to honor that commitment I made in the privacy of my own mind. I'm going to tell it like it is. I'm going to give you the raw, unvarnished truth. You really don't deserve it, the way you've been carrying on. But, fine chap that I am, I'm nonetheless going to give you what you've been angling for."

Carlo's Case
Good Citizen or Artful Equivocator?

"First, to the question of my supporting ISABELLE in 1983: the answer is, *yes, I did.* When I met privately with Wallenmeyer, I told him I thought it was better to get the project done than to stop it in midstream. I told him that it was bad to set a precedent of canceling a big project that had gone so far. I told him it was bad politically, and it was bad for all physicists, everywhere. I told him that it would be highly beneficial to his program were a U.S. lab to gain the experience of running a two-ring collider. I told him that it would be equally worthwhile and advantageous for the American high-energy program to have experimentalists working with the unique kind of particle events that such a collider would provide, *jets* in particular. Boy, was he pleased to hear all this! He was taking notes furiously. I could even see the beginnings of a smile sneaking through. Then we got to the technical matters, and abruptly things took a full one hundred and eighty degree turn.

"The two big technical questions-de-jour were: One, was the machine design workable, and more, was it optimal? And two, were the current ISABELLE magnets the right ones to use, and were they practical to make in large numbers? On these questions, as it ended up, I said virtually nothing. But I'm compelled to emphasize to you that it wasn't for lack of trying. I know that the picture I'm painting doesn't sound too believable. But, I assure you that it's so. Here's the way it went: Whenever a technical issue would enter the discussion that cast the slightest doubt on ISABELLE as it was, Wallenmeyer always managed to change the subject. Make no mistake about it: It was quite deliberate. He just didn't seem to want to delve into such matters or press such points. That put me in a very tough spot: Did he really want to know about any technical problems in ISABELLE? Did he really want to know if any changes might help the project? Did he really want to know how much such changes might cost and how long they might delay the project's completion? Did he really want to know what I thought about the machine design at all? Presumably not!

"Given that the ISABELLE project meant so much to the future of high-energy physics, and the fact that I had a lot to say about whether its design was reasonable or could be improved, you can understand that I didn't give up easily, but tried to squeeze the subject in. Going about it in a roundabout way, I used every gimmick I had in my arsenal: I spoke in generalities about possible delays and cost overruns. I hinted at probable start-up difficulties. At one point, I even said it could be a nightmare. But all I got were blank stares, non-sequiter-like responses, and eventually subject-changing. Maybe going about it in that circuitous and oblique manner was a mistake. Perhaps I should've been more direct. Perhaps I should've been stubborn and persistent. But it was his show. After all, I was but his guest, invited to help him. The agenda was his to make as he saw fit. I was there to answer his questions and give my views when asked. I couldn't just up and hit him between the eyes. Besides, it all happened so fast. Anyway, in the end, all my efforts to say the things I wanted to say about the ISABELLE design were in vain. Knowing how things transpired, it's obvious that I didn't have the effect of changing his mind in the least. My suspicion, in hindsight, is that *the deal was in*: His mind was made up from the very start that there was to be no change from what BNL wanted. And, you know, no matter how persuasive you might be, you can't impact a closed mind.

"Now, Mickey, you brought up the proposal made by Leon and Bob to use Fermilab magnets in ISABELLE. On that point I want to tell you as precisely and bluntly as I can what I actually said: I told Bill in no uncertain terms that, given the nature and the number of W events that we were getting at CERN, the Fermilab-type magnets, because they would allow the generation of more than sufficient collision energy, would be perfectly suitable as replacements to the magnets already incorporated in the existing ISABELLE design. True, by then it was too late for ISABELLE to be first to get the W. I'd already announced its discovery. Still, it would've been good for ISABELLE to get running as quickly as was humanly possible. But as soon as I alluded to the Fermilab magnets, Bill seemed to clam up. I got the impression that it was somehow threatening to him. I should've expected what happened then. But I was just a little slow on the uptake, and once again I was caught unawares and surprised out of my mind. Imagine, I wasn't asked to elaborate on the point: to lay down some details as to why I felt the ISABELLE tunnel should be filled with Fermilab magnets and to explain why I disapproved of what BNL was doing. As it happened, it was almost as if I hadn't brought up the topic at all. Wallenmeyer simply ignored anything I said about it. Then, to top it all off, when I wasn't asked about what I thought the chances were of the then-constituted ISABELLE design working, I knew it was useless to pursue talk of the design any further. So I simply dropped the subject of the machine entirely.

"Moving on, I have to tell you Mickey that I'm beginning to get the hang of how your mind works. I can prove it to you by telling you right now what you're thinking." Carlo had a mischievous, yet playful expression on his round, red face, as he mimicked Mickey's thoughts in a mocking tone: "*Hah! I've got it. Carlo actually wanted this meeting with Bill to come out exactly as it did. Sure, he even maneuvered the discussion so that Wallenmeyer would reject his support of the Fermilab magnet scheme and simply follow ISABELLE and BNL down the road to ruin. That's what he really wanted – to see the U.S. flounder and fall.* Well, Mickey, maybe you've got a point there. Maybe in the dark recesses of my mind I was happy to see the U.S. pursuing an almost sure-fire road to misery and failure. But, to go any further along those lines, I'm afraid I'll have to direct you to Doctor Freud."

Carlo stopped for a moment, seeming to take some ironic pleasure in having owned up to the possibility that he could actually embrace such a devious concealed motive. However, he wasn't ready to share his thoughts and feelings about it more than he already had. Maybe he hadn't explored it any further than that. On the other hand, maybe there simply wasn't any more to tell. In any case, the fact is that he'd admitted harboring a hidden secret, and what a juicy one it was. Unfortunately, he just wouldn't elaborate on it any further. Then, in the blink of an eye, Carlo completely changed course and altered his tone to suit the conclusion of his ISABELLE remarks. Proceeding in a matter-of-fact style, he gave his last words on the subject: "Taking everything into account, I gave Bill my considered opinion that ISABELLE should not be canceled. That's it! Simple, wouldn't you say? With that, I trust that I've taken care of your first question. So now let me get on with the second one."

Carlo's Case
Competition in the Marketplace, That's the Ticket!

"To begin with, does anyone in the least doubt that the instruments of Big Science are getting bigger and more costly? Furthermore, is there any doubt that this will only intensify as we move into the future? No, I imagine no one questions these trends. Even more, I'm surely not too far off in presuming that we all take these as self-evident truths. Getting bigger is just a fact of life in our modern world, and it's my guess that it's in our best interest to come to terms with it. So, I ask you, what does this mean for high-energy experimentation? Surely there's no mystery here: There'll simply be fewer experimental setups built and fewer experiments. It follows then, by straightforward rational deduction, that making the same types of big machines and big experimental pieces of equipment in different places – systems that do much the same thing – is just throwing good money down the rat-hole. Anyway, if we don't constrain ourselves, certainly our governments will make sure that we don't act in so foolish and extravagant a manner. Fashioning twin facilities in this new age of bigness is simply a luxury science can't afford.

"So where do we stand? Well, the fact of the matter is that accelerator facilities have already gotten to the point that duplicate machines are passé. Therefore, I contend that we must change our ways of doing business. We can't just continue to compete in the same way as we've done all these years, where we build a similar machine on each side of the Atlantic and then run like hell to get the golden goose first. Now, remember, I didn't say that competition is out the window, only that duplication is. Sure, competitiveness is only human. It's just that, for the next colliders, and on into the future, competition must and will take on a different form.

"Let's look a little more closely at this new state of affairs. Consider the scenario where one country or region invests a substantial amount of capital in a facility, while the others, for one reason or another, don't. Think of it: One has expended a lot of its resources and the others remain free of this cost. You must admit that it is hardly fair for all the countries and regions interested to have open access to do experiments at that facility totally free of obligation. There has to be some sort of quid pro quo. You've got to give in order to get. That's what makes the socio-economic world go round. But if any given country can't compete at the level of offering its own facility in return for using another's, then what? Can anyone suggest a better mechanism than requiring a payment of one kind or another? After all, isn't that exactly the kind of situation money was invented for?

"Turning to another scenario, suppose there were complementary facilities in two separate areas roughly equal in value and cost. Rather than going through the time and effort consumed in the bureaucratic process of each paying the other, they might simply choose the open facility route and waive the *access fees*. Since there are no apparent cost transfers, an outsider might well have the impression that he was witnessing a system with free and open access. Not so! What's happening is that payments are indeed being made; but rather than in hard cash, it is in the form of compensation-in-kind. In case you haven't noticed, let me point out that this is essentially the manner in which high energy facilities have been functioning on an international scale for nigh onto four decades. Unfortunately, with the coming of the super machines, times have changed. We must simply face the reality that complementary or duplicate facilities are a luxury of the past, and can be no more. In the present time, as the twenty-first century dawns, the *access fee* issue that was always there, lurking unseen in the background, has found its way to the surface and is now visible for all to see.

"You know it really pisses me off the way all those idealists are going around pinning a label on me, identifying me as the one who conjured up and put into practice the *access fee* they consider to be such a dastardly thing. What a bunch of phonies! Using an *access fee* is quite a natural thing for men to do. I didn't plan it. There was nothing sinister behind it. It is nothing but a quirk of history that it came to Big Science with such a bang at the time and place it did. It's just that when it occurred, it was I who happened to be in the driver's seat.

"How laughable it is the way they hearken back to the post World War II period when America was handing out free chocolates and other goodies to all! What nonsense! How can they compare the state of the world then, when Europe was devastated and in ruins, with the state the world's in now? The analogy is hollow, misleading, and specious. Look, Europe and America are now on an essentially equal footing, and the economy has become global and highly competitive. That's the reality! Today's world is a far cry from the forties. We're living in a time of delicate, perhaps even unstable economic equilibrium. If one side were to give away candy bars in this day and age, it might just be giving away the whole store.

"And that's exactly the way it is with Big Science! So, when you look at the situation in a realistic manner, what alternative is there for science but to imitate the hardhearted market place: place your bet on hard-nosed negotiating, and charge whatever the prevailing conditions demand? Unless someone can come up with a better solution, and I challenge anyone to do so, levying what you call an *entrance fee* seems quite a proper and fair procedure. It's simply part of man's social nature. Besides, it's been going on all the time anyway.

"Getting back to Americans being such goody-goodies way back when, although I shouldn't be preaching to you, especially in these final minutes, I must emphasize that today we're living in a new era: The past is over and done with, and it is futile to try to keep it alive. Living in the present must be the rule for our fast-changing science. Resisting the inevitable and holding back progress, trying to recover the *good old days*, can only risk having the whole edifice we've spent so many years building come crashing down on us. Come to think of it, you don't really believe those days back then were that good anyway, do you?"

Carlo's Case
Paying the Price

"OK, it's about time I took on your extra-credit questions. All in all, I think you got it right. Yes, I got shot down. Yes, part of the reason was that I sought to widen CERN's mission and outlook to include things like the world's certain-to-come power shortage. Yes, another reason was my brash, overbearing personality. Yes, another was that I would bulldoze right over anybody standing in my way. Yes, another was that I made a lot of enemies along the way, obviously, too many. Yes, for all these reasons, I did become a CERN persona-non-grata, or should I say DG-non-grata. And, as you know, in the end, I paid the price.

"On the *why-I-had-to-go* question, let me add a footnote for clarification. Although not too dissimilar from what you said, it has somewhat of a different flavor and emphasis. You see, the men of CERN, to their very core, from the highest member-state representatives to the lowliest technicians, wanted their lab to be solely a high-energy one. On that they were unified. It was to be nothing else. Period! The very thought of moving into a practical field like nuclear energy and being responsible for solving real world problems filled those in charge with high anxiety.

"However, I marched to the beat of my own drummer and didn't abide by this viewpoint. I wanted CERN to move in this direction, away from pure science toward the applied kind. I pushed for it. I insisted on it. I was actually in the process of doing it, regardless of what anybody else thought. I'm sure you can appreciate that to those really leading the CERN parade, my obstinacy and my actions were intolerable. So, I think, when push came to shove, they had to rid themselves of me at the very first opportunity they could, before I moved them irrevocably on a course they simply didn't want to be on. Yes, that obviously played a role, maybe even a big one." Carlo paused as if meditating, and then smiled with a touch of naughtiness, "On the whole, they probably just didn't like my style." With that, Carlo Rubbia, great scientist and great man, straightened his spine, leaned backward in his chair, laid the palms of his clasped hands, with fingers intertwined, on the back of his head, and laughed heartily. In this manner did *Carlo the Magnificent* finish his delivery with the flourish expected of an Italian romantic!

* * * * *

Day's End

Mickey was struck dumb and didn't have a clue about what to do. The only thing he seemed to be certain of was that this special day was rapidly coming to an end. Stunned and sitting motionlessly, a mixture of feelings rushed through him: relief that the day went so well, but also a profound sadness because something he so desperately and irrationally wanted to hold on to was fast fading away, dissolving before his very eyes. However, that moment at day's end was one for doing, not thinking. There was simply no time for reflection. The hour set for his departure was speedily approaching. There was no appealing that reality. There would be no extensions. The end was marked in stone and was unalterable. Mickey had no choice but to face up to it: It would be as it was preset and agreed to. In a flash of whimsy, he wondered whether there was a pumpkin in his future.

Just then, Mickey was jarred out of his momentary paralysis by the shifting and stirring around him. He looked up and saw the famous four men he'd spent the last two and a half hours with getting up from the table. They acted in a surprisingly casual manner: stretching, gabbing, and even yawning. Following their lead, Mickey also rose. He gazed at them, and involuntarily, from the bottom of his heart, a smile materialized. He felt his face becoming flushed as well as some sweat being released onto his brow. He was now running fully on instinct. In a natural and deliberate manner, he approached each of the four men in turn. Teary-eyed, he gratefully hugged each of them in a gracious gesture of goodbye. What a sublimely warm and sorrowfully sweet parting of the ways it was! Not a single word was spoken.

Then, with amazing suddenness, a disorienting sequence of things came about: the blond, who'd brought Mickey to the annex, appeared from out of nowhere. She grasped his left hand tightly in hers, and swiftly whisked him out the door he'd come through earlier. The quick turn of events both dazed and unnerved him; and his free will seemed to be switched off. Even though his mind screamed *no*, his body, sheep-like, seemed to be responding to the will of a prior understanding. He wanted to stop the flow of time so that he could think things through, but there was precious little chance of that. His time had run out! As he passed through the doorway, he looked back, hoping – almost expecting – to see four smiling faces. But the alcove was empty. Stepping into the garden patio, the blond was at his side, holding his hand, and directing his every move. It was then he knew for sure that it was all over.

Exiting the Mountain Retreat

The Blond Takes Charge

Dark was settling in as Mickey and his sleek partner moved smartly along the patio walkway. To his left, he could still see some brightness in the western sky on the far side of the mountain range where the sun still shone. Elsewhere the brilliance of the stars filled the night. The awesome panorama reminded him of man's insignificant place in the scheme of things; but, at the same time, of how lucky he was to be favored with life, the most resplendent gift the gods can give. He followed the blond as they walked quickly northward past the back of the Moulin Rouge. Then they proceeded down an extension of the walkway, heading across a lawn toward a wooded area.

Beginning to relax, Mickey relished his view of the blond striding along with such determination, such confidence in the perfection of her carriage, such certainty of purpose, and such grace of deportment and movement. Moving blindly, he tried to imitate her rhythm, but fell a few paces back. But then something quite curious took place in Mickey's mind. A line was somehow crossed: It was as if he'd become hypnotized. Later, he would try to understand or explain how and why he fell under the spell of this captivating jewel, this *beau idéal*. But with little success! Still, the fact remains: Although surrendering himself in such a manner was not typical of Mickey, he did nonetheless fall for this to-die-for, statuesque goddess. And what, you might ask, did this imply? What ensued was that while in the grip of this trance-like state, there was generated in him an uncanny sense of serenity and security that quickly overspread his being. But that wasn't the whole of it. So magnetic was his attraction, so compelling was his subconscious urge to place himself in her hands, that he yielded to her his full trust.

When the seductively pretty mademoiselle reached the edge of the grass, she turned and flirtatiously wagged a finger in playful reproach at Mickey's sluggish pace. With her hands placed girlishly on her hips and her shoulders tilted back, feigning a supercilious air, she made a mocking gesture as if to say, *well, why are you so slow*? Accompanying this theatrical chiding was such an endearing and enticing smile that Mickey couldn't do other than melt into willing compliance. Thus, he speeded up, and in doing so became hers to direct. Mickey marveled that such a natural, everyday sequence of acts could generate such a potent emotional impact on him. But it did. In this way, he became what so many had before him: a man smitten by a sweet woman cum girl. As such, he became free and easy, released from the many cares simmering inside him. If perchance there still remained the least amount of incipient anxiety in him, it was scotched well before it could materialize. As he approached her, with her smiling face awaiting him, she stretched out her arms, turned, and grasped his left arm as she had done a few hours earlier. So, arm in arm, they strutted with child-like abandon into the tree-filled tract behind the cafés on the north side of the *boulevard*.

Fearlessly, the couple entered a shadowy passageway, lit mainly by the moonlight shining through the trees. As Mickey's eyes became accustomed to the dark, he began to make out that they were gliding smoothly along a narrow clay pathway with dim lights at foot level along both sides. A little hunched over, cautiously eyeing the branches whistling past close to their heads, the pair hustled along. Every now and then Mickey could see a full moon through the breaks in the brush above. Although he should've been frazzled and sweating bullets in that spooky environment he'd set foot in, this brief excursion in the woods only served to reinforce the composed disposition, the peace of mind, and the devil-may-care sangfroid Mickey first came to feel once the blond took charge. So it was that all the fatiguing tension and mental strain of his wonder-filled afternoon happening simply faded away and vanished into thin air.

Mickey wondered at the incongruity of his reaction to the situation he was in: he didn't know where he was; his skin felt clammy; thorns were brushing his cheeks; and he hadn't the faintest idea of where he was going. Where were the concerns, the distress, the apprehension, the agitation, and the sinking stomach? Where indeed? They should've been there, but they weren't. As it was, for no reason he could figure out, he instead was exhilarated and euphoric. With poise and self-confidence abounding, although there were no logical grounds for him to be feeling that way, he was ready to take on whatever the future held in store.

Could it really have been the presence of the blond beauty that changed him from a sad sack to an I-can-do-anything romantic? *Naw*! Mickey thought. Then, for a brief interval, rationality returned to him. From front to back, top to bottom, he pondered over everything that had taken place since he left the Moulin Rouge with her. He reckoned that it couldn't be all these ultimately commonplace acts of life that turned his mind around. After all, their purpose was merely to get him from one place to another. No, the basis for such an attitude transformation had to be something that carried meaning and consequence for him, something that held some gravitas – yes, something that mattered deeply to him. Then he suddenly glommed onto the reason it had to be. How could he have missed it? Surely, it was because of the dazzling success of his day in wonderland. That's right! It had to be! The blond didn't cause the change; she only triggered it. Of course, there wasn't any doubt about it.

At that insightful instant, he grasped the full extent of the holiness of what had truly happened to him. Yes, this was the day that for Mickey was that once-in-a-lifetime, not-to-be-forgotten flash of grace in the vast eternity of time. Recognizing that it was incumbent on him not to let it slip from his mind and so consign it to oblivion, he knew he had to commit it to memory. So he began to do so, trying with all his might, with everything he could muster. However, just then, before he could pursue this undertaking any further, the forest boundary appeared and his nature interlude came to an abrupt end.

It's a Hideaway!

As the pair exited the trail into a grassy area, the blond released her hold on Mickey and, walking in front of him, moved a little ahead. They stepped onto a reddish brick crosswalk, and Mickey chuckled imperceptibly as the Wizard's yellow brick road came to mind. Looking ahead, he did a double take as he saw before him a wide roadway about fifteen yards from the wood's edge. *There really is a way to get in and out of this off-the-beaten-track compound*, he thought. Was this how he had arrived there, he wondered? If so, his memory of it was blank. Yet it was possible. Peering at the road intently, he deduced that it did in fact look wide enough to be a thoroughfare. This being the case, he was much amused at the notion that this could really be the *boulevard* taking you to where *broken dreams* had their resting place. *Stop this nonsense*, he chided himself! If he was to have any chance to discover his whereabouts, he knew that he would have to get more serious and bring to an end this quite unhelpful whimsicality.

Where was he anyway? Although disoriented, he made an effort to find some clues. He noticed that the street, lighted by lamps with a bright, silver-like glow, was empty as far as he could see in both directions, east and west he surmised. Squinting so as to see as far as he could, he could detect not a trace of either buildings or people. Only isolation and emptiness prevailed. However, at the roadside right in front of him was stationed a prestigious-looking black stretch limo parked at the end of the brick path. It seemed to Mickey to be the type of vehicle you'd use for VIPs. *How about that*, he thought, *I'm a VIP*. Standing beside the limo was a medium height muscular man, obviously the driver, holding open the curbside rear door. He had a ruddy face with strong bony features. His official-looking gray flat-topped cap with black visor covered most of his black, brilliantined hair; and, along with his black tie, he was wearing a dark suit with a high-buttoned jacket. As Mickey came closer to the car, he caught a glimpse of the wide sidewalk at the end of the brick pathway. When he was almost there, still a slight distance behind the blond, Mickey noticed that standing a couple of feet in front of the limo driver was Virginia Holt.

Virginia welcomed the newly arrived pair approaching her. She nodded to the young blond, and extended her arms toward Mickey, clasping her hands around his arms in a kind of semi-hug. She was smiling as she greeted him amiably and graciously with the comment: "Bon soir, glad to see you again." Mickey was somewhat taken aback by her warmth and cordiality. In trying to respond in kind, he returned the smile. Unfortunately for him, the words accompanying the gesture came out a jumble. Virginia was a little unsure of what Mickey said, but she believed it sounded like, *moi aussi*.

Mickey could kick himself for being nervous at a time like that. Bloody anxiety! It prevented him from exhibiting that suave manner and assured self-control he so wanted to project. From then on, he knew he would be seen as a bumbling academic. What a bummer! Well, there's nothing that could be done about it now, he thought, you just have to take things as they come. He was thankful, however, that Virginia appeared to be in a relaxed mood, revealing a bonhomie and genial spirit Mickey wasn't privy to in his first encounter with her. She turned toward the blond and said something to her that Mickey missed. Seeing Virginia in a tête-à-tête with her younger associate, most likely her assistant, Mickey grabbed the opportunity to take up his preoccupation with the *boulevard*.

Mickey noted that toward the east, the direction in which the limo was pointing, the road split into a divided highway about a hundred yards away. Soon after that, the sole visible in-out artery curved slightly northward into the darkness and out of sight. Following the road and looking upward, Mickey could see that the road had to be heading right into a distant mountain range to the north that up to then he had been totally oblivious of. With that added piece of information, he quickly figured out that the east and west mountain ranges were linked by a northern range, which implied an extensive, connected chain. Looking first to the north, then to the east, and then west, he realized that the mountains he had just become aware of formed the northern wall of a natural rampart that shielded the village enclave from the outside world. Even though he couldn't establish for sure the existence of a southern range, he felt quite confident in inferring that such a wall was there. That would then complete the total mountainous confinement of this mysterious fairy-tale world where past dreams are relived. *Wow*! Mickey thought. *This is a place deliberately designed to ensure absolute seclusion and privacy. Now, who could've imagined such a thing?* Suddenly, a feeling of puzzlement mixed with awe overtook him: *Who actually makes it work? Who controls it? Certainly not the two women who appear to run it! Then who?*

The Toast

Mickey turned his head, and found himself looking into Virginia's fascinating and enticing dark eyes. Her face was bursting with sensuousness and graced with an alluring smile. Her voice had that special feminine quality to it, filled with temptation and promise. To his utter relief, she was *poles apart* from what she was like in their afternoon encounter. Still, she spoke in a manner perfectly befitting the occasion, with just the right dose of polite formality: She told him that her *Petit Village* was especially pleased to have him as a guest, and asked if his day was productive and to his complete satisfaction. A smile began to take shape on Mickey's face as he nodded in the affirmative. But apparently he hesitated just a bit too long. Before he could shape and express an answer that adequately described his appreciation for the opportunity given him, before he could utter a sound, Virginia interjected a follow-up. With highly engaging graciousness, she went on to tell him that the village would welcome a future opportunity to serve his needs and wishes. The surprise of that last remark really put a clamper on Mickey's usual tendency to be talkative – perhaps long-winded would be more accurate! He wanted to say, *when*? But he was suffering from some kind of shock and couldn't get the word out. Whatever the reason, the fact is that he found himself speechless in the presence of this tantalizing, exciting super-beauty. The best he could do was to bow his head slightly to show his appreciation.

Yes indeed, Mickey was very much taken by Virginia, by her exquisite charm, by her mesmerizing magnetism. Thereby under her spell, what wouldn't he do for her? And this was exactly the way she wanted it. Oh yes, she knew well of the susceptibility of vulnerable men to women's captivating allure. Control is what she sought, and control is what she got. At this time extended conversation was not in the cards, and she had prepared perfectly for how to gain that end. Mickey was meant to wait silently for the next act in the drama to unfold, and that is what he did. In the meantime, echoing in his mind was the thought of whether she truly meant that little bombshell she let out moments before. What ecstasy, what a thrill it would be if he were actually permitted some day to return to this place as close to paradise as men can aspire to come!

Virginia turned her head to face the blond, and in a low and pleasing voice introduced her, "Mickey, this is Elise." Wide-eyed, Mickey took a step toward Elise, looked at her straight-on and, finding his capacity to speak returned, slowly and confidently articulated a winning observation: "What a perfect name for so lovely a companion; but I must complain that our time together has been far too brief." Finally he knew her name, Mickey thought.

Then, before Mickey could savor his witty opening remark to the woman he now knew as Elise, all grew silent. Without direction, the three spontaneously formed a small circle and took each other's hands. It was as if they were trying to protect each other from the black void engulfing them in the valley of dreams. So was ushered in a tender and magical moment. No words were spoken, but it was evident that in their brief time together, they'd come to share a bond of fondness and affection for each other. Elise took a step forward toward the center of the circle and looked dreamily straight up into the night sky. Sweet, youthful, and wonderfully desirable, she shone as dazzlingly as the most brilliant star in the sky. Human, yes, but she was a radiant source of luminous brightness that lit up the bleak and dark emptiness that was a perfectly appropriate backdrop for the gateway to the *Boulevard of Broken Dreams*. They held each other ever so tightly, as the mountains encircling them loomed menacingly. As it turned out, Elise's mystically reverential ceremonial-like performance was the climax of this flash of transcendence that swept over them. Then suddenly the moment was gone. How fleeting it was! It was over almost before it started. Later Mickey was to question whether the whole episode was real or only imagined. Can one truly trust one's memory of such a deliriously spiritual moment? Actually, when you come to think of it: does it really matter whether it was fact or fiction? Of course it matters; and Mickey was always to believe in his heart that it did indeed happen.

The limo driver appeared to relay a signal to Virginia, who moved the few steps toward him. She conferred with him briefly and then returned. She then motioned for Mickey to follow her into the limo. Elise seemed to sense a cue and entered close behind Mickey. The driver stood outside waiting. Once the three were inside, the scene there was right out of a romantic novel. Mickey was seated between two fascinating women of mystery. He was starry-eyed and at a loss as to what it all meant. *Anything's possible*, he thought. Virginia, to his left, pressed a button and a tray flipped out of the partition between the front and back sections of the limo. On the tray, locked in metal strips were wineglasses and a bottle of Chateauneuf-du-Pap. Virginia released them and the driver opened the door on her side and popped the cork. While pouring the three glasses to the brim, Virginia said, "I want to propose a toast." Smiling and sitting at the edge of the car's backseat, Elise and Mickey turned to face Virginia. As all three raised their glasses, Virginia continued, "We at *Le Petit Village* honor the *Players* for their achievements on the stage. However, recognizing that all who are human must in the end meet their destinies *avec tristesse*, we offer solace to the few who have tempted the gods and risked their souls. *Aux Joueurs*." And so in ironic amusement and delight they drank to the *Players*, their inspirational feats of the spirit, and their ultimate ends in sadness.

Virginia continually refilled the glasses. A second bottle was opened as the party continued. They laughed; they moved their bodies about; they intermittently touched; and they gazed at each other with smiling faces. There were sounds of clanking glasses; there were sounds of their shifting about; there were sounds of sighing and the like; and there were sounds of merriment, of joviality, and of fun. Wordlessly, the three sipped the wine and surrendered to their mirth until the emptying of the second bottle signaled the arrival of parting time. The driver noiselessly opened the left rear door, cleaned the tray, and lifted it back into its slot. He then walked around the car and opened the right rear door.

Rather than immediately exiting, Elise instead edged her upper body toward Mickey. She held his head firmly and slowly pressed her full-bodied moist lips onto his right cheek. As the warmth of her touches and her sweet reassuring fragrance penetrated and overspread his being, he felt as if he were riding the sky on a soft bed of clouds. Here was the scholar, the technocrat, the man of science, and the intellectual trapped in the net of a romantic illusion. But to Mickey, at that instant, it was nothing less than a heaven-sent experience to be savored. For a time, he tried to say something. But soon he gave up. Relieved of the capacity to think clearly, he willingly surrendered himself to the moment and to the divine Elise, the sparkling enchantress who held on her lips the wishes, the dreams, and the promise of eternity. She lingered awhile, as Mickey, having lost his bearings, bathed in her aura. But, as do all things of finite lifetime, this happening had to end. Only too quickly, the last tick of the clock sounded. Elise murmured, "Bonne nuit, à bientôt." During all the time she spent with Mickey that day, these were the only words that flowed between those lovely lips. As she spoke them, soft and low, she gracefully backed away and stepped out onto the pavement. Mickey, transfixed, watched longingly as she moved up the brick path in a spirited gait and disappeared into the nature trail.

Virginia seemed pleased with the way things were going. Looking fresh and clearly in charge, she waited for Mickey to regain his composure. When he did, she asked if he was satisfied and happy, and whether there was anything else he needed that came to mind. Mickey answered unthinkingly that he was very happy and that nothing more could be done for him. He wanted to say how much he appreciated her efforts and how she was perfection personified. But, still a bit bewildered by all that was taking place, he couldn't access the words in his overloaded, befuddled brain. In this way, the urge to express these as well as other thoughts simply passed on. There was no getting around it. Uncharacteristically, Mickey was quite off balance. Unquestioning and compliant, he just wasn't his usual self. In direct contrast, Virginia, self-assured and obviously experienced in matters relating to human feelings, knew exactly what she was doing, and was in full command of the situation. Sticking to the schedule set for her, while at the same time remaining unhurried and maintaining an intimate and gracious solicitousness, she told him the ride back would last through the night and he would arrive on Long Island in the early morning. She continued, "If you must contact the driver, knock on the glass panel. You may call him by his given name, Ron. But I really doubt that any such contact will be necessary. So sit back, relax, and enjoy the ride; and you'll be home in no time."

Just then the door on her side opened. Virginia moved to the front edge of her seat and turned toward Mickey. With an endearingly appealing smile, she nudged closer to him, and looked tenderly into his eyes. Sitting there face-to-face, only a few inches apart, he stared at her and felt a profound yearning for something he knew not what. He had an inclination to stretch out and hold her, but he was paralyzed. He gazed into her dark eyes. In the cloudiness of a dazed stupor, he was deluded into imagining her to be a true goddess. Of course, there was nothing to that. She indeed was real flesh and blood, as she soon proved. He could see a few tears on her cheeks as she stroked the right side of his head and gently moved her soft lips, in all their fullness, toward his left cheek. She kissed him affectionately, ever so slowly. He could feel her heartbeat, her deep breathing, and her thrilling body close to his. To Mickey, her scents were nothing short of bliss. Then, without warning, she whispered, "Au revoir, mon cher." With that she backed out of the limo as Mickey followed her every move with longing in his heart. In quick succession, both rear doors were closed, the driver took his place, the engine began to purr, and the car pulled away from the curb, moving quickly eastward. Mickey looked back, and his last image of *Le Petit Village* was Virginia standing on the *boulevard*, waving goodbye.

Going Home

Mickey was spent. He sat in the back seat dazed and immobilized, as the car sped along the highway toward the mountains to the northeast. He stayed motionless for a long while. When finally he was able to compose himself, the memory sectors of his mind were in overload: images and thoughts were flashing through so fast that he couldn't latch onto any of them. He tried the well-known rational approach of taking one thought at a time, but it was no use. *Well, c'est la vie*, he thought, persuading himself that for now it would be best simply to become resigned to his plight and to *just let it be*. But he resolved that at the first opportunity he would set down a record of what truly happened on that extraordinary day. As the dark tunnel engulfed him and he began to doze off, he thought, *what a story it's going to make!*

9. Dinner with Izzie

Mickey and Izzie

They met at the turn of the century, just as civilization was entering a new millennium - the third since the birth of Christ marked the starting point for man's destined journey into the modern world of industry and technology. This coming together of these two men from opposite ends of the science totem pole was not an earth-shaking event. It was merely two and a half hours of spirited discussion. Yet it meant the world to Mickey. Brief as it was, he had this time alone with Izzie. There was no interference from outsiders. That's the way it was set up. It was just the two of them: man-to-man, face-to-face. Or, perhaps the encounter would better be described as toe-to-toe. *Imagine*, Mickey remembered thinking, *what a coup*! Actually, it was highly unlikely that these two would ever meet, considering the large chasm between their standings in the science community. But, to Mickey's good fortune, America is a country with the distinction that such things did indeed happen, because it is a land where class distinction is fuzzy, and class separation weak, no doubt the weakest it's ever been in man's long and tortuous social history.

Izzie was a man of immense stature, in stark and humorous contrast to his meager height. Still, even standing only five feet tall, he had an intense presence, as merits a man of consequence. He simply oozed distinction and prestige. After all, he was a genius; he was a virtuoso; he was a star. His peerless, world-beating quality radiated from every part of his being: from the way he walked, from the way he talked, from the way he carried himself, from his air of supreme confidence, and from his secure sense of self as number one. When Izzie entered a room, true, you might at first think him to be quite ordinary. But, in no time flat, you'd have to be pretty dense not to perceive those commanding and dominating waves of social power emanating from his peasant-stock stubby build. Yes, he was physically small, but he shone like the brightest star in the sky.

When you initially caught sight of Izzie, here was the well-dressed Herr Doctor Professor. Yet there was no confusing him with the stodgy, formal, and ivory-towered expectation that such a label brings to mind. His sparkling eyes glowed through his old-fashioned horn-rimmed glasses; his biting tongue reflected that of a man who had lived to his fullest capacity both in academia and on the street; and his wry smile evinced an ironic sense of humor shaped by his experience, his pride, and his appreciation of life. A man of great resolve and purpose, not one easily denied what he sought, Izzie walked through life's corridors leaving in his wake a long string of triumphs and achievements. With his brilliant mind ever churning at full-tilt, he earned his way to fulfillment, esteem, and fame. As for the rest of us, we are all the better for what he did to deserve these gifts of honor.

Izzie was something of a chameleon: a man of many guises, who appeared in a variety of widely differing functions – all requiring specialized and advanced competence and capabilities. First and foremost, he was a teacher and a scientist. As a nuclear physicist, he was nonpareil, and his work garnered for him the Nobel Prize in 1944. He was a statesman at ease in the presence of no less than the U.S. President, this being his playing level at the game of advice and influence. Also down to earth, he did his duty in the World War II effort as one of that breed of soldier-physicists who formed spontaneously to defend the motherland and build the bomb. It was that experience that shaped in him a new capability and a new role: After the war, he became Rabi, the manager and the builder. He was of that rare class of men who have the capacity to build an institution. How extraordinary he was: taking his idea from its conceptualization to its place on the drawing board and then to its palpable glorious existence. So, you see, there's more to Rabi than meets the eye. OK, chance happened to place him in a little frame, but who would deign to question what a *big man* he became?

Almost diametrically Izzie's opposite, Mickey, physically a lot bigger, was substantially smaller in status and scientific track record. Yet, peculiarly enough, the two had much in common. In many ways, they were rather alike. They both loved science and were willing to give much of their lives to further it. They were both scientists, although Mickey was nowhere near being a Nobelist. They were both builders of management systems, but, far from Izzie's crowning institution-creation, Mickey could only eke out a somewhat small administrative structure. Izzie created a national laboratory from the ground up. Mickey could never match this and aimed far lower. Still, he crafted and gave rise to a uniquely original education-centered organization within the already existing national lab system. No doubt many would consider it only a minor accomplishment; but Mickey reeked with pride over his advanced accelerator school. Yes, it was small, but it was all his: his innovative conception; his implementation; and, once fashioned and running, his handiwork. You can't take that away from him!

So there you have it: Izzie and Mickey, big and little. True, there were many similarities between the two of them; however, frankly, these were only skin-deep. In the end, their dissimilarities far outweighed their similarities. That's the reality. There was a world of difference between them. While Izzie thought big, dreamed of institutions and such, as his destiny demanded, Mickey could only imagine building for the immediate benefit of the little people who populated those institutions, the class of people he knew and worked with, particularly the not-yet-polished up-and-coming young. Thus, even though Mickey and Izzie were after the same ends, and both strived to excel in the soaring grandeur of the world of science, their professional transits took them through widely divergent environs.

Try as he might, Mickey couldn't deny the reality staring at him. Different circles frequented! Different aspirations! Different levels reached! Different sorts of men become! It was simply inescapable! *Ay, there's the rub*! It was this disparity, this imbalance between them that could get in the way when they sat across from each other. So many differences! Such a wide chasm to bridge! Could it be done? That's what worried Mickey. That's what made him so devilishly apprehensive, so filled with misgivings, as he prepared to meet the *great Izzie*. Nonetheless, despite his being so unnerved, Mickey was thrilled to extravagant excess that he was to have the opportunity of going for it. It was his good luck that he had the nervy conceit and cheeky impertinence to imagine that he could find a way to talk on some sort of equal footing to one so much above him. Yes, it doesn't sound very promising. On the other hand, who knows? Mickey might be able to pull it off. Stranger things have happened. Maybe he could stand his ground. More than that, it could be exhilarating. Maybe even fun! In fact, if lady luck stuck with Mickey, he might even manage to get a little under Izzie's skin.

* * * * *

Le Petit Village Redux

It was an evening like any other when Mickey's joust with Izzie, the little big man, came about. It was only a few days since the arrangements had been made at *Le Petit Village*, but to Mickey the wait was an eternity. They met for dinner at a gourmet restaurant in upper Manhattan, *Le Chateau Repose*. Mickey had a funny feeling that the place must have some sort of affiliation with the sequestered haven he had visited just a few days earlier. Perhaps it was because he had never heard of the restaurant before. But why should he recognize it? He didn't really spend that much time in *the city*, and the borough was filled with *zillions* of restaurants. In any case, if there indeed were ties to the mountain retreat, that would at least be a logical explanation for why it was chosen. On the other hand, this place for elegant dining and spirited discourse was but a hop, skip, and a jump from Columbia, where Izzie had spent most of his productive life as scientist-without-equal, teacher, father figure, and shaper of young minds. That was surely another good reason for the choice of location. Then, to top it off, this place was especially fitting for their encounter because it was a scant 60 miles to the west of BNL: BNL was *the house that Izzie built*; it was all due to BNL that Mickey's path came to cross Izzie's; and it was because of the fall of BNL's ISABELLE that Mickey was driven, with single-minded determination, bordering on obsession, to make contact with the elusive Izzie and all the remembrances of things past this man of many faces retained. Anyway, for whatever reason the match was to be at Manhattan's *Le Chateau*, it was on its way: The time was set; the place was set; the agenda was set; the duelists of knowledge and reason, primed to grapple, were on the point of entering the arena; and the game of wits was about to begin.

With the moon lighting up the evening sky and a cool ocean breeze in the air, Mickey arrived in a Lincoln town car at half past seven and Izzie in a stretch limo a few minutes later. Izzie's insights into the human condition had always given him an edge on others; and on that special evening in Manhattan, he was true to form. Attired in an eye-catching, standout navy-blue suit and reddish tie, he was conspicuously spiffy. On that score, as on most others, there weren't many capable of outdoing him. Mickey, on the other hand, didn't put much stock in the idea of image making through wardrobe design. To him wearing apparel and garments were strictly utilitarian, and not accoutrements for influencing, perhaps even deceiving. So he shunned the whole notion and thought precious little, if any, about it. As it was, even for this occasion, Mickey was dressed in his usual casual manner. However, he did give in with the slight concession of dressing up just an itsy-bit, showing up in a tasteful outfit comprised of new black jeans, a silk shirt, and a light unbuttoned sports coat. As he walked into the restaurant, the field of combat as it were, he became concerned that the captain might not like his being tie-less. However, he needn't have worried because the captain, who knew people well, and above all knew his place, didn't react at all to what might well have been an awfully embarrassing faux pas. Thus, despite his lowbrow garb, Mickey managed to pass the upscale restaurant highbrow dress test. Although the captain was respectful enough to Mickey – no complaints there – as soon as Izzie came on the scene, he went through a full-scale conversion. What a radical shift in attitude it was! Overflowing with obsequiousness – without the least touch of inappropriateness – he simply fawned all over the man who counted. It was as if the captain knew he was in the presence of greatness.

After Izzie and Mickey greeted each other with smiles and handshakes, the captain led them to a quiet table for two at the rear of the dimly lit dining room. The location had the feel of isolation, being at least five yards from the nearest table. The soft lighting and quiet background music, a mixture of Mantovani and Mozart, provided a perfect atmosphere: What could be better to go along with the animated discussion Mickey was looking forward to – of course, sprinkled with savory delights to gratify the palate? As soon as the waiter arrived, they ordered immediately so as to minimize interruptions. But the strategy didn't work to Mickey's satisfaction because the waiter, as well as the maitre d', kept butting in to see that everything was as guest-perfect as it could be. Mickey was annoyed at this, and it showed in his face. But Izzie was as gracious as can be, and actually appeared to appreciate the attention. Obviously *Le Chateau's* stewards knew Izzie a lot better than Mickey did. The fact is that the way Mickey sized up the entire notion of serious talk in a meal's midst was quite wrong. You see, the logistics of serving, eating, and clearing up had no noticeable interfering effect. If anything, it enhanced the spirit of the discussion. But Mickey was a fast learner; and, in no time, taking his cue from Izzie, he became absorbed in the *Chateau's* cuisine they were about to partake of.

In the ordering department, Izzie stepped right in and took over. The menu turned out to be superfluous, since Izzie knew well the restaurant's offerings, and also knew exactly what he wanted. Actually, the choices were standard fare for a restaurant such as *Le Chateau*. To start, Izzie thought two brandies would hit the spot. He then suggested sharing a plate of mussels accompanied by Zinfandel Blanc. Mickey nodded in the affirmative, very pleased with the idea of splitting the mussels. This would then be followed by apple-Roquefort salads. For the entrées Mickey went with the duck à l'orange, while Izzie elected to go for the filet mignon, emphasizing that he favored it rare and juicy. To go along with the main course, Izzie requested his preference for a bottle of Chateauneuf-du-Pap. He whispered to the waiter that he would rather fancy a particular vintage year, if it were available. The waiter responded that for *the professor*, anything was possible. Izzie glanced at Mickey, remarking that the treat of this fabulous wine would indeed suit this memorable occasion. Although he didn't show it, hearing the name of that specific wine was something of a bombshell to Mickey, as he vividly recalled it as the *Le Petit Village* specialty. Yes, he thought, maybe his conjecture that the restaurant and the retreat were connected was actually right! But the reflection had nowhere to go, and so died on the vine. Izzie, oblivious of Mickey's dilemma, went right on to the dessert, selecting the crème brulé. Finally, Izzie topped the meal off with espresso and cognac. Throughout the ordering process, Mickey deferred to Izzie, who delighted in taking the initiative. Mickey, with his limited expertise in French cuisine and not familiar with the restaurant's specialties, felt comfortable, even pleased, with that arrangement. However, there was one trifling sour note for Mickey. Having been given the option of picking his own entrée, he chose the duck dish. But when later on the scrumptious-looking filet arrived at the table, boy, did he regret not having gone along with Izzie all the way! Ah well, nothing comes out absolutely perfect! All in all, however, the meal was delightful. But delicious and enjoyable as it was, it was but a minor distraction to the main event – although Mickey had to admit that it provided welcome breaks in the action, giving them time to think: Often, in fact, it was time that was sorely needed. Anyway, once the ordering was out of the way, wanting to squeeze in every moment of his allotted time, Mickey thought, *why not jump right in*?

* * * * *

Izzie Wants To Know Why

Just as Mickey was about to get his first words out, he noticed Izzie staring right at him, at the same time displaying a somewhat smug grin. Although the scene gave every appearance that Izzie was on top of things and ready to take over, in fact, he was only surveying the turf, fishing to find out exactly where he stood. Mickey hesitated, becoming increasingly unsure of himself as each second passed. Then, a bit piqued by the ensuing silence and his own lack of spunk, he thought: *Aw, the hell with it*! With that, Mickey returned to his resolve to get on with it. Thus, as it turned out, he was the one who got the ball rolling: "Because I don't want to waste any of our time together, I thought we could get the game under way on the double." Seeing no objection, Mickey dove right into the surf and started swimming, "I would like to go back to the beginning years of BNL because that's where I believe all the trouble-to-come got started." However, before he could get in another word, Izzie cut in: "Wait a minute, easy does it. Don't rush things. Keep in mind that everything must be taken in its own sweet time. So, before you get your engine all revved up for fast driving, first slow it down a bit and tell me why you wanted this meeting. And, frankly speaking, why did you pick on me?"

Mickey was caught off guard. He was supposed to be the one with the questioning prerogative, or so he believed. One thing he certainly didn't expect was for it to be pulled right out from under his very nose. With the adroitness of a seasoned pro, by his simple ploy, Izzie, from the get-go, demonstrated even in his post-corporeal years the quickness with which he could think and act. After that, there was no doubt who was really in charge. It was a tough position for Mickey to be in. But what was he to do about it? He couldn't just tell Izzie where to get off. Yet, if he simply allowed Izzie to run roughshod over him, there was a good chance he would lose this once-in-a-lifetime opportunity, the whole ball of wax. *Izzie questioning Mickey* – what a joke! What could Mickey, by any stretch of the imagination, tell *the great one*? So, was Izzie just stalling? Why was he there if he didn't want to talk, to open up? Why did he agree to meet with Mickey in the first place?

Mickey's mind raced a mile a minute trying to figure a way out of the quandary he was in. Then it hit him. All that frustration, that bafflement, and that disappointment! All that impatience and fretting about! All in vain! You see, it was nothing but his own damn vanity, pure and simple. Suddenly the clouds rolled by and the sky cleared. How dumb he was! Izzie's questions were right on. He deserved answers to them. Without the least doubt, Mickey shouldn't have been so cock-sure of himself. The fact is that he wasn't ready for Izzie's down-to-earth wisdom. He was caught with his pants down. That's the truth! He should've thoroughly planned for and readied himself to give Izzie succinct, rapid-fire, and to the point replies to his à propos *why* queries. But in his naïveté about what he was getting into and with whom he was dealing, he prepared squat. His self-conceit simply overpowered and blinded him. What poor reasoning and foresight he exhibited! What a stupid mess it put him in! But that was all water over the dam. At this point, he could only try to make the best of it. Maybe he could dig deep within himself and find the strength to adjust and adapt himself to the unanticipated circumstances he was in. Anyway, there was nothing to do but try. Who knows? Maybe he could come out of it with flying colors, proving to Izzie that here was a man to be reckoned with. So, hesitating only a bit in order to get his mind on this new and unexpected track, he ad-libbed a slow and deliberate statement of why he wanted the chance to challenge all the Players with the questions galore he'd put together, and why he particularly wanted to meet up with and have a head-to-head with Izzie, who was, after all, a key character – perhaps the single most crucial one – in the events of the past he wanted to reconstruct.

* * * * *

Mickey Explains That He Also Wants To Know Why, but a Why of a Different Color

"In my long affair with ISABELLE," Mickey began, "I became deeply attached to this ill-fated lady. Life, it seems, is not kind to the helpless at the mercy of ambitious men, bloated with swellheaded conceit and overbearing arrogance. Yet, when the project first began, BNL was filled with high hopes about the damsel's prospects. Great expectations permeated and saturated the air. Optimism flowed freely with the promise of a gratifying and glorious outcome. But they were counterfeit hopes, merely the pipe dreams of utopia-imagining fools. No, it wasn't meant to be. As a decade of labor passed, the promise turned to disappointment, and the hopes became blighted and turned to despair. The about-face was staggering – it slowly crept up on everybody. However, strangely, when the end came, hindsight made it appear that the transition was swift and sudden. But either way, it was an agonizing blow to the lab, severe, harsh, and cruel.

"As witness to this chain of events, seeing before my very eyes this radical turnaround of feelings, attitudes, and emotions, I'm sure you can appreciate how compelling it was to me. How intriguing it was! How I craved to find out how it all could've come about! How I sought to pry into the secret life of the dying lady! How I hungered to know why things took the course they did! Why did the ISABELLE project take the downhill course to oblivion? Why was it such an unmitigated failure? Why did

BNL just watch and let it happen? Why couldn't the fall of ISABELLE have been miraculously averted? Then there was the pivotal *why*, the *why* at the heart of the matter, the *sine qua non* of all of them: Why wasn't there a good and strong enough man to save the day, a knight in shining armor to enter, riding his gleaming white stallion, and reprieve the lady from her death sentence?

"These questions about the lady in distress haunted my thoughts. I became possessed, and was driven to exert myself to the fullest I could in pursuit of the truth, come what may. As I trod the rough and rocky truth-trail, more and more, I was led into the past, further and further back into its ever-increasing murkiness. In slogging through the mud, I came to see that the roots of the ISABELLE mystery were buried deep in a tightfisted and stingy past, a past determined to keep its well-guarded secrets hidden. It didn't take long for me to realize that, to discover what caused ISABELLE's sordid and inanely unnecessary expiration, I would have to find the means to coerce the past into disclosing its secrets. And that, as you no doubt know, is a tall order indeed, far easier said than done.

"The resistance that confronted me to having the details revealed was obstinate and unyielding. The usual means to learn about and understand things – reasoning through my observations, rational discourse with seemingly sane men, and using inference to glue it all together – proved futile. These standard methods of formulating history just didn't work. I was stumped and felt thoroughly defeated. The wall on whose other side might be the answers I sought appeared to be impregnable. As I came to know more of the thorny and demanding world I entered, the realm of the truth-search, I came to see the rocky shoals I'd have to maneuver through and was tempted to pull back, but I determined to persist and steeled myself to go on as far as I could.

"Actually, there was only one way I might win against such a formidable opponent as the past: I had to fight fire with fire. To break through the truth-barrier, I'd have to be as resolute as ever I was. If I was to free the past's secrets from their dungeon of confinement, I'd have to become as ruthless and as deceiving as the jailer was in keeping them from view. To compete with the past, I'd have to become as cunning as it was. I'd have to invent what was so effectively kept from me, and what was simply unobservable any longer, lost forever in the turbulent chaos of remembrances. And I persuaded myself that I could meet the test and do what was required of me. Thus, the hunt to ascertain what really happened became my mission, my passionate quest, and finally my obsession.

"Thus, upbeat and eager, full of spirit, and with bulldog tenacity to spur me on, I righteously mounted my moral high horse and set off in hot pursuit of not only who was behind it all but why and how, in days gone by, our dream was stolen and the life of the star-crossed lady ISABELLE taken. But, as filled with optimism as I was at the start, what a demoralizing and humbling ride it turned out to be! First, I found that the past has a bad habit of receding as it's approached. Then, at times, when it seemed I was catching up, it was only to be confronted with warning signs that read: *Keep out! Vexatious and confounding obstacles up ahead! And if any passerby overcomes these, beware that only disheartening and difficult to endure truths lie in wait.* But I didn't heed the signs. I stubbornly ignored all the cautionary alerts and admonishments, and chose to push on. I began with the obvious and made a thorough search of ISABELLE's past. But I could find nothing there of any significant value to me. The documentation was as cold as the public record generally is, wholly devoid of the hot human passions wherein are the true causes of things. Of course none of the people would talk: Either they knew nothing or were deliberately silent for their own private reasons. Yet, it wasn't all for naught, because I learned what proved to be a decisive lesson for me, to wit: *The skeletons – the reality that counts – are only to be found in their resident closets much further back in time*. So I was soon rummaging in the project's home base, peering into BNL's past; and from there I was inexorably drawn to the lab's origins, two to three decades earlier.

"To satisfy my urge to know about, to interpret, and possibly to explain the tragic events of those turbulent, inflamed, and impassioned times when ISABELLES's life ebbed away, I called upon the many involved people for enlightenment, in the hope of making some sense of their actions. Those still alive, I spoke with directly. The dead ones ended up speaking to me through what they left behind, both the palpable things I could dig up and via their voices that came through the memories of others. But all – bar none – were diligent in protecting their secrets, some to the point of purposefully drawing this innocent explorer down blind alleyways and into dead ends. However, despite their playing games with the truth, thereby making a consistent and plausible explanation harder to come by, I still persisted. And slowly but surely, step-by-step, some pictures of reality began to emerge. But these representations I was able to put together contained gaping holes and mysterious shadows lurking about. These nagging loose ends and missing links were critical impediments, fatal obstructions to lighting up the truth. How could I overcome that encumbering truth-handicap? How could I break through that seemingly impenetrable barrier that kept me from the knowledge I was seeking? Frankly, the answer was quite apparent, and I did finally get it. To understand the essence of what happened, I had to explore why this cast of characters acted in the manner it did. Thus was I drawn into the tangled web of intentions. As I wandered through this maze of smoke and mirrors, I wondered if this was the end of the line for me. Did any hope of success still remain? How was I to find a way to fathom the true minds of others, those alive and those dead? Yes, how indeed!

"No, I didn't give up. It's just not my nature. On the contrary, in the face of the seemingly impossible, my efforts multiplied. I strained my every nerve. I sweated blood. I left no stone unturned. I taxed myself to the breaking point. But it was in vain. Nothing seemed to come of it. I was as far away from discovery as when I lifted the first stone to start the dig by which I sought to free every *why* I could detect. *Give it up*, my mind urged. *Enough! You've already done everything possible. Let it be*! Then one day, as if sent by a choir of angels who saw my plight and pitied me, *Mister Serendipity* smiled on me. He took me by the hand and led me to gaze upon *Le Petit Village*. This magical venue was the only place left where I could turn in order to liberate the answers I needed to fill in the gaps in the puzzle. It was the dream I yearned for come to pass. Only in that wonderland of truth could I meet the Players and hear their intentions from their own lips. What luck! What a blessing! Here given to me free and without obligation was the gift of a lifetime. So I grabbed the star and held on for dear life as it took me on an excursion no one who didn't experience it could imagine or believe. Yet, it happened! And that, dear Izzie, is the story of my journey in search of the truth: That's why I desperately sought out the gang of performers in the drama; that's why I traveled beyond the limits of space and time to reach the mountain hideaway; and that's why I came to be here with you."

Mickey paused, unsure of whether or not he had gotten through to Izzie. Meanwhile, the man who'd been to the top of the mountain quietly listened to Mickey's justification for their meeting, and then seamlessly drifted into a mood of thoughtful reflection. However, in short order, Izzie looked up quizzically and reminded Mickey, with a hint of displeasure, that, although he did clarify why he sought to get together with all the actors in a truth-encouraging environment, he didn't address the second question of exactly why he picked Izzie. Somewhat embarrassed at the misstep, Mickey was fortunate to be only mildly flustered. Sure, he was rapped on the knuckles and scolded a bit, but he was quick enough to keep his *eye on the prize*: After all, he did have Izzie there and if *the man* wanted to let off some steam, so be it. That was a very small price to pay. Anyway, swiftly recovering his poise, Mickey's mind switched into high gear. How should he proceed? Whatever it was, it had to be fast, and it had to be firm and sure-footed. He certainly didn't want Izzie to see him bumbling about. It occurred to him that he should've gone into the fact that Izzie was central to Mickey's mission when he mentioned that the key to the whole ISABELLE affair and the lab's concurrent decline lay somewhere in BNL's origins. Too bad he hadn't!

But no harm was done. *Just be calm*, he thought. *Tackle the question head-on. Yes, that's the ticket. If that's what Izzie wants, then that's what he should have.* Feeling his self-assurance surging back, he started in: "Specifically why are *you* on the list, you asked? Sorry for overlooking that point. Maybe I skipped over it, involuntarily to be sure, because the reasons are so transparent and evident. They're axiomatic, and, in all likelihood, I simply took them for granted. Consider this: You're the lab's creator; you're its father; it was you who gave it its raison d'être and its potential to be the best; and it was you who made it what it was and what it ultimately became. You're a pivotal actor in the drama I'm seeking to recreate. You're imperative to a full understanding of any version of the BNL story. In the picture I've painted as a model for BNL's passage through history, you play perhaps the most decisive role, not only in the lab's rise in the fifties and sixties, but also in its declining fortunes in the seventies and eighties. If not you, whom shall I seek out to help put the finishing touches on the story and so bring it to an end? There's simply no alternative to you. I can only thank my lucky stars that – voilà – we are here."

* * * * *

Izzie Keeps Control of the Questioning

"Ah, fine," said a munching Izzie approvingly, "but pray have the patience to allow me to finish these last few mussels and to wash them down." So Izzie went at it, working the shells with a dexterity gained from much experience, while simultaneously managing the wineglass – no easy feat. In the meantime, Mickey found it hard to take his eyes off Izzie, and with a combination of awe and amusement, was riveted on *the man's* epicurean skill. But, even as time seemed to be Izzie's friend, as he idled about, it was most surely Mickey's enemy. He knew time was not about to wait for him, and Mickey, becoming increasingly concerned about the clock ticking away the minutes that were supposed to be his with Izzie, surreptitiously peeked at his watch. Poor Mickey! He didn't have a clue that Izzie's intent was to maneuver him into being off-balance. And artless Mickey, in the presence of one such as Izzie, fell for it hook, line, and sinker! Peering at Mickey, Izzie, seeing the younger man focusing on the table activity and on the time slipping away, was satisfied that this was the moment for him to make his move to keep his agenda on course. So, in an off-handed, plain-spoken, and natural manner – but don't for a second doubt that shrewd, crafty, and tactical cunningness lay behind this casual style – Izzie nonchalantly remarked: "Please excuse my preoccupation with these succulent mussels and this exquisitely palate-pleasing Zinfandel, but while I'm busy at that, why don't you give me a run-down on what you've found so far in your quest." Again Mickey was beaten to the punch! It began to dawn on him that if he were ever to take control as the interviewer, he'd have to assert himself a lot more than he had up to then. Izzie was certainly not a man easy to have the last word with. For Mickey to get what he wanted out of such a one, he'd have to change his ways *mucho*.

As Izzie's game plan began to sink in, Mickey had to admit that it had quite a bit of merit. In particular, Izzie's last request really wasn't out of line. *Reviewing the situation* would give them a starting point and a foundation for the ensuing discussion of the finer details. Why shouldn't Mickey open up about all he'd learned so far? Why shouldn't Izzie be brought up to snuff? Why shouldn't the two be on an equal footing? Wouldn't that make the give-and-take more effective and more interesting to both? Wouldn't the chance of any insights being born be that much the greater? *Yes*, Mickey thought, *I was clearly wrong. Izzie's way is far better*. He wondered why *he* didn't think of it. Was it because of modesty in the presence of such a big man as Izzie? Was it out of deference to *his highness* not to do too much of the talking? Was it because he wanted to hear more of what Izzie had to say? Well, whatever the reason, it was Izzie, not Mickey, who pitched the right approach, seemingly picking it right out of a hat. *OK*, Mickey conceded in his private thoughts, *chalk one up for Izzie*.

However, for Mickey, what happened wasn't only a vanity depressor. The situation that presented itself had a practical downside as well. Although it was the right way to go, Mickey found himself on the spot for a second time, and it was still early in the evening. You see, in double-quick time, he would have to come up with the preamble to serve as the prelude to the main event. Thus, caught flat-footed again, with no opportunity for preparation, he would have to present his case off-the-cuff. But Mickey, made of the right stuff, wasn't about to be stopped by this piddling obstacle. So, with the thought, *no use crying over spilt milk*, he screwed himself up to the task and determined to go ahead with his review of what he'd amassed during his travels. To that end, Mickey let his mind roam freely about what he'd learned so far. Sitting quietly and reflecting for a minute, while Izzie put away the mussels with abandon and sipped his wine, Mickey soon felt ready to face the man whom he'd adopted as teacher and taskmaster for the evening.

* * * * *

Mickey's Disturbing Findings
The Pain of Discovery

"What have I learned?" Mickey started, prolonging and drawing out each word, as if he were questioning himself. Staring into the distance behind Izzie, he chewed on it and mulled it over for a while, sweating bullets to find a handle to grab onto. "Frankly, the lesson that made the biggest impression on me is that most everything I've learned is tinged with fog and irony. Nothing is certain. There's nothing you can depend on without some misgivings, some reservations, and some qualms. In fact, some things I've come upon should only be brought into the open with bold-faced question marks attached to them. So, here I am, my mind filled with a plethora of indications and clues, an embarrassment of details, but none of them definite, none of them unquestionable. It therefore shouldn't surprise you, Izzie, at least not too much, that I'm having some difficulty finding a place to begin. Yet, there's a story to tell; and, damn it, nothing's going to stop me from lifting it from my brain and revealing it to you in all its at times hard-to-take rawness. I'm not sure exactly how I'm going to gain that end, but my instincts advise me to plunge right in. I guess that my best bet is to trust in these instincts, so here goes!

"The historical record includes the obvious facts that ISABELLE was created by politics in 1977 and died by it in 1983. Early on after the fall, perhaps because of this reality, most of the gossip surrounding the sorry business pointed to politics as the explanation of the whole mess. *Born by politics, kept alive by politics, and killed by politics, evidently politics is what makes the world of Big Science turn.* That's what most wanted to believe, and that's what they came to believe. Life was simple for those who surrendered to that view: With the right people in Washington behind you, you're a winner, and without them, you're a loser. It sounds right, but I tell you it's not. It's nothing more than a crock. As for me, you can be sure that I didn't buy it for a minute. No, how could I allow myself to be derailed by such simplistic bull? Now, don't get me wrong. I'm not saying that politics doesn't count. Of course it does. Who can deny that it gives projects the resources to get them off the ground, and that it pulls the rug out from under them when reality sets in and demands it? But, no matter how you slice it, politics didn't make ISABELLE lose its way during its long night of darkness. And, in the end, politics didn't willingly toss it into the junk heap. Only when Washington was forced into it was that done. Politics was only the instrument, not the cause. No, to explain what really happened to ISABELLE, forget politics! To uncover the truth about the sad lady thrown to the wolves, you have to delve deep into the swamp of the human drama. I'm well aware that such a place is not where most want to go. I know it's easier to believe that a clean democratic-like congressional vote did the deed in toto. But there's simply no escaping the as-sure-as-anything fact that it's in humanity's seedy and squalid underbelly where the inquiring mind must rummage and forage in if the true source of ISABELLE's fate is to be unearthed.

"In the six short years, from 1977 to 1983, that ISABELLE lived as a formal project, a lot happened. But my initiation took place much earlier. I started to work on ISABELLE in its pre-project days immediately following its conceptual origin in 1969.

Throughout its entire lifespan, I witnessed all the questionable goings-on, and tried to get hold of and digest every bit of what took place – bar none. In my day-to-day study of the details of the project, technical as well as managerial, I saw things that aroused and whipped up my craving to know even more. Thus spurred, I found myself flying off in every which direction. Being what I am, saddled with a voracious investigative appetite, I scurried along hungrily: discerning and absorbing all the things that were being done, both good and bad; fixing on who were the ones doing them; and even inferring reasons for the actions, some of which were transparent, some not so evident. Along the byways and pathways I traveled, sometimes there in front of me would be a particular piece of the puzzle, just sitting there like a pearl that when deeply peered at and caressed reveals its secrets. Such were moments to cherish. Unfortunately, they were rare. It wasn't much different from the fact that many an oyster must be laid open and exposed before one carrying a gem is discovered. Anyway, nothing could deter me. Demanding and grueling as the search was, on I went. Although it wasn't obvious as it was happening, inexorably I was drawn further and further back into the past. I came to discover that only by looking at things from that perspective, from way back when, was there a chance of laying my hands on the truth. Only then might my exhaustive probing and my gathering and culling of the evidence bear fruit. Surely it was there and only there that I might lay claim to those elusive missing pieces. Persuaded of this – in the end, not much more than an educated guess – I followed up and sent my mind to extract what it could from a past loathe to disclose what it knows.

"What came of all this, you ask? What came of this expeditionary trek into the past? What came of this reconnoitering, digging, ferreting out, and tracking down? What came of this project scrutinizing, people monitoring, searching for an angle, and brain-picking? What came of this evaluating and reevaluating, this analyzing and reanalyzing? Well, what I learned was dark and ominous. Yet, surprisingly, my ultimate breakthrough actually started out with a straightforward, uncomplicated, and not-too-menacing negative: Politics was not the determining factor in ISABELLE's premature end, and, more than that, was probably not even a very important one. No, something else was the primary cause, something far more insidious. But what was it? Perhaps I should've been more worldly and not so appalled and shaken up when I stumbled on the reason that proved to be the true one. But I must admit that I was stunned. You see, what I gleaned from my backward-in-time journey of discovery was that the project was destroyed from within through the insidious corruption that lay within BNL's internal managing apparatus. Yes, believe it or not, it was the infernal machinations of the lab's top guns, in cahoots with *the big names* running the physics community, that sent the sad lady ISABELLE to an untimely grave. I can see a tinge of doubt forming on your face, Izzie. I must tell you that I too reacted much like that. But, as it sank in, I came to appreciate that there's no doubt about it. Strange as it may seem at first, it was indeed they themselves that did them in!

"True, you might lay some blame at the doorstep of the funding agency's bureaucrats or other government honchos for not stepping in and forcing the lab to clean house and start anew. Or you might look askance at all those noble Nobels at the National Academy or the elected luminaries supposedly running the shows at the other societies and institutions for being remiss. All these men had many years in which to act.

Of course they could have, and they should have. But wait a minute! Try to look at it from their point of view. Isn't it a bit much to ask them to recklessly plow into technical and managerial territory they know so little about, and then ask them to tell the current ruling elite there how to run things? Yes, it is indeed too much to ask, far too much. Just think of it: If a man has a choice, then find me one so bold as to risk so much of his own personal circumstances for so thankless a task! At stake is his credibility! What if he should misstate the case? What if he should not get it exactly right? What if he should, while filled with uncertainty and self-doubt, interpret it to someone's dissatisfaction? As you well know, all of these possibilities, and perhaps even worse ones, are quite likely to occur. But wait, there's more: Contacts and associations made over decades would be placed in jeopardy. Friendships, both professional and personal, built up over the years would be threatened because impossible choices between community and friend would have to be made. And finally, whatever proposals were to be proffered would in all likelihood demand that prior formal and informal agreements and commitments entered into be abrogated. No, this type of risk-taking cannot be expected from *modern institutional man*. It's a hero that's needed, one willing to risk the stormy road traveled by the highly vulnerable *whistle-blower*; and such a man is hard to find. And what of poor ISABELLE, waiting and hoping for the appearance on the horizon of a white knight with the sense of purpose and strength of character to take on the stacked deck and save her? Oh, woe was she! She waited in vain, for such a one wasn't likely to appear. And none did!

"What about me, I sense you asking? Well, Izzie, I did the best I could. With naïvete as my sole ally, I spoke out with all the strength I could find in me. I badgered and harassed anyone who would listen. But no one heard. Only silence greeted my pleadings. So, in time, I withdrew; and from the sidelines I watched and took in the ensuing drama being enacted. With no influence, powerless to alter fate's will, I sought at least to know and understand what I could glean. How innocent I was! How could one of my ilk appreciate the pain of discovery? Nonetheless, it was thrust upon me anyway. And so it was that as my disturbing findings unfolded before me, I came to learn the sad and true ways of the world of Big Science."

Mickey's Disturbing Findings
An Inexorable Course

Mickey looked closely at Izzie, trying to discern if he was getting ready to interrupt. But Izzie made no eye contact. He was staring off into the dimness at the far end of the room. Mickey presumed him to be deep in thought, and chose to take this as a green light to go on: "I've been thinking about how people behave when trouble rears its ugly head. They observe it. They recognize it. They speculate: Maybe a foul-up of one kind or another has taken place. Maybe some sort of deception is beginning to emerge. Maybe it's already in the works. Maybe it's already grown into a grand deception. Maybe a full-fledged conspiracy has been born. OK, so suppose it's happened, and someone's become aware of it. Well, I can tell you that knowing about it is one thing. Doing something about it is an altogether different matter. Imagine your garden-variety top dog coming upon a situation that is all but begging for intervention. First, he assesses if there is any danger or risk attached to stepping in, confronting the actors, or any such thing. If he comes up with a *yes*, what's your guess as to what he might do? No problem here! Holding his tongue or getting fitted for blinders always has been and still remains his favored option. Believe it: Almost whatever trouble comes into his line of sight, he'll disregard it, neglect it, deliberately ignore it, or even try to convince himself it's really not there at all. He'll mind his own business. He'll use every trick in the book to keep himself disengaged from it. He'll run as fast as he can from it. *See no evil, hear no evil, speak no evil*, that's his motto. And why does he behave this way? Because taking care of *number one* is his prime concern! That's what worries him and gives him cause for alarm. That's what motivates and drives his deeds, his rationales, and his conduct. Yes indeed, heroes are hard to come by. The capacity of the vast majority of people for excuses, sophistry, and rationalization appears to know no bounds.

"Take ISABELLE. A straightforward case, one that on the face of it seems sound enough, can be made that it was purely the lab's business and none of anybody else's: After all, it was BNL and BNL alone that bore the responsibility and was fully accountable for the project's conception and its realization. If it went well, then fine and good, BNL would get well-deserved accolades. But, if things went awry, then it would be BNL that would have to face the music. It would be the lab that would be raked over the tormenting, harrowing fiery coals. Although that argument is quite right, there are the fine-print obligations to consider. BNL didn't just take ISABELLE and fly off on its own with it. It was funded, supported, and given the mandate to do it by the government and the science community to which it had to answer. There was an understanding between the parties. The lab was favored with the trust of the community and the largesse of the government. There was a contractual agreement – *you give this and I'll do that* – and there was a covenant among scientist-colleagues. No, the lab was not acting alone at all. In truth, BNL and its Director had the duty to fulfill their promise of providing Big Science the chance to make its dreams come true.

"Unfortunately, the arrangement was flawed from the get-go. What was anybody to do if the lab screwed up, wouldn't own up, and wouldn't do the right thing? Who could step in and do something about it? Nobody! The bureaucrats? Sure, I'll believe it when I see it! The politicians would be up in arms. Those opening their mouths would fast get the shaft themselves. Showing their dirty laundry in public! They'd be crucified. Well, what about the community? Ha! The men of the community just don't know enough to effectively intercede. Besides, for the most part, they're gutless. Smart, yes! But lionhearted, no! More like fainthearted, wimpy, and yellow-bellied! So who might walk into the lion's den to attempt to save the day, you ask? Not a soul, I tell you! Somehow this possibility never occurred to anyone. And when it comes to bigness, such a form of blindness is not that unlikely. In any case, when it came to ISABELLE, the chance of such a thing taking place was simply overlooked and not taken into account. Clearly the top men at the funding agency and in the community were asleep at the switch and found wanting. What a thing to escape their notice! Sure, they could've squeezed through, if only BNL carried its weight. But it didn't. The possibility that everyone disregarded actually came to pass.

"So now what were the community and the government to do about it? Well, as it happened, they started off by doing nothing. They gave the lab time to work out its problems, and then more time, and then even more. Who wanted to enter the fray and put their own necks on the line? You guessed it: *not a one*. But no amount of time seemed enough. So on went the game. But surely, at some point, somebody had to say: this far and no further. If BNL was not able to bring the project off and so fulfill its obligation, then there was simply no alternative but to end it. Yes, ISABELLE would have to be put to rest. But how was this to be done, who was to do it, and when? Ah, those are the questions!

"Then, as it happened, the tide began to shift. Finally, after years of just letting things slide – and there being not a chance in the world of a hero entering in time to save the woeful lady – the move against BNL's wavering project was at last made. A vacillating and hesitant community at long last formed a long-overdue consensus and did something. Too bad it waited so long. You see, when the action came, it was late in the day, too late. By then, the plummeting descent from a dazzling log aflame to a dimming, dying ember had run its course. As it turned out, the culminating climax was the ruinous collapse of a once distinguished, a once-celebrated BNL and the tragic deathblow to its disgraced, dishonored, and infamous project ISABELLE. What was there to do for the lab but to fall into tears and despair, while its offspring was discarded and made to take *the big sleep*?

"Izzie, you can't imagine how many times I've asked myself why it had to be that way. Looking back, I've come to the view that somewhere in time the lab lost its way. It wandered aimlessly in a wilderness populated by incipient failures, all oblivious of the trying and desperate times that awaited them. As it was hiding its head in the sand, BNL continued on its relentlessly downhill and catastrophic course. The facts were all plain to see, at least for anyone who cared to look. The lab didn't honor its pledge to provide the world of Big Science with a new machine of wonders; the lab's captain would not or could not steer the ship through the treacherous currents of the modern technological world; and BNL appeared ready to take the entire Big Physics world down with it. Then there was poor ISABELLE itself. Oh, what a sorry state the project was in during the early eighties. As much as it might have been wished for, there was no modern-day *Don Quixote* on hand to ride in to save her honor. Thus, the helpless lab followed its destiny, written years before. With no one able to halt its faltering self-destructiveness or to give it aid and comfort in its hour of need, BNL kept on its course toward the icebergs that, if reached, would crack it up. The lab was doomed; and the situation was intolerable. Conditions were dire, and something had to be done, if not to save BNL, then at least to salvage what remained of American Big Science. It was then and only then that a process of reclamation was begun. Punishment had to be meted out; the air had to be cleared; and reconstruction had to be gotten underway. And so it was."

Mickey's Disturbing Findings Conspiracy

So far in Mickey's portrayal of how and why American Big Physics took the turns it did, going from good to bad to worse as the decades of the latter half of the twentieth century rolled by, he recoiled at the idea of tagging real people. Gambling on personification, he relied on expressions like: *the community did this*, or *the lab wanted that*. OK, perhaps that's not such a bad way to start out, to give the overview – the big picture. But, when it comes right down to it, communities and labs don't act, it's the people running the show that do the doing. Mickey knew that, and so did Izzie. So, continuing that line of attack any further would certainly be counter-productive. It would be as if he were trying to pull the wool over Izzie's eyes. God forbid! Mickey certainly didn't want to treat Izzie in such a disrespectful manner. Besides, Izzie was a down-to-earth man, a man with a brilliant mind and a penetrating insight. He just wouldn't take it much longer anyway. So Mickey came to the view that he couldn't tiptoe around the matter anymore, and would simply have to name names.

With that settled in his mind, Mickey thought hard and quick about how he could articulate precisely the action taken by the community against ISABELLE, and naturally against BNL as well. Frankly, that meant finding the words to express who did what to whom, and why. Mickey knew that by injecting real names into his account, he'd have to speak openly and candidly. He'd have to be precise and accurate in his formulations, his inferences, and his deductions. After all, he didn't want to appear wet behind the ears in front of Izzie. In fact, if truth be told, he really wanted to impress the old man. Thus, persuaded to his satisfaction that the actors had to become part of his rendering of the drama, although he had almost no time to consider exactly how he would characterize them, he proceeded with his story, trusting that his instincts would carry him through.

"How did it happen?" Mickey began. "How was ISABELLE finally taken out of her misery? Who had the wherewithal, and who had the balls to step forward and be counted? Here was the situation: After more than three decades in which a system of collegiality ruled over the formation and the phenomenal development and growth of American Big Physics, when the eighties arrived, this quite legitimate system of governance was beginning to exhibit the classic symptoms of cracking up. To be blunt, it was falling apart at the seams. And what of the cause? Anybody who could see beyond his nose recognized that BNL was the culprit. Holding a hell of a lot of good cards – political alliances and community obligations – and cashing in chips right and left, this cancerous impediment was strangling and choking off the life-blood of the high-energy enterprise. Arrogantly foisting the gluttonous, resource-devouring ISABELLE on a wimpy, cowardly, and out-of-gas community, the lab was eating away the very capacity of Big Physics to move forward, and even to survive.

"Then a kind of visionary event, a wonder of wonders, took place. From out of nowhere, there spontaneously arose a group of men with guts galore. Filled with child-like eagerness, they were champing at the bit to challenge the entrenched Establishment, and, unbidden, to attempt to remove the burden from the community's back. Their springing up signaled that change was in the wind. A new ruling clique would soon come into being, the protective Guardians of Big Science, that would stand ready to defend a newly empowered high-energy physics from enemies within and enemies at the gate. Once having replaced the old fogies, they would then be the ones to wield the whip, wear the crown, and exercise sovereignty over the high-energy dominion. They would be self-appointed justice-enforcing marshals of order and freedom combined. They would be avengers and saviors all at once. They would be conspirators with the do-good, well-meaning intention of setting things right. They would be the Big Science Vigilantes. And, as it happened, they prevailed.

"The Vigilantes weren't friends of BNL, yet neither were they hating-type enemies. However, they were ready and willing to fight the good fight to stop the lab's seemingly limitless appetite from eating anymore into the community's limited resources. It's actually hard to say why they chose to act at all: Why were they willing to take on such a chancy venture? Why were they willing to wager all they'd earned by placing themselves squarely in the line of fire? Why were they willing to risk big-time by banking on the trust and loyalty of their fellow conspirators? Why were they willing to put their hard-won careers in hazardous jeopardy? What vexed questions! How perplexing! How, I ask you, Izzie, can you plumb the depths of such men's minds to fathom what was driving them? Perhaps they were truly men of honor. But then, perhaps they were mere opportunists. Frankly, when push comes to shove, who can tell? Who can figure it out? But wait a minute! We're not merely groping in the dark without any handle to hold on to. There is a small glimmer of light. Shining through is the ultimate aim they were striving for. Could it really be that there was a streak of altruism in them? Was it all done to save the lab from destroying itself? Was it all done to rid the community of the unfit and injurious men at BNL's helm?

"OK, let's buy that that's what they wanted to achieve. If so, then there's no denying that they were on the right track. But it's one thing to want something, quite another to get it done. What was vague was exactly how this laudable destination was to be reached. The prerequisites for the needed actions weren't a piece of cake: The men to achieve such ends most assuredly had to be brainy, quick, and persuasive; they had to be sharp-witted, shrewd, and crafty; they had to be ruthless; they had to be brilliant, ingenious, and chock-full of insights; and they had to have connections to real power. These are tall orders to fill. But, despite the low likelihood of success when they started, once on the move, they proved that they were certainly the right men for the job. Believe it or not, they found the needle in the haystack. Unlikely, true! But they did it! They managed to hit upon just the right way to achieve the ends they sought. Wouldn't you agree? Wouldn't you say that they got what they wanted and at the same time what was good for all?"

Mickey's Disturbing Findings
An Exposé of a Sort

"Izzie, I'm sure you're wondering who I've cast in this drama of men felled by hubris and betrayal, and others uplifted by pride and dreams. The drama itself came to pass because ISABELLE was doomed by fate never to see the light of day. It was a sorry tale of a dream denied. In this age-old story of wrong and right, there were bad guys with black hats, riding dark black horses; and there were good guys with white hats, entering on shiny white stallions as the denouement approached. But who were these men? Who were the bad guys, the ones who drove poor Lady ISABELLE into the silent, sun-less earth six feet under? And who were the good guys, those just and relentless, legitimate and courageous, ruthless and predatory Vigilantes, the ones who brought back order into the chaotic world of American Big Physics? Well, Izzie, this being an exposé of a sort, clearly naming names is what I must do. So I will now lay before you the cast of characters, the roles these men played, and my version of how the drama unfolded.

"First let's look at the actors who took down the project, men who took on the guise of being its upholders and champions: At the top of the list, there was Vineyard, BNL's Director, who stood pat and did diddly. I would guess that he hadn't the least appreciation of the mess he and the lab were in. So he just sat idly by while ISABELLE simmered and then burned. Then came Samios, Sanford and Rau, the other three members of the feckless gang of four. With their technical and managerial knowledge and the direct access they had to every bit of project information, these were men who could've and should've done something about the terrible things going on. They had ready-at-hand and close contact with the entire accelerator staff and knew better than anybody else the wretched, vulnerable, and defenseless state that ISABELLE was in. But why, I ask you, did they keep all this so valuable info to themselves? Could they have been unaware of its importance? Could they really have been such fools? I've often wondered if they even talked to each other about the appalling state of affairs. On the other hand, if they had their wits about them, then why didn't they appropriately apprise the Director that extreme action was in order? That was their job. Why wasn't the lab's Board of Directors duly informed? Why weren't the DOE and the high-energy community told of the true circumstances? Could it be that the three of them weren't able to stomach admitting outright that they were in the wrong from the start? Did they imagine that the consequences of doing that might be more than they could tolerate? Did they come to believe that their careers, built over many years of great and winning effort, might go down the drain if word of the true nature of the situation got out? Could it be that they couldn't face what they'd done, and so were blinded through their own self-deception? Were they blocked from telling all by their arrogance of pride? What an enigma! What a dilemma!

"I wish, Izzie, that I could answer all these provocative questions. Too Bad! I'm in the dark. I just can't penetrate any further. But that's life! Sometimes things you're trying to figure out get to be so ambiguous or so obscure – they acquire such an uncertain nature – that whether they're true or false can't be discerned to any satisfactory degree of likelihood. They become lost in the web of deceit and self-deception, and confound all reason. From there, attempts at recall are nothing but fruitless endeavors. Thus, in time, such things that have transpired leave man's jurisdiction of learning and comprehension, and become unknowable.

"Oddly enough, with the combined power Samios, Sanford, and Rau held at the lab, these three men could easily have maneuvered to change things and to right the wrongs. Even if the project ended up not being what they originally promised, still there was a very good chance they might've been considered heroes for saving the day. Unfortunately, they didn't act. They did zip. They just sat on their fannies, either thinking the problems they were swimming in were overrated, or that a miracle would come to them from out of the clear blue sky. Thus, although there were many who believed in these men, who believed that they would carry the lab out of its misery and bring back the glory days of yore, it was but false hope. Alas, that they represented a solution turned out to be only an illusion.

"In reality, although in lesser positions than the Director, in my judgment, the three deserved more of the blame than the technically bamboozled, managerially undiscerning, and unprepared and ill-advised Vineyard. Actually, puzzling as it is, in some difficult-to-grasp, strange way, all these four men of science seemed totally oblivious of the hard times they were about to experience. Although I don't exactly know why, I feel heavyhearted, wistful pangs of melancholy for the tall, aristocratic, and gentlemanly Vineyard. As it was, regretfully, as the deadly tide of vengeance began to swallow up the lab and to take its toll, he was the first to go under.

"As soon as Vineyard was out of the way in 1981, in came Samios. That's the day he always dreamed of. He sought it out, put his all into the quest, and now was finally on the throne. However, because his reason for being there was to turn the lab around, it behooves us to ask whether or not he actually did. There were in fact a lot of opinions about this making the gossip circuit at the time. Some thought he was making a good start and on his way. Some actually thought he was on the move and getting closer and closer. Some even imagined that he'd already gotten there. Shiny new magnets were put on display. *A new day is dawning*, Mister Samios proclaimed. However, when all was said and done, with a closer look, it was nothing but flimflam, mere fakery. In reality, what he produced was a phony show, with a lot of smooth talk and false façades. It was no more than ostentatious show biz. Yes, there was a flurry of activity at the lab, but all of it was inconsequential. Modifying the magnet design didn't begin to address the real problem that a whole project overhaul was in order. Besides, making what ended up being a minor alteration and doing it in 1982 and 1983 was a straightforward case of too little, too late. In the end, what Nick did in the two years he had before ISABELLE's run-in with destiny was all a sham, two-faced cock-and-bull, and a whopper of prevarication. It was *the big lie* in spades.

"What about Sanford and Rau? What happened to them? Lacking the strength of character to take the reins, and fearing for their skins as well, they hid in the shadows and tried to become invisible. But that strategy didn't work: After the fall of ISABELLE in 1983, they came to be among the first to suffer in the blame game. They were stonewalled, shunned, and casually cast aside as would puppets of no value anymore. They would thenceforth have to go it alone and make their own way. Yes, Nick, throwing them the old sucker punches down below, as was Nick's way, really gave it to them big-time. Well, such are the deserts of playing the high-stakes game and losing.

"During Nick's two-year window of opportunity to pull ISABELLE out of its ruinous spiraling-toward-oblivion dive, there were many scientists who might've acted, who might've at least taken a stab at getting BNL to change its course. But Nick the seemingly invincible man firmly ensconced in the seat of power, Nick the ruthless despot, wasn't the type to suffer those who didn't toe his line. And all were aware of his cold-blooded and merciless brutality. So who was there who would dare oppose him and risk crucifixion? Everybody knew the boss-man was vindictive and grudge-bearing. Everybody knew of his tendency to mete out quick, awful, and irrevocable punishment. There was no appeal. He was enforcer, jury, and judge of his kangaroo court. There was simply no way to escape the long arm of his lawless rule and *retributive justice*. Only if you could run from the lab by getting hold of a protector could you find succor. But few had that luxury. So, as it was, everybody was cowed and bowed before his highness. Up and down the chain of command, throughout the lab's hierarchy, all were in a constant state of apprehensiveness and disquiet. They knew well that if the finger were to be pointed at them, then they were in for a rough, only-few-could-take ride. So scientists at the lab developed the habit of walking in the shadows and staying out of the limelight, trying to be invisible. That's not an environment conducive to encouraging ingenuity and insights, which the lab sorely needed.

"Who were these unfortunate men-become-chickens? There were the supposedly powerful experimentalists looking forward to using the new collider they were promised. These *users* were university men of the stature of Sandweiss of Yale and Willis and Baltay of Columbia. The BNL *users* were of the likes of Ozaki and Lindenbaum. Then there were the accelerator physicists who were supposed to be building the machine. They were at a loss and didn't know what to do. They were men of the caliber of Courant, Palmer, Shutt, Parzen, Hahn, and oh so many others. All of these men from throughout the high-energy community seemed to have become frozen stiff, stopped cold by this squirt of an emperor who indeed was wearing no clothes at all. While Nick went around the country, especially Washington, selling his tainted, defective wares with empty assurances, the best these intimidated, scaredy-cat powder-puffs could muster up was to repeat time and time again the party line that they could see light at the end of the tunnel. Unfortunately, there was no light, only a stand-in mirage.

"What about AUI, you ask? Well, its President, Bob Hughes, was taking his usual siesta, as he was wont to do whenever a crisis appeared on the scene. What a joke it all was! AUI was the boss. It signed the contract with the government, a contract that said the government would provide the money and AUI would deliver the goods. But did it? Hardly! Formally, AUI managed the lab. It bore the fiscal responsibility and was accountable to generate the facilities it said it would. I know Izzie that you were deeply involved with AUI. But I have this urge to be honest and candid about this. I must tell you what I believe to be the truth: When trouble showed up at AUI's doorstep, Hughes simply stepped out, put up the *gone fishing* sign, and left. So much for AUI!

"As if all this weren't enough, there's even more. I ask you, Izzie: Where was the multitude of others who stood to benefit from the project? Where were they when BNL needed them so desperately? Where were the political cream of the crop – congressmen from New York and others committed to Big Science? Where were the funding agency officials – Wallenmeyer, Deutsch, and the others up and down the DOE line? Where were the best-of-the-best, the crowning scientists of the National Academy? Where were the standout, top-of-the-rung scientific minds at the American Physical Society? Where were all the professors, the superstars at the top universities – at Harvard, Stanford, Berkeley, Chicago, MIT, Illinois, Wisconsin, Texas, and the many others? Frankly, the only one-size-fits-all answer I could come up with is that they were scared out of their wits! They must've guessed that ISABELLE was cracking up, no matter what Nick and the rest of the insiders were telling them. So they held back and remained on the fence, choosing to minimize their risk by not investing too much of themselves – their time, their reputations, and their capital – in this unsheltered venture.

"Now honestly Izzie, given the predicament these men found themselves in, could you blame them? Surely, to step up and be counted would've been the right thing to do. But why voluntarily insert their necks in what appeared very much to be nooses? Why stick their noses into the whole squalid, sordid and damned affair? Why board a sinking ship? Why not just stay on the sidelines, playing it safe, ingenuously giving voice to the obvious hard times ahead and to an unlikely brighter future for Big Science? And that's what they did. They stayed out of the whole blooming mess. True, a few might've tried to give some well-needed advice to Vineyard and then to Samios, when he succeeded poor George. But it was to no avail. The truth was that George couldn't hear, and Nick wouldn't listen. You see, the two Directors, their minds impaired and enfeebled by the strain and tension of the stress they were under, were far gone. Objectivity and reality had already abandoned them; and what remained were only pride and the belief in castles-in-the-air and the stuff of dreams that can never be. As for the great majority of the lab's falsely professed friends, they were playing the don't-ask – don't-tell game. Except for the whispering gossip, they were silent. In this way, ISABELLE went without much resistance – alas, in truth, it was with nary a murmur."

Mickey's Disturbing Findings
The Vigilantes

For a moment, Mickey lost his train of thought. What was Izzie thinking about? There were no comments from him, no interruptions. After those nasty things from the past that Mickey aggressively brought out, he really expected some rapid rejoinder from the old man, maybe even an irritated one of outrage and infuriation. But none came, at least not as yet.

Mickey's mind was racing a mile a minute. Did Izzie regret his role in what happened to ISABELLE and to the lab so dear to him? Did he silently resent Mickey's intrusion into those long past affairs? Could he have possibly agreed with what Mickey was stating and implying? Did he perhaps concur with the gist of it? Did he have his own different version? Was he ready with material that would trash Mickey's model? Mickey was dying to know. But he hadn't the least suspicion of what was going on in Izzie's head; and Izzie wasn't the sort to divulge, by facial expressions, what he didn't want others to know. Over the years, he'd learned well the value and usefulness of being in control of his image and his appearance. Actually, Izzie was just gazing ahead, as if at a picture in his mind's eye. His outward look revealed nothing of how he felt about the things that were being said. *Quel dommage*, Mickey thought.

Then, suddenly, Mickey became aware of the lull that had come about and, knowing that it was his performance going on, thought to himself: *Get a grip on yourself. If you're feeling the heat and can't take it, if you're running out of story-telling steam, or if you're getting nervous, you can calm down and rest later. Now's not the time. So just get cracking and move along*! As it happened, Mickey took his good advice to himself, sipped a little water to moisten his dry throat, and carried on.

"Well, I've done with the BNL bunch. If I was a little tough on them, I'm sure you'll appreciate that I was in the thick of things at the time. I did so want ISABELLE to come off. I tried with all I had to make them change course. And who should know better what was technically needed than the one who did most of the detailed conceptual design? But, unfortunately, as you've already heard, they just wouldn't listen. They turned a deaf ear, not only to me, but also to all of us change-seekers. Anyway, that's all past. Let me now turn the coin over and look at the other side of the death of ISABELLE. On this side is where high hopes and great expectations enter the story, where the darkness of ISABELLE's fate gets transformed into the radiance of renewed faith, with the promise of an incredibly spectacular, intoxicating, and giddy-feeling future. So I turn now to the redeemers, the emancipators, the bringers of salvation, and the rescuers of the American high-energy endeavor – yes, the Vigilantes.

"The Vigilantes arose spontaneously, drawn into the power vacuum that came from the breakdown of the American Big Physics Establishment. You see, the high-energy world was moving fast and furiously into the realm of high technology and the management of bigness. This trend soon caused the old and aging Establishment to lose the capability of ruling effectively. Thus, order vanished, and the jungle began its infringement on Big Physics territory, threatening to overwhelm it.

"Some recognized that this just couldn't be allowed to happen. High-energy science was simply too valuable an enterprise to let slip away into dog-eat-dog chaos. The one who saw first how perilous the conditions were was Columbia's determined and energetic Leon Lederman, one of the stars that rose out of your elite coterie of students. In the fifties and sixties he was an experimental user *par excellence*, and a BNL man through and through. But over the years he did a full one hundred and eighty degree turn. Starting the seventies as a staunch supporter of BNL, as the decade wore on he came to realize that he'd stood unquestioningly behind the lab for far too long. BNL was falling behind and it wasn't long before it was brandishing merely old-hat stuff. Fermilab and CERN were both boasting much higher energy beams than BNL. They were also working to the bone toward a new-world future, as BNL kept lagging further and further in the rear. Perhaps it was seeing the three labs side by side that did the trick for Leon, allowing him to see the light. Frankly, it's hard to know exactly when it happened, but at some point Leon crossed a threshold. He found he just couldn't take any more of BNL's managerial incompetence and intransigence, the unwillingness or inability of its guys at the top to see the truth of their position. From then on he began to see BNL as a loser, and abandoned any hope he might've held for its future.

"It was in such a state of mind that Master Lederman did what he believed was the right thing to do: He turned on BNL. Of course, he could easily have just let it go. He could easily have just left it to others to fix the BNL mess and simply cast his lot elsewhere. But Leon was a far bigger man than that. He couldn't just put his tail between his legs and run from his duty as a science citizen. No, BNL was jeopardizing the viability and continuance of the entire Big Science enterprise and he couldn't just shirk his responsibility to do something about it. The plain fact is that, because of its ineptness and incapability of adapting to the new technological world of bigness, BNL simply had to be stopped from infecting the whole high-energy field. So, driven to the wall, Leon became the first of the Vigilantes.

"Although he may have been the most unwavering in his belief that BNL's time at the top of the high-energy game was over, he wasn't alone. No, by the early eighties, the opposition to ISABELLE was beginning to be visible, and there were even signs of a growing trend. As it turned out, there were two other resolute and single-minded individuals who were eager to team up with him to stop the menacing beast from the east. Together, the three of them shaped a formidable alliance. Besides Leon, the other two were Doug Pewitt, John Deutsch's deputy at the DOE, and Jay Keyworth, Reagan's science advisor. During the period 1981 to 1983, acting in concert and firm in their convictions, they won the day and rid the field of the burdensome ISABELLE.

"Fortunately for the three daring men of action, there were a host of bystanders who agreed with the Vigilantes. Under the right conditions, these sideliners might well be made to play in the game. But they simply didn't have the courage to be part of the initial strike force. *To remain safe* was their main concern, and *Silence is Golden* was their motto for survival. With their jobs at stake, most of them were afraid to get too deeply involved or even be associated with the all-out, no-appeal vendetta against BNL. They did, however, provide much needed moral support for the unsavory and disagreeable undertaking. As it happened, towards the end of the affair, many actually began to show their true faces and speak their true minds. Thus, moral support finally became transformed into open, active support. That was indeed important, because key to the execution of ISABELLE was the verdict of the 1983 HEPAP Sub-panel, and these were the men doing the voting. How exciting it was! How sad it was! Anyway, when the ballots were marked and counted, ISABELLE was doomed.

"In the wake of the death-ensuing ordeal, after the action subsided and the drama was done, in the final summation, it was the triumvirate of Doug, Jay and Leon that masterminded the plot and administered the killing blows. However, at the same time as launching their avenging strikes, the Vigilantes also afforded the American high-energy venture the opportunity of a lifetime, giving it a future worthy of the talent, brains, erudition, and wisdom it possessed. The entire strategy – maneuvers worthy of a Machiavelli – was brilliant. Starting with Pewitt's lightning punch at the DOE review of 1981 followed by the Keyworth-Lederman near fatal pummeling dealt out at Snowmass '82, the triple-threat team did what had to be done; and it culminated in the conspiracy to sell ISABELLE down the river – to trade its parasitic blood sucking for Reagan's *Excellence* in the palpable stamp of the SSC.

"Over the year following Snowmass '82, BNL put up a gritty fight for the survival of ISABELLE, but it was to no avail. The course was set at that destiny-making summer in the mountains of Colorado, the community spoke by its vote in the early summer of 1983, and so it was that ISABELLE took its last breath. There was simply no changing what the fates cooked up. Some BNL-supporting die-hards believed up until the last minute that there was still a chance. But it was nothing but a delusion, a trick of the mind that comes when you can't bear the clear and present danger, the imminent reality. You see, the conspiracy was on course; and the decision was by then already made by the unseen men higher up. There was indeed a good show put on as the summer sun of 1983 took its place in the sky. Still, despite the close vote, which was in reality a wily ruse, a bit of deceitful chicanery to soothe the all but fallen spirits of the losers, ISABELLE was put away in the rough and tumble of the double-barreled HEPAP '83 meeting in Washington and then at Columbia's Nevis lab. About three months later, the ceremonial burial announcement came somberly from Washington on a gray October day. Finally, it was official: ISABELLE was dead! For many, ISABELLE's departure was a cheery time, a time to look ahead to a future of would-be pioneers piercing the frontier. But at the lab, shock and sadness filled the air, for mighty ISABELLE had struck out."

Mickey's Disturbing Findings
Star-Crossed Lady

Breathing a little fast, Mickey paused in his monologue. Izzie, a feeling and perceptive man, recognizing Mickey's discomfort, sat by sympathetically, commiserating with Mickey, and looking much the concerned father. When Mickey's heart rate subsided, with only a little more to say, he went on: "Sorry about that! Where was I? Yes, I reached the place in my story where ISABELLE became a fallen lady. Alas! The fabulous, glory-bound dream lived her last days as a distressed damsel damned never to become the radiant light that was the original inspired conception. She was doomed to continue on only in the memories of the men who brought her to her fate. No doubt, with the benefit of hindsight, ISABELLE's stewards would've done things a lot differently. But life offers but one chance. You grab hold and make good use of the opportunity, or poof, it's gone. And so it was that ISABELLE was frittered away, and all who salute science can do naught but mourn her loss. So the dance is done, the orchestra has left, and the lights have dimmed. The stage is empty and the tale's *finis*."

Mickey stopped abruptly for theatrical effect. So much did he like the way he finished up, he wanted to just leave it at that. But he knew he couldn't. There was still one little thing he had to take care of. It was only a formality, but still, it needed saying. Having given such a long exposition, a very brief pulling together of what he tried to say was called for. It simply had to be done. So, in quick order, he plowed right into it: "Let me give you the short answer of what I've learned: My journey has shown me the dark side of a lab in the throes of failure. The story has many sides and many players. And – just as in the fable Rashomon – it can be looked at in many ways. So you can well appreciate that giving an account of what transpired has been quite a challenge. But I must tell you that my entire affair with ISABELLE – both her life and my search for its meaning – has been a gripping, enthralling, and riveting experience.

"As I've explored this way and that, that way and this, there's one point that hits me right in the eyes, one thing that stands out loud and clear. In searching for the truth, I've been led to the single inescapable view that the lab itself must bear the lion's share of the blame for what happened. I can even take that a step further. To carve out a straightforward and uncomplicated encapsulation of that provocative conclusion I've come to, it is this: Only BNL's Director – and, mark you, the Director alone – had the wherewithal and the power to change the course of events and save ISABELLE from its ultimate ruination. Thus it was solely Vineyard and then Samios, when he took the hot seat, who could've turned things around. I'm not saying it would have been an easy thing to do. Far from it! It needed guts; political savvy; vaulting hunger; a will of iron; and a ruthless resolve and determination to come out on top. It needed the amalgamation of a robust, lusty ambition with a calm, accommodating, give-and-take spirit; a combination of moderation and don't-give-an-inch stubbornness; and Machiavellian deceptiveness, cunningness, and wile. It needed all these things and more, but, unfortunately, these Directors were men who simply didn't have what it takes, and, without the right kind of men to guide the lab, the poor ISABELLE, lady of misfortune that she was, didn't stand a chance."

* * * * *

Izzie On Stage
A Desire to Tell of Days Long Gone

As Mickey finished his impromptu speech on the ISABELLE affair, he was utterly spent. How odd, he thought, that a sedentary activity – just talking – could cause an overwhelming physical exhaustion to permeate through his entire body. While in such a state, one thing was sure: He desperately needed a brief spell to recover. So it was just perfect for him that the headwaiter and his assistants were all milling about. Having removed the empty salad plates, there was a flurry of busyness as they cleaned the table, preparing it for the entrées, which were already on their way. By the time they arrived, Mickey, free from troubling words and troubling notions for that short spell, found himself refreshed, reinvigorated, and braced for the dialectic contest soon to resume.

That looks scrumptious, fit for kings, Izzie blurted out, as the waiters placed the delectable-looking main courses in front of them. *What a spread*, he added, his face lighting up as he glimpsed what awaited them. Izzie's filet, served above an adjustable burner, was cut into thick slices and soaked in a buttery herbed sauce, while Mickey's duck was served over wild rice encircled by a rich array of colorful grilled vegetables. For a while, at least, the mouth-watering food took their minds off the aborted ISABELLE, rude awakenings, disillusionment, and dashed hopes. But, despite Izzie's playing of the wag, the farceur, pattering on about the array of gustatory delights lying ahead, he, in reality, took advantage of the opportunity that the break in the action afforded him to ponder Mickey's provocative remarks.

With the aplomb and efficiency of top-notch professionals, the waiters did what had to be done *one-two-three*. Then, as they receded into the background, Izzie raised his wineglass and proposed a toast to *Le Petit Village*: *May it continue to flourish.* While they drank, Mickey wistfully remembered his day of breathless wonder and ineffable mystery spent in that enchanted valley to the west.

The ritual done, Izzie sat back in his chair with his head slightly tilted toward the ceiling and his thumbs holding his suspenders, like an old-time party boss. If you added a cigar and a smoke-filled room, you could have mistaken this for a days-of-yore political wheeling-dealing scene. But that it was not. On the contrary, it was quite the opposite. Truth was the keynote here, not political machinations and trickery. And soon that reality became evident, when, without the least warning, Izzie sat up and bent forward in his chair. Almost instantaneously, Izzie's humor dramatically altered, and the climate – the temperament – at the table turned from one of good-fellowship and conviviality to sobriety, touched with a little somber coloring. Looking straight into Mickey's eyes, Izzie began to speak. From the first words he uttered, it was clear that he'd cast off his joker's mask in order to don the grim and tristful one better matched to his radically transformed mood.

"I can't get away from the impression that you're pointing the finger of blame in my direction," said Izzie. There was an atypical melancholy in his voice, mixed in with a touching remorse. It almost appeared that some sort of oral apologia was in the offing. He went on: "However, don't jump to the conclusion that I'm censuring you for that. In a sense you're quite right to hold me at some fault. I'm most assuredly accountable at some level for what happened to BNL and ISABELLE; and to the extent that I am, I most certainly deserve a degree of reproach. But before you move too far too fast and lay it all squarely at my feet, let me relate some matters that I hope may soften your hard stance. Now understand that I'm only too well aware that what I have to say may or may not alter the model you've shaped of the past. Neither may it get you to modify your opinion of the lab. It may not even cause you to think a little better of me. However, having already put so much into this expedition of yours, and having so conscientiously sought me out, I think you deserve to know, and it behooves me to tell you, how I perceived and understood what took place.

"I must tell you that your stubborn pursuit of what really took ISABELLE from us intrigues me no end – so much so in fact that for myself, as much as for you, I am determined to attempt to express what up to now I've locked away in disused cells of sleeping memories. Thus, I feel ready to go even further than you might've expected. As much as I'm able to, as much as I can recall to my consciousness, I intend to try to disclose what was in my heart and in my mind as my influence, control, and power over BNL and community matters were diminishing, moving ever downward until they were entirely lost. You see, youthful enthusiasm and energy can't be kept forever. Aging is, after all, inevitable. So it was that I, as all of humankind eventually must, came to feel its consequences. But I'm getting a little ahead of myself. Let me start at the beginning."

A Good Director's Hard to Find

"I guess you're right about Directors. They do stand at the lab's influence fulcrum, and always have. Thus, if you're going to pick a single person who can make a lab a big thing or a dud, then surely he's the one. But you've already surmised that. So what can I offer? Actually, if you want to know something about how the BNL Directors came to be who they were, you've come to the right man. Frankly speaking – but don't go spreading this around – I picked them. Now hold on, I'm not saying that I picked them all. Of course I didn't. But I did start the ball rolling. And don't minimize the importance of that! Now you might ask, *how so*? Well, the situation with the class of BNL Directors is that they seem to follow some set of rules akin to a natural law. Once such a law is the governing agent, the only thing remaining free to select is the starting condition. Everything else ensues from that. Well, the succession process for Directors is not exactly a physical law, but if you think about the process and if you accumulate a lot of experience with it at close quarters, I believe you'd be surprised how close it is to being regulated by some kind of prescriptive formula. In any case, by observing the train of Directors over the years, I'm persuaded that there's simply no other way to look at it. Believe it or not, there really is a guiding principle for the succession of Directors. And that's what I want to tell you about. So let's go all the way back to the lab's origins after *the war*, when I was kinglike for matters relating to the lab. I was top man then, and for about a decade and a half after. If anyone put the first few Directors in office, it was I. From then on, if my theory's right, and I do think it is, the Directors that came afterwards were a foregone conclusion. Of course it's not quite that simple. But let me tell you my story, and you'll see what I mean.

"When our Northeast laboratory came to life, all charged-up, with vitality to burn, and with the-sky's-the-limit imaginings, it was an experience to remember. It was an awakening for all of us involved. It inspired us. It stirred our spirits. It set our souls on fire. We were all infected by the vision before us. But for those of us who were its founding fathers, it was more like a divine image. So, I ask you, Mickey, who could've noticed that one little dark spot in the glare of such radiance? Who could hold us accountable, who could rake us over the coals, for not immediately registering the significance of it? How were we to know that it would mean so much to the lab's future? And what was it? Well, actually it was no more than that we encountered a hell of a lot of resistance in getting someone to become the lab Director.

"This matter of installing a Director seemed like such a piddling thing to us at the time. We, those of us with the job of getting the lab off the ground, just sloughed it off as a quirk of the times. In the excitement of our quick and thrilling success in instilling the world of what came to be Big Science into the remains of Camp Upton, we saw the problem as being but a minor hindrance, a little hitch, a scant stone in our path to be easily shunted aside. We would get to it in due course, we thought. But, as we all now know with the benefit of hindsight, we were wrong! Yes, as it turned out, it was a big problem, with profound, cutting, and cruel consequences. It was a problem that needed thorough and painstakingly diligent tending. It was a problem that badly required immediate attention. How could we have been so dumb, you ask? The straight from the shoulders answer is that it was due to our being almost completely devoid of experience in institution building, and our pitiful lack of management foresight.

"You know, Mickey, even though what I'm telling you is quite true, even though what happened and why is exactly how I'm going to describe it, I'm still dismayed and mystified by it all. Who would've believed then that such deficiencies as we had could've ended up causing us so much agony and so much loss? Yet, these trifling and no-account shortcomings, as they then seemed to us to be, did just that. It's true that there finally came a day when we were able to comprehend the error of our ways. But by then the days of reckoning were already upon us. By then it was far too late. Would that we had been smarter and known better!"

The First Bona Fide Director

"Mickey, consider our situation back around 1947. The *Great War* of the forties was over. We had in our grip the go-ahead from Groves in Washington to build this once-in-a-lifetime lab dedicated to physics research. We found the site we finally all agreed upon. We were ecstatic – on cloud nine. But now we needed a Director. Who should we choose? Naturally, it would be the most illustrious, the most celebrated, the most renowned, and the most accomplished scientist America could offer up. He would be a man who could look the world square in the face, with defiance in his heart; and a man who could march ahead fearlessly toward the world's end and into eternity. That's the stouthearted mettle we were seeking. That's the paladin we wanted. A champion among scientists! A champion among men! This man could be no less. Remember, we were the *Physicists*! We smashed the atom apart and came to fathom its secrets. No, we were not mere men. We were close to being gods!

"Scientists that we were, pragmatic men, we treated the matter at hand much as a straightforward systematic study in analytical logic, with sweet reason as our secret weapon. Our problem: We had to find a Director. OK, so we wrote a few names down on a piece of paper. Needless to say, they were the best of the best. Then we contacted them; and that's when the shit hit the fan! To our utter surprise and consternation, what we got was one refusal after another. That's when a bit of alarm began to set in. Nonetheless, being cocky men, we weren't about to be deterred by our first setback. So we lowered our sights a little, devised a longer list this time, and started in again to get the task done. Still luck evaded us. Things just weren't going our way. However, our capacity for rationalization seemed endless, and we kept slogging ahead. It was about then that some desperation began to seep in as our self-assuredness began to edge southward. You see, the stature of the candidates kept declining the further we went; and not only didn't we have the type of man we wanted, we didn't have a man at all. As we crept along the chain of names, we knew we'd eventually get to an acceptance of a sort, but by then, we'd be many stature levels down from where we originally imagined we'd be. No, this wasn't at all the way we'd envisioned the finding of a Director to be. We thought they'd jump at such an opportunity, that they'd be flying at us, importuning us to install them. But they didn't. They stayed away in droves. They just didn't want it.

"The refusal reasons we got were plausible enough. Their rejection stories were simply articulated, straightforward and unsubtle, and easy to empathize with. During their wartime efforts, obliged to focus on highly advanced, sophisticated, and difficult problems of physics and engineering, they just became too exhausted for words. The secrecy their work entailed just wearied and drained them that much more. Many of them worked as project managers and administrators, and, having had their fill of that, certainly didn't want any more of it. Mostly heard, as if it were a rehearsed notion among them, was the necessity of relieving the pressures of those unnerving war years. Why would they want to replace one stressful set of circumstances with another? No, it was simply too soon.

"At that time, what these men of science were really seeking was a return to their pre-war years. What they really wanted and what they were driven to get back to was their teaching and basic research. The war was behind them. They served it well: with pride and dignity, and with unprecedented achievement. They did their duty and more. Now they wanted to reclaim their well-deserved lives as professors. Academia was the world where they felt secure and at ease, the world in which they knew how to maneuver, and the world they were attracted and devoted to. That's where they had a hankering to be, and that's where they were determined to go.

"Who would deny that the excuses for a more peaceful university life were levelheaded and reasonable ones? Who would doubt these men's right to go back to the life they were ripped from when their call to arms came, when they were whisked off to Los Alamos and other locales to become soldiers of science? Sure, I understood. After all, didn't I want the same thing? It was easy for me to identify with them. But somehow a few others and I were marching to a different drummer. We seemed to have a higher calling. You see, what came to be Big Physics was beckoning to us, and it was irresistible, an offer we couldn't refuse. Too bad the others didn't see that bright star we were aiming for.

"However, for our new lab to fly, we had to have a Director, and we had to have him on the double. So we began to twist arms. We used every trick in the book. We appealed to their presumed instinct to see science flourish in the future. *Without you*, we said, *who knows*? We implored them to think of the young. What would they do without new nuclear physics research facilities? We pointed to the fact that the new lab would open up hitherto undreamed of avenues, incredible and mind-blowing research of a magnitude and nature unavailable to universities-sans-lab. We pleaded with them not to be the cause for the loss of our one chance to have the American government fund science facilities of previously unheard of size and cost. *Now's the time*, we insisted. *Let's grab the opportunity; we're depending on you*, we added. But somehow it all fell on deaf ears. The ploy simply wasn't working. Then, at the moment when getting somewhere with this or the other tactics we'd devised appeared futile, we hit upon just the right means for just the right man. The man was Philip Morse of MIT. The way we got him was not with high-sounding phrases. He knew them all well, and, even more, appreciated their validity. But we reached him with the rather practical proviso that his tenure as Director would be as short as possible. *Yes, the job will be temporary, just long enough to find a full-fledged, full-term Director*, we conceded. Thus, in that somewhat mundane manner, we persuaded Morse to take on the job.

"You understand that this wasn't the best way to pick someone for such a challenging position. Giving a new lab the kick and thrust to get moving is not run-of-the-mill business. And getting it to move fast and in just the right direction is more like being in *Marlboro Country* – not for the weak-willed or weak-spirited. So the fact that we ended up with such a reluctant man wasn't exactly an auspicious beginning. But we were young, innocent, and sure of ourselves then. Nothing could faze us. We were filled with the cockiness often found in those of little experience. I know that now it all seems devoid of common sense. But it was different then. The confidence we had was simply boundless. Nothing could stop us! And look, facts are facts! We had our first Director. Morse was on board. Now the world was our oyster. It was all systems go! True, it was a little foolish. But we were young men overflowing with the pride of having our way. So we laughed: *We did it*!

"Of course there was that itsy-bitsy point that Morse's acceptance was a conditional one. But what did that matter? *Not to worry*, we trusted. Not for a minute did we imagine that this could ever amount to an impediment that we couldn't overcome. However, as it turned out, Morse had an agenda of his own. He was a sharp man with much experience to back him up. No one, and I mean no one, could play nonchalantly with Phil! You couldn't hoodwink a man such as he. He wanted it to be absolutely clear right from the start that his role as Director would be an abbreviated one, a year at most he kept repeating over and over again. He obviously didn't put much stock in our promise, because every chance he got, he would remind us, especially me, that we had given our solemn pledge, presumed by him to be our word of honor.

"Ostensibly, we went along with his wish for early relief. Almost from the day he took his chair in the Director's office, we went through the appropriate motions in search of a successor. However, if truth be told, our hearts weren't in it. I'd guess that in our subconscious minds, we really wanted to keep Morse precisely where he was. Naïvely, we thought that, having been roped in, he would change his mind. But that was a misjudgment on our part of Morse's character. No, he stuck to his guns and wouldn't budge, not an inch. In fact, he kept pushing and pushing to be released, as if he understood that we weren't giving our all to ensure his being a short-termer. Then, after he had served about a year, lo and behold, a successor was identified. To be accurate, it was Morse who actually pinpointed him, imposing the man on us in the manner of an implied ultimatum. *Take him, or I'm out the door anyway*, he seemed to be saying. At first glance, the new guy was a letdown, and we weren't satisfied one bloody bit. But what were we to do? We were going to lose Morse in any case. So, when push came to shove, we gave in and accepted his choice. Therefore, in the end, our vaunted principle of going for the peerless, quintessential scientist, the crème de la crème, el primo himself, reluctantly was abandoned. Once again, pragmatism threw principle out the window.

"How inconsiderate of Morse to give us the old *one-two*! First he leaves, and then he leaves us with Leland Haworth. How disagreeable that was! And what a bind he put us in! After dragging Haworth out of his post at the University of Illinois, he gave us not a stitch of time to do anything but accept the man and resign ourselves to it. Boy, were we taken? When you consider his stature in the physics community, Haworth certainly wasn't a man we would've picked if he were put through the wringer of the selection process. In fact, probably, he wouldn't even have made the list. Oh, he was all right as physicists go, but he wasn't *a man among men*, one who stood out among all others, one who shook the science world.

"Once the new man was settled on, things were set in motion and there was speedy change. We weren't too happy about it, but there it is. Morse soon fled the scene and Leland arrived on site raring to go. In such a manner did Haworth become BNL's first bona fide Director. As it happened, Leland was a man who really wanted the job and was willing to give it his all. As time passed and we came to see him in action, it began to dawn on us that our original judgment of him was, to put it mildly, all wet. The truth was that he was a good man, indeed, a very good man. He had a lot of moxie, and ended up being a Director that was as close as you could get to a sterling one. For more than a decade he ran the lab strongly and fairly. He was capable of carrying it through its formative years with consummate managerial skill. Frankly speaking, it was his expertise at guiding and captaining the BNL ship that made it a true winner, a smash hit. As I think about it, I almost can't believe how fortunate we were that, despite our being four-flushed by Morse, fate saw fit to hand over to us such a man as Leland was.

"Yes, Haworth turned out to be a gem of a Director: In a rather short time, he got the reactor done. Then, without skipping a beat, he had the Cosmotron built and producing physics. That machine was the first of the operating weak-focusing synchrotrons, setting loose a plethora of new elementary particles. I'll have you know that he built that accelerator contrary to my advice, which was to go for a higher energy one that Berkeley eventually built. How mistaken I was. The West Coast Bevatron, even though it was the first machine to find and study the anti-proton, wasn't much more than a dinosaur in disguise. Now you understand, Mickey, that I was something of a tyrant in my youthful days. Going against my wishes wasn't for the fainthearted. In fact, there weren't many who could. But Leland turned out to be one of the few who got away with it. He fought me tooth and nail, and he won. Even more, he turned out to be right. No doubt, there was something very classy about that man. Yes, he was indeed good!

"Added to his accomplished ability in building machines, he was a top-notch manager of people. Over the years, he undertook and carried off the delicate and praiseworthy task of satisfying the insatiable experimenters. That's tough enough in itself. But while he was doing that, he was also encouraging an atmosphere at the lab that gave the staff high incentive to work toward developing technologies for the future. This was a balancing act of the highest order. Yet, he pulled it off.

"As if all that weren't enough for one man, as the fifties progressed, he went for the gold and got it. He would go where no man had gone before, and take BNL with him. However, to reach those heights: he had to expend great effort; he had to have deep psychological insight; he had to have a commanding and compelling ability to persuade; he had to be able to take the heat from the many experimenters who felt they weren't getting their fair share anymore; he had to have unequaled technical judgment; and he had to have an uncanny manner of juggling money and people that would gain for him the end he sought. I gather you wouldn't be shocked if I told you that he had all these things. And with them, he reaped for all of us the reward of a lifetime. It was his tour de force.

"To realize his dream, Leland had to squeeze resources from wherever he could lay his hands on them. It was to be for a future unimagined by anyone before – one he believed to be worth the raging, venomous, unruly, mindless, and explosive resistance he encountered at the lab. The money had to come from somewhere. But from where would he take it? Each potential source said, *OK, get it, but not from me*! Nonetheless, he pushed ahead. He did the seemingly impossible, taking from the Cosmotron experimenters to give to the new rapidly advancing accelerator technology. Yes, he grabbed *user* money – the Director's prerogative – and, in so doing, made a lot of enemies along the way. But what came of it all was indeed awesome! As it happened, he oversaw the invention of the new synchrotron principle of strong focusing; and then – his pièce de résistance – he incorporated the new concept into the super-duper accelerator, the AGS that came to be – excuse the slight exaggeration – the father of high-energy physics."

The First Succession: Haworth to Goldhaber

There was a brief silence as Izzie was reminded of that remarkable era in BNL's life when the AGS came upon the scene. *It was quite a time*, he thought. Mickey, meanwhile, was gripped by a feeling of sorrow at seeing the old man in such a sad, meditative mood, seemingly on the verge of tears. But Mickey could think of nothing to do, so he just sat still, waiting for Izzie to pull himself together. Then, as quickly as the episode began, Izzie's sinking heart and low spirits, instigated by a nostalgic remembrance, simply vanished. It was a magical moment, as Izzie's face broke out into a mischievous grin, his typical liveliness and zest for living returning in full force. With a hungry craving, he lifted a juicy piece of filet and put it slowly into his mouth. He chewed the tempting morsel lustily. Then he took a gulp of wine, leaned back, and breathed a contented sigh. Remaining in that position, he said nothing for over a minute. *What might he conceivably have on his mind*, wondered Mickey? *Yes, it had to be. It had to be the Haworth to Goldhaber succession.* As it turned out, Mickey was right; and he didn't have long to wait to hear it from Izzie's own lips. With a suddenness that jolted Mickey, the pause ended. Izzie straightened his back, peered into Mickey's eyes, and began to speak.

"In trying to generate a picture of just how the Goldhaber accession came about, my mind meandered a bit, back to the lab's beginnings in the late forties. There was an immediacy then to the whole process of installing a Director for the fledgling lab. We were rushed into getting it done ASAP. Those go-getters in the war office, especially that hard and ruthless tiger Groves, were on pins and needles, ready to pounce on us if they had to. So we had to pull the man of the hour out of a hat, and fast. A good thing for us there was Morse! But the guys in Washington knew he was only an interim Director. They insisted that the real thing had to be put in place. Their impatience grew daily, and the pressure on us mounted correspondingly. Sure, we had Morse sitting in Director's chair, but finding a quick replacement was part of the deal we made. We had no choice but to act. Unfortunately, looking around, there simply wasn't anybody else of his caliber that we could finger. So the months passed and the stress we were under kept rising. Yes, it was a really hard time for us.

"Then, mostly through pure unadulterated luck – of course, I shouldn't forget that little dab of Morse's perseverance as well – Haworth simply materialized before us. At first, because his stature level was much reduced compared to that of Morse, in the immediate wake of his arrival, there was no satisfaction and peace of mind for us, no optimism or high hopes. How were we to know at the time that in reality the stars were shining on us? You see, it turned out that he was just the man we needed, coming to us at just the right moment, and for a position made to order for him. As a result, it wasn't too long after that we found ourselves relieved of our anxious concerns, our frayed nerves, and the hounding harassment we were experiencing from the money-givers in the capitol. Anyway, seeing that these guys who held the purse strings were comfortable, even pleased, with the new arrangement, and by then feeling quite good about Haworth ourselves, why should we complain? And we didn't! In fact, I, like the others who gave birth to BNL, came to be hypnotized into a false sense of being safe and slipup-proof. And why shouldn't we have felt that way? Haworth's knack for running the lab happened to be full of skill, full of mastery, and slick as a whistle. Thus, after performing his magic over the years, in our minds he became the ingenious virtuoso, and we became the brilliant and gilt-edged decision-makers. However, Mickey, I have to admit to you that I shouldn't have been so complacent. To be candid, something in me made me blind to the true reality before me. I just didn't appreciate that, a little more than a dozen years later, Haworth's succession would be as hard as his accession.

"Why was I so dense, you ask? For such a supposedly smart man, how could I have been so dim-witted? To be honest and straight with you, I must confess that, along the way, I succumbed to that tired and overrated advice: *if it ain't broke, don't fix it.* But it was the wrong aphorism for the spot we were in. Nonetheless, maybe because it was such an easy rule to follow – just do nothing – we stuck with it, and so paid the price. As it turned out, without an effective fix in place, the obvious came about, and the second lab transition gave us the same headache as the first. In all those years, we simply didn't learn a damned thing. The succession problem was staring us in the face. We'd already been through it. But still we convinced ourselves that there was nothing to worry about, and nothing that we had to do to prepare for the next transition of power that would inevitably be confronting us. So we ignored the whole business and simply let it go. And what was the result of this negligence? Well, we were forced to relive the entire distressing experience of the dozen or so years earlier.

"So there we were. The fifties were rapidly coming to an end. With Haworth now in the same role Morse had a dozen years earlier, we rewound the tape and played the same scene over again. However, there was a little difference this time. When Morse left, he'd glommed onto Haworth and rammed him down our throats, while, when Haworth left, he distanced himself from taking part in any of the succession business. Thinking about it, that really wasn't of much account. Who would've listened to Haworth anyway? You see, no matter that he'd done so much for high-energy science, we men running the show took scant notice of it. What foolish dolts we were! We judged him mediocre from the start, and, being know-it-all elitist scientists set in our ways, nothing could change our minds. But, leaving aside that minor matter of being involved in the succession itself, the match between what transpired in the cases of the two men ditching us and going their own way was uncanny. As Morse did, Haworth insisted, professing sound personal reasons, that he had to go with the least possible delay, setting a date that he asserted he had to adhere to. However, just as we had in the instance of Morse's hasty exit, at first we didn't believe Haworth really meant it. We kept trying to persuade him to stay on till we could arrange for a right and proper replacement. But, as a matter of fact, we simply couldn't accomplish it. Yes, we talked to a lot of people clearly of the right caliber, but none would buy our sales pitch. So, once again, we were left in the lurch. Now Mickey, try to grasp the predicament we got ourselves into: Haworth was on his way out the door, and we had no one of stature high enough for us wrapped up, ready to move in. What a god-awful mess! What were we to do?

"Although Haworth left on short notice and couldn't be persuaded to stay on even for a little while, I can't really lay any of the blame on his doorstep. Circumstances just piled up on him: His wife became very ill and he wasn't in great medical shape either; he had an offer from Ramsey for a job at the AEC with the hope of the top position at the NSF a while later; and he was being outrageously and hysterically – and in my admittedly after-the-fact opinion, undeservedly – harassed by the *users* at the Cosmotron. No, when he chose to depart BNL for better climes, there is no doubt that he acted in good faith and understandably did what he had to do. At least that's the way I see it now. If there has to be a scapegoat for the plight we were in, he's certainly not the one.

"In all probability, it was our own hard-headedness, our stupidity, and our inability to learn from past experience that left us holding the bag. That's right! We can't just claim that it was circumstances that put us in the position we found ourselves in. No, we can't simply slough off our responsibility as the leaders of the pack. There was so much hanging in the balance, but unfortunately we were found wanting. We were derelict in our duty. I'd even go further and say that we were reprehensible. It's a funny thing, Mickey, but our guilt didn't escape our subconscious; but only much later did it come to the fore, making its way to our conscious minds. No, in the end we weren't spared the awful regrets. We weren't given the luxury of getting off scot-free. At least that's the way it was for me.

"You know, Mickey, I've often thought about Leland in his last days at the lab. Poor man! Try to picture the tight spot he was in, being all alone with nary a friend of consequence around. There he was, the magician finding that he was having quite a bit of trouble keeping all the tossed balls up in the air at the same time. Meanwhile, facing him were the experimenters, with foul deeds on their minds and wickedness in their hearts, sensing his weakness and closing in on him looking for a kill. Don't you think we should've interceded on Leland's behalf when the *users* had it in for him? Don't you think we should've found a way to provide him with the help he needed when he needed it most? Sad to say, we weren't sensitive enough to what Leland was trying to do. Probably, although it pains me to say it, we secretly supported the experimenters. What a deplorable and distasteful speculation that is!

"Anyway, the die was cast. We lost Haworth and had no one that measured up to step in. The claim that events conspired against us is not the least convincing. Be assured that I myself am not at all persuaded by it. Look, you can't just sit around and wait for random chance to save you when trouble arrives. You've got to move into the thick of things. You've got to get off your butt and make things happen. You've got to be proactive as they say nowadays. In hindsight, it seems so obvious. We should've stepped into the breach earlier. We should've had the foresight to sense what was coming. We should've been pragmatic and smart enough to identify one or perhaps even more candidates who fit our criteria, and have them waiting in the wings. We should've done what had to be done. We should've given the candidates some of what they sought. We should've compromised. We should've been better negotiators. OK, it wasn't a snap to do all these things. But in fact we did none of them. Somehow we fell for the patently ridiculous notion that finding and installing a new Director is not such a tough proposition. *Just wait for the right guy to come along*, we thought. How could we have been such simpletons? Didn't anything stick from that frightfully frustrating period that eventually wound up giving us Haworth? The truth is that finding the right man simply can't be done when time is not on your side. You better believe it! For, who doubts that *procrastination is the thief of time*? Anyway, in the end, we waited far too long and refused to make any deals. We played with fire again and this time got burnt. What ignorant managers we were! What arrogant fools!

"Thus, there we were with our inaction this time coming back to bite us. Yes, history repeated itself, as again we couldn't find a person made of *the right stuff* to be the Director. But this time it was far worse. You see hitting upon and acquiring anyone was much harder the second time around. So much at the lab had already been carried out and put in place, thereby greatly limiting the freedom for a new Director to institute his own ideas. What could we offer any potential candidates? The great technological adventure seemed to be over. As far as anyone could see, it would be nothing but a maintenance operation. What then could we make appealing enough to stir a man's imagination? Why should any man worth his salt take on such a mundane job? Why should he sacrifice a life of meaning that he already had, merely to be a caretaker for what others had conceived, fashioned, and put into action? In fact, it was a lost cause. Thus, when the dust settled, we'd looked around the lab doing the *eeny-meeny-miny-mo* bit, picking a man just there for the taking. After all, we made him an offer he couldn't refuse. Yes, we ended up with someone far less in quality than we wished for and far less than the lab's then totally unforeseen future was to demand."

Gazing into Izzie's eyes gave Mickey the impression that the old man was overflowing with regret. Actually, Mickey wasn't far off the mark, as became evident when Izzie began to speak again. There was a gloomy sort of melancholy in his voice, a sorrowful, hard-to-take trembling. It must have been hard for him to go on; but trouper that he was, Izzie, with dignity written all over him, persisted: "What a mistake we made giving Goldhaber the *thumbs-up* sign! Just around the next bend lay undreamed of opportunities that the likes of such a man would never be able to recognize and grasp. When it came to management, Goldhaber was a technician, not an innovator. He thought he'd be given options; then say *yes* to this one and *no* to that one. If perchance *this* didn't work out, he could always revert to *that*. It was just a straightforward application of logic and practical reasoning out. And Goldhaber was quite well equipped to handle that kind of matter. But when it came to the challenge of seeing ahead, of identifying, however hazily, what was not palpably before him, of sensing the changing currents in the wind, he was but a novice, a babe in the woods.

"Goldhaber had another shortcoming. He hadn't a whit of insight into the constant delicate balancing act required of a good Director, not to mention a great one: of giving the experimenters their due but no more than that, while at the same time providing the lab's technologists with what they needed to pursue their mandate for the future. As a Director, you might well be confronted with a dilemma needing the judgment of a Solomon. Consider this: The experimenters, rife with influence, are breathing down your neck for more resources. The high-energy community is seeking a brand new, advanced, heretofore-never-done facility that only the lab's technologists can work through and maybe bring to fruition. You have inadequate resources for both. The spotlight is on you, and all are looking to you for answers. The pressure begins to mount. Everyone's depending on you. Which one will you choose: the present or the future? You have to decide. You have to act: Now! Well, Mickey, what would you do? What do you imagine a good Director would do? Hypothetically, what choice would you predict Maurice would make?

"Unbeknownst to anyone at the time, this is exactly the sticky situation BNL was headed into. Would that we had known! If we had, I venture to say that we never would have asked Goldhaber to serve as Director. No matter what it took, we'd have found a better way. You see, that quandary is no job for a lightweight; and, sad to say, Goldhaber was a lightweight. Because the experimenters had the louder voices and the longer stretch, and because he was of their breed, he gave them the lion's share of the cash. *The future be damned*, was effectively his reaction! The rationalization for doing this was a real doozer. Listen: *The AGS simply has to keep churning out data. That's what we're here for. The future can wait. It'll take care of itself.* To be honest, at the time the Board and all the BNL hangers-on bought the argument, including me. Yes, Mickey, I must admit that as the sixties opened I was as shortsighted as the rest of the BNL crowd, fully committed to experimental work over technology development. And what's the lesson of all this? Well, it's no more than that when a lightweight finds himself face-to-face with a heavyweight's problem, he almost always ends up doing the wrong thing. He has an overwhelming urge to hide his head in the sand. He won't even know he's doing it. He prances around with a fool's bravado, and because he is the Director, a grand science mogul, no one who sees the truth – and there were some of those – will tell him that things are going to pot and bound to crack up. So it was that Goldhaber set the lab's course firmly on the path toward its appointment with hardship and ruination."

The Inevitable Course to Paramount Power and the Consequences

"Although I didn't covet or strive for it, during the forties and fifties I became BNL's center of power. Believe it or not, I was almost like a science-style Godfather. My say held sway. I ruled like a king. So, suppose you were to ask: Who single-handedly chose and put in place the first few BNL Directors? I would answer without the least hesitation that it was my doing. However, as the sixties came and wore on, it was my time for ebbing. I was on the wane. By the time Goldhaber got the hang of his new job, and really took command of things, my influence on lab matters that counted had all but dissipated. You wouldn't believe how swiftly the impact I had declined. Anyway, with me gone, there was a power vacuum left to fill. Can you guess who stepped into it? Of course you can. It was none other than the Directors. Who else? I, who built the lab from scratch and knew it inside and out, was effectively gone. All the others connected with or hanging around the lab were on the periphery of the real action. What did they know of the lab's guts? So it was that from Goldhaber onward, a lineage of all-powerful BNL Directors was established, one that was to last for almost four decades.

"Looking back on the early days, I now realize that in principle the Director always had an awful lot of power, way too much for his own good and everybody else's. But, not realizing its dark, threatening consequences, that's in fact the way we set it up. That's the way we wanted it: We wanted action from him – on the spot. We wanted him to get the job done, sooner rather than later, and no excuses. And how was that to be accomplished? Why, by giving him free reign, of course. So that's what we did. There was no fuss made about it. There was no resistance put up by the Board, or by the BNL staff, or by the *user* community. Everyone simply bought into it. It seemed harmless enough. Thus, by our own design, the Director came to wield unquestioned, exceptional, and hard-to-match jurisdiction over an unseemly wide spectrum of lab activities: he managed the lab budget and personnel matters with no one of consequence to contest him; he exerted an unhealthy weight in determining the availability of experimental facilities and slots; and he held no small measure of influence and authority in the choice of new facilities. In short, he'd become very powerful in the science world. What that meant was that if you wanted to do something in Big Physics, he, and only he, was the man you had to play cards with.

"Unfortunately, when the lab system first got started, we lacked the astuteness to foresee the disagreeable, the adverse, and the detrimental consequences of the centralization of power. Well, we were young then, and we supposed that we had everything in hand. How wrong we were! Compared to what we imagined that we were establishing, what an utterly different picture was actually shaping up! Would you believe it? We expected the universities to become the dominant entity in an open, rational, and fair decision-making process. In this way we would build the best facilities and provide experimental access to the most deserving. Yes, it would be a distributed power system – placing the power in the universities, where it belonged, where we all came from. We were secure in our belief that they had the will and the clout to check any dictatorial tendencies that might begin to show up in the Director. To be sure, we didn't have the least doubt that the universities were the right ones to set the rules and run the show. Their prestige, their authoritativeness, their sphere of influence, and their capacity to be open-minded, evenhanded, and just made them precisely what was needed. Surely such pillars of the science community could play the parts of the true power behind the throne. But things didn't turn out the way we envisioned they would. As it happened, once I withered away, with amazing speed the Director became both the lab dictator and the Big Physics satrap, while the universities ended up being his mandarins. How ironic! It was exactly the opposite we were gunning for. We wanted the universities to be the ones on top, while the lab Director, though having a free hand in running the lab, would nonetheless be beholden to the universities and obliged to follow their counsel and guidance. But it seems that life has its way of twisting our designs. Too bad! It could've been so good!

"Well, what we desired, and what we wanted to materialize, is neither here nor there. The reality is that in the last few decades, the BNL Director has become packed with power. But that, Mickey, is a far cry from how it was in the early years. This is true in spite of the fact that the power potential was always there. It's just that, in the forties and fifties, the power was suppressed, the potential thereby unrealized. I guess you're wondering precisely why the Director's incipient power wasn't used right away. Since all men tend to use whatever power they have, why didn't Haworth? Yes, why didn't Haworth show his teeth?

"Actually, there are a few possible reasons for this: Maybe it was because the power of the Director's position had just been granted; and the knack of using that power just wasn't there. Yes, a lot of time and experience were still needed for the full force of the Director's power to reach the realm of adopted practice. Or, more likely, maybe it was because in those days so many politically savvy, standout, and top-rate university men were directly involved in the workings of the lab – and that means right in the middle of the day-to-day actions and operations, from top to bottom. Thus, they tended to hold back the just-under-the-surface desire for a man to snatch the whole ball of wax. Although it wasn't sustainable in the long run, for a time this substantial intimidation factor kept the Director curbed so that he couldn't run off on his own steam sans constraints.

"Another possible reason for the wolf in the Director being kept at bay perhaps had to do with me. Maybe it was my dominating presence and vulnerability-inducing influence – the trepidation, the timidity, and the cold feet that I instilled in many a man – that did the trick. I'm sure you wouldn't dispute that I was among the toughest and most tenacious of the men keeping the Director on a leash, under some kind of restraint. Yes, it could've well been me.

"I know it sounds a little hokey, but if you really want to know why we took on that onerous task of shackling and reining in the Director, it was because, as representatives of the universities, we were there to serve. We inserted ourselves voluntarily. We did it – and I kid you not – out of pure love for physics. However, as you might well have expected, our dedication and devotion to this duty didn't last. You can understand that, can't you?

"Just try to imagine how it was! We had no official positions; and we had no formal responsibility or accountability. Thus it became part-time work for us. Then, slowly but surely, other things in our lives began to take more and more precedence. Furthermore, we were getting on in years and noticeably slowing down. I gather all this is straightforward organization sociology, and not too much of a surprise to you. Therefore, you no doubt can easily see that, although the type of collateral involvement we had within the lab could well make a man appear to be a VIP and a mover-and-shaker, that image in reality is only skin-deep. But life teaches us that such things that are peripheral to the vital part of a man's life can't last too long. Inevitably they simply fade away. And so it was that this lab connection we had did just that! Without any sense of immediate obligation to energize us into action, with the high risks attached to actually doing anything, and without substantive self-interest to spur us on, over time we became but spectators. True, we had the illusion that we were actors in the show. But, eventually, the myth that we were real powerbrokers was revealed to all, even ourselves. Thus, our masks were ripped off. As for the Director, his tethers were thereby removed. Any constraints, hindrances, or inhibitions melted away. Resistance, dissent, and bold-faced opposition vanished. Then, finally, what happened became crystal clear: The full potential of the BNL Director as the unchallenged ruling bigwig was unloosed.

"As it happened, Goldhaber was the first of the unbound, unfettered, no-one-to-answer-to, free-to-do-as-you-wish Directors. By being first, he was the one to set the standard for the BNL Directors that came after him. When you give a man a big say in who his successor is to be, you shouldn't be too surprised to find that his choice will be some kind of carbon copy of himself or, more likely, a man of lesser quality. I'm afraid, Mickey, that's what happened at BNL. Goldhaber turned out to be a mediocre headman. It therefore followed that the succession generated only mediocrity, if not worse. No, there was no stopping it: The result of Goldhaber and what he wrought for the lab's future was that BNL moved relentlessly and uncontrollably downhill. Under the prevailing conditions, there wasn't and there couldn't have been any Director to reverse the trend that was set. So, as unchangeable destiny foretold and as it turned out, the next two Directors, Vineyard and Samios, just ensured that the decline of the lab initiated by Goldhaber continued on course.

"The three Directors, Goldhaber, Vineyard, and Samios, were men formed, for the most part, out of the same mold; and they came up the BNL ladder in much the same way. They were stars in the Physics Department, and, via that route, ascended to the throne. Their closeness and their similar professional histories made them natural successors. Vineyard was Goldhaber's lieutenant and Samios was Vineyard's. Could the outcome have been any other than it was? Not on your life! It was plain as day. For over 35 years, the three ruled the BNL roost; and together they took ISABELLE to the dung heap, and the lab to the brink of disaster.

"What a pity for BNL that these three Directors were in office just when history beckoned high-energy physics to make its mark on the world of science. The lab, eager to be part of this knowledge-feast on the horizon, put forth the idea for ISABELLE,

BNL's collider that would help pry open one of the doors that guarded the universe's secrets. What a challenge! What an adventure! However, the whole ISABELLE episode was a fiasco, more a farce than a drama. In getting the expedition off the ground, Goldhaber was tentative; and he started it off on the wrong track by placing the collider on a starvation diet. Vineyard latched onto the political angle, and actually was pushing the project ahead quite nicely; but he fell apart on the technical side and eventually set ISABELLE ablaze. Then, Samios entered the scene to douse Vineyard's flames; but, deaf to the good advice he was getting, he wound up applying the final and unkindest cut, and thereby sealing ISABELLE's doom. What a sad tale it is! ISABELLE was untimely ripped and died a sour death; and BNL, which began as a temple that was to foster communication with the gods, ended up as a house for the breeding of mediocrity."

Guilty With an Explanation

"Yes, Mickey, I can't escape it. It was a bad show at the end. Such a radical turnaround! Who would've expected it? Going from smash hit to floperoo, from showstopper to turkey, from boom to bust, from prosperity to destitution, and from winner to loser! And it all happened in one fell swoop, in merely a decade or so. In the beginning, I and the others who made BNL a going concern were thoroughly entranced and totally preoccupied with our newfound physics toys, mainly the Cosmotron and the AGS. We were determined to do things right for ourselves and for our time. We instinctively understood that this was our opportunity to enter the ring. We could hear the bell clanging and stood ready to accept fate's challenge to come out fighting. We sensed in our bones that *the postman only rings but once*, and you can be sure we weren't gonna pass up our one shot at the stars.

"But there was something we entirely forgot about. Frankly, we didn't give the least consideration to trying to set things properly in place for future generations. It simply didn't occur to us. If we'd been more perceptive about what might come later on, we might've built in stronger checks and balances: particularly limiting the power of the Director, and making doubly sure that the succession wouldn't just be a parade of the same men with slightly altered stripes. Well, whatever the reasons, we just didn't think ahead. We simply screwed up. Maybe we thought that we'd be there forever, shaping and manipulating, picking the Directors, peering over their shoulders, certifying their actions, making sure they were doing things right, bringing in the fix when things went awry, and always encouraging them to take the chances necessary to keep the lab a great one. And it worked! At least it worked for a while. But, as all things must, that time came to an end too. When the inevitable bad news came that we were in trouble, it was too late because by then we were too old and tired to do anything about it.

"I recognize that I'm using *we* quite loosely, as if there really were others involved. Well, let me set the record straight: My intention is that, for the most part, you infer it to be the *royal we*, Izzie alone, rather than the plural. I want no misunderstanding about that. I am not casting blame elsewhere. There's simply no way for me to avoid the large measure of responsibility that I bear for BNL's slide down to the depths. And I accept it. You see, in the end, I must fess up to what I've sown. And I do: *Mea Culpa*!

"Looking back it's easy to second-guess yourself, and I'm no different. I often wonder whether I could've done things differently so that the lab's outcome wouldn't have been what it was. Many questions keep coming back to haunt me: Did I not have the necessary strength in the late fifties to help Haworth and back him up when things got rough for him? Did I have to support the unsuitable Goldhaber rising to the throne? As the opposition was not so formidable then in the sixties, was I really too old to get in there and do battle for a future worthy of the illustrious, ennobled BNL? Did I really just become too tired and uninvolved to stop the Directors starting with Goldhaber from steamrolling over all in their path? At least when I had the chance, might I have been able to break that awful inbred chain of Goldhaber to Vineyard to Samios that led the lab into misfortune and calamity? Some questions, don't you think? However, in answer to them, even though I know full well that it's highly unsatisfying, I can only say lamely: Maybe yes and maybe no. I guess, in the end, I did what I did. And that's that! There's nothing more I can say or do. I simply must leave it to future generations to make what they will of it and cast their judgments upon me.

"Yet one of those questions does actually give me some pause. At that crucial period of BNL's life, after Haworth departed, could I have done something that would've altered BNL's future for the better? You can be sure I've struggled mightily with that one. But, as many times as I go over it, I still have no better answer than that I'd just lost the will to win. As much as my heart and soul wanted me to step in and work it out right, there wasn't an ounce of oomph left in me. I was getting on and becoming excruciatingly tired of all the wrangling and the hassles. The desire to mix it up seemed to be sapped from me. There was just no fight that remained. In fact I was too energy-drained even to get in the ring. Thus, since all of us must eventually exit the field of play, I happened to choose that particular circumstance and moment to let go and leave things to others.

"I must tell you, Mickey, that at the time it made sense for me to pull out voluntarily, before my body forced it on me anyway. Certainly I had undeniable signs that my moment of reckoning with age was not far away. In any case, I did it then and that's that. Still, I sometimes think about having done it when I did. I really can't say why. Of course, I always come up with: *yes, you did the right thing*, and *no, you couldn't have done it any better*. But, I know that I'm just playing the game people commonly play of trying to rationalize away their weaknesses, mistakes, and deficiencies. Yet, knowing it doesn't stop me from playing on. Not unlike others, I persist in trying, as strenuously as I can, to justify my past deeds and motives. You see, Mickey, it's a consolation to me to believe that with all I did and all I intended, I remained pure in heart and spirit. Would you deny a little peace of mind to an old man?"

As Izzie came to the end of his commentary on BNL's decline and his part in it, his muscles seemed to tighten as if he were feeling cold, and his face darkened. After his closing words, his head tilted downward and he appeared to be wrapped in some melancholy or disconcerting thought. The old man looked older than ever, as he remained speechless for a brief interval. Was he reminiscing? Mickey wondered.

Obviously, a kind of sadness overtook him. Perhaps it came about as a result of shame, of self-reproach, or of self-condemnation. Or, perhaps Izzie was trying to find a route to repentance. Whatever it was, Mickey only wished he had it in him to console Izzie. But he didn't, and so just sat and waited it out.

As it happened, Mickey needn't have been at all concerned, and really didn't have long to wait. As quickly as the mood came upon Izzie, it left him, and he again became the carefree puck, with his whimsical, clownish, beaming face. *Whew*, thought Mickey, as relief entered and permeated his entire body. For a moment there, an almost perfect moment, he was able to settle down and found himself overcome by the sheer pleasure of relaxation. All was quiet. And it stayed that way for a minute or so, Mickey remaining loose and calm, and Izzie, still cheery-looking, staring off into a far corner of the dining room. Then abruptly it was over.

Actually it was a good thing the intervals of soul-searching and silent recovery had ended since there still remained a lot of talking to be done. However, that would have to wait just a bit longer; for it was quite clear that the two of them needed a little more time away from their intense dialogue. No doubt, this was just the right moment for a break, and both simultaneously understood as much. Without a word spoken, Izzie rose and made his way to the washroom, followed closely by Mickey. As they proceeded into the darkness of the large room, the dim alcove was left in an eerie silence – the strangeness of the scene heightened by the two men's unfinished entrées just sitting on the table colorfully and undisturbed, in Felliniesque fashion.

* * * * *

An Interlude
An Act Not Meant To Be Seen

Being first to return to the table, Mickey stared at the duck in front of him, sorely tempted to put it on the filet warmer just a few inches away. *Why not*, he thought? Reaching over, carefully carrying his last piece clasped between his knife and fork, he placed it on a clear spot at the edge of the tray. After a minute, it was sizzling, and he surreptitiously put the duck back on his plate. At that moment, he sensed an almost inaudible sound. Turning his head and looking up, there to his surprise was Izzie, who'd silently returned and stumbled on this telltale, droll little scene. Izzie stared down at the red-faced, seemingly crushed younger man, wagging his finger at him, all the while wearing a sly and all-knowing fatherly smile. Mickey felt like a wet-behind-the-ears, humiliated kid caught with his hand in the cookie jar. "Now don't you go giving this a second thought," Izzie whispered in a reassuring tone, "we all indulge ourselves at times by returning to the rebellious days of our youth, when we were full of pranks and pratting about." With that, Izzie took his seat and looked with gusto at the remaining couple of pieces of his red and tender-looking, savory filet. *Yummie*, he thought! So, the two men, with relish, set about to finish off their delectable meats, Mickey still blushing from the not entirely unpleasant experience.

Actually, this embarrassing, nabbed-in-the-act chance occurrence triggered an emotional moment to flash through Mickey's mind from his early teens. The incident that he resurrected was itself of little consequence in the long run. Nonetheless, uncalled for, still it rushed into his consciousness. In his clear-as-a-bell reconstruction, there again arose within him that irrational panic he'd felt as an impressionable, vulnerable adolescent. What an enigmatic and wondrous organ is this mind of ours that permits the reliving of an occurrence that played itself out so long ago.

In those days long gone, Mickey's life was mostly driven by the macho and libidinous spirits that ruled within him. He found that he could derive some vicarious satisfaction for the urges within him from the possession of titillating girlie magazines as well as the sports ones that hooked him into identifying with the pros and the jocks. Anyway, there he was in the late afternoon of a weekend day aching with a yen that could only be appeased by getting his hands on some of those synthetic imitations of life. Did he simply go out and buy them? Not a chance! Not wily young Mickey! No, he had a far more clever design up his sleeve.

Then, there it was, that time from the oh-so-distant past. With his mind's projector beginning to roll, the scene began. Mickey was standing at the corner of an intersection of two busy thoroughfares. People were milling about and the roads were dense with cars and the mass transit of the time. Moments before, Mickey had lifted a few magazines of his heart's desire from the cigar store situated right on the corner of the streets, Queen Mary Road and Decarie Boulevard, in Montreal's Snowdon district. They were tucked under his jacket; but, even for a fat kid, he appeared clownish and somewhat gross, his pot appearing far too big for his body. Just minutes before, he'd walked quickly out of the store, and he was ever so anxious to get rolling. For his getaway, he used the number 29 streetcar, which stopped immediately in front of the store. With a nonchalance that came hard to him, he boarded just as the doors were about to close. He was thrilled; yet, he couldn't seem to control the agitation building in him. His face was flushed. He was almost there, almost on his way, heading for home, scot-free, with his booty. Although this wasn't the first time he'd done such a thing, the excitement, the tingling, and the surge of apprehension and dread were still there. He was so sure that he had hit pay dirt once again. But this time, it wasn't like all the others. This time, he wasn't going to get away with it. This time, he would learn his lesson. Blocking the electric vehicle from moving by inserting his immense stubby hands in the tram's doorway, Joe Black, the store's owner and Mickey's father's good friend, suddenly appeared and screamed out, "Hey there, don't you have something that doesn't belong to you?" Caught! Surprised, Mickey's arms relaxed, and the magazines fell from inside his jacket to the streetcar's floor. How useless they were! What Mickey wanted so badly moments before he now just wanted to disappear! But they didn't. The evidence of his misdeed was solid and incontrovertible. So, Mickey would have to face the music, and his father as well. Even after so many years, Mickey could still feel the paralysis that overtook him at that timeless instant his secret life of crime was uncovered. He found it intriguing and fascinating that a moment of such anguish and distress should turn out fifty years later to seem a nostalgic one of not unhappy melancholy. How strange!

As this thought of the past returned to its original resting place in some dark recess of his mind, Mickey faced the present, a trifle ruffled and less than pleased that he'd again been caught doing something others weren't meant to see. Somehow he wanted Izzie to say or do something that would set him at ease. But, how silly that was! Izzie had already pooh-poohed the whole episode. For him, it was just a little fun, no big deal. He'd made Mickey the butt of a little joking around, and that was that. Nothing more! Izzie wasn't about to make a federal case out of Mickey's every-day, commonplace act. As far as Mickey was concerned, it was clear that Izzie wasn't going to be of any help. No, whatever was rubbing Mickey the wrong way, whatever was preying on him, whatever was pinching his ass, he would have to pick the relief he sought out of a hat, or somehow find a way to get out of the funk he was in on his own. But, how to achieve that end, that was the question?

Mickey's Toast

Well, it wasn't reason that finally did it. It just happened by itself. Poof! Just like that! Mickey just stood up, still blushing and holding his half-filled wineglass. He'd found a way out of the rut he was in. He simply smiled and raised his glass in a toast to the wonders of *Le Petit Village*: "Izzie, to you and your little village. By a welcome quirk of fate I was invited to partake of its rare offerings and stumbled onto the chance of a lifetime. That's something I will forever be thankful for. I don't really know how I got there, and I haven't a clue about where it fits into the universe I still inhabit, but its lucky discovery was for me no less than a godsend. That whoever runs the place permitted me to see you here privately in *the Big Apple* is more than I could ever have hoped for. Although words alone cannot adequately convey my appreciation of the village and its ways, I fervently pray that they survive and endure. And to the men of *Le Petit Village*, and especially to you, I give my best wishes in the heartfelt hope that you will persist and linger on. With all the zeal that's in me, from my innermost being, I beg you and whoever might be listening that you continue to defy the world's natural laws, and go on assisting man as he stretches to his limits to better understand the meaning and the vastness of eternity." Izzie nodded agreement and smiled enigmatically, but spoke not a word. How odd it was! Here were two men, two scientists, whose beliefs revolved around imagining that romance, dreams, and a world beyond our ken are actually manifestations of true reality. It was quite a sight. They just stood there marveling at the wondrous nature of things around them, from the miniscule particles to the grand universe, and from an act of dastardly betrayal to one of pure love. It was in that frame of mind that they both drank of the wonderful juice of the gods.

Time seemed to stop for Mickey as he thought of the others he met on the boulevard and what a treat their company was. Yes, that was some shindig! What a blast! No, it wasn't a time he'd soon forget. Seeing them all in a concentrated way – those cardinals among men who together fashioned and gave rise to the glorious realm of Big Physics – seeing them in an atmosphere where civilized discourse held sway and past actions and thoughts were openly and willingly disclosed evoked impressions and sentiments in Mickey that he didn't know were in him. During the talkfest, that sweet banquet of their minds, he came to feel an unexpectedly intense affection for these most precious paragons of Big Science. This new emotional coloring he experienced was quite a stretch from how he felt about them in that time long gone, when his own uncertainties, anticipations, forebodings, hopes, and fears governed the swiftly passing days. Then the self ruled, and his inclinations and disposition toward others leaned more to being dispassionate and distant. But during their discussions on that stirring afternoon, Mickey's emotional bent toward these men, who sought to know the essence of heaven and earth, took a decided turn and became far softer and friendlier. His caring for them and, as it turned out, theirs for him replaced the pervasive, all-too-common mood of indifference to others; and gone from them was the self-serving, dominating power of advancing one's own career. It was almost as if a family of friends had taken shape that day.

Love Thine Enemy?

Oddly enough, Mickey's brotherly affection for the men who came to the *Le Petit Village* party applied to all of them, and even extended to the dreaded, dreadful, and once-despised Nick. To Mickey, Nick was something akin to sticky paper clinging to you, something to be discarded, but that you can't dislodge. In an analogous way, Nick always seemed to return to Mickey's conscious thoughts. Mickey just couldn't rid himself of that tiresome *Greek* and get the man off his mind. But, on that day, it all changed, and Nick – even Nick – became a sympathetic chord vibrating in Mickey's being.

Trying to see the big picture, Mickey spent a lot of time going around in circles, wondering endlessly about what impact his crossing both paths and swords with Nick had. What did it actually mean to him? Was it his misfortune or his good fortune to have Nick as a central figure in his professional life? As with most such questions, there are two sides. On the one hand, by attacking Mickey the way he did, Nick ended up forcing Mickey to seek help from others. That's how Mickey got to know all the mucketymucks. So, by Nick acting in his inimitable ugly and unseemly manner, Mickey achieved far more than he otherwise would have: He got to deal with the real big guys, the men who ran the community, including the non-BNL lab Directors. However, on the other hand, there was a price Mickey had to pay for this: Nick also caused him a great deal of pain over the years, pitilessly increasing Mickey's stress and strain by harassing him at every opportunity, as well as grossly and unfairly decreasing his financial compensation over almost two decades. So there you have it, two opposing impacts, one good, the other bad. One might well wonder whether the feelings generated by such painful hurts can ever be overcome. Well, in the abstract, it's hard to know. But, in Mickey's case, eventually he did manage to find a way to reconcile them.

It happened during the meetings at *Le Petit Village*. Somehow, although Mickey's conviction wasn't as firm as with the other *Players* at the *village of the valley*, the fact was that he came to like this man, Nick, the man who was his tormentor, the bane of his professional life, his crown of thorns. Well, if not like him, then certainly to empathize with him, and to sympathize with his late-in-his-professional-life plight. But how could that be? How could Mickey come to *like* this man who treated him so shoddily for almost two decades? What a mystery! Still, that's the way life is on this planet earth.

OK, that's the way it was: Nick continually abused Mickey over the years, yet Mickey emerged from it all liking the man. One can accept this at face value. After all, it's a fact. Nevertheless, it's not reasonable. It's just not satisfying. So, in the end, the question lying a thin-skin layer under the surface simply must be asked: Why didn't Mickey utterly detest the loathsome Nick, and gloat at what happened to him? Why would Mickey find a soft spot in his heart for a man who did him such wrongs? Well, maybe Mickey just felt sorry for what became of him: Nick, the mean, ornery, and malicious ogre and Mickey's erstwhile nemesis, was now a pathetic, pony-tailed also-ran washout – a flop and a bum – trying desperately and unsuccessfully to find a place in a world that rejected him. But there's another way of looking at it, having more to do with Mickey himself than with what happened to Nick. Maybe Mickey, as his life's experiences accumulated, came to believe that holding grudges, hating, and looking for revenge didn't serve him well. Rather than attaining satisfaction or justice, as he first imagined implementing such feelings might bring him to, he came to see that they only tended to make him and other people malevolent themselves. He came to see that by encouraging such thoughts, he would only become much like the object of his contempt and enmity. As with others who'd actually taken that road, he came to see that in the end, it would only make him an unhappy man. *Hey*! Mickey thought, *maybe this turn-the-other-cheek stuff may make some sense after all.*

As Mickey's mind wandered on about Nick, Izzie, settled at the table and, ready to resume, interrupted, "I hate to disturb your reverie again, but won't you let me in on it?" "Oh, so sorry," Mickey stammered, "I was thinking of how to phrase my next question for you – actually, to be precise, it's really my first." Answering with a little white lie allowed him to preempt Izzie should Izzie have wanted to continue to control the questioning. Mickey smiled inwardly at this after-the-fact excuse he made up. It pleased him no end to get the better of the *Master* once in a while. However, there was a downside to the accomplishment this time: Getting the best of Izzie at his game, beating him to the punch, meant that it was Mickey's turn to step up to the plate. Now he had to come up with a good question double-quick. Izzie sensed Mickey's lie and felt a little jokester's glee at the discomfort of his younger companion. Thoughts of what to ask raced through Mickey's mind while Izzie waited with continued amusement at Mickey's hesitancy and uneasiness. What to do? With no time to think, Mickey had to simply pick a topic at random and run with it. If that's the way it had to be, then so be it. But, unfortunately, just when it suited him least, his mind went totally blank. There was absolutely nothing left for him to do but depend on his instincts. He'd have to depend on the great deal of preparing he did in getting ready for this much sought-after get-together with Izzie. And he'd have to depend on all the thought he'd given over the years to the subject at hand. But time was up. The curtain rose. Action! Still not knowing what would emerge, Mickey began to speak.

* * * * *

Mickey On Mickey
A Brief Bio

In that no-time-consuming instant between opening his mouth and the words flowing out, Mickey deduced that Izzie wouldn't be familiar with Mickey's background in science, especially taking account of the big difference in the company they'd kept. And that's what turned out to be the gist of Mickey's opening, a brief biographical rundown: "When I started studying physics seriously in the late fifties at McGill University in Montreal, much in vogue with my generation was learning about those now-you-see-them-now-you-don't mysterious littler-than-little specks emanating from the atom that we came to know as elementary particles. You see, Izzie, even then I had some sort of a link to you. For, without those magic particles streaming out of the Cosmotron facility, who knows what academic field I might've been drawn to? As it was, I donned the flashy, glitzy moniker of particle theorist. With partial differential equations and Feynman diagrams dancing around in my head, I became overcome by the incredible, spellbinding conception that the world followed the dictates of abstract mathematical symbols. What an absurd, what a crazy notion it seems at first glance! Yet, what an inspirational one it becomes on second thought! What a crowning insight! To think that it's true: You can actually represent the nature of the inner world of the universe on a piece of paper. It's nothing less than mind-boggling, and too astounding for words. The seductiveness of it all was just too much to pass up. I simply had to become part of it, and so I did.

"Since the United States afforded prospects to work in the forefront of physics that were simply unavailable in Canada, PhD in hand, I packed my bags and took off for the land of milk and honey. I thereby became part of the migration of the young, the restless, and the ambitious to cross the border to where opportunity seemed limitless. I did realize that helping to drain Canada of its brainpower wasn't the nicest or most patriotic thing to do, but my nationalistic impulses at the time were weak. In fact, it seemed like quite a natural thing to do. The truth is that, whatever it meant to the land of my birth, I never regretted doing it. With optimism and pride, I adopted the U.S., along with its freedom, its boldness, and the chance to be the best that I could be.

"The first step I took in the U.S. was to accept a post-doc research appointment at the University of Illinois in 1964. As I was completing that and looking for a follow-up position, I came to appreciate that the theory of particle beams, distinct from the study of the individual particles themselves, was an intriguing and challenging subject in its own right. Luckily for me, the field of particle accelerators – atom smashers as they are inaccurately but commonly called – was blossoming at the time and was both appealing and attractive. So I went for it. True, the study of beams didn't immediately capture the imagination, as did that of particles alone, where you might get to the roots of the universe and perhaps win a Nobel Prize, but still it had plenty of rewards. Actually, as it happened, I derived immense satisfaction from my research on beams: how you could give them life, shape them, split them, transform them into new guises, alter their nature in flight, make them live longer, direct them, and, in sum, utterly control them. Yes indeed, I really relished my role in the designing of an accelerator, with the endless discussions of the pros and cons of doing it this way or that. By the way, I also got a naughty and playful kick out of provoking the staid and conservative types with some far-out, at times even insane ideas. Frankly, these guys weren't too adept at arguing such issues effectively, and so they'd inevitably resort to: *You can't do that, it'll cost too much.* So you can see, Izzie, not only did I consider myself doing work of substantial consequence, but I was also quite cozy with it, and had a lot of fun in the bargain.

"The fact of the matter is that the first step of generating and crafting the beams is indeed a vital link in the entire high-energy enterprise. Would anyone question that if you don't have high-quality beams fashioned just so, then studying particles wouldn't get very far? Come to think of it, would there be a field of high-energy physics at all? What I'm saying is that without first understanding and building the accelerators to generate powerful enough beams – that is, high intensity and high energy – frankly, particle research would be nothing much to speak of. In that case, all those would-be Nobelists could kiss their prizes goodbye. On the other hand, *Nobel Dreams* don't dance in the minds of accelerator physicists. So, as one myself, when all was said and done, the best I could hope for was a helping-hand consolation prize. Still, that's what I chose to do; and, as it turned out, it was just what the doctor ordered.

"To start my affair with particle beams, I read all the review literature on the subject that I could lay my hands on. During this pursuit of learning as much as was humanly possible and as fast as I could, it was my good fortune that I came across a few research papers that had my destiny written all over them. As I perused these particular ones, delving into every detail, I was stunned at what was accomplished. My jaws dropped. *That's really something to crow about, something worthy of center stage*, I thought. Not only was it a sensational showstopper, but this was also a class act. It was a masterstroke, played to the hilt; and it ended up with every *i* dotted and ever *t* crossed. It was a smash hit, through and through. The articles dealt with the remarkable discovery at BNL of a new principle that would allow the design of accelerators in which particle beams could reach unprecedented, unimaginably high energies. My heart skipped a beat. *This could revolutionize physics*, I thought. *Yes*, I asked myself, *why not beam theory for me*?

"Once what was taking place at BNL sank in, things began to happen fast. In January of 1966, I went to New York for the annual meeting of the American Physical Society. During the conference, a couple of high-level BNL accelerator scientists, Arie Van Steenbergen and George Wheeler, were recruiting physicists to come to the lab to work on an upgrade of their awesome, thrilling AGS, built a few years earlier. At the time, it was a buyer's market, but I can tell you, Izzie, I was an easy sell. After a brief interview, there was an offer for a job made, a slight hesitation on my part just for show, and then an acceptance. That was it. In the matter of the smaller part of an hour, I was transformed from a particle theorist to an accelerator physicist. For me, it was a chance sent from heaven. It was exactly what I was looking for. I didn't have a doubt that this was just my speed. Overflowing with enthusiasm for what lay ahead, I was just itching to get started.

"So it was that in the fall of that year, I found myself at the lab on the eastern part of Long Island, discovering the wonderful world of accelerators. Once at BNL, I marveled at its brilliant, out-of-this-world AGS, a monument to man's ingenuity and to his bravura flair for building magical things. That machine was the first of the big synchrotrons; and, from then on, it seemed that the sky was the limit. These masterful instruments came to be my calling and my mission, and they came to be my ardent and impassioned vocation. In short, they came to be my life's work.

"When I made this career move into accelerators, it had every appearance of being simply a transition from doing particle research to doing accelerator research. In fact, that's exactly what I believed to be the case. But the truth was that something very different from that awaited me. It was quite unanticipated; but, in the end, it turned out to be a valuable, all-to-the-good dividend for me. What was it, you ask? Well, when I came on the scene, I simply hadn't the least inkling of the wide array of occupations, undertakings, matters, and concerns – all in addition to the pure accelerator science – that pervaded, even dominated, the field. Yet, there it was, clear as the nose on your face. Because I became acutely interested in all of it, and got intensely involved in anything and everything I could glom onto, it greatly broadened my horizons of human enterprise, and gave me entry to the emerging venture into Big Science.

"In taking the road I did, I was brought face-to-face with the many aspects of the Big Physics endeavor: with designing accelerators and colliders; with frontier technology; with massive particle detection experiments; with the people and teamwork behind the challenges of the accelerators and the experiments; with the sophisticated engineering required to build these ever enlarging beam machines; and with the unforeseen management impediments and hurdles intrinsic to organizing for bigness. Suddenly, before I knew what was happening, I became not only an academic-style scientist, but also a builder of sorts. On the need to make these big things work – and work well – I was a physicist. To ensure their continued evolution and growth into the future, I was a builder. So earnest and excited was I that before long I was knee-deep in the massive and complex intricacies of the large-scale, sweeping accelerator enterprise.

"To understand more of the business of accelerators, and to help me become a better scientist-cum-builder, I sought help from academia, as was my way. To learn about the nature of organizations, and the psychology and sociology of the teams working in them, I went so far as to earn an MBA from Hofstra in 1971, working at nights and on weekends to gain the degree. With that under my belt, I began to fashion a deeper and better understanding of the constantly evolving institutional framework – involving the expanding national lab system, the university establishment, and the industrial sector – that was being put in place and molded to develop and bring into being these technological marvels of bigness. I was simply enthralled by the massive undertaking that was happening right before my very eyes; and being so determined a young man, I was willing to put everything I had and more into the game. I have to tell you, Izzie, it was a fantastic time for me, more than I can say. True, I worked myself to the bone, but, frankly, I loved every minute of it."

* * * * *

An Expedition of Discovery
The Devil Plays His Hand

Izzie looked at Mickey inquisitively, perhaps a little impatiently, wondering where he was headed. But he said nothing. He let it be Mickey's call all the way. Mickey, uncharacteristically uncertain of himself, knew he had to carry on. "Izzie, allow me to switch gears now and get on with my version of the ISABELLE affair. Early on, to be precise, in 1969, I became one of the primary designers of the big collider just arriving on the drawing board. Quickly the years rushed by. Oh, how exciting my accelerator work was! How engaging and absorbing! How it turned me on! It simply swept me up and consumed me. Strange as it sounds, so much was I part of ISABELLE that it soon became part of me. Then, at some point in the seventies, I came to fear that its collapse was a real and distinct possibility. The passage of time only served to strengthen that conviction. I'm not sure I truly trusted my words, but at the time I would repeat to my associates, *it could come crashing down around us, you know*! Sad to say, as one of them later remarked to me, I was indeed a prophet.

"You see, one day, the unimaginable happened! ISABELLE was dealt a mortal blow and unceremoniously sent to the *valley of the shadows*. What a tragedy! What a waste! *Big Failure* had suddenly reared its ugly, fearful face. What a perplexing phenomenon this was! Inexorably, I was drawn closer to it, in the hope that I might come to find some sense in it. How and why might such a thing come to pass? It was at that very instant that some sort of threshold was crossed. Just as these two questions came to be articulated in my consciousness, I found myself hooked. From that moment, there was no turning back. The questions plagued me. They overtook my very being. *How* and *why*? I kept asking myself. Eventually, a figment of an idea began to form in me. I developed a growing suspicion, which sometimes seemed like a certainty, that something had happened way back in the past that shaped the course of events and determined the bad things going on at BNL. More than that, somehow that was what precipitated the terrible outcome that was to follow – the deplorable and egregious, the notorious and the scandalous, and the lamentable and woeful death of ISABELLE.

"Over time, and with increasing frequency, I found myself embarked on thought-excursions back into the past, groping in the dark, probing and searching for clues, resolved to unearth the roots of ISABELLE's fate. I became a man mission-bound. I reconnoitered. I spied. I pried. I rummaged in every nook and cranny. I left no stone unturned. And the more I marched along the avenue in the *parade of ghosts*, the more convinced I became that I was on the right track. Just a little farther back, I would tell myself. There, around the next turn in the road. That's where could be found hiding the answers to unravel the ISABELLE mystery. That's where I could ascertain the basis and the rationale behind the doomed lady's fall. Then, after many false turns taken, after meny blind alleys stumbled into, it happened. A breakthrough! An opening! Yes, maybe all my effort was time well spent. OK, perhaps it wasn't the *Eureka-I've-found-it* answer I'd hoped for, but it indeed was a start.

"Here's the story: During one of my mind-expeditions into the sixties, I became struck by the strife-ridden contest for resources between BNL's running of experiments and its doing accelerator R&D. At first I was shocked and appalled at this revelation. Weren't the experimenters and the designers and builders of the accelerators all supposed to be part of the same team embracing the same ends? Weren't they in it together? Build the facility. Get it in tip-top shape, the most reliable, and highest-performing it could be. Get the most out of it that's earthly possible. Gather the data at full tilt. Dig into it full-blast. Interpret it till everyone falls. Win the game, that's what has to be done. But it can only be done by working in concert. Isn't it as clear as a deep blue sky on a cloudless day? Of course! Then why on earth would these two groups, all men of science, be drawing swords against each other? Why should they be perpetually wrangling and grappling? Why should they want to mistreat and abuse each other? Why would they maul each other? Wouldn't that end up causing injury to both sides? Wouldn't that end up poisoning the waters both groups live in? Then, to top it all off, wouldn't that, as sure as anything, result in damaging the lab itself? Yet, as obvious as the impact of this self-destructiveness was, it didn't have the least shadow of deterrence. That intense urge to hurt in all these men simply couldn't be defrayed. It was close to being unbelievable. Their conduct was undeniable: they did fight, they did harm each other, they did draw blood, and they did cause the lab to totter. As we all now know, years later, with all the votes cast and the tally made, BNL was brought as close to the brink as imaginable, close to falling into the pit from where there is no return.

"In psychological lingo, these men of science were behaving contrary to their collective interest as well as their own self-interests. Yes, they'd come to take a course down the road of irrationality. Although I knew very well about these ruinous and self-annihilating tendencies that it's possible for men to possess and exhibit, I never really had first-hand contact with them. Then, to see it all take place right before my very eyes among scientists shocked and confounded me far beyond my expectations. However, to understand more of this sorry self-destructive display, I had to be cool and logical, even while staring straight into the face of unreason. And so, with rationality as my companion, I continued on my mission of discovery.

"To get to the bottom of this sordid ISABELLE business, I delved into the whole matter with resolute, unshrinking, and cast-iron determination. Despite the devils dancing before me, even though it was irrationality I was digging into, I found, a little surprisingly, that a rational, analytic approach was still possible. So I went to it. And what did I learn? I came to see that the picture of these scientists and their actions was a manifestation of a more general lab problem, actually, one that can be seen in all manner of organizations. It was no more and no less than the result of the trade-off between present operations and future development. Yes, the present and the future were at it once again, just as they have been throughout man's history.

"The question before the lab in the sixties was simply this: With the fixed resources it had, how much should it allocate for the present and how much for the future? What a wrenching dilemma BNL had! On the one hand, there was this *out of sight*, smashing facility on site, along with proposals galore to do experiments with it. On the other hand, the demand for future high-energy facilities was rising at a remarkably rapid clip. This fact meant that for the lab to participate in the romance of the imagined time to come, it was necessary to focus on accelerator and technology R&D in order to develop the machines on the horizon. So the pressure mounted: The current experimenters screamed, *If you want to take full advantage of the prized beauty we've got and win more of the big Nobels, you've gotta give us more of the loot.* The builders, equally vociferously, proclaimed, *If you want a future that'll fill you with pride, if you want to keep ahead of the growing pack closing in, we've gotta be given the financial means to reach the finish line first*.

"Meanwhile, the entire high-energy enterprise was booming. There was competition for the AGS from CERN; and there was competition to build new, forefront facilities coming from all over the place. Everybody seemed to want a crack at it. Then there was the inspired, forward-looking Ramsey Panel that, from BNL's vantage point, served only to fan the competitive flames. What a face of the future the panel drew: whopping high-energy synchrotrons and the bold proposal that the U.S. begin to build high-energy proton colliders that would revolutionize the field, and change just about everything extant. What a bright and optimistic picture was conceived and augured! It was breathtaking. Surely, it was the best of times for physics. Yet, hold on, for the lab, it was also the worst of times. Yes, there's no doubt that the men who ran the lab wanted to be part of the glory that lay ahead. But they knew that they also had to do the bread-and-butter stuff *here and now*. Did they have what it takes to make the right choices and impart just the right balance? Did they have the guts, the quickness of wit, the management bag of tricks, the political prowess, the diplomatic know-how, and the mastery over their own house to capture it all? In short, did they have the *right stuff*?

"Unfortunately, the spark that could've ignited BNL and given it all to the lab just wasn't there. Something was missing, and it wasn't money. You see, in the mid-sixties, physics was flying high. It was in a phase of soaring growth, and resources were plentiful. Economics-wise, the situation was perfect: demand was high and so was supply. As for the lab, it was nothing if not flush with money. If anything, BNL actually had an embarrassment of riches. However, with all these funds, there came the inevitable reality that there were many ways of using the resources. Exactly how should the divvying up go? It should've been no problem. The people responsible for making the scientific and financial decisions simply had tough choices to make. So what else is new? Isn't that what the high and mighty are paid the big bucks to do? Shouldn't they have been smart enough to come up with the right answers? Shouldn't it be expected that there reside a little wisdom in the bunch of them?

"Anyway, Izzie, comb through your memory and try to bring back what they actually did. Frankly, I can't think of a better way to express it than that they put their thumbs in their mouths and cried: *We haven't enough cash.* Over and over again, they repeated the plaintive plea, even though it was a patent falsehood. It seemed as if they wanted it to appear as if there were a shortage of funds. It was most unnatural, almost as if they wanted to lose any claim on the future. But why would they play such a risky and hazardous game of deception? Well, perhaps it was an elaborate form of self-deception, giving them an excuse for not doing what they greatly feared: forgetting about any more rewards for their bold exploits of the past, getting down to the real business at hand of demanding designs, tough decisions, delicate negotiations, and competing to the point of ruthlessness to win. Or perhaps it was for the internal consumption of the lab: because, being power-hungry men, this bit of fakery gave them the chance to play God, allowing them to pompously puff up their egos and be the ones to choose the winners and the losers. Either way, it was a sorry show. What can be said of them except that they were just a gang of good-for-nothings, each one only looking out for *number one*? So it was that, in the end, the irrational BNL moguls got what the devil in them sought – their self-generated defeat. And the champagne days of dreams and Nobels had become but a distant remembrance."

Driven to Indict

Mickey paused to catch his breath, somewhat unsure of himself, and none too pleased that he was saying all this to Izzie, one of the key men supposed to be minding the store. Was it really right for him to be talking in such a manner to Izzie, the king? Was it right to confront anyone that way? Perhaps backing off a bit would be a better approach. Compromise a little! Be sensible! Think it over! Be more confident of the ground you're treading on! But Mickey didn't seem able to restrain himself. He had to get all this off his chest; and nothing – no, nothing – could sidetrack him from telling it like it is. Undoubtedly, these pent-up feelings had accumulated so long in him that the pressure build-up was too much for him to bear; and these beliefs and impressions just had to be released. Wondering in a brief instant of rationality how Izzie was going to react, he sighed, and thought, *Que sera, sera.*

As it turned out, not only was that not the end of Mickey's tirade, it had but scratched the surface. It was only the beginning. What Mickey found was that not a thing, not being reasonable, not any uncertainty in what he was saying, not any concern and affection for the man who was the butt of his assaults, nothing could make him break off and desist. There was still a lot more to be put to Izzie, questions far more pointed, far more provocative, far more accusing, and far more condemning; and come hell or high water, he would go on. It was as if he were under some kind of nothing-he-could-do-about-it spell. He wasn't able to think straight. With all reason abandoned, there was simply no arresting what he'd started. A driven man, Mickey had no choice but to go on with his indictment. Thus, clearly out of control, and with the hardnosed, aggressive, belligerent, and utterly inflexible course he'd adopted being unstoppable, he continued on his no-holds-barred line of attack.

"It's strange how innocuous the whole present-versus-future matter sounds in the euphemistic language of administrators. All the lab was doing was optimally dividing up the resources it had available. How could something seemingly so bland and inoffensive mean so much to so many? How could it fix the course of BNL history? Indeed, how could it determine the fate of the high-energy business far off into the distant future? Yet, there you have it. An action here leads to an effect there, which, in turn, leads to another action, then another effect, and so on, thus establishing no less than history itself. Thus, if you change the source action, that just about changes all that follows. Of course, this is true about everything in this tantalizing world of ours. It's just that some source actions result in picayune consequences, while some shape and govern the course of men's destinies. OK, but what about BNL? What I seem to have come upon, what I'm conjecturing, is that what BNL did during those moment-of-truth, linchpin few years some forty years ago, was one of the biggies. It took Big Physics on a road widely divergent from where it might've gone had the choices made been different. That's not to judge that what could've been, on the whole, would be better. But one thing I do say unhesitatingly: It sure as hell would've been better for BNL.

"I guess it's time to get down to brass tacks. So far we've established that how to divide up the resources BNL had in that decisive period in the mid-sixties was one of the biggest issues facing the lab's decision-makers. Well, how exactly was it done? To put it bluntly, the BNL experimental program was allotted with a surfeit of resources almost to the point of engorgement, while the program for future accelerators was squeezed and starved, forced to survive from hand to mouth. If there was one man who made it happen that way, it was none other than the ruler of the kingdom, Director Goldhaber, Mister Moneybags himself. Ostensibly, the onus was on him, the keeper of the mint, to find just the proper balance for sharing BNL's resources, that is, to provide each side with the optimum proportion to suit the lab's circumstances. That was a prodigious duty to place on the shoulders of any man. But putting such a burdensome responsibility on Goldhaber, a man clearly not worthy of such far-reaching trust, was high-order bad news. It didn't bode well for the lab. The truth is that as a result of the actions he took, the dark clouds began to gather over BNL, and what lay in store was indeed ominous.

"Frankly, Izzie, there's something about the whole picture that bothers me to my very core. The fact is that I simply don't believe that it was Goldhaber alone who conceived and put in place the policy. I don't believe that it was he alone who set the priorities. And I don't believe that he had the backbone to make such mighty decisions without a powerful mind guiding him, egging him on, and backing him up. Just think of it: That policy was designed to have present operations take precedence over technology development for the future. To come up with that and to make it stick, the true policy-maker had to have a lot more power and be much more of a man than Goldhaber. Now, let me be clear about this. I don't question that Goldhaber believed in the policy. How could he not have? Especially when you consider how he put it into practice with such gusto! It's just that I don't for a minute imagine that he could've been the originator. No, he never could've or would've done it on his own. He simply didn't have the gutsy pluck to go that far by himself. There just had to be a masked man standing behind the scenes pulling the strings."

Again Mickey stopped and hesitated. Now, for sure, he'd gone too far, he thought. But Izzie didn't appear to be offended or outraged. No, not at all! At least he gave no such indication. So Mickey continued on his merry way: "Izzie, I hope you don't take from what I've said that I think of Goldhaber as some sort of blob, with no mind of his own. Not at all! You see, despite my inference of a secret and far more powerful figure behind Goldhaber, it was Goldhaber who was at the front lines, running BNL, making the day-to-day decisions, and ensuring that they were implemented. Indeed, he was policy-architect, enforcer, prosecutor, jury, the judge who sent down the sentences, and the executioner who carried them out all rolled into one. Still, on the major question of the day – experiments versus accelerator technology – even as he sat in his plush chair in his ornate, extravagant, and unseemly-for-a-scientist office, he was merely an instrument used by some invisible power. What a sad state of affairs for him! Here was Goldhaber, the *Big Man* of Upton, with the key science concern of his generation on tap, and he wasn't free to think it out on his own and possibly do the right thing. Rather he was compelled to obediently follow the command of a higher authority, to wimp-like jump through the hoop like a trained seal.

"So it was that on his generation's foremost Big Physics issue for the country and for BNL, Goldhaber excessively favored running experiments over accelerator technology development, opting for the present over the future. That's a fact indelibly written on the *did-do* side of the ledger! But how about comparing that with what's on the *should-do* side. What he should've done was to progressively increase technology resources at the expense of current experimentation. Such action would've ensured that as the present became the past, the lab would've been ready and waiting for the sure-footed future to arrive, well prepared to be the front-runner when it did. However, Goldhaber didn't do what should've been done. And that is also a fact! So, there, in a nutshell, you have a compelling and irresistible case against the man in the Director's office based on the mustn't-be-violated *should-do – did-do* paradigm. According to the paradigm, when it comes to situations where such question-pairs are applied, it's best if the responses to the two of them are identical, and worst if they're diametrically opposed. Putting Goldhaber to the test, you can't but conclude that he failed miserably on his response. Naturally, I must add that the man in the shadows behind the Director is equally, perhaps more blameworthy; and he deserves precisely the same failing grade. And those, Izzie, are also facts!"

Justice Is Served

"As it turned out, the choice made of going all-out for AGS experimentation at the expense of new accelerator development was to haunt the lab. Years later, the devastating consequences of the loss of technology know-how began to be felt with a vengeance. BNL's technical management faltered badly, and the ability to be competitive, to be a player in the high-stakes high-energy game, all but vanished. The lab soon found that it couldn't successfully master the superconducting technology to build the new high-energy colliders, which, in the seventies, became the rage. In spite of the lack of the needed expertise, BNL tried anyway but, not unexpectedly, fell flat on its face. So it was that ISABELLE came and went: People and time were wasted; lots of money was thrown down the drain; and the lab came as close as imaginable to the pit of oblivion. Yes, for decades after those heyday sixties, the lab floundered, bouncing about in the turbulent waters without a port-of-call. It is a lesson worth learning. Who can tell when the past will return to claim its deadly due? For BNL, as for all who embrace the devil's bargain, payment was exacted harshly, unexpectedly, and way too soon.

"I've often asked myself why Goldhaber did what he did. With all his experience at the lab and in life, with his brilliant mind, and with his abundant knowledge of history and the human condition, he must've known full well that he was betting on the wrong horse. Furthermore, some at the lab were absolutely appalled at his passionate partiality for experimentation and his blatant repudiation of accelerator technology. They actually told him so in no uncertain terms. Even some of his buddies advised him that he might be going too far. With all that, he had to know he was in the midst of a big mistake. OK, so maybe he didn't altogether appreciate the colossal blunder in the making. Maybe he thought he was risking only a minor gaffe. But, surely, for the sake of the lab's future and of leaving a legacy of his own that he could be proud of, he should've admitted that the BNL ship might be going astray, and so steer it on the rational middle course that the situation at hand demanded. That's really all that was being asked of him: just a little common sense. However, any talk was just a waste of time. There was simply no changing him. He was determined to plunge ahead into the hellish waters of vanity and abandoned reason. And, since he was the commander-in-chief, that's the way it was.

"But why, Izzie? Why wouldn't Goldhaber listen to reason? Why was he so irrational? There has to be an answer. And perhaps there is. Perhaps it's much simpler than the deep-rooted one I'm stretching for. Perhaps it was just that the army of glory-seeking experimenters descending on the lab in the sixties simply overwhelmed him. Perhaps he was star-struck by the emerging big names of physics appearing at his doorstep. Perhaps, dazzled by the frontier-breaking cutting-edge experiments done at the AGS in those early days, he was hoping for some repeat performances that would shine on him. Or perhaps he was intimidated by the avalanche of proposals submitted to the lab by the multitude of would-be stars. Could anyone really expect him to have given a blunt *no* to either the *big boys* or the ones on the way? I don't think so.

"Actually, closer inspection does naught but reinforce that pride and its consequences was a major ingredient in the mix of motives that drove the weak man who was way out of his depth. The reality of the time is inescapable: Everyone who was anyone wanted to get in on the action because there was gold in *them thar hills*. Of course, since BNL was far and above the foremost hill, that was the place to be. Yes, the me-too spirit was abroad in the land of science; and the knocking on Goldhaber's door was continuous and persistent. In such a manner did the community of high-energy experimenters speak with an unambiguous voice; and Goldhaber, the team player, heard it loud and clear.

"Now I ask you, Izzie, is it possible that I've stumbled on the answer? Was it simply that Goldhaber entered a pressure-cooker and couldn't avoid the consequent stress? After all, it is well known that the resulting syndrome of tension and nervous strain is common among those who have to make tough decisions. Feeling the heat, could you really blame him for having squeezed in one more experiment when a bigwig-experimenter came to call? Could you expect any different from a man in a state of high anxiety? It's much like the ticket counter clerk who always has a ticket available if you happen to be the President. When you're in the line of fire and your back is against the wall, can you be faulted for giving up the ticket under the counter to *Mister Big*?

"I must say that this little analysis does indeed seem plausible. Giving in, as Goldhaber did – taking the path of least resistance – surely relieved his stress a little. Unfortunately, there were just too many such arrivals at his gate. You see, every time he gave in, further encouraging others to come, a little less of the lab's funds was left for future technology. It reminds me of the farmer who, strapped for cash, gave his cow a little less food each day, believing that a negligibly small reduction couldn't matter much. So, having chosen his priorities, he went blithely along, sure in the tactic he'd chosen; and, lo and behold, each day he was quite right. But one dark day, he awoke to find his cow dead of starvation.

"Understand that this is a story about a farmer who didn't have much common sense. But truly Izzie, how can you look at a highbrow scientist falling into such a trap as anything other than gross incompetence? The principle involved is transparent, school-boy stuff: If you keep adding up small changes of the same type, then eventually the sum will become something big. Unfortunately, these small changes are masked by much larger day-to-day fluctuations, and so are not so straightforward to detect, their importance not so easily recognized. However, that they invariably do add up, that disaster could well be accompanying the next sunrise, is something that anyone with a little common sense should be able to figure out. OK, you might be inclined to forgive the farmer in the parable, but a scientist! How could he conceivably miss it? Phenomena of such a type are all pervasive in science.

"I do admit that perhaps dealing with such things in a man's life as a scientist simply doesn't carry over into his daily life, or, in Goldhaber's case, his life as a manager. In any case, surely you should expect a man who's at the forefront of nuclear physics and also runs a great American national laboratory to be able to glean the connection. Frankly, Izzie, it strains credulity that Goldhaber failed to spot and grasp the urgent consequences of starving BNL's technology effort; and doing so even as he was staring at the Ramsey Panel report before him. Isn't it bothersome that a man with a soaring IQ could be so dense? And adding to the puzzling nature of the whole business, there's the question of the guy pulling the strings from behind the screen. What about him? Why didn't he step in and do something about it? What's your take on that, Izzie?

"What else can be said other than that BNL's future was in the hands of damn fools! And at their head was Goldhaber. But, I ask you, Izzie: of what good is a man leading a charge toward the unknown frontier if he's wearing blinders? It's really hard to believe that this man, who'd reached so high, really committed such a bonehead foul-up. It almost makes you wanna cry! God only knows what was on his mind as he was lousing things up so!

"Anyway, Izzie, you're well acquainted with what ensued. Actually, you didn't have to be a rocket scientist, as they say, to have predicted how things would play out. In time, there was a severe loss of accelerator expertise at the lab, leading to a gradual but relentless decline in the lab's ability to do first-rate, top-of-the-line technology development. Now, the dire nature of this for a technology-based national lab can't be exaggerated. Giving it to you straight, as a result of Goldhaber's dimwitted wrongheadedness, the superconducting magnet program ossified and the ISABELLE design became a joke among non-BNL accelerator builders. How could anyone with an ounce of realism in him deny it? The situation was grim and ominous, and the project a disaster waiting to happen; and, short of godly intervention, there was no way for the inevitable to be avoided. Thus, sadly, in the early eighties, the lab paid the price for its carefree days of squandering resources that should've been put to better use preparing for the future. True, the penalty was stiff. Still, although it pains me to say it, the punishment did indeed fit the crime; and, in the end, justice was properly served."

Fallen Star

"Today, when I think of what transpired during the first few years of the eighties and by comparison imagine what might've been, I still feel embittered, galled, and chagrined. Yes, it certainly was a dirty business. You know, Izzie, whenever I think about the whole rotten affair, as I do quite often, your name keeps cropping up. So many questions pop into my head, but unfortunately so few answers accompany them. Where were you in those heady days of the sixties? What was the role you played? Where did you fit in? Weren't you there in the middle of the mess? Weren't you in the thick of things, with power to spare? Didn't you see what was going on? But where do I go from there? Only you can help me out. You see, to me, you're much like Churchill's mystery wrapped in an enigma. However, there's one thing I'm confident of: You certainly knew better than to simply allow the lab to keep sliding on thin ice, as it was doing. Yet, if that's true, why didn't you put your foot down and demand change, and then follow through to ensure that things were actually turned around?

"Don't you remember the time back in the fifties, when Haworth was Director and you were the unchallenged political force behind the lab? It's all in the record of the time. With you two leading the pack, swiftly came the reactor and the Cosmotron. The Cosmotron was a super machine, something to write home about. Fantastic new particles seemed to appear daily. The rash of discoveries filled everyone with wonder and awe, and urged them on to shoot the moon and give their all for an even more thrilling and marvelously mysterious future. Take note, Izzie, that while these experiments were running, and the stars, new and old, were shining brightly, accelerator technology was also flourishing. The lab more resembled *Boom Town, USA* than anything else. True, the experimenters weren't all happy campers; and they harassed the generous and stouthearted Haworth almost to the point of a full-scale rebellion. But the dynamic duo of Haworth and Rabi was up to its job, magnificently unbeatable. Thus, out of the fifties came BNL, the lab that had no match. It was the one that paved the way for Big Physics to enter upon the stage; and it was the one that fashioned and made a reality of the high-energy enterprise. Not only did the lab escort to the dance of the wacky, madcap particles the best experimenters imaginable – a host of future stars – but it presented the world of science with the future-making AGS, ready and able to take Big Physics to regions of unimaginable energy, realms where dreams abound and fame and fortune are to be had.

"Then came the sixties, Izzie. The god's honest truth about that decade was that it was a superb and celebrated time for the lab; but only – and I mean, only – because of what you and Haworth did in the fifties. Doesn't it go without saying that you possessed that ineffable vision thing, allowing you to figure out just the right balance of resources between present experiments and future accelerators? Once having said that, I find myself stumped and stupefied. My reasoning power simply won't carry me from Izzie of the fifties to Izzie of the sixties. Alas, I'm stuck only with puzzles, conjectures, and so – you guessed it – more questions. Why, Izzie, why didn't you do in the sixties exactly what you did in the fifties, the things that would've properly prepared the lab and given it a leg up for the oh-so-challenging seventies? Considering the man you were, how can I believe other than that you truly might've altered the course of BNL's history, indeed, of the entire history of the high-energy field? That being the case, wasn't it worth taking a crack at it, giving it your best shot? So, why didn't you? Why didn't you step in; and, if you had to kick butt, why not? Why didn't you make the lab do what was right? After all, you'd done exactly that only a few years earlier. Besides, even in the sixties, you were the man behind the scenes. You were the one calling the shots. Intervening and preventing the debacle that was to come had to be right down your alley. You see, I can't imagine anything that would persuade me that your energy was sapped. That excuse holds no water with me. So tell me, Izzie: Why oh why didn't you do the right thing?"

* * * * *

An apparition appears

Mickey took a deep breath and stopped talking, so ending his thinly disguised anti-Izzie monologue. After that grueling diatribe of censure – coming that close to accusing and condemning Izzie of being either a party to BNL's decline or at best a fellow-traveler – Mickey was all played out. He'd raked Izzie over the coals, but in so doing, found that he'd only burned himself out. His tank was empty; he was clean out of gas. However, it wasn't for naught that he suffered through the ordeal. True, he didn't at all consider the possible consequences of what he was doing. True, he totally ignored the common sense use of pleasantries, not to mention politeness. True, he threw caution to the wind. But he ended up doing what he'd wanted to do. Headlong he'd flown toward his big in-your-face question, *why'd you do it, Izzie*? Yes, he actually went through with it, and, look, he survived it all still in one piece.

But what about Izzie? With such insinuations and provocations leveled at him, how would he react? Would he still be fair-minded, composed, impartial, and tranquil of temper? Would he still be the man Mickey came to admire and feel so affectionate toward? Would he give Mickey the benefit of the doubt? Would he be able to forgive Mickey if Mickey had erred? Would he be able to go on? Well, there was nothing Mickey could do about it, so he put all these unknowns out of his mind. The ball was now in Izzie's court, and what would next ensue was entirely up to him. As for Mickey, he would simply have to take whatever came.

At least for the moment, Mickey was quite content to have the situation out of his hands. He was fatigued and weary, and welcomed the strain-free respite. *Leave it to Izzie*, he thought. All worn out, Mickey sat still, with his head bowed. So it was that he became filled with a pensive wistfulness and nostalgia. Perhaps seeking some psychic energy replenishment from somewhere within his mind, he reminisced about days gone by. As much as he tried to arrest or at least to suppress it, his mood was somber. He just couldn't prevent the dispiritedness and blueness that overcame him. A blanket of sadness fell upon him.

The silence lingered for a while. Izzie, for his part, became oblivious of his dinner guest as he stared at the room's darkened interior above Mickey's right shoulder. There, in the blackness, Izzie could just make out what he perceived to be a candle flickering, as if in a mild breeze. *No, it isn't real*, he thought. *It can't be*! You see, he hadn't seen it when he scrutinized the entire room upon his arrival. And Izzie simply wasn't the type to allow such a thing to get by him. *What then is it*, he persisted in asking himself? Was his mind playing a trick on him? Hypnotized by its faint glow, he gazed at it intently. Just then, there appeared the full shape of a shadowy figure visible through the flame. Izzie almost jumped out of his chair, leaning forward and squinting, trying desperately to make it out. He stretched out his left arm as far as he could towards the apparition. He so wanted to reach and perhaps touch it, in the hope of finding out its true nature. Unable to, he peered at it suspiciously. He felt in his inner being, somewhere in his subconscious, that he knew it. Instinctively appreciating that time was not on his side, he urgently, frantically tried to detect some sign of recognition. For a brief moment, identifying the vision became an obsession. But the spirit only approached closer to the flame and then ebbed from it, continuing in this manner for a while, disappointingly evading any disclosure. Izzie's thoughts became jumbled, and his emotions took over, bubbling to the boiling point. A passionate yearning, non-specific, built within him, threatening to explode. Then suddenly, with Izzie's mind in a highly aroused, over-stimulated state of turmoil, the grayish image and wax-dripping candle dissolved and turned to naught. Thus, as it came, without any apparent rhyme or reason, so the haunting moment passed. Only emptiness – the bleak chill of nothingness – was left behind.

Izzie relaxed his tense, hunched-over shoulders. Then, somewhat dejected, he bent his head downward. Although for quite different reasons, for a brief spell, the two men manifested similarly cheerless, woebegone poses. Suddenly, in a demonstration of singular strength of character and matchless self-control, Izzie abruptly altered his frame of mind. To all appearances, this was triggered by no more than seeing the bowl of colorful berries and melon chunks on the table. Somehow, in the wink of an eye, that sight clicked his mind out of its low-spirited state and into one of buoyancy, lightheartedness, and lively optimism. It's hard to know exactly why this radical transition took place. But perhaps Izzie was reminded that it was only through a special favor of the gods that he was there in the first place. It was only because of their beneficence that he was able to partake of all this appealingly luscious food and drink and to muse about old times. So, if they wanted this mood-shift from him in return, how could he not comply with the wishes of the omnipotent rulers of all that is?

As it turned out, therefore, insofar as Izzie was concerned, Mickey had nothing at all to worry about. *The man* was truly a *mensch*! Anyway, with Izzie's regained high spirits in place, he lifted a delectable raspberry and put it in his mouth, squeezing it and slowly releasing its juices onto his palate. How he appreciated and enjoyed to the fullest its aroma and texture, much in the manner of a connoisseur. His face glowed with delight; and, his visage belying his words, he pronounced in a scolding, yet somewhat playful manner: "Well, we haven't got all night. Let's move on. What do you say, Mickey, eh?" With the mood pendulum having swung to its high point once again, Mickey, his vigor and positive spirits also restored, perked up: "I'd say that's an offer no sane man would pass up." Immediately, he followed it with the quip, "But I believe it's your turn at bat. Isn't that right?" "Well, you'll never find me refusing a chance to swing," came Izzie's retort. "But, just one second," he added, "I do believe I'll have a spoonful of my crème and one of those luscious strawberries first."

Professor Izzie Does His Thing
Teaching a Lesson

With the mood of colloquy and hot-blooded give-and-take reestablished, Izzie straightened up and started with the intention of relating his account of BNL's *accelerator-builder versus experimenter* war of the sixties. But before he did that, he just couldn't resist his urge to teach. "Now, Mickey, before I begin, I want to clarify something. I trust you weren't expecting uncomplicated, *yes-no* type answers to your mass of multi-faceted, knotty questions, especially to those nagging ones, *Izzie, why didn't you make everyone toe the line? Why didn't you set things right?* For if you were, let me set you straight right away: Be assured that you will most certainly not get anything even resembling clear-cut and undemanding simplicity from me. It just ain't gonna happen! Got it! Going that route, you wouldn't get anywhere near the truth anyway. OK, with that out of the way, let's get the show on the road.

"Since your major concern appears to be why I didn't do something, what's to stop me from specifying that it was due to this or that. I can easily pick out one of a number of reasons and designate it as the genuine one. Of course, I might also be tempted to claim the ever-popular *all-of-the-above*. Is that what you want? Suppose I simply repeat what I already indicated to you a little while ago. Suppose I insist that it was because I was getting on and tired of the arguing, persuading, intimidating and especially the acts of ruthlessness required of the power-hungry, mighty men. Would that satisfy you? Or suppose I veer away from that explanation and say that it was because I made a personal commitment to spend more time on my teaching and writing. Wouldn't you admit that these are essential things that must be done, that our field simply can't do without them? Just think a little! If we want physics to continue thriving we must educate and nourish future generations to carry on. If we want the public to keep supporting us, we must carefully and deliberately explain to them – the politicians and the men-on-the-street, the taxpayers – what we are doing and why it is vital that they continue subsidizing us, bolstering us, and going to bat for us. Don't you agree? Would that satisfy you? Suppose I say it was because in the late fifties, with the AGS right around the corner, I relinquished my power over the everyday life at the lab since – and I'm confident that you concur – *new blood must have its chance*. Isn't this transparent? Everything passes. The succession of generations is inevitable and inexorable. It's a fact of life. You see, I knew well that my time was coming to a close. So why not elect then to make my move? Certainly it's better to do it sooner than too late. Sure, it's harrowing to just pick up and leave, but why prolong an agony sure to come? It's sure as hell that if I had held on longer, then – becoming slower and, to be honest, less involved and interested – I could easily have become a problem myself. Why should I have done that? Why should I have made things harder for the lab than they already were? Why should I have compounded the other obstacles and troubles already there? So I chose instead to take the road of reason and went while I was still a welcome sight. It's not unlike the smart father who accepts the inevitable breaking of the cord and lets his son fly at an early stage. Surely you appreciate that it's better if he does so before rifts ensue and his son forces the issue. By procrastinating too long, as men's experiences tell us, the father must suffer that much more. Under such conditions, when the rupture and parting of the ways does finally come, what await him are only unpleasantness, estrangement, discord, jarring conflict, bad blood, and enmity. Now, why would I want to imitate a foolish father? So I didn't. Anyway, would that satisfy you? Would any of the three satisfy you? Would my becoming *old and tired* satisfy you? Would the beckoning attractive alternative of *teaching and writing* satisfy you? Would the inevitability of the *accession of the young* reason satisfy you? Would all of them?

"Thus, there you have it. I've given you three pretty down-to-earth and well-thought-out reasons for making myself scarce, for getting out of the rat race, and, yes, for abandoning the ship. To be up-front, what I've told you is not simply an academic exercise. All these three reasons actually applied in my case. What happened is that one by one they entered my consciousness, forcefully prodding me to *let go*. At first I wasn't too comfortable with what they demanded of me. So I thought hard, and ran them through my mind over and over. Then it hit me! That light bulb lit up in my head, and I knew what I had to do. Perhaps if there'd been fewer than three pragmatic and well-grounded reasons, it might not have come to me and I might not have acted as I did. But the combination of all three was simply too compelling, too persuasive to ignore. So I followed my insight and my reasoning, and began withdrawing from the political field of play. Soon taking my leave didn't seem like such a bad course at all. There was even something quite desirable about it.

"To be honest, Mickey, there's another, quite different side to the story. You've been presuming all along that my departure was purely voluntary. But, in actuality, it may not have been that way at all. What would you say if I told you that my departure was in reality a forced one? No, I wasn't pushed over a cliff or anything of that sort. It was quite a bit subtler than that. Nonetheless, the message given me was unambiguous. In fact, the more I think about it, the clearer the picture becomes. You can well appreciate that I didn't want to believe it, and for a time refused to acknowledge it. But, as it happened, it was a done deal. There was no choice offered me. Listen! And believe it! By the time the sixties arrived, I'd already been defanged by the new BNL crowd. No one was really listening to me any more. Yes, I could've continued on, playing the fool, but don't you think it was more sober-thinking and wiser of me to back off and just fade away? Anyway, that's what I did. It wasn't a happy ending. But how many of those have you come across? When you get old, that's the way it is. One way or another, having to get out is an inevitability. However, when all is said and done, I guess I have no complaints. After all, I was allowed to save face by giving the appearance that I was doing it of my own volition."

At that point, Izzie stopped speaking. It was as if he'd concluded. *Is that it*, Mickey thought? *No, it can't be. He's gotta have something up his sleeve.* It's true that when Izzie broke off, it could well have meant that he'd finished up. However, Mickey preferred to take the optimistic view that it was simply an interim closing, with far more to come. How unsatisfying it would've been if it turned out he was wrong, and Izzie's commentary up to then was indeed the sum total of his response to Mickey's complex of queries. No, it couldn't be. He wanted more from Izzie, a lot more. Although Mickey wasn't as yet sure, as time passed, a feeling of being cheated began to grow in him.

Meanwhile, across the table, Izzie was clearly bemused by Mickey's reaction of puzzlement and concern. He appeared to be gleefully enjoying himself. There he was, casually looking about the room, fussing about with his napkin, pouring himself a little wine, and just about getting ready to do the same for Mickey. The two seemed to be having a strange conversation, with gestures replacing words as the means of communication. Neither man was either willing or ready to break the silence.

If you looked carefully at the two of them, you would easily construe that Izzie, with his mind-game in progress, was merely playing around with Mickey. Well, if his objective was to unbalance the younger man, he most certainly was pulling it off. Making eye contact, Izzie stared at Mickey with a glare sure to unnerve him. Doubtlessly, he recognized in Mickey's demeanor an unmistakable discomfort and vexation at what was going on. *Good*, he thought, *it couldn't be better*. With things going his way, he let Mickey stew for a while. Time passed quickly for Izzie, but much more slowly for Mickey. Mickey was at his wit's end; but just before he could get any words out, Izzie decided to put an end to his little game, and his face broke out in a reassuring smile. So it was that Mickey was beaten to the punch yet again, as Izzie quickly restarted his vocal engine and took off.

"You look a little displeased and worried. But you needn't be, for surely you don't think I planned to rest my case here and leave you hanging essentially answerless. You know I wouldn't do a thing like that. Frankly, it frets me to think that you might see me in that light, even a little. The truth is that you've entirely misconstrued the situation. I'm only trying to ensure that you've learned something from all this: to wit, that you now regret using all those *why* questions. You see, by doing that, you merely opened the door to evasive responses. True, people will always be evasive if they want to be, no matter how you phrase your questioning. But the type of questioning you used particularly lent itself to logical evasion. The result speaks for itself: First, you gave me an easy way out and, second, you didn't get what you came for. Now, isn't that right? However, to show you what a nice fellow I can be, out of the goodness of my heart, for this one time, I'm going to let you take back what you've done. Normally, people aren't given a second chance; but, because you're so earnest in your quest for the truth, I'm going to give you this gift. You see, after all, there *is* an importance in being earnest. Seriously though, let this present I'm offering you commemorate our unique and very special evening here *on the town*. However, I do hope that you've been taught a lesson, and that, in the future, you won't make a habit of such carelessness."

Only a B-plus

"Before I dive into the topic on the table, the trials and tribulations of BNL, I really should lay out some ground rules to give some sort of order to our exchange of views and our dialectic airing of the complex issues involved. You will admit that a substantial change in how we're going about this give and take of ours is called for. To put it mildly, the approach you settled on, with those sophomoric *why* questions, was not a very useful one for the exercise at hand, our little labor of love. If only you'd gone in the direction of asking for my opinion of your analysis, now that would've struck a chord in me. It would've given me a solid core to grab hold of. It would've allowed me some solid material to dig into. I could've searched out its good points and its bad ones, and then derive the pleasure of making mincemeat of it if that's what it merited. You see, it would've made it that much more likely for me to say something meaningful, something meaty about BNL's escapades and follies. Yes, I certainly would've bitten the bait if you'd taken that line. Actually, that approach has something even more to commend it. It would've awakened the teacher in me. I really don't see how you missed that. It's me, Mickey. It's what I am. It's what my world revolves around. You should've thought of that. How it would've softened me! I'd surely have become putty in your hands. Well, all this going on about your wrong steps and gaffes, and how you might've done better isn't really getting us anywhere. So let's get to the nub of things. How should we move forward? How should we get to where we want to be? Since up to now we've gone your way, why not give mine a try? Take a look at my agenda, and see how it grabs you: First we scrap your questions; and second we take it that you're asking me for my views on your analysis. I gather that you'll agree to that, and if so, I stand ready to begin. Going once! Going twice! OK, hearing no objection, I'm off to the races.

"Being first and foremost a teacher, I will answer you in the manner of one. To start, I should tell you that, since the moment you began speaking, I've been assessing and judging everything you've said. Now, taking all the factors I use for grading into account, I give you a mark of B-plus. Your analysis is indeed very good. I'm sure you're well aware of that, and, on that basis, you probably were expecting an A-plus. Unfortunately, you dropped the ball on some of the major criteria, and so you don't deserve that distinguished honor. I imagine you're anxious to know more about my evaluation of your work, and particularly how I came to my appraisal. So, no doubt you'll be happy to know that I intend to give you the specific reasons that led to my finding. That, by the way, is more than I've done for most of my students. However, you'll have to wait a few minutes for the details. Right now, I must attend to more urgent business. You see, nature's calling, and I surely don't have to tell you that she won't be denied. The fact is that a man of my age, with a slightly enlarged prostate gland, must respond to the demands of his bladder's whims ASAP. So, if you'll permit an old man to take a quick break, I will return before you can say *Jackie Robinson*." With that, Izzie rose and disappeared into the shadows. Except for the flurry of muddled phrases and thoughts whizzing through Mickey's mind, Izzie's absence left a lull, a kind of empty suspension, in the dim debating corner where Mickey now sat alone.

Mickey made good use of the few free moments he had by reflecting on Izzie, the world-beating gem of physics, and Izzie, the man who derived amusement and delight from the simple pleasures of food, drink, and discourse. Whether in one guise or another, it was always an experience and an occasion-to-remember to see him in action. Here was a man who came to physics when the giants of the likes of Bohr, Planck, Einstein, Heisenberg, and Fermi roamed the playing field. Yet, despite the formidable array of European competition, he discovered a niche for himself. An American through and through, he managed to find a way to put his adopted nation on the physics-map, and rose to the top as a trailblazer as well as a genius-caliber scientist. Then, when his country called, he answered as a physicist-soldier, helping to keep America the land of the free. And when his science called, he was up to the task, building an institution, BNL, to house the first of the out-of-this-world instruments of Big Physics in the attempt to unlock the tightly held secrets of the gods. Thus, he carried himself to the heights of the stars. Still, his down-to-earth humanity shone through. A noble peer of the realm he became, but a man of the people he always remained. Reveling, going out on a lark, having a high time, and doing his high jinks number, were all part of life's merry-go-round he rode with gusto. Yes, he was a man to be reckoned with, a teacher, a statesman, a philosopher, a builder, and one of the guys. What can be said of such a one as he, except that he was a man among men! Just then, however, Mickey's bittersweet thoughts of the old gentleman were cut short as Izzie returned, sporting a wide grin. He sat down, nodded to Mickey in a friendly manner, took on a more serious and sedate demeanor, and, without any sort of preamble, got right down to business.

"Here's how I arrived at your B-plus: Since your analysis was pretty good – I actually like it a lot – I started you off with an A grade. However, you exhibited very poor judgment in using the *why* questions so frequently – to be more precise, ad nauseum – that I was compelled to reduce your grade to an A-minus. Now don't be too self-satisfied and smug just yet. You get a further downgrade because you either didn't know about, or you misunderstood, or you blundered in ignoring, or you misread something that's evident as well as key and essential to your analysis. As I'll make clearer to you later, this doesn't require a wholesale change in your reasoning. But it puts quite a different slant on the vital question: Was there or was there not a conscious policy determination or some manner of conspiracy underlying the brawling mêlée over the competing budget allocations for accelerator technology and experimental running? For that oversight, for not better clarifying your evidence about that crucial matter, your grade goes down to a B-plus. Well, that's it! If it's any consolation to you, let me tell you: coming from me that's a pretty good grade."

In Defense of a Failed Policy

"What I'd like to do next, Mickey, is give you my perspective on BNL after it reached its peak performance level sometime in the sixties, particularly what it made of its runaway high-energy dash for glory. Here's my plan of attack: What I'd like to do is paint a picture of what lay behind the ruinous and irremediable occurrences that overwhelmed the lab in its second two decades, establishing a radically altered character, and permanently, discordantly, and harshly determining the shape of its future. Frankly Mickey, just as you do, I believe the decade of the sixties was a decisive turning point for the lab, its defining moment and the climax of its life drama. So let's zoom in on it and see what we find. The central reality of BNL then was that it was a fabulous time, a time of mythic proportions, and a time that witnessed the belief-defying success of its experimental program. The lab was a place bursting with the fruits of heaven's secrets, ready to be picked and ripe for the taking. However, in an ironic twist of fate, the lab's future was not going to be determined by all these glorious goings-on. Rather it was to be decided and shaped by the ongoing budget war, inherited from the fifties, that flared into an agonizing, crippling, and far-reaching destructive struggle for power. On its face, the choice confronting the lab management seemed innocuous enough. Was it to be technology for the future or experiments for the present? But, in the end, the decision made tore the lab apart, leaving it with shattered hopes and futureless.

"In a nutshell, that is your analysis of the consequences of the experiment versus technology lab policy. In hindsight, how could anyone dispute your common sense logic? However, I must tell you that, in living through it all, the right choice to make was not as transparent as you imply. In fact, there is a defense to be made for the policy followed. Although you're undoubtedly too dogmatic and mulish to keep an open mind and listen to reason, I'll go ahead and give you the argument anyway.

"A major component of the bitter experiment-technology free-for-all at the lab, one that you, by the way, didn't emphasize in your analysis, was the escalating cost of doing experiments. Not only were the instruments getting bigger and bigger, but the demand for more of them was growing seemingly without limit. Then, as if that weren't enough of a headache for the already burden-filled lab management, ingenious ideas for new types of detectors were springing up all over the place like wildflowers. You see, the potential offered by doing experiments was simply irresistible. Hope and possibilities for exciting new discoveries filled the air with a surge of enthusiasm and anticipation. Free expression, inventiveness, creative power, and fertile, imaginative thought were everywhere. What was going on was the *experiment romp*, a dance to the joys of discovery. Experimenters and theorists alike flocked to the lab in teeming numbers. All the stars poured in, and many new young ones were able to establish themselves as such virtually overnight. It was truly a time of optimism and exuberance, a time I'll never forget. Do you really think it was possible not to allow them to follow their bliss, and so give them a blank check? I think Goldhaber and his troupe would've been beaten to a pulp and lynched if they were even thinking otherwise.

"I tell you, Mickey, it was a thrilling time. It was especially so for me, seeing my painstaking efforts and handiwork in giving birth to the lab being transformed into a hitherto unimaginable world of ardent, eager men of zeal as well as one of boundless fulfillment and success after success after success. And there was even more to fill my vanity to the point of overflowing. In the midst of this experimental welling up and gushing forth, this time for Big Physics to loudly and stridently assert itself, there was an extra-special treat for me: seeing so many of my students playing strategic and vital roles in this all-but-miraculous explosion of knowledge. There they were: so free-spirited, so full of life, and so self-reliant. They'd become such self-sufficient young men, running wild and sowing their oats; and they'd developed wills of their own, these new men of science, going their own way, bearing fruit at a rate hitherto unseen. They were productive beyond my wildest dreams. Yes, they'd grown into men, these children of mine. They'd gone beyond their teacher. They'd replaced me. Well, why not? They were, after all, *the future*. More importantly, for all intents and purposes, they had made themselves *the present* as well."

Leaving the Rat Race

"Mickey – and I say this exactly as it happened to me – it was then, at the very time that I was riding high on top of the world, that I made up my mind to leave the field of battle. Yes, I left the potential fame and stardom, but naturally also the certain trials and tribulations, to the new generation, the one that I helped foster and cultivate. You see, my time for the nerve-wracking and energy-sapping work of management and politics was up. My ability to muster up on demand deal-making, exploits, masterstrokes, and all such manner of actions needed in my way of doing things was conspicuously beginning to fail me. So I asked myself why I shouldn't take this emergence of the dedicated young as an opportunity to change course and devote my remaining years to my first loves, science itself and education. Still being young enough to advise graduate students, teach courses, enlighten the public, and even do a little research on my own, I couldn't have found a more perfect time to do it. So, I went for it.

"To be frank, there was a little more to it than the unassailable reasoning I've been spouting. At the lab, big trouble was obviously brewing. With other labs, highly competitive ones, quickly thrusting forward, and BNL itself butting heads with Washington, only hard days ahead could be the result. What it all meant was that money was sure to be tight. Thus, the battle of the lab budget was about to ensue. Now, I'd been through my share of budget battles in my day, so I knew first-hand the stress that they induced. Having come to sense and feel that I wasn't the spring chicken I used to be, and so, this time around, I might not be able to handle the nervous stomachs, the excessive irritations, and the taxing tension, I withdrew, leaving others to shoulder the burden. I admit that it wasn't a willful and thought-out course and, presuming it happened that way, that it was certainly the doing of my subconscious. But that's the nature of the beast. Your subconscious will sit back and let all manner of rational excuses induce you to consciously act, while it goes about its business directing the real action via subtle messages into the decisive conscious sectors of your mind. Yes, it indeed could've been that way. I might well have just wanted to slip away from it all and escape the ordeals and *tsures* sure-to-come.

"In looking back, I probably should've been more careful about who was going to fill my shoes. I probably should've insisted that it be one of the young, a man with fire in his belly, a thick skin, and a head on his shoulders. But, sad to say, I missed the gravity of doing that. More, I missed the urgency of doing it sooner rather than later. In my defense though, I should point out that it's not that easy to pick the right man. Even if you think you've done it, it's years later till you find out if you were on target. Then, more often than not, after the wait, it's only to discover that you were wrong in the first place.

"In my case, the situation was particularly complicated. It was far more than a straightforward succession. Formally, my rank was Chairman of the BNL Board of

Trustees, which provided me with the base from where I could operate. Not only did it afford me access to the lab and thence to politicians, men of industry, and government bureaucrats, but it also gave me a lot of leverage over the lab Director. Remember the government contract for running the lab was with AUI, the lab being the operating organ. Thus, in principle, I was the responsible party, the man to be held accountable, although in practice the Director was the chief officer in charge, the CEO so to speak. That was exactly the way it was designed to be, the way it was on the books, the way we organized it at the beginning back in 1947. The Director gave the orders and I provided the oversight. So you see, as the outside world knew it, I was but peripheral to the chain of command.

"However, that wasn't at all an accurate indication of who really carried the weight and had the clout. No, in many ways, I was the true boss and had the last word; and, let me be crystal-clear about this, that didn't happen because of my chairmanship. Well, how then, you ask? It was that, over the years, using my position and title to give me entry to the men who held the purse strings and carried their fearsome, intimidating batons, I slowly accumulated authority and learned to wield widespread influence. By building a network of people who would listen to me, heed me, act on my behalf, and do my bidding, I spun a web of power. More often than not, these people became beholden to me. When I put something to them, usually it was an offer they could ill afford to refuse. Thus, through manipulative skill and Machiavellian machinations, I set up a system that made the lab responsive to my will. How on earth could I have found someone to replace me with the capability for that sort of thing?

"Frankly speaking, right from the start, I knew deep down that it was a lost cause. Yes, it was quite clear that the whole business of finding a successor for me was an exercise in futility. Sure, you could easily find a new Chairman of the Board. But that meant squat. That wasn't a replacement for me. All that would do is give far more power to the lab Director. Too bad! But what has to be has to be, I guess. So, what it all came down to was that I simply didn't care any more. All I wanted to do was get my ass out of there. Does that make me a selfish and ugly sort of a man? Probably! But, you see, I had this blind urge to get back to my happy haven at Columbia. I knew that was always the place I could go to rest my weary soul. I just felt that I'd done my share and a little peace and quiet surely wasn't too much to ask in return. Anyway, that's the way it was. You can judge me as you will. But, in the end, I abandoned my post, cavalierly left a power vacuum behind me, and, to top it off, believe it or not, I gambled on chance to fill the hole I left and remedy the clumsy handling of my succession."

The Promise

Izzie remained motionless for a while, appearing to be a bit disheartened. Having no words that could come close to being some sort of consolation for him, Mickey just watched in silence. You could hear a pin drop. Then, suddenly, the man-cum-chameleon snapped out of it and braced up, his outlook refreshed and vital again. "OK, where were we? Ah, yes, the experiment-accelerator war that simmered just under the surface as the sixties opened, but then came hurtling out with a vengeance as the decade progressed.

Of course, you were right to guess that its origins derived from the fifties, when a clear distinction between funds for experimental running and funds for accelerator technology was established, and the means and scale for the distribution of these funds set in place. At that time, portioning out the money was done fairly and smartly, no matter that many whiningly complained about their share. The fact is that Haworth and I ensured that it be done right – exploit the present, but don't forget to prepare for the future.

"In the sixties, however, satisfaction with the system set up declined almost to the vanishing point, and the experiment-accelerator story that emerged had an inauspicious air about it, portending dark days ahead. Once the AGS started churning out protons at an unimaginable rate, discontentment in the two factions about their cash flow came to reign and the stage was set for battle. Well you know what happened. You said as much yourself. In one corner of the combat zone was a new group of accelerator specialists that was beginning to emerge and come into its own. Their mandate was to make a post-AGS future for the lab. Many were newly hired for that purpose. I believe you were such a one, Mickey. Anyway, quite rightly, they expected that the resources to allow them to do their jobs would be forthcoming. But things didn't turn out that way. In the other corner, standing in opposition to the accelerator builders, were the experimenters, and it was with them that the real power at the lab resided. They also sought funds, which in their case were to uncover nature's mysteries and thereby bestow greatness on both BNL and Big Physics. But to accomplish that, to discover the pot of gold, more experiments were needed, and more elaborate ones too. That meant they wanted mucho bucks to cover the ever-increasing experimental costs. However, there just wasn't enough hard and ready cash to please both sides. What to do! One thing I felt certain of: the experimenters had to be denied some, even as they pleaded for more. Yes, to do it right, the guys at the top had to give the newly forming group of design experts, builders, and technologists the wherewithal to envision an out-of-this-world dream machine, and to erect out of the earth the palpable reality of it. Only in such a way, providing this undertaking with both imagination and cash in sufficient doses, could BNL's future be shaped and its grandeur sustained.

"What a choice to put into the hands of the lab's top guns! If you think about the origins of these men, you have to realize that they were first and foremost interested in the experimental results. That's where their hearts lay. Thus, their duty to the lab and its future demanded that they refuse the appeals of their close friends, their own kind. No, they didn't ask to play such an onerous role. The task just fell on them. So what were they to do? Would they go the Cosmotron route, or would they choose a different approach? Would they choose *friend or country*? Of course, we all know what transpired. Goldhaber gave the experimenters all they wanted, and ended up decimating the accelerator effort at the lab. What a shortsighted, blockheaded, asinine, and klutzy way to go! Well, such is life! No doubt, the man did what he had to do! He just lacked the capability of looking over the next hill and seeing the dark clouds gathering.

"You know, Mickey, I remember well the experience at the Cosmotron. That's where Haworth and I determined the optimum funding division between experimentation and accelerator building. I can tell you in no uncertain terms that the experimenters weren't too happy with our choice of the dividing line. They thought, and proclaimed vociferously, that too much was being put into the development of the upcoming AGS. Now – keeping in mind that under the plan we chose, they were to get far less than they'd asked for and anticipated – this didn't shock us. So we continued on course and persevered. We did what had to be done, and certainly no excuses need be made for the amounts of money we gave each side. The fact that the AGS came into being speaks for itself. Besides, we were simply applying one of the prime principles of planning and organization, thinking of the collective interest by performing the delicate and ultimately thankless balancing act of allocating for the present without sacrificing the future. True, the experimenters grumbled a lot, but eventually they more or less accepted the compromise. However, perhaps how we got them to go along and comply left something to be desired. Apparently, they came away with the notion that a promise had been made them to the effect that when the AGS got going, a budget correction would follow in which they would get more. I'm not sure exactly what was said. But I do know for sure that such a promise was not explicitly made. However, I have to admit that the communication was vague, and deliberately so. After all, our goal was only to calm them down so they could live with what they were given. Frankly, when all is said and done, I believe there was some kind of misunderstanding. Unfortunately for the lab, that misunderstanding was to lead to a lot of trouble in the decade ahead."

Technology or Bust

Izzie took a brief moment to consider how best to proceed. Taking a sip of wine, he went on: "The experimenters didn't know it while they were grabbing all they could get and squeezing accelerators dry, but the high-energy funding arena was to greatly expand as the sixties ticked away. Soon BNL wouldn't be the only big game in town. In 1964, a signal event occurred for the national labs pursuing high-energy beam facilities. There was the issuance of the Ramsey Panel report that recommended that America set about constructing a series of new accelerators at unprecedented energies. That same year, going along at full tilt was the experiment milking of the AGS. Even after the report was hot off the presses, BNL kept at it for all it was worth, with nary a pause. As a result, by allowing its expertise in accelerator R&D to decline as much as it did, the lab was ill prepared to be a realistic contender for such projects. So it was that the BNL experimenters may well have won their petty war with their easily beaten weak accelerator brothers at the lab, but at the same time the lab itself lost its belated bid for the big synchrotron being planned by the AEC. What the internal BNL squabble ended up doing was to ensure the birth a few years later of a new lab – Fermilab."

"As the sixties came to a close, it became clear that the BNL strategy for that decade was a grave blunder, an all-around loser. Pumping the maximum money it could into AGS experiments, and holding accelerator R&D down to the lowest level possible, actually just short of killing it off entirely, was a patently ass-backward approach to modern Big Physics. If only Goldhaber and the rest of his mob would've had a little common sense and foresight, they might've been able to figure out what was really going on. You see, while all this crap was taking place, at the highest government levels it was decided that the AEC should substantially increase high-energy facilities in the U.S. The competition was on, but BNL just couldn't hack it. So, within a few years, Fermilab rose up out of the farmlands west of Chicago. But, even though the new lab's accelerator enjoyed an energy level that was more than ten times that of the AGS, it was just the beginning of the energy party. Scientists all over the country caught the bug, and began to dream the impossible dream. They believed they could go to any heights. Only the sky was the limit. They *kvelled* as their wishes danced in their minds' eyes. The next step was to go for it. So they pushed off the starting point double quick, anxious to let 'er rip. However, they'd gotten just a little ahead of themselves. In their rush to get moving, they'd overlooked a point of over-riding urgency. Something was missing. The fact is that to go any further, new technology was a prerequisite, an absolute must. To realize the visions of the Ramsey Panel, to open the door to the really high-energy accelerators imagined, what the country needed was a massive dose of inventive accelerator R&D to develop the compulsory technologies, particularly superconductivity technology and colliding beam technology. Without that, no one was going anywhere."

Money Makes the World Go Round

"The Commissioners at the AEC were forward-looking men – one of whom, by the way, was my old pal Haworth. They saw the future, and their vision was for an unprecedented upward surge in particle collision energy. For their part, their responsibility was to arrange for the total high-energy budget to go up, and to ensure that funding for the future became the highest priority and remained that way. *Deceptively simple, wouldn't you say, Mickey*? Well, despite the resistance they met up with in the halls of power, they managed to find a way to get more money. But there was a catch. It was to be directed primarily at building new accelerators; and that fly in the ointment proved to be a viper in the Big Physics body politic. You see, the high-energy budget went up, but not nearly enough, not by a long shot. What the AEC slipped up on was that a big increase for current experimentation at the AGS was getting to the point of urgency. There just had to be more funds to finance the burgeoning area of particle detectors. But the AEC number one mandate was higher energy accelerators, and their bent was to stick fast to it. The present-future problem was therefore sloughed off by the AEC and laid squarely at BNL's doorstep.

"From the lab's perspective, its immediate obligation was to exploit the AGS to the fullest by ensuring that experimentation was the best that it could be. Wasn't that the natural course? Wasn't that the right thing to do? Since the AGS was there pumping for gold, what choice did BNL have but to make accelerator R&D second in priority? Because of the clashing objectives, because they were at cross-purposes with the AEC, the lab's top men and loads of university experimenters flew off to Washington time after time, begging for more cash. But the Commissioners wouldn't listen. BNL's budget would indeed rise some, only not nearly enough to allow the lab to do justice to both current experiments and accelerator R&D. True, the AEC did give a little. What the commissioners chose to do was to allow the lab Director his prerogative of deciding for himself how to allocate the money. You've gotta admit that that's some tough position to be put in. The Director and his advisors would have to figure out themselves how best to use what they were given, an amount clearly smaller than needed.

"As it happened, throughout the sixties, the AEC chose to give only a little of its increased budget to BNL, an amount it considered to be fair. The lion's share of new money available was set aside for future construction and its associated R&D; and this, in the spirit of free competition, was to be made available to others eyeing the prize. The Commissioners were determined to go through with their plan for the future; and, when it came to taking account of BNL's plight, they just looked the other way. So it seemed that BNL was smack behind the eight ball! You do see the bind the lab was in, Mickey, don't you? Could it really have done other than shift money out of accelerator development? I ask you: If you were in the Director's shoes, what would you have done?

"So it was that BNL would have to decide for itself how much to use to support future machines and how much to sink into its high-flying experimental program. I'm sure you see what I'm driving at. In the fifties, we at the lab thought strongly in terms of accelerator development. That was the natural thing to do then. The machines were the primary reason for the lab in the first place; and the experimenters, although dissatisfied, came to accept it, albeit some had rebellion on their minds. However, when the sixties came, an entirely different raison d'être – exploiting the machines – began to express itself with a hitherto unseen force. Maybe it was just that the experiments became bigger and a lot more money was needed. Anyway, the result was that circumstances conspired to make the present-future budget balance, fixed in the previous decade, unacceptable any more. You better believe that there was trouble ahead.

"Here's what happened: In the early sixties, the fiery spirit engendered by the AGS creation spurred accelerator development at BNL, impelling it forward with a rapid thrust. In fact, at the rate it was moving, it was far outpacing the more modestly rising lab budget increase. Thus, if BNL was to remain competitive in the fast-growing accelerator R&D area, given its mandated modest budget rise, it would have to violate the apparent accord arrived at between the experimenters and the previous administration, iffy as that agreement was. At the same time, the experimenters, holding all the cards, together with the high-potency clout to match, were adamant: there was to be no revision. They wanted a substantial increase, and they aimed to get it. It was a case of an immovable object meeting an irresistible force, and something had to give. And it did!

"You know, Mickey, I often think about that time and wonder if money, simply more of it, could've saved BNL from all the grief that followed. Here was the AGS unexpectedly pouring out a glut of beam intensity; and it was being done in record time, coming much earlier than anyone anticipated or planned for. Suddenly, all kinds of new experiments became possible. Experimental slots came into extremely high demand, and bigger and better detectors were called for. The cost to do these newly conceived AGS experiments ran right through the roof. Compared to that, the Cosmotron experience was peanuts. Who could have told in advance that this was going to take place? Still, it didn't have to be such a big deal. All that was required was some cash to pour in, and things would then go on humming along, ever upward, unraveling mystery after mystery. Yes, it was that simple, just money, money, and money! Yet, for some strange reason, the AEC saw fit to hold BNL funding down and instead spread the loot around. What a blow! Even with Haworth as one of the commissioners, they were determined to pursue that policy. I still can't believe what they did. I still find it devilishly hard to fathom.

"As if all that weren't enough, even more pressure came bearing down on poor Goldhaber and his unprepared lot. The experimental competition coming from the CERN PS was also swiftly heating up. The American experimenters found themselves in a pressure-cooker. Actually, for them, that was a place devoutly to be wished for. It was exciting and provoked the best in them. It fostered ingenuity, inventiveness, and brilliance. However, for Goldhaber, although it must've filled him with pride and satisfaction to see what was going on, the stress must've reached a level almost too much to bear. So, what do you imagine his response to all this was? OK, perhaps it's a no-brainer. Of course, without thinking, he taxed everybody at the lab, including accelerator R&D, and just jammed into the experimental program as much money as he could lay his hands on. Now, Mickey, do you really expect that he could have foreseen what future for BNL the course he took augured?"

Questions of Priority

"In the end, combining the unquestioned lab top priority of exploiting the AGS to the fullest with the competitiveness, the natural ambitions, and the great influence and power possessed by the experimenters, especially the stars, a substantial money shift out of accelerator development was inescapable. If the AEC had only responded more generously to BNL's pleas, it certainly would've lessened the shift, and might even have avoided the rough and bitter ride the lab was in for. It most surely would've alleviated the bloodletting. But I guess it seemed to the Commissioners and their advisors that no amount of cash would've appeased the hungry beast inside the lab. Thus, the AEC, not willing to put all its eggs in one basket, and, besides, having other fish to fry, refused to go along. Finally, when the dust settled, the picture that appeared was indeed a dark one: the experimenters had their way, accelerator development at BNL began its inexorable decline, and the AEC turned its back on BNL and looked elsewhere for greener pastures.

"This seems like a good place to return for just a moment to our roles of me the teacher and you the student. During your analysis, you referred to a war between the experimenters and the builders. Well, Mickey, that's exactly what I've been dealing with. Yes, the war you were trying to come to grips with was indeed a real one. At the point I've reached in my account, the war was on and getting hot and ugly. And you were quite right: Things looked awfully bad for accelerator R&D. But contrary to your claims, there were no scheming stratagems. Absolutely none! I can't emphasize enough that it was not by the will of a thinker or a visionary that the BNL accelerator effort fell to such lowly and degrading depths. No, Mickey, there were no conspiracies. Not a one! It was simply the prevailing conditions of the times. I know it feels highly unsatisfactory that occurrences so chock-full of consequences, of suffering and pain, should come down to the luck of the draw. But, my dear young man, that's often the way life is. Yes, in this case – that meant so very much to you and me – it was a particular circumstance – a concert of weak men playing their own separate instruments and in whose minds psychological pressures and mental strain piled up – that proved to be the villain of the piece. That's where you veered off course and went wrong in your analysis. Too bad! Because that's why your grade went down to a B-plus!"

This seemed to Izzie like a good spot to stop. He chewed on that proposition for a while. However, as he ran through it, he was reminded that he still had a lot more to say. So, after grabbing a berry and playfully popping it into his mouth with a toss, he went on: "I have a feeling that we've both had enough of generalities. I gather it's time to dig under the surface and get down to the real nitty-gritty, the gory details: Who were the actors in the drama? What roles did they play? And what happened to them? So let's hop to it. This is where I believe we stand. So far, we've determined that the transition in the lab's accelerator-experiment policy was a done deal fixed in favor of the experimenters. When it was over, the change had been accomplished via a shift in the way the lab's high-energy funding was divided up. But now let's get the camera's zoom lens into the act and go over that again in close-up. Once the new policy was agreed to and accepted by the lab's top echelon in the Director's office, by the Board, and by the BNL-linked science gurus in the community – meaning that the policy was firmly entrenched – the time was ripe to put it into effect. That's when an ugly little hitch came to call.

"Since there were three divisions – the Experimental Support Division, the Accelerator Operations Division, and the Accelerator R&D Division – all under Green's aegis in the Accelerator Department (AD), Goldhaber thought the desired budget transfer would be straightforward, easy pickings. He conjectured that all it would require was a minor accounting adjustment, adding money to the experimental support division while subtracting it from accelerator R&D. And he was right. It was really that easy. But, hold on: There was a big stumbling block that first had to be overcome. Before Goldhaber could reach his goal, Green, who stood smack-dab in his path, would have to be bowled over.

"You see, Mickey, the lab's organization was designed to be a set of academic-style departments, with the chairmen having close to dictatorial authority. That was to prevent a strong centralization of power in the Director's office. Anyway, once Green was given his budget, Goldhaber would have to go through a lot of manipulating, finagling, and arm-twisting to get Green to do what was contrary to the man's wishes. Since Green was obstinate to the nth degree, he wasn't about to be casually walked all over. He knew what his rights as Chairman were. In particular, he knew he had the last word in dividing up his AD budget. If Goldhaber wanted him to do the dirty work, he would outright refuse. He just wouldn't do it. At least, he'd resist with all his might and with every fiber in him. And that's the way things transpired. Goldhaber tried every trick in the book: pressuring Green by holding up his budget allocation, causing him no end of grief; getting every leading light of physics he could think of to give him an earful to get him to acquiesce – and that, by the way, included me; and even going around Green by pushing money to the extent that he could through the Physics Department budget. But this strategy just didn't work. The Director was stymied. The truth is that Goldhaber underestimated Green's intransigence as well as his smarts. When push came to shove, he would have to go the distance, first threatening Green, and then finding the means to remove him from office. And, because Green was so mulish, and Goldhaber so stressed and desperate, that's the way it actually went down.

"On reflection, Green must've been struck by the irony that the entrance of the AGS on the scene – his crowning perfection – had the queer and startling consequence of threatening to sap the strength and integrity of the accelerator effort of his department. That the lab's top management was willing to unthinkingly and recklessly sacrifice future machine technology most surely whacked those rose-colored glasses off his long, bony nose. It must've utterly perplexed him and shaken him to his roots to see these top people so carelessly and indifferently dismissing the dreams of so many about fantastic and wondrous things to come. *Welcome to the real world, Mister Green*, I might well have said to him over a cognac and a *Lucky Strike*!

"Frankly, Mickey, I did indeed take the side of the experimenters, at least during the first half of those fateful sixties. You see why, don't you? They were of my ilk. I was one of them. Besides, all they wanted was what we all wanted – to get a crack at netting one of those elusive little devils roaming the heavens. However, as time passed and I looked more closely at the things going on: when I saw what was being done to the lab's accelerator undertaking; when I saw what all this was doing to slim Ken; when I saw how the lab was being ripped asunder; and when I saw BNL's future being buried even before it had a chance to show itself; yes, I wavered. But by then, as you know, I was out of the wheeling-and-dealing game. Thus, all I could do was watch the show, sympathize with Green, and shed some tears for my very own BNL. Still, my marbles hadn't forsaken me, and so what was happening didn't escape me. Let me tell you, Mickey, it's no picnic seeing it all before you, wanting to get in there and do something about it, but not having the capacity to. No, it's truly a discouraging comedown!

"As it turned out, Green wasn't the pushover Goldhaber thought he was; and, even though he had virtually no one backing him up, even though he stood all alone, Green made an honest-to-goodness fight out of it. It turned out to be another example of an irresistible force meeting an immovable object; and, as the song tells us, in such a situation *something's gotta give*. But, I must say, it was a humdinger of a match. In one corner was Goldhaber, the heavyweight with the authority of the big-man Director. In the other corner stood the obstinate and idealistic Green, only a lightweight, but a man who, for the moment, was holding onto the purse strings as tightly as he could. So, as they hopped about readying themselves for the big event, the million-dollar questions were: Who would come out on top, what would his opponent look like after his fall, and what would the consequences be for the lab? Well, I tell you, Mickey, the answers had unpropitious, even menacing stamps plastered all over them. Although he kept in their swinging till he could hardly remain standing, the long shot underdog took a bloody beating. But no one could've withstood the pounding he took. So, in the end, Green fell, and, as a manager, would never be heard from again. When the KO pronouncement came, Goldhaber basked in his brief moment as ascendant winner and conquering hero. Swiftly, the experimenters were up on their feet, cheering their champ and his resounding victory. There stood a man with a mission who simply couldn't be denied. Yet the truth of the matter is that it wasn't really a happy day either for Accelerator R&D or for BNL's future. No, that bitter fight represented a turning point for the lab. From there on, going back was not possible anymore. And only hard times lay ahead!

"Soon after the decade of the seventies arrived, Goldhaber began to realize the pinch he was in: Where was the lab going now? And what was he to do about the competition from Fermilab? Yes, it was quite a predicament he had on his hands. To come to some sort of resolution, without it blowing up in his face, required: subtlety of thought; managerial know-how, including the wisdom to pull it off; and sensitivity and empathy for others. That, Mickey, certainly doesn't fit the man who was then in the hot seat. When you think about it, giving that knotty set of issues facing BNL to a man like Goldhaber was scandalously dim-witted, a management gaffe of the highest order. But alas I must admit that it was my doing that put him there in the first place. That's what I agreed to when the succession unexpectedly came up as the sixties unfolded. Somehow, it just didn't occur to me then that it might be on his watch that the Director would be confronted with matters of such pith and import. I know, Mickey! You don't have to say it. It's true: I should've been able to foresee that possibility. Unfortunately, I just didn't. In my defense, weak as it is, I feel compelled to tell you that back then I did in fact try to get a new face with a strong and influential character, a man who could stand up firmly and unflinchingly to the experimenter-stars. But it's quite obvious that my efforts along those lines bore no fruit. Zilch! All I got were *no, no, and no*! So, up against the wall, I reluctantly acquiesced and accepted the inevitable. Thus it was that Goldhaber ascended to become BNL's second *true* Director.

"To the lab's grim misfortune, Goldhaber was a weak Director who could only stand and fight when the power-laden experimenters were propping him up. He was also a shilly-shallying and irresolute type who couldn't bear up and carry on very well under pressure. In hindsight, I regret that he was chosen. Having to face up to the seemingly limitless and insistent pleas and petitions that continually flowed from the demanding stars, there was simply no way that he should've been the one picked. You see, first, he was too chummy with the BNL users and the university experimenters. These were his colleagues and friends. Isn't it apparent that it was natural for him to have a decided tendency to give them just about everything they'd push for? Then, second, he had an inner nature that made him not much better than a brown-noser. So, instead of being a mediator between experimenters and technologists, as he should've been, he became an advocate of the *user-stars*. Even if there was an instance of a slight hesitation on his part, all they had to do was to flash their political clout in front of him, and he would immediately and easily succumb, giving them all he could, the entire kit 'n caboodle, if that's what they wished. How could I have missed staring at me these two glaring reasons that spoke so eloquently against him? Anyway, I did, and so Goldhaber became the man on the throne and BNL became an experimenter's paradise, accelerators and the future be damned!

"As for Green, he was doubly a loser. Goldhaber not only gave him the heave-ho as boss-man of accelerator R&D, but he also made the BNL accelerator R&D effort – that Green had so assiduously built up – wasteful, barren, and thoroughly unproductive. How did he do this? By callously cutting its money supply, of course! You see, money had to be found for the *in-house* BNL groups and for the *out-house* star-groups (as the university *users* were jokingly referred to). And where was this money to come from except out of the hide of accelerator R&D! If you want my opinion, Goldhaber didn't really understand what he was doing. Nonetheless, he did it, he caved in and ended up giving the whole store to the *users*. To his powerful friends, *in-housers* and *out-housers* alike, his generosity went well beyond bountiful. But what else could you expect from a weakling? Frankly, Mickey, the man was nothing but a mouse in a suit and tie.

"Actually, as we two sit here and ponder the type of person Goldhaber was and what he did, can't you almost perceive a glimmer of some sense and logic behind his behavior? Consider this. There's one thing we can certainly count on: he had an abiding proclivity for understanding physics and so a deep-seated, steadfast and staunch leaning toward experiments – there's no doubt about that. But, Mickey, think about what that really could imply. Suppose that all along he was planning to go back to his life as a physicist, living with the *users*, his colleagues and friends. That's plausible, isn't it? In fact, he used to say it all the time. It was expected of him. What else was he to do when he vacated the Director's chair? Doesn't the rest follow? How better to prepare for that time than to do what he did? Now if that truly were the right interpretation, what a laugh it would be! What a twist that would give to the whole Goldhaber story! What a hoot! By siding with the experimenters, by ingratiating himself with them, the man was simply setting up his future. Actually, mulling it over, doesn't it catch fire? OK, maybe he didn't actually plan it to the last detail. Maybe he didn't articulate the scheme in his mind. But that it was sitting there in his subconscious all the time seems to me to be a veritable certainty. Mickey, how could it be otherwise? Ha! What a joke! When all is said and done, when you add it all up, I guess he wasn't as naïve about the ways of the real world as I presumed he was."

No Good Came of It

Izzie felt a keen sense of self-satisfaction, the kind that takes shape after an experience of self-induced enlightenment. However, smug and overflowing with self-esteem as he was, it did make an impression on him that only now, in the midst of making a thorough evaluation of what the sixties wrought, did he come to the realization that Goldhaber might've acted out of sheer self-interest. Why hadn't it occurred to him before? Probably it was because he thought so little of the man that the occasion to dig into the intricate details just never seemed to come up. Or perhaps he simply didn't give Goldhaber much thought at all, certainly not enough to delve into what motivated him. Thus, with stars on their minds and stars filling the sky on that cool, clear evening, and as his gabfest with Mickey kept rolling right along, Izzie found himself most amused as he came to appreciate that there was more than a touch of irony in the fact that here he was seduced and ensnared by a *why* question, just the thing he was upbraiding and berating Mickey for. Nonetheless, Izzie didn't feel the least inclination to suppress the glow within him, the kind that comes from a discovery you've made. He went over it once again: *Why did Goldhaber act as he did?* That was the question. *Why, out of self-interest, of course*, came the inner reply! How obvious! How trivial it seemed now! Naturally, he should've come to it long before. But, what did that matter? He finally got it, and that's what really counted. So he sat quietly for a short spell, allowing the new notion to sink in and permeate through that inquisitive mind of his. How pleased he was with himself – how cocky – to have come upon that insight!

However, this wasn't at all the right moment to play with such a thought and be able to have much fun with it. He knew full well that this was neither the time nor the place to contemplate gossipy-type matters, even one as juicy as this one. The business at hand awaited him. And time was galloping forward without the merest regard for Izzie's immediate wish to think things through. *Just let it go*, his inner voice advised. And he did!

Peering at Mickey, who was spilling over with *shpilkes*, Izzie was sorely tempted to play the mischievous boy by just letting him sit there and stew. But, to Mickey's good fortune, Izzie decided against it. *The show must go on*, he thought. And, without hesitation, he switched course from self-absorption to the reasoning-feast duel, which was, after all, why he was there. *OK, where was I*? Izzie asked himself. He'd already given Mickey *the Izzie take* on BNL's past as well as on how the lab's past impacted its future. Now, what remained to be done was only to recap, solidify, and tie all the pieces together. *So, on with it*, he thought.

"I guess it's about time to wind up the story of the sixties and what it did to our once-shining lab. But before we do, now that I've come to a better appreciation of Goldhaber's hidden incentive, perhaps it's worth revisiting just one last time. Armed with my newfound understanding, how about if I give a quick look, focusing on the *Battle of the Decade*, the Green-Goldhaber fight to the finish?

"As that critical, turning-point decade neared its close, the AEC threw BNL into the throes of a severe budget squeeze, leaving the lab to fend for itself. With insufficient funds, the choice of who to feed and who not to feed had to be made. With the lab's priority to give out-and-out preference to experimenters over builders firmly fixed and irreversible, misguided as this policy was, there wasn't a ghost of a chance that Goldhaber wouldn't implement it. He just didn't have the spunk or the gumption for that. No question about it, it was going to be: *experiments first, accelerator R&D last*! And that was that! If truth be told, that's what he wanted in his heart of hearts anyway. Thus, being who he was, he plowed ahead, come what may. Without the will to counter his experimentalist friends, he came up with a scheme devised to cater to their every whim, to wholly favor them, and, in the end, to gratify them to the utmost. Determined to give them all they wanted, he set about to drain accelerator R&D dry, to crush this weakest link in the lab's accelerator enterprise chain. Unfortunately for Goldhaber, it wasn't going to be as easy as he first imagined. Standing in his way, guarding the till he was ready to rob, was AD Chairman Green. So, to win, Goldhaber was going to have to slog it out in the mud, and, in so doing, dirty both his hands and his soul.

"Green was a man of quite a different sort from Goldhaber. Far from playing the sap for the stars, the blatant characteristic that marked Goldhaber, Green was a rough and tough gladiator, a samurai who stood his ground for what was right. So, even though he was behind the eight ball, even though the odds were stacked heavily in favor of *the appeaser*, Green wasn't about to lie down and let Goldhaber loot his AD castle, at least not without mustering, with all he had, some defiant and never-say-die resistance. However, he couldn't count on much beyond himself. The truth is that Green was all alone. Along the lab hierarchy, none, nary a one, would side with him. As for the disordered and disheartened men of the AD, they were a motley crew to be sure, certainly not a bunch to be depended on in a fix. Yet, despite all he faced, Green didn't know the meaning of surrender. He would stand fast and stick it out to the bitter end. So it was that, with daring bravado and nothing more, Green took on Goldhaber's raw power with little else but his scrappy know-how.

"Green knew the practical ins and outs of the lab. He knew the things that had to get done, how to put them into effect, and how to sustain them to completion. He knew precisely the right people to seek out for what he had to accomplish. Yes, he'd been quite a manager. Over the years, he'd greased the wheels, and, on the day-to-day level of running things at the lab, these men who made things happen came unquestioningly to respond to his needs. And who could fault them? Green certainly had the gift of persuasion. But what turned out to count the most for him in his contentious dispute with Goldhaber was his unique mastery of the AD budget. In matters of controlling, manipulating, and playing with money, his touch, his flair, and his artistry were unequaled. No doubt, without the many budget tricks Green had up his sleeves, Goldhaber would've easily been able to run roughshod over him. Yes, Green would surely have been brought to his knees and humbled before the bell ending the first round rang. However, with his slick and nimble dexterity when it came to the flow of cash, he managed to go the distance with a man who strode *BNL-country* having behind him the potent clout of the muscle-packed *users* and the BNL-supporting contingent of power-laden men running the high-energy community. Thus, it so happened that because Goldhaber was a novice at the money game, and because he naïvely failed to take Green's obstinate personality seriously into account, he couldn't escape the blood feud that erupted, the divisiveness that followed in its wake, and the extreme experimenter-builder polarization that ultimately ensued at the lab.

"What a bitter pill it must've been for Green to swallow! What a sad picture of a proud man it was! There was Green, all alone; and there was Goldhaber, with all the big boys squarely behind him. So much hostility! So much resentment! So much all-round suffering! Surely it needn't have been that way. Surely they could've worked something out. But the reality was that they simply weren't able to. Their fates were sealed, and they were destined to play out their hands. Anyway, the outcome of the contest didn't leave much to the imagination. As it happened, when the troubles and pains of the self-defeating and lab-crushing match-up wended its course and finally subsided, when the dust settled, Green was found wobbling on hellishly shaky ground, brought to ruin, while Goldhaber, in stark contrast, was prancing about, his hands held high in victory.

"However, as all winners eventually learn, when you beat somebody up, there is a price to pay. And this case was no exception. Now Goldhaber was probably willing to pay some, but, if you ask me, he didn't truly appreciate how big the full price would be in the long run. What happened was really quite simple. The lab, sans Green, floundered in mastering and developing the accelerator technology it had to have in order to compete. So, downhill it went. How sad! As it turned out, within a couple of years, Goldhaber, in an ironic imitation of Green's fate, was also shown the door.

"Looking back, I think you'd have to say that Goldhaber wasn't really a bad man. No, I don't think so. In fact, what else could you infer about him than that he was rather innocent in the ways of the world? But those realities are neither here nor there. The truth is that his character was incorrigibly flawed. Selfish and lacking in generosity, *number one* inevitably came first. As his second term moved along, he came to recognize that his stint at the top had but a short time left, and soon he'd be gone from the spotlight. Thus, thinking primarily of himself, it seemed self-evident for him to cozy up to and stick as close as possible to the *users* – his chums, his cronies, and his collaborators-to-be. If BNL happened to bleed or even be nailed to the cross, it wouldn't much affect him personally. No, if any flack came from what he'd done, it would be somebody else that would have to bear the brunt of the repercussions. And by then he'd be far from the battle zone, safe in his world of dancing symbols. Others would be left to face the music and clean up the mess.

"Well, Mickey, you know the rest of the story: first came the profound decline of the lab's once-vaunted accelerator expertise; then came the demise of poor ISABELLE; and finally there came an all-too-bleak future for the lab that once had it all. No, it's not much of a happy ending, is it Mickey, eh?"

Intrigue or Happenstance?

There was quiet at the dinner table. In parallel, both men mused over days long departed. Reflecting on what was and what could've been, each in his own way had to confront the impeaching eyes of responsibility glaring at them. There was no escaping their self-accusations and self-judgment. Still, they couldn't change things. There was no alternative but to accept the roles they'd played and the deeds they'd done, and move on. That's life! Just leave well enough alone. You can't do it over again. One chance is what you get, and that's that! Then, on the other side of the coin, there was another way at looking at blameworthiness: Why condemn yourself when you don't really comprehend *how* and *why* it all occurred? So, wrapped up in the confusion so characteristic of reminiscing, they remained cogitating, seeking explanations, and trying to pinpoint their own parts – perhaps guilt – in the drama that transpired in those bygone years.

Mickey was first to make the break from his introspective façade. There in front of him was his delectable-looking crème brulé. Without the need of conscious brain-direction, he lifted his dessert spoon and sat picking away at it. While he waited for Izzie to return from his inner realm, he thought he might spend the time considering what *the man* had already divulged. Yes, Mickey thought, why not use the time he had to try to see things a little more clearly? Unfortunately, his brain wasn't in a very compliant mode. His mind just couldn't focus, couldn't fix on anything in particular. It was just a jumble of swirling sequences that prevented him from selecting one to investigate, scrutinize, and dissect. So he soon gave up the effort and waited contentedly, savoring his good fortune that Izzie would open up as much as he had. Yes, to be favored by *the great one's* most private thoughts, now that's something to crow about.

Meanwhile, Izzie, who had an uncanny ability to compartmentalize his emotions, suddenly looked up with the mischievous, jester-like grin Mickey had come to know so well. Without any lead-in or preamble, Izzie clicked right into high gear. Switching into his teacher mode, he went on with his take on the history preceding ISABELLE's fall: "On the accelerator-experiment policy question you've so often mentioned, I'd say you essentially got it right. Yes, an understanding did indeed develop and evolve among those in the Director's office and us at AUI. But before you jump to any conclusions too fast, I can tell you point-blank that the idea of shifting substantial funds from accelerator R&D to the experimental program was never formally articulated and certainly never written down. However, like many things in life that depend primarily on circumstance and on who has the momentary power, it nevertheless came to be an operative policy. Now, Mickey, I don't want to belabor this more than is necessary, but I do want to ensure that you get this policy business right. So let me spell it out for you one last time: Yes, the practice of stuffing money into experiments did take hold. But, mark you, it wasn't contrived or planned. It was only after tests of its staying power had taken place that we began to feel comfortable with it. *Hey, this works*, we undoubtedly thought, *we must be on the right track*. So we continued doing more and more of it, till it seemed to be quite the natural thing. Only then were we able to see things in their larger context. Only then were we able to recognize it for what it was – a de facto policy shift.

"Now, from your advantageous position, looking backward after the fact, you saw the policy shift as the result of an accelerator-experiment war where the winners looted and pillaged and the losers anteed up or had their ears boxed, or worse. True, that might be a good way to record the history. Hindsight does offer the advantages of giving us insights and of building cause-effect cases. It might even be a good way to commit the whole episode to memory. But as to what actually took place – what led to this record – I'm afraid you haven't hit a bulls-eye. You see, it didn't happen as simply as *plan the policy* and *implement it*. As a matter of fact, the vital if not critical factors came from chancy circumstances and whims of the moment. Since most of these went unrecorded, how could the formal, unembellished story be the correct one, the true one? That's simple to answer. It couldn't be right and it isn't right.

"Nonetheless, once the policy became history, it took on the character of being timeless and irreversible. How nice to look at it as simply as authoritative decision-making, firm planning, and incontestable implementation. That would surely surround it with an unmistakable air of finality. But think, Mickey, if it were that straightforward, then why should it be so tough to turn around? No, that isn't it at all. If you really want to know why it became so strong, listen: It was because so many people worked for it to come about, so many benefited from it, and so many small things were done to make it operational. Yes, it was the accumulation of these many smallish things that made going back a practical impossibility for mortal men. Voilà! Irreversibility! Much like the Second Law of Thermodynamics! Well, take it or leave it, that's my version of the story: The policy did ultimately come about. But, Mickey, there was no sinister back-room conspiracy. Take it from me: that's the truth. And who better than I should know?"

A Yellow Leaf Blowin' In the Wind

"Well, I've just about run out of steam on the subject of the sixties at the lab. Yet, I can't stop without giving you a brief comment on a question you've brought up in various forms and guises. True, it's a *why* question, so my inclination would normally be to ignore it. But, because of your persistence, because of the deep emotion you exhibit in expressing it, and because you appear to be so disappointed in me, I'm going to set aside my objection in this instance and try to satisfy your wish for an answer. In a nutshell, the question asks why I didn't do something *to stop the car from plunging over the cliff.* Rephrasing it, I presume I'm being asked why I didn't prevent the BNL experimenters from all but wiping out accelerator technology expertise at the lab.

"To start, let me lay out two unequivocal points: First, there was no formally established policy to favor experimenters; and, second, I didn't intervene even as the BNL accelerator enterprise was being torn down. OK, these are the facts. Now I'll impart to you as best I can my involvement, my impressions, and my intentions as this war – this accelerator-experiment war – was running its course. You well know that it wasn't the kind of war with two armies in spiffy uniforms fighting it out on a battlefield. Rather, it was more like a barroom brawl, started by loud-mouthed ruffians and greased by the power of the suit-and-tie types in the background. There was no organization behind it. It was merely men acting out of their own selfish interests. So, you see, if I were to enter the fray, it wouldn't be abstractions – ideas, agreements, documents, and the like – that I'd be for or against, but real people, flesh and blood. And I'd have to go after them one by one. In fact, as it happened, most of the men committing those base and shameful deeds, the acts that ultimately brought BNL to the edge of that cliff, were my colleagues and old friends. So, there you have it: I knew they were doing wrong. I knew that, for the good of the lab, I should do something about it. Still, God forgive me, I didn't. I guess it's time to tell you why!

"To do that, I'd like to outline the story for you, spicing it up with a little color here and there to account for why I didn't step in. As the drama unfolds, try to envision the main characters – the generals, so to speak. They were Haworth, Green, and Goldhaber; and, of course, I shouldn't forget myself. Sometime in 1959, Haworth and Green formulated and put together the expanded and unified Accelerator Department, with Green as Chairman. Green always claimed that, along with its formation, he'd struck a budget deal with Haworth and me, whereby the AD would be assured of equal priority with the experimental program. I wouldn't argue with that because, to tell the truth, I sort of recall it that way too. Getting to Goldhaber, I'm not quite sure of any role he played in the agreement. Straining my memory a little, I'd say he wasn't really implicated in the negotiation at all. Yes, come to think of it, in all likelihood, not considered a key player then, he was deliberately kept in the dark about it. As for me, I was a party to everything that was going on. In fact, my concurrence was essential, and I went along with all of it. But it was a private understanding. Nothing was put in writing. It was strictly a gentlemen's agreement, no more, no less than a *handshake*. It's not really a bad way to do business; but when a situation arises where fulfillment of the past obligation made is asked for, and furthermore if an intervening succession has occurred, then watch out! And that's exactly what transpired here.

"When Goldhaber took over as Director in 1961, the Green-Haworth pact conflicted head-on with his basic ideas on how the lab should be run. Thus, since there was no document to force him to do so, he wasn't about to voluntarily honor it. Could you blame him for just ignoring it? As for me, I'm sad to have to admit that even though I knew that an agreement along those lines was indeed entered into, I failed in my duty to intercede on behalf of the builders and their dreams of the future.

"Frankly, in retrospect, I'm not sure my butting in would've been effective anyway. The best I could do was to try to influence Goldhaber. But that would surely have been useless. You see, Goldhaber didn't have either the will or the stomach for the fight with experimenters that, beyond a shadow of a doubt, would've ensued. So, as you rightly surmised, I stayed out of the whole sordid business. On the other hand, when you implied that my entering the conflict would've helped, in my opinion, you weren't even in the ballpark.

"Now don't get me wrong: I didn't just say to myself that since I couldn't persuade Goldhaber to adopt a different philosophy, then forget it. Not at all! I did in fact think about it quite a bit, and actually came to have a passing glimpse into a forbidding future. But remember that, in the sixties, BNL's surface was lacquered in glory, and, blinded by it all, the dark thought passed quickly. In any case, with a golden age engulfing us, who cared about any possible decay occurring beyond our minds' radar screens? Who'd believe it, anyway? You know: *out of sight, out of mind.* Yes, the good times appeared to be splendidly rolling along, and everybody, without a care, carried on as if things were just hunky-dory. So, confronted with this reality, I knew instinctively that it would be futile to take any substantive action even if I could've brought it to my consciousness and figured out what to do. OK, you could call all this stuff rationalizing. Actually, I wouldn't argue with that assessment. Nonetheless, it's all the truth; it's the way my mind was working at the time.

"Frankly speaking, Mickey, what I haven't yet emphasized is that there was a higher truth about me then that wasn't evident to most. As hard as it was for me to face, the reality was that, as the sixties moved on, my influence was in a steady and inexorable decline, waning rapidly. My aging, my growing frailty had come home to roost. I didn't just come out and admit it. I even tried to hide it from my own consciousness. But it was no use. It was in every fiber of my being. It was in all my sensations and in all that I did. My feelings told it to me in every way, even if I didn't allow myself to think it. Believe it or not, more than anything else, it was that sense – that inner recognition – of my mortality, which caused my lack of action. Mickey, I ask you to look back with an open and clear mind. What could a decaying man have done? What could a man already written off have done? Who listens to an old man, a fallen leaf blowin' in the wind?"

A Judgment Call

Peering into Mickey's skeptical and suspicious eyes, Izzie knew he wasn't being convincing enough for the doubting Thomas sitting across from him. "Mickey, your demeanor speaks volumes," he began, "I guess you didn't buy the old-and-tired *shtick*. I get the distinct feeling that you're stuck on some starry-eyed, idealistic image of me, and just can't let go of it. I must tell you that, with all those things you said about me, so full of praise and adulation, you certainly do have a smooth and honeyed tongue. But, give it to me straight, do you really believe all that mumbo jumbo, all that high-sounding *narrishkeit*? C'mon, admit it! You were just gilding the lily, weren't you?" Mickey was blushing from ear to ear. He started to respond, but something stopped him, and he thought better of it. He lowered his head, out of Izzie's gaze, and tried to compose himself.

In the meantime, Izzie, always pleased to fluster his debating opponent, formed a smile and went on: "Look, Mickey, I simply wasn't the man you painted. Your portrait of me was most assuredly warped. I must say that your flights of fancy about me, despite some of that harsh criticism you sprinkled in, were rather cute and charming. Frankly, it was flattering. But, in all honesty, it's only in your imagination. It just wasn't how my life was, not in the least. To describe me accurately, I was a scientist – a research man – and a teacher – a molder of young minds. That's it! That's what I yearned for throughout my life, and, lucky me, that's what I got. True, I played in other of life's arenas. I dabbled as a statesman in the *Big Atomic War* and I perhaps gave Big Physics the push it needed by helping to institutionalize BNL. But, truly my young man, that was it. Now don't get me wrong. I find your way of looking at things highly endearing. I really wish I were the man you talk about. But, honestly, it wasn't me. It just wasn't me."

The old man's words trailed off as he immersed himself in a state of all-absorbing meditation. Mickey was also pondering, wondering whether Izzie was on target or not. Oh, he didn't doubt Izzie's sincerity, not for a minute. It's just that so much time had passed, and there was so much intervening rationalizing going on. Could Izzie really remember the truth about how he was in those years a half a century before? Mickey thought not. Actually, he saw Izzie's downplaying of his deeds as a form of not-fully-believed modesty. Perhaps he was trying to offset the remorse he felt at some of the things he did, or more precisely didn't do, as his BNL days were closing down. Then again, perhaps there was some sort of unwillingness to accept Mickey's full *Izzie-package* – that Izzie was a man nonpareil – and so rejected its key ingredients. *Why not? It isn't such an unlikely inference*, Mickey thought. In any case, just because Izzie said something didn't make it so. Yes, Mickey could still take his own version as the right one. So, in the end, it came down to choosing: Which one was it to be? When Mickey added up all the details, comparing what he knew with what Izzie contended, he wasn't about to change his mind. In fact, contrasting the two versions side by side made it abundantly clear to Mickey that his version of Izzie's story was far and away the more credible one.

And what a picture of *the man* Mickey's version offered up! It gave his life rich and deep-rooted meaning, and raised his soul high above those of other men. That's indeed what Mickey's exploration had uncovered. And that's the right way for Izzie to be remembered. The more he considered the issue, the more persuaded he became. Thus, when all is said and done, to Mickey, Izzie would never be merely a professor in his ivory tower – a man who took a few tentative steps into the cold, forbidding world, only to quickly return to his safe haven. No, Izzie would always be the man whose footprints stuck in the places he strode through, the man who could change the minds of Presidents, and the man who could build an institution from the ground up. Yes, he was some man, this Izzie!

War!

Izzie's considerations on what happened in the sixties and the consequences that came of it seemed to be at an end. But just before he gave up the floor, a thought suddenly leaped into his consciousness. Compelled by his nature, he simply couldn't hold it in. Facing upward and away from Mickey, with a questioning look on his face, Izzie just let it spill out: "You know, Mickey, spurred on by all those provocations you've hurled at me, I've been chewing over what our unforgivable failure to invest adequately in accelerator technology meant, not only for BNL's future, but for the future of high-energy physics.

"Try to picture with me what it was like, Mickey, back then, about four decades ago. Right before our eyes, new high-energy technology was sprouting and accelerators were on the verge of explosive growth. Who could've doubted that reality? It was so obvious. Yet, for strange reasons that still escape me, it bypassed us at BNL. Not only didn't we invest more in technology, we actually invested less. What a calamity that was! We lost the opportunity of a lifetime. Imagine, missing the *pièce de résistance* of the sixties: the founding and masterful shaping of Fermilab, followed quickly by its rapid rise to *Number One* and stardom! Wilson, who built and cultivated that upstart antagonist lab in the Midwest, was a giant among men and a formidable foe. He sped onward and forward, leaving us at BNL to taste the dust as he ran hungrily by us. What fools we were that we didn't see this early enough! *Quel misfortune* that we so underestimated Wilson, a master among builders! That little accelerator-experimenter war at our East Coast lab, the one we've been speaking so much of, gave Wilson just the opening he never dreamed we'd be dumb enough to give him. So, while we were asleep at the wheel, he stepped right in and made his dramatic and dazzling mark on the world of Big Physics.

"However, the consequences of our misjudgments and misdeeds of the sixties didn't end with Fermilab. Although it was a new era full of dreams and wild aspirations, both labs were busy planting the seeds that were eventually to bloom into full-fledged hostilities and malignancy in the form of the cutthroat and no-quarter-given BNL-Fermilab war. Fueled by the government's continued support of both labs, even though each one had a similar if not identical mandate, the war lasted much longer than anyone anticipated, wasting the American high-energy proton labs and throwing them into full-blown, unprecedented failures. I, for one, didn't see it coming. If only I had. If only others had. Then, perhaps, things might've been different for American Big Physics. Perhaps we would've dodged the ISABELLE bullet. Perhaps we would've won the race for the W. Perhaps we would've come through on the SSC, carrying us ever closer to the gods. Yes, it could've happened. We might've somehow seen the need to become unified as a field, and figured out how to do it. If early enough, we might've nipped the destructive conflagration in the bud by arriving at the solution to bring the new high-energy synchrotron to the East Coast, thereby instituting a *greater BNL*, an American-style CERN. OK, I know: I'm just dreaming. It's all pie-in-the-sky mind-meanderings. I'm just an old man imagining a world that simply wasn't. But what can I do? I am an old man. You know, Mickey, to be open and candid with you, I still haven't come to terms with that awful misjudgment I made back in the sixties of not insisting that the Green-Haworth agreement be honored. I simply don't know how to forgive myself for it. Well, I guess we all have to live with what we've done. But there's one thing I do know: Mark my words, the outcome that was the bitter BNL-Fermilab insanity is not over yet – not by a long shot."

* * * * *

The Return of a Distant Sentiment

Izzie's mood swings were indeed mysterious, as swift as thought-travel itself: from down-in-the-dumps to sitting-on-top-of-the-world and tossing-out-quips in the time it takes the nerve signals to navigate their way along the shortest-route pathway. How quick was the transformation of his mind from a *downer* into an *upper*! So, even though he had been pretty low just a wink and a nod before, he was ready to show his stuff. Lickety-split, with élan and gusto, he fashioned a naughty grin as he glanced at the few remaining zesty pieces of fruit. Happy and carefree, wide-eyed and childlike, he grasped a juicy morsel of melon between his forefinger and thumb. At that very moment, a waiter was extending his arms in the act of removing the almost empty fruit plate. "Don't take this, my good man," Izzie mildly chided the waiter, as he placed the little square carefully in his mouth. His face glowed with satisfaction as he took pleasure in the sweet flowing nectar. Mickey watched, much enjoying Izzie's performance, and ever so relieved and encouraged at this return from his brooding self-absorption. The two lingered in stillness, contented and glad to be where they were.

However, Izzie's coming back was rather short-lived. Within minutes of his apparent return, Izzie's thoughts were suddenly drawn far away from the present, floating back to a time long ago. The muscles in his face contracted noticeably as his mind struggled to fix on the precise moment he was craving. He felt so close to discovery. Yet the picture stayed unfound, as his mind's kaleidoscope kept on turning. No, he couldn't quite capture either the happening or the emotion that was evoked who knows when. Yet there was something about the experience that he was able to glom onto. Somehow he could sense that it was a moment of sadness, the bittersweet kind of sadness experienced by the young. But what was it all about? Why was there this ache in his heart now at what had happened so long ago? Why was he reliving the sentiment of a time gone by? Did that feeling he had then of sorrow or melancholy come as a result of a disquieting observation? Did he learn something unanticipated? Was it a moment of bewilderment as he was becoming aware of the strange predicament of life itself? Yes, that's a good question! How old was he then? Did it occur at birth, or in infancy, or in adolescence? Did it happen later than that? Could it have been in response to an insight he had? *Damn it*, Izzie thought, *what was it*? Oh, how he wanted to catch hold of it! And he almost did! But, alas, eluding his mental grasp, it lay just beyond his reach. Then, as quickly as it came, the opportunity to seize and fasten upon that moment from so long ago passed from his mind. A relaxed state then overtook him as he shut his eyes. Thinking of nothing in particular, he took a little catnap.

Across from Izzie, Mickey was puzzled by Izzie's abrupt withdrawal into himself. However, having been thrown into some confusion, flustered by Izzie's elaborate recounting of BNL in the sixties, he needed a bit of time to settle himself anyway. So Izzie's momentary fading away was not entirely unwelcome. In fact, the few minutes that he was afforded served him well, allowing him to recover his poise. Thus, resigned to biding his time while Izzie weathered the inner storm he was going through, Mickey wondered how the remainder of the evening would go. He especially tried to imagine how it would end. But how could he get very far on that score? What chance did he have to be able to foresee the future involving such a wild and unpredictable, such a constantly metamorphosing man as Izzie? Not much, to be sure! So, as it happened, there was simply nothing he could do but wait and see. What else was possible? Nothing! Yes, the wait-and-see game plan was all he had.

As the two men sat deep in their own thoughts, the waiters quietly cleared the table and brought the espresso and cognac. That appeared to do the trick for Izzie. Lifting his head, just the sight of these palate-gratifying juices brought him out of his reverie. Izzie eyed the brandy with unconcealed delight. Then he slowly, deliberately lifted the snifter containing the promise of sheer, unadulterated pleasure, and, using a well-practiced sequence of sips, unrushed and relishing every drop, he emptied it. His cheeks reddened and he smacked his lips with joy. Then he sat still, savoring the all-too-short moment.

Thus reinvigorated, Izzie said in a lusty voice, "Yes, a little schnapps to help us reach the finish line, don't you think?" Mickey could do no less than imitate his teacher and new friend. So, he too partook of the cognac. Izzie, having in this manner brought the discussion back to life, then set the stage for the evening's finale: "I believe we have time for you to take one more shot at me. I feel like a million bucks, so bring on your biggest cannons and fire away." Mickey was taken aback by Izzie's renewed enthusiasm and energy. He wondered where he would find his own second wind. The wine and cognac had left him a little tired and light-headed, and he so wanted to rest a while. But that was out of the question. He had a big issue he still wanted to bring up. How could he let this precious opportunity go to waste? No way! He knew he simply had to collect himself and get ready for action. He had to do it, no matter that he was tired and would like nothing better than to lay his head back, shut his eyes, and take a little trip to dreamland. But how? How was he to rid himself of his sudden nervousness?

Without thinking and without excusing himself, automaton-like, Mickey stood up and left the table. He walked briskly to the washroom, and splashed his face with cold water. *Wow*, he thought, *that did it! That hit the spot! That's just what I needed*! It appeared that *Lady Luck* was still with him, holding his hand and leading him on. Yes, that simple act certainly worked wonders. It was amazing! When he returned, he was refreshed and animated. *OK Izzie, I'm ready to go all the way*, Mickey thought. He felt unbeatable.

Mickey sat down and looked straight at Izzie, who was staring right back at him, sporting a slight, knowing grin. Although slightly unnerved by this ploy, Mickey didn't flinch. Casually, he apologized for leaving the table so impulsively, with such lack of proper decorum. Then he breathed deeply a few times, and lo, he was feeling on top of things again. In one of those non-time-consuming moments, he wondered what caused him to perk up so. Maybe it was just pure and simple vanity. Of course that's what it must be: Izzie was so darned eager and sure of himself, Mickey just couldn't leave the battlefield and allow *the man* to get the better of him. On the other hand, who was Mickey compared to Izzie? How could Mickey hope to compete with such an eminent man of renown?

Undoubtedly, all these thoughts were no more than Mickey's pride and imagination running wild. Or perhaps the true reason for this mind-meandering was that he just wanted so badly to find the right way to squeeze everything he could out of this dinner with Izzie. In any case, having found his second wind, Mickey felt ready to take on the master once more. So the two of them, having regrouped, were again on the verge of going at it. Taking his cue from Izzie, Mickey dove into this last chance he was to have at Izzie. In a clear and carefully intoned voice, phrasing each syllable precisely and deliberately as if weighing each word's potential impact, he began to speak.

The Nature of R&D
The Man Atop the Project

"In exploring the history of R&D projects, I've found certain generalities or principles that seem to shape their characters and determine their outcomes. These principles can be expressed in terms of rules that might be used as guides for project heads. To use them that way, you can express them in the form of a list, with each entry saying in effect, *If you want to succeed, do this or that.* That sounds great, doesn't it? It's precisely what every lab Director's looking for. Just hand over a sheet to the top project man with these *what-to-do* rules plastered on it, tell him to follow them, and your job's done. More than that, you might even presume that the project's done. Whoa! Not so fast! Hold on! There's a catch. You know: Nothing's that simple and straightforward. And certainly not projects! There's gotta be a hitch somewhere. And, of course, there is.

"OK, so what's the joker hiding in this *rule-deck* of mine? It's just this: I'm not – absolutely not – implying for a second that just anybody can take these rules, apply them, and – voilà – success! Perish the thought! No, the fly in the ointment is that the guy in charge has to be part of a particular elite class of man. He must be a special and unique type. And finding him ain't gonna be easy!

"In *management country*, people talk of the characteristics required of a leader. Well, although a project head should roughly conform to them, he must have far more than these run-of-the-mill traits. In my way of looking at it, the man-in-charge must boast certain rather uncommon and unnatural attitudes and ways of thinking that allow him, when some atypical or irregular situation calls for it, to act with determination, with cleverness, with all his wits at his disposal, and with dispatch. He must have the discipline and the self-command to act in ways that in other situations might well make him wince. Thus, for my set of *how-to-succeed* rules to work, the project's commander-in-chief must learn, adopt, and stick by these unusual attitudes and manner of thought – that is, unless, in the rare circumstance, he has an in-his-blood bent toward them. Thus a top-notch project leader needs not only to follow the rules laid down for him – not a great intellectual or practical feat by any stretch of the imagination – but also to build within himself the sometimes hard-to-take but absolutely essential attitudes. What I'm saying is that he'll have to change himself in ways that for most people will almost certainly fly in the face of their inner disposition and tendencies. And that, Izzie, as you well know, is a hell of a difficult thing to do.

"Now let me get down to brass tacks and be more specific about all of this. What is it that our *Little Caesar* must be prepared for? For the good of the project, he must be ready to do things against his own wishes, or against his natural inclinations, or against his friends, or even against his workaday principles of conduct accumulated over a lifetime. He must be ready to face up to and live with criticisms and attacks on his credibility and honesty. He must be ready to accept blame properly due others. He must be ready to be silent when speaking out would be his natural instinct, or vice versa. He must be ready to be secretive and at times deceitful. He must be ready to resort to lies and betrayal when demanded of him. He must be ready to be ruthless in gaining the desired end result – the project completion, on time and on budget. Izzie, what manner of man is capable of all this? One thing for sure, it doesn't describe just anyone. In fact, I ask you: Is there anyone you know who actually behaves that way in the course of living his daily life? I certainly don't, and I imagine you don't either. No doubt, he's of a rare breed. So, how then do you find such a difficult to detect and uncommon man?

"Consider yourself to be a Director seeking out just such a man to take over a project at your lab. Of course, you could try to grab one coming off an assignment where he showed he was made of the *right stuff*. But he'd surely be a tough one to steal away. I wouldn't count on that to resolve your dilemma. Well, I guess that unless you've got someone tucked away in your backyard, there's no alternative but to get out on the street and start looking. And what is it that you can expect to find out there? Only this: Some men simply can't or won't do what has to be done. Some are just not capable of the adjustment demanded of them. Some fool themselves, try, and end up falling flat on their faces. No doubt about it, nothing but disappointment is what you're sure to encounter out there in the real world. The truth is that only very few men are suited for a serious crack at a tough project. When it comes down to the crunch, if you want such a man, then better resign yourself to the fact that you won't just pick him off a tree, not a man from this one-in-a-hundred strain.

"OK, it's not easy. Well, what else is new? But you can't get discouraged before you even begin. You just have to get off your ass and find him. Anyway, here's what has to be done: Assemble a batch of men who want the job, haven't proved themselves yet, don't exactly appreciate what it really entails, but still think they can do it. Then, out of that group, what you have to do is to pick the one who's willing and able to change, to be transformed into the model project manager. That's some tall order, to be sure. You can imagine that choosing *Mister Right* out of the party you've managed to gather together is much like finding a needle in a haystack. Go ahead! Snatch him out of the pack! Which one of them is that special man who's ready to assume, practice, polish, and embrace attitudes he'd most likely shun in his daily life? Sure, he may well say that he's able to do what you're asking of him, but these are only empty words. Does he really mean it? Will he try to change? Will he do whatever's called for? Will he go all out? Will he succeed in the end? No, you can't avoid the trying difficulty of the job. And you can't avoid the uncertainty you'll inevitably be left with after you've made the choice. But if you're a Director in search of the right man, that's what you'll have to go through.

"Despite the daunting task it is, the acid test crucial for any project is hunting down and coming up with the perfect project chieftain. That means: whatever's standing in your way, you have to mow it down and get the guy. However, that's easier said than done. Since the one you really want is in such short supply, how could going about it in the standard way of filling an open position work? Bluntly said, it can't! So, what else can you do but try something unique and unusual, something imaginative and ingenious, some rare and off-the-beaten-track approach? And, pray, what is that? Why, you have to custom-make him yourself! You've got to create the man you're going to place atop the project with your own hands, shaping him to your immediate needs. I grant you it's not something to delegate. You'll surely have to get your hands a little soiled. But that's what it'll take, and more, it requires lots of man-hours of effort. However, only then, when out of a novice you can concoct the man who fits the bill, will you give yourself the best shot at hitting the jackpot. Only with the right man will the job get done right. If you don't have him, then both the project and the lab are just out of luck."

The Four Rules

The rules that Mickey built up over the years were neither profound nor unknown. Yes, he was quite aware of this. Still, his staunch tendency toward the didactic spurred him on to bring them together in one place, and set them down as if preparing them for a textbook. Since these *rules according to Mickey* had a scholastic tenor, clearly academic in character, he couldn't resist the temptation to lay them before *Herr Professor*, the master university-man. So, all worked up, more than a mite nervous in anticipation of Izzie's judgment of them, Mickey got started on a sketch of his rules: "I guess this is as good a time as any to get on with my set of four rules for running R&D projects, designed specifically for the project head working in concert with his boss, the lab Director." Mickey hesitated, his hands quivering. Why was he so jittery? Perhaps he was apprehensive about Izzie's reaction to the rules that he'd devoted so many years of effort to working out and compiling. Anyway, there was no turning back now. So, he alternately tightened and relaxed the muscles of his body a few times, then started in.

"*Rule number one*: Be bold technically. Unearth the newest technologies and push them toward the frontier and beyond. Lure the topmost scientific and engineering minds in the world, the best of the best. Don't accept less than the highest performance. Go as far as you can go, and then some! Shoot for the moon!

"*Rule number two*: Compete aggressively. Take on all comers, the bigger the better. Be fearless. *Toujours l'audace*! Use your full arsenal of tricks and invent some never seen before. Fight to the finish, till you fall. Don't give any ground, not an inch. Be ruthless if you absolutely have to – none of that kid stuff. Don't retreat except for tactical reasons. Be generous if it's at all possible, keeping in mind that you may need allies in times ahead. Focus on recruiting – it's good men that make the world go round. Be assiduous in bringing in the young, ensure that they're made to feel welcome, and give them their chance to shine. Don't engage in any private arrangements with other labs, unless it gets you where you want to go; project deals and personnel understandings are *verboten*. Always remember that your institution comes first. But, before you give your all to it, be convinced that it's the best it can be.

"*Rule number three*: Always seek to stay ahead of those who represent the government. The best way to do that is to make sure any authorized project gets done on schedule and within its agreed upon budget. There's no substitute for being on the ball and doing things well. Be responsive to government edicts and requests, but stand your ground when you're in the right. Keep in mind that a major lab function is to buffer its projects from any unnecessary bureaucratic interference. However, when you happen to be in opposition to the government on what's needed or on what's to be done, better check carefully that your ground is firm, technically and politically, lest you take the project down with useless, contentious bickering, your vanity dashed in parallel. Be cooperative with government men but be wary of their true motives. Your goals and theirs may not at all times be in synch. Still, trust is not out of the question. You see, once committed to your project, they depend on you as much as the reverse. So, although they do have a tendency to behave like bullies, don't be afraid of them. Since you know more about your organization than they do, there's no reason to allow them to push you around. Always bear in mind that you're the experts, and that they're more likely than not just a bunch of low-grade administrators and bureaucrats. (Do you recall, Izzie, how Pief used to refer to these scientists-turned-bureaucrats or scientist-trained-bureaucrats as men who epitomized the revenge of the mediocre students?)

"Remember that the government and the lab have entered into a transaction grounded in a legally underwritten contractual obligation. From this, isn't it as plain as day that honesty is the best policy? So, even though R&D is a vague, nebulous, and fuzzy business and science is made up of highly exclusive knowledge, thereby giving the labs a big edge in performance claims, still, unimpeachable results and clear, squeaky-clean reporting should be the order of the day. Strict adherence to promises made must never be compromised. Always beware of the temptation to take shortcuts using personal contacts with government officers – eschew them religiously unless you're awfully sure of yourself. Be warned that these officials may be with you one minute, but agin' you the next!

"Don't succumb to excessive dependence on the government. Self-reliance and self-sufficiency are best for projects because the government will only hold them back and slow you up. So stay clear and do things yourself as much as is humanly possible. And, for goodness sake, stay out of big trouble, and always keep a low profile. You see, when the going gets too rough – say, you need some substantial additional cash, or some congressmen get up on their hind legs – the government will drop a project like a hot potato, if that's what suits it and if you're overly dependent. Now, you don't want that to happen to your project, do you?

"If a lab has more than one project going on, any lab Director worth his salt is duty-bound to protect all of them and to ensure their completion and success. But if you happen to be in such a position, don't forget that you must also be straight with the government as to whether you can handle them all. It's a tall order and may not be goofproof, but, as best as you possibly can, always be frank about the resources that are needed to get all the lab's projects done successfully – let there be no monkey business on that score. And be especially sure to get that notion of low-balling costs out of your head.

"*Rule number four*: Bring the public with you. Court your local politicians because their reach extends from the highest powers of government to the families next door. They want to support you – be assured of that. And it's not only because they want to get re-elected. That's not all they're thinking about. Remember that they're very smart men. They're most assuredly astute enough to sense that science is the wave of the future and they want to ride that wave. They certainly don't want to miss the parade of technology into the twenty-first century. Also keep in mind that politicians, neighbors, and the extended lab community are proud of you and bask in the glories of their lab's new scientific discoveries and the new technologies conceived and developed there. But, if politicians are to support you in the halls of power, you must make them look good at home. It's *the people* that keep them in office, so be especially careful to please your neighbors. Show them that you care, be frank with them, and give them the respect they deserve.

"So there it is, Izzie, four simply stated rules: Be bold technically. Compete aggressively. Stay ahead of the government. And bring the public with you."

The Rules Rule

"Obviously, Izzie, you must be familiar with these rules, because, as a matter of fact, they're yours. They can all be generated from the example you set with your leadership of BNL from its inception right after the war until it reached the big time with the AGS in 1961. You were a go-getter from the get-go. What a thrilling man you were! A perfect fit for the transcendent, spectacular, and awe-inspiring times! What a killer-diller you were! What a pusher and achiever! What a statesman! Oh yes, you were a statesman, a real one, not that wishy-washy type from the diplomatic service. You stood tall, above it all; and smooth-tongued, you made it all happen, you made the BNL of the sixties the extraordinary place it was. You were a man with a mind that could move mountains; and you were possessed of those outstanding practical insights that get things to happen. You had the right contacts, and you had at your fingertips the right buttons to press. Then, using everything you had, you put the icing on the cake: you made BNL a distinguished, renowned, and splendid institution. Your magic was divine, your exhibition of remarkable feats of accomplishment out-of-this-world.

"How brilliant it was of you to choose Haworth! What foresight to be able to see his future worth! OK, in that instance, you had a *little bit o' luck* lending you some assistance. But having *Mister Serendipity* on your side is nothing to sneeze at. On the contrary, it's something to be thankful for. Actually, isn't it great when such a thing happens to you, when chance walks with you, hand-in-hand? You know, sometimes you've gotta have a little help from the gods.

"Izzie, my hat's off to you. You were a true leader, a born leader, and although you depended on good fortune here and there, I've often wondered whether *Lady Luck* doesn't smile more often on the great, the master spirits of the age. However, there was a hidden downside to your sunny days at BNL. As with all such men who rise above the others, you became indispensable to the lab. It came to depend on you to an inordinate degree. Slowly but surely it habituated itself to your presence; and, in the end, without you, it was just an ordinary, run-of-the-mill place. Even worse, when you left the stage, within a decade the lab simply fell apart. Would you agree with that cause-effect scenario? Or perhaps you'd contend that the confluence of occurrences – the departure of your power and genius from BNL and the breakdown and collapse of *the house that Izzie built* – was mere coincidence. Methinks if you're wont to choose the latter, it would be but false modesty.

"However, the facts are clearly evident. Once you left, the lab was ripped apart to its very core. Things kept going downhill, from bad to worse, until the catastrophes hit – and boy did they hit hard! In the early eighties, the ISABELLE fiasco knocked off BNL's wings and sent the lab into a tailspin. It recovered in mediocrity for about a decade and a half. But then, in the mid-nineties, the *Tritium Affair* wreaked havoc with this once flowering place of forefront science, and took BNL to the edge of ruination.

"Why, you might ask? Why did the lab have to sink so low? Well, circumstance certainly did play its part. But I still keep coming back to the explanation being that you weren't there. That's right! You weren't there to navigate the lab through the storms. You weren't there to keep it on track when the winds veered it off course. You weren't there to keep it from smashing into the icebergs lying in wait ahead, just out of view. You weren't there to keep morale up when the stark power emanating from the dark gathering clouds was sapping it dry. And then – the pièce de résistance – you weren't there to guide it to the heights, to make it once again the envy of the Big Science world. Was it you, entirely you, that made the difference? Of course, it was. Somehow, I imagine a young Izzie clone materializing to take hold of the lab in the sixties. And, yes, I do believe that would've made a difference. You'd have ensured that *the four rules* were held to, just as you had in the past when you were in your prime. Yes, you'd have seen to it that *The Rules Ruled.* Anyway, there's one thing I can guarantee: nobody could persuade me other than that you'd have made a big difference."

Following the Rules Sans Izzie?

"To better appreciate how BNL came to such a low ebb, let's examine how, when you were out of the picture, the behavior, decisions, and actions of the lab's bosses stacked up against my four management rules for projects.

"*Rule one*: Was the lab bold technically? As a matter of fact, the opposite was closer to the truth. ISABELLE just dragged on interminably, with nary a sign of a technologically true light at the end of the tunnel. The lab's superconducting-magnet-makers worked themselves to the bone, but the design contained an unfixable defect. So, not surprisingly, they kept coming up with duds. At the same time, the project cost-estimate kept rising, threatening to go right through the roof. You can well understand that the government was leery of fully committing itself; and the backing of the high-energy community began to wane, as the physicists got edgier and testier with the passing days. Thus, by the time ISABELLE got off the drawing board in the late seventies, flawed even then, the project was technically obsolete, scientifically uninteresting, and pretty meager in support. As it happened, two other labs, Fermilab in the U.S. and CERN in Switzerland, took up the torch for high-energy physics and were racing by, leaving BNL lagging in the rear. In the end, technically outdated, ISABELLE had nothing to offer that couldn't be done quicker, better, and cheaper elsewhere.

"*Rule two*: Did the lab compete aggressively? The short answer is *no*! Actually, the situation was much worse than you would imagine from that simple, awful two-letter word. In truth, it was a sorry sight to behold. The inferior and utterly inadequate management that characterized the sixties and seventies left BNL totally unprepared for the demands of the new world of Big Physics, which, ironically, BNL had spearheaded with its brilliant AGS. Yes, it was on the shoulders of the BNL invention of *strong focusing* that high-energy physics was advancing by leaps and bounds. But BNL stood still, unable to answer the call. Not only was ISABELLE superfluous and wasteful, but also this great lab you'd built from scratch was slowly being drained of its life-blood. The accelerator staff became stagnant, there being no recruitment to speak of. As for ISABELLE, it became something of a laughing stock, and was an embarrassment to both the lab and the country. Nobody needed or wanted it. Still, without rhyme or reason, the lab management stuck to its guns. How ridiculous! With nothing of quality to sell, how could BNL be expected to compete at all, much less think about competing aggressively?

"*Rule three*: Did the lab comply with the admonition to stay ahead of the government? No, it did not. The truth is that it flouted this rule's dire warning not to become too cozy with the government. By not heeding this good advice, the lab exposed itself to the whims of an unreliable ally. It was worse than you could imagine. The BNL brass, clearly without a firm grip on how defenseless and vulnerable it would make them, egregiously violated the rule's most cautionary clause: *do not become dependent on the government*. On the other hand, what else could the lab do? Possessing nothing but a non-product, there wasn't a chance in hell of it competing on a legitimate level, so it chose instead to sell its soul to the government. By doing this, using what appeared to be ingenious political skill, the much-underestimated BNL Director, George Vineyard, managed to keep project and R&D funds flowing in without any honest-to-goodness workable project in hand. Although hard to accept, that such a thing could happen in our open society is actually quite easily explained by the mendacity of a few and, most importantly, by the popular ignorance of *Science & Technology*, both in the Congress and in the public-at-large. It's really quite simple: There was just no one minding the Washington money-store but the bad guys. However, what the lab's top men, especially the Director, either forgot about or deceived themselves about was the other side of the government-lab arrangement coin: *What the government giveth, the government can take away.* As it turned out, this time, the Director went too far out on a limb. For a decade, Vineyard kept working his miracles. But, unbeknownst to him, as the decade of the eighties approached, the DOE was getting ready to let him and BNL take the fall and *swing in the wind.* So it was that in the early eighties the lab suffered the fate brought on by its Director's misguided pact with the untrustworthy devil. What ensued for BNL was the ultimate penalty: In 1983, when it suited it to do so, the government dropped ISABELLE like a hot potato.

"*Rule four*: Did the lab *bring the public with it*? Here, as with the other three rules, BNL gets a failing grade. To be fair, the management did pay attention to the standard sort of public relations expected of a U.S. national lab. In fact, perhaps too much valuable time was devoted to that stuff. There were the constant tours for politicians and visiting dignitaries, the routine Sunday tours for the public, and a steady stream of talks to local students about what science the lab was doing and about possible careers. A big showpiece was the lab's trendy summer programs, one for high-school science teachers and another for high-school students. In addition, the lab participated in a variety of other education programs on both local and national levels, with quite a lot of fanfare made over the ones for minority students and for gifted university students, these being all the rage in the eighties and nineties.

"But underneath this surface veneer, this picture of a lab that really cared, the top brass were possessed of a far different inclination. As for the public, the men running the lab just thought of these people as bothersome commoners that had to be tolerated. Such folks had absolutely no value for the grand mission of science; however, since they elected the guys that coughed up the cash, they simply had to be countenanced and endured. Then there were the politicians. Yes, the lab's men of science were obsequious enough in the presence of the power-packed politicos, whom they needed so much. But, deep down, they thought these men, who walked the government halls of power and held the purse strings, uncultivated, ordinary types, much inferior to the elite scientist class, with its high-minded nobility. Thus, the men steering the BNL ship violated a pivotal *Rule four* attitude-tenet. You see, they respected neither the public nor its representatives.

"For the bad judgment exhibited by the lab's bosses, and for the grave dereliction of their duty, BNL had to pay dearly. At the start, the incident that precipitated the dirty business didn't seem to be much of a big deal. One day in late 1996, it became known to the public that there was a small radiation leak from an old, poorly maintained BNL nuclear reactor. OK, such things happen. It could be fixed. After all, it's only a matter of a few bucks. But then, wholly unexpectedly, all hell broke loose. As it happened, the lab's managers were willfully ignoring it, and had been for many years. And worse, the leak was spreading outside the lab. Everyone was up in arms when that little bit of info came out. What contemptuous disrespect this was for the lab's neighbors, each of whom had his life's savings wrapped up in his little house bordering the site! But BNL had to face even more bad news. How imprudent and reckless the Director was for not informing the important DOE officials and politicians early enough, certainly well prior to the media's getting hold of it. What arrogance, alienating the likes of U.S. Senator Al D'Amato and U.S. Representative for the lab's congressional district, Mike Forbes! When brought together, what a deadly concoction these three items – *re* neighbors, media, and politicians – came to form. So it happened that, in 1997, not long after the public disclosure of the lab's wrongdoing, this triple-threat combination precipitated the eruption of the infamous *Tritium Affair*.

"The whole matter appeared to be such a small thing at the beginning. Just a mistake! Just a bit of carelessness! However, the management's inattentiveness to it ended up bringing the lab to its knees and didn't come very far from wiping BNL off the science map. Fortunately, that scary possibility brought forth some cool heads. With their rationality and political savvy working fast and furious, and acting with expert precision, they prevailed. Yes, this small group of men – from the lab, from the BNL-friendly universities, and from the government – succeeded in saving the lab and avoiding the worst. Nevertheless, the affair took its toll: It culminated in the firing of Associated Universities Inc. (AUI), the lab's managing contractor, and in the harsh and ominous summary dismissal of Samios, the Director, from the big-name, power-filled position he'd so eagerly sought and secured fifteen years earlier. What a heavy price this was to pay for such a seemingly inconsequential offense. But that, as we now know, was the going rate then for the sin of the arrogance of power. Thus, as it turned out, the then new U.S. Secretary of Energy in President Clinton's cabinet, Federico Pena, tossed AUI and the Director out on their ears. With these two BNL hubs of influence and order gone, only a power-vacuum was left. Everybody there felt as if the earth had opened up beneath them, and, in free-fall, they were flying down into emptiness. And from outside the lab looking in, with solid science dissipated, true men dispatched, and dreams dissolved, all that one could see was a false image of phony bravado."

Mickey's voice trailed off in a show of melancholy disappointment and blighted hope that he hadn't anticipated in the least. It appears that he cared a lot more for the beleaguered lab than he wished to admit. However, apparently having learned from Izzie, he allowed this down mood to last only some seconds. Thus, regaining his composure, he readied himself to wrap up the matter of *Mickey's rules* vis-à-vis post-Izzie BNL: "So, Izzie, what more is there to say? You stuck by the *rules*, and came out a grand-prize winner. To BNL's misfortune, without you, the lab's brass just couldn't hack it. They lacked your foresight, and ignored the *rules*. Leaving these *rules* to rot by the wayside, the lab indeed fared badly. When all is said and done, BNL, the gleam in your eyes, ended up the big loser. Too bad! A story that starts out so auspiciously, by all rights, shouldn't close out with such an agonizing, heartbreaking finale. On the other hand, come to think of it, in real life, isn't that the way it usually goes?"

Two Sweet and Simply Stated Questions

When Mickey finished his little performance on his *rules* bit, his face lit up, and pride streamed through every pore of his skin. But this self-satisfaction was slightly premature. He wasn't quite through yet. He still had to give Izzie some explicit questions. That was the way Mickey chose to play the game, and follow through he would. That meant there remained some thinking to do. *Don't dilly-dally; go to it*: he told himself. Then, it hit him! Why not just follow the master's directions and make it simple? Of course, that's the way to go. So, Mickey, pretty pleased with himself, looked up, staring right into Izzie's face, and laid his questions before *the man*. "I guess it's question time again. Actually, Izzie, I have just two for you. And I hope you'll take note that I've learned my lesson and am indeed following the advice you gave me earlier in the evening with regard to phrasing queries. Here's the first one. I've presumed all along that it was you who made the critical difference between BNL having it all and BNL tripping over itself, almost biting the dust. So, Izzie, what's your take on this point? Do you believe there's any validity to my surmise? As for number two, it's just this: What are your views on my analysis claiming a direct correlation between BNL's not practicing my *four rules* and its decline and near-fall? Well, that's it. Straightforward and succinct, wouldn't you say? OK, now it's your turn. So, whenever you're ready!"

Reflections On a King Among Men

For a time, silence pervaded the little alcove in *Le Chateau*. But Mickey's mind was swirling. It pained him that he just couldn't resist trying to put Izzie on the spot. What was going on in that head of his? Indeed, why did he have to slip in that first question? What compelled him to do it? Wasn't the second one enough? Certainly, if Izzie wanted to address that delicate issue of whether he should've or could've been there when BNL sorely needed him, he didn't need Mickey to keep prodding him to do it over and over again. Mickey's allusions to it throughout the evening most assuredly didn't escape him. So why did Mickey feel it necessary to stick it to Izzie yet again? It was just too much – enough is enough. But somehow, Mickey couldn't stop himself. Clearly, something dark in his subconscious was the driving force, and it simply wouldn't be denied. What made it especially puzzling was that he'd come to feel a deep affection for this sharp-witted and brainy devilish little man. Why then would Mickey want to be confrontational with him? In fact, during these brief couple of hours they'd spent together, he'd grown so close to *the man* that he felt akin to a brother. Yes, no doubt about it, Mickey's behavior was baffling to any rational way of thinking – mystifying indeed.

This is ridiculous! Mickey thought. *I've simply got to stop this self-doubting*. To be sure, Mickey was quite right. It would most assuredly be the prudent thing to do. Thoughts of the kind he was having only served to unnerve him. *Be calm and relax*, he wisely advised himself, *just breathe deeply for a bit*. And he tried. *That's the ticket*, he reassured himself.

However, self-persuasion just wasn't working. Mickey could still detect his right hand shaking a bit. Meanwhile, father time was continuing on his inexorable course, moving nearer and nearer to *closing time*. With the clock swiftly ticking away, he realized that simply waiting for a spontaneous recovery or the thought-method weren't really options anymore. Then, what was perhaps a saving idea popped up in his head. Recalling how he'd quickly changed his mood before, he again attempted the technique of moving about the room for a spell, stretching his legs, so to say. So he got up, walked a few feet from the table, and there tried to get a grip on himself.

As Mickey maneuvered around in a small space some ten yards from the table, his thoughts wandered back to the late twenties and thirties, where he caught a glimpse of young Izzie: In his mind's eye, he could make out this brash, ambitious, and so-sure-of-himself American in Europe. Even in the presence of greats of the likes of Bohr, Pauli, Heisenberg, and Dirac, the cocky American pushed his way in and made himself felt. Mickey recalled having read that the legendary physicists of the old country were possessed of uppity natures, and pranced about with their noses in the air. From the heights where they sat – these physics princes – they looked down contemptuously at the young American upstarts who had the effrontery to imagine themselves the intellectual equals of the European pillars of the age. Then and there, Izzie, eyeing these swollen-headed, patronizing, and imperious egocentrics, made the decision to become the speaker for his generation of scientists just beginning to assert itself in free America, where he and others like him believed that anything and everything was possible. To counter the Europeans' lordly posture, he made a vow that the challenge of his life would be to lead and meld the young Americans, men with endless spirit, desire, and energy, into the thick of the electrifying new physics rising up – this fresh modern way of viewing the world.

Yes, that was the kind of man Izzie was. No little stuff for him! He was a man who thought big, a man who would claim and have it all. When this image of Izzie took shape in Mickey's mind, he marveled at the fact that this whippersnapper, brimming with self-confidence but unfortunately little else when compared to those European intellectual giants, believed that he could put an end to the second-class status of American physics. That was some challenge that Izzie hoisted on himself. It was certainly something worth working for and giving one's life to attain. However, even for a real man like Izzie, it had written all over it: *Ha! You're gonna fall flat on your face. Who the hell do you think you are, anyway*? Yet, despite the improbability of it all, his dream of making American physicists the equals of Europeans – even surpassing them – became reality. And it was Izzie who made it happen! What a man this was: A man with the gall to *dream the impossible dream*, and then to actually bring it to fruition. Yes, he was truly a man of action, a man indelibly stamped with the mark of greatness.

Then, suddenly, as mysteriously as they began, these rambling thoughts came to a close. The episode of picturing Izzie when he was young abruptly ended. Slowly Mickey returned to the table, noticing that his hand wasn't shaking anymore. When he reached his chair, Izzie was waiting patiently and sympathetically. As it happened, Izzie sensed that Mickey was troubled, and chose to give him some breathing space. So, during this brief interlude, Izzie did no more than follow Mickey's every movement with an understanding gaze. As always, Izzie was on top of things. Little if anything fell outside of his field of perception. In contrast, Mickey was a mite confused and had an apologetic air as he sat down and looked at Izzie questioningly. "I hope there's enough time for you to answer," he said feebly. Izzie smiled a fatherly smile, with a touch of amusement showing on his face: "Of course there's enough time. Did you really think I would allow you that diversion – that inattention to the matters we're here for – if there weren't?" It was a simple and innocuous remark, but it served its purpose of lightening things up. And, for Mickey, it did the trick. He was in control of himself again, composed and cool. Soon the mood at the table would return to its intellectually invigorating and spirited, yet friendly and gracious character.

* * * * *

The Last Word
Turning the Tables

With Mickey's bout of agitation having taken its course – perhaps it was due to some qualms at the evening's end closing in – Izzie cleared his throat and began his last remarks. "I see from your second question that you've learned a little from our tête à tête. As for your first one, allow me to rephrase it to see if I understand exactly what you're driving at. What I gather you're saying is this: There is evidence that BNL thrived in one period and bombed in another. Correlated with this is my presence in the up period and my absence in the down one. And what you're really asking is whether there is a causal link between the circumstances of my presence and absence with the lab's rise and fall. Well, without a means of solid, independent confirmation, either path you take – yeah or nay – is a disputable and dicey proposition at best. Now, you do appreciate that since it involves me personally, it makes it that much harder for me to be thoroughly objective about it. Nonetheless, don't fret or be too concerned. Be assured, I'll definitely give you my take on it. However, I do want a little time to let it sink in. So, I'll simply attack *number two* first, and, while I'm responding to that question, I'll give free rein to some part of my brain to be active on *number one*. Thus, in the end – not to worry – I'll come through for you. Anyway, let's move on to your analysis of the rules for the optimum running of projects and how your analysis relates to BNL's ignominious passage from boom to bust.

"However, before jumping in, Mickey, before immersing ourselves in the nitty-gritty of your questions, I want to tell you how impressed I am with your scholarly leanings in the area of organization. It was quite a show you put on, laying out for me in such detail the nature of lab leadership. I must say that I very much appreciate your lesson in formal management. It's something that, over my life, I've been remiss in getting to. Yet, despite that lack, as I was listening to your *four rules*, it stimulated thoughts and ideas of a similar nature that I myself have had in the past. But, unfortunately, it simply never occurred to me to try to put them in such an orderly form and give them such an academic flavor as you managed to come up with. I certainly should've tried. I'm not sure I could've reached your standard, but at least I should've gone for it. Yet, when all is said and done, I didn't. It's strange! I can't really figure out why.

"Actually, as I think about the subject of management now, a possible explanation does indeed come to me of why I didn't take the prescriptive character of running a lab as seriously as I might have. You see, even though I'm a professor and a teacher to my very core, I never really thought of management and administration as a genuine university discipline. How could I have been so unobservant? All around me, the best universities in the world were showcasing their Business Schools, each and every one having professors of distinguished credentials and high renown. You know, my dear Columbia has one such department of celebrated merit. Still, despite the presence of these many university business departments screaming at me, I nonetheless missed the reality of it all. I simply didn't see it: Management just appeared to me to be something you did rather than something you went to the university for. What I believed, when I was young and in my prime, was that subjects like physics, economics, literature, history, and electrical engineering typified academia. But business? Of course, I should've been more open-minded. I should've recognized that business, over the twentieth century, clearly became a dignified academic calling of the stature of other university disciplines such as psychology, sociology, political science, and such. But, somehow, I didn't. I guess you are what you are.

"Frankly, if I'd been more receptive to the subject, it might well have had a substantial impact on my life vis-à-vis BNL. Knowing more about academic-style management – with its structural framework, its rules, and its prescriptions – would surely have afforded me more insight on how to deal with the lab much better than I did during those fateful sixties. I wouldn't argue much against it if you were to fault me on that score. But really Mickey, who would presume to judge another on such matters? Who would be so bold as to cast the first stone? Anyway, there you have it. The facts are before you. You can make of them what you will.

"OK, let's get down to business with your *four rules*: The bottom line is that I like them a lot, and give you high marks for your characterization of how labs should be led. What more can I say? You've earned about as close to an A grade as anybody's about to get from me. And I applaud you for it. However, although it may not be apparent to you, the truth is that you've done a lot more than merely get an exceedingly high mark for your analytic work. Somehow, your elucidating account of optimal managing greatly piqued my interest in the subject, so much so that you've got me roused up about it too. So, voilà, here I am ready to get into the action. Yes, believe it or not, I have a few ideas that you might be interested in hearing. So, without objection, and in keeping with the climate of informality we've established here, I'd very much like to try them out on you. What I've done is to attempt to extract from your *rules* a couple of overriding notions, which to me capture the spirit of what you're trying to say. I guess if you can lecture me on management, it's only right and proper that I return the favor and do the same for you. Wish me luck!

"Looking a little more closely and carefully at the *rules*, you can hardly mistake a common thread that runs through all of them, a particular thematic drift that's well encapsulated by the colloquial expression: *It's the staff, stupid*! Now Mickey, *ain't that the truth*! Yes, it's the people of the organization that are the decisive units, the ones that spell the difference between an up-lab and a down-lab, between success and failure. They make it all work. And when I say staff, I mean the staff from top to bottom, from the Board of Trustees and the Director, with his inside clique and his chief associates, on down the hierarchical chain. Actually, let me qualify that. As a matter of fact, you don't have to be concerned with every person composing the complete lab staff. The men in charge of the place are quite sufficient. You see, if the top people are of high quality, then this feature will work its way down. Of course, the reverse is also true: Low quality on top will, in time, wend its way down to the floor where the work gets done. In the last analysis, it's this characteristic of an organization that the best begets the best and the worst begets the worst that explains why it's so vital to get the very best men to run things.

"Thus, it seems that all you need are high-class men in the Director's office, men with integrity, men who can be trusted, and men who are willing to do what it takes to get the job done. How striking and odd is the simplicity of this apparent fact. Indeed, it is very curious. It almost sounds too easy to be true. But, of course, it's not easy at all. To find the right men for the top jobs is a great deal more difficult than it seems at first blush. If you delve deeper into the nature of the people fit for such work, as you've so correctly pointed out, you find that the ability to be ruthless when it's needed is a necessary ingredient in the mix. This requirement of leaders raises hackles in those not familiar with how labs or organizations in general work. Such types imagine that a lab will be just fine with only *Mister Nice Guys* in charge. They just don't like it, and won't have it otherwise. But that doesn't change the reality one little bit. What it does mean, however, is that if people divorced from life in the real organization are picking the leaders, then watch out!

"So we've come to the simple notion that when choosing a man for a leadership position, if you want to do it right, you've somehow gotta figure out if he's capable of ruthlessness. It's this unsavory component of what a top dog must be made of that brings out loud and clear the subtlety of trying to figure out how to find such a one. Who's gonna tell you that he's a ruthless type? Men just don't go around wearing signs on their sleeves that say: *Sure, I can be ruthless*. So, if you're a chooser, how can you know if you truly have the right man in hand, even when the two of you are looking at each other eye to eye? The fact is that, even if the man before you can be ruthless, his tendency is to hide it as far from view as he's able to. Confronted with that, what's to be done?

"OK, let me jump over that issue and go a step further. Take the hypothetical case in which I grant that you've discovered the means to glom onto your interviewee's secret of ruthless-capability. So, suppose that one fine day a man appears, and it's uncovered that he could be sufficiently ruthless. Still, hold on! That's not the end of the search. Not by a long shot! After finding that out about him, it has yet to be determined whether he's honest and trustworthy enough. What a combination to be looking for! Honesty, trustworthiness, and ruthlessness, all in the same man! Now, clearly it's quite unlikely that an à priori determination of that can be made. Still, let's continue on, taking the search-game just a little further. Even if you had such a man, is that enough? Is the contest of wits over? Can you claim victory? Unfortunately not! No, not even then!

"I can imagine you wondering, *what more can be asked for*? Well, as a matter of fact, you'd still like to know whether the man could be honest at the right time and ruthless at the right time. I know it's probably silly to demand that, for how could that be uncovered before you see the guy in action? Well, by now, I wouldn't blame you if concession weren't very far from your consciousness. I quite agree. Reaching that level of question, you'd be well advised to start thinking of throwing in the towel of logical decision-making, accepting the reality that you'll probably have to go the rest of the way on automatic pilot.

"OK, Mickey, that's my stab at proving to you that I did indeed learn a little from your fine exposition on lab management, and especially from those revealing and instructive *four rules*. You've actually reversed our student-teacher roles, and I have to tell you, it's quite a bit of fun to be a student once again. But I wouldn't like it very much if you made a habit of it," Izzie added, wearing his trademark naughty grin.

Without skipping a beat, Izzie kept on going: "I guess it's about time I got to your question about how BNL measured up to your demanding regimen of project and lab *dos and don'ts*. As you were putting the lab through the wringer in contrasting what BNL actually did with the prescriptions embodied in your *rules*, what struck me most about it was how right you were. Zooming in on one key factor, to be blunt, in the matter of choosing Directors, the best way I can think of expressing BNL's shoddy performance is that it sucked, to use the lingo of today's youth. True, I was unworthily lucky with Haworth. But after that the lab's course was downhill all the way. What a ghastly and thoroughly unpleasant show it was! To add to the woe, the government's manner of science oversight made things so much worse. Think of it! So bloody slow to act, the government simply allowed BNL to keep eating away at itself. And this went on for many a year more than it should have. It just boggles the mind when you realize how long the lab was permitted to remain in the self-destruct mode. Anyway, as implied by the *rules*, the staff unfailingly went on deteriorating with each passing day. On and on it went, till, in the end, both the technical and managerial staffs reached the point of total incompetence. And what was the end result of all this? As accurately predicted in *Rule Three*, it was the miserable and distressing tragedy of ISABELLE! True, after that – the lab, having gone down about as far as it could go – there was some measurable improvement. But the glue used to try to get *Humpty-Dumpty* together again could only go so far. You see, the lab's destiny was already cast in stone. Sad as it was, BNL was never able to come even close to equaling what it was in those fabulous fifties."

That Vision Thing

Izzie paused, thoughtfully considering just how to proceed. But it was only for a brief period. Then, as soon as he found the words to express the idea he had up his sleeve, he started up his engine and began to speak: "Although what I'm going to talk about now is not directly responsive to your questions, it's quite in the spirit of the discussion of management theory that we've veered into. What I'd like to do is to lay on the table a trait in a leader-to-be that's much sought after. Some would say it's absolutely imperative that he possess it. However, as you might expect, it's one that's awfully troublesome and tricky to discern or even detect in a man. Mickey, I give you that abundantly bandied about notion, *vision* – the extraordinary faculty that only few men can boast, allowing them to conceive, sculpt, and implement that distinctive and imaginative idea specially suited to his lab, and to give the lab the best possible shot at a smashingly splendid, bravissimo future. Wow! What a guy! All I have to say is, good luck in finding him. Even if he were standing right in front of you, how would you know he had this *vision thing* in him before he went into action and exhibited it? You simply wouldn't. OK, smart guy, go and choose someone who's done something on that scale before. Do you really think that'll help? Hardly! I ask you, how many people do you know who've done two things of real significance in their lives? Not many, I should think! So, in the end, the search for the perfect man is just a crap game, like so many other things in this life of ours. You throw the dice, pray, and wait for fate to do the rest.

"Personally, I'm not so sure that this *vision thing* is all it's cracked up to be. As I see it, it's too abstract. It lays the strategic emphasis on thinking things through and making prior choices. I have no problem with that. Really, it's great! However, it may not be what'll lift your lab to the sky. As a matter of fact, in many cases, perhaps most, you already know what needs doing. What's crying out for attention is how to do it and actually doing it! No, in my view, it's another type of man you should be looking for. What you need is someone with *chutzpah* and smarts in the ways of the real world. What you need is a practical man who's ready to take a shot at things. What you need is a man who knows when to push, yet also knows when to pull back. What you need is a man who knows when to hold and when to fold. And what you need is a man who's charming, yet one who's hard as a rock underneath the skin. Yes, that's my kind of man!

"Implausible as it might be, if, out of the blue, such a man as I've imagined materializes at your doorstep, then you'd do well to grab him. Forget the *vision* thing! Just don't worry about it! If he's got the *right stuff*, he'll tailor and frame the *vision*, and lick it into shape once he's on board and in the thick of things. You see, *vision* isn't part of a person's makeup. It isn't divorced from the action. Actually, the two, *vision* and action, are intermingled: one feeds on the other. They reinforce, enrich, sharpen, and strengthen each other. The fact is that *vision* is a mysterious thing that comes from the circumstances a man finds himself engulfed in. That's just the way it is: There's no *vision* without doing. They're really two faces of the same coin; and, if you tear them apart, then you'll be left with scant value. The *vision* will become insipid, flat, and stale; and the action will become mere floundering about and of utterly no consequence. Mickey, don't you think I've hit upon the answer to the *vision* riddle? It has to be. Yes, by itself, it's nothing but a vapid and unworldly ethos. However, when mixed with deeds and undertakings, it comes alive. Once you see that, isn't it obvious who the ideal man is that you should glom onto to lead your lab? Isn't he simply a man of action with the potential to model and mold a *vision*? Not that knowing that makes it any easier to collar such a man, but wouldn't you agree?

"Let's zoom in on this connection between *vision* and action. A question you might ask is, what actually glues them together? Well, it's ideas, of course. And there's certainly no dearth of those. In fact, good ideas are all around us. All you have to do is move about a lot, listen, and absorb them. I'm not kidding! Anywhere you turn, there they are. You can actually pick them out of the air. They're a dime-a-dozen commodity. Sometimes it's worthwhile having a bull-session with some appropriate staffers so as to ensure that you haven't missed something that might come back to bite you. But, in the end, ideas on almost anything are free and available for the taking. Nothing else is needed but keeping your wide-open ears to the ground.

"So, I ask you, Mickey, if ideas are all around waiting to be nabbed, why do you need any special *vision*? Well, with that question, I must admit that the cat's out of the bag. In truth, you do need it – that is, if that's the name you want to give to good judgment. You see, even though many ideas may be floating about, it's knowing when you've found the right one that really counts. Once that's done, it's time for *action* to enter the picture. That means shaping the idea into a concrete and meaningful reality. So it's simple, eh, Mickey? Having vision is the capacity of picking out the right idea; and being action-oriented is bringing that idea to life. It's having these two qualities that makes for a visionary man, a man worthy to lead a lab.

"When all is said and done, the man you've installed at the top needn't have a pre-formed *vision* of his own. Not at all! He can take one idea from here, one from there, and pretty soon, after bringing them to palpable fruition, he'll have built his own *vision* for the lab. Do you see what I mean? What you want is a type that doesn't necessarily have a *vision* before taking center stage, but one that can concoct and construct *visions* from the air. Maybe that's the big secret: A visionary man is a man who can latch onto ideas, assemble them into his *vision*, and generate the right approach for the lab to take – the one that fits the existing time and circumstances. The ideas – the raw material – that go into making *visions* are fungible. Indeed the *visions* themselves, as long as substantial actions haven't been taken and mucho money spent, are painlessly and handily transferable from one location to another. That's right! Any *vision's* place of origin and the sources of the ideas it contains don't matter a whit. Of course, when made into the real thing by concrete actions, *visions* will look quite different in different places. But, in the end, who cares where a *vision* came from or in whose mind it originated? Well, perhaps stuffy historians might, but that's about it. It's the *vision* realized in the form of a tangible reality that makes the front page. That's what'll be of any consequence. Yes, when it's there for all to see, real and manifest, that's the ticket, that's what's truly worthy enough to strive for, to give your all for."

Izzie stopped to catch his breath. In a bit of a dither, he found he'd speeded up his delivery. Not that he was in a hurry, or anything like that. As a matter of fact, he still had a few more minutes, so why rush? No, it's just that he was stirred up, maybe over-stimulated, by this whole management issue. However, as soon as he realized what was happening, he knew he had to slow down, if not to keep his own thoughts in order, then certainly to ensure that the picture he was trying to paint was as clear as could be. So he tried to cool off some by sitting still for a moment.

As Izzie began to relax somewhat, thoughts of the evening emerged in his mind. What an unexpected delight it was turning out to be! Although at first he wasn't overjoyed with the assignment, now, as it was winding down, he was coming to see the whole experience – the food, the drink, and especially all this talk of leadership and organization – as quite exhilarating and enlivening, and, indeed, rather pleasurable. To be sure, if he had his druthers, he'd just go on all night. But, alas, he was given a very particular time slot for this Gotham dinner, and he had no choice but to stick to it. That's what the powers that be at *Le Petit Village* had authorized, and there was simply no alternative to compliance. Thus, he plunged onward.

"There's still something else to add to my reasoning in the matter of *vision*, action, and their linkages. Although it's quite true that a bona-fide leader has to have some sort of *vision*, there's actually a lot more to it than that, even more than making it come to life. You see, he also has to have the know-how to make others embrace it. After all, he can't just waltz into the action-phase half-cocked. There's much he needs before going ahead: He needs government money and approval. He needs community concurrence and support. And he also needs his own staff to be foursquare behind him. If the lab's workers don't have their hearts in it, you can bet it's not gonna get anywhere fast. So, even though the leader – in the case of a national lab, its Director – must adopt and come to have a *vision* for the lab's future, you can be sure that, if he can't sell it, then it's not worth a dime. If he can't persuade others, then it simply won't happen. And if it isn't implemented, what's the use of a *vision* sitting in the backroom of someone's mind? How much would you pay for that?

"Suppose that while a particular *vision* is evolving, you find that the time and place aren't right for it. My guess is that, if that happened, the *vision* would become totally without value, and you couldn't even give it away. That's probably what transpired at BNL, and ended up kicking off the whole squalid, distasteful ISABELLE affair. That project, damned to hell not long after it began, was the *vision* of Vineyard, Goldhaber, Samios, and a few others. It seemed to be the right *vision* for BNL in the early seventies. However, in time, circumstances changed, and the *vision* became obsolete. The doomed project just couldn't wriggle out of its sticky web of entanglements and reach the finish line. With *vision* and action in dire opposition, could the end be far off? So it was that, as the seventies ended and the eighties began, the *vision* became but an idealized one, existing only in the minds of the BNL bosses. True, there were a lot of mortar and bricks – meaning a great deal of money was invested – but it was all to no avail. Such an awful waste of precious resources it was. What it all came down to was that the lab brass just didn't have the capability of translating the ISABELLE *vision* into reality.

"As it happened, the *vision* that was ISABELLE remained a theoretical one, never able to graduate to the phase of completion in concrete. So, because the project simply couldn't be made into a manifest *vision*, when the dust settled, the *vision* was dead, and only rubble remained. Thus, you see, in the real world, where *vision* and action go along in parallel, risk becomes the keynote. If the action can't be made to fit the *vision*, then there could be all hell to pay. And BNL had to learn about the harsh and grim nature of reality the hard way. Unfortunately, you see, Goldhaber, Vineyard, and then Samios were blind to the cold, brutal truth that their project, their *vision*, lost its purpose – its raison d'être – somewhere along the way and would never come to pass. They just couldn't see it. Mickey, I still find it so hard to accept. Such smart men! Anyway, because of their shortcomings, all at BNL paid a heavy price for the ISABELLE *vision* gone awry.

"With that, I've said about all I have to say on the subject of leadership and *vision*. And, to tell the truth, I've exhausted myself in the process. Just one last remark about it: I'd like you to know that the teacher has indeed learned much from the student tonight. You awakened a spirit in me for a subject that was in deep slumber in my mind for far too long. So, I humbly thank you for that. I only hope that, in return, I was able to give you an equally valuable gift."

Closing Time

Izzie realized it was *closing time*, and knew that the end of the affair was almost at hand. But first there was one loose end to take care of. "I imagine, that it's about time I got to your first question," he said. "I take it that you want to know what part I played in BNL's rise in the fifties and fall in the sixties and seventies. Now, Mickey, you know very well that during our evening's discussion we've been through all of this before. Actually, I've already answered you on this issue in elaborate detail while responding to a question you asked earlier. I've also made reference to my role in BNL's affairs over the years in many of the other things I've said over the course of our discussion. Still, you persist in asking about it. Obviously, you're not satisfied with my replies. That does indeed trigger some distress in me, particularly in view of how close we seem to have become. Anyway, since a couple of minutes remain, I'll try one last time. If you find it sufficiently reassuring, all well and good. Then, I can rest easy. On the other hand, if you're not persuaded, then so be it. Sure, I'll feel a little discontented about it. However, I'll get over it after a while, knowing that I tried my best to tell you the truth; and confident that, in the future, when your mind takes you back to this evening, you'll remember my words and come to understand me better – perhaps even forgive me.

"When I look back at those days long ago, I can't escape the disappointment I feel about the way I behaved and the things I did. Yes, I am blameworthy. Yes, I am culpable. Yes, if I could take it all back, and do it over again – doing it right, this time – I would certainly do so without the least hesitation. But this life of ours gives you only one shot at it. And I had mine. Whatever my chances were, so they were. Whatever I did, so I did. And that's that! But, Mickey, be assured that I've been perfectly straight with you, and haven't hidden or held anything back. You have everything, warts and all. Yes, I've told you my many faults that, in retrospect, I perceive so clearly, so unequivocally, so undeniably, and so regretfully. I find myself at fault for giving up my influence too early. I find myself at fault for not choosing a successor to Haworth who could measure up to the impending times. I find myself at fault for not stepping in and speaking out even after my power had waned. I find myself at fault specifically for not forcing an issue over Green's dismissal, for not helping him to hold on to his pivotal post as AD Chairman. I find myself at fault for being such a jackass in not foreseeing the post-AGS boom. I find myself at fault for not sensing the fast-approaching era of Big Physics. I find myself at fault for wanting too much the adulation of those I should've been confronting, for the sin of vanity. I find myself at fault for walking away, without fighting the good fight. I find myself at fault for wearying of the incessant squabbling and wrangling. And I find myself at fault for getting old and tired."

Izzie looked out into the darkness of the dining room, as if he were expecting to see something. His head was tilted slightly upward as he stared out a nearby window toward the star-filled heavens. Could he have been seeking something? Was it commiseration? Was it compassion? Was it forgiveness? Was it absolution? Or was it some form of exoneration? He stayed in that motionless pose for a brief spell, maybe a minute. Then, abruptly, his mood roller coaster went through a minimum and started going up again.

The transition was astonishing to behold. In no time flat, *the man* went from being downcast and dispirited to being the hardheaded, straight-thinking, unsentimental, and pragmatic *Professor Izzie*.

Paying no heed to the little scene that had just taken place, and in a tone that was sober and realistic, the professor started speaking: "Frankly, Mickey, after Haworth, the following BNL Directors lacked any real-life *vision*. Still, it wasn't their failings alone that brought BNL down to the depths of a living hell. As sure as anything, for my misjudgments and delinquent inactions, I must also share in the blame of what transpired. At one time, decades ago, endowed with the strength of a lion, I could shape the succession of Directors. But as timed passed by with unanticipated rapidity, I allowed that gift of power the gods allotted me to flow out of my being and slip away. From there, the slide to attendant lackey, to be called forth at the whim of the current power-holders to do his little dance, was quick and irrevocable. Try as I might, Mickey, there's simply no denying what really happened. The evidence speaks loud and clear. Yes, I have much to account for. In fact, if I had to grade myself, I'd merit no more than a B grade, and it would be that high primarily because of the early years, when I shook up the world of physics.

"Actually," Izzie continued, "there isn't much more to tell you. Fortune smiled on me with the Haworth selection. But the fickle *Lady Luck* vanished when I made the next choice. Sure, I should've done better. But I just didn't take the whole succession matter seriously enough. I thought I'd be around, looking over Goldhaber's shoulders, ensuring that he didn't waver or go too far astray. How was I to know that once he was sitting in his big Director's chair, I would become, with uncanny swiftness, a has-been power-boss? Yet I did. One day I was of weighty consequence, and the next I was nothing. Suddenly it was all over for me. Pfft! Just like that! I woke up one morning. The sun was shining brightly. The earth was spinning on its axis. People were going about their business. Physicists were hard at work. But Izzie the powerhouse was no more. Yes, my power was lost – lost through neglect, lost by encroaching age, lost to the wind, but unmistakably lost. So, like Macarthur's old soldier, I just faded away."

The Finale
The First Toast

Mickey gazed at Izzie, who was thoroughly wrapped up in his thoughts of things past, of what he'd seen, of what he'd been through, and of what might've been. For his part, Mickey's mind was overloaded with a profusion of confused, haphazard impulses, which every now and then produced a nostalgic phrase or two. He could hear the strains of a few random lines from that old ballad he'd listened to over and over again on his long obsolete Fleetwood phonograph: *The party's over. It's time to call it a day. All dreams must end. Now you must wake up. The party's over, it's all over, my friend.* Thus, rapt in reverie, they both sat in silence and remembered the old days.

As for Izzie, he appeared wounded and beaten. Was remorse hounding him? Was it regret or self-reproach? Was it his conscience coming back to haunt him? He appeared full of shame, and seemed to be inconsolable. But, if it was all or any of these things, the whole episode of self-engrossment didn't last long enough for Mickey to think it through and perhaps get a grip on it. There was just something in Izzie's makeup that impelled him to take life as it comes, and not let anything get him down. He had this much-to-be-envied capacity to simply take things as they are. In short order, he could just shrug off the distresses, the embarrassments, the grievances, and the afflictions that life happened to carry his way. How lucky for him to have been born under such a highly benevolent and felicitous star! And so it was that he was able to overcome and rise above the dark memories of bygone days. Thus recouping, the unconquerable Izzie rebounded and returned.

"Well, Mickey, let's look on the bright side of things. We're here, aren't we? And we're having a ball! You know, I was just pondering what might be the root-cause that brought us here tonight. Don't you think it's devilishly ironic that the ultimate reason we've gotten together like this is because we're both so intimately and inextricably linked to BNL? Because of the tightly knit bonds we've both forged with the lab! Because of our devotion to everything it stands for! Because of the common heritage it has brought to us! Because of how much of our lives each of us has invested in it! And because it's the lab we've both come to *love to hate*, yet also *hate but still love*! Yes, if truth be told, *we've grown accustomed to the place*. We've come to have a deep attachment and affection for the assailed and harried institution that it is. So, to mark this remarkable and splendid occasion, I propose that we give a hearty toast to the illustrious and celebrated lab that BNL once was, and might yet become again. May it go on to the twenty-first century with better prospects, grander aspirations, more hopefulness and higher achievement than it ended the twentieth with! May it come to shine even more brilliantly than it did in its early years, when it electrified the physics world!" And, with those wish-filled and dream-imbued words, the two men drank of the red wine, as if to seal in blood their mutual acceptance of as well as their complicity in the lab's fortune and destiny.

The Second Toast
Suddenly It Was All Over

The two men sat silently. They both emptied their glasses with what appeared to be great reluctance. It was as if by drinking slowly enough, they could prolong the evening. They seemed to want to hold time in abeyance, to obstruct the clock. So they procrastinated. They tarried. They lingered. But, when all was done, there was no postponing the inevitable. You simply can't put off *Father Time*. Thus, time took its course until the moment arrived when action could not be delayed any longer. Just then, at the last instant, when any further holdup was no longer an option, Izzie stood up and walked to the other side of the table toward Mickey. The younger man rose to face him. Although he didn't want it to be, Mickey knew that this was the prelude to the evening's end.

Izzie smiled warmly, and clasped Mickey's extended right hand with both of his. Then, he reached out and squeezed Mickey's arms, just short of hugging him. Filling the two empty glasses with the last of the *red* in the bottle, Izzie lifted both goblets and handed one to Mickey. In a final toast, with a mixture of peaceful resignation and a melancholy heart, Izzie said in a tear-tinted voice: "Mickey, this last drink is for you. And, of course, with my thanks to *Le Petit Village* for making you available! You've been a perfect dinner partner. You've given me a delightful and challenging evening, and quite an intellectual run for it, to be sure. I doff my cap to you for being able to stand up so well to such a seasoned and tenacious attack-dog as me. May you continue to derive satisfaction from your work till your last breath! May you have a life filled with good omens! Finally, may luck walk with you and the stars speak for you always! To our evening together and to you!" So they drank and emptied their glasses to the very last drop.

After the toast, for a wonderfully strange instant, time seemingly stood still. Mickey moved nary a muscle. He was stunned: in a state of confused, bewildered disorientation and breathless awe. *What a wonderful life*, he thought, *to be permitted such a marvelous and miraculous, such a phenomenal and transcendent evening*! But, like all things in this world, as was the entire evening, this mysterious moment was fleetingly transient. Eventually, it had to be let go. So it was that the formality of the end began. As if from out of nowhere, the captain appeared. He stood next to Mickey and, with the aplomb of those who know their place, almost imperceptibly motioned to Mickey to follow him into the darkened area of the room. How swiftly it happened! Suddenly it was all over! Although Mickey knew it was coming, still, the end seemed to sneak up on him. With all the preparation he'd made for it, he still wasn't ready for such quick finality. In the blink of an eye, it was done. The present had become the past. In the meantime, as Mickey was being escorted out, Izzie sat down, took a small sip of cognac, leaned back in his chair, and closed his eyes.

The Apparition Reveals Itself

Izzie relaxed in solitude in the empty room while awaiting his departure hour. He was at peace, alone in the city he cared so much for, and near the university he gave such a large chunk of his life to. All was quiet. This, in fact, was in stark contrast to the swirling flurry of thoughts and feelings engulfing his mind. Nerve impulses raced speedily through his brain, as he recalled the times of yore. Coming and going much like scenes flashing by in a film, he could visualize many of the people who helped mold what he was: his family, his friends, his students, and the supermen of physics who afforded him his calling and his career. Events that fashioned him also came and went, flitting swiftly by. But, over and over, he kept returning to the lab he founded and instilled life in when he was in his prime. BNL had empowered him, and endowed him with a mighty potency only the few who confer life are privileged to experience. However – akin to children brought into this world – in the end, his lab drained his blood from him and left him isolated. *As you come, so shall you go*! That's simply the way things are in this life of ours! Yet, far from feeling the cold chill of despondency that might've been expected to come from recalling his fall from the great heights of stardom, far from feeling the tristful melancholia that might be expected to accompany the remembrances of his youth, Izzie found himself blanketed in serenity and tranquility. Thus, as it happened, these thoughts of times past came to him without the stinging twinges of regret, but rather with a composed amusement, and, strangely, an ironic sense of grandeur. For a moment, overtaken by a lucid stillness, he calmly rejoiced in the life he'd lived.

The dim lights made for a pervasive orange glow in the air around him. It was as if circumstances had conspired to infuse in that place a curiously eerie nature exactly suited for strange happenings. Yes, it was quite the right time for ghosts of times past to appear. And so it was! Without announcement, without any heralding of entry, and without a harbinger to tell of its coming, there it was: the image that evoked such yearning in him earlier, now materializing right before his very eyes. He strained to discern its identity, to see through the shadows surrounding it and so make out this smoky figure. Finally, the air around it cleared, and it came into focus. So manifest, so palpable was it that it was as if the past had merged with the present. The apparition that crystallized, from so many years past, was his mother's exquisitely divine face. Oh, how sorrowful it appeared to be! Poor fair and loving creature! Those tears – sparsely sprinkled about and sparkling on her rosy cheeks, slipping from her wide-open and sad, dark eyes – opened a gaping wound in Izzie's aching heart. He stretched his hands outward as far as he could, craving to touch the love of his life. And she came to him and entered his being. Again, as it was long ago, he felt the warmth of her protective body. He tingled all over as her smooth skin brushed against his, and as her soft, full breasts pressed against his tiny frame. Intently, he watched her beautiful mouth, as her lips shaped those words he knew so well: *Hush my child. Don't be afraid. I'm here. Be still and rest awhile.*

finis

Postscript

Decline and fall is always with us. It's as certain as death and taxes. Just as the organs of a man's body begin to malfunction and eventually shut down as he inexorably ages, so do the men comprising the component parts of the body of an enterprise eventually wither and fail. And, as the organization men fall, so does the organization itself.

You might ask about the nature of an organization as it proceeds on its downward spiral. What characterizes it? Can the bitter end be seen coming? Can we intercede to interrupt and check its course? Can we reverse what appears certain? Can we enter and save the day? Or must we stand by, helpless in the face of some form of natural law? It is a conundrum. You might also want to know something of the consequences. What forms do they take? How far do they extend into the future and how long do they last? Can they be identified, isolated, and expunged? Can they be foreseen and avoided? Or must we accept them too, powerless to alter the inevitable? Finally, you might wonder about the past, and how it relentlessly reappears to haunt us. Can we ever be rid of the ghosts of old failures, not known about or guessed at by the newly arrived, and conveniently forgotten by the veterans of the wars that made them? Must the sins of the fathers unendingly be visited on their unsuspecting sons?

One thing you can count on is that you will not casually stumble on answers to such questions. If anything is to be unearthed, much digging must come first, with not the least promise that the truth, so deeply buried by ungenerous and coldhearted sentinels, will be revealed. However, if you'll forego prescriptions for future conduct, and settle for understanding what has already taken place, then all is not hopeless. In fact, it is with just such a limited objective that I embarked on my journey of discovery. With the path to knowledge that I chose to follow – marrying social ideas and contemporary history with science and technology and government patronage, and probing deeply into the minds of the *Players* – I did happen upon an explanation fitting the dire chain of events experienced by the physicist-dreamers of the 20th century. Can I then declare success in my endeavor? Perhaps! But the truth is that my tales tell only of the trials and tribulations of a few who are but grains of sand on the sweeping landscape of human experience. And, frankly speaking, that was all I sought to do. Thus, if it so happens that I've also cast a little light on *how* and *why* men of all stripes and organizations from all spheres fall, then my considerable efforts would carry an extra dividend and be that much more worthwhile.

As for purging humanity of the all but unstoppable ruinous fall, I'm afraid I cannot claim to have punctured that seemingly impenetrable wall to any significant degree. Still, what a welcome consolation it would be for me if my stories serve as a warning to all that our lives are susceptible to the descent into failure, and without knowing much of what we do, we all tend to walk close to the edge. As it was, the men in my story did indeed take such perilous walks. Some would say they strayed closer to the brink than they should have. Nonetheless, on the whole, in their small, circumscribed world of science and technology, they were men who strove to fly among the gods in the heavens, and they were men who reached the heights of greatness, succeeding well beyond what their modest beginnings had foretold. But, like all who give everything they have for the glory of man and the accompanying honor and renown, they found that they had limits; and when they had gone too far, as their destinies demanded, there was no turning back. And they had to face the truth that lies on the midnight side of starry-eyed youth and alluring fame. Still, once the last chapter has been written and all is said and done, these men were the salt of the earth, and my hat's off to them, one and all.

ADDENDUM

Cast of Characters
The Players
Supporting Cast
Incidental Characters
Glossary of Terms
Acronyms
Timeline
Author's Bio

Cast of Characters

The Players

Goldhaber, Maurice. Distinguished Scientist, BNL. Director, BNL, 1961-1973. National Medal of Science 1983.

Green, George Kenneth. Senior Scientist, BNL. Builder of the Alternating Gradient Synchrotron (AGS) 1960. Organizer and Chairman, BNL Accelerator Department, 1960-1970. Conceptualized BNL's NSLS in the mid seventies. Died, 1977.

Haworth, Leland. Professor of Physics, University of Illinois. Director, BNL, 1948-1961. Atomic Energy Commissioner, 1961-1963. Director, National Science Foundation, 1963-1969. Died, 1979.

Lederman, Leon M. Professor of Physics, Columbia University. Director, Fermi National Accelerator Laboratory, 1979-1989. Nobel Prize for Physics 1988.

Rabi, Isidor Isaac. Professor of Physics, Columbia University. Incorporating Trustee, Associated Universities Inc. 1946. Board of Trustees, AUI, 1946-1976. Founding father of AUI and BNL. Nobel Prize for Physics 1944. Died, 1988.

Rubbia, Carlo. Professor of Physics, Harvard University. Director-General, CERN, 1989-1994. Nobel Prize for Physics 1984.

Samios, Nicholas P. Distinguished Scientist, BNL. Director, BNL, 1982-1997. Discoverer of Omega-Minus Particle 1968.

Vineyard, George H. Distinguished Scientist, BNL. Director, BNL, 1973-1982. President-Elect, American Physical Society, 1987. Died, 1987.

Wilson, Robert R. Professor of Physics, Cornell University. Founding Director and Builder, Fermi National Accelerator Laboratory, 1967-1978. Died, 2000.

Mickey. Scientist, BNL. Founding Director, U.S. Particle Accelerator School, 1980-1998. Founder, Beam Physics Topical Group, American Physical Society, 1986, which became the Division of Physics of Beams (DPB) in 1989.

Supporting Cast

Adams, Sir John. *Father* of the giant particle accelerators that catapulted CERN to the top of the field of high-energy physics. An extraordinary accelerator designer, engineer, scientist, and administrator, he, more than any other person, shaped CERN into what it is – stamping it with his own personality. He served as the CERN Director-General (with Leon Van Hove) from 1971 to 1975. At the same time, he led the design and construction of the SPS. As Executive Director-General from 1976 to 1980, he saw to it that LEP was approved and set firmly on the road to success. He died in 1984.

Baltay, Charles. Professor of Physics, Columbia, Stanford, and Yale Universities.

Blewett, John. Arrived at BNL in 1947 and rose to become a Senior Scientist. Made significant contributions to the Cosmotron and AGS accelerators. Predicted synchrotron radiation at General Electric in 1946 and invented AG focusing for linear accelerators in 1952. He died in April 2000.

Chasman, Renate W. Senior Scientist, BNL. Rena Chasman came to BNL in 1963, where she moved from particle experimentation to accelerator theory, enticed by the glamour and potential of the BNL-discovered principle of AG focusing. She began working with the group preparing to build the 200-MeV Linac to replace the 50-MeV Linac serving as injector to the AGS. Soon she was named Chief Theorist of the *200-MeV Linac Group*, and promoted to the rank of BNL Senior Scientist. Working with John Blewett, she made many important contributions to the ISABELLE design in the seventies. Upset by the shabby treatment of her mentors, Ken Green and John Blewett, when Ken began to design a synchrotron radiation source for BNL, Chasman joined him in the effort. They soon devised a new magnetic focusing method, which allowed for maximal synchrotron radiation from the ring's bending magnets, and made space available along the ring's circumference for wigglers and undulators. Their invention is called the *Chasman-Green Magnetic Lattice*. It was subsequently used in BNL's NSLS, in the ALS at LBNL, as well as in some European labs. Diagnosed with cancer in 1972, Rena continued to work until she died in October 1977. After her death, the Brookhaven Women in Science initiated the Renate W. Chasman scholarship to encourage participation in science by women.

D'Amato, Alfonse M. Al D'Amato was elected to the U.S. Senate from New York in November 1980. After serving three terms, he lost to Democrat Charles Schumer in 1998. In 1997 and 1998, D'Amato was among the first to call for the permanent closure of the aging and damaged nuclear reactor – BNL's HFBR – leaking tritium into Long Island's groundwater. In the end, he got his way; but before this victory was realized, he lost his Senate seat. Right-on as he was, did his angry and harsh rhetoric against a New York based scientific institution play a role in his defeat? Probably some!

Deutch, John, M. Professor of Chemistry, Institute Professor, Dean of Science, and Provost, MIT. Director, Office of Energy Research, and Undersecretary, U.S.

Department of Energy, 1977-1980. Director U.S. Intelligence Agency, 1994-1995. Director of Central Intelligence (DCI), 1995-1996.

Forbes, Michael P. Forbes was elected to the U.S. House of Representatives in 1994, beating the Democratic junior incumbent in New York's First Congressional District, where BNL is located. During his second term, in 1997 and 1998, the lab's tritium fiasco broke wide open. In calling for an end to the HFBR, Forbes was one of the most ferocious of BNL's opponents. As it was, unrelated events and his own character contrived to cut his congressional career short. He was a bitter opponent of the Newt Gingrich *insurgency*; and, in July 1998, he defected from the Republican Party. Forbes was a man of conscience, who would not compromise. Not surprisingly, he made many enemies and, like D'Amato, in the 1998 election, lost his seat in Congress.

Keyworth, George A., II. Came to Los Alamos National Laboratory as a scientist in 1968, and rose to be the Director of the Physics Division. Science Advisor to President Reagan, and Director of the White House Office of Science and Technology Policy, 1981-1986. National Medal of Science, 1985. In 1986, he founded and became Chairman of the Keyworth Company, dedicated to developing growth strategies in the private sector.

Leiss, James E. Director, Office of High Energy and Nuclear Physics, U.S. Department of Energy, 1979-1985. Leiss began his career in 1954 as a physicist at the National Bureau of Standards in Washington, D.C. He worked on the 180-MeV Electron Synchrotron and its conversion to the country's first dedicated light source. He soon became Head of the Radiation Physics Division. In the early sixties, Jim designed and took charge of the 300-MeV Electron Linear Accelerator. By the seventies, he was Director of the Center for Radiation Research. In his 25 years at the *Bureau*, Leiss became an expert in accelerator technology, and served on assessment and recommendation committees. In the late seventies, John Deutsch, the Director of the DOE's Office of Energy Research, offered him the position of Director of the Office of High Energy and Nuclear Physics. Deutsch created this post to help him deal with detailed technical and financial matters in the rapidly growing High Energy and Nuclear Physics Divisions – particularly having to disentangle Wallenmeyer's budgetary shenanigans. Once Leiss was on board, Deutch delegated such matters to him. The reluctant Leiss had an even tougher assignment than he imagined because the ISABELLE mess was looming just ahead. As it turned out, Leiss was the right man for the job. In the midst of this massive failure, he helped keep high-energy physics going. Then, early in the country's thinking about the SSC, he went a good way toward strengthening the national lab culture for *building bigger and better*. However, when details of what the SSC was to be began to emerge, he saw trouble ahead for the big project. Beginning to feel his advancing age, he knew he'd be unable to withstand the pressures sure to come, and retired in 1985.

Lofgren, Edward J. Associate Director, Lawrence Berkeley National Laboratory. He retired in 1981 with the title, Associate Director Emeritus. He was a leading figure in the life of the Bevatron, a major party to the Berkeley-BNL Gentlemen's Agreement, and the Director of the Design Study for a multi-hundred-GeV accelerator facility in the sixties. When built, this design became the Fermilab facility.

McMillan, Edwin M. Professor of Physics, University of California at Berkeley. Director, Berkeley Radlab, 1958-1973. Discovered the principle of *Phase Stability*, thereby inventing acceleration in radio-frequency fields, opening the door to synchrotrons, 1945. *Atoms for Peace Prize*, 1963. Nobel Prize for Chemistry, 1951. Died, 1991.

Morse, Philip McCord. Professor of Physics, MIT. The father of Operations Research in the U.S. The author of landmark textbooks in physics. The first Director of BNL, 1947. In 1977, his autobiography was published, "In at the Beginnings: A Physicist's Life." Died, 1985.

Panofski, Wolfgang (Pief). Professor of Physics, Stanford University. Founding Director, Stanford Linear Accelerator Center, 1961-1984. U.S. President's Science Advisory Committee (PSAC), 1960-1964. President, American Physical Society, 1975. Chairman, SSC Board of Overseers, 1984-1993.

Peña, Federico F. After being a practicing Lawyer, serving in the Colorado State House of Representatives and as mayor of the City and County of Denver, and founding an investment firm, Peña became the eighth U.S. Secretary of Energy in 1997. He came to DOE at a critical time: Republicans were preparing an attempt to eliminate the department; and controversy was at a high pitch over disposal of civilian and defense nuclear waste, cleanup of weapons sites, energy deregulation, and surplus plutonium and enriched uranium elimination. Another issue was U.S. participation in international Big Science undertakings, specifically fusion research and CERN's LHC high-energy project. He was also confronted with Washington innuendo about his being appointed by Clinton solely because he was Hispanic. It was in this atmosphere, before he could get a grip on his job, that the tritium fiasco at BNL erupted. The adverse fallout from the bold and reasonable decisions Peña made vis-à-vis BNL and criticism about other matters took a heavy toll on him. In April 1998, he announced that he would resign effective June 30.

Pewitt, Douglas. Chairman of the Board, CEO, and Managing Director, AeroFon, a wireless communications company, San Diego. Deputy Director, Office of Energy Research, under John Deutch and his successor, from about 1979 to 1984. Associate Director and Acting Manager, SSC Lab, from about 1989 to 1993.

Ramsey, Norman F. Professor of Physics, Harvard University. Executive Secretary of AUI, set up to establish Brookhaven National Laboratory, 1946. First President of URA, formed to launch Fermilab, 1966-1981. President, American Physical Society, 1979. Chairman of President Kennedy's panel (the Ramsey Panel), 1963-1964. Nobel Prize in Physics, 1989.

Reagan, Ronald W. President, United States, 1981-1989. He restored American confidence and optimism in growth and progress. Through his "Presidential Initiative," he approved and funded the SSC project in 1987. He also approved the "Trivelpiece Initiative" to foster future science at U.S. national labs across the country.

Schwitters, Roy F. Professor of Physics, Harvard University and the University of Texas at Austin. Director of the Superconducting Super Collider Laboratory, 1989-1993.

Temple, L. Edward, Jr. In 1975, with a background in engineering and nuclear power reactors, Temple's first position at DOE was in the San Francisco Operations Office. In 1977, he moved to DOE headquarters near Washington, DC, where he served in the Comptroller's Office. In 1980, he transferred to OER, where he quickly became the successor to Phil McGee as Director of the Construction Management Division. Over a ten-year period, he developed a Project Management System that continues to be a model today for OER's management of its construction projects. After he left DOE in 1991, he held high-level project management positions at three of OER's national labs – ANL, ORNL, and Fermilab.

Trivelpiece, Alvin W. Director, Oak Ridge National Laboratory, 1989-2000. Director of the DOE's Office of Energy Research under President Reagan, 1981-1987. Conceived, organized, and carried out the "Trivelpiece Initiative," which called for the development and construction of scientific facilities at national labs across the country. This was a major step forward for U.S. Big Science; and also served to calm the nerves of scientists across the nation, concerned that the SSC would eat away their futures.

Van der Meer, Simon. Engineering physicist at CERN. He conceived the technique of *Stochastic Cooling* of particle beams, and polished his thinking on the idea at the ISR in the early to mid-seventies. In 1976, after Rubbia's inspiration for a proton-antiproton collider, Simon began to work on a method to accumulate and concentrate antiproton beams, which are very dilute when produced. Within a few years, the CERN Antiproton Accumulator (AA), using Simon's *Stochastic Cooling*, became a reality. This provided the key to Rubbia's plan to collide protons and antiprotons in the SPS. From conception to fulfillment, the entire project took only about three years, culminating in the discovery of the W and Z bosons, announced by Rubbia in 1983. Van der Meer and Rubbia were jointly awarded the Nobel Prize for Physics in 1984. It has been said of the pair's achievement that *Van der Meer made it possible, and Rubbia made it happen.*

Van Hove, Léon. Senior Physicist and Director-General (1976-1980), CERN. Van Hove came to CERN in 1961 to do research in theoretical physics. He was appointed CERN's Director-General in 1976. In his few short years at the helm, by getting the proton-antiproton collider and the LEP electron-positron collider on their way, Van Hove gave CERN the impetus it needed to become *number one* in world high-energy physics. After these remarkable administrative accomplishments, in 1980 Van Hove returned to a less stressful life – doing physics research, encouraging the younger generation, and becoming an ambassador for internationalism in science. Over the next decade, he became a shining beacon for European high-energy physics. He was active up to the end, when he succumbed to cancer in September 1990 at age 66.

Wallenmeyer, William A. Senior Physicist, U.S. Division of Research, Atomic Energy Commission, 1962-1964. Director, U.S. Division of High Energy Physics in the AEC, ERDA, and DOE, 1964-1988. President, Southeastern Universities Research Association, 1988. Fathered U.S. Big Physics through its rise and fall.

Incidental Characters

Ambro, Jerome Anthony, Jr. Elected to the U.S. House of Representatives from the 3rd Congressional District of New York in November 1974, he served three terms, from January 1975 to January 1981, but was defeated in 1980, when the Democrats went down with Carter as Reagan, broadcasting his optimistic vision for America, was swept into office. During Ambro's tenure in the House, his association with BNL was very strong. Influential in S&T, he was Vineyard's man in Washington. Vineyard and Ambro were quite a duo, but when Ambro lost, Vineyard lost his guardian star. Ambro died in 1993.

Barton, Mark Q. Senior Scientist, BNL. Arriving at BNL in 1955, he devoted his professional career to the operation and development of accelerators, in the fifties at the Cosmotron and the sixties at the AGS. In 1974 Vineyard appointed Mark to be Chairman of the Accelerator Department. In 1978 Jim Sanford, Director of the ISABELLE Project, named Barton Head of the ISABELLE Accelerator Division. After the project's fall, Barton led the mass 1983 exodus from ISABELLE to the National Synchrotron Light Source. Mark was Deputy Chairman of the NSLS Department for a few years, but soon felt it was time for a change. He did some research for the U.S. Defense Department on possible uses of particle beams in Reagan's *Star Wars* program. He also became interested in Compact Light Sources for industrial use. In 1987, he went on leave from BNL to IBM to help the company in its acquisition of a small storage ring for x-ray lithography. But that effort was not a success, and he soon retired.

Bentsen, Lloyd Millard, Jr. Elected as a Democrat to the U.S. Senate in 1970, he served four terms, but then left the Senate to become President Clinton's Secretary of the Treasury from January 1993 to December 1994. In 1988, he was the Democratic candidate for Vice-President. As one of the most powerful Senators from 1971 to 1993, he was able to deliver the Senate vote in favor of the Texas Supercollider in 1987, just as Jim Wright was able to deliver the House vote. But the big project was not to be. Persistent cost escalations and delay-after-delay forced it into another critical vote by the Congress in 1993. However, by then the two Texas powerhouse Congressmen were gone; and, without them, the SSC took the fall into oblivion.

Bethe, Hans. Professor of Physics, Cornell University. During World War II, contributed to the development of microwave radar at MIT and the creation of the first atomic bomb at Los Alamos. Developed a theory of the deuteron molecule in 1934 and explained the Lamb shift in 1947. He was awarded the 1967 Nobel Prize for Physics for his work on nuclear reactions, leading to his discovery of the reactions that supply the energy in stars. He was born in 1906.

Blewett, Hildred. In 1947, Hildred and her husband, John, arrived at BNL. As a scientist, she was party to the design and construction of both the Cosmotron and AGS. However, she had both professional and personal problems at BNL. Seeing opportunities across the sea, she left for CERN in the early sixties.

Blume, Martin. Editor-in-Chief, American Physical Society; and Senior Scientist, BNL. During his years at the lab, he was a condensed-matter theorist, the first Chairman of the National Synchrotron Light Source Department, and Deputy Director under Director Nick Samios. In 1996, he took on his role at the APS when *intellectual property* and *paper-versus-electronic-publishing* were the burning questions of the day, as they still are. These are challenging issues, just right for Blume's shrewd, pragmatic, and gung-ho spirit. Although the change he made does seem straightforward, still, the question remains: Was it pure luck that he took a leave of absence from BNL less than a year before the tritium fiasco, or was it Marty's foresight?

Bohr, Niels Henrik David. Professor of Physics, University of Copenhagen (1916), and Founding Director of the Institute for Theoretical Physics (1920). Bohr had the revolutionary idea that classical laws alone cannot explain atomic processes. Using the new Quantum Theory, in conjunction with his postulate that electrons move around the atomic nucleus in restricted orbits, he was able to explain how the atom absorbs and emits energy. For that work, he won the Nobel Prize for Physics in 1922. Bohr visited the U.S. in 1938 and 1939, and told American scientists of his belief that the uranium atom could be split into approximately equal halves, liberating a lot of energy. This was soon verified at Columbia University. Bohr returned to Denmark, but in 1943 he fled when the Nazis occupied it. After working at Los Alamos on the atomic bomb, he returned to Denmark in 1945. He died there in 1962.

Bush, George Herbert Walker. U.S. President, 1989-1993. Unable to withstand discontent at home from a faltering economy, rising violence in inner cities, and continued high-deficit spending, he lost his bid for reelection to Democrat William Clinton. Bush's untimely departure from active politics – another Texan biting the dust – was one more nail in the coffin of the SSC!

Bush, Vannevar. Professor of Electrical Engineering, MIT. Director, Office of Scientific Research and Development during World War II, 1941-1945. Among his many achievements during the war was the adaptation of microwave radar for use in submarine warfare. Asked by President Roosevelt in 1944, he prepared a report, "Science – The Endless Frontier," transmitted to President Harry Truman in July 1945. Bush recommended the speedy formation of a National Research Foundation, but it was not immediately implemented. Congressional haggling pushed it off until the National Science Foundation, a variation on his ideas, was created in 1950. Today, Bush's idea that the government support the country's "best" basic research of all kinds (weapons research included) – as determined by scientists themselves – remains a sterling promise for scientific progress.

Clinton, William Jefferson. U.S. President, 1993-2001. Although the country fared well under Clinton, high-energy physics didn't. Standing on the sidelines and not lifting a finger to help, he watched as the SSC was beaten to a pulp and then done away with by Congress in October 1993. Given Clinton's lukewarm support for basic research during his time in office, perhaps he even agreed with the action taken.

Collins, George. Senior Scientist, BNL. Member, original Board of Trustees, Associated Universities, Inc (1946-1950). Collins came to BNL from the University of

Rochester in 1950 to be the first Chairman of the Cosmotron Department. Although the Cosmotron opened a new world of elementary particles, in a few years it began to exhibit signs of aging. With the experiments becoming more sophisticated, the demand for running time going up, and the machine reliability going down, Collins became overwhelmed. In 1957, he spent a quiet semester in Europe. But on his return he found the Cosmotron about ready to give out. The pressure on Collins mounted, and in 1960 he was relieved of responsibility for the Cosmotron, and moved to the Physics Department, where he continued doing experiments until he retired in 1971. He died in December 2001.

Cool, Rodney. Professor of Physics, Rockefeller University (1970), and Senior Scientist, BNL. Cool began his career as a high-energy nuclear physics experimentalist at BNL, using beams from the Cosmotron, and then from the AGS. With the start-up of the AGS imminent, in 1961 he was made Associate Director for High Energy Physics, with the responsibility of seeing to it that the experimenters got whatever they wanted. In 1970, seeing that the competition between experimentation and accelerator development was getting out of hand, Cool accepted the offer of a professorship at Rockefeller University.

Courant, Ernest D. Senior Scientist and BSA-AUI Distinguished Scientist, BNL. Ernest came to BNL in 1947 and in the 21st century he's still calculating and computing, imagining and analyzing accelerators for the future. Without Ernest, there wouldn't have been any high-energy physics because all the big machines stemmed from his 1952 idea that "if you can't do two things together, you do one after the other," which formed the basis of the AG principle that he and two colleagues – M. Stanley Livingston and Hartland Snyder – discovered. For over five decades Ernest has been devoted to assisting in the birth of high-energy synchrotrons and colliders all over the world. In 1976 he was elected to the National Academy of Sciences and in 1986 he received the DOE's Enrico Fermi Award. When he retired from BNL in 1990, he was honored with the title of AUI Distinguished Scientist. Too bad he didn't recognize and point out the design flaws in ISABELLE, his one false step.

Cronin, James. Professor of Physics, University of Chicago. Nobel Prize for Physics, 1980, with Val Fitch, for the 1963 discovery at BNL's AGS of the violation of CP, one of nature's seemingly inviolate principles.

Dirac, Paul Adrien Maurice. Professor of Mathematics, Cambridge University (1932-1969), and Professor of Physics, Florida State University (1971-1984). Paul Dirac was one of the great men of physics. During the 1920s, strongly impacted by the work of Heisenberg and Schrödinger on their new Quantum Theory, he realized that the Schrödinger wave equation could be factored to represent two separate ones. This implied that the wave equation described the state and motion of two particles, not one. In a 1928 paper, Dirac, through mathematical conceptualization, foresaw the existence of the antiparticle. Demonstrating Dirac's prediction in 1932, C. D. Anderson discovered the antiparticle to the electron, known as the positron. For his brilliant mathematical insight – fashioning the Dirac equation – Dirac was awarded the 1933 Nobel Prize in Physics jointly with Erwin Schrödinger. A giant among scientists, Dirac was indispensable in the making of 20th century physics. He moved to the United States in 1969, and died in Florida in October 1984.

Dirksen, Everett McKinley. In 1932, Dirksen was elected as a Republican from Illinois to the U.S. House of Representatives for the first of eight terms. In 1950, he was voted in as a Senator from Illinois and in 1959 became the minority leader. Dirksen was a pragmatist and did what he believed was best for the nation and for his state. Because of their chummy relationship when they were both Senators, and because they were similar types of realistic men, he and Democratic President Johnson were able to work closely together. It was probably Dirksen's capacity to make deals and work with Johnson that allowed Fermilab to move forward politically, and paved the way for its site to be located in Illinois. Their joint announcement in 1967 that Fermilab was in, and in Illinois, was a super example of political realism. Dirksen died in 1969.

Einstein, Albert. In the early 1900s, as a young man, he conceived the Special Theory of Relativity, and explained the photoelectric effect. For this and other work, he was later awarded two Nobel Prizes for Physics. By 1913, Einstein had won international fame. In 1914, he became Professor of Physics as well as Director of Theoretical Physics at the Kaiser Wilhelm Institute. However, because of danger and fear aroused by the Nazis, in 1933 he accepted a post at the Institute for Advanced Study at Princeton University, which he held until his death in 1955. Although a pacifist, at the request of a group of friends and scientists, in 1939 Einstein wrote to President Franklin D, Roosevelt, stressing the urgency of investigating the possible use of atomic energy in bombs. Presumably, this induced FDR to set up the Manhattan Project. Einstein has become a model of the true scientist. Perhaps he was the greatest of them all.

Fermi, Enrico. Professor of Physics, Columbia University and the University of Chicago. Discovered "Fermi Statistics" that govern "spin-1/2" particles in 1926. Directed a classical series of experiments (under a Chicago football stadium) that led to the atomic pile and the first controlled nuclear chain reaction in December 1942. A leader in the development of the atomic bomb for the Manhattan Project. He was awarded the 1938 Nobel Prize for Physics for his work on "artificial" radioactivity produced by slow neutron bombardment. He died in Chicago in November 1954.

Fitch, Val. Professor of Physics, Princeton University. Nobel Prize for Physics 1980 with James Cronin for their 1963 discovery.

Fricken, Raymond. Deputy Director, Division of High Energy Physics, DOE. After receiving his doctoral degree in physics from Louisiana State University in 1963, Fricken went to work for Bill Wallenmeyer at the AEC. High-energy physics was then in its infancy, and the age of the big accelerators was just dawning. Under Bill's guidance, Ray learned the ins and outs of the U.S. National Laboratory system. He became expert in how to allocate a fixed amount of money optimally to satisfy the needs of experimental work, developing new technologies, and building better facilities. Ray became Wallenmeyer's right-hand man, and eventually Deputy Director of DOE's Division of High Energy Physics. In 1987, when the SSC arrived, to Wallenmeyer's chagrin, it wasn't added to his DOE empire. Wallenmeyer left the DOE, and Fricken's association with him ended. In 1989 Fricken was transferred to the Washington SSC

Office. The years he spent there were grueling ones. With the boss-man, Joe Cipriano, at the SSC site in Texas, trying to administer the SSC from Washington was a nightmare. Yet Ray remained a hard working and loyal government servant. He stuck it out until his 30 years of service were up, retiring in 1993.

Galvin, Robert W. Galvin was the force behind the start of the Motorola Company in 1940, and a senior officer in the company from 1959 to 1990. National Medal of Technology, 1991. Past Chairman and member, Universities Research Association Board of Trustees. Chairman, Task Force on Alternative Futures for the Department of Energy National Laboratories – *The Galvin Commission* – 1994-1995.

Gell-Mann, Murray. Millikan Professor of Physics Emeritus, California Institute of Technology. Professor and Co-Chairman of the Science Board of the Santa Fe Institute, founded in 1984 so that select scientists could have the opportunity and the environment to think freely and let their minds go where they will. Gell-Mann's theory of the *Eightfold-Way* brought order to the chaos of the experimental discovery of some 100 elementary particles; and led to the concept of *Quarks* confined within the many hadronic particles, as well as to a theory of *Strong Interactions*. For this work, he was awarded the Nobel Prize for Physics in 1969. At the Santa Fe Institute, he has stretched his mind to encompass the multitude of earthly matters confronting science and man. He has become the quintessential *science-man of the world*.

Gore, Albert. In 1992, Al Gore became the 45th Vice-President of the United States. Before coming to the Executive branch, he served his Tennessee constituents in Congress as a Democrat for 16 years, in the House from 1976 to 1984, and in the Senate from 1984 to 1992, when he resigned to run for Vice-President on the Clinton ticket. After two terms as Vice-President, he ran for President in November 2000, losing to George W. Bush.

Groves, Leslie R. In 1942-45, General Groves was Director of the Manhattan Project and engineered the development of the atomic bomb. He wisely chose J. Robert Oppenheimer to be the Director of the Los Alamos Laboratory, where the *bomb* was constructed. Groves reported to General George Marshall, the Army Chief of Staff, and wrote the order to deliver the bomb to be dropped on Japan. In 1944, Groves was promoted to major General. He continued to play a leading role in the atomic establishment until his retirement in the late forties. He died in July 1970.

Hahn, Harald. Senior Scientist, BNL. Hahn came to BNL in 1960, and spent his early years working on the AGS radio-frequency (RF) system, the design of an RF separator for the extracted beam, and research on the microwave properties of superconducting cavities. In 1973, after Rau took over as Chairman of the Accelerator Department, he appointed Hahn to be Head of the AD's Advanced Accelerator Development Division (AADD), replacing John Blewett. In 1975, a separate ISABELLE Division was formed within the AD, led by Hahn, and the magnet group built a full-scale prototype that exceeded its design field specification. In 1977 the government approved and funded the ISABELLE Project. In 1978 Vineyard named Jim Sanford, who'd returned to BNL in 1976 as Associate Director for ISABELLE, Project Head, and Hahn was relegated to a lower position. After ISABELLE died of the "too-little – too-late" disease, the coming of RHIC should have given Hahn another chance to fly, but again he was passed over, and performed only low-level administrative functions.

Heisenberg, Werner. Heisenberg was best known for his conception of the *Uncertainty Principle* – the idea that there is an intrinsic indeterminacy in the motion of particles in the subatomic realm. In 1926, he formulated his *Quantum Theory*, which accurately described how the atom really worked. For this and other work, he won the Nobel Prize for Physics in 1932. He was Professor of Physics at the universities of Leipzig (1927-1941) and Berlin (1942-1945). In 1958, he became the Director of the Max Planck Institute in Munich. Early in his career, he was a close associate of Niels Bohr, but he fell out of favor with Bohr as a result of the controversy surrounding his apparently pro-Nazi activities in the unsuccessful German attempt to build an atomic bomb during World War II. He died in 1976.

Holifield, Chet. Holifield was elected to the U.S. House of Representatives in 1942, and served his California District for 16 terms. He specialized in nuclear energy issues from the birth of the Atomic Age until he retired in 1973. He led Congress in legislating the creation of the Atomic Energy Commission in 1946; and, as Chairman of the Joint Committee on Atomic Energy, he played a major role in the formation and growth of the country's National Laboratory system, as well as in the nation's military and peacetime nuclear programs and policies. Recognizing the advantages of a civilian authority to manage the peacetime uses of Atomic Energy, he was instrumental in blocking a postwar plan to put the military in sole control. This helped make America an international leader by promoting world partnerships and opening the door to rapid advances in the nuclear field. In the sixties, when a fabulous new American synchrotron was envisaged, the Holifield-Dirksen-Ramsey-Seaborg-Wilson combine brought Fermilab into being. With Holifield as his man in Washington, Wilson became a Big Science man-of-power, but when Holifield left Congress in 1973, Wilson's days of glory were numbered. Holifield died in 1995 at the age of 91.

Hudis, Jerome. Senior Scientist, BNL, and Vice-President and Secretary, Associated Universities, Inc. Jerry Hudis joined BNL's Chemistry Department in 1952. His research focused primarily on high-energy nuclear reactions and x-ray photoelectron spectroscopy. In July 1977, Hudis became Chairman of the Chemistry Department; and in 1981, Vineyard made him Assistant Director for Scientific Staff Policy. In that capacity, he had oversight over the Office of Scientific Personnel and the Office of University Programs. He also established a new Office of Research and Technology Assessment to assess the lab's programs in order to identify technologies that might be used by industries (i.e. Technology Transfer), to disseminate information about lab research programs, and to provide technical assistance to state and local governments. In 1985, Hudis was made Vice-President for Programmatic Affairs and Secretary of AUI, leaving the lab after 33 years. At AUI, he served under President Robert Hughes until 1996, when Bob retired. In 1997, the Tritium Affair exploded, and AUI was fired as the DOE contractor for the operation of BNL. Thus the longtime Hudis connection to BNL was fully severed.

Hughes, Robert E. President of Associated Universities, Inc. Bob Hughes was Professor of Chemistry at the University of Pennsylvania for 10 years and at Cornell University for 18 years before joining AUI as its President in October 1980. He had a distinguished scientific career, performing research in x-ray crystallography, crystal and molecular structure, antibiotics, and the physical chemistry of macromolecules. During his university years, he interacted with the U.S. President's Office of Scientific Policy and the NSF, the right credentials for the top job at AUI. Hughes came to AUI just as BNL was on the threshold of hard times. Three years later the DOE killed ISABELLE, and the road back to productive life for the lab was long and tough. But Bob had the staying power to see BNL revived and returned to scientific normalcy. In the fall of 1996, after 16 years of service, President Hughes retired from AUI. Although in 1983 he had suffered through the snuffing out of ISABELLE, by departing AUI when he did, he was saved from the convulsions at the lab due to the tritium leaks.

Jackson, John David. Professor of Physics, University of California, Berkeley. A brilliant research physicist, his imaginative explorations have carried him through a diverse array of subjects. Also a gifted writer and teacher, his graduate textbook, *Classical Electrodynamics*, was first published by Wiley in 1962, with 2nd and 3rd editions released in 1975 and 1998. Although a theorist, Jackson is a well-rounded physicist, and has helped resolve practical physics issues confronting the science community. He was asked by Vineyard to assist in the BNL struggle to manufacture a workable superconducting magnet. Dave spent a few months one summer around 1980 trying to figure out what was wrong. He probed every angle, and identified the problem: limitations in the magnet coil design, specifically the braid-style wire. But his conclusions were ignored, as were those of others. Soon Dave left the lab and went on with his life as a professor and community advisor. He retired in 1993 as Emeritus Professor at Berkeley, but he's still teaching and doing research, and he's added physics history to his menu as well.

Johnsen, Kjell. Senior Physicist, CERN and Professor of Physics, University of Bergen, Norway. Johnsen arrived at CERN in 1952. He worked with John Adams' group designing an AG synchrotron. In 1959, Kjell was part of the PS commissioning team. In 1962, he headed a group studying future facilities and promoted the daring idea of colliding proton beams. The CERN Council approved this proposal in 1965, with Johnsen as Director of the Construction Department – and the ISR was started up five years later. In 1979 Kjell went to BNL as Deputy Head of the ISABELLE Project, and a year later was made the project's Technical Director. He had full responsibility for the design, R&D, and construction of ISABELLE. Having control over both collider and magnet design, he could've altered the bleak course that unfolded, but instead he let things slide, until the end came in 1983. Disgraced and embarrassed, Johnsen returned to CERN. There he turned his attention to accelerator education and initiated the CERN Accelerator School in 1983, but soon handed over the reins to Phil Bryant. In the two decades since, he's just faded away.

Johnson, Lyndon B. As U.S. President, 1963-1968, Johnson did much for the country and for high-energy physics. Without his ability to work effectively with Republican strongman Everett Dirksen, who knows whether Fermilab would now exist? He died in 1973.

Kennedy, John F. President, United States, 1961-1963. Assassinated November 1963.

Lawrence, Ernest Orlando. Professor of Physics, University of California at Berkeley. Nobel Prize for Physics 1939. Invented and developed the Cyclotron. Formed Berkeley Radlab, 1931, becoming the founder of the Lawrence Berkeley National Laboratory. First lab Director to 1958.

Lee, Wonyong. Professor of Physics, Columbia University.

Leipuner, Laurence B. Senior scientist, BNL. Leipuner came to BNL in 1955 as a physics Research Associate. He worked in the Cosmotron Department as an experimenter in Bob Adair's group. When the AGS became a reality in 1960, Larry stuck with the Cosmotron; and, when Lyle Smith left for the AGS Division, Leipuner became Head of the AD's Cosmotron Division until it disbanded in 1967. He then moved to the Physics Department and continued to do *fixed-target* experiments at both BNL and Fermilab until he retired in October 2001. In the late eighties he did a short stint in DOE's SSC Office as a BNL *detailee*. While there, he tried to persuade the SSC top management that conflict with the DOE was counter-productive, but his efforts were to no avail.

Lindenbaum, Sam J. Professor of Physics, City College of New York (1970), and Senior Scientist, BNL (1963). He was one of the early physicists who recognized the need for big, complex, high technology detectors for high-energy particle experiments. In 1971 he and Satoshi Ozaki led the construction of the BNL Multi-Particle Spectrometer (MPS), served by beam from the AGS. Able to handle a massive amount of experimental data simultaneously, the MPS became a user facility; and many research groups took full advantage of it. Science politics attracted Lindenbaum in the seventies and in 1976 he spent more than a year in Washington as Deputy for Scientific Affairs in ERDA's Division of High Energy Physics. He spoke with great conviction for the spin-off value of high-energy physics for society-at-large and became a staunch backer of ISABELLE. But as the project sank, Lindenbaum faded from the front lines.

Livdahl, Philip V. Physicist and Administrator, Fermi National Accelerator Laboratory. From 1957 to 1971, Livdahl gained wide experience in the ins and outs of national labs at Argonne National Laboratory, working in the Linac area and in experimental planning and operations. In 1971, he arrived at Fermilab during its early days and rose to be Deputy Head of the Accelerator Division in 1976. When Bob Wilson was dismissed as lab Director in June 1978, Phil was made Acting Director. He kept the lab going for about a year, until Leon Lederman became Director in 1979, when Phil was made Deputy Director. Livdahl's job was to work closely with DOE officials on administrative matters, while ensuring that lab actions were in compliance with government orders and edicts. He served well until he retired in October 1987.

Lowenstein, Derek I. Senior Scientist and Chairman, Collider Accelerator Department, BNL. Lowenstein's tenure at BNL was at a time of turmoil and swift change. An opportunist, he not only survived, but thrived. He arrived in 1973, and became Head of the Experimental Planning Division of the Accelerator Department (AD) in 1977. When Mark Barton, then AD Chairman, left for ISABELLE, the AGS became leaderless. Even when BNL and ERDA decided to shut down the AGS experimental program by the early eighties – the scheduled turn-on time for ISABELLE – Derek stuck with the old machine, destined for the lowly role of injector for the new collider. But Lowenstein didn't feel right about the ISABELLE design, and he fought to keep the AGS on track and its experiments going full blast. With no one else eager to step in, he became the AGS de facto leader, and in 1981 he was made Deputy AD Chairman. This was the year that began ISABELLE's deathwatch, which ended in October 1983. So, Lowenstein turned out to be right, and from there it was up, up, and away for him. In 1984, the deal to abolish AGS experiments was abrogated, and he was appointed Chairman of the new AGS Department. When RHIC came on the scene, Lowenstein sensed that it would eventually gravitate to his camp. He was right again! Through the eighties and nineties, the AGS kept going strong, and when RHIC was ready to run, the lab unified the nuclear and high-energy accelerator effort into a combined AGS-RHIC department, the Collider Accelerator Department, and Derek was made Chairman. By the 21st century, Derek was the top accelerator man at BNL.

McDaniel, Boyce D. Professor of Physics, Cornell University. Also, Director of the Cornell Lab for Nuclear Studies (LNS) from 1967 to 1985, when he retired as Emeritus Professor. He worked with Bob Wilson at Los Alamos during World War II and at the Cornell LNS after the war, where they built one electron synchrotron after another. After Wilson left to become builder and Director of Fermilab, McDaniel took over the Cornell lab. In 1976, he proposed upgrading the existing 10-GeV synchrotron (CESR) into an 8-GeV electron-positron storage ring. He threw himself into making it work, and it did, but even he didn't anticipate the treasure trove of science that it uncovered. Today the CESR collider is a foremost B-Factory, a tribute to Mac's inventive mind. He died on May 15, 2002, at age 84.

Mills, Frederick E. Senior Physicist, Fermilab. Mills started his career in physics in 1956 at the Midwestern Universities Research Association (MURA), where he rose to be Director. While there, he supervised the design and construction of a 240-MeV electron storage ring as a source of synchrotron radiation. In 1966, he became Professor of Physics at the University of Wisconsin, and was the Director of its Physical Sciences Laboratory. In 1970 he entered the hornet's nest at BNL initiated by Green's forced resignation as Chairman of the Accelerator Department. Taking over the Chairmanship, he was apparently unaware of the existing political morass. Fred was excited about the potential for new physics results using high-energy proton-proton storage rings, and fitted perfectly into the ISA program now under his supervision. This program was based on superconducting magnets, exactly what Fred was looking for. Incidentally, it was Mills who added *BELLE* to ISA, forming ISABELLE – beautiful ISA. However, Fred had underestimated the political infighting at the lab and couldn't last long in that environment. After 2-1/2 years, he was relieved of his administrative duties by Vineyard and he soon returned to Fermilab, where he worked on accelerator physics. He retired in the nineties.

Oppenheimer, J. Robert. Professor of Physics and Director of the Institute for Advanced Studies, Princeton. In June 1942, he was appointed Director of the Manhattan Project. He was one of the great scientific leaders of the twentieth century. Yet, he always had grave misgivings of what the atomic bomb – his creation – had wrought on the world. He died in 1967.

Palmer, Robert B. Senior Scientist, BNL. Bob Palmer is a physicist of the highest rank, whose contributions run the gamut of the high-energy enterprise. His scientific work stretches from conceiving, designing, and developing both accelerators and detectors to originating and executing experimental particle research. On the experimental side, he co-discovered (with Nick Samios and Ralph Shutt) the omega-minus particle in the sixties, played a role in the discovery of neutral currents at CERN in the early seventies, helped in the production of the first charmed baryon at BNL in 1975, and participated in the observation of direct single photons at CERN in 1978. On the accelerator side, he demonstrated the nature of the inverse free-electron laser in 1972, proposed longitudinal stochastic cooling by the now-called Palmer method in 1973, and invented the grating laser accelerator in 1980. From 1980 to 1983, Palmer and his BNL team developed practical and workable superconducting magnets for the CBA (formerly ISABELLE), and in the early nineties, when the SSC staff had trouble increasing their magnet's aperture by 25%, he stepped in and worked it out. In the nineties, he was engrossed in linear electron-positron colliders and in the tantalizing idea of a muon collider. The APS awarded Palmer the Panofsky Prize in 1993 for the omega-minus high-energy experiment and the Wilson Prize in 1999 for his work on accelerators and beams, and BNL gave him its R&D award in 1997 *for his many contributions to accelerator and detector concepts and technology.*

Pauli, Wolfgang. Professor of Theoretical Physics: University of Michigan, 1931-1940; Princeton University, 1940-1945; Federal Institute of Technology, Zurich, 1945-1958. Recognized that the two-valued spin variable characterizing the electron is exclusionary in nature. This momentous discovery is embodied in what is known as the Pauli Exclusion Principle. He won the Nobel Prize for Physics in 1945. He died in Zurich in 1958.

Percy, Charles Harting. *Chuck* Percy was elected to the U.S. Senate in November 1966 as an Illinois Republican. He served three terms, but was defeated in the 1984 election. Although foreign matters were his forte, he understood the importance of local business and of bringing federal projects to his state. Toward the end of his last term, the DOE placed on the table a new accelerator project for Nuclear Physics. Proposals were submitted to a DOE Technical Review Committee, the major ones from the Southeastern Universities Research Association (SURA) and from Argonne National Lab (ANL) in Illinois. In 1983 the committee chose the SURA proposal, and in 1984 DOE, following the committee's recommendation, selected a site in Virginia. Percy was livid. In a public speech after the decision was made, he chided the committee as well as taking the DOE to task, roughly saying: *The Technical Review Committee is perhaps best qualified to determine the winning proposal, but choosing the site is none of the committee's business. That's the province of politicians. Why Virginia? Why not Illinois? Chuck* was hopping mad but was surely on the right track.

Pevsner, Aihud. Professor of Physics, John Hopkins University. Pevsner was a high-energy physics experimentalist. He served on the AUI Board of Trustees, and was a steadfast and ever-loyal friend of BNL.

Planck, Max Karl Ernst Ludwig. Professor of Physics, Berlin University, 1889-1926. President, Kaiser Wilhelm Society, 1926-1937. He deduced the relationship between the energy and the frequency of particle radiation, based on the revolutionary idea that the energy emitted could take on only discrete values or "quanta." He designated the universal constant connecting the two by the letter *h*, now called *Planck's Constant*. This work marked a turning point in the history of Physics. He was awarded the Nobel Prize for Physics in 1918. He died at Göttingen in October 1947.

Rau, Ronald R. Senior Scientist, BNL. Rau came to BNL in 1956 to be an experimenter in elementary particle physics. He took part in the development and construction of BNL's bubble chambers, and used them to do experiments with beam first from the Cosmotron and then from the AGS. Rau was appointed Chairman of the Physics Department in 1966, and Associate Director for High Energy Physics in 1970. When George Vineyard became BNL Director in 1973, the Accelerator Department was in disarray, while, at the same time, BNL was preparing to launch ISABELLE. To set things straight, Vineyard threw out Fred Mills and called in Rau. Between 1973 and 1981, Ronnie made myriad changes. To get the staff ready for the big collider, he ousted Blewett and brought in a host of new faces, among them Mark Barton, Jim Sanford, Paul Reardon, Kjell Johnsen, D. Hywel White, and Bill Willis. It was a massive changing of the guard. But it was all in vain, because the dipole magnets – ISABELLE's Achilles' heel – kept failing. As a result, in 1981, Rau was removed as Associate Director. He took the fall, and two years later ISABELLE went down with him. A disillusioned man, Rau tried to go back to experimental physics, where he began. He went to DESY for a while to try to re-energize his career, but that didn't work, and he soon returned home. He retired in 1990.

Reardon, Paul J. Senior Scientist and Administrator. Reardon combined physics knowledge with managerial know-how, a much-needed skill in the age of big machines. He was at Fermilab from 1968 to 1975, as the lab was being built, went on to become the Project Manager for the Tokomak Fusion Test Reactor (TFTR) at Princeton's Plasma Physics Laboratory from 1975 to 1978, when he was named BNL's Associate Director for High Energy Facilities. Being an expert in the construction of large high technology facilities, the task of building ISABELLE seemed made to order for him. But ISABELLE was doomed. When RHIC was born out of ISABELLE's ashes, Reardon helped in its early development, but in 1986, he abruptly left BNL. After a few years of consulting, in early 1990 he went to Waxahachie to direct the technical design and construction of the SSC, but in January 1992, he chose to retire, thereby saving himself from the experience of the big project's demise.

Richter, Burton. Professor of Physics, Stanford University (1967 – present), and Director of the Stanford Linear Accelerator Center (1984-1999). In the early seventies, Richter spearheaded the construction of the electron-positron storage ring, SPEAR – at low cost and in record time. From that collider sprang the *November Revolution* of 1974

– the discovery of a new heavy particle (with mass about 3 GeV). From its decay products, the existence of a new kind of quark – the *quark with charm* – was established, setting the stage for what is now called *The Standard Model* of the elementary particles. For this work, Richter shared the 1976 Nobel Prize for Physics with Sam Ting, who made the same discovery in an independent experiment at BNL, using the AGS. In the late seventies, Burt's inspirations in accelerator S&T led him to proclaim the end of the era of circular electron colliders and the onset of the age of the Linear Collider. He devised the hybrid Stanford Linear Collider (a linac to accelerate the electrons and positrons, and a ring to bring them into collision), thereby demonstrating that linear colliders were feasible. Still, a true linear collider has yet to be built. Because of the *big money* involved, Burt is now taking the international-collaboration route. That's a hard road, but if anyone can fashion a political package that will make a linear collider happen, it's Burt!

Rutherford, Ernest (1st Baron Rutherford). Rutherford's studies of radioactivity led him to the discovery of the atomic nucleus. For that and other work, he was awarded the 1908 Nobel Prize for Chemistry. In 1911, he described the atom as a small, heavy nucleus surrounded by orbital electrons. Niels Bohr adopted this nuclear model of the atom; and, combining it with the new *Quantum Theory*, Bohr provided the basic description of the atom that is still accepted today. In 1919, Rutherford became Professor of Physics at Cambridge University, as well as the Director of the Cavendish Laboratory. He was knighted in 1914, and elevated to the peerage in 1931. Rutherford died in 1937.

Sandweiss, Jack. Professor of Physics, Yale University. Sandweiss has been on the Yale faculty since 1957, becoming a tenured professor in 1964. His focus has been high-energy physics experiments, but he is a physicist of the *old-style unified* kind, with wide-ranging knowledge. During the seventies, he became embroiled in the *rise and fall* of ISABELLE. Having widespread influence, he could have steered the project away from the fatal course it was on. However, even though his scientific insights and his access to lab information not easily available made him aware of the risks in the chosen design, he stood back and let things ride. After ISABELLE was gone, Jack worked on free-electron lasers (FELs) for a while, did experiments at the AGS and at Fermilab, delved into experimentation for BNL's RHIC project, and recently has joined Sam Ting's program of experiments on the collisions of highly energetic particles coming from the outer regions of the universe by launching an experimental facility into space.

Sanford, James R. Senior Scientist, BNL. From 1962 to 1969 Sanford was Head of the Division for Experimental Planning for the AGS research program. In 1969, he became Associate Director of the fledgling Fermilab, responsible for the experimental program. When he left in 1976, he returned to BNL as Associate Director for ISABELLE, and became head of the project when it was approved by ERDA a year later. Sanford predicted that ISABELLE would be completed by 1983, and would be able to handle at least 12 experimental groups simultaneously. These were fighting words, but he focused too much on the experimental program-to-be, and the collider itself went to pot! Ironically, his projected date for starting the experimental program was the year when ISABELLE was cancelled. A few years later, the SSC came along, and Sanford, not the man he once was, accepted a low-level administrative position. But again disappointment befell him when the SSC was stopped in 1993. He tried to return to BNL, but the truth is, *you can't go home again*, and soon after, he retired.

Schlesinger, James R. Professor of Political Economics, University of Virginia, 1955-1963. Director of Strategic Studies, the Rand Corporation, 1963-1969. Chairman, U.S. Atomic Energy Commission, 1971. Director, Central Intelligence Agency, 1973. Secretary of Defense in Nixon Administration, 1973-1975. First Secretary of Energy in Carter Administration, 1977-1979. Senior Advisor, Lehman Brothers, Kuhn Loeb Inc., New York City. He continues to write and speak publicly, particularly on National Security matters.

Seaborg, Glenn Theodore. University Professor of Chemistry, University of California at Berkeley (1945). From 1942 to 1946, he headed the plutonium effort for the Manhattan Project at the University of Chicago Metallurgical Laboratory. After the war, he became Director of LBNL, and in 1958 Director Emeritus, when he was made Chancellor of the University. For his work on heavy elements, he shared the 1951 Nobel Prize for Chemistry with Ed McMillan. Appointed by President Kennedy, he was Chairman of the Atomic Energy Commission from 1961 until 1971. This was a critical period for physics. Once the Ramsey Panel of 1963 challenged the U.S. to think big, it was up to the AEC to act. Under Seaborg, the AEC approved the construction of Fermilab, ushering in American Big Physics. After leaving the AEC, Seaborg continued to serve science and the nation as an advisor. He also wrote prodigiously. Tributes to him abounded over the years. In 1997, to honor him for the many elements he had discovered, the one with atomic number 106 was named Seaborgium, the first time an element was named for a living person. Seaborg died in February 1999 at age 86.

Schwartz, Mel. Professor of Physics, Columbia University. With Leon Lederman and Jack Steinberger, he was awarded the 1988 Nobel Prize for Physics for the 1962 discovery of a second neutrino, the muon neutrino, at BNL's AGS.

Shutt, Ralph P. Senior Scientist, BNL. Shutt came to BNL in 1947. He worked on cosmic radiation, and on high-energy nuclear experiments at the Cosmotron and the AGS. Around 1960, he conceived the 80-inch Bubble Chamber, which was built and ready to use by June 1963, when the first bubble tracks of charged secondary particles from the AGS were photographed in it. Among the many experiments at this facility was the discovery of the omega-minus particle, as predicted by the Gell-Mann theory of the *Eight-Fold Way*. Shutt became the lab authority on cryogenics and an administrative man of wisdom; and he is still at BNL, working away.

Smith, Lyle W. Senior Scientist, BNL. Lyle Smith joined the BNL staff in 1948. Within a few years, he became a leading figure in the Cosmotron Department. In 1960, when the Cosmotron was incorporated into the expanded Accelerator Department under Ken Green, Lyle was put in charge of the Cosmotron Division. In the coming years, with Lyle at the helm, the Cosmotron ran more smoothly than ever. But when he saw that the old machine's days were numbered, he moved to the AD's AGS Division. Focusing on the machine, he exhibited great skill, keeping the AGS running for experiments despite the disruptive effects of the Conversion Project. During the seventies, he spoke bluntly in defense of giving the AGS experimental program continued high priority, and became more and more fiery in his technical criticism of the ISABELLE Project. As the eighties opened and ISABELLE's troubles were mounting, Vineyard made Lyle a member of the *Gang of Five* (Vineyard, Rau, Sanford, Samios, and Smith) overseeing the big collider project. But Lyle's forthright, brusque manner didn't endear him to this high-level team. Before long, hotheaded Lyle was kicked out. When Derek Lowenstein was promoted to be Chairman of the new AGS Department – formally divorcing ISABELLE from the AGS – he chose Lyle to be his Deputy. But time was catching up with Lyle, and he retired from the lab in September 1984.

Steinberger, Jack. Professor of Physics, Columbia University and CERN. Nobel Prize for Physics 1988 with Mel Schwartz and Leon Lederman for their 1962 discovery of the muon neutrino.

Tigner, Maury. Professor of Physics, Cornell University. Over four decades, Tigner has contributed to the accelerator field as inventor, designer, and builder, and particularly in the development of superconducting radio-frequency systems. From 1977 to 1979, with Boyce McDaniel, he played a leading role in the design and construction of Cornell's CESR collider. In 1984 he was made Director of the SSC Central Design Group (CDG) at Berkeley's LBNL and served until 1989. The politics were intense, but despite the stress, he came up with a workable (although high cost) design. In 1989, hoping to be made Director of the new SSC Laboratory in Texas, he lost to Roy Schwitters. Tigner then returned to Cornell, and in June 2000, he was named Director of the Lab for Nuclear Studies (CLNS). Today, he runs the CLNS and continues to upgrade CESR's B-Factory capabilities.

Ting, Samuel C. C. Professor of Physics, MIT. Nobel Prize for Physics 1976 for the 1973 discovery of the J/psi particle at BNL's AGS. The prize was shared with Stanford University's Burton Richter, who simultaneously found the particle at SLAC's SPEAR Electron-Positron Collider. The discovery is referred to as the November revolution and set the stage for establishing the Standard Model for our universe's elementary particles.

Urey, Harold Clayton. Columbia University: Professor of Chemistry, 1934; Director of War Research, Atomic Bomb Project, 1940-1945. Professor of Chemistry, University of Chicago, 1945-1958. Professor-at-Large, University of California, 1958-1981. Discovered "heavy hydrogen" and conducted important research on isotopes. He was awarded the Nobel Prize for Chemistry in 1934. He died in 1981.

Van de Graaff, Robert Jemison. Professor of Physics, MIT (1934). He invented an electrostatic particle accelerator, now called the Van de Graaff generator. Introduced in 1931, it is widely used even today as the first stage of accelerator chains for high-energy machines. Van de Graaff died in 1967.

Weisskopf, Victor F. Professor of Physics, MIT. A stellar nuclear physicist and a model scientist for our time. Director-General CERN, 1961-1966. Provided the spark for CERN to spring ahead of the U.S. high-energy physics research program in the latter half of the twentieth century. International statesman of science, leader in the peaceful uses of atomic energy, and vigorous proponent of East-West scientific cooperation.

Wheeler, George W. Senior Scientist, BNL. Arriving at BNL from Yale University in October 1964, where he'd become a linac expert, he was instrumental in the design and construction of the 200-MeV Linac for the BNL Conversion Project, completed in 1968. The years that followed were a time of great stress for the lab, especially in the Accelerator Department. George worked on AGS operations and a variety of proposed projects. In April 1975, he abruptly left the lab.

Willis, William J. Professor of Physics, Columbia University. As a physics professor at Yale and a BNL physicist in the sixties and early seventies, Willis began his long high-energy physics career doing experiments at the AGS. He was influential in determining the initial design of ISABELLE, pushing for continuous beams, as in the ISR. Willis became an authority on big particle detectors for big colliders, and on experimentation with heavy ions. After spending 1973 to 1978 at CERN, he accepted the BNL offer to be Head of the Detector Division for the ISABELLE project. Since ISABELLE never made it, Willis, unsure of which course to take, vacillated between CERN and BNL. However, when RHIC came, he made the choice and returned to BNL. In 1990 he accepted a joint appointment as Columbia Professor and BNL Senior Scientist.

Wright, James Claude, Jr. U.S. Congressman. Wright was elected to the House of Representatives in 1954 as a Texas Democrat, and became House Majority Leader in 1976. After 16 terms, he was made Speaker of the House in 1987, but resigned in May 1989 amid charges of unethical conduct. Jim Wright's fall was an immense loss for Big Science. He was among the powerful men who brought the SSC to Texas, and kept the money flowing even as the project wobbled. As he and others like him left the stage, the SSC weakened and finally tumbled in 1993. When all is said and done, it was politics that took the life of the SSC, just as it took Jim Wright's career.

Glossary of Terms

Accelerator. An apparatus for accelerating charged particles to high energies by means of electric or electromagnetic fields. Accelerating times are on the order of seconds.

Accelerator Department. A department at a national accelerator laboratory made up of the staff responsible for planning, designing, building, and operating the lab's accelerator facilities. BNL's Accelerator Department formed in 1960 unified its accelerator expertise.

Advanced Light Source. A national synchrotron-radiation light source research facility at Lawrence Berkeley National Laboratory, funded by the DOE's Office of Basic Energy Sciences. Using 1- to 2-GeV electron beams in a storage ring, it is the world's brightest source of ultraviolet and soft x-ray beams, generating intense light for scientific and technological research. The facility started operating in 1993.

Advanced Neutron Source. This was a very high-power reactor-based neutron source proposed for research at ORNL in the original "Trivelpiece Initiative," but the project was never approved. It was replaced in the "Initiative" by the accelerator-based Spallation Neutron Source, now under construction.

Advanced Photon Source. A national synchrotron-radiation light source research facility at Argonne National Laboratory, funded by the DOE. Using a storage ring for 7-GeV beams of positrons (to avoid the degradation of electron beams by the trapping of dust particles and ions), it generates high brilliance x-ray beams used to carry out basic research in the academic and industrial sectors. The first x-ray beam was produced in March 1995.

Alternating Gradient Principle. When magnets are configured in sequence so that each alternate one has a magnetic field of the opposite gradient (the rate of change of the field outward from the center in the transverse direction), beams of particles can be kept to very small transverse size over large distances, like a narrow beam of light. Also referred to as the Strong Focusing Principle.

Alternating Gradient Synchrotron. A facility at BNL for high-energy physics research. This and the Proton Synchrotron at CERN were the first synchrotrons to use the Alternating Gradient Principle. First beam, July 1960.

American Association for the Advancement of Science. This, the world's largest scientific society, was founded in 1848. It now has 134,000 members, as well as 272 affiliates that serve 10 million members. The AAAS mission is to advance science and innovation throughout the world for the benefit of all people. Its objectives are to foster communication among scientists, engineers, and the public via meetings open to all; to enhance international cooperation in science and its applications by developing contacts and programs with foreign groups; to advance science unity by featuring work in a wide array of different sciences, including life sciences, physical sciences, and social sciences; to promote the responsible conduct and use of science and technology (S&T) by conducting lectures and discussions on ethics at its meetings and by taking positions on current issues; to run outreach programs in S&T education, in particular to aid schools in the teaching of modern science; to increase public understanding of S&T with programs that support science propagation in the media; to enhance the S&T workforce and infrastructure; and to strengthen the overall S&T enterprise by lobbying for the U.S. science budget by cultivating inventive ideas in its publications and at its meetings and by demonstrating to the public and its representatives how valuable S&T is for society-at-large. The AAAS, headquartered in Washington, DC, has a staff of 300, and it publishes the journal *Science*. Its motto is *Advancing Science and Serving Society.*

American Physical Society. The society's purpose is to advance and diffuse knowledge of physics in the belief that understanding the nature of the physical universe benefits mankind. The APS sponsors annual meetings of the full society; supports meetings of its various branches; and publishes physics journals – particularly, *Physical Review*, *Physical Review Letters*, and *Reviews of Modern Physics*. Recently, the APS has tried to bring together its disparate members into a unified group by attempting to counter the trend toward fragmentation into specialized factions. It also tries to educate the public about rapidly advancing physics results that seem obscure to the average person. Located in College Park, Maryland, the APS has more than 40,000 members worldwide. It was established in 1899.

Antiproton. An unstable elementary particle created by collisions of stable particles, protons and electrons. It annihilates when in contact with matter. Beams of antiprotons can be made and kept long enough for use in experiments when maintained in sufficiently high vacuum. Its charge is opposite to that of its partner proton. Referred to here as pbar.

Antiproton Accumulator. An accumulator and storage ring for about 3.5-GeV antiprotons, the AA was built at CERN as part of the proton-antiproton project to discover the W and Z particles and was operational by 1981. Using Van der Meer's method of stochastic cooling to compress the antiprotons, it took about a day of accumulation to obtain sufficient antiprotons to transfer to the PS, where acceleration to 26 GeV took place. Then the antiproton beam was injected into the SPS, where the proton beam awaited it for acceleration to the final collision energy. In contrast to the CERN AA, the Fermilab AA, with a circumference of about 474 meters, cools and accumulates antiprotons at about 8.9 GeV.

Argonne National Laboratory. Chartered in 1946, the nation's first national laboratory is in Illinois, about 25 miles southwest of Chicago. It is a multi-purpose lab operated by the University of Chicago for the Department of Energy. Its original purpose was to develop nuclear reactors for peaceful purposes. Over the years, its research has expanded to include many areas of science, engineering, and technology.

Associated Universities, Inc. This not-for-profit corporation, based in Washington DC, was founded in 1946 by a consortium of nine northeastern universities to manage a scientific facility for the federal government. Its purpose was to acquire land and to plan, construct, and operate this research laboratory, named BNL, which united the resources of universities, other research organizations, and the government. The vision for this organization, stemming from the Bush Report, was to create a national laboratory, funded by the government, too large, complex, and costly for a single university; and this lab was to be freely available on a competitive basis to all scientists without regard to affiliation. From 1947 to 1997, AUI managed BNL under contract with the government. In May 1997, claiming that AUI had violated safety standards, the DOE terminated the management contract.

Atomic Bomb. A bomb that derives its destructiveness from the release of nuclear energy, causing an unimaginable explosion and widespread radioactive contamination.

Atomic Energy Commission. Established in 1947 by congressional mandate for a larger federal role in atomic energy development, the AEC was led by five commissioners – scientists and others. It was unique in openly promoting and regulating a sensitive technology for non-military purposes, and it formulated American nuclear policies and programs. In 1975, it was incorporated into the Energy Research and Development Administration, later the Department of Energy.

Beam. A narrow directed flow of particles or radiation.

Beam Cooling. Beams are composed of particles with lots of space in between. The larger the average space between particles, the more dilute the beam. Beam cooling reduces the space between the particles, making the beam denser, and resulting in higher collision rates for experiments when such beams collide. Beam cooling requires highly sophisticated methods because beams have a natural tendency to get not smaller but larger due to like-charge electric repulsion. One mechanism for this type of enlarging process is intra-beam scattering.

Berkeley Lab. Short for Lawrence Berkeley National Laboratory, a part of the University of California at Berkeley and situated adjacent to its campus.

Berkeley-BNL Agreement. The *gentleman's agreement* entered into between the Berkeley Radlab and BNL whereby it was taken for granted that new accelerator facilities would alternate between the U.S. East and West Coasts.

Bevatron. This circular weak-focusing synchrotron, built by Lawrence at LBNL (then Lawrence Radiation Laboratory) in 1954, was about 150 yards in circumference, accelerating protons to 6-GeV energy, and was the last effective weak-focusing machine. The antiproton was discovered there in 1955, for which Segré and Chamberlain received the Nobel Prize for Physics in 1959.

B-Factory. This type of accelerator facility, designed to produce copious amounts of B-mesons for experimental study, is termed a "factory" because of its large numbers of collisions, its high reliability, and its smooth operation. The primary purpose of a B-factory is to pursue the question of why we live in a matter-dominated universe since, when the universe was created in the Big Bang, matter and anti-matter apparently were produced in equal amounts. If so, why didn't the particles and antiparticles annihilate on contact, leaving no matter for a palpable universe? The current theory on the question is that there was an exceedingly small imbalance in the matter-anti-matter ratio in primordial times that tipped the balance in favor of matter. The role of the B-factory is to substantiate this and to establish the mechanism for the tiny excess.

Big Science. An expression connoting the great increase in the size and cost of facilities and in the complexity of the technology used to conduct forefront scientific research.

Big Physics. Big Science, with reference to physics research.

Breeder Reactor. A nuclear reactor that creates more fissile material than it uses in the chain reaction.

Brookhaven National Laboratory. Established in 1947, BNL began as a multi-program national laboratory operated by Associated Universities Inc., originally for the AEC, and starting in the late seventies for the DOE. In 1997, the operating contractor was changed to Brookhaven Science Associates. BNL is situated on Long Island in Upton, New York, about 60 miles from New York City. Its mission is to carry out basic and applied research in long-term programs at the frontiers of science.

Bunched Beams. These are beams in accelerators or colliders that are configured, using radio-frequency electromagnetic fields, like a string of pearls. The string, circular or linear, represents the beam orbit, and each pearl represents a bunch of particles. Bunches can be squeezed tightly – the greater the bunch squeezing, the shorter they are, the larger the space between each one, and the higher the particle density. A beam is said to have a high bunching factor when the space between bunches is much larger than the length of each bunch. The higher the bunching factor, the better it is for experiments, producing more data for a given number of particles in the beam.

Bush Report. Requested by President Roosevelt in 1944, Vannevar Bush prepared the report *Science – The Endless Frontier* and transmitted it to President Truman in 1945. With a new vision of science and technology, it fundamentally altered the government's relationship to research and education in science and technology. Pragmatically integrating government, academia, and industry, it promised, via government support, to initiate a new era of basic research, scientific exploration, and technological innovation. From Roosevelt's letter to Bush of November 17, 1944: *New frontiers of the mind are before us, and if they are pioneered with the same vision, boldness, and drive with which we have waged war we can create a fuller and more fruitful employment and a fuller and more fruitful life.*

Cambridge Electron Accelerator. Constructed and operated jointly by Harvard University and MIT, and supported by the AEC as a research facility from 1962 to 1974, the CEA was used in pioneering research in the physics of high-energy interactions of electrons and photons. M. Stanley Livingston was its Director from 1962 to 1967, Karl Strauch from 1967 to 1974. With the growth of SLAC, particularly the construction of SPEAR in 1971, it became dispensable, and was shut down in 1974.

Central Design Group. The CDG, based at LBNL and managed by URA, was formed in the summer of 1984 as a prelude to the SSC, before site selection. The group was comprised of scientists, engineers, and administrators, and was directed by Maury Tigner, a Cornell University professor. At its peak, about 250 scientists and engineers participated. Completing a full conceptual design for the project, including magnet selection and a site-independent cost estimate, the CDG's end product was a Conceptual Design Report, published in 1986.

CERN. The European Organization for Nuclear Research was founded in 1954 as a joint venture of 12 Western European countries – later expanding to 20 countries. Located on the border between France and Switzerland outside Geneva, it is a unique model of international collaboration.

Collider. An apparatus containing two charged-particle beams configured so that they can collide at various places in their orbits. A proton collider is circular and an electron collider can be circular or linear. When one of the two beams is made up of particles and the other of the corresponding antiparticles, only one circular ring of magnets is needed to make up the collider; but if the two beams are both composed of particles (protons or electrons or heavy ions), then two rings are required to carry the beams in opposite directions.

Colliding Beam Accelerator. CBA was the name given to BNL's ISABELLE Project when Samios took over as lab Director after the disheartening and close-to-ruinous Temple Review in 1981. But the minor changes made were too little, too late. New name or old, the project was cancelled in 1983.

Colliding Beams. Beams contained within colliders are designed, at specific locations in their orbits, to smash into each other, liberating new particles. Large particle detectors surround the collision regions for the purpose of elementary particle research, i.e. identifying, analyzing, and studying the particles generated.

Conceptual Design Report. This generic expression for a facility design refers to two SSC-related reports: the site-independent CDG 1986 final report, and the site-specific CDR of the SSC laboratory completed in July 1990.

Continuous Beam. A beam of particles continuous in character, like a thick string.

Continuous Electron Beam Accelerator Facility. Recently CEBAF was renamed the Thomas Jefferson National Accelerator Facility.

Conversion Project. This mid-sixties project was an intensity upgrade of BNL's AGS that increased the number of protons per second going to fixed-target experiments by more than an order of magnitude – mainly by building a Linear Accelerator injector with twice the energy of the original one, going from 200 to 400 MeV. It was technically a success, but by choosing that option, the BNL top management prevented the lab from timely entering the new world of big accelerators and rapidly advancing technology.

Cornell Electron-positron Storage Ring. CESR is a circular electron-positron collider with a circumference of 768 meters, located 12 meters below ground level on the Cornell University campus. It can store circulating beams of particle energy 4.5 to 6 GeV per beam, thus generating head-on collisions with center-of-mass energies between 9 and 12 GeV. The products of these collisions are studied with a large and complex detector apparatus, called CLEO. Each of the two beams, moving in opposite directions, has 18 short bunches in a train. Electrostatic separators prevent the electron and positron bunches from colliding at any location other than the CLEO detector. With its high-rate production of B-mesons, the CESR-CLEO facility was the first designed to be a B-Factory.

Cornell High Energy Synchrotron Source. CHESS is a user-oriented national facility providing state-of-the-art synchrotron radiation for scientific study. It attracts a wide spectrum of experimental groups from universities, national labs, and industry, serving 400 to 500 scientists each year. It uses the high intensity photon flux flowing from the CESR ring, making the CESR facility a light source. CHESS was built in 1978-1980 as an x-ray facility parasitic to the CESR high-energy physics program.

Cornell University Lab for Nuclear Studies. CLNS is a Cornell University lab conducting research in accelerator physics at CESR, high-energy physics at CLEO, and synchrotron radiation at CHESS. The lab is supported by the National Science Foundation, and was recently renamed the Laboratory for Elementary Particle Physics.

Cosmotron. This machine was a circular weak-focusing proton synchrotron, about 75 yards in circumference, built at BNL prior to the invention of the AG Principle. It reached its full 3-GeV design energy in 1953. Parity violation was discovered there, for which T.D. Lee and C. N. Yang received the 1958 Nobel Prize for Physics. It was shut down in 1967.

Cyclotron. An apparatus for accelerating, in an electric field, charged atomic particles revolving in a magnetic field. The principle on which such machines are based limits their energies to the MeV range. Among other applications, cyclotrons are used in the radiation treatment of cancer.

Department of Energy. A cabinet level department of the U.S. government headed by the Secretary of Energy. Established by President Carter in 1977 to unify U.S. energy programs, the DOE assumed the responsibilities of the Federal Energy Administration, the Energy Research and Development Administration, the Federal Power Commission, and parts and programs of several other agencies.

Desertron. A proposal was made by Bob Wilson at Snowmass '82 to build a multi-TeV collider in the U.S. desert southwest. His idea was to use small, conventional magnets placed in shallow trenches in land far from where people lived. It would be run by remote control, so that the people in charge would not have to come near it while it was running. This machine, called the Desertron, was to be enormous in size but extremely low in cost. The high-energy community was intrigued by the idea, but rejected the details, choosing to utilize superconducting technology and go with the higher cost, conventionally designed SSC.

Deutsches Elektronen-Synchrotron. In 1959, by state treaty, the DESY foundation was established in Hamburg, Germany, to create the DESY lab, which today is one of the world's leading centers for accelerator-based research. With the mission to perform basic research in the natural sciences, its emphasis is on the development, construction, and operation of accelerators; particle physics research through the investigation of the fundamental properties of matter; and using synchrotron radiation for studies in the fields of physics, material sciences, chemistry, molecular biology, geophysics, and medicine. Its staff numbers about 1400. The lab has built a series of accelerators: the DESY electron synchrotron in 1964, the few-GeV electron-positron collider DORIS in 1974, the 15-Gev electron-positron collider PETRA in 1978, and the science world's first and only electron-proton collider HERA (6.3 kilometers long) in 1990. Experiments are done by 300 DESY scientists and several hundred other scientists working together in international groups.

Division of High Energy Physics. DHEP is a division of DOE's OER. Its mission is to fund the study of energy and matter at a fundamental level by investigating the elementary particles and the forces between them. It provides 90% of the federal funding for the country's HEP program, the remainder coming from the National Science Foundation.

Electron. An elementary particle that is stable except in collisions at high speeds with other elementary particles. Its mass is about 1/2000 that of a proton.

Electron Accelerator. A device that accelerates electron beams to higher energy, it can be circular or linear. Low energy electron linacs are built in massive quantities all over the world for use, among other things, in materials technology and the medical radiation treatment of cancer.

Electron Collider. An apparatus where two beams moving in opposite directions are made to collide. Usually one is an electron beam, the other a positron beam. Until recently the colliders were all circular, but, because of power limitations as the beam energy increases, future high-energy electron colliders will have to be linear colliders, where two head-to-head linacs shoot electrons or positrons at each other.

Electron Positron Collider. See Electron Collider.

Electron Proton Collider. A collider that has a ring storing protons of a particular energy and a separate ring storing electrons of an independently determined energy. The beams move in opposite directions, and, at one or more points along their orbits, magnets direct the beams toward the point of collision. The first high-energy electron-proton collider, HERA, was built more than a decade ago at DESY.

Elementary Particle. A subatomic particle, either non-decomposable or decomposable, produced from naturally occurring radioactive matter or as a byproduct of the high-speed collision of a beam with matter or with another beam.

Elementary Particle Experiments. Scientific experiments to explore the nature of the physical universe by measuring the properties and characteristics of elementary particles through particle collisions, generally by colliding beams from accelerators into dense fixed targets of matter or by using colliders. Naturally occurring cosmic rays are also sometimes used.

Energy Research. The Office of Energy Research (ER or OER) is the section in the DOE that supports basic research in the physical sciences, and also contributes to other fields, including computing, mathematics, and life sciences. OER also supports research in developing new energy sources, optimizing current energy resources, and cleaning up the waste resulting from energy production and use. Recently, OER has been renamed the Office of Science.

Energy Research and Development Administration. A U.S. government agency for the purpose of managing its programs for nuclear weapons, naval reactors, and energy development. Formed in 1975, it incorporated the AEC. It was incorporated into the DOE in 1977.

Environment, Safety, and Health. To ensure the safety and health of workers and the environment, the ES&H Division of DOE's OER formulates and issues guidelines and makes certain that they are followed. The guidelines concern radiation release, waste disposal, accident avoidance, and safely deploying the complex technologies used in OER's labs.

Environmental Impact Statement. An EIS is required by every project seeking U.S. government funding. The statement must include the environmental impact of the project: possible adverse effects and how to resolve them, and a comparison of the public's loss due to impacts on the environment with the public's gain from the project. Any irreversible loss must be declared, as well as less harmful alternatives given. The EIS process stems from the National Environmental Policy Act of 1969 (NEPA), congressional legislation that established a national policy for the environment.

Fermilab. Short for Fermi National Accelerator Laboratory.

Fermi National Accelerator Laboratory. Founded in 1967 and situated in Batavia, Illinois, west of Chicago, Fermilab is a national laboratory managed by Universities Associated, Inc. The first beam of 200-GeV protons passed through the lab's chain of accelerators in 1972.

Fixed Target. When beam is extracted from an accelerator at the energy required by a particular experiment, the beam is first smashed into a mass of stationary dense material, referred to as a fixed target. The high density optimizes the output of secondary particles. After the "secondaries" are produced, the needed type are separated out, focused into a beam, and transported for use in that experiment.

Galvin Commission. In 1994-1995, the Secretary of the DOE formed a task force, headed by Robert W. Galvin, to study alternative futures for the Department's laboratories. The Galvin Commission proposed a new modus operandi of Federal support for the labs, based on a private-style – *corporatized* – laboratory system. The recommendation was rejected.

Government Accounting Office. The GAO is an investigative arm of the U.S. Congress. It is the government's accountability watchdog over every federal program, activity, and function, evaluating programs, auditing expenditures, reporting its findings to the Congress, and offering recommendations. The GAO was a key player in assessing the poor performance of the SSC, determining that the project's management was fiscally irresponsible. Its final report was a major factor in cutting short the SSC's life.

Government Detailee. An individual, usually a scientist from a national laboratory, invited to spend a couple of years in a government agency. The purpose of this program is to cultivate an understanding in the science community of the role of the government's science administration.

Grumman Corporation. Grumman began in 1930 as a manufacturer of airplanes, and was a major defense contractor for the U.S. government, but later it moved into civilian technologies, including superconducting magnets. In 1977, Grumman contracted to produce a portion of ISABELLE's magnets. The first six magnets the company made were scrapped. With flawed magnets and an impractical design, ISABELLE too was a failure. In 1987, when RHIC construction began, Grumman again contracted to make some of the magnets. But this time the magnets were feasible, and the first working one was delivered to BNL in 1994. By 1996 the remaining hundred or so were tested at BNL and ready to be installed in the RHIC tunnel. When the Northrop Corporation acquired Grumman in 1994, it chose, after fulfilling its contract with BNL, to phase out its superconducting magnet effort, looking to Information Technology and related areas as the vision for the company's non-defense future.

Hadron. An elementary particle in the class that includes the proton, neutron, antiproton, and certain other short-lived particles. The electron and the muon are part of another class, that of leptons.

Hadron Electron Ring Accelerator. In the seventies, DESY scientists, looking to build a facility to explore uncharted territory settled on the idea of a *super electron microscope*. The outcome was HERA, the world's first storage ring facility to collide radically different types of particles – 30-GeV electrons and 900-GeV protons in a 6.3-kilometer tunnel 10 to 25 meters under the city of Hamburg. Construction began in 1984, with startup in 1990. Eleven countries participated in building the project. The mode of international cooperation used proved so effective that it now serves as a role model for the financing of large, international research projects – the so-called *HERA Model*.

Hanford Laboratories. The Hanford Site had two parts. The major part produced nuclear devices and material. The other part did nuclear-related R&D and was named the Hanford Laboratories. When the AEC decided to split off the R&D from the defense mission in 1964, Battelle submitted a proposal to run the Hanford Laboratories. Battelle was awarded the contract and assumed management in 1965. Under Battelle, the Hanford Laboratories became the Pacific Northwest National Laboratory, independent from Hanford Site operations.

Hanford Site. The Hanford Site is an approximately 560-square-mile tract of semi-arid land in southeastern Washington State. It was chosen by the U.S. Army Corps of Engineers in 1943 as the location for nuclear reactor and chemical processing facilities for the production, separation, and purification of plutonium for the Manhattan Project. After the war, plutonium production continued, but cutbacks were started in 1964, when serious pollution was uncovered. As a result, all the major facilities were shut down by 1989. In the late eighties, the focus at Hanford switched to environmental cleanup and restoration of the site, and in 1994 the DOE selected Bechtel Hanford Inc. as the Hanford Site Environmental Restoration Contractor.

Heavy Ion Accelerator. A Heavy Ion Accelerator is a machine – such as the Bevatron, the AGS, or the SPS – that accelerates a variety of ion beams, which are then extracted and smashed into fixed targets for experimental study. See also Heavy Ion Collisions.

Heavy Ion Collisions. Proton-proton colliders, with a straightforward upgrade – usually, vacuum improvements in the accelerator chain and the addition of a heavy ion source – can readily be made to accelerate and store heavy ions. RHIC is such a Heavy Ion Collider, with the capability of accelerating and storing gold ions, and thereby producing gold-on-gold heavy ion collisions.

HEPAP Sub-panel. A group formed by HEPAP to report on a specific matter such as project priorities, funding levels, and long-range planning for high-energy physics.

HEPAP Sub-panel – 1977. A HEPAP sub-panel was convened in the summer of 1977 at Woods Hole, Massachusetts, to assess competing proposals from BNL and Fermilab for a collider in the hundreds of GeV energy range, and to recommend the course of the country's high-energy program. The competition between the two labs was acrimonious; but Vineyard, through his political connections, got Congress to approve and fund BNL's proposal (ISABELLE) even as the meeting was in session. The sub-panel had no choice but to go along.

HEPAP Sub-panel – 1983. A HEPAP sub-panel met in June 1983 in Washington, DC, and later at Columbia's Nevis Laboratory, to decide the fate of ISABELLE. In Washington, the vote was a tie, but at Nevis, ISABELLE was given *thumbs-down* and the SSC given the green light.

High Energy Physics Advisory Panel. HEPAP is an advisory body to the DOE's Director of OER and the Assistant Director of NSF's Mathematical & Physical Sciences Directorate. Through periodic reviews of the national high-energy physics program and reports of its sub-panels – formed to analyze specific matters, such as strategies for long-range planning and current scientific priorities – HEPAP provides recommendations on funding levels and changes in programs to secure the U.S. a world leadership position and maintain it. Particularly, it proposes new projects and facility upgrades, and assesses the value of current facilities. The Chairman is appointed by the Secretary of Energy and the Director of the NSF.

International Committee for Future Accelerators. ICFA was created in 1976 by the International Union of Pure and Applied Physics (IUPAP) to facilitate international collaboration in the construction and use of accelerators for high-energy physics. Its purposes are to promote international collaboration in the construction and utilization of very high-energy accelerators; to organize world-inclusive meetings to publicize future plans for regional facilities and to plan for joint participation and use; and to organize workshops to study super high-energy accelerator complexes, foster R&D, and encourage new technologies. ICFA was formed because the growing energy, size, and cost of accelerators implied an eventual facility so large that only one could be built in the world. In 1979 it originally conceived an SSC-like facility as just such a project, but international collaboration broke down and the SSC was later pursued as an American project.

Intersecting Storage Accelerators. ISA was the original name of ISABELLE.

Intersecting Storage Rings. The CERN ISR was the first proton-proton collider. It used two counter-rotating high current continuous beams. It started operation in 1971, and was shut down in 1984.

ISABELLE. This ill-fated BNL proton-proton collider was started in 1978 and cancelled by the DOE in 1983 because it became obsolete before it could be completed.

KEK. See National Laboratory for High Energy Physics of Japan.

Large Electron-Positron Collider. LEP was a circular electron-positron collider at CERN. With a circumference of 27 kilometers, it was probably the largest that will ever be built. A further increase in energy would require an unreasonable increase in circumference because energy loss from synchrotron radiation increases sharply as the ring radius decreases. That is, without sufficient circumference enlargement, power requirements become prohibitive. This is the reasoning behind the shift in thinking from circular to linear electron-positron colliders. Originally conceived as an approximately 100 GeV per beam collider, LEP began at 50 GeV and was later upgraded to 90 GeV. Construction was begun in 1983 and experiments started in 1989. LEP was switched off in 2000 and dismantled to make room for the LHC.

Large Hadron Collider. The LHC, being built at CERN, is a proton-proton collider using highly advanced superconducting magnets, each designed to contain two parallel vacuum chambers along its length, one above the other, carrying beams moving in opposite directions. It will occupy the 27-kilometer LEP tunnel, colliding beams with energies around 7 TeV per beam. When operational, it will provide collisions of unsurpassed brightness. It will also be able to collide heavy-ion beams at energies thirty times that of RHIC. Experiments are planned to start by 2006.

Lawrence Berkeley National Laboratory. LBNL was started in 1931 by Ernest O. Lawrence for building cyclotrons, and was named the Radiation Laboratory or Berkeley Radlab in 1936. Initially privately funded, after World War II it became the foundation for a national laboratory managed for the government by the University of California.

Light Source. There are two types. A storage ring naturally curves beams of charged particles with bending magnets. When electron beams of various energies are bent, they radiate light –i.e. electromagnetic radiation – of varying frequency, which can be focused and used for experimentation. Another type of light source uses special magnets called wigglers and undulators that wave the particles "up and down" or "left to right." This causes radiation at frequencies determined by the nature of the motion induced by the magnet. In this way, linear accelerators can be used as light sources by attaching such devices to them. The frequencies used in light sources range through the ultraviolet and x-ray regions of the light spectrum.

Linac. Short for Linear Accelerator.

Linear Accelerator. An accelerator that uses radio-frequency electromagnetic fields (configured in rf-cavities) to accelerate particles along a straight path.

Linear Collider. A collider fashioned by having electrons or positrons in two separate linear accelerators, facing each other with the beams going in opposite directions. After exiting their respective machines, the two beams are made to smash into each other head-on, producing the particle collisions for experimentation.

Los Alamos National Laboratory. LANL, a DOE lab located in New Mexico but managed by the University of California, is one of the largest multidisciplinary institutions in the world. During the Manhattan Project, the first atomic bomb was made there, and when the "Cold War" was on, it was a weapons research lab. Today, it has a major role in managing the country's stockpile of nuclear weapons and in studying ways to reduce the threat of terrorism. LANL also does basic scientific research at its Neutron Science Center with neutron and meson beams from a high-power 800-MeV proton linac, and with a proton storage ring.

Mega-science. In the area of accelerator-based science, mega-science is a term – not widely used – that envisions grandiose laboratories on a world scale, with scientific facilities of enormous size and cost.

Magnet. A device producing a magnetic field in an enclosed evacuated space by using flowing electric currents in surrounding coils. Dipole magnets bend charged particle beams, and quadrupole magnets focus and concentrate them, allowing them to travel long distances without being enlarged. There are also low-field "permanent magnets" made out of naturally occurring magnetic material and not using electric currents.

Main Injector. The MI is a proton synchrotron, 2 miles in circumference, that began operation in 1999 as the approximately 150-GeV injector to Fermilab's Tevatron.

Ultimately, it is expected to result in a tenfold increase in the number of high-energy proton-antiproton collisions for Tevatron collider experiments.

Main Ring. The MR, built at Fermilab in 1972, was a 200-GeV accelerator with a circumference of about 4 miles. Eventually reaching 400 GeV, and stretching up to 500 GeV, the MR had the highest energy of its time. Leon Lederman's team of experimenters discovered the "bottom quark" there in 1977. After serving as the injector for the Tevatron for almost two decades, the MR was removed from the tunnel in 1998, when the Main Injector (MI) took over as the Tevatron's injector.

Manhattan Project. A secret U.S. project to build an atomic bomb before the Nazis did was initiated by President Roosevelt in 1941. Led by physicist J. Robert Oppenheimer and General Leslie Groves, it was a brilliant success. The Manhattan Project closed with the dropping of two atomic bombs on Japan and the end of World War II.

National Academy of Sciences. The NAS is a private, non-profit society of distinguished scientists and engineers, dedicated to the furtherance of science and technology and their use for the general welfare. Granted a charter by Congress in 1863, the Academy is required to advise the federal government on scientific and technical matters. Members and foreign associates of the Academy are elected in recognition of distinguished achievements in original research, and election is a high honor. The Academy has about 1900 members and 300 foreign associates, of whom more than 170 have won Nobel Prizes. It is governed by a Council comprised of twelve councilors and five officers, elected by the membership.

National Bureau of Standards. See National Institute of Standards and Technology.

National Institute of Standards and Technology. NIST, formerly the National Bureau of Standards founded in 1901, is a non-regulatory federal agency in the U.S. Commerce Department's Technology Administration. Its purposes are to develop measurement standards in manufacturing, to promote innovative technologies for broad national benefit, and to conduct research to advance the nation's technology infrastructure. From automated teller machines and atomic clocks to mammograms and semiconductors, innumerable products and services rely in some way on the technology effort and the measurements done by NIST. The institute has two locations: a 578-acre campus in Gaithersburg, Maryland, and a 208-acre campus in Boulder, Colorado. It employs about 3000 people, complemented by about 1600 guest researchers.

National Laboratory. In response to the 1945 Vannevar Bush Report, the U.S. government created the national laboratory system, a series of federal-government-supported Science and Technology labs for basic research and defense, located across the country. In the current era of Big Science and Big Weaponry, national labs for basic and applied research have become indispensable to the national welfare.

National Laboratory for High Energy Physics of Japan. Known as KEK, the Japanese National Laboratory for High Energy Physics was established in 1971 as a national center open to users from universities and other institutions around the world. KEK, located near Tokyo, was the first of thirteen "Inter-University Research Institutes" operated under Japan's Ministry of Education, Science, and Culture. A 12-GeV proton synchrotron was its first major facility in 1976, followed by a 30-GeV electron-positron colliding-beam accelerator, TRISTAN, in 1986. In the nineties, KEK was restructured, and its name was changed to the High Energy Accelerator Research Organization. TRISTAN ceased operation in 1995; highly sophisticated accelerator R&D was initiated, such as work toward an electron-positron Linear Collider; an x-ray light source - KEK's Photon Factory - and a B-Factory were put into operation; and in 2001 construction began on 3-GeV and 50-GeV synchrotrons to produce MW-power proton beams, with completion scheduled for 2007. KEK's staff numbers more than 600, and there are more than 100 foreign long-term visiting scientists. Hirotaka Sugawara, the Director-General and architect of the reorganization, sees KEK as a prototypical international laboratory on accelerator science and related fields, envisioning it as a model for the 21st century.

National Science Foundation. In 1950, Congress established the NSF to promote science; to advance the national health, prosperity, and welfare; to secure the national defense; and for other purposes.

National Synchrotron Light Source. The BNL NSLS is a facility for generating light in both the ultraviolet and x-ray parts of the spectrum. It is comprised of two separate sources. The vacuum ultraviolet (VUV) source, with its 0.8-GeV electron beam, began operations in late 1982, and the x-ray ring, with a 2.5 GeV electron beam circulating, was commissioned in 1984.

Nobel Prize. The first and most prestigious international award for excellence in areas of human endeavor, including physics, was founded by Alfred Nobel in 1901.

Nuclear Energy. The energy released from the interaction of the nuclei of certain elements such as uranium or plutonium. Depending on how it's executed, large-scale release in a chain reaction can lead to an atomic bomb or to nuclear power for electricity generation.

Nuclear Reactor. See Reactor.

Oak Ridge National Laboratory. Established in 1943 as the Clinton Laboratories, with the single mission of separating plutonium for the Manhattan Project, ORNL has evolved into a multi-purpose DOE lab conducting basic and applied R&D, with work ranging from S&T to pollution control to national security. It is managed by UT-Battelle, a limited liability partnership between the University of Tennessee and the Battelle Trust.

Office of Management and Budget. The OMB is a federal agency that assists the President in developing and executing his policy and programs. The OMB coordinates funding requests, and integrates them into a budget consistent with the legislation passed by Congress and signed by the President. Among its many duties the OMB evaluates lab projects, sets their priority in the federal budget, and makes recommendations about them to the President.

Office of Science. See Office of Energy Research.

Pacific Northwest National Laboratory. See Hanford Laboratories.

Particle Physics. The branch of physics that deals with the properties, relationships, and interactions of subatomic particles, e.g. protons and electrons.

Pbar. See Antiproton.

PEP Storage Ring. The Positron Electron Project (PEP) is an electron-positron storage ring facility at SLAC that can produce beam collisions with energies of about 30 GeV. Its construction was a collaborative effort of SLAC and LBNL, and the collider began operation in 1980. The experimental observation that the B-meson had a much longer lifetime than anticipated led SLAC to upgrade the PEP facility, PEP-II, designed to maximize the production of B-mesons. This B-Factory was built as a collaboration of SLAC, LBNL, and the Lawrence Livermore National Laboratory, and began operation in 1998.

Physichist. A pejorative term used (mainly in the seventies and eighties) by some accelerator physicists and engineers to describe an experimental user of accelerators who gratuitously considers himself to be a superior scientist.

Presidential Initiative. A process in which a major U.S. project is approved and directly funded by the Office of the President. Since funds to build the project are not specifically identified as such in any current science budget, these funds are properly referred to as "new money."

Proton. An elementary particle of about 1-GeV mass, stable except in high-speed collisions with other elementary particles.

Proton-Antiproton Project. The PA was a CERN project to generate antiprotons and to modify the 2.2-km-diameter SPS to produce proton-antiproton interactions at a collision energy of about 540 GeV. The two beams were injected into the SPS at 26 GeV and then accelerated to 270 GeV. The first proton-antiproton collision was observed in 1981. The W was discovered in January and the Z in May 1983.

Proton-Antiproton Collider. See Proton Collider.

Proton Collider. An apparatus in which two hadron (proton or antiproton) beams circulating in opposite directions are made to collide with each other. A single-ring collider allows proton-antiproton collisions. A two-ring collider allows proton-proton collisions as well.

Proton Synchrotron. An accelerator that uses sequential magnets to form a tube-like structure within a narrow circular tunnel, in contrast to a Cyclotron, where a single magnet encompasses the entire accelerating area, which is therefore bulky with iron and huge. The CERN accelerator using alternating-gradient magnets in the synchrotron mode (first beam November 1959) was called the PS.

Quark. Protons and neutrons, stable hadrons, are each made up of three quarks. Contrary to previous thought, quarks are the elemental constituents of matter. Since they have the strange property of being confined in hadrons, they can't be observed experimentally, only inferred. Quarks are trapped because the force between them gets stronger the more they try to pull away. In the veritable zoo of elementary particles, the stable protons and neutrons as well as the many with short lives, nanoseconds or less, are all formed from six elementary quarks. Ferreting out the evidence for this is a major achievement of high-energy physics.

Radlab or Berkeley Lab. Early names for Lawrence Berkeley National Laboratory.

Relativistic Heavy Ion Collider. RHIC is a BNL collider for heavy ions, such as gold. It was built in the tunnel meant for ISABELLE and used some of the old project's ancillary equipment. Construction began in 1991 and operation in 2000.

Ramsey Panel. In 1963, President John Kennedy commissioned a panel of science and technology experts, headed by Harvard professor Norman Ramsey, to recommend future research directions for particle physics and the technologies needed.

Reactor or Nuclear Reactor. An apparatus for producing energy by "splitting atoms" (more precisely, splitting atomic nuclei) through nuclear interactions that release excess energy (nuclear fission). Conditions are created that cause a chain reaction allowing large energy release, which can be used for particle experimentation or electric power generation.

Reactor, BNL Graphite Research Reactor. The BGRR, the first U.S. peacetime scientific research reactor, was built in 1950, and operated at 20 megawatts of power in 1958.

Reactor, BNL High Flux Beam Reactor. The HFBR was completed in 1965, and generated 30 to 60 megawatts of power for experimental use between 1965 and 1996.

Shoreham Nuclear Power Plant. In the mid-sixties, a high time for nuclear power, the Long Island Lighting Company (LILCO) began building its nuclear power plant in Shoreham, but anti-nuclear activists, filing endless protests based largely on a proclaimed impossibility of evacuating Long Island in an emergency, drove the cost to over $5 billion and delayed its completion. In the eighties, the plant won its operating license and passed its safety and power testing, but was never put into operation. In 1988, in the throes of severe anti-nuclear pressure, it was closed. The financial loss was borne by the investors, the customers, and federal taxpayers.

Snowmass '82. A three-week workshop was held under the auspices of the American Physical Society in Snowmass, Colorado, in the summer of 1982 for high-energy scientists to determine their future course. A proposal was made there for a very large collider, the Desertron, later transmuted into the SSC.

SLAC Large Detector. The SLD is a modern high-energy particle physics detector at SLAC, running at the SLC. It began operation in 1992. Using a polarized electron beam has allowed it to collect especially sensitive data on the Z boson.

SLAC Linear Collider. The SLC is a novel electron-positron machine built to serve as a test for upcoming linear colliders and as a facility capable of reaching the energy region where the Z particle could be produced and studied in detail. It began construction in 1983, and was completed in 1989. It began generating highly polarized electron beams in 1993.

Spallation Neutron Source. The SNS is an accelerator designed to accelerate high-power proton beams, extract them, and bombard them into a target to produce neutron beams for experiments. It is an alternative to a reactor as a neutron source. ORNL is currently building this powerful accelerator-based source for neutron scattering R&D, with its completion date scheduled for 2006.

SPEAR Storage Ring. The Stanford Positron Electron Accelerator Ring at SLAC uses counter-rotating beams circulating at energies up to 4 GeV. Completed in 1972, SPEAR became dedicated to synchrotron research in 1990. Its two great discoveries were the psi particle in 1974, which set off the "November revolution" and for which Burton Richter and Sam Ting (for a simultaneous experiment at BNL) were awarded the 1976 Nobel Prize in Physics, and the tau lepton in 1976, which validated the triumvirate of leptons necessary for the current theory of elementary particles, the three leptons being the electron, the muon, and, finally, the tau. Today, SPEAR produces intense beams of synchrotron radiation in the ultraviolet and x-ray frequency range for basic and applied research in science, medicine, and other fields.

Sputnik. On October 4, 1957, the Russians launched the world's first satellite from the Baikonur cosmodrome in Kazakhstan, spurring America to scientific endeavors unmatched in history.

Stanford Linear Accelerator Center. SLAC is a DOE national laboratory established in 1962 and managed by Stanford University. Built to design, construct, and operate state-of-the-art electron accelerators and related experimental facilities for use in high-energy physics, particle astrophysics, and synchrotron radiation research, its mandate also includes R&D on new technologies and new sources for both high-energy particle beams and synchrotron radiation. It is the preeminent U.S. national laboratory for research using high-energy electron beams.

Stochastic Cooling. This electronic means of beam cooling uses wide-band amplifiers to "detect" small portions of a beam, and then quickly "kicks" them with kicker magnets to pre-set positions that make the beam denser. The method was originated by Van der Meer in 1968, and was used in the CERN Antiproton Accumulator, constructed in 1981-82. Because antiproton beams are very dilute when produced, they must be cooled before they can be used in experiments. Beams cooled in this way were used for the

CERN proton-antiproton collider experiments, and led to the observation of the W and Z bosons that resulted in the Nobel Prize for Rubbia and Van der Meer in 1984.

Storage Ring. A circular apparatus similar to an accelerator used to store particle beams for periods up to many hours.

Strategic Defense Initiative. The SDI, or *Star Wars*, is a government program of R&D for a space-based system to defend the U.S. from attack by strategic ballistic missiles, originated by President Ronald Reagan in 1983, with the advice and encouragement of Edward Teller, the "father" of the H-bomb.

Strong Focusing. A method of configuring magnets in a synchrotron that uses the alternating-gradient or strong-focusing principle. See Alternating Gradient Principle.

Supercollider. An extremely large proton collider using superconducting magnets. See SSC, LHC, and Proton Collider.

Superconducting Accelerator. An accelerator using superconducting magnets. To attain high-energy particles, the accelerator has to be a large synchrotron.

Superconducting Magnet. A magnet cooled with superconducting technology to permit the attainment of very high magnetic fields. This is because the heat produced in standard magnets made with copper coils is eliminated when the current in the specially designed coils is brought close to absolute zero temperature. With higher current in the coils, a higher magnetic field results.

Superconducting Super Collider. The idea of an American multi-TeV proton collider project originated at the Snowmass '82 conference. After the decision to build the SSC was made in January 1987, construction began, but, before completion, cost overruns and excessive delays caused the project to be canceled in 1993.

Superconducting Technology. ST refers to methods of cooling devices with super-cooled liquid helium; and when magnets and radio-frequency systems in accelerators are cooled down close to absolute zero (– 458 degrees F) their performance is enhanced.

Super Proton Synchrotron. The SPS is a proton synchrotron at CERN with a maximum energy of 400 GeV, started up in 1976. In 1979 CERN began the conversion of the SPS into the world's first proton-antiproton collider using Van der Meer's stochastic beam cooling system. The W boson was discovered in the converted SPS in 1983.

Synchrotron. A particle accelerator where the magnetic field, which restrains the particles in the beam to move in a circular path, and the radio-frequency system, which determines the speed of the particles in the beam, increase synchronously.

Temple Review. The Construction Management Support Division (CMSD) of the DOE's Office of Energy Research was formed in 1979 to provide OER with independent information and advice on the major research projects being constructed and operated at OER's national laboratories. The CMSD conducts technical, cost, schedule, and management reviews of OER construction projects and makes recommendations to the OER Director. In late 1981, Edward Temple took over as CMSD Director. In his ten years at the job, he developed an OER Project Management System that continues as a model today. A taskmaster, he was demanding of the project staff and determined to drag every detail out of them. He was persistent to the point of badgering to get at the truth. The term "Temple Review" was coined to reflect this tough style of reviewing.

Tevatron. This strong-focusing 4-mile-circumference synchrotron at Fermilab, made with 1000 superconducting magnets, with the capability of accelerating protons to about 1000 GeV (1 TeV) energy, was completed in 1983. In 1986 it was upgraded to a collider, storing counter-rotating beams of protons and antiprotons simultaneously. The top quark, partner of the bottom quark, was discovered there in 1995.

Texas National Research Laboratory Commission. The TNRLC was formed in 1987 to oversee Texas interests in the SSC. In 1990 it created a program to distribute to universities throughout the U.S. approximately $100 million in support of SSC-related R&D. The release of funds was based on extensive peer review. After the SSC was canceled, the money left over was distributed to worthy scientific and educational endeavors, following which the TNRLC was dissolved.

Thomas Jefferson National Accelerator Facility. TJNAF, or Jefferson Lab or JLab, was formerly the Continuous Electron Beam Accelerator Facility or CEBAF. It is a national laboratory for basic research in Newport News, Virginia, managed by a consortium of 59 universities, the Southeastern Universities Research Association (SURA). In 1987, construction of CEBAF's 4-GeV electron accelerator got underway. Superconducting radio-frequency technology was adopted for the electron accelerating system in the hope of a future upgrade to 12 GeV. In 1995, fixed-target experiments were started and the design electron beam energy was reached. In 1996, the lab decided to diversify and changed its name from CEBAF to Jefferson Lab. A Free-Electron Laser reaching 1.72 kilowatts power was built in 1999, and in 2001 construction began for a 10-kilowatt FEL. The lab's Founding Director, Hermann Grunder, left to become ANL Director in 2002.

Three-Lab Concept. An idea in the seventies, probably Bill Wallenmeyer's, that BNL, Fermilab, and SLAC would take turns in building accelerator facilities, to assure the thriving of all three. The policy was in trouble from the start, and, along with ISABELLE's grim expiration, was dead in the water by the eighties.

Three Mile Island. The Three Mile Island nuclear power reactor, in Harrisburg, Pennsylvania, was put into operation in September 1978. On March 28, 1979, equipment failure and human error caused a partial meltdown, the worst nuclear accident in U.S. history. A class action suit, instituted against Metropolitan Edison Company on behalf of all businesses and residents within 25 miles of the plant, lasted over 15 years. But the plaintiffs lacked adequate proof linking their claims with the "accident," and the case was dismissed in June 1996.

Tritium Affair. It all started in the early eighties, with a slow, small leak in the BNL HFBR that was left unattended. In 1997, when the public found this out, all hell broke loose. In the end, the affair had a drastic impact on the national lab system, significantly reducing science output.

Universities Research Association. A management organization formed in 1965 by the AEC and the NAS to build and operate the planned Fermilab.

U.S. Particle Accelerator School. USPAS conducts educational programs in the field of beams and their associated technologies. It presents university-level courses that universities cannot offer because accelerator research is mostly done at national labs, not universities, and the teachers therefore have to come from the labs. The courses are complemented by advanced technology textbooks, which USPAS encourages its teachers to write. The USPAS central Office at Fermilab administers the courses, which are hosted by various universities. The curriculum covers accelerator science and technology via dawn-to-dusk two-week courses equivalent to ten-week semester courses at universities. Between 1987 and 2002, the 27 programs at more than 20 universities have included about 300 courses. More than 2000 students have attended, most of them earning three semester hours of credit. A Master's Program using USPAS courses has been established with Indiana University. USPAS is governed by a consortium of eleven national labs, which provide much of the funding, the rest coming from the DOE.

Van de Graaff Electrostatic Accelerator. A machine generating electrostatic charge and then accelerating the charged particles – protons or electrons – to higher energy by having the particles drawn from a low voltage plate to one of high voltage. If the higher-energy particles are passed through a small opening, they form a beam. A Van de Graaff machine is usually the first accelerator in the chain required to attain today's high energies.

W and Z Bosons. These short-lived elementary particles, called intermediate vector bosons, form a triplet: a positive and a negative W and the neutral Z. The mass of each W is about 80 times the proton mass (almost 1 GeV) while the Z mass is about 90 times the proton mass. These bosons govern the weak interactions, such as the natural radioactive decay of cobalt-60. If the mass-less photon, which mediates the electromagnetic interactions, as in electricity, magnetism, radio waves, etc., is added to this trio of bosons, the quartet can be shown to govern a unified weak-electromagnetic interaction. Thus, two seemingly widely different phenomena – nuclear decay and electromagnetism – are really two faces of the same unified force. For conceptualizing and describing how this works, Glashow, Weinberg, and Salam were awarded the 1979 Nobel Prize for Physics.

Westinghouse Electric Company. The Westinghouse Electric Company started in 1886, and over the years went through myriad changes - in organization and product base. In 1937 it built the first industrial *atom smasher*. Today, it is a leader in the peaceful uses of nuclear power, with about 50% of the nuclear power plants in operation worldwide and about 60% in the United States based on Westinghouse technology. In the seventies, the company decided to try its hand at superconducting R&D. In 1977 it contracted with BNL to manufacture six superconducting dipoles for ISABELLE. But when they arrived at BNL a few years later, they were tested and failed to reach their engineering specifications. After ISABELLE was canceled, Westinghouse turned to the SSC in the late eighties, making a deal to build some of the big project's superconducting magnets. The first ones were delivered to Texas in May 1993, and were up to *specs*. But when the SSC was snuffed out in October 1993, manufacturing superconducting magnets at Westinghouse came to an end.

Z Particle. See W and Z Bosons.

Acronyms

AA. Antiproton Accumulator, CERN.
AAAS. American Association for the Advancement of Science.
AD. Accelerator Department.
AEC. Atomic Energy Commission.
AG. Alternating Gradient.
AGS. Alternating Gradient Synchrotron.
ALS. Advanced Light Source.
ANL. Argonne National Laboratory.
ANS. Advanced Neutron Source.
APS. American Physical Society.
APS. Advanced Photon Source.
AUI. Associated Universities, Inc.
BGRR. Brookhaven Graphite Research Reactor.
BNL. Brookhaven National Laboratory.
BSA. Brookhaven Science Associates.
CBA. Colliding Beam Accelerator (new name for ISABELLE).
CDG. Central Design Group for SSC.
CDR. Conceptual Design Report for SSC.
CEA. Cambridge Electron Accelerator.
CEBAF. Continuous Electron Beam Accelerator Facility (now TJNAF).
CERN. European Research Center for Nuclear Physics (now Particle Physics).
CESR. Cornell Electron Storage Ring.
CHESS. Cornell High Energy Synchrotron Source.
CLNS. Cornell Laboratory for Nuclear Studies.
CMSD. Construction Management Support Division of OER.
DESY. Deutsches Elektronen-Synchrotron (Hamburg, Germany).
DHEP. Division of High Energy Physics, DOE.
DOE. Department of Energy.
EIS. Environmental Impact Statement.
ER. Office of Energy Research, DOE.
ERDA. Energy Research and Development Administration.
ES&H. Environment, Safety, and Health.
eV. Electron-volt, a measure of energy:
BeV. Same as GeV,
GeV. 1000 MeV,
MeV. 1 Million eV,
TeV. 1000 GeV.
FNAL. Fermi National Accelerator Laboratory (Fermilab).
GAO. Government Accounting Office.
HEP. High Energy Physics.
HEPAP. High Energy Physics Advisory Panel.
HERA. Hadron Electron Ring Accelerator (DESY).
HFBR. High Flux Beam Reactor, BNL.
ICFA. International Committee for Future Accelerators.

ISA. Intersecting Storage Accelerators (later ISABELLE).
ISR. Intersecting Storage Rings, CERN.
KEK. National Laboratory for High Energy Physics of Japan (Tsukuba).
LANL. Los Alamos National Laboratory.
LBL. Lawrence Berkeley Laboratory.
LBNL. Lawrence Berkeley National Laboratory (LBL, Berkeley Lab, Radlab).
LEP. Large Electron-positron Collider.
LEPP. Laboratory for Elementary Particle Physics (new name for CLNS), Cornell.
LHC. Large Hadron Collider.
MI. Main Injector, Fermilab.
MIT. Massachusetts Institute of Technology.
MR. Main Ring, Fermilab.
NAS. National Academy of Sciences.
NBS. National Bureau of Standards (now NIST).
NIST. National Institute of Standards and Technology (formerly NBS).
NSF. National Science Foundation.
NSLS. National Synchrotron Light Source.
OER. See ER.
OMB. Office of Management and Budget.
ORNL. Oak Ridge National Laboratory.
PA. Proton Antiproton Project, CERN.
PD. Physics Department.
PEP. Positron Electron Project, SLAC.
PS. Proton Synchrotron, CERN.
R&D. Research and Development.
RHIC. Relativistic Heavy Ion Collider, BNL.
SDI. Strategic Defense Initiative (Star Wars).
SLAC. Stanford Linear Accelerator Center.
SLC. SLAC Linear Collider.
SLD. SLAC Large Detector.
SNS. Spallation Neutron Source.
SPEAR. Stanford Positron-Electron Accelerator Ring.
SPS. Super Proton Synchrotron.
SR. Synchrotron Radiation.
SSC. Superconducting Super Collider.
TJNAF. Thomas Jefferson National Accelerator Facility (formerly CEBAF).
TNRLC. Texas National Research Laboratory Commission.
URA. Universities Research Association, Inc.
USPAS. U.S. Particle Accelerator School.
UT. University of Tennessee.

Timeline

1942 Manhattan Project underway.
1945 Two atomic bombs dropped on Japan.
1946 Vannevar Bush Report issued.
1947 AUI created.
Upton, Long Island, NY chosen as BNL site.
1948 Haworth named first "true" BNL Director.
1950 BNL Graphite Research Reactor completed.
1952 AG Principle discovered at BNL.
CERN established.
Van de Graaff Electrostatic Accelerator came on-line.
Cosmotron began to operate, exceeding 1 GeV of particle energy.
1957 *Sputnik* launched into space by the Soviet Union.
1960 Collins deposed as Cosmotron Department Head.
Unified Accelerator Department formed at BNL.
AGS commissioned, performance greatly exceeding expectations.
1961 Haworth resigned.
Gerald Tape (Deputy Director) became Interim Director (for 6 months).
Goldhaber named BNL Director.
President Kennedy vows to have an American man on the moon by the end of the decade.
1964 Ramsey Panel Report issued.
1966 Mickey began his accelerator career at BNL.
1967 Batavia, Illinois, selected as site for Fermilab.
1969 Green ousted as BNL Accelerator Department Chairman.
1970 Mills arrived at BNL to take charge of the disillusioned Accelerator Dept.
1972 Fermilab Accelerator Complex completed and running.
Goldhaber resigned after being BNL Director for two terms.
1973 Vineyard replaced Goldhaber as BNL Director.
Vineyard removed Mills and installed Rau as Acting AD Chairman.
Idea conceived at ERDA for three national labs to alternate in the construction of American high-energy accelerator facilities.
1975 Three-Lab Concept implemented: first facility construction to be at SLAC, then BNL, then Fermilab.
1976 ICFA conceived and established at New Orleans meeting.
1977 HEPAP Subpanel to recommend high-energy accelerator construction met at Woods Hole, Massachusetts.
Vineyard's political maneuvering resulted in Congress appropriating $5 million to initiate ISABELLE construction in FY1978.
Rubbia, rebuffed by the U.S., persuaded CERN to build a p-pbar collider by modifying the SPS facility.
CERN welcomed Rubbia.
1978 Wilson *fired* by Deutsch.
Mickey awarded BNL tenure.

1979 After vacillating for about a year, Lederman accepted Fermilab Directorship. Mickey, disheartened at the inadequacy of the ISABELLE design and by BNL's obstinate unwillingness to change it, accepted a post at DOE as a national lab *detailee*.

1981 *Temple Review* of ISABELLE resulted in DOE imposing a "pause" in the project construction.
Vineyard forced to resign as BNL Director.
Pewitt took the initiative that led to the Congressional appropriation of $2 million for a Fermilab p-pbar collider, killing the *three-Lab concept*.
Mickey founded USPAS, with its first program hosted by Fermilab.

1982 Samios named Acting BNL Director, and soon named Director.
Sanford dismissed as ISABELLE Project Head, replaced by Reardon.
Rau sacked by Samios as leader of the ISABELLE magnet program, supplanted by Palmer and Shutt.
Landmark meeting at Snowmass altered the course of high-energy physics:
– Wilson laid out his imaginative way to build a big collider, the Desertron.
– Lederman challenged American Big Physics to build the biggest and the best.
– Rubbia claimed that the W particle probably had been seen at CERN.
– Keyworth and Lederman came to a *meeting of the minds* to trade the end of ISABELLE for a big, unprecedented American collider, dashing Samios' hope of saving the BNL project, and ending the dream for internationalism in Big Physics.

1983 Rubbia announced to the physics world the discovery of the W and Z particles.
HEPAP Subpanel formed to settle ISABELLE's future.
The panel gave the project *thumbs down*.
ISABELLE canceled by DOE.
Samios attacked USPAS by disallowing BNL funds to support its programs.
Enlisting Lederman's help, Mickey managed to save it.

1984 Giving the *go* sign for R&D on the SSC, DOE set up a national Central Design Group at LBNL.

1985 Traces of tritium, growing over time, measured in some BNL test wells.
Samios kept this information confidential.
Samios harassed Mickey by refusing to pay his salary to be the USPAS Director.
Lederman and Richter came to the rescue, each providing one-third of Mickey's salary. Samios acquiesced! USPAS saved once again!

1986 A site-independent Conceptual Design Report for the SSC project produced by the CDG.
BNL proposed the RHIC collider, utilizing the ISABELLE tunnel and cryogenic facility to keep the cost down.

1987	The SSC approved by President Reagan as a Presidential Initiative. The *Trivelpiece Initiative* conceived, recommending the construction of accelerator facilities at national labs across the U.S., thereby ensuring their futures even with the monster, money-eating SSC hovering. RHIC made part of the *Initiative*. An SSC site-selection committee organized under the auspices of the NAS.
1988	Texas site at Waxahachie chosen for the SSC project. Rubbia succeeded Herwig Schopper as CERN Director-General.
1990	SSC Conceptual Design for the Texas site completed. SSC Environmental Impact Statement accepted by the public and approved by the DOE.
1991	SSC construction started. Formal approval for the RHIC project given by DOE.
1992	SSC cost estimate seemed to have no upper limit. Congressional concerns intensified. *Nay* votes for the project continued to rise.
1993	Congress ordered that funding for SSC construction cease. Only shutdown funds appropriated. DOE canceled SSC. Rubbia forced to resign as CERN Director-General.
1997	Possibility of seepage of tritium from BNL into the Peconic River exposed to the public. Unreasonable fears of health threats spread throughout the lab's vicinity. Home valuations tumbled. *Tritium Affair* at the lab reached its peak: Samios forced by DOE to resign as BNL Director. Energy Secretary Peña fired AUI as contractor for BNL. BNL in total disarray, its future threatened.
2000	RHIC construction completed and collider successfully operated. BNL Director Marburger focused on health and safety in the lab and its environs, and on keeping the environment clean, thus giving the lab a new lease on life. CERN turned off LEP and readied its tunnel for LHC installation. With no American big accelerator project in sight, the U.S. need to invest one-half billion dollars in CERN's LHC strengthened.
2002	American high-energy physics drifted into stagnation. Financial and technical troubles at CERN made the LHC appear to be faltering: Its cost estimate kept rising and its completion date pushed forward.
2003	LHC was originally scheduled to begin component installation, but its double-aperture superconducting magnets remained in doubt.

Author's Bio
Mel Month

Mel Month received his PhD in Physics from McGill University in 1964 and his MBA from Hofstra University in 1971. In 1966, he joined Brookhaven National Laboratory, where he began a research career in the study of particle beams and accelerators. Recognizing the importance of management in accelerator laboratories as a result of their complexity, size and advanced technology, he turned his attention during the 1970s toward management areas. From 1979 to 1983, he served in Washington, DC, in the U.S. Department of Energy, helping in the administration of the High Energy Physics (HEP) Program. In 1980, after serving on an accelerator R&D DOE panel, he began to sense that real trouble was brewing for HEP. With academia in his background and in his heart, it wasn't much of a surprise that his solution for improving matters was to develop better education for the technology-dominated accelerator field. Soon after, he started the U.S. Particle Accelerator School (USPAS) and became its first Director. As part of his varied School activities, he initiated the Prize for Achievement in Accelerator Physics and Technology in 1985; and, in 1987, he began a new type of program in which students can take USPAS courses for graduate credit at universities across the country. In 1997, Indiana University, in partnership with USPAS, initiated a Master's Degree in Beam Physics and Technology, the first such program ever. In conjunction with his USPAS Directorship, he further increased his activity in service to the accelerator community: He initiated and served as editor for three unique series of textbooks - with the American Institute of Physics (AIP), World Scientific, and John Wiley & Sons. Then, in late 1985, he organized the American Physical Society (APS) Topical Group on Particle Beam Physics; and, as its secretary-treasurer, worked tirelessly toward enhancing the status of the Topical Group to an APS Division. In November 1989, his efforts paid off when the Topical Group actually became a Division. Over the years, he has published many articles on his physics research and on his management work. In the late 1990s, he wrote, with three colleagues, the book, Managing Science, Management for R&D Laboratories, published by John Wiley & Sons in 2000.

With this book, he has entered the arena of the historical novel, dealing with the rise and decline of American Big Science: including the tough times being encountered in this rapid-change high-technology world of ours, and the roles played by the foremost – but swiftly fading – top guns – the ones who made physics such a splendid enterprise in the first place.

Printed in the United States
16180LVS00003B/17